THE GREAT MASTERS LIBRARY

MARK TWAIN

THE GREAT MASTERS LIBRARY

MARK TWAIN

The Adventures of Tom Sawyer

The Adventures of Huckleberry Finn

Mark Twain's Sketches

Mark Twain's
(Burlesque) Autobiography

The Prince and the Pauper

A Connecticut Yankee
in King Arthur's Court

Roughing It

Unabridged

With illustrations by True Williams,
E.W. Kemble, Dan Beard and others

CHATHAM RIVER PRESS • NEW YORK

The material in this omnibus edition was previously published in separate volumes under the titles:
   The Adventures of Tom Sawyer
   The Adventures of Huckleberry Finn
   Mark Twain's Sketches, Old and New
   Mark Twain's (Burlesque) Autobiography
   The Prince and the Pauper
   A Connecticut Yankee in King Arthur's Court
   Roughing It

This edition published in 1986 by Chatham River Press, a division of Arlington House, Inc., distributed by Crown Publishers, Inc., 225 Park Avenue South, New York, New York 10003

Manufactured in the United States of America

Library of Congress Cataloging in Publication Data

Twain, Mark, 1835-1910.
   Mark Twain.

   Contents: The adventures of Tom Sawyer—The adventures of Huckleberry Finn—Mark Twain's sketches—[etc.]
   I. Title.
PS1302   1986   818'.409   86-9622
ISBN 0-517-61833-8

h g f e d c b a

CONTENTS

FOREWORD

Samuel Langhorne Clemens was born in 1835 and spent the majority of his childhood in Hannibal, Missouri, located on the Mississippi River. His father died when Clemens was twelve, and he was apprenticed to a printer—an experience that served him well in later life. In 1857, at age 22, he trained with Horace Bixby to be a riverboat pilot. On the Mississippi he met "all the different types of human nature that are to be found in fiction, biography or history," and the river was to be an important theme in his work.

It was from his experience on the Mississippi that Clemens took his nom de plume—Mark Twain, the call used by riverboat pilots when taking soundings of the river. The nom de plume was especially appropriate for Clemens, reflecting both his love of the Mississippi and his wry sense of humor.

The Adventures of Tom Sawyer, published in 1876, was a humorous and joyful look at boyhood, based on Twain's childhood in Hannibal. Tom is a true child, not the dandified Little Lord Fauntleroy popular with writers at the time. Noisy, dirty, crafty, and kind, Tom shines at his sneaky best when "allowing" his friends to pay for the privilege of whitewashing Aunt Polly's fence; shows his kindness in comforting Becky Thatcher when they are lost in the cave; and is his most thoughtless when he decides to remain "dead" so he can watch his own funeral. Tom is simultaneously a devil and a delight. Twain was thoroughly accurate in his memory of childhood and did not turn children into miniature adults, as was the fashion of the day.

For some, the best moment of *The Adventures of Tom Sawyer* is meeting Huckleberry Finn, who comes into his own in *The Adventures of Huckleberry Finn*, published in 1884. Though Twain begins the story with the warning "Persons attempting to find a motive in the narrative will be prosecuted; persons attempting to find a moral will be banished; persons attempting to find a plot will be shot," it is a classic, not just froth. Huck and Jim floating on a raft down the Mississippi, free from the constraints of society, is everyone's dream of freedom. Yet the novel is more complex; it is an indictment of the times—the evils of slavery, the hypocrisy of the "good Christian" people that the two encounter, and the problems that twelve-year-old Huck has in building his personal system of morality.

Ernest Hemingway wrote: "All modern literature comes from one book by Mark Twain called *Huckleberry Finn*.... There was nothing before, there has been nothing as good since." Yet today there is a controversy in some school systems about whether the book is fit for junior high and high school students, whether the book should be banned. The adversaries of the book isolate Twain's satirization of bigoted white attitudes toward blacks as offensive. Twain fully believed that bigoted attitude to be wrong, which is why it is satirized. "Nigger Jim" was not a name invented by Twain as a derisive tag, it was an ironic name for the one truly kind and good person in Huck's adventures. To deny young readers the pleasure of reading *The Adventures of Huckleberry Finn* is to deny them a great American classic.

Both *The Adventures of Huckleberry Finn* and *The Adventures of Tom Sawyer* were popular at their time of publication, and Twain wrote more about the pair several years later in *Tom Sawyer Abroad* (1894) and *Tom Sawyer, Detective* (1896). However, neither of these two works had the charm and verve of the first novels. This edition uses the same illustrations as were used when the first editions were offered to the public by subscription—the True Williams illustrations for *The Adventures of Tom Sawyer* and the E.W. Kemble illustrations for *The Adventures of Huckleberry Finn*.

However, Twain was first known for his short, humorous sketches—his story "The Notorious Jumping Frog of Calaveras County" (1865) launched his literary career. The sketches collected here, including "The Notorious Jumping Frog of Calaveras County," show Twain at his humorous best. Whether it is his account of his "first literary venture," his unusual "family tree" in *Mark Twain's (Burlesque) Autobiography*, or his disgruntled biography of Benjamin Franklin, Twain is always fresh, original, and invariably funny.

The Prince and the Pauper and *A Connecticut Yankee in King Arthur's Court* are representatives of Twain's historical novels. *The Prince and the Pauper* (1881) is the more lighthearted of the two novels, capitalizing on the chance resemblance of Tom Canty, a slum child, and Edward Tudor, the Prince of Wales in the mid 1500s. Twain satirizes Merrie Olde England, pointing out the barbarisms and injustices of the time.

A Connecticut Yankee in King Arthur's Court (1889) places Hank Morgan, a machine shop superintendent, in medieval England at the time of King Arthur and the Knights of the Round Table. Though still humorous due to the incongruous juxtaposition of the nineteenth century and medieval times, the book has a darker vision than Twain's earlier works. Morgan brings with him American industrialization, and instead of putting the knowledge to use to build utopia, he destroys his new world in a technological debacle.

Roughing It was written in Twain's youth, before he developed a harsher, more cynical humor. It is an account of the time Twain went west with his brother Orion when Orion became lieutenant governor of Nevada. *Roughing It* is a classic account of the post-1849 mining epoch in the West. Whether Twain is describing the pony express, his failed mining venture, his job as newspaper editor, or his subsequent trip to Hawaii, *Roughing It* is factual as well as entertaining. In a prefatory statement to the book, Twain writes, "Yes, take it all around there is quite a good deal of information in the book. I regret this very much; but really it cannot be helped: information appears to stew out naturally, like the precious ottar of roses out of the otter."

Mark Twain was our first truly American humorist, laying the foundation for other uniquely American humorists such as Ring Lardner, Dorothy Parker, and James Thurber. Twain blended the hardy pioneer spirit with his belief that "against the assault of laughter, nothing can stand." In his early works—*Roughing It*, *The Adventures of Tom Sawyer*, *The Adventures of Huckleberry Finn* and his sketches —he was more lighthearted, more convinced of the boundless growth and energy of the age, a belief that was a characteristic of the "gilded age" in which he lived.

Yet, as he grew older, he became less convinced of man's mutability. He suffered defeats, business ventures bankrupted him, his beloved daughter died, and his vision grew darker, as seen in his almost nihilistic work, *The Mysterious Stranger.* His youthful exuberance diminished, but he did not completely give up his hopes and illusions. In *Pudd'nhead Wilson* he wrote, "Don't part with your illusions. When they are gone you may still exist, but you have ceased to live." In all that he did, Mark Twain remained fully alive.

This collection of Twain's work, complete with the original illustrations by True Williams, E.W. Kemble, Dan Beard, and others, is a rich overview of his writing, an enjoyable experience both for those familiar with Mark Twain and those who are reading him for the first time.

ANNE FICKLEN

New York
1982

The Adventures of Tom Sawyer

Illustrated by True Williams

To
MY WIFE
This Book
Is
Affectionately Dedicated.

PREFACE

Most of the adventures recorded in this book really occurred; one or two were experiences of my own, the rest those of boys who were schoolmates of mine. Huck Finn is drawn from life; Tom Sawyer also, but not from an individual—he is a combination of the characteristics of three boys whom I knew, and therefore belongs to the composite order of architecture.

The odd superstitions touched upon were all prevalent among children and slaves in the West at the period of this story—that is to say, thirty or forty years ago.

Although my book is intended mainly for the entertainment of boys and girls, I hope it will not be shunned by men and women on that account, for part of my plan has been to try to pleasantly remind adults of what they once were themselves, and of how they felt and thought and talked, and what queer enterprises they sometimes engaged in.

THE AUTHOR.

HARTFORD, 1876.

Chapter I

"TOM!"

No answer.

"TOM!"

No answer.

"What's gone with that boy, I wonder? You TOM!"

No answer.

The old lady pulled her spectacles down and looked over them about the room; then she put them up and looked out under them. She seldom or never looked *through* them for so small a thing as a boy; they were her state pair, the pride of her heart, and were built for "style," not service—she could have seen through a pair of stove lids just as well. She looked perplexed for a moment, and then said, not fiercely, but still loud enough for the furniture to hear:

"Well, I lay if I get hold of you I'll—"

She did not finish, for by this time she was bending down and punching under the bed with the broom, and so she needed breath to punctuate the punches with. She resurrected nothing but the cat.

"I never did see the beat of that boy!"

She went to the open door and stood in it and looked out among the tomato vines and "jimpson" weeds that constituted the garden. No Tom. So she lifted up her voice at an angle calculated for distance, and shouted:

"Y-o-u-u Tom!"

There was a slight noise behind her and she turned just in time to seize a small boy by the slack of his roundabout and arrest his flight.

"There! I might 'a' thought of that closet. What you been doing in there?"

"Nothing."

"Nothing! Look at your hands. And look at your mouth. What *is* that truck?"

"*I* don't know, aunt."

"Well, *I* know. It's jam—that's what it is. Forty times I've said if you didn't let that jam alone I'd skin you. Hand me that switch."

The switch hovered in the air—the peril was desperate—

"My! Look behind you, aunt!"

The old lady whirled round, and snatched her skirts out of danger. The lad fled, on the instant, scrambled up the high board-fence, and disappeared over it.

His aunt Polly stood surprised a moment, and then broke into a gentle laugh.

"Hang the boy, can't I never learn anything? Ain't he played me tricks enough like that for me to be looking out for him by this time? But old fools is the biggest fools there is. Can't learn an old dog new tricks, as the saying is. But my goodness, he never plays them alike, two days, and how is a body to know what's coming? He 'pears to know just how long he can torment me before I get my dander up, and he knows if he can make out to put me off for a minute or make me laugh, it's all down again and I can't hit him a lick. I ain't doing my duty by that boy, and that's the Lord's truth, goodness knows. Spare the rod and spile the child, as the Good Book says. I'm a laying up sin and suffering for us both, *I* know. He's full of the Old Scratch, but laws-a-me! he's my own dead sister's boy, poor thing, and I ain't got the heart to lash him, somehow. Every time I let him off, my conscience does hurt me so, and every time I hit him my old heart most breaks. Well-a-well, man that is born of woman is of few days and full of trouble, as the Scripture says, and I reckon it's so. He'll play hookey this evening,* and I'll just be obleeged to make him work, tomorrow, to punish him. It's mighty hard to make him work Saturdays, when all the boys is having holiday, but he hates work more than he hates anything else, and I've *got* to do some of my duty by him, or I'll be the ruination of the child."

Tom did play hookey, and he had a very good time. He got back home barely in season to help Jim, the small colored boy, saw next-day's wood and split the kindlings before supper—at least he was there in time to tell his adventures to Jim while Jim did three-fourths of the work. Tom's younger brother (or rather, half-brother) Sid, was already through with his part of the work (picking up chips) for he was a quiet boy, and had no adventurous, troublesome ways.

While Tom was eating his supper, and stealing sugar as opportunity offered, Aunt Polly asked him questions that were full of guile, and very deep—for she wanted to trap him into damaging revealments. Like many other simple-hearted souls, it was her pet vanity to believe she was endowed with a talent for dark and mysterious diplomacy, and she loved to contemplate her most transparent devices as marvels of low cunning. Said she:

"Tom, it was middling warm in school, warn't it?"

"Yes'm."

"Powerful warm, warn't it?"

"Yes'm."

"Didn't you want to go in a-swimming, Tom?"

A bit of a scare shot through Tom—a touch of uncomfortable suspicion. He searched Aunt Polly's face, but it told him nothing. So he said:

"No'm—well, not very much."

The old lady reached out her hand and felt Tom's shirt, and said:

"But you ain't too warm now, though." And it flattered her to reflect that she had discovered that the shirt was dry without anybody knowing that that was what she had in her mind. But in spite of her, Tom knew where the wind lay, now. So he forestalled what might be the next move:

"Some of us pumped on our heads—mine's damp yet. See?"

Aunt Polly was vexed to think she had overlooked that bit of circumstantial evidence, and missed a trick. Then she had a new inspiration:

---

* South-western for "afternoon."

"Tom, you didn't have to undo your shirt collar where I sewed it, to pump on your head, did you? Unbutton your jacket!"

The trouble vanished out of Tom's face. He opened his jacket. His shirt collar was securely sewed.

"Bother! Well, go 'long with you. I'd made sure you'd played hookey and been a-swimming. But I forgive ye, Tom. I reckon you're a kind of a singed cat, as the saying is—better'n you look. *This* time."

She was half sorry her sagacity had miscarried, and half glad that Tom had stumbled into obedient conduct for once.

But Sidney said:

"Well, now, if I didn't think you sewed his collar with white thread, but it's black."

"Why I did sew it with white! Tom!"

But Tom did not wait for the rest. As he went out at the door he said:

"Siddy, I'll lick you for that."

In a safe place Tom examined two large needles which were thrust into the lappels of his jacket, and had thread bound about them—one needle carried white thread and the other black. He said:

"She'd never noticed if it hadn't been for Sid. Confound it! sometimes she sews it with white, and sometimes she sews it with black. I wish to geeminy she'd stick to one or t'other—*I* can't keep the run of 'em. But I bet you I'll lam Sid for that. I'll learn him!"

He was not the Model Boy of the village. He knew the model boy very well though—and loathed him.

Within two minutes, or even less, he had forgotten all his troubles. Not because his troubles were one whit less heavy and bitter to him than a man's are to a man, but because a new and powerful interest bore them down and drove them out of his mind for the time—just as men's misfortunes are forgotten in the excitement of new enterprises. This new interest was a valued novelty in whistling, which he had just acquired from a negro, and he was suffering to practice it undisturbed. It consisted in a peculiar bird-like turn, a sort of liquid warble, produced by touching the tongue to the roof of the mouth at short intervals in the midst of the music—the reader probably remembers how to do it, if he has ever been a boy. Diligence and attention soon gave him the knack of it, and he strode down the street with his mouth full of harmony and his soul full of gratitude. He felt much as an astronomer feels who has discovered a new planet—no doubt, as far as strong, deep, unalloyed pleasure is concerned, the advantage was with the boy, not the astronomer.

The summer evenings were long. It was not dark, yet. Presently Tom checked his whistle. A stranger was before him—a boy a shade larger than himself. A new comer of any age or either sex was an impressive curiosity in the poor little shabby village of St. Petersburg. This boy was well-dressed, too—well-dressed on a week-day. This was simply astounding. His cap was a dainty thing, his close-buttoned blue cloth roundabout was new and natty, and so were his pantaloons. He had shoes on—and it was only Friday. He even wore a necktie, a bright bit of ribbon. He had a citified air about him that ate into Tom's vitals. The more Tom stared at the splendid marvel, the higher he turned up his nose at his finery and the shabbier and shabbier his own outfit seemed to him to grow. Neither boy spoke. If one moved, the other moved—but only sidewise, in a circle; they kept face to face and eye to eye all the time. Finally Tom said:

"I can lick you!"

"I'd like to see you try it."

"Well, I can do it."

"No you can't, either."

"Yes I can."

"No you can't."

"I can."

"You can't."

"Can!"

"Can't!"

An uncomfortable pause. Then Tom said:

"What's your name?"

"'Tisn't any of your business, maybe."

"Well I 'low I'll *make* it my business."

"Well why don't you?"

"If you say much I will."

"Much—much—*much*. There now."

"Oh, you think you're mighty smart, *don't* you? I could lick you with one hand tied behind me, if I wanted to."

"Well why don't you *do* it? You *say* you can do it."

"Well I *will*, if you fool with me."

"Oh yes—I've seen whole families in the same fix."

"Smarty! You think you're *some*, now, *don't* you? Oh what a hat!"

"You can lump that hat if you don't like it. I dare you to knock it off—and anybody that'll take a dare will suck eggs."

"You're a liar!"

"You're another."

"You're a fighting liar and dasn't take it up."

"Aw—take a walk!"

"Say—if you give me much more of your sass I'll take and bounce a rock off'n your head."

"Oh, of *course* you will."

"Well I *will*."

"Well why don't you *do* it then? What do you keep *saying* you will for? Why don't you *do* it? It's because you're afraid."

"I *ain't* afraid."

"You are."

"I ain't."

"You are."

Another pause, and more eyeing and sidling around each other. Presently they were shoulder to shoulder. Tom said:

"Get away from here!"

"Go away yourself!"

"I won't."

"*I* won't either."

So they stood, each with a foot placed at an angle as a brace, and both shoving with might and main, and glowering at each other with hate. But neither could get an advantage. After struggling till both were hot and flushed, each relaxed his strain with watchful caution, and Tom said:

"You're a coward and a pup. I'll tell my big brother on you, and he can thrash you with his little finger, and I'll make him do it, too."

"What do I care for your big brother? I've got a brother that's bigger than he is—and what's more, he can throw him over that fence, too." [Both brothers were imaginary.]

"That's a lie."

"*Your* saying so don't make it so."

Tom drew a line in the dust with his big toe, and said:

"I dare you to step over that, and I'll lick you till you can't stand up. Anybody that'll take a dare will steal sheep."

The new boy stepped over promptly, and said:

"Now you said you'd do it, now let's see you do it."

"Don't you crowd me now; you better look out."

"Well, you *said* you'd do it—why don't you do it?"

"By jingo! for two cents I *will* do it."

The new boy took two broad coppers out of his pocket and held them out with derision. Tom struck them to the ground. In an instant both boys were rolling and tumbling in the dirt, gripped together like cats; and for the space of a minute they tugged and tore at each other's hair and clothes, punched and scratched each other's noses, and covered themselves with dust and glory. Presently the confusion took form and through the fog of battle Tom appeared, seated astride the new boy, and pounding him with his fists.

"Holler 'nuff!" said he.

The boy only struggled to free himself. He was crying,—mainly from rage.

"Holler 'nuff!"—and the pounding went on.

At last the stranger got out a smothered "'Nuff!" and Tom let him up and said:

"Now that'll learn you. Better look out who you're fooling with next time."

The new boy went off brushing the dust from his clothes, sobbing, snuffling, and occasionally looking back and shaking his head and threatening what he would do to Tom the "next time he caught him out." To which Tom responded with jeers, and started off in high feather, and as soon as his back was turned the new boy snatched up a stone, threw it and hit him between the shoulders and then turned tail and ran like an antelope. Tom chased the traitor home, and thus found out where he lived. He then held a position at the gate for some time, daring the enemy to come outside, but the enemy only made faces at him through the window and declined. At last the enemy's mother appeared, and called Tom a bad, vicious, vulgar child, and ordered him away. So he went away; but he said he "'lowed" to "lay" for that boy.

He got home pretty late, that night, and when he climbed cautiously in at the window, he uncovered an ambuscade, in the person of his aunt; and when she saw the state his clothes were in her resolution to turn his Saturday holiday into captivity at hard labor became adamantine in its firmness.

Chapter II

SATURDAY MORNING WAS come, and all the summer world was bright and fresh, and brimming with life. There was a song in every heart; and if the heart was young the music issued at the lips. There was cheer in every face and a spring in every step. The locust trees were in bloom and the fragrance of the blossoms filled the air. Cardiff Hill, beyond the village and above it, was green with vegetation, and it lay just far enough away to seem a Delectable Land, dreamy, reposeful, and inviting.

Tom appeared on the sidewalk with a bucket of whitewash and a long-handled brush. He surveyed the fence, and all gladness left him and a deep melancholy settled down upon his spirit. Thirty yards of board fence nine feet high. Life to him seemed hollow, and existence but a burden. Sighing he dipped his brush and passed it along the topmost plank; repeated the operation; did it again; compared the insignificant whitewashed streak with the far-reaching continent of unwhitewashed fence, and sat down on a tree-box discouraged. Jim came skipping out at the gate with a tin pail, and singing "Buffalo Gals." Bringing water from the town pump had always been hateful work in Tom's eyes, before, but now it did not strike him so. He remembered that there was company at the pump. White, mulatto, and negro boys and girls were always there waiting their turns, resting, trading playthings, quarreling, fighting, skylarking. And he remembered that although the pump was only a hundred and fifty yards off, Jim never got back with a bucket of water under an hour—and even then somebody generally had to go after him. Tom said:

"Say, Jim, I'll fetch the water if you'll whitewash some."

Jim shook his head and said:

"Can't, Mars Tom. Ole missis, she tole me I got to go an' git dis water an' not stop foolin' roun' wid anybody. She say she spec' Mars Tom gwine to ax me to whitewash, an' so she tole me go 'long an' 'tend to my own business— she 'lowed *she'd* 'tend to de whitewashin'."

"Oh, never you mind what she said, Jim. That's the way she always talks.
Gimme the bucket—I won't be gone only a minute. *She* won't ever know."

"Oh, I dasn't Mars Tom. Ole missis she'd take an' tar de head off'n me.
'Deed she would."

"*She!* She never licks anybody—whacks 'em over the head with her thimble—
and who cares for that, I'd like to know. She talks awful, but talk don't hurt—
anyways it don't if she don't cry. Jim, I'll give you a marvel. I'll give you a
white alley!"

Jim began to waver.

"White alley, Jim! And it's a bully taw."

"My! Dat's a mighty gay marvel, *I* tell you! But Mars Tom I's powerful
'fraid ole missis—"

"And besides, if you will I'll show you my sore toe."

Jim was only human—this attraction was too much for him. He put down his
pail, took the white alley, and bent over the toe with absorbing interest while
the bandage was being unwound. In another moment he was flying down the
street with his pail and a tingling rear, Tom was whitewashing with vigor, and
Aunt Polly was retiring from the field with a slipper in her hand and triumph in
her eye.

But Tom's energy did not last. He began to think of the fun he had planned
for this day, and his sorrows multiplied. Soon the free boys would come tripping
along on all sorts of delicious expeditions, and they would make a world of fun
of him for having to work—the very thought of it burnt him like fire. He got
out his worldly wealth and examined it—bits of toys, marbles, and trash; enough
to buy an exchange of *work*, maybe, but not half enough to buy so much as half
an hour of pure freedom. So he returned his straightened means to his pocket,
and gave up the idea of trying to buy the boys. At this dark and hopeless moment
an inspiration burst upon him! Nothing less than a great, magnificent inspiration.

He took up his brush and went tranquilly to work. Ben Rogers hove in sight
presently—the very boy, of all boys, whose ridicule he had been dreading. Ben's
gait was the hop-skip-and-jump—proof enough that his heart was light and his
anticipations high. He was eating an apple, and giving a long, melodious whoop,
at intervals, followed by a deep-toned ding-dong-dong, ding-dong-dong, for he

TENDIN' TO BUSINESS.

was personating a steamboat. As he drew near, he slackened speed, took the middle of the street, leaned far over to starboard and rounded to ponderously and with laborious pomp and circumstance—for he was personating the "Big Missouri," and considered himself to be drawing nine feet of water. He was boat, and captain, and engine-bells combined, so he had to imagine himself standing on his own hurricane-deck giving the orders and executing them:

"Stop her, sir! Ting-a-ling-ling!" The headway ran almost out and he drew up slowly toward the side-walk.

"Ship up to back! Ting-a-ling-ling!" His arms straightened and stiffened down his sides.

"Set her back on the stabboard! Ting-a-ling-ling! Chow! ch-chow-wow! Chow!" His right hand, meantime, describing stately circles,—for it was representing a forty-foot wheel.

"Let her go back on the labboard! Ting-a-ling-ling! Chow-ch-chow-chow!" The left hand began to describe circles.

"Stop the stabboard! Ting-a-ling-ling! Stop the labbord! Come ahead on the stabboard! Stop her! Let your outside turn over slow! Ting-a-ling-ling! Chow-ow-ow! Get out that head-line! *Lively* now! Come—out with your spring-line— what're you about there! Take a turn round that stump with the bight of it! Stand by that stage, now—let her go! Done with the engines, sir! Ting-a-ling-ling! *Sh't! s'h't! sh't!*" (trying the gauge-cocks.)

Tom went on whitewashing—paid no attention to the steamboat. Ben stared a moment and then said:

"Hi-*yi! You're* up a stump, ain't you!"

No answer. Tom surveyed his last touch with the eye of an artist; then he gave his brush another gentle sweep and surveyed the result, as before. Ben ranged up alongside of him. Tom's mouth watered for the apple, but he stuck to his work. Ben said:

"Hello, old chap, you got to work, hey?"

Tom wheeled suddenly and said:

"Why it's you Ben! I warn't noticing."

"Say—*I'm* going in a swimming, *I* am. Don't you wish you could? But of course you'd druther *work*—wouldn't you? Course you would!"

Tom contemplated the boy a bit, and said:

"What do you call work?"

"Why ain't *that* work?"

Tom resumed his whitewashing, and answered carelessly:

"Well, maybe it is, and maybe it aint. All I know, is, it suits Tom Sawyer."

"Oh come, now, you don't mean to let on that you *like* it?"

The brush continued to move.

"Like it? Well I don't see why I oughtn't to like it. Does a boy get a chance to whitewash a fence every day?"

That put the thing in a new light. Ben stopped nibbling his apple. Tom swept his brush daintily back and forth—stepped back to note the effect—added a touch here and there—criticised the effect again—Ben watching every move and getting more and more interested, more and more absorbed. Presently he said:

"Say, Tom, let *me* whitewash a little."

Tom considered, was about to consent; but he altered his mind:

"No—no—I reckon it wouldn't hardly do, Ben. You see, Aunt Polly's awful particular about this fence—right here on the street, you know—but if it was

'AIN'T THAT WORK?

the back fence I wouldn't mind and *she* wouldn't. Yes, she's awful particular about this fence; it's got to be done very careful; I reckon there ain't one boy in a thousand, maybe two thousand, that can do it the way it's got to be done.

"No—is that so? Oh come, now—lemme just try. Only just a little—I'd let *you*, if you was me, Tom."

"Ben, I'd like to, honest injun; but Aunt Polly—well Jim wanted to do it, but she wouldn't let him; Sid wanted to do it, and she wouldn't let Sid. Now don't you see how I'm fixed? If you was to tackle this fence and anything was to happen to it—"

"Oh, shucks, I'll be just as careful. Now lemme try. Say—I'll give you the core of my apple."

"Well, here—. No, Ben, now don't. I'm afeard—"

"I'll give you *all* of it!"

Tom gave up the brush with reluctance in his face but alacrity in his heart. And while the late steamer "Big Missouri" worked and sweated in the sun, the retired artist sat on a barrel in the shade close by, dangled his legs, munched his apple, and planned the slaughter of more innocents. There was no lack of material; boys happened along every little while; they came to jeer, but remained to whitewash. By the time Ben was fagged out, Tom had traded the next chance to Billy Fisher for a kite, in good repair; and when *he* played out, Johnny Miller bought in for a dead rat and a string to swing it with—and so on, and so on, hour after hour. And when the middle of the afternoon came, from being a poor poverty-stricken boy in the morning, Tom was literally rolling in wealth. He had beside the things before mentioned, twelve marbles, part of a jews-harp, a piece of blue bottle-glass to look through, a spool cannon, a key that wouldn't unlock anything, a fragment of chalk, a glass stopper of a decanter, a tin soldier, a couple of tadpoles, six fire-crackers, a kitten with only one eye, a brass door-knob, a dog-collar—but no dog—the handle of a knife, four pieces of orange-peel, and a dilapidated old window-sash.

He had had a nice, good, idle time all the while—plenty of company—and the fence had three coats of whitewash on it! If he hadn't run out of whitewash, he would have bankrupted every boy in the village.

Tom said to himself that it was not such a hollow world, after all. He had discovered a great law of human action, without knowing it—namely, that in order to make a man or a boy covet a thing, it is only necessary to make the thing difficult to attain. If he had been a great and wise philosopher, like the writer of this book, he would now have comprehended that Work consists of whatever a body is *obliged* to do, and that Play consists of whatever a body is not obliged to do. And this would help him to understand why constructing artificial flowers or performing on a treadmill is work, while rolling ten-pins or climbing Mont Blanc is only amusement. There are wealthy gentlemen in England who drive four-horse passenger-coaches twenty or thirty miles on a daily line, in the summer, because the privilege costs them considerable money; but if they were offered wages for the service, that would turn it into work and then they would resign.

The boy mused a while over the substantial change which had taken place in his worldly circumstances, and then wended toward head-quarters to report.

Chapter III

TOM PRESENTED HIMSELF before Aunt Polly, who was sitting by an open window in a pleasant rearward apartment, which was bed-room, breakfast-room, dining-room, and library, combined. The balmy summer air, the restful quiet, the odor of the flowers, and the drowsing murmur of the bees had had their effect, and she was nodding over her knitting—for she had no company but the cat, and it was asleep in her lap. Her spectacles were propped up on her gray head for safety. She had thought that of course Tom had deserted long ago, and she wondered at seeing him place himself in her power again in this intrepid way. He said: "Mayn't I go and play now, aunt?"

"What, a'ready? How much have you done?"

"It's all done, aunt."

"Tom, don't lie to me—I can't bear it."

"I ain't, aunt; it *is* all done."

Aunt Polly placed small trust in such evidence. She went out to see for herself; and she would have been content to find twenty per cent of Tom's statement true. When she found the entire fence whitewashed, and not only whitewashed but elaborately coated and recoated, and even a streak added to the ground, her astonishment was almost unspeakable. She said:

"Well, I never! There's no getting round it, you *can* work when you're a mind to, Tom." And then she diluted the compliment by adding, "But it's powerful seldom you're a mind to, I'm bound to say. Well, go 'long and play; but mind you get back sometime in a week, or I'll tan you."

She was so overcome by the splendor of his achievement that she took him into the closet and selected a choice apple and delivered it to him, along with an improving lecture upon the added value and flavor a treat took to itself when it came without sin through virtuous effort. And while she closed with a happy scriptural flourish, he "hooked" a doughnut.

Then he skipped out, and saw Sid just starting up the outside stairway that led to the back rooms on the second floor. Clods were handy and the air was full of them in a twinkling. They raged around Sid like a hail-storm; and before

Aunt Polly could collect her surprised faculties and sally to the rescue, six or seven clods had taken personal effect, and Tom was over the fence and gone. There was a gate, but as a general thing he was too crowded for time to make use of it. His soul was at peace, now that he had settled with Sid for calling attention to his black thread and getting him into trouble.

Tom skirted the block, and came round into a muddy alley that led by the back of his aunt's cow-stable. He presently got safely beyond the reach of capture and punishment, and hasted toward the public square of the village, where two "military" companies of boys had met for conflict, according to previous appointment. Tom was General of one of these armies, Joe Harper (a bosom friend,) General of the other. These two great commanders did not condescend to fight in person—that being better suited to the still smaller fry—but sat together on an eminence and conducted the field operations by orders delivered through aides-de-camp. Tom's army won a great victory, after a long and hard-fought battle. Then the dead were counted, prisoners exchanged, the terms of the next disagreement agreed upon and the day for the necessary battle appointed; after which the armies fell into line and marched away, and Tom turned homeward alone.

As he was passing by the house where Jeff Thatcher lived, he saw a new girl in the garden—a lovely little blue-eyed creature with yellow hair plaited into two long tails, white summer frock and embroidered pantalettes. The fresh-crowned hero fell without firing a shot. A certain Amy Lawrence vanished out of his heart and left not even a memory of herself behind. He had thought he loved her to distraction, he had regarded his passion as adoration; and behold it was only a poor little evanescent partiality. He had been months winning her; she had confessed hardly a week ago; he had been the happiest and the proudest boy in the world only seven short days, and here in one instant of time she had gone out of his heart like a casual stranger whose visit is done.

He worshiped this new angel with furtive eye, till he saw that she had discovered him; then he pretended he did not know she was present, and began to "show off" in all sorts of absurd boyish ways, in order to win her admiration. He kept up this grotesque foolishness for some time; but by and by, while he was in the midst of some dangerous gymnastic performances, he glanced aside and saw

AFTER THE BATTLE.

that the little girl was wending her way toward the house. Tom came up to the
fence and leaned on it, grieving, and hoping she would tarry yet a while longer.
She halted a moment on the steps and then moved toward the door. Tom heaved
a great sigh as she put her foot on the threshold. But his face lit up, right away,
for she tossed a pansy over the fence a moment before she disappeared.

The boy ran around and stopped within a foot or two of the flower, and then
shaded his eyes with his hand and began to look down street as if he had
discovered something of interest going on in that direction. Presently he picked
up a straw and began trying to balance it on his nose, with his head tilted far
back; and as he moved from side to side, in his efforts, he edged nearer and
nearer toward the pansy; finally his bare foot rested upon it, his pliant toes closed
upon it, and he hopped away with the treasure and disappeared round the corner.
But only for a minute—only while he could button the flower inside his jacket,
next his heart—or next his stomach, possibly, for he was not much posted in
anatomy, and not hypercritical, anyway.

He returned, now, and hung about the fence till nightfall, "showing off," as
before; but the girl never exhibited herself again, though Tom comforted himself
a little with the hope that she had been near some window, meantime, and been
aware of his attentions. Finally he rode home reluctantly, with his poor head
full of visions.

All through supper his spirits were so high that his aunt wondered "what had
got into the child." He took a good scolding about clodding Sid, and did not
seem to mind it in the least. He tried to steal sugar under his aunt's very nose,
and got his knuckles rapped for it. He said:

"Aunt, you don't whack Sid when he takes it."

"Well, Sid don't torment a body the way you do. You'd be always into that
sugar if I warn't watching you."

Presently she stepped into the kitchen, and Sid, happy in his immunity, reached
for the sugar-bowl—a sort of glorying over Tom which was well-nigh unbearable.
But Sid's fingers slipped and the bowl dropped and broke. Tom was in ecstasies.
In such ecstasies that he even controlled his tongue and was silent. He said to
himself that he would not speak a word, even when his aunt came in, but would
sit perfectly still till she asked who did the mischief; and then he would tell,

and there would be nothing so good in the world as to see that pet model "catch it." He was so brim-full of exultation that he could hardly hold himself when the old lady came back and stood above the wreck discharging lightnings of wrath from over her spectacles. He said to himself, "Now it's coming!" And the next instant he was sprawling on the floor! The potent palm was uplifted to strike again when Tom cried out:

"Hold on, now, what 'er you belting *me* for?—Sid broke it!"

Aunt Polly paused, perplexed, and Tom looked for healing pity. But when she got her tongue again, she only said:

"Umf! Well, you didn't get a lick amiss, I reckon. You been into some other audacious mischief when I wasn't around, like enough."

Then her conscience reproached her, and she yearned to say something kind and loving; but she judged that this would be construed into a confession that she had been in the wrong, and discipline forbade that. So she kept silence, and went about her affairs with a troubled heart. Tom sulked in a corner and exalted his woes. He knew that in her heart his aunt was on her knees to him, and he was morosely gratified by the consciousness of it. He would hang out no signals, he would take notice of none. He knew that a yearning glance fell upon him, now and then, through a film of tears, but he refused recognition of it. He pictured himself lying sick unto death and his aunt bending over him beseeching one little forgiving word, but he would turn his face to the wall, and die with that word unsaid. Ah, how would she feel then? And he pictured himself brought home from the river, dead, with his curls all wet, and his sore heart at rest. How she would throw herself upon him, and how her tears would fall like rain, and her lips pray God to give her back her boy and she would never, never abuse him any more! But he would lie there cold and white and make no sign—a poor little sufferer, whose griefs were at an end. He so worked upon his feelings with the pathos of these dreams, that he had to keep swallowing, he was so like to choke; and his eyes swam in a blur of water, which overflowed when he winked, and ran down and trickled from the end of his nose. And such a luxury to him was this petting of his sorrows, that he could not bear to have any worldly cheeriness or any grating delight intrude upon it; it was too sacred for such contact; and so, presently, when his cousin Mary danced in, all alive with the joy of seeing home again after an age-long visit of one week to the country, he got up and moved in clouds and darkness out at one door as she brought song and sunshine in at the other.

He wandered far from the accustomed haunts of boys, and sought desolate places that were in harmony with his spirit. A log raft in the river invited him, and he seated himself on its outer edge and contemplated the dreary vastness of the stream, wishing, the while, that he could only be drowned, all at once and unconsciously, without undergoing the uncomfortable routine devised by nature. Then he thought of his flower. He got it out, rumpled and wilted, and it mightily increased his dismal felicity. He wondered if *she* would pity him if she knew? Would she cry, and wish that she had a right to put her arms around his neck and comfort him? Or would she turn coldly away like all the hollow world? This picture brought such an agony of pleasureable suffering that he worked it over and over again in his mind and set it up in new and varied lights, till he wore it threadbare. At last he rose up sighing and departed in the darkness.

About half past nine or ten o'clock he came along the deserted street to where the Adored Unknown lived; he paused a moment; no sound fell upon his listening ear; a candle was casting a dull glow upon the curtain of a second-story window. Was the sacred presence there? He climbed the fence, threaded his stealthy way through the plants, till he stood under that window; he looked up at it long, and with emotion; then he laid him down on the ground under it, disposing himself upon his back, with his hands clasped upon his breast and holding his poor wilted flower. And thus he would die—out in the cold world, with no shelter over his homeless head, no friendly hand to wipe the death-damps from his brow, no loving face to bend pityingly over him when the great agony came. And thus *she* would see him when she looked out upon the glad morning, and oh! would she drop one little tear upon his poor, lifeless form, would she heave one little sigh to see a bright young life so rudely blighted, so untimely cut down?

The window went up, a maid-servant's discordant voice profaned the holy calm, and a deluge of water drenched the prone martyr's remains!

The strangling hero sprang up with a relieving snort. There was a whiz as of a missile in the air, mingled with the murmur of a curse, a sound as of shivering glass followed, and a small, vague form went over the fence and shot away in the gloom.

Not long after, as Tom, all undressed for bed, was surveying his drenched garments by the light of a tallow dip, Sid woke up; but if he had any dim idea of making any "references to allusions," he thought better of it and held his peace, for there was danger in Tom's eye.

Tom turned in without the added vexation of prayers, and Sid made mental note of the omission.

Chapter IV

THE SUN ROSE upon a tranquil world, and beamed down upon the peaceful village like a benediction. Breakfast over, Aunt Polly had family worship; it began with a prayer built from the ground up of solid courses of Scriptural quotations, welded together with a thin mortar of originality; and from the summit of this she delivered a grim chapter of the Mosaic Law, as from Sinai.

Then Tom girded up his loins, so to speak, and went to work to "get his verses." Sid had learned his lesson days before. Tom bent all his energies to the memorizing of five verses, and he chose part of the Sermon on the Mount, because he could find no verses that were shorter. At the end of half an hour Tom had a vague general idea of his lesson, but no more, for his mind was traversing the whole field of human thought, and his hands were busy with distracting recreations. Mary took his book to hear him recite, and he tried to find his way through the fog:

"Blessed are the—a—a—"

"Poor"—

"Yes—poor; blessed are the poor—a—a—"

"In spirit—"

"In spirit; blessed are the poor in spirit, for they—they—"

"*Theirs*—"

"For *theirs*. Blessed are the poor in spirit, for *theirs* is the kingdom of heaven. Blessed are they that mourn, for they—they—"

"Sh—"

"For they—a—"

"S, H, A—"

"For they S, H—Oh I don't know what it is!"

"*Shall!*"

"Oh, *shall!* for they shall—for they shall—a—a—shall mourn—a—a—blessed are they that shall—they that—a—they that shall mourn, for they shall—a— shall *what*? Why don't you tell me Mary?—what do you want to be so mean for?"

"Oh, Tom, you poor thick-headed thing, I'm not teasing you. I wouldn't do that. You must go and learn it again. Don't you be discouraged, Tom, you'll manage it—and if you do, I'll give you something ever so nice. There, now, that's a good boy."

"All right! What is it, Mary, tell me what it is."

"Never you mind, Tom. You know if I say it's nice, it *is* nice."

"You bet you that's so, Mary. All right, I'll tackle it again."

And he did "tackle it again"—and under the double pressure of curiosity and prospective gain, he did it with such spirit that he accomplished a shining success. Mary gave him a bran-new "Barlow" knife worth twelve and a half cents; and the convulsion of delight that swept his system shook him to his foundations. True, the knife would not cut anything, but it was a "sure-enough" Barlow, and there was inconceivable grandeur in that—though where the western boys ever got the idea that such a weapon could possibly be counterfeited to its injury, is an imposing mystery and will always remain so, perhaps. Tom contrived to scarify the cupboard with it, and was arranging to begin on the bureau, when he was called off to dress for Sunday-School.

Mary gave him a tin basin of water and a piece of soap, and he went outside the door and set the basin on a little bench there; then he dipped the soap in the water and laid it down; turned up his sleeves; poured out the water on the ground, gently, and then entered the kitchen and began to wipe his face diligently on the towel behind the door. But Mary removed the towel and said:

"Now ain't you ashamed, Tom. You mustn't be so bad. Water won't hurt you."

Tom was a trifle disconcerted. The basin was refilled, and this time he stood over it a little while, gathering resolution; took in a big breath and began. When he entered the kitchen presently, with both eyes shut and groping for the towel with his hands, an honorable testimony of suds and water was dripping from his face. But when he emerged from the towel, he was not yet satisfactory, for the clean territory stopped short at his chin and his jaws, like a mask; below and beyond this line there was a dark expanse of unirrigated soil that spread downward in front and backward around his neck. Mary took him in hand, and when she was done with him he was a man and a brother, without distinction of color, and his saturated hair was neatly brushed, and its short curls wrought into a dainty and symmetrical general effect. [He privately smoothed out the curls, with labor and difficulty, and plastered his hair close down to his head; for he held curls to be effeminate, and his own filled his life with bitterness.] Then Mary got out a suit of his clothing that had been used only on Sundays during two years—they were simply called his "other clothes"—and so by that we know the size of his wardrobe. The girl "put him to rights" after he had dressed himself; she buttoned his neat roundabout up to his chin, turned his vast shirt collar down over his shoulders, brushed him off and crowned him with his speckled straw hat. He now looked exceedingly improved and uncomfortable. He was fully as uncomfortable as he looked; for there was a restraint about whole clothes and cleanliness that galled him. He hoped that Mary would forget his shoes, but the hope was blighted; she coated them thoroughly with tallow, as was the custom, and brought them out. He lost his temper and said he was always being made to do everything he didn't want to do. But Mary said, persuasively:

"Please, Tom—that's a good boy."

So he got into the shoes snarling. Mary was soon ready, and the three children set out for Sunday-school—a place that Tom hated with his whole heart; but Sid and Mary were fond of it.

Sabbath-school hours were from nine to half past ten; and then church service. Two of the children always remained for the sermon voluntarily, and the other always remained too—for stronger reasons. The church's high-backed, uncushioned pews would seat about three hundred persons; the edifice was but a small, plain affair, with a sort of pine board tree-box on top of it for a steeple. At the door Tom dropped back a step and accosted a Sunday-dressed comrade:

"Say, Billy, got a yaller ticket?"

"Yes."

"What'll you take for her?"

"What'll you give?"

"Piece of lickrish and a fish-hook."

"Less see 'em."

Tom exhibited. They were satisfactory, and the property changed hands. Then Tom traded a couple of white alleys for three red tickets, and some small trifle or other for a couple of blue ones. He waylaid other boys as they came, and went on buying tickets of various colors ten or fifteen minutes longer. He entered the church, now, with a swarm of clean and noisy boys and girls, proceeded to his seat and started a quarrel with the first boy that came handy. The teacher, a grave, elderly man, interfered; then turned his back a moment and Tom pulled a boy's hair in the next bench, and was absorbed in his book when the boy turned around; stuck a pin in another boy, presently, in order to hear him say "Ouch!" and got a new reprimand from his teacher. Tom's whole class were of a pattern—restless, noisy, and troublesome. When they came to recite their lessons, not one of them knew his verses perfectly, but had to be prompted all along. However, they worried through, and each got his reward—in small blue tickets, each with a passage of Scripture on it; each blue ticket was pay for two verses of the recitation. Ten blue tickets equalled a red one, and could be exchanged for it; ten red tickets equalled a yellow one: for ten yellow tickets the Superintendent gave a very plainly bound Bible, (worth forty cents in those easy times,) to the pupil. How many of my readers would have the industry and application to memorize two thousand verses, even for a Doré Bible? And yet Mary had acquired two Bibles in this way—it was the patient work of two years—and a boy of German parentage had won four or five. He once recited three thousand verses without stopping; but the strain upon his mental faculties was too great, and he was little better than an idiot from that day forth—a grievous misfortune for the school, for on great occasions, before company, the

Superintendent (as Tom expressed it) had always made this boy come out and "spread himself." Only the older pupils managed to keep their tickets and stick to their tedious work long enough to get a Bible, and so the delivery of one of these prizes was a rare and noteworthy circumstance; the successful pupil was so great and conspicuous for that day that on the spot every scholar's heart was fired with a fresh ambition that often lasted a couple of weeks. It is possible that Tom's mental stomach had never really hungered for one of those prizes, but unquestionably his entire being had for many a day longed for the glory and the eclat that came with it.

In due course the Superintendent stood up in front of the pulpit, with a closed hymn book in his hand and his forefinger inserted between its leaves, and commanded attention. When a Sunday-school Superintendent makes his customary little speech, a hymn-book in the hand is as necessary as is the inevitable sheet of music in the hand of a singer who stands forward on the platform and sings a solo at a concert—though why, is a mystery: for neither the hymn-book nor the sheet of music is ever referred to by the sufferer. This Superintendent was a slim creature of thirty-five, with a sandy goatee and short sandy hair; he wore a stiff standing-collar whose upper edge almost reached his ears and whose sharp points curved forward abreast the corners of his mouth—a fence that compelled a straight lookout ahead, and a turning of the whole body when a side view was required; his chin was propped on a spreading cravat which was as broad and as long as a bank note, and had fringed ends; his boot toes were turned sharply up, in the fashion of the day, like sleigh-runners—an effect patiently and laboriously produced by the young men by sitting with their toes pressed against a wall for hours together. Mr. Walters was very earnest of mien, and very sincere and honest at heart; and he held sacred things and places in such reverence, and so separated them from worldly matters, that unconsciously to himself his Sunday-school voice had acquired a peculiar intonation which was wholly absent on week-days. He began after this fashion:

"Now children, I want you all to sit up just as straight and pretty as you can and give me all your attention for a minute or two. There—that is it. That is the way good little boys and girls should do. I see one little girl who is looking out of the window—I am afraid she thinks I am out there somewhere—perhaps up in one of the trees making a speech to the little birds. [Applausive titter.] I want to tell you how good it makes me feel to see so many bright, clean little faces assembled in a place like this, learning to do right and be good." And so forth and so on. It is not necessary to set down the rest of the oration. It was of a pattern which does not vary, and so it is familiar to us all.

The latter third of the speech was marred by the resumption of fights and other recreations among certain of the bad boys, and by fidgetings and whisperings that extended far and wide, washing even to the bases of isolated and incorruptible rocks like Sid and Mary. But now every sound ceased suddenly, with the subsidence of Mr. Walters' voice, and the conclusion of the speech was received with a burst of silent gratitude.

A good part of the whispering had been occasioned by an event which was more or less rare—the entrance of visitors; lawyer Thatcher, accompanied by a very feeble and aged man; a fine, portly, middle-aged gentleman with iron-gray hair; and a dignified lady who was doubtless the latter's wife. The lady was leading a child. Tom had been restless and full of chafings and repinings; conscience-smitten, too—he could not meet Amy Lawrence's eye, he could not brook her

loving gaze. But when he saw this small new-comer his soul was all ablaze with
bliss in a moment. The next moment he was "showing off" with all his might—
cuffing boys, pulling hair, making faces—in a word, using every art that seemed
likely to fascinate a girl and win her applause. His exaltation had but one alloy—
the memory of his humiliation in this angel's garden—and that record in sand
was fast washing out, under the waves of happiness that were sweeping over it
now.

The visitors were given the highest seat of honor, and as soon as Mr. Walters'
speech was finished, he introduced them to the school. The middle-aged man
turned out to be a prodigious personage—no less a one than the county judge—
altogether the most august creation these children had ever looked upon—and
they wondered what kind of material he was made of—and they half wanted to
hear him roar, and were half afraid he might, too. He was from Constantinople,
twelve miles away—so he had traveled, and seen the world—these very eyes
had looked upon the county court house—which was said to have a tin roof.
The awe which these reflections inspired was attested by the impressive silence
and the ranks of staring eyes. This was the great Judge Thatcher, brother of
their own lawyer. Jeff Thatcher immediately went forward, to be familiar with
the great man and be envied by the school. It would have been music to his soul
to hear the whisperings:

"Look at him, Jim! He's a going up there. Say—look! he's a going to shake
hands with him—he *is* shaking hands with him! By jings, don't you wish you
was Jeff?"

Mr. Walters fell to "showing off," with all sorts of official bustlings and
activities giving orders, delivering judgments, discharging directions here, there,
everywhere that he could find a target. The librarian "showed off"—running
hither and thither with his arms full of books and making a deal of the splutter
and fuss that insect authority delights in. The young lady teachers "showed
off"—bending sweetly over pupils that were lately being boxed, lifting pretty
warning fingers at bad little boys and patting good ones lovingly. The young
gentlemen teachers "showed off" with small scoldings and other little displays
of authority and fine attention to discipline—and most of the teachers, of both
sexes, found business up at the library, by the pulpit; and it was business that
frequently had to be done over again two or three times, (with much seeming
vexation.) The little girls "showed off" in various ways, and the little boys
"showed off" with such diligence that the air was thick with paper wads and
the murmur of scufflings. And above it all the great man sat and beamed a
majestic judicial smile upon all the house, and warmed himself in the sun of his
own grandeur—for he was "showing off," too.

There was only one thing wanting, to make Mr. Walters' ecstacy complete,
and that was a chance to deliver a Bible-prize and exhibit a prodigy. Several
pupils had a few yellow tickets, but none had enough—he had been around
among the star pupils inquiring. He would have given worlds, now, to have that
German lad back again with a sound mind.

And now at this moment, when hope was dead, Tom Sawyer came forward
with nine yellow tickets, nine red tickets, and ten blue ones, and demanded a
Bible. This was a thunderbolt out of a clear sky. Walters was not expecting an
application from this source for the next ten years. But there was no getting
around it—here were the certified checks, and they were good for their face.
Tom was therefore elevated to a place with the Judge and the other elect, and

the great news was announced from head-quarters. It was the most stunning surprise of the decade, and so profound was the sensation that it lifted the new hero up to the judicial one's altitude, and the school had two marvels to gaze upon in place of one. The boys were all eaten up with envy—but those that suffered the bitterest pangs were those who perceived too late that they themselves had contributed to this hated splendor by trading tickets to Tom for the wealth he had amassed in selling whitewashing privileges. These despised themselves, as being the dupes of a wily fraud, a guileful snake in the grass.

The prize was delivered to Tom with as much effusion as the Superintendent could pump up under the circumstances; but it lacked somewhat of the true gush, for the poor fellow's instinct taught him that there was a mystery here that could not well bear the light, perhaps; it was simply preposterous that *this* boy had warehoused two thousand sheaves of Scriptural wisdom on his premises—a dozen would strain his capacity, without a doubt.

Amy Lawrence was proud and glad, and she tried to make Tom see it in her face—but he wouldn't look. She wondered; then she was just a grain troubled; next a dim suspicion came and went—came again; she watched; a furtive glance told her worlds—and then her heart broke, and she was jealous, and angry, and the tears came and she hated everybody. Tom most of all, (she thought.)

Tom was introduced to the Judge; but his tongue was tied, his breath would hardly come, his heart quaked—partly because of the awful greatness of the man, but mainly because he was *her* parent. He would have liked to fall down and worship him, if it were in the dark. The Judge put his hand on Tom's head and called him a fine little man, and asked him what his name was. The boy stammered, gasped, and got it out:

"Tom."

"Oh, no, not Tom—it is—"

"Thomas."

"Ah, that's it. I thought there was more to it, maybe. That's very well. But you've another one I daresay, and you'll tell it to me, won't you?"

"Tell the gentleman your other name, Thomas," said Walters, "and say *sir*.—You mustn't forget your manners."

"Thomas Sawyer—sir."

TOM AS A SUNDAY-SCHOOL HERO.

"That's it! That's a good boy. Fine boy. Fine, manly little fellow. Two thousand verses is a great many—very, very great many. And you never can be sorry for the trouble you took to learn them; for knowledge is worth more than anything there is in the world; it's what makes great men and good men; you'll be a great man and a good man yourself, some day, Thomas, and then you'll look back and say, It's all owing to the precious Sunday-school privileges of my boyhood—it's all owing to my dear teachers that taught me to learn—it's all owing to the good Superintendent, who encouraged me, and watched over me, and gave me a beautiful Bible—a splendid elegant Bible, to keep and have it all for my own, always—it's all owing to right bringing up! That is what you will say, Thomas—and you wouldn't take any money for those two thousand verses—no indeed you wouldn't. And now you wouldn't mind telling me and this lady some of the things you've learned—no, I know you wouldn't—for we are proud of little boys that learn. Now no doubt you know the names of all the twelve disciples. Won't you tell us the names of the first two that were appointed?"

Tom was tugging at a button hole and looking sheepish. He blushed, now, and his eyes fell. Mr. Walters' heart sank within him. He said to himself, it is not possible that the boy can answer the simplest question—why *did* the Judge ask him? Yet he felt obliged to speak up and say;

"Answer the gentleman, Thomas—don't be afraid."

Tom still hung fire.

"Now I know you'll tell *me*" said the lady. "The names of the first two disciples were—"

"DAVID AND GOLIAH!"

Let us draw the curtain of charity over the rest of the scene.

Chapter V

ABOUT HALF-PAST TEN the cracked bell of the small church began to ring, and presently the people began to gather for the morning sermon. The Sunday school children distributed themselves about the house and occupied pews with their parents, so as to be under supervision. Aunt Polly came, and Tom and Sid and Mary sat with her—Tom being placed next the aisle, in order that he might be as far away from the open window and the seductive outside summer scenes as possible. The crowd filed up the aisles: the aged and needy postmaster, who had seen better days; the mayor and his wife—for they had a mayor there, among other unnecessaries; the justice of the peace; the widow Douglas, fair, smart and forty, a generous, good-hearted soul and well-to-do, her hill mansion the only palace in the town, and the most hospitable and much the most lavish in the matter of festivities that St. Petersburg could boast; the bent and venerable Major and Mrs. Ward; lawyer Riverson, the new notable from a distance; next the belle of the village, followed by a troop of lawn-clad and ribbon-decked young heart-breakers; then all the young clerks in town in a body—for they had stood in the vestibule sucking their cane-heads, a circling wall of oiled and simpering admirers, till the last girl had run their gauntlet; and last of all came the Model Boy, Willie Mufferson, taking as heedful care of his mother as if she were cut glass. He always brought his mother to church, and was the pride of all the

matrons. The boys all hated him, he was so good. And besides, he had been
"thrown up to them" so much. His white handkerchief was hanging out of his
pocket behind, as usual on Sundays—accidentally. Tom had no handkerchief,
and he looked upon boys who had, as snobs.

The congregation being fully assembled, now, the bell rang once more, to
warn laggards and stragglers, and then a solemn hush fell upon the church which
was only broken by the tittering and whispering of the choir in the gallery. The
choir always tittered and whispered all through service. There was once a church
choir that was not ill-bred, but I have forgotten where it was, now. It was a
great many years ago, and I can scarcely remember anything about it, but I think
it was in some foreign country.

The minister gave out the hymn, and read it through with a relish, in a peculiar
style which was much admired in that part of the country. His voice began on
a medium key and climbed steadily up till it reached a certain point, where it
bore with strong emphasis upon the topmost word and then plunged down as if
from a spring-board:

Shall I be car-ri-ed to the skies, on flow'ry *beds*

of ease,

Whilst others fight to win the prize, and sail thro' *blood-*

-y seas?

He was regarded as a wonderful reader. At church "sociables" he was always
called upon to read poetry; and when he was through, the ladies would lift up
their hands and let them fall helplessly in their laps, and "wall" their eyes, and
shake their heads, as much as to say, "Words cannot express it; it is too beautiful,
too beautiful for this mortal earth."

After the hymn had been sung, the Rev. Mr. Sprague turned himself into a
bulletin board, and read off "notices" of meetings and societies and things till
it seemed that the list would stretch out to the crack of doom—a queer custom
which is still kept up in America, even in cities, away here in this age of abundant
newspapers. Often, the less there is to justify a traditional custom, the harder it
is to get rid of it.

And now the minister prayed. A good, generous prayer, it was, and went into
details: it pleaded for the church, and the little children of the church; for the
other churches of the village; for the village itself; for the county; for the State;
for the State officers; for the United States; for the churches of the United States;
for Congress; for the President; for the officers of the Government; for poor
sailors, tossed by stormy seas; for the oppressed millions groaning under the
heel of European monarchies and Oriental despotisms; for such as have the light
and the good tidings, and yet have not eyes to see nor ears to hear withal; for
the heathen in the far islands of the sea; and closed with a supplication that the
words he was about to speak might flnd grace and favor, and be as seed sown
in fertile ground, yielding in time a grateful harvest of good. Amen.

There was a rustling of dresses, and the standing congregation sat down. The
boy whose history this book relates did not enjoy the prayer, he only endured
it—if he even did that much. He was restive all through it; he kept tally of the

details of the prayer, unconsciously—for he was not listening, but he knew the ground of old, and the clergyman's regular route over it—and when a little trifle of new matter was interlarded, his ear detected it and his whole nature resented it; he considered additions unfair, and scoundrelly. In the midst of the prayer a fly had lit on the back of the pew in front of him and tortured his spirit by calmly rubbing its hands together, embracing its head with its arms, and polishing it so vigorously that it seemed to almost part company with the body, and the slender thread of a neck was exposed to view; scraping its wings with its hind legs and smoothing them to its body as if they had been coat tails; going through its whole toilet as tranquilly as if it knew it was perfectly safe. As indeed it was; for as sorely as Tom's hands itched to grab for it they did not dare—he believed his soul would be instantly destroyed if he did such a thing while the prayer was going on. But with the closing sentence his hand began to curve and steal forward; and the instant the "Amen" was out the fly was a prisoner of war. His aunt detected the act and made him let it go.

The minister gave out his text and droned along monotonously through an argument that was so prosy that many a head by and by began to nod—and yet it was an argument that dealt in limitless fire and brimstone and thinned the predestined elect down to a company so small as to be hardly worth the saving. Tom counted the pages of the sermon; after church he always knew how many pages there had been, but he seldom knew anything else about the discourse. However, this time he was really interested for a little while. The minister made a grand and moving picture of the assembling together of the world's hosts at the millennium when the lion and the lamb should lie down together and a little child should lead them. But the pathos, the lesson, the moral of the great spectacle were lost upon the boy; he only thought of the conspicuousness of the principal character before the on-looking nations; his face lit with the thought, and he said to himself that he wished he could be that child, if it was a tame lion.

Now he lapsed into suffering again, as the dry argument was resumed. Presently he bethought him of a treasure he had and got it out. It was a large black beetle with formidable jaws—a "pinch-bug," he called it. It was in a percussion-cap box. The first thing the beetle did was to take him by the finger. A natural fillip followed, the beetle went floundering into the aisle and lit on its back, and the hurt finger went into the boy's mouth. The beetle lay there working its helpless legs, unable to turn over. Tom eyed it, and longed for it; but it was safe out of his reach. Other people uninterested in the sermon, found relief in the beetle, and they eyed it too. Presently a vagrant poodle dog came idling along, sad at heart, lazy with the summer softness and the quiet, weary of captivity, sighing for change. He spied the beetle; the drooping tail lifted and wagged. He surveyed the prize; walked around it; smelt at it from a safe distance; walked around it again; grew bolder, and took a closer smell; then lifted his lip and made a gingerly snatch at it, just missing it; made another, and another; began to enjoy the diversion; subsided to his stomach with the beetle between his paws, and continued his experiments; grew weary at last, and then indifferent and absent-minded. His head nodded, and little by little his chin descended and touched the enemy, who seized it. There was a sharp yelp, a flirt of the poodle's head, and the beetle fell a couple of yards away, and lit on its back once more. The neighboring spectators shook with a gentle inward joy, several faces went behind fans and handkerchiefs, and Tom was entirely happy. The dog looked foolish, and probably felt so; but there was resentment in his heart, too, and a craving for revenge. So he went to the beetle and began a wary attack on it again; jumping at it from every point of a circle, lighting with his fore paws within an inch of the creature, making even closer snatches at it with his teeth, and jerking his head till his ears flapped again. But he grew tired once more, after a while; tried to amuse himself with a fly but found no relief; followed an ant around, with his nose close to the floor, and quickly wearied of that; yawned, sighed, forgot the beetle entirely, and sat down on it! Then there was a wild yelp of agony and the poodle went sailing up the aisle; the yelps continued, and so did the dog; he crossed the house in front of the altar; he flew down the other aisle; he crossed before the doors; he clamored up the home-stretch; his anguish grew with his progress, till presently he was but a woolly comet moving in its orbit with the gleam and the speed of light. At last the frantic sufferer sheered from its course, and sprang into its master's lap; he flung it out of the window, and the voice of distress quickly thinned away and died in the distance.

By this time the whole church was red-faced and suffocating with suppressed laughter, and the sermon had come to a dead stand-still. The discourse was resumed presently, but it went lame and halting, all possibility of impressiveness being at an end; for even the gravest sentiments were constantly being received with a smothered burst of unholy mirth, under cover of some remote pew-back, as if the poor parson had said a rarely facetious thing. It was a genuine relief to the whole congregation when the ordeal was over and the benediction pronounced.

Tom Sawyer went home quite cheerful, thinking to himself that there was some satisfaction about divine service when there was a bit of variety in it. He had but one marring thought; he was willing that the dog should play with his pinch-bug, but he did not think it was upright in him to carry it off.

Chapter VI

MONDAY MORNING FOUND Tom Sawyer miserable. Monday morning always found him so—because it began another week's slow suffering in school. He generally began that day with wishing he had had no intervening holiday, it made the going into captivity and fetters again so much more odious.

Tom lay thinking. Presently it occurred to him that he wished he was sick; then he could stay home from school. Here was a vague possibility. He canvassed his system. No ailment was found, and he investigated again. This time he thought he could detect colicky symptoms, and he began to encourage them with considerable hope. But they soon grew feeble, and presently died wholly away. He reflected further. Suddenly he discovered something. One of his upper front teeth was loose. This was lucky; he was about to begin to groan, as a "starter," as he called it, when it occurred to him that if he came into court with that argument, his aunt would pull it out, and that would hurt. So he thought he would hold the tooth in reserve for the present, and seek further. Nothing offered for some little time, and then he remembered hearing the doctor tell about a certain thing that laid up a patient for two or three weeks and threatened to make him lose a finger. So the boy eagerly drew his sore toe from under the sheet and held it up for inspection. But now he did not know the necessary symptoms.

However, it seemed well worth while to chance it, so he fell to groaning with considerable spirit.

But Sid slept on unconscious.

Tom groaned louder, and fancied that he began to feel pain in the toe.

No result from Sid.

Tom was panting with his exertions by this time. He took a rest and then swelled himself up and fetched a succession of admirable groans.

Sid snored on.

Tom was aggravated. He said, "Sid, Sid!" and shook him. This course worked well, and Tom began to groan again. Sid yawned, stretched, then brought himself up on his elbow with a snort, and began to stare at Tom. Tom went on groaning. Sid said:

"Tom! Say, Tom!" [No response.] "Here Tom! *Tom!* What is the matter, Tom?" And he shook him and looked in his face anxiously.

Tom moaned out:

"O don't, Sid. Don't joggle me."

"Why what's the matter Tom? I must call auntie."

"No—never mind. It'll be over by and by, maybe. Don't call anybody."

"But I must! *Don't* groan so, Tom, it's awful. How long you been this way?"

"Hours. Ouch! O don't stir so, Sid, you'll kill me."

"Tom, why didn't you wake me sooner? O, Tom, *don't!* It makes my flesh crawl to hear you. Tom, what *is* the matter?"

"I forgive you everything, Sid. [Groan.] Everything you've ever done to me. When I'm gone—"

"O, Tom, you ain't dying are you? Don't, Tom—O, don't. Maybe—"

"I forgive everybody, Sid. [Groan.] Tell 'em so, Sid. And Sid, you give my window-sash and my cat with one eye to that new girl that's come to town, and tell her—"

But Sid had snatched his clothes and gone. Tom was suffering in reality, now, so handsomely was his imagination working, and so his groans had gathered quite a genuine tone.

Sid flew down stairs and said:

"O, Aunt Polly, come! Tom's dying!"

"Dying!"

"Yes'm. Don't wait—come quick!"

"Rubbage! I don't believe it!"

But she fled up stairs, nevertheless, with Sid and Mary at her heels. And her face grew white, too, and her lip trembled. When she reached the bedside she gasped out:

"You Tom! Tom, what's the matter with you?"

"O, auntie, I'm—"

"What's the matter with you—what *is* the matter with you, child?"

"O auntie, my sore toe's mortified!"

The old lady sank down into a chair and laughed a little, then cried a little, then did both together. This restored her and she said:

"Tom, what a turn you did give me. Now you shut up that nonsense and climb out of this."

The groans ceased and the pain vanished from the toe. The boy felt a little foolish, and he said:

"Aunt Polly it *seemed* mortified, and it hurt so I never minded my tooth at all."

"Your tooth, indeed! What's the matter with your tooth?"

"One of them's loose, and it aches perfectly awful."

"There, there, now, don't begin that groaning again. Open your mouth. Well—your tooth *is* loose, but you're not going to die about that. Mary get me a silk thread, and a chunk of fire out of the kitchen."

Tom said:

"O, please auntie, don't pull it out. It don't hurt any more. I wish I may never stir if it does. Please don't, auntie. *I* don't want to stay home from school."

"Oh, you don't, don't you? So all this row was because you thought you'd get to stay home from school and go a fishing? Tom, Tom, I love you so, and you seem to try every way you can to break my old heart with your outrageousness." By this time the dental instruments were ready. The old lady made one end of the silk thread fast to Tom's tooth with a loop and tied the other to the bed-post. Then she seized the chunk of fire and suddenly thrust it almost into the boy's face. The tooth hung dangling by the bedpost, now.

But all trials bring their compensations. As Tom wended to school after breakfast, he was the envy of every boy he met because the gap in his upper row of teeth enabled him to expectorate in a new and admirable way. He gathered quite a following of lads interested in the exhibition; and one that had cut his finger and had been a centre of fascination and homage up to this time, now found himself suddenly without an adherent, and shorn of his glory. His heart was heavy, and he said with a disdain which he did not feel, that it wasn't anything to spit like Tom Sawyer; but another boy said "Sour grapes!" and he wandered away a dismantled hero.

Shortly Tom came upon the juvenile pariah of the village, Huckleberry Finn, son of the town drunkard. Huckleberry was cordially hated and dreaded by all the mothers of the town, because he was idle, and lawless, and vulgar and bad— and because all their children admired him so, and delighted in his forbidden society, and wished they dared to be like him. Tom was like the rest of the respectable boys, in that he envied Huckleberry his gaudy outcast condition, and was under strict orders not to play with him. So he played with him every time

DENTISTRY.

he got a chance. Huckleberry was always dressed in the cast-off clothes of full-grown men, and they were in perennial bloom and fluttering with rags. His hat was a vast ruin with a wide crescent lopped out of its brim; his coat, when he wore one, hung nearly to his heels and had the rearward buttons far down the back; but one suspender supported his trousers; the seat of the trousers bagged low and contained nothing; the fringed legs dragged in the dirt when not rolled up.

Huckleberry came and went, at his own free will. He slept on door-steps in fine weather and in empty hogsheads in wet; he did not have to go to school or to church, or call any being master or obey anybody; he could go fishing or swimming when and where he chose, and stay as long as it suited him; nobody forbade him to fight; he could sit up as late as he pleased; he was always the first boy that went barefoot in the spring and the last to resume leather in the fall; he never had to wash, nor put on clean clothes; he could swear wonderfully. In a word, everything that goes to make life precious, that boy had. So thought every harassed, hampered, respectable boy in St. Petersburg.

Tom hailed the romantic outcast:

"Hello, Huckleberry!"

"Hello yourself, and see how you like it."

"What's that you got?"

"Dead cat."

"Lemme see him Huck. My, he's pretty stiff. Where'd you get him?"

"Bought him off'n a boy."

"What did you give?"

"I give a blue ticket and a bladder that I got at the slaughter house."

"Where'd you get the blue ticket?"

"Bought it off'n Ben Rogers two weeks ago for a hoop-stick."

"Say—what is dead cats good for, Huck?"

"Good for? Cure warts with."

"No! Is that so? I know something that's better."

"I bet you don't. What is it?"

"Why, spunk-water."

"Spunk-water! I wouldn't give a dern for spunk-water."

HUCKLEBERRY FINN.

"You wouldn't wouldn't you? D'you ever try it?"

"No, I hain't. But Bob Tanner did."

"Who told you so!"

"Why he told Jeff Thatcher, and Jeff told Johnny Baker, and Johnny told Jim Hollis, and Jim told Ben Rogers, and Ben told a nigger, and the nigger told me. There now!"

"Well, what of it? They'll all lie. Leastways all but the nigger. I don't know *him*. But I never see a nigger that *wouldn't* lie. Shucks! Now you tell me how Bob Tanner done it, Huck."

"Why he took and dipped his hand in a rotten stump where the rain water was."

"In the day time?"

"Certainly."

"With his face to the stump?"

"Yes. Least I reckon so."

"Did he *say* anything?"

"I don't reckon he did. I don't know."

"Aha! Talk about trying to cure warts with spunk-water such a blame fool way as that! Why that ain't a going to do any good. You got to go all by yourself, to the middle of the woods, where you know there's a spunk-water stump, and just as it's midnight you back up against the stump and jam your hand in and say:

> "Barley-corn, Barley-corn, injun-meal shorts,
> Spunk-water, spunk-water, swaller these warts."

and then walk away quick, eleven steps, with your eyes shut, and then turn around three times and walk home without speaking to anybody. Because if you speak the charm's busted."

"Well that sounds like a good way; but that ain't the way Bob Tanner done."

"No, sir, you can bet he didn't, becuz he's the wartiest boy in this town; and he wouldn't have a wart on him if he'd knowed how to work spunk-water. I've took off thousands of warts off of my hands that way Huck. I play with frogs so much that I've always got considerable many warts. Sometimes I take 'em off with a bean."

"Yes, bean's good. I've done that."

"Have you? What's your way?"

"You take and split the bean, and cut the wart so as to get some blood, and then you put the blood on one piece of the bean and take and dig a hole and bury it 'bout midnight at the cross-roads in the dark of the moon, and then you burn up the rest of the bean. You see that piece that's got the blood on it will keep drawing and drawing, trying to fetch the other piece to it, and so that helps the blood to draw the wart, and pretty soon off she comes."

"Yes that's it Huck—that's it; though when you're burying it if you say 'Down bean; off wart; come no more to bother me!' it's better. That's the way Jo Harper does, and he's been nearly to Coonville and most everywheres. But say—how do you cure 'em with dead cats?"

"Why you take your cat and go and get in the graveyard 'long about midnight when somebody that was wicked has been buried; and when it's midnight a devil will come, or maybe two or three, but you can't see 'em, you can only hear something like the wind, or maybe hear 'em talk; and when they're taking that feller away, you heave your cat after 'em and say 'Devil follow corpse, cat follow devil, warts follow cat, *I*'m done with ye!' That'll fetch *any* wart.''

"Sounds right. D'you ever try it, Huck?"

"No, but old mother Hopkins told me."

"Well I reckon it's so, then. Becuz they say she's a witch."

"Say! Why Tom I *know* she is. She witched pap. Pap says so his own self. He come along one day, and he see she was a witching him, so he took up a rock, and if she hadn't dodged, he'd a got her. Well that very night he rolled off'n a shed wher' he was a layin drunk, and broke his arm."

"Why that's awful. How did he know she was a witching him."

"Lord, pap can tell, easy. Pap says when they keep looking at you right stiddy, they're a witching you. Specially if they mumble. Becuz when they mumble they're saying the Lord's Prayer back-ards."

"Say, Hucky, when you going to try the cat?"

"To-night. I reckon they'll come after old Hoss Williams to-night."

"But they buried him Saturday. Didn't they get him Saturday night?"

"Why how you talk! How could their charms work till midnight?—and *then* it's Sunday. Devils don't slosh around much of a Sunday, I don't reckon."

"I never thought of that. That's so. Lemme go with you?"

"Of course—if you ain't afeard."

"Afeard! 'Tain't likely. Will you meow?"

"Yes—and you meow back, if you get a chance. Last time, you kep' me a meowing around till old Hays went to throwing rocks at me and says 'Dern that cat!' and so I hove a brick through his window—but don't you tell."

"I won't. I couldn't meow that night, becuz auntie was watching me, but I'll meow this time. Say—what's that?"

"Nothing but a tick."

"Where'd you get him?"

"Out in the woods."

"What'll you take for him?"

"I don't know. I don't want to sell him."

"All right. It's a mighty small tick, anyway."

"O, anybody can run a tick down that don't belong to them. I'm satisfied with it. It's a good enough tick for me."

"Sho, there's ticks a plenty. I could have a thousand of 'em if I wanted to."

"Well why don't you? Becuz you know mighty well you can't. This is a pretty early tick, I reckon. It's the first one I've seen this year."

"Say Huck—I'll give you my tooth for him."

"Less see it."

Tom got out a bit of paper and carefully unrolled it. Huckleberry viewed it wistfully. The temptation was very strong. At last he said:

"Is it genuwyne?"

Tom lifted his lip aud showed the vacancy.

"Well, all right," said Huckleberry, "it's a trade."

Tom enclosed the tick in the percussion-cap box that had lately been the pinch-bug's prison, and the boys separated, each feeling wealthier than before.

When Tom reached the little isolated frame School-house, he strode in briskly, with the manner of one who had come with all honest speed. He hung his hat on a peg and flung himself into his seat with business-like alacrity. The master, throned on high in his great splint-bottom arm-chair, was dozing, lulled by the drowsy hum of study. The interruption roused him.

"Thomas Sawyer!"

Tom knew that when his name was pronounced in full, it meant trouble.

"Sir!"

"Come up here. Now sir, why are you late again, as usual?"

Tom was about to take refuge in a lie, when he saw two long tails of yellow hair hanging down a back that he recognized by the electric sympathy of love; and by that form was *the only vacant place* on the girl's side of the school-house. He instantly said:

"I STOPPED TO TALK WITH HUCKLEBERRY FINN!"

The master's pulse stood still, and he stared helplessly. The buzz of study ceased. The pupils wondered if this fool-hardy boy had lost his mind. The master said:

"You—you did what?"

"Stopped to talk with Huckleberry Finn."

There was no mistaking the words.

"Thomas Sawyer, this is the most astounding confession I have ever listened to. No mere ferule will answer for this offence. Take off your jacket."

The master's arm performed until it was tired and the stock of switches notably diminished. Then the order followed:

"Now sir, go and sit with the *girls!* And let this be a warning to you."

The titter that rippled around the room appeared to abash the boy, but in reality that result was caused rather more by his worshipful awe of his unknown idol and the dread pleasure that lay in his high good fortune. He sat down upon the end of the pine bench and the girl hitched herself away from him with a toss of her head. Nudges and winks and whispers traversed the room, but Tom sat still, with his arms upon the long, low desk before him, and seemed to study his book.

By and by attention ceased from him, and the accustomed school murmur rose upon the dull air once more. Presently the boy began to steal furtive glances at the girl. She observed it, "made a mouth" at him and gave him the back of her head for the space of a minute. When she cautiously faced around again, a peach lay before her. She thrust it away. Tom gently put it back. She thrust it away, again, but with less animosity. Tom patiently returned it to its place. Then she let it remain. Tom scrawled on his slate, "Please take it—I got more." The girl glanced at the words, but made no sign. Now the boy began to draw something on the slate, hiding his work with his left hand. For a time the girl refused to notice; but her human curiosity presently began to manifest itself by hardly perceptible signs. The boy worked on, apparently unconscious. The girl made a sort of non-committal attempt to see, but the boy did not betray that he was aware of it. At last she gave in and hesitatingly whispered:

"Let me see it."

Tom partly uncovered a dismal caricature of a house with two gable ends to it and a cork-screw of smoke issuing from the chimney. Then the girl's interest began to fasten itself upon the work and she forgot everything else. When it was finished, she gazed a moment, then whispered:

"It's nice—make a man."

The artist erected a man in the front yard, that resembled a derrick. He could have stepped over the house; but the girl was not hypercritical; she was satisfied with the monster, and whispered:

"It's a beautiful man—now make me coming along."

Tom drew an hour-glass with a full moon and straw limbs to it and armed the spreading fingers with a portentous fan. The girl said:

"It's ever so nice—I wish I could draw."

"It's easy," whispered Tom, "I'll learn you."

"O, will you? When?"

"At noon. Do you go home to dinner?"

"I'll stay if you will."

"Good,—that's a whack. What's your name?"

"Becky Thatcher. What's yours? Oh, I know. It's Thomas Sawyer."

"That's the name they lick me by. I'm Tom when I'm good. You call me Tom, will you?"

"Yes."

Now Tom began to scrawl something on the slate, hiding the words from the girl. But she was not backward this time. She begged to see. Tom said:

"Oh it ain't anything."

"Yes it is."

"No it ain't. You don't want to see."

"Yes I do, indeed I do. Please let me."

"You'll tell."

"No I won't—deed and deed and double deed I won't."

"You won't tell anybody at all? Ever, as long as you live?"

"No I won't ever tell *any*body. Now let me."

"Oh, *you* don't want to see!"

"Now that you treat me so, I *will* see." And she put her small hand upon his and a little scuffle ensued, Tom pretending to resist in earnest but letting his hand slip by degrees till these words were revealed: "*I love you.*"

"O, you bad thing!" And she hit his hand a smart rap but reddened and looked pleased, nevertheless.

Just at this juncture the boy felt a slow, fateful grip closing on his ear, and a steady lifting impulse. In that vise he was borne across the house and deposited

TOM AS AN ARTIST.

in his own seat, under a peppering fire of giggles from the whole school. Then the master stood over him during a few awful moments, and finally moved away to his throne without saying a word. But although Tom's ear tingled, his heart was jubilant.

As the school quieted down Tom made an honest effort to study, but the turmoil within him was too great. In turn he took his place in the reading class and made a botch of it; then in the geography class and turned lakes into mountains, mountains into rivers, and rivers into continents, till chaos was come again; then in the spelling class, and got "turned down," by a succession of mere baby words till he brought up at the foot and yielded up the pewter medal which he had worn with ostentation for months.

Chapter VII

THE HARDER TOM tried to fasten his mind on his book, the more his ideas wandered. So at last, with a sigh and a yawn, he gave it up. It seemed to him that the noon recess would never come. The air was utterly dead. There was not a breath stirring. It was the sleepiest of sleepy days. The drowsing murmur of the five and twenty studying scholars, soothed the soul like the spell that is in the murmur of bees. Away off in the flaming sunshine, Cardiff Hill lifted its soft green sides through a shimmering veil of heat, tinted with the purple of distance; a few birds floated on lazy wing high in the air; no other living thing was visible but some cows, and they were asleep. Tom's heart ached to be free, or else to have something of interest to do to pass the dreary time. His hand wandered into his pocket and his face lit up with a glow of gratitude that was prayer, though he did not know it. Then furtively the percussion-cap box came out. He released the tick and put him on the long flat desk. The creature probably glowed with a gratitude that amounted to prayer, too, at this moment, but it was premature: for when he started thankfully to travel off, Tom turned him aside with a pin and made him take a new direction.

Tom's bosom friend sat next him, suffering just as Tom had been, and now he was deeply and gratefully interested in this entertainment in an instant. This bosom friend was Joe Harper. The two boys were sworn friends all the week, and embattled enemies on Saturdays. Joe took a pin out of his lappel and began to assist in exercising the prisoner. The sport grew in interest momently. Soon Tom said that they were interfering with each other, and neither getting the fullest benefit of the tick. So he put Joe's slate on the desk and drew a line down the middle of it from top to bottom.

"Now," said he, "as long as he is on your side you can stir him up and I'll let him alone; but if you let him get away and get on my side, you're to leave him alone as long as I can keep him from crossing over."

"All right, go ahead; start him up."

The tick escaped from Tom, presently, and crossed the equator. Joe harassed him a while, and then he got away and crossed back again. This change of base occurred often. While one boy was worrying the tick with absorbing interest, the other would look on with interest as strong, the two heads bowed together over the slate, and the two souls dead to all things else. At last luck seemed to settle and abide with Joe. The tick tried this, that, and the other course, and got as excited and as anxious as the boys themselves, but time and again just as he would have victory in his very grasp, so to speak, and Tom's fingers would be twitching to begin, Joe's pin would deftly head him off, and keep possession. At last Tom could stand it no longer. The temptation was too strong. So he reached out and lent a hand with his pin. Joe was angry in a moment. Said he:

"Tom, you let him alone."

"I only just want to stir him up a little, Joe."

"No, sir, it ain't fair; you just let him alone."

"Blame it, I ain't going to stir him much."

"Let him alone, I tell you!"

"I won't!"

"You shall—he's on my side of the line."

"Look here, Joe Harper, whose is that tick?"

"*I* don't care whose tick he is—he's on my side of the line, and you shan't touch him."

"Well I'll just bet I will, though. He's my tick and I'll do what I blame please with him, or die!"

A tremendous whack came down on Tom's shoulders, and its duplicate on Joe's; and for the space of two minutes the dust continued to fly from the two jackets and the whole school to enjoy it. The boys had been too absorbed to notice the hush that had stolen upon the school a while before when the master came tip-toeing down the room and stood over them. He had contemplated a good part of the performance before he contributed his bit of variety to it.

When school broke up at noon, Tom flew to Becky Thatcher, and whispered in her ear:

"Put on your bonnet and let on you're going home; and when you get to the corner, give the rest of 'em the slip, and turn down through the lane and come back. I'll go the other way and come it over 'em the same way."

So the one went off with one group of scholars, and the other with another. In a little while the two met at the bottom of the lane, and when they reached the school they had it all to themselves. Then they sat together, with a slate before them, and Tom gave Becky the pencil and held her hand in his, guiding it, and so created another surprising house. When the interest in art began to wane, the two fell to talking. Tom was swimming in bliss. He said:

"Do you love rats?"

"No! I hate them!"

"Well, I do too—*live* ones. But I mean dead ones, to swing round your head with a string."

"No, I don't care for rats much, anyway. What *I* like is chewing-gum."

"O, I should say so! I wish I had some now."

"Do you? I've got some. I'll let you chew it awhile, but you must give it back to me."

That was agreeable, so they chewed it turn about, and dangled their legs against the bench in excess of contentment.

"Was you ever at a circus?" said Tom.

"Yes, and my pa's going to take me again some time, if I'm good."

"I been to the circus three or four times—lots of times. Church ain't shucks to a circus. There's things going on at a circus all the time. I'm going to be a clown in a circus when I grow up."

"O, are you! That will be nice. They're so lovely, all spotted up."

"Yes, that's so. And they get slathers of money—most a dollar a day, Ben Rogers says. Say, Becky, was you ever engaged?"

"What's that?"

"Why, engaged to be married."

"No."

"Would you like to?"

"I reckon so. I don't know. What is it like?"

"Like? Why it ain't like anything. You only just tell a boy you won't ever have any body but him, ever ever *ever*, and then you kiss and that's all. Anybody can do it."

"Kiss? What do you kiss for?"

"Why that, you know, is to—well, they always do that."

"Everybody?"

"Why yes, everybody that's in love with each other. Do you remember what I wrote on the slate?"

"Ye—yes."

"What was it?"

"I shant tell you."

"Shall I tell *you*?"

"Ye—yes—but some other time."

"No, now."

"No, not now—to-morrow."

"O, no, *now*. Please Becky—I'll whisper it, I'll whisper it ever so easy."

Becky hesitating, Tom took silence for consent, and passed his arm about her waist and whispered the tale ever so softly, with his mouth close to her ear. And then he added:

"Now you whisper it to me—just the same."

She resisted, for a while, and then said:

"You turn your face away so you can't see, and then I will. But you mustn't ever tell anybody—*will* you, Tom? Now you won't, *will* you?"

"No, indeed indeed I won't. Now Becky."

He turned his face away. She bent timidly around till her breath stirred his curls and whispered, "I—love—you!"

Then she sprang away and ran around and around the desks and benches, with Tom after her, and took refuge in a corner at last, with her little white apron to her face. Tom clasped her about her neck and pleaded:

"Now Becky, it's all done—all over but the kiss. Don't you be afraid of that—it aint anything at all. Please, Becky."—And he tugged at her apron and the hands.

By and by she gave up, and let her hands drop; her face, all glowing with the struggle, came up and submitted. Tom kissed the red lips and said:

"Now it's all done, Becky. And always after this, you know, you ain't ever to love anybody but me, and you ain't ever to marry anybody but me, never never and forever. Will you?"

"No, I'll never love anybody but you, Tom, and I'll never marry anybody but you—and you ain't to ever marry anybody but me, either."

"Certainly. Of course. That's *part* of it. And always coming to school or when we're going home, you're to walk with me, when there ain't anybody looking—and you choose me and I choose you at parties, because that's the way you do when you're engaged.''

"It's so nice. I never heard of it before.''

"Oh its ever so gay! Why me and Amy Lawrence''—

The big eyes told Tom his blunder and he stopped, confused.

"O, Tom! Then I ain't the first you've ever been engaged to!''

The child began to cry. Tom said:

"O don't cry, Becky, I don't care for her any more.''

"Yes you do, Tom,—you know you do.''

Tom tried to put his arm about her neck, but she pushed him away and turned her face to the wall, and went on crying. Tom tried again, with soothing words in his mouth, and was repulsed again. Then his pride was up, and he strode away and went outside. He stood about, restless and uneasy, for a while, glancing at the door, every now and then, hoping she would repent and come to find him. But she did not. Then he began to feel badly and fear that he was in the wrong. It was a hard struggle with him to make new advances, now, but he nerved himself to it and entered. She was still standing back there in the corner, sobbing, with her face to the wall. Tom's heart smote him. He went to her and stood a moment, not knowing exactly how to proceed. Then he said hesitatingly:

"Becky, I—I don't care for anybody but you.''

No reply—but sobs. "Becky,''—pleadingly. "Becky, won't you say something?''

More sobs.

Tom got out his chiefest jewel, a brass knob from the top of an andiron, and passed it around her so that she could see it, and said:

"Please, Becky, won't you take it?''

She struck it to the floor. Then Tom marched out of the house and over the hills and far away, to return to school no more that day. Presently Becky began to suspect. She ran to the door; he was not in sight; she flew around to the play-yard; he was not there. Then she called:

"Tom! Come back Tom!''

She listened intently, but there was no answer. She had no companions but silence and loneliness. So she sat down to cry again and upbraid herself; and

VAIN PLEADING.

by this time the scholars began to gather again, and she had to hide her griefs and still her broken heart and take up the cross of a long, dreary, aching afternoon, with none among the strangers about her to exchange sorrows with.

Chapter VIII

TOM DODGED HITHER and thither through lanes until he was well out of the track of returning scholars, and then fell into a moody jog. He crossed a small "branch" two or three times, because of a prevailing juvenile superstition that to cross water baffled pursuit. Half an hour later he was disappearing behind the Douglas mansion on the summit of Cardiff Hill, and the school-house was hardly distinguishable away off in the valley behind him. He entered a dense wood, picked his pathless way to the centre of it, and sat down on a mossy spot under a spreading oak. There was not even a zephyr stirring; the dead noonday heat had even stilled the songs of the birds; nature lay in a trance that was broken by no sound but the occasional far-off hammering of a woodpecker, and this seemed to render the pervading silence and sense of loneliness the more profound. The boy's soul was steeped in melancholy; his feelings were in happy accord with his surroundings. He sat long with his elbows on his knees and his chin in his hands, meditating. It seemed to him that life was but a trouble, at best, and he more than half envied Jimmy Hodges, so lately released; it must be very peaceful, he thought, to lie and slumber and dream forever and ever, with the wind whispering through the trees and caressing the grass and the flowers over the grave, and nothing to bother and grieve about, ever any more. If he only had a clean Sunday-school record he could be willing to go, and be done with it all. Now as to this girl. What had he done? Nothing. He had meant the best in the world, and been treated like a dog—like a very dog. She would be sorry some day—maybe when it was too late. Ah, if he could only die *temporarily!*

But the elastic heart of youth cannot be compressed into one constrained shape long at a time. Tom presently began to drift insensibly back into the concerns of this life again. What if he turned his back, now, and disappeared mysteriously? What if he went away—ever so far away, into unknown countries beyond the seas—and never come back any more! How would she feel then! The idea of being a clown recurred to him now, only to fill him with disgust. For frivolity and jokes and spotted tights were an offense, when they intruded themselves upon a spirit that was exalted into the vague august realm of the romantic. No, he would be a soldier, and return after long years, all war-worn and illustrious. No—better still, he would join the Indians, and hunt buffaloes and go on the warpath in the mountain ranges and the trackless great plains of the Far West, and away in the future come back a great chief, bristling with feathers, hideous with paint, and prance into Sunday-school, some drowsy summer morning, with a blood-curdling war-whoop, and sear the eye-balls of all his companions with unappeasable envy. But no, there was something gaudier even than this. He would be a pirate! That was it! *Now* his future lay plain before him, and glowing with unimaginable splendor. How his name would fill the world, and make people shudder! How gloriously he would go plowing the dancing seas, in his long, low, black-hulled racer, the "Spirit of the Storm," with his grisly flag flying at the fore! And at the zenith of his fame, how he would suddenly appear at the old village and stalk into church, brown and weather-beaten, in his black velvet doublet and trunks, his great jack-boots, his crimson sash, his belt bristling with horse-pistols, his crime-rusted cutlass at his side, his slouch hat with waving plumes, his black flag unfurled, with the skull and cross-bones on it, and hear with swelling ecstasy the whisperings, "It's Tom Sawyer the Pirate!—the Black Avenger of the Spanish Main!"

Yes, it was settled; his career was determined. He would run away from home and enter upon it. He would start the very next morning. Therefore he must now begin to get ready. He would collect his resources together. He went to a rotten log near at hand and began to dig under one end of it with his Barlow knife. He soon struck wood that sounded hollow. He put his hand there and uttered this incantation impressively:

"What hasn't come here, *come!* What's here, *stay* here!"

Then he scraped away the dirt, and exposed a pine shingle. He took it up and disclosed a shapely little treasure-house whose bottom and sides were of shingles. In it lay a marble. Tom's astonishment was boundless! He scratched his head with a perplexed air, and said:

"Well, that beats anything!"

Then he tossed the marble away pettishly, and stood cogitating. The truth was, that a superstition of his had failed, here, which he and all his comrades had always looked upon as infallible. If you buried a marble with certain necessary incantations, and left it alone a fortnight, and then opened the place with the incantation he had just used, you would find that all the marbles you had ever lost had gathered themselves together there, meantime, no matter how widely they had been separated. But now, this thing had actually and unquestionably failed. Tom's whole structure of faith was shaken to its foundations. He had many a time heard of this thing succeeding, but never of its failing before. It did not occur to him that he had tried it several times before, himself, but could never find the hiding places afterwards. He puzzled over the matter some time, and finally decided that some witch had interfered and broken the charm. He thought he would satisfy himself on that point; so he searched around till he found a small sandy spot with a little funnel-shaped depression in it. He laid himself down and put his mouth close to this depression and called:

"Doodle-bug, doodle-bug, tell me what I want to know! Doodle-bug, doodle-bug tell me what I want to know!"

The sand began to work, and presently a small black bug appeared for a second and then darted under again in a fright.

"He dasn't tell! So it *was* a witch that done it. I just knowed it."

He well knew the futility of trying to contend against witches, so he gave up discouraged. But it occurred to him that he might as well have the marble he had just thrown away, and therefore he went and made a patient search for it. But he could not find it. Now he went back to his treasure-house and carefully placed himself just as he had been standing when he tossed the marble away; then he took another marble from his pocket and tossed it in the same way, saying:

"Brother go find your brother!"

He watched where it stopped, and went there and looked. But it must have fallen short or gone too far; so he tried twice more. The last repetition was successful. The two marbles lay within a foot of each other.

Just here the blast of a toy tin trumpet came faintly down the green aisles of the forest. Tom flung off his jacket and trousers, turned a suspender into a belt, raked away some brush behind the rotten log, disclosing a rude bow and arrow, a lath sword and a tin trumpet, and in a moment had seized these things and bounded away, bare legged, with fluttering shirt. He presently halted under a great elm, blew an answering blast, and then began to tip-toe and look warily out, this way and that. He said cautiously—to an imaginary company:

"Hold, my merry men! Keep hid till I blow."

Now appeared Joe Harper, as airily clad and elaborately armed as Tom. Tom called:

"Hold! Who comes here into Sherwood Forest without my pass?"

"Guy of Guisborne wants no man's pass. Who art thou that—that—"

"Dares to hold such language," said Tom, prompting—for they talked "by the book," from memory.

"Who art thou that dares to hold such language?"

"I, indeed! I am Robin Hood, as thy caitiff carcase soon shall know."

"Then art thou indeed that famous outlaw? Right gladly will I dispute with thee the passes of the merry wood. Have at thee!"

They took their lath swords, dumped their other traps on the ground, struck a fencing attitude, foot to foot, and began a grave, careful combat, "two up and two down." Presently Tom said:

"Now if you've got the hang, go it lively!"

So they "went it lively," panting and perspiring with the work. By and by Tom shouted:

"Fall! fall! Why don't you fall?"

"I shan't! Why don't you fall yourself? You're getting the worst of it."

"Why that ain't anything. *I* can't fall; that ain't the way it is in the book. The book says 'Then with one back-handed stroke he slew poor Guy of Guisborne.' You're to turn around and let me hit you in the back."

There was no getting around the authorities, so Joe turned, received the whack and fell.

"Now," said Joe, getting up, "You got to let me kill *you*. That's fair."

"Why I can't do that, it ain't in the book."

"Well it's blamed mean,—that's all."

"Well, say, Joe, you can be Friar Tuck or Much the miller's son and lam me with a quarter-staff; or I'll be the Sheriff of Nottingham and you be Robin Hood a little while and kill me."

This was satisfactory, and so these adventures were carried out. Then Tom became Robin Hood again, and was allowed by the treacherous nun to bleed his strength away through his neglected wound. And at last Joe, representing a whole tribe of weeping outlaws, dragged him sadly forth, gave his bow into his feeble hands, and Tom said, "Where this arrow falls, there bury poor Robin Hood under the greenwood tree." Then he shot the arrow and fell back and would have died but he lit on a nettle and sprang up too gaily for a corpse.

The boys dressed themselves, hid their accoutrements, and went off grieving that there were no outlaws any more, and wondering what modern civilization could claim to have done to compensate for their loss. They said they would rather be outlaws a year in Sherwood Forest than President of the United States forever.

DEATH OF ROBIN HOOD.

Chapter IX

AT HALF PAST nine, that night, Tom and Sid were sent to bed, as usual. They said their prayers, and Sid was soon asleep. Tom lay awake and waited, in restless impatience. When it seemed to him that it must be nearly daylight, he heard the clock strike ten! This was despair. He would have tossed and fidgeted, as his nerves demanded, but he was afraid he might wake Sid. So he lay still, and stared up into the dark. Everything was dismally still. By and by, out of the stillness, little, scarcely perceptible noises began to emphasize themselves. The ticking of the clock began to bring itself into notice. Old beams began to crack mysteriously. The stairs creaked faintly. Evidently spirits were abroad. A measured, muffled snore issued from Aunt Polly's chamber. And now the tiresome chirping of a cricket that no human ingenuity could locate, began. Next the ghastly ticking of a death-watch in the wall at the bed's head made Tom shudder— it meant that somebody's days were numbered. Then the howl of a far-off dog rose on the night air, and was answered by a fainter howl from a remoter distance. Tom was in an agony. At last he was satisfied that time had ceased and eternity begun; he began to doze, in spite of himself; the clock chimed eleven but he did not hear it. And then there came mingling with his half-formed dreams, a most melancholy caterwauling. The raising of a neighboring window disturbed him. A cry of "Scat! you devil!" and the crash of an empty bottle against the back of his aunt's woodshed brought him wide awake, and a single minute later he was dressed and out of the window and creeping along the roof of the "ell" on all fours. He "meow'd" with caution once or twice, as he went; then jumped to the roof of the woodshed and thence to the ground. Huckleberry Finn was there, with his dead cat. The boys moved off and disappeared in the gloom. At the end of half an hour they were wading through the tall grass of the graveyard.

It was a graveyard of the old-fashioned western kind. It was on a hill, about a mile and a half from the village. It had a crazy board fence around it, which leaned inward in places, and outward the rest of the time, but stood upright nowhere. Grass and weeds grew rank over the whole cemetery. All the old graves were sunken in, there was not a tombstone on the place; round-topped, worm-eaten boards staggered over the graves, leaning for support and finding none. "Sacred to the memory of" So-and-So had been painted on them once, but it could no longer have been read, on the most of them, now, even if there had been light.

A faint wind moaned through the trees, and Tom feared it might be the spirits of the dead, complaining at being disturbed. The boys talked little, and only under their breath, for the time and the place and the pervading solemnity and silence oppressed their spirits. They found the sharp new heap they were seeking, and ensconced themselves within the protection of three great elms that grew in a bunch within a few feet of the grave.

Then they waited in silence for what seemed a long time. The hooting of a distant owl was all the sound that troubled the dead stillness. Tom's reflections grew oppressive. He must force some talk. So he said in a whisper:

"Hucky, do you believe the dead people like it for us to be here?"

Huckleberry whispered:

"I wisht I knowed. It's awful solemn like, *ain't* it?"

"I bet it is."

There was a considerable pause, while the boys canvassed this matter inwardly. Then Tom whispered:

"Say, Hucky—do you reckon Hoss Williams hears us talking?"

"O' course he does. Least his sperrit does."

Tom, after a pause:

"I wish I'd said *Mister* Williams. But I never meant any harm. Everybody calls him Hoss."

"A body can't be too partic'lar how they talk 'bout these-yer dead people, Tom."

This was a damper, and conversation died again, Presently Tom seized his comrade's arm and said:

"Sh!"

"What is it, Tom?" And the two clung together with beating hearts.

"Sh! There 'tis again! Didn't you hear it?"

"I—"

"There! Now you hear it."

"Lord, Tom they're coming! They're coming, sure. What'll we do?"

"I dono. Think they'll see us?"

"O, Tom, they can see in the dark, same as cats. I wisht I hadn't come."

"O, don't be afeard. *I* don't believe they'll bother us. We ain't doing any harm. If we keep perfectly still, maybe they won't notice us at all."

"I'll try to, Tom, but Lord I'm all of a shiver."

"Listen!"

The boys bent their heads together and scarcely breathed. A muffled sound of voices floated up from the far end of the graveyard.

"Look! See there!" whispered Tom. "What is it?"

"It's devil-fire. O, Tom, this is awful."

Some vague figures approached through the gloom, swinging an old-fashioned tin lantern that freckled the ground with innumerable little spangles of light. Presently Huckleberry whispered with a shudder:

"It's the devils sure enough. Three of 'em! Lordy, Tom, we're goners! Can you pray?"

"I'll try, but don't you be afeard. They ain't going to hurt us. Now I lay me down to sleep, I—"

"Sh!"

"What is it, Huck?"

"They're *humans!* One of 'em is, anyway. One of 'em's old Muff Potter's voice."

"No—tain't so, is it?"

"I bet I know it. Don't you stir nor budge. *He* ain't sharp enough to notice us. Drunk, same as usual, likely—blamed old rip!"

"All right, I'll keep still. Now they're stuck. Can't find it. Here they come again. Now they're hot. Cold again. Hot again. Red hot! They're p'inted right, this time. Say Huck, I know another o' them voices; it's Injun Joe."

"That's so—that murderin' half-breed! I'd druther they was devils a dern sight. What kin they be up to?"

The whispers died wholly out, now, for the three men had reached the grave and stood within a few feet of the boys' hiding-place.

"Here it is," said the third voice; and the owner of it held the lantern up and revealed the face of young Dr. Robinson.

Potter and Injun Joe were carrying a handbarrow with a rope and a couple of shovels on it. They cast down their load and began to open the grave. The doctor put the lantern at the head of the grave and came and sat down with his back against one of the elm trees. He was so close the boys could have touched him.

"Hurry, men!" he said in a low voice; "the moon might come out at any moment."

They growled a response and went on digging. For some time there was no noise but the grating sound of the spades discharging their freight of mould and gravel. It was very monotonous. Finally a spade struck upon the coffin with a dull woody accent, and within another minute or two the men had hoisted it out on the ground. They pried off the lid with their shovels, got out the body and dumped it rudely on the ground. The moon drifted from behind the clouds and exposed the pallid face. The barrow was got ready and the corpse placed on it, covered with a blanket, and bound to its place with the rope. Potter took out a large spring-knife and cut off the dangling end of the rope and then said:

"Now the cussed thing's ready, Sawbones, and you'll just out with another five, or here she stays."

"That's the talk!" said Injun Joe.

"Look here, what does this mean?" said the doctor. "You required your pay in advance, and I've paid you."

"Yes, and you done more than that," said Injun Joe, approaching the doctor, who was now standing. "Five years ago you drove me away from your father's kitchen one night, when I come to ask for something to eat, and you said I warn't there for any good; and when I swore I'd get even with you if it took a hundred years, your father had me jailed for a vagrant. Did you think I'd forget? The Injun blood ain't in me for nothing. And now I've *got* you, and you got to *settle*, you know!"

He was threatening the doctor, with his fist in his face, by this time. The doctor struck out suddenly and stretched the ruffian on the ground. Potter dropped his knife, and exclaimed:

THE ADVENTURES OF TOM SAWYER

"Here, now, don't you hit my pard!" and the next moment he had grappled with the doctor and the two were struggling with might and main, trampling the grass and tearing the ground with their heels. Injun Joe sprang to his feet, his eyes flaming with passion, snatched up Potter's knife, and went creeping, catlike and stooping, round and round about the combatants, seeking an opportunity. All at once the doctor flung himself free, seized the heavy head board of Williams' grave and felled Potter to the earth with it—and in the same instant the half-breed saw his chance and drove the knife to the hilt in the young man's breast. He reeled and fell partly upon Potter, flooding him with his blood, and in the same moment the clouds blotted out the dreadful spectacle and the two frightened boys went speeding away in the dark.

Presently, when the moon emerged again, Injun Joe was standing over the two forms, contemplating them. The doctor murmured inarticulately, gave a long gasp or two and was still. The half-breed muttered:

"*That* score is settled—damn you."

Then he robbed the body. After which he put the fatal knife in Potter's open right hand, and sat down on thc dismantled coffin. Three—four—five minutes passed, and then Potter began to stir and moan. His hand closed upon the knife; he raised it, glanced at it, and let it fall, with a shudder. Then he sat up, pushing the body from him, and gazed at it, and then around him, confusedly. His eyes met Joe's.

"Lord, how is this, Joe?" he said.

"It's a dirty business," said Joe, without moving. "What did you do it for?"

"I! I never done it!"

"Look here! That kind of talk won't wash."

Potter trembled and grew white.

"I thought I'd got sober. I'd no business to drink to-night. But it's in my head yet—worse'n when we started here. I'm all in a muddle; can't recollect anything of it hardly. Tell me, Joe—*honest*, now, old feller—did I do it? Joe, I never meant to—'pon my soul and honor I never meant to, Joe. Tell me how it was Joe. O, it's awful—and him so young and promising."

"Why you two was scuffling, and he fetched you one with the head-board and you fell flat; and then up you come, all reeling and staggering, like, and snatched the knife and jammed it into him, just as he fetched you another awful clip—and here you've laid, as dead as a wedge till now."

"O, I didn't know what I was a doing. I wish I may die this minute if I did. It was all on account of the whisky; and the excitement, I reckon. I never used a weepon in my life before, Joe. I've fought, but never with weepons. They'll all say that. Joe, don't tell! Say you won't tell, Joe—that's a good feller. I always liked you Joe, and stood up for you, too. Don't you remember? You *won't* tell, *will* you Joe?" And the poor creature dropped on his knees before the stolid murderer, and clasped his appealing hands.

"No, you've always been fair and square with me, Muff Potter, and I won't go back on you.—There, now, that's as fair as a man can say."

"O, Joe, you're an angel. I'll bless you for this the longest day I live." And Potter began to cry.

"Come, now, that's enough of that. This ain't any time for blubbering. You be off yonder way and I'll go this. Move, now, and don't leave any tracks behind you."

MUFF POTTER OUTWITTED.

Potter started on a trot that quickly increased to a run. The half-breed stood looking after him. He muttered:

"If he's as much stunned with the lick and fuddled with the rum as he had the look of being, he won't think of the knife till he's gone so far he'll be afraid to come back after it to such a place by himself—chicken-heart!"

Two or three minutes later the murdered man, the blanketed corpse, the lidless coffin and the open grave were under no inspection but the moon's. The stillness was complete again, too.

Chapter X

THE TWO BOYS flew on and on, toward the village, speechless with horror. They glanced backward over their shoulders from time to time, apprehensively, as if they feared they might be followed. Every stump that started up in their path seemed a man and an enemy, and made them catch their breath; and as they sped by some outlying cottages that lay near the village, the barking of the aroused watch-dogs seemed to give wings to their feet.

"If we can only get to the old tannery, before we break down!" whispered Tom, in short catches between breaths, "I can't stand it much longer."

Huckleberry's hard pantings were his only reply, and the boys fixed their eyes on the goal of their hopes and bent to their work to win it. They gained steadily on it, and at last, breast to breast they burst through the open door and fell grateful and exhausted in the sheltering shadows beyond. By and by their pulses slowed down, and Tom whispered:

"Huckleberry, what do you reckon 'll come of this?"

"If Dr. Robinson dies, I reckon hanging 'll come of it."

"Do you though?"

"Why I *know* it, Tom."

Tom thought a while, then he said:

"Who'll tell? We?"

"What are you talking about? S'pose something happened and Injun Joe *didn't* hang? Why he'd kill us some time or other, just as dead sure as we're a laying here."

"That's just what I was thinking to myself, Huck."

"If anybody tells, let Muff Potter do it, if he's fool enough. He's generally drunk enough."

Tom said nothing—went on thinking. Presently he whispered:

"Huck, Muff Potter don't *know* it. How can he tell?"

"What's the reason he don't know it?"

"Because he'd just got that whack when Injun Joe done it. D' you reckon he could see anything? D' you reckon he knowed anything?"

"By hokey, that's so Tom!"

"And besides, look-a-here—maybe that whack done for *him*!"

"No, 'taint likely Tom. He had liquor in him; I could see that; and besides, he always has. Well when pap's full, you might take and belt him over the head with a church and you couldn't phase him. He says so, his own self. So it's the same with Muff Potter, of course. But if a man was dead sober, I reckon maybe that whack might fetch him; I dono."

After another reflective silence, Tom said:

"Hucky, you sure you can keep mum?"

"Tom, we *got* to keep mum. *You* know that. That Injun devil wouldn't make any more of drownding us than a couple of cats, if we was to squeak 'bout this and they didn't hang him. Now look-a-here, Tom, less take and swear to one another—that's what we got to do—swear to keep mum."

"I'm agreed. It's the best thing. Would you just hold hands and swear that we—"

"O, no, that wouldn't do for this. That's good enough for little rubbishy common things—specially with gals, cuz *they* go back on you anyway, and blab if they get in a huff—but there orter be writing 'bout a big thing like this. And blood."

Tom's whole being applauded this idea. It was deep, and dark, and awful; the hour, the circumstances, the surroundings, were in keeping with it. He picked up a clean pine shingle that lay in the moonlight, took a little fragment of "red keel" out of his pocket, got the moon on his work, and painfully scrawled these lines, emphasizing each slow down-stroke by clamping his tongue between his teeth, and letting up the pressure on the up-strokes:

> "Huck Finn and
> Tom Sawyer swears
> they will keep mum
> about this and they
> wish they may drop
> down dead in their
> tracks if they ever
> tell and Rot."

Huckleberry was filled with admiration of Tom's facility in writing, and the sublimity of his language. He at once took a pin from his lappel and was going to prick his flesh, but Tom said:

"Hold on! Don't do that. A pin's brass. It might have verdigrease on it."

"What's verdigrease?"

"It's p'ison. That's what it is. You just swaller some of it once—you'll see."

So Tom unwound the thread from one of his needles, and each boy pricked the ball of his thumb and squeezed out a drop of blood. In time, after many squeezes, Tom managed to sign his initials, using the ball of his little finger for a pen. Then he showed Huckleberry how to make an H and an F, and the oath was complete. They buried the shingle close to the wall, with some dismal ceremonies and incantations, and the fetters that bound their tongues were considered to be locked and the key thrown away.

A figure crept stealthily through a break in the other end of the ruined building, now, but they did not notice it.

"Tom," whispered Huckleberry, "does this keep us from *ever* telling—*always*?"

"Of course it does. It don't make any difference *what* happens, we got to keep mum. We'd drop down dead—don't *you* know that?"

"Yes, I reckon that's so."

They continued to whisper for some little time. Presently a dog set up a long, lugubrious howl just outside—within ten feet of them. The boys clasped each other suddenly, in an agony of fright.

"Which of us does he mean?" gasped Huckleberry.

"I dono—peep through the crack. Quick!"

"No, *you*, Tom!"

"I can't—I can't *do* it, Huck!"

"Please, Tom. There 'tis again!"

"O, lordy, I'm thankful!" whispered Tom. "I know his voice. It's Bull Harbison." *

"O, that's good—I tell you, Tom, I was most scared to death; I'd a bet anything it was a *stray* dog."

The dog howled again. The boys' hearts sank once more.

"O, my! that ain't no Bull Harbison!" whispered Huckleberry. "*Do*, Tom!"

Tom, quaking with fear, yielded, and put his eye to the crack. His whisper was hardly audible when he said:

"O, Huck, IT'S A STRAY DOG!"

"Quick, Tom, quick ! Who does he mean?"

"Huck, he must mean us both—we're right together."

"O, Tom, I reckon we're goners. I reckon there ain't no mistake 'bout where *I'll* go to. I been so wicked."

"Dad fetch it! This comes of playing hookey and doing everything a feller's

---

* If Mr. Harbison had owned a slave named Bull, Tom would have spoken of him as "Harbison's Bull," but a son or a dog of that name was "Bull Harbison."

told *not* to do. I might a been good, like Sid, if I'd a tried—but no, I wouldn't, of course. But if ever I get off this time, I lay I'll just *waller* in Sunday-schools!'' And Tom began to snuffle a little.

"*You* bad!'' and Huckleberry began to snuffle too. "Consound it, Tom Sawyer, you're just old pie, 'longside o'what *I* am. O, *lordy*, lordy, lordy, I wisht I only had half your chance.''

Tom choked off and whispered:

"Look, Hucky, look! He's got his *back* to us!''

Hucky looked, with joy in his heart.

"Well he has, by jingoes! Did he before?''

"Yes, he did. But I, like a fool, never thought. O, this is bully, you know. *Now* who can he mean?''

The howling stopped. Tom pricked up his ears.

"Sh! What's that?'' he whispered.

"Sounds like—like hogs grunting. No—it's somebody snoring, Tom.''

"That *is* it? Where 'bouts is it, Huck?''

"I bleeve it's down at 'tother end. Sounds so, anyway. Pap used to sleep there, sometimes, 'long with the hogs, but laws bless you, he just lifts things when *he* snores. Besides, I reckon he ain't ever coming back to this town any more.''

The spirit of adventure rose in the boys' souls once more.

"Hucky do you das't to go if I lead?''

"I don't like to, much. Tom, s'pose it's Injun Joe!''

Tom quailed. But presently the temptation rose up strong again and the boys agreed to try, with the understanding that they would take to their heels if the snoring stopped. So they went tip-toeing stealthily down, the one behind the other. When they had got to within five steps of the snorer, Tom stepped on a stick, and it broke with a sharp snap. The man moaned, writhed a little, and his face came into the moonlight. It was Muff Potter. The boys' hearts had stood still, and their hopes too, when the man moved, but their fears passed away now. They tip-toed out, through the broken weather-boarding, and stopped at a little distance to exchange a parting word. That long, lugubrious howl rose on the night air again! They turned and saw the strange dog standing within a few feet of where Potter was lying, and *facing* Potter, with his nose pointing heavenward.

"O, geeminy it's *him*!'' exclaimed both boys, in a breath.

"Say, Tom—they say a stray dog come howling around Johnny Miller's house, 'bout midnight, as much as two weeks ago; and a whippoorwill come in and lit on the bannisters and sung, the very same evening; and there ain't anybody dead there yet.''

"Well I know that. And suppose there ain't. Didn't Gracie Miller fall in the kitchen fire and burn herself terrible the very next Saturday?''

"Yes, but she ain't *dead*. And what's more, she's getting better, too.''

"All right, you wait and see. She's a goner, just as dead sure as Muff Potter's a goner. That's what the niggers say, and they know all about these kind of things, Huck.''

Then they separated, cogitating. When Tom crept in at his bedroom window, the night was almost spent. He undressed with excessive caution, and fell asleep congratulating himself that nobody knew of his escapade. He was not aware that the gently-snoring Sid was awake, and had been so for an hour.

When Tom awoke, Sid was dressed and gone. There was a late look in the light, a late sense in the atmosphere. He was startled. Why had he not been called—persecuted till he was up, as usual? The thought filled him with bodings. Within five minutes he was dressed and down stairs, feeling sore and drowsy. The family were still at table, but they had finished breakfast. There was no voice of rebuke; but there were averted eyes; there was a silence and an air of solemnity that struck a chill to the culprit's heart. He sat down and tried to seem gay, but it was up-hill work; it roused no smile, no response, and he lapsed into silence and let his heart sink down to the depths.

After breakfast his aunt took him aside, and Tom almost brightened in the hope that he was going to be flogged; but it was not so. His aunt wept over him and asked him how he could go and break her old heart so; and finally told him to go on, and ruin himself and bring her gray hairs with sorrow to the grave, for it was no use for her to try any more. This was worse than a thousand whippings, and Tom's heart was sorer now than his body. He cried, he pleaded for forgiveness, promised reform over and over again and then received his dismissal, feeling that he had won but an imperfect forgiveness and established but a feeble confidence.

He left the presence too miserable to even feel revengeful toward Sid; and so the latter's prompt retreat through the back gate was unnecessary. He moped to school gloomy and sad, and took his flogging, along with Joe Harper, for playing hooky the day before, with the air of one whose heart was busy with heavier woes and wholly dead to trifles. Then he betook himself to his seat, rested his elbows on his desk and his jaws in his hands and stared at the wall with the stony stare of suffering that has reached the limit and can no further go. His elbow was pressing against some hard substance. After a long time he slowly and sadly changed his position, and took up this object with a sigh. It was in a paper. He unrolled it. A long, lingering, colossal sigh followed, and his heart broke. It was his brass andiron knob!

This final feather broke the camel's back.

Chapter XI

CLOSE UPON THE hour of noon the whole village was suddenly electrified with the ghastly news. No need of the as yet undreamed-of telegraph; the tale flew from man to man, from group to group, from house to house, with little less than telegraphic speed. Of course the schoolmaster gave holiday for that afternoon; the town would have thought strangely of him if he had not.

A gory knife had been found close to the murdered man, and it had been recognized by somebody as belonging to Muff Potter—so the story ran. And it was said that a belated citizen had come upon Potter washing himself in the "branch" about one or two o'clock in the morning, and that Potter had at once sneaked off—suspicious circumstances, especially the washing, which was not a habit with Potter. It was also said that the town had been ransacked for this "murderer," (the public are not slow in the matter of sifting evidence and arriving at a verdict), but that he could not be found. Horsemen had departed down all the roads in every direction, and the Sheriff "was confident" that he would be captured before night.

All the town was drifting toward the graveyard. Tom's heart-break vanished and he joined the procession, not because he would not a thousand times rather go anywhere else, but because an awful, unaccountable fascination drew him on. Arrived at the dreadful place, he wormed his small body through the crowd and saw the dismal spectacle. It seemed to him an age since he was there before. Somebody pinched his arm. He turned, and his eyes met Huckleberry's. Then both looked elsewhere at once, and wondered if anybody had noticed anything in their mutual glance. But everybody was talking, and intent upon the grisly spectacle before them.

"Poor fellow!" "Poor young fellow!" "This ought to be a lesson to grave-robbers !" "Muff Potter'll hang for this if they catch him!" This was the drift of remark; and the minister said, "It was a judgment; His hand is here."

Now Tom shivered from head to heel; for his eye fell upon the stolid face of Injun Joe. At this moment the crowd began to sway and struggle, and voices shouted, "It's him! it's him! he's coming himself!"

"Who? Who?" from twenty voices.

"Muff Potter!"

"Hallo, he's stopped!—Look out, he's turning! Don't let him get away!"

People in the branches of the trees over Tom's head, said he wasn't trying to get away—he only looked doubtful and perplexed.

"Infernal impudence!" said a bystander; "wanted to come and take a quiet look at his work, I reckon—didn't expect any company."

The crowd fell apart, now, and the Sheriff came through, ostentatiously leading Potter by the arm. The poor fellow's face was haggard, and his eyes showed the fear that was upon him. When he stood before the murdered man, he shook as with a palsy, and he put his face in his hands and burst into tears.

"I didn't do it, friends," he sobbed; "'pon my word and honor I never done it."

"Who's accused you?" shouted a voice.

This shot seemed to carry home. Potter lifted his face and looked around him with a pathetic hopelessness in his eyes. He saw Injun Joe, and exclaimed:

"O, Injun Joe, you promised me you'd never—"

"Is that your knife?" and it was thrust before him by the Sheriff.

INJUN JOE'S TWO VICTIMS.

Potter would have fallen if they had not caught him and eased him to the ground. Then he said:

"Something told me 't if I didn't come back and get—" He shuddered; then waved his nerveless hand with a vanquished gesture and said, "Tell 'em, Joe, tell 'em—it ain't any use any more."

Then Huckleberry and Tom stood dumb and staring, and heard the stony-hearted liar reel off his serene statement, they expecting every moment that the clear sky would deliver God's lightnings upon his head, and wondering to see how long the stroke was delayed. And when he had finished and still stood alive and whole, their wavering impulse to break their oath and save the poor betrayed prisoner's life faded and vanished away, for plainly this miscreant had sold himself to Satan and it would be fatal to meddle with the property of such a power as that.

"Why didn't you leave? What did you want to come here for?" somebody said.

"I couldn't help it—I couldn't help it," Potter moaned. "I wanted to run away, but I couldn't seem to come anywhere but here." And he fell to sobbing again.

Injun Joe repeated his statement, just as calmly, a few minutes afterward on the inquest, under oath; and the boys, seeing that the lightnings were still withheld, were confirmed in their belief that Joe had sold himself to the devil. He was now become, to them, the most balefully interesting object they had ever looked upon, and they could not take their fascinated eyes from his face.

They inwardly resolved to watch him, nights, when opportunity should offer, in the hope of getting a glimpse of his dread master.

Injun Joe helped to raise the body of the murdered man and put it in a wagon for removal; and it was whispered through the shuddering crowd that the wound bled a little! The boys thought that this happy circumstance would turn suspicion in the right direction; but they were disappointed, for more than one villager remarked:

"It was within three feet of Muff Potter when it done it."

Tom's fearful secret and gnawing conscience disturbed his sleep for as much as a week after this; and at breakfast one morning Sid said:

"Tom, you pitch around and talk in your sleep so much that you keep me awake about half the time."

Tom blanched and dropped his eyes.

"It's a bad sign," said Aunt Polly, gravely. "What you got on your mind, Tom?"

"Nothing. Nothing 't I know of." But the boy's hand shook so that he spilled his coffee.

"And you do talk such stuff," Sid said. "Last night you said 'it's blood, it's blood, that's what it is!' You said that over and over. And you said, 'Don't torment me so—I'll tell!' Tell *what?* What is it you'll tell?"

Everything was swimming before Tom. There is no telling what might have happened, now, but luckily the concern passed out of Aunt Polly's face and she came to Tom's relief without knowing it. She said:

"Sho! It's that dreadful murder. I dream about it most every night myself. Sometimes I dream it's me that done it."

Mary said she had been affected much the same way. Sid seemed satisfied. Tom got out of the presence as quick as he plausibly could, and after that he complained of toothache for a week, and tied up his jaws every night. He never knew that Sid lay nightly watching, and frequently slipped the bandage free and then leaned on his elbow listening a good while at a time, and afterward slipped the bandage back to its place again. Tom's distress of mind wore off gradually and the toothache grew irksome and was discarded. If Sid really managed to make anything out of Tom's disjointed mutterings, he kept it to himself.

It seemed to Tom that his schoolmates never would get done holding inquests on dead cats, and thus keeping his trouble present to his mind. Sid noticed that Tom never was coroner at one of these inquiries, though it had been his habit to take the lead in all new enterprises; he noticed, too, that Tom never acted as a witness,—and that was strange; and Sid did not overlook the fact that Tom even showed a marked aversion to these inquests, and always avoided them when he could. Sid marveled, but said nothing. However, even inquests went out of vogue at last, and ceased to torture Tom's conscience.

Every day or two, during this time of sorrow, Tom watched his opportunity and went to the little grated jail-window and smuggled such small comforts through to the "murderer" as he could get hold of. The jail was a trifling little brick den that stood in a marsh at the edge of the village, and no guards were afforded for it; indeed it was seldom occupied. These offerings greatly helped to ease Tom's conscience.

The villagers had a strong desire to tar-and-feather Injun Joe and ride him on a rail, for body-snatching, but so formidable was his character that nobody could be found who was willing to take the lead in the matter, so it was dropped. He had been careful to begin both of his inquest-statements with the fight, without confessing the grave-robbery that preceded it; therefore it was deemed wisest not to try the case in the courts at present.

Chapter XII

ONE OF THE reasons why Tom's mind had drifted away from its secret troubles was, that it had found a new and weighty matter to interest itself about. Becky Thatcher had stopped coming to school. Tom had struggled with his pride a few days, and tried to "whistle her down the wind," but failed. He began to find himself hanging around her father's house, nights, and feeling very miserable. She was ill. What if she should die! There was distraction in the thought. He no longer took an interest in war, nor even in piracy. The charm of life was gone; there was nothing but dreariness left. He put his hoop away, and his bat; there was no joy in them any more. His aunt was concerned. She began to try all manner of remedies on him. She was one of those people who are infatuated with patent medicines and all new-fangled methods of producing health or mending it. She was an inveterate experimenter in these things. When something fresh in this line came out she was in a fever, right away, to try it; not on herself, for she was never ailing, but on anybody else that came handy. She was a subscriber for all the "Health" periodicals and phreneological frauds; and the solemn ignorance they were inflated with was breath to her nostrils. All the "rot" they contained about ventilation, and how to go to bed, and how to get up, and what to eat, and what to drink, and how much exercise to take, and what frame of mind to keep one's self in, and what sort of clothing to wear, was all gospel to her, and she never observed that her health-journals of the current month customarily upset everything they had recommended the month before. She was as simple-hearted and honest as the day was long, and so she was an easy victim. She gathered together her quack periodicals and her quack medicines, and thus armed with death, went about on her pale horse, metaphorically speaking, with "hell following after." But she never suspected that she was not an angel of healing and the balm of Gilead in disguise, to the suffering neighbors.

The water treatment was new, now, and Tom's low condition was a windfall to her. She had him out at daylight every morning, stood him up in the woodshed and drowned him with a deluge of cold water; then she scrubbed him down with a towel like a file, and so brought him to; then she rolled him up in a wet sheet and put him away under blankets till she sweated his soul clean and "the yellow stains of it came through his pores"—as Tom said.

Yet notwithstanding all this, the boy grew more and more melancholy and pale and dejected. She added hot baths, sitz baths, shower baths and plunges. The boy remained as dismal as a hearse. She began to assist the water with a slim oatmeal diet and blister plasters. She calculated his capacity as she would a jug's, and filled him up every day with quack cure-alls.

Tom had become indifferent to persecution by this time. This phase filled the old lady's heart with consternation. This indifference must be broken up at any cost. Now she heard of Pain-killer for the first time. She ordered a lot at once. She tasted it and was filled with gratitude. It was simply fire in a liquid form. She dropped the water treatment and everything else, and pinned her faith to Pain-killer. She gave Tom a tea-spoonful and watched with the deepest anxiety for the result. Her troubles were instantly at rest, her soul at peace again; for the "indifference" was broken up. The boy could not have shown a wilder, heartier interest, if she had built a fire under him.

Tom felt that it was time to wake up; this sort of life might be romantic enough, in his blighted condition, but it was getting to have too little sentiment and too much distracting variety about it. So he thought over various plans for relief, and finally hit upon that of professing to be fond of Pain-killer. He asked for it so often that he became a nuisance, and his aunt ended by telling him to help himself and quit bothering her. If it had been Sid, she would have had no misgivings to alloy her delight; but since it was Tom, she watched the bottle clandestinely. She found that the medicine did really diminish, but it did not occur to her that the boy was mending the health of a crack in the sitting-room floor with it.

One day Tom was in the act of dosing the crack when his aunt's yellow cat came along, purring, eyeing the teaspoon avariciously, and begging for a taste. Tom said:

"Don't ask for it unless you want it, Peter."

But Peter signified that he did want it.

"You better make sure."

Peter was sure.

"Now you've asked for it, and I'll give it to you, because there ain't anything mean about *me*; but if you find you don't like it, you musn't blame anybody but your own self."

Peter was agreeable. So Tom pried his mouth open and poured down the Pain-killer. Peter sprang a couple of yards in the air, and then delivered a war-whoop and set off round and round the room, banging against furniture, upsetting flower pots and making general havoc. Next he rose on his hind feet and pranced around, in a frenzy of enjoyment, with his head over his shoulder and his voice proclaiming his unappeasable happiness. Then he went tearing around the house again spreading chaos and destruction in his path. Aunt Polly entered in time to see him throw a few double summersets, deliver a final mighty hurrah, and sail through the open window, carrying the rest of the flower-pots with him. The old lady stood petrified with astonishment, peering over her glasses; Tom lay on the floor expiring with laughter.

"Tom, what on earth ails that cat?"

"*I* don't know, aunt," gasped the boy.

"Why I never see anything like it. What *did* make him act so?"

"Deed I don't know Aunt Polly; cats always act so when they're having a good time."

"They do, do they?" There was something in the tone that made Tom apprehensive.

"Yes'm. That is, I believe they do."

"You *do*?"

"Yes'm."

The old lady was bending down, Tom watching, with interest emphasized by anxiety. Too late he divined her "drift." The handle of the tell-tale tea-spoon was visible under the bed-valance. Aunt Polly took it, held it up. Tom winced, and dropped his eyes. Aunt Polly raised him by the usual handle—his ear—and cracked his head soundly with her thimble.

"Now, sir, what did you want to treat that poor dumb beast so, for?"

"I done it out of pity for him—because he hadn't any aunt."

"Hadn't any aunt!—you numscull. What has that got to do with it?"

"Heaps. Because if he'd a had one she'd a burnt him out herself! She'd a roasted his bowels out of him 'thout any more feeling than if he was a human!"

Aunt Polly felt a sudden pang of remorse. This was putting the thing in a new light; what was cruelty to a cat *might* be cruelty to a boy, too. She began to soften; she felt sorry. Her eyes watered a little, and she put her hand on Tom's

A GENERAL GOOD TIME.

head and said gently:

"I was meaning for the best, Tom. And Tom, it *did* do you good."

Tom looked up in her face with just a perceptible twinkle peeping through his gravity:

"I know you was meaning for the best, aunty, and so was I with Peter. It done *him* good, too. I never see him get around so since—"

"O, go 'long with you, Tom, before you aggravate me again. And you try and see if you can't be a good boy, for once, and you needn't take any more medicine."

Tom reached school ahead of time. It was noticed that this strange thing had been occurring every day latterly. And now, as usual of late, he hung about the gate of the school-yard instead of playing with his comrades. He was sick, he said, and he looked it. He tried to seem to be looking everywhere but whither he really was looking—down the road. Presently Jeff Thatcher hove in sight, and Tom's face lighted; he gazed a moment, and then turned sorrowfully away. When Jeff arrived, Tom accosted him, and "led up" warily to opportunities for remark about Becky, but the giddy lad never could see the bait. Tom watched and watched, hoping whenever a frisking frock came in sight, and hating the owner of it as soon as he saw she was not the right one. At last frocks ceased to appear, and he dropped hopelessly into the dumps; he entered the empty school house and sat down to suffer. Then one more frock passed in at the gate, and Tom's heart gave a great bound. The next instant he was out, and "going on" like an Indian; yelling, laughing, chasing boys, jumping over the fence at risk of life and limb, throwing hand-springs, standing on his head—doing all the heroic things he could conceive of, and keeping a furtive eye out, all the while, to see if Becky Thatcher was noticing. But she seemed to be unconscious of it all; she never looked. Could it be possible that she was not aware that he was there? He carried his exploits to her immediate vicinity; came war-whooping around, snatched a boy's cap, hurled it to the roof of the school-house, broke through a group of boys, tumbling them in every direction, and fell sprawling, himself, under Becky's nose, almost upsetting her—and she turned, with her nose in the air, and he heard her say. "Mf! some people think they're mighty smart—always showing off!"

Tom's cheeks burned. He gathered himself up and sneaked off, crushed and crestfallen.

Chapter XIII

TOM'S MIND WAS made up now. He was gloomy and desperate. He was a forsaken, friendless boy, he said; nobody loved him; when they found out what they had driven him to, perhaps they would be sorry; he had tried to do right and get along, but they would not let him; since nothing would do them but to be rid of him, let it be so; and let them blame *him* for the consequences—why shouldn't they? What right had the friendless to complain? Yes, they had forced him to it at last: he would lead a life of crime. There was no choice.

By this time he was far down Meadow Lane, and the bell for school to "take up" tinkled faintly upon his ear. He sobbed, now, to think he should never, never hear that old familiar sound any more—it was very hard, but it was forced on him; since he was driven out into the cold world, he must submit—but he forgave them. Then the sobs came thick and fast.

Just at this point he met his soul's sworn comrade, Joe Harper—hard-eyed, and with evidently a great and dismal purpose in his heart. Plainly here were "two souls with but a single thought." Tom, wiping his eyes with his sleeve, began to blubber out something about a resolution to escape from hard usage and lack of sympathy at home by roaming abroad into the great world never to return; and ended by hoping that Joe would not forget him.

But it transpired that this was a request which Joe had just been going to make of Tom, and had come to hunt him up for that purpose. His mother had whipped him for drinking some cream which he had never tasted and knew nothing about; it was plain that she was tired of him and wished him to go; if she felt that way, there was nothing for him to do but succumb; he hoped she would be happy, and never regret having driven her poor boy out into the unfeeling world to suffer and die.

As the two boys walked sorrowing along, they made a new compact to stand by each other and be brothers and never separate till death relieved them of their troubles. Then they began to lay their plans. Joe was for being a hermit, and living on crusts in a remote cave, and dying, some time, of cold, and want, and grief; but after listening to Tom, he conceded that there were some conspicuous advantages about a life of crime, and so he consented to be a pirate.

Three miles below St. Petersburg, at a point where the Mississippi river was a trifle over a mile wide, there was a long, narrow, wooded island, with a shallow bar at the head of it, and this offered well as a rendezvous. It was not inhabited; it lay far over toward the further shore, abreast a dense and almost wholly unpeopled forest. So Jackson's Island was chosen. Who were to be the subjects of their piracies, was a matter that did not occur to them. Then they hunted up Huckleberry Finn, and he joined them promptly, for all careers were one to him; he was indifferent. They presently separated to meet at a lonely spot on the river bank two miles above the village at the favorite hour—which was midnight. There was a small log raft there which they meant to capture. Each would bring hooks and lines, and such provision as he could steal in the most dark and mysterious way—as became outlaws. And before the afternoon was done, they had all managed to enjoy the sweet glory of spreading the fact that pretty soon the town would "hear something." All who got this vague hint were cautioned to "be mum and wait."

About midnight Tom arrived with a boiled ham and a few trifles, and stopped in a dense undergrowth on a small bluff overlooking the meeting-place. It was starlight, and very still. The mighty river lay like an ocean at rest. Tom listened a moment, but no sound disturbed the quiet. Then he gave a low, distinct whistle. It was answered from under the bluff. Tom whistled twice more; these signals were answered in the same way. Then a guarded voice said:

"Who goes there?"

"Tom Sawyer, the Black Avenger of the Spanish Main. Name your names."

"Huck Finn the Red-Handed, and Joe Harper the Terror of the Seas." Tom had furnished these titles, from his favorite literature.

"'Tis well. Give the countersign."

Two hoarse whispers delivered the same awful word simultaneously to the brooding night:

"BLOOD!"

Then Tom tumbled his ham over the bluff and let himself down after it, tearing both skin and clothes to some extent in the effort. There was an easy, comfortable path along the shore under the bluff, but it lacked the advantages of difficulty and danger so valued by a pirate.

The Terror of the Seas had brought a side of bacon, and had about worn himself out with getting it there. Finn the Red-Handed had stolen a skillet and a quantity of half-cured leaf tobacco, and had also brought a few corncobs to make pipes with. But none of the pirates smoked or "chewed" but himself. The Black Avenger of the Spanish Main said it would never do to start without some fire. That was a wise thought; matches were hardly known there in that day. They saw a fire smouldering upon a great raft a hundred yards above, and they went stealthily thither and helped themselves to a chunk. They made an imposing adventure of it, saying "Hist!" every now and then, and suddenly halting with finger on lip; moving with hands on imaginary dagger-hilts; and giving orders in dismal whispers that if "the foe" stirred, to "let him have it to the hilt," because "dead men tell no tales." They knew well enough that the raftsmen were all down at the village laying in stores or having a spree, but still that was no excuse for their conducting this thing in an unpiratical way.

They shoved off, presently, Tom in command, Huck at the after oar and Joe at the forward. Tom stood amidships, gloomy-browed, and with folded arms, and gave his orders in a low, stern whisper:

"Luff, and bring her to the wind!"

"Aye-aye, sir!"

"Steady, stead-y-y-y!"

"Steady it is, sir!"

"Let her go off a point!"

"Point it is, sir!"

As the boys steadily and monotonously drove the raft toward mid-stream it was no doubt understood that these orders were given only for "style," and were not intended to mean anything in particular.

"What sail's she carrying?"

"Courses, tops'ls and flying-jib, sir."

"Send the r'yals up! Lay out aloft, there, half a dozen of ye,—foretopmaststuns'l! Lively, now!"

"Aye-aye, sir!"

"Shake out that maintogalans'l! Sheets and braces! *Now*, my hearties!"

"Aye-aye, sir!"

"Hellum-a-lee—hard a port! Stand by to meet her when she comes! Port, port! *Now*, men! With a will! Stead-y-y-y!"

"Steady it is, sir!"

The raft drew beyond the middle of the river; the boys pointed her head right, and then lay on their oars. The river was not high, so there was not more than a two or three-mile current. Hardly a word was said during the next three-quarters of an hour. Now the raft was passing before the distant town. Two or three glimmering lights showed where it lay, peacefully sleeping, beyond the vague vast sweep of star-gemmed water, unconscious of the tremendous event that was happening. The Black Avenger stood still with folded arms, "looking his last" upon the scene of his former joys and his later sufferings, and wishing "she" could see him now, abroad on the wild sea, facing peril and death with dauntless heart, going to his doom with a grim smile on his lips. It was but a

ON BOARD THEIR FIRST PRIZE.

small strain on his imagination to remove Jackson's Island beyond eye-shot of the village, and so he "looked his last" with a broken and satisfied heart. The other pirates were looking their last, too; and they all looked so long that they came near letting the current drift them out of the range of the island. But they discovered the danger in time, and made shift to avert it. About two o'clock in the morning the raft grounded on the bar two hundred yards above the head of the island, and they waded back and forth until they had landed their freight. Part of the little raft's belongings consisted of an old sail, and this they spread over a nook in the bushes for a tent to shelter their provisions; but they themselves would sleep in the open air in good weather, as became outlaws.

They built a fire against the side of a great log twenty or thirty steps within the sombre depths of the forest, and then cooked some bacon in the frying-pan for supper, and used up half of the corn "pone" stock they had brought. It seemed glorious sport to be feasting in that wild free way in the virgin forest of an unexplored and uninhabited island, far from the haunts of men, and they said they never would return to civilization. The climbing fire lit up their faces and threw its ruddy glare upon the pillared tree trunks of their forest temple, and upon the varnished foliage and festooning vines.

When the last crisp slice of bacon was gone, and the last allowance of corn pone devoured, the boys stretched themselves out on the grass, filled with contentment. They could have found a cooler place, but they would not deny themselves such a romantic feature as the roasting camp-fire.

"*Ain't* it gay?" said Joe.

"It's *nuts!*" said Tom. "What would the boys say if they could see us?"

"Say? Well they'd just die to be here—hey Hucky!"

"I reckon so," said Huckleberry; "anyways *I*'m suited. I don't want nothing better'n this. I don't ever get enough to eat, gen'ally—and here they can't come and pick at a feller and bullyrag him so."

"It's just the life for me," said Tom. "You don't have to get up, mornings, and you don't have to go to school, and wash, and all that blame foolishness. You see a pirate don't have to do *anything*, Joe, when he's ashore, but a hermit *he* has to be praying considerable, and then he don't have any fun, anyway, all by himself that way."

"O yes, that's so," said Joe, "but I hadn't thought much about it, you know. I'd a good deal rather be a pirate, now that I've tried it."

"You see," said Tom, "people don't go much on hermits, now-a-days, like they used to in old times, but a pirate's always respected. And a hermit's got to sleep on the hardest place he can find, and put sack-cloth and ashes on his head, and stand out in the rain, and—"

"What does he put sack-cloth and ashes on his head for?" inquired Huck.

"*I* dono. But they've *got* to do it. Hermits always do. You'd have to do that if you was a hermit."

"Dern'd if I would," said Huck.

"Well what would you do?"

"I dono. But I wouldn't do that."

"Why Huck, you'd *have* to. How'd you get around it?"

"Why I just wouldn't stand it. I'd run away."

"Run away! Well you *would* be a nice old slouch of a hermit. You'd be a disgrace."

The Red-Handed made no response, being better employed. He had finished gouging out a cob, and now he fitted a weed stem to it, loaded it with tobacco, and was pressing a coal to the charge and blowing a cloud of fragrant smoke— he was in the full bloom of luxurious contentment. The other pirates envied him this majestic vice, and secretly resolved to acquire it shortly. Presently Huck said:

"What does pirates have to do?"

Tom said:

"Oh they have just a bully time—take ships, and burn them, and get the money and bury it in awful places in their island where there's ghosts and things to watch it, and kill everybody in the ships—make 'em walk a plank."

"And they carry the women to the island," said Joe; "they don't kill the women."

"No," assented Tom, "they don't kill the women—they're too noble. And the women's always beautiful, too."

"And don't they wear the bulliest clothes! Oh, no! All gold and silver and di'monds," said Joe, with enthusiasm.

"Who?" said Huck.

"Why the pirates."

Huck scanned his own clothing forlornly.

"I reckon I ain't dressed fitten for a pirate," said he, with a regretful pathos in his voice; "but I ain't got none but these."

But the other boys told him the fine clothes would come fast enough, after they should have begun their adventures. They made him understand that his poor rags would do to begin with, though it was customary for wealthy pirates to start with a proper wardrobe.

Gradually their talk died out and drowsiness began to steal upon the eyelids of the little waifs. The pipe dropped from the fingers of the Red-Handed, and he slept the sleep of the conscience-free and the weary. The Terror of the Seas and the Black Avenger of the Spanish Main had more difficulty in getting to sleep. They said their prayers inwardly, and lying down, since there was nobody there with authority to make them kneel and recite aloud; in truth they had a mind not to say them at all, but they were afraid to proceed to such lengths as that, lest they might call down a sudden and special thunderbolt from Heaven.

Then at once they reached and hovered upon the imminent verge of sleep—but an intruder came, now, that would not "down." It was conscience. They began to feel a vague fear that they had been doing wrong to run away; and next they thought of the stolen meat, and then the real torture came. They tried to argue it away by reminding conscience that they had purloined sweetmeats and apples scores of times; but conscience was not to be appeased by such thin plausibilities; it seemed to them, in the end, that there was no getting around the stubborn fact that taking sweetmeats was only "hooking," while taking bacon and hams and such valuables was plain simple *stealing*—and there was a command against that in the Bible. So they inwardly resolved that so long as they remained in the business, their piracies should not again be sullied with the crime of stealing. Then conscience granted a truce, and these curiously inconsistent pirates fell peacefully to sleep.

Chapter XIV

WHEN TOM AWOKE in the morning, he wondered where he was. He sat up and rubbed his eyes and looked around. Then he comprehended. It was the cool gray dawn, and there was a delicious sense of repose and peace in the deep pervading calm and silence of the woods. Not a leaf stirred; not a sound obtruded upon great Nature's meditation. Beaded dew-drops stood upon the leaves and grasses. A white layer of ashes covered the fire, and a thin blue breath of smoke rose straight into the air. Joe and Huck still slept.

Now, far away in the woods a bird called; another answered; presently the hammering of a woodpecker was heard. Gradually the cool dim gray of the morning whitened, and as gradually sounds multiplied and life manifested itself. The marvel of Nature shaking off sleep and going to work unfolded itself to the musing boy. A little green worm came crawling over a dewy leaf, lifting two-thirds of his body into the air from time to time and "sniffing around," then proceeding again—for he was measuring, Tom said; and when the worm approached him, of its own accord, he sat as still as a stone, with his hopes rising and falling, by turns, as the creature still came toward him or seemed inclined to go elsewhere; and when at last it considered a painful moment with its curved body in the air and then came decisively down upon Tom's leg and began a journey over him, his whole heart was glad—for that meant that he was going to have a new suit of clothes—without the shadow of a doubt a gaudy piratical uniform. Now a procession of ants appeared, from nowhere in particular, and went about their labors; one struggled manfully by with a dead spider five times as big as itself in its arms, and lugged it straight up a tree-trunk. A brown spotted lady-bug climbed the dizzy height of a grass blade, and Tom bent down close to it and said, "Lady-bug, lady-bug, fly away home, your house is on fire, your children's alone," and she took wing and went off to see about it—which did not surprise the boy, for he knew of old that this insect was credulous about conflagrations and he had practiced upon its simplicity more than once. A tumble-bug came next, heaving sturdily at its ball, and Tom touched the creature, to see it shut its legs against its body and pretend to be dead. The birds were fairly rioting by this time. A cat-bird, the northern mocker, lit in a tree over Tom's

head, and trilled out her imitations of her neighbors in a rapture of enjoyment;
then a shrill jay swept down, a flash of blue flame, and stopped on a twig almost
within the boy's reach, cocked his head to one side and eyed the strangers with
a consuming curiosity; a gray squirrel and a big fellow of the "fox" kind came
skurrying along, sitting up at intervals to inspect and chatter at the boys, for the
wild things had probably never seen a human being before and scarcely knew
whether to be afraid or not. All Nature was wide awake and stirring, now; long
lances of sunlight pierced down through the dense foliage far and near, and a
few butterflies came fluttering upon the scene.

Tom stirred up the other pirates and they all clattered away with a shout, and
in a minute or two were stripped and chasing after and tumbling over each other
in the shallow limpid water of the white sand-bar. They felt no longing for the
little village sleeping in the distance beyond the majestic waste of water. A
vagrant current or a slight rise in the river had carried off their raft, but this only
gratified them, since its going was something like burning the bridge between
them and civilization.

They came back to camp wonderfully refreshed, glad-hearted, and ravenous;
and they soon had the camp-fire blazing up again. Huck found a spring of clear
cold water close by, and the boys made cups of broad oak or hickory leaves,
and felt that water, sweetened with such a wild-wood charm as that, would be
a good enough substitute for coffee. While Joe was slicing bacon for breakfast,
Tom and Huck asked him to hold on a minute; they stepped to a promising nook
in the river bank and threw in their lines; almost immediately they had reward.
Joe had not had time to get impatient before they were back again with some
handsome bass, a couple of sun-perch and a small catfish—provisions enough
for quite a family. They fried the fish with the bacon and were astonished; for
no fish had ever seemed so delicious before. They did not know that the quicker
a fresh water fish is on the fire after he is caught the better he is; and they
reflected little upon what a sauce open air sleeping, open air exercise, bathing,
and a large ingredient of hunger makes, too.

They lay around in the shade, after breakfast, while Huck had a smoke, and
then went off through the woods on an exploring expedition. They tramped gaily
along, over decaying logs, through tangled underbrush, among solemn monarchs

THE PIRATES' BATH.

of the forest, hung from their crowns to the ground with a drooping regalia of grape-vines. Now and then they came upon snug nooks carpeted with grass and jeweled with flowers.

They found plenty of things to be delighted with but nothing to be astonished at. They discovered that the island was about three miles long and a quarter of a mile wide, and that the shore it lay closest to was only separated from it by a narrow channel hardly two hundred yards wide. They took a swim about every hour, so it was close upon the middle of the afternoon when they got back to camp. They were too hungry to stop to fish, but they fared sumptuously upon cold ham, and then threw themselves down in the shade to talk. But the talk soon began to drag, and then died. The stillness, the solemnity that brooded in the woods, and the sense of loneliness, began to tell upon the spirits of the boys. They fell to thinking. A sort of undefined longing crept upon them. This took dim shape, presently—it was budding home-sickness. Even Finn the Red-Handed was dreaming of his door-steps and empty hogsheads. But they were all ashamed of their weakness, and none was brave enough to speak his thought.

For some time, now, the boys had been dully conscious of a peculiar sound in the distance, just as one sometimes is of the ticking of a clock which he takes no distinct note of. But now this mysterious sound became more pronounced, and forced a recognition. The boys started, glanced at each other, and then each assumed a listening attitude. There was a long silence, profound and unbroken; then a deep, sullen boom came floating down out of the distance.

"What is it!" exclaimed Joe, under his breath.

"I wonder," said Tom in a whisper.

"Tain't thunder," said Huckleberry, in an awed tone, "becuz thunder—"

"Hark!" said Tom. "Listen—don't talk."

They waited a time that seemed an age, and then the same muffled boom troubled the solemn hush.

"Let's go and see."

They sprang to their feet and hurried to the shore toward the town. They parted the bushes on the bank and peered out over the water. The little steam ferry boat was about a mile below the village, drifting with the current. Her broad deck seemed crowded with people. There were a great many skiffs rowing

THE SEARCH FOR THE DROWNED.

about or floating with the stream in the neighborhood of the ferry boat, but the boys could not determine what the men in them were doing. Presently a great jet of white smoke burst from the ferry boat's side, and as it expanded and rose in a lazy cloud, that same dull throb of sound was borne to the listeners again.

"I know now!" exclaimed Tom; "somebody's drownded!"

"That's it!" said Huck; "they done that last summer, when Bill Turner got drownded; they shoot a cannon over the water, and that makes him come up to the top. Yes, and they take loaves of bread and put quicksilver in 'em and set 'em afloat, and wherever there's anybody that's drownded, they'll float right there and stop."

"Yes, I've heard about that," said Joe. "I wonder what makes the bread do that."

"Oh it ain't the bread, so much," said Tom; "I reckon it's mostly what they *say* over it before they start it out."

"But they don't say anything over it," said Huck. "I've seen 'em and they don't."

"Well that's funny," said Tom. "But maybe they say it to themselves. Of *course* they do. Anybody might know that."

The other boys agreed that there was reason in what Tom said, because an ignorant lump of bread, uninstructed by an incantation, could not be expected to act very intelligently when sent upon an errand of such gravity.

"By jings I wish I was over there, now," said Joe.

"I do too," said Huck. "I'd give heaps to know who it is."

The boys still listened and watched. Presently a revealing thought flashed through Tom's mind, and he exclaimed:

"Boys, I know who's drownded—it's us!"

They felt like heroes in an instant. Here was a gorgeous triumph; they were missed; they were mourned; hearts were breaking on their account; tears were being shed; accusing memories of unkindnesses to these poor lost lads were rising up, and unavailing regrets and remorse were being indulged; and best of all, the departed were the talk of the whole town, and the envy of all the boys, as far as this dazzling notoriety was concerned. This was fine. It was worth while to be a pirate, after all.

As twilight drew on, the ferry boat went back to her accustomed business and the skiffs disappeared. The pirates returned to camp. They were jubilant with vanity over their new grandeur and the illustrious trouble they were making. They caught fish, cooked supper and ate it, and then fell to guessing at what the village was thinking and saying about them; and the pictures they drew of the public distress on their account were gratifying to look upon—from their point of view. But when the shadows of night closed them in, they gradually ceased to talk, and sat gazing into the fire, with their minds evidently wandering elsewhere. The excitement was gone, now, and Tom and Joe could not keep back thoughts of certain persons at home who were not enjoying this fine frolic as much as they were. Misgivings came; they grew troubled and unhappy; a sigh or two escaped, unawares. By and by Joe timidly ventured upon a round-about "feeler" as to how the others might look upon a return to civilization—not right now, but—

Tom withered him with derision! Huck, being uncommitted, as yet, joined in with Tom, and the waverer quickly "explained," and was glad to get out of the scrape with as little taint of chicken-hearted home-sickness clinging to his garments as he could. Mutiny was effectually laid to rest for the moment.

As the night deepened, Huck began to nod, and presently to snore. Joe followed next. Tom lay upon his elbow motionless, for some time, watching the two intently. At last he got up cautiously, on his knees, and went searching among the grass and the flickering reflections flung by the camp-fire. He picked up and inspected several large semi-cylinders of the thin white bark of a sycamore, and finally chose two which seemed to suit him. Then he knelt by the fire and painfully wrote something upon each of these with his "red keel;" one he rolled up and put in his jacket pocket, and the other he put in Joe's hat and removed it to a little distance from the owner. And he also put into the hat certain school-boy treasures of almost inestimable value—among them a lump of chalk, an India rubber ball, three fish-hooks, and one of that kind of marbles known as a "sure 'nough crystal." Then he tip-toed his way cautiously among the trees till he felt that he was out of hearing, and straightway broke into a keen run in the direction of the sand-bar.

Chapter XV

A FEW MINUTES later Tom was in the shoal water of the bar, wading toward the Illinois shore. Before the depth reached his middle he was half way over; the current would permit no more wading, now, so he struck out confidently to swim the remaining hundred yards. He swam quartering up stream, but still was swept downward rather faster than he had expected. However, he reached the shore finally, and drifted along till he found a low place and drew himself out. He put his hand on his jacket pocket, found his piece of bark safe, and then struck through the woods, following the shore, with streaming garments. Shortly before ten o'clock he came out into an open place opposite the village, and saw the ferry boat lying in the shadow of the trees and the high bank. Everything was quiet under the blinking stars. He crept down the bank, watching with all his eyes, slipped into the water, swam three or four strokes and climbed into the skiff that did "yawl" duty at the boat's stern. He laid himself down under the thwarts and waited, panting.

Presently the cracked bell tapped and a voice gave the order to "cast off." A minute or two later the skiff's head was standing high up, against the boat's swell, and the voyage was begun. Tom felt happy in his success, for he knew it was the boat's last trip for the night. At the end of a long twelve or fifteen minutes the wheels stopped, and Tom slipped overboard and swam ashore in the dusk, landing fifty yards down stream, out of danger of possible stragglers.

He flew along unfrequented alleys, and shortly found himself at his aunt's back fence. He climbed over, approached the "ell" and looked in at the sitting-room window, for a light was burning there. There sat Aunt Polly, Sid, Mary, and Joe Harper's mother, grouped together, talking. They were by the bed, and the bed was between them and the door. Tom went to the door and began to softly lift the latch; then he pressed gently and the door yielded a crack; he continued pushing cautiously, and quaking every time it creaked, till he judged

he might squeeze through on his knees; and so he put his head through and
began, warily.

"What makes the candle blow so?" said Aunt Polly. Tom hurried up. "Why
that door's open, I believe. Why of course it is. No end of strange things now.
Go 'long and shut it, Sid."

Tom disappeared under the bed just in time. He lay and "breathed" himself
for a time, and then crept to where he could almost touch his aunt's foot.

"But as I was saying," said Aunt Polly, "he warn't *bad*, so to say—only
misch*ee*vous. Only just giddy, and harum-scarum, you know. He warn't any
more responsible than a colt. *He* never meant any harm, and he was the best-
hearted boy that ever was"—and she began to cry.

"It was just so with my Joe—always full of his devilment, and up to every
kind of mischief, but he was just as unselfish and kind as he could be—and laws
bless me, to think I went and whipped him for taking that cream, never once
recollecting that I throwed it out myself because it was sour, and I never to see
him again in this world, never, never, never, poor abused boy!" And Mrs.
Harper sobbed as if her heart would break.

"I hope Tom's better off where he is," said Sid, "but if he'd been better in
some ways—"

"*Sid!*" Tom felt the glare of the old lady's eye, though he could not see it.
"Not a word against my Tom, now that he's gone! God'll take care of *him*—
never you trouble *your*self, sir! Oh, Mrs. Harper, I don't know how to give him
up! I don't know how to give him up! He was such a comfort to me, although
he tormented my old heart out of me, 'most."

"The Lord giveth and the Lord hath taken away,—Blessed be the name of
the Lord! But it's *so* hard—Oh, it's so hard! Only last Saturday my Joe busted
a fire-cracker right under my nose and I knocked him sprawling. Little did I
know then, how soon—O, if it was to do over again I'd hug him and bless him
for it."

"Yes, yes, yes, I know just how you feel, Mrs. Harper, I know just exactly
how you feel. No longer ago than yesterday noon, my Tom took and filled the
cat full of Pain-Killer, and I did think the cretur would tear the house down.
And God forgive me, I cracked Tom's head with my thimble, poor boy, poor

WHAT TOM SAW.

dead boy. But he's out of all his troubles now. And the last words I ever heard him say was to reproach—''

But this memory was too much for the old lady, and she broke entirely down. Tom was snuffling, now, himself—and more in pity of himself than anybody else. He could hear Mary crying, and putting in a kindly word for him from time to time. He began to have a nobler opinion of himself than ever before. Still he was sufficiently touched by his aunt's grief to long to rush out from under the bed and overwhelm her with joy—and the theatrical gorgeousness of the thing appealed strongly to his nature, too, but he resisted and lay still.

He went on listening, and gathered by odds and ends that it was conjectured at first that the boys had got drowned while taking a swim; then the small raft had been missed; next, certain boys said the missing lads had promised that the village should ''hear something'' soon; the wise-heads had ''put this and that together'' and decided that the lads had gone off on that raft and would turn up at the next town below, presently; but toward noon the raft had been found, lodged against the Missouri shore some five or six miles below the village,— and then hope perished; they must be drowned, else hunger would have driven them home by nightfall if not sooner. It was believed that the search for the bodies had been a fruitless effort merely because the drowning must have occurred in mid-channel, since the boys, being good swimmers, would otherwise have escaped to shore. This was Wednesday night. If the bodies continued missing until Sunday, all hope would be given over, and the funerals would be preached on that morning. Tom shuddered.

Mrs. Harper gave a sobbing good-night and turned to go. Then with a mutual impulse the two bereaved women flung themselves into each other's arms and had a good, consoling cry, and then parted. Aunt Polly was tender far beyond her wont, in her good-night to Sid and Mary. Sid snuffled a bit and Mary went off crying with all her heart.

Aunt Polly knelt down and prayed for Tom so touchingly, so appealingly, and with such measureless love in her words and her old trembling voice, that he was weltering in tears again, long before she was through.

He had to keep still long after she went to bed, for she kept making broken-hearted ejaculations from time to time, tossing unrestfully, and turning over. But at last she was still, only moaning a little in her sleep. Now the boy stole out, rose gradually by the bedside, shaded the candle-light with his hand, and stood regarding her. His heart was full of pity for her. He took out his sycamore scroll and placed it by the candle. But something occurred to him, and he lingered considering. His face lighted with a happy solution of his thought; he put the bark hastily in his pocket. Then he bent over and kissed the faded lips, and straightway made his stealthy exit, latching the door behind him.

He threaded his way back to the ferry landing, found nobody at large there, and walked boldly on board the boat, for he knew she was tenantless except that there was a watchman, who always turned in and slept like a graven image. He untied the skiff at the stern, slipped into it, and was soon rowing cautiously up stream. When he had pulled a mile above the village, he started quartering across and bent himself stoutly to his work. He hit the landing on the other side neatly, for this was a familiar bit of work to him. He was moved to capture the skiff, arguing that it might be considered a ship and therefore legitimate prey for a pirate, but he knew a thorough search would be made for it and that might end in revelations. So he stepped ashore and entered the wood.

He sat down and took a long rest, torturing himself meantime to keep awake, and then started wearily down the home-stretch. The night was far spent. It was broad daylight before he found himself fairly abreast the island bar. He rested again until the sun was well up and gilding the great river with its splendor, and then he plunged into the stream. A little later he paused, dripping, upon the threshold of the camp, and heard Joe say:

"No, Tom's true-blue, Huck, and he'll come back. He won't desert. He knows that would be a disgrace to a pirate, and Tom's too proud for that sort of thing. He's up to something or other. Now I wonder what?"

"Well, the things is ours, anyway, ain't they?"

"Pretty near, but not yet, Huck. The writing says they are if he ain't back here to breakfast."

"Which he is!" exclaimed Tom, with fine dramatic effect, stepping grandly into camp.

A sumptuous breakfast of bacon and fish was shortly provided, and as the boys set to work upon it, Tom recounted (and adorned) his adventures. They were a vain and boastful company of heroes when the tale was done. Then Tom hid himself away in a shady nook to sleep till noon, and the other pirates got ready to fish and explore.

Chapter XVI

AFTER DINNER ALL the gang turned out to hunt for turtle eggs on the bar. They went about poking sticks into the sand, and when they found a soft place they went down on their knees and dug with their hands. Sometimes they would take fifty or sixty eggs out of one hole. They were perfectly round white things a trifle smaller than an English walnut. They had a famous fried-egg feast that night, and another on Friday morning.

After breakfast they went whooping and prancing out on the bar, and chased each other round and round, shedding clothes as they went, until they were naked, and then continued the frolic far away up the shoal water of the bar, against the stiff current, which latter tripped their legs from under them from time to time and greatly increased the fun. And now and then they stooped in a group and splashed water in each other's faces with their palms, gradually approaching each other, with averted faces to avoid the strangling sprays and finally gripping and struggling till the best man ducked his neighbor, and then they all went under in a tangle of white legs and arms and came up blowing, sputtering, laughing and gasping for breath at one and the same time.

When they were well exhausted, they would run out and sprawl on the dry, hot sand, and lie there and cover themselves up with it, and by and by break for the water again and go through the original performance once more. Finally it occurred to them that their naked skin represented flesh-colored "tights" very fairly; so they drew a ring in the sand and had a circus—with three clowns in it, for none would yield this proudest post to his neighbor.

Next they got their marbles and played "knucks" and "ring-taw" and "keeps" till that amusement grew stale. Then Joe and Huck had another swim, but Tom would not venture, because he found that in kicking off his trousers he had kicked his string of rattlesnake rattles off his ankle, and he wondered how he had escaped cramp so long without the protection of this mysterious charm. He did not venture again until he had found it, and by that time the other boys were tired and ready to rest. They gradually wandered apart, dropped into the "dumps," and fell to gazing longingly across the wide river to where the village lay drowsing in the sun. Tom found himself writing "BECKY" in the sand with his big toe; he scratched it out, and was angry with himself for his weakness. But he wrote it again, nevertheless; he could not help it. He erased it once more and then took himself out of temptation by driving the other boys together and joining them.

But Joe's spirits had gone down almost beyond resurrection. He was so homesick that he could hardly endure the misery of it. The tears lay very near the surface. Huck was melancholy, too. Tom was down-hearted, but tried hard not to show it. He had a secret which he was not ready to tell, yet, but if this mutinous depression was not broken up soon, he would have to bring it out. He said, with a great show of cheerfulness:

"I bet there's been pirates on this island before, boys. We'll explore it again. They've hid treasures here somewhere. How'd you feel to light on a rotten chest full of gold and silver—hey?"

But it roused only a faint enthusiasm, which faded out, with no reply. Tom tried one or two other seductions; but they failed, too. It was discouraging work. Joe sat poking up the sand with a stick and looking very gloomy. Finally he said:

"O, boys, let's give it up. I want to go home. It's so lonesome."

"Oh, no, Joe, you'll feel better by and by," said Tom. "Just think of the fishing that's here."

"I don't care for fishing. I want to go home."

"But Joe, there ain't such another swimming place anywhere."

"Swimming's no good. I don't seem to care for it, somehow, when there ain't anybody to say I shan't go in. I mean to go home."

"O, shucks! Baby! You want to see your mother, I reckon."

"Yes, I *do* want to see my mother—and you would too, if you had one. I ain't any more baby than you are." And Joe snuffled a little.

"Well, we'll let the cry-baby go home to his mother, *won't* we Huck? Poor thing—does it want to see its mother? And so it shall. *You* like it here, *don't* you Huck? We'll stay, won't we?"

Huck said "Y-e-s"—without any heart in it.

"I'll never speak to you again as long as I live," said Joe rising. "There now!" And he moved moodily away and began to dress himself.

"Who cares!" said Tom. "Nobody wants you to. Go 'long home and get laughed at. O, you're a nice pirate. Huck and me ain't cry-babies. We'll stay, won't we Huck? Let him go if he wants to. I reckon we can get along without him, per'aps."

But Tom was uneasy, nevertheless, and was alarmed to see Joe go sullenly on with his dressing. And then it was discomforting to see Huck eyeing Joe's preparations so wistfully, and keeping up such an ominous silence. Presently, without a parting word, Joe began to wade off toward the Illinois shore. Tom's heart began to sink. He glanced at Huck. Huck could not bear the look, and dropped his eyes. Then he said:

"I want to go, too, Tom. It was getting so lonesome anyway, and now it'll be worse. Let's us go too, Tom."

"I won't! You can all go, if you want to. I mean to stay."

"Tom, I better go."

"Well go 'long—who's hendering you."

Huck began to pick up his scattered clothes. He said:

"Tom, I wisht you'd come too. Now you think it over. We'll wait for you when we get to shore."

"Well you'll wait a blame long time, that's all."

Huck started sorrowfully away, and Tom stood looking after him, with a strong desire tugging at his heart to yield his pride and go along too. He hoped the boys would stop, but they still waded slowly on. It suddenly dawned on Tom that it was become very lonely and still. He made one final struggle with his pride, and then darted after his comrades, yelling:

"Wait! Wait! I want to tell you something!"

They presently stopped and turned around. When he got to where they were, he began unfolding his secret, and they listened moodily till at last they saw the "point" he was driving at, and then they set up a war-whoop of applause and said it was "splendid!" and said if he had told them at first, they wouldn't have started away. He made a plausible excuse; but his real reason had been the fear that not even the secret would keep them with him any very great length of time, and so he had meant to hold it in reserve as a last seduction.

The lads came gaily back and went at their sports again with a will, chattering all the time about Tom's stupendous plan and admiring the genius of it. After a dainty egg and fish dinner, Tom said he wanted to learn to smoke, now. Joe caught at the idea and said he would like to try, too. So Huck made pipes and filled them. These novices had never smoked anything before but cigars made of grape-vine and they "bit" the tongue and were not considered manly, anyway.

Now they stretched themselves out on their elbows and began to puff, charily, and with slender confidence. The smoke had an unpleasant taste, and they gagged a little, but Tom said:

"Why it's just as easy! If I'd a knowed *this* was all, I'd a learnt long ago."

"So would I," said Joe. "It's just nothing."

"Why many a time I've looked at people smoking, and thought well I wish I could do that; but I never thought I could," said Tom.

"That's just the way with me, hain't it Huck? You've heard me talk just that way—haven't you Huck? I'll leave it to Huck if I haven't."

"Yes—heaps of times," said Huck.

"Well I have too," said Tom; "O, hundreds of times. Once down by the slaughter-house. Don't you remember, Huck? Bob Tanner was there, and Johnny Miller, and Jeff Thatcher, when I said it. Don't you remember Huck, 'bout me saying that?"

"Yes, that's so," said Huck. "That was the day after I lost a white alley. No, 'twas the day before."

"There—I told you so," said Tom. "Huck recollects it."

"I bleeve I could smoke this pipe all day," said Joe. "*I* don't feel sick."

"Neither do I," said Tom. "*I* could smoke it all day. But I bet you Jeff Thatcher couldn't."

"Jeff Thatcher! Why he'd keel over just with two draws. Just let him try it once. *He'd* see!"

"I bet he would. And Johnny Miller—I wish I could see Johnny Miller tackle it once."

"O, dont *I!*" said Joe, "Why I bet you Johnny Miller couldn't any more do this than nothing. Just one little snifter would fetch *him.*"

"'Deed it would, Joe. Say—I wish the boys could see us now."

"So do I."

"Say—boys, don't say anything about it, and some time when they're around, I'll come up to you and say 'Joe, got a pipe? I want a smoke.' And you'll say, kind of careless like, as if it warn't anything, you'll say, 'Yes, I got my *old* pipe, and another one, but my tobacker ain't very good.' And I'll say, 'Oh, that's all right, if it's *strong* enough.' And then you'll out with the pipes, and we'll light up just as ca'm, and then just see 'em look!"

"By jings that'll be gay, Tom! I wish it was *now!*"

"So do I! And when we tell 'em we learned when we was off pirating, won't they wish they'd been along?"

"O, I reckon not! I'll just *bet* they will!"

So the talk ran on. But presently it began to flag a trifle, and grow disjointed. The silences widened; the expectoration marvelously increased. Every pore inside the boys' cheeks became a spouting fountain; they could scarcely bail out the cellars under their tongues fast enough to prevent an inundation; little overflowings down their throats occurred in spite of all they could do, and sudden retchings followed every time. Both boys were looking very pale and miserable, now. Joe's pipe dropped from his nerveless fingers. Tom's followed. Both fountains were going furiously and both pumps bailing with might and main. Joe said feebly:

"I've lost my knife. I reckon I better go and find it."

Tom said, with quivering lips and halting utterance:

"I'll help you. You go over that way and I'll hunt around by the spring. No, you needn't come, Huck—we can find it."

So Huck sat down again, and waited an hour. Then he found it lonesome, and went to find his comrades. They were wide apart in the woods, both very pale, both fast asleep. But something informed him that if they had had any trouble they had got rid of it.

They were not talkative at supper that night. They had a humble look, and when Huck prepared his pipe after the meal and was going to prepare theirs, they said no, they were not feeling very well—something they ate at dinner had disagreed with them.

About midnight Joe awoke, and called the boys. There was a brooding oppressiveness in the air that seemed to bode something. The boys huddled themselves together and sought the friendly companionship of the fire, though the dull dead heat of the breathless atmosphere was stifling. They sat still, intent and waiting. The solemn hush continued. Beyond the light of the fire everything was swallowed up in the blackness of darkness. Presently there came a quivering glow that vaguely revealed the foliage for a moment and then vanished. By and by another came, a little stronger. Then another. Then a faint moan came sighing through the branches of the forest and the boys felt a fleeting breath upon their cheeks, and shuddered with the fancy that the Spirit of the Night had gone by. There was a pause. Now a weird flash turned night into day and showed every little grass-blade, separate and distinct, that grew about their feet. And it showed three white, startled faces, too. A deep peal of thunder went rolling and tumbling down the heavens and lost itself in sullen rumblings in the distance. A sweep of chilly air passed by, rustling all the leaves and snowing the flaky ashes broadcast about the fire. Another fierce glare lit up the forest and an instant crash followed that seemed to rend the tree-tops right over the boys' heads. They clung together in terror, in the thick gloom that followed. A few big raindrops fell pattering upon the leaves.

"Quick! boys, go for the tent!" exclaimed Tom.

They sprang away, stumbling over roots and among vines in the dark, no two plunging in the same direction. A furious blast roared through the trees, making everything sing as it went. One blinding flash after another came, and peal on peal of deafening thunder. And now a drenching rain poured down and the rising hurricane drove it in sheets along the ground. The boys cried out to each other, but the roaring wind and the booming thunder-blasts drowned their voices utterly. However one by one they straggled in at last and took shelter under the tent, cold, scared, and streaming with water; but to have company in misery seemed something to be grateful for. They could not talk, the old sail flapped so furiously, even if the other noises would have allowed them. The tempest rose higher and higher, and presently the sail tore loose from its fastenings and went winging away on the blast. The boys seized each others' hands and fled, with many tumblings and bruises, to the shelter of a great oak that stood upon the river bank. Now the battle was at its highest. Under the ceaseless conflagration of lightning that flamed in the skies, everything below stood out in clean-cut and shadowless distinctness: the bending trees, the billowy river, white with foam, the driving spray of spume-flakes, the dim outlines of the high bluffs on the other side, glimpsed through the drifting cloud-rack and the slanting veil of rain. Every little while some giant tree yielded the fight and fell crashing through the younger growth; and the unflagging thunder-peals came now in ear-splitting explosive bursts, keen and sharp, and unspeakably appalling. The storm culminated in one matchless effort that seemed likely to tear the island to pieces, burn it up, drown it to the tree tops, blow it away, and deafen every creature in it, all at one and the same moment. It was a wild night for homeless young heads to be out in.

But at last the battle was done, and the forces retired with weaker and weaker threatenings and grumblings, and peace resumed her sway. The boys went back to camp, a good deal awed; but they found there was still something to be thankful for, because the great sycamore, the shelter of their beds, was a ruin, now, blasted by the lightnings, and they were not under it when the catastrophe happened.

Everything in camp was drenched, the camp-fire as well; for they were but heedless lads, like their generation, and had made no provision against rain. Here was matter for dismay, for they were soaked through and chilled. They were eloquent in their distress; but they presently discovered that the fire had eaten so far up under the great log it had been built against, (where it curved upward and separated itself from the ground,) that a hand-breadth or so of it had escaped wetting; so they patiently wrought until, with shreds and bark gathered from the under sides of sheltered logs, they coaxed the fire to burn again. Then they piled on great dead boughs till they had a roaring furnace and were glad-hearted once more. They dried their boiled ham and had a feast, and after that they sat by the fire and expanded and glorified their midnight adventure until morning, for there was not a dry spot to sleep on, anywhere around.

As the sun began to steal in upon the boys, drowsiness came over them and they went out on the sand-bar and lay down to sleep. They got scorched out by and by, and drearily set about getting breakfast. After the meal they felt rusty, and stiff-jointed, and a little homesick once more. Tom saw the signs, and fell to cheering up the pirates as well as he could. But they cared nothing for marbles, or circus, or swimming, or anything. He reminded them of the imposing secret, and raised a ray of cheer. While it lasted, he got them interested in a new device. This was to knock off being pirates, for a while, and be Indians for a change. They were attracted by this idea; so it was not long before they were stripped, and striped from head to heel with black mud, like so many zebras,—all of them chiefs, of course—and then they went tearing through the woods to attack an English settlement.

By and by they separated into three hostile tribes, and darted upon each other from ambush with dreadful war-whoops, and killed and scalped each other by thousands. It was a gory day. Consequently it was an extremely satisfactory one.

They assembled in camp toward supper time, hungry and happy; but now a difficulty arose—hostile Indians could not break the bread of hospitality together without first making peace, and this was a simple impossibility without smoking a pipe of peace. There was no other process that ever they had heard of. Two of the savages almost wished they had remained pirates. However, there was no other way; so with such show of cheerfulness as they could muster they called for the pipe and took their whiff as it passed, in due form.

And behold they were glad they had gone into savagery, for they had gained something; they found that they could now smoke a little without having to go and hunt for a lost knife; they did not get sick enough to be seriously uncomfortable. They were not likely to fool away this high promise for lack of effort. No, they practiced cautiously, after supper, with right fair success, and so they spent a jubilant evening. They were prouder and happier in their new acquirement than they would have been in the scalping and skinning of the Six Nations. We will leave them to smoke and chatter and brag, since we have no further use for them at present.

TERRIBLE SLAUGHTER.

Chapter XVII

BUT THERE WAS no hilarity in the little town that same tranquil Saturday afternoon. The Harpers, and Aunt Polly's family, were being put into mourning, with great grief and many tears. An unusual quiet possessed the village, although it was ordinarily quiet enough, in all conscience. The villagers conducted their concerns with an absent air, and talked little; but they sighed often. The Saturday holiday seemed a burden to the children. They had no heart in their sports, and gradually gave them up.

In the afternoon Becky Thatcher found herself moping about the deserted school-house yard, and feeling very melancholy. But she found nothing there to comfort her. She soliloquised:

"Oh, if I only had his brass andiron-knob again! But I haven't got anything now to remember him by." And she choked back a little sob.

Presently she stopped, and said to herself:

"It was right here. O, if it was to do over again, I wouldn't say that—I wouldn't say it for the whole world. But he's gone now; I'll never never never see him any more."

This thought broke her down and she wandered away, with the tears rolling down her cheeks. Then quite a group of boys and girls,—playmates of Tom's and Joe's—came by, and stood looking over the paling fence and talking in reverent tones of how Tom did so-and-so, the last time they saw him, and how Joe said this and that small trifle (pregnant with awful prophecy, as they could easily see now!)—and each speaker pointed out the exact spot where the lost lads stood at the time, and then added something like "and I was a standing just so—just as I am now, and as if you was him—I was as close as that—and he smiled, just this way—and then something seemed to go all over me, like,—awful, you know—and I never thought what it meant, of course, but I can see now!"

Then there was a dispute about who saw the dead boys last in life, and many claimed that dismal distinction, and offered evidences, more or less tampered with by the witness; and when it was ultimately decided who *did* see the departed last, and exchanged the last words with them, the lucky parties took upon themselves a sort of sacred importance, and were gaped at and envied by all the rest. One poor chap, who had no other grandeur to offer, said with tolerably manifest pride in the remembrance:

"Well, Tom Sawyer he licked me once."

But that bid for glory was a failure. Most of the boys could say that, and so that cheapened the distinction too much. The group loitered away, still recalling memories of the lost heroes, in awed voices.

When the Sunday-school hour was finished, the next morning, the bell began to toll, instead of ringing in the usual way. It was a very still Sabbath, and the mournful sound seemed in keeping with the musing hush that lay upon nature. The villagers began to gather, loitering a moment in the vestibule to converse in whispers about the sad event. But there was no whispering in the house; only the funereal rustling of dresses as the women gathered to their seats, disturbed the silence there. None could remember when the little church had been so full before. There was finally a waiting pause, an expectant dumbness, and then Aunt Polly entered, followed by Sid and Mary, and they by the Harper family, all in deep black, and the whole congregation, the old minister as well, rose reverently and stood, until the mourners were seated in the front pew. There was another communing silence, broken at intervals by muffled sobs, and then the minister spread his hands abroad and prayed. A moving hymn was sung, and the text followed: "I am the Resurrection and the Life."

As the service proceeded, the clergyman drew such pictures of the graces, the winning ways and the rare promise of the lost lads, that every soul there, thinking he recognized these pictures, felt a pang in remembering that he had persistently blinded himself to them, always before, and had as persistently seen only faults and flaws in the poor boys. The minister related many a touching incident in the lives of the departed, too, which illustrated their sweet, generous natures, and the people could easily see, now, how noble and beautiful those episodes were, and remembered with grief that at the time they occurred they had seemed rank rascalities, well deserving of the cowhide. The congregation became more and more moved, as the pathetic tale went on, till at last the whole company broke down and joined the weeping mourners in a chorus of anguished sobs, the preacher himself giving way to his feelings, and crying in the pulpit.

There was a rustle in the gallery, which nobody noticed; a moment later the church door creaked; the minister raised his streaming eyes above his handkerchief, and stood transfixed! First one and then another pair of eyes followed the minister's, and then almost with one impulse the congregation rose and stared while the three dead boys came marching up the aisle, Tom in the lead, Joe next, and Huck, a ruin of drooping rags, sneaking sheepishly in the rear! They had been hid in the unused gallery listening to their own funeral sermon!

Aunt Polly, Mary and the Harpers threw themselves upon their restored ones, smothered them with kisses and poured out thanksgivings, while poor Huck stood abashed and uncomfortable, not knowing exactly what to do or where to hide from so many unwelcoming eyes. He wavered, and started to slink away, but Tom seized him and said:

"Aunt Polly, it ain't fair. Somebody's got to be glad to see Huck."

"And so they shall. *I'm* glad to see him, poor motherless thing!" And the

TOM'S PROUDEST MOMENT.

loving attentions Aunt Polly lavished upon him were the one thing capable of making him more uncomfortable than he was before.

Suddenly the minister shouted at the top of his voice: "Praise God from whom all blessings flow—SING!—and put your hearts in it!"

And they did. Old Hundred swelled up with a triumphant burst, and while it shook the rafters Tom Sawyer the Pirate looked around upon the envying juveniles about him and confessed in his heart that this was the proudest moment of his life.

As the "sold" congregation trooped out they said they would almost be willing to be made ridiculous again to hear Old Hundred sung like that once more.

Tom got more cuffs and kisses that day—according to Aunt Polly's varying moods—than he had earned before in a year; and he hardly knew which expressed the most gratefulness to God and affection for himself.

Chapter XVIII

THAT WAS TOM'S great secret—the scheme to return home with his brother pirates and attend their own funerals. They had paddled over to the Missouri shore on a log, at dusk on Saturday, landing five or six miles below the village; they had slept in the woods at the edge of the town till nearly daylight, and had then crept through back lanes and alleys and finished their sleep in the gallery of the church among a chaos of invalided benches.

At breakfast, Monday morning, Aunt Polly and Mary were very loving to Tom, and very attentive to his wants. There was an unusual amount of talk. In the course of it Aunt Polly said:

"Well, I don't say it wasn't a fine joke, Tom, to keep everybody suffering 'most a week so you boys had a good time, but it is a pity you could be so hard-hearted as to let *me* suffer so. If you could come over on a log to go to your funeral, you could have come over and give me a hint some way that you warn't *dead*, but only run off."

"Yes, you could have done that, Tom," said Mary; "and I believe you would if you had thought of it."

"Would you Tom?" said Aunt Polly, her face lighting wistfully. "Say, now, would you, if you'd thought of it?"

"I—well I don't know. 'Twould a spoiled everything."

"Tom, I hoped you loved me that much," said Aunt Polly, with a grieved tone that discomforted the boy. "It would been something if you'd cared enough to *think* of it, even if you didn't *do* it."

"Now auntie, that ain't any harm," pleaded Mary; "it's only Tom's giddy way—he is always in such a rush that he never thinks of anything."

"More's the pity. Sid would have thought. And Sid would have come and *done* it, too. Tom, you'll look back, some day, when it's too late, and wish you'd cared a little more for me when it would have cost you so little."

"Now auntie, you know I do care for you," said Tom.

"I'd know it better if you acted more like it."

"I wish now I'd thought," said Tom, with a repentant tone; "but I dreamed about you, anyway. That's something, ain't it?"

"It ain't much—a cat does that much—but it's better than nothing. What did you dream?"

"Why Wednesday night I dreamt that you was sitting over there by the bed, and Sid was sitting by the wood-box, and Mary next to him."

"Well, so we did. So we always do. I'm glad your dreams could take even that much trouble about us."

"And I dreamt that Joe Harper's mother was here."

"Why, she *was* here! Did you dream any more?"

"O, lots. But it's so dim, now."

"Well, *try* to recollect—can't you?"

"Some how it seems to me that the wind—the wind blowed the—the—"

"Try harder, Tom! The wind did blow something. Come!"

Tom pressed his fingers on his forehead an anxious minute, and then said:

"I've got it now! I've got it now! It blowed the candle!"

"Mercy on us! Go on, Tom—go on!"

"And it seems to me that you said, 'Why I believe that that door—' "

"Go *on*, Tom!"

"Just let me study a moment—just a moment. Oh, yes—you said you believed the door was open."

"As I'm a sitting here, I did! Didn't I, Mary! Go on!"

"And then—and then—well I won't be certain, but it seems like as if you made Sid go and—and—"

"Well? Well? What did I make him do, Tom? What did I make him do?"

"You made him—you—O, you made him shut it."

"Well for the land's sake! I never heard the beat of that in all my days! Don't tell *me* there ain't anything in dreams, any more. Sereny Harper shall know of this before I'm an hour older. I'd like to see her get around *this* with her rubbage 'bout superstition. Go on, Tom!"

"Oh, it's all getting just as bright as day, now. Next you said I warn't *bad*, only mischeevous and harum-scarum, and not any more responsible than—than—I think it was a colt, or something."

"And so it was! Well, goodness gracious! Go on, Tom!"

"And then you began to cry."

TOM TRIES TO REMEMBER.

"So I did. So I did. Not the first time, neither. And then—"

"Then Mrs. Harper she began to cry, and said Joe was just the same and she wished she hadn't whipped him for taking cream when she'd throwed it out her own self—"

"Tom! The sperrit was upon you! You was a prophecying—that's what you was doing! Land alive, go on, Tom!"

"Then Sid he said—he said—"

"I don't think I said anything," said Sid.

"Yes you did, Sid," said Mary.

"Shut your heads and let Tom go on! What did he say, Tom?"

"He said—I *think* he said he hoped I was better off where I was gone to, but if I'd been better sometimes—"

"*There*, d'you hear that! It was his very words!"

"And you shut him up sharp."

"I lay I did! There must a been an angel there. There *was* an angel there, somewheres!"

"And Mrs. Harper told about Joe scaring her with a fire-cracker, and you told about Peter and the Pain-killer—"

"Just as true as I live!"

"And then there was a whole lot of talk 'bout dragging the river for us, and 'bout having the funeral Sunday, and then you and old Miss Harper hugged and cried, and she went."

"It happened just so! It happened just so, as sure as I'm a sitting in these very tracks. Tom you couldn't told it more like, if you'd a seen it! And *then* what? Go on, Tom?"

"Then I thought you prayed for me—and I could see you and hear every word you said. And you went to bed, and I was so sorry, that I took and wrote on a piece of sycamore bark, '*We ain't dead—we are only off being pirates,*' and put it on the table by the candle; and then you looked so good, laying there asleep, that I thought I went and leaned over and kissed you on the lips."

"Did you, Tom, *did* you! I just forgive you everything for that!" And she seized the boy in a crushing embrace that made him feel like the guiltiest of villains.

"It was very kind, even though it was only a—dream," Sid soliloquised just audibly.

"Shut up Sid! A body does just the same in a dream as he'd do if he was awake. Here's a big Milum apple I've been saving for you Tom, if you was ever found again—now go 'long to school. I'm thankful to the good God and Father of us all I've got you back, that's long-suffering and merciful to them that believe on Him and keep His word, though goodness knows I'm unworthy of it, but if only the worthy ones got His blessings and had His hand to help them over the rough places, there's few enough would smile here or ever enter into His rest when the long night comes. Go 'long Sid, Mary, Tom—take yourselves off—you've hendered me long enough."

The children left for school, and the old lady to call on Mrs. Harper and vanquish her realism with Tom's marvelous dream. Sid had better judgment than to utter the thought that was in his mind as he left the house. It was this: "Pretty thin—as long a dream as that, without any mistakes in it!"

What a hero Tom was become, now! He did not go skipping and prancing, but moved with a dignified swagger as became a pirate who felt that the public eye was on him. And indeed it was; he tried not to seem to see the looks or hear the remarks as he passed along, but they were food and drink to him. Smaller boys than himself flocked at his heels, as proud to be seen with him, and tolerated by him, as if he had been the drummer at the head of a procession or the elephant leading a menagerie into town. Boys of his own size pretended not to know he had been away at all; but they were consuming with envy, nevertheless. They would have given anything to have that swarthy sun-tanned skin of his, and his glittering notoriety; and Tom would not have parted with either for a circus.

At school the children made so much of him and of Joe, and delivered such eloquent admiration from their eyes, that the two heroes were not long in becoming insufferably "stuck-up." They began to tell their adventures to hungry listeners— but they only began; it was not a thing likely to have an end, with imaginations like theirs to furnish material. And finally, when they got out their pipes and went serenely puffing around, the very summit of glory was reached.

Tom decided that he could be independent of Becky Thatcher now. Glory was sufficient. He would live for glory. Now that he was distinguished, maybe she would be wanting to "make up." Well, let her—she should see that he could be as indifferent as some other people. Presently she arrived. Tom pretended not to see her. He moved away and joined a group of boys and girls and began to talk. Soon he observed that she was tripping gayly back and forth with flushed face and dancing eyes, pretending to be busy chasing school-mates, and screaming with laughter when she made a capture; but he noticed that she always made her captures in his vicinity, and that she seemed to cast a conscious eye in his direction at such times, too. It gratified all the vicious vanity that was in him; and so, instead of winning him it only "set him up" the more and made him the more diligent to avoid betraying that he knew she was about. Presently she gave over skylarking, and moved irresolutely about, sighing once or twice and glancing furtively and wistfully toward Tom. Then she observed that now Tom was talking more particularly to Amy Lawrence than to any one else. She felt a sharp pang and grew disturbed and uneasy at once. She tried to go away, but her feet were treacherous, and carried her to the group instead. She said to a girl almost at Tom's elbow—with sham vivacity:

"Why Mary Austin! you bad girl, why didn't you come to Sunday-school?"

"I did come—didn't you see me?"

"Why no! Did you? Where did you sit?"

"I was in Miss Peter's class, where I always go. I saw *you.*"

"Did you? Why it's funny I didn't see you. I wanted to tell you about the pic-nic."

'O, that's jolly. Who's going to give it?"

"My ma's going to let me have one."

"O, goody; I hope she'll let *me* come."

"Well she will. The pic-nic's for me. She'll let anybody come that I want, and I want you."

"That's ever so nice. When is it going to be?"

"By and by. Maybe about vacation."

"O, won't it be fun! You going to have all the girls and boys?"

"Yes, every one that's friends to me—or wants to be;" and she glanced ever so furtively at Tom, but he talked right along to Amy Lawrence about the terrible storm on the island, and how the lightning tore the great sycamore tree "all to flinders" while he was "standing within three feet of it."

"O, may I come?" said Gracie Miller.

"Yes."

"And me?" said Sally Rogers.

"Yes."

"And me, too?" said Susy Harper. "And Joe?"

"Yes."

And so on, with clapping of joyful hands till all the group had begged for invitations but Tom and Amy. Then Tom turned coolly away, still talking, and took Amy with him. Becky's lips trembled and the tears came to her eyes; she hid these signs with a forced gayety and went on chattering, but the life had gone out of the pic-nic, now, and out of everything else; she got away as soon as she could and hid herself and had what her sex call "a good cry." Then she sat moody, with wounded pride till the bell rang. She roused up, now, with a vindictive cast in her eye, and gave her plaited tails a shake and said she knew what *she'd* do.

At recess Tom continued his flirtation with Amy with jubilant self-satisfaction. And he kept drifting about to find Becky and lacerate her with the performance. At last he spied her, but there was a sudden falling of his mercury. She was sitting cosily on a little bench behind the school-house looking at a picture book with Alfred Temple—and so absorbed were they, and their heads so close together over the book that they did not seem to be conscious of anything in the world besides. Jealousy ran red hot through Tom's veins. He began to hate himself for throwing away the chance Becky had offered for a reconciliation. He called himself a fool, and all the hard names he could think of. He wanted to cry with vexation. Amy chatted happily along, as they walked, for her heart was singing, but Tom's tongue had lost its function. He did not hear what Amy was saying, and whenever she paused expectantly he could only stammer an awkward assent, which was as often misplaced as otherwise. He kept drifting to the rear of the school-house, again and again, to sear his eye-balls with the hateful spectacle there. He could not help it. And it maddened him to see, as he thought he saw, that Becky Thatcher never once suspected that he was even in the land of the living. But she did see, nevertheless; and she knew she was winning her fight, too, and was glad to see him suffer as she had suffered.

Amy's happy prattle became intolerable. Tom hinted at things he had to attend to; things that must be done; and time was fleeting. But in vain—the girl chirped on. Tom thought, "O hang her, ain't I ever going to get rid of her?" At last he *must* be attending to those things—and she said artlessly that she would be "around" when school let out. And he hastened away, hating her for it.

"Any other boy!" Tom thought, grating his teeth. "Any boy in the whole town but that Saint Louis smarty that thinks he dresses so fine and is aristocracy! O, all right, I licked you the first day you ever saw this town, mister, and I'll lick you again! You just wait till I catch you out! I'll just take and—"

And he went through the motions of thrashing an imaginary boy—pummeling the air, and kicking and gouging. "Oh, you do, do you? You holler 'nough, do you? Now, then, let that learn you!" And so the imaginary flogging was finished to his satisfaction.

Tom fled home at noon. His conscience could not endure any more of Amy's grateful happiness, and his jealousy could bear no more of the other distress.

Becky resumed her picture-inspections with Alfred, but as the minutes dragged along and no Tom came to suffer, her triumph began to cloud and she lost interest; gravity and absent-mindedness followed, and then melancholy; two or three times she pricked up her ear at a footstep, but it was a false hope; no Tom came. At last she grew entirely miserable and wished she hadn't carried it so far. When poor Alfred, seeing that he was losing her, he did not know how, and kept exclaiming: "O here's a jolly one! look at this!" she lost patience at last, and said, "Oh, don't bother me! I don't care for them!" and burst into tears, and got up and walked away.

Alfred dropped alongside and was going to try to comfort her, but she said: "Go away and leave me alone, can't you! I hate you!"

So the boy halted, wondering what he could have done—for she had said she would look at pictures all through the nooning—and she walked on, crying. Then Alfred went musing into the deserted school-house. He was humiliated and angry. He easily guessed his way to the truth—the girl had simply made a convenience of him to vent her spite upon Tom Sawyer. He was far from hating Tom the less when this thought occurred to him. He wished there was some way to get that boy into trouble without much risk to himself. Tom's spelling book fell under his eye. Here was his opportunity. He gratefully opened to the lesson for the afternoon and poured ink upon the page.

Becky, glancing in at a window behind him at the moment, saw the act, and moved on, without discovering herself. She started homeward, now, intending to find Tom and tell him; Tom would be thankful and their troubles would be healed. Before she was half way home, however, she had changed her mind. The thought of Tom's treatment of her when she was talking about her pic-nic came scorching back and filled her with shame. She resolved to let him get whipped on the damaged spelling-book's account, and to hate him forever, into the bargain.

Chapter XIX

TOM ARRIVED AT home in a dreary mood, and the first thing his aunt said to him showed him that he had brought his sorrows to an unpromising market:

"Tom, I've a notion to skin you alive!"

"Auntie, what have I done?"

"Well, you've done enough. Here I go over to Sereny Harper, like an old softy, expecting I'm going to make her believe all that rubbage about that dream, when lo and behold you she'd found out from Joe that you was over here and heard all the talk we had that night. Tom I don't know what is to become of a boy that will act like that. It makes me feel so bad to think you could let me go to Sereny Harper and make such a fool of myself and never say a word."

This was a new aspect of the thing. His smartness of the morning had seemed to Tom a good joke before, and very ingenious. It merely looked mean and shabby now. He hung his head and could not think of anything to say for a moment. Then he said:

"Auntie, I wish I hadn't done it—but I didn't think."

"O, child you never think. You never think of anything but your own selfishness.

You could think to come all the way over here from Jackson's island in the night to laugh at our troubles, and you could think to fool me with a lie about a dream; but you couldn't ever think to pity us and save us from sorrow.''

"Auntie, I know now it was mean, but I didn't mean to be mean. I didn't, honest. And besides I didn't come over here to laugh at you that night.''

"What did you come for, then?''

"It was to tell you not to be uneasy about us, because we hadn't got drowned.''

"Tom, Tom, I would be the thankfullest soul in this world if I could believe you ever had as good a thought as that, but you know you never did—and *I* know it, Tom.''

"Indeed and 'deed I did, auntie—I wish I may never stir if I didn't.''

"O, Tom, don't lie—don't do it. It only makes things a hundred times worse.''

"It ain't a lie, auntie, it's the truth. I wanted to keep you from grieving—that was all that made me come.''

"I'd give the whole world to believe that—it would cover up a power of sins Tom. I'd 'most be glad you'd run off and acted so bad. But it aint reasonable; because, why didn't you tell me, child?''

"Why, you see, auntie, when you got to talking about the funeral, I just got all full of the idea of our coming and hiding in the church, and I couldn't somehow bear to spoil it. So I just put the bark back in my pocket and kept mum.''

"What bark?''

"The bark I had wrote on to tell you we'd gone pirating. I wish, now, you'd waked up when I kissed you—I do, honest.''

The hard lines in his aunt's face relaxed and a sudden tenderness dawned in her eyes.

"*Did* you kiss me, Tom?''

"Why yes I did.''

"Are you sure you did, Tom?''

"Why yes I did, auntie—certain sure.''

"What did you kiss me for, Tom?''

"Because I loved you so, and you laid there moaning and I was so sorry.''

The words sounded like truth. The old lady could not hide a tremor in her voice when she said:

"Kiss me again, Tom!—and be off with you to school, now, and don't bother me any more.''

The moment he was gone, she ran to a closet and got out the ruin of a jacket which Tom had gone pirating in. Then she stopped, with it in her hand, and said to herself:

"No, I don't dare. Poor boy, I reckon he's lied about it—but it's a blessed, blessed lie, there's such comfort come from it. I hope the Lord—I *know* the Lord will forgive him, because it was such goodheartedness in him to tell it. But I don't want to find out it's a lie. I won't look.''

She put the jacket away, and stood by musing a minute. Twice she put out her hand to take the garment again, and twice she refrained. Once more she ventured, and this time she fortified herself with the thought: "It's a good lie—it's a good lie—I won't let it grieve me.'' So she sought the jacket pocket. A moment later she was reading Tom's piece of bark through flowing tears and saying: "I could forgive the boy, now, if he'd committed a million sins!''

TOM JUSTIFIED.

Chapter XX

THERE WAS SOMETHING about Aunt Polly's manner, when she kissed Tom, that swept away his low spirits and made him light-hearted and happy again. He started to school and had the luck of coming upon Becky Thatcher at the head of Meadow Lane. His mood always determined his manner. Without a moment's hesitation he ran to her and said:

"I acted mighty mean to-day, Becky, and I'm so sorry. I won't ever, ever do that way again, as long as ever I live—please make up, won't you?"

The girl stopped and looked him scornfully in the face:

"I'll thank you to keep yourself *to* yourself, Mr. Thomas Sawyer. I'll never speak to you again."

She tossed her head and passed on. Tom was so stunned that he had not even presence of mind enough to say "Who cares, Miss Smarty?" until the right time to say it had gone by. So he said nothing. But he was in a fine rage, nevertheless. He moped into the school-yard wishing she were a boy, and imagining how he would trounce her if she were. He presently encountered her and delivered a stinging remark as he passed. She hurled one in return, and the angry breach was complete. It seemed to Becky, in her hot resentment, that she could hardly wait for school to "take in," she was so impatient to see Tom flogged for the injured spelling-book. If she had had any lingering notion of exposing Alfred Temple, Tom's offensive fling had driven it entirely away.

Poor girl, she did not know how fast she was nearing trouble herself. The master, Mr. Dobbins, had reached middle age with an unsatisfied ambition. The darling of his desires was, to be a doctor, but poverty had decreed that he should be nothing higher than a village schoolmaster. Every day he took a mysterious book out of his desk and absorbed himself in it at times when no classes were reciting. He kept that book under lock and key. There was not an urchin in school but was perishing to have a glimpse of it, but the chance never came. Every boy and girl had a theory about the nature of that book; but no two theories were alike, and there was no way of getting at the facts in the case. Now, as Becky was passing by the desk, which stood near the door, she noticed that the key was in the lock! It was a precious moment. She glanced around; found herself alone, and the next instant she had the book in her hands. The title-page—Professor somebody's "Anatomy"—carried no information to her mind; so she began to turn the leaves. She came at once upon a handsomely engraved and colored frontispiece—a human figure, stark naked. At that moment a shadow fell on the page and Tom Sawyer stepped in at the door, and caught a glimpse of the picture. Becky snatched at the book to close it, and had the hard luck to tear the pictured page half down the middle. She thrust the volume into the desk, turned the key, and burst out crying with shame and vexation.

"Tom Sawyer, you are just as mean as you can be, to sneak up on a person and look at what they're looking at."

"How could *I* know you was looking at anything?"

"You ought to be ashamed of yourself Tom Sawyer; you know you're going to tell on me, and O, what shall I do, what shall I do! I'll be whipped, and I never was whipped in school."

Then she stamped her little foot and said:

"*Be* so mean if you want to! *I* know something that's going to happen. You just wait and you'll see! Hateful, hateful, hateful!"—and she flung out of the house with a new explosion of crying.

Tom stood still, rather flustered by this onslaught. Presently he said to himself:

"What a curious kind of a fool a girl is. Never been licked in school! Shucks. What's a licking! That's just like a girl—they're so thin-skinned and chicken hearted. Well, of course *I* ain't going to tell old Dobbins on this little fool, because there's other ways of getting even on her, that ain't so mean; but what of it? Old Dobbins will ask who it was tore his book. Nobody'll answer. Then he'll do just the way he always does—ask first one and then t'other, and when he comes to the right girl he'll know it, without any telling. Girls' faces always tell on them. They ain't got any back-bone. She'll get licked. Well, it's a kind of a tight place for Becky Thatcher, because there ain't any way out of it." Tom conned the thing a moment longer and then added: "All right, though; she'd like to see me in just such a fix—let her sweat it out!"

CAUGHT IN THE ACT.

Tom joined the mob of skylarking scholars outside. In a few moments the master arrived and school "took in." Tom did not feel a strong interest in his studies. Every time he stole a glance at the girls' side of the room Becky's face troubled him. Considering all things, he did not want to pity her, and yet it was all he could do to help it. He could get up no exultation that was really worthy the name. Presently the spelling-book discovery was made, and Tom's mind was entirely full of his own matters for a while after that. Becky roused up from her lethargy of distress and showed good interest in the proceedings. She did not expect that Tom could get out of his trouble by denying that he spilt the ink on the book himself; and she was right. The denial only seemed to make the thing worse for Tom. Becky supposed she would be glad of that, and she tried to believe she was glad of it, but she found she was not certain. When the worst came to the worst, she had an impulse to get up and tell on Alfred Temple, but she made an effort and forced herself to keep still—because, said she to herself, "he'll tell about me tearing the picture sure. I wouldn't say a word, not to save his life!"

Tom took his whipping and went back to his seat not at all broken-hearted, for he thought it was possible that he had unknowingly upset the ink on the spelling-book himself, in some skylarking bout—he had denied it for form's sake and because it was custom, and had stuck to the denial from principle.

A whole hour drifted by, the master sat nodding in his throne, the air was drowsy with the hum of study. By and by, Mr. Dobbins straightened himself up, yawned, then unlocked his desk, and reached for his book, but seemed undecided whether to take it out or leave it. Most of the pupils glanced up languidly, but there were two among them that watched his movements with intent eyes. Mr. Dobbins fingered his book absently for a while, then took it out and settled himself in his chair to read! Tom shot a glance at Becky. He had seen a hunted and helpless rabbit look as she did, with a gun leveled at its head. Instantly he forgot his quarrel with her. Quick—something must be done! done in a flash, too! But the very imminence of the emergency paralyzed his invention. Good!—he had an inspiration! He would run and snatch the book, spring through the door and fly. But his resolution shook for one little instant, and the chance was lost—the master opened the volume. If Tom only had the wasted opportunity back again! Too late. There was no help for Becky now, he said. The next moment the master faced the school. Every eye sunk under his gaze. There was that in it which smote even the innocent with fear. There was silence while one might count ten, the master was gathering his wrath. Then he spoke:

"Who tore this book?"

There was not a sound. One could have heard a pin drop. The stillness continued; the master searched face after face for signs of guilt.

"Benjamin Rogers, did you tear this book?"

A denial. Another pause.

"Joseph Harper, did you?"

Another denial. Tom's uneasiness grew more and more intense under the slow torture of these proceedings. The master scanned the ranks of boys—considered a while, then turned to the girls:

"Amy Lawrence?"

A shake of the head.

"Gracie Miller?"

The same sign.

"Susan Harper, did you do this?"

Another negative. The next girl was Becky Thatcher. Tom was trembling from head to foot with excitement and a sense of the hopelessness of the situation.

"Rebecca Thatcher," [Tom glanced at her face—it was white with terror,]—"did you tear—no, look me in the face"—[her hands rose in appeal]—"did you tear this book?"

A thought shot like lightning through Tom's brain. He sprang to his feet and shouted—"*I* done it!"

The school stared in perplexity at this incredible folly. Tom stood a moment, to gather his dismembered faculties; and when he stepped forward to go to his punishment the surprise, the gratitude, the adoratiom that shone upon him out of poor Becky's eyes seemed pay enough for a hundred floggings. Inspired by the splendor of his own act, he took without an outcry the most merciless flaying that even Mr. Dobbins had ever administered; and also received with indifference the added cruelty of a command to remain two hours after school should be dismissed—for he knew who would wait for him outside till his captivity was done, and not count the tedious time as loss, either.

Tom went to bed that night planning vengeance against Alfred Temple; for with shame and repentance Becky had told him all, not forgetting her own treachery; but even the longing for vengeance had to give way, soon, to pleasanter musings, and he fell asleep at last, with Becky's latest words lingering dreamily in his ear—

"Tom, how *could* you be so noble!"

Chapter XXI

VACATION WAS APPROACHING. The schoolmaster, always severe, grew severer and more exacting than ever, for he wanted the school to make a good showing on "Examination" day. His rod and his ferule were seldom idle now—at least among the smaller pupils. Only the biggest boys, and young ladies of eighteen and twenty escaped lashing. Mr. Dobbins's lashings were very vigorous ones, too; for although he carried, under his wig, a perfectly bald and shiny head, he had only reached middle age and there was no sign of feebleness in his muscle. As the great day approached, all the tyranny that was in him came to the surface; he seemed to take a vindictive pleasure in punishing the least shortcomings. The consequence was, that the smaller boys spent their days in terror and suffering and their nights in plotting revenge. They threw away no opportunity to do the master a mischief. But he kept ahead all the time. The retribution that followed every vengeful success was so sweeping and majestic that the boys always retired from the field badly worsted. At last they conspired together and hit upon a plan that promised a dazzling victory. They swore-in the sign-painter's boy, told him the scheme, and asked his help. He had his own reasons for being delighted, for the master boarded in his father's family and had given the boy ample cause to hate him. The master's wife would go on a visit to the country in a few days, and there would be nothing to interfere with the plan; the master always prepared himself for great occasions by getting pretty well fuddled, and the sign-painter's boy said that when the dominie had reached the proper condition on Examination Evening he would "manage the thing" while he napped in his chair; then he would have him awakened at the right time and hurried away to school.

In the fullness of time the interesting occasion arrived. At eight in the evening the schoolhouse was brilliantly lighted, and adorned with wreaths and festoons of foliage and flowers. The master sat throned in his great chair upon a raised platform, with his blackboard behind him. He was looking tolerably mellow. Three rows of benches on each side and six rows in front of him were occupied by the dignitaries of the town and by the parents of the pupils. To his left, back of the rows of citizens, was a spacious temporary platform upon which were seated the scholars who were to take part in the exercises of the evening; rows of small boys, washed and dressed to an intolerable state of discomfort; rows of gawky big boys; snow-banks of girls and young ladies clad in lawn and muslin and conspicuously conscious of their bare arms, their grandmothers' ancient trinkets, their bits of pink and blue ribbon and the flowers in their hair. All the rest of the house was filled with non-participating scholars.

The exercises began. A very little boy stood up and sheepishly recited, "You'd scarce expect one of my age to speak in public on the stage, etc"—accompanying himself with the painfully exact and spasmodic gestures which a machine might have used—supposing the machine to be a trifle out of order. But he got through safely, though cruelly scared, and got a fine round of applause when he made his manufactured bow and retired.

A little shame-faced girl lisped "Mary had a little lamb, etc.," performed a compassion-inspiring curtsy, got her meed of applause, and sat down flushed and happy.

Tom Sawyer stepped forward with conceited confidence and soared into the unquenchable and indestructible "Give me liberty or give me death" speech, with fine fury and frantic gesticulation, and broke down in the middle of it. A ghastly stage-fright siezed him, his legs quaked under him and he was like to choke. True, he had the manifest sympathy of the house—but he had the house's silence, too, which was even worse than its sympathy. The master frowned, and this completed the disaster. Tom struggled a while and then retired, utterly defeated. There was a weak attempt at applause, but it died early.

"The Boy stood on the Burning Deck" followed; also "The Assyrian Came Down," and other declamatory gems. Then there were reading exercises, and a spelling fight. The meager Latin class recited with honor. The prime feature of the evening was in order, now—original "compositions" by the young ladies. Each in her turn stepped forward to the edge of the platform, cleared her throat, held up her manuscript (tied with dainty ribbon), and proceeded to read, with labored attention to "expression" and punctuation. The themes were the same that had been illuminated upon similar occasions by their mothers before them, their grandmothers, and doubtless all their ancestors in the female line clear back to the Crusades. "Friendship" was one; "Memories of Other Days;" "Religion in History;" "Dream Land;" "The Advantages of Culture;" "Forms of Political Government Compared and Contrasted;" "Melancholy;" "Filial Love;" "Heart Longings," etc., etc.

A prevalent feature in these compositions was a nursed and petted melancholy; another was a wasteful and opulent gush of "fine language;" another was a tendency to lug in by the ears particularly prized words and phrases until they were worn entirely out; and a peculiarity that conspicuously marked and marred them was the inveterate and intolerable sermon that wagged its crippled tail at the end of each and every one of them. No matter what the subject might be, a brain-racking effort was made to squirm it into some aspect or other that the moral and religious mind could contemplate with edification. The glaring insincerity of these sermons was not sufficient to compass the banishment of the fashion from the schools, and it is not sufficient to-day; it never will be sufficient while the world stands, perhaps. There is no school in all our land where the young ladies do not feel obliged to close their compositions with a sermon; and you will find that the sermon of the most frivolous and least religious girl in the school is always the longest and the most relentlessly pious. But enough of this. Homely truth is unpalatable.

Let us return to the "Examination." The first composition that was read was one entitled "Is this, then, Life?" Perhaps the reader can endure an extract from it:

> "In the common walks of life, with what delightful emotions does the youthful mind look forward to some anticipated scene of festivity! Imagination is busy sketching rose-tinted pictures of joy. In fancy, the voluptuous votary of fashion sees herself amid the festive throng, 'the observed of all observers.' Her graceful form, arrayed in snowy robes, is whirling through the mazes of the joyous dance; her eye is brightest, her step is lightest in the gay assembly.
>
> "In such delicious fancies time quickly glides by, and the welcome hour arrives for her entrance into the elysian world, of which she has had such bright dreams. How fairy-like does every thing appear to her enchanted vision! each new scene is more charming than the last. But after a while she finds that beneath this goodly exterior, all is vanity: the flattery which once charmed her soul, now grates harshly upon her ear; the ball-room has lost its charms; and with wasted health and imbittered heart, she turns away with the conviction that earthly pleasures cannot satisfy the longings of the soul!"

And so forth and so on. There was a buzz of gratification from time to time during the reading, accompanied by whispered ejaculations of "How sweet!" "How eloquent!" "So true!" etc., and after the thing had closed with a peculiarly afflicting sermon the applause was enthusiastic.

Then arose a slim, melancholy girl, whose face had the "interesting" paleness that comes of pills and indigestion, and read a "poem." Two stanzas of it will do:

A MISSOURI MAIDEN'S FAREWELL TO ALABAMA.

ALABAMA, good-bye! I love thee well!
    But yet for awhile do I leave thee now!
Sad, yes, sad thoughts of thee my heart doth swell,
    And burning recollections throng my brow!
For I have wandered through thy flowery woods;
    Have roamed and read near Tallapoosa's stream;
Have listened to Tallassee's warring floods,
    And wooed on Coosa's side Aurora's beam.

> Yet shame I not to bear an o'er-full heart,
>   Nor blush to turn behind my tearful eyes;
> 'Tis from no stranger land I now must part,
>   'Tis to no strangers left I yield these sighs.
> Welcome and home were mine within this State,
>   Whose vales I leave—whose spires fade fast from me;
> And cold must be mine eyes, and heart, and tête,
>   When, dear Alabama! they turn cold on thee!

There were very few there who knew what "*tête*" meant, but the poem was very satisfactory, nevertheless.

Next appeared a dark complexioned, black eyed, black haired young lady, who paused an impressive moment, assumed a tragic expression and began to read in a measured, solemn tone.

A VISION.

Dark and tempestuous was night. Around the throne on high not a single star quivered; but the deep intonations of the heavy thunder constantly vibrated upon the ear; whilst the terrific lightning revelled in angry mood through the cloudy chambers of heaven, seeming to scorn the power exerted over its terror by the illustrious Franklin! Even the boisterous winds unanimously came forth from their mystic homes, and blustered about as if to enhance by their aid the wildness of the scene.

At such a time, so dark, so dreary, for human sympathy my very spirit sighed; but instead thereof,

"My dearest friend, my counsellor, my comforter and guide—
My joy in grief, my second bliss in joy," came to my side.

She moved like one of those bright beings pictured in the sunny walks of fancy's Eden by the romantic and young, a queen of beauty unadorned save by her own transcendent loveliness. So soft was her step, it failed to make even a sound, and but for the magical thrill imparted by her genial touch, as other unobtrusive beauties, she would have glided away unperceived—unsought. A strange sadness rested upon her features, like icy tears upon the robe of December, as she pointed to the contending elements without, and bade me contemplate the two beings presented.

This nightmare occupied some ten pages of manuscript and wound up with a sermon so destructive of all hope to non-Presbyterians that it took the first prize. This composition was considered to be the very finest effort of the evening. The mayor of the village, in delivering the prize to the author of it, made a warm speech in which he said that it was by far the most "eloquent" thing he had ever listened to, and that Daniel Webster himself might well be proud of it.

It may be remarked, in passing, that the number of compositions in which the word "beauteous" was over-fondled, and human experience referred to as "life's page," was up to the usual average.

Now the master, mellow almost to the verge of geniality, put his chair aside, turned his back to the audience, and began to draw a map of America on the blackboard, to exercise the geography class upon. But he made a sad business of it with his unsteady hand, and a smothered titter rippled over the house. He knew what the matter was and set himself to right it. He sponged out lines and re-made them; but he only distorted them more than ever, and the tittering was more pronounced. He threw his entire attention upon his work, now, as if determined not to be put down by the mirth. He felt that all eyes were fastened upon him; he imagined he was succeeding, and yet the tittering continued; it even manifestly increased. And well it might. There was a garret above, pierced with a scuttle over his head; and down through this scuttle came a cat, suspended around the haunches by a string; she had a rag tied about her head and jaws to keep her from mewing; as she slowly descended she curved upward and clawed at the string, she swung downward and clawed at the intangible air. The tittering rose higher and higher—the cat was within six inches of the absorbed teacher's head—down, down, a little lower, and she grabbed his wig with her desperate claws, clung to it and was snatched up into the garret in an instant with her trophy still in her possession! And how the light did blaze abroad from the master's bald pate—for the sign-painter's boy had *gilded* it!

That broke up the meeting. The boys were avenged. Vacation had come.

NOTE.—The pretended ''compositions'' quoted in this chapter are taken without alteration from a volume entitled ''Prose and Poetry, by a Western Lady''—but they are exactly and precisely after the school-girl pattern and hence are much happier than any mere imitations could be.

Chapter XXII

TOM JOINED THE new order of Cadets of Temperance, being attracted by the showy character of their ''regalia.'' He promised to abstain from smoking, chewing and profanity as long as he remained a member. Now he found out a new thing—namely, that to promise not to do a thing is the surest way in the world to make a body want to go and do that very thing. Tom soon found himself tormented with a desire to drink and swear; the desire grew to be so intense that nothing but the hope of a chance to display himself in his red sash kept him from withdrawing from the order. Fourth of July was coming; but he soon gave that up—gave it up before he had worn his shackles over forty-eight hours— and fixed his hopes upon old Judge Frazer, justice of the peace, who was apparently on his death-bed and would have a big public funeral, since he was so high an official. During three days Tom was deeply concerned about the Judge's condition and hungry for news of it. Sometimes his hopes ran high— so high that he would venture to get out his regalia and practice before the looking-glass. But the Judge had a most discouraging way of fluctuating. At last he was pronounced upon the mend—and then convalescent. Tom was disgusted; and felt a sense of injury, too. He handed in his resignation at once—and that night the Judge suffered a relapse and died. Tom resolved that he would never trust a man like that again.

The funeral was a fine thing. The Cadets paraded in a style calculated to kill the late member with envy. Tom was a free boy again, however—there was something in that. He could drink and swear, now—but found to his surprise

HAPPY FOR TWO DAYS.

that he did not want to. The simple fact that he could, took the desire away, and the charm of it.

Tom presently wondered to find that his coveted vacation was beginning to hang a little heavily on his hands.

He attempted a diary—but nothing happened during three days, and so he abandoned it.

The first of all the negro minstrel shows came to town, and made a sensation. Tom and Joe Harper got up a band of performers and were happy for two days.

Even the Glorious Fourth was in some sense a failure, for it rained hard, there was no procession in consequence, and the greatest man in the world (as Tom supposed) Mr. Benton, an actual United States Senator, proved an overwhelming disappointment—for he was not twenty-five feet high, nor even anywhere in the neighborhood of it.

A circus came. The boys played circus for three days afterward in tents made of rag carpeting—admission, three pins for boys, two for girls—and then circusing was abandoned.

A phrenologist and a mesmerizer came—and went again and left the village duller and drearier than ever.

There were some boys-and-girls' parties, but they were so few and so delightful that they only made the aching voids between ache the harder.

Becky Thatcher was gone to her Constantinople home to stay with her parents during vacation—so there was no bright side to life anywhere.

The dreadful secret of the murder was a chronic misery. It was a very cancer for permanency and pain.

Then came the measles.

During two long weeks Tom lay a prisoner, dead to the world and its happenings. He was very ill, he was interested in nothing. When he got upon his feet at last and moved feebly down town, a melancholy change had come over everything and every creature. There had been a "revival," and everybody had "got religion," not only the adults, but even the boys and girls. Tom went about, hoping against hope for the sight of one blessed sinful face, but disappointment crossed him everywhere. He found Joe Harper studying a Testament, and turned sadly away from the depressing spectacle. He sought Ben Rogers, and found him visiting the poor with a basket of tracts. He hunted up Jim Hollis, who called his attention to the precious blessing of his late measles as a warning. Every boy he encountered added another ton to his depression; and when, in desperation, he flew for refuge at last to the bosom of Huckleberry Finn and was received with a scriptural quotation, his heart broke and he crept home and to bed realizing that he alone of all the town was lost, forever and forever.

And that night there came on a terrific storm, with driving rain, awful claps of thunder and blinding sheets of lightning. He covered his head with the bedclothes and waited in a horror of suspense for his doom; for he had not the shadow of a doubt that all this hubbub was about him. He believed he had taxed the forbearance of the powers above to the extremity of endurance and that this was the result. It might have seemed to him a waste of pomp and ammunition to kill a bug with a battery of artillery, but there seemed nothing incongruous about the getting up such an expensive thunder storm as this to knock the turf from under an insect like himself.

By and by the tempest spent itself and died without accomplishing its object. The boy's first impulse was to be grateful, and reform. His second was to wait— for there might not be any more storms.

The next day the doctors were back; Tom had relapsed. The three weeks he spent on his back this time seemed an entire age. When he got abroad at last he was hardly grateful that he had been spared, remembering how lonely was his estate, how companionless and forlorn he was. He drifted listlessly down the street and found Jim Hollis acting as judge in a juvenile court that was trying a cat for murder, in the presence of her victim, a bird. He found Joe Harper and Huck Finn up an alley eating a stolen melon. Poor lads! they—like Tom— had suffered a relapse.

Chapter XXIII

AT LAST THE sleepy atmosphere was stirred—and vigorously: the murder trial came on in the court. It became the absorbing topic of village talk immediately. Tom could not get away from it. Every reference to the murder sent a shudder to his heart, for his troubled conscience and fears almost persuaded him that these remarks were put forth in his hearing as "feelers;" he did not see how he could be suspected of knowing anything about the murder, but still he could not be comfortable in the midst of this gossip. It kept him in a cold shiver all the time. He took Huck to a lonely place to have a talk with him. It would be some relief to unseal his tongue for a little while; to divide his burden of distress with another sufferer. Moreover, he wanted to assure himself that Huck had remained discreet.

"Huck, have you ever told anybody about—that?"

"'Bout what?"

"You know what."

"Oh—'course I haven't."

"Never a word?"

"Never a solitary word, so help me. What makes you ask?"

"Well, I was afeard."

"Why Tom Sawyer, we wouldn't be alive two days if that got found out. *You* know that."

Tom felt more comfortable. After a pause:

"Huck, they couldn't anybody get you to tell, could they?"

"Get me to tell? Why if I wanted that half-breed devil to drownd me they could get me to tell. They ain't no different way."

"Well, that's all right, then. I reckon we're safe as long as we keep mum. But let's swear again, anyway. It's more surer."

"I'm agreed."

So they swore again with dread solemnities.

"What is the talk around, Huck? I've heard a power of it."

"Talk? Well, it's just Muff Potter, Muff Potter, Muff Potter all the time. It keeps me in a sweat, constant, so's I want to hide som'ers."

"That's just the same way they go on round me. I reckon he's a goner. Don't you feel sorry for him, sometimes?"

"Most always—most always. He ain't no account; but then he hain't ever done anything to hurt anybody. Just fishes a little, to get money to get drunk on—and loafs around considerable; but lord we all do that—leastways most of us,—preachers and such like. But he's kind of good—he give me half a fish, once, when there warn't enough for two; and lots of times he's kind of stood by me when I was out of luck."

"Well, he's mended kites for me, Huck, and knitted hooks on to my line. I wish we could get him out of there."

"My! we couldn't get him out Tom. And besides, 'twouldn't do any good; they'd ketch him again."

"Yes—so they would. But I hate to hear 'em abuse him so like the dickens when he never done—that."

"I do too, Tom. Lord, I hear 'em say he's the bloodiest looking villain in this country, and they wonder he wasn't ever hung before."

"Yes, they talk like that, all the time. I've heard 'em say that if he was to get free they'd lynch him."

"And they'd do it, too."

The boys had a long talk, but it brought them little comfort. As the twilight drew on, they found themselves hanging about the neighborhood of the little isolated jail, perhaps with an undefined hope that something would happen that might clear away their difficulties. But nothing happened; there seemed to be no angels or fairies interested in this luckless captive.

The boys did as they had often done before—went to the cell grating and gave Potter some tobacco and matches. He was on the ground floor and there were no guards.

His gratitude for their gifts had always smote their consciences before—it cut deeper than ever, this time. They felt cowardly and treacherous to the last degree when Potter said:

"You've been mighty good to me, boys—better'n anybody else in this town. And I don't forget it, I don't. Often I says to myself, says I, 'I used to mend all the boys' kites and things, and show 'em where the good fishin' places was, and befriend 'em what I could, and now they've all forgot old Muff when he's in trouble; but Tom don't, and Huck don't—*they* don't forget him,' says I, 'and I don't forget them.' Well, boys, I done an awful thing—drunk and crazy at the time—that's the only way I account for it—and now I got to swing for it, and it's right. Right, and *best,* too I reckon—hope so, anyway. Well, we won't talk about that. I don't want to make *you* feel bad; you've befriended me. But what I want to say, is, don't *you* ever get drunk—then you won't ever get here. Stand a little furder west—so—that's it; it's a prime comfort to see faces that's friendly when a body's in such a muck of trouble, and there don't none come here but yourn. Good friendly faces—good friendly faces. Git up on one another's backs and let me touch 'em. That's it. Shake hands—yourn'll come through the bars, but mine's too big. Little hands, and weak—but they've helped Muff Potter a power, and they'd help him more if they could."

Tom went home miserable, and his dreams that night were full of horrors. The next day and the day after, he hung about the court room, drawn by an almost irresistible impulse to go in, but forcing himself to stay out. Huck was having the same experience. They studiously avoided each other. Each wandered away, from time to time, but the same dismal fascination always brought them back presently. Tom kept his ears open when idlers sauntered out of the court room, but invariably heard distressing news—the toils were closing more and more relentlessly around poor Potter. At the end of the second day the village talk was to the effect that Injun Joe's evidence stood firm and unshaken, and that there was not the slightest question as to what the jury's verdict would be.

Tom was out late, that night, and came to bed through the window. He was in a tremendous state of excitement. It was hours before he got to sleep. All the village flocked to the Court house the next morning, for this was to be the great day. Both sexes were about equally represented in the packed audience. After a long wait the jury filed in and took their places; shortly afterward, Potter, pale and haggard, timid and hopeless, was brought in, with chains upon him, and seated where all the curious eyes could stare at him; no less conspicuous was Injun Joe, stolid as ever. There was another pause, and then the judge arrived and the sheriff proclaimed the opening of the court. The usual whisperings among the lawyers and gathering together of papers followed. These details and accompanying delays worked up an atmosphere of preparation that was as impressive as it was fascinating.

Now a witness was called who testified that he found Muff Potter washing in the brook, at an early hour of the morning that the murder was discovered, and that he immediately sneaked away. After some further questioning, counsel for the prosecution said—

"Take the witness."

The prisoner raised his eyes for a moment, but dropped them again when his own counsel said—

"I have no questions to ask him."

The next witness proved the finding of the knife near the corpse. Counsel for the prosecution said:

"Take the witness."

"I have no questions to ask him," Potter's lawyer replied.

A third witness swore he had often seen the knife in Potter's possession.

"Take the witness."

Counsel for Potter declined to question him. The faces of the audience began to betray annoyance. Did this attorney mean to throw away his client's life without an effort?

Several witnesses deposed concerning Potter's guilty behavior when brought to the scene of the murder. They were allowed to leave the stand without being cross-questioned.

Every detail of the damaging circumstances that occurred in the graveyard upon that morning which all present remembered so well, was brought out by credible witnesses, but none of them were cross-examined by Potter's lawyer. The perplexity and dissatisfaction of the house expressed itself in murmurs and provoked a reproof from the bench. Counsel for the prosecution now said:

"By the oaths of citizens whose simple word is above suspicion, we have fastened this awful crime beyond all possibility of question, upon the unhappy prisoner at the bar. We rest our case here."

A groan escaped from poor Potter, and he put his face in his hands and rocked his body softly to and fro, while a painful silence reigned in the courtroom. Many men were moved, and many women's compassion testified itself in tears. Counsel for the defence rose and said:

"Your honor, in our remarks at the opening of this trial, we foreshadowed our purpose to prove that our client did this fearful deed while under the influence of a blind and irresponsible delirium produced by drink. We have changed our mind. We shall not offer that plea." [Then to the clerk]: "Call Thomas Sawyer!"

A puzzled amazement awoke in every face in the house, not even excepting Potter's. Every eye fastened itself with wondering interest upon Tom as he rose and took his place upon the stand. The boy looked wild enough, for he was badly scared. The oath was administered.

"Thomas Sawyer, where were you on the seventeenth of June, about the hour of midnight?"

Tom glanced at Injun Joe's iron face and his tongue failed him. The audience listened breathless, but the words refused to come. fter a few moments, however, the boy got a little of his strength back, and managed to put enough of it into his voice to make part of the house hear:

"In the graveyard!"

"A little bit louder, please. Don't be afraid. You were—"

"In the graveyard."

A contemptuous smile flitted across Injun Joe's face.

"Were you anywhere near Horse Williams's grave?"

"Yes, sir."

"Speak up—just a trifle louder. How near were you?"

"Near as I am to you."

"Were you hidden, or not?"

"I was hid."

"Where?"

"Behind the elms that's on the edge of the grave."

Injun Joe gave a barely perceptible start.

"Any one with you?"

"Yes, sir. I went there with—"

"Wait—wait a moment. Never mind mentioning your companion's name. We will produce him at the proper time. Did you carry anything there with you?"

Tom hesitated and looked confused.

"Speak out my boy—don't be diffident. The truth is always respectable. What did you take there?"

"Only a—a—dead cat."

There was a ripple of mirth, which the court checked.

"We will produce the skeleton of that cat. Now my boy, tell us everything that occurred—tell it in your own way—don't skip anything, and don't be afraid."

Tom began—hesitatingly at first, but as he warmed to his subject his words flowed more and more easily; in a little while every sound ceased but his own voice; every eye fixed itself upon him; with parted lips and bated breath the audience hung upon his words, taking no note of time, rapt in the ghastly fascinations of the tale. The strain upon pent emotion reached its climax when the boy said—

"—and as the doctor fetched the board around and Muff Potter fell, Injun Joe jumped with the knife and—"

Crash! Quick as lightning the half-breed sprang for a window, tore his way through all opposers, and was gone!

Chapter XXIV

TOM WAS A glittering hero once more—the pet of the old, the envy of the young. His name even went into immortal print, for the village paper magnified him. There were some that believed he would be President, yet, if he escaped hanging.

As usual, the fickle, unreasoning world took Muff Potter to its bosom and fondled him as lavishly as it had abused him before. But that sort of conduct is to the world's credit; therefore it is not well to find fault with it.

Tom's days were days of splendor and exultation to him, but his nights were seasons of horror. Injun Joe infested all his dreams, and always with doom in his eye. Hardly any temptation could persuade the boy to stir abroad after nightfall. Poor Huck was in the same state of wretchedness and terror, for Tom had told the whole story to the lawyer the night before the great day of the trial, and Huck was sore afraid that his share in the business might leak out, yet,

notwithstanding Injun Joe's flight had saved him the suffering of testifying in court. The poor fellow had got the attorney to promise secrecy, but what of that? Since Tom's harrassed conscience had managed to drive him to the lawyer's house by night and wring a dread tale from lips that had been sealed with the dismalest and most formidable of oaths, Huck's confidence in the human race was well nigh obliterated.

Daily Muff Potter's gratitude made Tom glad he had spoken; but nightly he wished he had sealed up his tongue.

Half the time Tom was afraid Injun Joe would never be captured; the other half he was afraid he would be. He felt sure he never could draw a safe breath again until that man was dead and he had seen the corpse.

Rewards had been offered, the country had been scoured, but no Injun Joe was found. One of those omniscient and awe-inspiring marvels, a detective, came up from St Louis, moused around, shook his head, looked wise, and made that sort of astounding success which members of that craft usually achieve. That is to say he "found a clew." But you can't hang a "clew" for murder and so after that detective had got through and gone home, Tom felt just as insecure as he was before.

The slow days drifted on, and each left behind it a slightly lightened weight of apprehension.

Chapter XXV

THERE COMES A time in every rightly constructed boy's life when he has a raging desire to go somewhere and dig for hidden treasure. This desire suddenly came upon Tom one day. He sallied out to find Joe Harper, but failed of success. Next he sought Ben Rogers; he had gone fishing. Presently he stumbled upon Huck Finn the Red-Handed. Huck would answer. Tom took him to a private place and opened the matter to him confidentially. Huck was willing. Huck was

TOM DREAMS.

always willing to take a hand in any enterprise that offered entertainment and required no capital, for he had a troublesome superabundance of that sort of time which is *not* money. "Where'll we dig?" said Huck.

"O, most anywhere."

"Why, is it hid all around?"

"No indeed it ain't. It's hid in mighty particular places, Huck—sometimes on islands, sometimes in rotten chests under the end of a limb of an old dead tree, just where the shadow falls at midnight; but mostly under the floor in ha'nted houses."

"Who hides it?"

"Why robbers, of course— who'd you reckon? Sunday-school sup'rintendents?"

"I don't know. If 'twas mine I wouldn't hide it; I'd spend it and have a good time."

"So would I. But robbers don't do that way. They always hide it and leave it there."

"Don't they come after it any more?"

"No, they think they will, but they generally forget the marks, or else they die. Anyway it lays there a long time and gets rusty; and by and by somebody finds an old yellow paper that tells how to find the marks—a paper that's got to be ciphered over about a week because it's mostly signs and hy'roglyphics."

"Hyro—which?"

"Hy'rogliphics—pictures and things, you know, that don't seem to mean anything."

"Have you got one of them papers, Tom?"

"No."

"Well then, how you going to find the marks?"

"I don't want any marks. They always bury it under a ha'nted house or on an island, or under a dead tree that's got one limb sticking out. Well, we've tried Jackson's Island a little, and we can try it again some time; and there's the old ha'nted house up the Still-House branch, and there's lots of dead-limb trees— dead loads of 'em."

"Is it under all of them?"

"How you talk! No!"

"Then how you going to know which one to go for?"

"Go for all of 'em!"

"Why Tom, it'll take all summer."

"Well, what of that? Suppose you find a brass pot with a hundred dollars in it, all rusty and gay, or a rotten chest full of di'monds. How's that?"

Huck's eyes glowed.

"That's bully. Plenty bully enough for me. Just you gimme the hundred dollars and I don't want no di'monds."

"All right. But I bet you *I* ain't going to throw off on di'monds. Some of 'em's worth twenty dollars apiece—there ain't any, hardly, but's worth six bits or a dollar."

"No! Is that so?"

"Cert'nly—anybody'll tell you so. Hain't you ever seen one, Huck?"

"Not as I remember."

"O, kings have slathers of them."

"Well, I don't know no kings, Tom."

"I reckon you don't. But if you was to go to Europe you'd see a raft of 'em hopping around."

"Do they hop?"

"Hop? —your granny! No!"

"Well what did you say they did, for?"

"Shucks, I only meant you'd *see* 'em—not hopping, of course—what do they want to hop for?—but I mean you'd just see 'em—scattered around, you know, in a kind of a general way. Like that old hump-backed Richard."

"Richard? What's his other name?"

"He didn't have any other name. Kings don't have any but a given name."

"No?"

"But they don't."

"Well, if they like it, Tom, all right; but I don't want to be a king and have only just a given name, like a nigger. But say—where you going to dig first?"

"Well, I don't know. S'pose we tackle that old dead-limb tree on the hill t'other side of Still-House branch?"

"I'm agreed."

So they got a crippled pick and a shovel, and set out on their three-mile tramp. They arrived hot and panting, and threw themselves down in the shade of a neighboring elm to rest and have a smoke.

"I like this," said Tom.

"So do I."

"Say, Huck, if we find a treasure here, what you going to do with your share?"

"Well I'll have pie and a glass of soda every day, and I'll go to every circus that comes along. I bet I'll have a gay time."

"Well ain't you going to save any of it?"

"Save it? What for?"

"Why so as to have something to live on, by and by."

"O, that ain't any use. Pap would come back to thish-yer town some day and get his claws on it if I didn't hurry up, and I tell you he'd clean it out pretty quick. What you going to do with yourn, Tom?"

"I'm going to buy a new drum, and a sure-'nough sword, and a red neck-tie and a bull pup, and get married."

"Married!"

"That's it."

"Tom, you—why you ain't in your right mind."

"Wait—you'll see."

"Well that's the foolishest thing you could do. Look at pap and my mother. Fight! Why they used to fight all the time. I remember, mighty well."

"That ain't anything. The girl I'm going to marry won't fight."

"Tom, I reckon they're all alike. They'll all comb a body. Now you better think 'bout this a while. I tell you you better. What's the name of the gal?"

"It ain't a gal at all—it's a girl."

"It's all the same, I reckon; some says gal, some says girl—both's right, like enough. Anyway, what's her name, Tom?"

"I'll tell you some time—not now."

"All right—that'll do. Only if you get married I'll be more lonesomer than ever."

"No you won't. You'll come and live with me. Now stir out of this and we'll go to digging."

They worked and sweated for half an hour. No result. They toiled another half hour. Still no result. Huck said:

"Do they always bury it as deep as this?"

"Sometimes—not always. Not generally. I reckon we haven't got the right place."

So they chose a new spot and began again. The labor dragged a little, but still they made progress. They pegged away in silence for some time. Finally Huck leaned on his shovel, swabbed the beaded drops from his brow with his sleeve, and said:

"Where you going to dig next, after we get this one?"

"I reckon maybe we'll tackle the old tree that's over yonder on Cardiff Hill back of the widow's."

"I reckon that'll be a good one. But won't the widow take it away from us Tom? It's on her land."

"*She* take it away! Maybe she'd like to try it once. Whoever finds one of these hid treasures, it belongs to him. It don't make any difference whose land it's on."

That was satisfactory. The work went on. By and by Huck said:—

"Blame it, we must be in the wrong place again. What do you think?"

"It *is* mighty curious Huck. I don't understand it. Sometimes witches interfere. I reckon maybe that's what's the trouble now."

"Shucks, witches ain't got no power in the daytime."

"Well, that's so. I didn't think of that. Oh, *I* know what the matter is! What a blamed lot of fools we are! You got to find out where the shadow of the limb falls at midnight, and that's where you dig!"

"Then consound it, we've fooled away all this work for nothing. Now hang it all, we got to come back in the night. It's an awful long way. Can you get out?"

"I bet I will. We've got to do it to night, too, because if some body sees these holes they'll know in a minute what's here and they'll go for it."

"Well, I'll come around and maow to night."

BUSINESS.

"All right. Let's hide the tools in the bushes."

The boys were there that night, about the appointed time. They sat in the shadow waiting. It was a lonely place, and an hour made solemn by old traditions. Spirits whispered in the rustling leaves, ghosts lurked in the murky nooks, the deep baying of a hound floated up out of the distance, an owl answered with his sepulchral note. The boys were subdued by these solemnities, and talked little. By and by they judged that twelve had come; they marked where the shadow fell, and began to dig. Their hopes commenced to rise. Their interest grew stronger, and their industry kept pace with it. The hole deepened and still deepened, but every time their hearts jumped to hear the pick strike upon something, they only suffered a new disappointment. It was only a stone or a chunk. At last Tom said:—

"It ain't any use, Huck, we're wrong again."

"Well but we *can't* be wrong. We spotted the shadder to a dot."

"I know it, but then there's another thing."

"What's that?"

"Why we only guessed at the time. Like enough it was too late or too early."

Huck dropped his shovel.

"That's it," said he. "That's the very trouble. We got to give this one up. We can't ever tell the right time, and besides this kind of thing's too awful, here this time of night with witches and ghosts a fluttering around so. I feel as if something's behind me all the time; and I'm afeard to turn around, becuz maybe there's others in front a-waiting for a chance. I been creeping all over, ever since I got here."

"Well, I've been pretty much so, too, Huck. They most always put in a dead man when they bury a treasure under a tree, to look out for it."

"Lordy!"

"Yes, they do. I've always heard that."

"Tom I don't like to fool around much where there's dead people. A body's bound to get into trouble with 'em, sure."

"I don't like to stir 'em up, either. S'pose this one here was to stick his skull out and say something!"

"Don't, Tom! It's awful."

"Well it just is. Huck, I don't feel comfortable a bit."

"Say, Tom, let's give this place up, and try somewheres else."

"All right, I reckon we better."

"What'll it be?"

Tom considered a while; and then said—

"The ha'nted house. That's it!"

"Blame it, I don't like ha'nted houses Tom. Why they're a dern sight worse'n dead people. Dead people might talk, maybe, but they don't come sliding around in a shroud, when you ain't noticing, and peep over your shoulder all of a sudden and grit their teeth, the way a ghost does. I couldn't stand such a thing as that, Tom—nobody could."

"Yes, but Huck, ghosts don't travel around only at night. They won't hender us from digging there in the day time."

"Well that's so. But you know mighty well people don't go about that ha'nted house in the day nor the night."

"Well, that's mostly because they don't like to go where a man's been murdered, anyway—but nothing's ever been seen around that house except in the night—just some blue lights slipping by the windows—no regular ghosts.''

"Well where you see one of them blue lights flickering around, Tom, you can bet there's a ghost mighty close behind it. It stands to reason. Becuz *you* know that they don't anybody but ghosts use 'em.''

"Yes, that's so. But anyway they don't come around in the daytime, so what's the use of our being afeared?''

"Well, all right. We'll tackle the ha'nted house if you say so—but I reckon it's taking chances.''

They had started down the hill by this time. There in the middle of the moonlit valley below them stood the ''ha'nted'' house, utterly isolated, its fences gone long ago, rank weeds smothering the very doorsteps, the chimney crumbled to ruin, the window-sashes vacant, a corner of the roof caved in. The boys gazed a while, half expecting to see a blue light flit past a window; then talking in a low tone, as befitted the time and the circumstances, they struck far off to the right, to give the haunted house a wide berth, and took their way homeward through the woods that adorned the rearward side of Cardiff Hill.

Chapter XXVI

ABOUT NOON THE next day the boys arrived at the dead tree; they had come for their tools. Tom was impatient to go to the haunted house; Huck was measurably so, also—but suddenly said—

"Lookyhere, Tom, do you know what day it is?''

Tom mentally ran over the days of the week, and then quickly lifted his eyes with a startled look in them—

"My! I never once thought of it, Huck!''

"Well I didn't neither, but all at once it popped onto me that it was Friday.''

"Blame it, a body can't be too careful, Huck. We might a got into an awful scrape, tackling such a thing on a Friday.''

"*Might!* Better say we *would!* There's some lucky days, maybe, but Friday ain't.''

"Any fool knows that. I don't reckon *you* was the first that found it out, Huck.''

"Well, I never said I was, did I? And Friday ain't all, neither. I had a rotten bad dream last night—dreampt about rats.''

"No! Sure sign of trouble. Did they fight?''

"No.''

"Well that's good, Huck. When they don't fight it's only a sign that there's trouble around, you know. All we got to do is to look mighty sharp and keep out of it. We'll drop this thing for today, and play. Do you know Robin Hood, Huck?''

"No. Who's Robin Hood?''

"Why he was one of the greatest men that was ever in England—and the best. He was a robber.''

"Cracky, I wisht I was. Who did he rob?''

"Only sheriffs and bishops and rich people and kings, and such like. But he never bothered the poor. He loved 'em. He always divided up with 'em perfectly square.''

"Well, he must 'a' been a brick.''

"I bet you he was, Huck. Oh, he was the noblest man that ever was. They ain't any such men now, I can tell you. He could lick any man in England, with one hand tied behind him; and he could take his yew bow and plug a ten cent piece every time, a mile and a half.''

"What's a *yew* bow?''

"*I* don't know. It's some kind of a bow, of course. And if he hit that dime only on the edge he would set down and cry—and curse. But we'll play Robin Hood—it's noble fun. I'll learn you.''

"I'm agreed.''

So they played Robin Hood all the afternoon, now and then casting a yearning eye down upon the haunted house and passing a remark about the morrow's prospects and possibilities there. As the sun began to sink into the west they took their way homeward athwart the long shadows of the trees and soon were buried from sight in the forests of Cardiff Hill.

On Saturday, shortly after noon, the boys were at the dead tree again. They had a smoke and a chat in the shade, and then dug a little in their last hole, not with great hope, but merely because Tom said there were so many cases where people had given up a treasure after getting down within six inches of it, and then somebody else had come along and turned it up with a single thrust of a shovel. The thing failed this time, however, so the boys shouldered their tools and went away feeling that they had not trifled with fortune but had fulfilled all the requirements that belong to the business of treasure-hunting.

When they reached the haunted house there was something so weird and grisly about the dead silence that reigned there under the baking sun, and something so depressing about the loneliness and desolation of the place, that they were afraid, for a moment, to venture in. Then they crept to the door and took a trembling peep. They saw a weed-grown, floorless room, unplastered, an ancient fireplace, vacant windows, a ruinous staircase; and here, there, and everywhere, hung ragged and abandoned cobwebs. They presently entered, softly, with quickened pulses, talking in whispers, ears alert to catch the slightest sound, and muscles tense and ready for instant retreat.

In a little while familiarity modified their fears and they gave the place a critical and interested examination, rather admiring their own boldness, and wondering at it, too. Next they wanted to look up stairs. This was something like cutting off retreat, but they got to daring each other, and of course there could be but one result—they threw their tools into a corner and made the ascent. Up there were the same signs of decay. In one corner they found a closet that promised mystery, but the promise was a fraud—there was nothing in it. Their courage was up now and well in hand. They were about to go down and begin work when—

"Sh!'' said Tom.

"What is it?'' whispered Huck, blanching with fright.

"Sh! . . . . . . There! Hear it?''

"Yes! . . . . . O, my! Let's run!''

"Keep still! Don't you budge! They're coming right toward the door.''

The boys stretched themselves upon the floor with their eyes to knot holes in the planking, and lay waiting, in a misery of fear.

"They've stopped . . . . . No—coming . . . . . Here they are. Don't whisper another word, Huck. My goodness, I wish I was out of this!"

Two men entered. Each boy said to himself: "There's the old deaf and dumb Spaniard that's been about town once or twice lately—never saw t'other man before."

"T'other" was a ragged, unkempt creature, with nothing very pleasant in his face. The Spaniard was wrapped in a *serapè;* he had bushy white whiskers; long white hair flowed from under his sombrero, and he wore green goggles. When they came in, "t'other" was talking in a low voice; they sat down on the ground, facing the door, with their backs to the wall, and the speaker continued his remarks. His manner became less guarded and his words more distinct as he proceeded:

"No," said he, "I've thought it all over, and I don't like it. It's dangerous."

"Dangerous!" grunted the "deaf and dumb" Spaniard,—to the vast surprise of the boys. "Milksop!"

This voice made the boys gasp and quake. It was Injun Joe's! There was silence for some time. Then Joe said:

"What's any more dangerous than that job up yonder—but nothing's come of it."

"That's different. Away up the river so, and not another house about. 'Twon't ever be known that we tried, anyway, long as we didn't succeed."

"Well, what's more dangerous than coming here in the day time!—anybody would suspicion us that saw us."

"*I* know that. But there warn't any other place as handy after that fool of a job. I want to quit this shanty. I wanted to yesterday, only it warn't any use trying to stir out of here, with those infernal boys playing over there on the hill right in full view."

"Those infernal boys," quaked again under the inspiration of this remark, and thought how lucky it was that they had remembered it was Friday and concluded to wait a day. They wished in their hearts they had waited a year.

The two men got out some food and made a luncheon. After a long and thoughtful silence, Injun Joe said:

"Look here, lad—you go back up the river where you belong. Wait there till you hear from me. I'll take the chances on dropping into this town just once more, for a look. We'll do that 'dangerous' job after I've spied around a little and think things look well for it. Then for Texas! We'll leg it together!"

This was satisfactory. Both men presently fell to yawning, and Injun Joe said:

"I'm dead for sleep! It's your turn to watch."

He curled down in the weeds and soon began to snore. His comrade stirred him once or twice and he became quiet. Presently the watcher began to nod; his head drooped lower and lower, both men began to snore now.

The boys drew a long, grateful breath. Tom whispered—

"Now's our chance—come!"

Huck said:

"I can't—I'd die if they was to wake."

Tom urged—Huck held back. At last Tom rose slowly and softly, and started alone. But the first step he made wrung such a hideous creak from the crazy floor that he sank down almost dead with fright. He never made a second attempt. The boys lay there counting the dragging moments till it seemed to them that time must be done and eternity growing gray; and then they were grateful to note that at last the sun was setting.

Now one snore ceased. Injun Joe sat up, stared around—smiled grimly upon his comrade, whose head was drooping upon his knees—stirred him up with his foot and said—

"Here! *You're* a watchman, ain't you! All right, though—nothing's happened."

"My! have I been asleep?"

"Oh, partly, partly. Nearly time for us to be moving, pard. What'll we do with what little swag we've got left?"

"I don't know—leave it here as we've always done, I reckon. No use to take it away till we start south. Six hundred and fifty in silver's something to carry."

"Well—all right—it won't matter to come here once more."

"No—but I'd say come in the night as we used to do—it's better."

"Yes; but look here; it may be a good while before I get the right chance at that job; accidents might happen; 'tain't in such a very good place; we'll just regularly bury it—and bury it deep."

"Good idea," said the comrade, who walked across the room, knelt down, raised one of the rearward hearthstones and took out a bag that jingled pleasantly. He subtracted from it twenty or thirty dollars for himself and as much for Injun Joe and passed the bag to the latter, who was on his knees in the corner, now, digging with his bowie knife.

The boys forgot all their fears, all their miseries in an instant. With gloating eyes they watched every movement. Luck!—the splendor of it was beyond all imagination! Six hundred dollars was money enough to make half a dozen boys rich! Here was treasure-hunting under the happiest auspices—there would not be any bothersome uncertainty as to where to dig. They nudged each other every moment—eloquent nudges and easily understood, for they simply meant—"O, but ain't you glad *now* we're here!"

Joe's knife struck upon something.

"Hello!" said he.

"What is it?" said his comrade.

"Half-rotten plank—no it's a box, I believe. Here—bear a hand and we'll see what it's here for. Never mind, I've broke a hole."

He reached his hand in and drew it out—

"Man, it's money!"

The two men examined the handful of coins. They were gold. The boys above were as excited as themselves, and as delighted.

Joe's comrade said—

"We'll make quick work of this. There's an old rusty pick over amongst the weeds in the corner the other side of the fire-place—I saw it a minute ago."

He ran and brought the boys' pick and shovel. Injun Joe took the pick, looked it over critically, shook his head, muttered something to himself, and then began to use it. The box was soon unearthed. It was not very large; it was iron bound and had been very strong before the slow years had injured it. The men contemplated the treasure a while in blissful silence.

"Pard, there's thousands of dollars here," said Injun Joe.

"'Twas always said that Murrel's gang used around here one summer," the stranger observed.

"I know it," said Injun Joe; "and this looks like it, I should say."

"*Now* you won't need to do that job."

HIDDEN TREASURES UNEARTHED.

The half-breed frowned. Said he—

"You don't know me. Least you don't know all about that thing. 'Tain't robbery altogether—it's *revenge!*" and a wicked light flamed in his eyes. I'll need your help in it. When it's finished—then Texas. Go home to your Nance and your kids, and stand by till you hear from me."

"Well—if you say so, what'll we do with this—bury it again?"

"Yes. [Ravishing delight overhead.] *No!* by the great Sachem, no! [Profound distress overhead.] I'd nearly forgot. That pick had fresh earth on it! [The boys were sick with terror in a moment.] What business has a pick and a shovel here? What business with fresh earth on them? Who brought them here—and where are they gone? Have you heard anybody?—seen anybody? What! bury it again and leave them to come and see the ground disturbed? Not exactly—not exactly. We'll take it to my den."

"Why of course! Might have thought of that before. You mean Number One?"

"No—Number Two—under the cross. The other place is bad—too common."

"All right. It's nearly dark enough to start."

Injun Joe got up and went about from window to window cautiously peeping out. Presently he said:

"Who could have brought those tools here? Do you reckon they can be up stairs?"

The boys' breath forsook them. Injun Joe put his hand on his knife, halted a moment, undecided, and then turned toward the stairway. The boys thought of the closet, but their strength was gone. The steps came creaking up the stairs— the intolerable distress of the situation woke the stricken resolution of the lads— they were about to spring for the closet, when there was a crash of rotten timbers and Injun Joe landed on the ground amid the *débris* of the ruined stairway. He gathered himself up cursing, and his comrade said:

"Now what's the use of all that? If it's anybody, and they're up there, let them *stay* there—who cares? If they want to jump down, now, and get into trouble, who objects? It will be dark in fifteen minutes—and then let them follow us if they want to. I'm willing. In my opinion, whoever hove those things in here caught a sight of us and took us for ghosts or devils or something. I'll bet they're running yet."

Joe grumbled a while; then he agreed with his friend that what daylight was left ought to be economized in getting things ready for leaving. Shortly afterward they slipped out of the house in the deepening twilight, and moved toward the river with their precious box.

Tom and Huck rose up, weak but vastly relieved, and stared after them through the chinks between the logs of the house. Follow? Not they. They were content to reach ground again without broken necks, and take the townward track over the hill. They did not talk much. They were too much absorbed in hating themselves—hating the ill luck that made them take the spade and the pick there. But for that, Injun Joe never would have suspected. He would have hidden the silver with the gold to wait there till his "revenge" was satisfied, and then he would have had the misfortune to find that money turn up missing. Bitter, bitter luck that the tools were ever brought there!

They resolved to keep a lookout for that Spaniard when he should come to town spying out for chances to do his revengeful job, and follow him to "Number Two," wherever that might be. Then a ghastly thought occurred to Tom:

"Revenge? What if he means *us*, Huck!"

"O, don't!" said Huck, nearly fainting.

They talked it all over, and as they entered town they agreed to believe that he might possibly mean somebody else—at least that he might at least mean nobody but Tom, since only Tom had testified.

Very, very small comfort it was to Tom to be alone in danger! Company would be a palpable improvement, he thought.

Chapter XXVII

THE ADVENTURE OF the day mightily tormented Tom's dreams that night. Four times he had his hands on that rich treasure and four times it wasted to nothingness in his fingers as sleep forsook him and wakefulness brought back the hard reality of his misfortune. As he lay in the early morning recalling the incidents of his great adventure, he noticed that they seemed curiously subdued and far away— somewhat as if they had happened in another world, or in a time long gone by. Then it occurred to him that the great adventure itself must be a dream! There was one very strong argument in favor of this idea—namely, that the quantity of coin he had seen was too vast to be real. He had never seen as much as fifty dollars in one mass before, and he was like all boys of his age and station in life, in that he imagined that all references to "hundreds" and "thousands" were mere fanciful forms of speech, and that no such sums really existed in the world. He never had supposed for a moment that so large a sum as a hundred dollars was to be found in actual money in any one's possession. If his notions of hidden treasure had been analyzed, they would have been found to consist of a handful of real dimes and a bushel of vague, splendid, ungraspable dollars.

But the incidents of his adventure grew sensibly sharper and clearer under the attrition of thinking them over, and so he presently found himself leaning to the impression that the thing might not have been a dream, after all. This uncertainty must be swept away. He would snatch a hurried breakfast and go and find Huck.

Huck was sitting on the gunwale of a flatboat, listlessly dangling his feet in the water and looking very melancholy. Tom concluded to let Huck lead up to the subject. If he did not do it, then the adventure would be proved to have been only a dream.

"Hello, Huck!"

"Hello, yourself."

Silence, for a minute.

"Tom, if we'd a left the blame tools at the dead tree, we'd 'a' got the money. O, ain't it awful!"

"'Tain't a dream, then, 'tain't a dream! Somehow I most wish it was. Dog'd if I don't, Huck."

"What ain't a dream?"

"Oh, that thing yesterday. I been half thinking it was."

"Dream! If them stairs hadn't broke down you'd 'a' seen how much dream it was! I've had dreams enough all night—with that patch-eyed Spanish devil going for me all through 'em—rot him!"

"No, not rot him. *Find* him! Track the money!"

"Tom, we'll never find him. A feller don't have only once chance for such a pile—and that one's lost. I'd feel mighty shaky if I was to see him, anyway."

"Well, so'd I; but I'd like to see him, anyway—and track him out—to his Number Two."

"Number Two—yes, that's it. I ben thinking 'bout that. But I can't make nothing out of it. What do you reckon it is?"

"I dono. It's too deep. Say, Huck—maybe it's the number of a house!"

"Goody! . . . . . . No, Tom, that ain't it. If it is, it ain't in this one-horse town. They ain't no numbers here."

"Well, that's so. Lemme think a minute. Here—it's the number of a room—in a tavern, you know!"

"O, that's the trick! They ain't only two taverns. We can find out quick."

"You stay here, Huck, till I come."

Tom was off at once. He did not care to have Huck's company in public places. He was gone half an hour. He found that in the best tavern, No. 2 had long been occupied by a young lawyer, and was still so occupied. In the less ostentatious house No. 2 was a mystery. The tavern-keeper's young son said it was kept locked all the time, and he never saw anybody go into it or come out of it except at night; he did not know any particular reason for this state of things; had had some little curiosity, but it was rather feeble; had made the most of the mystery by entertaining himself with the idea that that room was "ha'nted;" had noticed that there was a light in there the night before.

"That's what I've found out, Huck. I reckon that's the very No. 2 we're after."

"I reckon it is, Tom. Now what you going to do?"

"Lemme think."

Tom thought a long time. Then he said:

"I'll tell you. The back door of that No. 2 is the door that comes out into that little close alley between the tavern and the old rattle-trap of a brick store. Now you get hold of all the door-keys you can find, and I'll nip all of Auntie's and the first dark night we'll go there and try 'em. And mind you keep a lookout for Injun Joe, because he said he was going to drop into town and spy around once more for a chance to get his revenge. If you see him, you just follow him; and if he don't go to that No. 2, that ain't the place."

"Lordy I don't want to foller him by myself!"

"Why it'll be night, sure. He mightn't ever see you—and if he did, maybe he'd never think anything."

"Well, if it's pretty dark I reckon I'll track him. I dono—I dono. I'll try."

"You bet *I*'ll follow him, if it's dark, Huck. Why he might 'a' found out he couldn't get his revenge, and be going right after that money."

"It's so, Tom, it's so. I'll foller him; I will, by jingoes!"

"Now you're *talking!* Don't you ever weaken, Huck, and I won't."

Chapter XXVIII

THAT NIGHT TOM and Huck were ready for their adventure. They hung about the neighborhood of the tavern until after nine, one watching the alley at a distance and the other the tavern door. Nobody entered the alley or left it; nobody resembling the Spaniard entered or left the tavern door. The night promised to be a fair one; so Tom went home with the understanding that if a considerable degree of darkness came on, Huck was to come and "maow," whereupon he would slip out and try the keys. But the night remained clear, and Huck closed his watch and retired to bed in an empty sugar hogshead about twelve.

Tuesday the boys had the same ill luck. Also Wednesday. But Thursday night promised better. Tom slipped out in good season with his aunt's old tin lantern, and a large towel to blindfold it with. He hid the lantern in Huck's sugar hogshead and the watch began. An hour before midnight the tavern closed up and its lights (the only ones thereabouts) were put out. No Spaniard had been seen. Nobody had entered or left the alley. Everything was auspicious. The blackness of darkness reigned, the perfect stillness was interrupted only by occasional mutterings of distant thunder.

Tom got his lantern, lit it in the hogshead, wrapped it closely in the towel, and the two adventurers crept in the gloom toward the tavern. Huck stood sentry and Tom felt his way into the alley. Then there was a season of waiting anxiety that weighed upon Huck's spirits like a mountain. He began to wish he could see a flash from the lantern—it would frighten him, but it would at least tell him that Tom was alive yet. It seemed hours since Tom had disappeared. Surely he must have fainted; maybe he was dead; maybe his heart had burst under terror and excitement. In his uneasiness Huck found himself drawing closer and closer to the alley; fearing all sorts of dreadful things, and momentarily expecting some catastrophe to happen that would take away his breath. There was not much to take away, for he seemed only able to inhale it by thimblefuls, and his heart would soon wear itself out, the way it was beating. Suddenly there was a flash of light and Tom came tearing by him:

"Run!" said he; "run, for your life!"

He needn't have repeated it; once was enough; Huck was making thirty or forty miles an hour before the repetition was uttered. The boys never stopped till they reached the shed of a deserted slaughter-house at the lower end of the village. Just as they got within its shelter the storm burst and the rain poured down. As soon as Tom got his breath he said:

"Huck, it was awful! I tried two of the keys, just as soft as I could; but they seemed to make such a power of racket that I couldn't hardly get my breath I was so scared. They wouldn't turn in the lock, either. Well, without noticing what I was doing, I took hold of the knob, and open comes the door! It warn't locked! I hopped in, and shook off the towel, and, *great Cæsar's ghost!*''

''What!—what 'd you see, Tom!''

''Huck, I most stepped onto Injun Joe's hand!''

''No!''

''Yes! He was laying there, sound asleep on the floor, with his old patch on his eye and his arms spread out.''

''Lordy, what did you do? Did he wake up?''

''No, never budged. Drunk, I reckon. I just grabbed that towel and started!''

''I'd never 'a' thought of the towel, I bet!''

''Well, *I* would. My aunt would make me mighty sick if I lost it.''

''Say, Tom, did you see that box?''

''Huck I didn't wait to look around. I didn't see the box, I didn't see the cross. I didn't see anything but a bottle and a tin cup on the floor by Injun Joe; yes, and I saw two barrels and lots more bottles in the room. Don't you see, now, what's the matter with that ha'nted room?''

''How?''

''Why it's ha'nted with whisky! Maybe *all* the Temperance Taverns have got a ha'nted room, hey Huck?''

''Well I reckon maybe that's so. Who'd 'a' thought such a thing? But say, Tom, now's a mighty good time to get that box, if Injun Joe's drunk.''

''It is, that! You try it!''

Huck shuddered.

''Well, no—I reckon not.''

''And *I* reckon not, Huck. Only one bottle alongside of Injun Joe ain't enough. If there'd been three, he'd be drunk enough and I'd do it.''

There was a long pause for reflection, and then Tom said:

''Lookyhere, Huck, less not try that thing any more till we know Injun Joe's not in there. It's too scary. Now if we watch every night, we'll be dead sure to see him go out, some time or other, and then we'll snatch that box quicker'n lightning.''

THE HAUNTED ROOM.

"Well, I'm agreed, I'll watch the whole night long, and I'll do it every night, too, if you'll do the other part of the job."

"All right, I will. All you got to do is to trot up Hooper street a block and maow—and if I'm asleep, you throw some gravel at the window and that'll fetch me."

"Agreed, and good as wheat!"

"Now Huck, the storm's over, and I'll go home. It'll begin to be daylight in a couple of hours. You go back and watch that long, will you?"

"I said I would, Tom, and I will. I'll ha'nt that tavern every night for a year! I'll sleep all day and I'll stand watch all night."

"That's all right. Now where you going to sleep?"

"In Ben Rogers's hayloft. He let's me, and so does his pap's nigger man, Uncle Jake. I tote water for Uncle Jake whenever he wants me to, and any time I ask him he gives me a little something to eat if he can spare it. That's a mighty good nigger, Tom. He likes me, becuz I don't ever act as if I was above him. Sometimes I've set right down and eat *with* him. But you needn't tell that. A body's got to do things when he's awful hungry he wouldn't want to do as a steady thing."

"Well, if I don't want you in the day time, I'll let you sleep. I won't come bothering around. Any time you see something's up, in the night, just skip right around and maow."

Chapter XXIX

THE FIRST THING Tom heard on Friday morning was a glad piece of news— Judge Thatcher's family had come back to town the night before. Both Injun Joe and the treasure sunk into secondary importance for a moment, and Becky took the chief place in the boy's interest. He saw her and they had an exhausting good time playing "hi-spy" and "gully-keeper" with a crowd of their schoolmates. The day was completed and crowned in a peculiarly satisfactory way: Becky teased her mother to appoint the next day for the long-promised and long-delayed picnic, and she consented. The child's delight was boundless; and Tom's not more moderate. The invitations were sent out before sunset, and straightway the young folks of the village were thrown into a fever of preparation and pleasurable anticipation. Tom's excitement enabled him to keep awake until a pretty late hour, and he had good hopes of hearing Huck's "maow," and of having his treasure to astonish Becky and the pic-nickers with, next day; but he was disappointed. No signal came that night.

Morning came, eventually, and by ten or eleven o'clock a giddy and rollicking company were gathered at Judge Thatcher's, and everything was ready for a start. It was not the custom for elderly people to mar pic-nics with their presence. The children were considered safe enough under the wings of a few young ladies of eighteen and a few young gentlemen of twenty-three or thereabouts. The old steam ferry-boat was chartered for the occasion; presently the gay throng filed up the main street laden with provision baskets. Sid was sick and had to miss the fun; Mary remained at home to entertain him. The last thing Mrs. Thatcher said to Becky, was—

"You'll not get back till late. Perhaps you'd better stay all night with some of the girls that live near the ferry landing, child."

"Then I'll stay with Susy Harper, mamma."

"Very well. And mind and behave yourself and don't be any trouble."

Presently, as they tripped along, Tom said to Becky:

"Say—I'll tell you what we'll do. 'Stead of going to Joe Harper's we'll climb right up the hill and stop at the Widow Douglas's. She'll have ice cream! She has it most every day—dead loads of it. And she'll be awful glad to have us."

"O, that will be fun!"

Then Becky reflected a moment and said:

"But what will mamma say?"

"How'll she ever know?"

The girl turned the idea over in her mind, and said reluctantly:

"I reckon it's wrong—but—"

"But shucks! Your mother won't know, and so what's the harm? All she wants is that you'll be safe; and I bet you she'd 'a' said go there if she'd 'a' thought of it. I know she would!"

The widow Douglas's splendid hospitality was a tempting bait. It and Tom's persuasions presently carried the day. So it was decided to say nothing to anybody about the night's programme. Presently it occurred to Tom that maybe Huck might come this very night and give the signal. The thought took a deal of the spirit out of his anticipations. Still he could not bear to give up the fun at Widow Douglas's. And why should he give it up, he reasoned—the signal did not come the night before, so why should it be any more likely to come to-night? The sure fun of the evening outweighed the uncertain treasure; and boy like, he determined to yield to the stronger inclination and not allow himself to think of the box of money another time that day.

Three miles below town the ferry-boat stopped at the mouth of a woody hollow and tied up. The crowd swarmed ashore and soon the forest distances and craggy heights echoed far and near with shoutings and laughter. All the different ways of getting hot and tired were gone through with, and by and by the rovers straggled back to camp fortified with responsible appetites, and then the destruction of the good things began. After the feast there was a refreshing season of rest and chat in the shade of spreading oaks. By and by somebody shouted—

"Who's ready for the cave?"

Everybody was. Bundles of candles were procured, and straightway there was a general scamper up the hill. The mouth of the cave was up the hillside—an opening shaped like a letter A. Its massive oaken door stood unbarred. Within was a small chamber, chilly as an ice-house, and walled by Nature with solid limestone that was dewy with a cold sweat. It was romantic and mysterious to stand here in the deep gloom and look out upon the green valley shining in the sun. But the impressiveness of the situation quickly wore off, and the romping began again. The moment a candle was lighted there was a general rush upon the owner of it; a struggle and a gallant defense followed, but the candle was soon knocked down or blown out, and then there was a glad clamor of laughter and a new chase. But all things have an end. By and by the procession went filing down the steep descent of the main avenue, the flickering rank of lights dimly revealing the lofty walls of rock almost to their point of junction sixty feet overhead. This main avenue was not more than eight or ten feet wide. Every few steps other lofty and still narrower crevices branched from it on either hand—

for McDougal's cave was but a vast labyrinth of crooked aisles that ran into each other and out again and led nowhere. It was said that one might wander days and nights together through its intricate tangle of rifts and chasms, and never find the end of the cave; and that he might go down, and down, and still down, into the earth, and it was just the same—labyrinth underneath labyrinth, and no end to any of them. No man "knew" the cave. That was an impossible thing. Most of the young men knew a portion of it, and it was not customary to venture much beyond this known portion. Tom Sawyer knew as much of the cave as any one.

The procession moved along the main avenue some three-quarters of a mile, and then groups and couples began to slip aside into branch avenues, fly along the dismal corridors, and take each other by surprise at points where the corridors joined again. Parties were able to elude each other for the space of half an hour without going beyond the "known" ground.

By and by, one group after another came straggling back to the mouth of the cave, panting, hilarious, smeared from head to foot with tallow drippings, daubed with clay, and entirely delighted with the success of the day. Then they were astonished to find that they had been taking no note of time and that night was about at hand. The clanging bell had been calling for half an hour. However, this sort of close to the day's adventures was romantic and therefore satisfactory. When the ferry-boat with her wild freight pushed into the stream, nobody cared sixpence for the wasted time but the captain of the craft.

Huck was already upon his watch when the ferry-boat's lights went glinting past the wharf. He heard no noise on board, for the young people were as subdued and still as people usually are who are nearly tired to death. He wondered what boat it was, and why she did not stop at the wharf—and then he dropped her out of his mind and put his attention upon his business. The night was growing cloudy and dark. Ten o'clock came, and the noise of vehicles ceased, scattered lights began to wink out, all straggling foot passengers disappeared, the village betook itself to its slumbers and left the small watcher alone with the silence and the ghosts. Eleven o'clock came, and the tavern lights were put out; darkness everywhere, now. Huck waited what seemed a weary long time, but nothing happened. His faith was weakening. Was there any use? Was there really any use? Why not give it up and turn in?

A noise fell upon his ear. He was all attention in an instant. The alley door closed softly. He sprang to the corner of the brick store. The next moment two men brushed by him, and one seemed to have something under his arm. It must be that box! So they were going to remove the treasure. Why call Tom now? It would be absurd—the men would get away with the box and never be found again. No, he would stick to their wake and follow them; he would trust to the darkness for security from discovery. So communing with himself, Huck stepped out and glided along behind the men, cat-like, with bare feet, allowing them to keep just far enough ahead not to be invisible.

They moved up the river street three blocks, then turned to the left up a cross street. They went straight ahead, then, until they came to the path that led up Cardiff Hill; this they took. They passed by the old Welchman's house, half way up the hill without hesitating, and still climbed upward. Good, thought Huck, they will bury it in the old quarry. But they never stopped at the quarry. They passed on, up the summit. They plunged into the narrow path between the tall sumach bushes, and were at once hidden in the gloom. Huck closed up and shortened his distance, now, for they would never be able to see him. He trotted along a while; then slackened his pace, fearing he was gaining too fast; moved on a piece, then stopped altogether; listened; no sound; none, save that he seemed to hear the beating of his own heart. The hooting of an owl came from over the hill—ominous sound! But no footsteps. Heavens, was everything lost! He was about to spring with winged feet, when a man cleared his throat not four feet from him! Huck's heart shot into his throat, but he swallowed it again; and then he stood there shaking as if a dozen agues had taken charge of him at once, and so weak that he thought he must surely fall to the ground. He knew where he was. He knew he was within five steps of the stile leading into Widow Douglas's grounds. Very well, he thought, let them bury it there; it won't be hard to find.

Now there was a voice—a very low voice—Injun Joe's:

"Damn her, maybe she's got company—there's lights, late as it is."

"I can't see any."

This was that stranger's voice—the stranger of the haunted house. A deadly chill went to Huck's heart—this, then, was the "revenge" job! His thought was, to fly. Then he remembered that the Widow Douglas had been kind to him more than once, and maybe these men were going to murder her. He wished he dared venture to warn her; but he knew he didn't dare—they might come and catch him. He thought all this and more in the moment that elapsed between the stranger's remark and Injun Joe's next—which was—

"Because the bush is in your way. Now—this way—now you see, don't you?"

"Yes. Well there *is* company there, I reckon. Better give it up."

"Give it up, and I just leaving this country forever! Give it up and maybe never have another chance. I tell you again, as I've told you before, I don't care for her swag—you may have it. But her husband was rough on me—many times he was rough on me—and mainly he was the justice of the peace that jugged me for a vagrant. And that ain't all. It ain't a millionth part of it! He had me *horsewhipped!*—horsewhipped in front of the jail, like a nigger!—with all the town looking on! HORSEWHIPPED!—do you understand? He took advantage of me and died. But I'll take it out of *her*."

"Oh, don't kill her! Don't do that!"

"Kill? Who said anything about killing? I would kill *him* if he was here; but not her. When you want to get revenge on a woman you don't kill her—bosh! you go for her looks. You slit her nostrils—you notch her ears like a sow!"

"By God, that's—"

"Keep your opinion to yourself! It will be safest for you. I'll tie her to the bed. If she bleeds to death, is that my fault? I'll not cry, if she does. My friend, you'll help in this thing—for *my* sake—that's why you're here—I mightn't be able alone. If you flinch, I'll kill you. Do you understand that? And if I have to kill you, I'll kill her—and then I reckon nobody'll ever know much about who done this business."

"Well, if it's got to be done, let's get at it. The quicker the better—I'm all in a shiver."

"Do it *now?* And company there? Look here—I'll get suspicious of you, first thing you know. No—we'll wait till the lights are out—there's no hurry."

Huck felt that a silence was going to ensue—a thing still more awful than any amount of murderous talk; so he held his breath and stepped gingerly back; planted his foot carefully and firmly, after balancing, one-legged, in a precarious way and almost toppling over, first on one side and then on the other. He took another step back, with the same elaboration and the same risks; then another and another, and—a twig snapped under his foot! His breath stopped and he listened. There was no sound—the stillness was perfect. His gratitude was measureless. Now he turned in his tracks, between the walls of sumach bushes— turned himself as carefully as if he were a ship—and then stepped quickly but cautiously along. When he emerged at the quarry he felt secure, and so he picked up his nimble heels and flew. Down, down he sped, till he reached the Welchman's. He banged at the door, and presently the heads of the old man and his two stalwart sons were thrust from windows.

"What's the row there? Who's banging? What do you want?"

"Let me in—quick! I'll tell everything."

"Why who are you?"

"Huckleberry Finn—quick, let me in!"

"Huckleberry Finn, indeed! It ain't a name to open many doors, I judge! But let him in, lads, and let's see what's the trouble."

"Please don't ever tell *I* told you," were Huck's first words when he got in. "Please don't—I'd be killed, sure—but the Widow's been good friends to me sometimes, and I want to tell—I *will* tell if you'll promise you won't ever say it was me."

"By George he *has* got something to tell, or he wouldn't act so!" exclaimed the old man; "out with it and nobody here'll ever tell, lad."

Three minutes later the old man and his sons, well armed, were up the hill, and just entering the sumach path on tip-toe, their weapons in their hands. Huck accompanied them no further. He hid behind a great bowlder and fell to listening. There was a lagging, anxious silence, and then all of a sudden there was an explosion of firearms and a cry.

Huck waited for no particulars. He sprang away and sped down the hill as fast as his legs could carry him.

A ROUSING ACT.

Chapter XXX

AS THE EARLIEST suspicion of dawn appeared on Sunday morning, Huck came groping up the hill and rapped gently at the old Welchman's door. The inmates were asleep but it was a sleep that was set on a hair-trigger, on account of the exciting episode of the night. A call came from a window—

"Who's there!"

Huck's scared voice answered in a low tone:

"Please let me in! It's only Huck Finn!"

"It's a name that can open this door night or day, lad!—and welcome!"

These were strange words to the vagabond boy's ears, and the pleasantest he had ever heard. He could not recollect that the closing word had ever been applied in his case before. The door was quickly unlocked, and he entered. Huck was given a seat and the old man and his brace of tall sons speedily dressed themselves.

"Now my boy I hope you're good and hungry, because breakfast will be ready as soon as the sun's up, and we'll have a piping hot one, too—make yourself easy about that! I and the boys hoped you'd turn up and stop here last night."

"I was awful scared," said Huck, "and I run. I took out when the pistols went off, and I didn't stop for three mile. I've come now becuz I wanted to know about it, you know; and I come before daylight becuz I didn't want to run acrost them devils, even if they was dead."

"Well, poor chap, you do look as if you'd had a hard night of it—but there's a bed here for you when you've had your breakfast. No, they ain't dead, lad— we are sorry enough for that. You see we knew right where to put our hands on them, by your description; so we crept along on tip-toe till we got within fifteen feet of them—dark as a cellar that sumach path was—and just then I found I was going to sneeze. It was the meanest kind of luck! I tried to keep it back, but no use—'twas bound to come, and it did come! I was in the lead with my pistol raised, and when the sneeze started those scoundrels a-rustling to get out of the path, I sung out, 'Fire, boys!' and blazed away at the place where the rustling was. So did the boys. But they were off in a jiffy, those villains, and we after them, down through the woods. I judge we never touched them. They fired a shot apiece as they started, but their bullets whizzed by and didn't do us any harm. As soon as we lost the sound of their feet we quit chasing, and went down and stirred up the constables. They got a posse together, and went off to guard the river bank, and as soon as it is light the sheriff and a gang are going to beat up the woods. My boys will be with them presently. I wish we had some sort of description of those rascals—'twould help a good deal. But you couldn't see what they were like, in the dark, lad, I suppose?"

"O, yes, I saw them down town and follered them."

"Splendid! Describe them—describe them, my boy!"

"One's the old deaf and dumb Spaniard that's ben around here once or twice, and t'other's a mean looking ragged—"

"That's enough, lad, we know the men! Happened on them in the woods back of the widow's one day, and they slunk away. Off with you, boys, and tell the sheriff—get your breakfast to-morrow morning!''

The Welchman's sons departed at once. As they were leaving the room Huck sprang up and exclaimed:

''Oh, please don't tell *any*body it was me that blowed on them! Oh, please!''

''All right if you say it, Huck, but you ought to have the credit of what you did.''

''Oh, no, no! Please don't tell!''

When the young men were gone, the old Welchman said—

''They won't tell—and I won't. But why don't you want it known?''

Huck would not explain, further than to say that he already knew too much about one of those men and would not have the man know that he knew anything against him for the whole world—he would be killed for knowing it, sure.

The old man promised secrecy once more, and said:

''How did you come to follow these fellows, lad? Were they looking suspicious?''

Huck was silent while he framed a duly cautious reply. Then he said:

''Well, you see, I'm a kind of a hard lot,—least everybody says so, and I don't see nothing agin it—and sometimes I can't sleep much, on accounts of thinking about it and sort of trying to strike out a new way of doing. That was the way of it last night. I couldn't sleep, and so I come along up street 'bout midnight, a-turning it all over, and when I got to that old shackly brick store by the Temperance Tavern, I backed up agin the wall to have another think. Well, just then along comes these two chaps slipping along close by me, with something under their arm and I reckoned they'd stole it. One was a-smoking, and t'other one wanted a light; so they stopped right before me and the cigars lit up their faces and I see that the big one was the deaf and dumb Spaniard, by his white whiskers and the patch on his eye, and t'other one was a rusty, ragged looking devil.''

''Could you see the rags by the light of the cigars?''

This staggered Huck for a moment. Then he said:

''Well, I don't know—but somehow it seems as if I did.''

''Then they went on, and you—''

''Follered 'em—yes. That was it. I wanted to see what was up—they sneaked along so. I dogged 'em to the widder's stile, and stood in the dark and heard the ragged one beg for the widder, and the Spaniard swear he'd spile her looks just as I told you and your two—''

''What! The *deaf and dumb* man said all that!''

Huck had made another terrible mistake! He was trying his best to keep the old man from getting the faintest hint of who the Spaniard might be, and yet his tongue seemed determined to get him into trouble in spite of all he could do. He made several efforts to creep out of his scrape, but the old man's eye was upon him and he made blunder after blunder. Presently the Welchman said:

''My boy, don't be afraid of me. I wouldn't hurt a hair of your head for all the world. No—I'd protect you—I'd protect you. This Spaniard is not deaf and dumb; you've let that slip without intending it; you can't cover that up now. You know something about that Spaniard that you want to keep dark. Now trust me—tell me what it is, and trust me—I won't betray you.''

Huck looked into the old man's honest eyes a moment, then bent over and whispered in his ear—

'' 'Tain't a Spaniard—it's Injun Joe!''

The Welchman almost jumped out of his chair. In a moment he said:

"It's all plain enough, now. When you talked about notching ears and slitting noses I judged that that was your own embellishment, because white men don't take that sort of revenge. But an Injun! That's a different matter altogether."

During breakfast the talk went on, and in the course of it the old man said that the last thing which he and his sons had done, before going to bed, was to get a lantern and examine the stile and its vicinity for marks of blood. They found none, but captured a bulky bundle of—

"Of WHAT?"

If the words had been lightning they could not have leaped with a more stunning suddenness from Huck's blanched lips. His eyes were staring wide, now, and his breath suspended—waiting for the answer. The Welchman started—stared in return—three seconds—five seconds—ten—then replied—

"Of burglar's tools. Why what's the *matter* with you?"

Huck sank back, panting gently, but deeply, unutterably grateful. The Welchman eyed him gravely, curiously—and presently said—

"Yes, burglar's tools. That appears to relieve you a good deal. But what did give you that turn? What were *you* expecting we'd found?"

Huck was in a close place—the inquiring eye was upon him—he would have given anything for material for a plausible answer—nothing suggested itself— the inquiring eye was boring deeper and deeper—a senseless reply offered— there was no time to weigh it, so at a venture he uttered it—feebly:

"Sunday-school books, maybe."

Poor Huck was too distressed to smile, but the old man laughed loud and joyously, shook up the details of his anatomy from head to foot, and ended by saying that such a laugh was money in a man's pocket, because it cut down the doctor's bills like everything. Then he added:

"Poor old chap, you're white and jaded—you ain't well a bit—no wonder you're a little flighty and off your balance. But you'll come out of it. Rest and sleep will fetch you out all right, I hope."

Huck was irritated to think he had been such a goose and betrayed such a suspicious excitement, for he had dropped the idea that the parcel brought from the tavern was the treasure, as soon as he had heard the talk at the widow's stile. He had only *thought* it was not the treasure, however—he had not known that it wasn't—and so the suggestion of a captured bundle was too much for his self-possession. But on the whole he felt glad the little episode had happened, for now he knew beyond all question that that bundle was not *the* bundle, and so his mind was at rest and exceedingly comfortable. In fact everything seemed to be drifting just in the right direction, now; the treasure must be still in No. 2, the men would be captured and jailed that day, and he and Tom could seize the gold that night without any trouble or any fear of interruption.

Just as breakfast was completed there was a knock at the door. Huck jumped for a hiding place, for he had no mind to be connected even remotely with the late event. The Welchman admitted several ladies and gentlemen, among them the widow Douglas, and noticed that groups of citizens were climbing up the hill—to stare at the stile. So the news had spread.

The Welchman had to tell the story of the night to the visitors. The widow's gratitude for her preservation was outspoken.

"Don't say a word about it madam. There's another that you're more beholden to than you are to me and my boys, maybe, but he don't allow me to tell his name. We wouldn't have been there but for him.''

Of course this excited a curiosity so vast that it almost belittled the main matter—but the Welchman allowed it to eat into the vitals of his visitors, and through them be transmitted to the whole town, for he refused to part with his secret. When all else had been learned, the widow said:

''I went to sleep reading in bed and slept straight through all that noise. Why didn't you come and wake me?''

''We judged it warn't worth while. Those fellows warn't likely to come again—they hadn't any tools left to work with, and what was the use of waking you up and scaring you to death? My three negro men stood guard at your house all the rest of the night. They've just come back.''

More visitors came, and the story had to be told and re-told for a couple of hours more.

There was no Sabbath-school during day-school vacation, but everybody was early at church. The stirring event was well canvassed. News came that not a sign of the two villains had been yet discovered. When the sermon was finished, Judge Thatcher's wife dropped alongside of Mrs. Harper as she moved down the aisle with the crowd and said:

''Is my Becky going to sleep all day? I just expected she would be tired to death.''

''Your Becky?''

''Yes,'' with a startled look,—''didn't she stay with you last night?''

''Why, no.''

Mrs. Thatcher turned pale, and sank into a pew, just as Aunt Polly, talking briskly with a friend, passed by. Aunt Polly said:

''Good morning, Mrs. Thatcher. Good morning Mrs. Harper. I've got a boy that's turned up missing. I reckon my Tom staid at your house last night—one of you. And now he's afraid to come to church. I've got to settle with him.''

Mrs. Thatcher shook her head feebly and turned paler than ever.

''He didn't stay with us,'' said Mrs. Harper, beginning to look uneasy. A marked anxiety came into Aunt Polly's face.

''Joe Harper, have you seen my Tom this morning?''

''No'm.''

''When did you see him last?''

Joe tried to remember, but was not sure he could say. The people had stopped moving out of church. Whispers passed along, and a boding uneasiness took possession of every countenance. Children were anxiously questioned, and young teachers. They all said they had not noticed whether Tom and Becky were on board the ferry-boat on the homeward trip; it was dark; no one thought of inquiring if any one was missing. One young man finally blurted out his fear that they were still in the cave! Mrs. Thatcher swooned away. Aunt Polly fell to crying and wringing her hands.

The alarm swept from lip to lip, from group to group, from street to street, and within five minutes the bells were wildly clanging and the whole town was up! The Cardiff Hill episode sank into instant insignificance, the burglars were forgotten, horses were saddled, skiffs were manned, the ferry-boat ordered out, and before the horror was half an hour old, two hundred men were pouring down high-road and river toward the cave.

All the long afternoon the village seemed empty and dead. Many women visited Aunt Polly and Mrs. Thatcher and tried to comfort them. They cried with them, too, and that was still better than words. All the tedious night the town waited for news; but when the morning dawned at last, all the word that came was, "Send more candles—and send food." Mrs. Thatcher was almost crazed; and Aunt Polly also. Judge Thatcher sent messages of hope and encouragement from the cave, but they conveyed no real cheer.

The old Welchman came home toward daylight, spattered with candle grease, smeared with clay, and almost worn out. He found Huck still in the bed that had been provided for him, and delirious with fever. The physicians were all at the cave, so the Widow Douglas came and took charge of the patient. She said she would do her best by him, because, whether he was good, bad, or indifferent, he was the Lord's, and nothing that was the Lord's was a thing to be neglected. The Welchman said Huck had good spots in him, and the widow said—

"You can depend on it. That's the Lord's mark. He don't leave it off. He never does. Puts it somewhere on every creature that comes from his hands."

Early in the forenoon parties of jaded men began to straggle into the village, but the strongest of the citizens continued searching. All the news that could be gained was that remotenesses of the cavern were being ransacked that had never been visited before; that every corner and crevice was going to be thoroughly searched; that wherever one wandered through the maze of passages, lights were to be seen flitting hither and thither in the distance, and shoutings and pistol shots sent their hollow reverberations to the ear down the sombre aisles. In one place, far from the section usually traversed by tourists, the names "BECKY & TOM" had been found traced upon the rocky wall with candle smoke, and near at hand a grease-soiled bit of ribbon. Mrs. Thatcher recognized the ribbon and cried over it. She said it was the last relic she should ever have of her child; and that no other memorial of her could ever be so precious, because this one parted latest from the living body before the awful death came. Some said that now and then, in the cave, a far-away speck of light would glimmer, and then a glorious shout would burst forth and a score of men go trooping down the echoing aisle—and then a sickening disappointment always followed; the children were not there; it was only a searcher's light.

Three dreadful days and nights dragged their tedious hours along, and the

TOM'S MARK.

village sank into a hopeless stupor. No one had heart for anything. The accidental discovery, just made, that the proprietor of the Temperance Tavern kept liquor on his premises, scarcely fluttered the public pulse, tremendous as the fact was. In a lucid interval, Huck feebly led up to the subject of taverns, and finally asked—dimly dreading the worst—if anything had been discovered at the Temperance Tavern since he had been ill?

"Yes," said the widow.

Huck started up in bed, wild-eyed:

"What! What was it?"

"Liquor!—and the place has been shut up. Lie down, child—what a turn you did give me!"

"Only tell me just one thing—only just one—please! Was it Tom Sawyer that found it?"

The widow burst into tears. "Hush, husl!, child, hush! I've told you before, you must *not* talk. You are very, very sick!"

Then nothing but liquor had been found; there would have been a great powwow if it had been the gold. So the treasure was gone forever—gone forever! But what could she be crying about? Curious that she should cry.

These thoughts worked their dim way through Huck's mind, and under the weariness they gave him he fell asleep. The widow said to herself:

"There—he's asleep, poor wreck. Tom Sawyer find it! Pity but somebody could find Tom Sawyer! Ah, there ain't many left, now, that's got hope enough, or strength enough, either, to go on searching."

Chapter XXXI

NOW TO RETURN to Tom and Becky's share in the pic-nic. They tripped along the murky aisles with the rest of the company, visiting the familiar wonders of the cave—wonders dubbed with rather over-descriptive names, such as "The Drawing-Room," "The Cathedral," "Aladdin's Palace," and so on. Presently the hide-and-seek frolicking began, and Tom and Becky engaged in it with zeal until the exertion began to grow a trifle wearisome; then they wandered down a sinuous avenue holding their candles aloft and reading the tangled web-work of names, dates, post-office addresses and mottoes with which the rocky walls had been frescoed (in candle smoke.) Still drifting along and talking, they scarcely noticed that they were now in a part of the cave whose walls were not frescoed. They smoked their own names under an overhanging shelf and moved on. Presently they came to a place where a little stream of water, trickling over a ledge and carrying a limestone sediment with it, had, in the slow-dragging ages, formed a laced and ruffled Niagara in gleaming and imperishable stone. Tom squeezed his small body behind it in order to illuminate it for Becky's gratification. He found that it curtained a sort of steep natural stairway which was enclosed between narrow walls, and at once the ambition to be a discoverer seized him. Becky responded to his call, and they made a smoke-mark for future guidance, and started upon their quest. They wound this way and that, far down into the secret depths of the cave, made another mark, and branched off in search of novelties to tell the upper world about. In one place they found a spacious cavern, from whose ceiling depended a multitude of shining stalactites of the length and circumference of a man's leg; they walked all about it, wondering and admiring, and presently left it by one of the numerous passages that opened into it. This shortly brought them to a bewitching spring, whose basin was encrusted with a frost work of glittering crystals; it was in the midst of a cavern whose walls were supported by many fantastic pillars which had been formed by the joining of great stalactites and stalagmites together, the result of the ceaseless water-drip of centuries. Under the roof vast knots of bats had packed themselves together, thousands in a bunch; the lights disturbed the creatures and they came flocking down by hundreds, squeaking and darting furiously at the candles. Tom knew their ways and the danger of this sort of conduct. He seized Becky's hand and hurried her into the first corridor that offered; and none too soon, for a bat struck Becky's light out with its wing while she was passing out of the cavern. The bats chased the children a good distance; but the fugitives plunged into every new passage that offered, and at last got rid of the perilous things. Tom found a subterranean lake, shortly, which stretched its dim length away until its shape was lost in the shadows. He wanted to explore its borders, but concluded that it would be best to sit down and rest a while, first. Now, for the first time, the deep stillness of the place laid a clammy hand upon the spirits of the children. Becky said—

"Why, I didn't notice, but it seems ever so long since I heard any of the others."

"Come to think, Becky, we are away down below them—and I don't know how far away north, or south, or east, or whichever it is. We couldn't hear them here."

Becky grew apprehensive.

"I wonder how long we've been down here, Tom. We better start back."

"Yes, I reckon we better. P'raps we better."

"Can you find the way, Tom? It's all a mixed-up crookedness to me."

"I reckon I could find it—but then the bats. If they put both our candles out it will be an awful fix. Let's try some other way, so as not to go through there."

"Well. But I hope we won't get lost. It would be so awful!" and the girl shuddered at the thought of the dreadful possibilities.

They started through a corridor, and traversed it in silence a long way, glancing at each new opening, to see if there was anything familiar about the look of it; but they were all strange. Every time Tom made an examination, Becky would watch his face for an encouraging sign, and he would say cheerily—

"Oh, it's all right. This ain't the one, but we'll come to it right away!"

But he felt less and less hopeful with each failure, and presently began to turn off into diverging avenues at sheer random, in desperate hope of finding the one that was wanted. He still said it was "all right," but there was such a leaden dread at his heart, that the words had lost their ring and sounded just as if he had said, "All is lost!" Becky clung to his side in an anguish of fear, and tried hard to keep back the tears, but they would come. At last she said:

"O, Tom, never mind the bats, let's go back that way! We seem to get worse and worse off all the time."

Tom stopped.

"Listen!" said he.

Profound silence; silence so deep that even their breathings were conspicuous in the hush. Tom shouted. The call went echoing down the empty aisles and died out in the distance in a faint sound that resembled a ripple of mocking laughter.

"Oh, don't do it again, Tom, it is too horrid," said Becky.

"It is horrid, but I better, Becky; they *might* hear us, you know" and he shouted again.

The "might" was even a chillier horror than the ghostly laughter, it so confessed a perishing hope. The children stood still and listened; but there was no result. Tom turned upon the back track at once, and hurried his steps. It was but a little while before a certain indecision in his manner revealed another fearful fact to Becky—he could not find his way back!

"O, Tom, you didn't make any marks!"

"Becky I was such a fool! Such a fool! I never thought we might want to come back! No—I can't find the way. It's all mixed up."

"Tom, Tom, we're lost! we're lost! We never can get out of this awful place! O, why *did* we ever leave the others!"

She sank to the ground and burst into such a frenzy of crying that Tom was appalled with the idea that she might die, or lose her reason. He sat down by her and put his arms around her; she buried her face in his bosom, she clung to him, she poured out her terrors, her unavailing regrets, and the far echoes turned them all to jeering laughter. Tom begged her to pluck up hope again, and she said she could not. He fell to blaming and abusing himself for getting her into this miserable situation; this had a better effect. She said she would try to hope again, she would get up and follow wherever he might lead if only he would not talk like that any more. For he was no more to blame than she, she said.

So they moved on, again—aimlessly—simply at random—all they could do was to move, keep moving. For a little while, hope made a show of reviving—not with any reason to back it, but only because it is its nature to revive when the spring has not been taken out of it by age and familiarity with failure.

By and by Tom took Becky's candle and blew it out. This economy meant so much! Words were not needed. Becky understood, and her hope died again. She knew that Tom had a whole candle and three or four pieces in his pockets—yet he must economise.

By and by, fatigue began to assert its claims; the children tried to pay no

DESPAIR.

attention, for it was dreadful to think of sitting down when time was grown to be so precious; moving, in some direction, in any direction, was at least progress and might bear fruit; but to sit down was to invite death and shorten its pursuit.

At last Becky's frail limbs refused to carry her farther. She sat down. Tom rested with her, and they talked of home, and the friends there, and the comfortable beds and above all, the light! Becky cried, and Tom tried to think of some way of comforting her, but all his encouragements were grown threadbare with use, and sounded like sarcasms. Fatigue bore so heavily upon Becky that she drowsed off to sleep. Tom was grateful. He sat looking into her drawn face and saw it grow smooth and natural under the influence of pleasant dreams; and by and by a smile dawned and rested there. The peaceful face reflected somewhat of peace and healing into his own spirit, and his thoughts wandered away to by-gone times and dreamy memories. While he was deep in his musings, Becky woke up with a breezy little laugh—but it was stricken dead upon her lips, and a groan followed it.

"Oh, how *could* I sleep! I wish I never, never had waked! No! No, I don't, Tom! Don't look so! I won't say it again."

"I'm glad you've slept, Becky; you'll feel rested, now, and we'll find the way out."

"We can try, Tom; but I've seen such a beautiful country in my dream. I reckon we are going there."

"Maybe not, maybe not. Cheer up, Becky, and let's go on trying."

They rose up and wandered along, hand in hand and hopeless. They tried to estimate how long they had been in the cave, but all they knew was that it seemed days and weeks, and yet it was plain that this could not be, for their candles were not gone yet. A long time after this—they could not tell how long— Tom said they must go softly and listen for dripping water—they must find a spring. They found one presently, and Tom said it was time to rest again. Both were cruelly tired, yet Becky said she thought she could go on a little farther. She was surprised to hear Tom dissent. She could not understand it. They sat down, and Tom fastened his candle to the wall in front of them with some clay. Thought was soon busy; nothing was said for some time. Then Becky broke the silence:

"Tom, I am so hungry!"

Tom took something out of his pocket.

"Do you remember this?" said he.

Becky almost smiled.

"It's our wedding cake, Tom."

"Yes—I wish it was as big as a barrel, for it's all we've got."

"I saved it from the pic-nic for us to dream on, Tom, the way grown-up people do with wedding cake—but it'll be our—"

She dropped the sentence where it was. Tom divided the cake and Becky ate with good appetite, while Tom nibbled at his moiety. There was abundance of cold water to finish the feast with. By and by Becky suggested that they move on again. Tom was silent a moment. Then he said:

"Becky, can you bear it if I tell you something?"

Becky's face paled, but she thought she could.

"Well then, Becky, we must stay here, where there's water to drink. That little piece is our last candle!"

Becky gave loose to tears and wailings. Tom did what he could to comfort her but with little effect. At length Becky said:

"Tom!"

"Well, Becky?"

"They'll miss us and hunt for us!"

"Yes, they will! Certainly they will!"

"Maybe they're hunting for us now, Tom."

"Why I reckon maybe they are. I hope they are."

"When would they miss us, Tom?"

"When they get back to the boat, I reckon."

"Tom, it might be dark, then—would they notice we hadn't come?"

"I don't know. But anyway, your mother would miss you as soon as they got home."

A frightened look in Becky's face brought Tom to his senses and he saw that he had made a blunder. Becky was not to have gone home that night! The children became silent and thoughtful. In a moment a new burst of grief from Becky showed Tom that the thing in his mind had struck hers also—that the Sabbath morning might be half spent before Mrs. Thatcher discovered that Becky was not at Mrs. Harper's.

The children fastened their eyes upon their bit of candle and watched it melt slowly and pitilessly away; saw the half inch of wick stand alone at last; saw the feeble flame rise and fall, climb the thin column of smoke, linger at its top a moment, and then—the horror of utter darkness reigned!

How long afterward it was that Becky came to a slow consciousness that she was crying in Tom's arms, neither could tell. All that they knew was, that after what seemed a mighty stretch of time, both awoke out of a dead stupor of sleep and resumed their miseries once more. Tom said it might be Sunday, now—maybe Monday. He tried to get Becky to talk, but her sorrows were too oppressive, all her hopes were gone. Tom said that they must have been missed long ago, and no doubt the search was going on. He would shout and maybe some one would come. He tried it; but in the darkness the distant echoes sounded so hideously that he tried it no more.

The hours wasted away, and hunger came to torment the captives again. A portion of Tom's half of the cake was left; they divided and ate it. But they seemed hungrier than before. The poor morsel of food only whetted desire.

By and by Tom said:

"*Sh!* Did you hear that?"

Both held their breath and listened. There was a sound like the faintest, far-off shout. Instantly Tom answered it, and leading Becky by the hand, started groping down the corridor in its direction. Presently he listened again; again the sound was heard, and apparently a little nearer.

"It's them!" said Tom; "they're coming! Come along Becky—we're all right now!"

The joy of the prisoners was almost overwhelming. Their speed was slow, however, because pitfalls were somewhat common, and had to be guarded against. They shortly came to one and had to stop. It might be three feet deep, it might be a hundred—there was no passing it at any rate. Tom got down on his breast and reached as far down as he could. No bottom. They must stay there and wait until the searchers came. They listened; evidently the distant shoutings were growing more distant! a moment or two more and they had gone altogether. The heart-sinking misery of it! Tom whooped until he was hoarse, but it was of no use. He talked hopefully to Becky; but an age of anxious waiting passed and no sounds came again.

The children groped their way back to the spring. The weary time dragged on; they slept again, and awoke famished and woe-stricken. Tom believed it must be Tuesday by this time.

Now an idea struck him. There were some side passages near at hand. It would be better to explore some of these than bear the weight of the heavy time in idleness. He took a kite-line from his pocket, tied it to a projection, and he and Becky started, Tom in the lead, unwinding the line as he groped along. At the end of twenty steps the corridor ended in a "jumping-off place." Tom got down on his knees and felt below, and then as far around the corner as he could reach with his hands conveniently; he made an effort to stretch yet a little further to the right, and at that moment, not twenty yards away, a human hand, holding a candle, appeared from behind a rock! Tom lifted up a glorious shout, and instantly that hand was followed by the body it belonged to—Injun Joe's! Tom was paralyzed; he could not move. He was vastly gratified the next moment, to see the "Spaniard" take to his heels and get himself out of sight. Tom wondered that Joe had not recognized his voice and come over and killed him for testifying in court. But the echoes must have disguised the voice. Without doubt, that was it, he reasoned. Tom's fright weakened every muscle in his body. He said to himself that if he had strength enough to get back to the spring he would stay there, and nothing should tempt him to run the risk of meeting Injun Joe again. He was careful to keep from Becky what it was he had seen. He told her he had only shouted "for luck."

But hunger and wretchedness rise superior to fears in the long run. Another tedious wait at the spring and another long sleep brought changes. The children awoke tortured with a raging hunger. Tom believed that it must be Wednesday or Thursday or even Friday or Saturday, now, and that the search had been given over. He proposed to explore another passage. He felt willing to risk Injun Joe and all other terrors. But Becky was very weak. She had sunk into a dreary apathy and would not be roused. She said she would wait, now, where she was, and die—it would not be long. She told Tom to go with the kite-line and explore if he chose; but she implored him to come back every little while and speak to her; and she made him promise that when the awful time came, he would stay by her and hold her hand until all was over.

Tom kissed her, with a choking sensation in his throat, and made a show of being confident of finding the searchers or an escape from the cave; then he took the kite-line in his hand and went groping down one of the passages on his hands and knees, distressed with hunger and sick with bodings of coming doom.

Chapter XXXII

TUESDAY AFTERNOON CAME, and waned to the twilight. The village of St. Petersburg still mourned. The lost children had not been found. Public prayers had been offered up for them, and many and many a private prayer that had the petitioner's whole heart in it; but still no good news came from the cave. The majority of the searchers had given up the quest and gone back to their daily avocations, saying that it was plain the children could never be found. Mrs. Thatcher was very ill, and a great part of the time delirious. People said it was heartbreaking to hear her call her child, and raise her head and listen a whole minute at a time, then lay it wearily down again with a moan. Aunt Polly had drooped into a settled melancholy, and her gray hair had grown almost white. The village went to its rest on Tuesday night, sad and forlorn.

Away in the middle of the night a wild peal burst from the village bells, and in a moment the streets were swarming with frantic half-clad people, who shouted, "Turn out! turn out! they're found! they're found!" Tin pans and horns were added to the din, the population massed itself and moved toward the river, met the children coming in an open carriage drawn by shouting citizens, thronged around it, joined its homeward march, and swept magnificently up the main street roaring huzzah after huzzah!

The village was illuminated; nobody went to bed again; it was the greatest night the little town had ever seen. During the first half hour a procession of villagers filed through Judge Thatcher's house, seized the saved ones and kissed them, squeezed Mrs. Thatcher's hand, tried to speak but couldn't—and drifted out raining tears all over the place.

Aunt Polly's happiness was complete, and Mrs. Thatcher's nearly so. It would be complete, however, as soon as the messenger dispatched with the great news to the cave should get the word to her husband. Tom lay upon a sofa with an eager auditory about him and told the history of the wonderful adventure, putting in many striking additions to adorn it withal; and closed with a description of how he left Becky and went on an exploring expedition; how he followed two avenues as far as his kite-line would reach; how he followed a third to the fullest stretch of the kite-line, and was about to turn back when he glimpsed a far-off speck that looked like daylight; dropped the line and groped toward it, pushed his head and shoulders through a small hole and saw the broad Mississippi rolling by! And if it had only happened to be night he would not have seen that speck of daylight and would not have explored that passage any more! He told how he went back for Becky and broke the good news and she told him not to fret her with such stuff, for she was tired, and knew she was going to die, and

THE ESCAPE FROM THE CAVE.

wanted to. He described how he labored with her and convinced her; and how she almost died for joy when she had groped to where she actually saw the blue speck of daylight; how he pushed his way out at the hole and then helped her out; how they sat there and cried for gladness; how some men came along in a skiff and Tom hailed them and told them their situation and their famished condition; how the men didn't believe the wild tale at first, "because," said they, "you are five miles down the river below the valley the cave is in"—then took them aboard, rowed to a house, gave them supper, made them rest till two or three hours after dark and then brought them home.

Before day-dawn, Judge Thatcher and the handful of searchers with him were tracked out, in the cave, by the twine clews they had strung behind them, and informed of the great news.

Three days and nights of toil and hunger in the cave were not to be shaken off at once, as Tom and Becky soon discovered. They were bedridden all of Wednesday and Thursday, and seemed to grow more and more tired and worn, all the time. Tom got about, a little, on Thursday, was down town Friday, and nearly as whole as ever Saturday; but Becky did not leave her room until Sunday, and then she looked as if she had passed through a wasting illness.

Tom learned of Huck's sickness and went to see him on Friday, but could not be admitted to the bedroom; neither could he on Saturday or Sunday. He was admitted daily after that, but was warned to keep still about his adventure and introduce no exciting topic. The widow Douglas staid by to see that he obeyed. At home Tom learned of the Cardiff Hill event; also that the "ragged man's" body had eventually been found in the river near the ferry landing; he had been drowned while trying to escape, perhaps.

About a fortnight after Tom's rescue from the cave, he started off to visit Huck, who had grown plenty strong enough, now, to hear exciting talk, and Tom had some that would interest him, he thought. Judge Thatcher's house was on Tom's way, and he stopped to see Becky. The Judge and some friends set Tom to talking, and some one asked him ironically if he wouldn't like to go to the cave again. Tom said he thought he wouldn't mind it. The Judge said:

"Well, there are others just like you, Tom, I've not the least doubt. But we have taken care of that. Nobody will get lost in that cave any more."

"Why?"

"Because I had its big door sheathed with boiler iron two weeks ago, and triple-locked—and I've got the keys."

Tom turned as white as a sheet.

"What's the matter, boy! Here, run, somebody! Fetch a glass of water!"

The water was brought and thrown into Tom's face.

"Ah, now you're all right. What was the matter with you, Tom?"

"Oh, Judge, Injun Joe's in the cave!"

Chapter XXXIII

WITHIN A FEW minutes the news had spread, and a dozen skiff-loads of men were on their way to McDougal's cave, and the ferry-boat, well filled with passengers, soon followed. Tom Sawyer was in the skiff that bore Judge Thatcher.

When the cave door was unlocked a sorrowful sight presented itself in the dim twilight of the place. Injun Joe lay stretched upon the ground, dead, with his face close to the crack of the door, as if his longing eyes had been fixed, to the latest moment, upon the light and the cheer of the free world outside. Tom was touched, for he knew by his own experience how this wretch had suffered. His pity was moved, but nevertheless he felt an abounding sense of relief and security, now, which revealed to him in a degree which he had not fully appreciated before how vast a weight of dread had been lying upon him since the day he lifted his voice against this bloody-minded outcast.

Injun Joe's bowie knife lay close by, its blade broken in two. The great foundation-beam of the door had been chipped and hacked through, with tedious labor; useless labor, too, it was, for the native rock formed a sill outside it, and upon that stubborn material the knife had wrought no effect; the only damage done was to the knife itself. But if there had been no stony obstruction there the labor would have been useless still, for if the beam had been wholly cut away Injun Joe could not have squeezed his body under the door, and he knew it. So he had only hacked that place in order to be doing something—in order to pass the weary time—in order to employ his tortured faculties. Ordinarily one could find half a dozen bits of candle stuck around in the crevices of this vestibule, left there by tourists; but there were none now. The prisoner had searched them out and eaten them. He had also contrived to catch a few bats, and these, also, he had eaten, leaving only their claws. The poor unfortunate had starved to death. In one place near at hand, a stalagmite had been slowly growing up from the ground for ages, builded by the water-drip from a stalactite overhead. The captive had broken off the stalagmite, and upon the stump had placed a stone, wherein he had scooped a shallow hollow to catch the precious drop that fell once in every three minutes with the dreary regularity of a clock-tick—a dessert spoonful once in four and twenty hours. That drop was falling when the Pyramids were new; when Troy fell; when the foundations of Rome were laid; when Christ was crucified; when the Conqueror created the British empire; when Columbus sailed; when the massacre at Lexington was "news." It is falling now; it will still be falling when all these things shall have sunk down the afternoon of history, and the twilight of tradition, and been swallowed up in the thick night of oblivion. Has everything a purpose and a mission? Did this drop fall patiently during five thousand years to be ready for this flitting human insect's need? and has it another important object to accomplish ten thousand years to come? No matter. It is many and many a year since the hapless half-breed scooped out the stone to catch the priceless drops, but to this day the tourist stares longest at that pathetic stone and that slow dropping water when he comes to see the wonders of McDougal's cave. Injun Joe's cup stands first in the list of the cavern's marvels; even "Aladdin's Palace" cannot rival it.

Injun Joe was buried near the mouth of the cave; and people flocked there in boats and wagons from the towns and from all the farms and hamlets for seven miles around; they brought their children, and all sorts of provisions, and confessed that they had had almost as satisfactory a time at the funeral as they could have had at the hanging.

This funeral stopped the further growth of one thing—the petition to the Governor for Injun Joe's pardon. The petition had been largely signed; many tearful and eloquent meetings had been held, and a committee of sappy women been appointed to go in deep mourning and wail around the governor, and implore him to be a merciful ass and trample his duty under foot. Injun Joe was believed to have killed five citizens of the village, but what of that? If he had been Satan himself there would have been plenty of weaklings ready to scribble their names to a pardon-petition, and drip a tear on it from their permanently impaired and leaky water-works.

The morning after the funeral Tom took Huck to a private place to have an important talk. Huck had learned all about Tom's adventure from the Welchman and the widow Douglas, by this time, but Tom said he reckoned there was one thing they had not told him; that thing was what he wanted to talk about now. Huck's face saddened. He said:

"I know what it is. You got into No. 2 and never found anything but whisky. Nobody told me it was you; but I just knowed it must 'a' ben you, soon as I heard 'bout that whisky business; and I knowed you hadn't got the money becuz you'd 'a' got at me some way or other and told me even if you was mum to everybody else. Tom, something's always told me we'd never get holt of that swag."

"Why Huck, *I* never told on that tavern-keeper. *You* know his tavern was all right the Saturday I went to the pic-nic. Don't you remember you was to watch there that night?"

"Oh, yes! Why it seems 'bout a year ago. It was that very night that I follered Injun Joe to the widder's."

"*You* followed him?"

"Yes—but you keep mum. I reckon Injun Joe's left friends behind him, and I don't want 'em souring on me and doing me mean tricks. If it hadn't ben for me he'd be down in Texas now, all right."

Then Huck told his entire adventure in confidence to Tom, who had only heard of the Welchmen's part of it before.

"Well," said Huck, presently, coming back to the main question, "whoever nipped the whisky in No. 2, nipped the money too, I reckon—anyways it's a goner for us, Tom."

"Huck, that money wasn't ever in No. 2!"

"What!" Huck searched his comrade's face keenly. "Tom, have you got on the track of that money again?"

"Huck, it's in the cave!"

Huck's eyes blazed.

"Say it again, Tom!"

"The money's in the cave!"

"Tom,—honest injun, now—is it fun, or earnest?"

"Earnest, Huck—just as earnest as ever I was in my life. Will you go in there with me and help get it out?"

"I bet I will! I will if it's where we can blaze our way to it and not get lost."

"Huck, we can do that without the least little bit of trouble in the world."

"Good as wheat! What makes you think the money's—"

"Huck, you just wait till we get in there. If we don't find it I'll agree to give you my drum and everything I've got in the world. I will, by jings."

"All right—it's a whiz. When do you say?"

"Right now, if you say it. Are you strong enough?"

"Is it far in the cave? I ben on my pins a little, three or four days, now, but I can't walk more'n a mile, Tom—least I don't think I could."

"It's about five mile into there the way anybody but me would go, Huck, but there's a mighty short cut that they don't anybody but me know about. Huck, I'll take you right to it in a skiff. I'll float the skiff down there, and I'll pull it back again all by myself. You needn't ever turn your hand over.''

"Less start right off, Tom.''

"All right. We want some bread and meat, and our pipes, and a little bag or two, and two or three kite-strings, and some of these new fangled things they call lucifer matches. I tell you many's the time I wished I had some when I was in there before.''

A trifle after noon the boys borrowed a small skiff from a citizen who was absent, and got under way at once. When they were several miles below "Cave Hollow," Tom said:

"Now you see this bluff here looks all alike all the way down from the cave hollow—no houses, no wood-yards, bushes all alike. But do you see that white place up yonder where there's been a landslide? Well that's one of my marks. We'll get ashore, now.''

They landed.

"Now Huck, where we're a-standing you could touch that hole I got out of with a fishing-pole. See if you can find it.''

Huck searched all the place about, and found nothing. Tom proudly marched into a thick clump of sumach bushes and said—

"Here you are! Look at it, Huck; it's the snuggest hole in this country. You just keep mum about it. All along I've been wanting to be a robber, but I knew I'd got to have a thing like this, and where to run across it was the bother. We've got it now, and we'll keep it quiet, only we'll let Joe Harper and Ben Rogers in—because of course there's got to be a Gang, or else there wouldn't be any style about it. Tom Sawyer's Gang—it sounds splendid, don't it, Huck?''

"Well, it just does, Tom. And who'll we rob?''

"Oh, most anybody. Waylay people—that's mostly the way.''

"And kill them?''

"No—not always. Hive them in the cave till they raise a ransom.''

"What's a ransom?''

"Money. You make them raise all they can, off'n their friends; and after you've kept them a year, if it ain't raised then you kill them. That's the general way. Only you don't kill the women. You shut up the women, but you don't kill them. They're always beautiful and rich, and awfully scared. You take their watches and things, but you always take your hat off and talk polite. They ain't anybody as polite as robbers—you'll see that in any book. Well the women get to loving you, and after they've been in the cave a week or two weeks they stop crying and after that you couldn't get them to leave. If you drove them out they'd turn right around and come back. It's so in all the books.''

"Why it's real bully, Tom. I b'lieve it's better'n to be a pirate.''

"Yes, it's better in some ways, because it's close to home and circuses and all that.''

By this time everything was ready and the boys entered the hole, Tom in the lead. They toiled their way to the farther end of the tunnel, then made their spliced kite-strings fast and moved on. A few steps brought them to the spring and Tom felt a shudder quiver all through him. He showed Huck the fragment of candle-wick perched on a lump of clay against the wall, and described how he and Becky had watched the flame struggle and expire.

The boys began to quiet down to whispers, now, for the stillness and gloom of the place oppressed their spirits. They went on, and presently entered and followed Tom's other corridor until they reached the "jumping-off place." The candles revealed the fact that it was not really a precipice, but only a steep clay hill twenty or thirty feet high. Tom whispered—

"Now I'll show you something, Huck."

He held his candle aloft and said—

"Look as far around the corner as you can. Do you see that? There—on the big rock over yonder—done with candle smoke."

"Tom, its a *cross!*"

"*Now* where's your Number Two? '*Under the cross,*' hey? Right yonder's where I saw Injun Joe poke up his candle, Huck!"

Huck stared at the mystic sign a while, and then said with a shaky voice—

"Tom, less git out of here!"

"What! and leave the treasure?"

"Yes—leave it. Injun Joe's ghost is round about there, certain."

"No it ain't, Huck, no it ain't. It would ha'nt the place where he died—away out at the mouth of the cave—five mile from here."

"No, Tom, it wouldn't. It would hang round the money. I know the ways of ghosts, and so do you."

Tom began to fear that Huck was right. Misgivings gathered in his mind. But presently an idea occurred to him—

"Looky here, Huck, what fools we're making of ourselves! Injun Joe's ghost ain't a going to come around where there's a cross!"

The point was well taken. It had its effect.

"Tom I didn't think of that. But that's so. It's luck for us, that cross is. I reckon we'll climb down there and have a hunt for that box."

Tom went first, cutting rude steps in the clay hill as he descended. Huck followed. Four avenues opened out of the small cavern which the great rock stood in. The boys examined three of them with no result. They found a small recess in the one nearest the base of the rock, with a pallet of blankets spread down in it; also an old suspender, some bacon rind, and the well gnawed bones of two or three fowls. But there was no money box. The lads searched and re-searched this place, but in vain. Tom said:

"He said *under* the cross. Well, this comes nearest to being under the cross. It can't be under the rock itself, because that sets solid on the ground."

They searched everywhere once more, and then sat down discouraged. Huck could suggest nothing. By and by Tom said:

"Looky here, Huck, there's foot-prints and some candle grease on the clay about one side of this rock, but not on the other sides. Now what's that for? I bet you the money *is* under the rock. I'm going to dig in the clay."

"That ain't no bad notion, Tom!" said Huck with animation.

Tom's "real Barlow" was out at once, and he had not dug four inches before he struck wood.

"Hey, Huck!—you hear that?"

Huck began to dig and scratch now. Some boards were soon uncovered and removed. They had concealed a natural chasm which led under the rock. Tom got into this and held his candle as far under the rock as he could, but said he could not see to the end of the rift. He proposed to explore. He stooped and passed under; the narrow way descended gradually. He followed its winding course, first to the right, then to the left, Huck at his heels. Tom turned a short curve, by and by, and exclaimed—

"My goodness, Huck, looky here!"

It was the treasure box, sure enough, occupying a snug little cavern, along with an empty powder keg, a couple of guns in leather cases, two or three pairs of old moccasins, a leather belt, and some other rubbish well soaked with the water-drip.

"Got it at last!" said Huck, plowing among the tarnished coins with his hand. "My, but we're rich, Tom!"

"Huck, I always reckoned we'd get it. It's just too good to believe, but we *have* got it, sure! Say—let's not fool around here. Let's snake it out. Lemme see if I can lift the box."

It weighed about fifty pounds. Tom could lift it, after an awkward fashion, but could not carry it conveniently.

"I thought so," he said; *they* carried it like it was heavy, that day at the ha'nted house. I noticed that. I reckon I was right to think of fetching the little bags along."

The money was soon in the bags and the boys took it up to the cross-rock.

"Now less fetch the guns and things," said Huck.

"No, Huck—leave them there. They're just the tricks to have when we go to robbing. We'll keep them there all the time, and we'll hold our orgies there, too. It's an awful snug place for orgies."

"What's orgies?"

"*I* dono. But robbers always have orgies, and of course we've got to have them, too. Come along, Huck, we've been in here a long time. It's getting late, I reckon. I'm hungry, too. We'll eat and smoke when we get to the skiff."

They presently emerged into the clump of sumach bushes, looked warily out, found the coast clear, and were soon lunching and smoking in the skiff. As the sun dipped toward the horizon they pushed out and got under way. Tom skimmed up the shore through the long twilight, chatting cheerily with Huck, and landed shortly after dark.

"Now Huck," said Tom, "we'll hide the money in the loft of the widow's

"GOT IT AT LAST!"

wood-shed, and I'll come up in the morning and we'll count it and divide, and then we'll hunt up a place out in the woods for it where it will be safe. Just you lay quiet here and watch the stuff till I run and hook Benny Taylor's little wagon; I won't be gone a minute."

He disappeared, and presently returned with the wagon, put the two small sacks into it, threw some old rags on top of them, and started off, dragging his cargo behind him. When the boys reached the Welchman's house, they stopped to rest. Just as they were about to move on, the Welchman stepped out and said:

"Hallo, who's that?"

"Huck and Tom Sawyer."

"Good! Come along with me, boys, you are keeping everybody waiting. Here—hurry up, trot ahead—I'll haul the wagon for you. Why, it's not as light as it might be. Got bricks in it?—or old metal?"

"Old metal," said Tom.

"I judged so; the boys in this town will take more trouble and fool away more time, hunting up six bits' worth of old iron to sell to the foundry than they would to make twice the money at regular work. But that's human nature—hurry along, hurry along!"

The boys wanted to know what the hurry was about.

"Never mind; you'll see, when we get to the Widow Douglas's."

Huck said with some apprehension—for he was long used to being falsely accused—

"Mr. Jones, *we* haven't been doing nothing."

The Welchman laughed.

"Well, I don't know, Huck, my boy. I don't know about that. Ain't you and the widow good friends?"

"Yes. Well, she's ben good friends to me, any ways."

"All right, then. What do you want to be afraid for?"

This question was not entirely answered in Huck's slow mind before he found himself pushed, along with Tom, into Mrs. Douglas's drawing-room. Mr. Jones left the wagon near the door and followed.

The place was grandly lighted, and everybody that was of any consequence in the village was there. The Thatchers were there, the Harpers, the Rogerses, Aunt Polly, Sid, Mary, the minister, the editor, and a great many more, and all dressed in their best. The widow received the boys as heartily as any one could well receive two such looking beings. They were covered with clay and candle grease. Aunt Polly blushed crimson with humiliation, and frowned and shook her head at Tom. Nobody suffered half as much as the two boys did, however. Mr. Jones said:

"Tom wasn't at home, yet, so I gave him up; but I stumbled on him and Huck right at my door, and so I just brought them along in a hurry."

"And you did just right," said the widow:—"Come with me, boys."

She took them to a bed chamber and said:

"Now wash and dress yourselves. Here are two new suits of clothes—shirts, socks, everything complete. They're Huck's—no, no thanks, Huck—Mr. Jones bought one and I the other. But they'll fit both of you. Get into them. We'll wait—come down when you are slicked up enough."

Then she left.

Chapter XXXIV

HUCK SAID: "Tom, we can slope, if we can find a rope. The window ain't high from the ground."

"Shucks, what do you want to slope for?"

"Well I ain't used to that kind of a crowd. I can't stand it. I ain't going down there, Tom."

"O, bother! It ain't anything. I don't mind it a bit. I'll take care of you."

Sid appeared.

"Tom," said he, "Auntie has been waiting for you all the afternoon. Mary got your Sunday clothes ready, and everybody's been fretting about you. Say— ain't this grease and clay, on your clothes?"

"Now Mr. Siddy, you jist 'tend to your own business. What's all this blow-out about, anyway?"

"It's one of the widow's parties that she's always having. This time it's for the Welchman and his sons, on account of that scrape they helped her out of the other night. And say—I can tell you something, if you want to know."

"Well, what?"

"Why old Mr. Jones is going to try to spring something on the people here to-night, but I overheard him tell auntie to-day about it, as a secret, but I reckon it's not much of a secret *now*. Everybody knows—the widow, too, for all she tries to let on she don't. Mr. Jones was bound Huck should be here—couldn't get along with his grand secret without Huck, you know!"

"Secret about what, Sid?"

"About Huck tracking the robbers to the widow's. I reckon Mr. Jones was going to make a grand time over his surprise, but I bet you it will drop pretty flat."

Sid chuckled in a very contented and satisfied way.

"Sid, was it you that told?"

"O, never mind who it was. *Somebody* told—that's enough."

"Sid, there's only one person in this town mean enough to do that, and that's you. If you had been in Huck's place you'd 'a' sneaked down the hill and never told anybody on the robbers. You can't do any but mean things, and you can't bear to see anybody praised for doing good ones. There—no thanks, as the widow says"—and Tom cuffed Sid's ears and helped him to the door with several kicks. "Now go and tell auntie if you dare—and to-morrow you'll catch it!"

Some minutes later the widow's guests were at the supper table, and a dozen children were propped up at little side tables in the same room, after the fashion of that country and that day. At the proper time Mr. Jones made his little speech, in which he thanked the widow for the honor she was doing himself and his sons, but said that there was another person whose modesty—

And so forth and so on. He sprung his secret about Huck's share in the adventure in the finest dramatic manner he was master of, but the surprise it occasioned was largely counterfeit and not as clamorous and effusive as it might have been under happier circumstances. However, the widow made a pretty fair show of astonishment, and heaped so many compliments and so much gratitude upon Huck that he almost forgot the nearly intolerable discomfort of his new clothes in the entirely intolerable discomfort of being set up as a target for everybody's gaze and everybody's laudations.

The widow said she meant to give Huck a home under her roof and have him educated; and that when she could spare the money she would start him in business in a modest way. Tom's chance was come. He said:

"Huck don't need it. Huck's rich!"

Nothing but a heavy strain upon the good manners of the company kept back the due and proper complimentary laugh at this pleasant joke. But the silence was a little awkward. Tom broke it—

"Huck's got money. Maybe you don't believe it, but he's got lots of it. Oh, you needn't smile—I reckon I can show you. You just wait a minute."

Tom ran out of doors. The company looked at each other with a perplexed interest—and inquiringly at Huck, who was tongue-tied.

"Sid, what ails Tom?" said Aunt Polly. "He—well, there ain't ever any making of that boy out. I never—"

Tom entered, struggling with the weight of his sacks, and Aunt Polly did not finish her sentence. Tom poured the mass of yellow coin upon the table and said—

"There—what did I tell you? Half of it's Huck's and half of it's mine!"

The spectacle took the general breath away. All gazed, nobody spoke for a moment. Then there was a unanimous call for an explanation. Tom said he could furnish it, and he did. The tale was long, but brim full of interest. There was scarcely an interruption from anyone to break the charm of its flow. When he had finished, Mr. Jones said—

"I thought I had fixed up a little surprise for this occasion, but it don't amount to anything now. This one makes it sing mighty small, I'm willing to allow."

The money was counted. The sum amounted to a little over twelve thousand dollars. It was more than any one present had ever seen at one time before, though several persons were there who were worth considerably more than that in property.

TOM BACKS HIS STATEMENT.

Chapter XXXV

THE READER MAY rest satisfied that Tom's and Huck's windfall made a mighty stir in the poor little village of St. Petersburg. So vast a sum, all in actual cash, seemed next to incredible. It was talked about, gloated over, glorified, until the reason of many of the citizens tottered under the strain of the unhealthy excitement. Every "haunted" house in St. Petersburg and the neighboring villages was dissected, plank by plank, and its foundations dug up and ransacked for hidden treasure—and not by boys, but men—pretty grave, unromantic men, too, some of them. Wherever Tom and Huck appeared they were courted, admired, stared at. The boys were not able to remember that their remarks had possessed weight before; but now their sayings were treasured and repeated; everything they did seemed somehow to be regarded as remarkable; they had evidently lost the power of doing and saying commonplace things; moreover, their past history was raked up and discovered to bear marks of conspicuous originality. The village paper published biographical sketches of the boys.

The widow Douglas put Huck's money out at six per cent., and Judge Thatcher did the same with Tom's at Aunt Polly's request. Each lad had an income, now, that was simply prodigious—a dollar for every week-day in the year and half of the Sundays. It was just what the minister got—no, it was what he was promised—he generally couldn't collect it. A dollar and a quarter a week would board, lodge and school a boy in those old simple days—and clothe him and wash him, too, for that matter.

Judge Thatcher had conceived a great opinion of Tom. He said that no commonplace boy would ever have got his daughter out of the cave. When Becky told her father, in strict confidence, how Tom had taken her whipping at school, the Judge was visibly moved; and when she pleaded grace for the mighty lie which Tom had told in order to shift that whipping from her shoulders to his own, the Judge said with a fine outburst that it was a noble, a generous, a magnanimous lie—a lie that was worthy to hold up its head and march down through history breast to breast with George Washington's lauded Truth about the hatchet! Becky thought her father had never looked so tall and so superb as when he walked the floor and stamped his foot and said that. She went straight off and told Tom about it.

Judge Thatcher hoped to see Tom a great lawyer or a great soldier some day. He said he meant to look to it that Tom should be admitted to the National military academy and afterwards trained in the best law school in the country, in order that he might be ready for either career or both.

Huck Finn's wealth and the fact that he was now under the widow Douglas's protection, introduced him into society—no, dragged him into it, hurled him into it—and his sufferings were almost more than he could bear. The widow's servants kept him clean and neat, combed and brushed, and they bedded him nightly in unsympathetic sheets that had not one little spot or stain which he could press to his heart and know for a friend. He had to eat with knife and fork; he had to use napkin, cup and plate; he had to learn his book, he had to go to church; he had to talk so properly that speech was become insipid in his mouth; whithersoever he turned, the bars and shackles of civilization shut him in and bound him hand and foot.

He bravely bore his miseries three weeks, and then one day turned up missing. For forty-eight hours the widow hunted for him everywhere in great distress. The public were profoundly concerned; they searched high and low, they dragged the river for his body. Early the third morning Tom Sawyer wisely went poking among some old empty hogsheads down behind the abandoned slaughter-house, and in one of them he found the refugee. Huck had slept there; he had just breakfasted upon some stolen odds and ends of food, and was lying off, now, in comfort with his pipe. He was unkempt, uncombed, and clad in the same old ruin of rags that had made him picturesque in the days when he was free and happy. Tom routed him out, told him the trouble he had been causing, and urged him to go home. Huck's face lost its tranquil content, and took a melancholy cast. He said:

"Don't talk about it, Tom. I've tried it, and it don't work; it don't work, Tom. It ain't for me; I ain't used to it. The widder's good to me, and friendly; but I can't stand them ways. She makes me git up just at the same time every morning; she makes me wash, they comb me all to thunder; she won't let me sleep in the wood-shed; I got to wear them blamed clothes that just smothers me, Tom; they don't seem to any air git through 'em, somehow; and they're so rotten nice that I can't set down, nor lay down, nor roll around anywher's; I hain't slid on a cellar-door for—well, it 'pears to be years; I got to go to church and sweat and sweat—I hate them ornery sermons! I can't ketch a fly in there, I can't chaw, I got to wear shoes all Sunday. The widder eats by a bell; she goes to bed by a bell; she gits up by a bell—everything's so awful reg'lar a body can't stand it."

"Well, everybody does that way, Huck."

"Tom, it don't make no difference. I ain't everybody, and I can't *stand* it. It's awful to be tied up so. And grub comes too easy—I don't take no interest in vittles, that way. I got to ask, to go a-fishing; I got to ask, to go in a-swimming—dern'd if I hain't got to ask to do everything. Well, I'd got to talk so nice it wasn't no comfort—I'd got to go up in the attic and rip out a while, every day, to git a taste in my mouth, or I'd a died, Tom. The widder wouldn't

COMFORTABLE ONCE MORE.

let me smoke; she wouldn't let me yell, she wouldn't let me gape, nor stretch, nor scratch, before folks—'' [Then with a spasm of special irritation and injury],—''And dad fetch it, she prayed all the time! I never *see* such a woman! I *had* to shove, Tom—I just had to. And besides, that school's going to open, and I'd a had to go to it—well, I wouldn't stand *that*, Tom. Lookyhere, Tom, being rich ain't what it's cracked up to be. It's just worry and worry, and sweat and sweat, and a-wishing you was dead all the time. Now these clothes suits me, and this bar'l suits me, and I ain't ever going to shake 'em any more. Tom, I wouldn't ever got into all this trouble if it hadn't 'a' been for that money; now you just take my sheer of it along with your'n, and gimme a ten-center sometimes—not many times, becuz I don't give a dern for a thing 'thout it's tollable hard to git—and you go and beg off for me with the widder.''

''Oh, Huck, you know I can't do that. 'Taint fair; and besides if you'll try this thing just a while longer you'll come to like it.''

''Like it! Yes—the way I'd like a hot stove if I was to set on it long enough. No, Tom, I won't be rich, and I won't live in them cussed smothery houses. I like the woods, and the river, and hogsheads, and I'll stick to 'em, too. Blame it all! just as we'd got guns, and a cave, and all just fixed to rob, here this dern foolishness has got to come up and spile it all!''

Tom saw his opportunity—

''Lookyhere, Huck, being rich ain't going to keep me back from turning robber.''

''No! Oh, good-licks, are you in real dead-wood earnest, Tom?''

''Just as dead earnest as I'm a sitting here. But Huck, we can't let you into the gang if you ain't respectable, you know.''

Huck's joy was quenched.

''Can't let me in, Tom? Didn't you let me go for a pirate?''

''Yes, but that's different. A robber is more high-toned than what a pirate is—as a general thing. In most countries they're awful high up in the nobility—dukes and such.''

''Now Tom, hain't you always ben friendly to me? You wouldn't shet me out, would you, Tom? You wouldn't do that, now, *would* you, Tom?''

''Huck, I wouldn't want to, and I *don't* want to—but what would people say? Why they'd say, 'Mph! Tom Sawyer's Gang! pretty low characters in it!' They'd mean you, Huck. You wouldn't like that, and I wouldn't.''

Huck was silent for some time, engaged in a mental struggle. Finally he said:

''Well, I'll go back to the widder for a month and tackle it and see if I can come to stand it, if you'll let me b'long to the gang, Tom.''

''All right, Huck, it's a whiz! Come along, old chap, and I'll ask the widow to let up on you a little, Huck.''

''Will you Tom—now will you? That's good. If she'll let up on some of the roughest things, I'll smoke private and cuss private, and crowd through or bust. When you going to start the gang and turn robbers?''

''Oh, right off. We'll get the boys together and have the initiation to-night, maybe.''

''Have the which?''

''Have the initiation.''

''What's that?''

''It's to swear to stand by one another, and never tell the gang's secrets, even if you're chopped all to flinders, and kill anybody and all his family that hurts one of the gang.''

"That's gay—that's mighty gay, Tom, I tell you.''

"Well I bet it is. And all that swearing's got to be done at midnight, in the lonesomest, awfulest place you can find—a ha'nted house is the best, but they're all ripped up now.''

"Well, midnight's good, anyway, Tom.''

"Yes, so it is. And you've got to swear on a coffin, and sign it with blood.''

"Now that's something *like!* Why it's a million times bullier than pirating. I'll stick to the widder till I rot, Tom; and if I git to be a reg'lar ripper of a robber, and everybody talking 'bout it, I reckon she'll be proud she snaked me in out of the wet.''

CONCLUSION

So ENDETH THIS chronicle. It being strictly a history of a *boy*, it must stop here; the story could not go much further without becoming the history of a *man*. When one writes a novel about grown people, he knows exactly where to stop— that is, with a marriage; but when he writes of juveniles, he must stop where he best can.

Most of the characters that perform in this book still live, and are prosperous and happy. Some day it may seem worth while to take up the story of the younger ones again and see what sort of men and women they turned out to be; therefore it will be wisest not to reveal any of that part of their lives at present.

THE END.

Adventures of Huckleberry Finn

(Tom Sawyer's Comrade)

Illustrated by E.W. Kemble

NOTICE

Persons attempting to find a motive in this narrative will be prosecuted; persons attempting to find a moral in it will be banished; persons attempting to find a plot in it will be shot.

BY ORDER OF THE AUTHOR
PER G. G., CHIEF OF ORDNANCE

Explanatory

In this book a number of dialects are used, to wit: the Missouri negro dialect; the extremest form of the backwoods South-Western dialect; the ordinary "Pike-County" dialect; and four modified varieties of this last. The shadings have not been done in a hap-hazard fashion, or by guess-work; but pains-takingly, and with the trustworthy guidance and support of personal familiarity with these several forms of speech.

I make this explanation for the reason that without it many readers would suppose that all these characters were trying to talk alike and not succeeding.

The Author

A Note to the Reader: There are racial references and language in this story that may be offensive to the modern reader. He should be aware, however, that these do not reflect the attitudes of the publisher of this edition. Moreover, Mark Twain's original intention was one of irony, where the insults applied to Jim, the runaway slave, were meant to emphasize Jim's nobility and integrity, in contrast to those who cast the slurs. It is in this light that the story should be read.

E.W.Kemble
1884

HUCKLEBERRY FINN.

Chapter I

YOU DON'T KNOW about me, without you have read a book by the name of "The Adventures of Tom Sawyer," but that ain't no matter. That book was made by Mr. Mark Twain, and he told the truth, mainly. There was things which he stretched, but mainly he told the truth. That is nothing. I never seen anybody but lied, one time or another, without it was Aunt Polly, or the widow, or maybe Mary. Aunt Polly—Tom's Aunt Polly, she is—and Mary, and the Widow Douglas, is all told about in that book—which is mostly a true book; with some stretchers, as I said before.

Now the way that the book winds up, is this: Tom and me found the money that the robbers hid in the cave, and it made us rich. We got six thousand dollars apiece—all gold. It was an awful sight of money when it was piled up. Well, Judge Thatcher, he took it and put it out at interest, and it fetched us a dollar a day apiece, all the year round—more than a body could tell what to do with. The Widow Douglas, she took me for her son, and allowed she would sivilize me; but it was rough living in the house all the time, considering how dismal regular and decent the widow was in all her ways; and so when I couldn't stand it no longer, I lit out. I got into my old rags, and my sugar-hogshead again, and was free and satisfied. But Tom Sawyer, he hunted me up and said he was going to start a band of robbers, and I might join if I would go back to the widow and be respectable. So I went back.

The widow she cried over me, and called me a poor lost lamb, and she called me a lot of other names, too, but she never meant no harm by it. She put me in them new clothes again, and I couldn't do nothing but sweat and sweat, and feel all cramped up. Well, then, the old thing commenced again. The widow rung a bell for supper, and you had to come to time. When you got to the table you couldn't go right to eating, but you had to wait for the widow to tuck down her head and grumble a little over the victuals, though there warn't really anything the matter with them. That is, nothing only everything was cooked by itself. In a barrel of odds and ends it is different; things get mixed up, and the juice kind of swaps around, and the things go better.

After supper she got out her book and learned me about Moses and the Bulrushers; and I was in a sweat to find out all about him; but by-and-by she let it out that Moses had been dead a considerable long time; so then I didn't care no more about him; because I don't take no stock in dead people.

LEARNING ABOUT MOSES AND THE "BULRUSHERS."

Pretty soon I wanted to smoke, and asked the widow to let me. But she wouldn't. She said it was a mean practice and wasn't clean, and I must try to not do it any more. That is just the way with some people. They get down on a thing when they don't know nothing about it. Here she was a bothering about Moses, which was no kin to her, and no use to anybody, being gone, you see, yet finding a power of fault with me for doing a thing that had some good in it. And she took snuff too; of course that was all right, because she done it herself.

Her sister, Miss Watson, a tolerable slim old maid, with goggles on, had just come to live with her, and took a set at me now, with a spelling-book. She worked me middling hard for about an hour, and then the widow made her ease up. I couldn't stood it much longer. Then for an hour it was deadly dull, and I was fidgety. Miss Watson would say, "Don't put your feet up there, Huckleberry;" and "don't scrunch up like that, Huckleberry—set up straight;" and pretty soon she would say, "Don't gap and stretch like that, Huckleberry—why don't you try to behave?" Then she told me all about the bad place, and I said I wished I was there. She got mad, then, but I didn't mean no harm. All I wanted was to go somewheres; all I wanted was a change, I warn't particular. She said it was wicked to say what I said; said she wouldn't say it for the whole world; *she* was going to live so as to go to the good place. Well, I couldn't see no advantage in going where she was going, so I made up my mind I wouldn't try for it. But I never said so, because it would only make trouble, and wouldn't do no good.

Now she had got a start, and she went on and told me all about the good place. She said all a body would have to do there was to go around all day long with a harp and sing, forever and ever. So I didn't think much of it. But I never said so. I asked her if she reckoned Tom Sawyer would go there, and, she said, not by a considerable sight. I was glad about that, because I wanted him and me to be together.

Miss Watson she kept pecking at me, and it got tiresome and lonesome. By-and-by they fetched the niggers in and had prayers, and then everybody was off to bed. I went up to my room with a piece of candle and put it on the table. Then I set down in a chair by the window and tried to think of something cheerful, but it warn't no use. I felt so lonesome I most wished I was dead. The stars was shining, and the leaves rustled in the woods ever so mournful; and I heard an owl, away off, who-whooing about somebody that was dead, and a whippowill and a dog crying about somebody that was going to die; and the wind was trying to whisper something to me and I couldn't make out what it was, and so it made the cold shivers run over me. Then away out in the woods I heard that kind of a sound that a ghost makes when it wants to tell about something that's on its mind and can't make itself understood, and so can't rest easy in its grave and has to go about that way every night grieving. I got so down-hearted and scared, I did wish I had some company. Pretty soon a spider went crawling up my shoulder, and I flipped it off and it lit in the candle; and before I could budge it was all shriveled up. I didn't need anybody to tell me that that was an awful bad sign and would fetch me some bad luck, so I was scared and most shook the clothes off of me. I got up and turned around in my tracks three times and crossed my breast every time; and then I tied up a little lock of my hair with a thread to keep witches away. But I hadn't no confidence. You do that when you've lost a horse-shoe that you've found, instead of nailing it up over the door, but I hadn't ever heard anybody say it was any way to keep off bad luck when you'd killed a spider.

I set down again, a shaking all over, and got out my pipe for a smoke; for the house was all as still as death, now, and so the widow wouldn't know. Well, after a long time I heard the clock away off in the town go boom—boom—boom—twelve licks—and all still again—stiller than ever. Pretty soon I heard a twig snap, down in the dark amongst the trees—something was a stirring. I set still and listened. Directly I could just barely hear a "*me-yow! me-yow!*" down there. That was good! Says I, "*me-yow! me-yow!*" as soft as I could, and then I put out the light and scrambled out of the window onto the shed. Then I slipped down to the ground and crawled in amongst the trees, and sure enough there was Tom Sawyer waiting for me.

HUCK STEALING AWAY.

Chapter II

WE WENT TIP-TOEING along a path amongst the trees back towards the end of the widow's garden, stooping down so as the branches wouldn't scrape our heads. When we was passing by the kitchen I fell over a root and made a noise. We scrouched down and laid still. Miss Watson's big nigger, named Jim, was setting in the kitchen door; we could see him pretty clear, because there was a light behind him. He got up and stretched his neck out about a minute, listening. Then he says,

"Who dah?"

He listened some more; then he come tip-toeing down and stood right between us; we could a touched him, nearly. Well, likely it was minutes and minutes that there warn't a sound, and we all there so close together. There was a place on my ankle that got to itching; but I dasn't scratch it; and then my ear begun to itch; and next my back, right between my shoulders. Seemed like I'd die if I couldn't scratch. Well, I've noticed that thing plenty of times since. If you are with the quality, or at a funeral, or trying to go to sleep when you ain't sleepy— if you are anywheres where it won't do for you to scratch, why you will itch all over in upwards of a thousand places. Pretty soon Jim says:

"Say—who is you? Whar is you? Dog my cats ef I didn' hear sumf'n. Well, I knows what I's gwyne to do. I's gwyne to set down here and listen tell I hears it agin."

So he set down on the ground betwixt me and Tom. He leaned his back up against a tree, and stretched his legs out till one of them most touched one of mine. My nose begun to itch. It itched till the tears come into my eyes. But I dasn't scratch. Then it begun to itch on the inside. Next I got to itching underneath. I didn't know how I was going to set still. This miserableness went on as much as six or seven minutes; but it seemed a sight longer than that. I was itching in eleven different places now. I reckoned I couldn't stand it more'n a minute longer, but I set my teeth hard and got ready to try. Just then Jim begun to breathe heavy; next he begun to snore—and then I was pretty soon comfortable again.

Tom he made a sign to me—kind of a little noise with his mouth—and we went creeping away on our hands and knees. When we was ten foot off, Tom whispered to me and wanted to tie Jim to the tree for fun; but I said no; he might wake and make a disturbance, and then they'd find out I warn't in. Then Tom said he hadn't got candles enough, and he would slip in the kitchen and get some more. I didn't want him to try. I said Jim might wake up and come. But Tom wanted to resk it; so we slid in there and got three candles, and Tom laid five cents on the table for pay. Then we got out, and I was in a sweat to get away; but nothing would do Tom but he must crawl to where Jim was, on his hands and knees, and play something on him. I waited, and it seemed a good while, everything was so still and lonesome.

As soon as Tom was back, we cut along the path, around the garden fence, and by-and-by fetched up on the steep top of the hill the other side of the house. Tom said he slipped Jim's hat off of his head and hung it on a limb right over him, and Jim stirred a little, but he didn't wake. Afterwards Jim said the witches bewitched him and put him in a trance, and rode him all over the State, and then set him under the trees again and hung his hat on a limb to show who done it. And next time Jim told it he said they rode him down to New Orleans; and after that, every time he told it he spread it more and more, till by-and-by he said they rode him all over the world, and tired him most to death, and his back was all over saddle-boils. Jim was monstrous proud about it, and he got so he wouldn't hardly notice the other niggers. Niggers would come miles to hear Jim tell about it, and he was more looked up to than any nigger in that country. Strange niggers would stand with their mouths open and look him all over, same as if he was a wonder. Niggers is always talking about witches in the dark by the kitchen fire; but whenever one was talking and letting on to know all about such things, Jim would happen in and say, "Hm! What you know 'bout witches?" and that nigger was corked up and had to take a back seat. Jim always kept that five-center piece around his neck with a string and said it was a charm the devil give to him with his own hands and told him he could cure anybody with it and fetch witches whenever he wanted to, just by saying something to it; but he never told what it was he said to it. Niggers would come from all around there and give Jim anything they had, just for a sight of that five-center piece; but they wouldn't touch it, because the devil had had his hands on it. Jim was most ruined, for a servant, because he got so stuck up on account of having seen the devil and been rode by witches.

Well, when Tom and me got to the edge of the hill-top, we looked away down into the village and could see three or four lights twinkling, where there was sick folks, may be; and the stars over us was sparkling ever so fine; and down by the village was the river, a whole mile broad, and awful still and grand. We went down the hill and found Jo Harper, and Ben Rogers, and two or three more of the boys, hid in the old tanyard. So we unhitched a skiff and pulled down the river two mile and a half, to the big scar on the hillside, and went ashore.

We went to a clump of bushes, and Tom made everybody swear to keep the secret, and then showed them a hole in the hill, right in the thickest part of the bushes. Then we lit the candles and crawled in on our hands and knees. We went about two hundred yards, and then the cave opened up. Tom poked about amongst the passages and pretty soon ducked under a wall where you wouldn't a noticed that there was a hole. We went along a narrow place and got into a kind of room, all damp and sweaty and cold, and there we stopped. Tom says:

"Now we'll start this band of robbers and call it Tom Sawyer's Gang. Everybody that wants to join has got to take an oath, and write his name in blood."

Everybody was willing. So Tom got out a sheet of paper that he had wrote the oath on, and read it. It swore every boy to stick to the band, and never tell any of the secrets; and if anybody done anything to any boy in the band, whichever boy was ordered to kill that person and his family must do it, and he mustn't eat and he mustn't sleep till he had killed them and hacked a cross in their breasts, which was the sign of the band. And nobody that didn't belong to the band could use that mark, and if he did he must be sued; and if he done it again he must be killed. And if anybody that belonged to the band told the secrets, he must have his throat cut, and then have his carcass burnt up and the ashes scattered all around, and his name blotted off of the list with blood and never mentioned again by the gang, but have a curse put on it and be forgot, forever.

Everybody said it was a real beautiful oath, and asked Tom if he got it out

TOM SAWYER'S BAND OF ROBBERS.

of his own head. He said, some of it, but the rest was out of pirate books, and robber books, and every gang that was high-toned had it.

Some thought it would be good to kill the *families* of boys that told the secrets. Tom said it was a good idea, so he took a pencil and wrote it in. Then Ben Rogers says:

"Here's Huck Finn, he hain't got no family—what you going to do 'bout him?"

"Well, hain't he got a father?" says Tom Sawyer.

"Yes, he's got a father, but you can't never find him, these days. He used to lay drunk with the hogs in the tanyard, but he hain't been seen in these parts for a year or more."

They talked it over, and they was going to rule me out, because they said every boy must have a family or somebody to kill, or else it wouldn't be fair and square for the others. Well, nobody could think of anything to do—everybody was stumped, and set still. I was most ready to cry; but all at once I thought of a way, and so I offered them Miss Watson—they could kill her. Everybody said:

"Oh, she'll do, she'll do. That's all right. Huck can come in."

Then they all stuck a pin in their fingers to get blood to sign with, and I made my mark on the paper.

"Now," says Ben Rogers, "what's the line of business of this Gang?"

"Nothing only robbery and murder," Tom said.

"But who are we going to rob? houses—or cattle—or—"

"Stuff! stealing cattle and such things ain't robbery, it's burglary," says Tom Sawyer. "We ain't burglars. That ain't no sort of style. We are highwaymen. We stop stages and carriages on the road, with masks on, and kill the people and take their watches and money."

"Must we always kill the people?"

"Oh, certainly. It's best. Some authorities think different, but mostly it's considered best to kill them. Except some that you bring to the cave here and keep them till they're ransomed."

"Ransomed? What's that?"

"I don't know. But that's what they do. I've seen it in books; and so of course that's what we've got to do."

"But how can we do it if we don't know what it is?"

"Why blame it all, we've *got* to do it. Don't I tell you it's in the books? Do you want to go to doing different from what's in the books, and get things all muddled up?"

"Oh, that's all very fine to *say*, Tom Sawyer, but how in the nation are these fellows going to be ransomed if we don't know how to do it to them? that's the thing *I* want to get at. Now what do you *reckon* it is?"

"Well I don't know. But per'aps if we keep them till they're ransomed, it means that we keep them till they're dead."

"Now, that's something *like*. That'll answer. Why couldn't you said that before? We'll keep them till they're ransomed to death—and a bothersome lot they'll be, too, eating up everything and always trying to get loose."

"How you talk, Ben Rogers. How can they get loose when there's a guard over them, ready to shoot them down if they move a peg?"

"A guard. Well, that *is* good. So somebody's got to set up all night and never get any sleep, just so as to watch them. I think that's foolishness. Why can't a body take a club and ransom them as soon as they get here?"

"Because it ain't in the books so—that's why. Now Ben Rogers, do you want to do things regular, or don't you?—that's the idea. Don't you reckon that the people that made the books knows what's the correct thing to do? Do you reckon *you* can learn 'em anything? Not by a good deal. No, sir, we'll just go on and ransom them in the regular way."

"All right. I don't mind; but I say it's a fool way, anyhow. Say—do we kill the women, too?"

"Well, Ben Rogers, if I was as ignorant as you I wouldn't let on. Kill the women? No—nobody ever saw anything in the books like that. You fetch them to the cave, and you're always as polite as pie to them; and by-and-by they fall in love with you and never want to go home any more."

"Well, if that's the way, I'm agreed, but I don't take no stock in it. Mighty soon we'll have the cave so cluttered up with women, and fellows waiting to be ransomed, that there won't be no place for the robbers. But go ahead, I ain't got nothing to say."

Little Tommy Barnes was asleep, now, and when they waked him up he was scared, and cried, and said he wanted to go home to his ma, and didn't want to be a robber any more.

So they all made fun of him, and called him cry-baby, and that made him mad, and he said he would go straight and tell all the secrets. But Tom give him five cents to keep quiet, and said we would all go home and meet next week and rob somebody and kill some people.

Ben Rogers said he couldn't get out much, only Sundays, and so he wanted to begin next Sunday; but all the boys said it would be wicked to do it on Sunday, and that settled the thing. They agreed to get together and fix a day as soon as they could, and then we elected Tom Sawyer first captain and Jo Harper second captain of the Gang, and so started home.

I clumb up the shed and crept into my window just before day was breaking. My new clothes was all greased up and clayey, and I was dog-tired.

HUCK CREEPS INTO HIS WINDOW.

Chapter III

WELL, I GOT a good going-over in the morning, from old Miss Watson, on account of my clothes; but the widow she didn't scold, but only cleaned off the grease and clay and looked so sorry that I thought I would behave a while if I could. Then Miss Watson she took me in the closet and prayed, but nothing come of it. She told me to pray every day, and whatever I asked for I would get it. But it warn't so. I tried it. Once I got a fish-line, but no hooks. It warn't any good to me without hooks. I tried for the hooks three or four times, but somehow I couldn't make it work. By-and-by, one day, I asked Miss Watson to try for me, but she said I was a fool. She never told me why, and I couldn't make it out no way.

I set down, one time, back in the woods, and had a long think about it. I says to myself, if a body can get anything they pray for, why don't Deacon Winn get back the money he lost on pork? Why can't the widow get back her silver snuff-box that was stole? Why can't Miss Watson fat up? No, says I to myself, there ain't nothing in it. I went and told the widow about it, and she said the thing a body could get by praying for it was "spiritual gifts." This was too many for me, but she told me what she meant—I must help other people, and do everything I could for other people, and look out for them all the time, and never think about myself. This was including Miss Watson, as I took it. I went out in the woods and turned it over in my mind a long time, but I couldn't see no advantage about it—except for the other people—so at last I reckoned I wouldn't worry about it any more, but just let it go. Sometimes the widow would take me one side and talk about Providence in a way to make a body's mouth water; but maybe next day Miss Watson would take hold and knock it all down again. I judged I could see that there was two Providences, and a poor chap would stand considerable show with the widow's Providence, but if Miss Watson's got him there warn't no help for him any more. I thought it all out, and reckoned I would belong to the widow's, if he wanted me, though I couldn't make out how he was agoing to be any better off then than what he was before, seeing I was so ignorant and so kind of low-down and ornery.

Pap he hadn't been seen for more than a year, and that was comfortable for me; I didn't want to see him no more. He used to always whale me when he was sober and could get his hands on me; though I used to take to the woods most of the time when he was around. Well, about this time he was found in the river drowned, about twelve mile above town, so people said. They judged it was him, anyway; said this drowned man was just his size, and was ragged, and had uncommon long hair—which was all like pap—but they couldn't make nothing out of the face, because it had been in the water so long it warn't much like a face at all. They said he was floating on his back in the water. They took him and buried him on the bank. But I warn't comfortable long, because I happened to think of something. I knowed mighty well that a drownded man don't float on his back, but on his face. So I knowed, then, that this warn't pap, but a woman dressed up in a man's clothes. So I was uncomfortable again. I judged the old man would turn up again by-and-by, though I wished he wouldn't.

We played robber now and then about a month, and then I resigned. All the boys did. We hadn't robbed nobody, we hadn't killed any people, but only just pretended. We used to hop out of the woods and go charging down on hog-drovers and women in carts taking garden stuff to market, but we never hived any of them. Tom Sawyer called the hogs "ingots," and he called the turnips and stuff "julery" and we would go to the cave and pow-wow over what we had done and how many people we had killed and marked. But I couldn't see no profit in it. One time Tom sent a boy to run about town with a blazing stick, which he called a slogan (which was the sign for the Gang to get together), and then he said he had got secret news by his spies that next day a whole parcel of Spanish merchants and rich A-rabs was going to camp in Cave Hollow with two hundred elephants, and six hundred camels, and over a thousand "sumter" mules, all loaded down with di'monds, and they didn't have only a guard of four hundred soldiers, and so we would lay in ambuscade, as he called it, and kill the lot and scoop the things. He said we must slick up our swords and guns, and get ready. He never could go after even a turnip-cart but he must have the swords and guns all scoured up for it; though they was only lath and broom-sticks, and you might scour at them till you rotted and then they warn't worth a mouthful of ashes more than what they was before. I didn't believe we could lick such a crowd of Spaniards and A-rabs, but I wanted to see the camels and elephants, so I was on hand next day, Saturday, in the ambuscade; and when we got the word, we rushed out of the woods and down the hill. But there warn't no Spaniards and A-rabs, and there warn't no camels nor no elephants. It warn't anything but a Sunday-school picnic, and only a primer-class at that. We busted it up, and chased the children up the hollow; but we never got anything but some doughnuts and jam, though Ben Rogers got a rag doll, and Jo Harper got a hymn-book and a tract; and then the teacher charged in and made us drop everything and cut. I didn't see no di'monds, and I told Tom Sawyer so. He said there was loads of them there, anyway; and he said there was A-rabs there, too, and elephants and things. I said, why couldn't we see them, then? He said if I warn't so ignorant, but had read a book called "Don Quixote," I would know without asking. He said it was all done by enchantment. He said there was hundreds of soldiers there, and elephants and treasure, and so on, but we had enemies which he called magicians, and they had turned the whole thing into an infant Sunday school, just out of spite. I said, all right, then the thing for us to do was to go for the magicians. Tom Sawyer said I was a numskull.

"Why," says he, "a magician could call up a lot of genies, and they would hash you up like nothing before you could say Jack Robinson. They are as tall as a tree and as big around as a church."

"Well," I says, "s'pose we got some genies to help *us*—can't we lick the other crowd then?"

"How you going to get them?"

"I don't know. How do *they* get them?"

"Why they rub an old tin lamp or an iron ring, and then the genies come tearing in, with the thunder and lightning a-ripping around and the smoke a-rolling, and everything they're told to do they up and do it. They don't think nothing of pulling a shot tower up by the roots, and belting a Sunday-school superintendent over the head with it—or any other man."

"Who makes them tear around so?"

"Why, whoever rubs the lamp or the ring. They belong to whoever rubs the lamp or the ring, and they've got to do whatever he says. If he tells them to build a palace forty miles long, out of di'monds, and fill it full of chewing gum, or whatever you want, and fetch an emperor's daughter from China for you to marry, they've got to do it—and they've got to do it before sun-up next morning, too. And more—they've got to waltz that palace around over the country wherever you want it, you understand."

"Well," says I, "I think they are a pack of flatheads for not keeping the palace themselves 'stead of fooling them away like that. And what's more—if I was one of them I would see a man in Jericho before I would drop my business and come to him for the rubbing of an old tin lamp."

"How you talk, Huck Finn. Why, you'd *have* to come when he rubbed it, whether you wanted to or not."

"What, and I as high as a tree and as big as a church? All right, then; I *would* come; but I lay I'd make that man climb the highest tree there was in the country."

"Shucks, it ain't no use to talk to you, Huck Finn. You don't seem to know anything, somehow—perfect sap-head."

I thought all this over for two or three days, and then I reckoned I would see if there was anything in it. I got an old tin lamp and an iron ring and went out in the woods and rubbed and rubbed till I sweat like an Injun, calculating to build a palace and sell it; but it warn't no use, none of the genies come. So then I judged that all that stuff was only just one of Tom Sawyer's lies. I reckoned he believed in the A-rabs and the elephants, but as for me I think different. It had all the marks of a Sunday school.

Chapter IV

WELL, THREE OR four months run along, and it was well into the winter, now. I had been to school most all the time, and could spell, and read, and write just a little, and could say the multiplication table up to six times seven is thirty-five, and I don't reckon I could ever get any further than that if I was to live forever. I don't take no stock in mathematics, anyway.

At first I hated the school, but by-and-by I got so I could stand it. Whenever I got uncommon tired I played hookey, and the hiding I got next day done me good and cheered me up. So the longer I went to school the easier it got to be. I was getting sort of used to the widow's ways, too, and they warn't so raspy on me. Living in a house, and sleeping in a bed, pulled on me pretty tight, mostly, but before the cold weather I used to slide out and sleep in the woods, sometimes, and so that was a rest to me. I liked the old ways best, but I was getting so I liked the new ones, too, a little bit. The widow said I was coming along slow but sure, and doing very satisfactory. She said she warn't ashamed of me.

One morning I happened to turn over the salt-cellar at breakfast. I reached for some of it as quick as I could, to throw over my left shoulder and keep off the bad luck, but Miss Watson was in ahead of me, and crossed me off. She says, "Take your hands away, Huckleberry—what a mess you are always making." The widow put in a good word for me, but that warn't going to keep off the bad luck, I knowed that well enough. I started out, after breakfast, feeling worried and shaky, and wondering where it was going to fall on me, and what it was going to be. There is ways to keep off some kinds of bad luck, but this wasn't one of them kind; so I never tried to do anything, but just poked along low-spirited and on the watch-out.

I went down the front garden and clumb over the stile, where you go through the high board fence. There was an inch of new snow on the ground, and I seen somebody's tracks. They had come up from the quarry and stood around the stile a while, and then went on around the garden fence. It was funny they hadn't come in, after standing around so. I couldn't make it out. It was very curious, somehow. I was going to follow around, but I stooped down to look at the tracks first. I didn't notice anything at first, but next I did. There was a cross in the left boot-heel made with big nails, to keep off the devil.

I was up in a second and shinning down the hill. I looked over my shoulder every now and then, but I didn't see nobody. I was at Judge Thatcher's as quick as I could get there. He said:

"Why, my boy, you are all out of breath. Did you come for your interest?"

"No sir," I says; "is there some for me?"

"Oh, yes, a half-yearly is in, last night. Over a hundred and fifty dollars. Quite a fortune for you. You better let me invest it along with your six thousand, because if you take it you'll spend it."

"No sir," I says, "I don't want to spend it. I don't want it at all—nor the six thousand, nuther. I want you to take it; I want to give it to you—the six thousand and all."

He looked surprised. He couldn't seem to make it out. He says:

"Why, what can you mean, my boy?"

I says, "Don't you ask me no questions about it, please. You'll take it—won't you?"

He says:

"Well I'm puzzled. Is something the matter?"

"Please take it," says I, "and don't ask me nothing—then I won't have to tell no lies."

He studied a while, and then he says:

"Oho-o. I think I see. You want to *sell* all your property to me—not give it. That's the correct idea."

Then he wrote something on a paper and read it over, and says:

"There—you see it says 'for a consideration.' That means I have bought it of you and paid you for it. Here's a dollar for you. Now, you sign it."

So I signed it, and left.

Miss Watson's nigger, Jim, had a hair-ball as big as your fist, which had been took out of the fourth stomach of an ox, and he used to do magic with it. He said there was a spirit inside of it, and it knowed everything. So I went to him that night and told him pap was here again, for I found his tracks in the snow. What I wanted to know, was, what he was going to do, and was he going to stay? Jim got out his hair-ball, and said something over it, and then he held it up and dropped it on the floor. It fell pretty solid, and only rolled about an inch. Jim tried it again, and then another time, and it acted just the same. Jim got down on his knees and put his ear against it and listened. But it warn't no use; he said it wouldn't talk. He said sometimes it wouldn't talk without money. I told him I had an old slick counterfeit quarter that warn't no good because the brass showed through the silver a little, and it wouldn't pass nohow, even if the brass didn't show, because it was so slick it felt greasy, and so that would tell on it every time. (I reckoned I wouldn't say nothing about the dollar I got from the judge.) I said it was pretty bad money, but maybe the hair-ball would take it, because maybe it wouldn't know the difference. Jim smelt it, and bit it, and rubbed it, and said he would manage so the hair-ball would think it was good. He said he would split open a raw Irish potato and stick the quarter in between and keep it there all night, and next morning you couldn't see no brass, and it wouldn't feel greasy no more, and so anybody in town would take it in a minute, let alone a hair-ball. Well, I knowed a potato would do that, before, but I had forgot it.

Jim put the quarter under the hair-ball and got down and listened again. This time he said the hair-ball was all right. He said it would tell my whole fortune if I wanted it to. I says, go on. So the hair-ball talked to Jim, and Jim told it to me. He says:

"Yo' ole father doan' know, yit, what he's a-gwyne to do. Sometimes he spec he'll go 'way, en den agin he spec he'll stay. De bes' way is to res' easy en let de ole man take his own way. Dey's two angels hoverin' roun' 'bout him.

JIM LISTENING.

One uv 'em is white en shiny, en 'tother one is black. De white one gits him to go right, a little while, den de black one sail in en bust it all up. A body can't tell, yit, which one gwyne to fetch him at de las'. But you is all right. You gwyne to have considable trouble in yo' life, en considable joy. Sometimes you gwyne to git hurt, en sometimes you gwyne to git sick; but every time you's gwyne to git well agin. Dey's two gals flyin' 'bout you in yo' life. One uv 'em's light en 'tother one is dark. One is rich en 'tother is po'. You's gwyne to marry de po' one fust en de rich one by-en-by. You wants to keep 'way fum de water as much as you kin, en don't run no resk, 'kase it's down in de bills dat you's gwyne to git hung.''

When I lit my candle and went up to my room that night, there set pap, his own self!

Chapter V

I HAD SHUT the door to. Then I turned around, and there he was. I used to be scared of him all the time, he tanned me so much. I reckoned I was scared now, too; but in a minute I see I was mistaken. That is, after the first jolt, as you may say, when my breath sort of hitched—he being so unexpected; but right away after, I see I warn't scared of him worth bothering about.

He was most fifty, and he looked it. His hair was long and tangled and greasy, and hung down, and you could see his eyes shining through like he was behind vines. It was all black, no gray; so was his long, mixed-up whiskers. There warn't no color in his face, where his face showed; it was white; not like another man's white, but a white to make a body sick, a white to make a body's flesh crawl—a tree-toad white, a fish-belly white. As for his clothes—just rags, that was all. He had one ankle resting on 'tother knee; the boot on that foot was busted, and two of his toes stuck through, and he worked them now and then. His hat was laying on the floor; an old black slouch with the top caved in, like a lid.

I stood a-looking at him; he set there a-looking at me, with his chair tilted back a little. I set the candle down. I noticed the window was up; so he had clumb in by the shed. He kept a-looking me all over. By-and-by he says:

"Starchy clothes—very. You think you're a good deal of a big-bug, *don't* you?"

"Maybe I am, maybe I ain't," I says.

"Don't you give me none o' your lip," says he. "You've put on considerble many frills since I been away. I'll take you down a peg before I get done with you. You're educated, too, they say; can read and write. You think you're better'n your father, now, don't you, because he can't? *I'll* take it out of you. Who told you you might meddle with such hifalut'n foolishness, hey?—who told you you could?"

"The widow. She told me."

"The widow, hey?—and who told the widow she could put in her shovel about a thing that ain't none of her business?"

"Nobody never told her."

"Well, I'll learn her how to meddle. And looky here—you drop that school, you hear? I'll learn people to bring up a boy to put on airs over his own father and let on to be better'n what *he* is. You lemme catch you fooling around that school again, you hear? Your mother couldn't read, and she couldn't write, nuther, before she died. None of the family couldn't, before *they* died. *I* can't; and here you're a-swelling yourself up like this. I ain't the man to stand it— you hear? Say—lemme hear you read.''

I took up a book and begun something about General Washington and the wars. When I'd read about a half a minute, he fetched the book a whack with his hand and knocked it across the house. He says:

''It's so. You can do it. I had my doubts when you told me. Now looky here; you stop that putting on frills. I won't have it. I'll lay for you, my smarty; and if I catch you about that school I'll tan you good. First you know you'll get religion, too. I never see such a son.''

He took up a little blue and yaller picture of some cows and a boy, and says: ''What's this?''

''It's something they give me for learning my lessons good.''

He tore it up, and says—

''I'll give you something better—I'll give you a cowhide.''

He set there a-mumbling and a-rowling a minute, and then he says—

''Ain't you a sweet-scented dandy, though? A bed; and bedclothes; and a look'n-glass; and a piece of carpet on the floor—and your own father got to sleep with the hogs in the tanyard. I never see such a son. I bet I'll take some o' these frills out o' you before I'm done with you. Why there ain't no end to your airs—they say you're rich. Hey?—how's that?''

''They lie—that's how.''

''Looky here—mind how you talk to me; I'm a-standing about all I can stand, now—so don't gimme no sass. I've been in town two days, and I hain't heard nothing but about you bein' rich. I heard about it away down the river, too. That's why I come. You git me that money to-morrow—I want it.''

''I hain't got no money.''

''It's a lie. Judge Thatcher's got it. You git it. I want it.''

''I hain't got no money, I tell you. You ask Judge Thatcher; he'll tell you the same.''

''All right. I'll ask him; and I'll make him pungle, too, or I'll know the reason why. Say—how much you got in your pocket? I want it.''

''I hain't got only a dollar, and I want that to——''

''It don't make no difference what you want it for—you just shell it out.''

He took it and bit it to see if it was good, and then he said he was going down town to get some whisky; said he hadn't had a drink all day. When he had got out on the shed, he put his head in again, and cussed me for putting on frills and trying to be better than him; and when I reckoned he was gone, he come back and put his head in again, and told me to mind about that school, because he was going to lay for me and lick me if I didn't drop that.

Next day he was drunk, and he went to Judge Thatcher's and bullyragged him and tried to make him give up the money, but he couldn't, and then he swore he'd make the law force him.

The judge and the widow went to law to get the court to take me away from him and let one of them be my guardian; but it was a new judge that had just come, and he didn't know the old man; so he said courts mustn't interfere and separate families if they could help it; said he'd druther not take a child away from its father. So Judge Thatcher and the widow had to quit on the business.

That pleased the old man till he couldn't rest. He said he'd cowhide me till I was black and blue if I didn't raise some money for him. I borrowed three dollars from Judge Thatcher, and pap took it and got drunk and went a-blowing around and cussing and whooping and carrying on; and he kept it up all over town, with a tin pan, till most midnight; then they jailed him, and next day they had him before court, and jailed him again for a week. But he said *he* was satisfied; said he was boss of his son, and he'd make it warm for *him*.

When he got out the new judge said he was agoing to make a man of him. So he took him to his own house, and dressed him up clean and nice, and had him to breakfast and dinner and supper with the family, and was just old pie to him, so to speak. And after supper he talked to him about temperance and such things till the old man cried, and said he'd been a fool, and fooled away his life; but now he was agoing to turn over a new leaf and be a man nobody wouldn't be ashamed of, and he hoped the judge would help him and not look down on him. The judge said he could hug him for them words; so *he* cried, and his wife she cried again; pap said he'd been a man that had always been misunderstood before, and the judge said he believed it. The old man said that what a man wanted that was down, was sympathy; and the judge said it was so; so they cried again. And when it was bedtime, the old man rose up and held out his hand, and says:

"Look at it gentlemen, and ladies all; take ahold of it; shake it. There's a hand that was the hand of a hog; but it ain't so no more; it's the hand of a man that's started in on a new life, and 'll die before he'll go back. You mark them words—don't forget I said them. It's a clean hand now; shake it—don't be afeard."

So they shook it, one after the other, all around, and cried. The judge's wife she kissed it. Then the old man he signed a pledge—made his mark. The judge said it was the holiest time on record, or something like that. Then they tucked the old man into a beautiful room, which was the spare room, and in the night sometime he got powerful thirsty and clumb out onto the porch-roof and slid down a stanchion and traded his new coat for a jug of forty-rod, and clumb back

REFORMING THE DRUNKARD.

again and had a good old time; and towards daylight he crawled out again, drunk as a fiddler, and rolled off the porch and broke his left arm in two places and was most froze to death when somebody found him after sun-up. And when they come to look at that spare room, they had to take soundings before they could navigate it.

The judge he felt kind of sore. He said he reckoned a body could reform the ole man with a shot-gun, maybe, but he didn't know no other way.

Chapter VI

WELL, PRETTY SOON the old man was up and around again, and then he went for Judge Thatcher in the courts to make him give up that money, and he went for me, too, for not stopping school. He catched me a couple of times and thrashed me, but I went to school just the same, and dodged him or out-run him most of the time. I didn't want to go to school much, before, but I reckoned I'd go now to spite pap. That law trial was a slow business; appeared like they warn't ever going to get started on it; so every now and then I'd borrow two or three dollars off of the judge for him, to keep from getting a cowhiding. Every time he got money he got drunk; and every time he got drunk he raised Cain around town; and every time he raised Cain he got jailed. He was just suited— this kind of thing was right in his line.

He got to hanging around the widow's too much, and so she told him at last, that if he didn't quit using around there she would make trouble for him. Well, *wasn't* he mad? He said he would show who was Huck Finn's boss. So he watched out for me one day in the spring, and catched me, and took me up the river about three mile, in a skiff, and crossed over to the Illinois shore where it was woody and there warn't no houses but an old log hut in a place where the timber was so thick you couldn't find it if you didn't know where it was.

He kept me with him all the time, and I never got a chance to run off. We lived in that old cabin, and he always locked the door and put the key under his head, nights. He had a gun which he had stole, I reckon, and we fished and hunted, and that was what we lived on. Every little while he locked me in and went down to the store, three miles, to the ferry, and traded fish and game for whisky and fetched it home and got drunk and had a good time, and licked me. The widow she found out where I was, by-and-by, and she sent a man over to try to get hold of me, but pap drove him off with the gun, and it warn't long after that till I was used to being where I was, and liked it, all but the cowhide part.

It was kind of lazy and jolly, laying off comfortable all day, smoking and fishing, and no books nor study. Two months or more run along, and my clothes got to be all rags and dirt, and I didn't see how I'd ever got to like it so well at the widow's, where you had to wash, and eat on a plate, and comb up, and go to bed and get up regular, and be forever bothering over a book and have old Miss Watson pecking at you all the time. I didn't want to go back no more. I had stopped cussing, because the widow didn't like it; but now I took to it again because pap hadn't no objections. It was pretty good times up in the woods there, take it all around.

SOLID COMFORT.

But by-and-by pap got too handy with his hick'ry, and I could't stand it. I was all over welts. He got to going away so much, too, and locking me in. Once he locked me in and was gone three days. It was dreadful lonesome. I judged he had got drowned and I wasn't ever going to get out any more. I was scared. I made up my mind I would fix up some way to leave there. I had tried to get out of that cabin many a time, but I couldn't find no way. There warn't a window to it big enought for a dog to get through. I couldn't get up the chimbly, it was too narrow. The door was thick solid oak slabs. Pap was pretty careful not to leave a knife or anything in the cabin when he was away; I reckon I had hunted the place over as much as a hundred times; well, I was 'most all the time at it, because it was about the only way to put in the time. But this time I found something at last; I found an old rusty wood-saw without any handle; it was laid in between a rafter and the clapboards of the roof. I greased it up and went to work. There was an old horse-blanket nailed against the logs at the far end of the cabin behind the table, to keep the wind from blowing through the chinks and putting the candle out. I got under the table and raised the blanket and went to work to saw a section of the big bottom log out, big enough to let me through. Well, it was a good long job, but I was getting towards the end of it when I heard pap's gun in the woods. I got rid of the signs of my work, and dropped the blanket and hid my saw, and pretty soon pap come in.

Pap warn't in a good humor—so he was his natural self. He said he was down to town, and everything was going wrong. His lawyer said he reckoned he would win his lawsuit and get the money, if they ever got started on the trial; but then there was ways to put it off a long time, and Judge Thatcher knowed how to do it. And he said people allowed there'd be another trial to get me away from him and give me to the widow for my guardian, and they guessed it would win, this time. This shook me up considerable, because I didn't want to go back to the widow's any more and be so cramped up and sivilized, as they called it. Then the old man got to cussing, and cussed everything and everybody he could think of, and then cussed them all over again to make sure he hadn't skipped any, and after that he polished off with a kind of a general cuss all round, including a considerable parcel of people which he didn't know the names of, and so called them what's-his-name, when he got to them, and went right along with his cussing.

He said he would like to see the widow get me. He said he would watch out, and if they tried to come any such game on him he knowed of a place six or seven mile off, to stow me in, where they might hunt till they dropped and they couldn't find me. That made me pretty uneasy again, but only for a minute; I reckoned I wouldn't stay on hand till he got that chance.

The old man made me go to the skiff and fetch the things he had got. There was a fifty-pound sack of corn meal, and a side of bacon, ammunition, and a four-gallon jug of whisky, and an old book and two newspapers for wadding, besides some tow. I toted up a load, and went back and set down on the bow of the skiff to rest. I thought it all over, and I reckoned I would walk off with the gun and some lines, and take to the woods when I run away. I guessed I wouldn't stay in one place, but just tramp right across the country, mostly night times, and hunt and fish to keep alive, and so get so far away that the old man nor the widow couldn't ever find me any more. I judged I would saw out and leave that night if pap got drunk enough, and I reckoned he would. I got so full of it I didn't notice how long I was staying, till the old man hollered and asked me whether I was asleep or drownded.

I got the things all up to the cabin, and then it was about dark. While I was cooking supper the old man took a swig or two and got sort of warmed up, and went to ripping again. He had been drunk over in town, and laid in the gutter all night, and he was a sight to look at. A body would a thought he was Adam, he was just all mud. Whenever his liquor begun to work, he most always went for the govment. This time he says:

"Call this a govment! why, just look at it and see what it's like. Here's the law a-standing ready to take a man's son away from him—a man's own son, which he has had all the trouble and all the anxiety and all the expense of raising. Yes, just as that man has got that son raised at last, and ready to go to work and begin to do suthin' for *him* and give him a rest, the law up and goes for him. And they call *that* govment! That ain't all, nuther. The law backs that old Judge Thatcher up and helps him to keep me out o' my property. Here's what the law does. The law takes a man worth six thousand dollars and upards, and jams him into an old trap of a cabin like this, and lets him go round in clothes that ain't fitten for a hog. They call that govment! A man can't get his rights in a govment like this. Sometimes I've a mighty notion to just leave the country for good and all. Yes, and I *told* 'em so; I told old Thatcher so to his face. Lots of 'em heard me, and can tell what I said. Says I, for two cents I'd leave the blamed country and never come anear it agin. Them's the very words. I says, look at my hat—if you call it a hat—but the lid raises up and the rest of it goes down till it's below my chin, and then it ain't rightly a hat at all, but more like my head was shoved up through a jint o' stove-pipe. Look at it, says I—such a hat for me to wear—one of the wealthiest men in this town, if I could git my rights.

"Oh, yes, this is a wonderful govment, wonderful. Why, looky here. There was a free nigger there, from Ohio; a mulatter, most as white as a white man. He had the whitest shirt on you ever see, too, and the shiniest hat; and there ain't a man in that town that's got as fine clothes as what he had; and he had a gold watch and chain, and a silver-headed cane—the awfulest old gray-headed nabob in the State. And what do you think? they said he was a p'fessor in a

college, and could talk all kinds of languages, and knowed everything. And that
ain't the wust. They said he could *vote*, when he was at home. Well, that let
me out. Thinks I, what is the country a-coming to? It was 'lection day, and I
was just about to go and vote, myself, if I warn't too drunk to get there; but
when they told me there was a State in this country where they'd let that nigger
vote, I drawed out. I says I'll never vote agin. Them's the very words I said;
they all heard me; and the country may rot for all me—I'll never vote agin as
long as I live. And to see the cool way of that nigger—why, he wouldn't a give
me the road if I hadn't shoved him out o' the way. I says to the people, why
ain't this nigger put up at auction and sold?—that's what I want to know. And
what do you reckon they said? Why, they said he couldn't be sold till he'd been
in the State six months, and he hadn't been there that long yet. There, now—
that's a specimen. They call that a govment that can't sell a free nigger till he's
been in the State six months. Here's a govment that calls itself a govment, and
lets on to be a govment, and thinks it is a govment, and yet's got to set stock-
still for six whole months before it can take ahold of a prowling, thieving,
infernal, white-shirted free nigger, and——''

Pap was agoing on so, he never noticed where his old limber legs was taking
him to, so he went head over heels over the tub of salt pork, and barked both
shins, and the rest of his speech was all the hottest kind of language—mostly
hove at the nigger and the govment, though he give the tub some, too, all along,
here and there. He hopped around the cabin considerable, first on one leg and
then on the other, holding first one shin and then the other one, and at last he
let out with his left foot all of a sudden and fetched the tub a rattling kick. But
it warn't good judgment, because that was the boot that had a couple of his toes
leaking out of the front end of it; so now he raised a howl that fairly made a
body's hair raise, and down he went in the dirt, and rolled there, and held his
toes; and the cussing he done then laid over anything he had ever done previous.
He said so his own self, afterwards. He had heard old Sowberry Hagan in his
best days, and he said it laid over him, too; but I reckon that was sort of piling
it on, maybe.

After supper pap took the jug, and said he had enough whisky there for two
drunks and one delirium tremens. That was always his word. I judged he would
be blind drunk in about an hour, and then I would steal the key, or saw myself
out, one or 'tother. He drank, and drank, and tumbled down on his blankets,
by-and-by; but luck didn't run my way. He didn't go sound asleep, but was
uneasy. He groaned, and moaned, and thrashed around this way and that, for a
long time. At last I got so sleepy I couldn't keep my eyes open, all I could do,
and so before I knowed what I was about I was sound asleep, and the candle
burning.

I don't know how long I was asleep, but all of a sudden there was an awful
scream and I was up. There was pap, looking wild and skipping around every
which way and yelling about snakes. He said they was crawling up his legs; and
then he would give a jump and scream, and say one had bit him on the cheek—
but I couldn't see no snakes. He started and run round and round the cabin,
hollering ''take him off! take him off! he's biting me on the neck!'' I never see
a man look so wild in the eyes. Pretty soon he was all fagged out, and fell down
panting; then he rolled over and over, wonderful fast, kicking things every which
way, and striking and grabbing at the air with his hands, and screaming, and
saying there was devils ahold of him. He wore out, by-and-by, and laid still a

while, moaning. Then he laid stiller, and didn't make a sound. I could hear the owls and the wolves, away off in the woods, and it seemed terrible still. He was laying over by the corner. By-and-by he raised up, part way, and listened, with his head to one side. He says very low:

"Tramp—tramp—tramp; that's the dead; tramp—tramp—tramp; they're coming after me; but I won't go— Oh, they're here! don't touch me—don't! hands off— they're cold; let go— Oh, let a poor devil alone!"

Then he went down on all fours and crawled off begging them to let him alone, and he rolled himself up in his blanket and wallowed in under the old pine table, still a-begging; and then he went to crying. I could hear him through the blanket.

By-and-by he rolled out and jumped up on his feet looking wild, and he see me and went for me. He chased me round and round the place, with a clasp-knife, calling me the Angel of Death and saying he would kill me and then I couldn't come for him no more. I begged, and told him I was only Huck, but he laughed *such* a screechy laugh, and roared and cussed, and kept on chasing me up. Once when I turned short and dodged under his arm he made a grab and got me by the jacket between my shoulders, and I thought I was gone; but I slid out of the jacket quick as lightning, and saved myself. Pretty soon he was all tired out, and dropped down with his back against the door, and said he would rest a minute and then kill me. He put his knife under him, and said he would sleep and get strong, and then he would see who was who.

So he dozed off, pretty soon. By-and-by I got the old split-bottom chair and clumb up, as easy as I could, not to make any noise, and got down the gun. I slipped the ramrod down it to make sure it was loaded, and then I laid it across the turnip barrel, pointing towards pap, and set down behind it to wait for him to stir. And how slow and still the time did drag along.

Chapter VII

Gɪᴛ ᴜᴘ! what you 'bout!"

I opened my eyes and looked around, trying to make out where I was. It was after sun-up, and I had been sound asleep. Pap was standing over me, looking sour—and sick, too. He says—

"What you doin' with this gun?"

I judged he didn't know nothing about what he had been doing, so I says:

"Somebody tried to get in, so I was laying for him."

"Why didn't you roust me out?"

"Well I tried to, but I couldn't; I couldn't budge you."

"Well, all right. Don't stand there palavering all day, but out with you and see if there's a fish on the lines for breakfast. I'll be along in a minute."

He unlocked the door and I cleared out, up the river bank. I noticed some pieces of limbs and such things floating down, and a sprinkling of bark; so I knowed the river had begun to rise. I reckoned I would have great times, now, if I was over at the town. The June rise used to be always luck for me; because as soon as that rise begins, here comes cord-wood floating down, and pieces of log rafts—sometimes a dozen logs together; so all you have to do is to catch them and sell them to the wood yards and the sawmill.

I went along up the bank with one eye out for pap and 'tother one out for what the rise might fetch along. Well, all at once, here comes a canoe; just a beauty, too, about thirteen or fourteen foot long, riding high like a duck. I shot head first off of the bank, like a frog, clothes and all on, and struck out for the canoe. I just expected there'd be somebody laying down in it, because people often done that to fool folks, and when a chap had pulled a skiff out most to it they'd raise up and laugh at him. But it warn't so this time. It was a drift-canoe, sure enough, and I clumb in and paddled her ashore. Thinks I, the old man will be glad when he sees this—she's worth ten dollars. But when I got to shore pap wasn't in sight yet, and as I was running her into a little creek like a gully, all hung over with vines and willows, I struck another idea; I judged I'd hide her good, and then, stead of taking to the woods when I run off, I'd go down the river about fifty mile and camp in one place for good, and not have such a rough time tramping on foot.

It was pretty close to the shanty, and I thought I heard the old man coming, all the time; but I got her hid; and then I out and looked around a bunch of willows, and there was the old man down the path apiece just drawing a bead on a bird with his gun. So he hadn't seen anything.

When he got along, I was hard at it taking up a "trot" line. He abused me a little for being so slow, but I told him I fell in the river and that was what made me so long. I knowed he would see I was wet, and then he would be asking questions. We got five cat-fish off of the lines and went home.

While we laid off, after breakfast, to sleep up, both of us being about wore out, I got to thinking that if I could fix up some way to keep pap and the widow from trying to follow me, it would be a certainer thing than trusting to luck to get far enough off before they missed me; you see, all kinds of things might happen. Well, I didn't see no way for a while, but by-and-by pap raised up a minute, to drink another barrel of water, and he says:

"Another time a man comes a-prowling round here, you roust me out, you hear? That man warn't here for no good. I'd a shot him. Next time, you roust me out, you hear?"

Then he dropped down and went to sleep again—but what he had been saying give me the very idea I wanted. I says to myself, I can fix it now so nobody won't think of following me.

About twelve o'clock we turned out and went along up the bank. The river was coming up pretty fast, and lots of drift-wood going by on the rise. By-and-by, along comes part of a log raft—nine logs fast together. We went out with the skiff and towed it ashore. Then we had dinner. Anybody but pap would a waited and seen the day through, so as to catch more stuff; but that warn't pap's style. Nine logs was enough for one time; he must shove right over to town and sell. So he locked me in and took the skiff and started off towing the raft about half-past three. I judged he wouldn't come back that night. I waited till I reckoned he had got a good start, then I out with my saw and went to work on that log again. Before he was 'tother side of the river I was out of the hole; him and his raft was just a speck on the water away off yonder.

I took the sack of corn meal and took it to where the canoe was hid, and shoved the vines and branches apart and put it in; then I done the same with the side of bacon; then the whisky jug; I took all the coffee and sugar there was, and all the ammunition; I took the wadding; I took the bucket and gourd, I took a dipper and a tin cup, and my old saw and two blankets, and the skillet and the coffee-pot. I took fish-lines and matches and other things—everything that was worth a cent. I cleaned out the place. I wanted an axe, but there wasn't any, only the one out at the wood pile, and I knowed why I was going to leave that. I fetched out the gun, and now I was done.

I had wore the ground a good deal, crawling out of the hole and dragging out so many things. So I fixed that as good as I could from the outside by scattering dust on the place, which covered up the smoothness and the sawdust. Then I fixed the piece of log back into its place, and put two rocks under it and one against it to hold it there,—for it was bent up at that place, and didn't quite touch ground. If you stood four or five foot away and didn't know it was sawed, you wouldn't ever notice it; and besides, this was the back of the cabin and it warn't likely anybody would go fooling around there.

It was all grass clear to the canoe; so I hadn't left a track. I followed around to see. I stood on the bank and looked out over the river. All safe. So I took the gun and went up a piece into the woods and was hunting around for some birds, when I see a wild pig; hogs soon went wild in them bottoms after they had got away from the prairie farms. I shot this fellow and took him into camp.

I took the axe and smashed in the door—I beat it and hacked it considerable, a-doing it. I fetched the pig in and took him back nearly to the table and hacked into his throat with the ax, and laid him down on the ground to bleed—I say ground, because it *was* ground—hard packed, and no boards. Well, next I took an old sack and put a lot of big rocks in it,—all I could drag—and I started it from the pig and dragged it to the door and through the woods down to the river and dumped it in, and down it sunk, out of sight. You could easy see that something had been dragged over the ground. I did wish Tom Sawyer was there, I knowed he would take an interest in this kind of business, and throw in the fancy touches. Nobody could spread himself like Tom Sawyer in such a thing as that.

Well, last I pulled out some of my hair, and bloodied the ax good, and stuck it on the back side, and slung the ax in the corner. Then I took up the pig and held him to my breast with my jacket (so he couldn't drip) till I got a good piece below the house and then dumped him into the river. Now I thought of something else. So I went and got the bag of meal and my old saw out of the canoe and fetched them to the house. I took the bag to where it used to stand, and ripped a hole in the bottom of it with the saw, for there warn't no knives and forks on the place—pap done everything with his clasp-knife, about the cooking. Then I carried the sack about a hundred yards across the grass and through the willows east of the house, to a shallow lake that was five mile wide and full of rushes— and ducks too, you might say, in the season. There was a slough or a creek leading out of it on the other side, that went miles away, I don't know where, but it didn't go to the river. The meal sifted out and made a little track all the way to the lake. I dropped pap's whetstone there too, so as to look like it had been done by accident. Then I tied up the rip in the meal sack with a string, so it wouldn't leak no more, and took it and my saw to the canoe again.

It was about dark, now; so I dropped the canoe down the river under some willows that hung over the bank, and waited for the moon to rise. I made fast to a willow; then I took a bite to eat, and by-and-by laid down in the canoe to smoke a pipe and lay out a plan. I says to myself, they'll follow the track of

that sackful of rocks to the shore and then drag the river for me. And they'll
follow that meal track to the lake and go browsing down the creek that leads
out of it to find the robbers that killed me and took the things. They won't ever
hunt the river for anything but my dead carcass. They'll soon get tired of that,
and won't bother no more about me. All right; I can stop anywhere I want to.
Jackson's Island is good enough for me; I know that island pretty well, and
nobody ever comes there. And then I can paddle over to town, nights, and slink
around and pick up things I want. Jackson's Island's the place.

I was pretty tired, and the first thing I knowed, I was asleep. When I woke
up I didn't know where I was, for a minute. I set up and looked around, a little
scared. Then I remembered. The river looked miles and miles across. The moon
was so bright I could a counted the drift logs that went a slipping along, black
and still, hundred of yards out from shore. Everything was dead quiet, and it
looked late, and *smelt* late. You know what I mean—I don't know the words
to put it in.

I took a good gap and a stretch, and was just going to unhitch and start, when
I heard a sound away over the water. I listened. Pretty soon I made it out. It
was that dull kind of a regular sound that comes from oars working in rowlocks
when it's a still night. I peeped out through the willow branches, and there it
was—a skiff, away across the water. I couldn't tell how many was in it. It kept
a-coming, and when it was abreast of me I see there warn't but one man in it.
Thinks I, maybe it's pap, though I warn't expecting him. He dropped below
me, with the current, and by-and-by he come a-swinging up shore in the easy
water, and he went by so close I could a reached out the gun and touched him.
Well, it *was* pap, sure enough—and sober, too, by the way he laid to his oars.

I didn't lose no time. The next minute I was a-spinning down stream soft but
quick in the shade of the bank. I made two mile and a half, and then struck out
a quarter of a mile or more towards the middle of the river, because pretty soon
I would be passing the ferry landing and people might see me and hail me. I
got out amongst the drift-wood and then laid down in the bottom of the canoe
and let her float. I laid there and had a good rest and a smoke out of my pipe,
looking away into the sky, not a cloud in it. The sky looks ever so deep when
you lay down on your back in the moonshine; I never knowed it before. And

TAKING A REST.

how far a body can hear on the water such nights! I heard people talking at the ferry landing. I heard what they said, too, every word of it. One man said it was getting towards the long days and the short nights, now. 'Tother one said *this* warn't one of the short ones, he reckoned—and then they laughed, and he said it over again and they laughed again; then they waked up another fellow and told him, and laughed, but he didn't laugh; he ripped out something brisk and said let him alone. The first fellow said he 'lowed to tell it to his old woman—she would think it was pretty good; but he said that warn't nothing to some things he had said in his time. I heard one man say it was nearly three o'clock, and he hoped daylight wouldn't wait more than about a week longer. After that, the talk got further and further away, and I couldn't make out the words any more, but I could hear the mumble; and now and then a laugh, too, but it seemed a long ways off.

I was away below the ferry now. I rose up and there was Jackson's Island, about two mile and a half down stream, heavy-timbered and standing up out of the middle of the river, big and dark and solid, like a steamboat without any lights. There warn't any signs of the bar at the head—it was all under water, now.

It didn't take me long to get there. I shot past the head at a ripping rate, the current was so swift, and then I got into the dead water and landed on the side towards the Illinois shore. I run the canoe into a deep dent in the bank that I knowed about; I had to part the willow branches to get in; and when I made fast nobody could a seen the canoe from the outside.

I went up and set down on a log at the head of the island and looked out on the big river and the black driftwood, and away over to the town, three mile away, where there was three or four lights twinkling. A monstrous big lumber raft was about a mile up stream, coming along down, with a lantern in the middle of it. I watched it come creeping down, and when it was most abreast of where I stood I heard a man say, "Stern oars, there! heave her head to stabboard!" I heard that just as plain as if the man was by my side.

There was a little gray in the sky, now; so I stepped into the woods and laid down for a nap before breakfast.

Chapter VIII

THE SUN WAS up so high when I waked, that I judged it was after eight o'clock. I laid there in the grass and the cool shade, thinking about things and feeling rested and ruther comfortable and satisfied. I could see the sun out at one or two holes, but mostly it was big trees all about, and gloomy in there amongst them. There was freckled places on the ground where the light sifted down through the leaves, and the freckled places swapped abont a little, showing there was a little breeze up there. A couple of squirrels set on a limb and jabbered at me very friendly.

I was powerful lazy and comfortable—didn't want to get up and cook breakfast. Well, I was dozing off again, when I thinks I hears a deep sound of "boom!" away up the river. I rouses up and rests on my elbow and listens; pretty soon I hears it again. I hopped up and went and looked out at a hole in the leaves, and

I see a bunch of smoke laying on the water a long ways up—about abreast the ferry. And there was the ferry-boat full of people, floating along down. I knowed what was the matter, now. "Boom!" I see the white smoke squirt out of the ferry-boat's side. You see, they was firing cannon over the water, trying to make my carcass come to the top.

I was pretty hungry, but it warn't going to do for me to start a fire, because they might see the smoke. So I set there and watched the cannon-smoke and listened to the boom. The river was a mile wide, there, and it always looks pretty on a summer morning—so I was having a good enough time seeing them hunt for my remainders, if I only had a bite to eat. Well, then I happened to think how they always put quicksilver in loaves of bread and float them off because they always go right to the drownded carcass and stop there. So says I, I'll keep a lookout, and if any of them's floating around after me, I'll give them a show. I changed to the Illinois edge of the island to see what luck I could have, and I warn't disappointed. A big double loaf come along, and I most got it, with a long stick, but my foot slipped and she floated out further. Of course I was where the current set in the closest to the shore—I knowed enough for that. But by-and-by along comes another one, and this time I won. I took out the plug and shook out the little dab of quicksilver, and set my teeth in. It was "baker's bread"—what the quality eat—none of your low-down corn-pone.

I got a good place amongst the leaves, and set there on a log, munching the bread and watching the ferry-boat, and very well satisfied. And then something struck me. I says, now I reckon the widow or the parson or somebody prayed that this bread would find me, and here it has gone and done it. So there ain't no doubt but there is something in that thing. That is, there's something in it when a body like the widow or the parson prays, but it don't work for me, and I reckon it don't work for only just the right kind.

I lit a pipe and had a good long smoke and went on watching. The ferry-boat was floating with the current, and I allowed I'd have a chance to see who was aboard when she come along, because she would come in close, where the bread did. When she'd got pretty well along down towards me, I put out my pipe and went to where I fished out the bread, and laid down behind a log on the bank in a little open place. Where the log forked I could peep through.

By-and-by she come along, and she drifted in so close that they could a run out a plank and walked ashore. Most everybody was on the boat. Pap, and Judge Thatcher, and Bessie Thatcher, and Jo Harper, and Tom Sawyer, and his old Aunt Polly, and Sid and Mary, and plenty more. Everybody was talking about the murder, but the captain broke in and says:

"Look sharp, now; the current sets in the closest here, and maybe he's washed ashore and got tangled amongst the brush at the water's edge. I hope so, anyway."

I didn't hope so. They all crowded up and leaned over the rails, nearly in my face, and kept still, watching with all their might. I could see them first-rate, but they couldn't see me. Then the captain sung out:

"Stand away!" and the cannon let off such a blast right before me that it made me deef with the noise and pretty near blind with the smoke, and I judged I was gone. If they'd a had some bullets in, I reckon they'd a got the corpse they was after. Well, I see I warn't hurt, thanks to goodness. The boat floated on and went out of sight around the shoulder of the island. I could hear the booming, now and then, further and further off, and by-and-by after an hour, I didn't hear it no more. The island was three mile long. I judged they had got to the foot, and was giving it up. But they didn't yet a while. They turned around the foot of the island and started up the channel on the Missouri side, under steam, and booming once in a while as they went. I crossed over to that side and watched them. When they got abreast the head of the island they quit shooting and dropped over to the Missouri shore and went home to the town.

I knowed I was all right now. Nobody else would come a-hunting after me. I got my traps out of the canoe and made me a nice camp in the thick woods. I made a kind of tent out of my blankets to put my things under so the rain couldn't get at them. I catched a cat-fish and haggled him open with my saw, and towards sundown I started my camp fire and had supper. Then I set out a line to catch some fish for breakfast.

When it was dark I set by my camp fire smoking, and feeling pretty satisfied; but by-and-by it got sort of lonesome, and so I went and set on the bank and listened to the currents washing along, and counted the stars and drift-logs and rafts that come down, and then went to bed; there ain't no better way to put in time when you are lonesome; you can't stay so, you soon get over it.

And so for three days and nights. No difference—just the same thing. But the next day I went exploring around down through the island. I was boss of it; it all belonged to me, so to say, and I wanted to know all about it; but mainly I wanted to put in the time. I found plenty strawberries, ripe and prime; and green summer-grapes, and green razberries; and the green blackberries was just beginning to show. They would all come handy by-and-by, I judged.

Well, I went fooling along in the deep woods till I judged I warn't far from the foot of the island. I had my gun along, but I hadn't shot nothing; it was for protection; thought I would kill some game nigh home. About this time I mighty near stepped on a good sized snake, and it went sliding off through the grass and flowers, and I after it, trying to get a shot at it. I clipped along, and all of a sudden I bounded right on to the ashes of a camp fire that was still smoking.

My heart jumped up amongst my lungs. I never waited for to look further, but uncocked my gun and went sneaking back on my tip-toes as fast as ever I could. Every now and then I stopped a second, amongst the thick leaves, and listened; but my breath come so hard I couldn't hear nothing else. I slunk along another piece further, then listened again; and so on, and so on; if I see a stump, I took it for a man; if I trod on a stick and broke it, it made me feel like a person had cut one of my breaths in two and I only got half, and the short half, too.

When I got to camp I warn't feeling very brash, there warn't much sand in my craw; but I says, this ain't no time to be fooling around. So I got all my traps into my canoe again so as to have them out of sight, and I put out the fire and scattered the ashes around to look like an old last year's camp, and then clumb a tree.

I reckon I was up in the tree two hours; but I didn't see nothing, I didn't hear nothing—I only *thought* I heard and seen as much as a thousand things. Well, I couldn't stay up there forever; so at last I got down, but I kept in the thick woods and on the lookout all the time. All I could get to eat was berries and what was left over from breakfast.

By the time it was night I was pretty hungry. So when it was good and dark, I slid out from shore before moonrise and paddled over to the Illinois bank— about a quarter of a mile. I went out in the woods and cooked a supper, and I had about made up my mind I would stay there all night, when I hear a *plunkety-*

plunk, plunkety-plunk, and says to myself, horses coming; and next I hear people's voices. I got everything into the canoe as quick as I could, and then went creeping through the woods to see what I could find out. I hadn't got far when I hear a man say:

"We better camp here, if we can find a good place; the horses is about beat out. Let's look around."

I didn't wait, but shoved out and paddled away easy. I tied up in the old place, and reckoned I would sleep in the canoe.

I didn't sleep much. I couldn't, somehow, for thinking. And every time I waked up I thought somebody had me by the neck. So the sleep didn't do me no good. By-and-by I says to myself, I can't live this way; I'm agoing to find out who it is that's here on the island with me; I'll find it out or bust. Well, I felt better, right off.

So I took my paddle and slid out from shore just a step or two, and then let the canoe drop along down amongst the shadows. The moon was shining, and outside of the shadows it made it most as light as day. I poked along well onto an hour, everything still as rocks and sound asleep. Well by this time I was most down to the foot of the island. A little ripply, cool breeze begun to blow, and that was as good as saying the night was about done. I give her a turn with the paddle and brung her nose to shore; then I got my gun and slipped out and into the edge of the woods. I set down there on a log and looked out through the leaves. I see the moon go off watch and the darkness begin to blanket the river. But in a little while I see a pale streak over the tree-tops, and knowed the day was coming. So I took my gun and slipped off towards where I had run across that camp fire, stopping every minute or two to listen. But I hadn't no luck, somehow; I couldn't seem to find the place. But by-and-by, sure enough, I catched a glimpse of fire, away through the trees. I went for it, cautious and slow. By-and-by I was close enough to have a look, and there laid a man on the ground. It most give me the fan-tods. He had a blanket around his head, and his head was nearly in the fire. I set there behind a clump of bushes, in about six foot of him, and kept my eyes on him steady. It was getting gray daylight, now. Pretty soon he gapped, and stretched himself, and hove off the blanket, and it was Miss Watson's Jim! I bet I was glad to see him. says:

"Hello, Jim!" and skipped out.

He bounced up and stared at me wild. Then he drops down on his knees, and puts his hands together and says:

"Doan' hurt me—don't! I hain't ever done no harm to a ghos'. I awluz liked dead people, en done all I could for 'em. You go en git in de river agin, whah you b'longs, en doan' do nuffn to Ole Jim, 'at 'uz awluz yo' fren'."

Well, I warn't long making him understand I warn't dead. I was ever so glad to see Jim. I warn't lonesome, now. I told him I warn't afraid of *him* telling the people where I was. I talked along, but he only set there and looked at me; never said nothing. Then I says:

"It's good daylight. Le's get breakfast. Make up your camp fire good."

"What's de use er makin' up de camp fire to cook strawbries en sich truck? But you got a gun, hain't you? Den we kin git sumfn better den strawbries."

"Strawberries and such truck," I says. "Is that what you live on?"

"I couldn' git nuffn else," he says.

"Why, how long you been on the island, Jim?"

"I come heah de night arter you's killed."

"What, all that time?"

"Yes-indeedy."

"And ain't you had nothing but that kind of rubbage to eat?"

"No, sah—nuffn else."

"Well, you must be most starved, ain't you?"

"I reck'n I could eat a hoss. I think I could. How long you ben on de islan'?"

"Since the night I got killed."

"No! W'y, what has you lived on? But you got a gun. Oh, yes, you got a gun. Dat's good. Now you kill sumfn en I'll make up de fire."

So we went over to where the canoe was, and while he built a fire in a grassy open place amongst the trees, I fetched meal and bacon and coffee, and coffee-pot and frying-pan, and sugar and tin cups, and the nigger was set back considerable, because he reckoned it was all done with witchcraft. I catched a good big cat-fish, too, and Jim cleaned him with his knife, and fried him.

When breakfast was ready, we lolled on the grass and eat it smoking hot. Jim laid it in with all his might, for he was most about starved. Then when we had got pretty well stuffed, we laid off and lazied.

By-and-by Jim says:

"But looky here, Huck, who wuz it dat 'uz killed in dat shanty, ef it warn't you?"

Then I told him the whole thing, and he said it was smart. He said Tom Sawyer couldn't get up no better plan than what I had. Then I says:

"How do you come to be here, Jim, and how'd you get here?"

He looked pretty uneasy, and didn't say nothing for a minute. Then he says:

"Maybe I better not tell."

"Why, Jim?"

"Well, dey's reasons. But you wouldn' tell on me ef I 'uz to tell you, would you, Huck?"

"Blamed if I would, Jim."

"Well, I b'lieve you, Huck. I—I *run off.*"

"Jim!"

"But mind, you said you wouldn't tell—you know you said you wouldn't tell, Huck."

"Well, I did. I said I wouldn't, and I'll stick to it. Honest *injun* I will. People would call me a low down Ablitionist and despise me for keeping mum—but that don't make no difference. I ain't agoing to tell, and I ain't agoing back there anyways. So now, le's know all about it."

"Well, you see, it 'uz dis way. Ole Missus—dat's Miss Watson—she pecks on me all de time, en treats me pooty rough, but she awluz said she wouldn' sell me down to Orleans. But I noticed dey wuz a nigger trader roun' de place considable, lately, en I begin to git oneasy. Well, one night I creeps to de do', pooty late, en de do' warn't quite shet, en I hear ole missus tell de widder she gwyne to sell me down to Orleans, but she didn' want to, but she could git eight hund'd dollars for me, en it 'uz sich a big stack o' money she couldn' resis'. De widder she try to git her to say she wouldn' do it, but I never waited to hear de res'. I lit out mighty quick, I tell you.

"I tuck out en shin down de hill en 'spec to steal a skift 'long de sho' som'ers 'bove de town, but dey wuz people a-stirrin' yit, so I hid in de ole tumble-down cooper shop on de bank to wait for everybody to go 'way. Well, I wuz dah all night. Dey wuz somebody roun' all de time. 'Long 'bout six in de mawnin', skifts begin to go by, en 'bout eight er nine every skift dat went 'long wuz talkin' 'bout how yo' pap come over to de town en say you's killed. Dese las' skifts wuz full o' ladies en genlmen agoin' over for to see de place. Sometimes dey'd pull up at de sho' en take a res' b'fo' dey started acrost, so by de talk I got to know all 'bout de killin'. I 'uz powerful sorry you's killed, Huck, but I ain't no mo', now.

"I laid dah under de shavins all day. I 'uz hungry, but I warn't afeared; bekase I knowed ole missus en de widder wuz goin' to start to de camp-meetn' right arter breakfas' en be gone all day, en dey knows I goes off wid de cattle 'bout daylight, so dey wouldn' 'spec to see me roun' de place, en so dey wouldn' miss me tell arter dark in de evenin'. De yuther servants wouldn' miss me, kase dey'd shin out en take holiday, soon as de ole folks 'uz out'n de way.

"Well, when it come dark I tuck out up de river road, en went 'bout two mile er more to whah dey warn't no houses. I'd made up my mine 'bout what I's agwyne to do. You see ef I kep' on tryin' to git away afoot, de dogs 'ud track me; ef I stole a skift to cross over, dey'd miss dat skift, you see, en dey'd know 'bout whah I'd lan' on de yuther side en whah to pick up my track. So I says, a raff is what I's arter; it doan' *make* no track.

"I see a light a-comin' roun' de p'int, bymeby, so I wade' in en shove' a log ahead o' me, en swum more'n half-way acrost de river, en got in 'mongst de drift-wood, en kep' my head down low, en kinder swum agin de current tell de raff come along. Den I swum to de stern uv it, en tuck aholt. It clouded up en 'uz pooty dark for a little while. So I clumb up en laid down on de planks. De men 'uz all 'way yonder in de middle, whah de lantern wuz. De river wuz arisin' en dey wuz a good current; so I reck'n'd 'at by fo' in de mawnin' I'd be twenty-five mile down de river, en den I'd slip in, jis' b'fo' daylight, en swim asho' en take to de woods on de Illinoi side.

"But I didn' have no luck. When we 'uz mos' down to de head er de islan', a man begin to come aft wid de lantern. I see it warn't no use fer to wait, so I slid overboad, en struck out fer de islan'. Well, I had a notion I could lan' mos' anywhers, but I couldn't—bank too bluff. I 'uz mos' to de foot er de islan' b'fo' I foun' a good place. I went into de woods en jedged I wouldn' fool wid raffs no mo', long as dey move de lantern roun' so. I had my pipe en a plug er dog-leg, en some matches in my cap, en dey warn't wet, so I 'uz all right."

"And so you ain't had no meat nor bread to eat all this time? Why didn't you get mud-turkles?"

"How you gwyne to git'm? You can't slip up on um en grab um; en how's a body gwyne to hit um wid a rock? How could a body do it in de night? en I warn't gwyne to show mysef on de bank in de daytime."

"Well, that's so. You've had to keep in the woods all the time, of course. Did you hear 'em shooting the cannon?"

"Oh, yes. I knowed dey was arter you. I see um go by heah; watched um thoo de bushes."

Some young birds come along, flying a yard or two at a time and lighting. Jim said it was a sign it was going to rain. He said it was a sign when young chickens flew that way, and so he reckoned it was the same way when young birds done it. I was going to catch some of them, but Jim wouldn't let me. He said it was death. He said his father laid mighty sick once, and some of them catched a bird, and his old granny said his father would die, and he did.

And Jim said you musn't count the things you are going to cook for dinner, because that would bring bad luck. The same if you shook the table-cloth after sundown. And he said if a man owned a bee-hive, and that man died, the bees must be told about it before sun-up next morning, or else the bees would all weaken down and quit work and die. Jim said bees wouldn't sting idiots; but I didn't believe that, because I had tried them lots of times myself, and they wouldn't sting me.

I had heard about some of these things before, but not all of them. Jim knowed all kinds of signs. He said he knowed most everything. I said it looked to me like all the signs was about bad luck, and so I asked him if there warn't any good-luck signs. He says:

"Mighty few—an ' *dey* ain' no use to a body. What you want to know when good luck's a-comin' for? want to keep it off?'' And he said: "Ef you's got hairy arms en a hairy breas', it's a sign dat you's agwyne to be rich. Well, dey's some use in a sign like dat, 'kase it's so fur ahead. You see, maybe you's got to be po' a long time fust, en so you might git discourage' en kill yo'sef 'f you didn' know by de sign dat you gwyne to be rich bymeby.''

"Have you got hairy arms and a hairy breast, Jim?''

"What's de use to ax dat question? don' you see I has?''

"Well, are you rich?''

"No, but I ben rich wunst, and gwyne to be rich agin. Wunst I had foteen dollars, but I tuck to specalat'n', en got busted out.''

"What did you speculate in, Jim?''

"Well, fust I tackled stock.''

"What kind of stock?''

"Why, live stock. Cattle, you know. I put ten dollars in a cow. But I ain' gwyne to resk no mo' money in stock. De cow up 'n' died on my han's.''

"So you lost the ten dollars.''

"No, I didn' lose it all. I on'y los' 'bout nine of it. I sole de hide en taller for a dollar en ten cents.''

"You had five dollars and ten cents left. Did you speculate any more?''

"Yes. You know dat one-laigged nigger dat b'longs to old Misto Bradish? well, he sot up a bank, en say anybody dat put in a dollar would git fo' dollars mo' at de en' er de year. Well, all de niggers went in, but dey didn' have much. I wuz de on'y one dat had much. So I stuck out for mo' dan fo' dollars, en I said 'f I didn' git it I'd start a bank mysef. Well o' course dat nigger want' to keep me out er de business, bekase he say dey warn't business 'nough for two banks, so he say I could put in my five dollars en he pay me thirty-five at de en' er de year.

"So I done it. Den I reck'n'd I'd inves' de thirty-five dollars right off en keep things a-movin'. Dey wuz a nigger name' Bob, dat had ketched a wood-flat, en his marster didn' know it; en I bought it off'n him en told him to take de thirty-five dollars when de en' er de year come; but somebody stole de wood-flat dat night, en nex' day de one-laigged nigger say de bank 's busted. So dey didn' none uv us git no money.''

"What did you do with the ten cents, Jim?''

"Well, I 'uz gwyne to spen' it, but I had a dream, en de dream tole me to give it to a nigger name' Balum—Balum's Ass dey call him for short, he's one er dem chuckle-heads, you know. But he's lucky, dey say, en I see I warn't lucky. De dream say let Balum inves' de ten cents en he'd make a raise for me. Well, Balum he tuck de money, en when he wuz in church he hear de preacher

say dat whoever give to de po' len' to de Lord, en boun' to git his money back
a hund'd times. So Balum he tuck en give de ten cents to de po', en laid low
to see what wuz gwyne to come of it.''

"Well, what did come of it, Jim?''

"Nuffn' never come of it. I couldn' manage to k'leck dat money no way; en
Balum he couldn'. I ain' gwyne to len' no mo' money 'dout I see de security.
Boun' to git yo' money back a hund'd times, de preacher says! Ef I could git
de ten *cents* back, I'd call it squah, en be glad er de chanst.''

"Well, it's all right, anyway, Jim, long as you're going to be rich again some
time or other.''

"Yes—en I's rich now, come to look at it. I owns mysef, en I's wuth eight
hund'd dollars. I wisht I had de money, I wouldn' want no mo'.''

Chapter IX

I WANTED TO go and look at a place right about the middle of the island, that
I'd found when I was exploring; so we started, and soon got to it, because the
island was only three miles long and a quarter of a mile wide.

This place was a tolerable long steep hill or ridge, about forty foot high. We
had a rough time getting to the top, the sides was so steep and the bushes so
thick. We tramped and clumb around all over it, and by-and-by found a good
big cavern in the rock, most up to the top on the side towards Illinois. The
cavern was as big as two or three rooms bunched together, and Jim could stand
up straight in it. It was cool in there. Jim was for putting our traps in there,
right away, but I said we didn't want to be climbing up and down there all the
time.

Jim said if we had the canoe hid in a good place, and had all the traps in the
cavern, we could rush there if anybody was to come to the island, and they
would never find us without dogs. And besides, he said them little birds had
said it was going to rain, and did I want the things to get wet?

EXPLORING THE CAVE.

So we went back and got the canoe and paddled up abreast the cavern, and lugged all the traps up there. Then we hunted up a place close by to hide the canoe in, amongst the thick willows. We took some fish off of the lines and set them again, and begun to get ready for dinner.

The door of the cavern was big enough to roll a hogshead in, and on one side of the door the floor stuck out a little bit and was flat and a good place to build a fire on. So we built it there and cooked dinner.

We spread the blankets inside for a carpet, and ate our dinner in there. We put all the other things handy at the back of the cavern. Pretty soon it darkened up and begun to thunder and lighten; so the birds was right about it. Directly it begun to rain, and it rained like all fury, too, and I never see the wind blow so. It was one of these regular summer storms. It would get so dark that it looked all blue-black outside, and lovely; and the rain would thrash along by so thick that the trees off a little ways looked dim and spider-webby; and here would come a blast of wind that would bend the trees down and turn up the pale underside of the leaves; and then a perfect ripper of a gust would follow along and set the branches to tossing their arms as if they was just wild; and next, when it was just about the bluest and blackest—*fst!* it was as bright as glory and you'd have a little glimpse of tree-tops a-plunging about, away off yonder in the storm, hundreds of yards further than you could see before; dark as sin again in a second, and now you'd hear the thunder let go with an awful crash and then go rumbling, grumbling, tumbling down the sky towards the under side of the world, like rolling empty barrels down stairs, where it's long stairs and they bounce a good deal, you know.

"Jim, this is nice," I says. "I wouldn't want to be nowhere else but here. Pass me along another hunk of fish and some hot corn-bread."

"Well, you wouldn't a ben here, 'f it hadn't a ben for Jim. You'd a ben down dah in de woods widout any dinner, en gittn' mos' drownded, too, dat you would, honey. Chickens knows when its gwyne to rain, en so do de birds, chile."

The river went on raising and raising for ten or twelve days, till at last it was over the banks. The water was three or four foot deep on the island in the low places and on the Illinois bottom. On that side it was a good many miles wide; but on the Missouri side it was the same old distance across—a half a mile— because the Missouri shore was just a wall of high bluffs.

Daytimes we paddled all over the island in the canoe. It was mighty cool and shady in the deep woods even if the sun was blazing outside. We went winding in and out amongst the trees; and sometimes the vines hung so thick we had to back away and go some other way. Well, on every old broken-down tree, you could see rabbits, and snakes, and such things; and when the island had been overflowed a day or two, they got so tame, on account of being hungry, that you could paddle right up and put your hand on them if you wanted to; but not the snakes and turtles—they would slide off in the water. The ridge our cavern was in, was full of them. We could a had pets enough if we'd wanted them.

One night we catched a little section of a lumber raft—nice pine planks. It was twelve foot wide and about fifteen or sixteen foot long, and the top stood above water six or seven inches, a solid level floor. We could see saw-logs go by in the daylight, sometimes, but we let them go; we didn't show ourselves in daylight.

Another night, when we was up at the head of the island, just before daylight, here comes a frame house down, on the west side. She was a two-story, and tilted over, considerable. We paddled out and got aboard—clumb in at an up-stairs window. But it was too dark to see yet, so we made the canoe fast and set in her to wait for daylight.

The light begun to come before we got to the foot of the island. Then we looked in at the window. We could make out a bed, and a table, and two old chairs, and lots of things around about on the floor; and there was clothes hanging against the wall. There was something laying on the floor in the far corner that looked like a man. So Jim says:

"Hello, you!"

But it didn't budge. So I hollered again, and then Jim says:

"De man ain't asleep—he's dead. You hold still—I'll go en see."

He went and bent down and looked, and says:

"It's a dead man. Yes, indeedy; naked, too. He's ben shot in de back. I reck'n he's ben dead two er three days. Come in, Huck, but doan' look at his face—it's too gashly."

I didn't look at him at all. Jim throwed some old rags over him, but he needn't done it; I didn't want to see him. There was heaps of old greasy cards scattered around over the floor, and old whisky bottles, and a couple of masks made out of black cloth; and all over the walls was the ignorantest kind of words and pictures, made with charcoal. There was two old dirty calico dresses, and a sun-bonnet, and some women's under-clothes, hanging against the wall, and some men's clothing, too. We put the lot into the canoe; it might come good. There was a boy's old speckled straw hat on the floor; I took that too. And there was a bottle that had had milk in it; and it had a rag stopper for a baby to suck. We would a took the bottle, but it was broke. There was a seedy old chest, and an old hair trunk with the hinges broke. They stood open, but there warn't nothing left in them that was any account. The way things was scattered about, we reckoned the people left in a hurry and warn't fixed so as to carry off most of their stuff.

We got an old tin lantern, and a butcher knife without any handle, and a bran-new Barlow knife worth two bits in any store, and a lot of tallow candles, and a tin candlestick, and a gourd, and a tin cup, and a ratty old bed-quilt off the

JIM SEES A DEAD MAN.

bed, and a reticule with needles and pins and beeswax and buttons and thread and all such truck in it, and a hatchet and some nails, and a fish-line as thick as my little finger, with some monstrous hooks on it, and a roll of buckskin, and a leather dog-collar, and a horse-shoe, and some vials of medicine that didn't have no label on them; and just as we was leaving I found a tolerable good curry-comb, and Jim he found a ratty old fiddle-bow, and a wooden leg. The straps was broke off of it, but barring that, it was a good enough leg, though it was too long for me and not long enough for Jim, and we couldn't find the other one, though we hunted all around.

And so, take it all around, we made a good haul. When we was ready to shove off, we was a quarter of a mile below the island, and it was pretty broad day; so I made Jim lay down in the canoe and cover up with the quilt, because if he set up, people could tell he was a nigger a good ways off. I paddled over to the Illinois shore, and drifted down most a half a mile doing it. I crept up the dead water under the bank, and hadn't no accidents and didn't see nobody. We got home all safe.

Chapter X

AFTER BREAKFAST I wanted to talk about the dead man and guess out how he come to be killed, but Jim didn't want to. He said it would fetch bad luck; and besides, he said, he might come and ha'nt us; he said a man that warn't buried was more likely to go a-ha'nting around than one that was planted and comfortable. That sounded pretty reasonable, so I didn't say no more; but I couldn't keep from studying over it and wishing I knowed who shot the man, and what they done it for.

We rummaged the clothes we'd got, and found eight dollars in silver sewed up in the lining of an old blanket overcoat. Jim said he reckoned the people in that house stole the coat, because if they'd a knowed the money was there they wouldn't a left it. I said I reckoned they killed him, too; but Jim didn't want to talk about that. I says:

"Now you think it's bad luck; but what did you say when I fetched in the snake-skin that I found on the top of the ridge day before yesterday? You said it was the worst bad luck in the world to touch a snake-skin with my hands. Well, here's your bad luck! We've raked in all this truck and eight dollars besides. I wish we could have some bad luck like this every day, Jim."

"Never you mind, honey, never you mind. Don't you git too peart. It's a-comin'. Mind I tell you, it's a-comin'."

It did come, too. It was a Tuesday that we had that talk. Well, after dinner Friday, we was laying around in the grass at the upper end of the ridge, and got out of tobacco. I went to the cavern to get some, and found a rattlesnake in there. I killed him, and curled him up on the foot of Jim's blanket, ever so natural, thinking there'd be some fun when Jim found him there. Well, by night I forgot all about the snake, and when Jim flung himself down on the blanket while I struck a light, the snake's mate was there, and bit him.

He jumped up yelling, and the first thing the light showed was the varmint curled up and ready for another spring. I laid him out in a second with a stick, and Jim grabbed pap's whisky jug and begun to pour it down.

He was barefooted, and the snake bit him right on the heel. That all comes of my being such a fool as to not remember that wherever you leave a dead snake its mate always comes there and curls around it. Jim told me to chop off the snake's head and throw it away, and then skin the body and roast a piece of it. I done it, and he eat it and said it would help cure him. He made me take off the rattles and tie them around his wrist, too. He said that that would help. Then I slid out quiet and throwed the snakes clear away amongst the bushes; for I warn't going to let Jim find out it was all my fault, not if I could help it.

Jim sucked and sucked at the jug, and now and then he got out of his head and pitched around and yelled; but every time he come to himself he went to sucking at the jug again. His foot swelled up pretty big, and so did his leg; but by-and-by the drunk begun to come, and so I judged he was all right; but I'd druther been bit with a snake than pap's whisky.

Jim was laid up for four days and nights. Then the swelling was all gone and he was around again. I made up my mind I wouldn't ever take aholt of a snake-skin again with my hands, now that I see what had come of it. Jim said he reckoned I would believe him next time. And he said that handling a snake-skin was such awful bad luck that maybe we hadn't got to the end of it yet. He said he druther see the new moon over his left shoulder as much as a thousand times than take up a snake-skin in his hand. Well, I was getting to feel that way myself, though I've always reckoned that looking at the new moon over your left shoulder is one of the carelessest and foolishest things a body can do. Old Hank Bunker done it once, and bragged about it; and in less than two years he got drunk and fell off of the shot tower and spread himself out so that he was just a kind of a layer, as you may say; and they slid him edgeways between two barn doors for a coffin, and buried him so, so they say, but I didn't see it. Pap told me. But anyway, it all come of looking at the moon that way, like a fool.

Well, the days went along, and the river went down between its banks again; and about the first thing we done was to bait one of the big hooks with a skinned rabbit and set it and catch a cat-fish that was as big as a man, being six foot two inches long, and weighed over two hundred pounds. We couldn't handle him, of course; he would a flung us into Illinois. We just set there and watched him rip and tear around till he drownded. We found a brass button in his stomach, and a round ball, and lots of rubbage. We split the ball open with the hatchet, and there was a spool in it. Jim said he'd had it there a long time, to coat it over so and make a ball of it. It was as big a fish as was ever catched in the Mississippi, I reckon. Jim said he hadn't ever seen a bigger one. He would a been worth a good deal over at the village. They peddle out such a fish as that by the pound in the market house there; everybody buys some of him; his meat's as white as snow and makes a good fry.

Next morning I said it was getting slow and dull, and I wanted to get a stirring up, some way. I said I reckoned I would slip over the river and find out what was going on. Jim liked that notion; but he said I must go in the dark and look sharp. Then he studied it over and said, couldn't I put on some of them old things and dress up like a girl? That was a good notion, too. So we shortened up one of the calico gowns and I turned up my trowser-legs to my knees and got into it. Jim hitched it behind with the hooks, and it was a fair fit. I put on the sun-bonnet and tied it under my chin, and then for a body to look in and

"A FAIR FIT."

see my face was like looking down a joint of stove-pipe. Jim said nobody would know me, even in the daytime, hardly. I practiced around all day to get the hang of the things, and by-and-by I could do pretty well in them, only Jim said I didn't walk like a girl; and he said I must quit pulling up my gown to get at my britches pocket. I took notice, and done better.

I started up the Illinois shore in the canoe just after dark.

I started across to the town from a little below the ferry landing, and the drift of the current fetched me in at the bottom of the town. I tied up and started along the bank. There was a light burning in a little shanty that hadn't been lived in for a long time, and I wondered who had took up quarters there. I slipped up and peeped in at the window. There was a woman about forty year old in there, knitting by a candle that was on a pine table. I didn't know her face; she was a stranger, for you couldn't start a face in that town that I didn't know. Now this was lucky, because I was weakening; I was getting afraid I had come; people might know my voice and find me out. But if this woman had been in such a little town two days she could tell me all I wanted to know; so I knocked at the door, and made up my mind I wouldn't forget I was a girl.

Chapter XI

"Come in," says the woman, and I did. She says:

"Take a cheer."

I done it. She looked me all over with her little shiny eyes, and says:

"What might your name be?"

"Sarah Williams."

"Where 'bouts do you live? In this neighborhood?"

"No'm. In Hookerville, seven mile below. I've walked all the way and I'm all tired out."

"Hungry, too, I reckon. I'll find you something."

"No'm, I ain't hungry. I was so hungry I had to stop two mile below here at a farm; so I ain't hungry no more. It's what makes me so late. My mother's down sick, and out of money and everything, and I come to tell my uncle Abner Moore. He lives at the upper end of the town, she says. I hain't ever been here before. Do you know him?''

"No; but I don't know everybody yet. I haven't lived here quite two weeks. It's a considerable ways to the upper end of the town. You better stay here all night. Take off your bonnet.''

"No," I says, "I'll rest a while, I reckon, and go on. I ain't afeard of the dark. ''

She said she wouldn't let me go by myself, but her husband would be in by-and-by, maybe in a hour and a half, and she'd send him along with me. Then she got to talking about her husband, and about her relations up the river, and her relations down the river, and about how much better off they used to was, and how they didn't know but they'd made a mistake coming to our town, instead of letting well alone—and so on and so on, till I was afeard *I* had made a mistake coming to her to find out what was going on in the town; but by-and-by she dropped onto pap and the murder, and then I was pretty willing to let her clatter right along. She told about me and Tom Sawyer finding the six thousand dollars (only she got it ten) and all about pap and what a hard lot he was, and what a hard lot I was, and at last she got down to where I was murdered. I says:

"Who done it? We've heard considerable about these goings on, down in Hookerville, but we don't know who 'twas that killed Huck Finn.''

"Well, I reckon there's a right smart chance of people *here* that'd like to know who killed him. Some thinks old Finn done it himself.''

"No—is that so?''

"Most everybody thought it at first. He'll never know how nigh he come to getting lynched. But before night they changed around and judged it was done by a runaway nigger named Jim.''

"Why *he*——''

I stopped. I reckoned I better keep still. She run on, and never noticed I had put in at all.

"The nigger run off the very night Huck Finn was killed. So there's a reward out for him—three hundred dollars. And there's a reward out for old Finn too—two hundred dollars. You see, he come to town the morning after the murder, and told about it, and was out with 'em on the ferry-boat hunt, and right away after he up and left. Before night they wanted to lynch him, but he was gone, you see. Well, next day they found out the nigger was gone; they found out he hadn't ben seen sence ten o'clock the night the murder was done. So then they put it on him, you see, and while they was full of it, next day back comes old Finn and went boo-hooing to Judge Thatcher to get money to hunt for the nigger all over Illinois with. The judge give him some, and that evening he got drunk and was around till after midnight with a couple of mighty hard looking strangers, and then went off with them. Well, he hain't come back sence, and they ain't looking for him back till this thing blows over a little, for people thinks now that he killed his boy and fixed things so folks would think robbers done it, and then he'd get Huck's money without having to bother a long time with a lawsuit. People do say he warn't any too good to do it. Oh, he's sly, I reckon. If he don't come back for a year, he'll be all right. You can't prove anything on him, you know; everything will be quieted down then, and he'll walk into Huck's money as easy as nothing.''

"Yes, I reckon so, 'm. I don't see nothing in the way of it. Has everybody quit thinking the nigger done it?"

"Oh, no, not everybody. A good many thinks he done it. But they'll get the nigger pretty soon, now, and maybe they can scare it out of him."

"Why, are they after him yet?"

"Well, you're innocent, ain't you! Does three hundred dollars lay round every day for people to pick up? Some folks thinks the nigger ain't far from here. I'm one of them—but I hain't talked it around. A few days ago I was talking with an old couple that lives next door in the log shanty, and they happened to say hardly anybody ever goes to that island over yonder that they call Jackson's Island. Don't anybody live there? says I. No, nobody, says they. I didn't say any more, but I done some thinking. I was pretty near certain I'd seen smoke over there, about the head of the island, a day or two before that, so I says to myself, like as not that nigger's hiding over there; anyway, says I, it's worth the trouble to give the place a hunt. I hain't seen any smoke sence, so I reckon maybe he's gone, if it was him; but husband's going over to see—him and another man. He was gone up the river; but he got back to-day and I told him as soon as he got here two hours ago."

I had got so uneasy I couldn't set still. I had to do something with my hands; so I took up a needle off of the table and went to threading it. My hands shook, and I was making a bad job of it. When the woman stopped talking, I looked up, and she was looking at me pretty curious, and smiling a little. I put down the needle and thread and let on to be interested—and I was, too—and says:

"Three hundred dollars is a power of money. I wish my mother could get it. Is your husband going over there to-night?"

"Oh, yes. He went up town with the man I was telling you of, to get a boat and see if they could borrow another gun. They'll go over after midnight."

"Couldn't they see better if they was to wait till daytime?"

"Yes. And couldn't the nigger see better, too? After midnight he'll likely be asleep, and they can slip around through the woods and hunt up his camp fire all the better for the dark, if he's got one."

"I didn't think of that."

The woman kept looking at me pretty curious, and I didn't feel a bit comfortable. Pretty soon she says:

"What did you say your name was, honey?"

"M—Mary Williams."

Somehow it didn't seem to me that I said it was Mary before, so I didn't look up; seemed to me I said it was Sarah; so I felt sort of cornered, and was afeared maybe I was looking it, too. I wished the woman would say something more; the longer she set still, the uneasier I was. But now she says:

"Honey, I thought you said it was Sarah when you first come in?"

"Oh, yes'm, I did. Sarah Mary Williams. Sarah's my first name. Some calls me Sarah, some calls me Mary."

"Oh, that's the way of it?"

"Yes'm."

I was feeling better, then, but I wished I was out of there, anyway. I couldn't look up yet.

Well, the woman fell to talking about how hard times was, and how poor they had to live, and how the rats was as free as if they owned the place, and so forth, and so on, and then I got easy again. She was right about the rats.

You'd see one stick his nose out of a hole in the corner every little while. She said she had to have things handy to throw at them when she was alone, or they wouldn't give her no peace. She showed me a bar of lead, twisted up into a knot, and said she was a good shot with it generly, but she'd wrenched her arm a day or two ago, and didn't know whether she could throw true, now. But she watched for a chance, and directly she banged away at a rat, but she missed him wide, and said "Ouch!" it hurt her arm so. Then she told me to try for the next one. I wanted to be getting away before the old man got back, but of course I didn't let on. I got the thing, and the first rat that showed his nose I let drive, and if he'd a stayed where he was he'd a been a tolerable sick rat. She said that that was first-rate, and she reckoned I would hive the next one. She went and got the lump of lead and fetched it back and brought along a hank of yarn, which she wanted me to help her with. I held up my two hands and she put the hank over them and went on talking about her and her husband's matters. But she broke off to say:

"Keep your eye on the rats. You better have the lead in your lap, handy."

So she dropped the lump into my lap, just at that moment, and I clapped my legs together on it and she went on talking. But only about a minute. Then she took off the hank and looked me straight in the face, but very pleasant, and says:

"Come, now—what's your real name?"

"Wh-what, mum?"

"What's your real name? Is it Bill, or Tom, or Bob?—or what is it?"

I reckon I shook like a leaf, and I didn't know hardly what to do. But I says:

"Please to don't poke fun at a poor girl like me, mum. If I'm in the way, here, I'll——"

"No, you won't. Set down and stay where you are. I ain't going to hurt you, and I ain't going to tell on you, nuther. You just tell me your secret, and trust me. I'll keep it; and what's more, I'll help you. So'll my old man, if you want him to. You see, you're a runaway 'prentice—that's all. It ain't anything. There ain't any harm in it. You've been treated bad, and you made up your mind to cut. Bless you, child, I wouldn't tell on you. Tell me all about it, now—that's a good boy."

So I said it wouldn't be no use to try to play it any longer, and I would just make a clean breast and tell her everything, but she mustn't go back on her promise. Then I told her my father and mother was dead, and the law had bound me out to a mean old farmer in the country thirty mile back from the river, and he treated me so bad I couldn't stand it no longer; he went away to be gone a couple of days, and so I took my chance and stole some of his daughter's old clothes, and cleared out, and I had been three nights coming the thirty miles; I traveled nights, and hid day-times and slept, and the bag of bread and meat I carried from home lasted me all the way and I had a plenty. I said I believed my uncle Abner Moore would take care of me, and so that was why I struck out for this town of Goshen."

"Goshen, child? This ain't Goshen. This is St. Petersburg. Goshen's ten mile further up the river. Who told you this was Goshen?"

"Why, a man I met at day-break this morning, just as I was going to turn into the woods for my regular sleep. He told me when the roads forked I must take the right hand, and five mile would fetch me to Goshen."

"He was drunk I reckon. He told you just exactly wrong."

"Well, he did act like he was drunk, but it ain't no matter now. I got to be moving along. I'll fetch Goshen before day-light."

"Hold on a minute. I'll put you up a snack to eat. You might want it."

So she put me up a snack, and says:

"Say—when a cow's laying down, which end of her gets up first? Answer up prompt, now—don't stop to study over it. Which end gets up first?"

"The hind end, mum."

"Well, then, a horse?"

"The for'rard end, mum."

"Which side of a tree does the most moss grow on?"

"North side."

"If fifteen cows is browsing on a hillside, how many of them eats with their heads pointed the same direction?"

"The whole fifteen, mum."

"Well, I reckon you *have* lived in the country. I thought maybe you was trying to hocus me again. What's your real name, now?"

"George Peters, mum."

"Well, try to remember it, George. Don't forget and tell me it's Elexander before you go, and then get out by saying it's George-Elexander when I catch you. And don't go about women in that old calico. You do a girl tolerable poor, but you might fool men, maybe. Bless you, child, when you set out to thread a needle, don't hold the thread still and fetch the needle up to it; hold the needle still and poke the thread at it—that's the way a woman most always does; but a man always does 'tother way. And when you throw at a rat or anything, hitch yourself up a tip-toe, and fetch your hand up over your head as awkard as you can, and miss your rat about six or seven foot. Throw stiff-armed from the shoulder, like there was a pivot there for it to turn on—like a girl; not from the wrist and elbow, with your arm out to one side, like a boy. And mind you, when a girl tries to catch anything in her lap, she throws her knees apart; she don't clap them together, the way you did when you catched the lump of lead. Why, I spotted you for a boy when you was threading the needle; and I contrived the other things just to make certain. Now trot along to your uncle, Sarah Mary Williams George Elexander Peters, and if you get into trouble you send word

SHE PUTS UP A SNACK.

to Mrs. Judith Loftus, which is me, and I'll do what I can to get you out of it. Keep the river road, all the way, and next time you tramp, take shoes and socks with you. The river road's a rocky one, and your feet'll be in a condition when you get to Goshen, I reckon.''

I went up the bank about fifty yards, and then I doubled on my tracks and slipped back to where my canoe was, a good piece below the house. I jumped in and was off in a hurry. I went up stream far enough to make the head of the island, and then started across. I took off the sun-bonnet, for I didn't want no blinders on, then. When I was about the middle, I hear the clock begin to strike; so I stops and listens; the sound come faint over the water, but clear—eleven. When I struck the head of the island I never waited to blow, though I was most winded, but I shoved right into the timber where my old camp used to be, and started a good fire there on a high-and-dry spot.

Then I jumped in the canoe and dug out for our place a mile and a half below, as hard as I could go. I landed, and slopped through the timber and up the ridge and into the cavern. There Jim laid, sound asleep on the ground. I roused him out and says:

"Git up and hump yourself, Jim! There ain't a minute to lose. They're after us!"

Jim never asked no questions, he never said a word; but the way he worked for the next half an hour showed about how he was scared. By that time everything we had in the world was on our raft and she was ready to be shoved out from the willow cove where she was hid. We put out the camp fire at the cavern the first thing, and didn't show a candle outside after that.

I took the canoe out from shore a little piece and took a look, but if there was a boat around I couldn't see it, for stars and shadows ain't good to see by. Then we got out the raft and slipped along down in the shade, past the foot of the island dead still, never saying a word.

Chapter XII

IT MUST A been close onto one o'clock when we got below the island at last, and the raft did seem to go mighty slow. If a boat was to come along, we was going to take to the canoe and break for the Illinois shore; and it was well a boat didn't come, for we hadn't ever thought to put the gun into the canoe, or a fishing-line or anything to eat. We was in ruther too much of a sweat to think of so many things. It warn't good judgment to put *everything* on the raft.

If the men went to the island, I just expect they found the camp fire I built, and watched it all night for Jim to come. Anyways, they stayed away from us, and if my building the fire never fooled them it warn't no fault of mine. I played it as low-down on them as I could.

When the first streak of day begun to show, we tied up to a tow-head in a big bend on the Illinois side, and hacked off cotton-wood branches with the hatchet and covered up the raft with them so she looked like there had been a cave-in in the bank there. A tow-head is a sand-bar that has cotton-woods on it as thick as harrow-teeth.

We had mountains on the Missouri shore and heavy timber on the Illinois

ON THE RAFT.

side, and the channel was down the Missouri shore at that place, so we warn't afraid of anybody running across us. We laid there all day and watched the rafts and steamboats spin down the Missouri shore, and up-bound steamboats fight the big river in the middle. I told Jim all about the time I had jabbering with that woman; and Jim said she was a smart one, and if she was to start after us herself *she* wouldn't set down and watch a camp fire—no, sir, she'd fetch a dog. Well, then, I said, why couldn't she tell her husband to fetch a dog? Jim said he bet she did think of it by the time the men was ready to start, and he believed they must a gone up town to get a dog and so they lost all that time, or else we wouldn't be here on a tow-head sixteen or seventeen mile below the village—no, indeedy, we would be in that same old town again. So I said I didn't care what was the reason they didn't get us, as long as they didn't.

When it was beginning to come on dark, we poked our heads out of the cotton-wood thicket and looked up, and down, and across; nothing in sight; so Jim took up some of the top planks of the raft and built a snug wigwam to get under in blazing weather and rainy, and to keep the things dry. Jim made a floor for the wigwam, and raised it a foot or more above the level of the raft, so now the blankets and all the traps was out of the reach of steamboat waves. Right in the middle of the wigwam we made a layer of dirt about five or six inches deep with a frame around it for to hold it to its place; this was to build a fire on in sloppy weather or chilly; the wigwam would keep it from being seen. We made an extra steering oar, too, because one of the others might get broke, on a snag or something. We fixed up a short forked stick to hang the old lantern on; because we must always light the lantern whenever we see a steamboat coming down stream, to keep from getting run over; but we wouldn't have to light it for upstream boats unless we see we was in what they call a "crossing;" for the river was pretty high yet, very low banks being still a little under water; so up-bound boats didn't always run the channel, but hunted easy water.

This second night we run between seven and eight hours, with a current that was making over four mile an hour. We catched fish, and talked, and we took a swim now and then to keep off sleepiness. It was kind of solemn, drifting down the big still river, laying on our backs looking up at the stars, and we didn't ever feel like talking loud, and it warn't often that we laughed, only a little kind of a low chuckle. We had mighty good weather, as a general thing, and nothing ever happened to us at all, that night, nor the next, nor the next.

Every night we passed towns, some of them away up on black hillsides, nothing but just a shiny bed of lights, not a house could you see. The fifth night we passed St. Louis, and it was like the whole world lit up. In St. Petersburg they used to say there was twenty or thirty thousand people in St. Louis, but I never believed it till I see that wonderful spread of lights at two o'clock that still night. There warn't a sound there; everybody was asleep.

Every night, now, I used to slip ashore, towards ten o'clock, at some little village, and buy ten or fifteen cents' worth of meal or bacon or other stuff to eat; and sometimes I lifted a chicken that warn't roosting comfortable, and took him along. Pap always said, take a chicken when you get a chance, because if you don't want him yourself you can easy find somebody that does, and a good deed ain't ever forgot. I never see pap when he didn't want the chicken himself, but that is what he used to say, anyway.

Mornings, before daylight, I slipped into corn fields and borrowed a watermelon, or a mushmelon, or a punkin, or some new corn, or things of that kind. Pap always said it warn't no harm to borrow things, if you was meaning to pay them back, sometime; but the widow said it warn't anything but a soft name for stealing, and no decent body would do it. Jim said he reckoned the widow was partly right and pap was partly right; so the best way would be for us to pick out two or three things from the list and say we wouldn't borrow them any more—then he reckoned it wouldn't be no harm to borrow the others. So we talked it over all one night, drifting along down the river, trying to make up our minds whether to drop the watermelons, or the cantelopes, or the mushmelons, or what. But towards daylight we got it all settled satisfactory, and concluded to drop crabapples and p'simmons. We warn't feeling just right, before that, but it was all comfortable now. I was glad the way it come out, too, because crabapples ain't ever good, and the p'simmons wouldn't be ripe for two or three months yet.

We shot a water-fowl, now and then, that got up too early in the morning or didn't go to bed early enough in the evening. Take it all around, we lived pretty high.

The fifth night below St. Louis we had a big storm after midnight, with a power of thunder and lightning, and the rain poured down in a solid sheet. We stayed in the wigwam and let the raft take care of itself. When the lightning glared out we could see a big straight river ahead, and high rocky bluffs on both sides. By-and-by says I, "Hel-*lo*, Jim, looky yonder!" It was a steamboat that had killed herself on a rock. We was drifting straight down for her. The lightning showed her very distinct. She was leaning over, with part of her upper deck above water, and you could see every little chimbly-guy clean and clear, and a chair by the big bell, with an old slouch hat hanging on the back of it when the flashes come.

Well, it being away in the night, and stormy, and all so mysterious-like, I felt just the way any other boy would a felt when I see that wreck laying there so mournful and lonesome in the middle of the river. I wanted to get aboard of her and slink around a little, and see what there was there. So I says:

"Le's land on her, Jim."

But Jim was dead against it, at first. He says:

"I doan' want to go fool'n 'long er no wrack. We's doin' blame' well, en we better let blame' well alone, as de good book says. Like as not dey's a watchman on dat wrack.''

"Watchman your grandmother," I says; "there ain't nothing to watch but the texas and the pilot-house; and do you reckon anybody's going to resk his life for a texas and a pilot-house such a night as this, when it's likely to break up and wash off down the river any minute?" Jim couldn't say nothing to that, so he didn't try. "And besides," I says, "we might borrow something worth having, out of the captain's stateroom. Seegars, *I* bet you—and cost five cents apiece, solid cash. Steamboat captains is always rich, and get sixty dollars a month, and *they* don't care a cent what a thing costs, you know, long as they want it. Stick a candle in your pocket; I can't rest, Jim, till we give her a rummaging. Do you reckon Tom Sawyer would ever go by this thing? Not for pie, he wouldn't. He'd call it an adventure—that's what he'd call it; and he'd land on that wreck if it was his last act. And wouldn't he throw style into it?—wouldn't he spread himself, nor nothing? Why, you'd think it was Christopher C'lumbus discovering Kingdom-Come. I wish Tom Sawyer *was* here.''

Jim he grumbled a little, but give in. He said we mustn't talk any more than we could help, and then talk mighty low. The lightning showed us the wreck again, just in time, and we fetched the starboard derrick, and made fast there.

The deck was high out, here. We went sneaking down the slope of it to labboard, in the dark, towards the texas, feeling our way slow with our feet, and spreading our hands out to fend off the guys, for it was so dark we couldn't see no sign of them. Pretty soon we struck the forward end of the skylight, and clumb onto it; and the next step fetched us in front of the captain's door, which was open, and by Jimminy, away down through the texas-hall we see a light! and all in the same second we seem to hear low voices in yonder!

Jim whispered and said he was feeling powerful sick, and told me to come along. I says, all right; and was going to start for the raft; but just then I heard a voice wail out and say:

"Oh, please don't, boys; I swear I won't ever tell!''

Another voice said, pretty loud:

"It's a lie, Jim Turner. You've acted this way before. You always want more'n your share of the truck, and you've always got it, too, because you've swore 't if you didn't you'd tell. But this time you've said it jest one time too many. You're the meanest, treacherousest hound in this country.''

By this time Jim was gone for the raft. I was just a-biling with curiosity; and I says to myself, Tom Sawyer wouldn't back out now, and so I won't either; I'm agoing to see what's going on here. So I dropped on my hands and knees, in the little passage, and crept aft in the dark, till there warn't but about one stateroom betwixt me and the cross-hall of the texas. Then, in there I see a man stretched on the floor and tied hand and foot, and two men standing over him, and one of them had a dim lantern in his hand and the other one had a pistol. This one kept pointing the pistol at the man's head on the floor and saying—

"I'd *like* to! And I orter, too, a mean skunk!''

The man on the floor would shrivel up, and say: "Oh, please don't, Bill—I hain't ever goin' to tell.''

And every time he said that, the man with the lantern would laugh, and say:

"'Deed you *ain't!* You never said no truer thing 'n that, you bet you.'' And once he said: "Hear him beg! and yit if we hadn't got the best of him and tied him, he'd a killed us both. And what *for?* Jist for noth'n. Jist because we stood on our *rights*—that's what for. But I lay you ain't agoin' to threaten nobody any more, Jim Turner. Put *up* that pistol, Bill.''

Bill says:

"I don't want to, Jake Packard. I'm for killin' him—and didn't he kill old Hatfield jist the same way—and don't he deserve it?''

"But I don't *want* him killed, and I've got my reasons for it.''

"Bless yo' heart for them words, Jake Packard! I'll never forgit you, long's I live!'' says the man on the floor, sort of blubbering.

Packard didn't take no notice of that, but hung up his lantern on a nail, and started towards where I was, there in the dark, and motioned Bill to come. I crawfished as fast as I could, about two yards, but the boat slanted so that I couldn't make very good time; so to keep from getting run over and catched I crawled into a stateroom on the upper side. The man come a-pawing along in the dark, and when Packard got to my stateroom, he says:

"Here—come in here.''

And in he come, and Bill after him. But before they got in, I was up in the upper berth, cornered, and sorry I come. Then they stood there, with their hands on the ledge of the berth, and talked. I couldn't see them, but I could tell where they was, by the whisky they'd been having. I was glad I didn't drink whisky; but it wouldn't made much difference, anyway, because most of the time they couldn't a treed me because I didn't breathe. I was too scared. And besides, a body *couldn't* breathe, and hear such talk. They talked low and earnest. Bill wanted to kill Turner. He says:

"He's said he'll tell, and he will. If we was to give both our shares to him *now*, it wouldn't make no difference after the row, and the way we've served him. Shore's you're born, he'll turn State's evidence; now you hear *me*. I'm for putting him out of his troubles.''

"So'm I,'' says Packard, very quiet.

"Blame it, I'd sorter begun to think you wasn't. Well, then, that's all right. Les' go and do it.''

"Hold on a minute; I hain't had my say yit. You listen to me. Shooting's good, but there's quieter ways if the thing's *got* to be done. But what *I* say, is this; it ain't good sense to go court'n around after a halter, if you can git at what you're up to in some way that's jist as good and at the same time don't bring you into no resks. Ain't that so?''

"You bet it is. But how you goin' to manage it this time?''

"Well, my idea is this: we'll rustle around and gether up whatever pickins we've overlooked in the staterooms, and shove for shore and hide the truck. Then we'll wait. Now I say it ain't agoin' to be more 'n two hours befo' this wrack breaks up and washes off down the river. See? He'll be drownded, and won't have nobody to blame for it but his own self. I reckon that's a considerble sight better'n killin' of him. I'm unfavorable to killin' a man as long as you can git around it; it ain't good sense, it ain't good morals. Ain't I right?''

"Yes—I reck'n you are. But s'pose she *don't* break up and wash off?''

"Well, we can wait the two hours, anyway, and see, can't we?''

"All right, then; come along.''

So they started, and I lit out, all in a cold sweat, and scrambled forward. It was dark as pitch there; but I said in a kind of a coarse whisper, "Jim!'' and he answered up, right at my elbow, with a sort of a moan, and I says:

"Quick, Jim, it ain't no time for fooling around and moaning; there's a gang of murderers in yonder, and if we don't hunt up their boat and set her drifting down the river so these fellows can't get away from the wreck, there's one of 'em going to be in a bad fix. But if we find their boat we can put *all* of 'em in a bad fix—for the Sheriff'll get 'em. Quick—hurry! I'll hunt the labboard side, you hunt the stabboard. You start at the raft, and——"

"Oh, my lordy, lordy! *Raf'?* Dey ain' no raf' no mo', she done broke loose en gone!—'en here we is!"

Chapter XIII

WELL, I CATCHED my breath and most fainted. Shut up on a wreck with such a gang as that! But it warn't no time to be sentimentering. We'd *got* to find that boat, now—had to have it for ourselves. So we went a-quaking and shaking down the stabboard side, and slow work it was, too—seemed a week before we got to the stern. No sign of a boat. Jim said he didn't believe he could go any further—so scared he hadn't hardly any strength left, he said. But I said come on, if we get left on this wreck, we are in a fix, sure. So on we prowled, again. We struck for the stern of the texas, and found it, and then scrabbled along forwards on the skylight, hanging on from shutter to shutter, for the edge of the skylight was in the water. When we got pretty close to the cross-hall door, there was the skiff, sure enough! I could just barely see her. I felt ever so thankful. In another second I would a been aboard of her; but just then the door opened. One of the men stuck his head out, only about a couple of foot from me, and I thought I was gone; but he jerked it in again, and says:

"Heave that blame lantern out o' sight, Bill!"

He flung a bag of something into the boat, and then got in himself, and set down. It was Packard. Then Bill *he* come out and got in. Packard says, in a low voice:

"All ready—shove off!"

I couldn't hardly hang onto the shutters, I was so weak. But Bill says:

"Hold on—'d you go through him?"

"No. Didn't you?"

"No. So he's got his share o' the cash, yet."

"Well, then, come along—no use to take truck and leave the money."

"Say—won't he suspicion what we're up to?"

"Maybe he won't. But we got to have it anyway. Come along."

So they got out and went in.

The door slammed to, because it was on the careened side; and in a half second I was in the boat, and Jim come a tumbling after me. I out with my knife and cut the rope, and away we went!

We didn't touch an oar, and we didn' speak nor whisper, nor hardly even breathe. We went gliding swift along, dead silent, past the tip of the paddle-box, and past the stern; then in a second or two more we was a hundred yards below the wreck, and the darkness soaked her up, every last sign of her, and we was safe, and knowed it.

When we was three or four hundred yards down stream, we see the lantern show like a little spark at the texas door, for a second, and we knowed by that

that the rascals had missed their boat, and was beginning to understand that they
was in just as much trouble, now, as Jim Turner was.

Then Jim manned the oars, and we took out after our raft. Now was the first
time that I begun to worry about the men—I reckon I hadn't had time to before.
I begun to think how dreadful it was, even for murderers, to be in such a fix.
I says to myself, there ain't no telling but I might come to be a murderer myself,
yet, and then how would *I* like it? So says I to Jim:

"The first light we see, we'll land a hundred yards below it or above it, in a
place where it's a good hiding-place for you and the skiff, and then I'll go and
fix up some kind of a yarn, and get somebody to go for that gang and get them
out of their scrape, so they can be hung when their time comes."

But that idea was a failure; for pretty soon it begun to storm again, and this
time worse than ever. The rain poured down, and never a light showed; everybody
in bed, I reckon. We boomed along down the river, watching for lights and
watching for our raft. After a long time the rain let up, but the clouds staid, and
the lightning kept whimpering, and by-and-by a flash showed us a black thing
ahead, floating, and we made for it.

It was the raft, and mighty glad was we to get aboard of it again. We seen a
light, now, away down to the right, on shore. So I said I would go for it. The
skiff was half full of plunder which that gang had stole, there on the wreck. We
hustled it onto the raft in a pile, and I told Jim to float along down, and show
a light when he judged he had gone about two mile, and keep it burning till I
come; then I manned my oars and shoved for the light. As I got down towards
it, three or four more showed—up on a hillside. It was a village. I closed in
above the shore-light, and laid on my oars and floated. As I went by, I see it
was a lantern hanging on the jackstaff of a double-hull ferry-boat. I skimmed
around for the watchman, a-wondering whereabouts he slept; and by-and-by I
found him roosting on the bitts, forward, with his head down between his knees.
I give his shoulder two or three little shoves, and begun to cry.

He stirred up, in a kind of a startlish way; but when he see it was only me,
he took a good gap and stretch, and then he says:

"Hello, what's up? Don't cry, bub. What's the trouble?"

I says:

"Pap, and mam, and sis, and——"

Then I broke down. He says:

"Oh, dang it, now, *don't* take on so, we all has to have our troubles and
this'n 'll come out all right. What's the matter with 'em?"

"They're—they're—are you the watchman of the boat?"

"Yes," he says, kind of pretty-well-satisfied like. "I'm the captain and the
owner, and the mate, and the pilot, and watchman, and head deck-hand; and
sometimes I'm the freight and passengers. I ain't as rich as old Jim Hornback,
and I can't be so blame' generous and good to Tom, Dick and Harry as what
he is, and slam around money the way he does; but I've told him a many a time
't I wouldn't trade places with him; for, says I, a sailor's life's the life for me,
and I'm derned if *I'd* live two mile out o' town, where there ain't nothing ever
goin' on, not for all his spondulicks and as much more on top of it. Says I—"

I broke in and says:

"They're in an awful peck of trouble, and——"

"*Who* is?"

"Why, pap, and mam, and sis, and Miss Hooker; and if you'd take your ferry-boat and go up there——"

"Up where? Where are they?"

"On the wreck."

"What wreck?"

"Why, there ain't but one."

"What, you don't mean the *Walter Scott?*"

"Yes."

"Good land! what are they doin' *there*, for gracious sakes?"

"Well, they didn't go there a-purpose."

"I bet they didn't! Why, great goodness, there ain't no chance for 'em if they don't git off mighty quick! Why, how in the nation did they ever git into such a scrape?"

"Easy enough. Miss Hooker was a-visiting, up there to the town——"

"Yes, Booth's Landing—go on."

"She was a-visiting, there at Booth's Landing, and just in the edge of the evening she started over with her nigger woman in the horse-ferry, to stay all night at her friend's house, Miss What-you-may-call-her, I disremember her name, and they lost their steering-oar, and swung around and went a-floating down, stern-first, about two mile, and saddle-baggsed on the wreck, and the ferry man and the nigger woman and the horses was all lost, but Miss Hooker she made a grab and got aboard the wreck. Well, about an hour after dark, we come along down in our trading-scow, and it was so dark we didn't notice the wreck till we was right on it; and so *we* saddle-baggsed; but all of us was saved but Bill Whipple—and oh, he *was* the best cretur!—I most wish't it had been me, I do."

"My George! It's the beatenest thing I ever struck. And *then* what did you all do?"

"Well, we hollered and took on, but it's so wide there, we couldn't make nobody hear. So pap said somebody got to get ashore and get help somehow. I was the only one that could swim, so I made a dash for it, and Miss Hooker she said if I didn't strike help sooner, come here and hunt up her uncle, and he'd fix the thing. I made the land about a mile below, and been fooling along ever since, trying to get people to do something, but they said, 'What, in such a night and such a current? there ain't no sense in it; go for the steam-ferry.' Now if you'll go, and ——"

"By Jackson, I'd *like* to, and blame it I don't know but I will; but who in the dingnation's agoin' to *pay* for it? Do you reckon your pap——"

"Why *that's* all right. Miss Hooker she told me, *particular*, that her uncle Hornback——"

"Great guns! is *he* her uncle? Looky here, you break for that light over yonder-way, and turn out west when you git there, and about a quarter of a mile out you'll come to the tavern; tell 'em to dart you out to Jim Hornback's and he'll foot the bill. And don't you fool around any, because he'll want to know the news. Tell him I'll have his niece all safe before he can get to town. Hump yourself, now; I'm agoing up around the corner here, to roust out my engineer."

I struck for the light, but as soon as he turned the corner I went back and got into my skiff and bailed her out and then pulled up shore in the easy water about six hundred yards, and tucked myself in among some woodboats; for I couldn't rest easy till I could see the ferry-boat start. But take it all around, I was feeling ruther comfortable on accounts of taking all this trouble for that gang, for not many would a done it. I wished the widow knowed about it. I judged she would be proud of me for helping these rapscallions, because rapscallions and dead beats is the kind the widow and good people takes the most interest in.

Well, before long, here comes the wreck, dim and dusky, sliding along down! A kind of cold shiver went through me, and then I struck out for her. She was very deep, and I see in a minute there warn't much chance for anybody being alive in her. I pulled all around her and hollered a little, but there wasn't any answer; all dead still. I felt a little bit heavy-hearted about the gang, but not much, for I reckoned if they could stand it, I could.

Then here comes the ferry-boat; so I shoved for the middle of the river on a long down-stream slant; and when I judged I was out of eye-reach, I laid on my oars, and looked back and see her go and smell around the wreck for Miss Hooker's remainders, because the captain would know her uncle Hornback would want them; and then pretty soon the ferry-boat give it up and went for shore, and I laid into my work and went a-booming down the river.

It did seem a powerful long time before Jim's light showed up; and when it did show, it looked like it was a thousand mile off. By the time I got there the sky was beginning to get a little gray in the east; so we struck for an island, and hid the raft, and sunk the skiff, and turned in and slept like dead people.

Chapter XIV

BY-AND-BY, WHEN WE got up, we turned over the truck the gang had stole off of the wreck, and found boots, and blankets, and clothes, and all sorts of other things, and a lot of books, and a spyglass, and three boxes of seegars. We hadn't ever been this rich before, in neither of our lives. The seegars was prime. We laid off all the afternoon in the woods talking, and me reading the books, and having a general good time. I told Jim all about what happened inside the wreck, and at the ferry-boat; and I said these kinds of things was adventures; but he

WE TURNED IN AND SLEPT.

said he didn't want no more adventures. He said that when I went in the texas and he crawled back to get on the raft and found her gone, he nearly died; because he judged it was all up with *him*, anyway it could be fixed; for if he didn't get saved he would get drownded; and if he did get saved, whoever saved him would send him back home so as to get the reward, and then Miss Watson would sell him South, sure. Well, he was right; he was most always right; he had an uncommon level head, for a nigger.

I read considerable to Jim about kings, and dukes, and earls, and such, and how gaudy they dressed, and how much style they put on, and called each other your majesty, and your grace, and your lordship, and so on, 'stead of mister; and Jim's eyes bugged out, and he was interested. He says:

"I didn' know dey was so many un um. I hain't hearn 'bout none un um, skasely, but ole King Sollermun, onless you counts dem kings dat's in a pack er k'yards. How much do a king git?"

"Get?" I says; "why, they get a thousand dollars a month if they want it; they can have just as much as they want; everything belongs to them."

"*Ain'* dat gay? En what dey got to do, Huck?"

"*They* don't do nothing! Why how you talk. They just set around."

"No—is dat so?"

"Of course it is. They just set around. Except maybe when there's a war; then they go to the war. But other times they just lazy around; or go hawking— just hawking and sp— Sh!—d' you hear a noise?"

We skipped out and looked; but it warn't nothing but the flutter of a steamboat's wheel, away down coming around the point; so we come back.

"Yes," says I, "and other times, when things is dull, they fuss with the parlyment; and if everybody don't go just so he whacks their heads off. But mostly they hang round the harem."

"Roun' de which?"

"Harem."

"What's de harem?"

"The place where he keep his wives. Don't you know about the harem? Solomon had one; he had about a million wives."

"Why, yes, dat's so; I—I'd done forgot it. A harem's a bo'd'n-house, I reck'n. Mos' likely dey has rackety times in de nussery. En I reck'n de wives quarrels considable; en dat 'crease de racket. Yit dey say Sollermun de wises' man dat ever live'. I doan' take no stock in dat. Bekase why: would a wise man want to live in de mids' er sich a blimblammin' all de time? No—'deed he wouldn't. A wise man 'ud take en buil' a biler-factry; en den he could shet *down* de biler-factry when he want to res'."

"Well, but he *was* the wisest man, anyway; because the widow she told me so, her own self."

"I doan k'yer what de widder say, he *warn't* no wise man, nuther. He had some er de dad-fetchedes' ways I ever see. Does you know 'bout dat chile dat he 'uz gwyne to chop in two?"

"Yes, the widow told me all about it."

"*Well*, den! Warn' dat de beatenes' notion in de worl'? You jes' take en look at it a minute. Dah's de stump, dah—dat's one er de women: heah's you—dat's de yuther one; I's Sollermun; en dish-yer dollar bill's de chile. Bofe un you claims it. What does I do? Does I shin aroun' mongs' de neighbors en fine out which un you de bill *do* b'long to, en han' it over to de right one, all safe en soun', de way dat anybody dat had any gumption would? No—I take en whack de bill in *two*, en give half un it to you, en de yuther half to de yuther woman. Dat's de way Sollermun was gwyne to do wid de chile. Now I want to ast you: what's de use er dat half a bill?—can't buy noth'n wid it. En what use is a half a chile? I would'n give a dern for a million un um.''

''But hang it, Jim, you've clean missed the point—blame it, you've missed it a thousand mile.''

''Who? Me? Go 'long. Doan' talk to *me* 'bout yo' pints. I reck'n I knows sense when I sees it; en dey ain' no sense in sich doin's as dat. De 'spute warn't 'bout a half a chile, de 'spute was 'bout a whole chile; en de man dat think he kin settle a 'spute 'bout a whole chile wid a half a chile, doan' know enough to come in out'n de rain. Doan' talk to me 'bout Sollermun, Huck, I knows him by de back.''

''But I tell you you don't get the point.''

''Blame de pint! I reck'n I knows what I knows. En mine you, de *real* pint is down furder—it's down deeper. It lays in de way Sollermun was raised. You take a man dat's got on'y one er two chillen; is dat man gwyne to be waseful o' chillen? No, he ain't; he can't 'ford it. *He* know how to value 'em. But you take a man dat's got 'bout five million chillen runnin' roun' de house, en it's diffunt. *He* as soon chop a chile in two as a cat. Dey's plenty mo'. A chile er two, mo' er less, warn't no consekens to Sollermun, dad fetch him!''

I never see such a nigger. If he got a notion in his head once, there warn't no getting it out again. He was the most down on Solomon of any nigger I ever see. So I went to talking about other kings, and let Solomon slide. I told about Louis Sixteenth that got his head cut off in France long time age; and about his little boy the dolphin, that would a been a king, but they took and shut him up in jail, and some say he died there.

''Po' little chap.''

''But some says he got out and got away, and come to America.''

''Dat's good! But he'll be pooty lonesome—dey ain' no kings here, is dey, Huck?''

''No.''

''Den he cain't git no situation. What he gwyne to do?''

THE STORY OF '' SOLLERMUN.''

"Well, I don't know. Some of them gets on the police, and some of them learns people how to talk French."

"Why, Huck, doan' de French people talk de same way we does?"

"*No*, Jim; you couldn't understand a word they said—not a single word."

"Well, now, I be ding-busted! How do dat come?"

"*I* don't know; but it's so. I got some of their jabber out of a book. Spose a man was to come to you and say *Polly-voo-franzy*—what would you think?"

"I wouldn' think nuff'n; I'd take en bust him over de head. Dat is, if he warn't white. I wouldn't 'low no nigger to call me dat."

"Shucks, it ain't calling you anything. It's only saying do you know how to talk French."

"Well, den, why couldn't he *say* it?"

"Why, he *is* a-saying it. That's a Frenchman's *way* of saying it."

"Well, it's a blame' ridicklous way, en I doan' want to hear no mo' 'bout it. Dey ain' no sense in it."

"Looky here, Jim; does a cat talk like we do?"

"No, a cat don't."

"Well, does a cow?"

"No, a cow don't, nuther."

"Does a cat talk like a cow, or a cow talk like a cat?"

"No, dey don't."

"It's natural and right for 'em to talk different from each other, ain't it?"

"'Course."

"And ain't it natural and right for a cat and a cow to talk different from *us?*"

"Why, mos' sholy it is."

"Well, then, why ain't it natural and right for a *Frenchman* to talk different from us? You answer me that."

"Is a cat a man, Huck?"

"No."

"Well, den, dey ain't no sense in a cat talkin' like a man. Is a cow a man?—er is a cow a cat?"

"No, she ain't either of them."

"Well, den, she ain' got no business to talk like either one er the yuther of 'em. Is a Frenchman a man?"

"Yes."

"*Well*, den! Dad blame it, why doan' he *talk* like a man? You answer me *dat!*"

I see it warn't no use wasting words—you can't learn a nigger to argue. So I quit.

Chapter XV

WE JUDGED THAT three nights more would fetch us to Cairo, at the bottom of Illinois, where the Ohio River comes in, and that was what we was after. We would sell the raft and get on a steamboat and go way up the Ohio amongst the free States, and then be out of trouble.

Well, the second night a fog begun to come on, and we made for a tow-head to tie to, for it wouldn't do to try to run in fog; but when I paddled ahead in the canoe, with the line, to make fast, there warn't anything but little saplings to tie to. I passed the line around one of them right on the edge of the cut bank, but there was a stiff current, and the raft come booming down so lively she tore it out by the roots and away she went. I see the fog closing down, and it made me so sick and scared I couldn't budge for most a half a minute it seemed to me—and then there warn't no raft in sight; you couldn't see twenty yards. I jumped into the canoe and run back to the stern and grabbed the paddle and set her back a stroke. But she didn't come. I was in such a hurry I hadn't untied her. I got up and tried to untie her, but I was so excited my hands shook so I couldn't hardly do anything with them.

As soon as I got started I took out after the raft, hot and heavy, right down the tow-head. That was all right as far as it went, but the tow-head warn't sixty yards long, and the minute I flew by the foot of it I shot out into the solid white fog, and hadn't no more idea which way I was going than a dead man.

Thinks I, it won't do to paddle; first I know I'll run into the bank or a tow-head or something; I got to set still and float, and yet it's mighty fidgety business to have to hold your hands still at such a time. I whooped and listened. Away down there, somewheres, I hears a small whoop, and up comes my spirits. I went tearing after it, listening sharp to hear it again. The next time it come, I see I warn't heading for it but heading away to the right of it. And the next time, I was heading away to the left of it—and not gaining on it much, either, for I was flying around, this way and that and 'tother, but it was going straight ahead all the time.

I did wish the fool would think to beat a tin pan, and beat it all the time, but he never did, and it was the still places between the whoops that was making the trouble for me. Well, I fought along, and directly I hears the whoop *behind* me. I was tangled good, now. That was somebody else's whoop, or else I was turned around.

I throwed the paddle down. I heard the whoop again; it was behind me yet, but in a different place; it kept coming, and kept changing its place, and I kept answering, till by-and-by it was in front of me again and I knowed the current had swung the canoe's head down stream and I was all right, if that was Jim and not some other raftsman hollering. I couldn't tell nothing about voices in a fog, for nothing don't look natural nor sound natural in a fog.

The whooping went on, and in about a minute I come a booming down on a cut bank with smoky ghosts of big trees on it, and the current throwed me off to the left and shot by, amongst a lot of snags that fairly roared, the current was tearing by them so swift.

In another second or two it was solid white and still again. I set perfectly still, then, listening to my heart thump, and I reckon I didn't draw a breath while it thumped a hundred.

I just give up, then I knowed what the matter was. That cut bank was an island, and Jim had gone down 'tother side of it. It warn't no tow-head, that you could float by in ten minutes. It had the big timber of a regular island; it might be five or six mile long and more than a half a mile wide.

I kept quiet, with my ears cocked, about fifteen minutes, I reckon. I was floating along, of course, four or five mile an hour; but you don't ever think of that. No, you *feel* like you are laying dead still on the water; and if a little glimpse of a snag slips by, you don't think to yourself how fast *you're* going, but you catch your breath and think, my! how that snag's tearing along. If you think it ain't dismal and lonesome out in a fog that way, by yourself, in the night, you try it once—you'll see.

Next, for about a half an hour, I whoops now and then; at last I hears the answer a long ways off, and tries to follow it, but I couldn't do it, and directly I judged I'd got into a nest of tow-heads, for I had little dim glimpses of them on both sides of me, sometimes just a narrow channel between; and some that I couldn't see, I knowed was there, because I'd hear the wash of the current against the old dead brush and trash that hung over the banks. Well, I warn't long losing the whoops, down amongst the tow-heads; and I only tried to chase them a little while, anyway, because it was worse than chasing a Jack-o-lantern. You never knowed a sound dodge around so, and swap places so quick and so much.

I had to claw away from the bank pretty lively, four or five times, to keep from knocking the islands out of the river; and so I judged the raft must be butting into the bank every now and then, or else it would get further ahead and clear out of hearing—it was floating a little faster than what I was.

Well, I seemed to be in the open river again, by-and-by, but I couldn't hear no sign of a whoop nowheres. I reckoned Jim had fetched up on a snag, maybe, and it was all up with him. I was good and tired, so I laid down in the canoe and said I wouldn't bother no more. I didn't want to go to sleep, of course; but I was so sleepy I couldn't help it; so I thought I would take just one little cat-nap.

But I reckon it was more than a cat-nap, for when I waked up the stars was shining bright, the fog was all gone, and I was spinning down a big bend stern first. First I didn't know where I was; I thought I was dreaming; and when things begun to come back to me, they seemed to come up dim out of last week.

It was a monstrous big river here, with the tallest and the thickest kind of timber on both banks; just a solid wall, as well as I could see, by the stars. I looked away down stream, and seen a black speck on the water. I took out after it; but when I got to it it warn't nothing but a couple of saw-logs made fast together. Then I see another speck, and chased that; then another, and this time I was right. It was the raft.

ASLEEP ON THE RAFT.

When I got to it Jim was setting there with his head down between his knees, asleep, with his right arm hanging over the steering oar. The other oar was smashed off, and the raft was littered up with leaves and branches and dirt. So she'd had a rough time.

I made fast and laid down under Jim's nose on the raft, and begun to gap, and stretch my fists out against Jim, and says:

"Hello, Jim, have I been asleep? Why didn't you stir me up?"

"Goodness gracious, is dat you, Huck? En you ain' dead—you ain' drownded—you's back agin? It's too good for true, honey, it's too good for true. Lemme look at you, chile, lemme feel o' you. No, you ain' dead! you's back agin, 'live en soun', jis de same ole Huck—de same ole Huck, thanks to goodness!"

"What's the matter with you, Jim? You been a drinking?"

"Drinkin'? Has I ben a drinkin'? Has I had a chance to be a drinkin'?"

"Well, then, what makes you talk so wild?"

"How does I talk wild?"

"*How?* why, hain't you been talking about my coming back, and all that stuff, as if I'd been gone away?"

"Huck—Huck Finn, you look me in de eye; look me in de eye. *Hain't* you ben gone away?"

"Gone away? Why, what in the nation do you mean? *I* hain't been gone anywheres. Where would I go to?"

"Well, looky here, boss, dey's sumf'n wrong, dey is. Is I *me*, or who *is* I? Is I heah, or whah *is* I? Now dat's what I wants to know?"

"Well, I think you're here, plain enough, but I think you're a tangle-headed old fool, Jim."

"I is, is I? Well you answer me dis. Didn't you tote out de line in de canoe, fer to make fas' to de tow-head?"

"No, I didn't. What tow-head? I hain't seen no tow-head."

"You hain't seen no tow-head? Looky here—didn't de line pull loose en de raf' go a hummin' down de river, en leave you en de canoe behine in de fog?"

"What fog?"

"Why *de* fog. De fog dat's ben aroun' all night. En didn't you whoop, en didn't I whoop, tell we got mix' up in de islands en one un us got los' en 'tother one was jis' as good as los', 'kase he didn' know whah he wuz? En didn't I bust up agin a lot er dem islands en have a turrible time en mos' git drownded? Now ain' dat so, boss—ain' it so? You answer me dat."

"Well, this is too many for me, Jim. I hain't seen no fog, nor no islands, nor no troubles, nor nothing. I been setting here talking with you all night till you went to sleep about ten minutes ago, and I reckon I done the same. You couldn't a got drunk in that time, so of course you've been dreaming."

"Dad fetch it, how is I gwyne to dream all dat in ten minutes?"

"Well, hang it all, you did dream it, because there didn't any of it happen."

"But Huck, it's all jis' as plain to me as——"

"It don't make no difference how plain it is, there ain't nothing in it. I know, because I've been here all the time."

Jim didn't say nothing for about five minutes, but set there studying over it. Then he says:

"Well, den, I reck'n I did dream it, Huck; but dog my cats ef it ain't de powerfullest dream I ever see. En I hain't ever had no dream b'fo' dat's tired me like dis one."

"Oh, well, that's all right, because a dream does tire a body like everything, sometimes. But this one was a staving dream—tell me all about it, Jim."

So Jim went to work and told me the whole thing right through, just as it happened, only he painted it up considerable. Then he said he must start in and "'terpret" it, because it was sent for a warning. He said the first tow-head stood for a man that would try to do us some good, but the current was another man that would get us away from him. The whoops was warnings that would come to us every now and then, and if we didn't try hard to make out to understand them they'd just take us into bad luck, 'stead of keeping us out of it. The lot of tow-heads was troubles we was going to get into with quarrelsome people and all kinds of mean folks, but if we minded our business and didn't talk back and aggravate them, we would pull through and get out of the fog and into the big clear river, which was the free States, and wouldn't have no more trouble.

It had clouded up pretty dark just after I got onto the raft, but it was clearing up again, now.

"Oh, well, that's all interpreted well enough, as far as it goes, Jim," I says; "but what does *these* things stand for?"

It was the leaves and rubbish on the raft, and the smashed oar. You could see them first rate, now.

Jim looked at the trash, and then looked at me, and back at the trash again. He had got the dream fixed so strong in his head that he couldn't seem to shake it loose and get the facts back into its place again, right away. But when he did get the thing straightened around, he looked at me steady, without ever smiling, and says:

"What do dey stan' for? I's gwyne to tell you. When I got all wore out wid work, en wid de callin' for you, en went to sleep, my heart wuz mos' broke bekase you wuz los', en I didn' k'yer no mo' what become er me en de raf'. En when I wake up en fine you back agin', all safe en soun', de tears come en I could a got down on my knees en kiss' yo' foot I's so thankful. En all you wuz thinkin 'bout wuz how you could make a fool uv ole Jim wid a lie. Dat truck dah is *trash;* en trash is what people is dat puts dirt on de head er dey fren's en makes 'em ashamed."

Then he got up slow, and walked to the wigwam, and went in there, without saying anything but that. But that was enough. It made me feel so mean I could almost kissed *his* foot to get him to take it back.

It was fifteen minutes before I could work myself up to go and humble myself to a nigger—but I done it, and I warn't ever sorry for it afterwards, neither. I didn't do him no more mean tricks, and I wouldn't done that one if I'd a knowed it would make him feel that way.

Chapter XVI

WE SLEPT MOST all day, and started out at night, a little ways behind a monstrous long raft that was as long going by as a procession. She had four long sweeps at each end, so we judged she carried as many as thirty men, likely. She had five big wigwams aboard, wide apart, and an open camp fire in the middle, and a tall flag-pole at each end. There was a power of style about her. It *amounted* to something being a raftsman on such a craft as that.

We went drifting down into a big bend, and the night clouded up and got hot. The river was very wide, and was walled with solid timber on both sides; you couldn't see a break in it hardly ever, or a light. We talked about Cairo, and wondered whether we would know it when we got to it. I said likely we wouldn't, because I had heard say there warn't but about a dozen houses there, and if they didn't happen to have them lit up, how was we going to know we was passing a town? Jim said if the two big rivers joined together there, that would show. But I said maybe we might think we was passing the foot of an island and coming into the same old river again. That disturbed Jim—and me too. So the question was, what to do? I said, paddle ashore the first time a light showed, and tell them pap was behind, coming along with a trading-scow, and was a green hand at the business, and wanted to know how far it was to Cairo. Jim thought it was a good idea, so we took a smoke on it and waited.

There warn't nothing to do, now, but to look out sharp for the town, and not pass it without seeing it. He said he'd be mighty sure to see it, because he'd be a free man the minute he seen it, but if he missed it he'd be in the slave country again and no more show for freedom. Every little while he jumps up and says:

"Dah she is!"

But it warn't. It was Jack-o-lanterns, or lightning-bugs; so he set down again, and went to watching, same as before. Jim said it made him all over trembly and feverish to be so close to freedom. Well, I can tell you it made me all over trembly and feverish, too, to hear him, because I begun to get it through my head that he *was* most free—and who was to blame for it? Why, *me*. I couldn't get that out of my conscience, no how nor no way. It got to troubling me so I couldn't rest; I couldn't stay still in one place. It hadn't ever come home to me before, what this thing was that I was doing. But now it did; and it staid with me, and scorched me more and more. I tried to make out to myself that *I* warn't to blame, because *I* didn't run Jim off from his rightful owner; but it warn't no use, conscience up and says, every time, "But you knowed he was running for

" IT AMOUNTED TO SOMETHING BEING A RAFTSMAN."

his freedom, and you could a paddled ashore and told somebody.'' That was so—I couldn't get around that, noway. That was where it pinched. Conscience says to me, ''What had poor Miss Watson done to you, that you could see her nigger go off right under your eyes and never say one single word? What did that poor old woman do to you, that you could treat her so mean? Why, she tried to learn you your book, she tried to learn you your manners, she tried to be good to you every way she knowed how. *That's* what she done.''

I got to feeling so mean and so miserable I most wished I was dead. I fidgeted up and down the raft, abusing myself to myself, and Jim was fidgeting up and down past me. We neither of us could keep still. Every time he danced around and says, ''Dah's Cairo!'' it went through me like a shot, and I thought if it *was* Cairo I reckoned I would die of miserableness.

Jim talked out loud all the time while I was talking to myself. He was saying how the first thing he would do when he got to a free State he would go to saving up money and never spend a single cent, and when he got enough he would buy his wife, which was owned on a farm close to where Miss Watson lived; and then they would both work to buy the two children, and if their master wouldn't sell them, they'd get an Ab'litionist to go and steal them.

It most froze me to hear such talk. He wouldn't ever dared to talk such talk in his life before. Just see what a difference it made in him the minute he judged he was about free. It was according to the old saying, ''give a nigger an inch and he'll take an ell.'' Thinks I, this is what comes of my not thinking. Here was this nigger which I had as good as helped to run away, coming right out flat-footed and saying he would steal his children—children that belonged to a man I didn't even know; a man that hadn't ever done me no harm.

I was sorry to hear Jim say that, it was such a lowering of him. My conscience got to stirring me up hotter than ever, until at last I says to it, ''Let up on me— it ain't too late, yet—I'll paddle ashore at the first light, and tell.'' I felt easy, and happy, and light as a feather, right off. All my troubles was gone. I went to looking out sharp for a light, and sort of singing to myself. By-and-by one showed. Jim sings out:

''We's safe, Huck, we's safe! Jump up and crack yo' heels, dat's de good ole Cairo at las', I jis knows it!''

I says:

''I'll take the canoe and go see, Jim. It mightn't be, you know.''

He jumped and got the canoe ready, and put his old coat in the bottom for me to set on, and give me the paddle; and as I shoved off, he says:

''Pooty soon I'll be a-shout'n for joy, en I'll say, it's all on accounts o' Huck; I's a free man, en I couldn't ever ben free ef it hadn' ben for Huck; Huck done it. Jim won't ever forgit you, Huck; you's de bes' fren' Jim's ever had; en you's de *only* fren' ole Jim's got now.''

I was paddling off, all in a sweat to tell on him; but when he says this, it seemed to kind of take the tuck all out of me. I went along slow then, and I warn't right down certain whether I was glad I started or whether I warn't. When I was fifty yards off, Jim says:

''Dah you goes, de ole true Huck; de on'y white genlman dat ever kep' his promise to ole Jim.''

Well, I just felt sick. But I says, I *got* to do it—I can't get *out* of it. Right then, along comes a skiff with two men in it, with guns, and they stopped and I stopped. One of them says:

"What's that, yonder?"

"A piece of a raft," I says.

"Do you belong on it?"

"Yes, sir."

"Any men on it?"

"Only one, sir."

"Well, there's five niggers run off to-night, up yonder above the head of the bend. Is your man white or black?"

I didn't answer up prompt. I tried to, but the words wouldn't come. I tried, for a second or two, to brace up and out with it, but I warn't man enough—hadn't the spunk of a rabbit. I see I was weakening; so I just give up trying, and up and says—

"He's white."

"I reckon we'll go and see for ourselves."

"I wish you would," says I, "because it's pap that's there, and maybe you'd help me tow the raft ashore where the light is. He's sick—and so is mam and Mary Ann."

"Oh, the devil! we're in a hurry, boy. But I s'pose we've got to. Come—buckle to your paddle, and let's get along."

I buckled to my paddle and they laid to their oars. When we had made a stroke or two, I says:

"Pap'll be mighty much obleeged to you, I can tell you. Everybody goes away when I want them to help me tow the raft ashore, and I can't do it by myself."

"Well, that's infernal mean. Odd, too. Say, boy, what's the matter with your father?"

"It's the—a—the—well, it ain't anything, much."

They stopped pulling. It warn't but a mighty little ways to the raft, now. One says:

"Boy, that's a lie. What *is* the matter with your pap? Answer up square, now, and it'll be the better for you."

"I will, sir, I will, honest—but don't leave us, please. It's the—the—gentlemen, if you'll only pull ahead, and let me heave you the head-line, you won't have to come a-near the raft—please do."

"Set her back, John, set her back!" says one. They backed water. "Keep away, boy—keep to looard. Confound it, I just expect the wind has blowed it to us. Your pap's got the small-pox, and you know it precious well. Why didn't you come out and say so? Do you want to spread it all over?"

"Well," says I, a-blubbering, "I've told everybody before, and then they just went away and left us."

"Poor devil, there's something in that. We are right down sorry for you, but we—well, hang it, we don't want the small-pox, you see. Look here, I'll tell you what to do. Don't you try to land by yourself, or you'll smash everything to pieces. You float along down about twenty miles and you'll come to a town on the left-hand side of the river. It will be long after sun-up, then, and when you ask for help, you tell them your folks are all down with chills and fever. Don't be a fool again, and let people guess what is the matter. Now we're trying to do you a kindness; so you just put twenty miles between us, that's a good boy. It wouldn't do any good to land yonder where the light is—it's only a wood-yard. Say—I reckon your father's poor, and I'm bound to say he's in pretty hard luck. Here—I'll put a twenty dollar gold piece on this board, and you get it when it floats by. I feel mighty mean to leave you, but my kingdom! it won't do to fool with small-pox, don't you see?''

"Hold on, Parker," says the other man, "here's a twenty to put on the board for me. Good-bye, boy, you do as Mr. Parker told you, and you'll be all right.''

"That's so, my boy—good-bye, good-bye. If you see any runaway niggers, you get help and nab them, and you can make some money by it.''

"Good-bye, sir," says I, "I won't let no runaway niggers get by me if I can help it.''

They went off, and I got aboard the raft, feeling bad and low, because I knowed very well I had done wrong, and I see it warn't no use for me to try to learn to do right; a body that don't get *started* right when he's little, ain't got no show—when the pinch comes there ain't nothing to back him up and keep him to his work, and so he gets beat. Then I thought a minute, and says to myself, hold on,—spose you'd a done right and give Jim up; would you felt better than what you do now? No, says I, I'd feel bad—I'd feel just the same way I do now. Well, then, says I, what's the use you learning to do right, when it's troublesome to do right and ain't no trouble to do wrong, and the wages is just the same? I was stuck. I couldn't answer that. So I reckoned I wouldn't bother no more about it, but after this always do whichever come handiest at the time.

I went into the wigwam; Jim warn't there. I looked all around; he warn't anywhere. I says:

"Jim!"

"Here I is, Huck. Is dey out o' sight yit? Don't talk loud.''

He was in the river, under the stern oar, with just his nose out. I told him they was out of sight, so he come aboard. He says:

"I was a-listenin' to all de talk, en I slips into de river en was gwyne to shove for sho' if dey come aboard. Den I was gwyne to swim to de raf' agin when dey was gone. But lawsy, how you did fool 'em, Huck! Dat *wuz* de smartes' dodge! I tell you, chile, I 'speck it save' ole Jim—ole Jim ain't gwyne to forgit you for dat, honey.''

Then we talked about the money. It was a pretty good raise, twenty dollars apiece. Jim said we could take deck passage on a steamboat now, and the money would last us as far as we wanted to go in the free States. He said twenty mile more warn't far for the raft to go, but he wished we was already there.

Towards daybreak we tied up, and Jim was mighty particular about hiding the raft good. Then he worked all day fixing things in bundles, and getting all ready to quit rafting.

That night about ten we hove in sight of the lights of a town away down in a left-hand bend.

I went off in the canoe, to ask about it. Pretty soon I found a man out in the river with a skiff, setting a trot-line. I ranged up and says:

"Mister, is that town Cairo?''

"Cairo? no. You must be a blame' fool.''

"What town is it, mister?''

"If you want to know, go and find out. If you stay here botherin' around me for about a half a minute longer, you'll get something you won't want.''

I paddled to the raft. Jim was awful disappointed, but I said never mind, Cairo would be the next place, I reckoned.

We passed another town before daylight, and I was going out again; but it was high ground, so I didn't go. No high ground about Cairo, Jim said. I had forgot it. We laid up for the day, on a tow-head tolerable close to the left-hand bank. I begun to suspicion something. So did Jim. I says:

"Maybe we went by Cairo in the fog that night."

He says:

"Doan' less' talk about it, Huck. Po' niggers can't have no luck. I awluz 'spected dat rattle-snake skin warn't done wid it's work."

"I wish I'd never seen that snake-skin, Jim—I do wish I'd never laid eyes on it."

"It ain't yo' fault, Huck; you didn' know. Don't you blame yo'self 'bout it."

When it was daylight, here was the clear Ohio water in shore, sure enough, and outside was the old regular Muddy! So it was all up with Cairo.

We talked it all over. It wouldn't do to take to the shore; we couldn't take the raft up the stream, of course. There warn't no way but to wait for dark, and start back in the canoe and take the chances. So we slept all day amongst the cotton-wood thicket, so as to be fresh for the work, and when we went back to the raft about dark the canoe was gone!

We didn't say a word for a good while. There warn't anything to say. We both knowed well enough it was some more work of the rattle-snake skin; so what was the use to talk about it? It would only look like we was finding fault, and that would be bound to fetch more bad luck—and keep on fetching it, too, till we knowed enough to keep still.

By-and-by we talked about what we better do, and found there warn't no way but just to go along down with the raft till we got a chance to buy a canoe to go back in. We warn't going to borrow it when there warn't anybody around, the way pap would do, for that might set people after us.

So we shoved out, after dark, on the raft.

Anybody that don't believe yet, that it's foolishness to handle a snake-skin, after all that that snake-skin done for us, will believe it now, if they read on and see what more it done for us.

The place to buy canoes is off of rafts laying up at shore. But we didn't see no rafts laying up; so we went along during three hours and more. Well, the night got gray, and ruther thick, which is the next meanest thing to fog. You can't tell the shape of the river, and you can't see no distance. It got to be very late and still, and then along comes a steamboat up the river. We lit the lantern, and judged she would see it. Up-stream boats didn't generly come close to us; they go out and follow the bars and hunt for easy water under the reefs; but nights like this they bull right up the channel against the whole river.

We could hear her pounding along, but we didn't see her good till she was close. She aimed right for us. Often they do that and try to see how close they can come without touching; sometimes the wheel bites off a sweep, and then the pilot sticks his head out and laughs, and thinks he's mighty smart. Well, here she comes, and we said she was going to try to shave us; but she didn't seem to be sheering off a bit. She was a big one, and she was coming in a hurry, too, looking like a black cloud with rows of glow-worms around it; but all of a sudden she bulged out, big and scary, with a long row of wide-open furnace doors shining like red-hot teeth, and her monstrous bows and guards hanging right over us. There was a yell at us, and a jingling of bells to stop the engines, a pow-wow of cussing, and whistling of steam—and as Jim went overboard on one side and I on the other, she come smashing straight through the raft.

I dived—and I aimed to find the bottom, too, for a thirty-foot wheel had got to go over me, and I wanted it to have plenty of room. I could always stay under water a minute; this time I reckon I staid under water a minute and a half. Then I bounced for the top in a hurry, for I was nearly busting. I popped out to my arm-pits and blowed the water out of my nose, and puffed a bit. Of course there was a booming current; and of course that boat started her engines again ten seconds after she stopped them, for they never cared much for raftsmen; so now she was churning along up the river, out of sight in the thick weather, though I could hear her.

I sung out for Jim about a dozen times, but I didn't get any answer; so I grabbed a plank that touched me while I was "treading water," and struck out for shore, shoving it ahead of me. But I made out to see that the drift of the current was towards the left-hand shore, which meant that I was in a crossing; so I changed off and went that way.

It was one of these long, slanting, two-mile crossings; so I was a good long time in getting over. I made a safe landing, and clum up the bank. I couldn't see but a little ways, but I went poking along over rough ground for a quarter of a mile or more, and then I run across a big old-fashioned double log house before I noticed it. I was going to rush by and get away, but a lot of dogs jumped out and went to howling and barking at me, and I knowed better than to move another peg.

Chapter XVII

IN ABOUT HALF a minute somebody spoke out of a window, without putting his head out, and says:

"Be done, boys! Who's there?"

I says:

"It's me."

"Who's me?"

"George Jackson, sir."

"What do you want?"

"I don't want nothing, sir. I only want to go along by, but the dogs won't let me."

"What are you prowling around here this time of night, for—hey?"

"I warn't prowling around, sir; I fell overboard off of the steamboat."

"Oh, you did, did you? Strike a light there, somebody. What did you say your name was?"

"George Jackson, sir. I'm only a boy."

"Look here; if you're telling the truth, you needn't be afraid—nobody'll hurt you. But don't try to budge; stand right where you are. Rouse out Bob and Tom, some of you, and fetch the guns. George Jackson, is there anybody with you?"

"No, sir, nobody."

I heard the people stirring around in the house, now, and see a light. The man sung out:

"Snatch that light away, Betsy, you old fool—ain't you got any sense? Put it on the floor behind the front door. Bob, if you and Tom are ready, take your places."

"All ready."

"Now, George Jackson, do you know the Shepherdsons?"

"No, sir—I never heard of them."

"Well, that may be so, and it mayn't. Now, all ready. Step forward, George Jackson. And mind, don't you hurry—come mighty slow. If there's anybody with you, let him keep back—if he shows himself he'll be shot. Come along, now. Come slow; push the door open, yourself—just enough to squeeze in, d' you hear?"

I didn't hurry, I couldn't if I'd a wanted to. I took one slow step at a time, and there warn't a sound, only I thought I could hear my heart. The dogs were as still as the humans, but they followed a little behind me. When I got to the three log door-steps, I heard them unlocking and unbarring and unbolting. I put my hand on the door and pushed it a little and a little more, till somebody said, "There, that's enough—put your head in." I done it, but I judged they would take it off.

The candle was on the floor, and there they all was, looking at me, and me at them, for about a quarter of a minute. Three big men with guns pointed at me, which made me wince, I tell you; the oldest, gray and about sixty, the other two thirty or more—all of them fine and handsome—and the sweetest old gray-headed lady, and back of her two young women which I couldn't see right well. The old gentleman says:

"There—I reckon it's all right. Come in."

As soon as I was in, the old gentleman he locked the door and barred it and bolted it, and told the young men to come in with their guns, and they all went in a big parlor that had a new rag carpet on the floor, and got together in a corner that was out of range of the front windows—there warn't none on the side. They held the candle, and took a good look at me, and all said, "Why *he* ain't a Shepherdson—no, there ain't any Shepherdson about him." Then the old man said he hoped I wouldn't mind being searched for arms, because he didn't mean no harm by it—it was only to make sure. So he didn't pry into my pockets, but only felt outside with his hands, and said it was all right. He told me to make myself easy and at home, and tell all about myself; but the old lady says:

"Why bless you, Saul, the poor thing's as wet as he can be; and don't you reckon it may be he's hungry?"

"True for you, Rachel—I forgot."

So the old lady says:

"Betsy" (this was a nigger woman), "you fly around and get him something to eat, as quick as you can, poor thing; and one of you girls go and wake up Buck and tell him— Oh, here he is himself. Buck, take this little stranger and get the wet clothes off from him and dress him up in some of yours that's dry."

Buck looked about as old as me—thirteen or fourteen or along there, though he was a little bigger than me. He hadn't on anything but a shirt, and he was very frowsy-headed. He come in gaping and digging one fist into his eyes, and he was dragging a gun along with the other one. He says:

"Ain't they no Shepherdsons around?"

They said, no, 'twas a false alarm.

"Well," he says, "if they'd a ben some, I reckon I'd a got one."

They all laughed, and Bob says:

"Why, Buck, they might have scalped us all, you've been so slow in coming."

"Well, nobody come after me, and it ain't right. I'm always kep' down; I don't get no show."

"Never mind, Buck, my boy," says the old man, "you'll have show enough, all in good time, don't you fret about that. Go 'long with you now, and do as your mother told you."

When we got up stairs to his room, he got me a coarse shirt and a roundabout and pants of his, and I put them on. While I was at it he asked me what my name was, but before I could tell him, he started to telling me about a blue jay and a young rabbit he had catched in the woods day before yesterday, and he asked me where Moses was when the candle went out. I said I didn't know; I hadn't heard about it before, no way.

"Well, guess," he says.

"How'm I going to guess," says I, "when I never heard tell about it before?"

"But you can guess, can't you? It's just as easy."

"*Which* candle?" I says.

"Why, any candle," he says.

"I don't know where he was," says I; "where was he?"

"Why he was in the *dark!* That's where he was!"

"Well, if you knowed where he was, what did you ask me for?"

"Why, blame it, it's a riddle, don't you see? Say, how long are you going to stay here? You got to stay always. We can just have booming times—they don't have no school now. Do you own a dog? I've got a dog—and he'll go in the river and bring out chips that you throw in. Do you like to comb up, Sundays, and all that kind of foolishness? You bet I don't, but ma she makes me. Confound these ole britches, I reckon I'd better put 'em on, but I'd ruther not, it's so warm. Are you all ready? All right—come along, old hoss."

Cold corn-pone, cold corn-beef, butter and butter-milk—that is what they had for me down there, and there ain't nothing better that ever I've come across yet. Buck and his ma and all of them smoked cob pipes, except the nigger woman, which was gone, and the two young women. They all smoked and talked, and I eat and talked. The young women had quilts around them, and their hair down their backs. They all asked me questions, and I told them how pap and me and all the family was living on a little farm down at the bottom of Arkansaw, and my sister Mary Ann run off and got married and never was heard of no more, and Bill went to hunt them and he warn't heard of no more, and Tom and Mort died, and then there warn't nobody but just me and pap left, and he was just trimmed down to nothing, on account of his troubles; so when he died I took what there was left, because the farm didn't belong to us, and started up the river, deck passage, and fell overboard; and that was how I come to be here. So they said I could have a home there as long as I wanted it. Then it was most daylight, and everybody went to bed, and I went to bed with Buck, and when I waked up in the morning, drat it all, I had forgot what my name was. So I laid there about an hour trying to think, and when Buck waked up, I says:

"Can you spell, Buck?"

"Yes," he says.

"I bet you can't spell my name," says I.

"I bet you what you dare I can," says he.

"All right," says I, "go ahead."

"G-o-r-g-e J-a-x-o-n—there now," he says.

"Well," says I, "you done it, but I didn't think you could. It ain't no slouch of a name to spell—right off without studying."

I set it down, private, because somebody might want *me* to spell it, next, and so I wanted to be handy with it and rattle it off like I was used to it.

It was a mighty nice family, and a mighty nice house, too. I hadn't seen no house out in the country before that was so nice and had so much style. It didn't have an iron latch on the front door, nor a wooden one with a buckskin string, but a brass knob to turn, the same as houses in a town. There warn't no bed in the parlor, not a sign of a bed; but heaps of parlors in towns has beds in them. There was a big fireplace that was bricked on the bottom, and the bricks was kept clean and red by pouring water on them and scrubbing them with another brick; sometimes they washed them over with red water-paint that they call Spanish-brown, same as they do in town. They had big brass dog-irons that could hold up a saw-log. There was a clock on the middle of the mantel-piece, with a picture of a town painted on the bottom half of the glass front, and a round place in the middle of it for the sun, and you could see the pendulum swing behind it. It was beautiful to hear that clock tick; and sometimes when one of these peddlers had been along and scoured her up and got her in good shape, she would start in and strike a hundred and fifty before she got tuckered out. They wouldn't took any money for her.

Well, there was a big outlandish parrot on each side of the clock, made out of something like chalk, and painted up gaudy. By one of the parrots was a cat made of crockery, and a crockery dog by the other; and when you pressed down on them they squeaked, but didn't open their mouths nor look different nor interested. They squeaked through underneath. There was a couple of big wild-turkey-wing fans spread out behind those things. On a table in the middle of the room was a kind of a lovely crockery basket that had apples and oranges and peaches and grapes piled up in it which was much redder and yellower and prettier than real ones is, but they warn't real because you could see where pieces had got chipped off and showed the white chalk or whatever it was, underneath.

This table had a cover made out of beautiful oil-cloth, with a red and blue spread-eagle painted on it, and a painted border all around. It come all the way from Philadelphia, they said. There was some books too, piled up perfectly exact, on each corner of the table. One was a big family Bible, full of pictures. One was "Pilgrim's Progress," about a man that left his family it didn't say why. I read considerable in it now and then. The statements was interesting, but tough. Another was "Friendship's Offering," full of beautiful stuff and poetry; but I didn't read the poetry. Another was Henry Clay's Speeches, and another was Dr. Gunn's Family Medicine, which told you all about what to do if a body was sick or dead. There was a Hymn Book, and a lot of other books. And there was nice split-bottom chairs, and perfectly sound, too—not bagged down in the middle and busted, like an old basket.

They had pictures hung on the walls—mainly Washingtons and Lafayettes, and battles, and Highland Marys, and one called "Signing the Declaration." There was some that they called crayons, which one of the daughters which was dead made her own self when she was only fifteen years old. They was different from any pictures I ever see before; blacker, mostly, than is common. One was a woman in a slim black dress, belted small under the arm-pits, with bulges like a cabbage in the middle of the sleeves, and a large black scoop-shovel bonnet with a black veil, and white slim ankles crossed about with black tape, and very wee black slippers, like a chisel, and she was leaning pensive on a tombstone on her right elbow, under a weeping willow, and her other hand hanging down her side holding a white handkerchief and a reticule, and underneath the picture it said "Shall I Never See Thee More Alas." Another one was a young lady with her hair all combed up straight to the top of her head, and knotted there in front of a comb like a chair-back, and she was crying into a handkerchief and had a dead bird laying on its back in her other hand with its heels up, and underneath the picture it said "I Shall Never Hear Thy Sweet Chirrup More Alas." There was one where a young lady was at a window looking up at the moon, and tears running down her cheeks; and she had an open letter in one hand with black sealing-wax showing on one edge of it, and she was mashing a locket with a chain to it against her mouth, and underneath the picture it said "And Art Thou Gone Yes Thou Art Gone Alas." These was all nice pictures, I reckon, but I didn't somehow seem to take to them, because if ever I was down a little, they always give me the fan-tods. Everybody was sorry she died, because she had laid out a lot more of these pictures to do, and a body could see by what she had done what they had lost. But I reckoned, that with her disposition, she was having a better time in the graveyard. She was at work on what they said was her greatest picture when she took sick, and every day and every night it was her prayer to be allowed to live till she got it done, but she never got the chance. It was a picture of a young woman in a long white gown, standing on the rail of a bridge all ready to jump off, with her hair all down her back, and looking up to the moon, with the tears running down her face, and she had two arms folded across her breast, and two arms stretched out in front, and two more reaching up towards the moon—and the idea was, to see which pair would look best and then scratch out all the other arms; but, as I was saying, she died before she got her mind made up, and now they kept this picture over the head of the bed in her room, and every time her birthday come they hung flowers on it. Other times it was hid with a little curtain. The young woman in the picture had a kind of a nice sweet face, but there was so many arms it made her look too spidery, seemed to me.

This young girl kept a scrap-book when she was alive, and used to paste obituaries and accidents and cases of patient suffering in it out of the *Presbyterian Observer*, and write poetry after them out of her own head. It was very good poetry. This is what she wrote about a boy by the name of Stephen Dowling Bots that fell down a well and was drownded:

ODE TO STEPHEN DOWLING BOTS,
DEC'D.

And did young Stephen sicken,
And did young Stephen die?
And did the sad hearts thicken,
And did the mourners cry?

No; such was not the fate of
Young Stephen Dowling Bots;

Though sad hearts round him thickened,
'Twas not from sickness' shots.

No whooping-cough did rack his frame,
Nor measles drear, with spots;
Not these impaired the sacred name
Of Stephen Dowling Bots.

Despised love struck not with woe
That head of curly knots,
Nor stomach troubles laid him low,
Young Stephen Dowling Bots.

O no. Then list with tearful eye,
Whilst I his fate do tell.
His soul did from this cold world fly,
By falling down a well.

They got him out and emptied him;
Alas it was too late;
His spirit was gone for to sport aloft
In the realms of the good and great.

If Emmeline Grangerford could make poetry like that before she was fourteen, there ain't no telling what she could a done by-and-by. Buck said she could rattle off poetry like nothing. She didn't ever have to stop to think. He said she would slap down a line, and if she couldn't find anything to rhyme with it she would just scratch it out and slap down another one, and go ahead. She warn't particular, she could write about anything you choose to give her to write about, just so it was sadful. Every time a man died, or a woman died, or a child died, she would be on hand with her "tribute" before he was cold. She called them tributes. The neighbors said it was the doctor first, then Emmeline, then the undertaker—the undertaker never got in ahead of Emmeline but once, and then

"THEY GOT HIM OUT AND EMPTIED HIM."

she hung fire on a rhyme for the dead person's name, which was Whistler. She warn't ever the same, after that; she never complained, but she kind of pined away and did not live long. Poor thing, many's the time I made myself go up to the little room that used to be hers and get out her poor old scrapbook and read in it when her pictures had been aggravating me and I had soured on her a little. I liked all that family, dead ones and all, and warn't going to let anything come between us. Poor Emmeline made poetry about all the dead people when she was alive, and it didn't seem right that there warn't nobody to make some about her, now she was gone; so I tried to sweat out a verse or two myself, but I couldn't seem to make it go, somehow. They kept Emmeline's room trim and nice and all the things fixed in it just the way she liked to have them when she was alive, and nobody ever slept there. The old lady took care of the room herself, though there was plenty of niggers, and she sewed there a good deal and read her Bible there, mostly.

Well, as I was saying about the parlor, there was beautiful curtains on the windows: white, with pictures painted on them, of castles with vines all down the walls, and cattle coming down to drink. There was a little old piano, too, that had tin pans in it, I reckon, and nothing was ever so lovely as to hear the young ladies sing, "The Last Link is Broken" and play "The Battle of Prague" on it. The walls of all the rooms was plastered, and most had carpets on the floors, and the whole house was whitewashed on the outside.

It was a double house, and the big open place betwixt them was roofed and floored, and sometimes the table was set there in the middle of the day, and it was a cool, comfortable place. Nothing couldn't be better. And warn't the cooking good, and just bushels of it too!

Chapter XVIII

COL. GRANGERFORD WAS a gentleman, you see. He was a gentleman all over; and so was his family. He was well born, as the saying is, and that's worth as much in a man as it is in a horse, so the Widow Douglass said, and nobody ever denied that she was of the first aristocracy in our town; and pap he always said it, too, though he warn't no more quality than a mud-cat, himself. Col. Grangerford was very tall and very slim, and had a darkish-paly complexion, not a sign of red in it anywheres; he was clean-shaved every morning, all over his thin face, and he had the thinnest kind of lips, and the thinnest kind of nostrils, and a high nose, and heavy eyebrows, and the blackest kind of eyes, sunk so deep back that they seemed like they was looking out of caverns at you, as you may say. His forehead was high, and his hair was black and straight, and hung to his shoulders. His hands was long and thin, and every day of his life he put on a clean shirt and a full suit from head to foot made out of linen so white it hurt your eyes to look at it; and on Sundays he wore a blue tail-coat with brass buttons on it. He carried a mahogany cane with a silver head to it. There warn't no frivolishness about him, not a bit, and he warn't ever loud. He was as kind as he could be—you could feel that, you know, and so you had confidence. Sometimes he smiled, and it was good to see; but when he straightened himself up like a liberty-pole, and the lightning begun to flicker out from under his eyebrows you wanted to climb a tree first, and find out what the matter was afterwards. He didn't ever have to tell anybody to mind their manners—everybody was always good mannered where he was. Everybody loved to have him around, too; he was sunshine most always—I mean he made it seem like good weather. When he turned into a cloud-bank it was awful dark for a half a minute and that was enough; there wouldn't nothing go wrong again for a week.

When him and the old lady come down in the morning, all the family got up out of their chairs and give them good-day, and didn't set down again till they had set down. Then Tom and Bob went to the sideboard where the decanters was, and mixed a glass of bitters and handed it to him, and he held it in his hand and waited till Tom's and Bob's was mixed, and then they bowed and said "Our duty to you, sir, and madam;" and *they* bowed the least bit in the world and said thank you, and so they drank, all three, and Bob and Tom poured a spoonful of water on the sugar and the mite of whisky or apple brandy in the bottom of their tumblers, and give it to me and Buck, and we drank to the old people too.

Bob was the oldest, and Tom next. Tall, beautiful men with very broad shoulders and brown faces, and long black hair and black eyes. They dressed in white linen from head to foot, like the old gentleman, and wore broad Panama hats.

Then there was Miss Charlotte, she was twenty-five, and tall and proud and grand, but as good as she could be, when she warn't stirred up; but when she was, she had a look that would make you wilt in your tracks, like her father. She was beautiful.

So was her sister, Miss Sophia, but it was a different kind. She was gentle and sweet, like a dove, and she was only twenty.

Each person had their own nigger to wait on them—Buck, too. My nigger had a monstrous easy time, because I warn't used to having anybody do anything for me, but Buck's was on the jump most of the time.

This was all there was of the family, now; but there used to be more—three sons; they got killed; and Emmeline that died.

The old gentleman owned a lot of farms, and over a hundred niggers. Sometimes a stack of people would come there, horseback, from ten or fifteen mile around, and stay five or six days, and have such junketings round about and on the river, and dances and picnics in the woods, day-times, and balls at the house, nights. These people was mostly kin-folks of the family. The men brought their guns with them. It was a handsome lot of quality, I tell you.

There was another clan of aristocracy around there—five or six families— mostly of the name of Shepherdson. They was as high-toned, and well born, and rich and grand, as the tribe of Grangerfords. The Shepherdsons and the Grangerfords used the same steamboat landing, which was about two mile above our house; so sometimes when I went up there with a lot of our folks I used to see a lot of the Shepherdsons there, on their fine horses.

One day Buck and me was away out in the woods, hunting, and heard a horse coming. We was crossing the road. Buck says:

"Quick! Jump for the woods!"

We done it, and then peeped down the woods through the leaves. Pretty soon a splendid young man come galloping down the road, setting his horse easy and looking like a soldier. He had his gun across his pommel. I had seen him before. It was young Harney Shepherdson. I heard Buck's gun go off at my ear, and

Harney's hat tumbled off from his head. He grabbed his gun and rode straight to the place where we was hid. But we didn't wait. We started through the woods on a run. The woods warn't thick, so I looked over my shoulder, to dodge the bullet, and twice I seen Harney cover Buck with his gun; and then he rode away the way he come—to get his hat, I reckon, but I couldn't see. We never stopped running till we got home. The old gentleman's eyes blazed a minute—'twas pleasure, mainly, I judged—then his face sort of smoothed down, and he says, kind of gentle:

"I don't like that shooting from behind a bush. Why didn't you step into the road, my boy?"

"The Shepherdsons don't, father. They always take advantage."

Miss Charlotte she held her head up like a queen while Buck was telling his tale, and her nostrils spread and her eyes snapped. The two young men looked dark, but never said nothing. Miss Sophia she turned pale, but the color come back when she found the man warn't hurt.

Soon as I could get Buck down by the corn-cribs under the trees by ourselves, I says:

"Did you want to kill him, Buck?"

"Well, I bet I did."

"What did he do to you?"

"Him? He never done nothing to me."

"Well, then, what did you want to kill him for?"

"Why nothing—only it's on account of the feud."

"What's a feud?"

"Why, where was you raised? Don't you know what a feud is?"

"Never heard of it before—tell me about it."

"Well," says Buck, "a feud is this way. A man has a quarrel with another man, and kills him; then that other man's brother kills *him;* then the other brothers, on both sides, goes for one another; then the *cousins* chip in—and by-and-by everybody's killed off, and there ain't no more feud. But it's kind of slow, and takes a long time."

"Has this one been going on long, Buck?"

"Well I should *reckon!* it started thirty year ago, or som'ers along there. There was trouble 'bout something and then a lawsuit to settle it; and the suit went agin one of the men, and so he up and shot the man that won the suit—which he would naturally do, of course. Anybody would."

"What was the trouble about, Buck?—land?"

"I reckon maybe—I don't know."

"Well, who done the shooting?—was it a Grangerford or a Shepherdson?"

"Laws, how do *I* know? it was so long ago."

"Don't anybody know?"

"Oh, yes, pa knows, I reckon, and some of the other old folks; but they don't know, now, what the row was about in the first place."

"Has there been many killed, Buck?"

"Yes—right smart chance of funerals. But they don't always kill. Pa's got a few buck-shot in him; but he don't mind it 'cuz he don't weigh much anyway. Bob's been carved up some with a bowie, and Tom's been hurt once or twice."

"Has anybody been killed this year, Buck?"

"Yes, we got one and they got one. 'Bout three months ago, my cousin Bud, fourteen year old, was riding through the woods, on t'other side of the river.

and didn't have no weapon with him, which was blame' foolishness, and in a lonesome place he hears a horse a-coming behind him, and sees old Baldy Shepherdson a-linkin' after him with his gun in his hand and his white hair a-flying in the wind; and 'stead of jumping off and taking to the brush, Bud 'lowed he could outrun him; so they had it, nip and tuck, for five mile or more, the old man a-gaining all the time; so at last Bud seen it warn't any use, so he stopped and faced around so as to have the bullet holes in front, you know, and the old man he rode up and shot him down. But he didn't git much chance to enjoy his luck, for inside of a week our folks laid *him* out.''

"I reckon that old man was a coward, Buck."

"I reckon he *warn't* a coward. Not by a blame' sight. There ain't a coward amongst them Shepherdsons—not a one. And there ain't no cowards amongst the Grangerfords, either. Why, that old man kep' up his end in a fight one day, for a half an hour, against three Grangerfords, and come out winner. They was all a-horseback; he lit off of his horse and got behind a little wood-pile, and kep' his horse before him to stop the bullets; but the Grangerfords staid on their horses and capered around the old man, and peppered away at him, and he peppered away at them. Him and his horse both went home pretty leaky and crippled, but the Grangerfords had to be *fetched* home—and one of 'em was dead, and another died the next day. No, sir, if a body's out hunting for cowards, he don't want to fool away any time amongst them Shepherdsons, becuz they don't breed any of that *kind*.''

Next Sunday we all went to church, about three mile, everybody a-horseback. The men took their guns along, so did Buck, and kept them between their knees or stood them handy against the wall. The Shepherdsons done the same. It was pretty ornery preaching—all about brotherly love, and such-like tiresomeness; but everybody said it was a good sermon, and they all talked it over going home, and had such a powerful lot to say about faith, and good works, and free grace, and preforeordestination, and I don't know what all, that it did seem to me to be one of the roughest Sundays I had run across yet.

About an hour after dinner everybody was dozing around, some in their chairs and some in their rooms, and it got to be pretty dull. Buck and a dog was stretched out on the grass in the sun, sound asleep. I went up to our room, and judged I would take a nap myself. I found that sweet Miss Sophia standing in her door, which was next to ours, and she took me in her room and shut the door very soft, and asked me if I liked her, and I said I did; and she asked me if I would do something for her and not tell anybody, and I said I would. Then she said she'd forgot her Testament, and left it in the seat at church, between two other books and would I slip out quiet and go there and fetch it to her, and not say nothing to nobody. I said I would. So I slid out and slipped off up the road, and there warn't anybody at the church, except maybe a hog or two, for there warn't any lock on the door, and hogs likes a puncheon floor in summer-time because it's cool. If you notice, most folks don't go to church only when they've got to; but a hog is different.

Says I to myself something's up—it ain't natural for a girl to be in such a sweat about a Testament; so I give it a shake, and out drops a little piece of paper with *''Half-past two''* wrote on it with a pencil. I ransacked it, but couldn't find anything else. I couldn't make anything out of that, so I put the paper in the book again, and when I got home and up stairs, there was Miss Sophia in her door waiting for me. She pulled me in and shut the door; then she looked

"AND ASKED ME IF I LIKED HER."

in the Testament till she found the paper, and as soon as she read it she looked glad; and before a body could think, she grabbed me and give me a squeeze, and said I was the best boy in the world, and not to tell anybody. She was mighty red in the face, for a minute, and her eyes lighted up and it made her powerful pretty. I was a good deal astonished, but when I got my breath I asked her what the paper was about, and she asked me if I had read it, and I said no, and she asked me if I could read writing, and I told her "no, only coarse-hand," and then she said the paper warn't anything but a book-mark to keep her place, and I might go and play now.

I went off down to the river, studying over this thing, and pretty soon I noticed that my nigger was following along behind. When we was out of sight of the house, he looked back and around a second, and then comes a-running, and says:

"Mars Jawge, if you'll come down into de swamp, I'll show you a whole stack o' water-moccasins."

Thinks I, that's mighty curious; he said that yesterday. He oughter know a body don't love water-moccasins enough to go around hunting for them. What is he up to anyway? So I says—

"All right, trot ahead."

I followed a half a mile, then he struck out over the swamp and waded ankle deep as much as another half mile. We come to a little flat piece of land which was dry and very thick with trees and bushes and vines, and he says—

"You shove right in dah, jist a few steps, Mars Jawge, dah's whah dey is. I's seed 'm befo', I don't k'yer to see 'em no mo'."

Then he slopped right along and went away, and pretty soon the trees hid him. I poked into the place a-ways, and come to a little open patch as big as a bedroom, all hung around with vines, and found a man laying there asleep— and by jings it was my old Jim!

I waked him up, and I reckoned it was going to be a grand surprise to him to see me again, but it warn't. He nearly cried, he was so glad, but he warn't surprised. Said he swum along behind me, that night, and heard me yell every time, but dasn't answer, because he didn't want nobody to pick *him* up, and take him into slavery again. Says he—

"I got hurt a little, en couldn't swim fas', so I wuz a considable ways behine you, towards de las'; when you landed I reck'ned I could ketch up wid you on de lan' 'dout havin' to shout at you, but when I see dat house I begin to go slow. I 'uz off too fur to hear what dey say to you—I wuz 'fraid o' de dogs—but when it 'uz all quiet agin, I knowed you's in de house, so I struck out for de woods to wait for day. Early in de mawnin' some er de niggers come along, gwyne to de fields, en dey tuck me en showed me dis place, whah de dogs can't track me on accounts o' de water, en dey brings me truck to eat every night, en tells me how you's a gitt'n along."

"Why didn't you tell my Jack to fetch me here sooner, Jim?"

"Well, 'twarn't no use to 'sturb you, Huck, tell we could do sumfn—but we's all right, now. I ben a-buyin' pots en pans en vittles, as I got a chanst, en a patchin' up de raf', nights, when——"

"*What* raft, Jim?"

"Our ole raf'."

"You mean to say our old raft warn't smashed all to flinders?"

"No, she warn't. She was tore up a good deal—one en' of her was—but dey warn't no great harm done, on'y our traps was mos' all los'. Ef we hadn' dive' so deep en swum so fur under water, en de night hadn' ben so dark, en we warn't so sk'yerd, en ben sich punkin-heads, as de sayin' is, we'd a seed de raf'. But it's jis' as well we didn't, 'kase now she's all fixed up agin mos' as good as new, en we's got a new lot o' stuff, too, in de place o' what 'uz los'."

"Why, how did you get hold of the raft again, Jim—did you catch her?"

"How I gwne to ketch her, en I out in de woods? No, some er de niggers foun' her ketched on a snag, along heah in de ben', en dey hid her in a crick, 'mongst de willows, en dey wuz so much jawin' 'bout which un 'um she b'long to de mos', dat I come to heah 'bout it pooty soon, so I ups en settles de trouble by tellin' 'um she don't b'long to none uv um, but to you en me; en I ast 'm if dey gwyne to grab a young white genlman's propaty, en git a hid'n for it? Den I gin 'm ten cents apiece, en dey 'uz mighty well satisfied, en wisht some mo' raf's 'ud come along en make 'm rich agin. Dey's mighty good to me, dese niggers is, en whatever I wants 'm to do fur me, I doan' have to ast 'm twice, honey. Dat Jack's a good nigger, en pooty smart."

"Yes, he is. He ain't ever told me you was here; told me to come, and he'd show me a lot of water-moccasins. If anything happens, *he* ain't mixed up in it. He can say he never seen us together, and it'll be the truth."

I don't want to talk much about the next day. I reckon I'll cut it pretty short. I waked up about dawn, and was agoing to turn over and go to sleep again, when I noticed how still it was—didn't seem to be anybody stirring. That warn't usual. Next I noticed that Buck was up and gone. Well, I gets up, a-wondering, and goes down stairs—nobody around; everything as still as a mouse. Just the same outside; thinks I, what does it mean? Down by the wood-pile I comes across my Jack, and says:

"What's it all about?"

Says he:

"Don't you know, Mars Jawge?"

"No," says I, "I don't."

"Well, den, Miss Sophia's run off! 'deed she has. She run off in de night, sometime—nobody don't know jis' when—run off to git married to dat young Harney Shepherdson, you know—leastways, so dey 'spec. De fambly foun' it out, 'bout half an hour ago—maybe a little mo'—en' I *tell* you dey warn't no time los'. Sich another hurryin' up guns en hosses *you* never see! De women folks has gone for to stir up de relations, en ole Mars Saul en de boys tuck dey guns en rode up de river road for to try to ketch dat young man en kill him 'fo' he kin git acrost de river wid Miss Sophia. I reck'n dey's gwyne to be mighty rough times.''

''Buck went off 'thout waking me up.''

''Well I reck'n he *did!* Dey warn't gwyne to mix you up in it. Mars Buck he loaded up his gun en 'lowed he's gwyne to fetch home a Shepherdson or bust. Well, dey'll be plenty un 'm dah, I reck'n, en you bet you he'll fetch one ef he gits a chanst.''

I took up the river road as hard as I could put. By-and-by I begin to hear guns a good ways off. When I come in sight of the log store and the wood-pile where the steamboats lands, I worked along under the trees and brush till I got to a good place, and then I clumb up into the forks of a cotton-wood that was out of reach, and watched. There was a wood-rank four foot high, a little ways in front of the tree, and first I was going to hide behind that; but maybe it was luckier I didn't.

There was four or five men cavorting around on their horses in the open place before the log store, cussing and yelling, and trying to get at a couple of young chaps that was behind the wood-rank alongside of the steamboat landing—but they couldn't come it. Every time one of them showed himself on the river side of the wood-pile he got shot at. The two boys was squatting back to back behind the pile, so they could watch both ways.

By-and-by the men stopped cavorting around and yelling. They started riding towards the store; then up gets one of the boys, draws a steady bead over the wood-rank, and drops one of them out of his saddle. All the men jumped off of their horses and grabbed the hurt one and started to carry him to the store; and that minute the two boys started on the run. They got half-way to the tree I was in before the men noticed. Then the men see them, and jumped on their horses and took out after them. They gained on the boys, but it didn't do no good, the boys had too good a start; they got to the wood-pile that was in front of my tree, and slipped in behind it, and so they had the bulge on the men again.

" BEHIND THE WOOD-PILE."

One of the boys was Buck, and the other was a slim young chap about nineteen years old.

The men ripped around awhile, and then rode away. As soon as they was out of sight, I sung out to Buck and told him. He didn't know what to make of my voice coming out of the tree, at first. He was awful surprised. He told me to watch out sharp and let him know when the men come in sight again; said they was up to some devilment or other—wouldn't be gone long. I wished I was out of that tree, but I dasn't come down. Buck begun to cry and rip, and 'lowed that him and his cousin Joe (that was the other young chap) would make up for this day, yet. He said his father and his two brothers was killed, and two or three of the enemy. Said the Shepherdsons laid for them, in ambush. Buck said his father and brothers ought to waited for their relations—the Shepherdsons was too strong for them. I asked him what was become of young Harney and Miss Sophia. He said they'd got across the river and was safe. I was glad of that; but the way Buck did take on because he didn't manage to kill Harney that day he shot at him—I hain't ever heard anything like it.

All of a sudden, bang! bang! bang! goes three or four guns—the men had slipped around through the woods and come in from behind without their horses! The boys jumped for the river—both of them hurt—and as they swum down the current the men run along the bank shooting at them and singing out, "Kill them, kill them!" It made me so sick I most fell out of the tree. I ain't agoing to tell *all* that happened—it would make me sick again if I was to do that. I wished I hadn't ever come ashore that night, to see such things. I ain't ever going to get shut of them—lots of times I dream about them.

I staid in the tree till it begun to get dark, afraid to come down. Sometimes I heard guns away off in the woods; and twice I seen little gangs of men gallop past the log store with guns; so I reckoned the trouble was still agoing on. I was mighty down-hearted; so I made up my mind I wouldn't ever go anear that house again, because I reckoned I was to blame, somehow. I judged that that piece of paper meant that Miss Sophia was to meet Harney somewheres at half-past two and run off; and I judged I ought to told her father about that paper and the curious way she acted, and then maybe he would a locked her up and this awful mess wouldn't ever happened.

When I got down out of the tree, I crept along down the river bank a piece, and found the two bodies laying in the edge of the water, and tugged at them till I got them ashore; then I covered up their faces, and got away as quick as I could. I cried a little when I was covering up Buck's face, for he was mighty good to me.

It was just dark, now. I never went near the house, but struck through the woods and made for the swamp. Jim warn't on his island, so I tramped off in a hurry for the crick, and crowded through the willows, red-hot to jump aboard and get out of that awful country—the raft was gone! My souls, but I was scared! I couldn't get my breath for most a minute. Then I raised a yell. A voice not twenty-five foot from me, says—

"Good lan'! is dat you, honey? Doan' make no noise."

It was Jim's voice—nothing ever sounded so good before. I run along the bank a piece and got aboard, and Jim he grabbed me and hugged me, he was so glad to see me. He says—

"Laws bless you, chile, I 'uz right down sho' you's dead agin. Jack's been heah, he say he reck'n you's ben shot, kase you didn' come home no mo'; so

I's jes' dis minute a startin' de raf' down towards de mouf er de crick, so's to be all ready for to shove out en leave soon as Jack comes agin en tells me for certain you *is* dead. Lawsy, I's mighty glad to git you back agin, honey.''

I says—

''All right—that's mighty good; they won't find me, and they'll think I've been killed, and floated down the river—there's something up there that'll help them to think so—so don't you lose no time, Jim, but just shove off for the big water as fast as ever you can.''

I never felt easy till the raft was two mile below there and out in the middle of the Mississippi. Then we hung up our signal lantern, and judged that we was free and safe once more. I hadn't had a bite to eat since yesterday; so Jim he got out some corn-dodgers and buttermilk, and pork and cabbage, and greens— there ain't nothing in the world so good, when it's cooked right—and whilst I eat my supper we talked, and had a good time. I was powerful glad to get away from the feuds, and so was Jim to get away from the swamp. We said there warn't no home like a raft, after all. Other places do seem so cramped up and smothery, but a raft don't. You feel mighty free and easy and comfortable on a raft.

Chapter XIX

TWO OR THREE days and nights went by; I reckon I might say they swum by, they slid along so quiet and smooth and lovely. Here is the way we put in the time. It was a monstrous big river down there—sometimes a mile and a half wide; we run nights, and laid up and hid day-times; soon as night was most gone, we stopped navigating and tied up—nearly always in the dead water under a towhead ; and then cut young cottonwoods and willows and hid the raft with them. Then we set out the lines. Next we slid into the river and had a swim, so as to freshen up and cool off; then we set down on the sandy bottom where the water was about knee deep, and watched the daylight come. Not a sound, anywheres—perfectly still—just like the whole world was asleep, only sometimes the bull-frogs a-cluttering, maybe. The first thing to see, looking away over the water, was a kind of dull line—that was the woods on t'other side—you couldn't make nothing else out; then a pale place in the sky; then more paleness, spreading around; then the river softened up, away off, and warn't black any more, but gray; you could see little dark spots drifting along, ever so far away—trading scows, and such things; and long black streaks—rafts; sometimes you could hear a sweep screaking; or jumbled up voices, it was so still, and sounds come so far; and by-and-by you could see a streak on the water which you know by the look of the streak that there's a snag there in a swift current which breaks on it and makes that streak look that way; and you see the mist curl up off of the water, and the east reddens up, and the river, and you make out a log cabin in the edge of the woods, away on the bank on t'other side of the river, being a wood-yard, likely, and piled by them cheats so you can throw a dog through it anywheres; then the nice breeze springs up, and comes fanning you from over there, so cool and fresh, and sweet to smell, on account of the woods and the flowers; but sometimes not that way, because they've left dead fish laying around, gars, and such, and they do get pretty rank; and next you've got the full day, and everything smiling in the sun, and the song-birds just going it!

A little smoke couldn't be noticed, now, so we would take some fish off of the lines, and cook up a hot breakfast. And afterwards we would watch the lonesomeness of the river, and kind of lazy along, and by-and-by lazy off to sleep. Wake up, by-and-by, and look to see what done it, and maybe see a steamboat, coughing along up stream, so far off towards the other side you couldn't tell nothing about her only whether she was stern-wheel or side-wheel; then for about an hour there wouldn't be nothing to hear nor nothing to see— just solid lonesomeness. Next you'd see a raft sliding by, away off yonder, and maybe a galoot on it chopping, because they're most always doing it on a raft; you'd see the ax flash, and come down—you don't hear nothing; you see that ax go up again, and by the time it's above the man's head, then you hear the *k'chunk!*—it had took all that time to come over the water. So we would put in the day, lazying around, listening to the stillness. Once there was a thick fog, and the rafts and things that went by was beating tin pans so the steamboats wouldn't run over them. A scow or a raft went by so close we could hear them talking and cussing and laughing—heard them plain; but we couldn't see no sign of them; it made you feel crawly, it was like spirits carrying on that way in the air. Jim said he believed it was spirits; but I says:

"No, spirits wouldn't say, 'dern the dern fog.'"

Soon as it was night, out we shoved; when we got her out to about the middle, we let her alone, and let her float wherever the current wanted her to; then we lit the pipes, and dangled our legs in the water and talked about all kinds of things—we was always naked, day and night, whenever the mosquitoes would let us—the new clothes Buck's folks made for me was too good to be comfortable, and besides I didn't go much on clothes, no-how.

Sometimes we'd have that whole river all to ourselves for the longest time. Yonder was the banks and the islands, across the water; and maybe a spark— which was a candle in a cabin window—and sometimes on the water you could see a spark or two—on a raft or a scow, you know; and maybe you could hear a fiddle or a song coming over from one of them crafts. It's lovely to live on a raft. We had the sky, up there, all speckled with stars, and we used to lay on our backs and look up at them, and discuss about whether they was made, or only just happened—Jim he allowed they was made, but I allowed they happened; I judged it would have took too long to *make* so many. Jim said the moon could a *laid* them; well, that looked kind of reasonable, so I didn't say nothing against it, because I've seen a frog lay most as many, so of course it could be done. We used to watch the stars that fell, too, and see them streak down. Jim allowed they'd got spoiled and was hove out of the nest.

Once or twice of a night we would see a steamboat slipping along in the dark, and now and then she would belch a whole world of sparks up out of her chimbleys, and they would rain down in the river and look awful pretty; then she would turn a corner and her lights would wink out and her pow-wow shut off and leave the river still again; and by-and-by her waves would get to us, a long time after she was gone, and joggle the raft a bit, and after that you wouldn't hear nothing for you couldn't tell how long, except maybe frogs or something.

After midnight the people on shore went to bed, and then for two or three hours the shores was black—no more sparks in the cabin windows. These sparks was our clock—the first one that showed again meant morning was coming, so we hunted a place to hide and tie up, right away.

One morning about day-break, I found a canoe and crossed over a chute to the main shore—it was only two hundred yards—and paddled about a mile up a crick amongst the cypress woods, to see if I couldn't get some berries. Just as I was passing a place where a kind of a cow-path crossed the crick, here comes a couple of men tearing up the path as tight as they could foot it. I thought I was a goner, for whenever anybody was after anybody I judged it was *me*— or maybe Jim. I was about to dig out from there in a hurry, but they was pretty close to me then, and sung out and begged me to save their lives—said they hadn't been doing nothing, and was being chased for it—said there was men and dogs a-coming. They wanted to jump right in, but I says—

"Don't you do it. I don't hear the dogs and horses yet; you've got time to crowd through the brush and get up the crick a little ways; then you take to the water and wade down to me and get in—that'll throw the dogs off the scent."

They done it, and soon as they was aboard I lit out for our tow-head, and in about five or ten minutes we heard the dogs and the men away off, shouting. We heard them come along towards the crick, but couldn't see them; they seemed to stop and fool around a while; then, as we got further and further away all the time, we couldn't hardly hear them at all; by the time we had left a mile of woods behind us and struck the river, everything was quiet, and we paddled over to the tow-head and hid in the cotton-woods and was safe.

One of these fellows was about seventy, or upwards, and had a bald head and very gray whiskers. He had an old battered-up slouch hat on, and a greasy blue woolen shirt, and ragged old blue jeans britches stuffed into his boot tops, and home-knit galluses—no, he only had one. He had an old long-tailed blue jeans coat with slick brass buttons, flung over his arm, and both of them had big fat ratty-looking carpet-bags.

The other fellow was about thirty and dressed about as ornery. After breakfast we all laid off and talked, and the first thing that come out was that these chaps didn't know one another.

"What got you into trouble?" says the baldhead to t'other chap.

"Well, I'd been selling an article to take the tartar off the teeth—and it does take it off, too, and generly the enamel along with it—but I staid about one night longer than I ought to, and was just in the act of sliding out when I ran across you on the trail this side of town, and you told me they were coming, and begged me to help you to get off. So I told you I was expecting trouble myself and would scatter out *with* you. That's the whole yarn—what's yourn?"

"Well, I'd ben a-runnin' a little temperance revival thar, 'bout a week, and was the pet of the women-folks, big and little, for I was makin' it mighty warm for the rummies, I *tell* you, and takin' as much as five or six dollars a night— ten cents a head, children and niggers free—and business a growin' all the time; when somehow or another a little report got around, last night, that I had a way of puttin' in my time with a private jug, on the sly. A nigger rousted me out this mornin', and told me the people was getherin' on the quiet, with their dogs and horses, and they'd be along pretty soon and give me 'bout half an hour's start, and then run me down, if they could; and if they got me they'd tar and feather me and ride me on a rail, sure. I didn't wait for no breakfast—I warn't hungry."

"Old man," says the young one, "I reckon we might double-team it together; what do you think?"

"I ain't undisposed. What's your line—mainly?"

"Jour printer, by trade; do a little in patent medicines; theatre-actor—tragedy, you know; take a turn at mesmerism and phrenology when there's a chance; teach singing-geography school for a change; sling a lecture, sometimes—oh, I do lots of things—most anything that comes handy, so it ain't work. What's your lay?"

"I've done considerble in the doctoring way in my time, Layin' on o' hands is my best holt—for cancer, and paralysis, and sich things; and I k'n tell a fortune pretty good, when I've got somebody along to find out the facts for me. Preachin's my line, too; and workin' camp-meetin's; and missionaryin around."

Nobody never said anything for a while; then the young man hove a sigh and says—

"Alas!"

"What're you alassin' about?" says the baldhead.

"To think I should have lived to be leading such a life, and be degraded down into such company." And he begun to wipe the corner of his eye with a rag.

"Dern your skin, ain't the company good enough for you?" says the baldhead, pretty pert and uppish.

"Yes, it *is* good enough for me; it's as good as I deserve; for who fetched me so low, when I was so high? *I* did myself. I don't blame *you,* gentlemen— far from it; I don't blame anybody. I deserve it all. Let the cold world do its worst; one thing I know—there's a grave somewhere for me. The world may go on just as its always done, and take everything from me—loved ones, property, everything—but it can't take that. Some day I'll lie down in it and forget it all, and my poor broken heart will be at rest." He went on a-wiping.

"Drot your pore broken heart," says the baldhead;" what are you heaving your pore broken heart at *us* f'r? *We* hain't done nothing."

"No, I know you haven't. I ain't blaming you, gentlemen. I brought myself down—yes, I did it myself. It's right I should suffer—perfectly right—I don't make any moan."

"Brought you down from whar? Whar was you brought down from?"

"Ah, you would not believe me; the world never beieves—let it pass—'tis no matter. The secret of my birth——"

"The secret of your birth? Do you mean to say——"

"Gentlemen," says the young man, very solemn, "I will reveal it to you, for I feel I may have confidence in you. By rights I am a duke!"

Jim's eyes bugged out when he heard that; and I reckon mine did, too. Then the baldhead says: "No! you can't mean it?"

"Yes. My great-grandfather, eldest son of the Duke of Bridgewater, fled to this country about the end of the last century, to breathe the pure air of freedom; married here, and died, leaving a son, his own father dying about the same time. The second son of the late duke seized the title and estates—the infant real duke was ignored. I am the lineal descendant of that infant—I am the rightful Duke of Bridgewater; and here am I, forlorn, torn from my high estate, hunted of men, despised by the cold world, ragged, worn, heart-broken, and degraded to the companionship of felons on a raft!"

Jim pitied him ever so much, and so did I. We tried to comfort him, but he said it warn't much use, he couldn't be much comforted; said if we was a mind

"BY RIGHTS I AM A DUKE!"

to acknowledge him, that would do him more good than most anything else; so we said we would, if he would tell us how. He said we ought to bow, when we spoke to him, and say "Your Grace," or "My Lord," or "Your Lordship"—and he wouldn't mind it if we called him plain "Bridgewater," which he said was a title, anyway, and not a name; and one of us ought to wait on him at dinner, and do any little thing for him he wanted done.

Well, that was all easy, so we done it. All through dinner Jim stood around and waited on him, and says, "Will yo' Grace have some o' dis, or some o' dat?" and so on, and a body could see it was mighty pleasing to him.

But the old man got pretty silent, by-and-by—didn't have much to say, and didn't look pretty comfortable over all that petting that was going on around that duke. He seemed to have something on his mind. So, along in the afternoon, he says:

"Looky here, Bilgewater," he says, "I'm nation sorry for you, but you ain't the only person that's had troubles like that."

"No?"

"No, you ain't, You ain't the only person that's ben snaked down wrongfully out'n a high place."

"Alas!"

"No, you ain't the only person that's had a secret of his birth." And by jings, *he* begins to cry.

"Hold! What do you mean?"

"Bilgewater, kin I trust you?" says the old man, still sort of sobbing.

"To the bitter death!" He took the old man by the hand and squeezed it, and says, "The secret of your being: speak!"

"Bilgewater, I am the late Dauphin!"

You bet you Jim and me stared, this time. Then the duke says:

"You are what?"

"Yes, my friend, it is too true—your eyes is lookin' at this very moment on the pore disappeared Dauphin, Looy the Seventeen, son of Looy the the Sixteen and Marry Antonette."

"You! At your age! No! You mean you're the late Charlemagne; you must be six or seven hundred years old, at the very least."

"Trouble has done it, Bilgewater, trouble has done it; trouble has brung these gray hairs and this premature balditude. Yes, gentlemen, you see before you, in blue jeans and misery, the wanderin', exiled, trampled-on and sufferin' rightful King of France."

Well, he cried and took on so, that me and Jim didn't know hardly what to do, we was so sorry—and so glad and proud we'd got him with us, too. So we set in, like we done before with the duke, and tried to comfort *him*. But he said it warn't no use, nothing but to be dead and done with it all could do him any good; though he said it often made him feel easier and better for a while if people treated him according to his rights, and got down on one knee to speak to him, and alway's called him "Your Majesty," and waited on him first at meals, and didn't set down in his presence till he asked them. So Jim and me set to majestying him, and doing this and that and t'other for him, and standing up till he told us we might set down. This done him heaps of good, and so he got cheerful and comfortable. But the duke kind of soured on him, and didn't look a bit satisfied with the way things was going; still, the king acted real friendly towards him, and said the duke's great-grandfather and all the other Dukes of Bilgewater was a good deal thought of by *his* father and was allowed to come to the palace considerable; but the duke staid huffy a good while, till by-and-by the king says:

"Like as not we got to be together a blamed long time, on this h-yer raft, Bilgewater, and so what's the use o' your bein' sour? It'll only make things oncomfortable. It ain't my fault I warn't born a duke, it ain't your fault you warn't born a king—so what's the use to worry? Make the best o' things the way you find 'em, says I—that's my motto. This ain't no bad thing that we've struck here—plenty grub and an easy life—come, give us your hand, Duke, and less all be friends."

The duke done it, and Jim and me was pretty glad to see it. It took away all the uncomfortableness, and we felt mighty good over it, beeause it would a been a miserable business to have any unfriendliness on the raft; for what you want, above all things, on a raft, is for everybody to be satisfied, and feel right and kind towards the others.

It didn't take me long to make up my mind that these liars warn't no kings nor dukes, at all, but just low-down humbugs and frauds. But I never said nothing, never let on; kept it to myself; it's the best way; then you don't have no quarrels, and don't get into no trouble. If they wanted us to call them kings and dukes, I hadn't no objections, 'long as it would keep peace in the family; and it warn't no use to tell Jim, so I didn't tell him. If I never learnt nothing else out of pap, I learnt that the best way to get along with his kind of people is to let them have their own way.

Chapter XX

THEY ASKED US considerable many questions; wanted to know what we covered up the raft that way for, and laid by in the day-time instead of running—was Jim a runaway nigger? Says I—

"Goodness sakes, would a runaway nigger run *south*?"

No, they allowed he wouldn't. I had to account for things some way, so I says:

"My folks was living in Pike County, in Missouri, where I was born, and they all died off but me and pa and my brother Ike. Pa, he 'lowed he'd break up and go down and live with Uncle Ben, who's got a little one-horse place on the river forty-four mile below Orleans. Pa was pretty poor, and had some debts; so when he'd squared up there warn't nothing left but sixteen dollars and our nigger, Jim. That warn't enough to take us fourteen hundred mile, deck passage nor no other way. Well, when the river rose, pa had a streak of luck one day; he ketched this piece of a raft; so we reckoned we'd go down to Orleans on it. Pa's luck didn't hold out; a steamboat run over the forrard corner of the raft, one night, and we all went overboard and dove under the wheel; Jim and me come up, all right, but pa was drunk, and Ike was only four years old, so they never come up no more. Well, for the next day or two we had considerable trouble, because people was always coming out in skiffs and trying to take Jim away from me, saying they believed he was a runaway nigger. We don't run day-times no more, now; nights they don't bother us."

The duke says—

"Leave me alone to cipher out a way so we can run in the day-time if we want to. I'll think the thing over—I'll invent a plan that'll fix it. We'll let it alone for to-day, because of course we don't want to go by that town yonder in daylight—it mightn't be healthy."

Towards night it begun to darken up and look like rain; the heat lightning was squirting around, low down in the sky, and the leaves was beginning to shiver—it was going to be pretty ugly, it was easy to see that. So the duke and the king went to overhauling our wigwam, to see what the beds was like. My bed was a straw tick—better than Jim's, which was a corn-shuck tick; there's always cobs around about in a shuck tick, and they poke into you and hurt; and when you roll over, the dry shucks sound like you was rolling over in a pile of dead leaves; it makes such a rustling that you wake up. Well, the duke allowed he would take my bed; but the king allowed he wouldn't. He says—

"I should a reckoned the difference in rank would a sejested to you that a

ON THE RAFT.

corn-shuck bed warn't just fitten for me to sleep on. Your Grace'll take the shuck bed yourself.''

Jim and me was in a sweat again, for a minute, being afraid there was going to be some more trouble amongst them; so we was pretty glad when the duke says—

"'Tis my fate to be always ground into the mire under the iron heel of oppression. Misfortune has broken my once haughty spirit; I yield, I submit; 'tis my fate. I am alone in the world—let me suffer; I can bear it.''

We got away as soon as it was good and dark. The king told us to stand well out towards the middle of the river, and not show a light till we got a long ways below the town. We come in sight of the little bunch of lights by-and-by—that was the town, you know—and slid by, about a half a mile out, all right. When we was three-quarters of a mile below, we hoisted up our signal lantern; and about ten o'elock it come on to rain and blow and thunder and lighten like everything; so the king told us to both stay on watch till the weather got better; then him and the duke crawled into the wigwam and turned in for the night. It was my watch below, till twelve, but I wouldn't a turned in, anyway, if I'd had a bed; because a body don't see such a storm as that every day in the week, not by a long sight. My souls, how the wind did scream along! And every second or two there'd come a glare that lit up the white-caps for a half a mile around, and you'd see the islands looking dusty through the rain, and the trees thrashing around in the wind; then comes a *h-wack!*—bum! bum! bumble-umble-um-bum-bum-bum-bum—and the thunder would go rumbling and grumbling away, and quit—and then *rip* comes another flash and another sockdolager. The waves most washed me off the raft, sometimes, but I hadn't any clothes on, and didn't mind. We didn't have no trouble about snags; the lightning was glaring and flittering around so constant that we could see them plenty soon enough to throw her head this way or that and miss them.

I had the middle watch, you know, but I was pretty sleepy by that time, so Jim he said he would stand the first half of it for me; he was always mighty good, that way, Jim was. I crawled into the wigwam, but the king and the duke had their legs sprawled around so there warn't no show for me; so I laid outside—I didn't mind the rain, because it was warm, and the waves warn't running so high, now. About two they come up again, though, and Jim was going to call me, but he changed his mind because he reckoned they warn't high enough yet to do any harm; but he was mistaken about that, for pretty soon all of a sudden along comes a regular ripper, and washed me overboard. It most killed Jim a-laughing. He was the easiest nigger to laugh that ever was, anyway.

I took the watch, and Jim he laid down and snored away; and by-and-by the storm let up for good and all; and the first cabin-light that showed, I rousted him out and we slid the raft into hiding-quarters for the day.

The king got out an old ratty deck of cards, after breakfast, and him and the duke played seven-up a while, five cents a game. Then they got tired of it, and allowed they would "lay out a campaign," as they called it. The duke went down into his carpet-bag and fetched up a lot of little printed bills, and read them out loud. One bill said "The celebrated Dr. Armand de Montalban of Paris," would "lecture on the Science of Phrenology" at such and such a place, on the blank day of blank, at ten cents admission, and "furnish charts of character at twenty-five cents apiece." The duke said that was *him*. In another bill he was the "world renowned Shaksperean tragedian, Garrick the Younger, of Drury

Lane, London.'' In other bills he had a lot of other names and done other wonderful things, like finding water and gold with a ''divining rod,'' ''dissipating witch-spells,'' and so on. By-and-by he says—

''But the histrionic muse is the darling. Have you ever trod the boards, Royalty?''

''No,'' says the king.

''You shall, then, before you're three days older, Fallen Grandeur,'' says the duke. ''The first good town we come to, we'll hire a hall and do the sword-fight in Richard III and the balcony scene in Romeo and Juliet. How does that strike you?''

''I'm in, up to the hub, for anything that will pay, Bilgewater, but you see I don't know nothing about play-actn', and hain't ever seen much of it. I was too small when pap used to have 'em at the palace. Do you reckon you can learn me?''

''Easy!''

''All right. I'm jist a-freezn' for something fresh, anyway. Less commence, right away.''

So the duke he told him all about who Romeo was, and who Juliet was, and said he was used to being Romeo, so the king could be Juliet.

''But if Juliet's such a young gal, Duke, my peeled head and my white whiskers is goin' to look oncommon odd on her, maybe.''

''No, don't you worry—these country jakes won't ever think of that, Besides, you know, you'll be in costume, and that makes all the difference in the world; Juliet's in a balcony, enjoying the moonlight before she goes to bed, and she's got on her night-gown and her ruffled night-cap. Here are the costumes for the parts.''

He got out two or three curtain-calico suits, which he said was meedyevil armor for Richard III and t'other chap, and a long white cotton night-shirt and a ruffled night-cap to match. The king was satisfied; so the duke got out his book and read the parts over in the most splendid spread-eagle way, prancing around and acting at the same time, to show how it had got to be done; then he give the book to the king and told him to get his part by heart.

There was a little one-horse town about three mile down the bend, and after dinner the duke said he had ciphered out his idea about how to run in daylight without it being dangersome for Jim; so he allowed he would go down to the town and fix that thing. The king allowed he would go too, and see if he couldn't strike something. We was out of coffee, so Jim said I better go along with them in the canoe and get some.

When we got there, there warn't nobody stirring; streets empty, and perfectly dead and still, like Sunday. We found a sick nigger sunning himself in a back yard, and he said everybody that warn't too young or too sick or too old, was gone to camp-meeting, about two mile back in the woods. The king got the directions, and allowed he'd go and work that camp-meeting for all it was worth, and I might go, too.

The duke said what he was after was a printing office. We found it; a little bit of a concern, up over a carpenter shop—carpenters and printers all gone to the meeting, and no doors locked. It was a dirty, littered-up place, and had ink marks, and handbills with pictures of horses and runaway niggers on them, all over the walls. The duke shed his coat and said he was all right, now. So me and the king lit out for the camp-meeting.

We got there in about a half an hour, fairly dripping, for it was a most awful hot day. There was as much as a thousand people there, from twenty mile around. The woods was full of teams and wagons, hitched everywheres, feeding out of the wagon troughs and stomping to keep off the flies. There was sheds made out of poles and roofed over with branches, where they had lemonade and gingerbread to sell, and piles of watermelons and green corn and such-like truck.

The preaching was going on under the same kinds of sheds, only they was bigger and held crowds of people. The benches was made out of outside slabs of logs, with holes bored in the round side to drive sticks into for legs. They didn't have no backs. The preachers had high platforms to stand on, at one end of the sheds. The women had on sunbonnets; and some had linsey-woolsey frocks, some gingham ones, and a few of the young ones had on calico. Some of the young men was barefooted, and some of the children didn't have on any clothes but just a tow-linen shirt. Some of the old women was knitting, and some of the young folks was courting on the sly.

The first shed we come to, the preacher was lining out a hymn. He lined out two lines, everybody sung it, and it was kind of grand to hear it, there was so many of them and they done it in such a rousing way; then he lined out two more for them to sing—and so on. The people woke up more and more, and sung louder and louder; and towards the end, some begun to groan, and some begun to shout. Then the preacher begun to preach; and begun in earnest, too; and went weaving first to one side of the platform and then the other, and then a leaning down over the front of it, with his arms and his body going all the time, and shouting his words out with all his might; and every now and then he would hold up his Bible and spread it open, and kind of pass it around this way and that, shouting, "It's the brazen serpent in the wilderness! Look upon it and live!" And people would shout out, "Glory!—A-a-men!" And so he went on, and the people groaning and crying and saying amen:

"Oh, come to the mourners' bench! come, black with sin! (*amen!*) come, sick and sore! (*amen!*) come, lame and halt, and blind! (*amen!*) come, pore and needy, sunk in shame! (*a-a-men!*) come all that's worn, and soiled, and suffering!— come with a broken spirit! come with a contrite heart! come in your rags and sin and dirt! the waters that cleanse is free, the door of heaven stands open— oh, enter in and be at rest!" (*a-a-men! glory, glory hallelujah!*)

And so on. You couldn't make out what the preacher said, any more, on account of the shouting and crying. Folks got up, everywheres in the crowd, and worked their way, just by main strength, to the mourners' bench, with the tears running down their faces; and when all the mourners had got up there to the front benches in a crowd, they sung, and shouted, and flung themselves down on the straw, just crazy and wild.

Well, the first I knowed, the king got agoing; and you could hear him over everybody; and next he went a-charging up on to the platform and the preacher he begged him to speak to the people, and he done it. He told them he was a pirate—ben a pirate for thirty years, out in the Indian Ocean, and his crew was thinned out considerable, last spring, in a fight, and he was home now, to take out some fresh men, and thanks to goodness he'd been robbed last night, and put ashore off of a steamboat without a cent, and he was glad of it, it was the blessedest thing that ever happened to him, because he was a changed man now, and happy for the first time in his life; and poor as he was, he was going to start right off and work his way back to the Indian Ocean and put in the rest of his life trying to turn the pirates into the true path; for he could do it better than anybody else, being acquainted with all the pirate crews in that ocean; and though it would take him a long time to get there, without money, he would get there anyway, and every time he convinced a pirate he would say to him, "Don't you thank me, don't you give me no credit, it all belongs to them dear people in Pokeville camp-meeting, natural brothers and benefactors of the race—and that dear preacher there, the truest friend a pirate ever had!"

And then he busted into tears, and so did everybody. Then somebody sings out, "Take up a collection for him, take up a collection!" Well, a half a dozen made a jump to do it, but somebody sings out, "Let *him* pass the hat around!" Then everybody said it, the preacher too.

So the king went all through the crowd with his hat, swabbing his eyes, and blessing the people and praising them and thanking them for being so good to the poor pirates away off there; and every little while the prettiest kind of girls, with the tears running down their cheeks, would up and ask him would he let them kiss him, for to remember him by; and he always done it; and some of them he hugged and kissed as many as five or six times—and he was invited to stay a week; and everybody wanted him to live in their houses, and said they'd think it was an honor; but he said as this was the last day of the camp-meeting he couldn't do no good, and besides he was in a sweat to get to the Indian Ocean right off and go to work on the pirates.

When we got back to the raft and he come to count up, he found he had collected eighty-seven dollars and seventy-five cents. And then he had fetched away a three-gallon jug of whisky, too, that he found under a wagon when we was starting home through the woods. The king said, take it all around, it laid over any day he'd ever put in in the missionarying line. He said it warn't no use talking, heathens don't amount to shucks, alongside of pirates, to work a camp-meeting with.

The duke was thinking *he'd* been doing pretty well, till the king come to show up, but after that he didn't think so so much. He had set up and printed off two little jobs for farmers, in that printing office—horse bills—and took the money, four dollars. And he had got in ten dollars worth of advertisements for the paper, which he said he would put in for four dollars if they would pay in advance—so they done it. The price of the paper was two dollars a year, but he took in three subscriptions for half a dollar apiece on condition of them paying him in advance; they were going to pay in cord-wood and onions, as usual, but he said he had just bought the concern and knocked down the price as low as he could afford it, and was going to run it for cash. He set up a little piece of poetry, which he made, himself, out of his own head—three verses—kind of sweet and saddish— the name of it was, "Yes, crush, cold world, this breaking heart"— and he left that all set up and ready to print in the paper and didn't charge nothing for it. Well, he took in nine dollars and a half, and said he'd done a pretty square day's work for it.

Then he showed us another little job he'd printed and hadn't charged for, because it was for us. It had a picture of a runaway nigger, with a bundle on a stick, over his shoulder, and "$200 reward" under it. The reading was all about Jim, and just described him to a dot. It said he run away from St. Jacques' plantation, forty mile below New Orleans, last winter, and likely went north, and whoever would catch him and send him back, he could have the reward and expenses.

"Now," says the duke, "after to-night we can run in the daytime if we want to. Whenever we see anybody coming, we can tie Jim hand and foot with a rope, and lay him in the wigwam and show this handbill and say we captured him up the river, and were too poor to travel on a steamboat, so we got this little raft on credit from our friends and are going down to get the reward. Handcuffs and chains would look still better on Jim, but it wouldn't go well with the story of us being so poor. Too much like jewelry. Ropes are the correct thing—we must preserve the unities, as we say on the boards."

We all said the duke was pretty smart, and there couldn't be no trouble about running daytimes. We judged we could make miles enough that night to get out of the reach of the pow-wow we reckoned the duke's work in the printing office was going to make in that little town—then we could boom right along, if we wanted to.

We laid low and kept still, and never shoved out till nearly ten o'clock; then we slid by, pretty wide away from the town, and didn't hoist our lantern till we was clear out of sight of it.

When Jim called me to take the watch at four in the morning, he says—

"Huck, does you reck'n we gwyne to run acrost any mo' kings on dis trip?"

"No," I says, "I reckon not."

"Well," says he, "dat's all right, den. I doan' mine one er two kings, but dat's enough. Dis one's powerful drunk, en de duke ain' much better."

I found Jim had been trying to get him to talk French, so he could hear what it was like; but he said he had been in this country so long, and had so much trouble, he'd forgot it.

Chapter XXI

IT WAS AFTER sun-up, now, but we went right on, and didn't tie up. The king and the duke turned out, by-and-by, looking pretty rusty; but after they'd jumped overboard and took a swim, it chippered them up a good deal. After breakfast the king he took a seat on a corner of the raft, and pulled off his boots and rolled up his britches, and let his legs dangle in the water, so as to be comfortable, and lit his pipe, and went to getting his Romeo and Juliet by heart. When he had got it pretty good, him and the duke begun to practice it together. The duke had to learn him over and over again, how to say every speech ; and he made him sigh, and put his hand on his heart, and after while he said he done it pretty well; "only," he says, "you mustn't bellow out *Romeo!* that way, like a bull— you must say it soft, and sick, and languishy, so—R-o-o-meo! that is the idea; for Juliet's a dear sweet mere child of a girl, you know, and she don't bray like a jackass."

Well, next they got out a couple of long swords that the duke made out of oak laths, and begun to practice the sword-fight—the duke called himself Richard III.; and the way they laid on, and pranced around the raft was grand to see. But by-and-by the king tripped and fell overboard, and after that they took a rest, and had a talk about all kinds of adventures they'd had in other times along the river.

After dinner, the duke says:

"Well, Capet, we'll want to make this a first-class show, you know, so I guess we'll add a little more to it. We want a little something to answer encores with, anyway."

"What's onkores, Bilgewater?"

The duke told him, and then says:

"I'll answer by doing the Highland fling or the sailor's hornpipe; and you— well, let me see—oh, I've got it—you can do Hamlet's soliloquy."

"Hamlet's which?"

"Hamlet's soliloquy, you know; the most celebrated thing in Shakespeare. Ah, it's sublime, sublime! Always fetches the house. I haven't got it in the book—I've only got one volume—but I reckon I can piece it out from memory. I'll just walk up and down a minute, and see if I can call it back from recollection's vaults."

So he went to marching up and down, thinking, and frowning horrible every now and then; then he would hoist up his eyebrows; next he would squeeze his hand on his forehead and stagger back and kind of moan; next he would sigh, and next he'd let on to drop a tear. It was beautiful to see him. By-and-by he got it. He told us to give attention. Then he strikes a most noble attitude, with one leg shoved forwards, and his arms stretched away up, and his head tilted back, looking up at the sky; and then he begins to rip and rave and grit his teeth; and after that, all through his speech he howled, and spread around, and swelled up his chest, and just knocked the spots out of any acting ever *I* see before. This is the speech—I learned it, easy enough, while he was learning it to the king:

> To be, or not a be; that is the bare bodkin
> That makes calamity of so long life;
> For who would fardels bear, till Birnam Wood do come to Dunsinane,
> But that the fear of something after death
> Murders the innocent sleep,
> Great nature's second course,
> And makes us rather sling the arrows of outrageous fortune
> Than fly to others that we know not of.
> There's the respect must give us pause:
> Wake Duncan with thy knocking! I would thou couldst;
> For who would bear the whips and scorns of time,
> The oppressor's wrong, the proud man's contumely,
> The law's delay, and the quietus which his pangs might take,
> In the dead waste and middle of the night, when churchyards yawn
> In customary suits of solemn black,
> But that the undiscovered country from whose bourne no traveler returns,
> Breathes forth contagion on the world,
> And thus the native hue of resolution, like the poor cat i' the adage,
> Is sicklied o'er with care,
> And all the clouds that lowered o'er our housetops,
> With this regard their currents turn away,
> And lose the name of action.
> 'Tis a consummation devoutly to be wished. But soft you, the fair Ophelia:
> Ope not thy ponderous and marble jaws,
> But get thee to a nunnery—go!

Well, the old man he liked that speech, and he mighty soon got it so he could do it first rate. It seemed like he was just born for it; and when he had his hand in and was excited, it was perfectly lovely the way he would rip and tear and rair up behind when he was getting it off.

The first chance we got, the duke he had some show bills printed; and after that, for two or three days as we floated along, the raft was a most uncommon lively place, for there warn't nothing but sword-fighting and rehearsing—as the duke called it—going on all the time. One morning, when we was pretty well down the State of Arkansaw, we come in sight of a little one-horse town in a big bend; so we tied up about three-quarters of a mile above it, in the mouth of a crick which was shut in like a tunnel by the cypress trees, and all of us but Jim took the canoe and went down there to see if there was any chance in that place for our show.

We struck it mighty lucky; there was going to be a circus there that afternoon, and the country people was already beginning to come in, in all kinds of old shackly wagons, and on horses. The circus would leave before night, so our show would have a pretty good chance. The duke he hired the court house, and we went around and stuck up our bills. They read like this:

Shaksperean Revival ! ! !

Wonderful Attraction !

For One Night Only !

The world renowned tragedians,

David Garrick the younger, of Drury Lane Theatre, London,

and

Edmund Kean the elder, of the Royal Haymarket Theatre, White-
chapel, Pudding Lane, Piccadilly, London, and the

Royal Continental Theatres, in their sublime

Shaksperean Spectacle entitled

The Balcony Scene

in

Romeo and Juliet ! ! !

Romeo . . . . .Mr.Garrick.

Juliet . . . . Mr. Kean.

Assisted by the whole strengh of the company !

New costumes, new scenery, new appointments !

Also :

The thrilling, masterly, and blood curdling

Broad-sword conflict

In Richard III. ! ! !

Richard III . . . . Mr. Garrick.

Richmond . . . . Mr. Kean.

also:

(by special request,)

Hamlet's Immortal Soliloquy ! !

By the Illustrious Kean !

Done by him 300 consecutive nights in Paris !

For One Night Only,

On account of imperative European engagements !

Admission 25 cents ; children and servants, 10 cents.

Then we went loafing around the town. The stores and houses was most all old shackly dried-up frame concerns that hadn't ever been painted; they was set up three or four foot above ground on stilts, so as to be out of reach of the water when the river was overflowed. The houses had little gardens around them, but they didn't seem to raise hardly anything in them but jimpson weeds, and sunflowers, and ash-piles, and old curled-up boots and shoes, and pieces of bottles, and rags, and played-out tin-ware. The fences was made of different kinds of boards, nailed on at different times; and they leaned every which-way, and had gates that didn't generly have but one hinge—a leather one. Some of the fences had been whitewashed, some time or another, but the duke said it was in Clumbus's time, like enough. There was generly hogs in the garden, and people driving them out.

All the stores was along one street. They had white-domestic awnings in front, and the country people hitched their horses to the awning-posts. There was empty dry-goods boxes under the awnings, and loafers roosting on them all day long, whittling them with their Barlow knives; and chawing tobacco, and gaping and yawning and stretching—a mighty ornery lot. They generly had on yellow straw hats most as wide as an umbrella, but didn't wear no coats nor waistcoats; they called one another Bill, and Buck, and Hank and Joe and Andy, and talked lazy and drawly, and used considerable many cuss-words. There was as many as one loafer leaning up against every awning-post, and he most always had his hands in his britches pockets, except when he fetched them out to lend a chaw of tobacco or scratch. What a body was hearing amongst them, all the time was—

"Gimme a chaw 'v tobacker, Hank."

"Cain't—I hain't got but one chaw left. Ask Bill."

Maybe Bill he gives him a chaw; maybe he lies and says he ain't got none. Some of them kinds of loafers never has a cent in the world, nor a chaw of tobacco of their own. They get all their chawing by borrowing—they say to a fellow, "I wisht you'd len' me a chaw, Jack, I jist this minute give Ben Thompson the last chaw I had"—which is a lie, pretty much every time; it don't fool nobody but a stranger; but Jack ain't no stranger, so he says—

"*You* give him a chaw, did you? so did your sister's cat's grandmother. You pay me back the chaws you've awready borry'd off'n me, Lafe Buckner, then I'll loan you one or two ton of it, and won't charge you no back intrust, nuther."

"Well, I *did* pay you back some of it wunst."

"Yes, you did—'bout six chaws. You borry'd store tobacker and paid back nigger-head."

Store tobacco if flat black plug, but these fellows mostly chaws the natural leaf twisted. When they borrow a chaw, they don't generly cut it off with a knife, but they set the plug in between their teeth, and gnaw with their teeth and tug at the plug with their hands till they get it in two—then sometimes the one that owns the tobacco looks mournful at it when it's handed back, and says, sarcastic—

"Here, gimmie the *chaw*, and you take the *plug*."

All the streets and lanes was just mud, they warn't nothing else *but* mud—mud as black as tar, and nigh about a foot deep in some places; and two or three inches deep in *all* the places. The hogs loafed and grunted around, everywheres. You'd see a muddy sow and a litter of pigs come lazying along the street and whollop herself right down in the way, where folks had to walk around her, and she'd stretch out, and shut her eyes, and wave her ears, whilst the pigs was milking her, and look as happy as if she was on salary. And pretty soon you'd hear a loafer sing out, "Hi! *so* boy! sick him, Tige!" and away the sow would go, squealing most horrible, with a dog or two swinging to each ear, and three or four dozen more a-coming; and then you would see all the loafers get up and watch the thing out of sight, and laugh at the fun and look grateful for the noise. Then they'd settle back again till there was a dog-fight. There couldn't anything wake them up all over, and make them happy all over, like a dog-fight—unless it might be putting turpentine on a stray dog and setting fire to him, or tying a tin pan to his tail and see him run himself to death.

On the river front some of the houses was sticking out over the bank, and they was bowed and bent, and about ready to tumble in. The people had moved out of them. The bank was caved away under one corner of some others, and that corner was hanging over. People lived in them yet, but it was dangersome, because sometimes a strip of land as wide as a house caves in at a time. Sometimes a belt of land a quarter of a mile deep will start in and cave along and cave along till it all caves into the river in one summer. Such a town as that has to be always moving back, and back, and back, because the river's always gnawing at it.

The nearer it got to noon that day, the thicker and thicker was the wagons and horses in the streets, and more coming all the time. Families fetched their dinners with them, from the country, and eat them in the wagons. There was considerable whiskey drinking going on, and I seen three fights. By-and-by somebody sings out—

"Here comes old Boggs!—in from the country for his little old monthly drunk—here he comes, boys!"

All the loafers looked glad—I reckoned they was used to having fun out of Boggs. One of them says—

"Wonder who he's a gwyne to chaw up this time. If he'd a chawed up all the men he's ben a gwyne to chaw up in the last twenty year, he'd have considerble ruputation, now."

Another one says, "I wisht old Boggs'd threaten me, 'cuz then I'd know I warn't gwyne to die for a thousan' year."

Boggs comes a-tearing along on his horse, whooping and yelling like an Injun, and singing out—

"Cler the track, thar. I'm on the waw-path, and the price uv coffins is a gwyne to raise."

He was drunk, and weaving about in his saddle; he was over fifty year old, and had a very red face. Everybody yelled at him, and laughed at him, and sassed him, and he sassed back, and said he'd attend to them and lay them out in their regular turns, but he couldn't wait now, because he'd come to town to kill old Colonel Sherburn, and his motto was, "meat first, and spoon vittles to top off on."

He see me, and rode up and says—

"Whar'd you come f'm, boy? You prepared to die?"

Then he rode on. I was scared; but a man says—

"He don't mean nothing; he's always a carryin' on like that, when he's drunk. He's the best-naturedest old fool in Arkansaw—never hurt nobody, drunk nor sober."

Boggs rode up before the biggest store in town and bent his head down so he could see under the curtain of the awning, and yells—

"Come out here, Sherburn! Come out and meet the man you've swindled. You're the houn' I'm after, and I'm a gwyne to have you, too!"

And so he went on, calling Sherburn everything he could lay his tongue to, and the whole street packed with people listening and laughing and going on. By-and-by a proud-looking man about fifty-five—and he was a heap the best dressed man in that town, too—steps out of the store, and the crowd drops back on each side to let him come. He says to Boggs, mighty ca'm and slow—he says:

"I'm tired of this; but I'll endure it till one o'clock. Till one o'clock, mind— no longer. If you open your mouth against me only once, after that time, you can't travel so far but I will find you."

Then he turns and goes in. The crowd looked mighty sober; nobody stirred, and there warn't no more laughing. Boggs rode off blackguarding Sherburn as loud as he could yell, all down the street; and pretty soon back he comes and stops before the store, still keeping it up. Some men crowded around him and tried to get him to shut up, but he wouldn't; they told him it would be one o'clock in about fifteen minutes, and so he *must* go home—he must go right away. But it didn't do no good. He cussed away, with all his might, and throwed his hat down in the mud and rode over it, and pretty soon away he went a-raging down the street again, with his gray hair a-flying. Everybody that could get a chance at him tried their best to coax him off of his horse so they could lock him up and get him sober; but it warn't no use—up the street he would tear again, and give Sherburn another cussing. By-and-by somebody says—

"Go for his daughter!—quick, go for his daughter; sometimes he'll listen to her. If anybody can persuade him, she can."

So somebody started on a run. I walked down street a ways, and stopped. In about five or ten minutes, here comes Boggs again—but not on his horse. He was a-reeling across the street towards me, bareheaded, with a friend on both sides of him aholt of his arms and hurrying him along. He was quiet, and looked uneasy; and he warn't hanging back any, but was doing some of the hurrying himself. Somebody sings out—

"Boggs!"

A LITTLE MONTHLY DRUNK.

I looked over there to see who said it, and it was that Colonel Sherburn. He was standing perfectly still, in the street, and had a pistol raised in his right hand—not aiming it, but holding it out with the barrel tilted up towards the sky. The same second I see a young girl coming on the run, and two men with her. Boggs and the men turned round, to see who called him, and when they see the pistol the men jumped to one side, and the pistol barrel come down slow and steady to a level—both barrels cocked. Boggs throws up both of his hands, and says, "O Lord, don't shoot!" Bang! goes the first shot, and he staggers back clawing at the air—bang! goes the second one, and he tumbles backwards onto the ground, heavy and solid, with his arms spread out. That young girl screamed out, and comes rushing, and down she throws herself on her father, crying, and saying, "Oh, he's killed him, he's killed him!" The crowd closed up around them, and shouldered and jammed one another, with their necks stretched, trying to see, and people on the inside trying to shove them back, and shouting, "Back, back! give him air, give him air!"

Colonel Sherburn he tossed his pistol onto the ground, and turned around on his heels and walked off.

They took Boggs to a little drug store, the crowd pressing around, just the same, and the whole town following, and I rushed and got a good place at the window, where I was close to him and could see in. They laid him on the floor, and put one large Bible under his head, and opened another one and spread it on his breast—but they tore open his shirt first, and I seen where one of the bullets went in. He made about a dozen long gasps, his breast lifting the Bible up when he drawed in his breath, and letting it down again when he breathed it out—and after that he laid still; he was dead. Then they pulled his daughter away from him, screaming and crying, and took her off. She was about sixteen, and very sweet and gentle-looking, but awful pale and scared.

Well, pretty soon the whole town was there, squirming and scrouging and pushing and shoving to get at the window and have a look, but people that had the places wouldn't give them up, and folks behind them was saying all the time, "Say, now, you've looked enough, you fellows; 'taint right and 'taint fair, for you to stay thar all the time, and never give nobody a chance; other folks has their rights as well as you."

There was considerable jawing back, so I slid out, thinking maybe there was going to be trouble. The streets was full, and everybody was excited. Everybody that seen the shooting was telling how it happened, and there was a big crowd packed around each one of these fellows, stretching their necks and listening. One long lanky man, with long hair and a big white fur stove-pipe hat on the back of his head, and a crooked-handled cane, marked out the places on the ground where Boggs stood, and where Sherburn stood, and the people following him around from one place to t'other and watching everything he done, and bobbing their heads to show they understood, and stooping a little and resting their hands on their thighs to watch him mark the places on the ground with his cane; and then he stood up straight and stiff where Sherburn had stood, frowning and having his hat-brim down over his eyes, and sung out, "Boggs!" and then fetched his cane down slow to a level, and says "Bang!" staggered backwards, says "Bang!" again, and fell down flat on his back. The people that had seen the thing said he done it perfect; said it was just exactly the way it all happened. Then as much as a dozen people got out their bottles and treated him.

Well, by-and-by somebody said Sherburn ought to be lynched. In about a minute everybody was saying it; so away they went, mad and yelling, and snatching down every clothes-line they come to, to do the hanging with.

Chapter XXII

THEY SWARMED UP the street towards Sherburn's house, a-whooping and yelling and raging like Injuns, and everything had to clear the way or get run over and tromped to mush, and it was awful to see. Children was heeling it ahead of the mob, screaming and trying to get out of the way; and every window along the road was full of women's heads, and there was nigger boys in every tree, and bucks and wenches looking over every fence; and as soon as the mob would get nearly to them they would break and skaddle back out of reach. Lots of the women and girls was crying and taking on, scared most to death.

They swarmed up in front of Sherburn's palings as thick as they could jam together, and you couldn't hear yourself think for the noise. It was a little twenty-foot yard. Some sung out ''Tear down the fence! tear down the fence!'' Then there was a racket of ripping and tearing and smashing, and down she goes, and the front wall of the crowd begins to roll in like a wave.

Just then Sherburn steps out on to the roof of his little front porch, with a double-barrel gun in his hand, and takes his stand, perfectly ca'm and deliberate, not saying a word. The racket stopped, and the wave sucked back.

Sherburn never said a word—just stood there, looking down. The stillness was awful creepy and uncomfortable. Sherburn run his eye slow along the crowd; and wherever it struck, the people tried a little to outgaze him, but they couldn't; they dropped their eyes and looked sneaky. Then pretty soon Sherburn sort of laughed; not the pleasant kind, but the kind that makes you feel like when you are eating bread that's got sand in it.

Then he says, slow and scornful:

''The idea of *you* lynching anybody! It's amusing. The idea of you thinking you had pluck enough to lynch a *man!* Because you're brave enough to tar and feather poor friendless cast-out women that come along here, did that make you

SHERBURN STEPS OUT.

think you had grit enough to lay your hands on a *man?* Why, a *man's* safe in the hands of ten thousand of your kind—as long as it's day-time and you're not behind him.

"Do I know you? I know you clear through. I was born and raised in the South, and I've lived in the North; so I know the average all around. The average man's a coward. In the North he lets anybody walk over him that wants to, and goes home and prays for a humble spirit to bear it. In the South one man, all by himself, has stopped a stage full of men, in the day-time, and robbed the lot. Your newspapers call you a brave people so much that you think you *are* braver than any other people—whereas you're just as brave, and no braver. Why don't your juries hang murderers? Because they're afraid the man's friends will shoot them in the back, in the dark—and it's just what they *would* do.

"So they always acquit; and then a *man* goes in the night, with a hundred masked cowards at his back, and lynches the rascal. Your mistake is, that you didn't bring a man with you; that's one mistake, and the other is that you didn't come in the dark, and fetch your masks. You brought *part* of a man—Buck Harkness, there—and if you hadn't had him to start you, you'd a taken it out in blowing.

"You didn't want to come. The average man don't like trouble and danger. *You* don't like trouble and danger. But if only *half* a man—like Buck Harkness, there—shouts 'Lynch him, lynch him!' you're afraid to back down—afraid you'll be found out to be what you are—*cowards*—and so you raise a yell and hang yourselves onto that half-a-man's coat tail, and come raging up here, swearing what big things you're going to do. The pitifulest thing out is a mob; that's what an army is—a mob; they don't fight with courage that's born in them, but with courage that's borrowed from their mass, and from their officers. But a mob without any *man* at the head of it, is *beneath* pitifulness. Now the thing for *you* to do, is to droop your tails and go home and crawl in a hole. If any real lynching's going to be done, it will be done in the dark, Southern fashion; and when they come they'll bring their masks, and fetch a *man* along. Now *leave*—and take your half-a-man with you"—tossing his gun up across his left arm and cocking it, when he says this.

The crowd washed back sudden, and then broke all apart and went tearing off every which way, and Buck Harkness he heeled it after them, looking tolerable cheap. I could a staid, if I'd a wanted to, but I didn't want to.

I went to the circus, and loafed around the back side till the watchman went by, and then dived in under the tent. I had my twenty-dollar gold piece and some other money, but I reckoned I better save it, because there ain't no telling how soon you are going to need it, away from home and amongst strangers, that way. You can't be too careful. I ain't opposed to spending money on circuses, when there ain't no other way, but there ain't no use in *wasting* it on them.

It was a real bully circus. It was the splendidest sight that ever was, when they all come riding in, two and two, a gentleman and lady, side by side, the men just in their drawers and under-shirts, and no shoes nor stirrups, and resting their hands on their thighs, easy and comfortable—there must a' been twenty of them—and every lady with a lovely complexion, and perfectly beautiful, and looking just like a gang of real sure-enough queens, and dressed in clothes that cost millions of dollars, and just littered with diamonds. It was a powerful fine sight; I never see anything so lovely. And then one by one they got up and stood, and went a-weaving around the ring so gentle and wavy and graceful, the men looking ever so tall and airy and straight, with their heads bobbing and skimming along, away up there under the tent-roof, and every lady's rose-leafy dress flapping soft and silky around her hips, and she looking like the most loveliest parasol.

And then faster and faster they went, all of them dancing, first one foot stuck out in the air and then the other, the horses leaning more and more, and the ring-master going round and round the centre-pole, cracking his whip and shouting "hi!—hi!" and the clown cracking jokes behind him; and by-and-by all hands dropped the reins, and every lady put her knuckles on her hips and every gentleman folded his arms, and then how the horses did lean over and hump themselves! And so, one after the other they all skipped off into the ring, and made the sweetest bow I ever see, and then scampered out, and everybody clapped their hands and went just about wild.

Well, all through the circus they done the most astonishing things; and all the time that clown carried on 'so it most killed the people. The ring-master couldn't ever say a word to him but he was back at him quick as a wink with the funniest things a body ever said; and how he ever *could* think of so many of them, and so sudden and so pat, was what I couldn't noway understand. Why, I couldn't a thought of them in a year. And by-and-by a drunk man tried to get into the ring—said he wanted to ride; said he could ride as well as anybody that ever was. They argued and tried to keep him out, but he wouldn't listen, and the whole show come to a standstill. Then the people begun to holler at him and make fun of him, and that made him mad, and he begun to rip and tear; so that stirred up the people, and a lot of men begun to pile down off of the benches and swarm towards the ring, saying, "Knock him down! throw him out!" and one or two women begun to scream. So, then, the ring-master he made a little speech, and said he hoped there wouldn't be no disturbance, and if the man would promise he wouldn't make no more trouble, he would let him ride, if he thought he could stay on the horse. So everybody laughed and said all right, and the man got on. The minute he was on, the horse begun to rip and tear and jump and cavort around, with two circus men hanging onto his bridle trying to hold him, and the drunk man hanging onto his neck, and his heels flying in the air every jump, and the whole crowd of people standing up shouting and laughing till the tears rolled down. And at last, sure enough, all the circus men could do, the horse broke loose, and away he went like the very nation, round and round the ring, with that sot laying down on him and hanging to his neck, with first one leg hanging most to the ground on one side, and then t'other one on t'other side, and the people just crazy. It warn't funny to me, though; I was all of a tremble to see his danger. But pretty soon he struggled up astraddle and grabbed the bridle, a-reeling this way and that; and the next miuute he sprung up and dropped the bridle and stood! and the horse agoing like a house afire too. He just stood up there, a-sailing around as easy and comfortable as if he warn't ever drunk in his life—and then he begun to pull off his clothes and sling them. He shed them so thick they kind of clogged up the air, and altogether he shed seventeen suits. And then, there he was, slim and handsome, and dressed the gaudiest and prettiest you ever saw, and he lit into that horse with his whip and made him fairly hum—and finally skipped off, and made his bow and danced off to the dressing-room, and everybody just a-howling with pleasure and as-tonishment.

Then the ring-master he see how he had been fooled, and he *was* the sickest ring-master you ever see, I reckon. Why, it was one of his own men! He had got up that joke all out of his own head, and never let on to nobody. Well, I felt sheepish enough, to be took in so, but I wouldn't a been in that ring-master's place, not for a thousand dollars. I don't know; there may be bullier circuses than what that one was, but I never struck them yet. Anyways it was plenty good enough for *me;* and wherever I run across it, it can have all of *my* custom, every time.

Well, that night we had *our* show; but there warn't only about twelve people there; just enough to pay expenses. And they laughed all the time, and that made the duke mad; and everybody left, anyway, before the show was over, but one boy which was asleep. So the duke said these Arkansaw lunkheads couldn't come up to Shakspeare; what they wanted was low comedy—and may be something ruther worse than low comedy, he reckoned. He said he could size their style. So next morning he got some big sheets of wrapping-paper and some black paint, and drawed off some handbills and stuck them up all over the village. The bills said:

AT THE COURT HOUSE!
FOR 3 NIGHTS ONLY!
The World-Renouned Tragedians
DAVID GARRICK THE YOUNGER!
AND
EDMUND KEAN THE ELDER!
Of the London and Continental
Theatres,
In their Thrilling Tragedy of
THE KING'S CAMELOPARD
OR
THE ROYAL NONESUCH!!!
Admission 50 cents.

Then at the bottom was the biggest line of all—which said:

LADIES AND CHILDREN NOT ADMITTED.

"There," says he, "if that line don't fetch them, I dont know Arkansaw!"

Chapter XXIII

WELL, ALL DAY him and the king was hard at it, rigging up a stage, and a curtain, and a row of candles for footlights; and that night the house was jam full of men in no time. When the place couldn't hold no more, the duke he quit tending door and went around the back way and come onto the stage and stood up before the curtain, and made a little speech, and praised up this tragedy, and said it was the most thrillingest one that ever was; and so he went on a-bragging about the tragedy and about Edmund Kean the Elder, which was to play the main principal part in it; and at last when he'd got everybody's expectations up high enough, he rolled up the curtain, and the next minute the king come a-prancing out on all fours, naked; and he was painted all over, ring-streaked-and-striped, all sorts of colors, as splendid as a rainbow. And—but never mind the rest of his outfit, it was just wild, but it was awful funny. The people most killed themselves laughing; and when the king got done capering, and capered off behind the scenes, they roared and clapped and stormed and haw-hawed till he come back and done it over again; and after that, they made him do it another time. Well, it would a made a cow laugh to see the shines that old idiot cut.

Then the duke he lets the curtain down, and bows to the people, and says the great tragedy will be performed only two nights more, on accounts of pressing London engagements, where the seats is all sold aready for it in Drury Lane; and then he makes them another bow, and says if he has succeeded in pleasing them and instructing them, he will be deeply obleeged if they will mention it to their friends and get them to come and see it.

Twenty people sings out:

"What, is it over? Is that *all?*"

The duke says yes. Then there was a fine time. Everybody sings out "sold," and rose up mad, and was agoing for that stage and them tragedians. But a big fine-looking man jumps up on a bench, and shouts:

"Hold on! Just a word, gentlemen." They stopped to listen. "We are sold—mighty badly sold. But we don't want to be the laughing-stock of this whole town, I reckon, and never hear the last of this thing as long as we live. *No.* What we want, is to go out of here quiet, and talk this show up, and sell the *rest* of the town! Then we'll all be in the same boat. Ain't that sensible?" ("You bet it is!—the jedge is right!" everybody sings out.) "All right, then—not a word about any sell. Go along home, and advise everybody to come and see the tragedy."

Next day you couldn't hear nothing around that town but how splendid that show was. House was jammed again, that night, and we sold this crowd the same way. When me and the king and the duke got home to the raft, we all had a supper; and by-and-by, about midnight, they made Jim and me back her out and float her down the middle of the river and fetch her in and hide her about two mile below town.

The third night the house was crammed again—and they warn't new-comers, this time, but people that was at the show the other two nights. I stood by the duke at the door, and I see that every man that went in had his pockets bulging, or something muffled up under his coat—and I see it warn't no perfumery neither, not by a long sight. I smelt sickly eggs by the barrel, and rotten cabbages, and such things; and if I know the signs of a dead cat being around, and I bet I do, there was sixty-four of them went in. I shoved in there for a minute, but it was too various for me, I couldn't stand it. Well, when the place couldn't hold no more people, the duke he give a fellow a quarter and told him to tend door for him a minute, and then he started around for the stage door, I after him; but the minute we turned the corner and was in the dark, he says:

"Walk fast, now, till you get away from the houses, and then shin for the raft like the dickens was after you!" I done it, and he done the same. We struck the raft at the same time, and in less than two seconds we was gliding down stream, all dark and still, and edging towards the middle of the river, nobody saying a word. I reckoned the poor king was in for a gaudy time of it with the audience; but nothing of the sort; pretty soon he crawls out from under the wigwam, and says:

"Well, how'd the old thing pan out this time, Duke ?"

He hadn't been up town at all.

We never showed a light till we was about ten mile below that village.

Then we lit up and had a supper, and the king and the duke fairly laughed their bones loose over the way they'd served them people. The duke says:

"Greenhorns, flatheads! *I* knew the first house would keep mum and let the rest of the town get roped in; and I knew they'd lay for us the third night, and consider it was *their* turn now. Well, it *is* their turn, and I'd give something to know how much they'd take for it. I *would* just like to know how they're putting in their opportunity. They can turn it into a picnic, if they want to—they brought plenty provisions."

Them rapscallions took in four hundred and sixty-five dollars in that three nights. I never see money hauled in by the wagon-load like that, before.

By-and-by, when they was asleep and snoring. Jim says:

"Don't it 'sprise you, de way dem kings carries on, Huck?"

"No," I says, "it don't."

"Why don't it, Huck?"

"Well, it don't, because it's in the breed. I reckon they're all alike."

"But, Huck, dese kings o' ourn is regular rapscallions; dat's jist what dey is; dey's reglar rapscallions."

"Well, that's what I'm a-saying; all kings is mostly rapseallions, as fur as I can make out."

"Is dat so?"

"You read about them once—you'll see. Look at Henry the Eight; this'n's a Sunday-School Superintendent to *him*. And look at Charles Second, and Louis Fourteen, and Louis Fifteen, and James Second, and Edward Second, and Richard Third, and forty more; besides all them Saxon heptarchies that used to rip around so in old times and raise Cain. My, you ought to seen old Henry the Eight when he was in bloom. He *was* a blossom. He used to marry a new wife every day, and chop off her head next morning. And he would do it just as indifferent as if he was ordering up eggs. 'Fetch up Nell Gwynn,' he says. They fetch her up. Next morning, 'Chop off her head!' And they chop it off. 'Fetch up Jane Shore,' he says; and up she comes. Next morning 'Chop off her head'—and they chop it off. 'Ring up Fair Rosamun.' Fair Rosamun answers the bell. Next morning, 'Chop off her head.' And he made every one of them tell him a tale every night; and he kept that up till he had hogged a thousand and one tales that way, and then he put them all in a book, and called it Domesday Book—which was a good name and stated the case. You don't know kings, Jim, but I know them; and this old rip of ourn is one of the cleanest I've struck in history. Well, Henry he takes a notion he wants to get up some trouble with this country. How does he go at it—give notice?—give the country a show? No. All of a sudden he heaves all the tea in Boston Harbor overboard, and whacks out a declaration of independence, and dares them to come on. That was *his* style—he never give anybody a chance. He had suspicions of his father, the Duke of Wellington. Well, what did he do?—ask him to show up? No—drownded him in a butt of mamsey, like a cat. Spose people left money laying around where he was— what did he do? He collared it. Spose he contracted to do a thing; and you paid him, and didn't set down there and see that he done it—what did he do? He always done the other thing. Spose he opened his mouth—what then? If he didn't shut it up powerful quick, he'd lose a lie, every time. That's the kind of a bug Henry was; and if we'd a had him along 'stead of our kings, he'd a fooled that town a heap worse than ourn done. I don't say that ourn is lambs, because they ain't, when you come right down to the cold facts; but they ain't nothing to *that* old ram, anyway. All I say is, kings is kings, and you got to make allowances. Take them all around, they're a mighty ornery lot. It's the way they're raised.''

"But dis one do *smell* so like de nation, Huck.''

"Well, they all do, Jim. *We* can't help the way a king smells; history don't tell no way.''

"Now de duke, he's a tolerble likely man, in some ways.''

"Yes, a duke's different. But not very different. This one's a middling hard lot, for a duke. When he's drunk, there ain't no near-sighted man could tell him from a king.''

"Well, anyways, I doan' hanker for no mo' un um, Huck. Dese is all I kin stan'.''

"It's the way I feel, too, Jim. But we've got them on our hands, and we got to remember what they are, and make allowances. Sometimes I wish we could hear of a country that's out of kings.''

What was the use to tell Jim these warn't real kings and dukes? It wouldn't a done no good; and besides, it was just as I said; you couldn't tell them from the real kind.

I went to sleep, and Jim didn't call me when it was my turn. He often done that. When I waked up, just at day-break, he was setting there with his head down betwixt his knees, moaning and mourning to himself. I didn't take notice, nor let on. I knowed what it was about. He was thinking about his wife and his children, away up yonder, and he was low and homesick; because he hadn't ever been away from home before in his life; and I do believe he cared just as much for his people as white folks does for their'n. It don't seem natural, but I reckon it's so. He was often moaning and mourning that way, nights, when he judged I was asleep, and saying, "Po' little 'Lizabeth! po' little Johnny! its mighty hard; I spec' I ain't ever gwyne to see you no mo', no mo'!'' He was a mighty good nigger, Jim was.

But this time I somehow got to talking to him about his wife and young ones; and by-and-by he says:

"What makes me feel so bad dis time, 'uz bekase I hear sumpn over yonder on de bank like a whack, er a slam, while ago, en it mine me er de time I treat my little 'Lizabeth so ornery. She warn't on'y 'bout fo' year ole, en she tuck de sk'yarlet-fever, en had a powful rough spell; but she got well, en one day she was a-stannin' aroun', en I says to her, I says:

"Shet de do'.''

"She never done it; jis' stood dah, kiner smilin' up at me. It make me mad; en I says agin, mighty loud, I says:

" 'Doan' you hear me?—shet de do'!''

"She jis' stood de same way, kiner smilin' up. I was a-bilin'! I says:

" 'I lay I *make* you mine!'

"En wid dat I fetch' her a slap side de head dat sont her a-sprawlin'. Den I went into de yuther room, en 'uz gone 'bout ten minutes; en when I come back, dah was dat do' a-stanuin' open *yit,* en dat chile stannin' mos' right in it, a-lookin' down and mournin', en de tears runnin' down. My, but I *wuz* mad, I was agwyne for de chile, but jis' den—it was a do' dat open innerds—jis' den, 'long come de wind en slam it to, behine de chile, ker-*blam!*—en my lan', de chile never move'! My breff mos' hop outer me; en I feel so—so—I doan' know *how* I feel. I crope out, all a-tremblin', en crope aroun' en open de do' easy en slow, en poke my head in behine de chile, sof'en still, en all uv a sudden, I says *pow!* jis' as loud as I could yell. *She never budge!* Oh, Huck, I bust out a-cryin' en grab her up in my arms, en say, 'Oh, de po' little thing! de Lord God Amighty fogive po' ole Jim, kaze he never gwyne to fogive hisself as long's he live!' Oh, she was plumb deef en dumb, Huck, plumb deef en dnmb—en I'd ben a-treat'n her so!''

Chapter XXIV

NEXT DAY, TOWARDS night, we laid up under a little willow tow-head out in the middle, where there was a village on each side of the river, and the duke and the king begun to lay out a plan for working them towns. Jim he spoke to the duke, and said he hoped it wouldn't take but a few hours, because it got mighty heavy and tiresome to him when he had to lay all day in the wigwam tied with the rope. You see, when we left him all alone we had to tie him, because if anybody happened on him all by himself and not tied, it wouldn't look much like he was a runaway nigger, you know. So the duke said it *was* kind of hard to have to lay roped all day, and he'd cipher out some way to get around it.

He was uncommon bright, the duke was, and he soon struck it. He dressed Jim up in King Lear's outfit—it was a long curtain-calico gown, and a white horse-hair wig and whiskers; and then he took his theatre-paint and painted Jim's face and hands and ears and neck all over a dead dull solid blue, like a man that's been drownded nine days. Blamed if he warn't the horriblest looking outrage I ever see. Then the duke took and wrote out a sign on a shingle so—

Sick Arab—but harmless when not out of his head.

And he nailed that shingle to a lath, and stood the lath up four or five foot in front of the wigwam. Jim was satisfied. He said it was a sight better than laying tied a couple of years every day and trembling all over every time there was a sound. The duke told him to make himself free and easy, and if anybody ever come meddling around, he must hop out of the wigwam, and carry on a little, and fetch a howl or two like a wild beast, and he reckoned they would light out and leave him alone. Which was sound enough judgment; but you take the average man, and he wouldn't wait for him to howl. Why, he didn't only look like he was dead, he looked considerable more than that.

These rapscallions wanted to try the Nonesuch again, because there was so much money in it, but they judged it wouldn't be safe, because maybe the news might a worked along down by this time. They couldn't hit no project that suited, exactly; so at last the duke said he reckoned he'd lay off and work his brains an hour or two and see if he couldn't put up something on the Arkansaw village; and the king he allowed he would drop over to t'other village, without any plan, but just trust in Providence to lead him the profitable way—meaning the devil, I reckon. We had all bought store clothes where we stopped last; and now the king put his'n on, and he told me to put mine on. I done it, of course. The king's duds was all black, and he did look real swell and starchy. I never knowed how clothes could change a body before. Why, before, he looked like the orneriest old rip that ever was; but now, when he'd take off his new white beaver and make a bow and do a smile, he looked that grand and good and pious that you'd say he had walked right out of the ark, and maybe was old Leviticus himself. Jim cleaned up the canoe, and I got my paddle ready. There was a big steamboat laying at the shore away up under the point, about three mile above town—been there a couple of hours, taking on freight. Says the king:

"Seein' how I'm dressed, I reckon maybe I better arrive down from St. Louis or Cincinnati, or some other big place. Go for the steamboat, Huckleberry; we'll come down to the village on her."

I didn't have to be ordered twice, to go and take a steamboat ride. I fetched the shore a half a mile above the village, and then went scooting along the bluff bank in the easy water. Pretty soon we come to a nice innocent-looking young country jake setting on a log swabbing the sweat off of his face, for it was powerful warm weather; and he had a couple of big carpet-bags by him.

"Run her nose in shore," says the king. I done it. "Wher' you bound for, young man?"

"For the steamboat; going to Orleans."

"Git aboard," says the king. "Hold on a minute, my servant'll he'p you with them bags. Jump out and he'p the gentleman, Adolphus"—meaning me, I see.

I done so, and then we all three started on again. The young chap was mighty thankful; said it was tough work toting his baggage such weather. He asked the king where he was going, and the king told him he'd come down the river and landed at the other village this morning, and now he was going up a few mile to see an old friend on a farm up there. The young fellow says:

"When I first see you I says to myself, 'It's Mr. Wilks, sure, and he come mighty near getting here in time.' But then I says again, 'No, I reckon it ain't him, or else he wouldn't be paddling up the river.' You *ain't* him, are you?"

"No, my name's Blodgett—Elexander Blodgett—*Reverend* Elexander Blodgett, I spose I must say, as I'm one o' the Lord's poor servants. But still I'm jist as

ADOLPHUS.

able to be sorry for Mr. Wilks for not arriving in time, all the same, if he's missed anything by it—which I hope he hasn't."

"Well, he don't miss any property by it, because he'll get that all right; but he's missed seeing his brother Peter die—which he mayn't mind, nobody can tell as to that—but his brother would a give anything in this world to see *him* before he died; never talked about nothing else all these three weeks; hadn't seen him since they was boys together—and hadn't ever seen his brother William at all—that's the deef and dumb one—William ain't more than thirty or thirty-five. Peter and George was the only ones that come out here; George was the married brother; him and his wife both died last year. Harvey and William's the only ones that's left now; and, as I was saying, they haven't got here in time."

"Did anybody send 'em word?"

"Oh, yes; a month or two ago, when Peter was first took; because Peter said then that he sorter felt like he warn't going to get well this time. You see, he was pretty old, and George's g'yirls was too young to be much company for him, except Mary Jane the red-headed one; and so he was kinder lonesome after George and his wife died, and didn't seem to care much to live. He most desperately wanted to see Harvey—and William too, for that matter—because he was one of them kind that can't bear to make a will. He left a letter behind for Harvey, and said he'd told in it where his money was hid, and how he wanted the rest of the property divided up so George's g'yirls would be all right—for George didn't leave nothing. And that letter was all they could get him to put a pen to."

"Why do you reckon Harvey don't come? Wher' does he live?"

"Oh, he lives in England—Sheffield—preaches there—hasn't ever been in this country. He hasn't had any too much time—and besides he mightn't a got the letter at all, you know."

"Too bad, too bad he couldn't a lived to see his brothers, poor soul. You going to Orleans, you say?"

"Yes, but that ain't only a part of it. I'm going in a ship, next Wednesday, for Ryo Janeero, where my uncle lives."

"It's a pretty long journey. But it'll be lovely; I wisht I was agoing. Is Mary Jane the oldest? How old is the others?"

"Mary Jane's nineteen, Susan's fifteen, and Joanna's about fourteen—that's the one that gives herself to good works and has a hare-lip."

"Poor things! to be left alone in the cold world so."

"Well, they could be worse off. Old Peter had friends, and they ain't going to let them come to no harm. There's Hobson, the Babtis' preacher; and Deacon Lot Hovey, and Ben Rucker, and Abner Shackleford, and Levi Bell, the lawyer; and Dr. Robinson, and their wives, and the widow Bartley, and—well, there's a lot of them; but these are the ones that Peter was thickest with, and used to write about sometimes, when he wrote home; so Harvey'll know where to look for friends when he get's here."

Well, the old man he went on asking questions till he just fairly emptied that young fellow. Blamed if he didn't inquire about everybody and everything in that blessed town, and all about all the Wilkses; and about Peter's business—which was a tanner; and about George's—which was a carpenter; and about Harvey's—which was a dissentering minister; and so on, and so on. Then he says:

"What did you want to walk all the way up to the steamboat for?"

"Because she's a big Orleans boat, and I was afeard she mightn't stop there. When they're deep they won't stop for a hail. A Cincinnati boat will, but this is a St. Louis one."

"Was Peter Wilks well off?"

"Oh, yes, pretty well off. He had houses and land, and it's reckoned he left three or four thousand in cash hid up som'ers."

"When did you say he died?"

"I didn't say, but it was last night."

"Funeral to-morrow, likely?"

"Yes, 'bout the middle of the day."

"Well, it's all terrible sad; but we've all got to go one time or another. So what we want to do is to be prepared; then we're all right."

"Yes, sir, it's the best way. Ma used to always say that."

When we struck the boat, she was about done loading, and pretty soon she got off. The king never said nothing about going aboard, so I lost my ride, after all. When the boat was gone, the king made me paddle up another mile to a lonesome place, and then he got ashore, and says:

"Now hustle back, right off, and fetch the duke up here, and the new carpet-bags. And if he's gone over to t'other side, go over there and git him. And tell him to git himself up regardless. Shove along, now."

I see what *he* was up to; but I never said nothing, of course. When I got back with the duke, we hid the canoe and then they set down on a log, and the king told him everything, just like the young fellow had said it—every last word of it. And all the time he was a doing it, he tried to talk like an Englishman; and he done it pretty well too, for a slouch. I can't imitate him, and so I ain't agoing to try to; but he really done it pretty good. Then he say's:

"How are you on the deef and dumb, Bilgewater?"

The duke said, leave him alone for that; said he had played a deef and dumb person on the histrionic boards. So then they waited for a steamboat.

About the middle of the afternoon a couple of little boats come along, but they didn't come from high enough up the river; but at last there was a big one, and they hailed her. She sent out her yawl, and we went aboard, and she was from Cincinnati; and when they found we only wanted to go four or five mile, they was booming mad, and give us a cussing, and said they wouldn't land us. But the king was ca'm. He says:

"If gentlemen kin afford to pay a dollar a mile apiece, to be took on and put off in a yawl, a steamboat kin afford to carry 'em, can't it?"

So they softened down and said it was all right; and when we got to the village, they yawled us ashore. About two dozen men flocked down, when they see the yawl a coming; and when the king says—

"Kin any of you gentlemen tell me wher' Mr. Peter Wilks lives?" they give a glance at one another, and nodded their heads, as much as to say, "What d' I tell you?" Then one of them says, kind of soft and gentle:

"I'm sorry, sir, but the best we can do is to tell you where he *did* live yesterday evening."

Sudden as winking, the ornery old cretur went all to smash, and fell up against the man, and put his chin on his shoulder, and cried down his back, and says:

"Alas, alas, our poor brother—gone, and we never got to see him; oh, it's too, *too* hard!"

Then he turns around, blubbering, and makes a lot of idiotic signs to the duke on his hands, and blamed if *he* didn't drop a carpet-bag and bust ont a-crying. If they warn't the beatenest lot, them two frauds, that ever I struck.

Well, the men gethered around, and sympathized with them, and said all sorts of kind things to them, and carried their carpet-bags up the hill for them, and let them lean on them and cry, and told the king all about his brother's last moments, and the king he told it all over again on his hands to the duke, and both of them took on about that dead tanner like they'd lost the twelve disciples. Well, if ever I struck anything like it, I'm a nigger. It was enough to make a body ashamed of the human race.

Chapter XXV

THE NEWS WAS all over town in two minutes, and you could see the people tearing down on the run, from every which way, some of them putting on their coats as they come. Pretty soon we was in the middle of a crowd, and the noise of the tramping was like a soldier-march. The windows and dooryards was full; and every minute somebody would say, over a fence:

"Is it *them?*"

And somebody trotting along with the gang would answer back and say,

"You bet it is."

When we got to the house, the street in front of it was packed, and the three girls was standing in the door. Mary Jane *was* red-headed, but that don't make no difference, she was most awful beautiful, and her face and her eyes was all lit up like glory, she was so glad her uncles was come. The king he spread his arms, and Mary Jane she jumped for them, and the hare-lip jumped for the duke, and there they *had* it! Everybody most, leastways women, cried for joy to see them meet again at last and have such good times.

Then the king he hunched the duke, private—I see him do it—and then he looked around and see the coffin, over on two chairs; so then, him and the duke, with a hand across each other's shoulder, and t'other hand to their eyes walked slow and solemn over there, everybody dropping back to give them room, and all the talk and noise stopping, people saying "Sh!" and all the men taking their hats off and drooping their heads, so you could a heard a pin fall. And when they got there, they bent over and looked in the coffin, and took one sight, and then they bust out a crying so you could a heard them to Orleans, most; and then they put their arms around each other's necks, and hung their chins over each other's shoulders; and then for three minutes, or maybe four, I never see two men leak the way they done. And mind you, everybody was doing the same; and the place was that damp I never see anything like it. Then one of them got on one side of the coffin, and t'other on t'other side, and they kneeled down and rested their foreheads on the coffin, and let on to pray all to theirselves. Well, when it come to that, it worked the crowd like you never see anything like it, and so everybody broke down and went to sobbing right out loud—the poor girls, too; and every woman, nearly, went up to the girls, without saying a word, and kissed them, solemn, on the forehead, and then put their hand on their head, and looked up towards the sky, with the tears running down, and then busted out and went off sobbing and swabbing, and give the next woman a show. I never see anything so disgusting.

Well, by-and-by the king he gets up and comes forward a little, and works himself up and slobbers out a speech, all full of tears and flapdoodle about its being a sore trial for him and his poor brother to lose the diseased, and to miss seeing diseased alive, after the long journey of four thousand mile, but it's a trial that's sweetened and sanctified to us by this dear sympathy and these holy tears, and so he thanks them out of his heart and out of his brother's heart, because out of their mouths they can't, words being too weak and cold, and all that kind of rot and slush, till it was just sickening; and then he blubbers out a pious goody-goody Amen, and turns himself loose and goes to crying fit to bust.

And the minute the words was out of his mouth somebody over in the crowd struck up the doxolojer, and everybody joined in with all their might, and it just warmed you up and made you feel as good as church letting out. Music *is* a good thing; and after all that soul-butter and hogwash, I never see it freshen up things so, and sound so honest and bully.

Then the king begins to work his jaw again, and says how him and his nieces would be glad if a few of the main principal friends of the family would take supper here with them this evening, and help set up with the ashes of the diseased; and says if his poor brother laying yonder could speak, he knows who he would name, for they was names that was very dear to him, and mentioned often in his letters; and so he will name the same, to-wit, as follows, vizz:—Rev. Mr. Hobson, and Deacon Lot Hovey, and Mr. Ben Rucker, and Abner Shackleford, and Levi Bell, and Dr. Robinson, and their wives, and the widow Bartley.

Rev. Hobson and Dr. Robinson was down to the end of the town, a-hunting together; that is, I mean the doctor was shipping a sick man to t'other world, and the preacher was pinting him right. Lawyer Bell was away up to Louisville on some business. But the rest was on hand, and so they all come and shook hands with the king and thanked him and talked to him; and then they shook hands with the duke, and didn't say nothing but just kept a-smiling and bobbing their heads like a passel of sapheads whilst he made all sorts of signs with his hands and said "Goo-goo—goo-goo-goo," all the time, like a baby that can't talk.

So the king he blatted along, and managed to inquire about pretty much everybody and dog in town, by his name, and mentioned all sorts of little things that happened one time or another in the town, or to George's family, or to Peter; and he always let on that Peter wrote him the things, but that was a lie, he got every blessed one of them out of that young flathead that we canoed up to the steamboat.

Then Mary Jane she fetched the letter her father left behind, and the king he read it out loud and cried over it. It give the dwelling-house and three thousand dollars, gold, to the girls; and it give the tanyard (which was doing a good business), along with some other houses and land (worth about seven thousand), and three thousand dollars in gold to Harvey and William, and told where the six thousand cash was hid, down cellar. So these two frauds said they'd go and fetch it up, and have everything square and above-board; and told me to come with a candle. We shut the cellar door behind us, und when they found the bag they spilt it out on the floor, and it was a lovely sight, all them yallerboys. My, the way the king's eyes did shine! He slaps the duke on the shoulder, and says:

"Oh, *this* ain't bully, nor noth'n! Oh, no, I reckon not! Why, Biljy, it beats the Nonesuch, *don't* it!''

The duke allowed it did. They pawed the yaller-boys, and sifted them through their fingers and let them jingle down on the floor; and the king says:

"It ain't no use talkin'; bein' brothers to a rich dead man, and representatives of furrin heirs that's got left, is the line for you and me, Bilge. Thish-yer comes of trust'n to Providence. It's the best way, in the long run. I've tried 'em all, and ther' ain't no better way.''

Most everybody would a been satisfied with the pile, and took it on trust; but no, they must count it. So they counts it, and it comes out four hundred and fifteen dollars short. Says the king:

"Dern him, I wonder what he done with that four hunderd and fifteen dollars?''

They worried over that a while, and ransacked all around for it. Then the duke says:

"Well, he was a pretty sick man, and likely he made a mistake—I reckon that's the way of it. The best way's to let it go, and keep still about it. We can spare it.''

"Oh, shucks, yes, we can *spare* it. I don't k'yer noth'n 'bout that—it's the *count* I'm thinkin' about. We want to be awful square and open and above-board here, you know. We want to lug this h-yer money up stairs and count it before everybody—then ther' ain't noth'n suspicious. But which the dead man says ther's six thous'n dollars, you know, we don't want to——''

"Hold on,'' say's the duke, "Less make up the deffsit''—and he begun to haul out yaller-boys out of his pocket.

"It's a most amaz'n' good idea, duke—you *have* got a rattlin' clever head on you,'' says the king. "Blest if the old Nonesuch ain't a heppin' us out agin''—and *he* begun to haul out yaller-jackets and stack them up.

It most busted them, but they made up the six thousand clean and clear.

"Say,'' says the duke, "I got another idea. Le's go up stairs and count this money, and then take and *give it to the girls.*''

"Good land, duke, lemme hug you! It's the most dazzling idea 'at ever a man struck. You have cert'nly got the most astonishin' head I ever see. Oh, this is the boss dodge, there ain't no mistake 'bout it. Let 'em fetch along their suspicions now, if they want to—this'll lay 'em out.''

When we got up stairs, everybody gethered around the table, and the king he counted it and stacked it up, three hundred dollars in a pile—twenty elegant little piles. Everybody looked hungry at it, and licked their chops. Then they raked it into the bag again, and I see the king begin to swell himself up for another speech. He says:

"Friends all, my poor brother that lays yonder, has done generous by them that's left behind in the vale of sorrers. He has done generous by these-yer poor little lambs that he loved and sheltered, and that's left fatherless and motherless. Yes, and we that knowed him, knows that he would a done *more* generous by 'em if he hadn't ben afeard o' woundin' his dear William and me. Now, *wouldn't* he? Ther' ain't no question 'bout it, in *my* mind. Well, then—what kind o' brothers would it be, that'd stand in his way at sech a time? And what kind o' uncles would it be that'd rob—yes, *rob*—sech poor sweet lambs as these 'at he loved so, at sech a time? If I know William—and I *think* I do—he—well, I'll jest ask him.'' He turns around and begins to make a lot of signs to the duke with his hands; and the duke he looks at him stupid and leather-headed a while, then all of a sudden he seems to catch his meaning, and jumps for the king, goo-gooing with all his might for joy, and hugs him about fifteen times before he lets up. Then the king says, "I knowed it; I reckon *that*'ll convince anybody the way *he* feels about it. Here, Mary Jane, Susan, Joanner, take the money— take it *all*. It's the gift of him that lays yonder, cold but joyful."

Mary Jane she went for him, Susan and the hare-lip went for the duke, and then such another hugging and kissing I never see yet. And everybody crowded up with the tears in their eyes, and most shook the hands off of them frauds, saying all the time:

"You *dear* good souls!—how *lovely!*—how *could* you!"

Well, then, pretty soon all hands got to talking about the diseased again, and how good he was, and what a loss he was, and all that; and before long a big iron-jawed man worked himself in there from outside, and stood a listening and looking, and not saying anything; and nobody saying anything to him either, because the king was talking and they was all busy listening. The king was saying—in the middle of something he'd started in on—

"—they bein' partickler friends o' the diseased. That's why they're invited here this evenin'; but to-morrow we want *all* to come—everybody; for he respected everybody, he liked everybody. and so it's fitten that his funeral orgiess h'd be public."

And so he went a-mooning on and on, liking to hear himself talk, and every little while he fetched in his funeral orgies again, till the duke he couldn't stand it no more; so he writes on a little serap of paper, "*obsequies,* you old fool," and folds it up and goes to goo-gooing and reaching it over people's heads to him. The king he reads it, and puts it in his pocket, and says:

"Poor William, afflicted as he is, his *heart's* aluz right. Asks me to invite everybody to come to the funeral—wants me to make 'em all welcome. But he needn't a worried—it was jest what I was at."

Then he weaves along again, perfectly ca'm, and goes to dropping in is funeral orgies again every now and them, just like he done before. And when he done it the third time, he says:

"I say orgies, not because it's the common term, because it ain't-obsequies bein' the comnion term—but because orgies is the right term. Obsequies ain't used in England no more, now—it's gone out. We say orgies now, in England. Orgies is better, because it means the thing you're after, more exact. It's a word that's made up out'n the Greek *orgo,* outside, open, abroad; and the Hebrew *jeesum,* to plant, cover up; hence in*ter.* So, you see, funeral orgies is an open er public funeral."

He was the *worst* I ever struck. Well, the iron-jawed man he laughed right in his face. Everybody was shocked. Everybody says, "Why *doctor!*" and Abner Shackleford says:

"Why, Robinson, hain't you heard the news? This is Harvey Wilks."

The king he smiled eager, and shoved out his flapper, and says:

"*Is* it my poor brother's dear good friend and physician? I——"

"Keep your hands off of me!" says the doctor. "*You* talk like an Englishman— *don't* you? It's the worse imitation I ever heard. *You* Peter Wilks's brother. You're a fraud, that's what you are!"

Well, how they all took on! They crowded around the doctor, and tried to quiet him down, and tried to explain to him, and tell him how Harvey'd showed in forty ways that he *was* Harvey, and knowed everybody by name, and the names of the very dogs, and begged and *begged* him not to hurt Harvey's feelings and the poor girls' feelings, and all that; but it warn't no use, he stormed right along, and said any man that pretended to be an Englishman and couldn't imitate the lingo no better than what he did, was a fraud and a liar. The poor girls was hanging to the king and crying; and all of a sudden the doctor ups and turns on *them*. He says:

"I was your father's friend, and I'm your friend; and I warn you *as* a friend, and an honest one, that wants to protect you and keep you out of harm and trouble, to turn your backs on that scoundrel, and have nothing to do with him, the ignorant tramp, with his idiotic Greek and Hebrew as he calls it. He is the thinnest kind of an impostor—has come here with a lot of empty names and facts which he has picked up somewheres, and you take them for *proofs,* and are helped to fool yourselves by these foolish friends here, who ought to know better. Mary Jane Wilks, you know me for your friend, and for your unselfish friend, too. Now listen to me; turn this pitiful rascal out—I *beg* you to do it; Will you?"

Mary Jane straightened herself up, and my, but she was handsome! She says:

"*Here* is my answer." She hove up the bag of money and put it in the king's hands, and says, "Take this six thousand dollars, and invest for me and my sisters any way you want to, and don't give us no receipt for it."

Then she put her arm around the king on one side, and Susan and the hare-lip done the same on the other. Everybody clapped their hands and stomped on the floor like a perfect storm, whilst the king held up his head and smiled proud. The doctor says:

"All right, I wash *my* hands of the matter. But I warn you all that a time's coming when you're going to feel sick whenever you think of this day"—and away he went.

"All right, doctor," says the king, kinder mocking him, "we'll try and get 'em to send for you"—which made them all laugh, and they said it was a prime good hit.

THE BAG OF MONEY.

Chapter XXVI

WELL WHEN THEY was all gone, the king he asks Mary Jane how they was off for spare rooms, and she said she had one spare room, which would do for Uncle William, and she'd give her own room to Uncle Harvey, which was a little bigger, and she would turn into the room with her sisters and sleep on a cot; and up garret was a little cubby, with a pallet in it. The king said the cubby would do for his valley—meaning me.

So Mary Jane took us up, and she showed them their rooms, which was plain but nice. She said she'd have her frocks and a lot of other traps took out of her room if they was in Uncle Harvey's way, but he said they warn't. The frocks was hung along the wall, and before them was a curtain made out of calico that hung down to the floor. There was an old hair trunk in one corner, and a guitar box in another, and all sorts of little knick-knacks and jimcracks around, like girls brisken up a room with. The king said it was all the more homely and more pleasanter for these fixings, and so don't disturb them. The duke's room was pretty small, but plenty good enough, and so was my cubby.

That night they had a big supper, and all them men and women was there, and I stood behind the king and the duke's chairs and waited on them, and the niggers waited on the rest. Mary Jane she set at the head of the table, with Susan along side of her, and said how bad the biscuits was, and how mean the preserves was, and how ornery and tough the fried chickens was—and all that kind of rot, the way women always do for to force out compliments; and the people all knowed everything was tip-top, and said so—said "How *do* you get biscuits to brown so nice?" and "Where, for the land's sake *did* you get these amaz'n pickles?" and all that kind of humbug talky-talk, just the way people always does at a supper, you know.

And when it was all done, me and the hare-lip had supper in the kitchen off of the leavings, whilst the others was helping the niggers clean up the things. The hare-lip she got to pumping me about England, and blest if I didn't think the ice was getting mighty thin, sometimes. She says:

"Did you ever see the king?"

"Who? William Fourth? Well, I bet I have—he goes to our church." knowed he was dead years ago, but I never let on. So when I says he goes to our church, she says:

"What—regular?"

"Yes—regular. His pew's right over opposite ourn—on 'tother side the pulpit."

"I thought he lived in London?"

"Well, he does. Where *would* he live?"

"But I thought *you* lived in Sheffield?"

I see I was up a stump. I had to let on to get choked with a chicken bone, so as to get time to think how to get down again. Then I says:

"I mean he goes to our church regular when he's in Sheffield. That's only in the summer-time, when he comes there to take the sea baths."

"Why, how you talk—Sheffield ain't on the sea."

"Well, who said it was?"

"Why, you did."

"I *didn't*, nuther."

"You did!"

"I didn't."

"You did."

"I never said nothing of the kind."

"Well, what *did* you say, then?"

"Said he come to take the sea *baths*—that's what I said."

"Well, then! how's he going to take the sea baths if it ain't on the sea?"

"Looky here," I says; "did you ever see any Congress water?"

" Yes."

"Well, did you have to go to Congress to get it?"

" Why, no."

"Well, neither does William Fourth have to go to the sea to get a sea bath."

"How does he get it, then?"

"Gets it the way people down here gets Congress-water—in barrels. There in the palace at Sheffield they've got furnaces, and he wants his water hot. They can't bile that amouut of water away off there at the sea. They haven't got no conveniences for it."

"Oh, I see, now. You might a said that in the first place and saved time."

When she said that, I see I was out of the woods again, and so I was comfortable and glad. Next, she says:

"Do you go to church, too?"

" Yes—regular."

"Where do you set?"

"Why, in our pew."

"*Whose* pew?"

"Why, *ourn*—your Uncle Harvey's."

"His'n? What does *he* want with a pew?"

"Wants it to set in. What did you *reckon* he wanted with it?"

"Why, I thought he'd be in the pulpit."

Rot him, I forgot he was a preacher. I see I was up a stump again, so I played another chicken bone and got another think. Then I says:

"Blame it, do you suppose there ain't but one preacher to a church?"

"Why, what do they want with more?"

"What!—to preach before a king? I never see such a girl as you. They don't have no less than seventeen."

"Seventeen! My land! Why, I wouldn't set out such a string as that, not if I *never* got to glory. It must take 'em a week."

"Shucks, they don't *all* of 'em preach the same day—only *one* of 'em."

"Well, then, what does the rest of 'em do?"

"Oh, nothing much. Loll around, pass the plate—and one thing or another. But mainly they don't do nothing."

"Well, then, what are they *for?*"

"Why, they're for *style*. Don't you know nothing?"

"Well, I don't *want* to know no such foolishness as that. How is servants treated in England? Do they treat 'em better 'n we treat our niggers?"

"*No!* A servant ain't nobody there. They treat them worse than dogs."

"Don't they give 'em holidays, the way we do, Christmas and New Year's week, and Fourth of July?"

"Oh, just listen! A body could tell *you* hain't ever been to England, by that.

Why, Hare-l—why, Joanna, they never see a holiday from year's end to year's end; never go to the circus, nor theatre, nor nigger shows, nor nowheres.''

"Nor church?"

"Nor church."

"But *you* always went to church."

Well, I was gone up again. I forgot I was the old man's servant. But next minute I whirled in on a kind of an explanation how a valley was different from a common servant, and *had* to go to church whether he wanted to or not, and set with the family, on account of it's being the law. But I didn't do it pretty good, and when I got done I see she warn't satisfied. She says:

"Honest injun, now, hain't you been telling me a lot of lies?"

"Honest injun," says I.

"None of it at all?"

"None of it at all. Not a lie in it," says I.

"Lay your hand on this book and say it."

I see it warn't nothing but a dictionary, so I laid my hand on it and said it. So then she looked a little better satisfied, and says:

"Well, then, I'll believe some of it; but I hope to gracious if I'll believe the rest."

"What is it you won't believe, Joe?" says Mary Jane, stepping in with Susan behind her. "It ain't right nor kind for you to talk so to him, and him a stranger and so far from his people. How would you like to be treated so?"

"That's always your way, Maim—always sailing in to help somebody before they're hurt. I hain't done nothing to him. He's told some stretchers, I reckon; and I said I wouldn't swallow it all; and that's every bit and grain I *did* say. I reckon he can stand a little thing like that, can't he?"

"I don't care whether 'twas little or whether 'twas big, he's here in our house and a stranger, and it wasn't good of you to say it. If you was in his place, it would make you feel ashamed; and so you oughtn't to say a thing to another person that will make *them* feel ashamed."

"Why, Maim, he said—"

"It don't make no difference what he *said*— that ain't the thing. The thing is for you to treat him *kind,* and not be saying things to make him remember he ain't in his own country and amongst his own folks."

I says to myself, *this* is a girl that I'm letting that old reptile rob her of her money!

Then Susan *she* waltzed in; and if you'll believe me, she did give Hare-lip hark from the tomb!

Says I to myself, And this is *another* one that I'm letting him rob her of her money!

Then Mary Jane she took another inning, and went in sweet and lovely again—which was her way—but when she got done there warn't hardly anything left o' poor Hare-lip. So she hollered.

"All right, then," says the other girls, "you just ask his pardon."

She done it, too. And she done it beautiful. She done it so beautiful it was good to hear; and I wished I could tell her a thousand lies, so she could do it again.

I says to myself, this is *another* one that I'm letting him rob her of her money. And when she got through, they all jest laid theirselves out to make me feel at home and know I was amongst friends. I felt so ornery and low down and mean, that I says to myself, My mind's made up; I'll hive that money for them or bust.

So then I lit out—for bed, I said, meaning some time or another. When I got by myself, I went to thinking the thing over. I says to myself, shall I go to that doctor, private, and blow on these frauds? No—that won't do. He might tell who told him; then the king and the duke would make it warm for me. Shall I go, private, and tell Mary Jane? No—I dasn't do it. Her face would give them a hint, sure; they've got the money, and they'd slide right out and get away with it. If she was to fetch in help, I'd get mixed up in the business, before it was done with, I judge. No, there ain't no good way but one. I got to steal that money, somehow; and I got to steal it some way that they won't suspicion that I done it. They've got a good thing, here; and they ain't agoing to leave till they've played this family and this town for all they're worth, so I'll find a chance time enough. I'll steal it, and hide it; and by-and-by, when I'm away down the river, I'll write a letter and tell Mary Jane where it's hid. But I better hive it tonight, if I can, because the doctor maybe hasn't let up as much as he lets on he has; he might scare them out of here, yet.

So, thinks I, I'll go and search them rooms. Up stairs the hall was dark, but I found the duke's room, and started to paw around it with my hands but I recollected it wouldn't be much like the king to let anybody else take care of that money but his own self; so then I went to his room and begun to paw around there. But I see I couldn't do nothing without a candle and I dasn't light one, of course. So I judged I'd got to do the other thing—lay for them, and eavesdrop. About that time, I hears their footsteps coming, and was going to skip under the bed; I reached for it, but it wasn't where I thought it would be; but I touched the curtain that hid Mary Jane's frocks, so I jumped in behind that and snuggled in amongst the gowns, and stood there perfectly still.

They come in and shut the door; and the first thing the duke done was to get down and look under the bed. Then I was glad I hadn't found the bed when I wanted it. And yet, you know, it's kind of natural to hide under the bed when you are up to anything private. They sets down, then, and the king says:

"Well, what is it? and cut it middlin' short, because it's better for us to be down there a whoopin'-up the mournin', than up here givin' 'em a chance to talk us over."

"Well, this is it, Capet. I ain't easy; I ain't comfortable. That doctor lays on my mind. I wanted to know your plans. I've got a notion, and I think it's a sound one."

"What is it, duke?"

"That we better glide out of this, before three in the morning, and clip it down the river with what we've got. Specially, seeing we got it so easy—*given* back to us, flung at our heads, as you may say, when of course we allowed to have to steal it back. I'm for knocking off and lighting out."

That made me feel pretty bad. About an hour or two ago, it would a been a little different, but now it made me feel bad and disappointed. The king rips out and says:

"What! And not sell out the rest o' the property? March off like a passel o' fools and leave eight or nine thous'n' dollars' worth o' property layin' around jest sufferin' to be scooped in?—and all good salable stuff, too."

The duke he grumbled; said the bag of gold was enough, and he didn't want to go no deeper—didn't want to rob a lot of orphans of *everything* they had.

"Why, how you talk!" says the king. "We shan't rob 'em of nothing at all but jest this money. The people that *buys* the property is the suff'rers; because as soon's it's found out 'at we didn't own it—which won't be long after we've slid—the sale won't be valid, and it'll all go back to the estate. These-yer orphans'll git their house back agin, and that's enough for *them;* they're young and spry, and k'n easy earn a livin'. *They* ain't agoing to suffer. Why, jest think—there's thous'n's and thous'n's that ain't nigh so well off. Bless you, *they* ain't got noth'n to complain of."

Well, the king he talked him blind; so at last he give in, and said all right, but said he believed it was blame foolishness to stay, and that doctor hanging over them. But the king says:

"Cuss the doctor! What do we k'yer for *him?* Hain't we got all the fools in town on our side? and ain't that a big enough majority in any town?"

So they got ready to go down stairs again. The duke says:

"I don't think we put that money in a good place."

That cheered me up. I'd begun to think I warn't going to get a hint of no kind to help me. The king says:

"Why?"

"Because Mary Jane'll be in mourning from this out; and first you know the nigger that does up the rooms will get an order to box these duds up and put 'em away; and do you reckon a nigger can run across money and not borrow some of it?"

"Your head's level, agin, duke," says the king; and he come a fumbling under the curtain two or three foot from where I was. I stuck tight to the wall, and kept mighty still, though quivery; and I wondered what them fellows would say to me if they catched me; and I tried to think what I'd better do if they did catch me. But the king he got the bag before I could think more than about a half a thought, and he never suspicioned I was around. They took and shoved the bag through a rip in the straw tick that was under the feather bed, and crammed it in a foot or two amongst the straw and said it was all right, now, because a nigger only makes up the feather bed, and don't turn over the straw tick only about twice a year, and so it warn't in no danger of getting stole, now.

But I knowed better. I had it out of there before they was half-way down stairs. I groped along up to my cubby, and hid it there till I could get a chance to do better. I judged I better hide it outside of the house somewheres, because if they missed it they would give the house a good ransacking. I knowed that very well. Then I turned in, with my clothes all on; but I couldn't a gone to sleep, if I'd a wanted to, I was in such a sweat to get through with the business. By-and-by I heard the king and the duke come up; so I rolled off of my pallet and laid with my chin at the top of my ladder and waited to see if anything was going to happen. But nothing did.

So I held on till all the late sounds had quit and the early ones hadn't begun, yet; and then I slipped down the ladder.

Chapter XXVII

I CREPT TO their doors and listened; they was snoring, so I tip-toed along, and got down stairs all right. There warn't a sound anywheres. I peeped through a crack of the dining-room door, and see the men that was watching the corpse all sound asleep on their chairs. The door was open into the parlor, where the corpse was laying, and there was a candle in both rooms. I passed along, and the parlor door was open; but I see there warn't nobody in there but the remainders of Peter; so I shoved on by; but the front door was locked, and the key wasn't there. Just then I heard somebody coming down the stairs, back behind me. I run in the parlor, and took a swift look around, and the only place I see to hide the bag was in the coffin. The lid was shoved along about a foot, showing the dead man's face down in there, with a wet cloth over it, and his shroud on. I tucked the money-bag in under the lid, just down beyond where his hands was crossed, which made me creep, they was so cold, and then I run back across the room and in behind the door.

The person coming was Mary Jane. She went to the coffin, very soft, and kneeled down and looked in; then she put up her handkerchief and I see she begun to cry, though I couldn't hear her, and her back was to me. I slid out, and as I passed the dining-room I thought I'd make sure them watchers hadn't seen me; so I looked through the crack and everything was all right. They hadn't stirred.

I slipped up to bed, feeling ruther blue, on accounts of the thing playing out that way after I had took so much trouble and run so much resk about it. Says I, if it could stay where it is, all right; because when we get down the river a hundred mile or two, I could write back to Mary Jane, and she could dig him up again and get it; but that ain't the thing that's going to happen; the thing that's going to happen is, the money'll be found when they come to screw on the lid. Then the king'll get it again, and it'll be a long day before he gives anybody another chance to smouch it from him. Of course I *wanted* to slide

HUCK TAKES THE MONEY.

A CRACK IN THE DINING-ROOM DOOR.

down and get it out of there, but I dasn't try it. Every minute it was getting earlier, now, and pretty soon some of them watchers would begin to stir, and I might get catched—catched with six thousand dollars in my hands that nobody hadn't hired me to take care of. I don't wish to be mixed up in no such business as that, I says to myself.

When I got down stairs in the morning, the parlor was shut up, and the watchers was gone. There warn't nobody around but the family and the widow Bartley and our tribe. I watched their faces to see if anything had been happening, but I couldn't tell.

Towards the middle of the day the undertaker come, with his man, and they set the coffin in the middle of the room on a couple of chairs, and then set all our chairs in rows, and borrowed more from the neighbors till the hall and the parlor and the dining-room was full. I see the coffin lid was the way it was before, but I dasn't go to look in under it, with folks around.

Then the people begun to flock in, and the beats and the girls took seats in the front row at the head of the coffin, and for a half an hour the people filed around slow, in single rank, and looked down at the dead man's face a minute, and some dropped in a tear, and it was all very still and solemn, only the girls and the beats holding handkerchiefs to their eyes and keeping their heads bent, and sobbing a little. There warn't no other sound but the scraping of the feet on the floor, and blowing noses—because people always blows them more at a funeral than they do at other places except church.

When the place was packed full, the undertaker he slid around in his black gloves with his softy soothering ways, putting on the last touches, and getting people and things all ship-shape and comfortable, and making no more sound than a cat. He never spoke; he moved people around, he squeezed in late ones, he opened up passage-ways, and done it all with nods, and signs with his hands. Then he took his place over against the wall. He was the softest, glidingest, stealthiest man I ever see; and there warn't no more smile to him than there is to a ham.

They had borrowed a melodeum—a sick one; and when everything was ready, a young woman set down and worked it, and it was pretty skreeky and colicky, and everybody joined in and sung, and Peter was the only one that had a good thing, according to my notion. Then the Reverend Hobson opened up, slow and solemn, and begun to talk; and straight off the most outrageous row busted out in the cellar a body ever heard; it was only one dog, but he made a most powerful racket, and he kept it up, right along; the parson he had to stand there, over the coffin, and wait—you couldn't hear yourself think. It was right down awkward, and nobody didn't seem to know what to do. But pretty soon they see that long-legged undertaker make a sign to the preacher as much as to say, "Don't yon worry—just depend on me." Then he stooped down and begun to glide along the wall, just his shoulders showing over the people's heads. So he glided along, and the pow-wow and racket getting more and more outrageous all the time; and at last, when he had gone around two sides of the room, he disappears down cellar. Then, in about two seconds we heard a whack, and the dog he finished up with a most amazing howl or two, and then everything was dead still, and the parson begun his solemn talk where he left off. In a minute or two here comes this undertaker's back and shoulders gliding along the wall again; and so he glided, and glided, around three sides of the room, and then rose up, and shaded his mouth with his hands, and stretched his neck out towards the preacher, over the people's heads, and says, in a kind of a coarse whisper, *"He had a rat!"* Then he drooped down and glided along the wall again to his place. You could see it was a great satisfaction to the people, because naturally they wanted to know. A little thing like that don't cost nothing, and it's just the little things that makes a man to be looked up to and liked. There warn't no more popular man in town than what that undertaker was.

Well, the funeral sermon was very good, but pison long and tiresome; and then the king he shoved in and got off some of his usual rubbage, and at last the job was through, and the undertaker begun to sneak up on the coffin with his screw-driver. I was in a sweat then, and watched him pretty keen. But he never meddled at all; just slid the lid along, as soft as mush, and screwed it down tight and fast. So there I was! I didn't know whether the money was in there, or not. So, says I, spose somebody has hogged that bag on the sly?—now how do *I* know whether to write to Mary Jane or not? 'Spose she dug him up and didn't find nothing—what would she think of me? Blame it, I says, I might get hunted up and jailed; I'd better lay low and keep dark, and not write at all; the thing's awful mixed, now; trying to better it, I've worsened it a hundred times, and I wish to goodness I'd just let it alone, dad fetch the whole business!

They buried him, and we come back home, and I went to watching faces again I couldn't help it, and I couldn't rest easy. But nothing come of it; the faces didn't tell me nothing.

The king he visited around, in the evening, and sweetened every body up, and made himself ever so friendly; and he give out the idea that his congregation over in England would be in a sweat about him, so he must hurry and settle up the estate right away, and leave for home. He was very sorry he was so pushed, and so was everybody; they wished he could stay longer, but they said they could see it couldn't be done. And he said of course him and William would take the girls home with them; and that pleased everybody too, because then the girls would be well fixed, and amongst their own relations; and it pleased the girls, too—tickled them so they clean forgot they ever had a trouble in the world; and told him to sell out as quick as he wanted to, they would be ready. Them poor things was that glad and happy it made my heart ache to see them getting fooled and lied to so, but I didn't see no safe way for me to chip in and change the general tune.

Well, blamed if the king didn't bill the house and the niggers and all the property for auction straight off—sale two days after the funeral; but anybody could buy private beforehand if they wanted to.

So the next day after the funeral, along about noontime, the girls' joy got the first jolt; a couple of nigger traders come along, and the king sold them the niggers reasonable, for three-day drafts as they called it, and away they went, the two sons up the river to Memphis, and their mother down the river to Orleans. I thought them poor girls and them niggers would break their hearts for grief; they cried around each other, and took on so it most made me down sick to see it. The girls said they hadn't ever dreamed of seeing the family separated or sold away from the town. I can't ever get it out of my memory, the sight of them poor miserable girls and niggers hanging around each other's necks and crying; and I reckon I couldn't a stood it all but would a had to bust out and tell on our gang if I hadn't knowed the sale warn't no account and the niggers would be back home in a week or two.

The thing made a big stir in the town, too, and a good many come out flat-footed and said it was scandalous to separate the mother and the children that way. It injured the frauds some; but the old fool he bulled right along, spite of all the duke could say or do, and I tell you the duke was powerful uneasy.

Next day was auction day. About broad-day in the morning, the king and the duke come up in the garret and woke me up, and I see by their look that there was trouble. The king says:

"Was you in my room night before last?"

"No, your majesty"—which was the way I always called him when nobody but our gang warn't around.

"Was you in there yisterday er last night?"

"No, your majesty."

"Honor bright, now—no lies."

"Honor bright, your majesty, I'm telling you the truth. I hain't been anear your room since Miss Mary Jane took you and the duke and showed it to you."

The duke says:

"Have you seen anybody else go in there?"

"No, your grace, not as I remember, I believe."

"Stop and think."

I studied a while, and see my chance, then I says:

"Well, I see the niggers go in there several times."

Both of them give a little jump; and looked like they hadn't ever expected it, and then like they had. Then the duke says:

"What, all of them?"

"No—leastways not all at once. That is, I don't think I ever see them all come out at once but just one time."

"Hello—when was that?"

"It was the day we had the funeral. In the morning. It warn't early, because I overslept. I was just starting down the ladder, and I see them."

"Well, go on, go on—what did they do? How'd they act?"

"They didn't do nothing. And they didn't act anyway, much, as fur as I see. They tip-toed away; so I seen, easy enough, that they'd shoved in there to do up your majesty's room, or something, sposing you was up; and found you *warn't* up, and so they was hoping to slide out of the way of trouble without waking you up, if they hadn't already waked you up.''

"Great guns, *this* is a go!" says the king; and both of them looked pretty sick, and tolerable silly. They stood there a thinking and scratching their heads, a minute, and then the duke he bust into a kind of a little raspy chuckle, and says:

"It does beat all, how neat the niggers played their hand. They let on to be *sorry* they was going out of this region! and I believed they *was* sorry. And so did you, and so did everybody. Don't ever tell *me* any more that a nigger ain't got any histrionic talent. Why, the way they played that thing, it would fool *anybody*. In my opinion there's a fortune in 'em. If I had capital and a theatre, I wouldn't want a better lay out than that—and here we've gone and sold 'em for a song. Yes, and ain't privileged to sing the song, yet. Say, where *is* that song?—that draft."

"In the bank for to be collected. Where *would* it be?"

"Well, *that's* all right then, thank goodness."

Says I, kind of timid-like:

"Is something gone wrong?"

The king whirls on me and rips out:

"None o' your business! You keep your head shet, and mind y'r own affairs— if you got any. Long as you're in this town, don't you forget *that,* you hear?" Then he says to the duke, "We got to jest swaller it, and say noth'n: mum's the word for *us*."

As they was starting down the ladder, the duke he chuckles again, and says:

"Quick sales *and* small profits! It's a good business—yes."

The king snarls around on him and says,

"I was trying to do for the best, in sellin' 'm out so quick. If the profits has turned out to be none, lackin' considable, and none to carry, is it my fault any more'n it's yourn?"

"Well, *they'd* be in this house yet, and we *wouldn't* if I could a got my advice listened to."

The king sassed back, as much as was safe for him, and then swapped around and lit into *me* again. He give me down the banks for not coming and *telling* him I see the niggers come out of his room acting that way—said any fool would a *knowed* something was up. And then waltzed in and cussed *himself* a while; and said it all come of him not laying late and taking his natural rest that morning, and he'd be blamed if he'd ever do it again. So they went off a jawing; and I felt dreadful glad I'd worked it all off onto the niggers and yet hadn't done the niggers no harm by it.

Chapter XXVIII

By-and-by it was getting-up time; so I come down the ladder and started for down stairs, but as I come to the girls' room, the door was open, and I see Mary Jane setting by her old hair trunk, which was open and she'd been packing things in it—getting ready to go to England. But she had stopped now, with a folded gown in her lap, and had her face in her hands, crying. I felt awful bad to see it; of course anybody would. I went in there, and says:

"Miss Mary Jane, you can't abear to see people in trouble, and *I* can't—most always. Tell me about it."

So she done it. And it was the niggers—I just expected it. She said the beautiful trip to England was most about spoiled for her; she didn't know *how* she was ever going to be happy there, knowing the mother and the children warn't ever going to see each other no more—and then busted out bitterer than ever, and flung up her hands, and says

"Oh, dear, dear, to think they ain't *ever* going to see each other any more!"

"But they *will*—and inside of two weeks—and I *know* it!" says I.

Laws it was out before I could think!—and before I could budge, she throws her arms around my neck, and told me to say it *again,* say it *again,* say it *again!*

I see I had spoke too sudden, and said too much, and was in a close place. I asked her to let me think a minute; and she set there, very impatient and excited, and handsome, but looking kind of happy and eased-up, like a person that's had a tooth pulled out. So I went to studying it out. I says to myself, I reckon a body that ups and tells the truth when he is in a tight place, is taking considerable many resks, though I ain't had no experience, and can't say for certain; but it looks so to me, anyway; and yet here's a case where I'm blest if it don't look to me like the truth is better, and actuly *safer,* than a lie. I must lay it by in my mind, and think it over some time or other, it's so kind of strange and unregular. I never see nothing like it. Well, I says to myself at last, I'm agoing to chance it; I'll up and tell the truth this time, though it does seem most like setting down on a kag of powder and touching it off just to see where you'll go to. Then I says:

"Miss Mary Jane, is there any place out of town a little ways, where you could go and stay three or four days?"

"Yes—Mr. Lothrop's. Why?"

"Never mind why, yet. If I'll tell you how I know the niggers will see each other again—inside of two weeks—here in this house—and *prove* how I know it—will you go to Mr. Lothrop's and stay four days?"

"Four days!" she says; "I'll stay a year!"

IN TROUBLE.

"All right," I says, "I don't want nothing more out of *you* than just your word—I druther have it than another man's kiss-the-Bible." She smiled, and reddened up very sweet, and I says, "If you don't mind it, I'll shut the door—and bolt it."

Then I come back and set down again, and says:

"Don't you holler. Just set still, and take it like a man. I got to tell the truth, and you want to brace up, Miss Mary, because it's a bad kind, and going to be hard to take, but there ain't no help for it. These uncles of yourn ain't no uncles at all—they're a couples of frauds—regular dead-beats. There, now we're over the worst of it—you can stand the rest middling easy."

It jolted her up like everything, of course; but I was over the shoal water now, so I went right along, her eyes a blazing higher and higher all the time, and told her every blame thing, from where we first struck that young fool going up to the steamboat, clear through to where she flung herself onto the kings breast at the front door and he kissed her sixteen or seventeen times—and then up she jumps, with her face afire like sunset, and says:

"The brute! Come—don't waste a minute—not a *second*—we'll have them tarred and feathered, and flung in the river!"

Says I:

"Cert'nly. But do you mean, *before* you go to Mr. Lothrop's, or——"

"Oh," she says, "what am I *thinking* about!" she says, and set right down again. "Don't mind what I said—please don't—you *won't*, now, *will* you?" Laying her silky hand on mind in that kind of a way that I said I would die first. "I never thought, I was so stirred up," she says; "now go on, and I won't do so any more. You tell me what to do, and whatever you say, I'll do it."

"Well," I says, "it's a rough gang, them two frauds, and I'm fixed so I got to travel with them a while longer, whether I want to or not—I druther not tell you why—and if you was to blow on them this town would get me out of their claws, and I'd be all right, but there'd be another person that you don't know about who'd be in big trouble. Well, we got to save *him,* hain't we? Of course. Well, then, we won't blow on them."

Saying them words put a good idea in my head. I see how maybe I could get me and Jim rid of the frauds; get them jailed here, and then leave. But I didn't want to run the raft in day-time, without anybody aboard to answer questions but me; so I didn't want the plan to begin working till pretty late to-night. I says:

"Miss Mary Jane, I'll tell you what we'll do—and you won't have to stay at Mr. Lothrop's so long, nuther. How fur is it?"

"A little short of four miles—right out in the country, back here."

"Well, that'll answer. Now you go along out there, and lay low till nine or half-past, to-night, and then get them to fetch you home again—tell them you've thought of something. If you get here before eleven, put a candle in this window, and if I don't turn up, wait *til* eleven, and *then* if I don't turn up it means I'm gone, and out of the way, and safe. Then you come out and spread the news around, and get these beats jailed."

"Good," she says, "I'll do it."

"And if it just happens so that I don't get away, but get took up along with them, you must up and say I told you the whole thing beforehand, and you must stand by me all you can."

"Stand by you, indeed I will. They sha'n't touch a hair of your head!" she says, and I see her nostrils spread and her eyes snap when she said it, too.

"If I get away, I sha'n't be here," I says, "to prove these rapscallions ain't your uncles, and I couldn't do it if I *was* here. I could swear they was beats and bummers, that's all; though that's worth something. Well, there's others can do that better than what I can—and they're people that ain't going to be doubted as quick as I'd be. I'll tell you how to find them. Gimme a pencil and a piece of paper, There—'*Royal Nonesuch, Bricksville.*' Put it away, and don't lose it. When the court wants to find out something about these two, let them send up to Bricksville and say they've got the men that played the Royal Nonesuch, and ask for some witnesses—why, you'll have that entire town down here before you can hardly wink, Miss Mary. And they'll come a-biling, too."

I judged we had got everything fixed about right, now. So I says:

"Just let the auction go right along, and don't worry. Nobody don't have to pay for the things they buy till a whole day after the auction, on accounts of the short notice, and they ain't going out of this till they get that money—and the way we've fixed it the sale ain't going to count, and they ain't going to *get* no money. It's just like the way it was with the niggers—it warn't no sale, and the niggers will be back before long. Why, they can't collect the money for the *niggers,* yet—they're in the worst kind of a fix, Miss Mary."

"Well," she says, "I'll run down to breakfast now, and then I'll start straight for Mr. Lothrop's."

"'Deed, *that* ain't the ticket, Miss Mary Jane," I says, "by no manner of means; go *before* breakfast."

"Why?"

"What did you reckon I wanted you to go at all for, Miss Mary?"

"Well, I never thought—and come to think, I don't know. What was it?"

"Why, it's because you ain't one of these leather-face people. I don't want no better book that what your face is. A body can set down and read it off like coarse print. Do you reckon you can go and face your uncles, when they come to kiss you good-morning, and never——"

"There, there, don't! Yes, I'll go before breakfast—I'll be glad to. And leave my sisters with them?"

"Yes—never mind about them. They've got to stand it yet a while. They might suspicion something if all of you was to go. I don't want you to see them, nor your sisters, nor nobody in this town—if a neighbor was to ask how is your uncles this morning, your face would tell something. No, you go right along, Miss Mary Jane, and I'll fix it with all of them. I'll tell Miss Susan to give your love to your uncles and say you've went away for a few hours for to get a little rest and change, or to see a friend; and you'll be back to-night or early in the morning."

"Gone to see a friend is all right, but I won't have my love given to them."

"Well, then, it sha'n't be." It was well enough to tell *her* so—no harm in it. It was only a little thing to do, and no trouble; and it's the little things that smoothes people's roads the most, down here below; it would make Mary Jane comfortable, and it wouldn't cost nothing. Then I says: "There's one more thing—that bag of money."

"Well, they've got that; and it makes me feel pretty silly to think *how* they got it."

"No, you're out, there. They hain't got it."

"Why, who's got it?"

"I wish I knowed, but I don't. I *had* it, because I stole it from them: and I stole it to give to you; and I know where I hid it, but I'm afraid it ain't there no more. I'm awful sorry, Miss Mary Jane, I'm just as sorry as I can be; but I done the best I could; I did, honest. I come nigh getting caught, and I had to shove it into the first place I come to, and run—and it warn't a good place."

"Oh, stop blaming yourself—it's too bad to do it, and I won't allow it—you couldn't help it; it wasn't you fault. Where did you hide it?"

I didn't want to set her to thinking about her troubles again; and I couldn't seem to get my mouth to tell her what would make her see that corpse laying in the coffin with that bag of money on his stomach. So for a minute I didn't say nothing—then I says:

"I'd rather not *tell* you where I put it, Miss Mary Jane, if you don't mind letting me off; but I'll write it for you on a piece of paper, and you can read it along the road to Mr. Lothrop's, if you want to. Do you reckon that'll do?"

"Oh, yes."

So I wrote: "I put it in the coffin. It was in there when you was crying there, away in the night. I was behind the door, and I was mighty sorry for you, Miss Mary Jane."

It made my eyes water a little, to remember her crying there all by herself in the night, and them devils laying there right under her own roof, shaming her and robbing her; and when I folded it up and give it to her, I see the water come into her eyes, too; and she shook me by the hand, hard, and says:

"*Good*-bye—I'm going to do everything just as you've told me; and if I don't ever see you again, I sha'n't ever forget you, and I'll think of you a many and a many a time, and I'll *pray* for you, too!"—and she was gone.

Pray for me! I reckoned if she knowed me she'd take a job that was more nearer her size. But I bet she done it, just the same—she was just that kind. She had the grit to pray for Judus if she took the notion—there warn't no back down to her, I judge. Yon may say what you want to, but in my opinion she had more sand in her than any girl I ever see; in my opinion she was just full of sand. It sounds like flattery, but it ain't no flattery. And when it comes to beauty—and goodness too—she lays over them all. I hain't ever seen her since that time that I see her go out of that door; no, I hain't ever seen her since, but I reckon I've thought of her a many and a many a million times, and of her saying she would pray for me; and if ever I'd a thought it would do any good for me to pray for *her*, blamed if I wouldn't a done it or bust.

Well, Mary Jane she lit out the back way, I reckon; because nobody see her go. When I struck Susan and the hare-lip, I says:

"What's the name of them people over on t'other side of the river that you. all goes to see sometimes?"

They says:

"There's several; but it's the Proctors, mainly."

"That's the name," I says; "I most forgot it. Well, Miss Mary Jane she told me to tell you she's gone over there in a dreadful hurry—one of them's sick."

"Which one?"

"I don't know; leastways I kinder forget; but I think it's——"

"Sakes alive, I hope it ain't *Hanner?*"

"I'm sorry to say it," I says, "but Hanner's the very one."

"My goodness—and she so well only last week! Is she took bad?"

"It ain't no name for it. They set up with her all night, Miss Mary Jane said, and they don't think she'll last many hours."

"Only think of that, now! What's the matter with her!"

I couldn't think of anything reasonable, right off that way, so I says:

"Mumps."

"Mumps your granny! They don't set up with people that's got the mumps."

"They don't, don't they? You better bet they do with *these* mumps. These mumps is different. It's a new kind, Miss Mary Jane said."

"How's it a new kind?"

"Because it's mixed up with other things."

"What other things?"

"Well, measles, and whooping-cough, and erysiplas, and consumption, and yaller janders, and brain fever, and I don't know what all."

"My land! And they call it the *mumps?*"

"That's what Miss Mary Jane said."

"Well, what in the nation do they call it the *mumps* for?"

"Why, because it *is* the mumps. That's what it starts with."

"Well, ther' ain't no sense in it. A body might stump his toe, and take pison, and fall down the well, and break his neck, and bust his brains out, and somebody come along and ask what killed him, and some numskull up and say, 'Why, he stumped his *toe.*' Would ther' be any sense in that? *No.* And ther' ain't no sense in *this,* nuther. Is it ketching?"

"Is it *ketching?* Why, how you talk. Is a *harrow* catching?—in the dark? If you don't hitch onto one tooth, you're bound to on another, ain't you? And you can't get away with that tooth without fetching the whole harrow along, can you? Well, these kind of mumps is a kind of a harrow, as you may say—and it ain't no slouch of a harrow, nuther, you come to get it hitched on good."

"Well, it's awful, *I* think," says the hare-lip. "I'll go to Uncle Harvey and—"

"Oh, yes," I says, "I *would.* Of *course* I would. I wouldn't lose no time."

"Well, why wouldn't you?"

"Just look at it a minute, and maybe you can see. Hain't your uncles obleeged to get along home to England as fast as they can? And do you reckon they'd be mean enough to go off and leave you to go all that journey by yourselves? *You* know they'll wait for you. So fur, so good. Your uncle Harvey's a preacher, ain't he? Very well, then; is a *preacher* going to deceive a steamboat clerk? is he going to deceive a *ship clerk?*—so as to get them to let Miss Mary Jane go aboard? Now *you* know he ain't. What *will* he do, then? Why, he'll say, 'It's a great pity, but my church matters has got to get along the best way they can; for my niece has been exposed to the dreadful pluribus-unum mumps, and so it's my bounden duty to set down here and wait the three months it takes to show on her if she's got it.' But never mind, if you think it's best to tell your uncle Harvey——"

"Shucks, and stay fooling around here when we could all be having good times in England whilst we was waiting to find out whether Mary Jane's got it or not? Why, you talk like a muggins."

"Well, anyway, maybe you better tell some of the neighbors."

"Listen at that, now. You do beat all, for natural stupidness. Can't you *see* that *they'd* go and tell? Ther' ain't no way but just to not tell anybody at *all.*"

"Well, maybe you're right—yes, I judge you *are* right."

"But I reckon we ought to tell Uncle Harvey she's gone out a while, anyway, so he wont be uneasy about her?"

"Yes, Miss Mary Jane she wanted you to do that. She says, 'Tell them to give Uncle Harvey and William my love and a kiss, and say I've run over the river to see Mr.—Mr.—what *is* the name of that rich family your uncle Peter used to think so much of?—I mean the one that——"

"Why, you must mean the Apthorps, ain't it?"

"Of course; bother them kind of names, a body can't ever seem to remember them, half the time, somehow. Yes, she said, say she has run over for to ask the Apthorps to be sure and come to the auction and buy this house, because she allowed her uncle Peter would ruther they had it than anybody else; and she's going to stick to them till they say they'll come, and then, if she ain't too tired, she's coming home; and if she is, she'll be home in the morning anyway. She said, don't say nothing about the Proctors, but only about the Apthorps—which'll be perfectly true, because she *is* going there to speak about their buying the house; I know it, because she told me so, herself."

"All right," they said and cleared out to lay for their uncles, and give them the love and the kisses, and tell them the message.

Everything was all right now. The girls wouldn't say nothing because they wanted to go to England; and the king and the duke would ruther Mary Jane was off working for the auction than around in reach of Doctor Robinson. I felt very good; I judged I had done it pretty neat—I reckoned Tom Sawyer couldn't a done it no neater himself. Of course he would a throwed more style into it, but I can't do that very handy, not being brung up to it.

Well, they held the auction in the public square, along towards the end of the afternoon, and it strung along, and strung along, and the old man he was on hand and looking his level pisonest, up there longside of the auctioneer, and chipping in a little Scripture, now and then, or a little goody-goody saying, of some kind, and the duke he was around goo-gooing for sympathy all he knowed how, and just spreading himself generly.

But by-and-by the thing dragged through, and everything was sold. Everything but a little old trifling lot in the graveyard. So they'd got to work *that* off—I never see such a giraftt as the king was for wanting to swallow *everything*. Well,

THE AUCTION.

whilst they was at it, a steamboat landed, and in about two minutes up comes a crowd a whooping and yelling and laughing and carrying on, and singing out:

"*Here's* your opposition line! here's your two sets o' heirs to old Peter Wilks— and you pays your money and you takes your choice!"

Chapter XXIX

THEY WAS FETCHING a very nice looking old gentleman along, and a nice looking younger one, with his right arm in a sling. And my souls, how the people yelled, and laughed, and kept it up. But I didn't see no joke about it, and I judged it would strain the duke and the king some to see any. I reckoned they'd turn pale. But no, nary a pale did *they* turn. The duke he never let on he suspicioned what was up, but just went a goo-gooing around, happy and satisfied, like a jug that's googling out buttermilk; and as for the king, he just gazed and gazed down sorrowful on them newcomers like it give him the stomach-ache in his very heart to think there could be such frauds and rascals in the world. Oh, he done it admirable. Lots of the principal people gethered around the king, to let him see they was on his side. That old gentleman that had just come looked all puzzled to death. Pretty soon he begun to speak, and I see, straight off, he pronounced *like* an Englishman, not the king's way, though the king's *was* pretty good, for an imitation. I can't give the old gent's words, nor I can't imitate him; but he turned around to the crowd, and says, about like this:

"This is a surprise to me which I wasn't looking for; and I'll acknowledge, candid and frank, I ain't very well fixed to meet it and answer it; for my brother and me has had misfortunes, he's broke his arm, and our baggage got put off at a town above here, last night in the night by a mistake. I am Peter Wilks's brother Harvey, and this is his brother William, which can't hear nor speak— and can't even make signs to amount to much, now 't he's only got one hand to work them with. We are who we say we are; and in a day or two, when I get the baggage, I can prove it. But, up till then, I won't say nothing more, but go to the hotel and wait."

So him and the new dummy started off; and the king he laughs, and blethers out:

"Broke his arm—*very* likely *ain't* it?—and very convenient, too, for a fraud that's got to make signs, and hain't learnt how. Lost their baggage! That's *mighty* good!—and mighty ingenious—under the *circumstances!*"

So he laughed again; and so did everybody else, except three or four, or maybe half a dozen. One of these was that doctor; another one was a sharp looking gentleman, with a carpet-bag of the old-fashioned kind made out of carpet-stuff, that had just come off of the steamboat and was talking to him in a low voice, and glancing towards the king now and then and nodding their heads—it was Levi Bell, the lawyer that was gone up to Louisville; and another one was a big rough husky that come along and listened to all the old gentleman said, and was listening to the king now. And when the king got done, this husky up and says:

"Say, looky here; if you are Harvey Wilks, when'd you come to this town?"

"The day before the funeral, friend," says the king.

"But what time o' day?"

"In the evenin'—'bout an hour er two before sundown."

"*How'd* you come?"

"I come down on the *Susan Powell,* from Cincinnati."

"Well, then, how'd you come to be up at the Pint in the *mornin'*—in a canoe?"

"I warn't up at the Pint in the mornin'."

"It's a lie."

Several of them jumped for him and begged him not to talk that way to an old man and a preacher.

"Preacher be hanged, he's a fraud and a liar. He was up at the Pint that mornin'. I live up there, don't I? Well, I was up there, and he was up there. I *see* him there. He come in a canoe, along with Tim Collins and a boy."

The doctor he up and says: "Would you know the boy again if you was to see him, Hines?"

"I reckon I would, but I don't know. Why, yonder he is, now. I know him perfectly easy."

It was me he pointed at. The doctor says:

"Neighbors, I don't know whether the new couple is frauds or not; but if *these* two ain't frauds, I am an idiot, that's all. I think it's our duty to see that they don't get away from here till we've looked into this thing. Come along, Hines; come along, the rest of you. We'll take these fellows to the tavern and affront them with t'other couple, and I reckon we'll find out *something* before we get through."

It was nuts for the crowd, though maybe not for the king's friends; so we all started. It was about sundown. The doctor he led me along by the hand, and was plenty kind enough, but he never let *go* my hand.

We all got in a big room in the hotel, and lit up some candles, and fetched in the new couple. First, the doctor says:

"I don't wish to be too hard on these two men, but *I* think they're frauds, and they may have complices that we don't know nothing about. If they have, won't the complices get away with that bag of gold Peter Wilks left? It ain't unlikely. If these men ain't frauds, they won't object to sending for that money and letting us keep it till they prove they're all right—ain't that so?"

THE DOCTOR LEADS HUCK.

Everybody agreed to that. So I judged they had our gang in a pretty tight place, right at the outstart. But the king he only looked sorrowful, and says:

"Gentlemen, I wish the money was there, for I ain't got no disposition to throw anything in the way of a fair, open, out-and-out investigation o' this misable business; but alas, the money ain't there; you k'n send and see, if you want to."

"Where is it, then?"

"Well, when my niece give it to me to keep for her, I took and hid it inside o' the straw tick o' my bed, not wishin' to bank it for the few days we'd be here, and considerin' the bed a safe place, we not bein' used to niggers, and suppos'n' 'em honest, like servants in England. The niggers stole it the very next mornin' after I had went down stairs; and when I sold 'em, I hadn't missed the money yit, so they got clean away with it. My servant here k'n tell you 'bout it gentlemen."

The doctor and several said "Shucks!" and I see nobody didn't altogether believe him. One man asked me if I see the niggers steal it. I said no, but I see them sneaking out of the room and hustling away, and I never thought nothing, only I reckoned they was afraid they had waked up my master and was trying to get away before he made trouble with them. That was all they asked me. Then the doctor whirls on me and says:

"Are *you* English too?"

I says yes; and him and some others laughed, and said, "Stuff!"

Well, then they sailed in on the general investigation, and there we had it, up and down, hour in, hour out, and nobody never said a word about supper, nor ever seemed to think about it—and so they kept it up, and kept it up; and it *was* the worst mixed-up thing you ever see. They made the king tell his yarn, and they made the old gentleman tell his'n; and anybody but a lot of prejudiced chuckleheads would a *seen* that the old gentleman was spinning truth and t'other one lies. And by-and-by they had me up to tell what I knowed. The king he give me a left-handed look out of the corner of his eye, and so I knowed enough to talk on the right side. I begun to tell about Sheffield, and how we lived there, and all about the English Wilkses, and so on; but I didn't get pretty fur till the doctor begun to laugh; and Levi Bell, the lawyer, says:

"Set down, my boy, I wouldn't strain myself, if I was you. I reckon you ain't used to lying, it don't seem to come handy; what you want is practice. You do it pretty awkward."

I didn't care nothing for the compliment, but I was glad to be let off, anyway.

The doctor he started to say something, and turns and says:

"If you'd been in town at first, Levi Bell——"

The king broke in and reached out his hand, and says:

"Why is this my poor dead brother's old friend that he's wrote so often about?"

The lawyer and him shook hands, and the lawyer smiled and looked pleased, and they talked right along a while, and then got to one side and talked low; and at last the lawyer speaks up and says:

"That'll fix it. I'll take the order and send it, along with your brother's, and then they'll know it's all right."

So they got some paper and a pen, and the king he set down and twisted his head to one side, and chawed his tongue, and scrawled off something; and then they give the pen to the duke—and then for the first time, the duke looked sick.

But he took the pen and wrote. So then the lawyer turns to the new old gentleman and says:

"You and your brother please write a line or two and sign your names."

The old gentleman wrote, but nobody couldn't read it. The lawyer looked powerful astonished, and says:

"Well, it beats *me*"—and snaked a lot of old letters out of his pocket, and examined them, and then examined the old man's writing, and then *them* again; and then says: "These old letters is from Harvey Wilks; and here's *these* two's handwritings, and anybody can see *they* didn't write them" (the king and the duke looked sold and foolish, I tell you, to see how the lawyer had took them in), "and here's *this* old gentleman's handwriting, and anybody can tell, easy enough, *he* didn't write them—fact is, the scratches he makes ain't properly *writing*, at all. Now here's some letters from——"

The new old gentleman says:

"If you please, let me explain. Nobody can read my hand but my brother there—so he copies for me. It's *his* hand you've got there, not mine."

"*Well!*" says the lawyer, "this *is* a state of things. I've got some of William's letters too; so if you'll get him to write a line or so we can com——"

"He *can't* write with his left hand," says the old gentleman. "If he could use his right hand, you would see that he wrote his own letters and mine too. Look at both, please—they're by the same hand."

The lawyer done it, and says:

"I believe it's so—and if it ain't so, there's a heap stronger resemblance than I'd noticed before, anyway. Well, well, well! I thought we was right on the track of a slution, but it's gone to grass, partly. But anyway, one thing is proved—*these* two ain't either of 'em Wilkses"—and he wagged his head towards the king and the duke.

Well, what do you think?—that muleheaded old fool wouldn't give in *then!* Indeed he wouldn't. Said it warn't no fair test. Said his brother William was the cussedest joker in the world, and hadn't *tried* to write—*he* see William was going to play one of his jokes the minute he put the pen to paper. And so he warmed up and went warbling and warbling right along, till he was actuly beginning to believe what he was saying, *himself*—but pretty soon the new old gentleman broke in, and says:

"I've thought of something. Is there anybody here that helped to lay out my br—helped to lay out the late Peter Wilks for burying?"

"Yes," says somebody, "me and Ab Turner done it. We're both here."

Then the old man turns towards the king, and says:

"Peraps this gentleman can tell me what was tatooed on his breast?"

Blamed if the king didn't have to brace up mighty quick, or he'd a squshed down like a bluff bank that the river has cut under, it took him so sudden—and mind you, it was a thing that was calculated to make most *anybody* sqush to get fetched such a solid one as that without any notice—because how was *he* going to know what was tatooed on the man? He whitened a little; he couldn't help it; and it was mighty still in there, and everybody bending a little forwards and gazing at him. Says I to myself, *Now* he'll throw up the sponge—there ain't no more use. Well, did he? A body can't hardly believe it, but he didn't. I reckon he thought he'd keep the thing up till he tired them people out, so they'd thin out, and him and the duke could break loose and get away. Anyway, he set there, and pretty soon he begun to smile, and says:

"Mf! It's a *very* tough question, *ain't* it! Yes, sir, I k'n tell you what's tatooed on his breast. It's jest a small, thin, blue arrow—that's what it is; and if you don't look clost, you can't see it. *Now* what do you say—hey?"

Well, *I* never see anything like that old blister for clean out-and-out cheek.

The new old gentleman turns brisk towards Ab Turner and his pard, and his eye lights up like he judged he'd got the king *this* time, and says:

"There—you've heard what he said! Was there any such mark on Peter Wilks's breast?"

Both of them spoke up and says:

"We didn't see no such mark."

"Good!" says the old gentleman. "Now, what you *did* see on his breast was a small dim P, and a B (which is an initial he dropped when he was young), and a W, with dashes between them, so: P—B—W"—and he marked them that way on a piece of paper. "Come—ain't that what you saw?"

Both of them spoke up again, and says:

"No, we *didn't*. We never seen any marks at all."

Well, everybody *was* in a state of mind, now; and they sings out

"The whole *bilin'* of 'm 's frauds! Le's duck 'em! le's drown 'em! le's ride 'em on a rail!" and everybody was whooping at once, and there was a rattling pow-wow. But the lawyer he jumps on the table and yells, and says:

"Gentlemen—gentlemen! Hear me just a word—just a *single* word—if you PLEASE! There's one way yet—let's go and dig up the corpse and look."

That took them.

"Hooray!" they all shouted, and was starting right off; but the lawyer and the doctor sung out:

"Hold on, hold on! Collar all these four men and the boy, and fetch *them* along, too!"

"We'll do it!" they all shouted: "and if we don't find them marks we'll lynch the whole gang!"

I *was* scared, now, I tell you. But there warn't no getting away, you know. They gripped us all, and marched us right along, straight for the graveyard, which was a mile and a half down the river, and the whole town at our heels, for we made noise enough, and it was only nine in the evening.

As we went by our house I wished I hadn't sent Mary Jane out of town; because now if I could tip her the wink, she'd light out and save me, and blow on our dead-beats.

Well, we swarmed along down the river road, just carrying on like wild-cats; and to make it more scary, the sky was darking up, and the lightning beginning to wink and flitter, and the wind to shiver amongst the leaves. This was the most awful trouble and most dangersome I ever was in; and I was kinder stunned; everything was going so different from what I had allowed for; stead of being fixed so I could take my own time, if I wanted to, and see all the fun, and have Mary Jane at my back to save me and set me free when the close-fit come, here was nothing in the world betwixt me and sudden death but just them tatoo-marks. If they didn't find them—

I couldn't bear to think about it; and yet, somehow, I couldn't think about nothing else. It got darker and darker, and it was a beautiful time to give the crowd the slip; but that big husky had me by the wrist—Hines—and a body might as well try to give Goliar the slip. He dragged me right along, he was so excited; and I had to run to keep up.

When they got there they swarmed into the graveyard and washed over it like an overflow. And when they got to the grave, they found they had about a hundred times as many shovels as they wanted, but nobody hadn't thought to fetch a lantern. But they sailed into digging, anyway, by the flicker of the lightning, and sent a man to the nearest house a half a mile off, to borrow one.

So they dug and dug, like everything; and it got awful dark, and the rain started, and the wind swished and swushed along, and the lightning come brisker and brisker, and the thunder boomed; but them people never took no notice of it, they was so full of this business; and one minute you could see everything and every face in that big crowd, and the shovelfuls of dirt sailing up out of the grave, and the next second the dark wiped it all out, and you couldn't see nothing at all.

At last they got out the coffin, and begun to unscrew the lid, and then such another crowding, and shouldering, and shoving as there was, to scrouge in and get a sight, you never see; and in the dark, that way, it was awful. Hines he hurt my wrist dreadful, pulling and tugging so, and I reckon he clean forgot I was in the world, he was so excited and panting.

All of a sudden the lightning let go a perfect sluice of white glare, and somebody sings out:

"By the living jingo, here's the bag of gold on his breast!"

Hines let out a whoop, like everybody else, and dropped my wrist and give a big surge to bust his way in and get a look, and the way I lit out and shinned for the road in the dark, there ain't nobody can tell.

I had the road all to myself, and I fairly flew—leastways I had it all to myself except the solid dark, and the now-and-then glares, and the buzzing of the rain, and the thrashing of the wind, and the splitting of the thunder; and sure as you are born I did clip it along!

When I struck the town, I see there warn't nobody out in the storm, so I never hunted for no back streets, but humped it straight through the main one; and when I begun to get towards our house I aimed my eye and set it. No light there; the house all dark—which made me feel sorry and disappointed, I didn't know why. But at last, just as I was sailing by, *flash* comes the light in Mary Jane's window! and my heart swelled up sudden, like to bust; and the same second the house and all was behind me in the dark, and wasn't ever going to be before me no more in this world. She *was* the best girl I ever see, and had the most sand.

The minute I was far enough above the town to see I could make the towhead, I begun to look sharp for a boat to borrow; and the first time the lightning showed me one that wasn't chained, I snatched it and shoved. It was a canoe, and warn't fastened with nothing but a rope. The towhead was a rattling big distance off, away out there in the middle of the river, but I didn't lose no time; and when I struck the raft at last, I was so fagged I would a just laid down to blow and gasp if I could afforded it. But I didn't. As I sprung aboard I sung out:

"Out with you Jim, and set her loose! Glory be to goodness, we're shut of them!"

Jim lit out, and was a coming for me with both arms spread, he was so full of joy; but when I glimpsed him in the lightning, my heart shot up in my mouth, and I went overboard backwards; for I forgot he was old King Lear and a drownded A-rab all in one, and it most scared the livers and lights out of me.

But Jim fished me out, and was going to hug me and bless me, and so on, he was so glad I was back and we was shut of the king and the duke, but I says:

"Not now—have it for breakfast, have it for breakfast! Cut loose and let her slide!"

So, in two seconds, away we went, a sliding down the river, and it *did* seem so good to be free again and all by ourselves on the big river and nobody to bother us. I had to skip around a bit, and jump up and crack my heels a few times, I couldn't help it; but about the third crack, I noticed a sound that I knowed mighty well—and held my breath and listened and waited—and sure enough, when the next flash busted out over the water, here they come!—and just a laying to their oars and making their skiff hum! It was the king and the duke.

So I wilted right down onto the planks, then, and give up; and it was all I could do to keep from crying.

Chapter XXX

WHEN THEY GOT aboard, the king went for me, and shook me by the collar, and says:

"Tryin' to give us the slip, was ye, you pup! Tired of our company—hey?"

I says:

"No, your majesty, we warn't—*please* don't, your majesty!"

"Quick, then, and tell us what *was* your idea, or I'll shake the insides out o' you!"

"Honest, I'll tell you everything, just as it happened, your majesty. The man that had aholt of me was very good to me, and kept saying he had a boy about as big as me that died last year, and he was sorry to see a boy in such a dangerous fix; and when they was all took by surprise by finding the gold, and made a rush for the coffin, he lets go of me and whispers, 'Heel it, now, or they'll hang ye, sure!' and I lit out. It didn't seem no good for *me* to stay—I couldn't do

"JIM LET OUT."

THE KING SHAKES HUCK.

nothing, and I didn't want to be hung if I could get away. So I never stopped running till I found the canoe; and when I got here I told Jim to hurry, or they'd catch me and hang me yet, and said I was afeard you and the duke wasn't alive, now, and I was awful sorry, and so was Jim, and was awful glad when we see you coming, you may ask Jim if I didn't."

Jim said it was so; and the king told him to shut up, and said, "Oh, yes, it's *mighty* likely!" and shook me up again, and said he reckoned he'd drownd me. But the duke says:

"Leggo the boy, you old idiot! Would *you* a done any different? Did you inquire around for *him,* when you got loose? *I* don't remember it."

So the king let go of me, and begun to cuss that town and everybody in it. But the duke says:

"You better a blame sight give *yourself* a good cussing, for you're the one that's entitled to it most. You hain't done a thing, from the start, that had any sense in it, except coming out so cool and cheeky with that imaginary blue-arrow mark. That *was* bright—it was right down bully; and it was the thing that saved us. For if it hadn't been for that, they'd a jailed us till them Englishmen's baggage come—and then—the penitentiary, you bet! But that trick took 'em to the graveyard, and the gold done us a still bigger kindness; for if the excited fools hadn't let go all holts and made that rush to get a look, we'd a slept in our cravats to-night—cravats warranted to *wear,* too—longer than *we'd* need 'em.''

They was still a minute—thinking—then the king says, kind of absent-minded like:

"Mf! And we reckoned the *niggers* stole it!"

That made me squirm!

"Yes," says the duke, kinder slow, and deliberate, and sarcastic, "*We* did."

After about a half a minute, the king drawls out:

" Least ways—*I* did."

The duke says, the same way:

"On the contrary—*I* did."

The king kind of ruffles up, and says:

"Looky here, Bilgewater, what'r you referrin' to?"

The duke says, pretty brisk:

"When it comes to that maybe you'll let me ask, what was *you* referring to?"

"Shucks!" says the king, very sarcastic; "but *I* don't know—maybe you was asleep, and didn't know what you was about."

The duke bristles right up, now, and says:

"Oh, let *up* on this cussed nonsense—do you take me for a blame' fool? Don't you reckon *I* know who hid that money in that coffin?"

"*Yes,* sir! I know you *do* know—because you done it yourself!"

"It's a lie!"—and the duke went for him. The king sings out:

"Take y'r hands off!—leggo my throat!—I take it all back!"

The duke says:

"Well, you just own up, first that you *did* hide that money there, intending to give me the slip one of these days, and come back and dig it up, and have it all to yourself."

"Wait jest a minute, duke—answer me this one question, honest and fair; if you didn't put the money there, say it, and I'll b'lieve you, and take back everything I said."

"You old scoundrel, I didn't, and you know I didn't. There, now!"

"Well, then, I b'lieve you. But answer me only jest this one more—now *don't* git mad; didn't you have it in your *mind* to hook the money and hide it?"

The duke never said nothing for a little bit; then he says:

"Well—I don't care if I *did,* I didn't *do* it, anyway. But you not only had it in mind to do it, but you *done* it."

"I wisht I may never die if I done it, duke, and that's honest. I won't say I warn't *goin'* to do it, because I *was;* but you—I mean somebody—got in ahead o' me."

"It's a lie! You done it, and you got to *say* you done it, or——"

The king begun to gurgle, and then he gasps out:

"'Nough!—*I own up!*"

I was very glad to hear him say that, it made me feel much more easier than what I was feeling before. So the duke took his hands off, and says:

"If you ever deny it again, I'll drown you. It's *well* for you to set there and blubber like a baby—it's fitten for you, after the way you've acted. I never see such an old ostrich for wanting to gobble everything—and I a trusting you all the time, like you was my own father. You ought to been ashamed of yourself to stand by and hear it saddled onto a lot of poor niggers and you never say a word for 'em. It makes me feel ridiculous to think I was soft enough to *believe* that rubbage. Cuss you, I can see, now, why you was so anxious to make up the deffesit—you wanted to get what money I'd got out of the Nonesuch and one thing or another, and scoop it *all!*"

The king says, timid, and still a snuffling:

"Why, duke, it was you that said make up the deffersit, it warn't me."

"Dry up! I don't want to hear no more *out* of you!" says the duke. "And *now* you see what you *got* by it. They've got all their own money back, and all of *ourn* but a shekel or two, *besides.* G'long to bed—and don't you deffersit *me* no more deffersits, long's *you* live!"

So the king sneaked into the wigwam, and took to his bottle for comfort; and before long the duke tackled *his* bottle; and so in about a half an hour they was as thick as thieves again, and the tighter they got, the lovinger they got; and went off a snoring in each other's arms. They both got powerful mellow, but I noticed the king didn't get mellow enough to forget to remember to not deny about hiding the money-bag again. That made me feel easy and satisfied. Of course when they got to snoring, we had a long gabble, and I told Jim everything.

Chapter XXXI

WE DASN'T STOP again at any town, for days and days; kept right along down the river. We was down south in the warm weather, now, and a mighty long ways from home. We begun to come to trees with Spanish moss on them, hanging down from the limbs like long gray beards. It was the first I ever see it growing, and it made the woods look solemn and dismal. So now the frauds reckoned they was out of danger, and they begun to work the villages again.

First they done a lecture on temperance; but they didn't make enough for them both to get drunk on. Then in another village they started a dancing school; but they didn't know no more how to dance than a kangaroo does; so the first prance they made, the general public jumped in and danced them out of town. Another time they tried a go at yellocution; but they didn't yellocute long till the audience got up and give them a solid good cussing and made them skip out. They tackled missionarying, and mesmerizering, and doctoring, and telling fortunes, and a little of everything; but they couldn't seem to have no luck. So at last they got just about dead broke, and laid around the raft, as she floated along, thinking, and thinking, and never saying nothing, by the half a day at a time, and dreadful blue and desperate.

And at last they took a change, and begun to lay their heads together in the wigwam and talk low and confidential two or three hours at a time. Jim and me got uneasy. We didn't like the look of it. We judged they was studying up some kind of worse deviltry than ever. We turned it over and over, and at last we made up our minds they was going to break into somebody's house or store, or was going into the counterfeit-money business, or something. So then we was pretty scared, and made up an agreement that we wouldn't have nothing in the world to do with such actions, and if we ever got the least show we would give them the cold shake, and clear out and leave them behind. Well, early one morning we hid the raft in a good safe place about two mile below a little bit of a shabby village, named Pikesville, and the king he went ashore, and told us all to stay hid whilst he went up to town and smelt around to see if anybody had got any wind of the Royal Nonesuch there yet. ("House to rob, you *mean*," says I to myself; "and when you get through robbing it you'll come back here and wonder what's become of me and Jim and the raft—and you'll have to take it out in wondering.") And he said if he warn't back by midday, the duke and me would know it was all right, and we was to come along.

So we staid where we was. The duke he fretted and sweated around, and was in a mighty sour way. He scolded us for everything, and we couldn't seem to do nothing right; he found fault with every little thing. Something was a-brewing, sure. I was good and glad when midday come and no king; we could have a change, anyway—and maybe a chance for *the* change, on top of it. So me and the duke went up to the village, and hunted around there for the king, and by-and-by we found him in the back room of a little low doggery, very tight, and

a lot of loafers bullyragging him for sport, and he a cussing and threatening
with all his might, and so tight he couldn't walk, and couldn't do nothing to
them. The duke he begun to abuse him for an old fool, and the king begun to
sass back; and the minute they was fairly at it, I lit out, and shook the reefs out
of my hind legs, and spun down the river road like a deer—for I see our chance;
and I made up my mind that it would be a long day before they ever see me
and Jim again. I got down there all out of breath but loaded up with joy, and
sung out—

"Set her loose, Jim, we're all right, now!"

But there warn't no answer, and nobody come out of the wigwam. Jim was
gone! I set up a shout—and then another—and then another one; and run this
way and that in the woods, whooping and screeching; but it warn't no use—old
Jim was gone. Then I set down and cried; I couldn't help it. But I couldn't set
still long. Pretty soon I went out on the road, trying to think what I better do,
and I run across a boy walking, and asked him if he'd seen a strange nigger,
dressed so and so, and he says:

"Yes."

"Whereabouts?" says I.

"Down to Silas Phelps's place, two mile below here. He's a runaway nigger,
and they've got him. Was you looking for him?"

"You bet I ain't! I run across him in the woods about an hour or two ago,
and he said if I hollered he'd cut my livers out—and told me to lay down and
stay where I was; and I done it. Been there ever since; afeard to come out."

"Well," he says, "you needn't be afeard no more, becuz they've got him.
He run off f'm down South, som'ers."

"It's a good job they got him."

"Well, I *reckon!* There's two hunderd dollars reward on him. It's like picking
up money out'n the road."

"Yes, it is—and *I* could a had it if I'd been big enough; I see him *first.* Who
nailed him?"

"It was an old fellow—a stranger—and he sold out his chance in him for
forty dollars, becuz he's got to go up the river and can't wait. Think o' that,
now! You bet *I'd* wait, if it was seven year."

"That's me, every time," says I. "But maybe his chance ain't worth no more
than that, if he'll sell it so cheap. Maybe there's something ain't straight about
it."

"But it *is,* though—straight as a string. I see the handbill myself. It tells all
about him, to a dot—paints him like a picture, and tells the plantation he's frum,
below Newr*leans.* No-sirree-*bob,* they ain't no trouble 'bout *that* speculation,
you bet you. Say, gimme a chaw tobacker, won't ye?"

I didn't have none, so he left. I went to the raft, and set down in the wigwam
to think. But I couldn't come to nothing. I thought till I wore my head sore,
but I couldn't see no way out of the trouble. After all this long journey, and
after all we'd done for them scoundrels, here was it all come to nothing, everything
all busted up and ruined, because they could have the heart to serve Jim such a
trick as that, and make him a slave again all his life, and amongst strangers,
too, for forty dirty dollars.

Once I said to myself it would be a thousand times better for Jim to be a slave
at home where his family was, as long as he'd *got* to be a slave, and so I'd
better write a letter to Tom Sawyer and tell him to tell Miss Watson where he

was. But I soon give up that notion, for two things: she'd be mad and disgusted at his rascality and ungratefulness for leaving her, and so she'd sell him straight down the river again; and if she didn't, everybody naturally despises an ungrateful nigger, and they'd make Jim feel it all the time, and so he'd feel ornery and disgraced. And then think of *me!* It would get all around, that Huck Finn helped a nigger to get his freedom; and if I was to ever see anybody from that town again, I'd be ready to get down and lick his boots for shame. That's just the way: a person does a low-down thing, and then he don't want to take no consequences of it. Thinks as long as he can hide it, it ain't no disgrace. That was my fix exactly. The more I studied about this, the more my conscience went to grinding me, and the more wicked and low-down and ornery I got to feeling. And at last, when it hit me all of a sudden that here was the plain hand of Providence slapping me in the face and letting me know my wickedness was being watched all the time from up there in heaven, whilst I was stealing a poor old woman's nigger that hadn't ever done me no harm, and now was showing me there's One that's always on the lookout, and ain't agoing to allow no such miserable doings to go only just so fur and no further, I most dropped in my tracks I was so scared. Well, I tried the best I could to kinder soften it up somehow for myself, by saying I was brung up wicked, and so I warn't so much to blame; but something inside of me kept saying, "There was the Sunday school, you could a gone to it; and if you'd a done it they'd a learnt you, there, that people that acts as I'd been acting about that nigger goes to everlasting fire."

It made me shiver. And I about made up my mind to pray; and see if I couldn't try to quit being the kind of a boy I was, and be better. So I kneeled down. But the words wouldn't come. Why wouldn't they? It warn't no use to try and hide it from Him. Nor from *me,* neither. I knowed very well why they wouldn't come. It was because my heart warn't right; it was because I warn't square; is was because I was playing double. I was letting *on* to give up sin, but away inside of me I was holding on to the biggest one of all. I was trying to make my mouth *say* I would do the right thing and the clean thing, and go and write to that nigger's owner and tell where he was; but deep down in me I knowed it was a lie—and He knowed it. You can't pray a lie—I found that out.

So I was full of trouble, full as I could be; and didn't know what to do. At last I had an idea; and I says, I'll go and write the letter—and *then* see if I can pray. Why, it was astonishing, the way I felt as light as a feather, right straight off, and my troubles all gone. So I got a piece of paper and a pencil, all glad and excited, and set down and wrote:

> Miss Watson your runaway nigger Jim is down here two mile below Pikesville and Mr. Phelps has got him and he will give him up for the reward if you send.   HUCK FINN

I felt good and all washed clean of sin for the first time I had ever felt so in my life, and I knowed I could pray now. But I didn't do it straight off, but laid the paper down and set there thinking—thinking how good it was all this happened so, and how near I come to being lost and going to hell. And went on thinking. And got to thinking over our trip down the river; and I see Jim before me, all the time, in the day, and in the night-time, sometimes moonlight, sometimes storms, and we a floating along, talking, and singing, and laughing. But somehow

I couldn't seem to strike no places to harden me against him, but only the other kind. I'd see him standing my watch on top of his'n, stead of calling me, so I could go on sleeping; and see him how glad he was when I come back out of the fog; and when I come to him again in the swamp, up there where the feud was; and such-like times; and would always call me honey, and pet me, and do everything he could think of for me, and how good he always was; and at last I struck the time I saved him by telling the men we had small-pox aboard, and he was so grateful, and said I was the best friend old Jim ever had in the world, and the *only* one he's got now; and then I happened to look around, and see that paper.

It was a close place. I took it up, and held it in my hand. I was a trembling, because I'd got to decide, forever, betwixt two things, and I knowed it. I studied a minute, sort of holding my breath, and then says to myself:

"All right, then, I'll *go* to hell"—and tore it up.

It was awful thoughts, and awful words, but they was said. And I let them stay said; and never thought no more about reforming. I shoved the whole thing out of my head; and said I would take up wickedness again, which was in my line, being brung up to it, and the other warn't. And for a starter, I would go to work and steal Jim out of slavery again; and if I could think up anything worse, I would do that, too; because as long as I was in, and in for good, I might as well go the whole hog.

Then I set to thinking over how to get at it, and turned over considerable many ways in my mind; and at last fixed up a plan that suited me. So then I took the bearings of a woody island that was down the river a piece, and as soon as it was fairly dark I crept out with my raft and went for it, and hid it there, and then turned in. I slept the night through, and got up before it was light, and had my breakfast, and put on my store clothes, and tied up some others and one thing or another in a bundle, and took the canoe and cleared for shore. I landed below where I judged was Phelps's place, and hid my bundle in the woods, and then filled up the canoe with water, and loaded rocks into her and sunk her where I could find her again when I wanted her, about a quarter of a mile below a little steam sawmill that was on the bank.

THINKING.

Then I struck up the road, and when I passed the mill I see a sign on it, "Phelps's Sawmill," and when I come to the farm-houses, two or three hundred yards further along, I kept my eyes peeled, but didn't see nobody around, though it was good daylight, now. But I didn't mind, because I didn't want to see nobody just yet—I only wanted to get the lay of the land. According to my plan, I was going to turn up there from the village, not from below. So I just took a look, and shoved along, straight for town. Well, the very first man I see, when I got there, was the duke. He was sticking up a bill for the Royal Nonesuch— three-night performance—like that other time. *They* had the cheek, them frauds! I was right on him, before I could shirk. He looked astonished, and says:

"Hel-*lo!* Where'd *you* come from?" Then he says, kind of glad and eager, "Where's the raft?—got her in a good place?"

I says:

"Why, that's just what I was agoing to ask your grace."

Then he didn't look so joyful—and says:

"What was your idea for asking *me?*" he says.

"Well," I says, "when I see the king in that doggery yesterday, I says to myself, we can't get him home for hours, till he's soberer; so I went a loafing around town to put in the time, and wait. A man up and offered me ten cents to help him pull a skiff over the river and back to fetch a sheep, and so I went along; but when we was dragging him to the boat, and the man left me aholt of the rope and went behind him to shove him along, he was too strong for me, and jerked loose and run, and we after him. We didn't have no dog, and so we had to chase him all over the country till we tired him out. We never got him till dark, then we feteched him over, and I started down for the raft. When I got there and see it was gone, I says to myself, 'they've got into trouble and had to leave; and they've took my nigger, which is the only nigger I've got in the world, and now I'm in a strange country, and ain't got no property no more, nor nothing, and no way to make my living;' so I set down and cried. I slept in the woods all night. But what *did* become of the raft then?—and Jim, poor Jim!"

"Blamed if *I* know—that is, what's become of the raft. That old fool had made a trade and got forty dollars, and when we found him in the doggery the loafers had matched half dollars with him and got every cent but what he'd spent for whisky; and when I got him home late last night and found the raft gone, we said, 'That little rascal has stole our raft and shook us, and run off down the river.' "

"I wouldn't shake my *nigger,* would I?—the only nigger I had in the world, and the only property."

"We never thought of that. Fact is, I reckon we'd come to consider him *our* nigger; yes, we did consider him so—goodness knows we had trouble enough for him. So when we see the raft was gone, and we flat broke, there warn't anything for it but to try the Royal Nonesnch another shake. And I've pegged along ever since, dry as a powderhorn. Where's that ten cents? Give it here."

I had considerable money, so I give him ten cents, but begged him to spend it for something to eat, and give me some, because it was all the money I had, and I hadn't had nothing to eat since yesterday. He never said nothing. The next minute he whirls on me and says:

"Do you reckon that nigger would blow on us? We'd skin him if he done that!"

"How can he blow? Hain't he run off?"

"No! That old fool sold him, and never divided with me, and the money's gone."

"*Sold* him?" I says, and begun to cry; "why, he was *my* nigger, and that was my money. Where is he?—I want my nigger."

"Well, you can't *get* your nigger, that's all—so dry up your blubbering. Looky here—do you think *you'd* venture to blow on us? Blamed if I think I'd trust you. Why, if you *was* to blow on us——"

He stopped, but I never see the duke look so ugly out of his eyes before. I went on a-whimpering, and says:

"I don't want to blow on nobody; and I ain't got no time to blow, nohow. I got to turn out and find my nigger."

He looked kinder bothered, and stood there with his bills fluttering on his arm, thinking, and wrinkling up his forehead. At last he says:

"I'll tell you something. We got to be here three days. If you'll promise you won't blow, and won't let the nigger blow, I'll tell you where to find him."

So I promised, and he says:

"A farmer by the name of Silas Ph——" and then he stopped. Yon see he started to tell me the truth; but when he stopped, that way, and begun to study and think again, I reckoned he was changing his mind. And so he was. He wouldn't trust me; he wanted to make sure of having me out of the way the whole three days. So pretty soon he says: "The man that bought him is named Abram Foster—Abram G. Foster—and he lives forty mile back here in the country, on the road to Lafayette."

"All right," I says, "I can walk it in three days. And I'll start this very afternoon."

"No you won't, you'll start *now;* and don't you lose any time about it, neither, nor do any gabbling by the way. Just keep a tight tongue in your head and move right along, and then you won't get into trouble with *us,* d'ye hear?"

That was the order I wanted, and that was the one I played for. I wanted to be left free to work my plans.

"So clear out" he says; "and you can tell Mr. Foster whatever you want to. Maybe you can get him to believe that Jim *is* your nigger—some idiots don't require documents—leastways I've heard there's such down South here. And when you tell him the handbill and the reward's bogus, maybe he'll believe you when you explain to him what the idea was for getting 'em out. Go 'long, now, and tell him anything you want to; but mind you don't work your jaw any *between* here and there."

So I left, and struck for the back country. I didn't look around, but I kinder felt like he was watching me. But I knowed I could tire him out at that. I went straight out in the country as much as a mile, before I stopped; then I doubled back through the woods towards Phelps's. I reckoned I better start in on my plan straight off, without fooling around, because I wanted to stop Jim's mouth till these fellows could get away. I didn't want no trouble with their kind. I'd seen all I wanted to of them, and wanted to get entirely shut of them.

Chapter XXXII

WHEN I GOT there it was all still and Sunday-like, and hot and sunshiny—the hands was gone to the fields; and there was them kind of faint dronings of bugs and flies in the air that makes it seem so lonesome and like everybody's dead and gone; and if a breeze fans along and quivers the leaves, it makes you feel mournful, because you feel like it's spirits whispering—spirits that's been dead ever so many years—and you always think they're talking about *you*. As a general thing it makes a body wish *he* was dead, too, and done with it all.

Phelps's was one of these little one-horse cotton plantations; and they all look alike. A rail fence round a two-acre yard; a stile, made out of logs sawed off and up-ended, in steps, like barrels of a different length, to climb over the fence with, and for the women to stand on when they are going to jump onto a horse; some sickly grass-patches in the big yard, but mostly it was bare and smooth, like an old hat with the nap rubbed off; big double log house for the white folks—hewed logs, with the chinks stopped up with mud or mortar, and these mud-stripes been whitewashed some time or another; round-log kitchen, with a big broad, open but roofed passage joining it to the house; log smoke-house back of the kitchen; three little log nigger-cabins in a row t'other side the smokehouse; one little hut all by itself away down against the back fence, and some out-buildings down a piece the other side; ash-hopper, and big kettle to bile soap in, by the little hut; bench by the kitchen door, with bucket of water and a gourd; hound asleep there, in the sun; more hounds asleep, round about; about three shade-trees away off in a corner; some currant bushes and gooseberry bushes in one place by the fence; outside of the fence a garden and a water-melon patch; then the cotton fields begins; and after the fields, the woods.

I went around and clumb over the back stile by the ash-hopper, and started for the kitchen. When I got a little ways, I heard the dim hum of a spinning-wheel wailing along up and sinking along down again; and then I knowed for certain I wished I was dead—for that *is* the lonesomest sound in the whole world.

I went right along, not fixing up any particular plan, but just trusting to Providence to put the right words in my mouth when the time come; for I'd noticed that Providence always did put the right words in my mouth, if I left it alone.

When I got half-way, first one hound and then another got up and went for me, and of course I stopped and faced them, and kept still. And such another pow-wow as they made! In a quarter of a minute I was a kind of a hub of a wheel, as you may say—spokes made out of dogs—circle of fifteen of them packed together around me, with their necks and noses stretched up towards me, a barking and howling; and more a coming; you could see them sailing over fences and around corners from everywheres.

A nigger woman come tearing out of the kitchen with a rolling-pin in her hand, singing out, "Begone! *you* Tige! you Spot! begone, sah!" and she fetched first one and then another of them a clip and sent him howling, and then the rest followed; and the next second, half of them come back, wagging their tails around me and making friends with me. There ain't no harm in a hound, nohow.

And behind the woman comes a little nigger girl and two little nigger boys, without anything on but tow-linen shirts, and they hung onto their mother's gown, and peeped out from behind her at me, bashful, the way they always do. And here comes the white woman running from the house, about forty-five or fifty year old, bareheaded, and her spinning-stick in her hand; and behind her comes her little white children, acting the same way the little niggers was doing. She was smiling all over so she could hardly stand—and says:

"It's *you,* at last!—*ain't* it?"

I out with a "Yes'm," before I thought.

She grabbed me and hugged me tight; and then gripped me by both hands and shook and shook; and the tears come in her eyes, and run down over; and she couldn't seem to hug and shake enough, and kept saying, "You don't look as much like your mother as I reckoned you would, but law sakes, I don't care for that, I'm *so* glad to see you! Dear, dear, it does seem like I could eat you up! Childern, it's your cousin Tom!—tell him howdy."

But they ducked their heads, and put their fingers in their mouths, and hid behind her. So she run on:

"Lize, hurry up and get him a hot breakfast, right away—or did you get your breakfast on the boat?"

I said I had got it on the boat. So then she started for the house, leading me by the hand, and the children tagging after. When we got there, she set me down in a split-bottomed chair, and set herself down on a little low stool in front of me, holding both of my hands, and says:

"Now I can have a *good* look at you; and laws-a-me, I've been hungry for it a many and a many a time, all these long years, and it's come at last! We been expecting you a couple of days and more. What's kep' you?—boat get aground?"

"Yes'm—she——"

"Don't say yes'm—say Aunt Sally. Where'd she get aground?"

I didn't rightly know what to say, because I didn't know whether the boat would be coming up the river or down. But I go a good deal on instinct; and my instinct said she would be coming up—from down towards Orleans. That did'nt help me much, though; for I didn't know the names of bars down that

SHE HUGGED HIM TIGHT.

way. I see I'd got to invent a bar, or forget the name of the one we got aground on—or— Now I struck an idea, and fetched it out:

"It warn't the grounding—that didn't keep us back but a little. We blowed out a cylinder-head."

"Good gracious! anybody hurt?"

"No'm. Killed a nigger."

"Well, it's lucky; because sometimes people do get hurt. Two years ago last Christmas, your uncle Silas was coming up from Newrleans on the old *Lally Rook,* and she blowed out a cylinder-head and crippled a man. And I think he died afterwards. He was a Babtist. Your uncle Silas knowed a family in Baton Rouge that knowed his people very well. Yes, I remember, now he *did* die. Mortification set in, and they had to amputate him. But it didn't save him. Yes, it was mortification—that was it. He turned blue all over, and died in the hope of a glorious resurrection. They say he was a sight to look at. Your uncle's been up to the town every day to fetch you. And he's gone again, not more'n an hour ago; he'll be back any minute, now. You must a met him on the road, didn't you?—oldish man, with a——"

"No, I didn't see nobody, Aunt Sally. The boat landed just at daylight, and I left my baggage on the wharf-boat and went looking around the town and out a piece in the country, to put in the time and not get here too soon; and so I come down the back way."

"Who'd you give the baggage to?"

"Nobody."

"Why, child, it'll be stole!"

"Not where *I* hid it I reckon it won't," I says.

"How'd you get your breakfast so early on the boat?"

It was kinder thin ice, but I says:

"The captain see me standing around, and told me I better have something to eat before I went ashore; so he took me in the texas to the officers' lunch, and give me all I wanted."

I was getting so uneasy I couldn't listen good. I had my mind on the children all the time; I wanted to get them out to one side, and pump them a little, and find out who I was. But I couldn't get no show, Mrs. Phelps kept it up and run on so. Pretty soon she made the cold chills streak all down my back, because she says:

"But here we're a running on this way, and you hain't told me a word about Sis, nor any of them. Now I'll rest my works a little, and you start up yourn; just tell me *everything*—tell me all about 'm all—every one of 'm; and how they are, and what they're doing, and what they told you to tell me; and every last thing you can think of."

Well, I see I was up a stump—and up it good. Providence had stood by me this fur, all right, but I was hard and tight aground, now. I see it warn't a bit of use to try to go ahead—I'd *got* to throw up my hand. So I says to myself, here's another place where I got to resk the truth. I opened my mouth to begin; but she grabbed me and hustled me in behind the bed, and says:

"Here he comes! stick your head down lower—there, that'll do; you can't be seen, now. Don't you let on you're here. I'll play a joke on him. Childern, don't you say a word."

I see I was in a fix, now. But it warn't no use to worry; there warn't nothing to do but just hold still, and try and be ready to stand from under when the lightning struck.

I had just one little glimpse of the old gentleman when he come in, then the bed hid him. Mrs. Phelps she jumps for him and says:

"Has he come?"

"No," says her husband.

"Good-*ness* gracious!" she says, "what in the world *can* have become of him?"

"I can't imagine," says the old gentleman; "and I must say, it makes me dreadful uneasy."

"Uneasy!" she says "I'm ready to go distracted! He *must* a come; and you've missed him along the road. I *know* it's so—something *tells* me so."

"Why Sally, I *couldn't* miss him along the road—*you* know that."

"But oh, dear, dear, what *will* Sis say! He must a come! You must a missed him. He——"

"Oh, don't distress me any more'n I'm already distressed. I don't know what in the world to make of it. I'm at my wit's end, and I don't mind acknowledging 't I'm right down scared. But there's no hope that he's come; for he *couldn't* come and me miss him. Sally, it's terrible—just terrible—something's happened to the boat, sure!"

"Why, Silas: Look yonder!—up the road!—ain't that somebody coming?"

He sprung to the window at the head of the bed, and that give Mrs. Phelps the chance she wanted. She stooped down quick, at the foot of the bed, and give me a pull, and out I come; and when he turned back from the window, there she stood, a-beaming and a-smiling like a house afire, and I standing pretty meek and sweaty alongside. The old gentleman stared, and says:

"Why, who's that?"

"Who do you reckon 't is?"

"I haint no idea. Who *is* it?"

"It's *Tom Sawyer!*"

By jings, I most slumped though the floor. But there warn't no time to swap knives; the old man grabbed me by the hand and shook, and kept on shaking; and all the time, how the woman did dance around and laugh and cry; and then how they both did fire off questions about Sid, and Mary, and the rest of the tribe.

But if they was joyful, it warn't nothing to what I was; for it was like being born again, I was so glad to find out who I was. Well, they froze to me for two hours; and at last when my chin was so tired it couldn't hardly go, any more, I had told them more about my family—I mean the Sawyer family—than ever happened to any six Sawyer families. And I explained all about how we blowed out a cylinder-head at the mouth of White River and it took us three days to fix it. Which was all right, and worked first rate; because *they* didn't know but what it would take three days to fix it. If I'd a called it a bolt-head it would a done just as well.

Now I was feeling pretty comfortable all down one side, and pretty uncomfortable all up the other. Being Tom Sawyer was easy and comfortable; and it stayed easy and comfortable till by-and-by I hear a steamboat coughing along down the river——then I says to myself, spose Tom Sawyer come down on that boat?— and spose he steps in here, any minute, and sings out my name before I can throw him a wink to keep quiet? Well, I couldn't *have* it that way—it wouldn't do at all. I must go up the road and waylay him. So I told the folks I reckoned I would go up to the town and fetch down my baggage. The old gentleman was for going along with me, but I said no, I could drive the horse myself, and I druther he wouldn't take no trouble about me.

Chapter XXXIII

So I STARTED for town, in the wagon, and when I was half-way I see a wagon coming, and sure enough it was Tom Sawyer, and I stopped and waited till he come along. I says "Hold on!" and it stopped alongside, and his mouth opened up like a trunk, and staid so; and he swallowed two or three times like a person that's got a dry throat, and then says:

"I hain't ever done you no harm. You know that. So then, what you want to come back and ha'nt *me* for?"

I says:

"I hain't come back—I hain't been *gone*."

When he heard my voice, it righted him up some, but he warn't quite satisfied yet. He says:

"Don't you play nothing on me, because I wouldn't harm you. Honest injun, now, you ain't a ghost?"

"Honest injun, I ain't," I says.

"Well—I—I—well, that ought to settle it, of course; but I can't somehow seem to understand it, no way. Looky here, warn't you ever murdered *at all?*"

"No. I warn't ever murdered at all—I played it on them. You come in here and feel of me if you don't believe me."

So he done it; and it satisfied him; and he was that glad to see me again, he didn't know what to do. And he wanted to know all about it right off; because it was a grand adventure and mysterious, and so it hit him where he lived. But I said, leave it alone till by-and-by; and told his driver to wait, and we drove off a little piece, and I told him the kind of a fix I was in, and what did he

"IT WAS TOM SAWYER."

reckon we better do? He said, let him alone a minute, and don't disturb him. So he thought and thought, and pretty soon he says:

"It's all right, I've got it. Take my trunk in your wagon, and let on it's your'n; and you turn back and fool along slow, so as to get to the house about the time you ought to; and I'll go towards town a piece, and take a fresh start, and get there a quarter or a half an hour after you; and you needn't let on to know me, at first."

I says:

"All right; but wait a minute. There's one more thing—a thing that *nobody* don't know but me. And that is, there's a nigger here that I'm a trying to steal out of slavery—and his name is *Jim*—old Miss Watson's Jim."

He says:

"What! Why Jim is——"

He stopped and went to studying. I says:

"I know what you'll say. You'll say it's dirty low-down business; but what if it is?—I'm low down; and I'm agoing to steal him, and I want you to keep mum and not let on. Will you?"

His eye lit up, and he says:

"I'll *help* you steal him!"

Well, I let go all holts then, like I was shot. It was the most astonishing speech I ever heard—and I'm bound to say Tom Sawyer fell, considerable, in my estimation. Only I couldn't believe it. Tom Sawyer a *nigger stealer!*

"Oh, shucks," I says, "you're joking."

"I ain't joking, either."

"Well, then," I says, "joking or no joking, if you hear anything said about a runaway nigger, don't forget to remember that *you* don't know nothing about him, and *I* don't know nothing about him."

Then we took the trunk and put it in my wagon, and he drove off his way, and I drove mine. But of course I forgot all about driving slow, on accounts of being glad and full of thinking; so I got home a heap too quick for that length of a trip. The old gentleman was at the door, and he says:

"Why, this is wonderful. Who ever would a thought it was in that mare to do it. I wish we'd a timed her. And she hain't sweated a hair—not a hair. It's wonderful. Why, I wouldn't take a hunderd dollars for that horse now; I wouldn't, honest; and yet I'd a sold her for fifteen before, and thought 'twas all she was worth."

That's all he said. He was the innocentest, best old soul I ever see. But it warn't surprising; because he warn't only just a farmer, he was a preacher, too, and had a little one-horse log church down back of the plantation, which he built it himself at his own expense, for a church and school-house, and never charged nothing for his preaching, and it was worth it, too. There was plenty other farmer-preachers like that, and done the same way, down South.

In about half an hour Tom's wagon drove up to the front stile, and Aunt Sally she see it through the window because it was only about fifty yards, and says:

"Why, there's somebody come! I wonder who 'tis? Why, I do believe it's a stranger. Jimmy" (that's one of the children), "run and tell Lize to put on another plate for dinner."

Everybody made a rush for the front door, because, of course, a stranger don't come *every* year, and so he lays over the yaller fever, for interest, when he does come. Tom was over the stile and starting for the house; the wagon was spinning up the road for the village, and we was all bunched in the front door. Tom had his store clothes on, and an audience—and that was always nuts for Tom Sawyer. In them circumstances it warn't no trouble to him to throw in an amount of style that was suitable. He warn't a boy to meeky along up that yard like a sheep; no, he come ca'm and important, like the ram. When he got afront of us, he lifts his hat ever so gracious and dainty, like it was the lid of a box that had butterflies asleep in it and he didn't want to disturb them, and says:

"Mr. Archibald Nichols, I presume?"

"No, my boy," says the old gentleman, "I'm sorry to say't your driver has deceived you; Nichol's place is down a matter of three mile more. Come in, come in.

"Tom he took a look back over his shoulder, and says, "Too late—he's out of sight."

"Yes, he's gone, my son, and you must come in and eat your dinner with us; and then we'll hitch up and take you down to Nichols's."

"Oh, I can't make you so much trouble; I couldn't think of it. I'll walk—I don't mind the distance."

"But we won't *let* you walk—it wouldn't be Southern hospitality to do it. Come right in."

"Oh, *do*," says Aunt Sally; "it ain't a bit of trouble to us, not a bit in the world. You *must* stay. It's a long, dusty three mile, and we *can't* let you walk. And besides, I've already told 'em to put on another plate, when I see you coming; so you mustn't disappoint us. Come right in, and make yourself at home."

So Tom he thanked them very hearty and handsome, and let himself be persuaded, and come in; and when he was in, he said he was a stranger from Hicksville, Ohio, and his name was William Thompson—and he made another bow.

Well, he run on, and on, and on, making up stuff about Hicksville and everybody in it he could invent, and I getting a little nervous, and wondering how this was going to help me out of my scrape; and at last, still talking along, he reached over and kissed Aunt Sally right on the mouth, and then settled back again in his chair, comfortable, and was going on talking; but she jumped up and wiped it off with the back of her hand, and says:

"You owdacious puppy!"

He looked kind of hurt, and says:

"I'm surprised at you, m'am."

"You're s'rp— Why, what do you reckon *I* am? I've a good notion to take and—say, what do you mean by kissing me?"

He looked kind of humble, and says:

"I didn't mean nothing, m'am. I didn't mean no harm. I—I—thought you'd like it."

"Why, you born fool!" She took up the spinning-stick, and it looked like it was all she could do to keep from giving him a crack with it. "What made you think I'd like it?"

"Well, I don't know. Only, they—they—told me you would."

"*They* told you I would. Whoever told you's *another* lunatic. I never heard the beat of it. Who's *they*?"

"Why—everybody. They all said so, m'am."

It was all she could do to hold in; and her eyes snapped, and her fingers worked like she wanted to scratch him; and she says:

"Who's 'everybody?' Out with their names—or ther'll be an idiot short."

He got up and looked distressed, and fumbled his hat, and says:

"I'm sorry, and I warn't expecting it. They told me to. They all told me to. They all said kiss her; and said she'll like it. They all said it—every one of them. But I'm sorry, m'am, and I won't do it no more—I won't, honest."

"You won't, won't you? Well, I sh'd *reckon* you won't!"

"No'm, I'm honest about it; I won't ever do it again. Till you ask me."

"Till I *ask* you! Well, I never see the beat of it in my born days! I lay you'll be the Methusalem-numskull of creation before ever *I* ask you—or the likes of you."

"Well," he says, "it does surprise me so. I can't make it out, somehow. They said you would, and I thought you would. But—" He stopped and looked around slow, like he wished he could run across a friendly eye, somewhere's; and fetched up on the old gentleman's, and says, "Didn't *you* think she'd like me to kiss her, sir?"

"Why, no, I—I—well, no, I b'lieve I didn't."

Then he looks on around, the same way, to me—and says:

"Tom, didn't *you* think Aunt Sally'd open out her arms and say, 'Sid Sawyer——' "

"My land!" she says, breaking in and jumping for him, "you impudent young rascal, to fool a body so—" and was going to hug him, but he fended her off, and says:

"No, not till you've asked me, first."

So she didn't lose no time, but asked him; and hugged him and kissed him, over and over again, and then turned him over to the old man, and he took what was left. And after they got a little quiet again, she says:

"Why, dear me, I never see such a surprise. We warn't looking for *you,* at all, but only Tom. Sis never wrote to me about anybody coming but him."

"It's because it warn't *intended* for any of us to come but Tom," he says; "but I begged and begged, and at the last minute she let me come, too; so, coming down the river, me and Tom thought it would be a first-rate surprise for him to come here to the house first, and for me to by-and-by tag along and drop in and let on to be a stranger. But it was a mistake, Aunt Sally. This ain't no healthy place for a stranger to come."

"No—not impudent whelps, Sid. You ought to had your jaws boxed; I hain't been so put out since I don't know when. But I don't care, I don't mind the terms—I'd be willing to stand a thousand such jokes to have you here. Well, to think of that performance! I don't deny it, I was most petrified with astonishment when yon give me that smack."

We had dinner out in that broad open passage betwixt the house and the kitchen; and there was things enough on that table for seven families—and all hot, too; none of your flabby tough meat that's laid in a cupboard in a damp cellar all night and tastes like a hunk of old cold cannibal in the morning. Uncle Silas he asked a pretty long blessing over it, but it was worth it; and it didn't cool it a bit, neither, the way I've seen them kind of interruptions do, lots of times.

There was a considerable good deal of talk, all the afternoon, and me and Tom was on the lookout all the time, but it warn't no use, they didn't happen to say nothing about any runaway nigger and we was afraid to try to work up to it. But at supper, at night, one of the little boys say's:

"Pa mayn't Tom and Sid and me go to the show?"

"No," says the old man, "I reckon there ain't going to be any; and you couldn't go if there was; because the runaway nigger told Burton and me all about that scandalous show, and Burton said he would tell the people; so I reckon they've drove the owdacious loafers out of town before this time."

So there it was!—but I couldn't help it. Tom and me was to sleep in the same room and bed; so, being tired, we bid good-night and went up to bed, right after supper, and clumb out of the window and down the lightning-rod, and shoved for the town; for I didn't believe anybody was going to give the king and the duke a hint, and so, if I didn't hurry up and give them one they'd get into trouble sure.

On the road Tom he told me all about how it was reckoned I was murdered, and how pap disappeared, pretty soon, and didn't come back no more, and what a stir there was when Jim run away; and I told Tom all about our Royal Nonesuch rapscallions, and as much of the raft-voyage as I had time to; and as we struck into the town and up through the middle of it—it was as much as half-after eight, then—here comes a raging rush of people, with torches, and an awful whooping and yelling, and banging tin pans and blowing horns; and we jumped to one side to let them 'go by; and as they went by, I see they had the king and the duke astraddle of a rail—that is, I knowed it *was* the king and the duke, though they was all over tar and feathers, and didn't look like nothing in the world that was human—just looked like a couple of monstrous big soldier-plumes. Well, it made me sick to see it; and I was sorry for them poor pitiful rascals, it seemed like I couldn't ever feel any hardness against them any more in the world. It was a dreadful thing to see. Human beings *can* be awful cruel to one another.

We see we was too late—couldn't do no good. We asked some stragglers about it, and they said everybody went to the show looking very innocent; and laid low and kept dark till the poor old king was in the middle of his cavortings on the stage; then somebody give a signal, and the house rose up and went for them.

So we poked along back home, and I warn't feeling so brash as I was before, but kind of ornery, and humble, and to blame, somehow—though *I* hadn't done nothing. But that's always the way; it don't make no difference whether you do right or wrong, a person's conscience ain't got no sense, and just goes for him *anyway*. If I had a yaller dog that didn't know no more than a person's conscience does, I would pison him. It takes up more room than all the rest of a person's insides, and yet ain't no good, nohow. Tom Sawyer he says the same.

Chapter XXXIV

WE STOPPED TALKING, and got to thinking. By-and-by Tom says:

"Looky here, Huck, what fools we are to not think of it before! I bet I know where Jim is."

"No! Where?"

"In that hut down by the ash-hopper. Why looky here. When we was at dinner, didn't you see a nigger man go in there with some vittles ?''

"Yes."

"What did you think the vittles was for?"

"For a dog."

"So'd I. Well, it wasn't for a dog."

"Why?"

"Because part of it was watermelon."

"So it was—I noticed it. Well, it does beat all, that I never thought about a dog not eating watermelon. It shows how a body can see and don't see at the same time."

"Well, the nigger unlocked the padlock when he went in, and he locked it again when he come out. He fetched uncle a key, about the time we got up from table—same key, I bet. Watermelon shows man, lock shows prisoner; and it ain't likely there's two prisoners on such a little plantation, and where the people's all so kind and good. Jim's the prisoner. All right—I'm glad we found it out detective fashion; I wouldn't give shucks for any other way. Now you work your mind and study out a plan to steal Jim, and I will study out one, too; and we'll take the one we like the best."

What a head for just a boy to have! If I had Tom Sawyer's head, I wouldn't trade it off to be a duke, nor mate of a steamboat, nor clown in a circus, nor nothing I can think of. I went to thinking out a plan, but only just to be doing something; I knowed very well where the right plan was going to come from. Pretty soon, Tom says:

"Ready?"

"Yes," I says.

"All right—bring it out."

"My plan is this," I says. "We can easy find out if it's Jim in there. Then get up my canoe to-morrow night, and fetch my raft over from the island. Then the first dark night that comes, steal the key out of the old man's britches, after he goes to bed, and shove off down the river on the raft, with Jim, hiding daytimes and running nights, the way me and Jim used to do before. Wouldn't that plan work?"

VITTLES.

"*Work?* Why certainly, it would work, like rats a fighting. But it's too blame' simple; there ain't nothing *to* it. What's the good of a plan that ain't no more trouble than that? It's as mild as goose-milk. Why, Huck, it wouldn't make no more talk than breaking into a soap factory."

I never said nothing, because I warn't expecting nothing different; but I knowed mighty well that whenever he got *his* plan ready it wouldn't have none of them objections to it.

And it didn't. He told me what it was, and I see in a minute it was worth fifteen of mine, for style, and would make Jim just as free a man as mine would, and maybe get us all killed besides. So I was satisfied, and said we would waltz in on it. I needn't tell what it was, here, because I knowed it wouldn't stay the way it was. I knowed he would be changing it around, every which way, as we went along, and heaving in new bullinesses wherever he got a chance. And that is what he done.

Well, one thing was dead sure; and that was, that Tom Sawyer was in earnest and was actly going to help steal that nigger out of slavery. That was the thing that was too many for me. Here was a boy that was respectable, and well brung up; and had a character to lose; and folks at home that had characters; and he was bright and not leather-headed; and knowing and not ignorant; and not mean, but kind; and yet here he was, without any more pride, or rightness, or feeling, than to stoop to this business, and make himself a shame, and his family a shame, before everybody. I *couldn't* understand it, no way at all. It was outrageous, and I knowed I ought to just up and tell him so; and so be his true friend, and let him quit the thing right where he was, and save himself. And I *did* start to tell him; but he shut me up, and says:

"Don't you reckon I know what I'm about? Don't I generally know what I'm about?"

"Yes."

"Didn't I *say* I was going to help steal the nigger?"

"Yes."

"*Well* then."

That's all he said, and that's all I said. It warn't no use to say any more; because when he said he'd do a thing, he always done it. But *I* couldn't make out how he was willing to go into this thing; so I just let it go, and never bothered no more about it. If he was bound to have it so, *I* couldn't help it.

When we got home, the house was all dark and still; so we went on down to the hut by the ash-hopper, for to examine it. We went through the yard, so as to see what the hounds would do. They knowed us, and didn't make no more noise than country dogs is always doing when anything comes by in the night. When we got to the cabin, we took a look at the front and the two sides; and on the side I warn't acquainted with—which was the north side—we found a square window-hole, up tolerable high, with just one stout board nailed across it. I says:

"Here's the ticket. This hole's big enough for Jim to get through, if we wrench off the board."

Tom says:

"It's as simple as tit-tat-toe, three-in-a-row, and as easy as playing hooky. I should hope we can find a way that's a little more complicated than *that,* Huck Finn."

"Well then," I says, 'how'll it do to saw him out, the way I done before I was murdered, that time?"

"That's more *like*," he says, "It's real mysterious, and troublesome, and good," he says; "but I bet we can find a way that's twice as long. There ain't no hurry; le's keep on looking around."

Betwixt the hut and the fence, on the back side, was a lean-to, that joined the hut at the eaves, and was made out of plank. It was as long as the hut, but narrow—only about six foot wide. The door to it was at the south end, and was padlocked. Tom he went to the soap kettle, and searched around and fetched back the iron thing they lift the lid with; so he took it and prized out one of the staples. The chain fell down, and we opened the door and went in, and shut it, and struck a match, and see the shed was only built against the cabin and hadn't no connection with it; and there warn't no floor to the shed, nor nothing in it but some old rusty played-out hoes, and spades, and picks, and a crippled plow. The match went out, and so did we, and shoved in the staple again, and the door was locked as good as ever. Tom was joyful. He says:

"Now we're all right. We'll *dig* him out. It'll take about a week!"

Then we started for the house, and I went in the back door—you only have to pull a buckskin latch-string, they don't fasten the doors—but that warn't romantical enough for Tom Sawyer: no way would do him but he must climb up the lightning-rod. But after he got up half-way about three times, and missed fire and fell every time, and the last time most busted his brains out, he thought he'd got to give it up; but after he was rested, he allowed he would give her one more turn for luck, and this time he made the trip.

In the morning we was up at break of day, and down to the nigger cabins to pet the dogs and make friends with the nigger that fed Jim—if it *was* Jim that was being fed. The niggers was just getting through breakfast and starting for the fields; and Jim's nigger was piling up a tin pan with bread and meat and things; and whilst the others was leaving, the key come from the house.

This nigger had a good-natured, chuckle-headed face, and his wool was all tied up in little bunches with thread. That was to keep witches off. He said the witches was pestering him awful, these nights, and making him see all kinds of strange things, and hear all kinds of strange words and noises, and he didn't believe he was ever witched so long, before, in his life. He got so worked up, and got to running on so about his troubles, he forgot all about what he'd been agoing to do. So Tom says:

"What's the vittles for? Going to feed the dogs?"

The nigger kind of smiled around graduly over his face, like when you heave a brickbat in a mud puddle, and he says:

"Yes, Mars Sid, *a* dog. Cur'us dog, too. Does you want to go en look at 'im?"

"Yes."

I hunched Tom, and whispers:

"You going, right here in the day-break? *That* warn't the plan."

"No, it warn't—but it's the plan *now*."

So, drat him, we went along, but I didn't like it much. When we got in, we couldn't hardly see anything, it was so dark; but Jim was there, sure enough, and could see us; and he sings out:

"Why, *Huck!* En good *lan'!* ain' dat Misto Tom?"

I just knowed how it would be; I just expected it. *I* didn't know nothing to do; and if I had, I couldn't a done it; because that nigger busted in and says:

"Why, de gracious sakes! do he know you genlmen?"

We could see pretty well, now. Tom he looked at the nigger, steady and kind of wondering, and says:

"Does *who* know us?"

"Why, dish-yer runaway nigger."

"I don't reckon he does; but what put that into your head ?"

"What *put* it dar? Didn' he jis' dis minute sing out like he knowed you?"

Tom says, in a puzzled-up kind of way:

"Well, that's mighty curious. *Who* sung out? *When* did he sing out? *What* did he sing out?" And turns to me, perfectly c'am, and says, "Did *you* hear anybody sing out?"

Of course there warn't nothing to be said but the one thing; so I say's:

"No; *I* ain't heard nobody say nothing."

Then he turns to Jim, and looks him over like he never see him before; and says:

"Did you sing out?"

"No, sah," says Jim; "*I* hain't said nothing, sah."

"Not a word?"

"No, sah, I hain't said a word."

"Did you ever see us before?"

"No, sah; not as I knows on."

So Tom turns to the nigger, which was looking wild and distressed, and says, kind of severe:

"What do you reckon's the matter with you, anyway? What made you think somebody sung out?"

"Oh, it's de dad-blame' witches, sah, en I wisht I was dead, I do. Dey's awluz at it, sah, en dey do mos' kill me, dey sk'yers me so. Please to don't tell nobody 'bout it sah, er ole Mars Silas he'll scole me; 'kase he say dey *ain't* no witches. I jis' wish to goodness he was heah now—*den* what would he say! I jis' bet he couldn' fine no way to git aroun' it dis time. But it's awluz jis' so; people dat's *sot,* stays sot; dey won't look into nothn' en fine it out f'r deyselves en when *you* fine it out en tell um 'bout it, dey doan' b'lieve you."

Tom give him a dime, and said we wouldn't tell nobody; and told him to buy some more thread to tie up his wool with; and then looks at Jim, and says:

"I wonder if Uncle Silas is going to hang this nigger. If I was to catch a nigger that was ungrateful enough to run away, *I* wouldn't give him up, I'd hang him." And whilst the nigger stepped to the door to look at the dime and bite it to see if it was good, he whispers to Jim, and says:

"Don't ever let on to know us. And if you hear any digging going on nights, it's us: we're going to set you free."

Jim only had time to grab us by the hand and squeeze it, then the nigger come back, and we said we'd come again some time if the nigger wanted us to; and he said he would, more particular if it was dark, because the witches went for him mostly in the dark, and it was good to have folks around then.

Chapter XXXV

IT WOULD BE most an hour, yet, till breakfast, so we left, and struck down into the woods; because Tom said we got to have *some* light to see how to dig by, and a lantern makes too much, and might get us into trouble; what we must have was a lot of them rotten chunks that's called fox-fire and just makes a soft kind of a glow when you lay them in a dark place. We fetched an armful and hid it in the weeds, and set down to rest, and Tom says, kind of dissatisfied:

"Blame it, this whole thing is just as easy and awkard as it can be. And so it makes it so rotten difficult to get up a difficult plan. There ain't no watchman to be drugged—now there *ought* to be a watchman. There ain't even a dog to give a sleeping-mixture to. And there's Jim chained by one leg, with a ten-foot chain, to the leg of his bed: why, all you got to do is to lift up the bedstead and slip off the chain. And Uncle Silas he trusts everybody; sends the key to the punkin-headed nigger, and don't send nobody to watch the nigger. Jim could a got out of that window hole before this, only there wouldn't be no use trying to travel with a ten-foot chain on his leg Why, drat it, Huck, it's the stupidest arrangement I ever see. You got to invent *all* the difficulties. Well, we can't help it, we got to do the best we can with the materials we've got. Anyhow, there's one thing—there's more honor in getting him out through a lot of difficulties and dangers, where there warn't one of them furnished to you by the people who it was their duty to furnish them, and you had to contrive them all out of your own head. Now look at just that one thing of the lantern. When you come down to the cold facts, we simply got to *let on* that a lantern's resky. Why, we could work with a torchlight procession if we wanted to, *I* believe. Now, whilst I think of it, we got to hunt up something to make a saw out of, the first chance we get."

"What do we want of a saw?"

"What do we *want* of it? Hain't we got to saw the leg of Jim's bed off, so as to get the chain loose?"

"Why, you just said a body could lift up the bedstead and slip the chain off."

"Well, if that ain't just like you, Huck Finn. You *can* get up the infant-schooliest ways of going at a thing. Why, hain't you ever read any books at all? —Baron Trenck, nor Casanova, nor Benvenuto Chelleeny, nor Henri IV., nor none of them heroes? Whoever heard of getting a prisoner loose in such an old-maidy way as that? No; the way all the best authorities does, is to saw the bed-leg in two, and leave it just so, and swallow the sawdust, so it can't be found, and put some dirt and grease around the sawed place so the very keenest seneskal can't see no sign of it's being sawed, and thinks the bed-leg is perfectly sound. Then, the night you're ready, fetch the leg a kick, down she goes; slip off your chain, and there you are. Nothing to do but hitch yonr rope-ladder to the battlements, shin down it, break your leg in the moat—because a rope-ladder nineteen foot too short, you know—and there's your horses and your trusty vassles, and they scoop you up and fling you across a saddle and away you go, to your native Langudoc, or Navarre, or wherever it is. It's gaudy, Huck. I wish there was a moat to this cabin. If we get time, the night of the escape, we'll dig one."

I says: "What do we want of a moat, when we're going to snake him out front under the cabin?''

But he never heard me. He had forgot me and everything else. He had his chin in his hand, thinking. Pretty soon, he sighs, and shakes his head; then sighs again, and say's:

"No, it wouldn't do—there ain't necessity enough for it."

"For what?" I says.

"Why, to saw Jim's leg off," he says.

"Good land!" I says, "why, there ain't *no* necessity for it. And what would you want to saw his leg off for, anyway?"

"Well, some of the best authorities has done it. They couldn't get the chain off, so they just cut their hand off, and shoved. And a leg would be better still. But we got to let that go. There ain't necessity enough in this case; and besides, Jim's a nigger and wouldn't understand the reasons for it, and how it's the custom in Europe; so we'll let it go. But there's one thing—he can have a rope-ladder; we can tear up our sheets and make him a rope-ladder easy enough. And we can send it to him in a pie; it's mostly done that way. And I've et worse pies."

"Why, Tom Sawyer, how you talk," I says; "Jim ain't got no use for a rope-ladder."

"He *has* got use for it, How *you* talk, you better say; you don't know nothing about it. He's *got* to have a rope ladder; they all do."

"What in the nation can he *do* with it?"

"*Do* with it? He can hide it in his bed, can't he? That's what they all do; and *he's* got to, too. Huck, you don't ever seem to want to do anything that's regular; you want to be starting something fresh all the time. Spose he *don't* do nothing with it? ain't it there in his bed, for a clew, after he's gone? and don't you reckon they'll want clews? Of course they will. And you wouldn't leave them any? That would be a *pretty* howdy-do, *wouldn't* it! I never heard of such a thing."

"Well," I says, "if it's in the regulations, and he's got to have it, all right, let him have it; because I don't wish to go back on no regulations; but there's one thing, Tom Sawyer—if we go to tearing up our sheets to make Jim a rope-ladder, we're going to get into trouble with Aunt Sally, just as sure as you're born. Now, the way I look at it, a hickry-bark ladder don't cost nothing, and don't waste nothing, and is just as good to load up a pie with, and hide in a straw tick, as any rag ladder you can start; and as for Jim, he ain't had no experience, and so *he* don't care what kind of a——"

"Oh, shucks, Huck Finn, if I was as ignorant as you, I'd keep still—that's what *I'd* do. Who ever heard of a state prisoner escaping by a hickry-bark ladder? Why, it's perfectly ridiculous."

"Well, all right, Tom, fix it your own way; but if you'll take my advice, you'll let me borrow a sheet off of the clothes-line."

He said that would do. And that give him another idea, and he says:

"Borrow a shirt, too."

"What do we want of a shirt, Tom?"

"Want it for Jim to keep a journal on."

"Journal your granny—*Jim* can't write."

"Spose he *can't* write—he can make marks on the shirt, can't he, if we make him a pen out of an old pewter spoon or a piece of an old iron barrel-hoop?"

"Why, Tom, we can pull a feather out of a goose and make him a better one; and quicker, too."

"*Prisoners* don't have geese running around the donjon-keep to pull pens out of, you muggins. They *always* make their pens out of the hardest, toughest, troublesomest piece of old brass candlestick or something like that they can get their hands on; and it takes them weeks and weeks, and months and months to file it out, too, because they've got to do it by rubbing it on the wall. *They* wouldn't use a goose-quill if they had it. It ain't regular."

"Well, then, what'll we make him the ink out of?"

"Many makes it out of iron-rust and tears; but that's the common sort and women; the best authorities uses their own blood. Jim can do that; and when he wants to send any little common ordinary mysterious message to let the world know where he's captivated, he can write it on the bottom of a tin plate with a fork and throw it out of the window. The Iron Mask always done that, and it's a blame' good way, too."

"Jim ain't got no tin plates. They feed him in a pan."

"That ain't anything; we can get him some."

"Can't nobody *read* his plates."

"That ain't got nothing to *do* with it, Huck Finn. All *he's* got to do is to write on the plate and throw it out. You don't *have* to be able to read it. Why, half the time you can't read anything a prisoner writes on a tin plate, or anywhere else."

"Well, then, what's the sense in wasting the plates?"

"Why, blame it all, it ain't the *prisoner's* plates."

"But it's *somebody's* plates, ain't it?"

"Well, spos'n it is? What does the *prisoner* care whose——"

He broke off there, because we heard the breakfast-horn blowing. So we cleared out for the house.

Along during that morning I borrowed a sheet and a white shirt off of the clothes-line; and I found an old sack and put them in it, and we went down and got the fox-fire, and put that in too. I called it borrowing, because that was what pap always called it; but Tom said it warn't borrowing, it was stealing. He said we was representing prisoners; and prisoners don't care how they get a thing so they get it, and nobody don't blame them for it, either. It ain't no crime in a prisoner to steal the thing he needs to get away with, Tom said; it's his right; and so, as long as we was representing a prisoner, we had a perfect right to steal anything on this place we had the least use for, to get ourselves out of prison with. He said if we warn't prisoners it would be a very different thing, and nobody but a mean ornery person would steal when he warn't a prisoner. So we allowed we would steal everything there was that come handy. And yet he made a mighty fuss, one day, after that, when I stole a watermelon out of the nigger patch and eat it; and he made me go and give the niggers a dime, without telling them what it was for. Tom said that what he meant was, we could steal anything we *needed*. Well, I says, I needed the watermelon. But he said I didn't need it to get out of prison with, there's where the difference was. He said if I'd a wanted it to hide a knife in, and smuggle it to Jim to kill the seneskal with, if would a been all right. So I let it go at that, though I couldn't see no advantage in my representing a prisoner, if I got to set down and chaw over a lot of gold-leaf distinctions like that, every time I see a chance to hog a watermelon.

Well, as I was saying, we waited that morning till everybody was settled down to business, and nobody in sight around the yard; then Tom he carried the sack into the lean-to whilst I stood off a piece to keep watch. By-and-by he come out, and we went and set down on the wood-pile, to talk. He says:

"Everything's all right, now, except tools: and that's easy fixed."

"Tools?" I says.

"Yes."

"Tools for what?"

"Why to dig with. We ain't agoing to *gnaw* him out, are we?"

"Ain't them old crippled picks and things in there good enough to dig a nigger out with?" I says.

He turns on me looking pitying enough to make a body cry, and says:

"Huck Finn, did you *ever* hear of a prisoner having picks and shovels, and all the modern conveniences in his wardrobe to dig himself out with? Now I want to ask you—if you got any reasonableness in you at all—what kind of a show would *that* give him to be a hero? Why, they might as well lend him the key, and done with it. Picks and shovels—why they wouldn't furnish 'em to a king."

"Well, then," I says, "if we don't want the picks and shovels, what do we want?"

"A couple of case-knives."

"To dig the foundations out from under that cabin with?"

"Yes."

"Confound it, it's foolish, Tom."

"It don't make no difference how foolish it is, it's the *right* way—and it's the regular way. And there ain't no *other* way, that ever I heard of, and I've read all the books that gives any information about these things. They always dig out with a case-knife—and not through dirt, mind you; generly it's through solid rock. And it takes them weeks and weeks and weeks, and for ever and ever. Why, look at one of them prisoners in the bottom dungeon of the Castle Deef, in the harbor of Marseilles, that dug himself out that way; how long was *he* at it, you reckon?"

"I don't know."

"Well, guess."

"I don't know. A month and a half?"

"*Thirty-seven year*—and he come out in China. *That's* the kind. I wish the bottom of *this* fortress was solid rock."

"*Jim* don't know nobody in China."

"What's *that* got to do with it? Neither did that other fellow. But you're always a-wandering off on a side issue. Why can't you stick to the main point?"

"All right—*I* don't care where he comes out, so he *comes* out; and Jim don't, either, I reckon. But there's one thing, anyway—Jim's too old to be dug out with a case-knife. He won't last."

"Yes he will *last*, too. You don't reckon it's going to take thirty-seven years to dig out through a dirt foundation, do you?"

"How long will it take, Tom?"

"Well, we can't resk being as long as we ought to, because it mayn't take very long for Uncle Silas to hear from down there by New Orleans. He'll hear Jim ain't from there. Then his next move will be to advertise Jim, or something like that. So we can't resk being as long digging him out as we ought to. By

rights I reckon we ought to be a couple of years; but we can't. Things being so
uncertain, what I recommend is this: that we really dig right in, as quick as we
can; and after that, we can *let on*, to ourselves, that we was at it thirty-seven
years. Then we can snatch him out and rush him away the first time there's an
alarm. Yes, I reckon that'll be the best way."

"Now, there's *sense* in that," I says. "Letting on don't cost nothing; letting
on ain't no trouble; and if it's any object, I don't mind letting on we was at it
a hundred fifty year. It wouldn't strain me none, after I got my hand in. So I'll
mosey along now, and smouch a couple of case-knives."

"Smouch three," he says; "we want one to make a saw out of."

"Tom, if it ain't unregular and irreligious to sejest it," I says, "there's an
old rusty saw-blade around yonder sticking under the weatherboarding behind
the smoke-house."

He looked kind of weary and discouraged-like, and says:

"It ain't no use to try to learn you nothing, Huck. Run along and smouch the
knives—three of them." So I done it.

Chapter XXXVI

AS SOON AS we reckoned everybody was asleep, that night, we went down the
lightning-rod, and shut ourselves up in the lean-to, and got out our pile of fox-
fire, and went to work. We cleared everything out of the way, about four or
five foot along the middle of the bottom log. Tom said he was right behind Jim's
bed now, and we'd dig in under it, and when we got through there couldn't
nobody in the cabin ever know there was any hole there, because Jim's counterpin
hung down most to the ground, and you'd have to raise it up and look under to
see the hole. So we dug and dug, with the case-knives, till most midnight; and
then we was dog-tired, and our hands was blistered, and yet you couldn't see
we'd done anything, hardly. At last I says: "This ain't no thirty-seven year job,

SMOUCHING THE KNIVES.

this is a thirty-eight year job, Tom Sawyer.''

He never said nothing. But he sighed, and pretty soon he stopped digging, and then for a good little while I knowed he was thinking. Then he says:

"It ain't no use, Huck, it ain't agoing to work. If we was prisoners it would, because then we'd have as many years as we wanted, and no hurry; and we wouldn't get but a few minutes to dig, every day, while they was changing watches, and so our hands wouldn't get blistered, and we could keep it up right along, year in and year out, and do it right, and the way it ought to be done.

But *we* can't fool along, we got to rush; we ain't got no time to spare. If we was to put it another night this way, we'd have to knock off for a week to let our hands get well—couldn't touch a case-knife with them sooner.''

"Well, then, what are we going to do, Tom?''

"I'll tell you. It ain't right, and it ain't moral, and I wouldn't like it to get out—but there ain't only just the one way; we got to dig him out with the picks, and *let on* it's case-knives.''

"*Now* you're *talking!*'' I says; "your head gets leveler and leveler all the time, Tom Sawyer,'' I says. "Picks is the thing, moral or no moral; and as for me, I don't care shucks for the morality of it, nohow. When I start in to steal a nigger, or a watermelon, or a Sunday-school book, I ain't no ways particular how it's done so it's done. What I want is my nigger; or what I want is my watermelon; or what I want is my Sunday school book; and if a pick's the handiest thing, that's the thing I'm going to dig that nigger or that watermelon or that Sunday-school book out with; and I don't give a dead rat what the authorities thinks about it nuther.''

"Well,'' he says, "there's excuse for picks and letting-on in a case like this; if it warn't so, I wouldn't approve of it, nor I wouldn't stand by and see the rules broke—because right is right, and wrong is wrong, and a body ain't got no business doing wrong when he ain't ignorant and knows better. It might answer for *you* to dig Jim out with a pick *without* any letting-on, because you don't know no better; but it wouldn't for me, because I do know better. Gimme a case-knife.''

He had his own by him, but I handed him mine. He flung it down, and says:

GOING DOWN THE LIGHTNING-ROD.

"Gimme a *case-knife.*"

I didn't know just what to do—but then I thought. I scratched around amongst the old tools, and got a pick-ax and give it to him, and he took it and went to work, and never said a word.

He was always just that particular. Full of principle

So then I got a shovel, and then we picked and shoveled, turn about, and made the fur fly. We stuck to it about a half an hour, which was as long as we could stand up; but we had a good deal of a hole to show for it. When I got up stairs, I looked out at the window and see Tom doing his level best with the lightning-rod, but he couldn't come it, his hands was so sore. At last he says:

"It ain't no use, it can't be done. What you reckon I better do? Can't you think up no way?"

"Yes," I says, "but I reckon it ain't regular. Come up the stairs, and let on it's a lightning-rod."

So he done it.

Next day Tom stole a pewter spoon and a brass candlestick in the house, for to make some pens for Jim out of, and six tallow candles; and I hung around the nigger cabins, and laid for a chance, and stole three tin plates. Tom said it wasn't enough; but I said nobody wouldn't ever see the plates that Jim throwed out, because they'd fall in the dog-fennel and jimpson weeds under the window-hole—then we could tote them back and he could use them over again. So Tom was satisfied. Then he says:

"Now, the thing to study out is, how to get the things to Jim."

"Take them in through the hole," I says, "when we get it done."

He only just looked scornful, and said something about nobody ever heard of such an idiotic idea, and then he went to studying. By-and-by he said he had ciphered out two or three ways, but there warn't no need to decide on any of them yet. Said we'd got to post Jim first.

That night we went down the lightning-rod a little after ten, and took one of the candles along, and listened under the window-hole, and heard Jim snoring; so we pitched it in, and it didn't wake him. Then we whirled in with the pick and shovel, and in about two hours and a half the job was done. We crept in under Jim's bed and into the cabin, and pawed around and found the candle and lit it, and stood over Jim a while, and found him looking hearty and healthy, and then we woke him up gentle and gradual. He was so glad to see us he most cried; and called us honey, and all the pet names he could think of; and was for having us hunt up a cold chisel to cut the chain off of his leg with, right away, and clearing out without losing any time. But Tom he showed him how unregular it would be, and set down and told him all about our plans, and how we could alter them in a minute any time there was an alarm; and not to be the least afraid, because we would see he got away, *sure.* So Jim he said it was all right, and we set there and talked over old times a while, and then Tom asked a lot of questions, and when Jim told him Uncle Silas come in every day or two to pray with him, and Aunt Sally come in to see if he was comfortable and had plenty to eat, and both of them was kind as they could be, Tom says:

"*Now* I know how to fix it. We'll send you some things by them."

I said, "Don't do nothing of the kind; it's one of the most jackass ideas I ever struck;" but he never paid no attention to me; went right on. It was his way when he'd got his plans set.

So he told Jim how we'd have to smuggle in the rope-ladder pie, and other large things, by Nat, the nigger that fed him, and he must be on the lookout, and not be surprised, and not let Nat see him open them; and we would put small things in uncle's coat pockets and he must steal them out; and we would tie things to aunt's apron strings or put them in her apron pocket, if we got a chance; and told him what they would be and what they was for. And told him how to keep a journal on the shirt with his blood, and all that. He told him everything. Jim he couldn't see no sense in the most of it, but he allowed we was white folks and knowed better than him; so he was satisfied, and said he would do it all just as Tom said.

Jim had plenty corn-cob pipes and tobacco; so we had a right down good sociable time; then we crawled out through the hole, and so home to bed, with hands that looked like they'd been chawed. Tom was in high spirits. He said it was the best fun he ever had in his life, and the most intellectural; and said if he only could see his way to it we would keep it up all the rest of our lives and leave Jim to our children to get out; for he believed Jim would come to like it better and better the more he got used to it. He said that in that way it could be strung out to as much as eighty year, and would be the best time on record. And he said it would make us all celebrated that had a hand in it.

In the morning we went out to the wood-pile and chopped up the brass candlestick into handy sizes, and Tom put them and the pewter spoon in his pocket. Then we went to the nigger cabins, and while I got Nat's notice off, Tom shoved a piece of candlestick into the middle of a corn-pone that was in Jim's pan, and we went along with Nat to see how it would work, and it just worked noble; when Jim bit into it it most mashed all his teeth out; and there warn't ever anything could a worked better. Tom said so himself. Jim he never let on but what it was only just a piece of rock or something like that that's always getting into bread, you know; but after that he never bit into nothing but what he jabbed his fork into it in three or four places, first.

And whilst we was a standing there in the dimmish light, here comes a couple of the hounds bulging in, from under Jim's bed; and they kept on piling in till there was eleven of them, and there warn't hardly room in there to get your breath. By jings, we forgot to fasten that lean-to door. The nigger Nat he only just hollered "witches!" once, and keeled over onto the floor amongst the dogs, and begun to groan like he was dying. Tom jerked the door open and flung out a slab of Jim's meat, and the dogs went for it, and in two seconds he was out himself and back again and shut the door, and I knowed he'd fixed the other door too. Then he went to work on the nigger, coaxing him and petting him, and asking him if he'd been imagining he saw something again. He raised up, and blinked his eyes around, and says:

"Mars Sid, you'll say I's a fool, but if I didn't b'lieve I see most a million dogs, er devils, er some'n, I wisht I may die right heah in dese tracks. I did, mos' sholy. Mars Sid, I felt um—I *felt* um, sah; dey was all over me. Dad fetch it, I jis' wisht I could git my han's on one er dem witches jis' wunst—on'y jis' wunst—it's all *I*'d ast. But mos'ly I wisht dey'd lemme 'lone, I does."

Tom says:

"Well, I tell you what *I* think. What makes them come here just at this runaway nigger's breakfast-time? It's because they're hungry; that's the reason. You make them a witch pie; that's the thing for *you* to do."

"But my lan', Mars Sid, how's *I* gwyne to make 'm a witch pie? I doan' know how to make it. I hain't ever hearn er sich a thing b'fo.'"

"Well, then, I'll have to make it myself."

"Will you do it, honey?—will you? I'll wusshup de groun' und' yo' foot, I will!"

"All right, I'll do it, seeing it's you, and you've been good to us and showed us the runaway nigger. But you got to be mighty careful. When we come around, you turn your back; and then whatever we've put in the pan, don't you let on you see it at all. And don't you look, when Jim unloads the pan—something might happen, I don't know what. And above all, don't you *handle* the witch-things."

"*Hannel* 'm Mars Sid? What *is* you a talkin' 'bout? I wouldn' lay de weight er my finger on um, not f'r ten hund'd thous'n' billion dollars, I wouldn't."

Chapter XXXVII

THAT WAS ALL fixed. So then we went away and went to the rubbage-pile in the back yard where they keep the old boots, and rags, and pieces of bottles, and wore-out tin things, and all such truck, and scratched around and found an old tin washpan and stopped up the holes as well as we could, to bake the pie in, and took it down cellar and stole it full of flour, and started for breakfast and found a couple of shingle-nails that Tom said would be handy for a prisoner to scrabble his name and sorrows on the dungeon walls with, and dropped one of them in Aunt Sally's apron pocket which was hanging on a chair, and t'other we stuck in the band of Uncle Silas's hat, which was on the bureau, because we heard the children say their pa and ma was going to the runaway nigger's house this morning, and then went to breakfast, and Tom dropped the pewter spoon in Uncle Silas's coat pocket, and Aunt Sally wasn't come yet, so we had to wait a little while.

And when she come she was hot, and red, and cross, and couldn't hardly wait for the blessing; and then she went to sluicing out coffee with one hand and cracking the handiest child's head with her thimble with the other, and says:

"I've hunted high, and I've hunted low, and it does beat all, what *has* become of your other shirt."

My heart fell down amongst my lungs and livers and things, and a hard piece of corn-crust started down my throat after it and got met on the road with a cough and was shot across the table and took one of the children in the eye and curled him up like a fishing-worm, and let a cry out of him the size of a war-whoop, and Tom he turned kinder blue around the gills, and it all amounted to a considerable state of things for about a quarter of a minute or as much as that, and I would a sold out for half price if there was a bidder. But after that we was all right again—it was the sudden surprise of it that knocked us so kind of cold. Uncle Silas he says:

"It's most uncommon curious, I can't understand it. I know perfectly well I took it *off*, because——"

"Because you hain't got but one *on*. Just *listen* at the man! *I* know you took it off, and know it by a better way than your wool-gethering memory, too, because it was on the clo'es-line yesterday—I see it there myself. But it's gone—that's the long and the short of it, and you'll just have to change to a red flann'l one till I can get time to make a new one. And it'll be the third I've made in two years; it just keeps a body on the jump to keep you in shirts; and whatever you do manage to *do* with 'm all, is more'n *I* can make out. A body'd think you *would* learn to take some sort of care of 'em, at your time of life.''

"I know it, Sally, and I do try all I can. But it oughtn't to be altogether my fault, beeause you know I don't see them nor have nothing to do with them except when they're on me; and I don't believe I've ever lost one of them *off* of me.''

"Well, it ain't *your* fault if you haven't, Silas—you'd a done it if you could, I reckon. And the shirt ain't all that's gone, nuther. Ther's a spoon gone; and *that* ain't all. There was ten, and now ther's only one. The calf got the shirt I reckon, but the calf never took the spoon, *that's* certain.''

"Why, what else is gone, Sally?''

"Ther's six *candles* gone—that's what. The rats could a got the candles, and I reckon they did; I wonder they don't walk off with the whole place, the way you're always going to stop their holes and don't do it; and if they warn't fools they'd sleep in your hair, Silas—*you'd* never find it out; but you can't lay the *spoon* on the rats, and that I *know*.''

"Well, Sally, I'm in fault, and I acknowledge it; I've been remiss; but I won't let to-morrow go by without stopping up them holes.''

"Oh, I wouldn't hurry, next year'll do. Matilda Angelina Araminta *Phelps!*''

Whack comes the thimble, and the child snatches her claws out of the sugar-bowl without fooling around any. Just then, the nigger woman steps onto the passage, and says:

"Missus, dey's a sheet gone.''

"A *sheet* gone! Well, for the land's sake!''

"I'll stop up them holes *to-day*,'' says Uncles Silas, looking sorrowful.

"Oh, *do* shet up !—spose the rats took the *sheet? Where's* it gone, Lize?''

"Clah to goodness I hain't no notion, Miss Sally. She wuz on de clo's-line yistiddy, but she done gone; she ain' dah no mo,' now.''

"I reckon the world *is* coming to an end. I *never* see the beat of it, in all my born days. A shirt, and a sheet, and a spoon, and six can——''

"Missus,'' comes a young yaller wench, "dey's a brass cannelstick miss'n.''

"Cler out from here, yon hussy, er I'll take a skillet to ye!''

Well, she was just a biling. I begun to lay for a chance; I reckoned I would sneak out and go for the woods till the weather moderated. She kept a raging right along, running her insurrection all by herself, and everybody else mighty meek and quiet; and at last Uncle Silas, looking kind of foolish, fishes up that spoon out of his pocket. She stopped, with her mouth open and her hands up; and as for me, I wished I was in Jeruslem or somewheres. But not long; because she says:

"It's *just* as I expected. So you had it in your pocket all the time; and like as not you've got the other things there, too. How'd it get there?''

"I reely don't know, Sally,'' he says, kind of apologizing, "or you know I would tell. I was a-studying over my text in Acts Seventeen, before breakfast, and I reckon I put it in there, not noticing, meaning to put my Testament in, and it must be so, because my Testament ain't in, but I'll go and see, and if the Testament is where I had it, I'll know I didn't put it in, and that will show that I laid the Testament down and took up the spoon, and——''

"Oh, for the land's sake! Give a body a rest! Go 'long now, the whole kit and biling of ye; and don't come nigh me again till I've got back my peace of mind."

I'd a heard her, if she'd a said it to herself, let alone speaking it out; and I'd a got up and obeyed her, if I'd a been dead. As we was passing through the setting-room, the old man he took up his hat, and the shingle-nail fell out on the floor, and he just merely picked it up and laid it on the mantel-shelf, and never said nothing, and went out. Tom see him do it, and remembered about the spoon, and says:

"Well, it ain't no use to send things by *him* no more, he ain't reliable." Then he says: "But he done us a good turn with the spoon, anyway, without knowing it, and so we'll go and do him one without *him* knowing it—stop up his rat-holes."

There was a noble good lot of them, down cellar, and it took us a whole hour, but we done the job tight and good, and ship-shape. Then we heard steps on the stairs, and blowed out our light, and hid; and here comes the old man, with a candle in one hand and a bundle of stuff in t'other, looking as absent-minded as year before last. He went a mooning around, first to one rat-hole and then another, till he'd been to them all. Then he stood about five minutes, picking tallow-drip off of his candle and thinking. Then he turns off slow and dreamy towards the stairs, saying:

"Well, for the life of me I can't remember when I done it. I could show her now that I warn't to blame on account of the rats. But never mind—let it go. I reckon it wouldn't do no good."

And so he went on a mumbling up stairs, and then we left. He was a mighty nice old man. And always is.

Tom was a good deal bothered about what to do for a spoon, but he said we'd got to have it; so he took a think. When he had ciphered it out, he told me how we was to do; then we went and waited around the spoon-basket till we see Aunt Sally coming, and then Tom went to counting the spoons and laying them out to one side, and I slid one of them up my sleeve, and Tom says:

"Why, Aunt Sally, there ain't but nine spoons, *yet*."

She says:

"Go 'long to your play, and don't bother me. I know better, I counted 'm myself."

"Well, I've counted them twice, Aunty, and *I* can't make but nine."

She looked out of all patience, but of course she come to count—anybody would.

"I declare to gracious ther' *ain't* but nine!" she says. "Why, what in the world—plague *take* the things, I'll count 'm again."

So I slipped back the one I had, and when she got done counting, she says:

"Hang the troublesome rubbage, ther's *ten,* now!" and she looked huffy and bothered both. But Tom says:

"Why, Aunty, *I* don't think there's ten."

"You numskull, didn't you see me *count* 'm?"

"I know, but—"

"Well, I'll count 'm *again*."

So I smouched one, and they come out nine same as the other time. Well, she *was* in a tearing way—just a trembling all over, she was so mad. But she counted and counted, till she got that addled she'd start to count-in the *basket* for a spoon, sometimes; and so, three times they come out right, and three times they come out wrong. Then she grabbed up the basket and slammed it across the house and knocked the cat galley-west; and she said cle'r out and let her have some peace, and if we come botherin around her again betwixt that and dinner, she'd skin us. So we had the odd spoon; and dropped it in her apron pocket whilst she was a giving us our sailing-orders, and Jim got it all right, along with her shingle-nail, before noon. We was very well satisfied with this business, and Tom allowed it was worth twice the trouble it took, because he said *now* she couldn't ever count them spoons twice alike again to save her life; and wouldn't believe she'd counted them right, if she *did;* and said that after she'd about counted her head off, for the next three days, he judged she'd give it up and offer to kill anybody that wanted her to ever count them any more.

So we put the sheet back on the line, that night, and stole one out of her closet; and kept on putting it back and stealing it again, for a couple of days, till she didn't know how many sheets she had, anymore, and said she didn't *care,* and warn't agoing to bullgag the rest of her soul out about it, and wouldn't count them again not to save her life, she druther die first.

So we was all right now, as to the shirt and the sheet and the spoon and the candles, by the help of the calf and the rats and the mixed-up counting; and as to the candlestick, it warn't no consequence, it would blow over by-and-by.

But that pie was a job; we had no end of trouble with that pie. We fixed it up away down in the woods, and cooked it there; and we got it done at last, and very satisfactory, too; but not all in one day; and we had to use up three washpans full of flour, before we got through, and we got burnt pretty much all over, in places, and eyes put out with the smoke; because, you see, we didn't want nothing but a crust, and we couldn't prop it up right, and she would always cave in. But of course we thought of the right way at last; which was to cook the ladder, too, in the pie. So then we laid in with Jim, the seeond night, and tore up the sheet all in little strings, and twisted them together, and long before daylight we had a lovely rope, that you could a hung a person with. We let on it took nine months to make it.

And in the forenoon we took it down to the woods, but it wouldn't go in the pie. Being made of a whole sheet, that way, there was rope enough for forty

IN A TEARING WAY.

pies, if we'd a wanted them, and plenty left over for soup, or sausage, or anything you choose. We could a had a whole dinner.

But we didn't need it. All we needed was just enough for the pie, and so we throwed the rest away. We didn't cook none of the pies in the washpan, afraid the solder would melt; but Uncle Silas he had a noble brass warming-pan which he thought considerable of, because it belonged to one of his ancestors with a long wooden handle that come over from England with William the Conqueror in the *Mayflower* or one of them early ships and was hid away up garret with a lot of other old pots and things that was valuable, not on account of being any account because they warn't, but on account of them being relicts, you know, and we snaked her out, private, and took her down there, but she failed on the first pies, because we didn't know how, but she come up smiling on the last one. We took and lined her with dough, and set her in the coals, and loaded her up with ragrope, and put on a dough roof, and shut down the lid, and put hot embers on top, and stood off five foot, with the long handle, cool and comfortable, and in fifteen minutes she turned out a pie that was a satisfaction to look at. But the person that et it would want to fetch a couple of kags of toothpicks along, for if that rope-ladder wouldn't cramp him down to business, I don't know nothing what I'm talking about, and lay him in enough stomach-ache to last him till next time, too.

Nat didn't look, when we put the witch-pie in Jim's pan; and we put the three tin plates in the bottom of the pan under the vittles; and so Jim got everything all right, and as soon as he was by himself he busted-into the pie and hid the rope-ladder inside of his straw tick, and scratched some marks on a tin plate and throwed it out of the window-hole.

Chapter XXXVIII

MAKING THEM PENS was a distressid-tough job, and so was the saw; and Jim allowed the inscription was going to be the toughest of all, That's the one which the prisoner has to scrabble on the wall. But we had to have it; Tom said we'd *got* to; there warn't no case of a state prisoner not scrabbling his inscription to leave behind, and his coat of arms.

"Look at Lady Jane Grey," he says; "look at Gilford Dudley; look at old Northumberland! Why, Huck, spose it *is* considerble trouble?—what you going to do?—how you going to get around it? Jim's *got* to do his inscription and coat of arms. They all do."

Jim says:

"Why, Mars Tom, I hain't got no coat o' arms; I hain't got nuffn but dish yer ole shirt, en you knows I got to keep de journal on dat."

"Oh, you don't understand, Jim; a coat of arms is very different."

"Well," I says, "Jim's right, anyway, when he says he hain't got no coat of arms, because he hain't."

"I reckon *I* knowed that," Tom says, "but you bet he'll have one before he goes out of this—because he's going out *right,* and there ain't going to be no flaws in his record."

So whilst me and Jim filed away at the pens on a brickbat apiece, Jim a

JIM'S COAT OF ARMS.

making his'n out of the brass and I making mine out of the spoon, Tom set to work to think out the coat of arms. By-and-by he said he'd struck so many good ones he didn't hardly know which to take, but there was one which he reckoned he'd decide on. He says:

"On the scutcheon we'll have a bend *or* in the dexter base, a saltire *murrey* in the fess, with a dog, couchant, for common charge, and under his foot a chain embattled, for slavery, with a chevron *vert* in a chief engrailed, and three invected lines on a field *azure,* with the nombril points rampant on a dancette indented; crest, a runaway nigger, *sable,* with his bundle over his shoulder on a bar sinister: and a couple of gules for supporters, which is you and me; motto, *Maggiore fretta, minore atto.* Got it out of a book—means, the more haste, the less speed."

"Geewhillikins," I says, "but what does the rest of it mean?"

"We ain't got no time to bother over that," he says, "we got to dig in like all git-out."

"Well, anyway," I says, "what's *some* of it? What's a fess?"

"A fess—fess is—*you* don't need to know what a fess is. I'll show him how to make it when he gets to it."

"Shucks, Tom," I says, "I think you might tell a person. What's a bar sinister?"

"Oh, *I* don't know. But he's got to have it. All the nobility does."

That was just his way. If it didn't suit him to explain a thing to you, he wouldn't do it. You might pump at him a week, it wouldn't make no difference.

He'd got all that coat of arms business fixed, so now he started in to finish up the rest of that part of the work, which was to plan out a mournful inscription—said Jim got to have one, like they all done. He made up a lot, and wrote them out on a paper, and read them off, so:

1. *Here a captive heart busted.*

2. *Here a poor prisoner, forsook by the world and friends, fretted out his sorrowful life.*

3. *Here a lonely heart broke, and a worn spirit went to its rest, after thirty-seven years of solitary captivity.*

4. *Here, homeless and friendless, after thirty-seven years of bitter captivity, perished a noble stranger, natural son of Louis XIV.*

Tom's voice trembled, whilst he was reading them, and he most broke down. When he got done, he couldn't no way make up his mind which one for Jim to scrabble onto the wall, they was all so good; but at last he allowed he would let him scrabble them all on. Jim said it would take him a year to scrabble such a lot of truck onto the logs with a nail, and he didn't know how to make letters, besides; but Tom said he would block them out for him, and then he wouldn't have nothing to do but just follow the lines. Then pretty soon he says:

"Come to think, the logs ain't agoing to do; they don't have log walls in a dungeon: we got to dig the inscriptions into a rock. We'll fetch a rock."

Jim said the rock was worse than the logs; he said it would take him such a pison long time to dig them into a rock, he wouldn't ever get out. But Tom said he would let me help him do it. Then he took a look to see how me and Jim was getting along with the pens. It was most pesky tedious hard work and slow, and didn't give my hands no show to get well of the sores, and we didn't seem to make no headway, hardly. So Tom says:

"I know how to fix it. We got to have a rock for the coat of arms and mournful inscriptions, and we can kill two birds with that same rock. There's a gaudy big grindstone down at the mill, and we'll smouch it, and carve the things on it, and file out the pens and the saw on it, too."

It warn't no slouch of an idea; and it warn't no slouch of a grindstone nuther; but we allowed we'd tackle it. It warn't quite midnight, yet, so we cleared out for the mill, leaving Jim at work. We smouched the grindstone, and set out to roll her home, but it was a most nation tough job. Sometimes, do what we could, we couldn't keep her from falling over, and she come mighty near mashing us, every time. Tom said she was going to get one of us, sure, before we got through. We got her half way; and then we was plumb played out, and most drownded with sweat. We see it warn't no use, we got to go and fetch Jim. So he raised up his bed and slid the chain off of the bed-leg, and wrapt it round and round his neck, and we crawled out through our hole and down there, and Jim and me laid into that grindstone and walked her along like nothing; and Tom superintended. He could out-superintend any boy I ever see. He knowed how to do everything.

Our hole was pretty big, but it warn't big enough to get the grindstone through; but Jim he took the pick and soon made it big enough. Then Tom marked out them things on it with the nail, and set Jim to work on them, with the nail for a chisel and an iron bolt from the rubbage in the lean-to for a hammer, and told him to work till the rest of his candle quit on him, and then he could go to bed, and hide the grindstone under his straw tick and sleep on it. Then we helped him fix his chain back on the bed-leg, and was ready for bed ourselves. But Tom thought of something, and says:

"You got any spiders in here, Jim?"

"No, sah, thanks to goodness I hain't, Mars Tom."

"All right, we'll get you some."

"But bless you, honey, I doan' *want* none. I's afeard un um. I jis' 's soon have rattlesnakes aroun'."

Tom thought a minute or two, and says:

"It's a good idea. And I reckon it's been done. It *must* a been done; it stands to reason. Yes, it's a prime good idea. Where could you keep it?"

"Keep what, Mars Tom?"

"Why, a rattlesnake."

"De goodness gracious alive, Mars Tom! Why, if dey was a rattlesnake to come in heah, I'd take en bust right out thoo dat log wall, I would, wid my head."

"Why, Jim, you wouldn't be afraid of it, after a little. You could tame it."

"*Tame* it!"

"Yes—easy enough. Every animal is grateful for kindness and petting, and they wouldn't *think* of hurting a person that pets them. Any book will tell you that. You try—that's all I ask; just try for two or three days. Why, you can get him so, in a little while, that he'll love you; and sleep with you; and won't stay away from you a minute; and will let you wrap him round your neck and put his head in your mouth."

"*Please*, Mars Tom—*doan'* talk so! I can't *stan'* it! He'd *let* me shove his head in my mouf—fer a favor, hain't it? I lay he'd wait a pow'ful long time 'fo' I *ast* him. En mo' en dat, I doan' *want* him to sleep wid me."

"Jim, don't act so foolish. A prisoner's *got* to have some kind of a dumb pet, and if a rattlesnake hain't ever been tried, why, there's more glory to be gained in your being the first to ever try it than any other way you could ever think of to save your life."

"Why, Mars Tom, I doan' *want* no sich glory. Snake take 'n bite Jim's chin off, den *whah* is de glory? No, sah, I doan' want no sich doin's."

"Blame it, can't you *try*? I only *want* you to try—you needn't keep it up if it don't work."

"But de trouble all *done*, ef de snake bite me while I's a tryin' him. Mars Tom, I's willin' to tackle mos' anything 'at ain't onreasonable, but ef you en Huck fetches a rattlesnake in heah for me to tame, I's gwyne to *leave*, dat's *shore*."

"Well, then, let it go, let it go, if you're so bullheaded about it. We can get you some garter-snakes and you can tie some buttons on their tails, and let on they're rattlesnakes, and I reckon that'll have to do."

"I k'n stan' *dem*, Mars Tom, but blame' 'f I couldn' get along widout um, I tell you dat. I never knowed b'fo', 't was so much bother and trouble to be a prisoner."

"Well, it *always* is, when it's done right. You got any rats around here?"

"No, sah, I hain't seed none."

"Well, we'll get you some rats."

"Why, Mars Tom, I doan' *want* no rats. Dey's de dad-blamedest creturs to sturb a body, en rustle roun' over 'im, en bite his feet, when he's tryin' to sleep, I ever see. No, sah, gimme g'yarter-snakes, 'f I's got to have 'm, but doan' gimme no rats, I ain' got no use f'r um, skasely."

"But Jim, you *got* to have 'em—they all do. So don't make no more fuss about it. Prisoners ain't ever without rats. There ain't no instance of it. And they train them, and pet them, and learn them tricks, and they get to be as sociable as flies. But you got to play music to them. You got anything to play music on?"

"I ain' got nuffn but a coase comb en a piece o' paper, en a juice-harp; but I reck'n dey wouldn' take no stock in a juice-harp."

"Yes they would. *They* don't care what kind of music 'tis. A jews-harp's plenty good enough for a rat. All animals likes music—in a prison they dote on it. Specially, painful music; and you can't get no other kind out of a jews-harp. It always interests them; they come out to see what's the matter with you. Yes, you're all right; you're fixed very well. You want to set on your bed, nights, before you go to sleep, and early in the mornings, and play your jews-harp; play The Last Link is Broken—that's the thing that'll scoop a rat, quicker'n anything else: and when you've played about two minutes, you'll see all the rats, and the snakes, and spiders, and things begin to feel worried about you, and come. And they'll just fairly swarm over you, and have a noble good time.''

"Yes, *dey* will, I reck'n, Mars Tom, but what kine er time is *Jim* havin'? Blest if I kin see de pint. But I'll do it ef I got to. I reck'n I better keep de animals satisfied, en not have no trouble in de house.''

Tom waited to think over, and see if there wasn't nothing else; and pretty soon he says:

"Oh—there's one thing I forgot. Could you raise a flower here, do you reckon?''

"I doan' know but maybe I could, Mars Tom; but it's tolable dark in heah, en I ain' got no use f'r no flower, nohow, en she'd be a pow'ful sight o' trouble.''

"Well, you try it, anyway. Some other prisoners has done it.''

"One er dem big cat-tail-lookin' mullen-stalks would grow in heah, Mars Tom, I reck'n, but she wouldn' be wuth half de trouble she'd coss.''

"Don't you believe it. We'll fetch you a little one, and you plant it in the corner, over there, and raise it. And don't call it mullen, call it Pitchiola—that's its right name, when it's in a prison. And you want to water it with your tears.''

"Why, I got plenty spring water, Mars Tom.''

"You don't *want* spring water; you want to water it with your tears. It's the way they always do.''

"Why, Mars Tom, I lay I kin raise one er dem mullen-stalks twyste wid spring water whiles another man's a *start'n* one wid tears.''

"That ain't the idea. You *got* to do it with tears.''

"She'll die on my han's, Mars Tom, she sholy will; kase I doan' skasely ever cry.''

So Tom was stumped. But he studied it over, and then said Jim would have to worry along the best he could with an onion. He promised he would go to the nigger cabins and drop one, private, in Jim's coffee-pot, in the morning. Jim said he would "jis' 's soon have tobacker in his coffee;'' and found so much fault with it, and with the work and bother of raising the mullen, and jews-harping the rats, and petting and flattering up the snakes and spiders and things, on top of all the other work he had to do on pens, and inscriptions, and journals, and things, which made it more trouble and worry and responsibility to be a prisoner than anything he ever undertook, that Tom most lost all patience with him; and said he was just loadened down with more gaudier chances than a prisoner ever had in the world to make a name for himself, and yet he didn't know enough to appreciate them, and they was just about wasted on him. So Jim he was sorry, and said he wouldn't behave so no more, and then me and Tom shoved for bed.

Chapter XXXIX

IN THE MORNING we went up to the village and bought a wire rat trap and fetched it down, and unstopped the best rat hole, and in about an hour we had fifteen of the bulliest kind of ones; and then we took it and put it in a safe place under Aunt Sally's bed. But while we was gone for spiders, little Thomas Franklin Benjamin Jefferson Elexander Phelps found it there, and opened the door of it to see if the rats would come out, and they did; and Aunt Sally she come in, and when we got back she was a standing on top of the bed raising Cain, and the rats was doing what they could to keep off the dull times for her. So she took and dusted us both with the hickry, and we was as much as two hours catching another fifteen or sixteen, drat that meddlesome cub, and they warn't the likeliest, nuther, because the first haul was the pick of the flock. I never see a likelier lot of rats than what that first haul was.

We got a splendid stock of sorted spiders, and bugs, and frogs, and caterpillars, and one thing or another; and we like-to got a hornet's nest, but we didn't. The family was at home. We didn't give it right up, but staid with them as long as we could; because we allowed we'd tire them out or they'd got to tire us out, and they done it. Then we got allycumpain and rubbed on the places, and was pretty near all right again, but couldn't set down convenient. And so we went for the snakes, and grabbed a couple of dozen garters and house-snakes, and put them in a bag, and put it in our room, and by that time it was supper time, and a rattling good honest day's work; and hungry?—oh, no, I reckon not! And there warn't a blessed snake up there, when we went back—we didn't half tie the sack, and they worked out, somehow, and left. But it didn't matter much, because they was still on the premises somewheres. So we judged we could get some of them again. No, there warn't no real scarcity of snakes about the house for a considerble spell. You'd see them dripping from the rafters and places, every now and then; and they generly landed in your plate, or down the back of your neck, and most of the time where you didn't want them. Well, they was handsome, and striped, and there warn't no harm in a million of them; but that never made no difference to Aunt Sally, she despised snakes, be the breed what they might, and she couldn't stand them no way you could fix it; and every time one of them flopped down on her, it didn't make no difference what she was doing, she would just lay that work down and light out. I never see such a woman. And you could hear her whoop to Jericho. You couldn't get her to take aholt of one of them with the tongs. And if she turned over and found one in bed, she would scramble out and lift a howl that you would think the house was afire. She disturbed the old man so, that he said he could most wish there hadn't ever been no snakes created. Why, after every last snake had been gone clear out of the house for as much as a week, Aunt Sally warn't over it yet; she warn't near over it; when she was setting thinking about something, you could touch her on the back of her neck with a feather and she would jump right out of her stockings. It was very curious. But Tom said all women was just so. He said they was made that way; for some reason or other.

We got a licking every time one of our snakes come in her way; and she allowed these lickings warn't nothing to what she would do if we ever loaded up the place again with them. I didn't mind the lickings, because they didn't amount to nothing; but I minded the trouble we had, to lay in another lot. But we got them laid in, and all the other things; and you never see a cabin as blithesome as Jim's was when they'd all swarm out for music and go for him. Jim didn't like the spiders, and the spiders didn't like Jim; and so they'd lay for him and make it mighty warm for him. And he said that between the rats, and the snakes, and the grindstone, there warn't no room in bed for him, skasely; and when there was, a body couldn't sleep, it was so lively, and it was always lively, he said, because *they* never all slept at one time, but took turn about, so when the snakes was asleep the rats was on deck, and when the rats turned in the snakes come on watch, so he always had one gang under him, in his way, and t'other gang having a circus over him, and if he got up to hunt a new place, the spiders would take a chance at him as he crossed over. He said if he ever got out, this time, he wouldn't ever be a prisoner again, not for a salary.

Well, by the end of three weeks, everything was in pretty good shape. The shirt was sent in early, in a pie, and every time a rat bit Jim he would get up and write a little in his journal whilst the ink was fresh; the pens was made, the inscriptions and so on was all carved on the grindstone; the bed-leg was sawed in two, and we had et up the sawdust, and it give us a most amazing stomach-ache. We reckoned we was all going to die, but didn't. It was the most undigestible sawdust I ever see; and Tom said the same. But as I was saying, we'd got all the work done, now, at last; and we was all pretty much fagged out, too, but mainly Jim. The old man had wrote a couple of times to the plantation below Orleans to come and get their runaway nigger, but hadn't got no answer, because there warn't no such plantation; so he allowed he would advertise Jim in the St. Louis and New Orleans papers; and when he mentioned the St. Louis ones, it give me the cold shivers, and I see we hadn't no time to lose. So Tom said, now for the nonnamous letters.

"What's them?" I says.

"Warnings to the people that something is up. Sometimes it's done one way, sometimes another. But there's always somebody spying around, that gives notice to the governor of the castle. When Louis XVI was going to light out of the Tooleries, a servant girl done it. It's a very good way, and so is the nonnamous

SAWDUST DIET.

letters. We'll use them both. And it's usual for the prisoner's mother to change clothes with him, and she stays in, and he slides out in her clothes. We'll do that too.''

''But looky here, Tom, what do we want to *warn* anybody for, that something's up? Let them find it out for themselves—it's their lookout.''

''Yes, I know; but you can't depend on them. It's the way they've acted from the very start—left us to do *everything*. They're so confiding and mullet-headed they don't take notice of nothing at all. So if we don't *give* them notice, there won't be nobody nor nothing to interfere with us, and so after all our hard work and trouble this escape 'll go off perfectly flat: won't amount to nothing—won't be nothing *to* it.''

''Well, as for me, Tom, that's the way I'd like.''

''Shucks,'' he says, and looked disgusted. So I says:

''But I ain't going to make no complaint. Anyway that suits you suits me. What you going to do about the servant-girl?''

''You'll be her. You slide in, in the middle of the night, and hook that yaller girl's frock.''

''Why, Tom, that'll make trouble next morning; because of course she prob'bly hain't got any but that one.''

''I know; but you don't want it but fifteen minutes, to carry the nonnamous letter and shove it under the front door.''

''All right, then, I'll do it; but I could carry it just as handy in my own togs.''

''You wouldn't look like a servant-girl *then*, would you?''

''No, but there won't be nobody to see what I look like, *anyway*.''

''That ain't got nothing to do with it. The thing for us to do, is just to do our *duty*, and not worry about whether anybody *sees* us do it or not. Hain't you got no principle at all?''

''All right, I ain't saying nothing; I'm the servant-girl. Who's Jim's mother?''

''I'm his mother. I'll hook a gown from Aunt Sally.''

''Well, then, you'll have to stay in the cabin when me and Jim leaves.''

''Not much. I'll stuff Jim's clothes full of straw and lay it on his bed to represent his mother in disguise, and Jim 'll take the nigger woman's gown off of me and wear it, and we'll all evade together. When a prisoner of style escapes, it's called an evasion. It's always called so when a king escapes, f'rinstance. And the same with a king's son; it don't make no difference whether he's a natural one or an unnatural one.''

So Tom he wrote the nonnamous letter, and I smouched the yaller wench's frock, that night, and put it on, and shoved it under the front door, the way Tom told me to. It said:

Beware. Trouble is brewing. Keep a sharp lookout. UNKNOWN FRIEND.

Next night we stuck a picture which Tom drawed in blood, of a skull and crossbones, on the front door; and next night another one of a coffin, on the back door. I never see a family in such a sweat. They couldn't a been worse scared if the place had a been full of ghosts laying for them behind everything and under the beds and shivering through the air. If a door banged, Aunt Sally she jumped, and said ''ouch!'' if anything fell, she jumped and said ''ouch!'' if you happened to touch her, when she warn't noticing, she done the same; she couldn't face noway and be satisfied, because she allowed there was something behind her every time—so she was always a whirling around, sudden, and saying "ouch," and before she'd get two-thirds around, she'd whirl back again, and say it again; and she was afraid to go to bed, but she dasn't set up. So the thing was working very well, Tom said; he said he never see a thing work more satisfactory. He said it showed it was done right.

So he said, now for the grand bulge! So the very next morning at the streak of dawn we got another letter ready, and was wondering what we better do with it, because we heard them say at supper they was going to have a nigger on watch at both doors all night. Tom he went down the lightning-rod to spy around; and the nigger at the back door was asleep, and he stuck it in the back of his neck and come back. This letter said:

> *Don't betray me, I wish to be your friend. There is a desprate gang of cutthroats from over in the Ingean Territory going to steal your runaway nigger to-night, and they have been trying to scare you so as you will stay in the house and not bother them. I am one of the gang, but have got relliggion and wish to quit it and lead a honest life again, and will betray the hellish design. They will sneak down from northards, along the fence, at midnight exact, with a false key, and go in the nigger's cabin to get him. I am to be off a piece and blow a tin horn if I see any danger; but stead of that, I will Ba like a sheep soon as they get in and not blow at all; then whilst they are getting his chains loose, you slip there and lock them in, and can kill them at your leisure. Don't do anything but just the way I am telling you, if you do they will suspicion something and raise whoopjamboreehoo. I do not wish any reward but to know I have done the right thing.*
>
> UNKNOWN FRIEND

Chapter XL

WE WAS FEELING pretty good, after breakfast, and took my canoe and went over the river a fishing, with a lunch, and had a good time, and took a look at the raft and found her all right, and got home late to supper, and found them in such a sweat and worry they didn't know which end they was standing on, and made us go right off to bed the minute we was done supper, and wouldn't tell us what the trouble was, and never let on a word about the new letter, but didn't need to, because we knowed as much about it as anybody did, and as soon as we was half up stairs and her back was turned, we slid for the cellar cubboard and loaded up a good lunch and took it up to our room and went to bed, and got up about half-past eleven, and Tom put on Aunt Sally's dress that he stole and was going to start with the lunch, but says:

"Where's the butter?"

"I laid out a hunk of it," I says, "on a piece of a corn-pone."

"Well, you *left* it laid out, then—it ain't here."

"We can get along without it," I says.

"We can get along *with* it, too," he says; "just you slide down cellar and fetch it. And then mosey right down the lightning-rod and come along. I'll go

FISHING.

and stuff the straw into Jim's clothes to represent his mother in disguise, and
be ready to *ba* like a sheep and shove soon as you get there.''

So out he went, and down cellar went I. The hunk of butter big as a person's
fist, was where I had left it, so I took up the slab of corn-pone with it on, and
blowed out my light, and started up stairs, very stealthy, and got up to the main
floor all right, but here comes Aunt Sally with a candle, and I clapped the truck
in my hat, and clapped my hat on my head, and the next second she see me;
and she says:

"You been down cellar?"

"Yes'm."

"What you been doing down there?"

"Noth'n."

"*Noth'n!*"

"No'm."

"Well, then, what possessed you to go down there, this time of night?"

"I don't know'm."

"You don't *know*? Don't answer me that way, Tom, I want to know what
you been *doing* down there?"

"I hain't been doing a single thing, Aunt Sally, I hope to gracious if I have."

I reckoned she'd let me go, now, and as a generl thing she would; but I spose
there was so many strange things going on she was just in a sweat about every
little thing that warn't yard-stick straight; so she says, very decided:

"You just march into that setting-room and stay there till I come. You been
up to something you no business to, and I lay I'll find out what it is before *I'm*
done with you."

So she went away as I opened the door and walked into the setting-room.
My, but there was a crowd there! Fifteen farmers, and every one of them had
a gun. I was most powerful sick, and slunk to a chair and set down. They was
setting around, some of them talking a little, in a low voice, and all of them
fidgety and uneasy, but trying to look like they warn't; but I knowed they was,
because they was always taking off their hats, and putting them on, and scratching
their heads, and changing their seats, and fumbling with their buttons. I warn't
easy myself but I didn't take my hat off, all the same.

I did wish Aunt Sally would come, and get done with me, and lick me, if she wanted to, and let me get away and tell Tom how we'd overdone this thing, and what a thundering hornet's nest we'd got ourselves into, so we could stop fooling around, straight off, and clear out with Jim before these rips got out of patience and come for us.

At last she come, and begun to ask me questions, but I *couldn't* answer them straight, I didn't know which end of me was up; because these men was in such a fidget now, that some was wanting to start right *now* and lay for them desperadoes, and saying it warn't but a few minutes to midnight; and others was trying to get them to hold on and wait for the sheep-signal; and here was aunty pegging away at the questions, and me a shaking all over and ready to sink down in my tracks I was that scared; and the place getting hotter and hotter, and the butter beginning to melt and run down my neck and behind my ears; and pretty soon, when one of them says, "*I'm* for going and getting in the cabin *first*, and right *now*, and catching them when they come," I most dropped; and a streak of butter come a trickling down my forehead, and Aunt Sally she see it, and turns white as a sheet, and says:

"For the land's sake what *is* the matter with the child!—he's got the brain fever as shore as you're born, and they're oozing out!"

And everybody runs to see, and she snatches off my hat, and out comes the bread, and what was left of the butter, and she grabbed me, and hugged me, and says:

"Oh, what a turn you did give me! and how glad and grateful I am it ain't no worse; for luck's against us, and it never rains but it pours, and when I see that truck I thought we'd lost you, for I knowed by the color and all, it was just like your brains would be if— Dear, dear, whyd'nt you *tell* me that was what you'd been down there for, *I* wouldn't a cared. Now cler out to bed, and don't lemme see no more of you till morning!"

I was up stairs in a second, and down the lightning-rod in another one, and shinning through the dark for the lean-to. I couldn't hardly get my words out, I was so anxious; but I told Tom as quick as I could, we must jump for it, now, and not a minute to lose—the house full of men, yonder, with guns!

His eyes just blazed; and he says:

"No!—is that so? *Ain't* it bully! Why, Huck, if it was to do over again, I bet I could fetch two hundred! If we could put it off till—"

"Hurry! *hurry!*" I says. "Where's Jim?"

"Right at your elbow; if you reach out your arm you can touch him. He's dressed, and everything's ready. Now we'll slide out and give the sheepsignal."

But then we heard the tramp of men, coming to the door, and heard them begin to fumble with the padlock; and heard a man say:

"I *told* you we'd be too soon; they haven't come—the door is locked. Here, I'll lock some of you into the cabin and you lay for 'em in the dark and kill 'em when they come; and the rest scatter around a piece, and listen if you can hear 'em coming."

So in they come, but couldn't see us in the dark, and most trod on us whilst we was hustling to get under the bed. But we got under all right, and out through the hole, swift but soft—Jim first, me next, and Tom last, which was according to Tom's orders. Now we was in the lean-to, and heard trampings close by outside. So we crept to the door, and Tom stopped us there and put his eye to the crack, but couldn't make out nothing, it was so dark; and whispered and said he would listen for the steps to get further, and when he nudged us Jim must glide out first, and him last. So he set his ear to the crack and listened, and listened, and listened, and the steps a scraping around, out there, all the time; and at last he nudged us, and we slid out, and stooped down, not breathing, and not making the least noise, and slipped stealthy towards the fence, in Injun file, and got to it, all right, and me and Jim over it; but Tom's britches catched fast on a splinter on the top rail, and then he hear the steps coming, so he had to pull loose, which snapped the splinter and made a noise; and as he dropped in our tracks and started, somebody sings out:

"Who's that? Answer, or I'll shoot!"

But we didn't answer; we just unfurled our heels and shoved. Then there was a rush, and a *bang, bang, bang!* and the bullets fairly whizzed around us! We heard them sing out:

"Here they are! They've broke for the river! after 'em, boys! And turn loose the dogs!"

So here they come, full tilt. We could hear them, because they wore boots, and yelled, but we didn't wear no boots, and didn't yell. We was in the path to the mill; and when they got pretty close onto us, we dodged into the bush and let them go by, and then dropped in behind them. They'd had all the dogs shut up, so they wouldn't scare off the robbers; but by this time somebody had let them loose, and here they come, making pow-wow enough for a million; but they was our dogs; so we stopped in our tracks till they catched up; and when they see it warn't nobody but us, and no excitement to offer them, they only just said howdy, and tore right ahead towards the shouting and clattering; and then we up steam again and whizzed along after them till we was nearly to the mill, and then struck up through the bush to where my canoe was tied, and hopped in and pulled for dear life towards the middle of the river, but didn't make no more noise than we was obleeged to. Then we struck out, easy and comfortable, for the island where my raft was; and we could hear them yelling and barking at each other all up and down the bank, till we was so far away the sounds got dim and died out. And when we stepped onto the raft, I says:

"*Now*, old Jim, you're a free man *again*, and I bet you won't ever be a slave no more."

"En a mighty good job it wuz, too, Huck. It 'uz planned beautiful, en it 'uz *done* beautiful; en dey ain't *nobody* kin git up a plan dat's mo' mixed-up en splendid den what dat one wuz."

We was all as glad as we could be, but Tom was the gladdest of all, because he had a bullet in the calf of his leg.

When me and Jim heard that, we didn't feel so brash as what we did before. It was hurting him considerble, and bleeding; so we laid him in the wigwam and tore up one of the duke's shirts for to bandage him, but he says:

"Gimmie the rags, I can do it myself. Don't stop, now; don't fool around here, and the evasion booming along so handsome; man the sweeps, and set her loose! Boys, we done it elegant!—'deed we did. I wish *we'd* a had the handling of Louis XVI, there wouldn't a been no 'Son of Saint Louis, ascend to heaven!' wrote down in *his* biography: no, sir, we'd a whooped him over the *border*— that's what we'd a done with *him*—and done it just as slick as nothing at all, too. Man the sweeps—man the sweeps!"

But me and Jim was consulting—and thinking. And after we'd thought a minute, I says:

"Say it, Jim."

So he says:

"Well, den, dis is de way it look to me, Huck. Ef it wuz *him* dat 'uz bein' sot free, en one er de boys wuz to git shot, would he say 'Go on en save me, nemmine 'bout a doctor f'r to save dis one? Is dat like Mars Tom Sawyer? Would he say dat? You *bet* he wouldn't! *Well*, den, is *Jim* gwyne to say it? No, sah—I doan' budge a step out'n dis place, 'dout a *doctor*; not if it's forty year!"

I knowed he was white inside, and I reckoned he'd say what he did say—so it was all right, now, and I told Tom I was agoing for a doctor. He raised considerble row about it, but me and Jim stuck to it and wouldn't budge; so he was for crawling out and setting the raft loose himself; but we wouldn't let him. Then he give us a piece of his mind—but it didn't do no good.

So when he see me getting the canoe ready, he says:

"Well, then, if you're bound to go, I'll tell you the way to do, when you get to the village. Shut the door, and blindfold the doctor tight and fast, and make him swear to be silent as the grave, and put a purse full of gold in his hand, and then take and lead him all around the back alleys and everywheres, in the dark, and then fetch him here in the canoe, in a roundabout way amongst the islands, and search him and take his chalk away from him, and don't give it back to him till you get him back to the village, or else he will chalk this raft so he can find it again. It's the way they all do."

So I said I would, and left, and Jim was to hide in the woods when he see the doctor coming, till he was gone again.

Chapter XLI

THE DOCTOR WAS an old man; a very nice, kind-looking old man, when I got him up. I told him me and my brother was over on Spanish Island hunting, yesterday afternoon, and camped on a piece of a raft we found, and about midnight he must a kicked his gun in his dreams, for it went off and shot him in the leg, and we wanted him to go over there and fix it and not say nothing about it, nor let anybody know, because we wanted to come home this evening, and surprise the folks.

"Who is your folks?" he says.

"The Phelpses, down yonder."

"Oh," he says. And after a minute, he says: "How'd you say he got shot?"

"He had a dream," I says, "and it shot him."

"Singular dream," he says.

So he lit up his lantern, and got his saddle-bags, and we started. But when he see the canoe, he didn't like the look of her—said she was big enough for one, but didn't look pretty safe for two. I says:

"Oh, you needn't be afeard, sir, she carried the three of us, easy enough."

"What three?"

"Why, me and Sid, and—and—and *the guns;* that's what I mean."

"Oh," he says.

But he put his foot on the gunnel, and rocked her; and shook his head, and said he reckoned he'd look around for a bigger one. But they was all locked and chained; so he took my canoe, and said for me to wait till he come back, or I could hunt around further, or maybe I better go down home and get them ready for the surprise, if I wanted to. But I said I didn't; so I told him just how to find the raft, and then he started.

I struck an idea, pretty soon. I says to myself, spos'n he can't fix that leg just in three shakes of a sheep's tail, as the saying is? spos'n it takes him three or four days? What are we going to do?—lay around there till he lets the cat out of the bag? No, sir, I know what *I'll* do. I'll wait, and when he comes back, if he says he's got to go any more, I'll get down there, too, if I swim; and we'll take and tie him, and keep him, and shove out down the river; and when Tom's done with him, we'll give him what it's worth, or all we got, and then let him get shore.

So then I crept into a lumber pile to get some sleep; and next time I waked up the sun was away up over my head! I shot out and went for the doctor's house, bnt they told me he'd gone away in the night, some time or other, and warn't back yet. Well, thinks I, that looks powerful bad for Tom, and I'll dig out for the island, right off. So away I shoved, and turned the corner, and nearly rammed my head into Uncle Silas's stomach! He says:

"Why, *Tom*! Where you been, all this time, you rascal?"

"I hain't been nowheres," I says, "only just hunting for the runaway nigger—me and Sid."

"Why, where ever did you go?" he says. "Your aunt's been mighty uneasy."

"She needn't," I says, "because we was all right. We followed the men and the dogs, but they out-run us, and we lost them; but we thought we heard them on the water, so we got a canoe and took out after them, and crossed over but couldn't find nothing of them; so we cruised along up-shore till we got kind of tired and beat out; and tied up the canoe and went to sleep, and never waked up till about an hour ago, then we paddled over here to hear the news, and Sid's at the post-office to see what he can hear, and I'm a branching out to get something to eat for us, and then we're going home."

So then we went to the post-office to get "Sid"; but just as I suspicioned, he warn't there; so the old man he got a letter out of the office, and we waited a while longer but Sid didn't come; so the old man said come along, let Sid foot it home, or canoe-it, when he got done fooling around—but we would ride. I couldn't get him to let me stay and wait for Sid; and he said there warn't no use in it, and I must come along, and let Aunt Sally see we was all right.

When we got home, Aunt Sally was that glad to see me she laughed and cried both, and hugged me, and give me one of them lickings of hern that don't amount to shucks, and said she'd serve Sid the same when he come.

And the place was plumb full of farmers and farmers' wives, to dinner; and such another clack a body never heard. Old Mrs. Hotchkiss was the worst; her tongue was agoing all the time. She says:

"Well, Sister Phelps, I've ransacked that-air cabin over an' I b'lieve the nigger was crazy. I says so to Sister Damrell—didn't I, Sister Damrell?—s'I, he's crazy, s'I—them's the very words I said. You all hearn me: he's crazy, s'I; everything shows it, s'I. Look at that-air grindstone, s'I; want to tell *me* 't any cretur 'ts in his right mind 's agoin' to scrabble all them crazy things onto a grindstone, s'I? Here sich 'n' sich a person busted his heart; 'n' here so 'n' so pegged along for thirty-seven year, 'n' all that—natcherl son o' Louis somebody, 'n' sich everlast'n rubbage. He's plumb crazy, s'I; it's what I says in the fust place, it's what I says in the middle, 'n' it's what I says last 'n' all the time—the nigger's crazy—crazy's Nebokoodneezer, s'I.''

"An' look at that-air ladder made out'n rags, Sister Hotchkiss,'' says old Mrs. Damrell, "what in the name o' goodness *could* he ever want of——''

"The very words I was a-sayin' no longer ago th'n this minute to Sister Utterback, 'n' she'll tell you so herself. Sh-she, look at that-air rag ladder, sh-she; 'n' s'I, yes, *look* at it, s'I—what *could* he a wanted of it, s'I. Sh-she, Sister Hotchkiss, sh-she——''

"But how in the nation'd they ever *git* that grindstone *in* there, *any*way? 'n' who dug that-air *hole?* 'n' who——''

"My very *words*, Brer Penrod! I was a-sayin'—pass that-air sasser o' m'lasses, won't ye?—I was a-sayin' to Sister Dunlap, jist this minute, how *did* they git that grindstone in there, s'I. Without *help*, mind you—'thout *help*! *Thar's* wher' 'tis. Don't tell *me*, s'I; there *wuz* help, s'I; 'n' ther' wuz a *plenty* help, too, s'I; ther's ben a *dozen* a-helpin' that nigger, 'n' I lay I'd skin every last nigger on this place, but *I'd* find out who done it, s'I; 'n' moreover; s'I——''

"A *dozen* says you!—*forty* couldn't a done everything that's been done. Look at them case-knife saws and things, how tedious they've been made; look at that bed-leg sawed off with 'm, a week's work for six men; look at that nigger made out'n straw on the bed; and look at——''

"You may *well* say it, Brer Hightower! It's jist as I was a-sayin' to Brer Phelps, his own self. S'e, what do *you* think of it, Sister Hotchkiss, s'e? think O' what, Brer Phelps, s'I? think o' that bed-leg sawed off that a way, s'e? *think* of it, s'I? I lay it never sawed *itself* off, s'I—somebody *sawed* it, s'I; that's my opinion, take it or leave it, it mayn't be no 'count, s'I, but sich as 't is, it's my opinion, s'I, 'n' if anybody k'n start a better one, s'I, let him *do* it, s'I, that's all. I says to Sister Dunlap, s'I——''

"Why, dog my cats, they must a ben a house-full o' niggers in there every night for four weeks, to a done all that work, Sister Phelps. Look at that shirt—every last inch of it kivered over with secret African writ'n done with blood! Must a ben a raft uv 'm at it right along, all the time, amost. Why, I'd give two doliars to have it read to me; 'n' as for the niggers that wrote it, I 'low I'd take 'n' lash 'm t'll——''

"People to *help* him, Brother Marples! Well, I reckon you'd *think* so, if you'd a been in this house for a while back. Why, they've stole everything they could lay their hands on—and we a watching, all the time, mind you. They stole that shirt right off o' the line! and as for that sheet they made the rag ladder out of ther' ain't no telling how many times they *didn't* steal that; and flour, and candles, and candlesticks, and spoons, and the old warming-pan, and most a thousand things that I disremember, now, and my new calico dress; and me, and Silas, and my Sid and Tom on the constant watch day *and* night, as I was a telling you, and not a one of us could catch hide nor hair, nor sight nor sound of them; and here at the last minute, lo and behold you, they slides right in under our noses, and fools us, and not only fools *us* but the Injun Territory robbers too, and actuly gets *away* with that nigger, safe and sound, and that with sixteen men and twenty-two dogs right on their very heels at that very time! I tell you, it just bangs anything I ever *heard* of. Why, *sperits* couldn't a done better, and been no smarter. And I reckon they must a *been* sperits—because, *you* know our dogs, and ther' ain't no better; well, them dogs never even got on the track of 'm, once! You explain *that* to me, if you can!—*any* of you!''

"Well, it does beat——"

"Laws alive, I never——"

"So help me, I wouldn't a be——"

"*House*-thieves as well as——"

"Goodnessgracioussakes, I'd a ben afeard to *live* in sich a——"

"'Fraid to *live!*—why, I was that scared I das'nt hardly go to bed, or get up, or lay down, or *set* down, Sister Ridgeway. Why, they'd steal the very—why, goodness sakes, you can guess what kind of a fluster *I* was in by the time midnight come, last night. I hope to gracious if I warn't afraid they'd steal some o' the family! I was just to that pass, I didn't have no reasoning faculties no more. It looks foolish enough, *now*, in the day-time; but I says to myself, there's my two poor boys asleep, 'way up stairs in that lonesome room, and I declare to goodness I was that uneasy 't I crep' up there and locked 'em in! I *did*. And anybody would. Because, you know, when you get scared, that way, and it keeps running on, and getting worse and worse, all the time, and your wits gets to addling, and you get to doing all sorts o' wild things, and by-and-by you think to yourself, spos'n *I* was a boy, and was away up there, and the door ain't locked, and you——" She stopped, looking kind of wondering, and then she turned her head around slow, and when her eye lit on me—I got up and took a walk.

Says I to myself, I can explain better how we come to not be in that room this morning, if I go out to one side and study over it a little. So I done it. But I dasn't go fur, or she'd a sent for me. And when it was late in the day, the people all went, and then I come in and told her the noise and shooting waked up me and "Sid," and the door was locked, and we wanted to see the fun, so we went down the lightning-rod, and both of us got hurt a little, and we didn't never want to try *that* no more. And then I went on and told her all what I told Uncle Silas before; and then she said she'd forgive us, and maybe it was all right enough anyway, and about what a body might expect of boys, for all boys was a pretty harum-scarum lot, as fur as she could see; and so, as long as no harm hadn't come of it, she judged she better put in her time being grateful we was alive and well and she had us still, stead of fretting-over what was past and done. So then she kissed me, and patted me on the head, and dropped into a kind of a brown study; and pretty soon jumps up, and says:

"Why, lawsamercy, it's most night, and Sid not come yet! What *has* become of that boy?"

I see my chance; so I skips up and says:

"I'll run right up to town and get him," I says.

"No you won't," she says. "You'll stay right where you are; *one's* enough to be lost at a time. If he ain't here to supper, your uncle 'll go."

Well, he warn't there to supper; so right after supper uncle went.

He come back about ten, a little bit uneasy; hadn't run across Tom's track. Aunt Sally was a good *deal* uneasy; but Uncle Silas he said there warn't no occasion to be—boys will be boys, he said, and you'll see this one turn up in the morning, all sound and right. So she had to be satisfied. But she said she'd set up for him a while, anyway, and keep a light burning, so he could see it.

And then when I went up to bed she come up with me and fetched her candle, and tucked me in, and mothered me so good I felt mean, and like I couldn't look her in the face; and she set down on the bed and talked with me a long time, and said what a splendid boy Sid was, and didn't seem to want to ever

AUNT SALLY TALKS TO HUCK.

stop talking about him; and kept asking me every now and then, if I reckoned he could a got lost, or hurt, or maybe drownded, and might be laying at this minute, somewheres, suffering or dead, and she not by him to help him, and so the tears would drip down, silent, and I would tell her that Sid was all right, and would be home in the morning, sure; and she would squeeze my hand, or maybe kiss me, and tell me to say it again, and keep on saying it, because it done her good, and she was in so much trouble. And when she was going away, she looked down in my eyes, so steady and gentle, and says:

"The door ain't going to be locked, Tom; and there's the window and the rod; but you'll be good, *won't* you? And you won't go? For *my* sake."

Laws knows I *wanted* to go, bad enough, to see about Tom, and was all intending to go; but after that, I wouldn't a went, not for kingdoms.

But she was on my mind, and Tom was on my mind; so I slept very restless. And twice I went down the rod, away in the night, and slipped around front, and see her setting there by her candle in the window with her eyes towards the road and the tears in them; and I wished I could do something for her, but I couldn't, only to swear that I wouldn't never do nothing to grieve her any more. And the third time, I waked up at dawn, and slid down, and she was there yet, and her candle was most out, and her old gray head was resting on her hand, and she was asleep.

Chapter XLII

THE OLD MAN was up town again, before breakfast, but couldn't get no track of Tom; and both of them set at the table, thinking, and not saying nothing, and looking mournful, and their coffee getting cold, and not eating anything. And by-and-by the old man says:

"Did I give you the letter?"

"What letter?"

"The one I got yesterday out of the post-office."

"No, you didn't give me no letter."

"Well, I must a forgot it."

So he rummaged his pockets, and then went off somewheres where he had laid it down, and fetched it, and give it to her. She says:

"Why, it's from St. Petersburg—it's from Sis."

I allowed another walk would do me good; but I couldn't stir. But before she could break it open, she dropped it and run—for she see something. And so did I. It was Tom Sawyer on a mattress; and that old doctor; and Jim, in *her* calico dress, with his hands tied behind him; and a lot of people. I hid the letter behind the first thing that come handy, and rushed. She flung herself at Tom, crying, and says:

"Oh, he's dead, he's dead, I know he's dead!"

And Tom he turned his head a little, and muttered something or other, which showed he warn't in his right mind; then she flung up her hands, and says:

"He's alive, thank God! And that's enough!" and she snatched a kiss of him, and flew for the house to get the bed ready, and scattering orders right and left at the niggers and everybody else, as fast as her tongue could go, every jump of the way.

I followed the men to see what they was going to do with Jim; and the old doctor and Uncle Silas followed after Tom into the house. The men was very huffy, and some of them wanted to hang Jim, for an example to all the other niggers around there, so they wouldn't be trying to run away, like Jim done, and making such a raft of trouble, and keeping a whole family scared most to death for days and nights. But the others said, don't do it, it wouldn't answer at all, he ain't our nigger, and his owner would turn up and make us pay for him, sure. So that cooled them down a little, because the people that's always the most anxious for to hang a nigger that hain't done just right, is always the very ones that ain't the most anxious to pay for him when they've got their satisfaction out of him.

They cussed Jim considerble, though, and give him a cuff or two, side the head, once in a while, but Jim never said nothing, and he never let on to know me, and they took him to the same cabin, and put his own clothes on him, and chained him again, and not to no bed-leg, this time, but to a big staple drove

TOM SAWYER WOUNDED.

into the bottom log, and chained his hands, too, and both legs, and said he warn't to have nothing but bread and water to eat, after this, till his owner come or he was sold at auction, because he didn't come in a certain length of time and filled up our hole, and said a couple of farmers with guns must stand watch around about the cabin every night, and a bull-dog tied to the door in the day-time; and about this time they was through with the job and was tapering off with a kind of generl good-bye cussing, and then the old doctor comes and takes a look, and says:

"Don't be no rougher on him than you're obleeged to, because he ain't a bad nigger. When I got to where I found the boy, I see I couldn't cut the bullet out without some help, and he warn't in no condition for me to leave, to go and get help; and he got a little worse and a little worse, and after a long time he went out of his head, and wouldn't let me come anigh him, any more, and said if I chalked his raft he'd kill me, and no end of wild foolishness like that, and I see I couldn't do anything at all with him; so I says, I got to have *help*, somehow; and the minute I says it, out crawls this nigger from somewheres, and says he'll help, and he done it, too, and done it very well. Of course I judged he must be a runaway nigger, and there I *was!* and there I had to stick, right straight along all the rest of the day, and all night. It was a fix, I tell you! I had a couple of patients with the chills, and of course I'd of liked to run up to town and see them, but I dasn't, because the nigger might get away, and then I'd be to blame; and yet never a skiff come close enough for me to hail. So there I had to stick, plumb till daylight this morning; and I never see a nigger that was a better nuss or faithfuller, and yet he was resking his freedom to do it, and was all tired out, too, and I see plain enough he'd been worked main hard, lately. I liked the nigger for that; I tell you, gentlemen, a nigger like that is worth a thousand dollars—and kind treatment, too. I had everything I needed, and the boy was doing as well there as he would a done at home—better, maybe, because it was so quiet; but there I *was*, with both of 'm on my hands; and there I had to stick, till about dawn this morning; then some men in a skiff come by, and as good luck would have it, the nigger was setting by the pallet with his head propped on his knees, sound asleep; so I motioned them in, quiet, and they slipped up on him and grabbed him and tied him before he knowed what he was about, and we never had no trouble. And the boy being in a kind of a flighty sleep, too, we muffled the oars and hitched the raft on, and towed her over very nice and quiet, and the nigger never made the least row nor said a word, from the start. He ain't no bad nigger, gentlemen; that's what I think about him."

Somebody says:

"Well, it sounds very good, doctor, I'm obleeged to say."

Then the others softened up a little, too, and I was mighty thankful to that old doctor for doing Jim that good turn; and I was glad it was according to my judgment of him, too; because I thought he had a good heart in him and was a good man, the first time I see him. Then they all agreed that Jim had acted very well, and was deserving to have some notice took of it, and reward. So every one of them promised, right out and hearty, that they wouldn't cuss him no more.

Then they come out and locked him up. I hoped they was going to say he could have one or two of the chains took off, because they was rotten heavy, or could have meat and greens with his bread and water, but they didn't think of it, and I reckoned it warn't best for me to mix in, but I judged I'd get the doctor's yarn to Aunt Sally, somehow or other, as soon as I'd got through the breakers that was laying just ahead of me. Explanations, I mean, of how I forgot to mention about Sid being shot, when I was telling how him and me put in that dratted night paddling around hunting the runaway nigger.

But I had plenty time. Aunt Sally she stuck to the sick-room all day and all night; and every time I see Uncle Silas mooning around, I dodged him.

Next morning I heard Tom was a good deal better, and they said Aunt Sally was gone to get a nap. So I slips to the sick-room, and if I found him awake I reckoned we could put up a yarn for the family that would wash. But he was sleeping, and sleeping very peaceful, too; and pale, not fire-faced the way he was when he come. So I set down and laid for him to wake. In about a half an hour, Aunt Sally comes gliding in, and there I was, up a stump again! She motioned me to be still, and set down by me, and begun to whisper, and said we could all be joyful now, because all the symptoms was first rate, and he'd been sleeping like that for ever so long, and looking better and peacefuller all the time, and ten to one he'd wake up in his right mind.

So we set there watching, and by-and-by he stirs a bit, and opened his eyes very natural, and takes a look, and says:

"Hello, why I'm at *home!* How's that? Where's the raft?"

"It's all right," I says.

"And *Jim?*"

"The same," I says, but couldn't say it pretty brash. But he never noticed, but says:

"Good! Splendid! *Now* we're all right and safe! Did you tell Aunty?"

I was going to say yes; but she chipped in and says:

"About what, Sid?"

"Why, about the way the whole thing was done."

"What whole thing?"

"Why, *the* whole thing. There ain't but one; how we set the runaway nigger free—me and Tom."

"Good land! Set the run— What *is* the child talking about! Dear, dear, out of his head again!"

"*No*, I ain't out of my HEAD; I know all what I'm talking about. We *did* set him free—me and Tom. We laid out to do it, and we *done* it. And we done it elegant, too." He'd got a start, and she never checked him up, just set and stared and stared, and let him clip along, and I see it warn't no use for *me* to put in. "Why, Aunty, it cost us a power of work—weeks of it—hours and hours, every night, whilst you was all asleep. And we had to steal candles, and the sheet, and the shirt, and your dress, and spoons, and tin plates, and case-knives, and the warming-pan, and the grindstone, and flour, and just no end of things, and you can't think what work it was to make the saws, and pens, and inscriptions, and one thing or another, and you can't think *half* the fun it was. And we had to make up the pictures of coffins and things, and nonnamous letters from the robbers, and get up and down the lightning-rod, and dig the hole into the cabin, and make the rope-ladder and send it in cooked up in a pie, and send in spoons and things to work with, in your apron pocket"——

"Mercy sakes!"

——"and load up the cabin with rats and snakes and so on, for company for Jim; and then you kept Tom here so long with the butter in his hat that you come near spoiling the whole business, because the men come before we was out of the cabin, and we had to rush, and they heard us and let drive at us, and I got my share, and we dodged out of the path and let them go by, and when the dogs come they warn't interested in us, but went for the most noise, and we got our canoe, and made for the raft, and was all safe, and Jim was a free man, and we done it all by ourselves, and *wasn't* it bully, Aunty!''

"Well, I never heard the likes of it in all my born days! So it was *you*, you little rapscallions, that's been making all this trouble, and turned everybody's wits clean inside out and scared us all most to death. I've as good a notion as ever I had in my life, to take it out o' you this very minute. To think, here I've been, night after night, a—*you* just get well once, you young scamp, and I lay I'll tan the Old Harry out o' both o' ye!''

But Tom, he *was* so proud and joyful, he just *couldn't* hold in, and his tongue just *went* it—she a-chipping in, and spitting fire all along, and both of them going it at once, like a cat-convention; and she says:

"*Well*, you get all the enjoyment you can out of it *now*, for mind I tell you if I catch you meddling with him again——''

"Meddling with *who?*'' Tom says, dropping his smile and looking surprised.

"With *who?* Why, the runaway nigger, of course. Who'd you reckon?''

Tom looks at me very grave, and says:

"Tom, didn't you just tell me he was all right? Hasn't he got away?''

"*Him?*'' says Aunt Sally; "the runaway nigger? 'Deed he hasn't. They've got him back, safe and sound, and he's in that cabin again, on bread and water, and loaded down with chains, till he's claimed or sold!''

Tom rose square up in bed, with his eye hot, and his nostrils opening and shutting like gills, and sings out to me:

"They hain't no *right* to shut him up! *Shove!*—and don't you lose a minute. Turn him loose! he ain't no slave; he's as free as any cretur that walks this earth!''

"What *does* the child mean?''

"I mean every word I *say*, Aunt Sally, and if somebody don't go, *I'll* go. I've knowed him all his life, and so has Tom, there. Old Miss Watson died two months ago, and she was ashamed she ever was going to sell him down the river, and *said* so; and she set him free in her will.''

"Then what on earth did *you* want to set him free for, seeing he was already free?''

"Well, that *is* a question, I must say; and *just* like women! Why, I wanted the *adventure* of it; and I'd a waded neck-deep in blood to—goodness alive, AUNT POLLY!''

If she warn't standing right there, just inside the door, looking as sweet and contented as an angel half-full of pie, I wish I may never!

Aunt Sally jumped for her, and most hugged the head off of her, and cried over her, and I found a good enough place for me under the bed, for it was getting pretty sultry for *us*, seemed to me. And I peeped out, and in a little while Tom's Aunt Polly shook herself loose and stood there looking across at Tom over her spectacles—kind of grinding him into the earth, you know. And then she says:

"Yes, you *better* turn y'r head away—I would if I was you, Tom.''

"Oh, deary me!'' says Aunt Sally; "*is* he changed so? Why, that ain't *Tom* it's Sid; Tom's—Tom's—why, where is Tom? He was here a minute ago.''

"You mean where's Huck *Finn*—that's what you mean! I reckon I hain't raised such a scamp as my Tom all these years, not to know him when I *see* him. That *would* be a pretty howdy-do. Come out from under that bed, Huck Finn.''

So I done it. But not feeling brash.

Aunt Sally she was one of the mixed-upest looking persons I ever see; except one, and that was Uncle Silas, when he come in, and they told it all to him. It kind of made him drunk, as you may say, and he didn't know nothing at all the rest of the day, and preached a prayer-meeting sermon that night that give him a rattling ruputation, because the oldest man in the world couldn't a understood it. So Tom's Aunt Polly, she told all about who I was, and what; and I had to up and tell how I was in such a tight place that when Mrs. Phelps took me for Tom Sawyer—she chipped in and says, ''Oh, go on and call me Aunt Sally, I'm used to it, now, and 'tain't no need to change''—that when Aunt Sally took me for Tom Sawyer, I had to stand it—there warn't no other way, and I knowed he wouldn't mind, because it would be nuts for him, being a mystery, and he'd make an adventure out of it and be perfectly satisfied. And so it turned out, and he let on to be Sid, and made things as soft as he could for me.

And his Aunt Polly she said Tom was right about old Miss Watson setting Jim free in her will; and so, sure enough, Tom Sawyer had gone and took all that trouble and bother to set a free nigger free! and I couldn't ever understand, before, until the minute and that talk, how he *could* help a body set a nigger free, with his bringing-up.

Well, Aunt Polly she said that when Aunt Sally wrote to her that Tom and *Sid* had come, all right and safe, she says to herself:

''Look at that, now! I might have expected it, letting him go off that way without anybody to watch him. So now I got to go and trapse all the way down the river, eleven hundred mile, and find out what that creetur's up to, *this* time; as long as I couldn't seem to get any answer out of you about it.''

''Why, I never heard nothing from you,'' says Aunt Sally.

''Well, I wonder! Why, I wrote to you twice, to ask you what you could mean by Sid being here.''

''Well, I never got em, Sis.''

Aunt Polly, she turns around slow and severe, and says:

''You, Tom!''

''Well—*what?''* he says, kind of pettish.

''Don't you what *me,* you impudent thing—hand out them letters.''

''What letters?''

''*Them* letters. I be bound, if I have to take aholt of you I'll——''

''They're in the trunk. There, now. And they're just the same as they was when I got them out of the office. I hain't looked into them, I hain't touched them. But I knowed they'd make trouble, and I thought if you warn't in no hurry, I'd——''

''Well, you *do* need skinning, there ain't no mistake about it. And I wrote another one to tell you I was coming; and I spose he——''

''No, it come yesterday; I hain't read it yet, but *it's* all right, I've got that one.''

I wanted to offer to bet two dollars she hadn't, but I reckoned maybe it was just as safe to not to. So I never said nothing.

CHAPTER THE LAST

THE FIRST TIME I catched Tom, private, I asked him what was his idea, time of the evasion?—what it was he'd planned to do if the evasion worked all right and he managed to set a nigger free that was already free before? And he said, what he had planned in his head, from the start, if we got Jim out all safe, was for us to run him down the river, on the raft, and have adventures plumb to the mouth of the river, and then tell him about his being free, and take him back up home on a steamboat, in style, and pay him for his lost time, and write word ahead and get out all the niggers around, and have them waltz him into town with a torchlight procession and a brass band, and then he would be a hero, and so would we. But I reckened it was about as well the way it was.

We had Jim out of the chains in no time, and when Aunt Polly and Uncle Silas and Aunt Sally found out how good he helped the doctor nurse Tom, they made a heap of fuss over him, and fixed him up prime, and give him all he wanted to eat, and a good time, and nothing to do. And we had him up to the sick-room; and had a high talk; and Tom give Jim forty dollars for being prisoner for us so patient, and doing it up so good, and Jim was pleased most to death, and busted out, and says:

"*Dah,* now, Huck, what I tell you?—what I tell you up dah on Jackson islan'? I *tole* you I got a hairy breas', en what's de sign un it; en I *tole* you I ben rich wunst, en gwineter to be rich *agin;* en it's come true; en heah she *is! Dah,* now! doan' talk to *me*—signs is *signs,* mine I tell you; en I knowed jis' 's well 'at I 'uz gwineter be rich agin as I's a stannin' heah dis minute!"

And then Tom he talked along, and talked along, and says, le's all three slide out of here, one of these nights, and get an outfit, and go for howling adventures amongst the Injuns, over in the Territory, for a couple of weeks or two; and I says, all right, that suits me, but I aint got no money for to buy the outfit, and I reckon I couldn't get none from home, because it's likely pap's been back before now, and got it all away from Judge Thatcher and drunk it up.

OUT OF BONDAGE.

"No he hain't," Tom says; "it's all there, yet—six thousand dollars and more; and your pap hain't ever been back since. Hadn't when I come away, anyhow."

Jim says, kind of solemn:

"He ain't a comin' back no mo', Huck."

I says:

"Why, Jim?"

"Nemmine why, Huck—but he ain't comin' back no mo'."

But I kept at him; so at last he says:

"Doan' you 'member de house dat was float'n down de river, en dey wuz a man in dah, kivered up, en I went in en unkivered him and didn' let you come in? Well, den' you k'n git yo' money when you wants it; kase dat wuz him."

Tom's most well, now, and got his bullet around his neck on a watch-guard for a watch, and is always seeing what time it is, and so there ain't nothing more to write about, and I am rotten glad of it, because if I'd a knowed what a trouble it was to make a book I wouldn't a tackled it and aint't agoing to no more. But I reckon I got to light out for the Territory ahead of the rest, because Aunt Sally she's going to adopt me and sivilize me and I can't stand it. I been there before.

THE END. YOURS TRULY, HUCK FINN

Mark Twain's Sketches

Illustrated by True Williams

THE NOTORIOUS JUMPING FROG

OF CALAVERAS* COUNTY

IN COMPLIANCE WITH the request of a friend of mine, who wrote me from the East, I called on good-natured, garrulous old Simon Wheeler, and inquired after my friend's friend, Leonidas W. Smiley, as requested to do, and I hereunto append the result. I have a lurking suspicion that *Leonidas W*. Smiley is a myth; that my friend never knew such a personage; and that he only conjectured that if I asked old Wheeler about him, it would remind him of his infamous *Jim* Smiley, and he would go to work and bore me to death with some exasperating reminiscence of him as long and as tedious as it should be useless to me. If that was the design, it succeeded.

I found Simon Wheeler dozing comfortably by the bar-room stove of the dilapidated tavern in the decayed mining camp of Angel's, and I noticed that

* Pronounced Cal-e-*va*-ras.

he was fat and bald-headed, and had an expression of winning gentleness and simplicity upon his tranquil countenance. He roused up, and gave me good-day. I told him a friend of mine had commissioned me to make some inquiries about a cherished companion of his boyhood named *Leonidas W*. Smiley—*Rev. Leonidas W.* Smiley, a young minister of the Gospel, who he had heard was at one time a resident of Angel's Camp. I added that if Mr. Wheeler could tell me anything about this Rev. Leonidas W. Smiley, I would feel under many obligations to him.

Simon Wheeler backed me into a corner and blockaded me there with his chair, and then sat down and reeled off the monotonous narrative which follows this paragraph. He never smiled, he never frowned, he never changed his voice from the gentle-flowing key to which he tuned his initial sentence, he never betrayed the slightest suspicion of enthusiasm; but all through the interminable narrative there ran a vein of impressive earnestness and sincerity, which showed me plainly that, so far from his imagining that there was anything ridiculous or funny about his story, he regarded it as a really important matter, and admired its two heroes as men of transcendent genius in *finesse*. I let him go on in his own way, and never interrupted him once.

"Rev. Leonidas W. H'm, Reverend Le—well, there was a feller here once by the name of *Jim* Smiley, in the winter of '49—or may be it was the spring of '50—I don't recollect exactly, somehow, though what makes me think it was one or the other is because I remember the big flume warn't finished when he first come to the camp; but any way, he was the curiosest man about always betting on anything that turned up you ever see, if he could get anybody to bet on the other side; and if he couldn't he'd change sides. Any way that suited the other man would suit *him*—any way just so's he got a bet, *he* was satisfied. But still he was lucky, uncommon lucky; he most always come out winner. He was always ready and laying for a chance; there couldn't be no solit'ry thing mentioned but that feller'd offer to bet on it, and take ary side you please, as I was just telling you. If there was a horse-race, you'd find him flush or you'd find him busted at the end of it; if there was a dog-fight, he'd bet on it; if there was a cat-fight, he'd bet on it; if there was a chicken-fight, he'd bet on it; why, if there was two birds setting on a fence, he would bet you which one would fly first; or if there was a camp-meeting, he would be there reg'lar to bet on Parson Walker, which he judged to be the best exhorter about here, and so he was too, and a good man. If he even see a straddle-bug start to go anywheres, he would bet you how long it would take him to get to—to wherever he was going to, and if you took him up, he would foller that straddle-bug to Mexico but what he would find out where he was bound for and how long he was on the road. Lots of the boys here has seen that Smiley, and can tell you about him. Why, it never made no difference to *him*—he'd bet on *any* thing—the dangdest feller. Parson Walker's wife laid very sick once, for a good while, and it seemed as if they warn't going to save her; but one morning he come in, and Smiley up and asked him how she was, and he said she was considable better—thank the Lord for his inf'nit mercy—and coming on so smart that with the blessing of Prov'dence she'd get well yet; and Smiley, before he thought says, "Well, I'll resk two-and-a-half she don't anyway."

Thish-yer Smiley had a mare—the boys called her the fifteen-minute nag, but that was only in fun, you know, because of course she was faster than that—and he used to win money on that horse, for all she was so slow and always had the asthma, or the distemper, or the consumption, or something of that kind. They used to give her two or three hundred yards' start, and then pass her under way; but always at the fag-end of the race she'd get excited and desperate-like, and come cavorting and straddling up, and scattering her legs around limber, sometimes in the air, and sometimes out to one side amongst the fences, and kicking up m-o-r-e dust and raising m-o-r-e racket with her coughing and sneezing and blowing her nose—and *always* fetch up at the stand just about a neck ahead, as near as you could cipher it down.

And he had a little small bull-pup, that to look at him you'd think he warn't worth a cent but to set around and look ornery and lay for a chance to steal something. But as soon as money was up on him he was a different dog; his under-jaw'd begin to stick out like the fo'castle of a steamboat, and his teeth would uncover and shine like the furnaces. And a dog might tackle him and bullyrag him, and bite him, and throw him over his shoulder two or three times, and Andrew Jackson—which was the name of the pup—Andrew Jackson would never let on but what *he* was satisfied, and hadn't expected nothing else—and the bets being doubled and doubled on the other side all the time, till the money was all up; and then all of a sudden he would grab that other dog jest by the j'int of his hind leg and freeze to it—not chaw, you understand, but only just grip and hang on till they throwed up the sponge, if it was a year. Smiley always come out winner on that pup, till he harnessed a dog once that didn't have no hind legs, because they'd been sawed off in a circular saw, and when the thing had gone along far enough, and the money was all up, and he come to make a snatch for his pet holt, he see in a minute how he'd been imposed on, and how the other dog had him in the door, so to speak, and he 'peared surprised, and then he looked sorter discouraged-like, and didn't try no more to win the fight, and so he got shucked out bad. He give Smiley a look, as much as to say his heart was broke, and it was *his* fault, for putting up a dog that hadn't no hind legs for him to take holt of, which was his main dependence in a fight, and then he limped off a piece and laid down and died. It was a good pup, was that Andrew Jackson, and would have made a name for hisself if he'd lived, for the stuff was in him and he had genius—I know it, because he hadn't no opportunities to speak of, and it don't stand to reason that a dog could make such a fight as he could under them circumstances if he hadn't no talent. It always makes me feel sorry when I think of that last fight of his'n, and the way it turned out.

Well, thish-yer Smiley had rat-tarriers, and chicken cocks, and tom-cats and all them kind of things, till you couldn't rest, and you couldn't fetch nothing for him to bet on but he'd match you. He ketched a frog one day, and took him home, and said he cal'lated to educate him; and so he never done nothing for three months but set in his back yard and learn that frog to jump. And you bet you he *did* learn him, too. He'd give him a little punch behind, and the next minute you'd see that frog whirling in the air like a doughnut—see him turn one summerset, or may be a couple, if he got a good start, and come down flat-footed and all right, like a cat. He got him up so in the matter of ketching flies, and kep' him in practice so constant, that he'd nail a fly every time as fur as he could see him. Smiley said all a frog wanted was education, and he could do 'most anything—and I believe him. Why, I've seen him set Dan'l Webster down here on this floor—Dan'l Webster was the name of the frog—and sing out, "Flies, Dan'l, flies!" and quicker'n you could wink he'd spring straight up and snake a fly off'n the counter there, and flop down on the floor ag'in as solid as a gob of mud, and fall to scratching the side of his head with his hind foot as indifferent as if he hadn't no idea he'd been doin' any more'n any frog might do. You never see a frog so modest and straightfor'ard as he was, for all he was so gifted. And when it come to fair and square jumping on a dead level, he could get over more ground at one straddle than any animal of his breed you ever see. Jumping on a dead level was his strong suit, you understand; and when it come to that, Smiley would ante up money on him as long as he had a red. Smiley was monstrous proud of his frog, and well he might be, for fellers that had traveled and been everywheres, all said he laid over any frog that ever *they* see.

Well, Smiley kep' the beast in a little lattice box, and he used to fetch him down town sometimes and lay for a bet. One day a feller—a stranger in the camp, he was—come acrost him with his box, and says:

"What might it be that you've got in the box?"

And Smiley says, sorter indifferent-like, "It might be a parrot, or it might be a canary, maybe, but it ain't—it's only just a frog."

And the feller took it, and looked at it careful, and turned it round this way and that, and says, "H'm—so 'tis. Well, what's *he* good for?"

"Well," Smiley says, easy and careless, "he's good enough for *one* thing, I should judge—he can outjump any frog in Calaveras county."

The feller took the box again, and took another long, particular look, and give it back to Smiley, and says, very deliberate, "Well," he says, "I don't see no p'ints about that frog that's any better'n any other frog."

"Maybe you don't," Smiley says. "Maybe you understand frogs and maybe you don't understand 'em; maybe you've had experience, and maybe you ain't only a amature, as it were. Anyways, I've got *my* opinion and I'll resk forty dollars that he can outjump any frog in Calaveras county."

And the feller studied a minute, and then says, kinder sad like, "Well, I'm only a stranger here, and I ain't got no frog; but if I had a frog, I'd bet you."

And then Smiley says, "That's all right—that's all right—if you'll hold my box a minute, I'll go and get you a frog." And so the feller took the box, and put up his forty dollars along with Smiley's, and set down to wait.

So he set there a good while thinking and thinking to hisself, and then he got the frog out and prized his mouth open and took a teaspoon and filled him full of quail shot—filled him pretty near up to his chin—and set him on the floor. Smiley he went to the swamp and slopped around in the mud for a long time, and finally he ketched a frog, and fetched him in, and give him to this feller, and says:

"Now, if you're ready, set him alongside of Dan'l, with his fore-paws just even with Dan'l's, and I'll give the word." Then he says, "One—two— three— *git!*" and him and the feller touched up the frogs from hehind, and the new frog hopped off lively, but Dan'l give a heave, and hysted up his shoulders—so— like a Frenchman, but it warn't no use—he couldn't budge; he was planted as solid as a church, and he couldn't no more stir than if he was anchored out. Smiley was a good deal surprised, and he was disgusted too, but he didn't have no idea what the matter was, of course.

The feller took the money and started away; and when he was going out at the door, he sorter jerked his thumb over his shoulder—so—at Dan'l, and says again, very deliberate, "Well," he says "*I* don't see no p'ints about that frog that's any better'n any other frog."

Smiley he stood scratching his head and looking down at Dan'l a long time, and at last he says, "I do wonder what in the nation that frog throw'd off for— I wonder if there ain't something the matter with him—he 'pears to look mighty baggy, somehow." And he ketched Dan'l by the nap of the neck, and hefted him, and says, "Why blame my cats if he don't weigh five pound!" and turned him upside down and he belched out a double handful of shot. And then he see how it was, and he was the maddest man—he set the frog down and took out after that feller, but he never ketched him. And——"

[Here Simon Wheeler heard his name called from the front yard, and got up to see what was wanted.] And turning to me as he moved away, he said: "Just set where you are, stranger, and rest easy—I ain't going to be gone a second."

But, by your leave, I did not think that a continuation of the history of the enterprising vagabond *Jim* Smiley would be likely to afford me much information concerning the Rev. *Leonidas W.* Smiley, and so I started away.

At the door I met the sociable Wheeler returning, and he button-holed me and re-commenced:

"Well, thish-yer Smiley had a yaller one-eyed cow that didn't have no tail, only jest a short stump like a bannanner, and——"

However, lacking both time and inclination, I did not wait to hear about the afflicted cow, but took my leave.

MY FIRST LITERARY VENTURE

I WAS A very smart child at the age of thirteen—an unusually smart child, I thought at the time. It was then that I did my first newspaper scribbling, and most unexpectedly to me it stirred up a fine sensation in the community. It did, indeed, and I was very proud of it, too. I was a printer's "devil," and a progressive and aspiring one. My uncle had me on his paper (the *Weekly Hannibal Journal*, two dollars a year in advance—five hundred subscribers, and they paid in cordwood, cabbages, and unmarketable turnips), and on a lucky summer's day he left town to be gone a week, and asked me if I thought I could edit one issue of the paper judiciously. Ah! didn't I want to try! Higgins was the editor on the rival paper. He had lately been jilted, and one night a friend found an open note on the poor fellow's bed, in which he stated that he could no longer endure life and had drowned himself in Bear Creek. The friend ran down there and discovered Higgins wading back to shore! He had concluded he wouldn't. The village was full of it for several days, but Higgins did not suspect it. I thought this was a fine opportunity. I wrote an elaborately wretched account of the whole matter, and then illustrated it with villainous cuts engraved on the bottoms of wooden type with a jack-knife—one of them a picture of Higgins wading out into the creek in his shirt, with a lantern, sounding the depth of the water with a walking-stick. I thought it was desperately funny, and was densely unconscious that there was any moral obliquity about such a publication. Being satisfied with this effort I looked around for other worlds to conquer, and it struck me that it would make good, interesting matter to charge the editor of a neighboring country paper with a piece of gratuitous rascality and "see him squirm."

I did it, putting the article into the form of a parody on the Burial of "Sir John Moore"—and a pretty crude parody it was, too.

Then I lampooned two prominent citizens outrageously—not because they had done anything to deserve it, but merely because I thought it was my duty to make the paper lively.

Next I gently touched up the newest stranger—the lion of the day, the gorgeous journeyman tailor from Quincy. He was a simpering coxcomb of the first water, and the "loudest" dressed man in the State. He was an inveterate woman-killer. Every week he wrote lushy "poetry" for the "Journal," about his newest conquest. His rhymes for my week were headed, "TO MARY IN H—L," meaning to Mary in Hannibal, of course. But while setting up the piece I was suddenly riven from head to heel by what I regarded as a perfect thunderbolt of humor, and I compressed it into a snappy foot-note at the bottom—thus:—"We will let this thing pass, just this once; but we wish Mr. J. Gordon Runnels to understand distinctly that we have a character to sustain, and from this time forth when he wants to commune with his friends in h—l, he must select some other medium than the columns of this journal!"

The paper came out, and I never knew any little thing attract so much attention as those playful trifles of mine.

For once the Hannibal Journal was in demand—a novelty it had not experienced before. The whole town was stirred. Higgins dropped in with a double-barrelled shot-gun early in the forenoon. When he found that it was an infant (as he called me) that had done him the damage, he simply pulled my ears and went away; but he threw up his situation that night and left town for good. The tailor came with his goose and a pair of shears; but he despised me too, and departed for the South that night. The two lampooned citizens came with threats of libel, and went away incensed at my insignificance. The country editor pranced in with a warwhoop next day, suffering for blood to drink; but he ended by forgiving me cordially and inviting me down to the drug store to wash away all animosity in a friendly bumper of "Fahnestock's Vermifuge." It was his little joke. My uncle was very angry when he got back—unreasonably so, I thought, considering what an impetus I had given the paper, and considering also that gratitude for his preservation ought to have been uppermost in his mind, inasmuch as by his delay

he had so wonderfully escaped dissection, tomahawking, libel, and getting his head shot off. But he softened when he looked at the accounts and saw that I had actually booked the unparalleled number of thirty-three new subscribers, and had the vegetables to show for it, cordwood, cabbage, beans, and unsalable turnips enough to run the family for two years!

A TRUE STORY

REPEATED WORD FOR WORD AS I HEARD IT.

IT WAS SUMMER time, and twilight. We were sitting on the porch of the farm-house, on the summit of the hill, and ''Aunt Rachel'' was sitting respectfully below our level, on the steps,—for she was our servant, and colored. She was of mighty frame and stature; she was sixty years old, but her eye was undimmed and her strength unabated. She was a cheerful, hearty soul, and it was no more trouble for her to laugh than it is for a bird to sing. She was under fire, now, as usual when the day was done. That is to say, she was being chaffed without mercy, and was enjoying it. She would let off peal after peal of laughter, and then sit with her face in her hands and shake with throes of enjoyment which she could no longer get breath enough to express. At such a moment as this a thought occurred to me, and I said:

''Aunt Rachel, how is it that you've lived sixty years and never had any trouble?''

She stopped quaking. She paused, and there was a moment of silence. She turned her face over her shoulder toward me, and said, without even a smile in her voice:—

''Misto C——, is you in 'arnest?''

It surprised me a good deal; and it sobered my manner and my speech, too. I said:—

Is one o' de ole Blue Hen's chickens, I is.

"Why, I thought—that is, I meant—why, you *can't* have had any trouble. I've never heard you sigh, and never seen your eye when there wasn't a laugh in it."

She faced fairly around, now, and was full of earnestness.

"Has I had any trouble? Misto C——, I's gwyne to tell you, den I leave it to you. I was bawn down 'mongst de slaves; I knows all 'bout slavery, 'case I ben one of 'em my own se'f. Well, sah, my ole man—dat's my husban'—he was lovin' an' kind to me, jist as kind as you is to yo' own wife. An' we had chil'en—seven chil'en—an' we loved dem chil'en jist de same as you loves yo' chil'en. Dey was black, but de Lord can't make no chil'en so black but what dey mother loves 'em an' wouldn't give 'em up, no, not for anything dat's in dis whole world.

"Well sah, I was raised in ole Fo'ginny, but my mother she was raised in Maryland; an' my *souls!* she was turrible when she'd git started! My *lan'!* but she'd make de fur fly! When she'd git into dem tantrums, she always had one word dat she said. She'd straighten herse'f up an' put her fists in her hips an' say, 'I want you to understan' dat I wa'nt bawn in de mash to be fool' by trash! I's one o' de ole Blue Hen's Chickens, *I* is!' 'Ca'se, you see, dat's what folks dat's bawn in Maryland calls deyselves, an' dey's proud of it. Well, dat was her word. I don't ever forgit it, beca'se she said it so much, an' beca'se she said it one day when my little Henry tore his wris' awful, and most busted his head, right up at de top of his forehead, an' de niggers didn't fly aroun' fas' enough to 'tend to him. An' when dey talk' back at her, she up an' she says, 'Look-a-heah!' she says, 'I want you niggers to understan' dat I wa'nt bawn in de mash to be fool' by trash! I's one o' de ole Blue Hen's Chickens, *I* is!' an' den she clar' dat kitchen an' bandage' up de chile herse'f. So I says dat word, too, when I's riled.

"Well, bymeby my ole mistis say she's broke, an' she' got to sell all the niggers on de place. An' when I heah dat dey gwyne to sell us all off at action in Richmon', oh de good gracious! I know what dat mean!"

Aunt Rachel had gradually risen, while she warmed to her subject, and now she towered above us, black against the stars.

"Dey put chains on us an' put us on a stan' as high as dis po'ch,—twenty foot high,—an' all de people stood aroun', crowds an' crowds. An' dey'd come up dah an' look at us all roun', an' squeeze our arm, an' make us git up an' walk, an' den say, 'Dis one too ole,' or 'Dis one lame,' or 'Dis one don't 'mount to much.' An' dey sole my ole man, an' took him away, an' dey begin to sell my chil'en an' take *dem* away, an' I begin to cry; an' de man say, 'Shet up yo' dam blubberin',' an' hit me on de mouf wid his han'. An' when de las' one was gone but my little Henry, I grab' *him* clost up to my breas' so, an' I ris up an' says, 'You shan't take him away,' I says; 'I'll kill de man dat tetches him!' I says. But my little Henry whisper an' say, 'I gwyne to run away, an' den I work an' buy yo' freedom.' Oh, bless de chile, he always so good! But dey got him—dey got him, de men did; but I took and tear de clo'es mos' off of 'em an' beat 'em over de head wid my chain; an' *dey* give it to *me*, too, but I didn't mine dat.

"Well, dah was my ole man gone, an' all my chil'en, all my seven chil'en— an' six of 'em I hain't set eyes on ag'in to dis day, an' dat's twenty-two year ago las' Easter. De man dat bought me b'long' in Newbern, an' he took me dah. Well, bymeby de years roll on an' de waw come. My marster he was a

Confedrit colonel, an' I was his family's cook. So when de Unions took dat town, dey all run away an' lef' me all by myse'f wid de other niggers in dat mons'us big house. So de big Union officers move in dah, an' dey ask me would I cook for *dem*. 'Lord bless you,' says I, 'dat's what I's *for*.'

"Dey wa'nt no small-fry officers, mine you, dey was de biggest dey *is;* an' de way dey made dem sojers mosey roun'! De Gen'l he tole me to boss dat kitchen; an' he say, 'If anybody come meddlin' wid you, you jist make 'em walk chalk; don't you be afeared,' he say; 'you's 'mong frens, now.'

"Well, I thinks to myse'f, if my little Henry ever got a chance to run away, he'd make to de Norf, o' course. So one day I comes in dah whar de big officers was, in de parlor, an' I drops a kurtchy, so, an' I up an' tole 'em 'bout my Henry, dey a-listenin' to my troubles jist de same as if I was white folks; an' I says, 'What I come for is beca'se if he got away and got up Norf whar you gemmen comes from, you might 'a' seen him, maybe, an' could tell me so as I could fine him ag'in; he was very little, an' he had a sk-yar on his lef' w'ris', an' at de top of his forehead.' Den dey look mournful, an' de Gen'l say, 'How long sence you los' him?' an' I say, 'Thirteen year.' Den de Gen'l say, 'He wouldn't be little no mo', now—he's a man!'

"I never thought o' dat befo'! He was only dat little feller to *me,* yit. I never thought 'bout him growin' up an' bein' big. But I see it den. None o' de gemmen had run acrost him, so dey couldn't do nothin' for me. But all dat time, do' *I* didn't know it, my Henry *was* run off to de Norf, years an' years, an' he was a barber, too, an' worked for hisse'f. An' bymeby, when de waw come' he ups an' he says: 'I's done barberin',' he says, 'I's gwyne to fine my ole mammy, less'n she's dead.' So he sole out an' went to whar dey was recruitin', an' hired hisse'f out to de colonel for his servant; an' den he went all froo de battles everywhah, huntin' for his ole mammy; yes indeedy, he'd hire to fust one officer an' den another, tell he'd ransacked de whole Souf; but you see *I* didn't know nuffin 'bout *dis*. How was *I* gwyne to know it?

"Well, one night we had a big sojer ball; de sojers dah at Newbern was always havin' balls an' carryin' on. Dey had 'em in my kitchen, heaps o' times, 'ca'se it was so big. Mine you, I was *down* on sich doin's; beca'se my place was wid de officers, an' it rasp me to have dem common sojers cavortin' roun' my kitchen like dat. But I alway' stood aroun' an' kep' things straight, I did; an' sometimes dey'd git my dander up, an' den I'd make 'em clar dat kitchen, mine I *tell* you!

"Well, one night—it was a Friday night—dey comes a whole plattoon f'm a *nigger* ridgment dat was on guard at de house,—de house was head-quarters, you know,—an' den I was jist a-*bilin'*! Mad? I was jist a-*boomin'*! I swelled aroun', an' swelled aroun'; I jist was a-itchin' for 'em to do somefin for to start me. An' dey was a-waltzin' an' a-dancin'! *my!* but dey was havin' a time! an' I jist a-swellin' an' a-swellin' up! Pooty soon, 'long comes *sich* a spruce young nigger a-sailin' down de room wid a yaller wench roun' de wais'; an' roun' an' roun' an' roun' dey went, enough to make a body drunk to look at 'em; an' when dey got abreas' o' me, dey went to kin' o' balancin' aroun' fust on one leg an' den on t'other, an' smilin' at my big red turban, an' makin' fun, an' I ups an' says '*Git* along w'id you!—rubbage!' De young man's face kin' o' changed, all of a sudden, for 'bout a second, but den he went to smilin' ag'in, same as he was befo'. Well, 'bout dis time, in comes some niggers dat played music and b'long' to de ban', an' dey *never* could git along widout puttin' on airs. An' de very fust air dey put on dat night, I lit into 'em! Dey laughed, an' dat made me wuss. De 'res o' de niggers got to laughin', an' den my soul *alive* but I was hot! My eye was jist a-blazin'! I jist straightened myself up, so,—jist as I is now, plum to de ceilin', mos',—an' I digs my fists into my hips, an' I says, 'Look-a-heah!' I says, 'I want you niggers to understan' dat I wa'nt bawn in de mash to be fool' by trash! I's one o' de ole Blue Hen's Chickens, *I* is!' an' den I see dat young man stan' a-starin' an' stiff, lookin' kin' o' up at de ceilin' like he fo'got somefin, an' couldn't 'member it no mo'. Well, I jist march' on dem niggers,—so, lookin' like a gen'l,—an' dey jist cave' away befo' me an' out at de do'. An' as dis young man was a-goin' out, I heah him say to another nigger, 'Jim,' he says, 'you go 'long an' tell de cap'n I be on han' 'bout eight o'clock in de mawnin'; dey's somefin on my mine,' he says; 'I don't sleep no mo' dis night. You go 'long,' he says, 'an' leave me by my own se'f.'

"Dis was 'bout one o'clock in de mawnin'. Well, 'bout seven, I was up an' on han', gittin' de officers' breakfast. I was a-stoopin' down by de stove,—jist so, same as if yo' foot was de stove,—an' I'd opened de stove do' wid my right han',—so, pushin' it back, jist as I pushes yo' foot,—an' I'd jist got de pan o' hot biscuits in my han' an' was 'bout to raise up, when I see a black face come aroun' under mine, an' de eyes a-lookin' up into mine, jist as I's a-lookin' up clost under yo' face now; an' I jist stopped *right dah,* an' never budged! jist gazed , an' gazed, so; an' de pan begin to tremble, an' all of a sudden I *knowed!* De pan drop' on de flo' an' I grab his lef' han' an' shove back his sleeve,—jist so, as I's doin' to you,—an' den I goes for his forehead an' push de hair back, so, an' 'Boy!' I says, 'if you an't my Henry, what is you doin' wid dis welt on yo' wris' an' dat sk-yar on yo' forehead? De Lord God ob heaven be praise', I got my own ag'in!'

"Oh, no, Misto C——, *I* hain't had no trouble. An' no *joy!*"

THE PETRIFIED MAN

Now, TO SHOW how really hard it is to foist a moral or a truth upon an unsuspecting public through a burlesque without entirely and absurdly missing one's mark, I will here set down two experiences of my own in this thing. In the fall of 1862, in Nevada and California, the people got to running wild about extraordinary petrifications and other natural marvels. One could scarcely pick up a paper without finding in it one or two glorified discoveries of this kind. The mania was becoming a little ridiculous. I was a bran-new local editor in Virginia City, and I felt called upon to destroy this growing evil; we all have our benignant fatherly moods at one time or another, I suppose. I chose to kill the petrifaction mania with a delicate, a very delicate satire. But maybe it was altogether too delicate, for nobody ever perceived the satire part of it at all. I put my scheme in the shape of the discovery of a remarkably petrified man.

I had had a temporary falling out with Mr. ——, the new coroner and justice of the peace of Humboldt, and thought I might as well touch him up a little at the same time and make him ridiculous, and thus combine pleasure with business. So I told, in patient belief-compelling detail, all about the finding of a petrified man at Gravelly Ford (exactly a hundred and twenty miles, over a breakneck mountain trail, from where —— lived); how all the savants of the immediate

neighborhood had been to examine it (it was notorious that there was not a living creature within fifty miles of there, except a few starving Indians, some crippled grasshoppers, and four or five buzzards out of meat and too feeble to get away); how those savants all pronounced the petrified man to have been in a state of complete petrifaction for over ten generations; and then, with a seriousness that I ought to have been ashamed to assume, I stated that as soon as Mr. —— heard the news he summoned a jury, mounted his mule, and posted off, with noble reverence for official duty, on that awful five days' journey, through alkali, sage-brush, peril of body, and imminent starvation, to *hold an inquest* on this man that had been dead and turned to everlasting stone for more than three hundred years! And then, my hand being ''in,'' so to speak, I went on, with the same unflinching gravity, to state that the jury returned a verdict that deceased came to his death from *protracted exposure.* This only moved me to higher flights of imagination, and I said that the jury, with that charity so characteristic of pioneers, then dug a grave, and were about to give the petrified man Christian burial, when they found that for ages a limestone sediment had been trickling down the face of the stone against which he was sitting, and this stuff had run under him and cemented him fast to the ''bed-rock;'' that the jury (they were all silver-miners) canvassed the difficulty a moment, and then got out their powder and fuse, and proceeded to drill a hole under him, in order to *blast him from his position,* when Mr. ——, ''with that delicacy so characteristic of him, forbade them, observing that it would be little less than sacrilege to do such a thing.''

From beginning to end the ''Petrified Man'' squib was a string of roaring absurdities, albeit they were told with an unfair pretence of truth that even imposed upon me to some extent, and I was in some danger of believing in my own fraud. But I really had no desire to deceive anybody, and no expectation of doing it. I depended on the way the petrified man was *sitting* to explain to the public that he was a swindle. Yet I purposely mixed that up with other things, hoping to make it obscure—and I did. I would describe the position of one foot, and then say his right thumb was against the side of his nose; then talk about his other foot, and presently come back and say the fingers of his right hand were spread apart; then talk about the back of his head a little, and return and say the left thumb was hooked into the right little finger; then ramble off about something else, and by and by drift back again and remark that the fingers of the left hand were spread like those of the right. But I was too ingenious. I mixed it up rather too much; and so all that description of the attitude, as a key to the humbuggery of the article, was entirely lost, for nobody but me ever discovered and comprehended the peculiar and suggestive position of the petrified man's hands.

As a *satire* on the petrifaction mania, or anything else, my Petrified Man was a disheartening failure; for everybody received him in innocent good faith, and I was stunned to see the creature I had begotten to pull down the wonder-business with, and bring derision upon it, calmly exalted to the grand chief place in the list of the genuine marvels our Nevada had produced. I was so disappointed at the curious miscarriage of my scheme, that at first I was angry, and did not like to think about it; but by and by, when the exchanges began to come in with the Petrified Man copied and guilelessly glorified, I began to feel a soothing secret satisfaction; and as my gentleman's field of travels broadened, and by the exchanges I saw that he steadily and implacably penetrated territory after territory, State after State, and land after land, till he swept the great globe and culminated in sublime and unimpeached legitimacy in the august London *Lancet,* my cup was full, and I said I was glad I had done it. I think that for about eleven months, as nearly as I can remember, Mr. ──'s daily mail-bag continued to be swollen by the addition of half a bushel of newspapers hailing from many climes with the Petrified Man in them, marked around with a prominent belt of ink. I sent them to him. I did it for spite, not for fun. He used to shovel them into his back yard and curse. And every day during all those months the miners, his constituents (for miners never quit joking a person when they get started), would call on him and ask if he could tell them where they could get hold of a paper with the Petrified Man in it. He could have accommodated a continent with them. I hated ── in those days, and these things pacified me and pleased me. I could not have gotten more real comfort out of him without killing him.

HISTORY REPEATS ITSELF

THE FOLLOWING I find in a Sandwich Island paper which some friend has sent me from that tranquil far-off retreat. The coincidence between my own experience and that here set down by the late Mr. Benton is so remarkable that I cannot forbear publishing and commenting upon the paragraph. The Sandwich Island paper says:—

> "How touching is this tribute of the late Hon. T. H. Benton to his mother's influence:—'My mother asked me never to use tobacco; I have never touched it from that time to the present day. She asked me not to gamble, and I have never gambled. I cannot tell who is losing in games that are being played. She admonished me, too, against liquor-drinking, and whatever capacity for endurance I have at present, and whatever usefulness I may have attained through life, I attribute to having complied with her pious and correct wishes. When I was seven years of age she

asked me not to drink, and then I made a resolution of total abstinence;
and that I have adhered to it through all time I owe to my mother.' "

I never saw anything so curious. It is almost an exact epitome of my own moral career—after simply substituting a grandmother for a mother. How well I remember my grandmother's asking me not to use tobacco, good old soul! She said, "You're at it again, are you, you whelp? Now, don't ever let me catch you chewing tobacco before breakfast again, or I lay I'll blacksnake you within an inch of your life!" I have never touched it at that hour of the morning from that time to the present day.

She asked me not to gamble. She whispered and said, "Put up those wicked cards this minute!—two pair and a jack, you numskull, and the other fellow's got a flush!"

I never have gambled from that day to this—never once—without a "cold deck" in my pocket. I cannot even tell who is going to lose in games that are being played unless I dealt myself.

When I was two years of age she asked me not to drink, and then I made a resolution of total abstinence. That I have adhered to it and enjoyed the beneficent effects of it through all time, I owe to my grandmother. I have never drunk a drop from that day to this of any kind of water.

THE LATE BENJAMIN FRANKLIN

["Never put off till to-morrow what you can do day after to-morrow just as well."—B. F.]

THIS PARTY WAS one of those persons whom they call Philosophers. He was twins, being born simultaneously in two different houses in the city of Boston. These houses remain unto this day, and have signs upon them worded in accordance with the facts. The signs are considered well enough to have, though not necessary, because the inhabitants point out the two birth-places to the stranger anyhow,

and sometimes as often as several times in the same day. The subject of this memoir was of a vicious disposition, and early prostituted his talents to the invention of maxims and aphorisms calculated to inflict suffering upon the rising generation of all subsequent ages. His simplest acts, also, were contrived with a view to their being held up for the emulation of boys for ever—boys who might otherwise have been happy. It was in this spirit that he became the son of a soap-boiler, and probably for no other reason than that the efforts of all future boys who tried to be anything might be looked upon with suspicion unless they were the sons of soap-boilers. With a malevolence which is without parallel in history, he would work all day, and then sit up nights, and let on to be studying algebra by the light of a smouldering fire, so that all other boys might have to do that also, or else have Benjamin Franklin thrown up to them. Not satisfied with these proceedings, he had a fashion of living wholly on bread and water, and studying astronomy at meal time—a thing which has brought affliction to millions of boys since, whose fathers had read Franklin's pernicious biography.

His maxims were full of animosity towards boys. Nowadays a boy cannot follow out a single natural instinct without tumbling over some of those everlasting aphorisms and hearing from Franklin on the spot. If he buys two cents' worth of peanuts, his father says, "Remember what Franklin has said, my son—'A groat a day's a penny a year;' " and the comfort is all gone out of those peanuts. If he wants to spin his top when he has done work, his father quotes, "Procrastination is the thief of time." If he does a virtuous action, he never gets any thing for it, because "Virtue is its own reward." And that boy is hounded to death and robbed of his natural rest, because Franklin said once, in one of his inspired flights of malignity—

> "Early to bed and early to rise
> Makes a man healthy and wealthy and wise."

As if it were any object to a boy to be healthy and wealthy and wise on such terms. The sorrow that that maxim has cost me through my parents' experimenting on me with it, tongue cannot tell. The legitimate result is my present state of general debility, indigence, and mental aberration. My parents used to have me up before nine o'clock in the morning, sometimes, when I was a boy. If they had let me take my natural rest, where would I have been now? Keeping store, no doubt, and respected by all.

And what an adroit old adventurer the subject of this memoir was! In order to get a chance to fly his kite on Sunday he used to hang a key on the string and let on to be fishing for lightning. And a guileless public would go home chirping about the "wisdom" and the "genius" of the hoary Sabbath-breaker. If anybody caught him playing "mumble-peg" by himself, after the age of sixty, he would immediately appear to be ciphering out how the grass grew—as if it was any of his business. My grandfather knew him well, and he says Franklin was always fixed—always ready. If a body, during his old age, happened on him unexpectedly when he was catching flies, or making mud pies, or sliding on a cellar-door, he would immediately look wise, and rip out a maxim, and walk off with his nose in the air and his cap turned wrong side before, trying to appear absent-minded and eccentric. He was a hard lot.

He invented a stove that would smoke your head off in four hours by the clock. One can see the almost devilish satisfaction he took in it by his giving it his name.

He was always proud of telling how he entered Philadelphia for the first time, with nothing in the world but two shillings in his pocket and four rolls of bread under his arm. But really, when you come to examine it critically, it was nothing. Anybody could have done it.

To the subject of this memoir belongs the honor of recommending the army to go back to bows and arrows in place of bayonets and muskets. He observed, with his customary force, that the bayonet was very well under some circumstances, but that he doubted whether it could be used with accuracy at a long range.

Benjamin Franklin did a great many notable things for his country, and made her young name to be honored in many lands as the mother of such a son. It is not the idea of this memoir to ignore that or cover it up. No; the simple idea of it is to snub those pretentious maxims of his, which he worked up with a great show of originality out of truisms that had become wearisome platitudes as early as the dispersion from Babel; and also to snub his stove, and his military inspirations, his unseemly endeavor to make himself conspicuous when he entered Philadelphia, and his flying his kite and fooling away his time in all sorts of such ways when he ought to have been foraging for soap-fat, or constructing candles. I merely desired to do away with somewhat of the prevalent calamitous idea among heads of families that Franklin *acquired* his great genius by working for nothing, studying by moonlight, and getting up in the night instead of waiting till morning like a Christian; and that this programme, rigidly inflicted, will make a Franklin of every father's fool. It is time these gentlemen were finding out that these execrable eccentricities of instinct and conduct are only the *evidences* of genius, not the *creators* of it. I wish I had been the father of my parents long enough to make them comprehend this truth, and thus prepare them to let their son have an easier time of it. When I was a child I had to boil soap, notwithstanding my father was wealthy, and I had to get up early and study geometry at breakfast, and peddle my own poetry, and do everything just as Franklin did, in the solemn hope that I would be a Franklin some day. And here I am.

CURING A COLD

It is a good thing, perhaps, to write for the amusement of the public, but it is a far higher and nobler thing to write for their instruction, their profit, their actual and tangible benefit. The latter is the sole object of this article. If it prove the means of restoring to health one solitary sufferer among my race, of lighting up once more the fire of hope and joy in his faded eyes, of bringing back to his dead heart again the quick, generous impulses of other days, I shall be amply rewarded for my labor; my soul will be permeated with the sacred delight a Christian feels when he has done a good, unselfish deed.

Having led a pure and blameless life, I am justified in believing that no man who knows me will reject the suggestions I am about to make, out of fear that I am trying to deceive him. Let the public do itself the honor to read my experience in doctoring a cold, as herein set forth, and then follow in my footsteps.

When the White House was burned in Virginia City, I lost my home, my happiness, my constitution, and my trunk. The loss of the two first-named articles was a matter of no great consequence, since a home without a mother or a sister, or a distant young female relative in it, to remind you, by putting your soiled linen out of sight and taking your boots down off the mantel-piece, that there are those who think about you and care for you, is easily obtained. And I cared nothing for the loss of my happiness, because not being a poet, it could not be possible that melancholy would abide with me long. But to lose a good constitution and a better trunk were serious misfortunes. On the day of the fire my constitution succumbed to a severe cold, caused by undue exertion in getting ready to do something. I suffered to no purpose, too, because the plan I was figuring at for the extinguishing of the fire was so elaborate that I never got it completed until the middle of the following week.

The first time I began to sneeze, a friend told me to go and bathe my feet in hot water and go to bed. I did so. Shortly afterwards, another friend advised me to get up and take a cold shower-bath. I did that also. Within the hour, another

friend assured me that it was policy to "feed a cold and starve a fever." I had both. So I thought it best to fill myself up for the cold, and then keep dark and let the fever starve awhile.

In a case of this kind, I seldom do things by halves; I ate pretty heartily; I conferred my custom upon a stranger who had just opened his restaurant that morning: he waited near me in respectful silence until I had finished feeding my cold, when he inquired if the people about Virginia City were much afflicted with colds? I told him I thought they were. He then went out and took in his sign.

I started down toward the office, and on the way encountered another bosom friend, who told me that a quart of salt water, taken warm, would come as near curing a cold as anything in the world. I hardly thought I had room for it, but I tried it anyhow. The result was surprising. I believed I had thrown up my immortal soul.

Now, as I am giving my experience only for the benefit of those who are troubled with the distemper I am writing about, I feel that they will see the propriety of my cautioning them against following such portions of it as proved inefficient with me, and acting upon this conviction, I warn them against warm salt water. It may be a good enough remedy, but I think it is too severe. If I had another cold in the head, and there were no course left me but to take either an earthquake or a quart of warm salt water, I would take my chances on the earthquake.

After the storm which had been raging in my stomach had subsided, and no more good Samaritans happening along, I went on borrowing handkerchiefs again and blowing them to atoms, as had been my custom in the early stages of my cold, until I came across a lady who had just arrived from over the plains, and who said she had lived in a part of the country where doctors were scarce, and had from necessity acquired considerable skill in the treatment of simple "family complaints." I knew she must have had much experience, for she appeared to be a hundred and fifty years old.

She mixed a decoction composed of molasses, aquafortis, turpentine, and various other drugs, and instructed me to take a wine-glass full of it every fifteen minutes. I never took but one dose; that was enough; it robbed me of all moral principle, and awoke every unworthy impulse of my nature. Under its malign influence my brain conceived miracles of meanness, but my hands were too feeble to execute them; at that time, had it not been that my strength had surrendered to a succession of assaults from infallible remedies for my cold, I am satisfied that I would have tried to rob the graveyard. Like most other people, I often feel mean, and act accordingly; but until I took that medicine I had never revelled in such supernatural depravity, and felt proud of it. At the end of two days I was ready to go to doctoring again. I took a few more unfailing remedies, and finally drove my cold from my head to my lungs.

I got to coughing incessantly, and my voice fell below zero; I conversed in a thundering base, two octaves below my natural tone; I could only compass my regular nightly repose by coughing myself down to a state of utter exhaustion, and then the moment I began to talk in my sleep, my discordant voice woke me up again.

My case grew more and more serious every day. Plain gin was recommended; I took it. Then gin and molasses; I took that also. Then gin and onions; I added the onions, and took all three. I detected no particular result, however, except that I had acquired a breath like a buzzard's.

I found I had to travel for my health. I went to Lake Bigler with my reportorial comrade, Wilson. It is gratifying to me to reflect that we traveled in considerable style; we went in the Pioneer coach, and my friend took all his baggage with him, consisting of two excellent silk handkerchiefs and a daguerreotype of his grandmother. We sailed and hunted and fished and danced all day, and I doctored my cough all night. By managing in this way, I made out to improve every hour in the twenty-four. But my disease continued to grow worse.

A sheet-bath was recommended. I had never refused a remedy yet, and it seemed poor policy to commence then; therefore I determined to take a sheet-bath, notwithstanding I had no idea what sort of arrangement it was. It was administered at midnight, and the weather was very frosty. My breast and back were bared, and a sheet (there appeared to be a thousand yards of it) soaked in ice-water, was wound around me until I resembled a swab for a Columbiad.

It is a cruel expedient. When the chilly rag touches one's warm flesh, it makes him start with sudden violence, and gasp for breath just as men do in the death agony. It froze the marrow in my bones, and stopped the beating of my heart. I thought my time had come.

Young Wilson said the circumstance reminded him of an anecdote about a negro who was being baptized, and who slipped from the parson's grasp, and came near being drowned. He floundered around, though, and finally rose up out of the water considerably strangled, and furiously angry, and started ashore at once, spouting water like a whale, and remarking, with great asperity, that "one o' dese days some gen'l'man's nigger gwyne to get killed wid jis' such dam foolishness as dis!"

Never take a sheet-bath—never. Next to meeting a lady acquaintance, who, for reasons best known to herself, don't see you when she looks at you, and don't know you when she does see you, it is the most uncomfortable thing in the world.

But, as I was saying, when the sheet-bath failed to cure my cough, a lady friend recommended the application of a mustard plaster to my breast. I believe that would have cured me effectually, if it had not been for young Wilson. When I went to bed, I put my mustard plaster—which was a very gorgeous one, eighteen inches square—where I could reach it when I was ready for it. But young Wilson got hungry in the night, and—here is food for the imagination.

After sojourning a week at Lake Bigler, I went to Steamboat Springs, and beside the steam baths, I took a lot of the vilest medicines that were ever concocted. They would have cured me, but I had to go back to Virginia City, where, notwithstanding the variety of new remedies I absorbed every day, I managed to aggravate my disease by carelessness and undue exposure.

I finally concluded to visit San Francisco, and the first day I got there, a lady at the hotel told me to drink a quart of whisky every twenty-four hours, and a friend up town recommended precisely the same course. Each advised me to take a quart; that made half a gallon. I did it, and still live.

Now, with the kindest motives in the world, I offer for the consideration of consumptive patients the variegated course of treatment I have lately gone through. Let them try it: if it don't cure, it can't more than kill them.

Mark Twain's
(Burlesque) Autobiography

A BURLESQUE AUTOBIOGRAPHY

TWO OR THREE persons having at different times intimated that if I would write an autobiography they would read it when they got leisure, I yield at last to this frenzied public demand, and herewith tender my history:

Ours is a noble old house, and stretches a long way back into antiquity. The earliest ancestor the Twains have any record of was a friend of the family by the name of Higgins. This was in the eleventh century, when our people were living in Aberdeen, county of Cork, England. Why it is that our long line has ever since borne the maternal name (except when one of them now and then took a playful refuge in an alias to avert foolishness), instead of Higgins, is a mystery which none of us has ever felt much desire to stir. It is a kind of vague, pretty romance, and we leave it alone. All the old families do that way.

Arthour Twain was a man of considerable note—a solicitor on the highway in William Rufus' time. At about the age of thirty he went to one of those fine old English places of resort called Newgate, to see about something, and never returned again. While there he died suddenly.

Augustus Twain seems to have made something of a stir about the year 1160. He was as full of fun as he could be, and used to take his old sabre and sharpen it up, and get in a convenient place on a dark night, and stick it through people as they went by, to see them jump. He was a born humorist. But he got to going too far with it; and the first time he was found stripping one of these parties, the authorities removed one end of him, and put it up on a nice high place on Temple Bar, where it could contemplate the people and have a good time. He never liked any situation so much or stuck to it so long.

Then for the next two hundred years the family tree shows a succession of soldiers—noble, high-spirited fellows, who always went into battle singing, right behind the army, and always went out a-whooping, right ahead of it.

This is a scathing rebuke to old dead Froissart's poor witticism that our family tree never had but one limb to it, and that that one stuck out at right angles, and bore fruit winter and summer.

Early in the fifteenth century we have Beau Twain, called "the Scholar." He wrote a beautiful, beautiful hand. And he could imitate anybody's hand so closely that it was enough to make a person laugh his head off to see it. He had infinite sport with his talent. But by and by he took a contract to break stone for a road, and the roughness of the work spoiled his hand. Still, he enjoyed life all the time he was in the stone business, which, with inconsiderable intervals, was some forty-two years. In fact, he died in harness. During all those long years he gave such satisfaction that he never was through with one contract a week till government gave him another. He was a perfect pet. And he was always a favorite with his fellow-artists, and was a conspicuous member of their benevolent secret society, called the Chain Gang. He always wore his hair short, had a preference for striped clothes, and died lamented by the government. He was a sore loss to his country. For he was so regular.

Some years later we have the illustrious John Morgan Twain. He came over to this country with Columbus in 1492, as a passenger. He appears to have been of a crusty, uncomfortable disposition. He complained of the food all the way over, and was always threatening to go ashore unless there was a change. He wanted fresh shad. Hardly a day passed over his head that he did not go idling about the ship with his nose in the air, sneering about the commander, and saying he did not believe Columbus knew where he was going to or had ever been there before. The memorable cry of "Land ho!" thrilled every heart in the ship but his. He gazed a while through a piece of smoked glass at the penciled line lying on the distant water, and then said: "Land be hanged,—it's a raft!"

When this questionable passenger came on board the ship, he brought nothing with him but an old newspaper containing a handkerchief marked "B. G.," one cotton sock marked "L. W. C." one woollen one marked "D. F." and a nightshirt marked "O. M. R." And yet during the voyage he worried more about his "trunk," and gave himself more airs about it, than all the rest of the passengers put together. If the ship was "down by the head," and would not steer, he would go and move his "trunk" further aft, and then watch the effect. If the ship was "by the stern," he would suggest to Columbus to detail some men to "shift that baggage." In storms he had to be gagged, because his wailings about his "trunk" made it impossible for the men to hear the orders. The man does not appear to have been openly charged with any gravely unbecoming thing, but it is noted in the ship's log as a "curious circumstance" that albeit he brought his baggage on board the ship in a newspaper, he took it ashore in four trunks, a queensware crate, and a couple of champagne baskets. But when he came back insinuating in an insolent, swaggering way, that some of his things were missing, and was going to search the other passengers' baggage, it was too much, and they threw him overboard. They watched long and wonderingly for him to come up, but not even a bubble rose on the quietly ebbing tide. But while every one was most absorbed in gazing over the side, and the interest was momentarily increasing, it was observed with consternation that the vessel was adrift and the anchor cable hanging limp from the bow. Then in the ship's dimmed and ancient log we find this quaint note:

> "In time it was discouvered y^t ye troblesome passenger hadde gonne
> downe and got ye anchor, and toke ye same and solde it to ye dam sauvages
> from ye interior, saying y^t he hadde *founde* it, ye sonne of a ghun!"

Yet this ancestor had good and noble instincts, and it is with pride that we call to mind the fact that he was the first white person who ever interested himself in the work of elevating and civilizing our Indians. He built a commodious jail and put up a gallows, and to his dying day he claimed with satisfaction that he had had a more restraining and elevating influence on the Indians than any other reformer that ever labored among them. At this point the chronicle becomes less frank and chatty, and closes abruptly by saying that the old voyager went to see his gallows perform on the first white man ever hanged in America, and while there received injuries which terminated in his death.

The great grandson of the "Reformer" flourished in sixteen hundred and something, and was known in our annals as "the old Admiral," though in history he had other titles. He was long in command of fleets of swift vessels, well armed and manned, and did great service in hurrying up merchantmen. Vessels which he followed and kept his eagle eye on, always made good fair time across the ocean. But if a ship still loitered in spite of all he could do, his indignation would grow till he could contain himself no longer—and then he would take that ship home where he lived and keep it there carefully, expecting the owners to come for it, but they never did. And he would try to get the idleness and sloth out of the sailors of that ship by compelling them to take invigorating exercise and a bath. He called it "walking a plank." All the pupils liked it. At any rate, they never found any fault with it after trying it. When the owners were late coming for their ships, the Admiral always burned them, so that the insurance money should not be lost. At last this fine old tar was cut down in the fulness of his years and honors. And to her dying day, his poor heart-broken widow believed that if he had been cut down fifteen minutes sooner he might have been resuscitated.

Charles Henry Twain lived during the latter part of the seventeenth century, and was a zealous and distinguished missionary. He converted sixteen thousand South Sea islanders, and taught them that a dog-tooth necklace and a pair of spectacles was not enough clothing to come to divine service in. His poor flock loved him very, very dearly; and when his funeral was over, they got up in a body (and came out of the restaurant) with tears in their eyes, and saying, one to another, that he was a good tender missionary, and they wished they had some more of him.

PAH-GO-TO-WAH-WAH-PUKKETEKEEWIS (Mighty-Hunter-with-a-Hog-Eye) TWAIN adorned the middle of the eighteenth century, and aided Gen. Braddock with all his heart to resist the oppressor Washington. It was this ancestor who fired seventeen times at our Washington from behind a tree. So far the beautiful romantic narrative in the moral story-books is correct; but when that narrative goes on to say that at the seventeenth round the awe-stricken savage said solemnly that that man was being reserved by the Great Spirit for some mighty mission, and he dared not lift his sacrilegious rifle against him again, the narrative seriously impairs the integrity of history. What he *did* say was:

"It ain't no (hic!) no use. 'At man's so drunk he can't stan' still long enough for a man to hit him. I (hic!) *I* can't 'ford to fool away any more am'nition on *him!*"

That was why he stopped at the seventeenth round, and it was a good plain matter-of-fact reason, too, and one that easily commends itself to us by the eloquent, persuasive flavor of probability there is about it.

I always enjoyed the story-book narrative, but I felt a marring misgiving that every Indian at Braddock's Defeat who fired at a soldier a couple of times (*two* easily grows to seventeen in a century), and missed him, jumped to the conclusion that the Great Spirit was reserving that soldier for some grand mission; and so I somehow feared that the only reason why Washington's case is remembered and the others forgotten is, that in his the prophecy came true, and in that of the others it didn't. There are not books enough on earth to contain the record of the prophecies Indians and other unauthorized parties have *made;* but one may carry in his overcoat pockets the record of all the prophecies that have been *fulfilled.*

I will remark here, in passing, that certain ancestors of mine are so thoroughly well known in history by their *aliases*, that I have not felt it to be worth while to dwell upon them, or even mention them in the order of their birth. Among these may be mentioned RICHARD BRINSLEY TWAIN, *alias* Guy Fawkes; JOHN WENTWORTH TWAIN, *alias* Sixteen-String Jack; WILLIAM HOGARTH TWAIN, *alias* Jack Sheppard; ANANIAS TWAIN, *alias* Baron Munchausen; JOHN GEORGE TWAIN, *alias* Capt. Kydd; and then there are George Francis Train, Tom Pepper, Nebuchadnezzar and Baalam's Ass—they all belong to our family, but to a branch of it somewhat distantly removed from the honorable direct line—in fact, a collateral branch, whose members chiefly differ from the ancient stock in that, in order to acquire the notoriety we have always yearned and hungered for, they have got into a low way of going to jail instead of getting hanged.

It is not well, when writing an autobiography, to follow your ancestry down too close to your own time—it is safest to speak only vaguely of your great-grandfather, and then skip from there to yourself, which I now do.

I was born without teeth—and there Richard III had the advantage of me; but I was born without a humpback, likewise, and there I had the advantage of *him.* My parents were neither very poor nor conspicuously honest.

But now a thought occurs to me. My own history would really seem so tame contrasted with that of my ancestors, that it is simply wisdom to leave it unwritten until I am hanged. If some other biographies I have read had stopped with the ancestry until a like event occurred, it would have been a felicitous thing for the reading public. How does it strike *you?*

The Prince and the Pauper

A Tale for Young People of All Ages

TO THOSE GOOD-MANNERED AND AGREEABLE CHILDREN,
SUSIE AND CLARA CLEMENS,
THIS BOOK
IS AFFECTIONATELY INSCRIBED
BY THEIR FATHER

THE quality of mercy . . .
                    is twice bless'd;
It blesseth him that gives, and him that takes;
'Tis mightiest in the mightiest: it becomes
The thronéd monarch better than his crown.

Merchant of Venice.

I WILL SET down a tale as it was told to me by one who had it of his father, which latter had it of *his* father, this last having in like manner had it of *his* father—and so on, back and still back, three hundred years and more, the fathers transmitting it to the sons and so preserving it. It may be history, it may be only a legend, a tradition. It may have happened, it may not have happened: but it *could* have happened. It may be that the wise and the learned believed it in the old days; it may be that only the unlearned and the simple loved it and credited it.

"LET HIM IN!"

Chapter I

THE BIRTH OF THE PRINCE AND THE PAUPER

IN THE ANCIENT city of London, on a certain autumn day in the second quarter of the sixteenth century, a boy was born to a poor family of the name of Canty, who did not want him. On the same day another English child was born to a rich family of the name of Tudor, who did want him. All England wanted him too. England had so longed for him, and hoped for him, and prayed God for him, that, now that he was really come the people went nearly mad for joy. Mere acquaintances hugged and kissed each other and cried. Everybody took a holiday, and high and low, rich and poor, feasted and danced and sang, and got very mellow; and they kept this up for days and nights together. By day, London was a sight to see, with gay banners waving from every balcony and housetop, and splendid pageants marching along. By night, it was again a sight to see, with its great bonfires at every corner, and its troops of revellers making merry around them. There was no talk in all England but of the new baby, Edward Tudor, Prince of Wales, who lay lapped in silks and satins, unconscious of all this fuss, and not knowing that great lords and ladies were tending him and watching over him—and not caring, either. But there was no talk about the other baby, Tom Canty, lapped in his poor rags, except among the family of paupers whom he had just come to trouble with his presence.

Chapter II

TOM'S EARLY LIFE

LET US SKIP a number of years.

London was fifteen hundred years old, and was a great town—for that day. It had a hundred thousand inhabitants—some think double as many. The streets were very narrow, and crooked, and dirty, especially in the part where Tom Canty lived, which was not far from London Bridge. The houses were of wood, with the second story projecting over the first, and the third sticking its elbows out beyond the second. The higher the houses grew, the broader they grew. They were skeletons of strong criss-cross beams, with solid material between, coated with plaster. The beams were painted red or blue or black, according to the owner's taste, and this gave the houses a very picturesque look. The windows were small, glazed with little diamond-shaped panes, and they opened outward, on hinges, like doors.

The house which Tom's father lived in was up a foul little pocket called Offal Court, out of Pudding Lane. It was small, decayed, and rickety, but it was packed full of wretchedly poor families. Canty's tribe occupied a room on the third floor. The mother and father had a sort of bedstead in the corner; but Tom, his grandmother, and his two sisters, Bet and Nan, were not restricted—they had all the floor to themselves, and might sleep where they chose. There were the remains of a blanket or two, and some bundles of ancient and dirty straw, but these could not rightly be called beds, for they were not organized; they were kicked into a general pile, mornings, and selections made from the mass at night, for service.

Bet and Nan were fifteen years old—twins. They were good-hearted girls, unclean, clothed in rags, and profoundly ignorant. Their mother was like them. But the father and the grandmother were a couple of fiends. They got drunk whenever they could; then they fought each other or anybody else who came in the way; they cursed and swore always, drunk or sober; John Canty was a thief, and his mother a beggar. They made beggars of the children, but failed to make thieves of them. Among, but not of, the dreadful rabble that inhabited the house, was a good old priest whom the King had turned out of house and home with a pension of a few farthings, and he used to get the children aside and teach them right ways secretly. Father Andrew also taught Tom a little Latin, and how to read and write; and would have done the same with the girls, but they were afraid of the jeers of their friends, who could not have endured such a queer accomplishment in them.

All Offal Court was just such another hive as Canty's house. Drunkenness, riot and brawling were the order, there, every night and nearly all night long. Broken heads were as common as hunger in that place. Yet little Tom was not unhappy. He had a hard time of it, but did not know it. It was the sort of time

* "WITH ANY MISERABLE CRUST."

that all the Offal Court boys had, therefore he supposed it was the correct and comfortable thing. When he came home empty handed at night, he knew his father would curse him and thrash him first, and that when he was done the awful grandmother would do it all over again and improve on it; and that away in the night his starving mother would slip to him stealthily with any miserable scrap or crust she had been able to save for him by going hungry herself, notwithstanding she was often caught in that sort of treason and soundly beaten for it by her husband.

No, Tom's life went along well enough, especially in summer. He only begged just enough to save himself, for the laws against mendicancy were stringent, and the penalties heavy; so he put in a good deal of his time listening to good Father Andrew's charming old tales and legends about giants and fairies, dwarfs and genii, and enchanted castles, and gorgeous kings and princes. His head grew to be full of these wonderful things, and many a night as he lay in the dark on his scant and offensive straw, tired, hungry, and smarting from a thrashing, he unleashed his imagination and soon forgot his aches and pains in delicious picturings to himself of the charmed life of a petted prince in a regal palace. One desire came in time to haunt him day and night: it was to see a real prince, with his own eyes. He spoke of it once to some of his Offal Court comrades; but they jeered him and scoffed him so unmercifully that he was glad to keep his dream to himself after that.

He often read the priest's old books and got him to explain and enlarge upon them. His dreamings and readings worked certain changes in him, by and by. His dream-people were so fine that he grew to lament his shabby clothing and his dirt, and to wish to be clean and better clad. He went on playing in the mud just the same, and enjoying it, too; but instead of splashing around in the Thames solely for the fun of it, he began to find an added value in it because of the washings and cleansings it afforded.

Tom could always find something going on around the Maypole in Cheapside, and at the fairs; and now and then he and the rest of London had a chance to see a military parade when some famous unfortunate was carried prisoner to the Tower, by land or boat. One summer's day he saw poor Anne Askew and three men burned at the stake in Smithfield, and heard an ex-Bishop preach a sermon to them which did not interest him. Yes, Tom's life was varied and pleasant enough, on the whole.

By and by Tom's reading and dreaming about princely life wrought such a strong effect upon him that he began to *act* the prince, unconsciously. His speech and manners became curiously ceremonious and courtly, to the vast admiration and amusement of his intimates. But Tom's influence among these young people began to grow, now, day by day; and in time he came to be looked up to, by them, with a sort of wondering awe, as a superior being. He seemed to know so much! and he could do and say such marvellous things! and withal, he was so deep and wise! Tom's remarks, and Tom's performances, were reported by the boys to their elders; and these, also, presently began to discuss Tom Canty, and to regard him as a most gifted and extraordinary creature. Full grown people brought their perplexities to Tom for solution, and were often astonished at the wit and wisdom of his decisions. In fact he was become a hero to all who knew him except his own family—these, only, saw nothing in him.

Privately, after a while, Tom organized a royal court! He was the prince; his special comrades were guards, chamberlains, equerries, lords and ladies in waiting, and the royal family. Daily the mock prince was received with elaborate ceremonials borrowed by Tom from his romantic readings; daily the great affairs of the mimic kingdom were discussed in the royal council, and daily his mimic highness issued decrees to his imaginary armies, navies, and viceroyalties.

After which, he would go forth in his rags and beg a few farthings, eat his poor crust, take his customary cuffs and abuse, and then stretch himself upon his handful of foul straw, and resume his empty grandeurs in his dreams.

And still his desire to look just once upon a real prince, in the flesh, grew upon him, day by day, and week by week, until at last it absorbed all other desires, and became the one passion of his life.

One January day, on his usual begging tour, he tramped despondently up and down the region round about Mincing Lane and Little East Cheap, hour after hour, bare-footed and cold, looking in at cook-shop windows and longing for the dreadful pork-pies and other deadly inventions displayed there—for to him these were dainties fit for the angels; that is, judging by the smell, they were— for it had never been his good luck to own and eat one. There was a cold drizzle of rain; the atmosphere was murky; it was a melancholy day. At night Tom reached home so wet and tired and hungry that it was not possible for his father and grandmother to observe his forlorn condition and not be moved—after their fashion; wherefore they gave him a brisk cuffing at once and sent him to bed. For a long time his pain and hunger, and the swearing and fighting going on in the building, kept him awake; but at last his thoughts drifted away to far, romantic lands, and he fell asleep in the company of jewelled and gilded princelings who lived in vast palaces, and had servants salaaming before them or flying to execute their orders. And then, as usual, he dreamed that *he* was a princeling himself.

All night long the glories of his royal estate shone upon him; he moved among great lords and ladies, in a blaze of light, breathing perfumes, drinking in delicious music, and answering the reverent obeisances of the glittering throng as it parted to make way for him, with here a smile, and there a nod of his princely head.

And when he awoke in the morning and looked upon the wretchedness about him, his dream had had its usual effect—it had intensified the sordidness of his surroundings a thousand fold. Then came bitterness, and heart-break, and tears.

Chapter III

TOM'S MEETING WITH THE PRINCE

TOM GOT UP hungry, and sauntered hungry away, but with his thoughts busy with the shadowy splendors of his night's dreams. He wandered here and there in the city, hardly noticing where he was going, or what was happening around him. People jostled him, and some gave him rough speech; but it was all lost on the musing boy. By and by he found himself at Temple Bar, the farthest from home he had ever travelled in that direction. He stopped and considered a moment, then fell into his imaginings again, and passed on outside the walls of London. The Strand had ceased to be a country-road then, and regarded itself as a street, but by a strained construction; for, though there was a tolerably compact row of houses on one side of it, there were only some scattering great buildings on the other, these being palaces of rich nobles, with ample and beautiful grounds stretching to the river,—grounds that are now closely packed with grim acres of brick and stone.

Tom discovered Charing Village presently, and rested himself at the beautiful cross built there by a bereaved king of earlier days; then idled down a quiet, lovely road, past the great cardinal's stately palace, toward a far more mighty and majestic palace beyond,—Westminster. Tom stared in glad wonder at the vast pile of masonry, the wide-spreading wings, the frowning bastions and turrets, the huge stone gateway, with its gilded bars and its magnificent array of colossal granite lions, and the other signs and symbols of English royalty. Was the desire of his soul to be satisfied at last? Here, indeed, was a king's palace. Might he not hope to see a prince now,—a prince of flesh and blood, if Heaven were willing?

At each side of the gilded gate stood a living statue, that is to say, an erect and stately and motionless man-at-arms, clad from head to heel in shining steel armor. At a respectful distance were many country folk, and people from the city, waiting for any chance glimpse of royalty that might offer. Splendid carriages, with splendid people in them and splendid servants outside, were arriving and departing by several other noble gateways that pierced the royal enclosure.

Poor little Tom, in his rags, approached, and was moving slow and timidly past the sentinels, with a beating heart and a rising hope, when all at once he caught sight through the golden bars of a spectacle that almost made him shout for joy. Within was a comely boy, tanned and brown with sturdy out-door sports and exercises, whose clothing was all of lovely silks and satins, shining with jewels; at his hip a little jewelled sword and dagger; dainty buskins on his feet, with red heels; and on his head a jaunty crimson cap, with drooping plumes fastened with a great sparkling gem. Several gorgeous gentlemen stood near,— his servants, without a doubt. Oh! he was a prince—a prince, a living prince, a real prince—without the shadow of a question; and the prayer of the pauper-boy's heart was answered at last.

Tom's breath came quick and short with excitement, and his eyes grew big with wonder and delight. Every thing gave way in his mind instantly to one desire: that was to get close to the prince, and have a good, devouring look at him. Before he knew what he was about, he had his face against the gate-bars. The next instant one of the soldiers snatched him rudely away, and sent him spinning among the gaping crowd of country gawks and London idlers. The soldier said,—

"Mind thy manners, thou young beggar!"

The crowd jeered and laughed; but the young prince sprang to the gate with his face flushed, and his eyes flashing with indignation, and cried out,—

"How dar'st thou use a poor lad like that! How dar'st thou use the King my father's meanest subject so! Open the gates, and let him in!"

You should have seen that fickle crowd snatch off their hats then. You should have heard them cheer, and shout, "Long live the Prince of Wales!"

The soldiers presented arms with their halberds, opened the gates, and presented again as the little Prince of Poverty passed in, in his fluttering rags, to join hands with the Prince of Limitless Plenty.

Edward Tudor said,—

"Thou lookest tired and hungry: thou'st been treated ill. Come with me."

Half a dozen attendants sprang forward to—I don't know what; interfere, no doubt. But they were waved aside with a right royal gesture, and they stopped stock still where they were, like so many statues. Edward took Tom to a rich apartment in the palace, which he called his cabinet. By his command a repast was brought such as Tom had never encountered before except in books. The prince, with princely delicacy and breeding, sent away the servants, so that his humble guest might not be embarrassed by their critical presence; then he sat near by, and asked questions while Tom ate.

"What is thy name, lad?"

"Tom Canty, an' it please thee, sir."

"'Tis an odd one. Where dost live?"

"In the city, please thee, sir. Offal Court, out of Pudding Lane."

"Offal Court! Truly 'tis another odd one. Hast parents?"

"Parents have I, sir, and a grand-dam likewise that is but indifferently precious to me, God forgive me if it be offence to say it—also twin sisters, Nan and Bet."

"Then is thy grand-dam not over kind to thee, I take it."

"Neither to any other is she, so please your Worship. She hath a wicked heart, and worketh evil all her days."

"Doth she mistreat thee?"

"There be times that she stayeth her hand, being asleep or overcome with drink; but when she hath her judgment clear again, she maketh it up to me with goodly beatings."

A fierce look came into the little prince's eyes, and he cried out,—

"What! Beatings?"

"Oh, indeed, yes, please you, sir."

"*Beatings!*—and thou so frail and little. Hard ye: before the night come, she shall hie her to the Tower. The King my father"—

"In sooth, you forget, sir, her low degree. The Tower is for the great alone."

"True, indeed. I had not thought of that. I will consider of her punishment. Is thy father kind to thee?"

"Not more than Gammer Canty, sir."

"Fathers be alike, mayhap. Mine hath not a doll's temper. He smiteth with a heavy hand, yet spareth me: he spareth me not always with his tongue, though, sooth to say. How doth thy mother use thee?"

"She is good, sir, and giveth me neither sorrow nor pain of any sort. And Nan and Bet are like to her in this."

"How old be these?"

"Fifteen, an' it please you, sir."

"The Lady Elizabeth, my sister, is fourteen, and the Lady Jane Grey, my cousin, is of mine own age, and comely and gracious withal; but my sister the Lady Mary, with her gloomy mien and— Look you: do thy sisters forbid their servants to smile, lest the sin destroy their souls?"

"They? Oh, dost think, sir, that *they* have servants?"

The little prince contemplated the little pauper gravely a moment, then said,—

"And prithee, why not? Who helpeth them undress at night? who attireth them when they rise?"

"None, sir. Wouldst have them take off their garment, and sleep without,— like the beasts?"

"Their garment! Have they but one?"

"Ah, good your worship, what would they do with more? Truly they have not two bodies each."

"It is a quaint and marvellous thought! Thy pardon, I had not meant to laugh. But thy good Nan and thy Bet shall have raiment and lackeys enow, and that soon, too: my cofferer shall look to it. No, thank me not; 'tis nothing. Thou speakest well; thou hast an easy grace in it. Art learned?"

"I know not if I am or not, sir. The good priest that is called Father Andrew taught me, of his kindness, from his books."

"Know'st thou the Latin?"

"But scantly, sir, I doubt."

"Learn it, lad: 'tis hard only at first. The Greek is harder; but neither these nor any tongues else, I think, are hard to the Lady Elizabeth and my cousin. Thou shouldst hear those damsels at it! But tell me of thy Offal Court. Hast thou a pleasant life there?"

"In truth, yes, so please you, sir, save when one is hungry. There be Punch-and-Judy shows, and monkeys,—oh, such antic creatures! and so bravely dressed!—and there be plays wherein they that play do shout and fight till all are slain, and 'tis so fine to see, and costeth but a farthing—albeit 'tis main hard to get the farthing, please your worship."

"Tell me more."

"We lads of Offal Court do strive against each other with the cudgel, like to the fashion of the 'prentices, sometimes."

The prince's eyes flashed. Said he,—

"Marry, that would I not mislike. Tell me more."

"We strive in races, sir, to see who of us shall be fleetest."

"That would I like also. Speak on."

"In summer, sir, we wade and swim in the canals and in the river, and each doth duck his neighbor, and spatter him with water, and dive and shout and tumble and"—

"'Twould be worth my father's kingdom but to enjoy it once! Prithee go on."

"We dance and sing about the Maypole in Cheapside; we play in the sand, each covering his neighbor up; and times we make mud pastry—oh, the lovely mud, it hath not its like for delightfulness in all the world!—we do fairly wallow in the mud, sir, saving your worship's presence."

"Oh, prithee, say no more, 'tis glorious! If that I could but clothe me in raiment like to thine, and strip my feet, and revel in the mud once, just once, with none to rebuke me or forbid, meseemeth I could forego the crown!"

"And if that I could clothe me once, sweet sir, as thou art clad—just once"—

"Oho, wouldst like it? Then so shall it be. Doff thy rags, and don these splendors, lad! It is a brief happiness, but will be not less keen for that. We will have it while we may, and change again before any come to molest."

A few minutes later the little Prince of Wales was garlanded with Tom's fluttering odds and ends, and the little Prince of Pauperdom was tricked out in the gaudy plumage of royalty. The two went and stood side by side before a great mirror, and lo, a miracle: there did not seem to have been any change made! They stared at each other, then at the glass, then at each other again. At last the puzzled princeling said,—

"What dost thou make of this?"

"Ah, good your worship, require me not to answer. It is not meet that one of my degree should utter the thing."

"Then will *I* utter it. Thou hast the same hair, the same eyes, the same voice and manner, the same form and stature, the same face and countenance, that I bear. Fared we forth naked, there is none could say which was you, and which the Prince of Wales. And, now that I am clothed as thou wert clothed, it seemeth I should be able the more nearly to feel as thou didst when the brute soldier— Hark ye, is not this a bruise upon your hand?"

"Yes; but it is a slight thing, and your worship knoweth that the poor man-at-arms"—

"Peace! It was a shameful thing and a cruel!" cried the little prince, stamping his bare foot. "If the King— Stir not a step till I come again! It is a command!"

In a moment he had snatched up and put away an article of national importance that lay upon a table, and was out at the door and flying through the palace grounds in his bannered rags, with a hot face and glowing eyes. As soon as he reached the great gate, he seized the bars, and tried to shake them, shouting,—

"Open! Unbar the gates!"

The soldier that had maltreated Tom obeyed promptly; and as the prince burst through the portal, half-smothered with royal wrath, the soldier fetched him a sounding box on the ear that sent him whirling to the roadway, and said,—

"Take that, thou beggar's spawn, for what thou got'st me from his Highness!"

The crowd roared with laughter. The prince picked himself out of the mud, and made fiercely at the sentry, shouting,—

"I am the Prince of Wales, my person is sacred; and thou shalt hang for laying thy hand upon me!"

The soldier brought his halberd to a present-arms and said mockingly,—

"I salute your gracious Highness." Then angrily, "Be off, thou crazy rubbish!"

Here the jeering crowd closed around the poor little prince, and hustled him far down the road, hooting him, and shouting, "Way for his royal Highness! way for the Prince of Wales!"

Chapter IV

THE PRINCE'S TROUBLES BEGIN

AFTER HOURS OF persistent pursuit and persecution, the little prince was at last deserted by the rabble and left to himself. As long as he had been able to rage against the mob, and threaten it royally, and royally utter commands that were good stuff to laugh at, he was very entertaining; but when weariness finally forced him to be silent, he was no longer of use to his tormentors, and they sought amusement elsewhere. He looked about him, now, but could not recognize the locality. He was within the city of London—that was all he knew. He moved on, aimlessly, and in a little while the houses thinned, and the passers-by were infrequent. He bathed his bleeding feet in the brook which flowed then where Farringdon street now is; rested a few moments, then passed on, and presently came upon a great space with only a few scattered houses in it, and a prodigious church. He recognized this church. Scaffoldings were about, everywhere, and swarms of workmen; for it was undergoing elaborate repairs. The prince took heart at once—he felt that his troubles were at an end, now. He said to himself, "It is the ancient Grey Friars' church, which the king my father hath taken from the monks and given for a home forever for poor and forsaken children, and new-named it Christ's Church. Right gladly will they serve the son of him who hath done so generously by them—and the more that that son is himself as poor and as forlorn as any that be sheltered here this day, or ever shall be."

He was soon in the midst of a crowd of boys who were running, jumping, playing at ball and leap-frog and otherwise disporting themselves, and right noisily, too. They were all dressed alike, and in the fashion which in that day prevailed among serving-men and 'prentices—that is to say, each had on the crown of his head a flat black cap about the size of a saucer, which was not useful as a covering, it being of such scanty dimensions, neither was it ornamental; from beneath it the hair fell, unparted, to the middle of the forehead, and was cropped straight around; a clerical band at the neck; a blue gown that fitted closely and hung as low as the knees or lower; full sleeves; a broad red belt; bright yellow stockings, gartered above the knees; low shoes with large metal buckles. It was a sufficiently ugly costume.

The boys stopped their play and flocked about the prince, who said with native dignity—

"Good lads, say to your master that Edward Prince of Wales desireth speech with him."

A great shout went up, at this, and one rude fellow said—

"Marry, art thou his grace's messenger, beggar?"

The prince's face flushed with anger, and his ready hand flew to his hip, but there was nothing there. There was a storm of laughter, and one boy said—

"Didst mark that? He fancied he had a sword—belike he is the prince himself."

This sally brought more laughter. Poor Edward drew himself up proudly and said—

"I am the prince; and it ill beseemeth you that feed upon the king my father's bounty to use me so."

This was vastly enjoyed, as the laughter testified. The youth who had first spoken, shouted to his comrades—

"SET UPON BY DOGS."

"Ho, swine, slaves, pensioners of his grace's princely father, where be your manners? Down on your marrow bones, all of ye, and do reverence to his kingly port and royal rags!"

With boisterous mirth they dropped upon their knees in a body and did mock homage to their prey. The prince spurned the nearest boy with his foot, and said fiercely—

"Take thou that, till the morrow come and I build thee a gibbet!"

Ah, but this was not a joke—this was going beyond fun. The laughter ceased on the instant, and fury took its place. A dozen shouted—

"Hale him forth! To the horse-pond, to the horse-pond! Where be the dogs? Ho, there, Lion! ho, Fangs!"

Then followed such a thing as England had never seen before—the sacred person of the heir to the throne rudely buffeted by plebeian hands, and set upon and torn by dogs.

As night drew to a close that day, the prince found himself far down in the close-built portion of the city. His body was bruised, his hands were bleeding, and his rags were all besmirched with mud. He wandered on and on, and grew more and more bewildered, and so tired and faint he could hardly drag one foot after the other. He had ceased to ask questions of any one, since they brought him only insult instead of information. He kept muttering to himself, "Offal court—that is the name; if I can but find it before my strength is wholly spent and I drop, then am I saved—for his people will take me to the palace and prove that I am none of theirs, but the true prince, and I shall have mine own again." And now and then his mind reverted to his treatment by those rude Christ's Hospital boys, and he said, "When I am king, they shall not have bread and shelter only, but also teachings out of books; for a full belly is little worth where the mind is starved, and the heart. I will keep this diligently in my remembrance, that this day's lesson be not lost upon me, and my people suffer thereby; for learning softeneth the heart and breedeth gentleness and charity."

The lights began to twinkle, it came on to rain, the wind rose, and a raw and gusty night set in. The houseless prince, the homeless heir to the throne of England, still moved on, drifting deeper into the maze of squalid alleys where the swarming hives of poverty and misery were massed together.

Suddenly a great drunken ruffian collared him and said—

"Out to this time of night again, and hast not brought a farthing home, I warrant me! If it be so, an' I do not break all the bones in thy lean body, then am I not John Canty, but some other."

The prince twisted himself loose, unconsciously brushed his profaned shoulder, and eagerly said—

"O, art *his* father, truly? Sweet heaven grant it be so—then wilt thou fetch him away and restore me!"

"*His* father? I know not what thou mean'st; I but know I am *thy* father, as thou shalt soon have cause to"—

"O, jest not, palter not, delay not!—I am worn, I am wounded, I can bear no more. Take me to the king my father, and he will make thee rich beyond thy wildest dreams. Believe me, man, believe me!—I speak no lie, but only the truth!—put forth thy hand and save me! I am indeed the Prince of Wales!"

The man stared down, stupefied, upon the lad, then shook his head and muttered—

"Gone stark mad as any Tom o' Bedlam!"—then collared him once more, and said with a coarse laugh and an oath, "But mad or no mad, I and thy Gammer Canty will soon find where the soft places in thy bones lie, or I'm no true man!"

With this he dragged the frantic and struggling prince away, and disappeared up a front court followed by a delighted and noisy swarm of human vermin.

Chapter V

TOM AS A PATRICIAN

TOM CANTY, LEFT alone in the prince's cabinet, made good use of his opportunity. He turned himself this way and that before the great mirror, admiring his finery; then walked away, imitating the prince's high-bred carriage, and still observing results in the glass. Next he drew the beautiful sword, and bowed, kissing the blade, and laying it across his breast, as he had seen a noble knight do, by way of salute to the lieutenant of the Tower, five or six weeks before, when delivering the great lords of Norfolk and Surrey into his hands for captivity. Tom played with the jewelled dagger that hung upon his thigh; he examined the costly and exquisite ornaments of the room; he tried each of the sumptuous chairs, and thought how proud he would be if the Offal Court herd could only peep in and see him in his grandeur. He wondered if they would believe the marvellous tale he should tell when he got home, or if they would shake their heads, and say his overtaxed imagination had at last upset his reason.

At the end of half an hour it suddenly occurred to him that the prince was gone a long time; then right away he began to feel lonely; very soon he fell to listening and longing, and ceased to toy with the pretty things about him; he grew uneasy, then restless, then distressed. Suppose some one should come, and catch him in the prince's clothes, and the prince not there to explain. Might they not hang him at once, and inquire into his case afterward? He had heard that the great were prompt about small matters. His fears rose higher and higher; and trembling he softly opened the door to the antechamber, resolved to fly and seek the prince, and, through him, protection and release. Six gorgeous gentlemen-servants and two young pages of high degree, clothed like butterflies, sprung to their feet, and bowed low before him. He stepped quickly back, and shut the door. He said,—

"Oh, they mock at me! They will go and tell. Oh! why came I here to cast away my life?"

He walked up and down the floor, filled with nameless fears, listening, starting at every trifling sound. Presently the door swung open, and a silken page said,—

"The Lady Jane Grey."

The door closed, and a sweet young girl, richly clad, bounded toward him. But she stopped suddenly, and said in a distressed voice,—

"Oh, what aileth thee, my lord?"

Tom's breath was nearly failing him; but he made shift to stammer out,—

"Ah, be merciful, thou! In sooth I am no lord, but only poor Tom Canty of Offal Court in the city. Prithee let me see the prince, and he will of his grace

"NEXT HE DREW THE SWORD."

restore to me my rags, and let me hence unhurt. Oh, be thou merciful, and save me!"

By this time the boy was on his knees, and supplicating with his eyes and uplifted hands as well as with his tongue. The young girl seemed horror-stricken. She cried out—

"O my lord, on thy knees?—and to *me!*"

Then she fled away in fright; and Tom, smitten with despair, sank down, murmuring—

"There is no help, there is no hope. Now will they come and take me."

Whilst he lay there benumbed with terror, dreadful tidings were speeding through the palace. The whisper, for it was whispered always, flew from menial to menial, from lord to lady, down all the long corridors, from story to story, from saloon to saloon, "The prince hath gone mad, the prince hath gone mad!" Soon every saloon, every marble hall, had its groups of glittering lords and ladies, and other groups of dazzling lesser folk, talking earnestly together in whispers, and every face had in it dismay. Presently a splendid official came marching by these groups, making solemn proclamation,—

"IN THE NAME OF THE KING.

Let none list to this false and foolish matter, upon pain of death, nor discuss the same, nor carry it abroad. In the name of the King!"

The whisperings ceased as suddenly as if the whisperers had been stricken dumb.

Soon there was a general buzz along the corridors, of "The prince! See, the prince comes!"

Poor Tom came slowly walking past the low-bowing groups, trying to bow in return, and meekly gazing upon his strange surroundings with bewildered and pathetic eyes. Great nobles walked upon each side of him, making him lean upon them, and so steady his steps. Behind him followed the court-physicians and some servants.

Presently Tom found himself in a noble apartment of the palace, and heard the door close behind him. Around him stood those who had come with him.

Before him, at a little distance, reclined a very large and very fat man, with a wide, pulpy face, and a stern expression. His large head was very gray; and his whiskers, which he wore only around his face, like a frame, were gray also. His clothing was of rich stuff, but old, and slightly frayed in places. One of his swollen legs had a pillow under it, and was wrapped in bandages. There was silence now; and there was no head there but was bent in reverence, except this man's. This stern-countenanced invalid was the dread Henry VIII. He said,— and his face grew gentle as he began to speak,—

"How now, my lord Edward, my prince? Hast been minded to cozen me, the good King, thy father, who loveth thee, and kindly useth thee, with a sorry jest?"

Poor Tom was listening, as well as his dazed faculties would let him, to the beginning of this speech; but when the words "me the good King" fell upon his ear, his face blanched, and he dropped as instantly upon his knees as if a shot had brought him there. Lifting up his hands, he exclaimed,—

"Thou the *King?* Then am I undone indeed!"

This speech seemed to stun the King. His eyes wandered from face to face aimlessly, then rested, bewildered, upon the boy before him. Then he said in a tone of deep disappointment,—

"Alack, I had believed the rumor disproportioned to the truth; but I fear me 'tis not so." He breathed a heavy sigh, and said in a gentle voice, "Come to thy father, child: thou art not well."

Tom was assisted to his feet, and approached the Majesty of England, humble and trembling. The King took the frightened face between his hands, and gazed earnestly and lovingly into it awhile, as if seeking some grateful sign of returning reason there, then pressed the curly head against his breast, and patted it tenderly. Presently he said,—

"Dost not know thy father, child? Break not mine old heart; say thou know'st me. Thou *dost* know me, dost thou not?"

"Yea: thou art my dread lord the King, whom God preserve!"

"True, true—that is well—be comforted, tremble not so; there is none here who would hurt thee; there is none here but loves thee. Thou art better now; thy ill dream passeth—is't not so? And thou knowest thyself now also—is't not so? Thou wilt not miscall thyself again, as they say thou didst a little while agone?"

"I pray thee of thy grace believe me, I did but speak the truth, most dread lord; for I am the meanest among thy subjects, being a pauper born, and 'tis by a sore mischance and accident I am here, albeit I was therein nothing blameful. I am but young to die, and thou canst save me with one little word. Oh speak it, sir!"

"Die? Talk not so, sweet prince—peace, peace, to thy troubled heart—thou shalt not die!"

Tom dropped upon his knees with a glad cry,—

"God requite thy mercy, oh my King, and save thee long to bless thy land!" Then springing up, he turned a joyful face toward the two lords in waiting, and exclaimed, "Thou hear'st it! I am not to die: the King hath said it!" There was no movement, save that all bowed with grave respect; but no one spoke. He hesitated, a little confused, then turned timidly toward the King, saying, "I may go now?"

"Go? Surely, if thou desirest. But why not tarry yet a little? Whither wouldst go?"

Tom dropped his eyes, and answered humbly,—

"Peradventure I mistook; but I did think me free, and so was I moved to seek again the kennel where I was born and bred to misery, yet which harboreth my mother and my sisters, and so is home to me; whereas these pomps and splendors whereunto I am not used—oh, please you, sir, to let me go!"

The King was silent and thoughtful a while, and his face betrayed a growing distress and uneasiness. Presently he said, with something of hope in his voice,—

"Perchance he is but mad upon this one strain, and hath his wits unmarred as toucheth other matter. God send it may be so! We will make trial."

Then he asked Tom a question in Latin, and Tom answered him lamely in the same tongue. The King was delighted, and showed it. The lords and doctors manifested their gratification also. The King said,—

"'Twas not according to his schooling and ability, but sheweth that his mind is but diseased, not stricken fatally. How say you, sir?"

The physician addressed bowed low, and replied,—

"It jumpeth with mine own conviction, sire, that thou hast divined aright."

The King looked pleased with this encouragement, coming as it did from so excellent authority, and continued with good heart,—

"Now mark ye all: we will try him further."

He put a question to Tom in French. Tom stook silent a moment, embarrassed by having so many eyes centred upon him, then said diffidently,—

"I have no knowledge of this tongue, so please your majesty."

The King fell back upon his couch. The attendants flew to his assistance; but he put them aside, and said,—

"Trouble me not—it is nothing but a scurvy faintness. Raise me! there, 'tis sufficient. Come hither, child; there, rest thy poor troubled head upon thy father's heart, and be at peace. Thou'lt soon be well; 'tis but a passing fantasy. Fear thou not; thou'lt soon be well." Then he turned toward the company: his gentle manner changed, and baleful lightnings began to play from his eyes. He said,—

"List ye all! This my son is mad; but it is not permanent. Over-study hath done this, and somewhat too much of confinement. Away with his books and teachers! see ye to it. Pleasure him with sports, beguile him in wholesome ways, so that his health come again." He raised himself higher still, and went on with energy, "He is mad; but he is my son, and England's heir; and, mad or sane, still shall he reign! And hear ye further, and proclaim it: whoso speaketh of this his distemper worketh against the peace and order of these realms, and shall to the gallows! . . . Give me to drink—I burn: This sorrow sappeth my strength. . . . There, take away the cup. . . . Support me. There, that is well. Mad, is he? Were he a thousand times mad, yet is he Prince of Wales, and I the King will confirm it. This very morrow shall he be installed in his princely dignity in due and ancient form. Take instant order for it, my lord Hertford."

One of the nobles knelt at the royal couch, and said,—

"The King's majesty knoweth that the Hereditary Great Marshal of England lieth attainted in the Tower. It were not meet that one attainted"—

"Peace! Insult not mine ears with his hated name. Is this man to live forever? Am I to be balked of my will? Is the prince to tarry uninstalled, because, forsooth, the realm lacketh an earl marshal free of treasonable taint to invest him with his honors? No, by the splendor of God! Warn my parliament to bring me Norfolk's doom before the sun rise again, else shall they answer for it grievously!''

Lord Hertford said,—

"The King's will is law;" and, rising, returned to his former place.

Gradually the wrath faded out of the old King's face, and he said,—

"Kiss me, my prince. There . . . what fearest thou? Am I not thy loving father?"

"Thou art good to me that am unworthy, O mighty and gracious lord: that in truth I know. But—but—it grieveth me to think of him that is to die, and"—

"Ah, 'tis like thee, 'tis like thee! I know thy heart is still the same, even though thy mind hath suffered hurt, for thou wert ever of a gentle spirit. But this duke standeth between thee and thine honors: I will have another in his stead that shall bring no taint to his great office. Comfort thee, my prince: trouble not thy poor head with this matter."

"But is it not I that speed him hence, my liege? How long might he not live, but for me?"

"Take no thought of him, my prince: he is not worthy. Kiss me once again, and go to thy trifles and amusements; for my malady distresseth me. I am aweary, and would rest. God with thine uncle Hertford and thy people, and come again when my body is refreshed."

Tom, heavy-hearted, was conducted from the presence, for this last sentence was a death-blow to the hope he had cherished that now he would be set free. Once more he heard the buzz of low voices exclaiming, "The prince, the prince comes!"

His spirits sank lower and lower as he moved between the glittering files of bowing courtiers; for he recognized that he was indeed a captive now, and might remain forever shut up in this gilded cage, a forlorn and friendless prince, except God in his mercy take pity on him and set him free.

And, turn where he would, he seemed to see floating in the air the severed head and the remembered face of the great Duke of Norfolk, the eyes fixed on him reproachfully.

His old dreams had been so pleasant; but this reality was so dreary!

Chapter VI

TOM RECEIVES INSTRUCTIONS

TOM WAS CONDUCTED to the principal apartment of a noble suite, and made to sit down—a thing which he was loath to do, since there were elderly men and men of high degree about him. He begged them to be seated, also, but they only bowed their thanks or murmured them, and remained standing. He would have insisted, but his "uncle" the earl of Hertford whispered in his ear—

"Prithee, insist not, my lord; it is not meet that they sit in thy presence."

The lord St. John was announced, and after making obeisance to Tom, he said—

"I come upon the king's errand, concerning a matter which requireth privacy.

Will it please your royal highness to dismiss all that attend you here, save my lord the earl of Hertford?''

Observing that Tom did not seem to know how to proceed, Hertford whispered him to make a sign with his hand and not trouble himself to speak unless he chose. When the waiting gentlemen had retired, lord St. John said—

"His majesty commandeth, that for due and weighty reasons of state, the prince's grace shall hide his infirmity in all ways that be within his power, till it be passed and he be as he was before. To wit, that he shall deny to none that he is the true prince, and heir to England's greatness; that he shall uphold his princely dignity, and shall receive, without word or sign of protest, that reverence and observance which unto it do appertain of right and ancient usage; that he shall cease to speak to any of that lowly birth and life his malady hath conjured out of the unwholesome imaginings of o'erwrought fancy; that he shall strive with diligence to bring unto his memory again those faces which he was wont to know—and where he faileth he shall hold his peace, neither betraying by semblance of surprise, or other sign, that he hath forgot; that upon occasions of state, whensoever any matter shall perplex him as to the thing he should do or the utterance he should make, he shall show nought of unrest to the curious that look on, but take advice in that matter of the lord Hertford, or my humble self, which are commanded of the king to be upon this service and close at call, till this commandment be dissolved. Thus saith the king's majesty, who sendeth greeting to your royal highness and prayeth that God will of His mercy quickly heal you and have you now and ever in his holy keeping."

The lord St. John made reverence and stood aside. Tom replied, resignedly—

"The king hath said it. None may palter with the king's command, or fit it to his ease, where it doth chafe, with deft evasions. The king shall be obeyed."

Lord Hertford said—

"Touching the king's majesty's ordainment concerning books and such like serious matters, it may peradventure please your highness to ease your time with lightsome entertainment, lest you go wearied to the banquet and suffer harm thereby."

Tom's face showed enquiring surprise; and a blush followed when he saw lord St. John's eyes bent sorrowfully upon him. His lordship said—

"Thy memory still wrongeth thee, and thou hast shown surprise—but suffer it not to trouble thee, for 'tis a matter that will not bide, but depart with thy mending malady. My lord of Hertford speaketh of the city's banquet which the king's majesty did promise two months flown, your highness should attend. Thou recallest it now?"

"It grieves me to confess it had indeed escaped me," said Tom, in a hesitating voice; and blushed again.

At that moment the lady Elizabeth and the lady Jane Grey were announced. The two lords exchanged significant glances, and Hertford stepped quickly toward the door. As the young girls passed him, he said in a low voice—

"I pray ye, ladies, seem not to observe his humors, nor show surprise when his memory doth lapse—it will grieve you to note how it doth stick at every trifle."

Meanwhile lord St. John was saying in Tom's ear—

"Please you sir, keep diligently in mind his majesty's desire. Remember all thou canst—*Seem* to remember all else. Let them not perceive that thou art much changed from thy wont, for thou knowest how tenderly thy old play-fellows bear thee in their hearts and how 'twould grieve them. Art willing, sir, that I remain?—and thine uncle?''

Tom signified assent with a gesture and a murmured word, for he was already learning, and in his simple heart was resolved to acquit himself as best he might, according to the king's command.

In spite of every precaution, the conversation among the young people became a little embarrassing, at times. More than once, in truth, Tom was near to breaking down and confessing himself unequal to his tremendous part; but the tact of the princess Elizabeth saved him, or a word from one or the other of the vigilant lords, thrown in apparently by chance, had the same happy effect. Once the little lady Jane turned to Tom and dismayed him with this question—

"Hast paid thy duty to the queen's majesty to-day, my lord?''

Tom hesitated, looked distressed, and was about to stammer out something at hazard, when lord St. John took the word and answered for him with the easy grace of a courtier accustomed to encounter delicate difficulties and to be ready for them—

"He hath indeed, madam, and she did greatly hearten him, as touching his majesty's condition; is it not so, your highness?''

Tom mumbled something that stood for assent, but felt that he was getting upon dangerous ground. Somewhat later it was mentioned that Tom was to study no more at present, whereupon her little ladyship exclaimed—

"'Tis a pity, 'tis such a pity! Thou wert proceeding bravely. But bide thy time in patience; it will not be for long. Thou'lt yet be graced with learning like thy father, and make thy tongue master of as many languages as his, good my prince.''

"My father!'' cried Tom, off his guard for the moment. "I trow he cannot speak his own so that any but the swine that wallow in the styes may tell his meaning; and as for learning of any sort soever''—

He looked up and encountered a solemn warning in my lord St. John's eyes.

He stopped, blushed, then continued low and sadly: "Ah, my malady persecuteth me again, and my mind wandereth. I meant the king's grace no irreverence.''

"We know it, sir,'' said the princess Elizabeth, taking her "brother's'' hand between her two palms, respectfully but caressingly; "trouble not thyself as to that. The fault is none of thine, but thy distemper's.''

"Thou'rt a gentle comforter, sweet lady,'' said Tom, gratefully, "and my heart moveth me to thank thee for't, an' I may be so bold.''

Once the giddy little lady Jane fired a simple Greek phrase at Tom. The princess Elizabeth's quick eye saw by the serene blankness of the target's front that the shaft was overshot; so she tranquilly delivered a return volley of sounding Greek on Tom's behalf, and then straightway changed the talk to other matters.

Time wore on pleasantly, and likewise smoothly, on the whole. Snags and sandbars grew less and less frequent, and Tom grew more and more at his ease, seeing that all were so lovingly bent upon helping him and overlooking his mistakes. When it came out that the little ladies were to accompany him to the Lord Mayor's banquet in the evening, his heart gave a bound of relief and delight, for he felt that he should not be friendless, now, among that multitude of strangers, whereas, an hour earlier, the idea of their going with him would have been an insupportable terror to him.

Tom's guardian angels, the two lords, had had less comfort in the interview than the other parties to it. They felt much as if they were piloting a great ship through a dangerous channel; they were on the alert constantly, and found their office no child's play. Wherefore, at last, when the ladies' visit was drawing to a close and the lord Guilford Dudley was announced, they not only felt that their charge had been sufficiently taxed for the present, but also that they themselves were not in the best condition to take their ship back and make their anxious voyage all over again. So they respectfully advised Tom to excuse himself, which he was very glad to do, although a slight shade of disappointment might have been observed upon my lady Jane's face when she heard the splendid stripling denied admittance.

There was a pause, now, a sort of waiting silence which Tom could not understand. He glanced at lord Hertford, who gave him a sign—but he failed to understand that, also. The ready Elizabeth came to the rescue with her usual easy grace. She made reverence and said,—

"Have we leave of the prince's grace my brother to go?"

Tom said—

"Indeed your ladyships can have whatsoever of me they will, for the asking; yet would I rather give them any other thing that in my poor power lieth, than leave to take the light and blessing of their presence hence. Give ye good den, and God be with ye!" Then he smiled inwardly at the thought, "'tis not for nought I have dwelt but among princes in my reading, and taught my tongue some slight trick of their broidered and gracious speech withal!"

When the illustrious maidens were gone, Tom turned wearily to his keepers and said—

"May it please your lordships to grant me leave to go into some corner and rest me?"

Lord Hertford said—

"So please your highness, it is for you to command, it is for us to obey. That thou shouldst rest, is indeed a needful thing, since thou must journey to the city presently."

He touched a bell, and a page appeared, who was ordered to desire the presence of Sir William Herbert. This gentleman came straightway, and conducted Tom to an inner apartment. Tom's first movement, there, was to reach for a cup of water; but a silk-and-velvet servitor seized it, dropped upon one knee, and offered it to him on a golden salver.

Next, the tired captive sat down and was going to take off his buskins, timidly asking leave with his eye, but another silk-and-velvet discomforter went down upon his knees and took the office from him. He made two or three further efforts to help himself, but being promptly forestalled each time, he finally gave up, with a sigh of resignation and a murmured "Beshrew me but I marvel they do not require to breathe for me also!" Slippered, and wrapped in a sumptuous robe, he laid himself down at last to rest, but not to sleep, for his head was too full of thoughts and the room too full of people. He could not dismiss the former, so they staid; he did not know enough to dismiss the latter, so they staid also, to his vast regret,—and theirs.

Tom's departure had left his two noble guardians alone. They mused a while, with much head-shaking and walking the floor, then lord St. John said—

"Plainly, what dost thou think?"

"Plainly, then, this. The king is near his end, my nephew is mad, mad will mount the throne, and mad remain. God protect England, since she will need it!''

''Verily it promiseth so, indeed. But . . . have you no misgivings as to . . . as to'' . . .

The speaker hesitated, and finally stopped. He evidently felt that he was upon delicate ground. Lord Hertford stopped before him, looked into his face with a clear, frank eye, and said—

''Speak on—there is none to hear but me. Misgivings as to what?''

''I am full loath to word the thing that is in my mind, and thou so near to him in blood, my lord. But craving pardon if I do offend, seemeth it not strange that madness could so change his port and manner!—not but that his port and speech are princely still, but that they *differ* in one unweighty trifle or another, from what his custom was aforetime. Seemeth it not strange that madness should filch from his memory his father's very lineaments; the customs and observances that are his due from such as be about him; and, leaving him his Latin, strip him of his Greek and French? My lord, be not offended, but ease my mind of its disquiet and receive my grateful thanks. It haunteth me, his saying he was not the prince, and so''—

''Peace, my lord, thou utterest treason! Hast forgot the king's command? Remember I am party to thy crime, if I but listen.''

St. John paled, and hastened to say—

''I was in fault, I do confess it. Betray me not, grant me this grace out of thy courtesy, and I will neither think nor speak of this thing more. Deal not hardly with me, sir, else am I ruined.''

''I am content, my lord. So thou offend not again, here or in the ears of others, it shall be as though thou hadst not spoken. But thou needst not have misgivings. He is my sister's son; are not his voice, his face, his form, familiar to me from his cradle? Madness can do all the odd conflicting things thou seest in him, and more. Dost not recall how that the old Baron Marley, being mad, forgot the favor of his own countenance that he had known for sixty years, and held it was another's; nay, even claimed he was the son of Mary Magdalene, and that his head was made of Spanish glass; and sooth to say, he suffered none to touch it, lest by mischance some heedless hand might shiver it. Give thy misgivings easement, good my lord. This is the very prince, I know him well— and soon will be thy king; it may advantage thee to bear this in mind and more dwell upon it than the other.''

After some further talk, in which the lord St. John covered up his mistake as well as he could by repeated protests that his faith was thoroughly grounded, now, and could not be assailed by doubts again, the lord Hertford relieved his fellow keeper, and sat down to keep watch and ward alone. He was soon deep in meditation. And evidently the longer he thought, the more he was bothered. By and by he began to pace the floor and mutter.

''Tush, he *must* be the prince! Will any he in all the land maintain there can be two, not of one blood and birth, so marvellously twinned? And even were it so, 'twere yet a stranger miracle that chance should cast the one into the other's place. Nay, 'tis folly, folly, folly!''

Presently he said—

''Now were he impostor and called himself prince, look you *that* would be natural; that would be reasonable. But lived ever an impostor yet, who, being called prince by the king, prince by the court, prince by all, *denied* his dignity and pleaded against his exaltation? *No!* By the soul of St. Swithin, no! This is the true prince, gone mad!''

Chapter VII

TOM'S FIRST ROYAL DINNER

SOMEWHAT AFTER ONE in the afternoon, Tom resignedly underwent the ordeal of being dressed for dinner. He found himself as finely clothed as before, but every thing different, every thing changed, from his ruff to his stockings. He was presently conducted with much state to a spacious and ornate apartment, where a table was already set for one. Its furniture was all of massy gold, and beautified with designs which well-nigh made it priceless, since they were the work of Benvenuto. The room was half filled with noble servitors. A chaplain said grace, and Tom was about to fall to, for hunger had long been constitutional with him, but was interrupted by my lord the Earl of Berkeley, who fastened a napkin about his neck; for the great post of Diaperers to the Princes of Wales was hereditary in this nobleman's family. Tom's cup-bearer was present, and forestalled all his attempts to help himself to wine. The Taster to his highness the Prince of Wales was there also, prepared to taste any suspicious dish upon requirement, and run the risk of being poisoned. He was only an ornamental appendage at this time, and was seldom called upon to exercise his function; but there had been times, not many generations past, when the office of taster had its perils, and was not a grandeur to be desired. Why they did not use a dog or a plumber seems strange; but all the ways of royalty are strange. My lord d'Arcy, First Groom of the Chamber, was there, to do goodness knows what; but there he was—let that suffice. The Lord Chief Butler was there, and stood behind Tom's chair, overseeing the solemnities, under command of the Lord Great Steward and the Lord Head Cook, who stood near. Tom had three hundred and eighty-four servants beside these; but they were not all in that room, of course, nor the quarter of them; neither was Tom aware yet that they existed.

All those that were present had been well drilled within the hour to remember that the prince was temporarily out of his head, and to be careful to show no surprise at his vagaries. These "vagaries" were soon on exhibition before them; but they only moved their compassion and their sorrow, not their mirth. It was a heavy affliction to them to see the beloved prince so stricken.

Poor Tom ate with his fingers mainly; but no one smiled at it, or even seemed to observe it. He inspected his napkin curiously, and with deep interest, for it was of a very dainty and beautiful fabric, then said with simplicity,—

"Prithee take it away, lest in mine unheedfulness it be soiled."

The Hereditary Diaperer took it away with reverent manner, and without word or protest of any sort.

Tom examined the turnips and the lettuce with interest, and asked what they were, and if they were to be eaten; for it was only recently that men had begun to raise these things in England in place of importing them as luxuries from Holland. His question was answered with grave respect, and no surprise manifested. When he had finished his dessert, he filled his pockets with nuts; but nobody appeared to be aware of it, or disturbed by it. But the next moment he was himself disturbed by it, and showed discomposure; for this was the only service he had been permitted to do with his own hands during the meal, and he did not doubt that ne had done a most improper and unprincely thing. At that moment the muscles of his nose began to twitch, and the end of that organ to lift and wrinkle. This continued, and Tom began to evince a growing distress. He looked appealingly, first at one and then another of the lords about him, and tears came into his eyes. They sprang forward with dismay in their faces, and begged to know his trouble. Tom said with genuine anguish,—

"I crave your indulgence: my nose itcheth cruelly. What is the custom and usage in this emergence? Prithee speed, for 'tis but a little time that I can bear it."

None smiled; but all were sore perplexed, and looked one to the other in deep tribulation for counsel. But behold, here was a dead wall, and nothing in English history to tell how to get over it. The Master of Ceremonies was not present: there was no one who felt safe to venture upon this uncharted sea, or risk the attempt to solve this solemn problem. Alas! there was no Hereditary Scratcher. Meantime the tears had overflowed their banks, and begun to trickle down Tom's cheeks. His twitching nose was pleading more urgently than ever for relief. At last nature broke down the barriers of etiquette: Tom lifted up an inward prayer for pardon if he was doing wrong, and brought relief to the burdened hearts of his court by scratching his nose himself.

His meal being ended, a lord came and held before him a broad, shallow, golden dish with fragrant rose-water in it, to cleanse his mouth and fingers with; and my lord the Hereditary Diaperer stood by with a napkin for his use. Tom gazed at the dish a puzzled moment or two, then raised it to his lips, and gravely took a draught. Then he returned it to the waiting lord, and said,—

"Nay, it likes me not, my lord: it hath a pretty flavor, but it wanteth strength."

This new eccentricity of the prince's ruined mind made all the hearts about him ache; but the sad sight moved none to merriment.

Tom's next unconscious blunder was to get up and leave the table just when the chaplain had taken his stand behind his chair and with uplifted hands, and

"TOM ATE WITH HIS FINGERS."

closed, uplifted eyes, was in the act of beginning the blessing. Still nobody seemed to perceive that the prince had done a thing unusual.

By his own request, our small friend was now conducted to his private cabinet, and left there alone to his own devices. Hanging upon hooks in the oaken wainscoting were the several pieces of a suit of shining steel armor, covered all over with beautiful designs exquisitely inlaid in gold. This martial panoply belonged to the true prince,—a recent present from Madam Parr the Queen. Tom put on the greaves, the gauntlets, the plumed helmet, and such other pieces as he could don without assistance, and for a while was minded to call for help and complete the matter, but bethought him of the nuts he had brought away from dinner, and the joy it would be to eat them with no crowd to eye him, and no Grand Hereditaries to pester him with undesired services; so he restored the pretty things to their several places, and soon was cracking nuts, and feeling almost naturally happy for the first time since God for his sins had made him a prince. When the nuts were all gone, he stumbled upon some inviting books in a closet, among them one about the etiquette of the English court. This was a prize. He lay down upon a sumptuous divan, and proceeded to instruct himself with honest zeal. Let us leave him there for the present.

Chapter VIII

THE QUESTION OF THE SEAL

ABOUT FIVE O'CLOCK Henry VIII. awoke out of an unrefreshing nap, and muttered to himself, "Troublous dreams, troublous dreams! Mine end is now at hand: so say these warnings, and my failing pulses do confirm it." Presently a wicked light flamed up in his eye, and he muttered, "Yet will not I die till *he* go before."

His attendants perceiving that he was awake, one of them asked his pleasure concerning the Lord Chancellor, who was waiting without.

"Admit him, admit him!" exclaimed the King eagerly.

The Lord Chancellor entered, and knelt by the King's couch, saying,—

"I have given order, and, according to the King's command, the peers of the realm, in their robes, do now stand at the bar of the House, where, having confirmed the Duke of Norfolk's doom, they humbly wait his majesty's further pleasure in the matter."

The King's face lit up with a fierce joy. Said he,—

"Lift me up! In mine own person will I go before my Parliament, and with mine own hand will I seal the warrant that rids me of"—

His voice failed; an ashen pallor swept the flush from his cheeks; and the attendants eased him back upon his pillows, and hurriedly assisted him with restoratives. Presently he said sorrowfully,—

"Alack, how have I longed for this sweet hour! and lo, too late it cometh, and I am robbed of this so coveted chance. But speed ye, speed ye! let others do this happy office sith 'tis denied to me. I put my great seal in commission: choose thou the lords that shall compose it, and get ye to your work. Speed ye, man! Before the sun shall rise and set again, bring me his head that I may see it."

"According to the King's command, so shall it be. Will 't please your majesty to order that the Seal be now restored to me, so that I may forth upon the business?"

"The Seal! Who keepeth the Seal but thou?"

"Please your majesty, you did take it from me two days since, saying it should no more do its office till your own royal hand should use it upon the Duke of Norfolk's warrant."

"Why, so in sooth I did: I do remember it. . . . What did I with it? . . . I am very feeble. . . . So oft these days doth my memory play the traitor with me. . . . 'Tis strange, strange"—

The King dropped into inarticulate mumblings, shaking his gray head weakly from time to time, and gropingly trying to recollect what he had done with the Seal. At last my lord Hertford ventured to kneel and offer information,—

"Sire, if that I may be so bold, here be several that do remember with me how that you gave the Great Seal into the hands of his highness the Prince of Wales to keep against the day that"—

"True, most true!" interrupted the King. "Fetch it! Go: time flieth!"

Lord Hertford flew to Tom, but returned to the King before very long, troubled and empty-handed. He delivered himself to this effect,—

"It grieveth me, my lord the King, to bear so heavy and unwelcome tidings; but it is the will of God that the prince's affliction abideth still, and he cannot recall to mind that he received the Seal. So came I quickly to report, thinking it were waste of precious time, and little worth withal, that any should attempt to search the long array of chambers and saloons that belong unto his royal high"—

A groan from the King interrupted my lord at this point. After a little while his majesty said, with a deep sadness in his tone,—

"Trouble him no more, poor child. The hand of God lieth heavy upon him, and my heart goeth out in loving compassion for him, and sorrow that I may not bear his burden on mine own old trouble-weighted shoulders, and so bring him peace."

He closed his eyes, fell to mumbling, and presently was silent. After a time he opened his eyes again, and gazed vacantly around until his glance rested upon the kneeling Lord Chancellor. Instantly his face flushed with wrath,—

"What, thou here yet! By the glory of God, an' thou gettest not about that traitor's business, thy mitre shall have holiday the morrow for lack of a head to grace withal!"

The trembling Chancellor answered,—

"Good your majesty, I cry you mercy! I but waited for the Seal."

"Man, hast lost thy wits? The small Seal which aforetime I was wont to take with me abroad lieth in my treasury. And, since the Great Seal hath flown away, shall not it suffice? Hast lost thy wits? Begone! And hark ye,—come no more till thou do bring his head."

The poor Chancellor was not long in removing himself from this dangerous vicinity; nor did the commission waste time in giving the royal assent to the work of the slavish Parliament, and appointing the morrow for the beheading of the premier peer of England, the luckless Duke of Norfolk.

Chapter IX

THE RIVER PAGEANT

AT NINE IN the evening the whole vast river-front of the palace was blazing with light. The river itself, as far as the eye could reach citywards, was so thickly covered with watermen's boats and with pleasure-barges, all fringed with colored lanterns, and gently agitated by the waves, that it resembled a glowing and limitless garden of flowers stirred to soft motion by summer winds. The grand terrace of stone steps leading down to the water, spacious enough to mass the army of a German principality upon, was a picture to see, with its ranks of royal halberdiers in polished armor, and its troops of brilliantly costumed servitors flitting up and down, and to and fro, in the hurry of preparation.

Presently a command was given, and immediately all living creatures vanished from the steps. Now the air was heavy with the hush of suspense and expectancy. As far as one's vision could carry, he might see the myriads of people in the boats rise up, and shade their eyes from the glare of lanterns and torches, and gaze toward the palace.

A file of forty or fifty state barges drew up to the steps. They were richly gilt, and their lofty prows and sterns were elaborately carved. Some of them were decorated with banners and streamers; some with cloth-of-gold and arras embroidered with coats-of-arms; others with silken flags that had numberless little silver bells fastened to them, which shook out tiny showers of joyous music whenever the breezes fluttered them; others of yet higher pretensions, since they belonged to nobles in the prince's immediate service, had their sides picturesquely fenced with shields gorgeously emblazoned with armorial bearings. Each state barge was towed by a tender. Besides the rowers, these tenders carried each a number of men-at-arms in glossy helmet and breastplate, and a company of musicians.

The advance-guard of the expected procession now appeared in the great gateway, a troop of halberdiers. "They were dressed in striped hose of black and tawny, velvet caps graced at the sides with silver roses, and doublets of murrey and blue cloth, embroidered on the front and back with the three feathers, the prince's blazon, woven in gold. Their halberd staves were covered with crimson velvet, fastened with gilt nails, and ornamented with gold tassels. Filing off on the right and left, they formed two long lines, extending from the gateway of the palace to the water's edge. A thick, rayed cloth or carpet was then unfolded, and laid down between them by attendants in the gold-and-crimson liveries of the prince. This done, a flourish of trumpets resounded from within. A lively prelude arose from the musicians on the water; and two ushers with white wands marched with a slow and stately pace from the portal. They were followed by an officer bearing the civic mace, after whom came another carrying the city's sword; then several sergeants of the city guard, in their full accoutrements, and with badges on their sleeves; then the garter king-at-arms, in his tabard; then several knights of the bath, each with a white lace on his sleeve; then their esquires; then the judges, in their robes of scarlet and coifs; then the lord high chancellor of England, in a robe of scarlet, open before, and purfled with minever;

then a deputation of aldermen, in their scarlet cloaks; and then the heads of the different civic companies, in their robes of state. Now came twelve French gentlemen, in splendid habiliments, consisting of pourpoints of white damask barred with gold, short mantles of crimson velvet lined with violet taffeta, and carnation-colored *hauts-de-chausses,* and took their way down the steps. They were of the suite of the French ambassador, and were followed by twelve cavaliers of the suite of the Spanish ambassador, clothed in black velvet, unrelieved by any ornament. Following these came several great English nobles with their attendants."

There was a flourish of trumpets within; and the prince's uncle, the future great Duke of Somerset, emerged from the gateway, arrayed in a "doublet of black cloth-of-gold, and a cloak of crimson satin flowered with gold, and ribanded with nets of silver." He turned, doffed his plumed cap, bent his body in a low reverence, and began to step backward, bowing at each step. A prolonged trumpet-blast followed, and a proclamation, "Way for the high and mighty, the Lord Edward, Prince of Wales!" High aloft on the palace walls a long line of red tongues of flame leaped forth with a thunder-crash: the massed world on the river burst into a mighty roar of welcome; and Tom Canty, the cause and hero of it all, stepped into view, and slightly bowed his princely head.

He was "magnificently habited in a doublet of white satin, with a front-piece of purple cloth-of-tissue, powdered with diamonds, and edged with ermine. Over this he wore a mantle of white cloth-of-gold, pounced with the triple-feather crest, lined with blue satin, set with pearls and precious stones, and fastened with a clasp of brilliants. About his neck hung the order of the Garter, and several princely foreign orders;" and wherever light fell upon him jewels responded with a blinding flash. O Tom Canty, born in a hovel, bred in the gutters of London, familiar with rags and dirt and misery, what a spectacle is this!

Chapter X

THE PRINCE IN THE TOILS

WE LEFT JOHN CANTY dragging the rightful prince into Offal Court, with a noisy and delighted mob at his heels. There was but one person in it who offered a pleading word for the captive, and he was not heeded: he was hardly even heard, so great was the turmoil. The prince continued to struggle for freedom, and to rage against the treatment he was suffering, until John Canty lost what little patience was left in him, and raised his oaken cudgel in a sudden fury over the prince's head. The single pleader for the lad sprang to stop the man's arm, and the blow descended upon his own wrist. Canty roared out,—

"Thou'lt meddle, wilt thou? Then have thy reward."

His cudgel crashed down upon the meddler's head: there was a groan, a dim form sank to the ground among the feet of the crowd, and the next moment it lay there in the dark alone. The mob pressed on, their enjoyment nothing disturbed by this episode.

Presently the prince found himself in John Canty's abode, with the door closed against the outsiders. By the vague light of a tallow candle which was thrust into a bottle, he made out the main features of the loathsome den, and also the occupants of it. Two frowsy girls and a middle-aged woman cowered against the wall in one corner, with the aspect of animals habituated to harsh usage, and expecting and dreading it now. From another corner stole a withered hag with streaming gray hair and malignant eyes. John Canty said to this one,—

"Tarry! There's fine mummeries here. Mar them not till thou'st enjoyed them; then let thy hand be heavy as thou wilt. Stand forth, lad. Now say thy foolery again, an' thou'st not forgot it. Name thy name. Who art thou?"

The insulted blood mounted to the little prince's cheek once more, and he lifted a steady and indignant gaze to the man's face, and said,—

"'Tis but ill-breeding in such as thou to command me to speak. I tell thee now, as I told thee before, I am Edward, Prince of Wales, and none other."

The stunning surprise of this reply nailed the hag's feet to the floor where she stood, and almost took her breath. She stared at the prince in stupid amazement, which so amused her ruffianly son, that he burst into a roar of laughter. But the effect upon Tom Canty's mother and sisters was different. Their dread of bodily injury gave way at once to distress of a different sort. They ran forward with woe and dismay in their faces, exclaiming,—

"O poor Tom, poor lad!"

The mother fell on her knees before the prince, put her hands upon his shoulders, and gazed yearningly into his face through her rising tears. Then she said,—

"O my poor boy! thy foolish reading hath wrought its woful work at last, and ta'en thy wit away. Ah! why didst thou cleave to it when I so warned thee 'gainst it? Thou'st broke thy mother's heart."

The prince looked into her face, and said gently,—

"Thy son is well, and hath not lost his wits, good dame. Comfort thee: let me to the palace where he is, and straightway will the King my father restore him to thee."

"The King thy father! O my child! unsay these words that be freighted with death for thee, and ruin for all that be near to thee. Shake off this grewsome dream. Call back thy poor wandering memory. Look upon me. Am not I thy mother that bore thee, and loveth thee?"

The prince shook his head, and reluctantly said,—

"God knoweth I am loath to grieve thy heart; but truly have I never looked upon thy face before."

The woman sank back to a sitting posture on the floor, and, covering her eyes with her hands, gave way to heartbroken sobs and wailings.

"Let the show go on!" shouted Canty. "What, Nan! what, Bet! Mannerless wenches! will ye stand in the prince's presence? Upon your knees, ye pauper scum, and do him reverence!"

He followed this with another horse-laugh. The girls began to plead timidly for their brother; and Nan said,—

"An' thou wilt but let him to bed, father, rest and sleep will heal his madness: prithee, do."

"Do, father," said Bet: "he is more worn than is his wont. To-morrow will he be himself again, and will beg with diligence, and come not empty home again."

This remark sobered the father's joviality, and brought his mind to business. He turned angrily upon the prince, and said,—

"The morrow must we pay two pennies to him that owns this hole; two pennies, mark ye,—all this money for a half-year's rent, else out of this we go. Show what thou'st gathered with thy lazy begging."

The prince said,—

"Offend me not with thy sordid matters. I tell thee again I am the King's son."

A sounding blow upon the prince's shoulder from Canty's broad palm sent him staggering into goodwife Canty's arms, who clasped him to her breast, and sheltered him from a pelting rain of cuffs and slaps by interposing her own person.

The frightened girls retreated to their corner; but the grandmother stepped eagerly forward to assist her son. The prince sprang away from Mrs. Canty, exclaiming,—

"Thou shalt not suffer for me, madam. Let these swine do their will upon me alone."

This speech infuriated the swine to such a degree that they set about their work without waste of time. Between them they belabored the boy right soundly, and then gave the girls and their mother a beating for showing sympathy for the victim.

"Now," said Canty, "to bed, all of ye. The entertainment has tired me."

The light was put out, and the family retired. As soon as the snorings of the head of the house and his mother showed that they were asleep, the young girls crept to where the prince lay, and covered him tenderly from the cold with straw and rags; and their mother crept to him also, and stroked his hair, and cried over him, whispering broken words of comfort and compassion in his ear the while. She had saved a morsel for him to eat, also; but the boy's pains had swept away all appetite,—at least for black and tasteless crusts. He was touched by her brave and costly defence of him, and by her commiseration; and he thanked her in very noble and princely words, and begged her to go to her sleep and try to forget her sorrows. And he added that the King his father would not let her loyal kindness and devotion go unrewarded. This return to his "madness" broke her heart anew, and she strained him to her breast again and again and then went back, drowned in tears, to her bed.

As she lay thinking and mourning, the suggestion began to creep into her mind that there was an undefinable something about this boy that was lacking in Tom Canty, mad or sane. She could not describe it, she could not tell just what it was, and yet her sharp mother-instinct seemed to detect it and perceive it. What if the boy were really not her son, after all? O, absurd! She almost smiled at the idea, spite of her griefs and troubles. No matter, she found that it was an idea that would not "down," but persisted in haunting her. It pursued her, it harassed her, it clung to her, and refused to be put away or ignored. At last she perceived that there was not going to be any peace for her until she should devise a test that should prove, clearly and without question, whether this lad was her son or not, and so banish these wearing and worrying doubts. Ah yes, this was plainly the right way out of the difficulty; therefore she set her wits to work at once to contrive that test. But it was an easier thing to propose than to accomplish. She turned over in her mind one promising test after another, but was obliged to relinquish them all—none of them were absolutely sure, absolutely perfect; and an imperfect one could not satisfy her. Evidently she was racking her head in vain—it seemed manifest that she must give the matter up.

While this depressing thought was passing through her mind, her ear caught the
regular breathing of the boy, and she knew he had fallen asleep. And while she
listened, the measured breathing was broken by a soft, startled cry, such as one
utters in a troubled dream. This chance occurrence furnished her instantly with
a plan worth all her labored tests combined. She at once set herself feverishly,
but noiselessly, to work, to relight her candle, muttering to herself, "Had I but
seen him *then,* I should have known! Since that day, when he was little, that
the powder burst in his face, he hath never been startled of a sudden out of his
dreams or out of his thinkings, but he hath cast his hand before his eyes, even
as he did that day; and not as others would do it, with the palm inward, but
always with the palm turned outward—I have seen it a hundred times, and it
hath never varied nor ever failed. Yes, I shall soon know, now!"

By this time she had crept to the slumbering boy's side, with the candle,
shaded, in her hand. She bent heedfully and warily over him, scarcely breathing,
in her suppressed excitement, and suddenly flashed the light in his face and
struck the floor by his ear with her knuckles. The sleeper's eyes sprung wide
open, and he cast a startled stare about him—but he made no special movement
with his hands.

The poor woman was smitten almost helpless with surprise and grief; but she
contrived to hide her emotions, and to soothe the boy to sleep again; then she
crept apart and communed miserably with herself upon the disastrous result of
her experiment. She tried to believe that her Tom's madness had banished this
habitual gesture of his; but she could not do it. "No," she said, "his *hands* are
not mad, they could not unlearn so old a habit in so brief a time. O, this is a
heavy day for me!"

Still, hope was as stubborn, now, as doubt had been before; she could not
bring herself to accept the verdict of the test; she must try the thing again—the
failure must have been only an accident; so she startled the boy out of his sleep
a second and a third time, at intervals—with the same result which had marked
the first test—then she dragged herself to bed, and fell sorrowfully asleep, saying,
"But I cannot give him up—O, no, I cannot, I cannot—he *must* be my boy!"

The poor mother's interruptions having ceased, and the prince's pains having
gradually lost their power to disturb him, utter weariness at last sealed his eyes
in a profound and restful sleep. Hour after hour slipped away, and still he slept
like the dead. Thus four or five hours passed. Then his stupor began to lighten.
Presently while half asleep and half awake, he murmured—

"Sir William!"

After a moment—

"Ho, Sir William Herbert! Hie thee hither, and list to the strangest dream
that ever . . . Sir William! Dost hear? Man, I did think me changed to a pauper,
and . . . Ho there! Guards! Sir William! What! is there no groom of the chamber
in waiting? Alack it shall go hard with"—

"What aileth thee?" asked a whisper near him. "Who art thou calling?"

"Sir William Herbert. Who art thou?"

"I? Who should I be, but thy sister Nan? O, Tom, I had forgot! Thou'rt mad
yet—poor lad thou'rt mad yet, would I had never woke to know it again! But
prithee master thy tongue, lest we be all beaten till we die!"

The startled prince sprang partly up, but a sharp reminder from his stiffened
bruises brought him to himself, and he sunk back among his foul straw with a
moan and the ejaculation—

"Alas, it was no dream, then!"

In a moment all the heavy sorrow and misery which sleep had banished were upon him again, and he realized that he was no longer a petted prince in a palace, with the adoring eyes of a nation upon him, but a pauper, an outcast, clothed in rags, prisoner in a den fit only for beasts, and consorting with beggars and thieves.

In the midst of his grief he began to be conscious of hilarious noises and shoutings, apparently but a block or two away. The next moment there were several sharp raps at the door; John Canty ceased from snoring and said—

"Who knocketh? What wilt thou?"

A voice answered—

"Know'st thou who it was thou laid thy cudgel on?"

"No. Neither know I, nor care."

"Belike thou'lt change thy note eftsoons. An' thou would save thy neck, nothing but flight may stead thee. The man is this moment delivering up the ghost. 'Tis the priest, Father Andrew!"

"God-a-mercy!" exclaimed Canty. He roused his family, and hoarsely commanded, "Up with ye all and fly—or bide where ye are and perish!"

Scarcely five minutes later the Canty household were in the street and flying for their lives. John Canty held the prince by the wrist, and hurried him along the dark way, giving him this caution in a low voice—

"Mind thy tongue, thou mad fool, and speak not our name. I will choose me a new name, speedily, to throw the law's dogs off the scent. Mind thy tongue, I tell thee!"

He growled these words to the rest of the family—

"If it so chance that we be separated, let each make for London bridge; whoso findeth himself as far as the last linen-draper's shop on the bridge, let him tarry there till the others be come, then will we flee into Southwark together."

At this moment the party burst suddenly out of darkness into light; and not only into light, but into the midst of a multitude of singing, dancing, and shouting people, massed together on the river frontage. There was a line of bonfires stretching as far as one could see, up and down the Thames; London bridge was illuminated; Southwark bridge likewise; the entire river was aglow with the flash and sheen of colored lights; and constant explosions of fireworks filled the skies with an intricate commingling of shooting splendors and a thick rain of dazzling sparks that almost turned night into day; everywhere were crowds of revellers; all London seemed to be at large.

John Canty delivered himself of a furious curse and commanded a retreat; but it was too late. He and his tribe were swallowed up in that swarming hive of humanity, and hopelessly separated from each other in an instant. We are not considering that the prince was one of his tribe; Canty still kept his grip upon him. The prince's heart was beating high with hopes of escape, now. A burly waterman, considerably exalted with liquor, found himself rudely shoved, by Canty, in his efforts to plough through the crowd; he laid his great hand on Canty's shoulder and said—

"Nay, whither so fast, friend? Dost canker thy soul with sordid business when all that be leal men and true make holiday?"

"Mine affairs are mine own, they concern thee not," answered Canty, roughly; "take away thy hand and let me pass."

"Sith that is thy humor, thou'lt *not* pass, till thou'st drunk to the Prince of Wales, I tell thee that," said the waterman, barring the way resolutely.

"Give me the cup, then, and make speed, make speed!"

Other revellers were interested by this time. They cried out—

"The loving-cup, the loving-cup! make the sour knave drink the loving-cup, else will we feed him to the fishes."

So a huge loving-cup was brought; the waterman, grasping it by one of its handles, and with his other hand bearing up the end of an imaginary napkin, presented it in due and ancient form to Canty, who had to grasp the opposite handle with one of his hands and take off the lid with the other, according to ancient custom. This left the prince hand-free for a second, of course. He wasted no time, but dived among the forest of legs about him and disappeared. In another moment he could not have been harder to find, under that tossing sea of life, if its billows had been the Atlantic's and he a lost sixpence.

He very soon realized this fact, and straightway busied himself about his own affairs without further thought of John Canty. He quickly realized another thing, too. To wit, that a spurious Prince of Wales was being feasted by the city in his stead. He easily concluded that the pauper lad, Tom Canty, had deliberately taken advantage of his stupendous opportunity and become a usurper.

Therefore there was but one course to pursue—find his way to the Guildhall, make himself known, and denounce the impostor. He also made up his mind that Tom should be allowed a reasonable time for spiritual preparation, and then be hanged, drawn and quartered, according to the law and usage of the day, in cases of high treason.

"HE WASTED NO TIME."

Chapter XI

AT GUILDHALL

THE ROYAL BARGE, attended by its gorgeous fleet, took its stately way down the Thames through the wilderness of illuminated boats. The air was laden with music; the river banks were beruffled with joy-flames; the distant city lay in a soft luminous glow from its countless invisible bonfires; above it rose many a slender spire into the sky, incrusted with sparkling lights, wherefore in their remoteness they seemed like jewelled lances thrust aloft; as the fleet swept along, it was greeted from the banks with a continuous hoarse roar of cheers and the ceaseless flash and boom of artillery.

To Tom Canty, half buried in his silken cushions, these sounds and this spectacle were a wonder unspeakably sublime and astonishing. To his little friends at his side, the princess Elizabeth and the lady Jane Grey, they were nothing.

Arrived at the Dowgate, the fleet was towed up the limpid Walbrook (whose channel has now been for two centuries buried out of sight under acres of buildings,) to Bucklersbury, past houses and under bridges populous with merrymakers and brilliantly lighted, and at last came to a halt in a basin where now is Barge Yard, in the centre of the ancient city of London. Tom disembarked, and he and his gallant procession crossed Cheapside and made a short march through the Old Jewry and Basinghall street to the Guildhall.

Tom and his little ladies were received with due ceremony by the Lord Mayor and the Fathers of the City, in their gold chains and scarlet robes of state, and conducted to a rich canopy of state at the head of the great hall, preceded by heralds making proclamation, and by the Mace and the City Sword. The lords and ladies who were to attend upon Tom and his two small friends took their places behind their chairs.

At a lower table the court grandees and other guests of noble degree were seated, with the magnates of the city; the commoners took places at a multitude of tables on the main floor of the hall. From their lofty vantage-ground, the giants Gog and Magog, the ancient guardians of the city, contemplated the spectacle below them with eyes grown familiar to it in forgotten generations. There was a bugle-blast and a proclamation, and a fat butler appeared in a high perch in the leftward wall, followed by his servitors bearing with impressive solemnity a royal Baron of Beef, smoking hot and ready for the knife.

After grace, Tom (being instructed) rose—and the whole house with him—and drank from a portly golden loving-cup with the princess Elizabeth; from her it passed to the lady Jane, and then traversed the general assemblage. So the banquet began.

By midnight the revelry was at its height. Now came one of those picturesque spectacles so admired in that old day. A description of it is still extant in the quaint wording of a chronicler who witnessed it:

"Space being made, presently entered a baron and an earl appareled after the Turkish fashion in long robes of bawdkin powdered with gold; hats on their heads of crimson velvet, with great rolls of gold, girded with two swords, called scimitars, hanging by great bawdricks of gold. Next came yet another baron and another earl, in two long gowns of yellow satin, traversed with white satin, and in every bend of white was a bend of crimson satin, after the fashion of Russia, with furred hats of gray on their heads; either of them having an hatchet in their hands, and boots with *pykes''* (points a foot long), "turned up. And after them came a knight, then the Lord High Admiral, and with him five nobles, in doublets of crimson velvet, voyded low on the back and before to the cannell-bone, laced on the breasts with chains of silver; and, over that, short cloaks of crimson satin, and on their heads hats after the dancers' fashion, with pheasants' feathers in them. These were appareled after the fashion of Prussia. The torch-bearers, which were about a hundred, were appareled in crimson satin and green, like Moors, their faces black. Next came in a *mommarye*. Then the minstrels, which were disguised, danced; and the lords and ladies did wildly dance also, that it was a pleasure to behold."

And while Tom, in his high seat, was gazing upon this "wild" dancing, lost in admiration of the dazzling commingling of kaleidoscopic colors which the whirling turmoil of gaudy figures below him presented, the ragged but real little prince of Wales was proclaiming his rights and his wrongs, denouncing the impostor, and clamoring for admission at the gates of Guildhall! The crowd enjoyed this episode prodigiously, and pressed forward and craned their necks to see the small rioter. Presently they began to taunt him and mock at him, purposely to goad him into a higher and still more entertaining fury. Tears of mortification sprung to his eyes, but he stood his ground and defied the mob right royally. Other taunts followed, added mockings stung him, and he exclaimed—

"I tell ye again, you pack of unmannerly curs, I am the prince of Wales! And all forlorn and friendless as I be, with none to give me word of grace or help me in my need, yet will not I be driven from my ground, but will maintain it!"

"Though thou be prince or no prince, 'tis all one, thou be'st a gallant lad, and not friendless neither! Here stand I by thy side to prove it; and mind I tell thee thou might'st have a worser friend than Miles Hendon and yet not tire thy legs with seeking. Rest thy small jaw, my child, I talk the language of these base kennel-rats like to a very native."

The speaker was a sort of Don Cæsar de Bazan in dress, aspect, and bearing. He was tall, trim-built, muscular. His doublet and trunks were of rich material, but faded and threadbare, and their gold-lace adornments were sadly tarnished; his ruff was rumpled and damaged; the plume in his slouched hat was broken and had a bedraggled and disreputable look; at his side he wore a long rapier in a rusty iron sheath; his swaggering carriage marked him at once as a ruffler of the camp. The speech of this fantastic figure was received with an explosion of jeers and laughter. Some cried, "'Tis another prince in disguise!" "'Ware thy tongue, friend, belike he is dangerous!" "Marry, he looketh it—mark his eye!" "Pluck the lad from him—to the horse-pond wi' the cub!"

Instantly a hand was laid upon the prince, under the impulse of this happy thought; as instantly the stranger's long sword was out and the meddler went to the earth under a sounding thump with the flat of it. The next moment a score of voices shouted "Kill the dog! kill him! kill him!" and the mob closed in on the warrior, who backed himself against a wall and began to lay about him with his long weapon like a madman. His victims sprawled this way and that, but the mob-tide poured over their prostrate forms and dashed itself against the champion with undiminished fury. His moments seemed numbered, his destruction certain, when suddenly a trumpet-blast sounded, a voice shouted, "Way for the king's messenger!" and a troop of horsemen came charging down upon the mob, who fled out of harm's reach as fast as their legs could carry them. The bold stranger caught up the prince in his arms, and was soon far away from danger and the multitude.

Return we within the Guildhall. Suddenly, high above the jubilant roar and thunder of the revel, broke the clear peal of a bugle-note. There was instant silence,—a deep hush; then a single voice rose—that of the messenger from the palace—and began to pipe forth a proclamation, the whole multitude standing, listening. The closing words, solemnly pronounced, were—

"The king is dead!"

The great assemblage bent their heads upon their breasts with one accord; remained so, in profound silence, a few moments; then all sunk upon their knees in a body, stretched out their hands toward Tom, and a mighty shout burst forth that seemed to shake the building—

"Long live the king!"

Poor Tom's dazed eyes wandered abroad over this stupefying spectacle, and finally rested dreamily upon the kneeling princesses beside him, a moment, then upon the earl of Hertford. A sudden purpose dawned in his face. He said, in a low tone, at lord Hertford's ear—

"Answer me truly, on thy faith and honor! Uttered I here a command, the which none but a king might hold privilege and prerogative to utter, would such commandment be obeyed, and none rise up to say me nay?"

"None, my liege, in all these realms. In thy person bides the majesty of England. Thou art the king—thy word is law."

Tom responded, in a strong, earnest voice, and with great animation—

"Then shall the king's law be law of mercy, from this day, and never more be law of blood! Up from thy knees and away! To the Tower and say the king decrees the duke of Norfolk shall not die!"

The words were caught up and carried eagerly from lip to lip far and wide over the hall, and as Hertford hurried from the presence, another prodigious shout burst forth—

"The reign of blood is ended! Long live Edward, king of England!"

"BEGAN TO LAY ABOUT HIM."

Chapter XII

THE PRINCE AND HIS DELIVERER

As SOON AS Miles Hendon and the little prince were clear of the mob, they struck down through back lanes and alleys toward the river. Their way was unobstructed until they approached London Bridge; then they ploughed into the multitude again, Hendon keeping a fast grip upon the prince's—no, the king's—wrist. The tremendous news was already abroad, and the boy learned it from a thousand voices at once—"The king is dead!" The tidings struck a chill to the heart of the poor little waif, and sent a shudder through his frame. He realized the greatness of his loss, and was filled with a bitter grief; for the grim tyrant who had been such a terror to others had always been gentle with him. The tears sprung to his eyes and blurred all objects. For an instant he felt himself the most forlorn, outcast, and forsaken of God's creatures—then another cry shook the night with its far-reaching thunders: "Long live King Edward the Sixth!" and this made his eyes kindle, and thrilled him with pride to his fingers' ends. "Ah," he thought, "how grand and strange it seems—I AM KING!"

Our friends threaded their way slowly through the throngs upon the Bridge. This structure, which had stood for six hundred years, and had been a noisy and populous thoroughfare all that time, was a curious affair, for a closely packed rank of stores and shops, with family quarters overhead, stretched along both sides of it, from one bank of the river to the other. The Bridge was a sort of town to itself; it had its inn, its beer houses, its bakeries, its haberdasheries, its food markets, its manufacturing industries, and even its church. It looked upon the two neighbors which it linked together—London and Southwark—as being well enough, as suburbs, but not otherwise particularly important. It was a close corporation, so to speak; it was a narrow town, of a single street a fifth of a mile long, its population was but a village population, and everybody in it knew all his fellow townsmen intimately, and had known their fathers and mothers before them—and all their little family affairs into the bargain. It had its aristocracy, of course—its fine old families of butchers, and bakers, and what-not, who had occupied the same old premises for five or six hundred years, and knew the great history of the Bridge from beginning to end, and all its strange legends; and who always talked bridgy talk, and thought bridgy thoughts, and lied in a long, level, direct, substantial bridgy way. It was just the sort of population to be narrow and ignorant and self-conceited. Children were born on the Bridge, were reared there, grew to old age and finally died without ever having set a foot upon any part of the world but London Bridge alone. Such people would naturally imagine that the mighty and interminable procession which moved through its street night and day, with its confused roar of shouts and cries, its neighings and bellowings and bleatings and its muffled thunder-tramp, was the one great thing in this world, and themselves somehow the proprietors of it. And so they were in effect—at least they could exhibit it from their windows, and did—for a consideration—whenever a returning king or hero gave it a fleeting splendor, for there was no place like it for affording a long, straight, uninterrupted view of marching columns.

Men born and reared upon the Bridge found life unendurably dull and inane, elsewhere. History tells of one of these who left the Bridge at the age of seventy-one and retired to the country. But he could only fret and toss in his bed; he could not go to sleep, the deep stillness was so painful, so awful, so oppressive. When he was worn out with it, at last, he fled back to his old home, a lean and haggard spectre, and fell peacefully to rest and pleasant dreams under the lulling music of the lashing waters and the boom and crash and thunder of London Bridge.

In the times of which we are writing, the Bridge furnished "object lessons" in English history, for its children—namely, the livid and decaying heads of renowned men impaled upon iron spikes atop of its gateways. But we digress.

Hendon's lodgings were in the little inn on the Bridge. As he neared the door with his small friend, a rough voice said—

"So, thou'rt come at last! Thou'lt not escape again, I warrant thee; and if pounding thy bones to a pudding can teach thee somewhat, thou'lt not keep us waiting another time, mayhap"—and John Canty put out his hand to seize the boy.

Miles Hendon stepped in the way, and said—

"Not too fast, friend. Thou art needlessly rough, methinks. What is the lad to thee?"

"If it be any business of thine to make and meddle in others' affairs, he is my son."

"'Tis a lie!" cried the little king, hotly.

"Boldly said, and I believe thee, whether thy small headpiece be sound or cracked, my boy. But whether this scurvy ruffian be thy father or no, 'tis all one, he shall not have thee to beat thee and abuse, according to his threat, so thou prefer to bide with me."

"I do, I do—I know him not, I loathe him, and will die before I will go with him."

"Then 'tis settled, and there is nought more to say."

"We will see, as to that!" exclaimed John Canty, striding past Hendon to get at the boy; "by force shall he"—

"If thou do but touch him, thou animated offal, I will spit thee like a goose!" said Hendon, barring the way and laying his hand upon his sword hilt. Canty drew back. "Now mark ye," continued Hendon, "I took this lad under my protection when a mob of such as thou would have mishandled him, mayhap killed him; dost imagine I will desert him now to a worser fate?—for whether thou art his father or no,—and sooth to say, I think it is a lie—a decent swift death were better for such a lad than life in such brute hands as thine. So go thy ways, and set quick about it, for I like not much bandying of words, being not over-patient in my nature."

John Canty moved off, muttering threats and curses, and was swallowed from sight in the crowd. Hendon ascended three flights of stairs to his room, with his charge, after ordering a meal to be sent thither. It was a poor apartment, with a shabby bed and some odds and ends of old furniture in it, and was vaguely lighted by a couple of sickly candles. The little king dragged himself to the bed and lay down upon it, almost exhausted with hunger and fatigue. He had been on his feet a good part of a day and a night, for it was now two or three o'clock in the morning, and had eaten nothing meantime. He murmured drowsily—

"Prithee call me when the table is spread," and sunk into a deep sleep immediately.

A smile twinkled in Hendon's eye, and he said to himself—

"By the mass, the little beggar takes to one's quarters and usurps one's bed with as natural and easy a grace as if he owned them—with never a by-your-leave or so-please-it-you, or anything of the sort. In his diseased ravings he called himself the prince of Wales, and bravely doth he keep up the character. Poor little friendless rat, doubtless his mind has been disordered with ill usage. Well, I will be his friend; I have saved him, and it draweth me strongly to him; already I love the bold-tongued little rascal. How soldier-like he faced the smutty rabble and flung back his high defiance! And what a comely, sweet and gentle face he hath, now that sleep hath conjured away its troubles and its griefs. I will teach him, I will cure his malady; yea, I will be his elder brother, and care for him and watch over him; and whoso would shame him or do him hurt, may order his shroud, for though I be burnt for it he shall need it!"

He bent over the boy and contemplated him with kind and pitying interest, tapping the young cheek tenderly and smoothing back the tangled curls with his great brown hand. A slight shiver passed over the boy's form. Hendon muttered—

"See, now, how like a man it was to let him lie here uncovered and fill his body with deadly rheums. Now what shall I do? 'twill wake him to take him up and put him within the bed, and he sorely needeth sleep."

He looked about for extra covering, but finding none, doffed his doublet and wrapped the lad in it, saying, "I am used to nipping air and scant apparel, 'tis little I shall mind the cold"—then walked up and down the room to keep his blood in motion, soliloquizing, as before.

"His injured mind persuades him he is prince of Wales; 'twill be odd to have a prince of Wales still with us, now that he that *was* the prince is prince no more, but king,—for this poor mind is set upon the one fantasy, and will not reason out that now it should cast by the prince and call itself the king. . . . If my father liveth still, after these seven years that I have heard naught from home in my foreign dungeon, he will welcome the poor lad and give him generous shelter for my sake; so will my good elder brother, Arthur; my other brother, Hugh—but I will crack his crown, an *he* interfere, the fox-hearted, ill-conditioned animal! Yes, thither will we fare—and straightway, too."

A servant entered with a smoking meal, disposed it upon a small deal table, placed the chairs, and took his departure, leaving such cheap lodgers as these to wait upon themselves. The door slammed after him, and the noise woke the boy, who sprung to a sitting posture, and shot a glad glance about him; then a grieved look came into his face and he murmured, to himself, with a deep sigh, "Alack, it was but a dream, woe is me." Next he noticed Miles Hendon's doublet—glanced from that to Hendon, comprehended the sacrifice that had been made for him, and said, gently—

"Thou art good to me, yes, thou art very good to me. Take it and put it on— I shall not need it more."

Then he got up and walked to the washstand in the corner, and stood there, waiting. Hendon said in a cheery voice—

"We'll have a right hearty sup and bite, now, for every thing is savory and smoking hot, and that and thy nap together will make thee a little man again, never fear!"

The boy made no answer, but bent a steady look, that was filled with grave surprise, and also somewhat touched with impatience, upon the tall knight of the sword. Hendon was puzzled, and said—

"What's amiss?"

"Good sir, I would wash me."

"O, is that all! Ask no permission of Miles Hendon for aught thou cravest. Make thyself perfectly free here, and welcome, with all that are his belongings."

Still the boy stood, and moved not; more, he tapped the floor once or twice with his small impatient foot. Hendon was wholly perplexed. Said he—

"Bless us, what is it?"

"Prithee pour the water, and make not so many words!"

Hendon, suppressing a horse-laugh, and saying to himself, "By all the saints, but this is admirable!" stepped briskly forward and did the small insolent's bidding; then stood by, in a sort of stupefaction, until the command, "Come—the towel!" woke him sharply up. He took up a towel, from under the boy's nose, and handed it to him, without comment. He now proceeded to comfort his own face with a wash, and while he was at it his adopted child seated himself at the table and prepared to fall to. Hendon despatched his ablutions with alacrity, then drew back the other chair and was about to place himself at table, when the boy said, indignantly—

"Forbear! Wouldst sit in the presence of the king?"

This blow staggered Hendon to his foundations. He muttered to himself, "Lo, the poor thing's madness is up with the time! it hath changed with the great change that is come to the realm, and now in fancy is he *king!* Good lack, I must humor the conceit, too—there is no other way—faith, he would order me to the Tower, else!"

And pleased with this jest, he removed the chair from the table, took his stand behind the king, and proceeded to wait upon him in the courtliest way he was capable of.

When the king ate, the rigor of his royal dignity relaxed a little, and with his growing contentment came a desire to talk. He said—

"I think thou callest thyself Miles Hendon, if I heard thee aright?"

"Yes, sire," Miles replied; then observed to himself, "If I *must* humor the poor lad's madness, I must sire him, I must majesty him, I must not go by halves, I must stick at nothing that belongeth to the part I play, else shall I play it ill and work evil to this charitable and kindly cause."

The king warmed his heart with a second glass of wine, and said—"I would know thee—tell me thy story. Thou hast a gallant way with thee, and a noble—art nobly born?"

"We are of the tail of the nobility, good your majesty. My father is a baronet—one of the smaller lords, by knight service *—Sir Richard Hendon, of Hendon Hall, by Monk's Holm in Kent."

"The name has escaped my memory. Go on—tell me thy story."

"'Tis not much, your majesty, yet perchance it may beguile a short half hour for want of a better. My father, Sir Richard, is very rich, and of a most generous nature. My mother died whilst I was yet a boy. I have two brothers: Arthur, my elder, with a soul like to his father's; and Hugh, younger than I, a mean spirit,

---

* He refers to the order of baronets, or baronettes,—the *barones minores,* as distinct from the parliamentary barons;—not, it need hardly be said, the baronets of later creation.

covetous, treacherous, vicious, underhanded—a reptile. Such was he from the cradle; such was he ten years past, when I last saw him—a ripe rascal at nineteen, I being twenty, then, and Arthur twenty-two. There is none other of us but the lady Edith, my cousin—she was sixteen, then—beautiful, gentle, good, the daughter of an earl, the last of her race, heiress of a great fortune and a lapsed title. My father was her guardian. I loved her and she loved me; but she was betrothed to Arthur from the cradle, and Sir Richard would not suffer the contract to be broken. Arthur loved another maid, and bade us be of good cheer and hold fast to the hope that delay and luck together would some day give success to our several causes. Hugh loved the lady Edith's fortune, though in truth he said it was herself he loved—but then 'twas his way, alway, to say the one thing and mean the other. But he lost his arts upon the girl: he could deceive my father, but none else. My father loved him best of us all, and trusted and believed him; for he was the youngest child and others hated him—these qualities being in all ages sufficient to win a parent's dearest love; and he had a smooth persuasive tongue, with an admirable gift of lying—and these be qualities which do mightily assist a blind affection to cozen itself. I was wild—in troth I might go yet farther and say *very* wild, though 'twas a wildness of an innocent sort, since it hurt none but me, brought shame to none, nor loss, nor had in it any taint of crime or baseness, or what might not beseem mine honorable degree.

"Yet did my brother Hugh turn these faults to good account—he seeing that our brother Arthur's health was but indifferent, and hoping the worst might work him profit were I swept out of the path—so,—but 'twere a long tale, good my liege, and little worth the telling. Briefly, then, this brother did deftly magnify my faults and make them crimes; ending his base work with finding a silken ladder in mine apartments—conveyed thither by his own means—and did convince my father by this, and suborned evidence of servants and other lying knaves, that I was minded to carry off my Edith and marry with her, in rank defiance of his will.

"Three years of banishment from home and England might make a soldier and a man of me, my father said, and teach me some degree of wisdom. I fought out my long probation in the continental wars, tasting sumptuously of hard knocks, privation and adventure; but in my last battle I was taken captive, and during the seven years that have waxed and waned since then, a foreign dungeon hath harbored me. Through wit and courage I won to the free air at last, and fled hither straight; and am but just arrived, right poor in purse and raiment, and poorer still in knowledge of what these dull seven years have wrought at Hendon Hall, its people and belongings. So please you, sir, my meagre tale is told."

"Thou hast been shamefully abused!" said the little king, with a flashing eye. "But I will right thee—by the cross will I! The king hath said it."

Then, fired by the story of Miles's wrongs, he loosed his tongue and poured the history of his own recent misfortunes into the ears of his astonished listener. When he had finished, Miles said to himself—

"Lo, what an imagination he hath! Verily this is no common mind; else, crazed or sane, it could not weave so straight and gaudy a tale as this out of the airy nothings wherewith it hath wrought this curious romaunt. Poor ruined little head, it shall not lack friend or shelter whilst I bide with the living. He shall never leave my side; he shall be my pet, my little comrade. And he shall be cured!—aye, made whole and sound—then will he make himself a name—and proud shall I be to say, 'Yes, he is mine—I took him, a homeless little ragamuffin, but I saw what was in him, and I said his name would be heard some day—behold him, observe him—was I right?''

The king spoke—in a thoughtful, measured voice—

"Thou didst save me injury and shame, perchance my life, and so my crown. Such service demandeth rich reward. Name thy desire, and so it be within the compass of my royal power, it is thine."

Ths fantastic suggestion startled Hendon out of his revery. He was about to thank the king and put the matter aside with saying he had only done his duty and desired no reward, but a wiser thought came into his head, and he asked leave to be silent a few moments and consider the gracious offer—an idea which the king gravely approved, remarking that it was best to be not too hasty with a thing of such great import.

Miles reflected during some moments, then said to himself, "Yes, that is the thing to do—by any other means it were impossible to get at it—and certes, this hour's experience has taught me 'twould be most wearing and inconvenient to continue it as it is. Yes, I will propose it; 'twas a happy accident that I did not throw the chance away." Then he dropped upon one knee and said—

"My poor service went not beyond the limit of a subject's simple duty, and therefore hath no merit; but since your majesty is pleased to hold it worthy some reward, I take heart of grace to make petition to this effect. Near four hundred years ago, as your grace knoweth, there being ill blood betwixt John, King of England, and the King of France, it was decreed that two champions should fight together in the lists, and so settle the dispute by what is called the arbitrament of God. These two kings, and the Spanish king, being assembled to witness and judge the conflict, the French champion appeared; but so redoubtable was he, that our English knights refused to measure weapons with him. So the matter, which was a weighty one, was like to go against the English monarch by default. Now in the Tower lay the lord de Courcy, the mightiest arm in England, stripped of his honors and possessions, and wasting with long captivity. Appeal was made to him; he gave assent, and came forth arrayed for battle; but no sooner did the Frenchman glimpse his huge frame and hear his famous name but he fled away, and the French king's cause was lost. King John restored de Courcy's

"HE DROPPED ON ONE KNEE."

titles and possessions, and said, 'Name thy wish and thou shalt have it, though it cost me half my kingdom;' whereat de Courcy, kneeling, as I do now, made answer, 'This, then, I ask, my liege; that I and my successors may have and hold the privilege of remaining covered in the presence of the kings of England, henceforth while the throne shall last.' The boon was granted, as your majesty knoweth; and there hath been no time, these four hundred years, that that line has failed of an heir; and so, even unto this day, the head of that ancient house still weareth his hat or helm before the king's majesty, without let or hindrance, and this none other may do.* Invoking this precedent in aid of my prayer, I beseech the king to grant to me but this one grace and privilege—to my more than sufficient reward—and none other, to wit: that I and my heirs, forever, may *sit* in the presence of the majesty of England!''

"Rise, Sir Miles Hendon, Knight," said the king, gravely—giving the accolade with Hendon's sword—"rise, and seat thyself. Thy petition is granted. Whilst England remains, and the crown continues, the privilege shall not lapse."

His majesty walked apart, musing, and Hendon dropped into a chair at table, observing to himself, "''Twas a brave thought, and hath wrought me a mighty deliverance; my legs are grievously wearied. An' I had not thought of that, I must have had to stand for weeks, till my poor lad's wits are cured." After a little, he went on, "And so I am become a knight of the Kingdom of Dreams and Shadows! A most odd and strange position, truly, for one so matter-of-fact as I. I will not laugh—no, God forbid, for this thing which is so substanceless to me is *real* to him. And to me, also, in one way, it is not a falsity, for it reflects with truth the sweet and generous spirit that is in him." After a pause: "Ah, what if he should call me by my fine title before folk!—there'd be a merry contrast betwixt my glory and my raiment! But no matter: let him call me what he will, so it please him; I shall be content."

Chapter XIII

THE DISAPPEARANCE OF THE PRINCE

A HEAVY DROWSINESS presently fell upon the two comrades. The king said—
"Remove these rags"—meaning his clothing.

Hendon disapparelled the boy without dissent or remark, tucked him up in bed, then glanced about the room, saying to himself, ruefully, "He hath taken my bed again, as before—marry, what shall *I* do?" The little king observed his perplexity, and dissipated it with a word. He said, sleepily—

"Thou wilt sleep athwart the door, and guard it." In a moment more he was out of his troubles, in a deep slumber.

"Dear heart, he should have been born a king!" muttered Hendon, admiringly; "he playeth the part to a marvel."

Then he stretched himself across the door, on the floor, saying contentedly—

* The lords of Kingsale, descendants of de Courcy, still enjoy this curious privilege.

"I have lodged worse for seven years; 'twould be but ill gratitude to Him above to find fault with this."

He dropped asleep as the dawn appeared. Toward noon he rose, uncovered his unconscious ward—a section at a time—and took his measure with a string. The king awoke, just as he had completed his work, complained of the cold, and asked what he was doing.

"'Tis done, now, my liege," said Hendon; "I have a bit of business outside, but will presently return; sleep thou again—thou needest it. There—let me cover thy head also—thou'lt be warm the sooner."

The king was back in dreamland before this speech was ended. Miles slipped softly out, and slipped as softly in again, in the course of thirty or forty minutes, with a complete second-hand suit of boy's clothing, of cheap material, and showing signs of wear; but tidy, and suited to the season of the year. He seated himself, and began to overhaul his purchase, mumbling to himself—

"A longer purse would have got a better sort, but when one has not the long purse one must be content with what a short one may do—

> " 'There was a woman in our town,
> In our town did dwell'—

"He stirred, methinks—I must sing in a less thunderous key; 'tis not good to mar his sleep, with this journey before him and he so wearied out, poor chap. . . . This garment—'tis well enough—a stitch here and another one there will set it aright. This other is better, albeit a stitch or two will not come amiss in it, likewise. . . . *These* be very good and sound, and will keep his small feet warm and dry—an odd new thing to him, belike, since he has doubtless been used to foot it bare, winters and summers the same. . . . Would thread were bread, seeing one getteth a year's sufficiency for a farthing, and such a brave big needle without cost, for mere love. Now shall I have the demon's own time to thread it!"

And so he had. He did as men have always done, and probably always will do, to the end of time—held the needle still, and tried to thrust the thread through the eye, which is the opposite of a woman's way. Time and time again the thread missed the mark, going sometimes on one side of the needle, sometimes on the other, sometimes doubling up against the shaft; but he was patient, having been through these experiences before, when he was soldiering. He succeeded at last, and took up the garment that had lain waiting, meantime, across his lap, and began his work.

"The inn is paid—the breakfast that is to come, included—and there is wherewithal left to buy a couple of donkeys and meet our little costs for the two or three days betwixt this and the plenty that awaits us at Hendon Hall—

> " 'She loved her hus'—

"Body o' me! I have driven the needle under my nail! . . . It matters little— 'tis not a novelty—yet 'tis not a convenience, neither. . . . We shall be merry there, little one, never doubt it! Thy troubles will vanish, there, and likewise thy sad distemper—

> " 'She loved her husband dearilee,
> But another man'—

"These be noble large stitches!"—holding the garment up and viewing it admiringly—"they have a grandeur and a majesty that do cause these small stingy ones of the tailor-man to look mightily paltry and plebeian—

> " 'She loved her husband dearilee,
> But another man he loved she,'—

"Marry, 'tis done—a goodly piece of work, too, and wrought with expedition. Now will I wake him, apparel him, pour for him, feed him, and then will we hie us to the mart by the Tabard inn in Southwark and—be pleased to rise, my liege!—he answereth not—what ho, my liege!—of a truth must I profane his sacred person with a touch, sith his slumber is deaf to speech. What!"

He threw back the covers—the boy was gone!

He stared about him in speechless astonishment for a moment; noticed for the first time that his ward's ragged raiment was also missing, then he began to rage and storm, and shout for the innkeeper.—At that moment a servant entered with the breakfast.

"Explain, thou limb of Satan, or thy time is come!" roared the man of war, and made so savage a spring toward the waiter that this latter could not find his tongue, for the instant, for fright and surprise. "Where is the boy?"

In disjointed and trembling syllables the man gave the information desired.

"You were hardly gone from the place, your worship, when a youth came running and said it was your worship's will that the boy come to you straight, at the bridge-end on the Southwark side. I brought him hither; and when he woke the lad and gave his message, the lad did grumble some little for being disturbed 'so early,' as he called it, but straightway trussed on his rags and went with the youth, only saying it had been better manners that your worship came yourself, not sent a stranger—and so"—

"And so thou'rt a fool!—a fool, and easily cozened—hang all thy breed! Yet mayhap no hurt is done. Possibly no harm is meant the boy. I will go fetch him. Make the table ready. Stay! the coverings of the bed were disposed as if one lay beneath them—happened that by accident?"

"I know not, good your worship. I saw the youth meddle with them—he that came for the boy."

"Thousand deaths! 'twas done to deceive me—'tis plain 'twas done to gain time. Hark ye! Was that youth alone?"

"All alone, your worship."

"Art sure?"

"Sure, your worship."

"Collect thy scattered wits—bethink thee—take time, man."

After a moment's thought, the servant said—

"When he came, none came with him; but now I remember me that as the two stepped into the throng of the Bridge, a ruffian-looking man plunged out from some near place; and just as he was joining them"—

"What *then?*—out with it!" thundered the impatient Hendon, interrupting.

"Just then the crowd lapped them up and closed them in, and I saw no more, being called by my master, who was in a rage because a joint that the scrivener had ordered was forgot, though I take all the saints to witness that to blame *me* for that miscarriage were like holding the unborn babe to judgment for sins com"—

"Out of my sight, idiot! Thy prating drives me mad! Hold! whither art flying? Canst not bide still an instant? Went they toward Southwark?"

"Even so, your worship—for, as I said before, as to that detestable joint, the babe unborn is no whit more blameless than"—

"Art here *yet!* And prating still? Vanish, lest I throttle thee!" The servitor vanished. Hendon followed after him, passed him, and plunged down the stairs two steps at a stride, muttering, "'Tis that scurvy villain that claimed he was his son. I have lost thee, my poor little mad master—it is a bitter thought—and I had come to love thee so! No! by book and bell, *not* lost! Not lost, for I will ransack the land till I find thee again. Poor child, yonder is his breakfast—and mine, but I have no hunger now—so, let the rats have it—speed, speed! that is the word!" As he wormed his swift way through the noisy multitudes upon the Bridge, he several times said to himself—clinging to the thought as if it were a particularly pleasing one—"He grumbled, but he *went*—he went, yes, because he thought Miles Hendon asked it, sweet lad—he would ne'er have done it for another, I know it well."

Chapter XIV

"LE ROI EST MORT—VIVE LE ROI"

TOWARD DAYLIGHT OF the same morning, Tom Canty stirred out of a heavy sleep and opened his eyes in the dark. He lay silent a few moments, trying to analyze his confused thoughts and impressions, and get some sort of meaning out of them, then suddenly he burst out in a rapturous guarded voice—

"I see it all, I see it all! Now God be thanked, I am indeed awake at last! Come, joy! vanish, sorrow! Ho, Nan! Bet! kick off your straw and hie ye hither to my side, till I do pour into your unbelieving ears the wildest madcap dream that ever the spirits of night did conjure up to astonish the soul of man withal! . . . Ho, Nan, I say! Bet!" . . .

A dim form appeared at his side, and a voice said—

"Wilt deign to deliver thy commands?"

"Commands? . . . O, woe is me, I know thy voice! Speak, thou—who am I?"

"Thou? In sooth, yesternight wert thou the prince of Wales, to-day art thou my most gracious liege, Edward, King of England."

Tom buried his head among his pillows, murmuring plaintively—

"Alack, it was no dream! Go to thy rest, sweet sir—leave me to my sorrows."

Tom slept again, and after a time he had this pleasant dream. He thought it was summer and he was playing, all alone, in the fair meadow called Goodman's Fields, when a dwarf only a foot high, with long red whiskers and a humped back, appeared to him suddenly and said, "Dig, by that stump." He did so, and found twelve bright new pennies—wonderful riches! Yet this was not the best of it; for the dwarf said—

"I know thee. Thou art a good lad and deserving; thy distresses shall end, for the day of thy reward is come. Dig here every seventh day, and thou shalt find always the same treasure, twelve bright new pennies. Tell none—keep the secret."

Then the dwarf vanished, and Tom flew to Offal Court with his prize, saying to himself, "Every night will I give my father a penny; he will think I begged it, it will glad his heart, and I shall no more be beaten. One penny every week the good priest that teacheth me shall have; mother, Nan and Bet the other four. We be done with hunger and rags, now, done with fears and frets and savage usage."

In his dream he reached his sordid home all out of breath, but with eyes dancing with grateful enthusiasm; cast four of his pennies into his mother's lap and cried out—

"They are for thee!—all of them, every one!—for thee and Nan and Bet—and honestly come by, not begged nor stolen!"

The happy and astonished mother strained him to her breast and exclaimed—

"It waxeth late—may it please your majesty to rise?"

Ah, that was not the answer he was expecting. The dream had snapped asunder—he was awake.

He opened his eyes—the richly clad First Lord of the Bedchamber was kneeling by his couch. The gladness of the lying dream faded away—the poor boy recognized that he was still a captive and a king. The room was filled with courtiers clothed in purple mantles—the mourning color—and with noble servants of the monarch. Tom sat up in bed and gazed out from the heavy silken curtains upon this fine company.

The weighty business of dressing began, and one courtier after another knelt and paid his court and offered to the little King his condolences upon his heavy loss, whilst the dressing proceeded. In the beginning, a shirt was taken up by the Chief Equerry in Waiting, who passed it to the First Lord of the Buckhounds, who passed it to the Second Gentleman of the Bedchamber, who passed it to the Head Ranger of Windsor Forest, who passed it to the Third Groom of the Stole, who passed it to the Chancellor Royal of the Duchy of Lancaster, who passed it to the Master of the Wardrobe, who passed it to Norroy King-at-Arms,

"WILT DEIGN TO DELIVER THY COMMANDS?"

who passed it to the Constable of the Tower, who passed it to the Chief Steward of the Household, who passed it to the Hereditary Grand Diaperer, who passed it to the Lord High Admiral of England, who passed it to the Archbishop of Canterbury, who passed it to the First Lord of the Bedchamber, who took what was left of it and put it on Tom. Poor little wondering chap, it reminded him of passing buckets at a fire.

Each garment in its turn had to go through this slow and solemn process; consequently Tom grew very weary of the ceremony; so weary that he felt an almost gushing gratefulness when he at last saw his long silken hose begin the journey down the line and knew that the end of the matter was drawing near. But he exulted too soon. The First Lord of the Bedchamber received the hose and was about to encase Tom's legs in them, when a sudden flush invaded his face and he hurriedly hustled the things back into the hands of the Archbishop of Canterbury with an astounded look and a whispered, "See, my lord!"— pointing to a something connected with the hose. The Archbishop paled, then flushed, and passed the hose to the Lord High Admiral, whispering, "See, my lord!" The Admiral passed the hose to the Hereditary Grand Diaperer, and had hardly breath enough in his body to ejaculate, "See, my lord!" The hose drifted backward along the line, to the Chief Steward of the Household, the Constable of the Tower, Norroy King-at-Arms, the Master of the Wardrobe, the Chancellor Royal of the Duchy of Lancaster, the Third Groom of the Stole, the Head Ranger of Windsor Forest, the Second Gentleman of the Bedchamber, the First Lord of the Buckhounds,—accompanied always with that amazed and frightened "See! see!"—till they finally reached the hands of the Chief Equerry in Waiting, who gazed a moment, with a pallid face, upon what had caused all this dismay, then hoarsely whispered, "Body of my life, a tag gone from a truss point!—to the Tower with the Head Keeper of the King's Hose!"—after which he leaned upon the shoulder of the First Lord of the Buckhounds to regather his vanished strength whilst fresh hose, without any damaged strings to them, were brought.

But all things must have an end, and so in time Tom Canty was in a condition to get out of bed. The proper official poured water, the proper official engineered the washing, the proper official stood by with a towel, and by and by Tom got safely through the purifying stage and was ready for the services of the Hairdresser-royal. When he at length emerged from this master's hands, he was a gracious figure and as pretty as a girl, in his mantle and trunks of purple satin, and purple-plumed cap. He now moved in state toward his breakfast room, through the midst of the courtly assemblage; and as he passed, these fell back, leaving his way free, and dropped upon their knees.

After breakfast he was conducted, with regal ceremony, attended by his great officers and his guard of fifty Gentlemen Pensioners bearing gilt battle-axes, to the throne-room, where he proceeded to transact business of state. His "uncle," lord Hertford, took his stand by the throne, to assist the royal mind with wise counsel.

The body of illustrious men named by the late king as his executors, appeared, to ask Tom's approval of certain acts of theirs—rather a form, and yet not wholly a form, since there was no Protector as yet. The Archbishop of Canterbury made report of the decree of the Council of Executors concerning the obsequies of his late most illustrious majesty, and finished by reading the signatures of the Executors, to-wit: the Archbishop of Canterbury; the Lord Chancellor of England; William

Lord St. John; John Lord Russell; Edward Earl of Hertford; John Viscount Lisle; Cuthbert Bishop of Durham—

Tom was not listening—an earlier clause of the document was puzzling him. At this point he turned and whispered to lord Hertford—

"What day did he say the burial hath been appointed for?"

"The 16th of the coming month, my liege."

"'Tis a strange folly. Will he keep?"

Poor chap, he was still new to the customs of royalty; he was used to seeing the forlorn dead of Offal Court hustled out of the way with a very different sort of expedition. However, the lord Hertford set his mind at rest with a word or two.

A secretary of state presented an order of the Council appointing the morrow at eleven for the reception of the foreign ambassadors, and desired the king's assent.

Tom turned an inquiring look toward Hertford, who whispered—

"Your majesty will signify consent. They come to testify their royal masters' sense of the heavy calamity which hath visited your grace and the realm of England."

Tom did as he was bidden. Another secretary began to read a preamble concerning the expenses of the late king's household, which had amounted to £28,000 during the preceding six months—a sum so vast that it made Tom Canty gasp; he gasped again when the fact appeared that £20,000 of this money were still owing and upaid;* and once more when it appeared that the king's coffers were about empty, and his twelve hundred servants much embarrassed for lack of the wages due them. Tom spoke out, with lively apprehension—

"We be going to the dogs, 'tis plain. 'Tis meet and necessary that we take a smaller house and set the servants at large, sith they be of no value but to make delay, and trouble one with offices that harass the spirit and shame the soul, they misbecoming any but a doll, that hath nor brains nor hands to help itself withal. I remember me of a small house that standeth over against the fish-market, by Billingsgate"—

A sharp pressure upon Tom's arm stopped his foolish tongue and sent a blush to his face; but no countenance there betrayed any sign that this strange speech had been remarked or given concern.

A secretary made report that forasmuch as the late king had provided in his will for conferring the ducal degree upon the earl of Hertford and raising his brother, Sir Thomas Seymour, to the peerage, and likewise Hertford's son to an earldom, together with similar aggrandizements to other great servants of the crown, the Council had resolved to hold a sitting on the 16th of February for the delivering and confirming of these honors; and that meantime, the late king not having granted, in writing, estates suitable to the support of these dignities, the Council, knowing his private wishes in that regard, had thought proper to grant to Seymour "£500 lands," and to Hertford's son "800 pound lands, and 300 pound of the next bishop's lands which should fall vacant,"—his present majesty being willing.*

Tom was about to blurt out something about the propriety of paying the late King's debts first, before squandering all this money; but a timely touch upon

---

* Hume.

his arm, from the thoughtful Hertford, saved him this indiscretion; wherefore he gave the royal assent, without spoken comment, but with much inward discomfort. While he sat reflecting, a moment, over the ease with which he was doing strange and glittering miracles, a happy thought shot into his mind: why not make his mother Duchess of Offal Court and give her an estate? But a sorrowful thought swept it instantly away: he was only a king in name, these grave veterans and great nobles were his masters; to them his mother was only the creature of a diseased mind; they would simply listen to his project with unbelieving ears, then send for the doctor.

The dull work went tediously on. Petitions were read, and proclamations, patents, and all manner of wordy, repetitious and wearisome papers relating to the public business; and at last Tom sighed pathetically and murmured to himself, "In what have I offended, that the good God should take me away from the fields and the free air and the sunshine, to shut me up here and make me a king and afflict me so?" Then his poor muddled head nodded a while, and presently dropped to his shoulder; and the business of the empire came to a stand-still for want of that august factor, the ratifying power. Silence ensued, around the slumbering child, and the sages of the realm ceased from their deliberations.

During the forenoon, Tom had an enjoyable hour, by permission of his keepers, Hertford and St. John, with the lady Elizabeth and the little lady Jane Grey; though the spirits of the princesses were rather subdued by the mighty stroke that had fallen upon the royal house; and at the end of the visit his "elder sister"—afterwards the "Bloody Mary" of history—chilled him with a solemn interview which had but one merit in his eyes, its brevity. He had a few moments to himself, and then a slim lad of about twelve years of age was admitted to his presence, whose clothing, except his snowy ruff and the laces about his wrists, was of black,—doublet, hose and all. He bore no badge of mourning but a knot of purple ribbon on his shoulder. He advanced hesitatingly, with head bowed and bare, and dropped upon one knee in front of Tom. Tom sat still and contemplated him soberly a moment. Then he said—

"Rise, lad. Who art thou? What wouldst have?"

The boy rose, and stood at graceful ease, but with an aspect of concern in his face. He said—

"Of a surety thou must remember me, my lord. I am thy whipping-boy."

"My *whipping*-boy?"

"The same, your grace. I am Humphrey—Humphrey Marlow."

Tom perceived that here was some one whom his keepers ought to have posted him about. The situation was delicate. What should he do?—pretend he knew this lad, and then betray by his every utterance, that he had never heard of him before? No, that would not do. An idea came to his relief: accidents like this might be likely to happen with some frequency, now that business urgencies would often call Hertford and St. John from his side, they being members of the council of executors; therefore perhaps it would be well to strike out a plan himself to meet the requirements of such emergencies. Yes, that would be a wise course—he would practice on this boy, and see what sort of success he might achieve. So he stroked his brow, perplexedly, a moment or two, and presently said—

"Now I seem to remember thee somewhat—but my wit is clogged and dim with suffering"—

"Alack, my poor master!" ejaculated the whipping-boy, with feeling; adding, to himself, "In truth 'tis as they said—his mind is gone—alas, poor soul! But misfortune catch me, how am I forgetting! they said one must not seem to observe that aught is wrong with him."

"'Tis strange how my memory doth wanton with me these days," said Tom. "But mind it not—I mend apace—a little clew doth often serve to bring me back again the things and names which had escaped me. [And not they, only, forsooth, but e'en such as I ne'er heard before—as this lad shall see.] Give thy business speech."

"'Tis matter of small weight, my liege, yet will I touch upon it an' it please your grace. Two days gone by, when your majesty faulted thrice in your Greek—in the morning lessons,—dost remember it?"

"Y-e-s—methinks I do. [It is not much of a lie—an' I had meddled with the Greek at all, I had not faulted simply thrice, but forty times.] Yes, I do recall it, now—go on."

—"The master, being wroth with what he termed such slovenly and doltish work, did promise that he would soundly whip me for it—and"—

"Whip *thee!*" said Tom, astonished out of his presence of mind. "Why should he whip *thee* for faults of mine?"

"Ah, your grace forgetteth again. He always scourgeth me, when thou dost fail in thy lessons."

"True, true—I had forgot. Thou teachest me in private—then if I fail, he argueth that thy office was lamely done, and"—

"O, my liege, what words are these? I, the humblest of thy servants, presume to teach *thee?*"

"Then where is thy blame? What riddle is this? Am I in truth gone mad, or is it thou? Explain—speak out."

"But good your majesty, there's nought that needeth simplifying.—None may visit the sacred person of the prince of Wales with blows; wherefore when he faulteth, 'tis I that take them; and meet it is and right, for that it is mine office and my livelihood."

Tom stared at the tranquil boy, observing to himself, "Lo, it is a wonderful thing,—a most strange and curious trade; I marvel they have not hired a boy to take my combings and my dressings for me—would heaven they would!—an' they will do this thing, I will take my lashings in mine own person, giving God thanks for the change." Then he said aloud—

"And hast thou been beaten, poor friend, according to the promise?"

"No, good your majesty, my punishment was appointed for this day, and peradventure it may be annulled, as unbefitting the season of mourning that is come upon us; I know not, and so have made bold to come hither and remind your grace about your gracious promise to intercede in my behalf"—

"With the master? To save thee thy whipping?"

"Ah thou dost remember!"

"My memory mendeth, thou seest. Set thy mind at ease—thy back shall go unscathed—I will see to it."

"O, thanks, my good lord!" cried the boy, dropping upon his knee again. "Mayhap I have ventured far enow; and yet" . . .

Seeing Master Humphrey hesitate, Tom encouraged him to go on, saying he was "in the granting mood."

"Then will I speak it out, for it lieth near my heart. Sith thou art no more prince of Wales but King, thou canst order matters as thou wilt, with none to say thee nay; wherefore it is not in reason that thou wilt longer vex thyself with dreary studies, but wilt burn thy books and turn thy mind to things less irksome. Then am I ruined, and mine orphan sisters with me!''

"Ruined? Prithee how?"

"My back is my bread, O my gracious liege! if it go idle, I starve. An' thou cease from study, mine office is gone, thou'lt need no whipping-boy. Do not turn me away!''

Tom was touched with this pathetic distress. He said, with a right royal burst of generosity—

"Discomfort thyself no further, lad. Thine office shall be permanent in thee and thy line, forever." They he struck the boy a light blow on the shoulder with the flat of his sword, exclaiming, "Rise, Humphrey Marlow, Hereditary Grand Whipping-Boy to the royal house of England! Banish sorrow—I will betake me to my books again, and study so ill that they must in justice treble thy wage, so mightily shall the business of thine office be augmented."

The grateful Humphrey responded fervidly—

"Thanks, O most noble master, this princely lavishness doth far surpass my most distempered dreams of fortune. Now shall I be happy all my days, and all the house of Marlow after me."

Tom had wit enough to perceive that here was a lad who could be useful to him. He encouraged Humphrey to talk, and he was nothing loath. He was delighted to believe that he was helping in Tom's "cure;" for always, as soon as he had finished calling back to Tom's diseased mind the various particulars of his experiences and adventures in the royal school-room and elsewhere about the palace, he noticed that Tom was then able to "recall" the circumstances quite clearly. At the end of an hour Tom found himself well freighted with very valuable information concerning personages and matters pertaining to the Court; so he resolved to draw instruction from this source daily; and to this end he would give order to admit Humphrey to the royal closet whenever he might come, provided the majesty of England was not engaged with other people. Humphrey had hardly been dismissed when my lord Hertford arrived with more trouble for Tom.

He said that the lords of the Council, fearing that some overwrought report of the king's damaged health might have leaked out and got abroad, they deemed it wise and best that his majesty should begin to dine in public after a day or two—his wholesome complexion and vigorous step, assisted by a carefully guarded repose of manner and ease and grace of demeanor, would more surely quiet the general pulse—in case any evil rumors *had* gone about—than any other scheme that could be devised.

Then the earl proceeded, very delicately, to instruct Tom as to the observances proper to the stately occasion, under the rather thin disguise of "reminding" him concerning things already known to him; but to his vast gratification it turned out that Tom needed very little help in this line—he had been making use of Humphrey in that direction, for Humphrey had mentioned that within a few days he was to begin to dine in public; having gathered it from the swift-winged gossip of the Court. Tom kept these facts to himself, however.

Seeing the royal memory so improved, the earl ventured to apply a few tests to it, in an apparently casual way, to find out how far its amendment had progressed. The results were happy, here and there, in spots—spots where Humphrey's tracks remained—and on the whole my lord was greatly pleased and encouraged. So encouraged was he, indeed, that he spoke up and said in a quite hopeful voice—

"Now am I persuaded that if your majesty will but tax your memory yet a little further, it will resolve the puzzle of the Great Seal—a loss which was of moment yesterday, although of none to-day, since its term of service ended with our late lord's life. May it please your grace to make the trial?"

Tom was at sea—a Great Seal was a something which he was totally unacquainted with. After a moment's hesitation he looked up innocently and asked—

"What was it like, my Lord?"

The earl started, almost imperceptibly, muttering to himself, "Alack, his wits are flown again!—it was ill wisdom to lead him on to strain them"—then he deftly turned the talk to other matters, with the purpose of sweeping the unlucky Seal out of Tom's thoughts—a purpose which easily succeeded.

Chapter XV

TOM AS KING

THE NEXT DAY the foreign ambassadors came, with their gorgeous trains; and Tom, throned in awful state, received them. The splendors of the scene delighted his eye and fired his imagination, at first, but the audience was long and dreary, and so were most of the addresses—wherefore, what began as a pleasure, grew into weariness and homesickness by and by. Tom said the words which Hertford put into his mouth from time to time, and tried hard to acquit himself satisfactorily, but he was too new to such things, and too ill at ease to accomplish more than a tolerable success. He looked sufficiently like a king, but he was ill able to feel like one. He was cordially glad when the ceremony was ended.

The larger part of his day was "wasted"—as he termed it, in his own mind— in labors pertaining to his royal office. Even the two hours devoted to certain princely pastimes and recreations were rather a burden to him, than otherwise, they were so fettered by restrictions and ceremonious observances. However he had a private hour with his whipping-boy which he counted clear gain, since he got both entertainment and needful information out of it.

The third day of Tom Canty's Kingship came and went much as the others had done, but there was a lifting of his cloud in one way—he felt less uncomfortable than at first; he was getting a little used to his circumstances and surroundings; his chains still galled, but not all the time; he found that the presence and homage of the great afflicted and embarrassed him less and less sharply with every hour that drifted over his head.

But for one single dread, he could have seen the fourth day approach without serious distress—the dining in public; it was to begin that day. There were greater matters in the programme—for on that day he would have to preside at a Council which would take his views and commands concerning the policy to be pursued toward various foreign nations scattered far and near over the great globe; on that day, too, Hertford would be formally chosen to the grand office of Lord Protector; other things of note were appointed for that fourth day, also, but to Tom they were all insignificant compared with the ordeal of dining all by himself with a multitude of curious eyes fastened upon him and a multitude of mouths whispering comments upon his performance,—and upon his mistakes, if he should be so unlucky as to make any.

Still, nothing could stop that fourth day, and so it came. It found poor Tom low-spirited and absent-minded, and this mood continued; he could not shake it off. The ordinary duties of the morning dragged upon his hands, and wearied him. Once more he felt the sense of captivity heavy upon him.

Late in the forenoon he was in a large audience chamber, conversing with the earl of Hertford and dully awaiting the striking of the hour appointed for a visit of ceremony from a considerable number of great officials and courtiers.

After a little while, Tom, who had wandered to a window and become interested in the life and movement of the great highway beyond the palace gates—and not idly interested, but longing with all his heart to take part in person in its stir and freedom—saw the van of a hooting and shouting mob of disorderly men, women and children of the lowest and poorest degree approaching from up the road.

"I would I knew what 'tis about!" he exclaimed, with all a boy's curiosity in such happenings.

"Thou art the king!" solemnly responded the earl, with a reverence. "Have I your grace's leave to act?"

"O blithely, yes! O gladly yes!" exclaimed Tom, excitedly, adding to himself with a lively sense of satisfaction, "In truth, being a king is not all dreariness— it hath its compensations and conveniences."

The earl called a page, and sent him to the captain of the guard with the order—

"Let the mob be halted, and inquiry made concerning the occasion of its movement. By the king's command!"

A few seconds later a long rank of the royal guards, cased in flashing steel, filed out at the gates and formed across the highway in front of the multitude. A messenger returned, to report that the crowd were following a man, a woman, and a young girl to execution for crimes committed against the peace and dignity of the realm.

Death—and a violent death—for these poor unfortunates! The thought wrung Tom's heart-strings. The spirit of compassion took control of him, to the exclusion of all other considerations; he never thought of the offended laws, or of the grief or loss which these three criminals had inflicted upon their victims, he could think of nothing but the scaffold and the grisly fate hanging over the heads of the condemned. His concern made him even forget, for the moment, that he was but the false shadow of a king, not the substance; and before he knew it he had blurted out the command—

"Bring them here!"

Then he blushed scarlet, and a sort of apology sprung to his lips; but observing that his order had wrought no sort of surprise in the earl or the waiting page, he suppressed the words he was about to utter. The page, in the most matter-of-course way, made a profound obeisance and retired backwards out of the room to deliver the command. Tom experienced a glow of pride and a renewed sense of the compensating advantages of the kingly office. He said to himself, "Truly it is like what I was used to feel when I read the old priest's tales, and did imagine mine own self a prince, giving law and command to all, saying 'Do this, do that,' whilst none durst offer let or hindrance to my will."

Now the doors swung open; one high-sounding title after another was announced, the personages owning them followed, and the place was quickly half filled with noble folk and finery. But Tom was hardly conscious of the presence of these people, so wrought up was he and so intensely absorbed in that other and more interesting matter. He seated himself, absently, in his chair of state, and turned his eyes upon the door with manifestations of impatient expectancy; seeing which, the company forebore to trouble him, and fell to chatting a mixture of public business and court gossip one with another.

In a little while the measured tread of military men was heard approaching, and the culprits entered the presence in charge of an under-sheriff and escorted by a detail of the king's guard. The civil officer knelt before Tom, then stood aside; the three doomed persons knelt, also, and remained so; the guard took position behind Tom's chair. Tom scanned the prisoners curiously. Something about the dress or appearance of the man had stirred a vague memory in him. "Methinks I have seen this man ere now . . . but the when or the where fail me"—such was Tom's thought. Just then the man glanced quickly up, and quickly dropped his face again, not being able to endure the awful port of sovereignty; but the one full glimpse of the face, which Tom got, was sufficient. He said to himself: "Now is the matter clear; this is the stranger that plucked Giles Witt out of the Thames, and saved his life, that windy, bitter, first day of the New Year—a brave good deed—pity he hath been doing baser ones and got himself in this sad case. . . . I have not forgot the day, neither the hour; by reason that an hour after, upon the stroke of eleven, I did get a hiding by the hand of Gammer Canty which was of so goodly and admired severity that all that went before or followed after it were but fondlings and caresses by comparison."

Tom now ordered that the woman and the girl be removed from the presence for a little time; then addressed himself to the under-sheriff, saying—

"Good sir, what is this man's offence?"

The officer knelt, and answered—

"So please your majesty, he hath taken the life of a subject by poison."

Tom's compassion for the prisoner, and admiration of him as the daring rescuer of a drowning boy, experienced a most damaging shock.

"The thing was proven upon him?" he asked.

"Most clearly, sire."

Tom sighed, and said—

"Take him away—he hath earned his death. 'Tis a pity, for he was a brave heart—na—na, I mean he hath the *look* of it!"

The prisoner clasped his hands together with sudden energy, and wrung them despairingly, at the same time appealing imploringly to the "King" in broken and terrified phrases—

"O my lord the king, an' thou canst pity the lost, have pity upon me! I am innocent—neither hath that wherewith I am charged been more than but lamely proved—yet I speak not of that; the judgment is gone forth against me and may not suffer alteration; yet in mine extremity I beg a boon, for my doom is more than I can bear. A grace, a grace, my lord the king! in thy royal compassion grant my prayer—give commandment that I be hanged!"

Tom was amazed. This was not the outcome he had looked for.

"Odds my life, a strange *boon!* Was it not the fate intended thee?"

"O good my liege, not so! It is ordered that I be *boiled alive!*"

The hideous surprise of these words almost made Tom spring from his chair. As soon as he could recover his wits he cried out—

"Have thy wish, poor soul! an' thou had poisoned a hundred men thou shouldst not suffer so miserable a death."

The prisoner bowed his face to the ground and burst into passionate expressions of gratitude—ending with—

"If ever thou shouldst know misfortune—which God forfend!—may thy goodness to me this day be remembered and requited!"

Tom turned to the earl of Hertford, and said—

"My lord, is it believable that there was warrant for this man's ferocious doom?"

"It is the law, your grace—for poisoners. In Germany coiners be boiled to death in *oil*—not cast in of a sudden, but by a rope let down into the oil by degrees, and slowly; first the feet, then the legs, then"—

"O prithee no more, my lord, I cannot bear it!" cried Tom, covering his eyes with his hands to shut out the picture. "I beseech your good lordship that order be taken to change this law—O, let no more poor creatures be visited with its tortures."

The earl's face showed profound gratification, for he was a man of merciful and generous impulses—a thing not very common with his class in that fierce age. He said—

"These your grace's noble words have sealed its doom. History will remember it to the honor of your royal house."

The under-sheriff was about to remove his prisoner; Tom gave him a sign to wait; then he said—

"Good sir, I would look into this matter further. The man has said his deed was but lamely proved. Tell me what thou knowest."

"If the king's grace please, it did appear upon the trial, that this man entered into a house in the hamlet of Islington where one lay sick—three witnesses say it was at ten of the clock in the morning and two say it was some minutes later—the sick man being alone at the time, and sleeping—and presently the man came forth again, and went his way. The sick man died within the hour, being torn with spasms and retchings."

"Did any see the poison given? Was poison found?"

"Marry, no, my liege."

"Then how doth one know there was poison given at all?"

"Please your majesty, the doctors testified that none die with such symptoms but by poison."

Weighty evidence, this—in that simple age. Tom recognized its formidable nature, and said—

"The doctor knoweth his trade—belike they were right. The matter hath an ill look for this poor man."

"Yet was not this all, your majesty; there is more and worse. Many testified that a witch, since gone from the village, none know whither, did foretell, and speak it privately in their ears, that the sick man *would die by poison*—and more, that a stranger would give it—a stranger with brown hair and clothed in a worn and common garb; and surely this prisoner doth answer woundily to the bill. Please your majesty to give the circumstance that solemn weight which is its due, seeing it was *foretold*."

This was an argument of tremendous force, in that superstitious day. Tom felt that the thing was settled; if evidence was worth anything, this poor fellow's guilt was proved. Still he offered the prisoner a chance, saying—

"If thou canst say aught in thy behalf, speak."

"Nought that will avail, my king. I am innocent, yet cannot I make it appear. I have no friends, else might I show that I was not in Islington that day; so also might I show that at that hour they name I was above a league away, seeing I was at Wapping Old Stairs; yea more, my King, for I could show, that whilst they say I was *taking* life, I was *saving* it. A drowning boy"—

"Peace! Sheriff, name the day the deed was done!"

"At ten in the morning, or some minutes later, the first day of the new year, most illustrious"—

"Let the prisoner go free—it is the king's will!"

Another blush followed this unregal outburst, and he covered his indecorum as well as he could by adding—

"It enrageth me that a man should be hanged upon such idle, hare-brained evidence!"

A low buzz of admiration swept through the assemblage. It was not admiration of the decree that had been delivered by Tom, for the propriety or expediency of pardoning a convicted poisoner was a thing which few there would have felt justified in either admitting or admiring—no, the admiration was for the intelligence and spirit which Tom had displayed. Some of the low-voiced remarks were to this effect—

"This is no mad king—he hath his wits sound."

"How sanely he put his questions—how like his former natural self was this abrupt, imperious disposal of the matter!"

"God be thanked his infirmity is spent! This is no weakling, but a king. He hath borne himself like to his own father."

The air being filled with applause, Tom's ear necessarily caught a little of it. The effect which this had upon him was to put him greatly at his ease, and also to charge his system with very gratifying sensations.

However, his juvenile curiosity soon rose superior to these pleasant thoughts and feelings; he was eager to know what sort of deadly mischief the woman and the little girl could have been about; so, by his command the two terrified and sobbing creatures were brought before him.

"What is it that these have done?" he inquired of the sheriff.

"Please your majesty, a black crime is charged upon them, and clearly proven; wherefore the judges have decreed, according to the law, that they be hanged. They sold themselves to the devil—such is their crime."

Tom shuddered. He had been taught to abhor people who did this wicked thing. Still, he was not going to deny himself the pleasure of feeding his curiosity, for all that; so he asked—

"Where was this done?—and when?"

"On a midnight, in December—in a ruined church, your majesty."

Tom shuddered again.

"Who was there present?"

"Only these two, your grace—and *that other*."

"Have these confessed?"

"Nay, not so, sire—they do deny it."

"Then prithee, how was it known?"

"Certain witnesses did see them wending thither, good your majesty; this bred the suspicion, and dire effects have since confirmed and justified it. In particular, it is in evidence that through the wicked power so obtained, they did invoke and bring about a storm that wasted all the region round about. Above forty witnesses have proved the storm; and sooth one might have had a thousand, for all had reason to remember it, sith all had suffered by it.''

"Certes this is a serious matter." Tom turned this dark piece of scoundrelism over in his mind a while, then asked—

"Suffered the woman, also, by the storm?''

Several old heads among the assemblage nodded their recognition of the wisdom of this question. The sheriff, however, saw nothing consequential in the inquiry; he answered, with simple directness—

"Indeed, did she, your majesty, and most righteously, as all aver. Her habitation was swept away, and herself and child left shelterless.''

"Methinks the power to do herself so ill a turn was dearly bought. She had been cheated, had she paid but a farthing for it; that she paid her soul, and her child's, argueth that she is mad; if she is mad she knoweth not what she doth, therefore sinneth not.''

The elderly heads nodded recognition of Tom's wisdom once more, and one individual murmured, "An' the king be mad himself, according to report, then is it a madness of a sort that would improve the sanity of some I wot of, if by the gentle providence of God they could but catch it.''

"What age hath the child?" asked Tom.

"Nine years, please your majesty.''

"By the law of England may a child enter into covenant and sell itself, my lord?" asked Tom, turning to a learned judge.

"The law doth not permit a child to make or meddle in any weighty matter, good my liege, holding that its callow wit unfitteth it to cope with the riper wit and evil schemings of them that are its elders. The *devil* may buy a child, if he so choose, and the child agree thereto, but not an Englishman—in this latter case the contract would be null and void.''

"It seemeth a rude unchristian thing, and ill contrived, that English law denieth privileges to Englishmen, to waste them on the devil!" cried Tom, with honest heat.

This novel view of the matter excited many smiles, and was stored away in many heads to be repeated about the court as evidence of Tom's originality as well as progress toward mental health.

The elder culprit had ceased from sobbing, and was hanging upon Tom's words with an excited interest and a growing hope. Tom noticed this, and it strongly inclined his sympathies toward her in her perilous and unfriended situation. Presently he asked—

"How wrought they, to bring the storm?''

"By pulling off their stockings, sire.''

This astonished Tom, and also fired his curiosity to fever heat. He said, eagerly—

"It is wonderful! Hath it always this dread effect?''

"Always, my liege—at least if the woman desire it, and utter the needful words, either in her mind or with her tongue.''

Tom turned to the woman, and said with impetuous zeal—

"Exert thy power—I would see a storm!''

There was a sudden paling of cheeks in the superstitious assemblage, and a general, though unexpressed, desire to get out of the place—all of which was lost upon Tom, who was dead to everything but the proposed cataclysm. Seeing a puzzled and astonished look in the woman's face, he added, excitedly—

"Never fear—thou shalt be blameless. More—thou shalt go free—none shall touch thee. Exert thy power."

"O, my lord the king, I have it not—I have been falsely accused."

"Thy fears stay thee. Be of good heart, thou shalt suffer no harm. Make a storm—it mattereth not how small a one—I require nought great or harmful, but indeed prefer the opposite—do this and thy life is spared—thou shalt go out free, with thy child, bearing the king's pardon, and safe from hurt or malice from any in the realm."

The woman prostrated herself, and protested, with tears, that she had no power to do the miracle, else she would gladly win her child's life, alone, and be content to lose her own, if by obedience to the king's command so precious a grace might be acquired.

Tom urged—the woman still adhered to her declarations. Finally he said—

"I think the woman hath said true. An' *my* mother were in her place and gifted with the devil's functions, she had not stayed a moment to call her storms and lay the whole land in ruins, if the saving of my forfeit life were the price she got! It is argument that other mothers are made in like mould. Thou art free, good wife—thou and thy child—for I do think thee innocent. *Now* thou'st nought to fear, being pardoned—pull off thy stockings!—an' thou canst make me a storm, thou shalt be rich!"

The redeemed creature was loud in her gratitude, and proceeded to obey, whilst Tom looked on with eager expectancy, a little marred by apprehension; the courtiers at the same time manifesting decided discomfort and uneasiness. The woman stripped her own feet and her little girl's also, and plainly did her best to reward the king's generosity with an earthquake, but it was all a failure and a disappointment. Tom sighed, and said—

"There, good soul, trouble thyself no further, thy power is departed out of thee. Go thy way in peace; and if it return to thee at any time, forget me not, but fetch me a storm."

Chapter XVI

THE STATE DINNER

THE DINNER HOUR drew near—yet strangely enough, the thought brought but slight discomfort to Tom, and hardly any terror. The morning's experiences had wonderfully built up his confidence; the poor little ash-cat was already more wonted to his strange garret, after four days' habit, than a mature person could have become in a full month. A child's facility in accommodating itself to circumstances was never more strikingly illustrated.

Let us privileged ones hurry to the great banqueting room and have a glance at matters there whilst Tom is being made ready for the imposing occasion. It is a spacious apartment, with gilded pillars and pilasters, and pictured walls and ceilings. At the door stand tall guards, as rigid as statues, dressed in rich and picturesque costumes, and bearing halberds. In a high gallery which runs all around the place is a band of musicians and a packed company of citizens of both sexes, in brilliant attire. In the centre of the room, upon a raised platform, is Tom's table. Now let the ancient chronicler speak:

"A gentleman enters the room bearing a rod, and along with him another bearing a table-cloth, which, after they have both kneeled three times with the utmost veneration, he spreads upon the table, and after kneeling again they both retire; then come two others, one with the rod again, the other with a salt-cellar, a plate, and bread; when they have kneeled as the others had done, and placed what was brought upon the table, they too retire with the same ceremonies performed by the first; at last come two nobles, richly clothed, one bearing a tasting-knife, who, after prostrating themselves in the most graceful manner, approach and rub the table with bread and salt, with as much awe as if the king had been present." *

So end the solemn preliminaries. Now, far down the echoing corridors we hear a bugle-blast, and the indistinct cry, "Place for the king! way for the king's most excellent majesty!" These sounds are momently repeated—they grow nearer and nearer—and presently, almost in our faces, the martial note peals and the cry rings out, "Way for the king!" At this instant the shining pageant appears, and files in at the door, with a measured march. Let the chronicler speak again:

"First come Gentlemen, Barons, Earls, Knights of the Garter, all richly dressed and bareheaded; next comes the Chancellor, between two, one of which carries the royal sceptre, the other the Sword of State in a red scabbard, studded with golden fleurs-de-lis, the point upwards; next comes the King himself—whom, upon his appearing, twelve trumpets and many drums salute with a great burst of welcome, whilst all in the galleries rise in their places, crying "God save the King!" After him come nobles attached to his person, and on his right and left march his guard of honor, his fifty Gentlemen Pensioners, with gilt battle-axes."

This was all fine and pleasant. Tom's pulse beat high and a glad light was in his eye. He bore himself right gracefully, and all the more so because he was

"A GENTLEMAN BEARING A ROD."

* Leigh Hunt's "The Town," p. 408, quotation from an early tourist.

not thinking of how he was doing it, his mind being charmed and occupied with
the blithe sights and sounds about him—and besides, nobody can be very ungraceful
in nicely-fitting beautiful clothes after he has grown a little used to them—
especially if he is for the moment unconscious of them. Tom remembered his
instructions, and acknowledged his greeting with a slight inclination of his plumed
head, and a courteous "I thank ye, my good people."

He seated himself at table, without removing his cap; and did it without the
least embarrassment; for to eat with one's cap on was the one solitary royal
custom upon which the kings and the Cantys met upon common ground, neither
party having any advantage over the other in the matter of old familiarity with
it. The pageant broke up and grouped itself picturesquely, and remained bareheaded.

Now, to the sound of gay music, the Yeomen of the Guard entered,—"the
tallest and mightiest men in England, they being selected in this regard"—but
we will let the chronicler tell about it:

"The Yeomen of the Guard entered, bareheaded, clothed in scarlet, with
golden roses upon their backs; and these went and came, bringing in each turn
a course of dishes, served in plate. These dishes were received by a gentleman
in the same order they were brought, and placed upon the table, while the taster
gave to each guard a mouthful to eat of the particular dish he had brought, for
fear of any poison."

Tom made a good dinner, notwithstanding he was conscious that hundreds of
eyes followed each morsel to his mouth and watched him eat it with an interest
which could not have been more intense if it had been a deadly explosive and
was expected to blow him up and scatter him all over the place. He was careful
not to hurry, and equally careful not to do any thing whatever for himself, but
wait till the proper official knelt down and did it for him. He got through without
a mistake—flawless and precious triumph.

When the meal was over at last and he marched away in the midst of his
bright pageant, with the happy noises in his ears of blaring bugles, rolling drums
and thundering acclamations, he felt that if he had seen the worst of dining in
public, it was an ordeal which he would be glad to endure several times a day
if by that means he could but buy himself free from some of the more formidable
requirements of his royal office.

Chapter XVII

FOO-FOO THE FIRST

MILES HENDON HURRIED along toward the Southwark end of the bridge, keeping
a sharp lookout for the persons he sought, and hoping and expecting to overtake
them presently. He was disappointed in this, however. By asking questions, he
was enabled to track them part of the way through Southwark; then all traces
ceased, and he was perplexed as to how to proceed. Still, he continued his efforts
as best he could during the rest of the day. Nightfall found him leg-weary, half
famished, and his desire as far from accomplishment as ever; so he supped at
the Tabard inn and went to bed, resolved to make an early start in the morning,
and give the town an exhaustive search. As he lay thinking and planning, he

presently began to reason thus: The boy would escape from the ruffian, his reputed father, if possible; would he go back to London and seek his former haunts? no, he would not do that, he would avoid recapture. What, then, would he do? Never having had a friend in the world, or a protector, until he met Miles Hendon, he would naturally try to find that friend again, provided the effort did not require him to go toward London and danger. He would strike for Hendon Hall, that is what he would do, for he knew Hendon was homeward bound and there he might expect to find him. Yes, the case was plain to Hendon—he must lose no more time in Southwark, but move at once through Kent, toward Monk's Holm, searching the wood and inquiring as he went. Let us return to the vanished little king, now.

The ruffian whom the waiter at the inn on the bridge saw "about to join" the youth and the king, did not exactly join them, but fell in close behind them and followed their steps. He said nothing. His left arm was in a sling, and he wore a large green patch over his left eye; he limped slightly, and used an oaken staff as a support. The youth led the king a crooked course through Southwark, and by and by struck into the high road beyond. The king was irritated, now, and said he would stop here—it was Hendon's place to come to him, not his to go to Hendon. He would not endure such insolence; he would stop where he was. The youth said—

"Thou'lt tarry here, and thy friend lying wounded in the wood yonder? So be it, then."

The king's manner changed at once. He cried out—

"Wounded? And who hath dared to do it? But that is apart; lead on, lead on! Faster, sirrah! art shod with lead? Wounded, is he? Now though the doer of it be a duke's son, he shall rue it!"

It was some distance to the wood, but the space was speedily traversed. The youth looked about him, discovered a bough sticking in the ground, with a small bit of rag tied to it, then led the way into the forest, watching for similar boughs and finding them at intervals: they were evidently guides to the point he was aiming at. By and by an open place was reached, where were the charred remains of a farm house, and near them a barn which was falling to ruin and decay. There was no sign of life anywhere, and utter silence prevailed. The youth entered the barn, the king following eagerly upon his heels. No one there! The king shot a surprised and suspicious glance at the youth, and asked—

"Where is he?"

A mocking laugh was his answer. The king was in a rage in a moment; he seized a billet of wood and was in the act of charging upon the youth when another mocking laugh fell upon his ear. It was from the lame ruffian, who had been following at a distance. The king turned and said angrily—

"Who art thou? What is thy business here?"

"Leave thy foolery," said the man, "and quiet thyself. My disguise is none so good that thou canst pretend thou knowest not thy father through it."

"Thou art not my father. I know thee not. I am the king. If thou hast hid my servant, find him for me, or thou shalt sup sorrow for what thou hast done."

John Canty replied, in a stern and measured voice—

"It is plain thou art mad, and I am loth to punish thee; but if thou provoke me, I must. Thy prating doth no harm here, where there are no ears that need to mind thy follies, yet is it well to practice thy tongue to wary speech, that it may do no hurt when our quarters change. I have done a murder, and may not tarry at home—neither shalt thou, seeing I need thy service. My name is changed, for wise reasons; it is Hobbs—John Hobbs; thine is Jack—charge thy memory accordingly. Now, then, speak. Where is thy mother? where are thy sisters? They came not to the place appointed—knowest thou whither they went?''

The king answered, sullenly—

''Trouble me not with these riddles. My mother is dead; my sisters are in the palace.''

The youth near by burst into a derisive laugh, and the king would have assaulted him, but Canty—or Hobbs, as he now called himself—prevented him, and said—

''Peace, Hugo, vex him not; his mind is astray, and thy ways fret him. Sit thee down, Jack, and quiet thyself; thou shalt have a morsel to eat, anon.''

Hobbs and Hugo fell to talking together, in low voices, and the king removed himself as far as he could from their disagreeable company. He withdrew into the twilight of the farther end of the barn, where he found the earthen floor bedded a foot deep with straw. He lay down here, drew straw over himself in lieu of blankets, and was soon absorbed in thinking. He had many griefs, but the minor ones were swept almost into forgetfulness by the supreme one, the loss of his father. To the rest of the world the name of Henry VIII. brought a shiver, and suggested an ogre whose nostrils breathed destruction and whose hand dealt scourgings and death; but to this boy the name brought only sensations of pleasure, the figure it invoked wore a countenance that was all gentleness and affection. He called to mind a long succession of loving passages between his father and himself, and dwelt fondly upon them, his unstinted tears attesting how deep and real was the grief that possessed his heart. As the afternoon wasted away, the lad, wearied with his troubles, sunk gradually into a tranquil and healing slumber.

After a considerable time—he could not tell how long—his senses struggled to a half-consciousness, and as he lay with closed eyes vaguely wondering where he was and what had been happening, he noted a murmurous sound, the sullen beating of rain upon the roof. A snug sense of comfort stole over him, which was rudely broken, the next moment, by a chorus of piping cackles and coarse laughter. It startled him disagreeably, and he unmuffled his head to see whence this interruption proceeded. A grim and unsightly picture met his eye. A bright fire was burning in the middle of the floor, at the other end of the barn; and around it, and lit weirdly up by the red glare, lolled and sprawled the motliest company of tattered gutter-scum and ruffians, of both sexes, he had ever read or dreamed of. There were huge, stalwart men, brown with exposure, long-haired, and clothed in fantastic rags; there were middle-sized youths, of truculent countenance, and similarly clad; there were blind mendicants, with patched or bandaged eyes; crippled ones, with wooden legs and crutches; there was a villain-looking peddler with his pack; a knife-grinder, a tinker, and a barber-surgeon, with the implements of their trades; some of the females were hardly-grown girls, some were at prime, some were old and wrinkled hags, and all were loud, brazen, foul-mouthed; and all soiled and slatternly; there were three sore-faced babies; there were a couple of starveling curs, with strings about their necks, whose office was to lead the blind.

The night was come, the gang had just finished feasting, an orgy was beginning, the can of liquor was passing from mouth to mouth. A general cry broke forth—

''A song! a song from the Bat and Dick Dot-and-go-One!''

One of the blind men got up, and made ready by casting aside the patches that sheltered his excellent eyes, and the pathetic placard which recited the cause of his calamity. Dot-and-go-One disencumbered himself of his timber leg and took his place, upon sound and healthy limbs, beside his fellow-rascal; then they roared out a rollicking ditty, and were re-enforced by the whole crew, at the end of each stanza, in a rousing chorus. By the time the last stanza was reached, the half-drunken enthusiasm had risen to such a pitch, that everybody joined in and sang it clear through from the beginning, producing a volume of villainous sound that made the rafters quake. These were the inspiring words:

> "Bien Darkmans then, Bouse Mort and Ken,
> The bien Coves bings awast,
> On Chates to trine by Rome Coves dine
> For his long lib at last.
> Bing'd out bien Morts and toure, and toure,
> Bing out of the Rome vile bine,
> And toure the Cove that cloy'd your duds,
> Upon the Chates to trine." *

Conversation followed; not in the thieves' dialect of the song, for that was only used in talk when unfriendly ears might be listening. In the course of it it appeared that "John Hobbs" was not altogether a new recruit, but had trained in the gang at some former time. His later history was called for, and when he said he had "accidentally" killed a man, considerable satisfaction was expressed; when he added that the man was a priest, he was roundly applauded, and had to take a drink with everybody. Old acquaintances welcomed him joyously, and new ones were proud to shake him by the hand. He was asked why he had "tarried away so many months." He answered—

"London is better than the country, and safer these late years, the laws be so bitter and so diligently enforced. An' I had not had that accident, I had staid there. I had resolved to stay, and never more venture country wards—but the accident has ended that."

He inquired how many persons the gang numbered now. The "Ruffler," or chief, answered—

"Five and twenty sturdy budges, bulks, files, clapperdogeons and maunders, counting the dells and doxies and other morts.* Most are here, the rest are wandering eastward, along the winter lay. We follow at dawn."

"I do not see the Wen among the honest folk about me. Where may he be?"

"Poor lad, his diet is brimstone, now, and over hot for a delicate taste. He was killed in a brawl, somewhere about midsummer."

"I sorrow to hear that; the Wen was a capable man, and brave."

"That was he, truly. Black Bess, his dell, is of us yet, but absent on the eastward tramp; a fine lass, of nice ways and orderly conduct, none ever seeing her drunk above four days in the seven."

"She was ever strict—I remember it well—a goodly wench and worthy all

---

* From "The English Rogue;" London, 1665.
* Canting terms for various kinds of thieves, beggars and vagabonds, and their female companions.

commendation. Her mother was more free and less particular; a troublesome and ugly tempered beldame, but furnished with a wit above the common.''

"We lost her through it. Her gift of palmistry and other sorts of fortune-telling begot for her at last a witch's name and fame. The law roasted her to death at a slow fire. It did touch me to a sort of tenderness to see the gallant way she met her lot—cursing and reviling all the crowd that gaped and gazed around her, whilst the flames licked upward toward her face and catched her thin locks and crackled about her old gray head—cursing them, said I?—cursing them! why an' thou shouldst live a thousand years thoud'st never hear so masterful a cursing. Alack, her art died with her. There be base and weakling imitations left, but no true blasphemy.''

The Ruffler sighed; the listeners sighed in sympathy; a general depression fell upon the company for a moment, for even hardened outcasts like these are not wholly dead to sentiment, but are able to feel a fleeting sense of loss and affliction at wide intervals and under peculiarly favoring circumstances—as in cases like to this, for instance, when genius and culture depart and leave no heir. However, a deep drink all round soon restored the spirits of the mourners.

"Have any others of our friends fared hardly?" asked Hobbs.

"Some—yes. Particularly new comers—such as small husbandmen turned shiftless and hungry upon the world because their farms were taken from them to be changed to sheep ranges. They begged, and were whipped at the cart's tail, naked from the girdle up, till the blood ran; then set in the stocks to be pelted; they begged again, were whipped again, and deprived of an ear; they begged a third time—poor devils, what else could they do?—and were branded on the cheek with a red hot iron, then sold for slaves; they ran away, were hunted down, and hanged. 'Tis a brief tale, and quickly told. Others of us have fared less hardly. Stand forth, Yokel, Burns, and Hodge—show your adornments!''

These stood up and stripped away some of their rags, exposing their backs, criss-crossed with ropy old welts left by the lash; one turned up his hair and showed the place where a left ear had once been; another showed a brand upon his shoulder—the letter V—and a mutilated ear; the third said—

"I am Yokel, once a farmer and prosperous, with loving wife and kids—now am I somewhat different in estate and calling; and the wife and kids are gone; mayhap they are in heaven, mayhap in—in the other place—but the kindly God be thanked, they bide no more in *England!* My good old blameless mother strove to earn bread by nursing the sick; one of these died, the doctors knew not how, so my mother was burnt for a witch, whilst my babes looked on and wailed. English law!—up, all, with your cups!—now altogether and with a cheer!—drink to the merciful English law that delivered *her* from the English hell! Thank you, mates, one and all. I begged, from house to house—I and the wife—bearing with us the hungry kids—but it was crime to be hungry in England—so they stripped us and lashed us through three towns. Drink ye all again to the merciful English law!—for its lash drank deep of my Mary's blood and its blessed deliverance came quick. She lies there, in the potter's field, safe from all harms. And the kids—well, whilst the law lashed me from town to town, they starved. Drink lads—only a drop—a drop to the poor kids, that never did any creature harm. I begged again—begged for a crust, and got the stocks and lost an ear—see, here bides the stump; I begged again, and here is the stump of the other to keep me minded of it. And still I begged again, and was sold for a slave—here on my cheek under this stain, if I washed it off, ye might see the red S the branding-iron left there! A SLAVE! Do ye understand that word! An English SLAVE!—that is he that stands before ye. I have run from my master, and when I am found— the heavy curse of heaven fall on the law of the land that hath commanded it!— I shall hang!''

A ringing voice came through the murky air—

''Thou shalt *not!*—and this day the end of that law is come!''

All turned, and saw the fantastic figure of the little king approaching hurriedly; as it emerged into the light and was clearly revealed, a general explosion of inquiries broke out:

''Who is it? *What* is it? Who art thou, manikin?''

The boy stood unconfused in the midst of all those surprised and questioning eyes, and answered with princely dignity—

''I am Edward, king of England.''

A wild burst of laughter followed, partly of derision and partly of delight in the excellence of the joke. The king was stung. He said sharply—

''Ye mannerless vagrants, is this your recognition of the royal boon I have promised?''

He said more, with angry voice and excited gesture, but it was lost in a whirlwind of laughter and mocking exclamations. ''John Hobbs'' made several attempts to make himself heard above the din, and at last succeeded—saying—

''Mates, he is my son, a dreamer, a fool, and stark mad—mind him not—he thinketh he *is* the king.''

''I *am* the king,'' said Edward, turning toward him, ''as thou shalt know to thy cost, in good time. Thou hast confessed a murder—thou shalt swing for it.''

''*Thou'lt* betray me?—*thou?* An' I get my hands upon thee''—

''Tut-tut!'' said the burly Ruffler, interposing in time to save the king, and emphasizing this service by knocking Hobbs down with his fist, ''hast respect for neither Kings *nor* Rufflers? An' thou insult my presence so again, I'll hang thee up myself.'' Then he said to his majesty, ''Thou must make no threats against thy mates, lad; and thou must guard thy tongue from saying evil of them elsewhere. *Be* king, if it please thy mad humor, but be not harmful in it. Sink the title thou hast uttered,—'tis treason; we be bad men, in some few trifling ways, but none among us is so base as to be traitor to his king; we be loving and loyal hearts, in that regard. Note if I speak truth. Now—all together: 'Long live Edward, king of England!' ''

''LONG LIVE EDWARD, KING OF ENGLAND!''

The response came with such a thundergust from the motley crew that the crazy building vibrated to the sound. The little king's face lighted with pleasure for an instant, and he slightly inclined his head and said with grave simplicity—

''I thank you, my good people.''

This unexpected result threw the company into convulsions of merriment. When something like quiet was presently come again, the Ruffler said, firmly, but with an accent of good nature—

''Drop it, boy, 'tis not wise, nor well. Humor thy fancy, if thou must, but choose some other title.''

A tinker shrieked out a suggestion—

''Foo-foo the First, King of the Mooncalves!''

The title ''took,'' at once, every throat responded, and a roaring shout went up, of—

"THRONE HIM."

"Long live Foo-foo the First, King of the Mooncalves!" followed by hootings, cat-calls, and peals of laughter.

"Hale him forth, and crown him!"

"Robe him!"

"Sceptre him!"

"Throne him!"

These and twenty other cries broke out at once; and almost before the poor little victim could draw a breath he was crowned with a tin basin, robed in a tattered blanket, throned upon a barrel, and sceptred with the tinker's soldering-iron. Then all flung themselves upon their knees about him and sent up a chorus of ironical wailings, and mocking supplications, whilst they swabbed their eyes with their soiled and ragged sleeves and aprons—

"Be gracious to us, O, sweet king!"

"Trample not upon thy beseeching worms, O noble majesty!"

"Pity thy slaves, and comfort them with a royal kick!"

"Cheer us and warm us with thy gracious rays, O flaming sun of sovereignty!"

"Sanctify the ground with the touch of thy foot, that we may eat the dirt and be ennobled!"

"Deign to spit upon us, O sire, that our children's children may tell of thy princely condescension, and be proud and happy forever!"

But the humorous tinker made the "hit" of the evening and carried off the honors. Kneeling, he pretended to kiss the king's foot, and was indignantly spurned; whereupon he went about begging for a rag to paste over the place upon his face which had been touched by the foot, saying it must be preserved from contact with the vulgar air, and that he should make his fortune by going on the highway and exposing it to view at the rate of a hundred shillings a sight. He made himself so killingly funny that he was the envy and admiration of the whole mangy rabble.

Tears of shame and indignation stood in the little monarch's eyes; and the thought in his heart was, "Had I offered them a deep wrong they could not be more cruel—yet have I proffered nought but to do them a kindness—and it is thus they use me for it!"

Chapter XVIII

THE PRINCE WITH THE TRAMPS

THE TROOP OF vagabonds turned out at early dawn, and set forward on their march. There was a lowering sky overhead, sloppy ground under foot, and a winter chill in the air. All gayety was gone from the company; some were sullen and silent, some were irritable and petulant, none were gentle-humored, all were thirsty.

The Ruffler put "Jack" in Hugo's charge, with some brief instructions, and commanded John Canty to keep away from him and let him alone; he also warned Hugo not to be too rough with the lad.

After a while the weather grew milder, and the clouds lifted somewhat. The troop ceased to shiver, and their spirits began to improve. They grew more and more cheerful, and finally began to chaff each other and insult passengers along the highway. This showed that they were awaking to an appreciation of life and its joys once more. The dread in which their sort was held was apparent in the fact that everybody gave them the road, and took their ribald insolences meekly, without venturing to talk back. They snatched linen from the hedges, occasionally, in full view of the owners, who made no protest, but only seemed grateful that they did not take the hedges, too.

By and by they invaded a small farm house and made themselves at home while the trembling farmer and his people swept the larder clean to furnish a breakfast for them. They chucked the housewife and her daughters under the chin whilst receiving the food from their hands, and made coarse jests about them, accompanied with insulting epithets and bursts of horse-laughter. They threw bones and vegetables at the farmer and his sons, kept them dodging all the time, and applauded uproariously when a good hit was made. They ended by buttering the head of one of the daughters who resented some of their familiarities. When they took their leave they threatened to come back and burn the house over the heads of the family if any report of their doings got to the ears of the authorities.

About noon, after a long and weary tramp, the gang came to a halt behind a hedge on the outskirts of a considerable village. An hour was allowed for rest, then the crew scattered themselves abroad to enter the village at different points to ply their various trades.—"Jack" was sent with Hugo. They wandered hither and thither for some time, Hugo watching for opportunities to do a stroke of business but finding none—so he finally said—

"I see nought to steal; it is a paltry place. Wherefore we will beg."

"*We*, forsooth! Follow thy trade—it befits thee. But *I* will not beg."

"Thou'lt not beg!" exclaimed Hugo, eying the king with surprise. "Prithee, since when hast thou reformed?"

"What dost thou mean?"

"Mean? Hast thou not begged the streets of London all thy life?"

"I? Thou idiot!"

"Spare thy compliments—thy stock will last the longer. Thy father says thou

429

hast begged all thy days. Mayhap he lied. Peradventure you will even make so bold as to *say* he lied,'' scoffed Hugo.

"Him *you* call my father? Yes, he lied."

"Come, play not thy merry game of madman so far, mate; use it for thy amusement, not thy hurt. An' I tell him this, he will scorch thee finely for it.''

"Save thyself the trouble. I will tell him.''

"I like thy spirit, I do in truth; but I do not admire thy judgment. Bone-rackings and bastings be plenty enow in this life, without going out of one's way to invite them. But a truce to these matters; *I* believe your father. I doubt not he can lie; I doubt not he *doth* lie, upon occasion, for the best of us do that; but there is no occasion here. A wise man does not waste so good a commodity as lying for nought. But come; sith it is thy humor to give over begging, wherewithal shall we busy ourselves? With robbing kitchens?''

The king said, impatiently—

"Have done with this folly—you weary me!''

Hugo replied, with temper—

"Now harkee, mate; you will not beg, you will not rob; so be it. But I will tell you what you *will* do. You will play decoy whilst *I* beg. Refuse, an' you think you may venture!''

The king was about to reply contemptuously, when Hugo said, interrupting—

"Peace! Here comes one with a kindly face. Now will I fall down in a fit. When the stranger runs to me, set you up a wail, and fall upon your knees, seeming to weep; then cry out as all the devils of misery were in your belly, and say, 'O, sir, it is my poor afflicted brother, and we be friendless; o' God's name cast through your merciful eyes one pitiful look upon a sick, forsaken and most miserable wretch; bestow one little penny out of thy riches upon one smitten of God and ready to perish!'—and mind you, keep you *on* wailing, and abate not till we bilk him of his penny, else shall you rue it.''

Then immediately Hugo began to moan, and groan, and roll his eyes, and reel and totter about; and when the stranger was close at hand, down he sprawled before him, with a shriek, and began to writhe and wallow in the dirt, in seeming agony.

"O dear, O dear!'' cried the benevolent stranger. "O poor soul, poor soul, how he doth suffer! There—let me help thee up.''

"O, noble sir, forbear, and God love you for a princely gentleman—but it giveth me cruel pain to touch me when I am taken so. My brother there will tell your worship how I am racked with anguish when these fits be upon me. A penny, dear sir, a penny, to buy a little food; then leave me to my sorrows.''

"A penny! thou shalt have three, thou hapless creature''—and he fumbled in his pocket with nervous haste and got them out. "There, poor lad, take them, and most welcome. Now come hither, my boy, and help me carry thy stricken brother to yon house, where''—

"I am not his brother,'' said the king, interrupting.

"What! not his brother?''

"O hear him!'' groaned Hugo, then privately ground his teeth. "He denies his own brother—and he with one foot in the grave!''

"Boy, thou art indeed hard of heart, if this is thy brother. For shame!—and he scarce able to move hand or foot. If he is not thy brother, who is he, then?''

"A beggar and a thief! He has got your money and has picked your pocket likewise. An' thou wouldst do a healing miracle, lay thy staff over his shoulders and trust Providence for the rest.''

But Hugo did not tarry for the miracle. In a moment he was up and off like the wind, the gentleman following after and raising the hue and cry lustily as he went. The king, breathing deep gratitude to Heaven for his own release, fled in the opposite direction and did not slacken his pace until he was out of harm's reach. He took the first road that offered, and soon put the village behind him. He hurried along, as briskly as he could, during several hours, keeping a nervous watch over his shoulder for pursuit; but his fears left him at last, and a grateful sense of security took their place. He recognized, now, that he was hungry; and also very tired. So he halted at a farm house; but when he was about to speak, he was cut short and driven rudely away. His clothes were against him.

He wandered on, wounded and indignant, and was resolved to put himself in the way of light treatment no more. But hunger is pride's master; so as the evening drew near, he made an attempt at another farm house; but here he fared worse than before; for he was called hard names and was promised arrest as a vagrant except he moved on promptly.

The night came on, chilly and overcast; and still the foot-sore monarch labored slowly on. He was obliged to keep moving, for every time he sat down to rest he was soon penetrated to the bone with the cold. All his sensations and experiences, as he moved through the solemn gloom and the empty vastness of the night, were new and strange to him. At intervals he heard voices approach, pass by, and fade into silence; and as he saw nothing more of the bodies they belonged to than a sort of formless drifting blur, there was something spectral and uncanny about it all that made him shudder. Occasionally he caught the twinkle of a light—always far away, apparently—almost in another world; if he heard the tinkle of a sheep's bell, it was vague, distant, indistinct; the muffled lowing of the herds floated to him on the night wind in vanishing cadences, a mournful sound; now and then came the complaining howl of a dog over viewless expanses of field and forest; all sounds were remote; they made the little king feel that all life and activity were far removed from him, and that he stood solitary, companionless, in the centre of a measureless solitude.

He stumbled along, through the grewsome fascinations of this new experience, startled occasionally by the soft rustling of the dry leaves overhead, so like human whispers they seemed to sound; and by and by he came suddenly upon the freckled light of a tin lantern near at hand. He stepped back into the shadows and waited. The lantern stood by the open door of a barn. The king waited some time—there was no sound, and nobody stirring. He got so cold, standing still, and the hospitable barn looked so enticing, that at last he resolved to risk everything and enter. He started swiftly and stealthily, and just as he was crossing the threshold he heard voices behind him. He darted behind a cask, within the barn, and stooped down. Two farm laborers came in, bringing the lantern with them, and fell to work, talking meanwhile. Whilst they moved about with the light, the king made good use of his eyes and took the bearings of what seemed to be a good sized stall at the further end of the place, purposing to grope his way to it when he should be left to himself. He also noted the position of a pile of horse blankets, midway of the route, with the intent to levy upon them for the service of the crown of England for one night.

By and by the men finished and went away, fastening the door behind them and taking the lantern with them. The shivering king made for the blankets, with as good speed as the darkness would allow; gathered them up and then groped his way safely to the stall. Of two of the blankets he made a bed, then covered himself with the remaining two. He was a glad monarch, now, though the blankets were old and thin, and not quite warm enough; and besides gave out a pungent horsy odor that was almost suffocatingly powerful.

Although the king was hungry and chilly, he was also so tired and so drowsy that these latter influences soon began to get the advantage of the former, and he presently dozed off into a state of semi-consciousness. Then, just as he was on the point of losing himself wholly, he distinctly felt something touch him! He was broad awake in a moment, and gasping for breath. The cold horror of that mysterious touch in the dark almost made his heart stand still. He lay motionless, and listened, scarcely breathing. But nothing stirred, and there was no sound. He continued to listen, and wait, during what seemed a long time, but still nothing stirred, and there was no sound. So he began to drop into a drowse once more, at last; and all at once he felt that mysterious touch again! It was a grisly thing, this light touch from this noiseless and invisible presence; it made the boy sick with ghostly fears. What should he do? That was the question; but he did not know how to answer it. Should he leave these reasonably comfortable quarters and fly from this inscrutable horror? But fly whither? He could not get out of the barn; and the idea of scurrying blindly hither and thither in the dark, within the captivity of the four walls, with this phantom gliding after him, and visiting him with that soft hideous touch upon cheek or shoulder at every turn, was intolerable. But to stay where he was, and endure this living death all night?—was that better? No. What, then, was there left to do? Ah, there was but one course; he knew it well—he must put out his hand and find that thing!

It was easy to think this; but it was hard to brace himself up to try it. Three times he stretched his hand a little way out into the dark, gingerly; and snatched it suddenly back, with a gasp—not because it had encountered any thing, but because he had felt so sure it was just *going* to. But the fourth time, he groped a little further, and his hand lightly swept against something soft and warm. This petrified him, nearly, with fright—his mind was in such a state that he could imagine the thing to be nothing else than a corpse, newly dead and still warm. He thought he would rather die than touch it again. But he thought this false thought because he did not know the immortal strength of human curiosity. In no long time his hand was tremblingly groping again—against his judgment, and without his consent—but groping persistently on, just the same. It encountered a bunch of long hair; he shuddered, but followed up the hair and found what seemed to be a warm rope; followed up the rope and found an innocent calf!— for the rope was not a rope at all, but the calf's tail.

The king was cordially ashamed of himself for having gotten all that fright and misery out of so paltry a matter as a slumbering calf; but he need not have felt so about it, for it was not the calf that frightened him but a dreadful non- existent something which the calf stood for; and any other boy, in those old superstitious times, would have acted and suffered just as he had done.

The king was not only delighted to find that the creature was only a calf, but delighted to have the calf's company; for he had been feeling so lonesome and friendless that the company and comradeship of even this humble animal was welcome. And he had been so buffeted, so rudely entreated by his own kind, that it was a real comfort to him to feel that he was at last in the society of a fellow creature that had at least a soft heart and a gentle spirit, whatever loftier attributes might be lacking. So he resolved to waive rank and make friends with the calf.

While stroking its sleek warm back—for it lay near him and within easy reach—it occurred to him that this calf might be utilized in more ways than one. Whereupon he re-arranged his bed, spreading it down close to the calf; then he cuddled himself up to the calf's back, drew the covers up over himself and his friend, and in a minute or two was as warm and comfortable as he had ever been in the downy couches of the regal palace of Westminster.

Pleasant thoughts came, at once; life took on a cheerfuller seeming. He was free of the bonds of servitude and crime, free of the companionship of base and brutal outlaws; he was warm, he was sheltered; in a word, he was happy. The night wind was rising; it swept by in fitful gusts that made the old barn quake and rattle, then its forces died down at intervals and went moaning and wailing around corners and projections—but it was all music to the king, now that he was snug and comfortable: let it blow and rage, let it batter and bang, let it moan and wail, he minded it not, he only enjoyed it. He merely snuggled the closer to his friend, in a luxury of warm contentment, and drifted blissfully out of consciousness into a deep and dreamless sleep that was full of serenity and peace. The distant dogs howled, the melancholy kine complained, and the winds went on raging, whilst furious sheets of rain drove along the roof; but the majesty of England slept on, undisturbed, and the calf did the same, it being a simple creature and not easily troubled by storms or embarrassed by sleeping with a king.

Chapter XIX

THE PRINCE WITH THE PEASANTS

When the king awoke in the early morning, he found that a wet but thoughtful rat had crept into the place during the night and made a cosey bed for itself in his bosom. Being disturbed, now, it scampered away. The boy smiled, and said, "Poor fool, why so fearful? I am as forlorn as thou. 'Twould be a shame in me to hurt the helpless, who am myself so helpless. Moreover, I owe you thanks for a good omen; for when a king has fallen so low that the very rats do make a bed of him, it surely meaneth that his fortunes be upon the turn, since it is plain he can no lower go."

He got up and stepped out of the stall, and just then he heard the sound of children's voices. The barn door opened and a couple of little girls came in. As soon as they saw him their talking and laughing ceased, and they stopped and stood still, gazing at him with strong curiosity; they presently began to whisper together, then they approached nearer, and stopped again to gaze and whisper. By and by they gathered courage and began to discuss him aloud. One said—

"He hath a comely face."

The other added—

"And pretty hair."

"But is ill clothed enow."

"And how starved he looketh."

They came still nearer, sidling shyly around and about him, examining him minutely from all points, as if he were some strange new kind of animal; but warily and watchfully, the while, as if they half feared he might be a sort of animal that would bite, upon occasion. Finally they halted before him, holding each other's hands, for protection, and took a good satisfying stare with their innocent eyes; then one of them plucked up all her courage and inquired with honest directness—

"Who art thou, boy?"

"I am the king," was the grave answer.

The children gave a little start, and their eyes spread themselves wide open and remained so during a speechless half minute. Then curiosity broke the silence—

"The *king?* What king?"

"The king of England."

The children looked at each other—then at him—then at each other again—wonderingly, perplexedly—then one said—

"Didst hear him, Margery?—he saith he is the king. Can that be true?"

"How can it be else but true, Prissy? Would he say a lie? For look you, Prissy, an' it were not true, it *would* be a lie. It surely would be. Now think on't. For all things that be not true, be lies—thou canst make nought else out of it."

It was a good tight argument, without a leak in it anywhere; and it left Prissy's half-doubts not a leg to stand on. She considered a moment, then put the king upon his honor with the simple remark—

"If thou art truly the king, then I believe thee."

"I am truly the king."

This settled the matter. His majesty's royalty was accepted without further question or discussion, and the two little girls began at once to inquire into how he came to be where he was, and how he came to be so unroyally clad, and whither he was bound, and all about his affairs. It was a mighty relief to him to pour out his troubles where they would not be scoffed at or doubted; so he told his tale with feeling, forgetting even his hunger for the time; and it was received with the deepest and tenderest sympathy by the gentle little maids. But when he got down to his latest experiences and they learned how long he had been without food, they cut him short and hurried him away to the farm house to find a breakfast for him.

The king was cheerful and happy, now, and said to himself, "When I am come to my own again, I will always honor little children, remembering how that these trusted me and believed in me in my time of trouble; whilst they that were older, and thought themselves wiser, mocked at me and held me for a liar."

The children's mother received the king kindly, and was full of pity; for his forlorn condition and apparently crazed intellect touched her womanly heart. She was a widow, and rather poor; consequently she had seen trouble enough to enable her to feel for the unfortunate. She imagined that the demented boy had wandered away from his friends or keepers; so she tried to find out whence he had come, in order that she might take measures to return him; but all her references to neighboring towns and villages, and all her inquiries in the same line, went for nothing—the boy's face, and his answers, too, showed that the

"TOOK A GOOD SATISFYING STARE."

things she was talking of were not familiar to him. He spoke earnestly and simply about court matters; and broke down, more than once, when speaking of the late king "his father;" but whenever the conversation changed to baser topics, he lost interest and became silent.

The woman was mightily puzzled; but she did not give up. As she proceeded with her cooking, she set herself to contriving devices to surprise the boy into betraying his real secret. She talked about cattle—he showed no concern; then about sheep—the same result—so her guess that he had been a shepherd boy was an error; she talked about mills; and about weavers, tinkers, smiths, trades and tradesmen of all sorts; and about Bedlam, and jails, and charitable retreats; but no matter, she was baffled at all points. Not altogether, either; for she argued that she had narrowed the thing down to domestic service. Yes, she was sure she was on the right track, now—he must have been a house servant. So she led up to that. But the result was discouraging. The subject of sweeping appeared to weary him; fire-building failed to stir him; scrubbing and scouring awoke no enthusiasm. Then the goodwife touched, with a perishing hope, and rather as a matter of form, upon the subject of cooking. To her surprise, and her vast delight, the king's face lighted at once! Ah, she had hunted him down at last, she thought; and she was right proud too, of the devious shrewdness and tact which had accomplished it.

Her tired tongue got a chance to rest, now; for the king's, inspired by gnawing hunger and the fragrant smells that came from the sputtering pots and pans, turned itself loose and delivered itself up to such an eloquent dissertation upon certain toothsome dishes, that within three minutes the woman said to herself, "Of a truth I was right—he hath holpen in a kitchen!" Then he broadened his bill of fare, and discussed it with such appreciation and animation, that the good-wife said to herself, "Good lack! how can he know so many dishes, and so fine ones withal? For these belong only upon the tables of the rich and great. Ah, now I see! ragged outcast as he is, he must have served in the palace before his reason went astray; yes, he must have helped in the very kitchen of the king himself! I will test him."

Full of eagerness to prove her sagacity, she told the king to mind the cooking a moment—hinting that he might manufacture and add a dish or two, if he chose—then she went out of the room and gave her children a sign to follow after. The king muttered—

"Another English king had a commission like to this, in a bygone time—it is nothing against my dignity to undertake an office which the great Alfred stooped to assume. But I will try to better serve my trust than he; for he let the cakes burn."

The intent was good, but the performance was not answerable to it; for this king, like the other one, soon fell into deep thinkings concerning his vast affairs, and the same calamity resulted—the cookery got burned. The woman returned in time to save the breakfast from entire destruction; and she promptly brought the king out of his dreams with a brisk and cordial tongue-lashing. Then, seeing how troubled he was, over his violated trust, she softened at once and was all goodness and gentleness toward him.

The boy made a hearty and satisfying meal, and was greatly refreshed and gladdened by it. It was a meal which was distinguished by this curious feature, that rank was waived on both sides; yet neither recipient of the favor was aware that it had been extended. The goodwife had intended to feed this young tramp with broken victuals in a corner, like any other tramp, or like a dog; but she was so remorseful for the scolding she had given him, that she did what she could to atone for it by allowing him to sit at the family table and eat with his betters, on ostensible terms of equality with them; and the king, on his side, was so remorseful for having broken his trust, after the family had been so kind to him, that he forced himself to atone for it by humbling himself to the family level, instead of requiring the woman and her children to stand and wait upon him while he occupied their table in the solitary state due his birth and dignity. It does us all good to unbend sometimes. This good woman was made happy all the day long by the applauses she got out of herself for her magnanimous condescension to a tramp; and the king was just as self-complacent over his gracious humility toward a humble peasant woman.

When breakfast was over, the housewife told the king to wash up the dishes. This command was a staggerer, for a moment, and the king came near rebelling; but then he said to himself, "Alfred the Great watched the cakes; doubtless he would have washed the dishes, too—therefore will I essay it."

He made a sufficiently poor job of it; and to his surprise, too, for the cleaning of wooden spoons and trenchers had seemed an easy thing to do. It was a tedious and troublesome piece of work, but he finished it at last. He was becoming impatient to get away on his journey now; however, he was not to lose this thrifty dame's society so easily. She furnished him some little odds and ends of employment, which he got through with after a fair fashion and with some credit. Then she set him and the little girls to paring some winter apples; but he was so awkward at this service, that she retired him from it and gave him a butcher knife to grind. Afterward she kept him carding wool until he began to think he had laid the good King Alfred about far enough in the shade for the present, in the matter of showy menial heroisms that would read picturesquely in story-books and histories, and so he was half minded to resign. And when, just after the noonday dinner, the goodwife gave him a basket of kittens to drown, he did resign. At least he was just going to resign—for he felt that he must draw the line somewhere, and it seemed to him that to draw it at kitten-drowning was about the right thing—when there was an interruption. The interruption was John Canty—with a peddler's pack on his back—and Hugo!

The King discovered these rascals approaching the front gate before they had had a chance to see him; so he said nothing about drawing the line, but took up his basket of kittens and stepped quietly out the back way, without a word. He left the creatures in an outhouse, and hurried on, into a narrow lane at the rear.

Chapter XX

THE PRINCE AND THE HERMIT

THE HIGH HEDGE hid him from the house, now; and so, under the impulse of a deadly fright, he let out all his forces and sped toward a wood in the distance. He never looked back until he had almost gained the shelter of the forest; then he turned and descried two figures in the distance. That was sufficient; he did not wait to scan them critically, but hurried on, and never abated his pace till he was far within the twilight depths of the wood. Then he stopped; being persuaded that he was now tolerably safe. He listened intently, but the stillness was profound and solemn—awful, even, and depressing to the spirits. At wide intervals his straining ear did detect sounds, but they were so remote, and hollow, and mysterious, that they seemed not to be real sounds, but only the moaning and complaining ghosts of departed ones. So the sounds were yet more dreary than the silence which they interrupted.

It was his purpose, in the beginning, to stay where he was, the rest of the day; but a chill soon invaded his perspiring body, and he was at last obliged to resume movement in order to get warm. He struck straight through the forest, hoping to pierce to a road presently, but he was disappointed in this. He travelled on and on; but the farther he went, the denser the wood became, apparently. The gloom began to thicken, by and by, and the king realized that the night was coming on. It made him shudder to think of spending it in such an uncanny place; so he tried to hurry faster, but he only made the less speed, for he could not now see well enough to choose his steps judiciously; consequently he kept tripping over roots and tangling himself in vines and briers.

And how glad he was when at last he caught the glimmer of a light! He approached it warily, stopping often to look about him and listen. It came from an unglazed window-opening in a little hut. He heard a voice, now, and felt a disposition to run and hide; but he changed his mind at once, for this voice was praying, evidently. He glided to the one window of the hut, raised himself on tip-toe, and stole a glance within. The room was small; its floor was the natural earth, beaten hard by use; in a corner was a bed of rushes and a ragged blanket or two; near it was a pail, a cup, a basin, and two or three pots and pans; there was a short bench and a three-legged stool; on the hearth the remains of a fagot fire were smouldering; before a shrine, which was lighted by a single candle, knelt an aged man, and on an old wooden box at his side, lay an open book and a human skull. The man was of large, bony frame; his hair and whiskers were very long and snowy white; he was clothed in a robe of sheepskins which reached from his neck to his heels.

"A holy hermit!" said the king to himself; "now am I indeed fortunate."

The hermit rose from his knees; the king knocked. A deep voice responded—

"Enter!—but leave sin behind, for the ground whereon thou shalt stand is holy!"

The king entered, and paused. The hermit turned a pair of gleaming, unrestful eyes upon him, and said—

"Who art thou?"

"I am the king," came the answer, with placid simplicity.

"Welcome, king!" cried the hermit, with enthusiasm. Then, bustling about with feverish activity, and constantly saying "Welcome, welcome," he arranged his bench, seated the king on it, by the hearth, threw some fagots on the fire, and finally fell to pacing the floor, with a nervous stride.

"Welcome! Many have sought sanctuary here, but they were not worthy, and were turned away. But a king who casts his crown away, and despises the vain splendors of his office, and clothes his body in rags, to devote his life to holiness and the mortification of the flesh—he is worthy, he is welcome!—here shall he abide all his days till death come." The king hastened to interrupt and explain, but the hermit paid no attention to him—did not even hear him, apparently, but went right on with his talk, with a raised voice and a growing energy. "And thou shalt be at peace here. None shall find out thy refuge to disquiet thee with supplications to return to that empty and foolish life which God hath moved thee to abandon. Thou shalt pray, here; thou shalt study the Book; thou shalt meditate upon the follies and delusions of this world, and upon the sublimities of the world to come; thou shalt feed upon crusts and herbs, and scourge thy body with whips, daily, to the purifying of thy soul. Thou shalt wear a hair shirt next thy skin; thou shalt drink water, only; and thou shalt be at peace; yes, wholly at peace; for whoso comes to seek thee shall go his way again, baffled; he shall not find thee, he shall not molest thee."

The old man, still pacing back and forth, ceased to speak aloud, and began to mutter. The king seized this opportunity to state his case; and he did it with an eloquence inspired by uneasiness and apprehension. But the hermit went on muttering, and gave no heed. And still muttering, he approached the king and said, impressively—

" 'Sh! I will tell you a secret!" He bent down to impart it, but checked himself, and assumed a listening attitude. After a moment or two he went on tiptoe to the window-opening, put his head out and peered around in the gloaming, then came tiptoeing back again, put his face down to the king's, and whispered—

"I am an archangel!"

The king started violently, and said to himself, "Would God I were with the outlaws again; for lo, now am I the prisoner of a madman!" His apprehensions were heightened, and they showed plainly in his face. In a low, excited voice, the hermit continued——

"I see you feel my atmosphere! There's awe in your face! None may be in this atmosphere and not be thus affected; for it is the very atmosphere of heaven. I go thither and return, in the twinkling of an eye. I was made an archangel on this very spot, it is five years ago, by angels sent from heaven to confer that awful dignity. Their presence filled this place with an intolerable brightness. And they knelt to me, king! yes, they knelt to me! for I was greater than they. I have walked in the courts of heaven, and held speech with the patriarchs. Touch my hand—be not afraid—touch it. There—now thou hast touched a hand which has been clasped by Abraham, and Isaac and Jacob! For I have walked in the golden courts, I have seen the Deity face to face!" He paused, to give this speech effect; then his face suddenly changed, and he started to his feet again, saying, with angry energy, "Yes, I am an archangel; *a mere archangel!*—I that might have been pope! It is verily true. I was told it from heaven in a dream, twenty years ago; ah, yes, I was to be pope!—and I *should* have been pope, for Heaven had said it—but the king dissolved my religious house, and I, poor obscure unfriended monk, was cast homeless upon the world, robbed of my mighty destiny!" Here he began to mumble again, and beat his forehead in futile rage, with his fist; now and then articulating a venomous curse, and now and then a pathetic "Wherefore I am nought but an archangel—I that should have been pope!"

So he went on, for an hour, whilst the poor little king sat and suffered. Then all at once the old man's frenzy departed, and he became all gentleness. His voice softened, he came down out of his clouds, and fell to prattling along so simply and so humanely, that he soon won the king's heart completely. The old devotee moved the boy nearer to the fire and made him comfortable; doctored his small bruises and abrasions with a deft and tender hand; and then set about preparing and cooking a supper—chatting pleasantly all the time, and occasionally stroking the lad's cheek or patting his head, in such a gently caressing way that in a little while all the fear and repulsion inspired by the archangel were changed to reverence and affection for the man.

This happy state of things continued while the two ate the supper; then, after a prayer before the shrine, the hermit put the boy to bed, in a small adjoining room, tucking him in as snugly and lovingly as a mother might; and so, with a parting caress, left him and sat down by the fire, and began to poke the brands about in an absent and aimless way. Presently he paused; then tapped his forehead several times with his fingers, as if trying to recall some thought which had escaped from his mind. Apparently he was unsuccessful. Now he started quickly up, and entered his guest's room, and said—

"Thou art king?"

"Yes," was the response, drowsily uttered.

"What king?"

"Of England."

"Of England! Then Henry is gone!"

"Alack, it is so. I am his son."

A black frown settled down upon the hermit's face, and he clenched his bony hands with a vindictive energy. He stood a few moments, breathing fast and swallowing repeatedly, then said in a husky voice—

"Dost know it was he that turned us out into the world houseless and homeless?"

There was no response. The old man bent down and scanned the boy's reposeful face and listened to his placid breathing. "He sleeps—sleeps soundly;" and the frown vanished away and gave place to an expression of evil satisfaction. A smile flitted acros the dreaming boy's features. The hermit muttered. "So—his heart is happy;" and he turned away. He went stealthily about the place, seeking here and there for something; now and then halting to listen, now and then jerking his head around and casting a quick glance toward the bed; and always muttering, always mumbling to himself. At last he found what he seemed to want—a rusty old butcher knife and a whetstone. Then he crept to his place by the fire, sat himself down, and began to whet the knife softly on the stone, still muttering, mumbling, ejaculating. The winds sighed around the lonely place, the mysterious voices of the night floated by out of the distances. The shining eyes of venturesome mice and rats peered out at the old man from cracks and coverts, but he went on with his work, rapt absorbed, and noted none of these things.

At long intervals he drew his thumb along the edge of his knife, and nodded his head with satisfaction. "It grows sharper," he said; "yes, it grows sharper."

He took no note of the flight of time, but worked tranquilly on, entertaining himself with his thoughts, which broke out occasionally in articulate speech:

"His father wrought us evil, he destroyed us—and is gone down into the eternal fires! Yes, down into the eternal fires! He escaped us—but it was God's will, yes it was God's will, we must not repine. But he hath not escaped the fires! no, he hath not escaped the fires, the consuming, unpitying, remorseless fires—and *they* are everlasting!"

And so he wrought; and still wrought; mumbling—chuckling a low rasping chuckle, at times—and at times breaking again into words:

"It was his father that did it all. I am but an archangel—but for him, I should be pope!"

The king stirred. The hermit sprang noiselessly to the bedside, and went down upon his knees, bending over the prostrate form with his knife uplifted. The boy stirred again; his eyes came open for an instant, but there was no speculation in them, they saw nothing; the next moment his tranquil breathing showed that his sleep was sound once more.

The hermit watched and listened, for a time, keeping his position and scarcely breathing; then he slowly lowered his arm, and presently crept away, saying,—

"It is long past midnight—it is not best that he should cry out, lest by accident some one be passing."

He glided about his hovel, gathering a rag here, a thong there, and another one yonder; then he returned, and by careful and gentle handling, he managed to tie the king's ankles together without waking him. Next he essayed to tie the wrists; he made several attempts to cross them, but the boy always drew one hand or the other away, just as the cord was ready to be applied; but at last, when the archangel was almost ready to despair, the boy crossed his hands himself, and the next moment they were bound. Now a bandage was passed under the sleeper's chin and brought up over his head and tied fast—and so

" THE NEXT MOMENT THEY WERE BOUND."

softly, so gradually, and so deftly were the knots drawn together and compacted, that the boy slept peacefully through it all without stirring.

Chapter XXI

HENDON TO THE RESCUE

THE OLD MAN glided away, stooping, stealthily, cat-like, and brought the low bench. He seated himself upon it, half his body in the dim and flickering light, and the other half in shadow; and so, with his craving eyes bent upon the slumbering boy, he kept his patient vigil there, heedless of the drift of time, and softly whetted his knife, and mumbled and chuckled; and in aspect and attitude he resembled nothing so much as a grizzly, monstrous spider, gloating over some hapless insect that lay bound and helpless in his web.

After a long while, the old man, who was still gazing,—yet not seeing, his mind having settled into a dreamy abstraction,—observed on a sudden, that the boy's eyes were open—wide open and staring!—staring up in frozen horror at the knife. The smile of a gratified devil crept over the old man's face, and he said, without changing his attitude or his occupation—

"Son of Henry the Eighth, hast thou prayed?"

The boy struggled helplessly in his bonds; and at the same time forced a smothered sound through his closed jaws, which the hermit chose to interpret as an affirmative answer to his question.

"Then pray again. Pray the prayer for the dying!"

A shudder shook the boy's frame, and his face blenched. Then he struggled again to free himself—turning and twisting himself this way and that; tugging frantically, fiercely, desperately—but uselessly—to burst his fetters: and all the while the old ogre smiled down upon him, and nodded his head, and placidly whetted his knife; mumbling, from time to time. "The moments are precious, they are few and precious—pray the prayer for the dying!"

The boy uttered a despairing groan, and ceased from his struggles, panting. The tears came, then, and trickled, one after the other, down his face; but this piteous sight wrought no softening effect upon the savage old man.

The dawn was coming, now; the hermit observed it, and spoke up sharply, with a touch of nervous apprehension in his voice—

"I may not indulge this ecstasy longer! The night is already gone. It seems but a moment—only a moment; would it had endured a year! Seed of the Church's spoiler, close thy perishing eyes, an' thou fearest to look upon" . . .

The rest was lost in inarticulate mutterings. The old man sunk upon his knees, his knife in his hand, and bent himself over the moaning boy—

Hark! There was a sound of voices near the cabin—the knife dropped from the hermit's hand; he cast a sheepskin over the boy and started up, trembling. The sounds increased, and presently the voices became rough and angry; then came blows, and cries for help; then a clatter of swift footsteps, retreating. Immediately came a succession of thundering knocks upon the cabin door, followed by—

"Hullo-o-o! Open! And despatch, in the name of all the devils!"

" HE SUNK UPON HIS KNEES, HIS KNIFE IN HAND. "

O, this was the blessedest sound that had ever made music in the king's ears; for it was Miles Hendon's voice!

The hermit, grinding his teeth in impotent rage, moved swiftly out of the bedchamber, closing the door behind him; and straightway the king heard a talk, to this effect, proceeding from the "chapel:"

"Homage and greeting, reverend sir! Where is the boy—*my* boy?"

"What boy, friend?"

"What boy! Lie me no lies, sir priest, play me no deceptions!—I am not in the humor for it. Near to this place I caught the scoundrels who I judged did steal him from me, and I made them confess; they said he was at large again, and they had tracked him to your door. They showed me his very footprints. Now palter no more; for look you, holy sir, an' thou produce him not— Where is the boy?"

"O, good sir, peradventure you mean the ragged regal vagrant that tarried here the night. If such as you take interest in such as he, know, then, that I have sent him of an errand. He will be back anon."

"How soon? How soon? Come, waste not the time—cannot I overtake him? How soon will he be back?"

"Thou needst not stir; he will return quickly."

"So be it then. I will try to wait. But stop!—*you* sent him of an errand?— you! Verily, this is a lie—he would not go. He would pull thy old beard, an' thou didst offer him such an insolence. Thou hast lied, friend; thou hast surely lied! He would not go for thee nor for any man."

"For any *man*—no; haply not. But I am not a man."

"*What!* Now o' God's name what art thou, then?"

"It is a secret—mark thou reveal it not. I am an archangel!"

There was a tremendous ejaculation from Miles Hendon—not altogether un-profane—followed by—

"This doth well and truly account for his complaisance! Right well I knew he would budge nor hand nor foot in the menial service of any mortal; but lord, even a king must obey when an archangel gives the word o' command! Let me—'sh! What noise was that?"

All this while the king had been yonder, alternately quaking with terror and trembling with hope; and all the while, too, he had thrown all the strength he could into his anguished moanings, constantly expecting them to reach Hendon's ear, but always realizing, with bitterness, that they failed, or at least made no impression. So this last remark of his servant came as comes a reviving breath from fresh fields to the dying; and he exerted himself once more, and with all his energy, just as the hermit was saying—

"Noise? I heard only the wind."

"Mayhap it was. Yes, doubtless that was it. I have been hearing it faintly all the—there it is again! It is not the wind! What an odd sound! Come, we will hunt it out!"

Now the king's joy was nearly insupportable. His tired lungs did their utmost—and hopefully, too—but the sealed jaws and the muffling sheepskin sadly crippled the effort. Then the poor fellow's heart sank, to hear the hermit say—

"Ah, it came from without—I think from the copse yonder. Come, I will lead the way."

The king heard the two pass out, talking; heard their footsteps die quickly away—then he was alone with a boding, brooding, awful silence.

It seemed an age till he heard the steps and voices approaching again—and this time he heard an added sound—the trampling of hoofs, apparently. Then he heard Hendon say—

"I will not wait longer. I *cannot* wait longer. He has lost his way in this thick wood. Which direction took he? Quick—point it out to me."

"He—but wait; I will go with thee."

"Good—good! Why, truly thou art better than thy looks. Marry I do think there's not another archangel with so right a heart as thine. Wilt ride? Wilt take the wee donkey that's for my boy, or wilt thou fork thy holy legs over this ill-conditioned slave of a mule that I have provided for myself?—and had been cheated in, too, had he cost but the indifferent sum of a month's usury on a brass farthing let to a tinker out of work."

"No—ride thy mule, and lead thine ass; I am surer on mine own feet, and will walk."

"Then prithee mind the little beast for me while I take my life in my hands and make what success I may toward mounting the big one."

Then followed a confusion of kicks, cuffs, tramplings and plungings, accompanied by a thunderous intermingling of volleyed curses, and finally a bitter apostrophe to the mule, which must have broken its spirit, for hostilities seemed to cease from that moment.

With unutterable misery the fettered little king heard the voices and footsteps fade away and die out. All hope forsook him, now, for the moment, and a dull despair settled down upon his heart. "My only friend is deceived and got rid of," he said; "the hermit will return and"— He finished with a gasp; and at once fell to struggling so frantically with his bonds again, that he shook off the smothering sheepskin.

And now he heard the door open! The sound chilled him to the marrow—already he seemed to feel the knife at his throat. Horror made him close his eyes; horror made him open them again—and before him stood John Canty and Hugo!

He would have said "Thank God!" if his jaws had been free.

A moment or two later his limbs were at liberty, and his captors each gripping him by an arm, were hurrying him with all speed through the forest.

Chapter XXII

A VICTIM OF TREACHERY

ONCE MORE "King Foo-foo the First" was roving with the tramps and outlaws, a butt for their coarse jests and dull-witted railleries, and sometimes the victim of small spitefulnesses at the hands of Canty and Hugo when the Ruffler's back was turned. None but Canty and Hugo really disliked him. Some of the others liked him, and all admired his pluck and spirit. During two or three days, Hugo, in whose ward and charge the king was, did what he covertly could to make the boy uncomfortable; and at night, during the customary orgies, he amused the company by putting small indignities upon him—always as if by accident. Twice he stepped upon the king's toes—accidentally—and the king, as became his royalty, was contemptuously unconscious of it and indifferent to it; but the third time Hugo entertained himself in that way, the king felled him to the ground with a cudgel, to the prodigious delight of the tribe. Hugo, consumed with anger and shame, sprang up, seized a cudgel, and came at his small adversary in a fury. Instantly a ring was formed around the gladiators, and the betting and cheering began. But poor Hugo stood no chance whatever. His frantic and lubberly 'prentice-work found but a poor market for itself when pitted against an arm which had been trained by the first masters of Europe in single-stick, quarter-staff, and every art and trick of swordsmanship. The little king stood, alert but at graceful ease, and caught and turned aside the thick rain of blows with a facility and precision which set the motley on-lookers wild with admiration; and every now and then, when his practised eye detected an opening, and a lightning-swift rap upon Hugo's head followed as a result, the storm of cheers and laughter that swept the place was something wonderful to hear. At the end of fifteen minutes, Hugo, all battered, bruised, and the target for a pitiless bombardment of ridicule, slunk from the field; and the unscathed hero of the fight was seized and borne aloft upon the shoulders of the joyous rabble to the place of honor beside the Ruffler, where with vast ceremony he was crowned King of the Game-Cocks; his meaner title being at the same time solemnly cancelled and annulled, and a decree of banishment from the gang pronounced against any who should henceforth utter it.

All attempts to make the king serviceable to the troop had failed. He had stubbornly refused to act; moreover he was always trying to escape. He had been thrust into an unwatched kitchen, the first day of his return; he not only came forth empty handed, but tried to rouse the housemates. He was sent out with a tinker to help him at his work; he would not work; moreover he threatened the tinker with his own soldering-iron; and finally both Hugo and the tinker found their hands full with the mere matter of keeping him from getting away. He delivered the thunders of his royalty upon the heads of all who hampered his liberties or tried to force him to service. He was sent out, in Hugo's charge, in company with a slatternly woman and a diseased baby, to beg; but the result was not encouraging—he declined to plead for the mendicants, or be a party to their cause in any way.

Thus several days went by; and the miseries of this tramping life, and the weariness and sordidness and meanness and vulgarity of it, became gradually and steadily so intolerable to the captive that he began at last to feel that his release from the hermit's knife must prove only a temporary respite from death, at best.

But at night, in his dreams, these things were forgotten, and he was on his throne, and master again. This, of course, intensified the sufferings of the awakening—so the mortifications of each succeeding morning of the few that passed between his return to bondage and the combat with Hugo, grew bitterer and bitterer, and harder and harder to bear.

The morning after that combat, Hugo got up with a heart filled with vengeful purposes against the king. He had two plans, in particular. One was to inflict upon the lad what would be, to his proud spirit and "imagined" royalty, a peculiar humiliation; and if he failed to accomplish this, his other plan was to put a crime of some kind upon the king and then betray him into the implacable clutches of the law.

In pursuance of the first plan, he proposed to put a "clime" upon the king's leg; rightly judging that that would mortify him to the last and perfect degree; and as soon as the clime should operate, he meant to get Canty's help, and *force* the king to expose his leg in the highway and beg for alms. "Clime" was the cant term for a sore, artificially created. To make a clime, the operator made a paste or poultice of unslaked lime, soap, and the rust of old iron, and spread it upon a piece of leather, which was then bound tightly upon the leg. This would presently fret off the skin, and make the flesh raw and angry-looking; blood was then rubbed upon the limb, which, being fully dried, took on a dark and repulsive color. Then a bandage of soiled rags was put on in a cleverly careless way which would allow the hideous ulcer to be seen and move the compassion of the passer-by.*

Hugo got the help of the tinker whom the king had cowed with the soldering-iron; they took the boy out on a tinkering tramp, and as soon as they were out of sight of the camp they threw him down and the tinker held him while Hugo bound the poultice tight and fast upon his leg.

The king raged and stormed, and promised to hang the two the moment the sceptre was in his hand again; but they kept a firm grip upon him and enjoyed his impotent struggling and jeered at his threats. This continued until the poultice began to bite; and in no long time its work would have been perfected, if there had been no interruption. But there was; for about this time the "slave" who had made the speech denouncing England's laws, appeared on the scene and put an end to the enterprise, and stripped off the poultice and bandage.

The king wanted to borrow his deliverer's cudgel and warm the jackets of the two rascals on the spot; but the man said no, it would bring trouble—leave the matter till night; the whole tribe being together, then, the outside world would not venture to interfere or interrupt. He marched the party back to camp and reported the affair to the Ruffler, who listened, pondered, and then decided that the king should not be again detailed to beg, since it was plain he was worthy of something higher and better—wherefore, on the spot he promoted him from the mendicant rank and appointed him to steal!

Hugo was overjoyed. He had already tried to make the king steal, and failed;

---

* From "The English Rogue;" London, 1665.

but there would be no more trouble of that sort, now, for of course the king would not dream of defying a distinct command delivered directly from headquarters. So he planned a raid for that very afternoon, purposing to get the king in the law's grip in the course of it; and to do it, too, with such ingenious strategy, that it should seem to be accidental and unintentional; for the King of the Game-Cocks was popular, now, and the gang might not deal over-gently with an unpopular member who played so serious a treachery upon him as the delivering him over to the common enemy, the law.

Very well. All in good time Hugo strolled off to a neighboring village with his prey; and the two drifted slowly up and down one street after another, the one watching sharply for a sure chance to achieve his evil purpose, and the other watching as sharply for a chance to dart away and get free of his infamous captivity forever.

Both threw away some tolerably fair-looking opportunities; for both, in their secret hearts, were resolved to make absolutely sure work this time, and neither meant to allow his fevered desires to seduce him into any venture that had much uncertainty about it.

Hugo's chance came first. For at last a woman approached who carried a fat package of some sort in a basket. Hugo's eyes sparkled with sinful pleasure as he said to himself, "Breath o' my life, an' I can but put *that* upon him, 'tis good-den and God keep thee, King of the Game-Cocks!" He waited and watched —outwardly patient, but inwardly consuming with excitement—till the woman had passed by, and the time was ripe; then said, in a low voice—"Tarry here till I come again," and darted stealthily after the prey.

The king's heart was filled with joy—he could make his escape, now, if Hugo's quest only carried him far enough away.

But he was to have no such luck. Hugo crept behind the woman, snatched the package, and came running back, wrapping it in an old piece of blanket which he carried on his arm. The hue and cry was raised in a moment, by the woman, who knew her loss by the lightening of her burden, although she had not seen the pilfering done. Hugo thrust the bundle into the king's hands without halting, saying,—

"Now speed ye after me with the rest, and cry 'Stop thief!' but mind ye lead them astray!"

The next moment Hugo turned a corner and darted down a crooked alley,— and in another moment or two he lounged into view again, looking innocent and indifferent, and took up a position behind a post to watch results.

The insulted king threw the bundle on the ground; and the blanket fell away from it just as the woman arrived, with an augmenting crowd at her heels; she seized the king's wrist with one hand, snatched up her bundle with the other, and began to pour out a tirade of abuse upon the boy while he struggled, without success, to free himself from her grip.

Hugo had seen enough—his enemy was captured and the law would get him, now—so he slipped away, jubilant and chuckling, and wended campwards, framing a judicious version of the matter to give to the Ruffler's crew as he strode along.

The king continued to struggle in the woman's grasp, and now and then cried out, in vexation—

"Unhand me, thou foolish creature; it was not I that bereaved thee of thy paltry goods."

"THE KING SPRANG TO HIS DELIVERER'S SIDE."

The crowd closed around, threatening the king and calling him names; a brawny blacksmith in leather apron, and sleeves rolled to his elbows, made a reach for him, saying he would trounce him well, for a lesson; but just then a long sword flashed in the air and fell with convincing force upon the man's arm, flat-side down, the fantastic owner of it remarking pleasantly at the same time—

"Marry, good souls, let us proceed gently, not with ill blood and uncharitable words. This is matter for the law's consideration, not private and unofficial handling. Loose thy hold from the boy, good-wife."

The blacksmith averaged the stalwart soldier with a glance, then went muttering away, rubbing his arm; the woman released the boy's wrist reluctantly; the crowd eyed the stranger unlovingly, but prudently closed their mouths. The king sprang to his deliverer's side, with flushed cheeks and sparkling eyes, exclaiming—

"Thou hast lagged sorely, but thou comest in good season, now, Sir Miles; carve me this rabble to rags!"

Chapter XXIII

THE PRINCE A PRISONER

HENDON FORCED BACK a smile, and bent down and whispered in the king's ear—

"Softly, softly, my prince, wag thy tongue warily—nay, suffer it not to wag at all. Trust in me—all shall go well in the end." Then he added, to himself: "*Sir* Miles! Bless me, I had totally forgot I was a knight! Lord how marvelous a thing it is, the grip his memory doth take upon his quaint and crazy fancies! . . . An empty and foolish title is mine, and yet it is something to have deserved it, for I think it is more honor to be held worthy to be a spectre-knight in his Kingdom of Dreams and Shadows, than to be held base enough to be an earl in some of the *real* kingdoms of this world."

The crowd fell apart to admit a constable, who approached and was about to lay his hand upon the king's shoulder, when Hendon said—

"Gently, good friend, withhold your hand—he shall go peaceably; I am responsible for that. Lead on, we will follow."

The officer led, with the woman and her bundle; Miles and the king followed after, with the crowd at their heels. The king was inclined to rebel; but Hendon said to him in a low voice—

"Reflect, sire—your laws are the wholesome breath of your own royalty; shall their source resist them, yet require the branches to respect them? Apparently one of these laws has been broken; when the king is on his throne again, can it ever grieve him to remember that when he was seemingly a private person he loyally sunk the king in the citizen and submitted to its authority?"

"Thou art right; say no more; thou shalt see that whatsoever the king of England requires a subject to suffer under the law, he will himself suffer while he holdeth the station of a subject."

When the woman was called upon to testify before the justice of the peace, she swore that the small prisoner at the bar was the person who had committed the theft; there was none able to show the contrary, so the king stood convicted. The bundle was now unrolled, and when the contents proved to be a plump little dressed pig, the judge looked troubled, whilst Hendon turned pale, and his body was thrilled with an electric shiver of dismay; but the king remained unmoved, protected by his ignorance. The judge meditated, during an ominous pause, then turned to the woman, with the question—

"What dost thou hold this property to be worth?"

The woman courtesied and replied—

"Three shillings and eightpence, your worship—I could not abate a penny and set forth the value honestly."

The justice glanced around uncomfortably upon the crowd, then nodded to the constable and said—

"Clear the court and close the doors."

It was done. None remained but the two officials, the accused, the accuser, and Miles Hendon. This latter was rigid and colorless, and on his forehead big drops of cold sweat gathered, broke and blended together, and trickled down

" GENTLY, GOOD FRIEND."

his face. The judge turned to the woman again, and said, in a compassionate voice—

"'Tis a poor ignorant lad, and mayhap was driven hard by hunger, for these be grievous times for the unfortunate; mark you, he hath not an evil face—but when hunger driveth—Good woman! dost know that when one steals a thing above the value of thirteen pence ha'penny the law saith he shall *hang* for it?"

The little king started, wide-eyed with consternation, but controlled himself and held his peace; but not so the woman. She sprang to her feet, shaking with fright, and cried out—

"O, good lack, what have I done! God-a-mercy, I would not hang the poor thing for the whole world! Ah, save me from this, your worship—what shall I do, what *can* I do?"

The justice maintained his judicial composure, and simply said—

"Doubtless it is allowable to revise the value, since it is not yet writ upon the record."

"Then in God's name call the pig eightpence, and heaven bless the day that freed my conscience of this awesome thing!"

Miles Hendon forgot all decorum in his delight; and surprised the king and wounded his dignity, by throwing his arms around him and hugging him. The woman made her grateful adieux and started away with her pig; and when the constable opened the door for her, he followed her out into the narrow hall. The justice proceeded to write in his record book. Hendon, always alert, thought he would like to know why the officer followed the woman out; so he slipped softly into the dusky hall and listened. He heard a conversation to this effect—

"It is a fat pig, and promises good eating; I will buy it of thee; here is the eightpence."

"Eightpence, indeed! Thou'lt do no such thing. It cost me three shillings and eightpence, good honest coin of the last reign, that old Harry that's just dead ne'er touched nor tampered with. A fig for thy eightpence!"

"Stands the wind in that quarter? Thou wast under oath, and so swore falsely when thou saidst the value was but eightpence. Come straightway back with me before his worship, and answer for the crime!—and then the lad will hang."

"There, there, dear heart, say no more, I am content. Give me the eightpence, and hold thy peace about the matter."

The woman went off crying; Hendon slipped back into the court room, and the constable presently followed, after hiding his prize in some convenient place. The justice wrote a while longer, then read the king a wise and kindly lecture, and sentenced him to a short imprisonment in the common jail, to be followed by a public flogging. The astounded king opened his mouth and was probably going to order the good judge to be beheaded on the spot; but he caught a warning sign from Hendon, and succeeded in closing his mouth again before he lost any thing out of it. Hendon took him by the hand, now made reverence to the justice, and the two departed in the wake of the constable toward the jail. The moment the street was reached, the inflamed monarch halted, snatched away his hand, and exclaimed—

"Idiot, dost imagine I will enter a common jail *alive?*"

Hendon bent down and said, somewhat sharply—

"*Will* you trust in me? Peace! and forbear to worsen our chances with dangerous speech. What God wills, will happen; thou canst not hurry it, thou canst not alter it; therefore wait, and be patient—'twill be time enow to rail or rejoice when what is to happen has happened.''

Chapter XXIV

THE ESCAPE

THE SHORT WINTER day was nearly ended. The streets were deserted, save for a few random stragglers, and these hurried straight along, with the intent look of people who were only anxious to accomplish their errands as quickly as possible and then snugly house themselves from the rising wind and the gathering twilight. They looked neither to the right nor to the left; they paid no attention to our party, they did not even seem to see them. Edward the Sixth wondered if the spectacle of a king on his way to jail had ever encountered such marvellous indifference before. By and by the constable arrived at a deserted market-square and proceeded to cross it. When he had reached the middle of it, Hendon laid his hand upon his arm, and said in a low voice—

"Bide a moment, good sir, there is none in hearing, and I would say a word to thee.''

"My duty forbids it, sir; prithee hinder me not, the night comes on.''

"Stay, nevertheless, for the matter concerns thee nearly. Turn thy back a moment and seem not to see; *let this poor lad escape.*''

"This to me, sir! I arrest thee in"—

"Nay, be not too hasty. See thou be careful and commit no foolish error"— then he shut his voice down to a whisper, and said in the man's ear—"the pig thou hast purchased for eightpence may cost thee thy neck, man!''

The poor constable, taken by surprise, was speechless, at first, then found his tongue and fell to blustering and threatening; but Hendon was tranquil, and waited with patience till his breath was spent; then said—

"I have a liking to thee, friend, and would not willingly see thee come to harm. Observe, I heard it all—every word. I will prove it to thee.'' Then he repeated the conversation which the officer and the woman had had together in the hall, word for word, and ended with—

"There—have I set it forth correctly? Should not I be able to set it forth correctly before the judge, if occasion required?''

The man was dumb with fear and distress, for a moment; then he rallied and said with forced lightness—

"'Tis making a mighty matter indeed, out of a jest; I but plagued the woman for mine amusement.''

"Kept you the woman's pig for amusement?''

The man answered sharply—

"Nought else, good sir—I tell thee 'twas but a jest.''

"I do begin to believe thee,'' said Hendon, with a perplexing mixture of mockery and half-conviction in his tone; "but tarry thou here a moment whilst I run and ask his worship—for nathless, he being a man experienced in law, in jests, in"—

He was moving away, still talking; the constable hesitated, fidgetted, spat out an oath or two, then cried out—

"Hold, hold, good sir—prithee wait a little—the judge! why man, he hath no more sympathy with a jest than hath a dead corpse!—come, and we will speak further. Ods body! I seem to be in evil case—and all for an innocent and thoughtless pleasantry. I am a man of family; and my wife and little ones— List to reason, good your worship; what wouldst thou of me?"

"Only that thou be blind and dumb and paralytic whilst one may count a hundred thousand—counting slowly," said Hendon, with the expression of a man who asks but a reasonable favor, and that a very little one.

"It is my destruction!" said the constable despairingly. "Ah, be reasonable, good sir; only look at this matter, on all its sides, and see how mere a jest it is—how manifestly and how plainly it is so. And even if one granted it were not a jest, it is a fault so small that e'en the grimmest penalty it could call forth would be but a rebuke and warning from the judge's lips."

Hendon replied with a solemnity which chilled the air about him—

"This jest of thine hath a name, in law,—wot you what it is?"

"I knew it not! Peradventure I have been unwise. I never dreamed it had a name—ah, sweet heaven, I thought it was original."

"Yes, it hath a name. In the law this crime is called *Non compos mentis lex talionis sic transit gloria Mundi.*"

"Ah, my God!"

"And the penalty is death!"

"God be merciful to me, a sinner!"

"By advantage taken of one in fault, in dire peril, and at thy mercy, thou hast seized goods worth above thirteen pence ha'penny, paying but a trifle for the same; and this, in the eye of the law, is constructive barratry, misprision of treason, malfeasance in office, *ad hominem expurgatis in statu quo*—and the penalty is death by the halter, without ransom, commutation, or benefit of clergy."

"Bear me up, bear me up, sweet sir, my legs do fail me! Be thou merciful— spare me this doom, and I will turn my back and see nought that shall happen."

"Good! now thou'rt wise and reasonable. And thou'lt restore the pig?"

"I will, I will indeed—nor ever touch another, though heaven send it and an archangel fetch it. Go—I am blind for thy sake—I see nothing. I will say thou didst break in and wrest the prisoner from my hands by force. It is but a crazy, ancient door—I will batter it down myself betwixt midnight and the morning."

"Do it, good soul, no harm will come of it; the judge hath a loving charity for this poor lad, and will shed no tears and break no jailer's bones for his escape."

Chapter XXV

HENDON HALL

AS SOON AS Hendon and the king were out of sight of the constable, his majesty was instructed to hurry to a certain place outside the town, and wait there, whilst Hendon should go to the inn and settle his account. Half an hour later the two friends were blithely jogging eastward on Hendon's sorry steeds. The king was warm and comfortable, now, for he had cast his rags and clothed himself in the second-hand suit which Hendon had bought on London Bridge.

Hendon wished to guard against over-fatiguing the boy; he judged that hard journeys, irregular meals, and illiberal measures of sleep would be bad for his crazed mind; whilst rest, regularity, and moderate exercise would be pretty sure to hasten its cure; he longed to see the stricken intellect made well again and its diseased visions driven out of the tormented little head; therefore he resolved to move by easy stages toward the home whence he had so long been banished, instead of obeying the impulse of his impatience and hurrying along night and day.

When he and the king had journeyed about ten miles, they reached a considerable village, and halted there for the night, at a good inn. The former relations were resumed; Hendon stood behind the king's chair, while he dined, and waited upon him; undressed him when he was ready for bed; then took the floor for his own quarters, and slept athwart the door, rolled up in a blanket.

The next day, and the next day after, they jogged lazily along talking over the adventures they had met since their separation, and mightily enjoying each other's narratives. Hendon detailed all his wide wanderings in search of the king, and described how the archangel had led him a fool's journey all over the forest, and taken him back to the hut, finally, when he found he could not get rid of him. Then—he said—the old man went into the bedchamber and came staggering back looking broken-hearted, and saying he had expected to find that the boy had returned and lain down in there to rest, but it was not so. Hendon had waited at the hut all day; hope of the king's return died out, then, and he departed upon the quest again.

"And old Sanctum Sanctorum *was* truly sorry your highness came not back," said Hendon; "I saw it in his face."

"Marry I will never doubt *that!*" said the King—and then told his own story; after which, Hendon was sorry he had not destroyed the archangel.

During the last day of the trip, Hendon's spirits were soaring. His tongue ran constantly. He talked about his old father, and his brother Arthur, and told of many things which illustrated their high and generous characters; he went into loving frenzies over his Edith, and was so gladhearted that he was even able to say some gentle and brotherly things about Hugh. He dwelt a deal on the coming meeting at Hendon Hall; what a surprise it would be to everybody, and what an outburst of thanksgiving and delight there would be.

It was a fair region, dotted with cottages and orchards, and the road led through broad pasture lands whose receding expanses, marked with gentle elevations and depressions, suggested the swelling and subsiding undulations of the sea.

"JOGGING EASTWARD ON SORRY STEEDS."

In the afternoon the returning prodigal made constant deflections from his course to see if by ascending some hillock he might not pierce the distance and catch a glimpse of his home. At last he was successful, and cried out excitedly—

"There is the village, my prince, and there is the Hall close by! You may see the towers from here; and that wood there—that is my father's park. Ah, *now* thou'lt know what state and grandeur be! A house with seventy rooms—think of that!—and seven and twenty servants! A brave lodging for such as we, is it not so? Come, let us speed—my impatience will not brook further delay."

All possible hurry was made; still, it was after three o'clock before the village was reached. The travellers scampered through it, Hendon's tongue going all the time. "Here is the church—covered with the same ivy—none gone, none added." "Yonder is the inn, the old Red Lion,—and yonder is the marketplace." "Here is the Maypole, and here the pump—nothing is altered; nothing but the people, at any rate; ten years make a change in people; some of these I seem to know, but none know me." So his chat ran on. The end of the village was soon reached; then the travellers struck into a crooked, narrow road, walled in with tall hedges, and hurried briskly along it for a half mile, then passed into a vast flower garden through an imposing gateway whose huge stone pillars bore sculptured armorial devices. A noble mansion was before them.

"Welcome to Hendon Hall, my king!" exclaimed Miles. "Ah, 'tis a great day! My father and my brother, and the lady Edith will be so mad with joy that they will have eyes and tongue for none but me in the first transports of the meeting, and so thou'lt seem but coldly welcomed—but mind it not; 'twill soon seem otherwise; for when I say thou art my ward, and tell them how costly is my love for thee, thou'lt see them take thee to their breasts for Miles Hendon's sake, and make their house and hearts thy home forever after!"

The next moment Hendon sprang to the ground before the great door, helped the king down, then took him by the hand and rushed within. A few steps brought him to a spacious apartment; he entered, seated the king with more hurry than ceremony, then ran toward a young man who sat at a writing table in front of a generous fire of logs.

"Embrace me, Hugh," he cried, "and say thou'rt glad I am come again! and call our father, for home is not home till I shall touch his hand, and see his face, and hear his voice once more!''

But Hugh only drew back, after betraying a momentary surprise, and bent a grave stare upon the intruder—a stare which indicated somewhat of offended dignity, at first, then changed, in response to some inward thought or purpose, to an expression of marvelling curiosity, mixed with a real or assumed compassion. Presently he said, in a mild voice—

''Thy wits seem touched, poor stranger; doubtless thou hast suffered privations and rude buffetings at the world's hands; thy looks and dress betoken it. Whom dost thou take me to be?''

''Take thee? Prithee for whom else than whom thou art? I take thee to be Hugh Hendon,'' said Miles, sharply.

The other continued, in the same soft tone—

''And whom dost thou imagine thyself to be?''

''Imagination hath nought to do with it! Dost thou pretend thou knowest me not for thy brother Miles Hendon?''

An expression of pleased surprise flitted across Hugh's face, and he exclaimed—

''What! thou art not jesting? can the dead come to life? God be praised if it be so! Our poor lost boy restored to our arms after all these cruel years! Ah, it seems too good to be true, it *is* too good to be true—I charge thee, have pity, do not trifle with me! Quick—come to the light—let me scan thee well!''

He seized Miles by the arm, dragged him to the window, and began to devour him from head to foot with his eyes, turning him this way and that, and stepping briskly around him and about him to prove him from all points of view; whilst the returned prodigal, all aglow with gladness, smiled, laughed, and kept nodding his head and saying—

''Go on, brother, go on, and fear not; thou'lt find nor limb nor feature that cannot bide the test. Scour and scan me to thy content, my dear old Hugh—I am indeed thy old Miles, thy same old Miles, thy lost brother, is't not so? Ah, 'tis a great day—I *said* 'twas a great day! Give me thy hand, give me thy cheek— lord, I am like to die of very joy!''

He was about to throw himself upon his brother; but Hugh put up his hand in dissent, then dropped his chin mournfully upon his breast, saying with emotion—

''Ah, God of his mercy give me strength to bear this grievous disappointment!''

Miles, amazed, could not speak, for a moment; then he found his tongue, and cried out—

''*What* disappointment? Am I not thy brother?''

Hugh shook his head sadly, and said—

''I pray heaven it may prove so, and that other eyes may find the resemblances that are hid from mine. Alack, I fear me the letter spoke but too truly.''

''What letter?''

''One that came from over sea, some six or seven years ago. It said my brother died in battle.''

''It was a lie! Call thy father—he will know me.''

''One may not call the dead.''

''Dead?'' Miles's voice was subdued, and his lips trembled. ''My father dead!—O, this is heavy news. Half my new joy is withered now. Prithee let me see my brother Arthur—he will know me; he will know me and console me.''

''He, also, is dead.''

''God be merciful to me, a stricken man! Gone,—both gone—the worthy taken and the worthless spared, in me! Ah! I crave your mercy!—do not say the lady Edith''—

"Is dead? No, she lives."

"Then, God be praised, my joy is whole again! Speed thee, brother—let her come to me! An' *she* say I am not myself,—but she will not; no, no, *she* will know me, I were a fool to doubt it. Bring her—bring the old servants; they, too, will know me."

"All are gone but five—Peter, Halsey, David, Bernard and Margaret."

So saying, Hugh left the room. Miles stood musing, a while, then began to walk the floor, muttering—

"The five arch villains have survived the two-and-twenty leal and honest— 'tis an odd thing."

He continued walking back and forth, muttering to himself; he had forgotten the king entirely. By and by his majesty said gravely, and with a touch of genuine compassion, though the words themselves were capable of being interpreted ironically—

"Mind not thy mischance, good man; there be others in the world whose identity is denied, and whose claims are derided. Thou hast company."

"Ah, my king," cried Hendon, coloring slightly, "do not thou condemn me—wait, and thou shalt see. I am no impostor—she will say it; you shall hear it from the sweetest lips in England. I an impostor? Why I know this old hall, these pictures of my ancestors, and all these things that are about us, as a child knoweth its own nursery. Here was I born and bred, my lord; I speak the truth; I would not deceive thee; and should none else believe, I pray thee do not *thou* doubt me—I could not bear it."

"I do not doubt thee," said the king, with a childlike simplicity and faith.

"I thank thee out of my heart!" exclaimed Hendon, with a fervency which showed that he was touched. The king added, with the same gentle simplicity—

"Dost thou doubt *me?*"

A guilty confusion seized upon Hendon, and he was grateful that the door opened to admit Hugh, at that moment, and saved him the necessity of replying.

A beautiful lady, richly clothed, followed Hugh, and after her came several liveried servants. The lady walked slowly, with her head bowed and her eyes fixed upon the floor. The face was unspeakably sad. Miles Hendon sprang forward, crying out—

"O, my Edith, my darling''—

But Hugh waved him back, gravely, and said to the lady—

"Look upon him. Do you know him?"

At the sound of Miles's voice the woman had started, slightly, and her cheeks had flushed; she was trembling, now. She stood still, during an impressive pause of several moments; then slowly lifted up her head and looked into Hendon's eyes with a stony and frightened gaze; the blood sank out of her face, drop by drop, till nothing remained but the gray pallor of death; then she said, in a voice as dead as the face, "I know him not!" and turned, with a moan and a stifled sob, and tottered out of the room.

Miles Hendon sank into a chair and covered his face with his hands. After a pause, his brother said to the servants—

"You have observed him. Do you know him?"

They shook their heads; then the master said—

"The servants know you not, sir. I fear there is some mistake. You have seen that my wife knew you not."

"Thy *wife!*" In an instant Hugh was pinned to the wall, with an iron grip about his throat. "O, thou fox-hearted slave, I see it all! Thou'st writ the lying letter thyself, and my stolen bride and goods are its fruit. There—now get thee gone, lest I shame mine honorable soldiership with the slaying of so pitiful a manikin!"

Hugh, red-faced, and almost suffocated, reeled to the nearest chair, and commanded the servants to seize and bind the murderous stranger. They hesitated, and one of them said—

"He is armed, Sir Hugh, and we are weaponless."

"Armed? What of it, and ye so many? Upon him, I say!"

But Miles warned them to be careful what they did, and added—

"Ye know me of old—I have not changed; come on, an' it like you."

This reminder did not hearten the servants much; they still held back.

"Then go, ye paltry cowards, and arm yourselves and guard the doors, whilst I send one to fetch the watch;" said Hugh. He turned, at the threshold, and said to Miles, "You'll find it to your advantage to offend not with useless endeavors at escape."

"Escape? Spare thyself discomfort, an' that is all that troubles thee. For Miles Hendon is master of Hendon Hall and all its belongings. He will remain—doubt it not."

Chapter XXVI

DISOWNED

THE KING SAT musing a few moments, then looked up and said—

" 'Tis strange—most strange. I cannot account for it."

"No, it is not strange, my liege. I know him, and this conduct is but natural. He was a rascal from his birth."

"O, I spake not of *him*, Sir Miles."

"Not of him? Then of what? What is it that is strange?"

"That the king is not missed."

"How? Which? I doubt I do not understand."

"Indeed! Doth it not strike you as being passing strange that the land is not filled with couriers and proclamations describing my person and making search for me? Is it no matter for commotion and distress that the head of the State is gone?—that I am vanished away and lost?"

"Most true, my king, I had forgot." Then Hendon sighed, and muttered to himself, "Poor ruined mind—still busy with its pathetic dream."

"But I have a plan that shall right us both. I will write a paper, in three tongues—Latin, Greek and English—and thou shalt haste away with it to London in the morning. Give it to none but my uncle, the lord Hertford; when he shall see it, he will know and say I wrote it. Then he will send for me."

"Might it not be best, my prince, that we wait, here, until I prove myself and make my rights secure to my domains? I should be so much the better able then to"—

The king interrupted him imperiously—

"Peace! What are thy paltry domains, thy trivial interests, contrasted with matters which concern the weal of a nation and the integrity of a throne!" Then he added, in a gentle voice, as if he were sorry for his severity, "Obey and have no fear; I will right thee, I will make thee whole—yes, more than whole. I shall remember, and requite."

So saying, he took the pen, and set himself to work. Hendon contemplated him lovingly, a while, then said to himself—

"An' it were dark, I should think it *was* a king that spoke; there's no denying it, when the humor's upon him he doth thunder and lighten like your true king— now where got he that trick? See him scribble and scratch away contentedly at his meaningless pot-hooks, fancying them to be Latin and Greek—and except my wit shall serve me with a lucky device for diverting him from his purpose, I shall be forced to pretend to post away to-morrow on this wild errand he hath invented for me."

The next moment Sir Miles's thoughts had gone back to the recent episode. So absorbed was he in his musings, that when the king presently handed him the paper which he had been writing, he received it and pocketed it without being conscious of the act. "How marvellous strange she acted," he muttered. "I think she knew me—and I think she did *not* know me. These opinions do conflict, I perceive it plainly; I cannot reconcile them, neither can I, by argument, dismiss either of the two, or even persuade one to outweigh the other. The matter standeth simply thus: she *must* have known my face, my figure, my voice, for how could it be otherwise? yet she *said* she knew me not, and that is proof perfect, for she cannot lie. But stop—I think I begin to see. Peradventure he hath influenced her—commanded her—compelled her, to lie. That is the solution! The riddle is unriddled. She seemed dead with fear—yes, she was under his compulsion. I will seek her; I will find her; now that he is away, she will speak her true mind. She will remember the old times when we were little playfellows together, and this will soften her heart, and she will no more betray me, but will confess me. There is no treacherous blood in her—no, she was always honest and true. She has loved me in those old days—this is my security; for whom one has loved, one cannot betray."

He stepped eagerly toward the door; at that moment it opened, and the lady Edith entered. She was very pale, but she walked with a firm step, and her carriage was full of grace and gentle dignity. Her face was as sad as before.

Miles sprang forward, with a happy confidence, to meet her, but she checked him with a hardly perceptible gesture, and he stopped where he was. She seated herself, and asked him to do likewise. Thus simply did she take the sense of old-comradeship out of him, and transform him into a stranger and a guest. The surprise of it, the bewildering unexpectedness of it, made him begin to question, for a moment, if he *was* the person he was pretending to be, after all. The lady Edith said—

"Sir, I have come to warn you. The mad cannot be persuaded out of their delusions, perchance; but doubtless they may be persuaded to avoid perils. I think this dream of yours hath the seeming of honest truth to you, and therefore is not criminal—but do not tarry here with it; for here it is dangerous." She looked steadily into Miles's face, a moment, then added, impressively, "It is the more dangerous for that you *are* much like what our lost lad must have grown to be, if he had lived.''

"Heavens, madame, but I *am* he!''

"I truly think you think it, sir. I question not your honesty in that—I but warn you, that is all. My husband is master in this region; his power hath hardly any limit; the people prosper or starve, as he wills. If you resembled not the man whom you profess to be, my husband might bid you pleasure yourself with your dream in peace; but trust me, I know him well, I know what he will do; he will say to all, that you are but a mad impostor, and straightway all will echo him.'' She bent upon Miles that same steady look once more, and added: "If you *were* Miles Hendon, and he knew it and all the region knew it—consider what I am saying, weigh it well—you would stand in the same peril, your punishment would be no less sure; he would deny you and denounce you, and none would be bold enough to give you countenance.''

"Most truly I believe it,'' said Miles, bitterly. "The power that can command one life-long friend to betray and disown another, and be obeyed, may well look to be obeyed in quarters where bread and life are on the stake and no cobweb ties of loyalty and honor are concerned.''

A faint tinge appeared for a moment in the lady's cheek, and she dropped her eyes to the floor; but her voice betrayed no emotion when she proceeded—

"I have warned you, I must still warn you, to go hence. This man will destroy you, else. He is a tyrant who knows no pity. I, who am his fettered slave, know this. Poor Miles, and Arthur, and my dear guardian, Sir Richard, are free of him, and at rest—better that you were with them than that you bide here in the clutches of this miscreant. Your pretensions are a menace to his title and possessions; you have assaulted him in his own house—you are ruined if you stay. Go—do not hesitate. If you lack money, take this purse, I beg of you, and bribe the servants to let you pass. O be warned, poor soul, and escape while you may.''

Miles declined the purse with a gesture, and rose up and stood before her.

"Grant me one thing,'' he said. "Let your eyes rest upon mine, so that I may see if they be steady. There—now answer me. Am I Miles Hendon?''

"No. I know you not.''

"Swear it!''

The answer was low, but distinct—

"I swear.''

"O, this passes belief!''

"Fly! Why will you waste the precious time? Fly and save yourself.''

At that moment the officers burst into the room and a violent struggle began; but Hendon was soon overpowered and dragged away. The king was taken, also, and both were bound, and led to prison.

Chapter XXVII

IN PRISON

THE CELLS WERE all crowded; so the two friends were chained in a large room where persons charged with trifling offenses were commonly kept. They had company, for there were some twenty manacled and fettered prisoners here, of both sexes and of varying ages,—an obscene and noisy gang. The king chafed bitterly over the stupendous indignity thus put upon his royalty, but Hendon was moody and taciturn. He was pretty thoroughly bewildered. He had come home, a jubilant prodigal, expecting to find everybody wild with joy over his return; and instead had got the cold shoulder and a jail. The promise and the fulfilment differed so widely, that the effect was stunning; he could not decide whether it was most tragic or most grotesque. He felt much as a man might who had danced blithely out to enjoy a rainbow, and got struck by lightning.

But gradually his confused and tormenting thoughts settled down into some sort of order, and then his mind centred itself upon Edith. He turned her conduct over, and examined it in all lights, but he could not make any thing satisfactory out of it. Did she know him?—or didn't she know him? It was a perplexing puzzle, and occupied him a long time; but he ended, finally, with the conviction that she did know him, and had repudiated him for interested reasons. He wanted to load her name with curses now; but this name had so long been sacred to him that he found he could not bring his tongue to profane it.

Wrapped in prison blankets of a soiled and tattered condition, Hendon and the king passed a troubled night. For a bribe the jailer had furnished liquor to some of the prisoners; singing of ribald songs, fighting, shouting, and carousing, was the natural consequence. At last, a while after midnight, a man attacked a woman and nearly killed her by beating her over the head with his manacles before the jailer could come to the rescue. The jailer restored peace by giving the man a sound clubbing about the head and shoulders—then the carousing

"CHAINED IN A LARGE ROOM."

ceased; and after that, all had an opportunity to sleep who did not mind the annoyance of the moanings and groanings of the two wounded people.

During the ensuing week, the days and nights were of a monotonous sameness, as to events; men whose faces Hendon remembered more or less distinctly, came, by day, to gaze at the ''impostor'' and repudiate and insult him; and by night the carousing and brawling went on, with symmetrical regularity. However, there was a change of incident at last. The jailer brought in an old man, and said to him—

''The villain is in this room—cast thy old eyes about and see if thou canst say which is he.''

Hendon glanced up, and experienced a pleasant sensation for the first time since he had been in the jail. He said to himself, ''This is Blake Andrews, a servant all his life in my father's family—a good honest soul, with a right heart in his breast. That is, formerly. But none are true, now; all are liars. This man will know me—and will deny me, too, like the rest.''

The old man gazed around the room, glanced at each face in turn, and finally said—

''I see none here but paltry knaves, scum o' the streets. Which is he?''

The jailer laughed.

''Here,'' he said; ''scan this big animal, and grant me an opinion.''

The old man approached, and looked Hendon over, long and earnestly, then shook his head and said—

''Marry, *this* is no Hendon—nor ever was!''

''Right! Thy old eyes are sound yet. An' I were Sir Hugh, I would take the shabby carle and''—

The jailer finished by lifting himself a-tip-toe with an imaginary halter, at the same time making a gurgling noise in his throat suggestive of suffocation. The old man said, vindictively—

''Let him bless God an' he fare no worse. An' *I* had the handling o' the villain, he should roast, or I am no true man!''

The jailer laughed a pleasant hyena laugh, and said—

''Give him a piece of thy mind, old man—they all do it. Thou'lt find it good diversion.''

Then he sauntered toward his ante-room and disappeared. The old man dropped upon his knees and whispered—

''God be thanked, thou'rt come again, my master! I believed thou wert dead these seven years, and lo, here thou art alive! I knew thee the moment I saw thee; and main hard work it was to keep a stony countenance and seem to see none here but tuppenny knaves and rubbish o' the streets. I am old and poor, Sir Miles; but say the word and I will go forth and proclaim the truth though I be strangled for it.''

''No,'' said Hendon; ''thou shalt not. It would ruin thee, and yet help but little in my cause. But I thank thee; for thou hast given me back somewhat of my lost faith in my kind.''

The old servant became very valuable to Hendon and the king; for he dropped in several times a day to ''abuse'' the former, and always smuggled in a few delicacies to help out the prison bill of fare; he also furnished the current news. Hendon reserved the dainties for the king; without them his majesty might not have survived, for he was not able to eat the coarse and wretched food provided by the jailer. Andrews was obliged to confine himself to brief visits, in order to avoid suspicion; but he managed to impart a fair degree of information each time—information delivered in a low voice, for Hendon's benefit, and interlarded with insulting epithets delivered in a louder voice, for the benefit of other hearers.

So, little by little, the story of the family came out. Arthur had been dead six years. This loss, with the absence of news from Hendon, impaired the father's health; he believed he was going to die, and he wished to see Hugh and Edith settled in life before he passed away; but Edith begged hard for delay, hoping for Miles's return; then the letter came which brought the news of Miles's death; the shock prostrated Sir Richard; he believed his end was very near, and he and Hugh insisted upon the marriage; Edith begged for and obtained a month's respite; then another, and finally a third; the marriage then took place, by the death-bed of Sir Richard. It had not proved a happy one. It was whispered about the country that shortly after the nuptials the bride found among her husband's papers several rough and incomplete drafts of the fatal letter, and had accused him of precipitating the marriage—and Sir Richard's death, too—by a wicked forgery. Tales of cruelty to the lady Edith and the servants were to be heard on all hands; and since the father's death Sir Hugh had thrown off all soft disguises and become a pitiless master toward all who in any way depended upon him and his domains for bread.

There was a bit of Andrews's gossip which the king listened to with a lively interest—

"There is rumor that the king is mad. But in charity forbear to say *I* mentioned it, for 'tis death to speak of it, they say."

His majesty glared at the old man and said—

"The king is *not* mad, good man—and thou'lt find it to thy advantage to busy thyself with matters that nearer concern thee than this seditious prattle."

"What doth the lad mean?" said Andrews, surprised at this brisk assault from such an unexpected quarter. Hendon gave him a sign, and he did not pursue his question, but went on with his budget—

"The late king is to be buried at Windsor in a day or two—the 16th of the month,—and the new king will be crowned at Westminster the 20th."

"Methinks they must needs find him first," muttered his majesty; then added, confidently, "but they will look to that—and so also shall I."

"In the name of"—

But the old man got no further—a warning sign from Hendon checked his remark. He resumed the thread of his gossip—

"Sir Hugh goeth to the coronation—and with grand hopes. He confidently looketh to come back a peer, for he is high in favor with the Lord Protector."

"What Lord Protector?" asked his majesty.

"His grace the Duke of Somerset."

"What Duke of Somerset?"

"Marry, there is but one—Seymour, Earl of Hertford."

The king asked, sharply—

"Since when is *he* a duke, and Lord Protector?"

"Since the last day of January."

"And prithee who made him so?"

"Himself and the Great Council—with help of the king."

His majesty started violently. "The *king!*" he cried. "*What* king, good sir?"

"What king, indeed! (God-a-mercy, what aileth the boy?) Sith we have but one, 'tis not difficult to answer—his most sacred majesty King Edward the

"THE KING!" HE CRIED. "WHAT KING?"

Sixth—whom God preserve! Yea, and a dear and gracious little urchin is he, too; and whether he be mad or no—and they say he mendeth daily—his praises are on all men's lips; and all bless him, likewise, and offer prayers that he may be spared to reign long in England; for he began humanely, with saving the old duke of Norfolk's life, and now is he bent on destroying the cruelest of the laws that harry and oppress the people."

This news struck his majesty dumb with amazement, and plunged him into so deep and dismal a revery that he heard no more of the old man's gossip. He wondered if the "little urchin" was the beggar-boy whom he left dressed in his own garments in the palace. It did not seem possible that this could be, for surely his manners and speech would betray him if he pretended to be the prince of Wales—then he would be driven out, and search made for the true prince. Could it be that the Court had set up some sprig of the nobility in his place? No, for his uncle would not allow that—he was all-powerful and could and would crush such a movement, of course. The boy's musings profited him nothing; the more he tried to unriddle the mystery the more perplexed he became, the more his head ached, and the worse he slept. His impatience to get to London grew hourly, and his captivity became almost unendurable.

Hendon's arts all failed with the king—he could not be comforted, but a couple of women who were chained near him, succeeded better. Under their gentle ministrations he found peace and learned a degree of patience. He was very grateful, and came to love them dearly and to delight in the sweet and soothing influence of their presence. He asked them why they were in prison, and when they said they were Baptists, he smiled, and inquired—

"Is that a crime to be shut up for, in a prison? Now I grieve, for I shall lose ye—they will not keep ye long for such a little thing."

They did not answer; and something in their faces made him uneasy. He said, eagerly—

"You do not speak—be good to me, and tell me—there will be no other punishment? Prithee tell me there is no fear of that."

They tried to change the topic, but his fears were aroused, and he pursued it—

"Will they scourge thee? No, no, they would not be so cruel! Say they would not. Come, they *will* not, will they?"

The women betrayed confusion and distress, but there was no avoiding an answer, so one of them said, in a voice choked with emotion—

"O, thou'lt break our hearts, thou gentle spirit! God will help us to bear our"—

"It is a confession!" the king broke in. "Then they *will* scourge thee, the stonyhearted wretches! But O, thou must not weep, I cannot bear it. Keep up thy courage—I shall come to my own in time to save thee from this bitter thing, and I will do it!"

When the king awoke in the morning, the women were gone.

"They are saved!" he said, joyfully; then added, despondently, "but woe is me!—for they were my comforters."

Each of them had left a shred of ribbon pinned to his clothing, in token of remembrance. He said he would keep these things always; and that soon he would seek out these dear good friends of his and take them under his protection.

Just then the jailer came in with some subordinates and commanded that the prisoners be conducted to the jail-yard. The king was overjoyed—it would be a blessed thing to see the blue sky and breathe the fresh air once more. He fretted and chafed at the slowness of the officers, but his turn came at last and he was released from his staple and ordered to follow the other prisoners, with Hendon.

The court or quadrangle, was stone-paved, and open to the sky. The prisoners entered it through a massive archway of masonry, and were placed in file, standing, with their backs against the wall. A rope was stretched in front of them, and they were also guarded by their officers. It was a chill and lowering morning, and a light snow which had fallen during the night whitened the great empty space and added to the general dismalness of its aspect. Now and then a wintry wind shivered through the place and sent the snow eddying hither and thither.

In the centre of the court stood two women, chained to posts. A glance showed the king that these were his good friends. He shuddered, and said to himself, "Alack, they are not gone free, as I had thought. To think that such as these should know the lash!—in England! Ay there's the shame of it—not in Heathenesse, but Christian England! They will be scourged; and I, whom they have comforted and kindly entreated, must look on and see the great wrong done; it is strange, so strange! that I, the very source of power in this broad realm, am helpless to protect them. But let these miscreants look well to themselves, for there is a day coming when I will require of them a heavy reckoning for this work. For every blow they strike now, they shall feel a hundred, then."

A great gate swung open and a crowd of citizens poured in. They flocked around the two women, and hid them from the king's view. A clergyman entered and passed through the crowd, and he also was hidden. The king now heard talking, back and forth, as if questions were being asked and answered, but he could not make out what was said. Next there was a deal of bustle and preparation, and much passing and repassing of officials through that part of the crowd that stood on the further side of the women; and whilst this proceeded a deep hush gradually fell upon the people.

Now, by command, the masses parted and fell aside, and the king saw a spectacle that froze the marrow in his bones. Fagots had been piled about the two women, and a kneeling man was lighting them!

The women bowed their heads, and covered their faces with their hands; the yellow flames began to climb upward among the snapping and crackling fagots, and wreaths of blue smoke to stream away on the wind; the clergyman lifted his hands and began a prayer—just then two young girls came flying through the great gate, uttering piercing screams, and threw themselves upon the women at the stake. Instantly they were torn away by the officers, and one of them was kept in a tight grip, but the other broke loose, saying she would die with her mother; and before she could be stopped she had flung her arms about her mother's neck again. She was torn away once more, and with her gown on fire. Two or three men held her, and the burning portion of her gown was snatched off and thrown flaming aside, she struggling all the while to free herself, and saying she would be alone in the world, now, and begging to be allowed to die with her mother. Both the girls screamed continually, and fought for freedom; but suddenly this tumult was drowned under a volley of heart-piercing shrieks of mortal agony,—the king glanced from the frantic girls to the stake, then turned away and leaned his ashen face against the wall, and looked no more. He said, "That which I have seen, in that one little moment, will never go out from my memory, but will abide there; and I shall see it all the days, and dream of it all the nights, till I die. Would God I had been blind!"

Hendon was watching the king. He said to himself, with satisfaction, "His disorder mendeth; he hath changed, and groweth gentler. If he had followed his wont, he would have stormed at these varlets, and said he was king, and commanded that the women be turned loose unscathed. Soon his delusion will pass away and be forgotten, and his poor mind will be whole again. God speed the day!"

That same day several prisoners were brought in to remain over night, who were being conveyed, under guard, to various places in the kingdom, to undergo punishment for crimes committed. The king conversed with these,—he had made it a point, from the beginning, to instruct himself for the kingly office by questioning prisoners whenever the opportunity offered—and the tale of their woes wrung his heart. One of them was a poor half-witted woman who had stolen a yard or two of cloth from a weaver—she was to be hanged for it. Another was a man who had been accused of stealing a horse; he said the proof had failed, and he had imagined that he was safe from the halter; but no—he was hardly free before he was arraigned for killing a deer in the king's park; this was proved against him, and now he was on his way to the gallows. There was a tradesman's apprentice whose case particularly distressed the king; this youth said he found a hawk, one evening, that had escaped from its owner, and he took it home with him, imagining himself entitled to it; but the court convicted him of stealing it, and sentenced him to death.

The king was furious over these inhumanities, and wanted Hendon to break jail and fly with him to Westminster, so that he could mount his throne and hold out his sceptre in mercy over these unfortunate people and save their lives. "Poor child," sighed Hendon, "these woful tales have brought his malady upon him again—alack, but for this evil hap, he would have been well in a little time."

Among these prisoners was an old lawyer—a man with a strong face and a dauntless mien. Three years past, he had written a pamphlet against the Lord Chancellor, accusing him of injustice, and had been punished for it by the loss of his ears in the pillory, and degradation from the bar, and in addition had been fined £3000 and sentenced to imprisonment for life. Lately he had repeated his offence; and in consequence was now under sentence to lose *what remained of his ears*, pay a fine of £5000 pounds, be branded on both cheeks, and remain in prison for life.

"These be honorable scars," he said, and turned back his gray hair and showed the mutilated stubs of what had once been his ears.

The king's eye burned with passion. He said—

"None believe in me—neither wilt thou. But no matter—within the compass of a month thou shalt be free; and more, the laws that have dishonored thee, and shamed the English name, shall be swept from the statute books. The world is made wrong, kings should go to school to their own laws, at times, and so learn mercy."

Chapter XXVIII

THE SACRIFICE

MEANTIME MILES WAS growing sufficiently tired of confinement and inaction. But now his trial came on, to his great gratification, and he thought he could welcome any sentence provided a further imprisonment should not be a part of it. But he was mistaken about that. He was in a fine fury when he found himself described as a "sturdy vagabond" and sentenced to sit two hours in the pillory for bearing that character and for assaulting the master of Hendon Hall. His pretensions as to brothership with his prosecutor, and rightful heirship to the Hendon honors and estates, were left contemptuously unnoticed, as being not even worth examination.

He raged and threatened, on his way to punishment, but it did no good; he was snatched roughly along, by the officers, and got an occasional cuff, besides, for his unreverent conduct.

The king could not pierce through the rabble that swarmed behind; so he was obliged to follow in the rear, remote from his good friend and servant. The king had been nearly condemned to the stocks, himself, for being in such bad company, but had been let off with a lecture and a warning, in consideration of his youth. When the crowd at last halted, he flitted feverishly from point to point around its outer rim, hunting a place to get through; and at last, after a deal of difficulty and delay, succeeded. There sat his poor henchman in the degrading stocks, the sport and butt of a dirty mob—he, the body servant of the king of England! Edward had heard the sentence pronounced, but he had not realized the half that it meant. His anger began to rise as the sense of this new indignity which had been put upon him sank home; it jumped to summer heat, the next moment, when he saw an egg sail through the air and crush itself against Hendon's cheek, and heard the crowd roar its enjoyment of the episode. He sprang across the open circle and confronted the officer in charge, crying—

"For shame! This is my servant—set him free! I am the—"

"O, peace!" exclaimed Hendon, in a panic, "thou'lt destroy thyself. Mind him not, officer, he is mad."

"Give thyself no trouble as to the matter of minding him, good man, I have small mind to mind him; but as to teaching him somewhat, to that I am well inclined." He turned to a subordinate and said, "Give the little fool a taste or two of the lash, to mend his manners."

"Half a dozen will better serve his turn," suggested Sir Hugh, who had ridden up, a moment before, to take a passing glance at the proceedings.

The king was seized. He did not even struggle, so paralyzed was he with the mere thought of the monstrous outrage that was proposed to be inflicted upon his sacred person. History was already defiled with the record of the scourging of an English king with whips—it was an intolerable reflection that he must furnish a duplicate of that shameful page. He was in the toils, there was no help for him: he must either take this punishment or beg for its remission. Hard conditions; he would take the stripes—a king might do that, but a king could not beg.

But meantime, Miles Hendon was resolving the difficulty. "Let the child go," said he; "ye hearless dogs, do ye not see how young and frail he is? Let him go—I will take his lashes."

"Marry, a good thought,—and thanks for it," said Sir Hugh, his face lighting with a sardonic satisfaction. "Let the little beggar go, and give this fellow a dozen in his place—an honest dozen, well laid on." The king was in the act of entering a fierce protest, but Sir Hugh silenced him with the potent remark, "Yes, speak up, do, and free thy mind—only, mark ye, that for each word you utter he shall get six strokes the more."

Hendon was removed from the stocks, and his back laid bare; and whilst the lash was applied the poor little king turned away his face and allowed unroyal tears to channel his cheeks unchecked. "Ah, brave good heart," he said to himself, "this loyal deed shall never perish out of my memory. I will not forget it—and neither shall *they!*" he added, with passion. Whilst he mused, his appreciation of Hendon's magnanimous conduct grew to greater and still greater dimensions in his mind, and so also did his gratefulness for it. Presently he said to himself, "Who saves his prince from wounds and possible death—and this he did for me—performs high service; but it is little—it is nothing!—O, less than nothing!—when 'tis weighed against the act of him who saves his prince from SHAME!"

Hendon made no outcry, under the scourge, but bore the heavy blows with soldierly fortitude. This, together with his redeeming the boy by taking his stripes for him, compelled the respect of even that forlorn and degraded mob that was gathered there; and its gibes and hootings died away, and no sound remained but the sound of the falling blows. The stillness that pervaded the place, when Hendon found himself once more in the stocks, was in strong contrast with the insulting clamor which had prevailed there so little a while before. The king came softly to Hendon's side, and whispered in his ear—

"Kings cannot ennoble thee, thou good, great soul, for One who is higher than kings hath done that for thee; but a king can confirm thy nobility to men." He picked up the scourge from the ground, touched Hendon's bleeding shoulders lightly with it, and whispered, "Edward of England dubs thee earl!"

Hendon was touched. The water welled to his eyes, yet at the same time the grisly humor of the situation and circumstances so undermined his gravity that it was all he could do to keep some sign of his inward mirth from showing outside. To be suddenly hoisted, naked and gory, from the common stocks to the Alpine altitude and splendor of an Earldom, seemed to him the last possibility in the line of the grotesque. He said to himself, "Now am I finely tinselled, indeed! The spectre-knight of the Kingdom of Dreams and Shadows is become a spectre-earl!—a dizzy flight for a callow wing! An' this go on, I shall presently be hung like a very may-pole with fantastic gauds and make-believe honors. But I shall value them, all valueless as they are, for the love that doth bestow them. Better these poor mock dignities of mine, that come unasked, from a clean hand and a right spirit, than real ones bought by servility from grudging and interested power."

The dreaded Sir Hugh wheeled his horse about, and as he spurred away, the living wall divided silently to let him pass, and as silently closed together again. And so remained; nobody went so far as to venture a remark in favor of the prisoner, or in compliment to him; but no matter, the absence of abuse was a sufficient homage in itself. A late comer who was not posted as to the present circumstances, and who delivered a sneer at the "impostor" and was in the act of following it with a dead cat, was promptly knocked down and kicked out, without any words, and then the deep quiet resumed sway once more.

Chapter XXIX

TO LONDON

WHEN HENDON'S TERM of service in the stocks was finished, he was released and ordered to quit the region and come back no more. His sword was restored to him, and also his mule and his donkey. He mounted and rode off, followed by the king, the crowd opening with quiet respectfulness to let them pass, and then dispersing when they were gone.

Hendon was soon absorbed in thought. There were questions of high import to be answered. What should he do? Whither should he go? Powerful help must be found, somewhere, or he must relinquish his inheritance and remain under the imputation of being an impostor besides. Where could he hope to find this powerful help? Where, indeed! It was a knotty question. By and by a thought occurred to him which pointed to a possibility—the slenderest of slender possibilities, certainly, but still worth considering, for lack of any other that promised any thing at all. He remembered what old Andrews had said about the young king's goodness and his generous championship of the wronged and unfortunate. Why not go and try to get speech of him and beg for justice? Ah, yes, but could so fantastic a pauper get admission to the august presence of a monarch? Never mind—let that matter take care of itself; it was a bridge that would not need to be crossed till he should come to it. He was an old campaigner, and used to inventing shifts and expedients; no doubt he would be able to find a way. Yes, he would strike for the capital. Maybe his father's old friend Sir Humphrey Marlow would help him—"good old Sir Humphrey, Head Lieutenant of the late king's kitchen, or stables, or something"—Miles could not remember just what or which. Now that he had something to turn his energies to, a distinctly defined object to accomplish, the fog of humiliation and depression which had settled down upon his spirits lifted and blew away, and he raised his head and looked about him. He was surprised to see how far he had come; the village was away behind him. The king was jogging along in his wake, with his head bowed; for he, too, was deep in plans and thinkings. A sorrowful misgiving clouded Hendon's new-born cheerfulness: would the boy be willing to go again to a city where, during all his brief life, he had never known any thing but ill usage and pinching want? But the question must be asked; it could not be avoided; so Hendon reined up, and called out—

"I had forgotten to inquire whither we are bound. Thy commands, my liege!"

"To London!"

Hendon moved on again, mightily contented with the answer—but astounded at it, too.

The whole journey was made without an adventure of importance. But it ended with one. About ten o'clock on the night of the 19th of February, they stepped upon London Bridge, in the midst of a writhing, struggling jam of howling and hurrahing people, whose beer-jolly faces stood out strongly in the glare from manifold torches—and at that instant the decaying head of some former duke or other grandee tumbled down between them, striking Hendon on the elbow and then bounding off among the hurrying confusion of feet. So evanescent and unstable are men's works, in this world!—the late good king is but three weeks dead and three days in his grave, and already the adornments which he took such pains to select from prominent people for his noble bridge are falling. A citizen stumbled over that head, and drove his own head into the back of somebody in front of him, who turned and knocked down the first person that came handy, and was promptly laid out himself by that person's friend. It was the right ripe time for a free fight, for the festivities of the morrow—Coronation Day—were already beginning; everybody was full of strong drink and patriotism; within five minutes the free fight was occupying a good deal of ground; within ten or twelve it covered an acre or so, and was become a riot. By this time Hendon and the king were hopelessly separated from each other and lost in the rush and turmoil of the roaring masses of humanity. And so we leave them.

Chapter XXX

TOM'S PROGRESS

Whilst the true King wandered about the land poorly clad, poorly fed, cuffed and derided by tramps one while, herding with thieves and murderers in a jail another, and called idiot and impostor by all impartially, the mock King Tom Canty enjoyed a quite different experience.

When we saw him last, royalty was just beginning to have a bright side for him. This bright side went on brightening more and more every day: in a very little while it was become almost all sunshine and delightfulness. He lost his fears; his misgivings faded out and died; his embarrassments departed, and gave place to an easy and confident bearing. He worked the whipping-boy mine to ever-increasing profit.

He ordered my Lady Elizabeth and my Lady Jane Grey into his presence when he wanted to play or talk, and dismissed them when he was done with them, with the air of one familiarly accustomed to such performances. It no longer confused him to have these lofty personages kiss his hand at parting.

He came to enjoy being conducted to bed in state at night, and dressed with intricate and solemn ceremony in the morning. It came to be a proud pleasure to march to dinner attended by a glittering procession of officers of state and gentlemen-at-arms; insomuch, indeed, that he doubled his guard of gentlemen-at-arms, and made them a hundred. He liked to hear the bugles sounding down the long corridors, and the distant voices responding, "Way for the King!"

He even learned to enjoy sitting in throned state in council, and seeming to be something more than the Lord Protector's mouth-piece. He liked to receive great ambassadors and their gorgeous trains, and listen to the affectionate messages they brought from illustrious monarchs who called him "brother." O happy Tom Canty, late of Offal Court!

He enjoyed his splendid clothes, and ordered more: he found his four hundred servants too few for his proper grandeur, and trebled them. The adulation of salaaming courtiers came to be sweet music to his ears. He remained kind and gentle, and a sturdy and determined champion of all that were oppressed, and he made tireless war upon unjust laws: yet upon occasion, being offended, he could turn upon an earl, or even a duke, and give him a look that would make him tremble. Once, when his royal "sister," the grimly, holy Lady Mary, set herself to reason with him against the wisdom of his course in pardoning so many people who would otherwise be jailed, or hanged, or burned, and reminded him that their august late father's prisons had sometimes contained as high as sixty thousand convicts at one time, and that during his admirable reign he had delivered seventy-two thousand thieves and robbers over to death by the executioner,* the boy was filled with generous indignation, and commanded her to go to her closet, and beseech God to take away the stone that was in her breast, and give her a human heart.

Did Tom Canty never feel troubled about the poor little rightful prince who had treated him so kindly, and flown out with such hot zeal to avenge him upon the insolent sentinel at the palace-gate? Yes; his first royal days and nights were pretty well sprinkled with painful thoughts about the lost prince, and with sincere longings for his return, and happy restoration to his native rights and splendors. But as time wore on, and the prince did not come, Tom's mind became more and more occupied with his new and enchanting experiences, and by little and little the vanished monarch faded almost out of his thoughts; and finally, when he did intrude upon them at intervals, he was become an unwelcome spectre, for he made Tom feel guilty and ashamed.

Tom's poor mother and sisters travelled the same road out of his mind. At first he pined for them, sorrowed for them, longed to see them, but later, the thought of their coming some day in their rags and dirt, and betraying him with their kisses, and pulling him down from his lofty place, and dragging him back to penury and degradation and the slums, made him shudder. At last they ceased to trouble his thoughts almost wholly. And he was content, even glad; for, whenever their mournful and accusing faces did rise before him now, they made him feel more despicable than the worms that crawl.

At midnight of the 19th of February, Tom Canty was sinking to sleep in his rich bed in the palace, guarded by his loyal vassals, and surrounded by the pomps of royalty, a happy boy; for to-morrow was the day appointed for his solemn

---

* Hume's England.

crowning as King of England. At that same hour, Edward, the true king, hungry and thirsty, soiled and draggled, worn with travel, and clothed in rags and shreds,—his share of the results of the riot,—was wedged in among a crowd of people who were watching with deep interest certain hurrying gangs of workmen who streamed in and out of Westminster Abbey, busy as ants: they were making the last preparation for the royal coronation.

Chapter XXXI

THE RECOGNITION PROCESSION

WHEN TOM CANTY awoke the next morning, the air was heavy with a thunderous murmur: all the distances were charged with it. It was music to him; for it meant that the English world was out in its strength to give loyal welcome to the great day.

Presently Tom found himself once more the chief figure in a wonderful floating pageant on the Thames; for by ancient custom the "recognition procession" through London must start from the Tower, and he was bound thither.

When he arrived there, the sides of the venerable fortress seemed suddenly rent in a thousand places, and from every rent leaped a red tongue of flame and a white gush of smoke; a deafening explosion followed, which drowned the shoutings of the multitude, and made the ground tremble; the flame-jets, the smoke, and the explosions, were repeated over and over again with marvellous celerity, so that in a few moments the old Tower disappeared in the vast fog of its own smoke, all but the very top of the tall pile called the White Tower: this, with its banners, stood out above the dense bank of vapor as a mountain-peak projects above a cloud-rack.

Tom Canty, splendidly arrayed, mounted a prancing war-steed, whose rich trappings almost reached to the ground; his "uncle," the Lord Protector Somerset, similarly mounted, took place in his rear; the King's Guard formed in single ranks on either side, clad in burnished armor; after the Protector followed a seemingly interminable procession of resplendent nobles attended by their vassals; after these came the lord mayor and the aldermanic body, in crimson velvet robes, and with their gold chains across their breasts; and after these the officers and members of all the guilds of London, in rich raiment, and bearing the showy banners of the several corporations. Also in the procession, as a special guard of honor through the city, was the Ancient and Honorable Artillery Company,— an organization already three hundred years old at that time, and the only military body in England possessing the privilege (which it still possesses in our day) of holding itself independent of the commands of Parliament. It was a brilliant spectacle, and was hailed with acclamations all along the line, as it took its stately way through the packed multitudes of citizens. The chronicler says, "The King, as he entered the city, was received by the people with prayers, welcomings, cries, and tender words, and all signs which argue an earnest love of subjects toward their sovereign; and the King, by holding up his glad countenance to such as stood afar off, and most tender language to those that stood nigh his Grace, showed himself no less thankful to receive the people's good will than

they to offer it. To all that wished him well, he gave thanks. To such as bade
'God save his Grace,' he said in return, 'God save you all!' and added that 'he
thanked them with all his heart.' Wonderfully transported were the people with
the loving answers and gestures of their King.''

In Fenchurch Street a ''fair child, in costly apparel,'' stood on a stage to
welcome his Majesty to the city. The last verse of his greeting was in these
words:

> ''Welcome, O King! as much as hearts can think;
>   Welcome again, as much as tongue can tell,—
> Welcome to joyous tongues, and hearts that will not shrink:
>   God thee preserve, we pray, and wish thee ever well.''

The people burst forth in a glad shout, repeating with one voice what the child
had said. Tom Canty gazed abroad over the surging sea of eager faces, and his
heart swelled with exultation; and he felt that the one thing worth living for in
this world was to be a king, and a nation's idol. Presently he caught sight, at a
distance, of a couple of his ragged Offal Court comrades,—one of them the lord
high admiral in his late mimic court, the other the first lord of the bedchamber
in the same pretentious fiction; and his pride swelled higher than ever. Oh, if
they could only recognize him now! What unspeakable glory it would be, if they
could recognize him, and realize that the derided mock king of the slums and
back alleys was become a real king, with illustrious dukes and princes for his
humble menials, and the English worlds at his feet! But he had to deny himself,
and choke down his desire, for such a recognition might cost more than it would
come to: so he turned away his head, and left the two soiled lads to go on with
their shoutings and glad adulations, unsuspicious of whom it was they were
lavishing them upon.

Every now and then rose the cry, ''A largess! a largess!'' and Tom responded
by scattering a handful of bright new coins abroad for the multitude to scramble
for.

The chronicler says, ''At the upper end of Gracechurch Street, before the sign
of the Eagle, the city had erected a gorgeous arch, beneath which was a stage,

'' WELCOME, O KING !''

which stretched from one side of the street to the other. This was a historical pageant, representing the King's immediate progenitors. There sat Elizabeth of York in the midst of an immense white rose, whose petals formed elaborate furbelows around her; by her side was Henry VII., issuing out of a vast red rose, disposed in the same manner: the hands of the royal pair were locked together, and the wedding-ring ostentatiously displayed. From the red and white roses proceeded a stem, which reached up to a second stage, occupied by Henry VIII., issuing from a red-and-white rose, with the effigy of the new king's mother, Jane Seymour, represented by his side. One branch sprang from this pair, which mounted to a third stage, where sat the effigy of Edward VI. himself, enthroned in royal majesty; and the whole pageant was framed with wreaths of roses, red and white.''

This quaint and gaudy spectacle so wrought upon the rejoicing people, that their acclamations utterly smothered the small voice of the child whose business it was to explain the thing in eulogistic rhymes. But Tom Canty was not sorry; for this loyal uproar was sweeter music to him than any poetry, no matter what its quality might be. Whithersoever Tom turned his happy young face, the people recognized the exactness of his effigy's likeness to himself, the flesh and blood counterpart; and new whirlwinds of applause burst forth.

The great pageant moved on, and still on, under one triumphal arch after another, and past a bewildering succession of spectacular and symbolical tableaux, each of which typified and exalted some virtue, or talent, or merit, of the little king's. ''Throughout the whole of Cheapside, from every penthouse and window, hung banners and streamers; and the richest carpets, stuffs, and cloth-of-gold tapestried the streets,—specimens of the great wealth of the stores within; and the splendor of this thoroughfare was equalled in the other streets, and in some even surpassed.''

''And all these wonders and these marvels are to welcome me—me!'' murmured Tom Canty.

The mock king's cheeks were flushed with excitement, his eyes were flashing, his senses swam in a delirium of pleasure. At this point, just as he was raising his hand to fling another rich largess, he caught sight of a pale, astounded face which was strained forward out of the second rank of the crowd, its intense eyes riveted upon him. A sickening consternation struck through him; he recognized his mother! and up flew his hand, palm outward, before his eyes,—that old involuntary gesture, born of a forgotten episode, and perpetuated by habit. In an instant more she had torn her way out of the press, and past the guards, and was at his side. She embraced his leg, she covered it with kisses, she cried, ''O my child, my darling!'' lifting toward him a face that was transfigured with joy and love. The same instant an officer of the King's Guard snatched her away with a curse, and sent her reeling back whence she came with a vigorous impulse from his strong arm. The words ''I do not know you, woman!'' were falling from Tom Canty's lips when this piteous thing occurred; but it smote him to the heart to see her treated so; and as she turned for a last glimpse of him, whilst the crowd was swallowing her from his sight, she seemed so wounded, so broken-hearted, that a shame fell upon him which consumed his pride to ashes, and withered his stolen royalty. His grandeurs were stricken valueless: they seemed to fall away from him like rotten rags.

The procession moved on, and still on, through ever augmenting splendors and ever augmenting tempests of welcome; but to Tom Canty they were as if they had not been. He neither saw nor heard. Royalty had lost its grace and sweetness; its pomps were become a reproach. Remorse was eating his heart out. He said, "Would God I were free of my captivity!"

He had unconsciously dropped back into the phraseology of the first days of his compulsory greatness.

The shining pageant still went winding like a radiant and interminable serpent down the crooked lanes of the quaint old city, and through the huzzaing hosts; but still the King rode with bowed head and vacant eyes, seeing only his mother's face and that wounded look in it.

"Largess, largess!" The cry fell upon an unheeding ear.

"Long live Edward of England!" It seemed as if the earth shook with the explosion; but there was no response from the King. He heard it only as one hears the thunder of the surf when it is blown to the ear out of a great distance, for it was smothered under another sound which was still nearer, in his own breast, in his accusing conscience,—a voice which kept repeating those shameful words, "I do not know you, woman!"

The words smote upon the King's soul as the strokes of a funeral bell smite upon the soul of a surviving friend when they remind him of secret treacheries suffered at his hands by him that is gone.

New glories were unfolded at every turning; new wonders, new marvels, sprung into view; the pent clamors of waiting batteries were released; new raptures poured from the throats of the waiting multitudes: but the King gave no sign, and the accusing voice that went moaning through his comfortless breast was all the sound he heard.

By and by the gladness in the faces of the populace changed a little, and became touched with a something like solicitude or anxiety: an abatement in the volume of applause was observable too. The lord protector was quick to notice these things: he was as quick to detect the cause. He spurred to the King's side, bent low in his saddle, uncovered, and said,—

"My liege, it is an ill time for dreaming. The people observe thy downcast head, thy clouded mien, and they take it for an omen. Be advised: unveil the sun of royalty, and let it shine upon these boding vapors, and disperse them. Lift up thy face, and smile upon the people."

So saying, the duke scattered a handful of coins to right and left, then retired to his place. The mock king did mechanically as he had been bidden. His smile had no heart in it, but few eyes were near enough or sharp enough to detect that. The noddings of his plumed head as he saluted his subjects were full of grace and graciousness; the largess which he delivered from his hand was royally liberal: so the people's anxiety vanished, and the acclamations burst forth again in as mighty a volume as before.

Still once more, a little before the progress was ended, the duke was obliged to ride forward, and make remonstrance. He whispered,—

"O dread sovereign! shake off these fatal humors: the eyes of the world are upon thee." Then he added with sharp annoyance, "Perdition catch that crazy pauper! 'twas she that hath disturbed your Highness."

The gorgeous figure turned a lustreless eye upon the duke, and said in a dead voice,—

"She was my mother!"

"My God!" groaned the protector as he reined his horse backward to his post, "the omen was pregnant with prophecy. He is gone mad again!"

"MY LIEGE, IT IS AN ILL TIME FOR DREAMING."

Chapter XXXII

CORONATION DAY

LET US GO backward a few hours, and place ourselves in Westminster Abbey, at four o'clock in the morning of this memorable Coronation Day. We are not without company; for although it is still night, we find the torch-lighted galleries already filling up with people who are well content to sit still and wait seven or eight hours till the time shall come for them to see what they may not hope to see twice in their lives—the coronation of a king. Yes, London and Westminster have been astir ever since the warning guns boomed at three o'clock, and already crowds of untitled rich folk who have bought the privilege of trying to find sitting-room in the galleries are flocking in at the entrances reserved for their sort.

The hours drag along, tediously enough. All stir has ceased for some time, for every gallery has long ago been packed. We may sit, now, and look and think at our leisure. We have glimpses, here and there and yonder, through the dim cathedral twilight, of portions of many galleries and balconies, wedged full with people, the other portions of these galleries and balconies being cut off from sight by intervening pillars and architectural projections. We have in view the whole of the great north transept—empty, and waiting for England's privileged ones. We see also the ample area or platform, carpeted with rich stuffs, whereon the throne stands. The throne occupies the centre of the platform, and is raised above it upon an elevation of four steps. Within the seat of the throne is enclosed a rough flat rock—the stone of Scone—which many generations of Scottish kings sat on to be crowned, and so it in time became holy enough to answer a like purpose for English monarchs. Both the throne and its footstool are covered with cloth of gold.

Stillness reigns, the torches blink dully, the time drags heavily. But at last the lagging daylight asserts itself, the torches are extinguished, and a mellow radiance suffuses the great spaces. All features of the noble building are distinct, now, but soft and dreamy, for the sun is lightly veiled with clouds.

At seven o'clock the first break in the drowsy monotony occurs; for on the stroke of this hour the first peeress enters the transept, clothed like Solomon for splendor, and is conducted to her appointed place by an official clad in satins and velvets, whilst a duplicate of him gathers up the lady's long train, follows after, and, when the lady is seated, arranges the train across her lap for her. He then places her footstool according to her desire, after which he puts her coronet where it will be convenient to her hand when the time for the simultaneous coronetting of the nobles shall arrive.

By this time the peeresses are flowing in in a glittering stream, and the satin-clad officials are flitting and glinting everywhere, seating them and making them comfortable. The scene is animated enough, now. There is stir and life, and shifting color everywhere. After a time, quiet reigns again; for the peeresses are all come, and are all in their places—a solid acre, or such a matter, of human flowers, resplendent in variegated colors, and frosted like a Milky Way with diamonds. There are all ages, here: brown, wrinkled, whitehaired dowagers who are able to go back, and still back, down the stream of time, and recall the crowning of Richard III. and the troublous days of that old forgotten age; and there are handsome middle-aged dames; and lovely and gracious young matrons; and gentle and beautiful young girls, with beaming eyes and fresh complexions, who may possibly put on their jewelled coronets awkwardly when the great time comes; for the matter will be new to them, and their excitement will be a sore hindrance. Still, this may not happen, for the hair of all these ladies has been arranged with a special view to the swift and successful lodging of the crown in its place when the signal comes.

We have seen that this massed array of peeresses is sown thick with diamonds, and we also see that it is a marvellous spectacle—but now we are about to be astonished in earnest. About nine, the clouds suddenly break away and a shaft of sunshine cleaves the mellow atmosphere, and drifts slowly along the ranks of ladies; and every rank it touches flames into a dazzling splendor of many-colored fires, and we tingle to our finger-tips with the electric thrill that is shot through us by the surprise and the beauty of the spectacle! Presently a special envoy from some distant corner of the Orient, marching with the general body of foreign ambassadors, crosses this bar of sunshine, and we catch our breath, the glory that streams and flashes and palpitates about him is so overpowering; for he is crusted from head to heel with gems, and his slightest movement showers a dancing radiance all around him.

Let us change the tense for convenience. The time drifted along,—one hour—two hours—two hours and a half; then the deep booming of artillery told that the king and his grand procession had arrived at last; so the waiting multitude rejoiced. All knew that a further delay must follow, for the king must be prepared and robed for the solemn ceremony; but this delay would be pleasantly occupied by the assembling of the peers of the realm in their stately robes. These were conducted ceremoniously to their seats, and their coronets placed conveniently at hand; and meanwhile the multitude in the galleries were alive with interest, for most of them were beholding for the first time, dukes, earls and barons, whose names had been historical for five hundred years. When all were finally seated, the spectacle from the galleries and all coigns of vantage was complete; a gorgeous one to look upon and to remember.

Now the robed and mitred great heads of the church, and their attendants, filed in upon the platform and took their appointed places; these were followed by the Lord Protector and other great officials, and these again by a steel-clad detachment of the Guard.

There was a waiting pause; then, at a signal, a triumphant peal of music burst forth, and Tom Canty, clothed in a long robe of cloth of gold, appeared at a door, and stepped upon the platform. The entire multitude rose, and the ceremony of the Recognition ensued.

Then a noble anthem swept the Abbey with its rich waves of sound; and thus heralded and welcomed, Tom Canty was conducted to the throne. The ancient ceremonies went on, with impressive solemnity, whilst the audience gazed; and as they drew nearer and nearer to completion, Tom Canty grew pale, and still paler, and a deep and steadily deepening woe and despondency settled down upon his spirits and upon his remorseful heart.

At last the final act was at hand. The Archbishop of Canterbury lifted up the crown of England from its cushion and held it out over the trembling mock-king's head. In the same instant a rainbow-radiance flashed along the spacious transept; for with one impulse every individual in the great concourse of nobles lifted a coronet and poised it over his or her head,—and paused in that attitude.

A deep hush pervaded the Abbey. At this impressive moment, a startling apparition intruded upon the scene—an apparition observed by none in the absorbed multitude, until it suddenly appeared, moving up the great central aisle. It was a boy, bare-headed, ill shod, and clothed in coarse plebeian garments that were falling to rags. He raised his hand with a solemnity which ill comported with his soiled and sorry aspect, and delivered this note of warning—

"I forbid you to set the crown of England upon that forfeited head. *I* am the king!"

In an instant several indignant hands were laid upon the boy; but in the same instant Tom Canty, in his regal vestments, made a swift step forward and cried out in a ringing voice—

"Loose him and forbear! He *is* the king!"

A sort of panic of astonishment swept the assemblage, and they partly rose in their places and stared in a bewildered way at one another and at the chief

"AND FELL ON HIS KNEES BEFORE HIM."

figures in this scene, like persons who wondered whether they were awake and in their senses, or asleep and dreaming. The Lord Protector was as amazed as the rest, but quickly recovered himself and exclaimed in a voice of authority—

"Mind not his Majesty, his malady is upon him again—seize the vagabond!"

He would have been obeyed, but the mock-king stamped his foot and cried out—

"On your peril! Touch him not, he is the king!"

The hands were withheld; a paralysis fell upon the house; no one moved, no one spoke; indeed no one knew how to act or what to say, in so strange and surprising an emergency. While all minds were struggling to right themselves, the boy still moved steadily forward, with high port and confident mien; he had never halted from the beginning; and while the tangled minds still floundered helplessly, he stepped upon the platform, and the mock-king ran with a glad face to meet him; and fell on his knees before him and said—

"O, my lord the king, let poor Tom Canty be first to swear fealty to thee, and say 'Put on thy crown and enter into thine own again!' "

The Lord Protector's eye fell sternly upon the new-comer's face; but straightway the sternness vanished away, and gave place to an expression of wondering surprise. This thing happened also to the other great officers. They glanced at each other, and retreated a step by a common and unconscious impulse. The thought in each mind was the same: "What a strange resemblance!"

The Lord Protector reflected a moment or two, in perplexity, then he said, with grave respectfulness—

"By your favor, sir, I desire to ask certain questions which"—

"I will answer them, my lord."

The duke asked him many questions about the court, the late king, the prince, the princesses,—the boy answered them correctly and without hesitating. He described the rooms of state in the palace, the late king's apartments, and those of the Prince of Wales.

It was strange; it was wonderful; yes, it was unaccountable—so all said that heard it. The tide was beginning to turn, and Tom Canty's hopes to run high, when the Lord Protector shook his head and said—

"It is true it is most wonderful—but it is no more than our lord the king likewise can do." This remark, and this reference to himself as still the king, saddened Tom Canty, and he felt his hopes crumbling from under him. "These are not *proofs*," added the Protector.

The tide was turning very fast, now, very fast indeed—but in the wrong direction; it was leaving poor Tom Canty stranded on the throne, and sweeping the other out to sea. The Lord Protector communed with himself—shook his head—the thought forced itself upon him, "It is perilous to the State and to us all, to entertain so fateful a riddle as this; it could divide the nation and undermine the throne." He turned and said—

"Sir Thomas, arrest this—No, hold!" His face lighted, and he confronted the ragged candidate with this question—

"Where lieth the Great Seal? Answer me this truly, and the riddle is unriddled; for only he that was Prince of Wales *can* so answer! On so trival a thing hang a throne and a dynasty!"

It was a lucky thought, a happy thought. That it was so considered by the great officials was manifested by the silent applause that shot from eye to eye around their circle in the form of bright approving glances. Yes, none but the

true prince could dissolve the stubborn mystery of the vanished Great Seal—
this forlorn little impostor had been taught his lesson well, but here his teachings
must fail, for his teacher himself could not answer *that* question—ah, very good,
very good indeed; now we shall be rid of this troublesome and perilous business
in short order! And so they nodded invisibly and smiled inwardly with satisfaction,
and looked to see this foolish lad stricken with a palsy of guilty confusion. How
surprised they were, then, to see nothing of the sort happen—how they marvelled
to hear him answer up promptly, in a confident and untroubled voice, and say—

"There is nought in this riddle that is difficult." Then, without so much as
a by-your-leave to anybody, he turned and gave this command, with the easy
manner of one accustomed to doing such things: "My lord St. John, go you to
my private cabinet in the palace—for none knoweth the place better than you—
and, close down to the floor, in the left corner remotest from the door that opens
from the antechamber, you shall find in the wall a brazen nail-head; press upon
it and a little jewel-closet will fly open which not even you do know of—no,
nor any soul else, in all the world but me and the trusty artisan that did contrive
it for me. The first thing that falleth under your eye will be the Great Seal—
fetch it hither."

All the company wondered at this speech, and wondered still more to see the
little mendicant pick out this peer without hesitancy or apparent fear of mistake,
and call him by name with such a placidly convincing air of having known him
all his life. The peer was almost surprised into obeying. He even made a movement
as if to go, but quickly recovered his tranquil attitude and confessed his blunder
with a blush. Tom Canty turned upon him and said, sharply—

"Why dost thou hesitate? Hast not heard the king's command? Go!"

The lord St. John made a deep obeisance—and it was observed that it was a
significantly cautious and non-committal one, it not being delivered at either of
the kings, but at the neutral ground about half way between the two—and took
his leave.

Now began a movement of the gorgeous particles of that official group which
was slow, scarcely perceptible, and yet steady and persistent—a movement such
as is observed in a kaleidoscope that is turned slowly, whereby the components
of one splendid cluster fall away and join themselves to another—a movement
which little by little, in the present case, dissolved the glittering crowd that stood
about Tom Canty and clustered it together again in the neighborhood of the new-
comer. Tom Canty stood almost alone. Now ensued a brief season of deep
suspense and waiting—during which even the few faint-hearts still remaining
near Tom Canty gradually scraped together courage enough to glide, one by
one, over to the majority. So at last Tom Canty, in his royal robes and jewels,
stood wholly alone and isolated from the world, a conspicuous figure, occupying
an eloquent vacancy.

Now the lord St. John was seen returning. As he advanced up the mid-aisle
the interest was so intense that the low murmur of conversation in the great
assemblage died out and was succeeded by a profound hush, a breathless stillness,
through which his footfalls pulsed with a dull and distant sound. Every eye was
fastened upon him as he moved along. He reached the platform, paused a
moment, then moved toward Tom Canty with a deep obeisance, and said—

"Sire, the Seal is not there!"

A mob does not melt away from the presence of a plague-patient with more
haste than the band of pallid and terrified courtiers melted away from the presence

of the shabby little claimant of the Crown. In a moment he stood all alone, without friend or supporter, a target upon which was concentrated a bitter fire of scornful and angry looks. The Lord Protector called out fiercely—

"Cast the beggar into the street, and scourge him through the town—the paltry knave is worth no more consideration!"

Officers of the guard sprang forward to obey, but Tom Canty waved them off and said—

"Back! Whoso touches him perils his life!"

The Lord Protector was perplexed, in the last degree. He said to the lord St. John—

"Searched you well?—but it boots not to ask that. It doth seem passing strange. Little things, trifles, slip out of one's ken, and one does not think it matter for surprise; but how a so bulky thing as the Seal of England can vanish away and no man be able to get track of it again—a massy golden disk"—

Tom Canty, with beaming eyes, sprang forward and shouted—

"Hold, that is enough! Was it round?—and thick?—and had it letters and devices graved upon it?—Yes? O, *now* I know what this Great Seal is that there's been such worry and pother about! An' ye had described it to me, ye could have had it three weeks ago. Right well I know where it lies; but it was not I that put it there—first."

"Who, then, my liege?" asked the Lord Protector.

"He that stands there—the rightful king of England. And he shall tell you himself where it lies—then you will believe he knew it of his own knowledge. Bethink thee, my king—spur thy memory—it was the last, the very *last* thing thou didst that day before thou didst rush forth from the palace, clothed in my rags, to punish the soldier that insulted me."

A silence ensued, undisturbed by a movement or a whisper, and all eyes were fixed upon the new-comer, who stood, with bent head and corrugated brow, groping in his memory among a thronging multitude of valueless recollections for one single little elusive fact, which, found, would seat him upon a throne—unfound, would leave him as he was, for good and all—a pauper and an outcast. Moment after moment passed—the moments built themselves into minutes—still the boy struggled silently on, and gave no sign. But at last he heaved a

"BETHINK THEE, MY KING."

sigh, shook his head slowly, and said, with a trembling lip and in a despondent voice—

"I call the scene back—all of it—but the Seal hath no place in it." He paused, then looked up, and said with gentle dignity, "My lords and gentlemen, if ye will rob your rightful sovereign of his own for lack of this evidence which he is not able to furnish, I may not stay ye, being powerless. But"—

"O, folly, O, madness, my king!" cried Tom Canty, in a panic, "wait!— think! Do not give up!—the cause is not lost! Nor *shall* be, neither! List to what I say—follow every word—I am going to bring that morning back again, every hap just as it happened. We talked—I told you of my sisters, Nan and Bet— ah, yes, you remember that; and about mine old grandam—and the rough games of the lads of Offal Court—yes, you remember these things also; very well, follow me still, you shall recall every thing. You gave me food and drink, and did with princely courtesy send away the servants, so that my low breeding might not shame me before them—ah, yes, this also you remember."

As Tom checked off his details, and the other boy nodded his head in recognition of them, the great audience and the officials stared in puzzled wonderment; the tale sounded like true history, yet how could this impossible conjunction between a prince and a beggar boy have come about? Never was a company of people so perplexed, so interested, and so stupefied, before.

"For a jest, my prince, we did exchange garments. Then we stood before a mirror; and so alike were we that both said it seemed as if there had been no change made—yes, you remember that. Then you noticed that the soldier had hurt my hand—look! here it is, I cannot yet even write with it, the fingers are so stiff. At this your Highness sprang up, vowing vengeance upon that soldier, and ran toward the door—you passed a table—that thing you call the Seal lay on that table—you snatched it up and looked eagerly about, as if for a place to hide it—your eye caught sight of"—

"There, 'tis sufficient!—and the dear God be thanked!" exclaimed the ragged claimant, in a mighty excitement. "Go, my good St. John,—in an arm-piece of the Milanese armor that hangs on the wall, thou'lt find the Seal!"

"Right, my king! right!" cried Tom Canty; "*now* the sceptre of England is thine own; and it were better for him that would dispute it that he had been born dumb! Go, my lord St. John, give thy feet wings!"

The whole assemblage was on its feet, now, and well nigh out of its mind with uneasiness, apprehension, and consuming excitement. On the floor and on the platform a deafening buzz of frantic conversation burst forth, and for some time nobody knew any thing or heard any thing or was interested in any thing but what his neighbor was shouting into his ear, or he was shouting into his neighbor's ear. Time—nobody knew how much of it—swept by unheeded and unnoted.—At last a sudden hush fell upon the house, and in the same moment St. John appeared upon the platform and held the Great Seal aloft in his hand. Then such a shout went up!

"Long live the true King!"

For five minutes the air quaked with shouts and the crash of musical instruments, and was white with a storm of waving handkerchiefs; and through it all a ragged lad, the most conspicuous figure in England, stood, flushed and happy and proud, in the centre of the spacious platform, with the great vassals of the kingdom kneeling around him.

Then all rose, and Tom Canty cried out—

"Now, O, my king, take these regal garments back, and give poor Tom, thy servant, his shreds and remnants again."

The Lord Protector spoke up—

"Let the small varlet be stripped and flung into the Tower."

But the new king, the true king, said—

"I will not have it so. But for him I had not got my crown again—none shall lay a hand upon him to harm him. And as for thee, my good uncle, my Lord Protector, this conduct of thine is not grateful toward this poor lad, for I hear he hath made thee a duke"—the Protector blushed—"yet he was not a king; wherefore, what is thy fine title worth, now? To-morrow you shall sue to me, *through him*, for its confirmation, else no duke, but a simple earl, shalt thou remain."

Under this rebuke, his grace the duke of Somerset retired a little from the front for the moment. The king turned to Tom, and said, kindly—

"My poor boy, how was it that you could remember where I hid the Seal when I could not remember it myself?"

"Ah, my king, that was easy, since I used it divers days."

"Used it,—yet could not explain where it was?"

"I did not know it was *that* they wanted. They did not describe it, your majesty."

"Then how used you it?"

The red blood began to steal up into Tom's cheeks, and he dropped his eyes and was silent.

"Speak up, good lad, and fear nothing," said the king. "How used you the Great Seal of England?"

Tom stammered a moment, in a pathetic confusion, then got it out—

"To crack nuts with!"

Poor child, the avalanche of laughter that greeted this, nearly swept him off his feet. But if a doubt remained in any mind that Tom Canty was not the king of England and familiar with the august appurtenances of royalty, this reply disposed of it utterly.

Meantime the sumptuous robe of state had been removed from Tom's shoulders to the king's, whose rags were effectually hidden from sight under it. Then the coronation ceremonies were resumed; the true king was anointed and the crown set upon his head, whilst cannon thundered the news to the city, and all London seemed to rock with applause.

Chapter XXXIII

EDWARD AS KING

MILES HENDON WAS picturesque enough before he got into the riot on London Bridge—he was more so when he got out of it. He had but little money when he got in, none at all when he got out. The pickpockets had stripped him of his last farthing.

But no matter, so he found his boy. Being a soldier, he did not go at his task in a random way, but set to work, first of all, to arrange his campaign.

What would the boy naturally do? Where would he naturally go? Well—argued Miles—he would naturally go to his former haunts, for that is the instinct of unsound minds, when homeless and forsaken, as well as of sound ones. Whereabouts were his former haunts? His rags, taken together with the low villain who seemed to know him and who even claimed to be his father, indicated that his home was in one or another of the poorest and meanest districts of London. Would the search for him be difficult, or long? No, it was likely to be easy and brief. He would not hunt for the boy, he would hunt for a crowd; in the centre of a big crowd or a little one, sooner or later, he should find his poor little friend, sure; and the mangy mob would be entertaining itself with pestering and aggravating the boy, who would be proclaiming himself king, as usual. Then Miles Hendon would cripple some of those people, and carry off his little ward, and comfort and cheer him with loving words, and the two would never be separated any more.

So Miles started on his quest. Hour after hour he tramped through back alleys and squalid streets, seeking groups and crowds, and finding no end of them, but never any sign of the boy. This greatly surprised him, but did not discourage him. To his notion, there was nothing the matter with his plan of campaign; the only miscalculation about it was that the campaign was becoming a lengthy one, whereas he had expected it to be short.

When daylight arrived, at last, he had made many a mile, and canvassed many a crowd, but the only result was that he was tolerably tired, rather hungry, and very sleepy. He wanted some breakfast, but there was no way to get it. To beg for it did not occur to him; as to pawning his sword, he would as soon have thought of parting with his honor; he could spare some of his clothes—yes, but one could as easily find a customer for a disease as for such clothes.

At noon he was still tramping—among the rabble which followed after the royal procession, now; for he argued that this regal display would attract his little lunatic powerfully. He followed the pageant through all its devious windings about London, and all the way to Westminster and the Abbey. He drifted here and there amongst the multitudes that were massed in the vicinity for a weary long time, baffled and perplexed, and finally wandered off, thinking, and trying to contrive some way to better his plan of campaign. By and by, when he came to himself out of his musings, he discovered that the town was far behind him and that the day was growing old. He was near the river, and in the country; it was a region of fine rural seats—not the sort of district to welcome clothes like his.

It was not at all cold; so he stretched himself on the ground in the lee of a hedge to rest and think. Drowsiness presently began to settle upon his senses; the faint and far-off boom of cannon was wafted to his ear, and he said to himself "The new king is crowned," and straightway fell asleep. He had not slept or rested, before, for more than thirty hours. He did not wake again until near the middle of the next morning.

He got up, lame, stiff, and half famished, washed himself in the river, stayed his stomach with a pint or two of water, and trudged off toward Westminster grumbling at himself for having wasted so much time. Hunger helped him to a new plan, now; he would try to get speech with old Sir Humphrey Marlow and borrow a few marks, and—but that was enough of a plan for the present; it would be time enough to enlarge it when this first stage should be accomplished.

Toward eleven o'clock he approached the palace; and although a host of showy people were about him, moving in the same direction, he was not inconspicuous—his costume took care of that. He watched these people's faces narrowly, hoping to find a charitable one whose possessor might be willing to carry his name to the old lieutenant—as to trying to get into the palace himself, that was simply out of the question.

Presently our whipping-boy passed him, then wheeled about and scanned his figure well, saying to himself, "An' that is not the very vagabond his majesty is in such a worry about, then am I an ass—though belike I was that before. He answereth the description to a rag—that God should make two such, would be to cheapen miracles, by wasteful repetition. I would I could contrive an excuse to speak with him."

Miles Hendon saved him the trouble; for he turned about, then, as a man generally will when somebody mesmerizes him by gazing hard at him from behind; and observing a strong interest in the boy's eyes, he stepped toward him and said—

"You have just come out from the palace; do you belong there?"

"Yes, your worship."

"Know you Sir Humphrey Marlow?"

The boy started, and said to himself, "Lord! mine old departed father!" Then he answered, aloud, "Right well, your worship."

"Good—is he within?"

"Yes," said the boy; and added, to himself, "within his grave."

"Might I crave your favor to carry my name to him, and say I beg to say a word in his ear?"

"I will despatch the business right willingly, fair sir."

"Then say Miles Hendon, son of Sir Richard, is here without—I shall be greatly bounden to you, my good lad."

The boy looked disappointed—"the king did not name him so," he said to himself—"but it mattereth not, this is his twin brother, and can give his majesty news of 'tother Sir-Odds-and-Ends, I warrant." So he said to Miles, "Step in there a moment, good sir, and wait till I bring you word."

Hendon retired to the place indicated—it was a recess sunk in the palace wall, with a stone bench in it—a shelter for sentinels in bad weather. He had hardly seated himself when some halberdiers, in charge of an officer, passed by. The officer saw him, halted his men, and commanded Hendon to come forth. He obeyed, and was promptly arrested as a suspicious character prowling within the precincts of the palace. Things began to look ugly. Poor Miles was going to explain, but the officer roughly silenced him, and ordered his men to disarm him and search him.

"God of his mercy grant that they find somewhat," said poor Miles; "I have searched enow, and failed, yet is my need greater than theirs."

Nothing was found but a document. The officer tore it open, and Hendon smiled when he recognized the "pot-hooks" made by his lost little friend that black day at Hendon Hall. The officer's face grew dark as he read the English paragraph, and Miles blenched to the opposite color as he listened.

"Another new claimant of the crown!" cried the officer. "Verily they breed like rabbits, to-day. Seize the rascal, men, and see ye keep him fast whilst I convey this precious paper within and send it to the king."

He hurried away, leaving the prisoner in the grip of the halberdiers.

"Now is my evil luck ended at last," muttered Hendon, "for I shall dangle at a rope's end for a certainty, by reason of that bit of writing. And what will become of my poor lad!—ah, only the good God knoweth.''

By and by he saw the officer coming again, in a great hurry; so he plucked his courage together, purposing to meet his trouble as became a man. The officer ordered the men to loose the prisoner and return his sword to him; then bowed respectfully, and said—

"Please you sir, to follow me.''

Hendon followed, saying to himself, "An' I were not travelling to death and judgment, and so must needs economize in sin, I would throttle this knave for his mock courtesy.''

The two traversed a populous court, and arrived at the grand entrance of the palace, where the officer, with another bow, delivered Hendon into the hands of a gorgeous official, who received him with profound respect and led him forward through a great hall, lined on both sides with rows of splendid flunkies (who made reverential obeisance as the two passed along, but fell into death-throes of silent laughter at our stately scare-crow the moment his back was turned,) and up a broad staircase, among flocks of fine folk, and finally conducted him into a vast room, clove a passage for him through the assembled nobility of England, then made a bow, reminded him to take his hat off, and left him standing in the middle of the room, a mark for all eyes, for plenty of indignant frowns, and for a sufficiency of amused and derisive smiles.

Miles Hendon was entirely bewildered. There sat the young king, under a canopy of state, five steps away, with his head bent down and aside, speaking with a sort of human bird of paradise—a duke, maybe; Hendon observed to himself that it was hard enough to be sentenced to death in the full vigor of life, without having this peculiarly public humiliation added. He wished the king would hurry about it—some of the gaudy people near by were becoming pretty offensive. At this moment the king raised his head slightly and Hendon caught a good view of his face. The sight nearly took his breath away!—He stood gazing at the fair young face like one transfixed; then presently ejaculated—

"Lo, the lord of the Kingdom of Dreams and Shadows on his throne!''

He muttered some broken sentences, still gazing and marvelling; then turned his eyes around and about, scanning the gorgeous throng and the splendid saloon, murmuring "But these are *real*—verily these are *real*—surely it is not a dream.''

He stared at the king again—and thought, "*Is* it a dream? . . . or *is* he the veritable sovereign of England, and not the friendless poor Tom o' Bedlam I took him for—who shall solve me this riddle?''

A sudden idea flashed in his eye, and he strode to the wall, gathered up a chair, brought it back, planted it on the floor, and sat down in it!

A buzz of indignation broke out, a rough hand was laid upon him, and a voice exclaimed,—

"Up, thou mannerless clown!—wouldst sit in the presence of the king?''

The disturbance attracted his majesty's attention, who stretched forth his hand and cried out—

"Touch him not, it is his right!''

The throng fell back, stupefied. The king went on—

"Learn ye all, ladies, lords and gentlemen, that this is my trusty and well beloved servant, Miles Hendon, who interposed his good sword and saved his prince from bodily harm and possible death—and for this he is a knight, by the king's voice. Also learn, that for a higher service, in that he saved his sovereign

stripes and shame, taking these upon himself, he is a peer of England, Earl of
Kent, and shall have gold and lands meet for the dignity. More—the privilege
which he hath just exercised is his by royal grant; for we have ordained that the
chiefs of his line shall have and hold the right to sit in the presence of the majesty
of England henceforth, age after age, so long as the crown shall endure. Molest
him not.''

Two persons, who, through delay, had only arrived from the country during
this morning, and had now been in this room only five minutes, stood listening
to these words and looking at the king, then at the scare-crow, then at the king
again, in a sort of torpid bewilderment. These were Sir Hugh and the Lady
Edith. But the new Earl did not see them. He was still staring at the monarch,
in a dazed way, and muttering—

''O, body o' me! *This* my pauper! This my lunatic! This is he whom *I* would
show what grandeur was, in my house of seventy rooms and seven and twenty
servants! This is he who had never known aught but rags for raiment, kicks for
comfort, and offal for diet! This is he whom *I* adopted and would make respectable!
Would God I had a bag to hide my head in!''

Then his manners suddenly came back to him, and he dropped upon his knees,
with his hands between the king's, and swore allegiance and did homage for his
lands and titles. Then he rose and stood respectfully aside, a mark still for all
eyes—and much envy, too.

Now the king discovered Sir Hugh, and spoke out, with wrathful voice and
kindling eye—

''Strip this robber of his false show and stolen estates, and put him under
lock and key till I have need of him.''

The late Sir Hugh was led away.

There was a stir at the other end of the room, now; the assemblage fell apart,
and Tom Canty, quaintly but richly clothed, marched down, between these living
walls, preceded by an usher. He knelt before the king, who said—

''I have learned the story of these past few weeks, and am well pleased with
thee. Thou hast governed the realm with right royal gentleness and mercy. Thou
hast found thy mother and thy sisters again? Good; they shall be cared for—and
thy father shall hang, if thou desire it and the law consent. Know, all ye that

''TOM ROSE AND KISSED THE KING'S HAND.''

hear my voice, that from this day, they that abide in the shelter of Christ's Hospital and share the king's bounty, shall have their minds and hearts fed, as well as their baser parts; and this boy shall dwell there, and hold the chief place in its honorable body of governors, during life. And for that he hath been a king, it is meet that other than common observance shall be his due; wherefore, note this his dress of state, for by it he shall be known, and none shall copy it; and wheresoever he shall come, it shall remind the people that he hath been royal, in his time, and none shall deny him his due of reverence or fail to give him salutation. He hath the throne's protection, he hath the crown's support, he shall be known and called by the honorable title of the King's Ward.''

The proud and happy Tom Canty rose and kissed the king's hand, and was conducted from the presence. He did not waste any time, but flew to his mother, to tell her and Nan and Bet all about it and get them to help him enjoy the great news.

Conclusion

JUSTICE AND RETRIBUTION

WHEN THE MYSTERIES were all cleared up, it came out, by confession of Hugh Hendon, that his wife had repudiated Miles by his command, that day at Hendon Hall—a command assisted and supported by the perfectly trustworthy promise that if she did not deny that he was Miles Hendon, and stand firmly to it, he would have her life; whereupon she said take it, she did not value it—and she would not repudiate Miles; then the husband said he would spare her life but have Miles assassinated! This was a different matter; so she gave her word and kept it.

Hugh was not prosecuted for his threats or for stealing his brother's estates and title, because the wife and brother would not testify against him—and the former would not have been allowed to do it, even if she had wanted to. Hugh deserted his wife and went over to the continent, where he presently died; and by and by the earl of Kent married his relict. There were grand times and rejoicings at Hendon village when the couple paid their first visit to the Hall.

Tom Canty's father was never heard of again.

The king sought out the farmer who had been branded and sold as a slave, and reclaimed him from his evil life with the Ruffler's gang, and put him in the way of a comfortable livelihood.

He also took that old lawyer out of prison and remitted his fine. He provided good homes for the daughters of the two Baptist women whom he saw burned at the stake, and roundly punished the official who laid the undeserved stripes upon Miles Hendon's back.

He saved from the gallows the boy who had captured the stray falcon, and also the woman who had stolen a remnant of cloth from a weaver; but he was too late to save the man who had been convicted of killing a deer in the royal forest.

He showed favor to the justice who had pitied him when he was supposed to have stolen a pig, and he had the gratification of seeing him grow in the public esteem and become a great and honored man.

As long as the king lived he was fond of telling the story of his adventures, all through, from the hour that the sentinel cuffed him away from the palace gate till the final midnight when he deftly mixed himself into a gang of hurrying workmen and so slipped into the Abbey and climbed up and hid himself in the Confessor's tomb, and then slept so long, next day, that he came within one of missing the Coronation altogether. He said that the frequent rehearsing of the precious lesson kept him strong in his purpose to make its teachings yield benefits to his people; and so, whilst his life was spared he should continue to tell the story, and thus keep its sorrowful spectacles fresh in his memory and the springs of pity replenished in his heart.

Miles Hendon and Tom Canty were favorites of the king, all through his brief reign, and his sincere mourners when he died. The good earl of Kent had too much good sense to abuse his peculiar privilege; but he exercised it twice after the instance we have seen of it before he was called from the world; once at the accession of Queen Mary, and once at the accession of Queen Elizabeth. A descendant of his exercised it at the accession of James I. Before this one's son chose to use the privilege, near a quarter of a century had elapsed, and the "privilege of the Kents" had faded out of most people's memories; so, when the Kent of that day appeared before Charles I. and his court and sat down in the sovereign's presence to assert and perpetuate the right of his house, there was a fine stir, indeed! But the matter was soon explained and the right confirmed. The last earl of the line fell in the wars of the Commonwealth fighting for the king, and the odd privilege ended with him.

Tom Canty lived to be a very old man, a handsome, white-haired old fellow, of grave and benignant aspect. As long as he lasted he was honored; and he was also reverenced, for his striking and peculiar costume kept the people reminded that "in his time he had been royal;" so, wherever he appeared the crowd fell apart, making way for him, and whispering, one to another, "Doff thy hat, it is the King's Ward!"—and so they saluted, and got his kindly smile in return— and they valued it, too, for his was an honorable history.

Yes, King Edward VI lived only a few years, poor boy, but he lived them worthily. More than once, when some great dignitary, some gilded vassal of the crown, made argument against his leniency, and urged that some law which he was bent upon amending was gentle enough for its purpose, and wrought no suffering or oppression which any one need mightily mind, the young king turned the mournful eloquence of his great compassionate eyes upon him and answered—

"What dost *thou* know of suffering and oppression? I and my people know, but not thou."

The reign of Edward VI was a singularly merciful one for those harsh times. Now that we are taking leave of him let us try to keep this in our minds, to his credit.

A Connecticut Yankee in King Arthur's Court

PREFACE

THE UNGENTLE LAWS and customs touched upon in this tale are historical, and the episodes which are used to illustrate them are also historical. It is not pretended that these laws and customs existed in England in the sixth century; no, it is only pretended that inasmuch as they existed in the English and other civilizations of far later times, it is safe to consider that it is no libel upon the sixth century to suppose them to have been in practice in that day also. One is quite justified in inferring that whatever one of these laws or customs was lacking in that remote time, its place was competently filled by a worse one.

The question as to whether there is such a thing as divine right of kings is not settled in this book. It was found too difficult. That the executive head of a nation should be a person of lofty character and extraordinary ability, was manifest and indisputable; that none but the Deity could select that head unerringly, was also manifest and indisputable; that the Deity ought to make that selection, then, was likewise manifest and indisputable; consequently, that He does make it, as claimed, was an unavoidable deduction. I mean, until the author of this book encountered the Pompadour, and Lady Castlemaine, and some other executive heads of that kind; these were found so difficult to work into the scheme, that it was judged better to take the other tack in this book (which must be issued this fall), and then go into training and settle the question in another book. It is, of course, a thing which ought to be settled, and I am not going to have anything particular to do next winter anyway.

MARK TWAIN.

A WORD OF EXPLANATION

IT WAS IN Warwick Castle that I came across the curious stranger whom I am going to talk about. He attracted me by three things: his candid simplicity, his marvelous familiarity with ancient armor, and the restfulness of his company—for he did all the talking. We fell together, as modest people will, in the tail of the herd that was being shown through, and he at once began to say things which interested me. As he talked along, softly, pleasantly, flowingly, he seemed to drift away imperceptibly out of this world and time, and into some remote era and old forgotten country; and so he gradually wove such a spell about me that I seemed to move among the specters and shadows and dust and mold of a gray antiquity, holding speech with a relic of it! Exactly as I would speak of my nearest personal friends or enemies, or my most familiar neighbors, he spoke of Sir Bedivere, Sir Bors de Ganis, Sir Launcelot of the Lake, Sir Galahad, and all the other great names of the Table Round—and how old, old, unspeakably old and faded and dry and musty and ancient he came to look as he went on! Presently he turned to me and said, just as one might speak of the weather, or any other common matter—

"You know about transmigration of souls; do you know about transposition of epochs—and bodies?"

I said I had not heard of it. He was so little interested—just as when people speak of the weather—that he did not notice whether I made him any answer or not. There was half a moment of silence, immediately interrupted by the droning voice of the salaried cicerone:

"Ancient hauberk, date of the sixth century, time of King Arthur and the Round Table; said to have belonged to the knight Sir Sagramor le Desirous; observe the round hole through the chain-mail in the left breast; can't be accounted for; supposed to have been done with a bullet since invention of firearms— perhaps maliciously by Cromwell's soldiers."

My acquaintance smiled—not a modern smile, but one that must have gone out of general use many, many centuries ago—and muttered apparently to himself:

"Wit ye well, *I saw it done*." Then, after a pause, added: "I did it myself."

By the time I had recovered from the electric surprise of this remark, he was gone.

All that evening I sat by my fire at the Warwick Arms, steeped in a dream of the olden time, while the rain beat upon the windows, and the wind roared about the eaves and corners. From time to time I dipped into old Sir Thomas Malory's enchanting book, and fed at its rich feast of prodigies and adventures, breathed in the fragrance of its obsolete names, and dreamed again. Midnight being come at length, I read another tale, for a nightcap—this which here follows, to wit:

HOW SIR LAUNCELOT SLEW TWO GIANTS, AND MADE A CASTLE FREE

Anon withal came there upon him two great giants, well armed, all save the heads, with two horrible clubs in their hands. Sir Launcelot put his shield afore him, and put the stroke away of the one giant, and with his sword he clave his head asunder. When his fellow saw that, he ran away as he were wood,[1] for fear of the horrible strokes, and Sir Launcelot after him with all his might, and smote him on the shoulder, and clave him to the middle. Then Sir Launcelot went into the hall, and there came afore him threescore ladies and damsels, and all kneeled unto him, and thanked God and him of their deliverance. For, sir, said they, the most part of us have been here this seven year their prisoners, and we have worked all manner of silk works for our meat, and we are all great

---

[1] Demented.

gentlewomen born, and blessed be the time, knight, that ever thou wert born; for thou hast done the most worship that ever did knight in the world, that will we bear record, and we all pray you to tell us your name, that we may tell our friends who delivered us out of prison. Fair damsels, he said, my name is Sir Launcelot du Lake. And so he departed from them and betaught them unto God. And then he mounted upon his horse, and rode into many strange and wild countries, and through many waters and valleys, and evil was he lodged. And at the last by fortune him happened against a night to come to a fair courtilage, and therein he found an old gentlewoman that lodged him with a good will, and there he had good cheer for him and his horse. And when time was, his host brought him into a fair garret over the gate to his bed. There Sir Launcelot unarmed him, and set his harness by him, and went to bed, and anon he fell on sleep. So, soon after there came one on horseback, and knocked at the gate in great haste. And when Sir Launcelot heard this he rose up, and looked out at the window, and saw by the moonlight three knights come riding after that one man, and all three lashed on him at once with swords, and that one knight turned on them knightly again and defended him. Truly, said Sir Launcelot, yonder one knight shall I help, for it were shame for me to see three knights on one, and if he be slain I am partner of his death. And therewith he took his harness and went out at a window by a sheet down to the four knights, and then Sir Launcelot said on high, Turn you knights unto me, and leave your fighting with that knight. And then they all three left Sir Kay, and turned unto Sir Launcelot, and there began great battle, for they alight all three, and strake many strokes at Sir Launcelot, and assailed him on every side. Then Sir Kay dressed him for to have holpen Sir Launcelot. Nay, sir, said he, I will none of your help, therefore as ye will have my help let me alone with them. Sir Kay for the pleasure of the knight suffered him for to do his will, and so stood aside. And then anon within six strokes Sir Launcelot had stricken them to the earth.

And then they all three cried, Sir Knight, we yield us unto you as man of might matchless. As to that, said Sir Launcelot, I will not take your yielding unto me, but so that ye yield you unto Sir Kay the seneschal, on that covenant I will save your lives and else not. Fair knight, said they, that were we loath to do; for as for Sir Kay we chased him hither, and had overcome him had ye not been; therefore, to yield us unto him it were no reason. Well, as to that, said Sir Launcelot, advise you well, for ye may choose whether ye will die or live, for an ye be yielden, it shall be unto Sir Kay. Fair knight, then they said, in saving our lives we will do as thou commandest us. Then shall ye, said Sir Launcelot, on Whitsunday next coming go unto the court of King Arthur, and there shall ye yield you unto Queen Guenever, and put you all three in her grace and mercy, and say that Sir Kay sent you thither to be her prisoners. On the morn Sir Launcelot arose early, and left Sir Kay sleeping; and Sir Launcelot took Sir Kay's armor and his shield and armed him, and so he went to the stable and took his horse, and took his leave of his host, and so he departed. Then soon after arose Sir Kay and missed Sir Launcelot; and then he espied that he had his armor and his horse. Now by my faith I know well that he will grieve some of the court of King

Arthur; for on him knights will be bold, and deem that it is I, and that will beguile them; and because of his armor and shield I am sure I shall ride in peace. And then soon after departed Sir Kay, and thanked his host.

As I laid the book down there was a knock at the door, and my stranger came in. I gave him a pipe and a chair, and made him welcome. I also comforted him with a hot Scotch whisky; gave him another one; then still another—hoping always for his story. After a fourth persuader, he drifted into it himself, in a quite simple and natural way:

THE STRANGER'S HISTORY

I am an American. I was born and reared in Hartford, in the state of Connecticut—anyway, just over the river, in the country. So I am a Yankee of the Yankees—and practical; yes, and nearly barren of sentiment, I suppose—or poetry, in other words. My father was a blacksmith, my uncle was a horse-doctor, and I was both, along at first. Then I went over to the great arms factory and learned my real trade; learned all there was to it; learned to make everything: guns, revolvers, cannon, boilers, engines, all sorts of labor-saving machinery. Why, I could make anything a body wanted—anything in the world, it didn't make any difference what; and if there wasn't any quick new-fangled way to make a thing, I could invent one—and do it as easy as rolling off a log. I became head superintendent; had a couple of thousand men under me.

Well, a man like that is a man that is full of fight—that goes without saying. With a couple of thousand rough men under one, one has plenty of that sort of amusement. I had, anyway. At last I met my match, aud I got my dose. It was during a misunderstanding conducted with crowbars with a fellow we used to call Hercules. He laid me out with a crusher alongside the head that made everything crack, and seemed to spring every joint in my skull and made it overlap its neighbor. Then the world went out in darkness, and I didn't feel anything more, and didn't know anything at all—at least for a while.

When I came to again, I was sitting under an oak tree, on the grass, with a whole beautiful and broad country landscape all to myself—nearly. Not entirely; for there was a fellow on a horse, looking down at me—a fellow fresh out of a picture-book. He was in old-time iron armor from head to heel, with a helmet on his head the shape of a nail-keg with slits in it; and he had a shield, and a sword, and a prodigious spear; and his horse had armor on, too, and a steel horn projecting from his forehead, and gorgeous red and green silk trappings that hung down all around him like a bedquilt, nearly to the ground.

"Fair sir, will ye just?" said this fellow.

"Will I which?"

"Will ye try a passage of arms for land or lady or for—"

"What are you giving me?" I said. "Get along back to your circus, or I'll report you."

Now what does this man do but fall back a couple of hundred yards and then come rushing at me as hard as he could tear, with his nail-keg bent down nearly to his horse's neck and his long spear pointed straight ahead. I saw he meant business, so I was up the tree when he arrived.

He allowed that I was his property, the captive of his spear. There was argument on his side—and the bulk of the advantage—so I judged it best to humor him. We fixed up an agreement whereby I was to go with him and he was not to hurt me. I came down, and we started away, I walking by the side of his horse. We marched comfortably along, through glades and over brooks which I could not remember to have seen before—which puzzled me and made me wonder—and yet we did not come to any circus or sign of a circus. So I gave up the idea of a circus, and concluded he was from an asylum. But we never came to an asylum—so I was up a stump, as you may say. I asked him how far we were from Hartford. He said he had never heard of the place; which I took to be a lie, but allowed it to go at that. At the end of an hour we saw a far-away town sleeping in a valley by a winding river; and beyond it on a hill, a vast gray fortress, with towers and turrets, the first I had ever seen out of a picture.

"Bridgeport?" said I, pointing.

"Camelot," said he.

My stranger had been showing signs of sleepiness. He caught himself nodding, now, and smiled one of those pathetic, obsolete smiles of his, and said:

"I find I can't go on; but come with me, I've got it all written out, and you can read it if you like."

In his chamber, he said: "First, I kept a journal; then by and by, after years, I took the journal and turned it into a book. How long ago that was!"

He handed me his manuscript, and pointed out the place where I should begin:

"Begin here—I've already told you what goes before." He was steeped in drowsiness by this time. As I went out at his door I heard him murmur sleepily: "Give you good den, fair sir."

I sat down by my fire and examined my treasure. The first part of it—the great bulk of it—was parchment, and yellow with age. I scanned a leaf particularly and saw that it was a palimpsest. Under the old dim writing of the Yankee historian appeared traces of a penmanship which was older and dimmer still— Latin words and sentences: fragments from old monkish legends, evidently. I turned to the place indicated by my stranger and began to read—as follows:

Chapter I

CAMELOT

"Camelot—Camelot," said I to myself. "I don't seem to remember hearing of it before. Name of the asylum, likely."

It was a soft, reposeful summer landscape, as lovely as a dream, and as lonesome as Sunday. The air was full of the smell of flowers, and the buzzing of insects, and the twittering of birds, and there were no people, no wagons, there was no stir of life, nothing going on. The road was mainly a winding path with hoof-prints in it, and now and then a faint trace of wheels on either side in the grass—wheels that apparently had a tire as broad as one's hand.

Presently a fair slip of a girl, about ten years old, with a cataract of golden hair streaming down over her shoulders, came along. Around her head she wore a hoop of flame-red poppies. It was as sweet an outfit as ever I saw, what there was of it. She walked indolently along, with a mind at rest, its peace reflected in her innocent face. The circus man paid no attention to her; didn't even seem to see her. And she—she was no more startled at his fantastic make-up than if she was used to his like every day of her life. She was going by as indifferently as she might have gone by a couple of cows; but when she happened to notice me, *then* there was a change! Up went her hands, and she was turned to stone; her mouth dropped open, her eyes stared wide and timorously, she was the picture of astonished curiosity touched with fear. And there she stood gazing, in a sort of stupefied fascination, till we turned a corner of the wood and were lost to her view. That she should be startled at me instead of at the other man, was too many for me; I couldn't make head or tail of it. And that she should seem to consider me a spectacle, and totally overlook her own merits in that respect, was another puzzling thing, and a display of magnanimity, too, that was surprising in one so young. There was food for thought here. I moved along as one in a dream.

As we approached the town, signs of life began to appear. At intervals we passed a wretched cabin, with a thatched roof, and about it small fields and garden patches in an indifferent state of cultivation. There were people, too; brawny men, with long, coarse, uncombed hair that hung down over their faces and made them look like animals. They and the women, as a rule, wore a coarse tow-linen robe that came well below the knee, and a rude sort of sandal, and

many wore an iron collar. The small boys and girls were always naked; but
nobody seemed to know it. All of these people stared at me, talked about me,
ran into the huts and fetched out their families to gape at me; but nobody ever
noticed that other fellow, except to make him humble salutation and get no
response for their pains.

In the town were some substantial windowless houses of stone scattered among
a wilderness of thatched cabins; the streets were mere crooked alleys, and unpaved;
troops of dogs and nude children played in the sun and made life and noise;
hogs roamed and rooted contentedly about, and one of them lay in a reeking
wallow in the middle of the main thoroughfare and suckled her family. Presently
there was a distant blare of military music; it came nearer, still nearer, and soon
a noble cavalcade wound into view, glorious with plumed helmets and flashing
mail and flaunting banners and rich doublets and horse-cloths and gilded spearheads;
and through the muck and swine, and naked brats, and joyous dogs, and shabby
huts, it took its gallant way, and in its wake we followed. Followed through
one winding alley and then another—and climbing, always climbing—till at last
we gained the breezy height where the huge castle stood. There was an exchange
of bugle-blasts; then a parley from the walls, where men-at-arms, in hauberk
and morion, marched back and forth with halberd at shoulder under flapping
banners with the rude figure of a dragon displayed upon them; and then the great
gates were flung open, the drawbridge was lowered, and the head of the cavalcade
swept forward under the frowning arches; and we, following, soon found ourselves
in a great paved court, with towers and turrets stretching up into the blue air on
all the four sides; and all about us the dismount was going on, and much greeting
and ceremony, and running to and fro, and a gay display of moving and intermingling
colors, and an altogether pleasant stir and noise and confusion.

Chapter II
KING ARTHUR'S COURT

THE MOMENT I got a chance I slipped aside privately and touched an ancient
common-looking man on the shoulder and said, in an insinuating, confidential
way:

"Friend, do me a kindness. Do you belong to the asylum, or are you just
here on a visit or something like that?"

He looked me over stupidly, and said:

"Marry, fair sir, me seemeth—"

"That will do," I said; "I reckon you are a patient."

I moved away, cogitating, and at the same time keeping an eye out for any
chance passenger in his right mind that might come along and give me some
light. I judged I had found one, presently; so I drew him aside and said in his
ear:

"If I could see the head keeper a minute—only just a minute—"

"Prithee do not let me."

"Let you *what*?"

"*Hinder* me, then, if the word please thee better." Then he went on to say

"THAT WILL DO," I SAID; "I RECKON YOU'RE A PATIENT."

he was an under-cook and could not stop to gossip, though he would like it another time; for it would comfort his very liver to know where I got my clothes. As he started away he pointed and said yonder was one who was idle enough for my purpose, and was seeking me besides, no doubt. This was an airy slim boy in shrimp-colored tights that made him look like a forked carrot; the rest of his gear was blue silk and dainty laces and ruffles; and he had long yellow curls, and wore a plumed pink satin cap tilted complacently over his ear. By his look, he was good-natured; by his gait, he was satisfied with himself. He was pretty enough to frame. He arrived, looked me over with a smiling and impudent curiosity; said he had come for me, and informed me that he was a page.

"Go 'long," I said; "you ain't more than a paragraph."

It was pretty severe, but I was nettled. However, it never fazed him; he didn't appear to know he was hurt. He began to talk aud laugh, in happy, thoughtless, boyish fashion, as we walked along, and made himself old friends with me at once; asked me all sorts of questions about myself and about my clothes, but never waited for an answer—always chattered straight ahead, as if he didn't know he had asked a question and wasn't expecting any reply, until at last he happened to mention that he was born in the beginning of the year 513.

It made the cold chills creep over me! I stopped, and said, a little faintly:

"Maybe I didn't hear you just right. Say it again—and say it slow. What year was it?"

"513."

"513! You don't look it! Come, my boy, I am a stranger and friendless; be honest and honorable with me. Are you in your right mind?"

He said he was.

"Are these other people in their right minds?"

He said they were.

"And this isn't an asylum? I mean, it isn't a place where they cure crazy people?"

He said it wasn't.

"Well, then," I said, "either I am a lunatic, or something just as awful has happened. Now tell me, honest and true, where am I?"

"IN KING ARTHUR'S COURT."

I waited a minute, to let that idea shudder its way home, and then said:

"And according to your notions, what year is it now?"

"528—nineteenth of June."

I felt a mournful sinking at the heart, and muttered: "I shall never see my friends again—never, never again. They will not be born for more than thirteen hundred years yet."

I seemed to believe the boy, I didn't know why. *Something* in me seemed to believe him—my consciousness, as you may say; but my reason didn't. My reason straighway began to clamor; that was natural. I didn't know how to go about satisfying it, because I knew that the testimony of men wouldn't serve— my reason would say they were lunatics, and throw out their evidence. But all of a sudden I stumbled on the very thing, just by luck. I knew that the only total eclipse of the sun in the first half of the sixth century occurred on the 21st of June, A.D. 528, O.S., and began at 3 minutes after 12 noon. I also knew that no total eclipse of the sun was due in what to *me* was the present year— *i.e.,* 1879. So, if I could keep my anxiety and curosity from eating the heart out of me for forty-eight hours, I should then find out for certain whether this boy was telling me the truth or not.

Wherefore, being a practical Connecticut man, I now shoved this whole problem clear out of my mind till its appointed day and hour should come, in order that I might turn all my attention to the circumstances of the present moment, and be alert and ready to make the most out of them that could be made. One thing at a time, is my motto—and just play that thing for all it is worth, even if it's only two pair and a jack. I made up my mind to two things: if it was still the nineteenth century and I was among lunatics and couldn't get away, I would presently boss that asylum or know the reason why; and if, on the other hand, it was really the sixth century, all right, I didn't want any softer thing: I would boss the whole country inside of three months; for I judged I would have the start of the best-educated man in the kingdom by a matter of thirteen hundred years and upward. I'm not a man to waste time after my mind's made up and there's work on hand; so I said to the page:

"Now, Clarence, my boy—if that might happen to be your name—I'll get you to post me up a little if you don't mind. What is the name of that apparition that brought me here?"

"My master and thine? That is the good knight and great lord Sir Kay the Seneschal, foster-brother to our liege the king."

"Very good; go on, tell me everything."

He made a long story of it; but the part that had immediate interest for me was this: He said I was Sir Kay's prisoner, and that in the due course of custom I would be flung into a dungeon and left there on scant commons until my friends ransomed me—unless I chanced to rot, first. I saw that the last chance had the best show, but I didn't waste any bother about that; time was too precious. The page said, further, that dinner was about ended in the great hall by this time, and that as soon as the sociability and the heavy drinking should begin, Sir Kay would have me in and exhibit me before King Arthur and his illustrious knights seated at the Table Round, and would brag about his exploit in capturing me, and would probably exaggerate the facts a little, but it wouldn't be good form for me to correct him, and not over-safe, either; and when I was done being exhibited, then ho for the dungeon; but he, Clarence, would find a way to come and see me every now and then, and cheer me up, and help me get word to my friends.

Get word to my friends! I thanked him; I couldn't do less; and about this time a lackey came to say I was wanted; so Clarence led me in and took me off to one side and sat down by me.

Well, it was a curious kind of spectacle, and interesting. It was an immense place, and rather naked—yes, and full of loud contrasts. It was very, very lofty; so lofty that the banners depending from the arched beams and girders away up there floated in a sort of twilight; there was a stone-railed gallery at each end, high up, with musicians in the one, and women, clothed in stunning colors, in the other. The floor was of big stone flags laid in black and white squares, rather battered by age and use, and needing repair. As to ornament, there wasn't any, strictly speaking; though on the walls hung some huge tapestries which were probably taxed as works of art; battle-pieces, they were, with horses shaped like those which children cut out of paper or create in gingerbread; with men on them in scale armor whose scales are represented by round holes—so that the man's coat looks as if it had been done with a biscuit-punch. There was a fireplace big enough to camp in; and its projecting sides and hood, of carved and pillared stonework, had the look of a cathedral door. Along the walls stood men-at-arms, in breastplate and morion, with halberds for their only weapon—rigid as statues; and that is what they looked like.

In the middle of this groined and vaulted public square was an oaken table which they called the Table Round. It was as large as a circus-ring; and around it sat a great company of men dressed in such various and splendid colors that it hurt one's eyes to look at them. They wore their plumed hats, right along, except that whenever one addressed himself directly to the king, he lifted his hat a trifle just as he was beginning his remark.

Mainly they were drinking—from entire ox horns; but a few were still munching bread or gnawing beef bones. There was about an average of two dogs to one man; and these sat in expectant attitudes till a spent bone was flung to them, and then they went for it by brigades and divisions, with a rush, and there ensued a fight which filled the prospect with a tumultuous chaos of plunging heads and bodies and flashing tails, and the storm of howlings and barkings deafened all speech for the time; but that was no matter, for the dog-fight was always a bigger interest anyway; the men rose, sometimes, to observe it the better and bet on it, and the ladies and the musicians stretched themselves out over their balusters with the same object; and all broke into delighted ejaculations from time to time. In the end, the winning dog stretched himself out comfortably with his bone between his paws, and proceeded to growl over it, and gnaw it, and grease the floor with it, just as fifty others were already doing; and the rest of the court resumed their previous industries and entertainments.

As a rule, the speech and behavior of these people were gracious and courtly; and I noticed that they were good and serious listeners when anybody was telling anything—I mean in a dog-fightless interval. And plainly, too, they were a childlike and innocent lot; telling lies of the stateliest pattern with a most gentle and winning naïveté, and ready and willing to listen to anybody else's lie, and believe it, too. It was hard to associate them with anything cruel or dreadful; and yet they dealt in tales of blood and suffering with a guileless relish that made me almost forget to shudder.

I was not the only prisoner present. There were twenty or more. Poor devils, many of them were maimed, hacked, carved, in a frightful way; and their hair, their faces, their clothing, were caked with black and stiffened drenchings of blood. They were suffering sharp physical pain, of course; and weariness, and hunger and thirst, no doubt; and at least none had given them the comfort of a wash, or even the poor charity of a lotion for their wounds; yet you never heard them utter a moan or a groan, or saw them show any sign of restlessness, or any disposition to complain. The thought was forced upon me: "The rascals— *they* have served other people so in their day; it being their own turn, now, they were not expecting any better treatment than this; so their philosophical bearing is not an outcome of mental training, intellectual fortitude, reasoning; it is mere animal training; they are white Indians."

Chapter III

KNIGHTS OF THE TABLE ROUND

MAINLY THE ROUND Table talk was monologues—narrative accounts of the adventures in which these prisoners were captured and their friends and backers killed and stripped of their steeds and armor. As a general thing—as far as I could make out—these murderous adventures were not forays undertaken to avenge injuries, nor to settle old disputes or sudden fallings out; no, as a rule they were simply duels between strangers—duels between people who had never even been introduced to each other, and between whom existed no cause of offense whatever. Many a time I had seen a couple of boys, strangers, meet by chance, and say simultaneously, "I can lick you," and go at it on the spot; but I had always imagined until now that that sort of thing belonged to children only, and was a sign and mark of childhood; but here were these big boobies sticking to it and taking pride in it clear up into full age and beyond. Yet there was something very engaging about these great simplehearted creatures, something attractive and lovable. There did not seem to be brains enough in the entire nursery, so to speak, to bait a fish-hook with; but you didn't seem to mind that, after a little, because you soon saw that brains were not needed in a society like that, and indeed would have marred it, hindered it, spoiled its symmetry— perhaps rendered its existence impossible.

There was a fine manliness observable in almost every face; and in some a certain loftiness and sweetness that rebuked your belittling criticisms and stilled them. A most noble benignity and purity reposed in the countenance of him they called Sir Galahad, and likewise in the king's also; and there was majesty and greatness in the giant frame and high bearing of Sir Launcelot of the Lake.

There was presently an incident which centered the general interest upon this Sir Launcelot. At a sign from a sort of master of ceremonies, six or eight of the prisoners rose and came forward in a body and knelt on the floor and lifted up their hands toward the ladies' gallery and begged the grace of a word with the queen. The most conspicuously situated lady in that massed flower-bed of feminine show and finery inclined her head by way of assent, and then the spokesman of the prisoners delivered himself and his fellows into her hands for free pardon, ransom, captivity, or death, as she in her good pleasure might elect; and this, as he said, he was doing by command of Sir Kay the Seneschal, whose prisoners they were, he having vanquished them by his single might and prowess in sturdy conflict in the field.

Surprise and astonishment flashed from face to face all over the house; the queen's gratified smile faded out at the name of Sir Kay, and she looked disappointed; and the page whispered in my ear with an accent and manner expressive of extravagant derision—

"Sir *Kay*, forsooth! Oh, call me pet names, dearest, call me a marine! In twice a thousand years shall the unholy invention of man labor at odds to beget the fellow to this majestic lie!"

Every eye was fastened with severe inquiry upon Sir Kay. But he was equal to the occasion. He got up and played his hand like a major—and took every trick. He said he would state the case exactly according to the facts; he would tell the simple straightforward tale, without comment of his own; "and then," said he, "if ye find glory and honor due, ye will give it unto him who is the mightiest man of his hands that ever bare shield or strake with sword in the ranks of Christian battle—even him that sitteth there!" and he pointed to Sir Launcelot. Ah, he fetched them; it was a rattling good stroke. Then he went on and told how Sir Launcelot, seeking adventures, some brief time gone by, killed seven giants at one sweep of his sword, and set a hundred and forty-two captive maidens free; and then went further, still seeking adventures, and found him (Sir Kay) fighting a desperate fight against nine foreign knights, and straightway took the battle solely into his own hands, and conquered the nine; and that night Sir Launcelot rose quietly, and dressed him in Sir Kay's armor and took Sir Kay's horse and gat him away into distant lands, and vanquished sixteen knights in one pitched battle and thirty-four in another; and all these and the former nine he made to swear that about Whitsuntide they would ride to Arthur's court and yield them to Queen Guenever's hands as captives of Sir Kay the Seneschal, spoil of his knightly prowess; and now here were these half-dozen, and the rest would be along as soon as they might be healed of their desperate wounds.

Well, it was touching to see the queen blush and smile, and look embarrassed, and happy, and fling furtive glances at Sir Launcelot that would have got him shot in Arkansas, to a dead certainty.

Everybody praised the valor and magnanimity of Sir Launcelot; and as for me, I was perfectly amazed, that one man, all by himself, should have been able to beat down and capture such battalions of practised fighters. I said as much to Clarence; but this mocking featherhead only said:

"An Sir Kay had had time to get another skin of sour wine into him, ye had seen the accompt doubled."

I looked at the boy in sorrow; and as I looked I saw the cloud of a deep despondency settle upon his countenance. I followed the direction of his eye, and saw that a very old and white-bearded man, clothed in a flowing black gown, had risen and was standing at the table upon unsteady legs, and feebly swaying his ancient head and surveying the company with his watery and wandering eye. The same suffering look that was in the page's face was observable in all the faces around—the look of dumb creatures who know that they must endure and make no moan.

"Marry, we shall have it again," sighed the boy; "that same old weary tale that he hath told a thousand times in the same words, and that he *will* tell till he dieth, every time he hath gotten his barrel full and feeleth his exaggeration-mill a-working. Would God I had died or I saw this day!''

''Who is it?''

''Merlin, the mighty liar and magician, perdition singe him for the weariness he worketh with his one tale! But that men fear him for that he hath the storms and the lightnings and all the devils that be in hell at his beck and call, they would have dug his entrails out these many years ago to get at that tale and squelch it. He telleth it always in the third person, making believe he is too modest to glorify himself—maledictions light upon him, misfortune be his dole! Good friend, prithee call me for evensong.''

The boy nestled himself upon my shoulder and pretended to go to sleep. The old man began his tale; and presently the lad was asleep in reality; so also were the dogs, and the court, the lackeys, and the files of men-at-arms. The droaning voice droned on; a soft snoring arose on all sides and supported it like a deep and subdued accompaniment of wind instruments. Some heads were bowed upon folded arms, some lay back with open mouths that issued unconscious music; the flies buzzed and bit, unmolested, the rats swarmed softly out from a hundred holes, and pattered about, and made themselves at home everywhere; and one of them sat up like a squirrel on the king's head and held a bit of cheese in its hands and nibbled it, and dribbled the crumbs in the king's face with naïve and impudent irreverence. It was a tranquil scene, and restful to the weary eye and the jaded spirit.

This was the old man's tale. He said:

''Right so the king and Merlin departed, and went until an hermit that was a good man and a great leech. So the hermit searched all his wounds and gave him good salves; so the king was there three days, and then were his wounds well amended that he might ride and go, and so departed. And as they rode, Arthur said, I have no sword. No force,[1] said Merlin, hereby is a sword that shall be yours an I may. So they rode till they came to a lake, the which was a fair water and broad, and in the midst of the lake Arthur was ware of an arm

'' THE FLIES BUZZED AND BIT UNMOLESTED.''

---

[1] No matter.

clothed in white samite, that held a fair sword in that hand. Lo, said Merlin, yonder is that sword that I spake of. With that they saw a damsel going upon the lake. What damsel is that? said Arthur. That is the Lady of the lake, said Merlin; and within that lake is a rock, and there in is as fair a place as any on earth, and richly beseen, and this damsel will come to you anon, and then speak ye fair to her that she will give you that sword. Anon withal came the damsel unto Arthur and saluted him, and he her again. Damsel, said Arthur, what sword is that, that yonder the arm holdeth above the water? I would it were mine, for I have no sword. Sir Arthur King, said the damsel, that sword is mine, and if ye will give me a gift when I ask it you, ye shall have it. By my faith, said Arthur, I will give you what gift ye will ask. Well, said the damsel, go ye into yonder barge and row yourself to the sword, and take it and the scabbard with you, and I will ask my gift when I see my time. So Sir Arthur and Merlin alight, and tied their horses to two trees, and so they went into the ship, and when they came to the sword that the hand held, Sir Arthur took it up by the handles, and took it with him. And the arm and the hand went under the water; and so they came unto the land and rode forth. And then Sir Arthur saw a rich pavilion. What signifieth yonder pavilion? It is the knight's pavilion, said Merlin, that ye fought with last, Sir Pellinore, but he is out, he is not there; he hath ado with a knight of yours, that hight Egglame, and they have fought together, but at the last Egglame fled, and else he had been dead, and he hath chased him even to Carlion, and we shall meet with him anon in the highway. That is well said, said Arthur, now have I a sword, now will I wage battle with him, and be avenged on him. Sir, ye shall not so, said Merlin, for the knight is weary of fighting and chasing, so that ye shall have no worship to have ado with him; also, he will not lightly be matched of one knight living; and therefore it is my counsel, let him pass, for he shall do you good service in short time, and his sons, after his days. Also ye shall see that day in short space ye shall be right glad to give him your sister to wed. When I see him, I will do as ye advise me, said Arthur. Then Sir Arthur looked on the sword, and liked it passing well. Whether liketh you better, said Merlin, the sword or the scabbard? Me liketh better the sword, said Arthur. Ye are more unwise, said Merlin, for the scabbard is worth ten of the sword, for while ye have the scabbard upon you ye shall never lose no blood, be ye never so sore wounded; therefore, keep well the scabbard always with you. So they rode into Carlion, and by the way they met with Sir Pellinore; but Merlin had done such a craft that Pellinore saw not Arthur, and he passed by without any words. I marvel, said Arthur, that the knight would not speak. Sir, said Merlin, he saw you not; for an he had seen you ye had not lightly departed. So they came unto Carlion, whereof his knights were passing glad. And when they heard of his adventures they marveled that he would jeopard his person so alone. But all men of worship said it was merry to be under such a chieftain that would put his person in adventure as other poor knights did.''

Chapter IV

SIR DINADAN THE HUMORIST

IT SEEMED TO me that this quaint lie was most simply and beautifully told; but then I had heard it only once, and that makes a difference; it was pleasant to the others when it was fresh, no doubt.

Sir Dinadan the Humorist was the first to awake, and he soon roused the rest with a practical joke of a sufficiently poor quality. He tied some metal mugs to a dog's tail and turned him loose, and he tore around and around the place in a frenzy of fright, with all the other dogs bellowing after him and battering and crashing against everything that came in their way and making altogether a chaos of confusion and a most deafening din and turmoil; at which every man and woman of the multitude laughed till the tears flowed, and some fell out of their chairs and wallowed on the floor in ecstasy. It was just like so many children. Sir Dinadan was so proud of his exploit that he could not keep from telling over and over again, to weariness, how the immortal idea happened to occur to him; and as is the way with humorists of his breed, he was still laughing at it after everybody else had got through. He was so set up that he concluded to make a speech—of course a humorous speech. I think I never heard so many old played-out jokes strung together in my life. He was worse than the minstrels, worse than the clown in the circus. It seemed peculiarly sad to sit here, thirteen hundred years before I was born, and listen again to poor, flat, worm-eaten jokes that had given me the dry gripes when I was a boy thirteen hundred years afterward. It about convinced me that there isn't any such thing as a new joke possible. Everybody laughed at these antiquities—but then they always do; I had noticed that, centuries later. However, of course the scoffer didn't laugh—I mean the boy. No, he scoffed; there wasn't anything he wouldn't scoff at. He said the most of Sir Dinadan's jokes were rotten and the rest were petrified. I said "petrified" was good; as I believed, myself, that the only right way to classify the majestic ages of some of those jokes was by geologic periods. But that neat idea hit the boy in a blank place, for geology hadn't been invented yet. However, I made a note of the remark, and calculated to educate the commonwealth up to it if I pulled through. It is no use to throw a good thing away merely because the market isn't ripe yet.

Now Sir Kay arose and began to fire up on his history-mill with me for fuel. It was time for me to feel serious, and I did. Sir Kay told how he had encountered me in a far land of barbarians, who all wore the same ridiculous garb that I did—a garb that was a work of enchantment, and intended to make the wearer secure from hurt by human hands. However, he had nullified the force of the enchantment by prayer, and had killed my thirteen knights in a three hours' battle, and taken me prisoner, sparing my life in order that so strange a curiosity as I was might be exhibited to the wonder and admiration of the king and the court. He spoke of me all the time, in the blandest way, as "this prodigious giant," and "this horrible sky-towering monster," and "this tusked and taloned man-devouring ogre," and everybody took in all this bosh in the naïvest way, and never smiled or seemed to notice that there was any discrepancy between these watered statistics and me. He said that in trying to escape from him I sprang into the top of a tree two hundred cubits high at a single bound, but he dislodged me wlth a stone the size of a cow, which "all-to brast" the most of my bones, and then swore me to appear at Arthur's court for sentence. He ended by condemning me to die at noon on the 21st; and was so little concerned about it that he stopped to yawn before he named the date.

I was in a dismal state by this time; indeed, I was hardly enough in my right mind to keep the run of a dispute that sprung up as to how I had better be killed, the possibility of the killing being doubted by some, because of the enchantment in my clothes. And yet it was nothing but an ordinary suit of fifteen-dollar slop-shops. Still, I was sane enough to notice this detail, to wit: many of the terms used in the most matter-of-fact way by this great assemblage of the first ladies and gentlemen in the land would have made a Comanche blush. Indelicacy is too mild a term to convey the idea. However, I had read *Tom Jones*, and *Roderick Random*, and other books of that kind, and knew that the highest and first ladies and gentlemen in England had remained little or no cleaner in their talk, and in the morals and conduct which such talk implies, clear up to a hundred years ago; in fact clear into our own nineteenth century—in which century, broadly speaking, the earliest samples of the real lady and real gentleman discoverable in English history—or in European history, for that matter—may be said to have made their appearance. Suppose Sir Walter, instead of putting the conversations into the mouths of his characters, had allowed the characters to speak for themselves? We should have had talk from Rebecca and Ivanhoe and the soft lady Rowena which would embarrass a tramp in our day. However, to the unconsciously indelicate all things are delicate. King Arthur's people were not aware that they were indecent, and I had presence of mind enough not to mention it.

They were so troubled about my enchanted clothes that they were mightily relieved, at last, when old Merlin swept the difficulty away for them with a common-sense hint. He asked them why they were so dull—why didn't it occur to them to strip me. In half a minute I was as naked as a pair of tongs! And dear, dear, to think of it: I was the only embarrassed person there. Everybody discussed me; and did it as unconcernedly as if I had been a cabbage. Queen Guenever was as naïvely interested as the rest, and said she had never seen anybody with legs just like mine before. It was the only compliment I got—if it was a compliment.

Finally I was carried off in one direction, and my perilous clothes in another. I was shoved into a dark and narrow cell in a dungeon, with some scant remnants for dinner, some moldy straw for a bed, and no end of rats for company.

Chapter V

AN INSPIRATION

I WAS SO tired that even my fears were not able to keep me awake long.

When I next came to myself, I seemed to have been asleep a very long time. My first thought was, "Well, what an astonishing dream I've had! I reckon I've waked only just in time to keep from being hanged or drowned or burned or something. . . . I'll nap again till the whistle blows, and then I'll go down to the arms factory and have it out with Hercules.''

But just then I heard the harsh music of rusty chains and bolts, a light flashed in my eyes, and that butterfly, Clarence, stood before me! I gasped with surprise; my breath almost got away from me.

''What!'' I said, ''you here yet? Go along with the rest of the dream! scatter!''

But he only laughed, in his light-hearted way, and fell to making fun of my sorry plight.

''All right,'' I said resignedly, ''let the dream go on; I'm in no hurry.''

''Prithee what dream?''

''What dream? Why, the dream that I am in Arthur's court—a person who never existed; and that I am talking to you, who are nothing but a work of the imagination.''

''Oh, la, indeed! and is it a dream that you're to be burned to-morrow? Ho-ho—answer me that!''

The shock that went through me was distressing. I now began to reason that my situation was in the last degree serious, dream or no dream; for I knew by past experience of the lifelike intensity of dreams, that to be burned to death, even in a dream, would be very far from being a jest, and was a thing to be avoided, by any means, fair or foul, that I could contrive. So I said beseechingly:

''Ah, Clarence, good boy, only friend I've got—for you *are* my friend, aren't you?—don't fail me; help me to devise some way of escaping from this place!''

''Now do but hear thyself! Escape? Why, man, the corridors are in guard and keep of men-at-arms.''

''No doubt, no doubt. But how many, Clarence? Not many, I hope?''

''Full a score. One may not hope to escape.'' After a pause—hesitatingly: ''and there be other reasons—and weightier.''

''Other ones? What are they?''

''Well, they say—oh, but I daren't, indeed I daren't!''

''Why, poor lad, what is the matter? Why do you blench? Why do you tremble so?''

''Oh, in sooth, there is need! I do want to tell you, but—''

''Come, come, be brave, be a man—speak out, there's a good lad!''

He hesitated, pulled one way by desire, the other way by fear; then he stole to the door and peeped out, listening; and finally crept close to me and put his mouth to my ear and told me his fearful news in a whisper, and with all the cowering apprehension of one who was venturing upon awful ground and speaking of things whose very mention might be freighted with death.

''Merlin, in his malice, has woven a spell about this dungeon, and there bides not the man in these kingdoms that would be desperate enough to essay to cross its lines with you! Now God pity me, I have told it! Ah, be kind to me, be merciful to a poor boy who means thee well; for an thou betray me I am lost!''

I laughed the only really refreshing laugh I had had for some time; and shouted:

''Merlin has wrought a spell! *Merlin*, forsooth! That cheap old humbug, that maundering old ass? Bosh, pure bosh, the silliest bosh in the world! Why, it does seem to me that of all the childish, idiotic, chuckle-headed, chicken-livered superstitions that ev—oh, damn Merlin!''

But Clarence had slumped to his knees before I had half finished, and he was like to go out of his mind with fright.

"Oh, beware! These are awful words! Any moment these walls may crumble upon us if you say such things. Oh call them back before it is too late!"

Now this strange exhibition gave me a good idea and set me to thinking. If everybody about here was so honestly and sincerely afraid of Merlin's pretended magic as Clarence was, certainly a superior man like me ought to be shrewd enough to contrive some way to take advantage of such a state of things. I went on thinking, and worked out a plan. Then I said:

"Get up. Pull yourself together; look me in the eye. Do you know why I laughed?"

"No—but for our blessed Lady's sake, do it no more."

"Well, I'll tell you why I laughed. Because I'm a magician myself."

"Thou!" The boy recoiled a step, and caught his breath, for the thing hit him rather sudden; but the aspect which he took on was very, very respectful. I took quick note of that; it indicated that a humbug didn't need to have a reputation in this asylum; people stood ready to take him at his word, without that. I resumed.

"I've known Merlin seven hundred years, and he—"

"Seven hun—"

"Don't interrupt me. He has died and come alive again thirteen times, and traveled under a new name every time: Smith, Jones, Robinson, Jackson, Peters, Haskins, Merlin—a new alias every time he turns up. I knew him in Egypt three hundred years ago; I knew him in India five hundred years ago—he is always blethering around in my way, everywhere I go; he makes me tired. He don't amount to shucks, as a magician; knows some of the old common tricks, but has never got beyond the rudiments, and never will. He is well enough for the provinces—one-night stands and that sort of thing, you know—but dear me, *he* oughtn't to set up for an expert—anyway not where there's a real artist. Now look here, Clarence, I am going to stand your friend, right along, and in return you must be mine. I want you to do me a favor. I want you to get word to the king that I am a magician myself—and the Supreme Grand High-yu-Muckamuck and head of the tribe, at that; and I want him to be made to understand that I am just quietly arranging a little calamity here that will make the fur fly in these realms if Sir Kay's project is carried out and any harm comes to me. Will you get that to the king for me?"

The poor boy was in such a state that he could hardly answer me. It was pitiful to see a creature so terrified, so unnerved, so demoralized. But he promised everything; and on my side he made me promise over and over again that I would remain his friend, and never turn against him or cast any enchantments upon him. Then he worked his way out, staying himself with his hand along the wall, like a sick person.

Presently this thought occurred to me: how heedless I have been! When the boy gets calm, he will wonder why a great magician like me should have begged a boy like him to help me get out of this place; he will put this and that together, and will see that I am a humbug.

I worried over that heedless blunder for an hour, and called myself a great many hard names, meantime. But finally it occurred to me all of a sudden that these animals didn't reason; that *they* never put this and that together; that all their talk showed that they didn't know a discrepancy when they saw it. I was at rest, then.

But as soon as one is at rest, in this world, off he goes on something else to worry about. It occurred to me that I had made another blunder: I had sent the boy off to alarm his betters with a threat—I intending to invent a calamity at my leisure; now the people who are the readiest and eagerest and willingest to swallow miracles are the very ones who are hungriest to see you perform them; suppose I should be called on for a sample? Suppose I should be asked to name my calamity? Yes, I had made a blunder; I ought to have invented my calamity first. "What shall I do? what can I say, to gain a little time?" I was in trouble again; in the deepest kind of trouble: . . . "There's a footstep!—they're coming. If I had only just a moment to think. . . . Good, I've got it. I'm all right."

You see, it was the eclipse. It came into my mind, in the nick of time, how Columbus, or Cortez, or one of those people, played an eclipse as a saving trump once, on some savages, and I saw my chance. I could play it myself, now; and it wouldn't be any plagiarism, either, because I should get it in nearly a thousand years ahead of those parties.

Clarence came in, subdued, distressed, and said:

"I hasted the message to our liege the king, and straightway he had me to his presence. He was frighted even to the marrow, and was minded to give order for your instant enlargement, and that you be clothed in fine raiment and lodged as befitted one so great; but then came Merlin and spoiled all; for he persuaded the king that you are mad, and know not whereof you speak; and said your threat is but foolishness and idle vaporing. They disputed long, but in the end, Merlin, scoffing, said, 'Wherefore hath he not *named* his brave calamity? Verily it is because he cannot.' This thrust did in a most sudden sort close the king's mouth, and he could offer naught to turn the argument; and so, reluctant, and full loth to do you the discourtesy, he yet prayeth you to consider his perplexed case, as noting how the matter stands, and name the calamity—if so be you have determined the nature of it and the time of its coming. Oh, prithee delay not; to delay at such a time were to double and treble the perils that already compass thee about. Oh, be thou wise—name the calamity!"

I allowed silence to accumulate while I got my impressiveness together, and then said:

"How long have I been shut up in this hole?"

"Ye were shut up when yesterday was well spent. It is nine of the morning now."

"No! Then I have slept well, sure enough. Nine in the morning now! And yet it is the very complexion of midnight, to a shade. This is the 20th, then?"

"The 20th—yes."

"And I am to be burned alive to-morrow." The boy shuddered.

"At what hour?"

"At high noon."

"Now then, I will tell you what to say." I paused, and stood over that cowering lad a whole minute in awful silence; then, in a voice deep, measured, charged with doom, I began, and rose by dramatically graded stages to my colossal climax, which I delivered in as sublime and noble a way as ever I did such a thing in my life: "Go back and tell the king that at that hour I will smother the whole world in the dead blackness of midnight; I will blot out the sun, and he shall never shine again; the fruits of the earth shall rot for lack of light and warmth, and the peoples of the earth shall famish and die, to the last man!"

I had to carry the boy out myself, he sunk into such a collapse. I handed him over to the soldiers, and went back.

Chapter VI

THE ECLIPSE

IN THE STILLNESS and the darkness, realization soon began to supplement knowledge. The mere knowledge of a fact is pale; but when you come to *realize* your fact, it takes on color. It is all the difference between hearing of a man being stabbed to the heart, and seeing it done. In the stillness and the darkness, the knowledge that I was in deadly danger took to itself deeper and deeper meaning all the time; a something which was realization crept inch by inch through my veins and turned me cold.

But it is a blessed provision of nature that at times like these, as soon as a man's mercury has got down to a certain point there comes a revulsion, and he rallies. Hope springs up, and cheerfulness along with it, and then he is in good shape to do something for himself, if anything can be done. When my rally came, it came with a bound. I said to myself that my eclipse would be sure to save me, and make me the greatest man in the kingdom besides; and straightway my mercury went up to the top of the tube, and my solicitudes all vanished. I was as happy a man as there was in the world. I was even impatient for to-morrow to come, I so wanted to gather in that great triumph and be the center of all the nation's wonder and reverence. Besides, in a business way it would be the making of me; I knew that.

Meantime there was one thing which had got pushed into the background of my mind. That was the half-conviction that when the nature of my proposed calamity should be reported to those superstitious people, it would have such an effect that they would want to compromise. So, by and by when I heard footsteps coming, that thought was recalled to me, and I said to myself, "As sure as anything, it's the compromise. Well, if it is good, all right, I will accept; but if it isn't, I mean to stand my ground and play my hand for all it is worth."

The door opened, and some men-at-arms appeared. The leader said:

"The stake is ready. Come!"

The stake! The strength went out of me, and I almost fell down. It is hard to get one's breath at such a time, such lumps come into one's throat, and such gaspings; but as soon as I could speak, I said:

"But this is a mistake—the execution is to-morrow."

"Order changed; been set forward a day. Haste thee!"

I was lost. There was no help for me. I was dazed, stupefied; I had no command over myself; I only wandered purposelessly about, like one out of his mind; so the soldiers took hold of me, and pulled me along with them, out of the cell and along the maze of underground corridors, and finally into the fierce glare of daylight and the upper world. As we stepped into the vast inclosed court of the castle I got a shock; for the first thing I saw was the stake, standing in the center, and near it the piled fagots and a monk. On all four sides of the court the seated multitudes rose rank above rank, forming sloping terraces that were rich with color. The king and the queen sat in their thrones, the most conspicuous figures there, of course.

To note all this, occupied but a second. The next second Clarence had slipped from some place of concealment and was pouring news into my ear, his eyes beaming with triumph and gladness. He said:

"'Tis through *me* the change was wrought! And main hard have I worked to do it, too. But when I revealed to them the calamity in store, and saw how mighty was the terror it did engender, then saw I also that this was the time to strike! Wherefore I diligently pretended, unto this and that and the other one, that your power against the sun could not reach its full until the morrow; and so if any would save the sun and the world, you must be slain to-day, while your enchantments are but in the weaving and lack potency. Odsbodikins, it was but a dull lie, a most indifferent invention, but you should have seen them seize it and swallow it, in the frenzy of their fright, as it were salvation sent from heaven; and all the while was I laughing in my sleeve the one moment, to see them so cheaply deceived, and glorifying God the next, that He was content to let the meanest of His creatures be His instrument to the saving of thy life. Ah, how happy has the matter sped! You will not need to do the sun a *real* hurt— ah, forget not that, on your soul forget it not! Only make a little darkness—only the littlest little darkness, mind, and cease with that. It will be sufficient. They will see that I spoke falsely—being ignorant, as they will fancy—and with the falling of the first shadow of that darkness you shall see them go mad with fear; and they will set you free and make you great! Go to thy triumph, now! But remember—ah, good friend, I implore thee remember my supplication, and do the blessed sun no hurt. For *my* sake, thy true friend."

I choked out some words through my grief and misery; as much as to say I would spare the sun; for which the lad's eyes paid me back with such deep and loving gratitude that I had not the heart to tell him his good-hearted foolishness had ruined me and sent me to my death.

As the soldiers assisted me across the court the stillness was so profound that if I had been blindfold I should have supposed I was in a solitude instead of walled in by four thousand people. There was not a movement perceptible in those masses of humanity; they were as rigid as stone images, and as pale; and dread sat upon every countenance. This hush continued while I was being chained to the stake; it still continued while the fagots were carefully and tediously piled about my ankles, my knees, my thighs, my body. Then there was a pause, and a deeper hush, if possible, and a man knelt down at my feet with a blazing torch; the multitude strained forward, gazing, and parting slightly from their seats without knowing it; the monk raised his hands above my head, and his eyes toward the blue sky, and began some words in Latin; in this attitude he droned on and on, a little while, and then stopped. I waited two or three moments; then looked up; he was standing there petrified. With a common impulse the multitude rose slowly up and stared into the sky. I followed their eyes; as sure as guns, there was my eclipse beginning! The life went boiling through my veins; I was a new man! The rim of black spread slowly into the sun's disk, my heart beat higher and higher, and still the assemblage and the priest stared into the sky, motionless. I knew that this gaze would be turned upon me, next. When it was, I was ready. I was in one of the most grand attitudes I ever struck, with my arm stretched up pointing to the sun. It was a noble effect. You could *see* the shudder sweep the mass like a wave. Two shouts rang out, one close upon the heels of the other:

"Apply the torch!"

"I forbid it!"

The one was from Merlin, the other from the king. Merlin started from his place—to apply the torch himself, I judged. I said:

"Stay where you are. If any man moves—even the king —before I give him leave, I will blast him with thunder, I will consume him with lightnings!"

The multitude sank meekly into their seats, and I was just expecting they would. Merlin hesitated a moment or two, and I was on pins and needles during that little while. Then he sat down, and I took a good breath; for I knew I was master of the situation now. The king said:

"Be merciful, fair sir, and essay no further in this perilous matter, lest disaster follow. It was reported to us that your powers could not attain unto their full strength until the morrow; but—"

"Your Majesty thinks the report may have been a lie? It *was* a lie."

That made an immense effect; up went appealing hands everywhere, and the king was assailed with a storm of supplications that I might be bought off at any price, and the calamity stayed. The king was eager to comply. He said:

"Name any terms, reverend sir, even to the halving of my kingdom; but banish this calamity, spare the sun!"

My fortune was made, I would have taken him up in a minute, but I couldn't stop an eclipse; the thing was out of the question. So I asked time to consider. The king said:

"How long—ah, how long, good sir? Be merciful; look, it groweth darker, moment by moment. Prithee how long?"

"Not long. Half an hour—maybe an hour."

There were a thousand pathetic protests, but I couldn't shorten up any, for I couldn't remember how long a total eclipse lasts. I was in a puzzled condition, anyway, and wanted to think. Something was wrong about that eclipse, and the fact was very unsettling. If this wasn't the one I was after, how was I to tell whether this was the sixth century, or nothing but a dream? Dear me, if I could only prove it was the latter! Here was a glad new hope. If the boy was right about the date, and this was surely the 20th, it *wasn't* the sixth century. I reached for the monk's sleeve, in considerable excitement, and asked him what day of the month it was.

Hang him, he said it was the *twenty-first*! It made me turn cold to hear him. I begged him not to make any mistake about it; but he was sure; he knew it was the 21st. So, that feather-headed boy had botched things again! The time of the day was right for the eclipse; I had seen that for myself, in the beginning, by the dial that was near by. Yes, I *was* in King Arthur's court, and I might as well make the most of it I could.

The darkness was steadily growing, the people becoming more and more distressed. I now said:

"I have reflected, Sir King. For a lesson, I will let this darkness proceed, and spread night in the world; but whether I blot out the sun for good, or restore it shall rest with you. These are the terms, to wit: You shall remain king over all your dominions, and receive all the glories and honors that belong to the kingship; but you shall appoint me your perpetual minister and executive, and give me for my services one per cent. of such actual increase of revenue over and above its present amount as I may succeed in creating for the state. If I can't live on that, I sha'n't ask anybody to give me a lift. Is it satisfactory?"

There was a prodigious roar of applause, and out of the midst of it the king's voice rose, saying: "Away with his bonds, and set him free! and do him homage, high and low, rich and poor, for he is become the king's right hand, is clothed with power and authority, and his seat is upon the highest step of the throne! Now sweep away this creeping night, and bring the light and cheer again, that all the world may bless thee.''

But I said:

"That a common man should be shamed before the world, is nothing; but it were dishonor to the *king* if any that saw his minister naked should not also see him delivered from his shame. If I might ask that my clothes be brought again—''

"They are not meet,'' the king broke in. "Fetch raiment of another sort; clothe him like a prince!''

My idea worked. I wanted to keep things as they were till the eclipse was total, otherwise they would be trying again to get me to dismiss the darkness, and of course I couldn't do it. Sending for the clothes gained some delay, but not enough. So I had to make another excuse. I said it would be but natural if the king should change his mind and repent to some extent of what he had done under excitement; therefore I would let the darkness grow awhile, and if at the end of a reasonable time the king had kept his mind the same, the darkness should be dismissed. Neither the king nor anybody else was satisfied with that arrangement, but I had to stick to my point.

It grew darker and darker and blacker and blacker, while I struggled with those awkward sixth-century clothes. It got to be pitch-dark, at last, and the multitude groaned with horror to feel the cold uncanny night breezes fan through the place and see the stars come out and twinkle in the sky. At last the eclipse was total, and I was very glad of it, but everybody else was in misery; which was quite natural. I said:

"The king, by his silence, still stands to the terms.'' Then I lifted up my hand—stood just so a moment—then I said, with the most awful solemnity: "Let the enchantment dissolve and pass harmless away!''

There was no response, for a moment, in that deep darkness and that graveyard hush. But when the silver rim of the sun pushed itself out, a moment or two later, the assemblage broke loose with a vast shout and came pouring down like a deluge to smother me with blessings and gratitude; and Clarence was not the last of the wash, to be sure.

Chapter VII

MERLIN'S TOWER

INASMUCH AS I was now the second personage in the kingdom, as far as political power and authority were concerned, much was made of me. My raiment was of silks and velvets and cloth-of-gold, and by consequence was very showy, also uncomfortable. But habit would soon reconcile me to my clothes; I was aware of that. I was given the choicest suite of apartments in the castle, after the king's. They were aglow with loud-colored silken hangings, but the stone floors had nothing but rushes on them for a carpet, and they were misfit rushes at that, being not all of one breed. As for conveniences, properly speaking, there weren't any. I mean *little* conveniences; it is the little conveniences that make the real comfort of life. The big oaken chairs, graced with rude carvings, were well enough, but that was the stopping-place. There was no soap, no matches, no looking-glass—except a metal one, about as powerful as a pail of water. And not a chromo. I had been used to chromos for years, and I saw now that without my suspecting it a passion for art had got worked into the fabric of my being, and was become a part of me. It made me homesick to look around over this proud and gaudy but heartless barrenness and remember that in our house in East Hartford, all unpretending as it was, you couldn't go into a room but you would find an insurance-chromo, or at least a three-color God-Bless-Our-Home over the door; and in the parlor we had nine. But here, even in my grand room of state, there wasn't anything in the nature of a picture except a thing the size of a bedquilt, which was either woven or knitted (it had darned places in it), and nothing in it was the right color or the right shape; and as for proportions, even Raphael himself couldn't have botched them more formidably, after all his practice on those nightmares they call his "celebrated Hampton Court cartoons." Raphael was a bird. We had several of his chromos; one was his "Miraculous Draught of Fishes," where he puts in a miracle of his own—puts three men into a canoe which wouldn't have held a dog without upsetting. I always admired to study R.'s art, it was so fresh and unconventional.

There wasn't even a bell or a speaking-tube in the castle. I had a great many servants, and those that were on duty lolled in the anteroom; and when I wanted one of them I had to go and call for him. There was no gas, there were no candles; a bronze dish half full of boarding-house butter with a blazing rag floating in it was the thing that produced what was regarded as light. A lot of these hung along the walls and modified the dark, just toned it down enough to make it dismal. If you went out at night, your servants carried torches. There were no books, pens, paper or ink, and no glass in the openings they believed to be window's. It is a little thing—glass is—until it is absent, then it becomes a big thing. But perhaps the worst of all was, that there wasn't any sugar, coffee, tea, or tobacco. I saw that I was just another Robinson Crusoe cast away on an uninhabited island, with no society but some more or less tame animals, and if I wanted to make life bearable I must do as he did—invent, contrive, create, reorganize things; set brain and hand to work, and keep them busy. Well, that was in my line.

One thing troubled me along at first—the immense interest which people took in me. Apparently the whole nation wanted a look at me. It soon transpired that the eclipse had scared the British world almost to death; that while it lasted the whole country, from one end to the other, was in a pitiable state of panic, and the churches, hermitages, and monkeries overflowed with praying and weeping poor creatures who thought the end of the world was come. Then had followed the news that the producer of this awful event was a stranger, a mighty magician at Arthur's court; that he could have blown out the sun like a candle, and was just going to do it when his mercy was purchased, and he then dissolved his enchantments, and was now recognized and honored as the man who had by his unaided might saved the globe from destruction and its peoples from extinction. Now if you consider that everybody believed that, and not only believed it, but never even dreamed of doubting it, you will easily understand that there was not a person in all Britain that would not have walked fifty miles to get a sight

"THERE WAS NO SOAP, NO MATCHES, NO LOOKING-GLASS"

of me. Of course I was all the talk—all other subjects were dropped; even the king became suddenly a person of minor interest and notoriety. Within twenty-four hours the delegations began to arrive, and from that time onward for a fortnight they kept coming. The village was crowded, and all the country-side. I had to go out a dozen times a day and show myself to these reverent and awestricken multitudes. It came to be a great burden, as to time and trouble, but of course it was at the same time compensatingly agreeable to be so celebrated and such a center of homage. It turned Brer Merlin green with envy and spite, which was a great satisfaction to me. But there was one thing I couldn't understand— nobody had asked for an autograph. I spoke to Clarence about it. By George! I had to explain to him what it was. Then he said nobody in the country could read or write but a few dozen priests. Land! think of that.

There was another thing that troubled me a little. Those multitudes presently began to agitate for another miracle. That was natural. To be able to carry back to their far homes the boast that they had seen the man who could command the sun, riding in the heavens, and be obeyed, would make them great in the eyes of their neighbors, and envied by them all; but to be able to also say they had seen him work a miracle themselves—why, people would come a distance to see *them*. The pressure got to be pretty strong. There was going to be an eclipse of the moon, and I knew the date and hour, but it was too far away. Two years. I would have given a good deal for license to hurry it up and use it now when there was a big market for it. It seemed a great pity to have it wasted so, and come lagging along at a time when a body wouldn't have any use for it, as like as not. If it had been booked for only a month away, I could have sold it short; but, as matters stood, I couldn't seem to cipher out any way to make it do me any good, so I gave up trying. Next, Clarence found that old Merlin was making himself busy on the sly among those people. He was spreading a report that I was a humbug, and that the reason I didn't accommodate the people with a miracle was because I couldn't. I saw that I must do something. I presently thought out a plan.

By my authority as executive I threw Merlin into prison—the same cell I had occupied myself. Then I gave public notice by herald and trumpet that I should be busy with affairs of state for a fortnight, but about the end of that time I would take a moment's leisure and blow up Merlin's stone tower by fires from heaven; in the mean time, whoso listened to evil reports about me, let him beware. Furthermore, I would perform but this one miracle at this time, and no more; if it failed to satisfy and any murmured, I would turn the murmurers into horses, and make them useful. Quiet ensued.

I took Clarence into my confidence, to a certain degree, and we went to work privately. I told him that this was a sort of miracle that required a trifle of preparation, and that it would be sudden death to ever talk about these preparations to anybody. That made his mouth safe enough. Clandestinely we made a few bushels of first-rate blasting-powder, and I superintended my armorers while they constructed a lightning-rod and some wires. This old stone tower was very massive—and rather ruinous, too, for it was Roman, and four hundred years old. Yes, and handsome, after a rude fashion, and clothed with ivy from base to summit, as with a shirt of scale mail. It stood on a lonely eminence, in good view from the castle, and about half a mile away.

Working by night, we stowed the powder in the tower—dug stones out, on the inside, and buried the powder in the walls themselves, which were fifteen feet thick at the base. We put in a peck at a time, in a dozen places. We could have blown up the Tower of London with these charges. When the thirteenth night was come we put up our lightning-rod, bedded it in one of the batches of powder, and ran wires from it to the other batches. Everybody had shunned that locality from the day of my proclamation, but on the morning of the fourteenth I thought best to warn the people, through the heralds, to keep clear away—a quarter of a mile away. Then added, by command, that at some time during the twenty-four hours I would consummate the miracle, but would first give a brief notice; by flags on the castle towers if in the daytime, by torch-baskets in the same places if at night.

Thunder-showers had been tolerably frequent of late, and I was not much afraid of a failure; still, I shouldn't have cared for a delay of a day or two; I should have explained that I was busy with affairs of state yet, and the people must wait.

Of course, we had a blazing sunny day—almost the first one without a cloud for three weeks; things always happen so. I kept secluded, and watched the weather. Clarence dropped in from time to time and said the public excitement was growing and growing all the time, and the whole country filling up with human masses as far as one could see from the battlements. At last the wind sprang up and a cloud appeared—in the right quarter, too, and just at nightfall. For a little while I watched that distant cloud spread and blacken, then I judged it was time for me to appear. I ordered the torch-baskets to be lit, and Merlin liberated and sent to me. A quarter of an hour later I ascended the parapet and there found the king and the court assembled and gazing off in the darkness toward Merlin's Tower. Already the darkness was so heavy that one could not see far; these people and the old turrets, being partly in deep shadow and partly in the red glow from the great torch-baskets overhead, made a good deal of a picture.

Merlin arrived in a gloomy mood. I said:

"You wanted to burn me alive when I had not done you any harm, and latterly you have been trying to injure my professional reputation. Therefore I am going to call down fire and blow up your tower, but it is only fair to give you a chance; now if you think you can break my enchantments and ward off the fires, step to the bat, it's your innings."

"I can, fair sir, and I will. Doubt it not."

He drew an imaginary circle on the stones of the roof, and burnt a pinch of powder in it, which sent up a small cloud of aromatic smoke, whereat everybody fell back and began to cross themselves and get uncomfortable. Then he began to mutter and make passes in the air with his hands. He worked himself up slowly and gradually into a sort of frenzy, and got to thrashing around with his arms like the sails of a windmill. By this time the storm had about reached us; the gusts of wind were flaring the torches and making the shadows swash about, the first heavy drops of rain were falling, the world abroad was black as pitch, the lightning began to wink fitfully. Of course, my rod would be loading itself now. In fact, things were imminent. So I said:

"You have had time enough. I have given you every advantage, and not interfered. It is plain your magic is weak. It is only fair that I begin now."

I made about three passes in the air, and then there was an awful crash and that old tower leaped into the sky in chunks, along with a vast volcanic fountain of fire that turned night to noonday, and showed a thousand acres of human beings groveling on the ground in a general collapse of consternation. Well, it rained mortar and masonry the rest of the week. This was the report; but probably the facts would have modified it.

It was an effective miracle. The great bothersome temporary population vanished. There were a good many thousand tracks in the mud the next morning, but they were all outward bound. If I had advertised another miracle I couldn't have raised an audience with a sheriff.

Merlin's stock was flat. The king wanted to stop his wages; he even wanted to banish him, but I interfered. I said he would be useful to work the weather, and attend to small matters like that, and I would give him a lift now and then when his poor little parlor magic soured on him. There wasn't a rag of his tower left, but I had the government rebuild it for him, and advised him to take boarders; but he was too high-toned for that. And as for being grateful, he never even said thank you. He was a rather hard lot, take him how you might; but then you couldn't fairly expect a man to be sweet that had been set back so.

Chapter VIII

THE BOSS

TO BE VESTED with enormous authority is a fine thing; but to have the onlooking world consent to it is a finer. The tower episode solidified my power, and made it impregnable. If any were perchance disposed to be jealous and critical before that, they experienced a change of heart, now. There was not any one in the kingdom who would have considered it good judgment to meddle with my matters.

I was fast getting adjusted to my situation and circumstances. For a time, I used to wake up, mornings, and smile at my "dream," and listen for the Colt's factory whistle; but that sort of thing played itself out, gradually, and at last I was fully able to realize that I was actually living in the sixth century, and in Arthur's court, not a lunatic asylum. After that, I was just as much at home in that century as I could have been in any other; and as for preference, I wouldn't have traded it for the twentieth. Look at the opportunities here for a man of knowledge, brains, pluck, and enterprise to sail in and grow up with the country. The grandest field that ever was; and all my own; not a competitor; not a man who wasn't a baby to me in acquirements and capacities; whereas, what would I amount to in the twentieth century? I should be foreman of a factory, that is about all; and could drag a seine down-street any day and catch a hundred better men than myself.

What a jump I had made! I couldn't keep from thinking about it, and contemplating it, just as one does who has struck oil. There was nothing back of me that could approach it, unless it might be Joseph's case; and Joseph's only approached it, it didn't equal it, quite. For it stands to reason that as Joseph's splendid financial ingenuities advantaged nobody but the king, the general public must have regarded him with a good deal of disfavor, whereas I had done my entire public a kindness in sparing the sun, and was popular by reason of it.

I was no shadow of a king; I was the substance; the king himself was the shadow. My power was colossal; and it was not a mere name, as such things have generally been, it was the genuine article. I stood here, at the very spring and source of the second great period of the world's history; and could see the trickling stream of that history gather and deepen and broaden, and roll its mighty tides down the far centuries; and I could note the upspringing of adventurers like myself in the shelter of its long array of thrones: De Montforts, Gavestons, Mortimers, Villierses; the war-making, campaign-directing wantons of France, and Charles the Second's scepter-wielding drabs; but nowhere in the procession was my full-sized fellow visible. I was a Unique; and glad to know that that fact could not be dislodged or challenged for thirteen centuries and a half, for sure.

Yes, in power I was equal to the king. At the same time there was another power that was a trifle stronger than both of us put together. That was the Church. I do not wish to disguise that fact. I couldn't, if I wanted to. But never mind about that, now; it will show up, in its proper place, later on. It didn't cause me any trouble in the beginning—at least any of consequence.

Well, it was a curious country, and full of interest. And the people! They were the quaintest and simplest and trustingest race; why, they were nothing but rabbits. It was pitiful for a person born in a wholesome free atmosphere to listen to their humble and hearty outpourings of loyalty toward their king and Church and nobility; as if they had any more occasion to love and honor king and Church and noble than a slave has to love and honor the lash, or a dog has to love and honor the stranger that kicks him! Why, dear me, *any* kind of royalty, howsoever modified, *any* kind of aristocracy, howsoever pruned, is rightly an insult; but if you are born and brought up under that sort of arrangement you probably never find it out for yourself, and don't believe it when somebody else tells you. It is enough to make a body ashamed of his race to think of the sort of froth that has always occupied its thrones without shadow of right or reason, and the seventh-rate people that have always figured as its aristocracies—a company of monarchs and nobles who, as a rule, would have achieved only poverty and obscurity if left, like their betters, to their own exertions.

The most of King Arthur's British nation were slaves, pure and simple, and bore that name, and wore the iron collar on their necks; and the rest were slaves in fact, but without the name; they imagined themselves men and freemen, and called themselves so. The truth was, the nation as a body was in the world for one object, and one only: to grovel before king and Church and noble; to slave for them, sweat blood for them, starve that they might be fed, work that they might play, drink misery to the dregs that they might be happy, go naked that they might wear silks and jewels, pay taxes that they might be spared from paying them, be familiar all their lives with the degrading language and postures of adulation that they might walk in pride and think themselves the gods of this world. And for all this, the thanks they got were cuffs and contempt; and so poor-spirited were they that they took even this sort of attention as an honor.

Inherited ideas are a curious thing, and interesting to observe and examine. I had mine, the king and his people had theirs. In both cases they flowed in ruts worn deep by time and habit, and the man who should have proposed to divert them by reason and argument would have had a long contract on his hands. For instance, those people had inherited the idea that all men without title and a long pedigree, whether they had great natural gifts and acquirements or hadn't, were creatures of no more consideration than so many animals, bugs, insects;

whereas I had inherited the idea that human daws who can consent to masquerade in the peacock shams of inherited dignities and unearned titles, are of no good but to be laughed at. The way I was looked upon was odd, but it was natural. You know how the keeper and the public regard the elephant in the menagerie: well, that is the idea. They are full of admiration of his vast bulk and his prodigious strength; they speak with pride of the fact that he can do a hundred marvels which are far and away beyond their own powers; and they speak with the same pride of the fact that in his wrath he is able to drive a thousand men before him. But does that make him one of *them?* No; the raggedest tramp in the pit would smile at the idea. He couldn't comprehend it; couldn't take it in; couldn't in any remote way conceive of it. Well, to the king, the nobles, and all the nation, down to the very slaves and tramps, I was just that kind of an elephant, and nothing more. I was admired, also feared; but it was as an animal is admired and feared. The animal is not reverenced, neither was I; I was not even respected. I had no pedigree, no inherited title; so in the king's and nobles' eyes I was mere dirt; the people regarded me with wonder and awe, but there was no reverence mixed with it; through the force of inherited ideas they were not able to conceive of anything being entitled to that except pedigree and lordship. There you see the hand of that awful power, the Roman Catholic Church. In two or three little centuries it had converted a nation of men to a nation of worms. Before the day of the Church's supremacy in the world, men were men, and held their heads up, and had a man's pride and spirit and independence; and what of greatness and position a person got, he got mainly by achievement, not by birth. But then the Church came to the front, with an ax to grind; and she was wise, subtle, and knew more than one way to skin a cat— or a nation; she invented "divine right of things," and propped it all around, brick by brick, with the Beatitudes—wrenching them from their good purpose to make them fortify an evil one; she preached (to the commoner) humility, obedience to superiors, the beauty of self-sacrifice; she preached (to the commoner) meekness under insult; preached (still to the commoner, always to the commoner) patience, meanness of spirit, non-resistance under oppression; and she introduced heritable ranks and aristocracies, and taught all the Christian populations of the earth to bow down to them and worship them. Even down to my birth-century that poison was still in the blood of Christendom, and the best of English commoners was still content to see his inferiors impudently continuing to hold a number of positions, such as lordships and the throne, to which the grotesque laws of his country did not allow him to aspire; in fact, he was not merely contented with this strange condition of things, he was even able to persuade himself that he was proud of it. It seems to show that there isn't anything you can't stand, if you are only born and bred to it. Of course that taint, that reverence for rank and title, had been in our American blood, too—I know that; but when I left America it had disappeared—at least to all intents and purposes. The remnant of it was restricted to the dudes and dudesses. When a disease has worked its way down to that level, it may fairly be said to be out of the system.

But to return to my anomalous position in King Arthur's kingdom. Here I was, a giant among pygmies, a man among children, a master intelligence among intellectual moles; by all rational measurement the one and only actually great man in that whole British world; and yet there and then, just as in the remote England of my birth-time, the sheep-witted earl who could claim long descent from a king's leman, acquired at second hand from the slums of London, was a better man than I was. Such a personage was fawned upon in Arthur's realm and reverently looked up to by everybody, even though his dispositions were as mean as his intelligence, and his morals as base as his lineage. There were times when *he* could sit down in the king's presence, but I couldn't. I could have got a title easily enough, and that would have raised me a large step in everybody's eyes; even in the king's, the giver of it. But I didn't ask for it; and I declined it when it was offered. I couldn't have enjoyed such a thing with my notions; and it wouldn't have been fair, anyway, because as far back as I could go, our tribe had always been short of the bar sinister. I couldn't have felt really and satisfactorily fine and proud and set-up over any title except one that should come from the nation itself, the only legitimate source; and such an one I hoped to win; and in the course of years of honest and honorable endeavor, I did win it and did wear it with a high and clean pride. This title fell casually from the lips of a blacksmith, one day, in a village, was caught up as a happy thought and tossed from mouth to mouth with a laugh and an affirmative vote; in ten days it had swept the kingdom, and was become as familiar as the king's name. I was never known by any other designation afterward, whether in the nation's talk or in grave debate upon matters of state at the council-board of the sovereign. This title, translated into modern speech, would be THE BOSS. Elected by the nation. That suited me. And it was a pretty high title. There were very few THE'S, and I was one of them. If you spoke of the duke, or the earl, or the bishop, how could anybody tell which one you meant? But if you spoke of The King or The Queen or The Boss, it was different.

Well, I liked the king, and *as* king I respected him—respected the office; at least respected it as much as I was capable of respecting any unearned supremacy; but as *men* I looked down upon him and his nobles—privately. And he and they liked me, and respected my office; but as an animal, without birth or sham title, they looked down upon me—and were not particularly private about it, either. I didn't charge for my opinion about them, and they didn't charge for their opinion about me: the account was square, the books balanced, everybody was satisfied.

Chapter IX

THE TOURNAMENT

THEY WERE ALWAYS having grand tournaments there at Camelot; and very stirring and picturesque and ridiculous human bull-fights they were, too, but just a little wearisome to the practical mind. However, I was generally on hand—for two reasons: a man must not hold himself aloof from the things which his friends and his community have at heart if he would be liked—especially as a statesman; and both as business man and statesman I wanted to study the tournament and see if I couldn't invent an improvement on it. That reminds me to remark, in passing, that the very first official thing I did, in my administration—and it was on the very first day of it, too—was to start a patent office; for I knew that a country without a patent office and good patent laws was just a crab, and couldn't travel any way but sideways or backwards.

Things ran along, a tournament nearly every week; and now and then the boys used to want me to take a hand—I mean Sir Launcelot and the rest—but I said I would by and by: no hurry yet, and too much government machinery to oil up and set to rights and start a-going.

We had one tournament which was continued from day to day during more than a week, and as many as five hundred knights took part in it, from first to last. They were weeks gathering. They came on horseback from everywhere; from the very ends of the country, and even from beyond the sea; and many brought ladies, and all brought squires and troops of servants. It was a most gaudy and gorgeous crowd, as to costumery, and very characteristic of the country and the time, in the way of high animal spirits, innocent indecencies of language, and happy-hearted indifference to morals. It was fight or look on, all day and every day; and sing, gamble, dance, carouse half the night every night. They had a most noble good time. You never saw such people. Those banks of beautiful ladies, shining in their barbaric splendors, would see a knight sprawl from his horse in the lists with a lance-shaft the thickness of your ankle clean through him and the blood spouting, and instead of fainting they would clap their hands and crowd each other for a better view; only sometimes one would dive into her handkerchief, and look ostentatiously broken-hearted, and then you could lay two to one that there was a scandal there somewhere and she was afraid the public hadn't found it out.

The noise at night would have been annoying to me ordinarily, but I didn't mind it in the present circumstances, because it kept me from hearing the quacks detaching legs and arms from the day's cripples. They ruined an uncommon good old crosscut saw for me, and broke the saw-buck, too, but I let it pass. And as for my ax—well, I made up my mind that the next time I lent an ax to a surgeon I would pick my century.

I not only watched this tournament from day to day, but detailed an intelligent priest from my Department of Public Morals and Agriculture, and ordered him to report it; for it was my purpose by and by, when I should have gotten the people along far enough, to start a newspaper. The first thing you want in a new country, is a patent office; then work up your school system; and after that, out with your paper. A newspaper has its faults, and plenty of them, but no matter, it's hark from the tomb for a dead nation, and don't you forget it. You can't resurrect a dead nation without it; there isn't any way. So I wanted to sample things, and be finding out what sort of reporter-material I might be able to rake together out of the sixth century when I should come to need it.

Well, the priest did very well, considering. He got in all the details, and that is a good thing in a local item: you see, he had kept books for the undertaker department of his church when he was younger, and there, you know, the money's in the details; the more details, the more swag: bearers, mutes, candles, prayers—everything counts; and if the bereaved don't buy prayers enough you mark up your candles with a forked pencil, and your bill shows up all right. And he had a good knack at getting in the complimentary thing here and there about a knight that was likely to advertise—no, I mean a knight that had influence; and he also had a neat gift of exaggeration, for in his time he had kept door for a pious hermit who lived in a sty and worked miracles.

Of course this novice's report lacked whoop and crash and lurid description, and therefore wanted the true ring; but its antique wording was quaint and sweet and simple, and full of the fragrances and flavors of the time, and these little

merits made up in a measure for its more important lacks. Here is an extract
from it:

> Then Sir Brian de les Isles and Grummore Grummorsum, knights of
> the castle, encountered with Sir Aglovale and Sir Tor, and Sir Tor smote
> down Sir Grummore Grummorsum to the earth. Then came Sir Carados
> of the dolorous tower, and Sir Turquine, knights of the castle, and there
> encountered with them Sir Percivale de Galis and Sir Lamorak de Galis,
> that were two brethren, and there encountered Sir Percivale and Sir
> Carados, and either brake their spears unto their hands, and then Sir
> Turquine with Sir Lamorak, and either of them smote down other, horse
> and all, to the earth, and either parties rescued other and horsed them
> again. And Sir Arnold, and Sir Gauter, knights of the castle, encountered
> with Sir Brandiles and Sir Kay, and these four knights encountered
> mightily, and brake their spears to their hands. Then came Sir Pertolope
> from the castle, and there encountered with him Sir Lionel, and there
> Sir Pertolope the green knight smote down Sir Lionel, brother to Sir
> Launcelot. All this was marked by noble heralds, who bare him best,
> and their names. Then Sir Bleobaris brake his spear upon Sir Gareth,
> but of that stroke Sir Bleobaris fell to the earth. When Sir Galihodin saw
> that, he bad Sir Gareth keep him, and Sir Gareth smote him to the earth.
> Then Sir Galihud gat a spear to avenge his brother, and in the same wise
> Sir Gareth served him, and Sir Dinadan and his brother La Cote Male
> Taile, and Sir Sagramor le Desirous, and Sir Dodinas le Savage; all these
> he bare down with one spear. When King Agwisance of Ireland saw Sir
> Gareth fare so he marveled what he might be, that one time seemed
> green, and another time, at his again coming, he seemed blue. And thus
> at every course that he rode to and fro he changed his color, so that there
> might neither king nor knight have ready cognizance of him. Then Sir
> Agwisance the King of Ireland encountered with Sir Gareth, and there
> Sir Gareth smote him from his horse, saddle and all. And then came
> King Carados of Scotland, and Sir Gareth smote him down horse and
> man. And in the same wise he served King Uriens of the land of Gore.
> And then there came in Sir Bagdemagus, and Sir Gareth smote him down
> horse and man to the earth. And Bagdemagus's son Meliganus brake a
> spear upon Sir Gareth mightily and knightly. And then Sir Galahault the
> noble prince cried on high, Knight with the many colors, well hast thou
> justed; now make thee ready that I may just with thee. Sir Gareth heard
> him, and he gat a great spear, and so they encountered together, and
> there the prince brake his spear; but Sir Gareth smote him upon the left
> side of the helm, that he reeled here and there, and he had fallen down
> had not his men recovered him. Truly, said King Arthur, that knight
> with the many colors is a good knight. Wherefore the king called unto
> him Sir Launcelot, and prayed him to encounter with that knight. Sir,
> said Launcelot, I may as well find in my heart for to forbear him at this
> time, for he hath had travail enough this day, and when a good knight
> doth so well upon some day, it is no good knight's part to let him of his
> worship, and, namely, when he seeth a knight hath done so great labor;
> for peradventure, said Sir Launcelot, his quarrel is here this day, and
> peradventure he is best beloved with this lady of all that be here, for I

see well he paineth himself and enforceth him to do great deeds, and therefore, said Sir Launcelot, as for me, this day he shall have the honor; though it lay in my power to put him from it, I would not.

There was an unpleasant little episode that day, which for reasons of state I struck out of my priest's report. You will have noticed that Garry was doing some great fighting in the engagement. When I say Garry I mean Sir Gareth. Garry was my private pet name for him; it suggests that I had a deep affection for him, and that was the case. But it was a private pet name only, and never spoken aloud to any one, much less to him; being a noble, he would not have endured a familiarity like that from me. Well, to proceed: I sat in the private box set apart for me as the king's minister. While Sir Dinadan was waiting for his turn to enter the lists, he came in there and sat down and began to talk; for he was always making up to me, because I was a stranger and he liked to have a fresh market for his jokes, the most of them having reached that stage of wear where the teller has to do the laughing himself while the other person looks sick. I had always responded to his efforts as well as I could, and felt a very deep and real kindness for him, too, for the reason that if by malice of fate he knew the one particular anecdote which I had heard oftenest and had most hated and most loathed all my life, he had at least spared it me. It was one which I had heard attributed to every humorous person who had ever stood on American soil, from Columbus down to Artemus Ward. It was about a humorous lecturer who flooded an ignorant audience with the killingest jokes for an hour and never got a laugh; and then when he was leaving, some gray simpletons wrung him gratefully by the hand and said it had been the funniest thing they had ever heard, and "it was all they could do to keep from laughin' right out in meetin'." That anecdote never saw the day that it was worth the telling; and yet I had sat under the telling of it hundreds and thousands and millions and billions of times, and cried and cursed all the way through. Then who can hope to know what my feelings were, to hear this armor-plated ass start in on it again, in the murky twilight of tradition, before the dawn of history, while even Lactantius might be referred to as "the late Lactantius," and the Crusades wouldn't be born for five hundred years yet? Just as he finished, the call-boy came; so, haw-hawing like a demon, he went rattling and clanking out like a crate of loose castings, and I knew nothing more. It was some minutes before I came to, and then I opened my eyes just in time to see Sir Gareth fetch him an awful welt, and I unconsciously out with the prayer, "I hope to gracious he's killed!" But by ill luck, before I had got half through with the words, Sir Gareth crashed into Sir Sagramor le Desirous and sent him thundering over his horse's crupper, and Sir Sagramor caught my remark and thought I meant it for *him*.

Well, whenever one of those people got a thing into his head, there was no getting it out again. I knew that, so I saved my breath, and offered no explanations. As soon as Sir Sagramor got well, he notified me that there was a little account to settle between us, and he named a day three or four years in the future; place of settlement, the lists where the offense had been given. I said I would be ready when he got back. You see, he was going for the Holy Grail. The boys all took a flier at the Holy Grail now and then. It was a several years' cruise. They always put in the long absence snooping around, in the most conscientious way, though none of them had any idea where the Holy Grail really was, and I don't think any of them actually expected to find it, or would have known what to do with it if he *had* run across it. You see, it was just the Northwest Passage of that day, as you may say; that was all. Every year expeditions went out holy grailing, and next year relief expeditions went out to hunt for *them*. There was worlds of reputation in it, but no money. Why, they actually wanted *me* to put in! Well, I should smile.

Chapter X

BEGINNINGS OF CIVILIZATION

THE ROUND TABLE soon heard of the challenge, and of course it was a good deal discussed, for such things interested the boys. The king thought I ought now to set forth in quest of adventures, so that I might gain renown and be the more worthy to meet Sir Sagramor when the several years should have rolled away. I excused myself for the present; I said it would take me three or four years yet to get things well fixed up and going smoothly; then I should be ready; all the chances were that at the end of that time Sir Sagramor would still be out grailing, so no valuable time would be lost by the postponement; I should then have been in office six or seven years, and I believed my system and machinery would be so well developed that I could take a holiday without its working any harm.

I was pretty well satisfied with what I had already accomplished. In various quiet nooks and corners I had the beginnings of all sorts of industries under way—nuclei of future vast factories, the iron and steel missionaries of my future civilization. In these were gathered together the brightest young minds I could find, and I kept agents out raking the country for more, all the time. I was training a crowd of ignorant folk into experts—experts in every sort of handiwork and scientific calling. These nurseries of mine went smoothly and privately along undisturbed in their obscure country retreats, for nobody was allowed to come into their precincts without a special permit—for I was afraid of the Church.

SOME OF THE BOYS GOING A GRAILING.

I had started a teacher-factory and a lot of Sunday-schools the first thing; as a result, I now had an admirable system of graded schools in full blast in those places, and also a complete variety of Protestant congregations all in a prosperous and growing condition. Everybody could be any kind of a Christian he wanted to; there was perfect freedom in that matter. But I confined public religious teaching to the churches and the Sunday-schools, permitting nothing of it in my other educational buildings. I could have given my own sect the preference and made everybody a Presbyterian without any trouble, but that would have been to affront a law of human nature: spiritual wants and instincts are as various in the human family as are physical appetites, complexions, and features, and a man is only at his best, morally, when he is equipped with the religious garment whose color and shape and size most nicely accommodate themselves to the spiritual complexion, angularities, and stature of the individual who wears it; and, besides, I was afraid of a united Church; it makes a mighty power, the mightiest conceivable, and then when it by and by gets into selfish hands, as it is always bound to do, it means death to human liberty and paralysis to human thought.

All mines were royal property, and there were a good many of them. They had formerly been worked as savages always work mines—holes grubbed in the earth and the mineral brought up in sacks of hide by hand, at the rate of a ton a day; but I had begun to put the mining on a scientific basis as early as I could.

Yes, I had made pretty handsome progress when Sir Sagramor's challenge struck me.

Four years rolled by—and then! Well, you would never imagine it in the world. Unlimited power *is* the ideal thing when it is in safe hands. The despotism of heaven is the one absolutely perfect government. An earthly despotism would be the absolutely perfect earthly government, if the conditions were the same, namely, the despot the perfectest individual of the human race, and his lease of life perpetual. But as a perishable perfect man must die, and leave his despotism in the hands of an imperfect successor, an earthly despotism is not merely a bad form of government, it is the worst form that is possible.

My works showed what a despot could do with the resources of a kingdom at his command. Unsuspected by this dark land, I had the civilization of the nineteenth century booming under its very nose! It was fenced away from the public view, but there it was, a gigantic and unassailable fact—and to be heard from, yet, if I lived and had luck. There it was, as sure a fact and as substantial a fact as any serene volcano, standing innocent with its smokeless summit in the blue sky and giving no sign of the rising hell in its bowels. My schools and churches were children four years before; they were grown up now; my shops of that day were vast factories now; where I had a dozen trained men then, I had a thousand now; where I had one brilliant expert then, I had fifty now. I stood with my hand on the cock, so to speak, ready to turn it on and flood the midnight world with light at any moment. But I was not going to do the thing in that sudden way. It was not my policy. The people could not have stood it; and, moreover, I should have had the Established Roman Catholic Church on my back in a minute.

No, I had been going cautiously all the while. I had had confidential agents trickling through the country some time, whose office was to undermine knighthood by imperceptible degrees, and to gnaw a little at this and that and the other superstition, and so prepare the way gradually for a better order of things. I was turning on my light one candlepower at a time, and meant to continue to do so.

I had scattered some branch schools secretly about the kingdom, and they were doing very well. I meant to work this racket more and more, as time wore on, if nothing occurred to frighten me. One of my deepest secrets was my West Point—my military academy. I kept that most jealously out of sight; and I did the same with my naval academy which I had established at a remote seaport. Both were prospering to my satisfaction.

Clarence was twenty-two now, and was my head executive, my right hand. He was a darling; he was equal to anything; there wasn't anything he couldn't turn his hand to. Of late I had been training him for journalism, for the time seemed about right for a start in the newspaper line; nothing big, but just a small weekly for experimental circulation in my civilization-nurseries. He took to it like a duck; there was an editor concealed in him, sure. Already he had doubled himself in one way; he talked sixth century and wrote nineteenth. His journalistic style was climbing, steadily; it was already up to the back settlement Alabama mark, and couldn't be told from the editorial output of that region either by matter or flavor.

We had another large departure on hand, too. This was a telegraph and a telephone; our first venture in this line. These wires were for private service only, as yet, and must be kept private until a riper day should come. We had a gang of men on the road, working mainly by night. They were stringing ground-wires; we were afraid to put up poles, for they would attract too much inquiry. Ground-wires were good enough, in both instances, for my wires were protected by an insulation of my own invention which was perfect. My men had orders to strike across country, avoiding roads, and establishing connection with any considerable towns whose lights betrayed their presence, and leaving experts in charge. Nobody could tell you how to find any place in the kingdom, for nobody ever went intentionally to any place, but only struck it by accident in his wanderings, and then generally left it without thinking to inquire what its name was. At one time and another we had sent out topographical expeditions to survey and map the kingdom, but the priests had always interfered and raised trouble. So we had given the thing up, for the present; it would be poor wisdom to antagonize the Church.

As for the general condition of the country, it was as it had been when I arrived in it, to all intents and purposes. I had made changes, but they were necessarily slight, and they were not noticeable. Thus far, I had not even meddled with taxation, outside of the taxes which provided the royal revenues. I had systematized those, and put the service on an effective and righteous basis. As a result, these revenues were already quadrupled, and yet the burden was so much more equally distributed than before, that all the kingdom felt a sense of relief, and the praises of my administration were hearty and general.

Personally, I struck an interruption, now, but I did not mind it, it could not have happened at a better time. Earlier it could have annoyed me, but now everything was in good hands and swimming right along. The king had reminded me several times, of late, that the postponement I had asked for, four years before, had about run out now. It was a hint that I ought to be starting out to seek adventures and get up a reputation of a size to make me worthy of the honor of breaking a lance with Sir Sagramor, who was still out grailing, but was being hunted for by various relief expeditions, and might be found any year, now. So you see I was expecting this interruption; it did not take me by surprise.

Chapter XI

THE YANKEE IN SEARCH OF ADVENTURES

THERE NEVER WAS such a country for wandering liars; and they were of both sexes. Hardly a month went by without one of these tramps arriving; and generally loaded with a tale about some princess or other wanting help to get her out of some far-away castle where she was held in captivity by a lawless scoundrel, usually a giant. Now you would think that the first thing the king would do after listening to such a novelette from an entire stranger, would be to ask for credentials— yes, and a pointer or two as to locality of castle, best route to it, and so on. But nobody ever thought of so simple and common-sense a thing as that. No, everybody swallowed these people's lies whole, and never asked a question of any sort or about anything. Well, one day when I was not around, one of these people came along—it was a she one, this time—and told a tale of the usual pattern. Her mistress was a captive in a vast and gloomy castle, along with forty-four other young and beautiful girls, pretty much all of them princesses; they had been languishing in that cruel captivity for twenty-six years; the masters of the castle were three stupendous brothers, each with four arms and one eye—the eye in the center of the forehead, and as big as a fruit. Sort of fruit not mentioned; their usual slovenliness in statistics.

Would you believe it? The king and the whole Round Table were in raptures over this preposterous opportunity for adventure. Every knight of the Table jumped for the chance, and begged for it; but to their vexation and chagrin the king conferred it upon me, who had not asked for it at all.

By an effort, I contained my joy when Clarence brought me the news. But he—he could not contain his. His mouth gushed delight and gratitude in a steady discharge—delight in my good fortune, gratitude to the king for this splendid mark of his favor for me. He could keep neither his legs nor his body still, but pirouetted about the place in an airy ecstasy of happiness.

On my side, I could have cursed the kindness that conferred upon me this benefaction, but I kept my vexation under the surface for policy's sake, and did what I could to let on to be glad. Indeed, I *said* I was glad. And in a way it was true; I was as glad as a person is when he is scalped.

Well, one must make the best of things, and not waste time with useless fretting, but get down to business and see what can be done. In all lies there is wheat among the chaff; I must get at the wheat in this case: so I sent for the girl and she came. She was a comely enough creature, and soft and modest, but, if signs went for anything, she didn't know as much as a lady's watch. I said:

"My dear, have you been questioned as to particulars?"

She said she hadn't.

"Well, I didn't expect you had, but I thought I would ask, to make sure; it's the way I've been raised. Now you mustn't take it unkindly if I remind you that as we don't know you, we must go a little slow. You may be all right, of course, and we'll hope that you are; but to take it for granted isn't business. *You* understand that. I'm obliged to ask you a few questions; just answer up fair and square, and don't be afraid. Where do you live, when you are at home?''

"In the land of Moder, fair sir.''

"Land of Moder. I don't remember hearing of it before. Parents living?''

"As to that, I know not if they be yet on live, sith it is many years that I have lain shut up in the castle.''

"Your name, please?''

"I hight the Demoiselle Alisande la Carteloise, an it please you.''

"Do you know anybody here who can identify you?''

"That were not likely, fair lord, I being come hither now for the first time.''

"Have you brought any letters—any documents—any proofs that you are trustworthy and truthful?''

"Of a surety, no; and wherefore should I? Have I not a tongue, and cannot I say all that myself?''

"But *your* saying it, you know, and somebody else's saying it, is different.''

"Different? How might that be? I fear me I do not understand.''

"Don't *understand?* Land of—why, you see—you see—why, great Scott, can't you understand a little thing like that? Can't you understand the difference between your—*why* do you look so innocent and idiotic!''

"I? In truth I know not, but an it were the will of God.''

"Yes, yes, I reckon that's about the size of it. Don't mind my seeming excited; I'm not. Let us change the subject. Now as to this castle, with forty-five princesses in it, and three ogres at the head of it, tell me—where is this harem?''

"Harem?''

"The *castle,* you understand; where is the castle?''

"Oh, as to that, it is great, and strong, and well beseen, and lieth in a far country. Yes, it is many leagues.''

"How many?''

"Ah, fair sir, it were woundily hard to tell, they are so many, and do so lap the one upon the other, and being made all in the same image and tincted with the same color, one may not know the one league from its fellow, nor how to count them except they be taken apart, and ye wit well it were God's work to do that, being not within man's capacity; for ye will note—''

"Hold on, hold on, never mind about the distance; *whereabouts* does the castle lie? What's the direction from here?''

"Ah, please you sir, it hath no direction from here; by reason that the road lieth not straight, but turneth evermore; wherefore the direction of its place abideth not, but is some time under the one sky and anon under another, whereso if ye be minded that it is in the east, and wend thitherward, ye shall observe that the way of the road doth yet again turn upon itself by the space of half a circle, and this marvel happing again and yet again and still again, it will grieve you that you have thought by vanities of the mind to thwart and bring to naught the will of Him that giveth not a castle a direction from a place except it pleaseth Him, and if it please Him not, will the rather that even all castles and all directions thereunto vanish out of the earth, leaving the places wherein they tarried desolate and vacant, so warning His creatures that where He will He will, and where He will not He—''

"Oh, that's all right, that's all right, give us a rest; never mind about the direction, *hang* the direction—I beg pardon, I beg a thousand pardons, I am not well to-day; pay no attention when I soliloquize, it is an old habit, an old, bad habit, and hard to get rid of when one's digestion is all disordered with eating food that was raised forever and ever before he was born; good land! a man can't keep his funtions regular on spring chickens thirteen hundred years old. But come—never mind about that; let's—have you got such a thing as a map of that region about you? Now a good map—"

"Is it peradventure that manner of thing which of late the unbelievers have brought from over the great seas, which, being boiled in oil, and an onion and salt added thereto, doth—"

"What, a map? What are you talking about? Don't you know what a map is? There, there, never mind, don't explain, I hate explanations; they fog a thing up so that you can't tell anything about it. Run along, dear; good day; show her the way, Clarence."

Oh, well, it was reasonably plain, now, why these donkeys didn't prospect these liars for details. It may be that this girl had a fact in her somewhere, but I don't believe you could have sluiced it out with a hydraulic; nor got it with the earlier forms of blasting, even; it was a case for dynamite. Why, she was a perfect ass; and yet the king and his knights had listened to her as if she had been a leaf out of the gospel. It kind of sizes up the whole party. And think of the simple ways of this court: this wandering wench hadn't any more trouble to get access to the king in his palace than she would have had to get into the poorhouse in my day and country. In fact, he was glad to see her, glad to hear her tale: with that adventure of hers to offer, she was as welcome as a corpse is to a coroner.

Just as I was ending up these reflections Clarence came back. I remarked upon the barren result of my efforts with the girl; hadn't got hold of a single point that could help me to find the castle. The youth looked a little surprised, or puzzled, or something, and intimated that he had been wondering to himself what I had wanted to ask the girl all those questions for.

"Why great guns," I said, "don't I want to find the castle? And how else would I go about it?"

"La, sweet your worship, one may lightly answer that, I ween. She will go with thee. They always do. She will ride with thee."

"Ride with me? Nonsense!"

"But of a truth she will. She will ride with thee. Thou shalt see."

"What? She browse around the hills and scour the woods with me—alone—and I as good as engaged to be married? Why, it's scandalous. Think how it would look."

My, the dear face that rose before me! The boy was eager to know all about this tender matter. I swore him to secrecy and then whispered her name—"Puss Flanagan." He looked disappointed, and said he didn't remember the countess. How natural it was for the little courtier to give her a rank. He asked me where she lived.

"In East Har—" I came to myself and stopped, a little confused; then I said, "Never mind, now; I'll tell you some time."

And might he see her? Would I let him see her some day?

It was but a little thing to promise—thirteen hundred years or so—and he so eager; so I said Yes. But I sighed; I couldn't help it. And yet there was no sense in sighing, for she wasn't born yet. But that is the way we are made: we don't reason, where we feel; we just feel.

My expedition was all the talk that day and that night, and the boys were very good to me, and made much of me, and seemed to have forgotten their vexation and disappointment, and come to be as anxious for me to hive those ogres and set those ripe old virgins loose as if it were themselves that had the contract. Well, they *were* good children—but just children, that is all. And they gave me no end of points about how to scout for giants, and how to scoop them in; and they told me all sorts of charms against enchantments, and gave me salves and other rubbish to put on my wounds. But it never occurred to one of them to reflect that if I was such a wonderful necromancer as I was pretending to be, I ought not to need salves or instructions, or charms against enchantments, and, least of all, arms and armor, on a foray of any kind—even against fire-spouting dragons, and devils hot from perdition, let alone such poor adversaries as these I was after, these commonplace ogres of the back settlements.

I was to have an early breakfast, and start at dawn, for that was the usual way; but I had the demon's own time with my armor, and this delayed me a little. It is troublesome to get into, and there is so much detail. First you wrap a layer or two of blanket around your body, for a sort of cushion and to keep off the cold iron; then you put on your sleeves and shirt of chain mail—these are made of small steel links woven together, and they form a fabric so flexible · that if you toss your shirt onto the floor, it slumps into a pile like a peck of wet fish-net; it is very heavy and is nearly the uncomfortablest material in the world for a nightshirt, yet plenty used it for that—tax-collectors, and reformers, and one-horse kings with a defective title, and those sorts of people; then you put on your shoes—flat-boats roofed over with interleaving bands of steel—and screw your clumsy spurs into the heels. Next you buckle your greaves on your legs, and your cuisses on your thighs; then come your back-plate and your breast-plate, and you begin to feel crowded; then you hitch onto the breast-plate the half-petticoat of broad overlapping bands of steel which hangs down in front but is scolloped out behind so you can sit down, and isn't any real improvement on an inverted coal-scuttle, either for looks or for wear, or to wipe your hands on; next you belt on your sword; then you put your stove-pipe joints onto your arms, your iron gauntlets onto your hands, your iron rat-trap onto your head, with a rag of steel web hitched onto it to hang over the back of your neck—and there you are, snug as a candle in a candle-mold. This is no time to dance. Well, a man that is packed away like that is a nut that isn't worth the cracking, there is so little of the meat, when you get down to it, by comparison with the shell.

The boys helped me, or I never could have got in. Just as we finished, Sir Bedivere happened in, and I saw that as like as not I hadn't chosen the most convenient outfit for a long trip. How stately he looked; and tall and broad and grand. He had on his head a conical steel casque that only came down to his ears, and for visor had only a narrow steel bar that extended down to his upper lip and protected his nose; and all the rest of him, from neck to heel, was flexible chain mail, trousers and all. But pretty much all of him was hidden under his outside garment, which of course was of chain mail, as I said, and hung straight from his shoulders to his ankles; and from his middle to the bottom, both before and behind, was divided, so that he could ride and let the skirts hang down on each side. He was going grailing, and it was just the outfit for it, too. I would have given a good deal for that ulster, but it was too late now to be fooling around. The sun was just up, the king and the court were all on hand to see me off and wish me luck; so it wouldn't be etiquette for me to tarry. You don't get on your horse yourself; no, if you tried it you would get disappointed. They carry you out, just as they carry a sunstruck man to the drug store, and put you on, and help get you to rights, and fix your feet in the stirrups; and all the while you do feel so strange and stuffy and like somebody else—like somebody that has been married on a sudden, or struck by lightning, or something like that, and hasn't quite fetched around yet, and is sort of numb, and can't just get his bearings. Then they stood up the mast they called a spear, in its socket by my left foot, and I gripped it with my hand; lastly they hung my shield around my neck, and I was all complete and ready to up anchor and get to sea. Everybody was as good to me as they could be, and a maid of honor gave me the stirrup-cup her own self. There was nothing more to do now, but for that damsel to get up behind me on a pillion, which she did, and put an arm or so around me to hold on.

And so we started, and everybody gave us a good-by and waved their hand-kerchiefs or helmets. And everybody we met, going down the hill and through the village, was respectful to us, except some shabby little boys on the outskirts. They said:

"Oh, what a guy!" And hove clods at us.

In my experience boys are the same in all ages. They don't respect anything, they don't care for anything or anybody. They say "Go up, baldhead" to the prophet going his unoffending way in the gray of antiquity; they sass me in the holy gloom of the Middle Ages; and I had seen them act the same way in Buchanan's administration; I remember, because I was there and helped. The prophet had his bears and settled with his boys; and I wanted to get down and settle with mine, but it wouldn't answer, because I couldn't have got up again. I hate a country without a derrick.

Chapter XII

SLOW TORTURE

STRAIGHT OFF, WE were in the country. It was most lovely and pleasant in those sylvan solitudes in the early cool morning in the first freshness of autumn. From hilltops we saw fair green valleys lying spread out below, with streams winding through them, and island groves of trees here and there, and huge lonely oaks scattered about and casting black blots of shade; and beyond the valleys we saw the ranges of hills, blue with haze, stretching away in billowy perspective to the horizon, with at wide intervals a dim fleck of white or gray on a wave-summit, which we knew was a castle. We crossed broad natural lawns sparkling with dew, and we moved like spirits, the cushioned turf giving out no sound of footfall; we dreamed along through glades in a mist of green light that got its tint from the sun-drenched roof of leaves overhead, and by our feet the clearest and coldest of runlets went frisking and gossiping over its reefs and making a sort of whispering music, comfortable to hear; and at times we left the world behind and entered into the solemn great deeps and rich gloom of the forest, where furtive wild things whisked and scurried by and were gone before you could even get your eye on the place where the noise was; and where only the earliest birds were turning out and getting to business with a song here and a quarrel yonder and a mysterious far-off hammering and drumming for worms on a tree-trunk away somewhere in the impenetrable remotenesses of the woods. And by and by out we would swing again into the glare.

About the third or fourth or fifth time that we swung out into the glare—it was along there somewhere, a couple of hours or so after sun-up—it wasn't as pleasant as it had been. It was beginning to get hot. This was quite noticeable. We had a very long pull, after that, without any shade. Now it is curious how progressively little frets grow and multiply after they once get a start. Things which I didn't mind at all, at first, I began to mind now—and more and more, too, all the time. The first ten or fifteen times I wanted my handkerchief I didn't seem to care; I got along, and said never mind, it isn't any matter, and dropped it out of my mind. But now it was different; I wanted it all the time; it was nag, nag, nag, right along, and no rest; I couldn't get it out of my mind; and so at last I lost my temper and said hang a man that would make a suit of armor without any pockets in it. You see I had my handkerchief in my helmet; and some other things; but it was that kind of a helmet that you can't take off by yourself. That hadn't occurred to me when I put it there; and in fact I didn't know it. I supposed it would be particularly convenient there. And so now, the thought of its being there, so handy and close by, and yet not get-at-able, made it all the worse and the harder to bear. Yes, the thing that you can't get is the thing that you want, mainly; every one has noticed that. Well, it took my mind off from everything else; took it clear off, and centered it in my helmet; and mile after mile, there it stayed, imagining the handkerchief, picturing the hand-kerchief; and it was bitter and aggravating to have the salt sweat keep trickling down into my eyes, and I couldn't get at it. It seems like a little thing, on paper, but it was not a little thing at all; it was the most real kind of misery. I would not say it if it was not so. I made up my mind that I would carry along a reticule next time, let it look how it might, and people say what they would. Of course these iron dudes of the Round Table would think it was scandalous, and maybe raise Sheol about it, but as for me, give me comfort first, and style afterward. So we jogged along, and now and then we struck a stretch of dust, and it would tumble up in clouds and get into my nose and make me sneeze and cry; and of coures I said things I oughtn't to have said, I don't deny that. I am not better than others.

We couldn't seem to meet anybody in this lonesome Britain, not even an ogre; and, in the mood I was in then, it was well for the ogre; that is, an ogre with a handkerchief. Most knights would have thought of nothing but getting his armor; but so I got his bandana, he could keep his hardware, for all of me.

Meantime, it was getting hotter and hotter in there. You see, the sun was beating down and warming up the iron more and more all the time. Well, when you are hot, that way, every little thing irritates you. When I trotted, I rattled like a crate of dishes, and that annoyed me; and moreover I couldn't seem to stand that shield slatting and banging, now about my breast, now around my back; and if I dropped into a walk my joints creaked and screeched in that wearisome way that a wheelbarrow does, and as we didn't create any breeze at that gait, I was like to get fried in that stove; and besides, the quieter you went the heavier the iron settled down on you and the more and more tons you seemed to weigh every minute. And you had to be always changing hands, and passing your spear over to the other foot, it got so irksome for one hand to hold it long at a time.

Well, you know, when you perspire that way, in rivers, there comes a time when you—when you—well, when you itch. You are inside, your hands are outside; so there you are; nothing but iron between. It is not a light thing, let it sound as it may. First it is one place; then another; then some more; and it goes on spreading and spreading, and at last the territory is all occupied, and nobody can imagine what you feel like, nor how unpleasant it is. And when it had got to the worst, and it seemed to me that I could not stand anything more, a fly got in through the bars and settled on my nose, and the bars were stuck and wouldn't work, and I couldn't get the visor up; and I could only shake my head, which was baking hot by this time, and the fly—well, you know how a fly acts when he has got a certainty—he only minded the shaking enough to change from nose to lip, and lip to ear, and buzz and buzz all around in there, and keep on lighting and biting, in a way that a person, already so distressed as I was, simply could not stand. So I gave in, and got Alisande to unship the helmet and relieve me of it. Then she emptied the conveniences out of it and fetched it full of water, and I drank and then stood up, and she poured the rest down inside the armor. One cannot think how refreshing it was. She continued to fetch and pour until I was well soaked and thoroughly comfortable.

It was good to have a rest—and peace. But nothing is quite perfect in this life, at any time. I had made a pipe awhile back, and also some pretty fair tobacco; not the real thing, but what some of the Indians use: the inside bark of the willow dried. These comforts had been in the helmet, and now I had them again, but no matches.

Gradually, as the time wore along, one annoying fact was borne in upon my understanding—that we were weather-bound. An armed novice cannot mount his horse without help and plenty of it. Sandy was not enough; not enough for me, anyway. We had to wait until somebody should come along. Waiting, in silence, would have been agreeable enough, for I was full of matter for reflection, and wanted to give it a chance to work. I wanted to try and think out how it was that rational or even half-rational men could ever have learned to wear armor, considering its inconveniences; and how they had managed to keep up such a fashion for generations when it was plain that what I had suffered to-day they had had to suffer all the days of their lives. I wanted to think that out; and moreover I wanted to think out some way to reform this evil and persuade the people to let the foolish fashion die out; but thinking was out of the question in the circumstances. You couldn't think, where Sandy was.

She was a quite biddable creature and good-hearted, but she had a flow of talk that was as steady as a mill, and made your head sore like the drays and wagons in a city. If she had had a cork she would have been a comfort. But you can't cork that kind; they would die. Her clack was going all day, and you would think something would surely happen to her works, by and by; but no, they never got out of order; and she never had to slack up for words. She could grind, and pump, and churn, and buzz by the week, and never stop to oil up or blow out. And yet the result was just nothing but wind. She never had any ideas, any more than a fog has. She was a perfect blatherskite; I mean for jaw, jaw, jaw, talk, talk, talk, jabber, jabber, jabber; but just as good as she could be. I hadn't minded her mill that morning, on account of having that hornets' nest of other troubles; but more than once in the afternoon I had to say:

"Take a rest, child; the way you are using up all the domestic air, the kingdom will have to go to importing it by to-morrow, and it's a low enough treasury without that."

Chapter XIII

FREEMEN

YES, IT IS strange how little a while at a time a person can be contented. Only a little while back, when I was riding and suffering what a heaven this peace, this rest, this sweet serenity in this secluded shady nook by this purling stream would have seemed, where I could keep perfectly comfortable all the time by pouring a dipper of water into my armor now and then; yet already I was getting dissatisfied; partly because I could not light my pipe—for, although I had long ago started a match factory, I had forgotten to bring matches with me—and partly because we had nothing to eat. Here was another illustration of the childlike improvidence of this age and people. A man in armor always trusted to chance for his food on a journey, and would have been scandalized at the idea of hanging a basket of sandwiches on his spear. There was probably not a knight of all the Round Table combination who would not rather have died than been caught carrying such a thing as that on his flagstaff. And yet there could not be anything more sensible. It had been my intention to smuggle a couple of sandwiches into my helmet, but I was interrupted in the act, and had to make an excuse and lay them aside, and a dog got them.

Night approached, and with it a storm. The darkness came on fast. We must camp, of course. I found a good shelter for the demoiselle under a rock, and went off and found another for myself. But I was obliged to remain in my armor, because I could not get it off by myself and yet could not allow Alisande to help, because it would have seemed so like undressing before folk. It would not have amounted to that in reality, because I had clothes on underneath; but the prejudices of one's breeding are not gotten rid of just at a jump, and I knew that when it came to stripping off that bobtailed iron petticoat I should be embarrassed.

With the storm came a change of weather; and the stronger the wind blew, and the wilder the rain lashed around, the colder and colder it got. Pretty soon, various kinds of bugs and ants and worms and things began to flock in out of the wet and crawl down inside my armor to get warm; and while some of them behaved well enough, and snuggled up amongst my clothes and got quiet, the majority were of a restless, uncomfortable sort, and never stayed still, but went on prowling and hunting for they did not know what; especially the ants, which went tickling along in wearisome procession from one end of me to the other by the hour, and are a kind of creatures which I never wish to sleep with again. It would be my advice to persons situated in this way, to not roll or thrash around, because this excites the interest of all the different sorts of animals and makes every last one of them want to turn out and see what is going on, and this makes things worse than they were before, and of course makes you objurgate harder, too, if you can. Still, if one did not roll and thrash around he would die; so perhaps it is as well to do one way as the other; there is no real choice. Even after I was frozen solid I could still distinguish that tickling, just as a corpse does when he is taking electric treatment. I said I would never wear armor after this trip.

All those trying hours whilst I was frozen and yet was in a living fire, as you may say, on account of that swarm of crawlers, that same unanswerable question kept circling and circling through my tired head: How do people stand this miserable armor? How have they managed to stand it all these generations? How can they sleep at night for dreading the tortures of next day?

When the morning came at last, I was in a bad enough plight: seedy, drowsy, fagged, from want of sleep; weary from thrashing around, famished from long fasting; pining for a bath, and to get rid of the animals; and crippled with rheumatism. And how had it fared with the nobly born, the titled aristocrat, the Demoiselle Alisande la Carteloise? Why, she was as fresh as a squirrel; she had slept like the dead; and as for a bath, probably neither she nor any other noble in the land had ever had one, and so she was not missing it. Measured by modern standards, they were merely modified savages, those people. This noble lady showed no impatience to get to breakfast—and that smacks of the savage, too. On their journeys those Britons were used to long fasts, and knew how to bear them; and also how to freight up against probable fasts before starting, after the style of the Indian and the anaconda. As like as not, Sandy was loaded for a three-day stretch.

We were off before sunrise, Sandy riding and I limping along behind. In half an hour we came upon a group of ragged poor creatures who had assembled to mend the thing which was regarded as a road. They were as humble as animals to me; and when I proposed to breakfast with them, they were so flattered, so overwhelmed by this extraordinary condescension of mine that at first they were not able to believe that I was in earnest. My lady put up her scornful lip and withdrew to one side; she said in their hearing that she would as soon think of eating with the other cattle—a remark which embarrassed these poor devils merely because it referred to them, and not because it insulted or offended them, for it didn't. And yet they were not slaves, not chattels. By a sarcasm of law and phrase they were freemen. Seven-tenths of the free population of the country were of just their class and degree: small "independent" farmers, artisans, etc.; which is to say, they were the nation, the actual Nation; they were about all of it that was useful, or worth saving, or really respectworthy, and to subtract them would have been to subtract the Nation and leave behind some dregs, some refuse, in the shape of a king, nobility and gentry, idle, unproductive, acquainted mainly with the arts of wasting and destroying, and of no sort of use or value in any rationally constructed world. And yet, by ingenious contrivance, this gilded minority, instead of being in the tail of the procession where it belonged, was marching head up and banners flying, at the other end of it; had elected itself to be the Nation, and these innumerable clams had permitted it so long that they had come at last to accept it as a truth; and not only that, but to believe it right and as it should be. The priests had told their fathers and themselves that this ironical state of things was ordained of God; and so, not reflecting upon how unlike God it would be to amuse himself with sarcasms, and especially such poor transparent ones as this, they had dropped the matter there and become respectfully quiet.

The talk of these meek people had a strange enough sound in a formerly American ear. They were freemen, but they could not leave the estates of their lord or their bishop without his permission; they could not prepare their own bread, but must have their corn ground and their bread baked at his mill and his bakery, and pay roundly for the same; they could not sell a piece of their own property without paying him a handsome percentage of the proceeds, nor buy a piece of somebody else's without remembering him in cash for the privilege; they had to harvest his grain for him gratis, and be ready to come at a moment's notice, leaving their own crop to destruction by the threatened storm; they had to let him plant fruit trees in their fields, and then keep their indignation to themselves when his heedless fruit-gatherers trampled the grain around the trees; they had to smother their anger when his hunting-parties galloped through their fields laying waste the result of their patient toil; they were not allowed to keep doves themselves, and when the swarms from my lord's dovecote settled on their crops they must not lose their temper and kill a bird, for awful would the penalty be; when the harvest was at last gathered, then came the procession of robbers to levy their blackmail upon it: first the Church carted off its fat tenth, then the king's commissioner took his twentieth, then my lord's people made a mighty inroad upon the remainder; after which, the skinned freeman had liberty to bestow the remnant in his barn, in case it was worth the trouble; there were taxes, and taxes, and taxes, and more taxes, and taxes again, and yet other taxes—upon this free and independent pauper, but none upon his lord the baron or the bishop, none upon the wasteful nobility or the all-devouring Church; if the baron would sleep unvexed, the freeman must sit up all night after his day's work and whip the ponds to keep the frogs quiet; if the freeman's daughter— but no, that last infamy of monarchical government is unprintable; and finally, if the freeman, grown desperate with his tortures, found his life unendurable under such conditions, and sacrificed it and fled to death for mercy and refuge, the gentle Church condemned him to eternal fire, the gentle law buried him at midnight at the crossroads with a stake through his back, and his master the baron or the bishop confiscated all his property and turned his widow and his orphans out of doors.

And here were these freemen assembled in the early morning to work on their lord the bishop's road three days each—gratis; every head of a family, and every son of a family, three days each, gratis, and a day or so added for their servants. Why, it was like reading about France and the French, before the ever memorable and blessed Revolution, which swept a thousand years of such villany away in one swift tidal wave of blood—one: a settlement of that hoary debt in the proportion of half a drop of blood for each hogshead of it that had been pressed by slow tortures out of that people in the weary stretch of ten centuries of wrong and shame and misery the like of which was not to be mated but in hell. There were two "Reigns of Terror," if we would but remember it and consider it; the one wrought murder in hot passion, the other in heartless cold blood; the one lasted mere months, the other had lasted a thousand years; the one inflicted death upon ten thousand persons, the other upon a hundred millions; but our shudders are all for the "horrors" of the minor Terror, the momentary Terror, so to speak; whereas, what is the horror of swift death by the ax compared with lifelong death from hunger, cold, insult, cruelty, and heartbreak? What is swift death by lightning compared with death by slow fire at the stake? A city cemetery could contain the coffins filled by that brief Terror which we have all been so diligently taught to shiver at and mourn over; but all France could hardly contain the coffins filled by that older and real Terror—that unspeakably bitter and awful Terror which none of us has been taught to see in its vastness or pity as it deserves.

These poor ostensible freemen who were sharing their breakfast and their talk with me, were as full of humble reverence for their king and Church and nobility as their worst enemy could desire. There was something pitifully ludicrous about it. I asked them if they supposed a nation of people ever existed, who, with a free vote in every man's hand, would elect that a single family and its descendants should reign over it forever, whether gifted or boobies, to the exclusion of all other families—including the voter's; and would also elect that a certain hundred families should be raised to dizzy summits of rank, and clothed on with offensive transmissible glories and privileges to the exclusion of the rest of the nation's families—*including his own.*

They all looked unhit, and said they didn't know; that they had never thought about it before, and it hadn't ever occurred to them that a nation could be so situated that every man *could* have a say in the government. I said I had seen one—and that it would last until it had an Established Church. Again they were all unhit—at first. But presently one man looked up and asked me to state that proposition again; and state it slowly, so it could soak into his understanding. I did it; and after a little he had the idea, and he brought his fist down and said *he* didn't believe a nation where every man had a vote would voluntarily get down in the mud and dirt in any such way; and that to steal from a nation its will and preference must be a crime and the first of all crimes. I said to myself:

"This one's a man. If I were backed by enough of his sort, I would make a strike for the welfare of this country, and try to prove myself its loyalest citizen by making a wholesome change in its system of government."

You see my kind of loyalty was loyalty to one's country, not to its institutions or its office-holders. The country is the real thing, the substantial thing, the eternal thing; it is the thing to watch over, and care for, and be loyal to; institutions are extraneous, they are its mere clothing, and clothing can wear out, become ragged, cease to be comfortable, cease to protect the body from winter, disease, and death. To be loyal to rags, to shout for rags, to worship rags, to die for rags—that is a loyalty of unreason, it is pure animal; it belongs to monarchy, was invented by monarchy; let monarchy keep it. I was from Connecticut, whose Constitution declares "that all political power is inherent in the people, and all free governments are founded on their authority and instituted for their benefit; and that they have *at all times* an undeniable and indefeasible right to *alter their form of government* in such a manner as they may think expedient."

Under that gospel, the citizen who thinks he sees that the commonwealth's political clothes are worn out, and yet holds his peace and does not agitate for a new suit, is disloyal; he is a traitor. That he may be the only one who thinks he sees this decay, does not excuse him; it is his duty to agitate anyway, and it is the duty of the others to vote him down if they do not see the matter as he does.

And now here I was, in a country where a right to say how the country should be governed was restricted to six persons in each thousand of its population. For the nine hundred and ninety-four to express dissatisfaction with the regnant system and propose to change it, would have made the whole six shudder as one man, it would have been so disloyal, so dishonorable, such putrid black treason. So to speak, I was become a stockholder in a corporation where nine hundred and ninety-four of the members furnished all the money and did all the work, and the other six elected themselves a permanent board of direction and took all the dividends. It seemed to me that what the nine hundred and ninety-four dupes needed was a new deal. The thing that would have best suited the circus side of my nature would have been to resign the Boss-ship and get up an insurrection and turn it into a revolution; but I knew that the Jack Cade or the Wat Tyler who tries such a thing without first educating his materials up to revolution grade is almost absolutely certain to get left. I had never been accustomed to getting left, even if I do say it myself. Wherefore, the "deal" which had been for some time working into shape in my mind was of a quite different pattern from the Cade-Tyler sort.

So I did not talk blood and insurrection to that man there who sat munching black bread with that abused and mistaught herd of human sheep, but took him aside and talked matter of another sort to him. After I had finished, I got him to lend me a little ink from his veins; and with this and a sliver I wrote on a piece of bark—

Put him in the Man-factory—

and gave it to him and said:

"Take it to the palace at Camelot and give it into the hands of Amyas le Poulet, whom I call Clarence, and he will understand."

"He is a priest, then," said the man, and some of the enthusiasm went out of his face.

"How—a priest? Didn't I tell you that no chattel of the Church, no bond-slave of pope or bishop can enter my Man-factory? Didn't I tell you that *you* couldn't enter unless your religion, whatever it might be, was your own free property?"

"Marry, it is so, and for that I was glad; wherefore it liked me not, and bred in me a cold doubt, to hear of this priest being there."

"But he isn't a priest, I tell you."

The man looked far from satisfied. He said:

"He is not a priest, and yet can read?"

"He is not a priest and yet can read—yes, and write, too, for that matter. I taught him myself." The man's face cleared. "And it is the first thing that you yourself will be taught in that Factory—"

"I? I would give blood out of my heart to know that art. Why, I will be your slave, your—"

"No you won't, you won't be anybody's slave. Take your family and go along. Your lord the bishop will confiscate your small property, but no matter, Clarence will fix you all right."

Chapter XIV

"DEFEND THEE, LORD"

I PAID THREE pennies for my breakfast, and a most extravagant price it was, too, seeing that one could have breakfasted a dozen persons for that money; but I was feeling good by this time, and I had always been a kind of spendthrift anyway; and then these people had wanted to give me the food for nothing, scant as their provision was, and so it was a grateful pleasure to emphasize my appreciation and sincere thankfulness with a good big financial lift where the money would do so much more good than it would in my helmet, where, these pennies being made of iron and not stinted in weight, my half-dollar's worth was a good deal of a burden to me. I spent money rather too freely in those days, it is true; but one reason for it was that I hadn't got the proportions of things entirely adjusted, even yet, after so long a sojourn in Britain—hadn't got along to where I was able to absolutely realize that a penny in Arthur's land and a couple of dollars in Connecticut were about one and the same thing: just twins, as you may say, in purchasing-power. If my start from Camelot could have been delayed a very few days I could have paid these people in beautiful new coins from our own mint, and that would have pleased me; and them, too, not less. I had adopted the American values exclusively. In a week or two now, cents, nickels, dimes, quarters, and half-dollars, and also a trifle of gold, would be trickling in thin but steady streams all through the commercial veins of the kingdom, and I looked to see this new blood freshen up its life.

The farmers were bound to throw in something, to sort of offset my liberality, whether I would or no; so I let them give me a flint and steel; and as soon as they had comfortably bestowed Sandy and me on our horse, I lit my pipe. When the first blast of smoke shot out through the bars of my helmet, all those people broke for the woods, and Sandy went over backward and struck the ground with a dull thud. They thought I was one of those fire-belching dragons they had heard so much about from knights and other professional liars. I had infinite trouble to persuade those people to venture back within explaining distance. Then I told them that this was only a bit of enchantment which would work harm to none but my enemies. And I promised, with my hand on my heart, that if all who felt no enmity toward me would come forward and pass before me they should see that only those who remained behind would be struck dead. The procession moved with a good deal of promptness. There were no casualties to report, for nobody had curiosity enough to remain behind to see what would happen.

I lost some time, now, for these big children, their fears gone, became so ravished with wonder over my awe-compelling fireworks that I had to stay there and smoke a couple of pipes out before they would let me go. Still the delay was not wholly unproductive, for it took all that time to get Sandy thoroughly wonted to the new thing, she being so close to it, you know. It plugged up her conversation-mill, too, for a considerable while, and that was a gain. But above all other benefits accruing, I had learned something. I was ready for any giant or any ogre that might come along, now.

We tarried with a holy hermit, that night, and my opportunity came about the middle of the next afternoon. We were crossing a vast meadow by way of short cut, and I was musing absently, hearing nothing, seeing nothing, when Sandy suddenly interrupted a remark which she had begun that morning, with the cry:

"Defend thee, lord!—peril of life is toward!"

And she slipped down from the horse and ran a little way and stood. I looked up and saw, far off in the shade of a tree, half a dozen armed knights and their squires; and straightway there was bustle among them and tightening of saddle-girths for the mount. My pipe was ready and would have been lit, if I had not been lost in thinking about how to banish oppression from this land and restore to all its people their stolen rights and manhood without disobliging anybody. I lit up at once, and by the time I had got a good head of reserved steam on, here they came. All together, too; none of those chivalrous magnanimities which one reads so much about—one courtly rascal at a time, and the rest standing by to see fair play. No, they came in a body, they came with a whir and a rush, they came like a volley from a battery; came with heads low down, plumes streaming out behind, lances advanced at a level. It was a handsome sight, a beautiful sight—for a man up a tree. I laid my lance in rest and waited, with my heart beating, till the iron wave was just ready to break over me, then spouted a column of white smoke through the bars of my helmet. You should have seen the wave go to pieces and scatter! This was a finer sight than the other one.

But these people stopped, two or three hundred yards away, and this troubled me. My satisfaction collapsed, and fear came; I judged I was a lost man. But Sandy was radiant; and was going to be eloquent; but I stopped her, and told her my magic had miscarried, somehow or other, and she must mount, with all despatch, and we must ride for life. No, she wouldn't. She said that my enchantment had disabled those knights; they were not riding on, because they couldn't; wait, they would drop out of their saddles presently, and we would get their horses and harness. I could not deceive such trusting simplicity, so I said it was a mistake; that when my fireworks killed at all, they killed instantly; no, the men would not die, there was something wrong about my apparatus, I couldn't tell what; but we must hurry and get away, for those people would attack us again, in a minute. Sandy laughed, and said:

"Lack-a-day, sir, they be not of that breed! Sir Launcelot will give battle to dragons, and will abide by them, and will assail them again, and yet again, and still again, until he do conquer and destroy them; and so likewise will Sir Pellinore and Sir Aglovale and Sir Carados, and mayhap others, but there be none else that will venture it, let the idle say what the idle will. And, la, as to yonder base rufflers, think ye they have not their fill, but yet desire more?"

"Well, then, what are they waiting for? Why don't they leave? Nobody's hindering. Good land, I'm willing to let bygones be bygones, I'm sure."

"Leave, is it? Oh, give thyself easement as to that. They dream not of it, no, not they. They wait to yield them."

"Come—really, is that 'sooth'—as you people say? If they want to, why don't they?"

"It would like them much; but an ye wot how dragons are esteemed, ye would not hold them blamable. They fear to come."

"Well, then, suppose I go to them instead, and—"

"Ah, wit ye well they would not abide your coming. I will go."

And she did. She was a handy person to have along on a raid. I would have considered this a doubtful errand, myself. I presently saw the knights riding away, and Sandy coming back. That was a relief. I judged she had somehow failed to get the first innings—I mean in the conversation; otherwise the interview wouldn't have been so short. But it turned out that she had managed the business well; in fact, admirably. She said that when she told those people I was The Boss, it hit them where they lived: "smote them sore with fear and dread" was her word; and then they were ready to put up with anything she might require. So she swore them to appear at Arthur's court within two days and yield them, with horse and harness, and be my knights henceforth, and subject to my command. How much better she managed that thing than I should have done it myself! She was a daisy.

Chapter XV

SANDY'S TALE

"AND SO I'M proprietor of some knights," said I, as we rode off. "Who would ever have supposed that I should live to list up assets of that sort. I sha'n't know what to do with them; unless I raffle them off. How many of them are there, Sandy?"

"Seven, please you, sir, and their squires."

"It is a good haul. Who are they? Where do they hang out?"

"Where do they hang out?"

"Yes, where do they live?"

"Ah, I understood thee not. That will I tell eftsoons." Then she said musingly, and softly, turning the words daintily over her tongue: "Hang they out—hang they out—where hang—where do they hang out; eh, right so; where do they hang out. Of a truth the phrase hath a fair and winsome grace, and is prettily worded withal. I will repeat it anon and anon in mine idlesse, whereby I may peradventure learn it. Where do they hang out. Even so! already it falleth trippingly from my tongue, and forasmuch as—"

"Don't forget the cowboys, Sandy."

"Cowboys?"

"Yes; the knights, you know: You were going to tell me about them. A while back, you remember. Figuratively speaking, game's called."

"Game—"

"Yes, yes, yes! Go to the bat. I mean, get to work on your statistics, and don't burn so much kindling getting your fire started. Tell me about the knights."

"I will well, and lightly will begin. So they two departed and rode into a great forest. And—"

"Great Scott!"

You see, I recognized my mistake at once. I had set her works a-going; it was my own fault; she would be thirty days getting down to those facts. And she generally began without a preface and finished without a result. If you interrupted her she would either go right along without noticing, or answer with a couple of words, and go back and say the sentence over again. So, interruptions only did harm; and yet I had to interrupt, and interrupt pretty frequently, too, in order to save my life; a person would die if he let her monotony drip on him right along all day.

"Great Scott!" I said in my distress. She went right back and began over again:

"So they two departed and rode into a great forest. And—"

"*Which* two?"

"Sir Gawaine and Sir Uwaine. And so they came to an abbey of monks, and there were well lodged. So on the morn they heard their masses in the abbey, and so they rode forth till they came to a great forest; then was Sir Gawaine ware in a valley by a turret, of twelve fair damsels, and two knights armed on great horses, and the damsels went to and fro by a tree. And then was Sir Gawaine ware how there hung a white shield on that tree, and ever as the damsels came by it they spit upon it, and some threw mire upon the shield—"

"Now, if I hadn't seen the like myself in this country, Sandy, I wouldn't believe it. But I've seen it, and I can just see those creatures now, parading before that shield and acting like that. The women here do certainly act like all possessed. Yes, and I mean your best, too, society's very choicest brands. The humblest hello-girl along ten thousand miles of wire could teach gentleness, patience, modesty, manners, to the highest duchess in Arthur's land."

"Hello-girl?"

"Yes, but don't you ask me to explain; it's a new kind of a girl; they don't have them here; one often speaks sharply to them when they are not the least in fault, and he can't get over feeling sorry for it and ashamed of himself in thirteen hundred years, it's such shabby mean conduct and so unprovoked; the fact is, no gentleman ever does it—though I—well, I myself, if I've got to confess—"

"Peradventure she—"

"Never mind her; never mind her; I tell you I couldn't ever explain her so you would understand."

"Even so be it, sith ye are so minded. Then Sir Gawaine and Sir Uwaine went and saluted them, and asked them why they did that despite to the shield. Sirs, said the damsels, we shall tell you. There is a knight in this country that owneth this white shield, and he is a passing good man of his hands, but he hateth all ladies and gentlewomen, and therefore we do all this despite to the shield. I will say you, said Sir Gawaine, it beseemeth evil a good knight to despise all ladies and gentlewomen, and peradventure though he hate you he hath some cause, and peradventure he loveth in some other places ladies and gentlewomen, and to be loved again, and he such a man of prowess as ye speak of—"

"Man of prowess—yes, that is the man to please them, Sandy. Man of brains—that is a thing they never think of. Tom Sayers—John Heenan—John L. Sullivan—pity but you could be here. You would have your legs under the Round Table and a 'Sir' in front of your names within the twenty-four hours; and you could bring about a new distribution of the married princesses and duchesses of the Court in another twenty-four. The fact is, it is just a sort of polished-up court of Comanches, and there isn't a squaw in it who doesn't stand ready at the dropping of a hat to desert to the buck with the biggest string of scalps at his belt."

—"and he be such a man of prowess as ye speak of, said Sir Gawaine. Now, what is his name? Sir, said they, his name is Marhaus the king's son of Ireland."

"Son of the king of Ireland, you mean; the other form doesn't mean anything. And look out and hold on tight, now, we must jump this gully. . . . There, we are all right now. This horse belongs in the circus; he is born before his time."

"I know him well," said Sir Uwaine, he is passing good knight as any is on live."

"*On live.* If you've got a fault in the world, Sandy, it is that you are a shade too archaic. But it isn't any matter."

—"for I saw him once proved at a justs where many knights were gathered, and that time there might no man withstand him. As, said Sir Gawaine, damsels, methinketh ye are to blame, for it is to suppose he that hung that shield there will not be long therefrom, and then may those knights match him on horseback, and that is more your worship than thus; for I will abide no longer to see a knight's shield dishonored. And therewith Sir Uwaine and Sir Gawaine departed a little from them, and then were they ware where Sir Marhaus came riding on a great horse straight toward them. And when the twelve damsels saw Sir Marhaus they fled into the turret as they were wild, so that some of them fell by the way. Then the one of the knights of the tower dressed his shield, and said on high, Sir Marhaus defend thee. And so they ran together that the knight brake his spear on Marhaus, and Sir Marhaus smote him so hard that he brake his neck and the horse's back—"

"Well, that is just the trouble about this state of things, it ruins so many horses."

"That saw the other knight of the turret, and dressed him toward Marhaus, and they went so eagerly together, that the knight of the turret was soon smitten down, horse and man, stark dead—"

"*Another* horse gone; I tell you it is a custom that ought to be broken up. I don't see how people with any feeling can applaud and support it."

"So these two knights came together with great random—"

I saw that I had been asleep and missed a chapter, but I didn't say anything. I judged that the Irish knight was in trouble with the visitors by this time, and this turned out to be the case.

—"that Sir Uwaine smote Sir Marhaus that his spear brast in pieces on the shield, and Sir Marhaus smote him so sore that horse and man he bare to the earth, and hurt Sir Uwaine on the left side—"

"The truth is, Alisande, the archaics are a little *too* simple; the vocabulary is too limited, and so, by consequence, descriptions suffer in the matter of variety; they run too much to level Saharas of fact, and not enough to picturesque detail; this throws about them a certain air of the monotonous; in fact the fights are all alike: a couple of people come together with great random—random is a good word, and so is exegesis, for that matter, and so is holocaust, and defalcation, and usufruct and a hundred others, but land! a body ought to discriminate—they come together with great random, and a spear is brast, and one party brake his shield and the other one goes down, horse and man, over his horse-tail and brake his neck, and then the next candidate comes randoming in, and brast *his* spear, and the other man brast his shield, and down *he* goes, horse and man, over his horse-tail, and brake *his* neck, and then there's another elected, and another and another and still another, till the material is all used up; and when you come to figure up results, you can't tell one fight from another, nor who whipped; and as a *picture*, of living, raging, roaring battle, sho! why, it's pale and noiseless—

just ghosts scuffling in a fog. Dear me, what would this barren vocabulary get out of the mightiest spectacle?—the burning of Rome in Nero's time, for instance? Why, it would merely say, 'Town burned down; no insurance; boy brast a window, fireman brake his neck!' Why, *that* ain't a picture!''

It was a good deal of a lecture, I thought, but it didn't disturb Sandy, didn't turn a feather; her steam soared steadily up again, the minute I took off the lid:

''Then Sir Marhaus turned his horse and rode toward Gawaine with his spear. And when Sir Gawaine saw that, he dressed his shield, and they aventred their spears, and they came together with all the might of their horses, that either knight smote other so hard in the midst of their shields, but Sir Gawaine's spear brake—''

''I knew it would.''

—''but Sir Marhaus's spear held; and therewith Sir Gawaine and his horse rushed down to the earth—''

''Just so—and brake his back.''

—''and lightly Sir Gawaine rose upon his feet and pulled out his sword, and dressed him toward Sir Marhaus on foot, and therewith either came unto other eagerly, and smote together with their swords, that their shields flew in cantels, and they bruised their helms and their hauberks, and wounded either other. But Sir Gawaine, fro it passed nine of the clock, waxed by the space of three hours ever stronger and stronger, and thrice his might was increased. All this espied Sir Marhaus, and had great wonder how his might increased, and so they wounded other passing sore; and then when it was come noon—''

The pelting sing-song of it carried me forward to scenes and sounds of my boyhood days:

''N-e-e-ew Haven! ten minutes for refreshments—knductr 'll strike the gong-bell two minutes before train leaves—passengers for the Shore line please take seats in the rear k'yar, this k'yar don't go no furder—*ahh*-pls, *aw*-rnjz, b'*nan*ners, *s-a-n-d*'ches, p——*op*-corn!''

—''and waxed past noon and drew toward evensong. Sir Gawaine's strength feebled and waxed passing faint, that unnethes he might dure any longer, and Sir Marhaus was then bigger and bigger—''

''Which strained his armor, of course; and yet little would one of these people mind a small thing like that.''

—''and so, Sir Knight, said Sir Marhaus, I have well felt that ye are a passing good knight, and a marvelous man of might as ever I felt any, while it lasteth, and our quarrels are not great, and therefore it were a pity to do you hurt, for I feel you are passing feeble. Ah, said Sir Gawaine, gentle knight, ye say the word that I should say. And therewith they took off their helms and either kissed other, and there they swore together either to love other as brethren—''

But I lost the thread there, and dozed off to slumber, thinking about what a pity it was that men with such superb strength—strength enabling them to stand up cased in cruelly burdensome iron and drenched with perspiration, and hack and batter and bang each other for six hours on a stretch—should not have been born at a time when they could put it to some useful purpose. Take a jackass, for instance: a jackass has that kind of strength, and puts it to a useful purpose, and is valuable to this world because he *is* a jackass; but a nobleman is not valuable because he is a jackass. It is a mixture that is always ineffectual, and should never have been attempted in the first place. And yet, once you start a mistake, the trouble is done and you never know what is going to come of it.

When I came to myself again and began to listen, I perceived that I had lost another chapter, and that Alisande had wandered a long way off with her people.

"And so they rode and came into a deep valley full of stones, and thereby they saw a fair stream of water; above thereby was the head of the stream, a fair fountain, and three damsels sitting thereby. In this country, said Sir Marhaus, came never knight since it was christened, but he found strange adventures—"

"This is not good form, Alisande. Sir Marhaus the king's son of Ireland talks like all the rest; you ought to give him a brogue, or at least a characteristic expletive; by this means one would recognize him as soon as he spoke, without his ever being named. It is a common literary device with the great authors. You should make him say, 'In this country, be jabers, came never knight since it was christened, but he found strange adventures, be jabers.' You see how much better that sounds."

"—came never knight but he found strange adventures, be jabers. Of a truth it doth indeed, fair lord, albeit 'tis passing hard to say, though peradventure that will not tarry but better speed with usage. And then they rode to the damsels, and either saluted other, and the eldest had a garland of gold about her head, and she was threescore winter of age or more—"

"The *damsel* was?"

"Even so, dear lord—and her hair was white under the garland—"

"Celluloid teeth, nine dollars a set, as like as not—the loose-fit kind, that go up and down like a portcullis when you eat, and fall out when you laugh."

"The second damsel was of thirty winter of age, with a circlet of gold about her head. The third damsel was but fifteen year of age—"

Billows of thought came rolling over my soul, and the voice faded out of my hearing!

Fifteen! Break—my heart! oh, my lost darling! Just her age who was so gentle, and lovely, and all the world to me, and whom I shall never see again! How the thought of her carries me back over wide seas of memory to a vague dim time, a happy time, so many, many centuries hence, when I used to wake in the soft summer mornings, out of sweet dreams of her, and say "Hello, Central!" just to hear her dear voice come melting back to me with a "Hello, Hank!" that was music of the spheres to my enchanted ear. She got three dollars a week, but she was worth it.

I could not follow Alisande's further explanation of who our captured knights were, now—I mean in case she should ever get to explaining who they were. My interest was gone, my thoughts were far away, and sad. By fitful glimpses of the drifting tale, caught here and there and now and then, I merely noted in a vague way that each of these three knights took one of these three damsels up behind him on his horse, and one rode north, another east, the other south, to seek adventures, and meet again and lie, after year and day. Year and day—and without baggage. It was of a piece with the general simplicity of the country.

The sun was now setting. It was about three in the afternoon when Alisande had begun to tell me who the cowboys were; so she had made pretty good progress with it—for her. She would arrive some time or other, no doubt, but she was not a person who could be hurried.

We were approaching a castle which stood on high ground; a huge, strong, venerable structure, whose gray towers and battlements were charmingly draped with ivy, and whose whole majestic mass was drenched with splendors flung from the sinking sun. It was the largest castle we had seen, and so I thought it might be the one we were after, but Sandy said no. She did not know who owned it; she said she had passed it without calling, when she went down to Camelot.

Chapter XVI

MORGAN LE FAY

IF KNIGHTS ERRANT were to be believed, not all castles were desirable places to seek hospitality in. As a matter of fact, knights errant were *not* persons to be believed—that is, measured by modern standards of veracity; yet, measured by the standards of their own time, and scaled accordingly, you got the truth. It was very simple: you discounted a statement ninety-seven per cent.; the rest was fact. Now after making this allowance, the truth remained that if I could find out something about a castle before ringing the door-bell—I mean hailing the warders—it was the sensible thing to do. So I was pleased when I saw in the distance a horseman making the bottom turn of the road that wound down from this castle.

As we approached each other, I saw that he wore a plumed helmet, and seemed to be otherwise clothed in steel, but bore a curious addition also—a stiff square garment like a herald's tabard. However, I had to smile at my own forgetfulness when I got nearer and read this sign on his tabard:

"Persimmons's Soap—All the Prime-Donne Use It."

That was a little idea of my own, and had several wholesome purposes in view toward the civilizing and uplifting of this nation. In the first place, it was a furtive, underhand blow at this nonsense of knight errantry, though nobody suspected that but me. I had started a number of these people out—the bravest knights I could get—each sandwiched between bulletin-boards bearing one device or another, and I judged that by and by when they got to be numerous enough they would begin to look ridiculous; and then, even the steel-clad ass that *hadn't* any board would himself begin to look ridiculous because he was out of the fashion.

Secondly, these missionaries would gradually, and without creating suspicion or exciting alarm, introduce a rudimentary cleanliness among the nobility, and from them it would work down to the people, if the priests could be kept quiet. This would undermine the Church. I mean would be a step toward that. Next, education—next, freedom—and then she would begin to crumble. It being my conviction that any Established Church is an established crime, an established slave-pen, I had no scruples, but was willing to assail it in any way or with any weapon that promised to hurt it. Why, in my own former day—in remote centuries not yet stirring in the womb of time—there were old Englishmen who imagined that they had been born in a free country: a "free" country with the Corporation Act and the Test still in force in it—timbers propped against men's liberties and dishonored consciences to shore up an Established Anachronism with.

My missionaries were taught to spell out the gilt signs on their tabards—the showy gilding was a neat idea, I could have got the king to wear a bulletin-board for the sake of that barbaric splendor—they were to spell out these signs and then explain to the lords and ladies what soap was; and if the lords and

ladies were afraid of it, get them to try it on a dog. The missionary's next move
was to get the family together and try it on himself; he was to stop at no
experiment, however desperate, that could convince the nobility that soap was
harmless; if any final doubt remained, he must catch a hermit—the woods were
full of them; saints they called themselves, and saints they were believed to be.
They were unspeakably holy, and worked miracles, and everybody stood in awe
of them. If a hermit could survive a wash, and that failed to convince a duke,
give him up, let him alone.

Whenever my missionaries overcame a knight errant on the road they washed
him, and when he got well they swore him to go and get a bulletin-board and
disseminate soap and civilization the rest of his days. As a consequence the
workers in the field were increasing by degrees, and the reform was steadily
spreading. My soap factory felt the strain early. At first I had only two hands;
but before I had left home I was already employing fifteen, and running night
and day; and the atmospheric result was getting so pronounced that the king
went sort of fainting and gasping around and said he did not believe he could
stand it much longer, and Sir Launcelot got so that he did hardly anything but
walk up and down the roof and swear, although I told him it was worse up there
than anywhere else, but he said he wanted plenty of air; and he was always
complaining that a palace was no place for a soap factory anyway, and said if
a man was to start one in his house he would be damned if he wouldn't strangle
him. There were ladies present, too, but much these people ever cared for that;
they would swear before children, if the wind was their way when the factory
was going.

This missionary knight's name was La Cote Male Taile, and he said that this
castle was the abode of Morgan le Fay, sister of King Arthur, and wife of King
Uriens, monarch of a realm about as big as the District of Columbia—you could
stand in the middle of it and throw bricks into the next kingdom. "Kings" and
"Kingdoms" were as thick in Britain as they had been in little Palestine in
Joshua's time, when people had to sleep with their knees pulled up because they
couldn't stretch out without a passport.

La Cote was much depressed, for he had scored here the worst failure of his
campaign. He had not worked off a cake; yet he had tried all the tricks of the
trade, even to the washing of a hermit; but the hermit died. This was, indeed,
a bad failure, for this animal would now be dubbed a martyr, and would take
his place among the saints of the Roman calendar. Thus made he his moan, this
poor Sir La Cote Male Taile, and sorrowed passing sore. And so my heart bled
for him, and I was moved to comfort and stay him. Wherefore I said:

"Forbear to grieve, fair knight, for this is not a defeat. We have brains, you
and I; and for such as have brains there are no defeats, but only victories.
Observe how we will turn this seeming disaster into an advertisement; an advertisement for our soap; and the biggest one, to draw, that was ever thought
of; an advertisement that will transform that Mount Washington defeat into a
Matterhorn victory. We will put on your bulletin-board, *'Patronized by the Elect.'*
How does that strike you?"

"Verily, it is wonderly bethought!"

"Well, a body is bound to admit that for just a modest little one-line ad., it's
a corker."

So the poor colporteur's griefs vanished away. He was a brave fellow, and
had done mighty feats of arms in his time. His chief celebrity rested upon the

events of an excursion like this one of mine, which he had once made with a
damsel named Maledisant, who was as handy with her tongue as was Sandy,
though in a different way, for her tongue churned forth only railings and insult,
whereas Sandy's music was of a kindlier sort. I knew his story well, and so I
knew how to interpret the compassion that was in his face when he bade me
farewell. He supposed I was having a bitter hard time of it.

Sandy and I discussed his story, as we rode along, and she said that La Cote's
bad luck had begun with the very beginning of that trip; for the king's fool had
overthrown him on the first day, and in such cases it was customary for the girl
to desert to the conqueror, but Maledisant didn't do it; and also persisted afterward
in sticking to him, after all his defeats. But, said I, suppose the victor should
decline to accept his spoil? She said that that wouldn't answer—he must. He
couldn't decline; it wouldn't be regular. I made a note of that. If Sandy's music
got to be too burdensome, some time, I would let a knight defeat me, on the
chance that she would desert to him.

In due time we were challenged by the warders, from the castle walls, and
after a parley admitted. I have nothing pleasant to tell about that visit. But it
was not a disappointment, for I knew Mrs. le Fay by reputation, and was not
expecting anything pleasant. She was held in awe by the whole realm, for she
had made everybody believe she was a great sorceress. All her ways were wicked,
all her instincts devilish. She was loaded to the eyelids with cold malice. All
her history was black with crime; and among her crimes murder was common.
I was most curious to see her; as curious as I could have been to see Satan. To
my surprise she was beautiful; black thoughts had failed to make her expression
repulsive, age had failed to wrinkle her satin skin or mar its bloomy freshness.
She could have passed for old Uriens' granddaughter, she could have been
mistaken for sister to her own son.

As soon as we were fairly within the castle gates we were ordered into her
presence. King Uriens was there, a kind-faced old man with a subdued look;
and also the son, Sir Uwaine le Blanchemains, in whom I was, of course,
interested on account of the tradition that he had once done battle with thirty
knights, and also on account of his trip with Sir Gawaine and Sir Marhaus,
which Sandy had been aging me with. But Morgan was the main attraction, the
conspicuous personality here; she was head chief of this household, that was
plain. She caused us to be seated, and then she began, with all manner of pretty
graces and graciousnesses, to ask me questions. Dear me, it was like a bird or
a flute, or something, talking. I felt persuaded that this woman must have been
misrepresented, lied about. She trilled along, and trilled along, and presently a
handsome young page, clothed like the rainbow, and as easy and undulatory of
movement as a wave, came with something on a golden salver, and, kneeling
to present it to her, overdid his graces and lost his balance, and so fell lightly
against her knee. She slipped a dirk into him in as matter-of-course a way as
another person would have harpooned a rat!

Poor child! he slumped to the floor, twisted his silken limbs in one great
straining contortion of pain, and was dead. Out of the old king was wrung an
involuntary ''O-h!'' of compassion. The look he got, made him cut it suddenly
short and not put any more hyphens in it. Sir Uwaine, at a sign from his mother,
went to the anteroom and called some servants, and meanwhile madame went
rippling sweetly along with her talk.

I saw that she was a good housekeeper, for while she talked she kept a corner of her eye on the servants to see that they made no balks in handling the body and getting it out; when they came with fresh clean towels, she sent back for the other kind; and when they had finished wiping the floor and were going, she indicated a crimson fleck the size of a tear which their duller eyes had overlooked. It was plain to me that La Cote Male Taile had failed to see the mistress of the house. Often, how louder and clearer than any tongue, does dumb circumstantial evidence speak.

Morgan le Fay rippled along as musically as ever. Marvelous woman. And what a glance she had: when it fell in reproof upon those servants, they shrunk and quailed as timid people do when the lightning flashes out of a cloud. I could have got the habit myself. It was the same with that poor old Brer Uriens; he was always on the ragged edge of apprehension; she could not even turn toward him but he winced.

In the midst of the talk I let drop a complimentary word about King Arthur, forgetting for the moment how this woman hated her brother. That one little compliment was enough. She clouded up like a storm; she called for her guards, and said:

"Hale me these varlets to the dungeons."

That struck cold on my ears, for her dungeons had a reputation. Nothing occurred to me to say—or do. But not so with Sandy. As the guard laid a hand upon me, she piped up with the tranquilest confidence, and said:

"God's wownds, dost thou covet destruction, thou maniac? It is The Boss!"

Now what a happy idea that was!—and so simple; yet it would never have occurred to me. I was born modest; not all over, but in spots; and this was one of the spots.

The effect upon madame was electrical. It cleared her countenance and brought back her smiles and all her persuasive graces and blandishments; but nevertheless she was not able to entirely cover up with them the fact that she was in a ghastly fright. She said:

"La, but do list to thine handmaid! as if one gifted with powers like to mine might say the thing which I have said unto one who has vanquished Merlin, and not be jesting. By mine enchantments I foresaw your coming, and by them I knew you when you entered here. I did but play this little jest with hope to surprise you into some display of your art, as not doubting you would blast the guards with occult fires, consuming them to ashes on the spot, a marvel much beyond mine own ability, yet one which I have long been childishly curious to see."

The guards were less curious, and got out as soon as they got permission.

Chapter XVII

A ROYAL BANQUET

MADAME, SEEING ME pacific and unresentful, no doubt judged that I was deceived by her excuse; for her fright dissolved away, and she was soon so importunate to have me give an exhibition and kill somebody, that the thing grew to be embarrassing. However, to my relief she was presently interrupted by the call to prayers. I will say this much for the nobility: that, tyrannical, murderous, rapacious, and morally rotten as they were, they were deeply and enthusiastically religious. Nothing could divert them from the regular and faithful performance of the pieties enjoined by the Church. More than once I had seen a noble who had gotten his enemy at a disadvantage, stop to pray before cutting his throat; more than once I had seen a noble, after ambushing and despatching his enemy, retire to the nearest wayside shrine and humbly give thanks, without even waiting to rob the body. There was to be nothing finer or sweeter in the life of even Benvenuto Cellini, that rough-hewn saint, ten centuries later. All the nobles of Britain, with their families, attended divine service morning and night daily, in their private chapels, and even the worst of them had family worship five or six times a day besides. The credit of this belonged entirely to the Church. Although I was no friend to that Catholic Church, I was obliged to admit this. And often, in spite of me, I found myself saying, "What would this country be without the Church?"

After prayers we had dinner in a great banqueting-hall which was lighted by hundreds of grease-jets, and everything was as fine and lavish and rudely splendid as might become the royal degree of the hosts. At the head of the hall, on a dais, was the table of the king, queen, and their son, Prince Uwaine. Stretching down the hall from this, was the general table, on the floor. At this, above the salt, sat the visiting nobles and the grown members of their families, of both sexes—the resident Court, in effect—sixty-one persons; below the salt sat minor officers of the household, with their principal subordinates: altogether a hundred and eighteen persons sitting, and about as many liveried servants standing behind their chairs, or serving in one capacity or another. It was a very fine show. In a gallery a band with cymbals, horns, harps, and other horrors, opened the proceedings with what seemed to be the crude first-draft or original agony of the wail known to later centuries as "In the Sweet Bye and Bye." It was new, and ought to have been rehearsed a little more. For some reason or other the queen had the composer hanged, after dinner.

After this music, the priest who stood behind the royal table said a noble long grace in ostensible Latin. Then the battalion of waiters broke away from their posts, and darted, rushed, flew, fetched and carried, and the mighty feeding began; no words anywhere, but absorbing attention to business. The rows of chops opened and shut in vast unison, and the sound of it was like to the muffled burr of subterranean machinery.

The havoc continued an hour and a half, and unimaginable was the destruction of substantials. Of the chief feature of the feast—the huge wild boar that lay stretched out so portly and imposing at the start—nothing was left but the semblance of a hoop-skirt; and he was but the type and symbol of what had happened to all the other dishes.

With the pastries and so on, the heavy drinking began—and the talk. Gallon after gallon of wine and mead disappeared, and everybody got comfortable, then happy, then sparklingly joyous—both sexes—and by and by pretty noisy. Men told anecdotes that were terrific to hear, but nobody blushed; and when the nub was sprung, the assemblage let go with a horse-laugh that shook the fortress. Ladies answered back with historiettes that would almost have made Queen Margaret of Navarre or even the great Elizabeth of England hide behind a handkerchief, but nobody hid here, but only laughed—howled, you may say. In pretty much all of these dreadful stories, ecclesiastics were the hardy heroes, but that didn't worry the chaplain any, he had his laugh with the rest; more than that, upon invitation he roared out a song which was of as daring a sort as any that was sung that night.

By midnight everybody was fagged out, and sore with laughing; and, as a rule, drunk; some weepingly, some affectionately, some hilariously, some quarrelsomely, some dead and under the table. Of the ladies, the worst spectacle was a lovely young duchess, whose wedding-eve this was; and indeed she was a spectacle, sure enough. Just as she was she could have sat in advance for the portrait of the young daughter of the Regent d'Orleans, at the famous dinner whence she was carried, foul-mouthed, intoxicated, and helpless, to her bed, in the lost and lamented days of the Ancient Régime.

Suddenly, even while the priest was lifting his hands, and all conscious heads were bowed in reverent expectation of the coming blessing, there appeared under the arch of the far-off door at the bottom of the hall an old and bent and white-haired lady, leaning upon a crutch-stick; and she lifted the stick and pointed it toward the queen and cried out:

"The wrath and curse of God fall upon you, woman without pity, who have slain mine innocent grandchild and made desolate this old heart that had nor chick, nor friend nor stay nor comfort in all this world but him!"

Everybody crossed himself in a grisly fright, for a curse was an awful thing to those people; but the queen rose up majestic, with the death-light in her eye, and flung back this ruthless command:

"Lay hands on her! To the stake with her!"

The guards left their posts to obey. It was a shame; it was a cruel thing to see. What could be done? Sandy gave me a look; I knew she had another inspiration. I said:

"Do what you choose."

She was up and facing toward the queen in a moment. She indicated me, and said:

"Madame, *he* saith this may not be. Recall the commandment, or he will dissolve the castle and it shall vanish away like the instable fabric of a dream!"

Confound it, what a crazy contract to pledge a person to! What if the queen—

But my consternation subsided there, and my panic passed off; for the queen, all in a collapse, made no show of resistance but gave a countermanding sign and sunk into her seat. When she reached it she was sober. So were many of the others. The assemblage rose, whiffed ceremony to the winds, and rushed for the door like a mob; overturning chairs, smashing crockery, tugging, struggling, shouldering, crowding—anything to get out before I should change my mind and puff the castle into the measureless dim vacancies of space. Well, well, well, they *were* a superstitious lot. It is all a body can do to conceive of it.

The poor queen was so scared and humbled that she was even afraid to hang the composer without first consulting me. I was very sorry for her—indeed, any one would have been, for she was really suffering; so I was willing to do anything that was reasonable, and had no desire to carry things to wanton extremities. I therefore considered the matter thoughtfully, and ended by having the musicians ordered into our presence to play that Sweet Bye and Bye again, which they did. Then I saw that she was right, and gave her permission to hang the whole band. This little relaxation of sternness had a good effect upon the queen. A statesman gains little by the arbitrary exercise of iron-clad authority upon all occasions that offer, for this wounds the just pride of his subordinates, and thus tends to undermine his strength. A little concession, now and then, where it can do no harm, is the wiser policy.

Now that the queen was at ease in her mind once more, and measurably happy, her wine naturally began to assert itself again, and it got a little the start of her. I mean it set her music going—her silver bell of a tongue. Dear me, she was a master talker. It would not become me to suggest that it was pretty late and that I was a tired man and very sleepy. I wished I had gone off to bed when I had the chance. Now I must stick it out; there was no other way. So she tinkled along and along, in the otherwise profound and ghostly hush of the sleeping castle, until by and by there came, as if from deep down under us, a far-away sound, as of a muffled shriek—with an expression of agony about it that made my flesh crawl. The queen stopped, and her eyes lighted with pleasure; she tilted her graceful head as a bird does when it listens. The sound bored its way up through the stillness again.

"What is it?" I said.

"It is truly a stubborn soul, and endureth long. It is many hours now."

"Endureth what?"

"The rack. Come—ye shall see a blithe sight. An he yield not his secret now, ye shall see him torn asunder."

What a silky smooth hellion she was; and so composed and serene, when the cords all down my legs were hurting in sympathy with that man's pain. Conducted by mailed guards bearing flaring torches, we tramped along echoing corridors, and down stone stairways dank and dripping, and smelling of mold and ages of imprisoned night—a chill, uncanny journey and a long one, and not made the shorter or the cheerier by the sorceress's talk, which was about this sufferer and his crime. He had been accused by an anonymous informer, of having killed a stag in the royal preserves. I said:

"Anonymous testimony isn't just the right thing, your Highness. It were fairer to confront the accused with the accuser."

"I had not thought of that, it being but of small consequence. But an I would, I could not, for that the accuser came masked by night, and told the forester, and straightway got him hence again, and so the forester knoweth him not."

"Then is this Unknown the only person who saw the stag killed?"

"Marry, *no* man *saw* the killing, but this Unknown saw this hardy wretch near to the spot where the stag lay, and came with right loyal zeal and betrayed him to the forester."

"So the Unknown was near the dead stag, too? Isn't it just possible that he did the killing himself? His loyal zeal—in a mask—looks just a shade suspicious. But what is your Highness's idea for racking the prisoner? Where is the profit?"

"He will not confess, else; and then were his soul lost. For his crime his life is forfeited by the law—and of a surety will I see that he payeth it!—but it were peril to my own soul to let him die unconfessed and unabsolved. Nay, I were a fool to fling me into hell for *his* accommodation."

"But, your Highness, suppose he has nothing to confess?"

"As to that, we shall see, anon. An I rack him to death and he confess not, it will peradventure show that he had indeed naught to confess—ye will grant that that is sooth? Then shall I not be damned for an unconfessed man that had naught to confess—wherefore, I shall be safe."

It was the stubborn unreasoning of the time. It was useless to argue with her. Arguments have no chance against petrified training; they wear it as little as the waves wear a cliff. And her training was everybody's. The brightest intellect in the land would not have been able to see that her position was defective.

As we entered the rack-cell I caught a picture that will not go from me; I wish it would. A native young giant of thirty or thereabouts lay stretched upon the frame on his back, with his wrists and ankles tied to ropes which led over windlasses at either end. There was no color in him; his features were contorted and set, and sweat-drops stood upon his forehead. A priest bent over him on each side; the executioner stood by; guards were on duty; smoking torches stood in sockets along the walls; in a corner crouched a poor young creature, her face drawn with anguish, a half-wild and hunted look in her eyes, and in her lap lay a little child asleep. Just as we stepped across the threshold the executioner gave his machine a slight turn, which wrung a cry from both the prisoner and the woman; but I shouted, and the executioner released the strain without waiting to see who spoke. I could not let this horror go on; it would have killed me to see it. I asked the queen to let me clear the place and speak to the prisoner privately; and when she was going to object I spoke in a low voice and said I did not want to make a scene before her servants, but I must have my way; for I was King Arthur's representative, and was speaking in his name. She saw she had to yield. I asked her to indorse me to these people, and then leave me. It was not pleasant for her, but she took the pill; and even went further than I was meaning to require. I only wanted the backing of her own authority; but she said:

"Ye will do in all things as this lord shall command. It is The Boss."

It was certainly a good word to conjure with: you could see it by the squirming of these rats. The queen's guards fell into line, and she and they marched away, with their torch-bearers, and woke the echoes of the cavernous tunnels with the measured beat of their retreating footfalls. I had the prisoner taken from the rack and placed upon his bed, and medicaments applied to his hurts, and wine given him to drink. The woman crept near and looked on, eagerly, lovingly, but timorously—like one who fears a repulse; indeed, she tried furtively to touch the man's forehead, and jumped back the picture of fright, when I turned unconsciously toward her. It was pitiful to see.

"Lord," I said, "stroke him, lass, if you want to. Do anything you're a mind to; don't mind me."

Why, her eyes were as grateful as an animal's, when you do it a kindness that it understands. The baby was out of her way and she had her cheek against the man's in a minute, and her hands fondling his hair, and her happy tears running down. The man revived, and caressed his wife with his eyes, which was all he could do. I judged I might clear the den, now, and I did; cleared it of all but the family and myself. Then I said:

"Now, my friend, tell me your side of this matter; I know the other side."

The man moved his head in sign of refusal. But the woman looked pleased—as it seemed to me—pleased with my suggestion. I went on:

"You know of me?"

"Yes. All do, in Arthur's realms."

"If my reputation has come to you right and straight, you should not be afraid to speak."

The woman broke in, eagerly:

"Ah, fair my lord, do thou persuade him! Thou canst an thou wilt. Ah, he suffereth so; and it is for me—for *me!* And how can I bear it? I would I might see him die—a sweet, swift death; oh, my Hugo, I cannot bear this one!''

And she fell to sobbing and groveling about my feet, and still imploring. Imploring what? The man's death? I could not quite get the bearings of the thing. But Hugo interrupted her and said:

"Peace! Ye wit not what ye ask. Shall I starve whom I love, to win a gentle death? I wend thou knewest me better.''

"Well,'' I said, "I can't quite make this out. It is a puzzle. Now—''

"An, dear my lord, an ye will but persuade him! Consider how these his tortures wound me! Oh, and he will not speak!—whereas, the healing, the solace that lie in a blessed swift death—''

"What *are* you maundering about? He's going out from here a free man and whole—he's not going to die.''

The man's white face lit up, and the woman flung herself at me in a most surprising explosion of joy, and cried out:

"He is saved!—for it is the king's word by the mouth of the king's servant—Arthur, the king whose word is gold!''

"Well, then you do believe I can be trusted, after all. Why didn't you before?''

"Who doubted? Not I, indeed; and not she.''

"Well, why wouldn't you tell me your story, then?''

"Ye had made no promise; else had it been otherwise.''

"I see, I see. . . . And yet I believe I don't quite see, after all. You stood the torture and refused to confess; which shows plain enough to even the dullest understanding that you had nothing to confess—''

"*I,* my lord? How so? It was I that killed the deer!''

"You *did?* Oh, dear, this is the most mixed-up business that ever—''

"Dear lord, I begged him on my knees to confess. but—''

"You *did!* It gets thicker and thicker. What did you want him to do that for?''

"Sith it would bring him a quick death and save him all this cruel pain.''

"Well—yes, there is reason in that. But *he* didn't want the quick death.''

"He? Why, of a surety he *did.*''

"Well, then, why in the world *didn't* he confess?''

"Ah, sweet sir, and leave my wife and chick without bread and shelter?''

"Oh, heart of gold, now I see it! The bitter law takes the convicted man's estate and beggars his widow and his orphans. They could torture you to death, but without conviction or confession they could not rob your wife and baby. You stood by them like a man; and *you*—true wife and true woman that you are—you would have bought him release from torture at cost to yourself of slow starvation and death—well, it humbles a body to think what your sex can do when it comes to self-sacrifice. I'll book you both for my colony; you'll like it there; it's a Factory where I'm going to turn groping and grubbing automata into *men.*''

Chapter XVIII

IN THE QUEEN'S DUNGEONS

WELL, I ARRANGED all that; and I had the man sent to his home. I had a great desire to rack the executioner; not because he was a good, painstaking and paingiving official—for surely it was not to his discredit that he performed his functions well—but to pay him back for wantonly cuffing and otherwise distressing that young woman. The priests told me about this, and were generously hot to have him punished. Something of this disagreeable sort was turning up every now and then. I mean, episodes that showed that not all priests were frauds and self-seekers, but that many, even the great majority, of these that were down on the ground among the common people, were sincere and right-hearted, and devoted to the alleviation of human troubles and sufferings. Well, it was a thing which could not be helped, so I seldom fretted about it, and never many minutes at a time; it has never been my way to bother much about things which you can't cure. But I did not like it, for it was just the sort of thing to keep people reconciled to an Established Church. We *must* have a religion—it goes without saying—but my idea is, to have it cut up into forty free sects, so that they will police each other, as had been the case in the United States in my time. Concentration of power in a political machine is bad; and an Established Church is only a political machine; it was invented for that; it is nursed, cradled, preserved for that; it is an enemy to human liberty, and does no good which it could not better do in a split-up and scattered condition. That wasn't law; it wasn't gospel: it was only an opinion—my opinion, and I was only a man, one man: so it wasn't worth any more than the pope's—or any less, for that matter.

Well, I couldn't rack the executioner, neither would I overlook the just complaint of the priests. The man must be punished somehow or other, so I degraded him from his office and made him leader of the band—the new one that was to be started. He begged hard, and said he couldn't play—a plausible excuse, but too thin; there wasn't a musician in the country that could.

The queen was a good deal outraged, next morning, when she found she was going to have neither Hugo's life nor his property. But I told her she must bear this cross; that while by law and custom she certainly was entitled to both the man's life and his property, there were extenuating circumstances, and so in Arthur the king's name I had pardoned him. The deer was ravaging the man's fields, and he had killed it in sudden passion, and not for gain; and he had carried it into the royal forest in the hope that that might make detection of the misdoer impossible. Confound her, I couldn't make her see that sudden passion is an extenuating circumstance in the killing of venison—or of a person—so I gave it up and let her sulk it out. I *did* think I was going to make her see it by remarking that her own sudden passion in the case of the page modified that crime.

"Crime!" she exclaimed, "How thou talkest! Crime, forsooth! Man, I am going to *pay* for him!"

Oh, it was no use to waste sense on her. Training—training is everything; training is all there is *to* a person. We speak of nature; it is folly; there is no

557

such thing as nature; what we call by that misleading name is merely heredity and training. We have no thoughts of our own, no opinions of our own; they are transmitted to us, trained into us. All that is original in us, and therefore fairly creditable or discreditable to us, can be covered up and hidden by the point of a cambric needle, all the rest being atoms contributed by, and inherited from, a procession of ancestors that stretches back a billion years to the Adam-clam or grasshopper or monkey from whom our race has been so tediously and ostentatiously and unprofitably developed. And as for me, all that I think about in this plodding sad pilgrimage, this pathetic drift between the eternities, is to look out and humbly live a pure and high and blameless life, and save that one microscopic atom in me that is truly *me:* the rest may land in Sheol and welcome for all I care.

No, confound her, her intellect was good, she had brains enough, but her training made her an ass—that is, from a many-centuries-later point of view. To kill the page was no crime—it was her right; and upon her right she stood, serenely and unconscious of offense. She was a result of generations of training in the unexamined and unassailed belief that the law which permitted her to kill a subject when she chose was a perfectly right and righteous one.

Well, we must give even Satan his due. She deserved a compliment for one thing; and I tried to pay it, but the words stuck in my throat. She had a right to kill the boy, but she was in no wise obliged to pay for him. That was law for some other people, but not for her. She knew quite well that she was doing a large and generous thing to pay for that lad, and that I ought in common fairness to come out with something handsome about it, but I couldn't—my mouth refused. I couldn't help seeing, in my fancy, that poor old grandma with the broken heart, and that fair young creature lying butchered, his little silken pomps and vanities laced with his golden blood. How could she *pay* for him! *Whom* could she pay? And so, well knowing that this woman, trained as she had been, deserved praise, even adulation, I was yet not able to utter it, trained as *I* had been. The best I could do was to fish up a compliment from outside, so to speak—and the pity of it was, that it was true:

"Madame, your people will adore you for this."

Quite true, but I meant to hang her for it some day, if I lived. Some of those laws were too bad, altogether too bad. A master might kill his slave for nothing: for mere spite, malice, or to pass the time—just as we have seen that the crowned head could do it with *his* slave, that is to say, anybody. A gentleman could kill a free commoner, and pay for him—cash or garden-truck. A noble could kill a noble without expense, as far as the law was concerned, but reprisals in kind were to be expected. *Any*body could kill *some*body, except the commoner and the slave; these had no privileges. If they killed, it was murder, and the law wouldn't stand murder. It made short work of the experimenter—and of his family, too, if he murdered somebody who belonged up among the ornamental ranks. If a commoner gave a noble even so much as a Damiens-scratch which didn't kill or even hurt, he got Damiens' dose for it just the same; they pulled him to rags and tatters with horses, and all the world came to see the show, and crack jokes, and have a good time; and some of the performances of the best people present were as tough, and as properly unprintable, as any that have been printed by the pleasant Casanova in his chapter about the dismemberment of Louis XV.'s poor awkward enemy.

I had had enough of this grisly place by this time, and wanted to leave, but

I couldn't, because I had something on my mind that my conscience kept prodding me about, and wouldn't let me forget. If I had the remaking of man, he wouldn't have any conscience. It is one of the most disagreeable things connected with a person; and although it certainly does a great deal of good, it cannot be said to pay, in the long run; it would be much better to have less good and more comfort. Still, this is only my opinion, and I am only one man; others, with less experience, may think differently. They have a right to their view, I only stand to this; I have noticed my conscience for many years, and I know it is more trouble and bother to me than anything else I started with. I suppose that in the beginning I prized it, because we prize anything that is ours; and yet how foolish it was to think so. If we look at it in another way, we see how absurd it is: if I had an anvil in me would I prize it? Of course not. And yet when you come to think, there is no real difference between a conscience and an anvil— I mean for comfort. I have noticed it a thousand times. And you could dissolve an anvil with acids, when you couldn't stand it any longer; but there isn't any way that you can work off a conscience—at least so it will stay worked off; not that I know of, anyway.

There was something I wanted to do before leaving, but it was a disagreeable matter, and I hated to go at it. Well, it bothered me all the morning. I could have mentioned it to the old king, but what would be the use?—he was but an extinct volcano; he had been active in his time, but his fire was out, this good while, he was only a stately ashpile now; gentle enough, and kindly enough for my purpose, without doubt, but not usable. He was nothing, this so-called king: the queen was the only power there. And she was a Vesuvius. As a favor, she might consent to warm a flock of sparrows for you, but then she might take that very opportunity to turn herself loose and bury a city. However, I reflected that as often as any other way, when you are expecting the worst, you get something that is not so bad, after all.

So I braced up and placed my matter before her royal Highness. I said I had been having a general jail-delivery at Camelot and among neighboring castles, and with her permission I would like to examine her collection, her bric-à-brac— that is to say, her prisoners. She resisted; but I was expecting that. But she finally consented. I was expecting that, too, but not so soon. That about ended my discomfort. She called her guards and torches, and we went down into the dungeons. These were down under the castle's foundations, and mainly were small cells hollowed out of the living rock. Some of these cells had no light at all. In one of them was a woman, in foul rags, who sat on the ground, and would not answer a question or speak a word, but only looked up at us once or twice, through a cobweb of tangled hair, as if to see what casual thing it might be that was disturbing with sound and light the meaningless dull dream that was become her life; after that, she sat bowed, with her dirtcaked fingers idly interlocked in her lap, and gave no further sign. This poor rack of bones was a woman of middle age, apparently; but only apparently; she had been there nine years, and was eighteen when she entered. She was a commoner, and had been sent here on her bridal night by Sir Breuse Sance Pité, a neighboring lord whose vassal her father was, and to which said lord she had refused what has since been called *le droit du seigneur;* and, moreover, had opposed violence to violence and spilt half a gill of his almost sacred blood. The young husband had interfered at that point, believing the bride's life in danger, and had flung the noble out into the midst of the humble and trembling wedding guests, in the parlor, and left him there astonished at this strange treatment, and implacably embittered against both bride and groom. The said lord being cramped for dungeon-room had asked the queen to accommodate his two criminals, and here in her bastile they had been ever since; hither, indeed, they had come before their crime was an hour old, and had never seen each other since. Here they were, kerneled like toads in the same rock; they had passed nine pitch-dark years within fifty feet of each other, yet neither knew whether the other was alive or not. All the first years, their only question had been—asked with beseechings and tears that might have moved stones, in time, perhaps, but hearts are not stones: "Is he alive?" "Is she alive?" But they had never got an answer; and at last that question was not asked any more—or any other.

I wanted to see the man, after hearing all this. He was thirty-four years old, and looked sixty. He sat upon a squared block of stone, with his head bent down, his forearms resting on his knees, his long hair hanging like a fringe before his face, and he was muttering to himself. He raised his chin and looked us slowly over, in a listless dull way, blinking with the distress of the torchlight, then dropped his head and fell to muttering again and took no further notice of us. There were some pathetically suggestive dumb witnesses present. On his wrists and ankles were cicatrices, old smooth scars, and fastened to the stone on which he sat was a chain with manacles and fetters attached; but this apparatus lay idle on the ground, and was thick with rust. Chains cease to be needed after the spirit has gone out of a prisoner.

I could not rouse the man; so I said we would take him to her, and see—to the bride who was the fairest thing in the earth to him, once—roses, pearls, and dew made flesh, for him; a wonder-work, the master-work of nature: with eyes like no other eyes, and voice like no other voice, and a freshness, and lithe young grace, and beauty, that belonged properly to the creatures of dreams— as he thought—and to no other. The sight of her would set his stagnant blood leaping; the sight of her—

But it was a disappointment. They sat together on the ground and looked dimly wondering into each other's faces awhile, with a sort of weak animal curiosity; then forgot each other's presence, and dropped their eyes, and you saw that they were away again and wandering in some far land of dreams and shadows that we know nothing about.

I had them taken out and sent to their friends. The queen did not like it much. Not that she felt any personal interest in the matter, but she thought it disrespectful to Sir Breuse Sance Pité. However, I assured her that if he found he couldn't stand it I would fix him so that he could.

I set forty-seven prisoners loose out of those awful rat-holes, and left only one in captivity. He was a lord, and had killed another lord, a sort of kinsman of the queen. That other lord had ambushed him to assassinate him, but this fellow had got the best of him and cut his throat. However, it was not for that that I left him jailed, but for maliciously destroying the only public well in one of his wretched villages. The queen was bound to hang him for killing her kinsman, but I would not allow it: it was no crime to kill an assassin. But I said I was willing to let her hang him for destroying the well; so she concluded to put up with that, as it was better than nothing.

Dear me, for what trifling offenses the most of those forty-seven men and women were shut up there! Indeed, some were there for no distinct offense at all, but only to gratify somebody's spite; and not always the queen's by any means, but a friend's. The newest prisoner's crime was a mere remark which he had made. He said he believed that men were about all alike, and one man as good as another, barring clothes. He said he believed that if you were to strip the nation naked and send a stranger through the crowd, he couldn't tell the king from a quack doctor, nor a duke from a hotel clerk. Apparently, here was a man whose brains had not been reduced to an ineffectual mush by idiotic training. I set him loose and sent him to the Factory.

Some of the cells carved in the living rock were just behind the face of the precipice, and in each of these an arrow-slit had been pierced outward to the daylight, and so the captive had a thin ray from the blessed sun for his comfort. The case of one of these poor fellows was particularly hard. From his dusky swallow's hole high up in that vast wall of native rock he could peer out through the arrow-slit and see his own home off yonder in the valley; and for twenty-two years he had watched it, with heartache and longing, through that crack. He could see the lights shine there at night, and in the daytime he could see figures go in and come out—his wife and children, some of them, no doubt, though he could not make out at that distance. In the course of years he noted festivities there, and tried to rejoice, and wondered if they were weddings or what they might be. And he noted funerals; and they wrung his heart. He could make out the coffin, but he could not determine its size, and so could not tell whether it was wife or child. He could see the procession form, with priests and mourners, and move solemnly away, bearing the secret with them. He had left behind him five children and a wife; and in nineteen years he had seen five funerals issue, and none of them humble enough in pomp to denote a servant. So he had lost five of his treasures; there must still be one remaining—one now infinitely, unspeakably precious—but *which* one? wife, or child? That was the question that tortured him, by night and by day, asleep and awake. Well, to have an interest, of some sort, and half a ray of light, when you are in a dungeon, is a great support to the body and preserver of the intellect. This man was in pretty good condition yet. By the time he had finished telling me his distressful tale, I was in the same state of mind that you would have been in yourself, if you have got average human curiosity; that is to say, I was as burning up as he was to find out which member of the family it was that was left. So I took him over home myself; and an amazing kind of a surprise party it was, too—typhoons and cyclones of frantic joy, and whole Niagaras of happy tears; and by George! we found the aforetime young matron graying toward the imminent verge of her half-century, and the babies all men and women, and some of them married and experimenting familywise themselves—for not a soul of the tribe was dead! Conceive of the ingenious devilishness of that queen: she had a special hatred for this prisoner, and she had *invented* all those funerals herself, to scorch his heart with; and the sublimest stroke of genius of the whole thing was leaving the family invoice a funeral *short,* so as to let him wear his poor old soul out guessing.

But for me, he never would have got out. Morgan le Fay hated him with her whole heart, and she never would have softened toward him. And yet his crime was committed more in thoughtlessness than deliberate depravity. He had said she had red hair. Well, she had; but that was no way to speak of it. When red-headed people are above a certain social grade their hair is auburn.

Consider it: among these forty-seven captives there were five whose names, offenses, and dates of incarceration were no longer known! One woman and four men—all bent, and wrinkled, and mind-extinguished patriarchs. They themselves had long ago forgotten these details; at any rate, they had mere vague theories about them, nothing definite and nothing that they repeated twice in the same way. The succession of priests whose office it had been to pray daily with the captives and remind them that God had put them there, for some wise purpose or other, and teach them that patience, humbleness, and submission to oppression was what He loved to see in parties of a subordinate rank, had traditions about these poor old human ruins, but nothing more. These traditions went but little way, for they concerned the length of the incarceration only, and not the names of the offenses. And even by the help of tradition the only thing that could be proven was that none of the five had seen daylight for thirty-five years: how much longer this privation had lasted was not guessable. The king and the queen knew nothing about these poor creatures, except that they were heirlooms, assets inherited, along with the throne, from the former firm. Nothing of their history had been transmitted with their persons, and so the inheriting owners had considered them of no value, and had felt no interest in them. I said to the queen:

"Then why in the world didn't you set them free?"

The question was a puzzler. She didn't know *why* she hadn't; the thing had never come up in her mind. So here she was, forecasting the veritable history of future prisoners of the Castle d'If, without knowing it. It seemed plain to me now, that with her training, those inherited prisoners were merely property—nothing more, nothing less. Well, when we inherit property, it does not occur to us to throw it away, even when we do not value it.

When I brought my procession of human bats up into the open world and the glare of the afternoon sun—previously blindfolding them, in charity for eyes so long untortured by light—they were a spectacle to look at. Skeletons, scarecrows, goblins, pathetic frights, every one; legitimatest possible children of Monarchy by the Grace of God and the Established Church. I muttered absently:

· "I *wish* I could photograph them!"

You have seen that kind of people who will never let on that they don't know the meaning of a new big word. The more ignorant they are, the more pitifully certain they are to pretend you haven't shot over their heads. The queen was just one of that sort, and was always making the stupidest blunders by reason of it. She hesitated a moment; then her face brightened up with sudden comprehension, and she said she would do it for me.

I thought to myself: She? why what can she know about photography? But it was a poor time to be thinking. When I looked around, she was moving on the procession with an ax!

Well, she certainly was a curious one, was Morgan le Fay. I have seen a good many kinds of women in my time, but she laid over them all for variety. And how sharply characteristic of her this episode was. She had no more idea than a horse of how to photograph a procession; but being in doubt, it was just like her to try to do it with an ax.

Chapter XIX

KNIGHT-ERRANTRY AS A TRADE

SANDY AND I were on the road again, next morning, bright and early. It was *so* good to open up one's lungs and take in whole luscious barrelfuls of the blessed God's untainted, dew-fashioned, woodland-scented air once more, after suffocating body and mind for two days and nights in the moral and physical stenches of that intolerable old buzzard-roost! I mean, for me: of course the place was all right and agreeable enough for Sandy, for she had been used to high life all her days.

Poor girl, her jaws had had a wearisome rest now for a while, and I was expecting to get the consequences. I was right; but she had stood by me most helpfully in the castle, and had mightily supported and reinforced me with gigantic foolishnesses which were worth more for the occasion than wisdoms double their size; so I thought she had earned a right to work her mill for a while, if she wanted to, and I felt not a pang when she started it up:

"Now turn we unto Sir Marhaus that rode with the damsel of thirty winter of age southward—"

"Are you going to see if you can work up another half-stretch on the trail of the cowboys, Sandy?"

"Even so, fair my lord."

"Go ahead, then. I won't interrupt this time, if I can help it. Begin over again; start fair, and shake out all your reefs, and I will load my pipe and give good attention."

"Now turn we unto Sir Marhaus that rode with the damsel of thirty winter of age southward. And so they came into a deep forest, and by fortune they were nighted, and rode along in a deep way, and at the last they came into a courtelage where abode the duke of South Marches, and there they asked harbor. And on the morn the duke sent unto Sir Marhaus, and bad him make him ready. And so Sir Marhaus arose and armed him, and there was a mass sung afore him, and he brake his fast, and so mounted on horseback in the court of the castle, there they should do the battle. So there was the duke already on horseback, clean-armed, and his six sons by him, and every each had a spear in his hand, and so they encountered, whereas the duke and his two sons brake their spears upon him, but Sir Marhaus held up his spear and touched none of them. Then came the four sons by couples, and two of them brake their spears, and so did the other two. And all this while Sir Marhaus touched them not. Then Sir Marhaus ran to the duke, and smote him with his spear that horse and man fell to the earth. And so he served his sons. And then Sir Marhaus alight down, and bad the duke yield him or else he would slay him. And then some of his sons recovered, and would have set upon Sir Marhaus. Then Sir Marhaus said to the duke, Cease thy sons, or else I will do the uttermost to you all. When the duke saw he might not escape the death, he cried to his sons, and charged them to yield them to Sir Marhaus. And they kneeled all down and put the pommels of their swords to the knight, and so he received them. And then they holp up their father, and so by their common assent promised unto Sir Marhaus never to be foes unto King Arthur, and thereupon at Whitsuntide after, to come he and his sons, and put them in the king's grace.[1]

"Even so standeth the history, fair Sir Boss. Now ye shall wit that that very duke and his six sons are they whom but few days past you also did overcome and send to Arthur's court!"

"Why, Sandy, you can't mean it!"

"An I speak not sooth, let it be the worse for me."

"Well, well, well—now who would ever have thought it? One whole duke and six dukelets; why, Sandy, it was an elegant haul. Knight-errantry is a most chuckle-headed trade, and it is tedious hard work, too, but I begin to see that there *is* money in it, after all, if you have luck. Not that I would ever engage in it as a business; for I wouldn't. No sound and legitimate business can be established on a basis of speculation. A successful whirl in the knight-errantry line—now what is it when you blow away the nonsense and come down to the cold facts? It's just a corner in pork, that's all, and you can't make anything else out of it. You're rich—yes—suddenly rich—for about a day, maybe a week; then somebody corners the market on *you,* and down goes your bucketshop; ain't that so, Sandy?"

"Whethersoever it be that my mind miscarrieth, bewraying simple language in such sort that the words do seem to come endlong and overthwart—"

"There's no use in beating about the bush and trying to get around it that way, Sandy, it's *so,* just as I say. I *know* it's so. And, moreover, when you come right down to the bed-rock, knight-errantry is *worse* than pork; for whatever happens, the pork's left, and so somebody's benefited anyway; but when the market breaks, in a knight-errantry whirl, and every knight in the pool passes in his checks, what have you got for assets? Just a rubbish-pile of battered corpses and a barrel or two of busted hardware. Can you call *those* assets? Give me pork, every time. Am I right?"

"An, peradventure my head being distraught by the manifold matters whereunto the confusions of these but late adventured haps and fortunings whereby not I alone nor you alone, but every each of us, meseemeth—"

"No, it's not your head, Sandy. Your head's all right, as far as it goes, but you don't know business; that's where the trouble is. It unfits you to argue about business, and you're wrong to be always trying. However, that aside, it was a good haul, anyway, and will breed a handsome crop of reputation in Arthur's court. And speaking of the cowboys, what a curious country this is for women and men that never get old. Now there's Morgan le Fay, as fresh and young as a Vassar pullet, to all appearances, and here is this old duke of the South Marches still slashing away with sword and lance at his time of life, after raising such a family as he has raised. As I understand it, Sir Gawaine killed seven of his sons, and still he had six left for Sir Marhaus and me to take into camp. And then there was that damsel of sixty winter of age still excursioning around in her frosty bloom— How old are you, Sandy?"

It was the first time I ever struck a still place in her. The mill had shut down for repairs, or something.

---

[1] The story is borrowed, language and all, from the *Morte d'Arthur.*—M. T.

Chapter XX

THE OGRE'S CASTLE

BETWEEN SIX AND nine we made ten miles, which was plenty for a horse carrying triple—man, woman, and armor; then we stopped for a long nooning under some trees by a limpid brook.

Right so came by and by a knight riding; and as he drew near he made dolorous moan, and by the words of it I perceived that he was cursing and swearing; yet nevertheless was I glad of his coming, for that I saw he bore a bulletin-board whereon in letters all of shining gold was writ:

"USE PETERSON'S PROPHYLACTIC TOOTH-BRUSH—ALL THE GO."

I was glad of his coming, for even by this token I knew him for knight of mine. It was Sir Madok de la Montaine, a burly great fellow whose chief distinction was that he had come within an ace of sending Sir Launcelot down over his horse-tail once. He was never long in a stranger's presence without finding some pretext or other to let out that great fact. But there was another fact of nearly the same size, which he never pushed upon anybody unasked, and yet never withheld when asked: that was, that the reason he didn't quite succeed was, that he was interrupted and sent down over horse-tail himself. This innocent vast lubber did not see any particular difference between the two facts. I liked him, for he was earnest in his work, and very valuable. And he was so fine to look at, with his broad mailed shoulders, and the grand leonine set of his plumed head, and his big shield with its quaint device of a gauntleted hand clutching a prophylactic tooth-brush, with motto: "*Try Noyoudont.*" This was a tooth-wash that I was introducing.

He was aweary, he said, and indeed he looked it; but he would not alight. He said he was after the stove-polish man; and with this he broke out cursing and swearing anew. The bulletin-boarder referred to was Sir Ossaise of Surluse, a brave knight, and of considerable celebrity on account of his having tried conclusions in a tournament once, with no less a Mogul than Sir Gaheris himself—although not successfully. He was of a light and laughing disposition, and to him nothing in this world was serious. It was for this reason that I had chosen him to work up a stove-polish sentiment. There were no stoves yet, and so there could be nothing serious about stove-polish. All that the agent needed to do was to deftly and by degrees prepare the public for the great change, and have them established in predilections toward neatness against the time when the stove should appear upon the stage.

Sir Madok was very bitter, and brake out anew with cursings. He said he had cursed his soul to rags; and yet he would not get down from his horse, neither would he take any rest, or listen to any comfort, until he should have found Sir Ossaise and settled this account. It appeared, by what I could piece together of the unprofane fragments of his statement, that he had chanced upon Sir Ossaise at dawn of the morning, and been told that if he would make a short cut across the fields and swamps and broken hills and glades, he could head off a company of travelers who would be rare customers for prophylactics and tooth-wash. With characteristic zeal Sir Madok had plunged away at once upon this quest, and after three hours of awful cross-lot riding had overhauled his game. And behold, it was the five patriarchs that had been released from the dungeons the evening before! Poor old creatures, it was all of twenty years since any one of them had known what it was to be equipped with any remaining snag or remnant of a tooth.

"Blank-blank-blank him," said Sir Madok, "an I do not stove-polish him an I may find him, leave it to me; for never no knight that hight Ossaise or aught else may do me this disservice and bide on live, an I may find him, the which I have thereunto sworn a great oath this day."

And with these words and others, he lightly took his spear and gat him thence. In the middle of the afternoon we came upon one of those very patriarchs ourselves, in the edge of a poor village. He was basking in the love of relatives and friends whom he had not seen for fifty years; and about him and caressing him were also descendants of his own body whom he had never seen at all till now; but to him these were all strangers, his memory was gone, his mind was stagnant. It seemed incredible that a man could outlast half a century shut up in a dark hole like a rat, but here were his old wife and some old comrades to testify to it. They could remember him as he was in the freshness and strength of his young manhood, when he kissed his child and delivered it to its mother's hands and went away into that long oblivion. The people at the castle could not tell within half a generation the length of time the man had been shut up there for his unrecorded and forgotten offense; but this old wife knew; and so did her old child, who stood there among her married sons and daughters trying to realize a father who had been to her a name, a thought, a formless image, a tradition, all her life, and now was suddenly concreted into actual flesh and blood and set before her face.

It was a curious situation; yet it is not on that account that I have made room for it here, but on account of a thing which seemed to me still more curious. To wit, that this dreadful matter brought from these downtrodden people no outburst of rage against these oppressors. They had been heritors and subjects of cruelty and outrage so long that nothing could have startled them but a kindness. Yes, here was a curious revelation, indeed, of the depth to which this people had been sunk in slavery. Their entire being was reduced to a monotonous dead level of patience, resignation, dumb uncomplaining acceptance of whatever might befall them in this life. Their very imagination was dead. When you can say that of a man, he has struck bottom, I reckon; there is no lower deep for him.

I rather wished I had gone some other road. This was not the sort of experience for a statesman to encounter who was planning out a peaceful revolution in his mind. For it could not help bringing up the unget-aroundable fact that, all gentle cant and philosophizing to the contrary notwithstanding, no people in the world ever did achieve their freedom by goody-goody talk and moral suasion: it being immutable law that all revolutions that will succeed must *begin* in blood, whatever may answer afterward. If history teaches anything, it teaches that. What this folk needed, then, was a Reign of Terror and a guillotine, and I was the wrong man for them.

Two days later, toward noon, Sandy began to show signs of excitement and feverish expectancy. She said we were approaching the ogre's castle. I was surprised into an uncomfortable shock. The object of our quest had gradually dropped out of my mind; this sudden resurrection of it made it seem quite a real and startling thing for a moment, and roused up in me a smart interest. Sandy's excitement increased every moment; and so did mine, for that sort of thing is catching. My heart got to thumping. You can't reason with your heart; it has its own laws, and thumps about things which the intellect scorns. Presently, when Sandy slid from the horse, motioned me to stop, and went creeping stealthily, with her head bent nearly to her knees, toward a row of bushes that bordered a declivity, the thumpings grew stronger and quicker. And they kept it up while she was gaining her ambush and getting her glimpse over the declivity; and also while I was creeping to her side on my knees. Her eyes were burning now, as she pointed with her finger, and said in a panting whisper:

"The castle! The castle! Lo, where it looms!"

What a welcome disappointment I experienced! I said:

"Castle? It is nothing but a pigsty; a pigsty with a wattled fence around it."

She looked surprised and distressed. The animation faded out of her face; and during many moments she was lost in thought and silent. Then:

"It was not enchanted aforetime," she said in a musing fashion, as if to herself. "And how strange is this marvel, and how awful—that to the one perception it is enchanted and dight in a base and shameful aspect; yet to the perception of the other it is not enchanted, hath suffered no change, but stands firm and stately still, girt with its moat and waving its banners in the blue air from its towers. And God shield us, how it pricks the heart to see again these gracious captives, and the sorrow deepened in their sweet faces! We have tarried along, and are to blame."

I saw my cue. The castle was enchanted to *me*, not to her. It would be wasted time to try to argue her out of her delusion, it couldn't be done; I must just humor it. So I said:

"This is a common case—the enchanting of a thing to one eye and leaving it in its proper form to another. You have heard of it before, Sandy, though you haven't happened to experience it. But no harm is done. In fact, it is lucky the way it is. If these ladies were hogs to everybody and to themselves, it would be necessary to break the enchantment, and that might be impossible if one failed to find out the particular process of the enchantment. And hazardous, too; for in attempting a disenchantment without the true key, you are liable to err, and turn your hogs into dogs, and the dogs into cats, the cats into rats, and so on, and end by reducing your materials to nothing finally, or to an odorless gas which you can't follow—which, of course, amounts to the same thing. But here, by good luck, no one's eyes but mine are under the enchantment, and so it is of no consequence to dissolve it. These ladies remain ladies to you, and to themselves, and to everybody else; and at the same time they will suffer in no way from my delusion, for when I know that an ostensible hog is a lady, that is enough for me, I know how to treat her."

"Thanks, oh, sweet my lord, thou talkest like an angel. And I know that thou wilt deliver them, for that thou art minded to great deeds and art as strong a knight of your hands and as brave to will and to do, as any that is on live."

"I will not leave a princess in the sty, Sandy. Are those three yonder that to my disordered eyes are starveling swineherds—"

"The ogres? Are *they* changed also? It is most wonderful. Now am I fearful; for how canst thou strike with sure aim when five of their nine cubits of stature are to thee invisible? Ah, go warily, fair sir; this is a mightier emprise than I wend.''

"You be easy, Sandy. All I need to know is, how *much* of an ogre is invisible; then I know how to locate his vitals. Don't you be afraid, I will make short work of these bunco-steerers. Stay where you are.''

I left Sandy kneeling there, corpse-faced but plucky and hopeful, and rode down to the pigsty, and struck up a trade with the swineherds. I won their gratitude by buying out all the hogs at the lump sum of sixteen pennies, which was rather above latest quotations. I was just in time; for the Church, the lord of the manor, and the rest of the tax-gatherers would have been along next day and swept off pretty much all the stock, leaving the swineherds very short of hogs and Sandy out of princesses. But now the tax people could be paid in cash, and there would be a stake left besides. One of the men had ten children; and he said that last year when a priest came and of his ten pigs took the fattest one for tithes, the wife burst out upon him, and offered him a child and said:

"Thou beast without bowels of mercy, why leave me my child, yet rob me of the wherewithal to feed it?''

How curious. The same thing had happened in the Wales of my day, under this same old Established Church, which was supposed by many to have changed its nature when it changed its disguise.

I sent the three men away, and then opened the sty gate and beckoned Sandy to come—which she did; and not leisurely, but with the rush of a prairie fire. And when I saw her fling herself upon those hogs, with tears of joy running down her cheeks, and strain them to her heart, and kiss them, and caress them, and call them reverently by grand princely names, I was ashamed of her, ashamed of the human race.

We had to drive those hogs home—ten miles; and no ladies were ever more fickle-minded or contrary. They would stay in no road, no path; they broke out through the brush on all sides, and flowed away in all directions, over rocks, and hills, and the roughest places they could find. And they must not be struck, or roughly accosted; Sandy could not bear to see them treated in ways unbecoming their rank. The troublesomest old sow of the lot had to be called my Lady, and your Highness, like the rest. It is annoying and difficult to scour around after hogs, in armor. There was one small countess, with an iron ring in her snout and hardly any hair on her back, that was the devil for perversity. She gave me a race of an hour, over all sorts of country, and then we were right where we had started from, having made not a rod of real progress. I seized her at last by the tail, and brought her along squealing. When I overtook Sandy she was horrified, and said it was in the last degree indelicate to drag a countess by her train.

We got the hogs home just at dark—most of them. The princess Nerovens de Morganore was missing, and two of her ladies in waiting: namely, Miss Angela Bohun, and the Demoiselle Elaine Courtemains, the former of these two being a young black sow with a white star in her forehead, and the latter a brown one with thin legs and a slight limp in the forward shank on the starboard side—a couple of the tryingest blisters to drive that I ever saw. Also among the missing were several mere baronesses—and I wanted them to stay missing; but no, all that sausage-meat had to be found; so servants were sent out with torches to scour the woods and hills to that end.

Of course, the whole drove was housed in the house, and, great guns!—well,

I never saw anything like it. Nor ever heard anything like it. And never smelt anything like it. It was like an insurrection in a gasometer.

Chapter XXI

THE PILGRIMS

WHEN I DID get to bed at last I was unspeakably tired; the stretching-out, and the relaxing of the long-tense muscles, how luxurious, how delicious! but that was as far as I could get—sleep was out of the question for the present. The ripping and tearing and squealing of the nobility up and down the halls and corridors was pandemonium come again, and kept me broad awake. Being awake, my thoughts were busy, of course; and mainly they busied themselves with Sandy's curious delusion. Here she was, as sane a person as the kingdom could produce; and yet, from my point of view she was acting like a crazy woman. My land, the power of training! of influence! of education! It can bring a body up to believe anything. I had to put myself in Sandy's place to realize that she was not a lunatic. Yes, and put her in mine, to demonstrate how easy it is to seem a lunatic to a person who has not been taught as you have been taught. If I had told Sandy I had seen a wagon, uninfluenced by enchantment, spin along fifty miles an hour; had seen a man, unequipped with magic powers, get into a basket and soar out of sight among the clouds; and had listened, without any necromancer's help, to the conversation of a person who was several hundred miles away, Sandy would not merely have supposed me to be crazy, she would have thought she knew it. Everybody around her believed in enchantments; nobody had any doubts; to doubt that a castle could be turned into a sty, and its occupants into hogs, would have been the same as my doubting among Connecticut people the actuality of the telephone and its wonders—and in both cases would be absolute proof of a diseased mind, an unsettled reason. Yes, Sandy was sane; that must be admitted. If I also would be sane—to Sandy—I must keep my superstitions about unenchanted and unmiraculous locomotives, balloons, and telephones, to myself. Also, I believed that the world was not flat, and hadn't pillars under it to support it, nor a canopy over it to turn off a universe of water that occupied all space above; but as I was the only person in the kingdom afflicted with such impious and criminal opinions, I recognized that it would be good wisdom to keep quiet about this matter, too, if I did not wish to be suddenly shunned and forsaken by everybody as a madman.

The next morning Sandy assembled the swine in the dining-room and gave them their breakfast, waiting upon them personally and manifesting in every way the deep reverence which the natives of her island, ancient and modern, have always felt for rank, let its outward casket and the mental and moral contents be what they may. I could have eaten with the hogs if I had had birth approaching my lofty official rank; but I hadn't, and so accepted the unavoidable slight and made no complaint. Sandy and I had our breakfast at the second table. The family were not at home. I said:

"How many are in the family, Sandy, and where do they keep themselves?"

"Family?"

"Yes."

"Which family, good my lord?"

"Why, this family; your own family."

"Sooth to say, I understand you not. I have no family."

"No family? Why, Sandy, isn't this your home?"

"Now how indeed might that be? I have no home."

"Well, then, whose house is this?"

"Ah, wit you well I would tell you an I knew myself."

"Come—you don't even know these people? Then who invited us here?"

"None invited us. We but came; that is all."

"Why, woman, this is a most extraordinary performance. The effrontery of it is beyond admiration. We blandly march into a man's house, and cram it full of the only really valuable nobility the sun has yet discovered in the earth, and then it turns out that we don't even know the man's name. How did you ever venture to take this extravagant liberty? I supposed, of course, it was your home. What will the man say?"

"What will he say? Forsooth what can he say but give thanks?"

"Thanks for what?"

Her face was filled with a puzzled surprise:

"Verily, thou troublest mine understanding with strange words. Do ye dream that one of his estate is like to have the honor twice in his life to entertain company such as we have brought to grace his house withal?"

"Well, no—when you come to that. No, it's an even bet that this is the first time he has had a treat like this."

"Then let him be thankful, and manifest the same by grateful speech and due humility; he were a dog, else, and the heir and ancestor of dogs."

To my mind, the situation was uncomfortable. It might become more so. It might be a good idea to muster the hogs and move on. So I said:

"The day is wasting, Sandy. It is time to get the nobility together and be moving."

"Wherefore, fair sir and Boss?"

"We want to take them to their home, don't we?"

"La, but list to him! They be of all the regions of the earth! Each must hie to her own home; wend you we might do all these journeys in one so brief life as He hath appointed that created life, and thereto death likewise with help of Adam, who by sin done through persuasion of his helpmeet, she being wrought upon and bewrayed by the beguilements of the great enemy of man, that serpent hight Satan, aforetime consecrated and set apart unto that evil work by overmastering spite and envy begotten in his heart through fell ambitions that did blight and mildew a nature erst so white and pure whenso it hove with the shining multitudes its brethren-born in glade and shade of that fair heaven wherein all such as native be to that rich estate and—"

"Great Scott!"

"My lord?"

"Well, you know we haven't got time for this sort of thing. Don't you see, we could distribute these people around the earth in less time than it is going to take you to explain that we can't. We mustn't talk now, we must act. You want to be careful; you mustn't let your mill get the start of you that way, at a time like this. To business now—and sharp's the word. Who is to take the aristocracy home?"

"Even their friends. These will come for them from the far parts of the earth."

This was lightning from a clear sky, for unexpectedness; and the relief of it was like pardon to a prisoner. She would remain to deliver the goods, of course.

"Well, then, Sandy, as our enterprise is handsomely and successfully ended, I will go home and report; and if ever another one—"

"I also am ready; I will go with thee."

This was recalling the pardon.

"How? You will go with me? Why should you?"

"Will I be traitor to my knight, dost think? That were dishonor. I may not part from thee until in knightly encounter in the field some overmatching champion shall fairly win and fairly wear me. I were to blame an I thought that that might ever hap."

"Elected for the long term," I sighed to myself. "I may as well make the best of it." So then I spoke up and said:

"All right; let us make a start."

While she was gone to cry her farewells over the pork, I gave that whole peerage away to the servants. And I asked them to take a duster and dust around a little where the nobilities had mainly lodged and promenaded; but they considered that that would be hardly worth while, and would moreover be a rather grave departure from custom, and therefore likely to make talk. A departure from custom—that settled it; it was a nation capable of committing any crime but that. The servants said they would follow the fashion, a fashion grown sacred through immemorial observance; they would scatter fresh rushes in all the rooms and halls, and then the evidence of the aristocratic visitation would be no longer visible. It was a kind of satire on Nature: it was the scientific method, the geologic method; it deposited the history of the family in a stratified record; and the antiquary could dig through it and tell by the remains of each period what changes of diet the family had introduced successively for a hundred years.

The first thing we struck that day was a procession of pilgrims. It was not going our way, but we joined it, nevertheless; for it was hourly being borne in upon me now, that if I would govern this country wisely, I must be posted in the details of its life, and not at second hand, but by personal observation and scrutiny.

This company of pilgrims resembled Chaucer's in this: that it had in it a sample of about all the upper occupations and professions the country could show, and a corresponding variety of costume. There were young men and old men, young women and old women, lively folk and grave folk. They rode upon mules and horses, and there was not a sidesaddle in the party; for this specialty was to remain unknown in England for nine hundred years yet.

It was a pleasant, friendly, sociable herd; pious, happy, merry and full of unconscious coarsenesses and innocent indecencies. What they regarded as the merry tale went the continual round and caused no more embarrassment than it would have caused in the best English society twelve centuries later. Practical jokes worthy of the English wits of the first quarter of the far-off nineteenth century were sprung here and there and yonder along the line, and compelled the delightedest applause; and sometimes when a bright remark was made at one end of the procession and started on its travels toward the other, you could note its progress all the way by the sparkling spray of laughter it threw off from its bows as it plowed along; and also by the blushes of the mules in its wake.

Sandy knew the goal and purpose of this pilgrimage, and she posted me. She said:

"They journey to the Valley of Holiness, for to be blessed of the godly hermits and drink of the miraculous waters and be cleansed from sin."

"Where is this watering-place?"

"It lieth a two-day journey hence, by the borders of the land that hight the Cuckoo Kingdom."

"Tell me about it. Is it a celebrated place?"

"Oh, of a truth, yes. There be none more so. Of old time there lived there an abbot and his monks. Belike were none in the world more holy than these; for they gave themselves to study of pious books, and spoke not the one to the other, or indeed to any, and ate decayed herbs and naught thereto, and slept hard, and prayed much, and washed never; also they wore the same garment until it fell from their bodies through age and decay. Right so came they to be known of all the world by reason of these holy austerities, and visited by rich and poor, and reverenced."

"Proceed."

"But always there was lack of water there. Whereas, upon a time, the holy abbot prayed, and for answer a great stream of clear water burst forth by miracle in a desert place. Now were the fickle monks tempted of the Fiend, and they wrought with their abbot unceasingly by beggings and beseechings that he would construct a bath; and when he was become aweary and might not resist more, he said have ye your will, then, and granted that they asked. Now mark thou what 'tis to forsake the ways of purity the which He loveth, and wanton with such as be worldly and an offense. These monks did enter into the bath and come thence washed as white as snow; and lo, in that moment His sign appeared, in miraculous rebuke! for His insulted waters ceased to flow, and utterly vanished away."

"They fared mildly, Sandy, considering how that kind of crime is regarded in this country."

"Belike; but it was their first sin; and they had been of perfect life for long, and differing in naught from the angels. Prayers, tears, torturings of the flesh, all was vain to beguile that water to flow again. Even processions; even burnt offerings; even votive candles to the Virgin, did fail every each of them; and all in the land did marvel."

"How odd to find that even this industry has its financial panics, and at times sees its assignats and greenbacks languish to zero, and everything come to a standstill. Go on, Sandy."

"And so upon a time, after year and day, the good abbot made humble surrender and destroyed the bath. And behold, His anger was in that moment appeased, and the waters gushed richly forth again, and even unto this day they have not ceased to flow in that generous measure."

"Then I take it nobody has washed since."

"He that would essay it could have his halter free; yes, and swiftly would he need it, too."

"The community has prospered since?"

"Even from that very day. The fame of the miracle went abroad into all lands. From every land came monks to join; they came even as the fishes come, in shoals; and the monastery added building to building, and yet others to these, and so spread wide its arms and took them in. And nuns came, also; and more again, and yet more; and built over against the monastery on the yon side of the vale, and added building to building, until mighty was that nunnery. And these were friendly unto those, and they joined their loving labors together, and together they built a fair great foundling asylum midway of the valley between.''

"You spoke of some hermits, Sandy."

"These have gathered there from the ends of the earth. A hermit thriveth best where there be multitudes of pilgrims. Ye shall not find no hermit of no sort wanting. If any shall mention a hermit of a kind he thinketh new and not to be found but in some far strange land, let him but scratch among the holes and caves and swamps that line that Valley of Holiness, and whatsoever be his breed, it skills not, he shall find a sample of it there.''

I closed up alongside of a burly fellow with a fat good-humored face, purposing to make myself agreeable and pick up some further crumbs of fact; but I had hardly more than scraped acquaintance with him when he began eagerly and awkwardly to lead up, in the immemorial way, to that same old anecdote—the one Sir Dinadan told me, what time I got into trouble with Sir Sagramor and was challenged of him on account of it. I excused myself and dropped to the rear of the procession, sad at heart, willing to go hence from this troubled life, this vale of tears, this brief day of broken rest, of cloud and storm, of weary struggle and monotonous defeat; and yet shrinking from the change, as remembering how long eternity is, and how many have wended thither who know that anecdote.

Early in the afternoon we overtook another procession of pilgrims; but in this one was no merriment, no jokes, no laughter, no playful ways, nor any happy giddiness, whether of youth or age. Yet both were here, both age and youth; gray old men and women, strong men and women of middle age, young husbands, young wives, little boys and girls, and three babies at the breast. Even the children were smileless; there was not a face among all these half a hundred people but was cast down, and bore that set expression of hopelessness which is bred of long and hard trials and old acquaintance with despair. They were slaves. Chains led from their fettered feet and their manacled hands to a sole-leather belt about their waists; and all except the children were also linked together in a file, six feet apart, by a single chain which led from collar to collar all down the line. They were on foot, and had tramped three hundred miles in eighteen days, upon the cheapest odds and ends of food, and stingy rations of that. They had slept in these chains every night, bundled together like swine. They had upon their bodies some poor rags, but they could not be said to be clothed. Their irons had chafed the skin from their ankles and made sores which were ulcerated and wormy. Their naked feet were torn, and none walked without a limp. Originally there had been a hundred of these unfortunates, but about half had been sold on the trip. The trader in charge of them rode a horse and carried a whip with a short handle and a long heavy lash divided into several knotted tails at the end. With this whip he cut the shoulders of any that tottered from weariness and pain, and straightened them up. He did not speak; the whip conveyed his desire without that. None of these poor creatures looked up as we rode along by; they showed no consciousness of our presence. And they made no sound but one; that was the dull and awful clank of their chains from end to end of the long file, as forty-three burdened feet rose and fell in unison. The file moved in a cloud of its own making.

All these faces were gray with a coating of dust. One has seen the like of this coating upon furniture in unoccupied houses, and has written his idle thought in it with his finger. I was reminded of this when I noticed the faces of some of those women, young mothers carrying babes that were near to death and freedom, how a something in their hearts was written in the dust upon their faces, plain to see, and lord, how plain to read! for it was the track of tears. One of these young mothers was but a girl, and it hurt me to the heart to read that writing, and reflect that it was come up out of the breast of such a child, a breast that ought not to know trouble yet, but only the gladness of the morning of life; and no doubt—

She reeled just then, giddy with fatigue, and down came the lash and flicked a flake of skin from her naked shoulder. It stung me as if I had been hit instead. The master halted the file and jumped from his horse. He stormed and swore at this girl, and said she had made annoyance enough with her laziness, and as this was the last chance he should have, he would settle the account now. She dropped on her knees and put up her hands and began to beg, and cry, and implore, in a passion of terror, but the master gave no attention. He snatched the child from her, and then made the men-slaves who were chained before and behind her throw her on the ground and hold her there and expose her body; and then he laid on with his lash like a madman till her back was flayed, she shrieking and struggling the while piteously. One of the men who was holding her turned away his face, and for this humanity he was reviled and flogged.

All our pilgrims looked on and commented—on the expert way in which the whip was handled. They were too much hardened by lifelong every-day familiarity with slavery to notice that there was anything else in the exhibition that invited comment. This was what slavery could do, in the way of ossifying what one may call the superior lobe of human feeling; for these pilgrims were kind-hearted people, and they would not have allowed that man to treat a horse like that.

I wanted to stop the whole thing and set the slaves free, but that would not do. I must not interfere too much and get myself a name for riding over the country's laws and the citizen's rights rough-shod. If I lived and prospered I would be the death of slavery, that I was resolved upon; but I would try to fix it so that when I became its executioner it should be by command of the nation.

Just here was the wayside shop of a smith; and now arrived a landed proprietor who had bought this girl a few miles back, deliverable here where her irons could be taken off. They were removed; then there was a squabble between the gentleman and the dealer as to which should pay the blacksmith. The moment the girl was delivered from her irons, she flung herself, all tears and frantic sobbings, into the arms of the slave who had turned away his face when she was whipped. He strained her to his breast, and smothered her face and the child's with kisses, and washed them with the rain of his tears. I suspected. I inquired. Yes, I was right; it was husband and wife. They had to be torn apart by force; the girl had to be dragged away, and she struggled and fought and shrieked like one gone mad till a turn of the road hid her from sight; and even after that, we could still make out the fading plaint of those receding shrieks. And the husband and father, with his wife and child gone, never to be seen by him again in life?—well, the look of him one might not bear at all, and so I turned away; but I knew I should never get his picture out of my mind again, and there it is to this day, to wring my heart-strings whenever I think of it.

We put up at the inn in a village just at nightfall, and when I rose next morning and looked abroad, I was ware where a knight came riding in the golden glory of the new day, and recognized him for knight of mine—Sir Ozana le Cure

Hardy. He was in the gentlemen's furnishing line, and his missionarying specialty was plug-hats. He was clothed all in steel, in the beautifulest armor of the time— up to where his helmet ought to have been; but he hadn't any helmet, he wore a shiny stove-pipe hat, and was as ridiculous a spectacle as one might want to see. It was another of my surreptitious schemes for extinguishing knighthood by making it grotesque and absurd. Sir Ozana's saddle was hung about with leather hat-boxes, and every time he overcame a wandering knight he swore him into my service and fitted him with a plug and made him wear it. I dressed and ran down to welcome Sir Ozana and get his news.

"How is trade?" I asked.

"Ye will note that I have but these four left; yet were they sixteen whenas I got me from Camelot."

"Why, you have certainly done nobly, Sir Ozana. Where have you been foraging of late?"

"I am but now come from the Valley of Holiness, please you sir."

"I am pointed for that place myself. Is there anything stirring in the monkery, more than common?"

"By the mass ye may not question it! . . . Give him good feed, boy, and stint it not, an thou valuest thy crown; so get ye lightly to the stable and do even as I bid. . . . Sir, it is parlous news I bring, and—be these pilgrims? Then ye may not do better, good folk, than gather and hear the tale I have to tell, sith it concerneth you, forasmuch as ye go to find that ye will not find, and seek that ye will seek in vain, my life being hostage for my word, and my word and message being these, namely: That a hap has happened whereof the like has not been seen no more but once this two hundred years, which was the first and last time that that said misfortune strake the holy valley in that form by commandment of the Most High whereto by reasons just and causes thereunto contributing, wherein the matter—"

"The miraculous fount hath ceased to flow!" This shout burst from twenty pilgrim mouths at once.

"Ye say well, good people. I was verging to it, even when ye spake."

"Has somebody been washing again?"

"Nay, it is suspected, but none believe it. It is thought to be some other sin, but none wit what."

"How are they feeling about the calamity?"

"None may describe it in words. The fount is these nine days dry. The prayers that did begin then, and the lamentations in sackcloth and ashes, and the holy processions, none of these have ceased nor night nor day; and so the monks and the nuns and the foundlings be all exhausted, and do hang up prayers writ upon parchment, sith that no strength is left in man to lift up voice. And at last they sent for thee, Sir Boss, to try magic and enchantment; and if you could not come, then was the messenger to fetch Merlin, and he is there these three days now, and saith he will fetch that water though he burst the globe and wreck its kingdoms to accomplish it; and right bravely doth he work his magic and call upon his hellions to hie them hither and help, but not a whiff of moisture hath he started yet, even so much as might qualify as mist upon a copper mirror an ye count not the barrel of sweat he sweateth betwixt sun and sun over the dire labors of his task; and if ye—"

Breakfast was ready. As soon as it was over I showed to Sir Ozana these words which I had written on the inside of his hat: *Chemical Department,*

Laboratory extension, Section G. Pxxp. Send two of first size, two of No. 3,
and six of No. 4, together with the proper complementary details—and two of
my trained assistants.'' And I said:

"Now get you to Camelot as fast as you can fly, brave knight, and show the
writing to Clarence, and tell him to have these required matters in the Valley
of Holiness with all possible despatch.''

"I will well, Sir Boss,'' and he was off.

Chapter XXII

THE HOLY FOUNTAIN

THE PILGRIMS WERE human beings. Otherwise they would have acted differently.
They had come a long and difficult journey, and now when the journey was
nearly finished, and they learned that the main thing they had come for had
ceased to exist, they didn't do as horses or cats or angle-worms would probably
have done—turn back and get at something profitable—no, anxious as they had
before been to see the miraculous fountain, they were as much as forty times
as anxious now to see the place where it had used to be. There is no accounting
for human beings.

We made good time; and a couple of hours before sunset we stood upon the
high confines of the Valley of Holiness, and our eyes swept it from end to end
and noted its features. That is, its large features. These were the three masses
of buildings. They were distant and isolated temporalities shrunken to toy con-
structions in the lonely waste of what seemed a desert—and was. Such a scene
is always mournful, it is so impressively still, and looks so steeped in death.
But there was a sound here which interrupted the stillness only to add to its
mournfulness; this was the faint far sound of tolling bells which floated fitfully
to us on the passing breeze, and so faintly, so softly, that we hardly knew
whether we heard it with our ears or with our spirits.

We reached the monastery before dark, and there the males were given lodging,
but the women were sent over to the nunnery. The bells were close at hand now,
and their solemn booming smote upon the ear like a message of doom. A
superstitious despair possessed the heart of every monk and published itself in
his ghastly face. Everywhere, these black-robed, soft-sandaled, tallow-visaged
specters appeared, flitted about and disappeared, noiseless as the creatures of a
troubled dream, and as uncanny.

The old abbot's joy to see me was pathetic. Even to tears; but he did the
shedding himself. He said:

"Delay not, son, but get to thy saving work. An we bring not the water back
again, and soon, we are ruined, and the good work of two hundred years must
end. And see thou do it with enchantments that be holy, for the Church will not
endure that work in her cause be done by devil's magic.''

"When I work, Father, be sure there will be no devil's work connected with
it. I shall use no arts that come of the devil, and no elements not created by the
hand of God. But is Merlin working strictly on pious lines?''

"Ah, he said he would, my son, he said he would, and took oath to make his promise good.''

"Well, in that case, let him proceed.''

"But surely you will not sit idle by, but help?''

"It will not answer to mix methods, Father, neither would it be professional courtesy. Two of a trade must not underbid each other. We might as well cut rates and be done with it; it would arrive at that in the end. Merlin has the contract; no other magician can touch it till he throws it up.''

"But I will take it from him; it is a terrible emergency and the act is thereby justified. And if it were not so, who will give law to the Church? The Church giveth law to all; and what she wills to do, that she may do, hurt whom it may. I will take it from him; you shall begin upon the moment.''

"It may not be, Father. No doubt, as you say, where power is supreme, one can do as one likes and suffer no injury; but we poor magicians are not so situated. Merlin is a very good magician in a small way, and has quite a neat provincial reputation. He is struggling along, doing the best he can, and it would not be etiquette for me to take his job until he himself abandons it.''

The abbot's face lighted.

"Ah, that is simple. There are ways to persuade him to abandon it.''

"No-no, Father, it skills not, as these people say. If he were persuaded against his will, he would load that well with a malicious enchantment which would balk me until I found out its secret. It might take a month. I could set up a little enchantment of mine which I call the telephone, and he could not find out its secret in a hundred years. Yes, you perceive, he might block me for a month. Would you like to risk a month in a dry time like this?''

"A month! The mere thought of it maketh me to shudder. Have it thy way, my son. But my heart is heavy with this disappointment. Leave me, and let me wear my spirit with weariness and waiting, even as I have done these ten long days, counterfeiting thus the thing that is called rest, the prone body making outward sign of repose where inwardly is none.''

Of course, it would have been best, all round, for Merlin to waive etiquette and quit and call it half a day, since he would never be able to start that water, for he was a true magician of the time; which is to say, the big miracles, the ones that gave him his reputation, always had the luck to be performed when nobody but Merlin was present; he couldn't start this well with all this crowd around to see; a crowd was as bad for a magician's miracle in that day as it was for a spiritualist's miracle in mine; there was sure to be some skeptic on hand to turn up the gas at the crucial moment and spoil everything. But I did not want Merlin to retire from the job until I was ready to take hold of it effectively myself; and I could not do that until I got my things from Camelot, and that would take two or three days.

My presence gave the monks hope, and cheered them up a good deal; insomuch that they ate a square meal that night for the first time in ten days. As soon as their stomachs had been properly reinforced with food, their spirits began to rise fast; when the mead began to go round they rose faster. By the time everybody was half-seas over, the holy community was in good shape to make a night of it; so we stayed by the board and put it through on that line. Matters got to be very jolly. Good old questionable stories were told that made the tears run down and cavernous mouths stand wide and the round bellies shake with laughter; and questionable songs were bellowed out in a mighty chorus that drowned the boom of the tolling bells.

At last I ventured a story myself; and vast was the success of it. Not right off, of course, for the native of those islands does not, as a rule, dissolve upon the early applications of a humorous thing; but the fifth time I told it, they began to crack in places; the eighth time I told it, they began to crumble; at the twelfth repetition they fell apart in chunks; and at the fifteenth they disintegrated, and I got a broom and swept them up. This language is figurative. Those islanders—well, they are slow pay at first, in the matter of return for your investment of effort, but in the end they make the pay of all other nations poor and small by contrast.

I was at the well next day betimes. Merlin was there, enchanting away like a beaver, but not raising the moisture. He was not in a pleasant humor; and every time I hinted that perhaps this contract was a shade too hefty for a novice he unlimbered his tongue and cursed like a bishop—French bishop of the Regency days, I mean.

Matters were about as I expected to find them. The ''fountain'' was an ordinary well, it had been dug in the ordinary way, and stoned up in the ordinary way. There was no miracle about it. Even the lie that had created its reputation was not miraculous; I could have told it myself, with one hand tied behind me. The well was in a dark chamber which stood in the center of a cut-stone chapel, whose walls were hung with pious pictures of a workmanship that would have made a chromo feel good; pictures historically commemorative of curative miracles which had been achieved by the waters when nobody was looking. That is, nobody but angels; they are always on deck when there is a miracle to the fore—so as to get put in the picture, perhaps. Angels are as fond of that as a fire company; look at the old masters.

The well-chamber was dimly lighted by lamps; the water was drawn with a windlass and chain by monks, and poured into troughs which delivered it into stone reservoirs outside in the chapel—when there was water to draw, I mean—and none but monks could enter the well-chamber. I entered it, for I had temporary authority to do so, by courtesy of my professional brother and subordinate. But he hadn't entered it himself. He did everything by incantations; he never worked his intellect. If he had stepped in there and used his eyes, instead of his disordered mind, he could have cured the well by natural means, and then turned it into a miracle in the customary way; but no, he was an old numskull, a magician who believed in his own magic; and no magician can thrive who is handicapped with a superstition like that.

I had an idea that the well had sprung a leak; that some of the wall stones near the bottom had fallen and exposed fissures that allowed the water to escape. I measured the chain—ninety-eight feet. Then I called in a couple of monks, locked the door, took a candle, and made them lower me in the bucket. When the chain was all paid out, the candle confirmed my suspicion; a considerable section of the wall was gone, exposing a good big fissure.

I almost regretted that my theory about the well's trouble was correct, because I had another one that had a showy point or two about it for a miracle. I remembered that in America, many centuries later, when an oil-well ceased to flow, they used to blast it out with a dynamite torpedo. If I should find this well dry and no explanation of it, I could astonish these people most nobly by having a person of no especial value drop a dynamite bomb into it. It was my idea to appoint Merlin. However, it was plain that there was no occasion for the bomb. One cannot have everything the way he would like it. A man has no business to be depressed by a disappointment, anyway; he ought to make up his mind to get even. That is what I did. I said to myself, I am in no hurry, I can wait; that bomb will come good yet. And it did, too.

When I was above ground again, I turned out the monks, and let down a fish-line; the well was a hundred and fifty feet deep, and there was forty-one feet of water in it! I called in a monk and asked:

"How deep is the well?"

"That, sir, I wit not, having never been told."

"How does the water usually stand in it?"

"Near to the top, these two centuries, as the testimony goeth, brought down to us through our predecessors."

It was true—as to recent times at least—for there was witness to it, and better witness than a monk; only about twenty or thirty feet of the chain showed wear and use, the rest of it was unworn and rusty. What had happened when the well gave out that other time? Without doubt some practical person had come along and mended the leak, and then had come up and told the abbot he had discovered by divination that if the sinful bath were destroyed the well would flow again. The leak had befallen again now, and these children would have prayed, and processioned, and tolled their bells for heavenly succor till they all dried up and blew away, and no innocent of them all would ever have thought to drop a fishline into the well or go down in it and find out what was really the matter. Old habit of mind is one of the toughest things to get away from in the world. It transmits itself like physical form and feature; and for a man, in those days, to have had an idea that his ancestors hadn't had, would have brought him under suspicion of being illegitimate. I said to the monk:

"It is a difficult miracle to restore water in a dry well, but we will try, if my brother Merlin fails. Brother Merlin is a very passable artist, but only in the parlor-magic line, and he may not succeed; in fact, is not likely to succeed. But that should be nothing to his discredit; the man that can do *this* kind of miracle knows enough to keep hotel."

"Hotel? I mind not to have heard—"

"Of hotel? It's what you call hostel. The man that can do this miracle can keep hostel. I can do this miracle; I shall do this miracle; yet I do not try to conceal from you that it is a miracle to tax the occult powers to the last strain."

"None knoweth that truth better than the brotherhood, indeed; for it is of record that aforetime it was parlous difficult and took a year. Natheless, God send you good success, and to that end will we pray."

As a matter of business it was a good idea to get the notion around that the thing was difficult. Many a small thing has been made large by the right kind of advertising. That monk was filled up with the difficulty of this enterprise; he would fill up the others. In two days the solicitude would be booming.

On my way home at noon, I met Sandy. She had been sampling the hermits. I said:

"I would like to do that myself. This is Wednesday. Is there a matinée?"

"A which, please you, sir?"

"Matinée. Do they keep open afternoons?"

"Who?"

"The hermits, of course."

"Keep open?"

"Yes, keep open. Isn't that plain enough? Do they knock off at noon?"

"Knock off?"

"Knock off?—yes, knock off. What is the matter with knock off? I never saw such a dunderhead; can't you understand anything at all? In plain terms, do they shut up shop, draw the game, bank the fires—"

"Shut up shop, draw—"

"There, never mind, let it go; you make me tired. You can't seem to understand the simplest thing."

"I would I might please thee, sir, and it is to me dole and sorrow that I fail, albeit sith I am but a simple damsel and taught of none, being from the cradle unbaptized in those deep waters of learning that do anoint with a sovereignty him that partaketh of that most noble sacrament, investing him with reverend state to the mental eye of the humble mortal, who by bar and lack of that great consecration seeth in his own unlearned estate but a symbol of that other sort of lack and loss which men do publish to the pitying eye with sackcloth trappings whereon the ashes of grief do lie bepowdered and bestrewn, and so, when such shall in the darkness of his mind encounter these golden phrases of high mystery, these shut-up-shops, and draw-the-game, and bank-the-fires, it is but by the grace of God that he burst not for envy of the mind that can beget, and tongue that can deliver so great and mellow-sounding miracles of speech, and if there do ensue confusion in that humbler mind, and failure to divine the meanings of these wonders, then if so be this miscomprehension is not vain but sooth and true, wit ye well it is the very substance of worshipful dear homage and may not lightly be misprized, nor had been, an ye had noted this complexion of mood and mind and understood that that I would I could not, and that I could not I might not, nor yet nor might *nor* could, nor might-not nor could-not, might be by advantage turned to the desired *would,* and so I pray you mercy of my fault, and that ye will of your kindness and your charity forgive it, good my master and most dear lord."

I couldn't make it all out—that is, the details—but I got the general idea; and enough of it, too, to be ashamed. It was not fair to spring those nineteenth-century technicalities upon the untutored infant of the sixth and then rail at her because she couldn't get their drift; and when she was making the honest best drive at it she could, too, and no fault of hers that she couldn't fetch the home plate; and so I apologized. Then we meandered pleasantly away toward the hermit holes in sociable converse together, and better friends than ever.

I was gradually coming to have a mysterious and shuddery reverence for this girl; nowadays whenever she pulled out from the station and got her train fairly started on one of those horizonless transcontinental sentences of hers, it was borne in upon me that I was standing in the awful presence of the Mother of the German Language. I was so impressed with this, that sometimes when she began to empty one of these sentences on me I unconsciously took the very attitude of reverence, and stood uncovered; and if words had been water, I had been drowned, sure. She had exactly the German way; whatever was in her mind to be delivered, whether a mere remark, or a sermon, or a cyclopedia, or the history of a war, she would get it into a single sentence or die. Whenever the literary German dives into a sentence, that is the last you are going to see of him till he emerges on the other side of his Atlantic with his verb in his mouth.

We drifted from hermit to hermit all the afternoon. It was a most strange menagerie. The chief emulation among them seemed to be, to see which could manage to be the uncleanest and most prosperous with vermin. Their manner and attitudes were the last expression of complacent self-righteousness. It was one anchorite's pride to lie naked in the mud and let the insects bite him and blister him unmolested; it was another's to lean against a rock, all day long, conspicuous to the admiration of the throng of pilgrims and pray; it was another's to go naked and crawl around on all fours; it was another's to drag about with him, year in and year out, eighty pounds of iron; it was another's to never lie down when he slept, but to stand among the thorn-bushes and snore when there were pilgrims around to look; a woman, who had the white hair of age, and no other apparel, was black from crown to heel with forty-seven years of holy abstinence from water. Groups of gazing pilgrims stood around all and every of these strange objects, lost in reverent wonder, and envious of the fleckless sanctity which these pious austerities had won for them from an exacting heaven.

By and by we went to see one of the supremely great ones. He was a mighty celebrity; his fame had penetrated all Christendom; the noble and the renowned journeyed from the remotest lands on the globe to pay him reverence. His stand was in the center of the widest part of the valley; and it took all that space to hold his crowds.

His stand was a pillar sixty feet high, with a broad platform on the top of it. He was now doing what he had been doing every day for twenty years up there— bowing his body ceaselessly and rapidly almost to his feet. It was his way of praying. I timed him with a stop-watch, and he made twelve hundred and forty-four revolutions in twenty-four minutes and forty-six seconds. It seemed a pity to have all this power going to waste. It was one of the most useful motions in mechanics, the pedal movement; so I made a note in my memorandum-book, purposing some day to apply a system of elastic cords to him and run a sewing-machine with it. I afterward carried out that scheme, and got five years' good service out of him; in which time he turned out upward of eighteen thousand first-rate tow-linen shirts, which was ten a day. I worked him Sundays and all; he was going, Sundays, the same as week-days, and it was no use to waste the power. These shirts cost me nothing but just the mere trifle for the materials— I furnished those myself, it would not have been right to make him do that— and they sold like smoke to pilgrims at a dollar and a half apiece, which was the price of fifty cows or a blooded race-horse in Arthurdom. They were regarded as a perfect protection against sin, and advertised as such by my knights everywhere, with the paint-pot and stencil-plate; insomuch that there was not a cliff or a boulder or a dead wall in England but you could read on it at a mile distance:

"Buy the only genuine St. Stylite; patronized by the Nobility. Patent applied for."

There was more money in the business than one knew what to do with. As it extended, I brought out a line of goods suitable for kings, and a nobby thing for duchesses and that sort, with ruffles down the forehatch and the running-gear clewed up with a featherstitch to leeward and then hauled aft with a backstay and triced up with a half-turn in the standing rigging forward of the weather-gaskets. Yes, it was a daisy.

But about that time I noticed that the motive power had taken to standing on one leg, and I found that there was something the matter with the other one; so I stocked the business and unloaded, taking Sir Bors de Ganis into camp financially along with certain of his friends; for the works stopped within a year, and the good saint got him to his rest. But he had earned it. I can say that for him.

When I saw him that first time—however, his personal condition will not quite bear description here. You can read it in the *Lives of the Saints*.

Chapter XXIII

RESTORATION OF THE FOUNTAIN

SATURDAY NOON I went to the well and looked on awhile. Merlin was still burning smoke-powders, and pawing the air, and muttering gibberish as hard as ever, but looking pretty downhearted, for of course he had not started even a perspiration in that well yet. Finally I said:

"How does the thing promise by this time, partner?"

"Behold, I am even now busied with trial of the powerfulest enchantment known to the princes of the occult arts in the lands of the East; an it fail me, naught can avail. Peace, until I finish."

He raised a smoke this time that darkened all the region, and must have made matters uncomfortable for the hermits, for the wind was their way, and it rolled down over their dens in a dense and billowy fog. He poured out volumes of speech to match, and contorted his body and sawed the air with his hands in a most extraordinary way. At the end of twenty minutes he dropped down panting, and about exhausted. Now arrived the abbot and several hundred monks and nuns, and behind them a multitude of pilgrims and a couple of acres of foundlings, all drawn by the prodigious smoke, and all in a grand state of excitement. The abbot inquired anxiously for results. Merlin said:

"If any labor of mortal might break the spell that binds these waters, this which I have but just essayed had done it. It has failed; whereby I do now know that that which I had feared is a truth established; the sign of this failure is, that the most potent spirit known to the magicians of the East, and whose name none may utter and live, has laid his spell upon this well. The mortal does not breathe, nor ever will, who can penetrate the secret of that spell, and without that secret none can break it. The water will flow no more forever, good Father. I have done what man could. Suffer me to go."

Of course this threw the abbot into a good deal of a consternation. He turned to me with the signs of it in his face, and said:

"Ye have heard him. Is it true?"

"Part of it is."

"Not all, then, not all! What part is true?"

"That that spirit with the Russian name has put his spell upon the well."

"God's wownds, then are we ruined!"

"Possibly."

"But not certainly? Ye mean, not certainly?"

"That is it."

"Wherefore, ye also mean that when he saith none can break the spell—"

"Yes, when he says that, he says what isn't necessarily true. There are conditions under which an effort to break it may have some chance—that is, some small, some trifling chance—of success.''

''The conditions—''

''Oh, they are nothing difficult. Only these: I want the well and the surroundings for the space of half a mile, entirely to myself from sunset to-day until I remove the ban—and nobody allowed to cross the ground but by my authority.''

''Are these all?''

''Yes.''

''And you have no fear to try?''

''Oh, none. One may fail, of course; and one may also succeed. One can try, and I am ready to chance it. I have my conditions?''

''These and all others ye may name. I will issue commandment to that effect.''

''Wait,'' said Merlin, with an evil smile. ''Ye wit that he that would break this spell must know that spirit's name?''

''Yes, I know his name.''

''And wit you also that to know it skills not of itself, but ye must likewise pronounce it? Ha-ha! Knew ye that?''

''Yes, I knew that, too.''

''You had that knowledge! Art a fool? Are ye minded to utter that name and die?''

''Utter it? Why certainly. I would utter it if it was Welsh.''

''Ye are even a dead man, then; and I go to tell Arthur.''

''That's all right. Take your gripsack and get along. The thing for *you* to do is to go home and work the weather, John W. Merlin.''

It was a home shot, and it made him wince; for he was the worst weather failure in the kingdom. Whenever he ordered up the danger-signals along the coast there was a week's dead calm, sure, and every time he prophesied fair weather it rained brickbats. But I kept him in the weather bureau right along, to undermine his reputation. However, that shot raised his bile, and instead of starting home to report my death, he said he would remain and enjoy it.

My two experts arrived in the evening, and pretty well fagged, for they had traveled double tides. They had pack-mules along, and had brought everything I needed—tools, pump, lead pipe, Greek fire, sheaves of big rockets, roman candles, colored fire sprays, electric apparatus, and a lot of sundries—everything necessary for the stateliest kind of a miracle. They got their supper and a nap, and about midnight we sallied out through a solitude so wholly vacant and complete that it quite overpassed the required conditions. We took possession of the well and its surroundings. My boys were experts in all sorts of things, from the stoning-up of a well to the constructing of a mathematical instrument. An hour before sunrise we had that leak mended in shipshape fashion, and the water began to rise. Then we stowed our fireworks in the chapel, locked up the place, and went home to bed.

Before the noon mass was over, we were at the well again; for there was a deal to do yet, and I was determined to spring the miracle before midnight, for business reasons: for whereas a miracle worked for the Church on a week-day is worth a good deal, it is worth six times as much if you get it in on a Sunday. In nine hours the water had risen to its customary level; that is to say, it was within twenty-three feet of the top. We put in a little iron pump, one of the first turned out by my works near the capital; we bored into a stone reservoir which stood against the outer wall of the well-chamber and inserted a section of lead pipe that was long enough to reach to the door of the chapel and project beyond the threshold, where the gushing water would be visible to the two hundred and fifty acres of people I was intending should be present on the flat plain in front of this little holy hillock at the proper time.

We knocked the head out of an empty hogshead and hoisted this hogshead to the flat roof of the chapel, where we clamped it down fast, poured in gunpowder till it lay loosely an inch deep on the bottom, then we stood up rockets in the hogshead as thick as they could loosely stand, all the different breeds of rockets there are; and they made a portly and imposing sheaf, I can tell you. We grounded the wire of a pocket electrical battery in that powder, we placed a whole magazine of Greek fire on each corner of the roof—blue on one corner, green on another, red on another, and purple on the last—and grounded a wire in each.

About two hundred yards off, in the flat, we built a pen of scantlings, about four feet high, and laid planks on it, and so made a platform. We covered it with swell tapestries borrowed for the occasion, and topped it off with the abbot's own throne. When you are going to do a miracle for an ignorant race, you want to get in every detail that will count; you want to make all the properties impressive to the public eye; you want to make matters comfortable for your head guest; then you can turn yourself loose and play your effects for all they are worth. I know the value of these things, for I know human nature. You can't throw too much style into a miracle. It costs trouble, and work, and sometimes money; but it pays in the end. Well, we brought the wires to the ground at the chapel, and then brought them under the ground to the platform, and hid the batteries there. We put a rope fence a hundred feet square around the platform to keep off the common multitude, and that finished the work. My idea was, doors open at ten-thirty, performance to begin at eleven-twenty-five sharp. I wished I could charge admission, but of course that wouldn't answer. I instructed my boys to be in the chapel as early as ten, before anybody was around, and be ready to man the pumps at the proper time, and make the fur fly. Then we went home to supper.

The news of the disaster to the well had traveled far by this time; and now for two or three days a steady avalanche of people had been pouring into the valley. The lower end of the valley was become one huge camp; we should have a good house, no question about that. Criers went the rounds early in the evening and announced the coming attempt, which put every pulse up to fever-heat. They gave notice that the abbot and his official suite would move in state and occupy the platform at ten-thirty, up to which time all the region which was under my ban must be clear; the bells would then cease from tolling, and this sign should be permission to the multitudes to close in and take their places.

I was at the platform and all ready to do the honors when the abbot's solemn procession hove in sight—which it did not do till it was nearly to the rope fence, because it was a starless black night and no torches permitted. With it came Merlin, and took a front seat on the platform; he was as good as his word for once. One could not see the multitudes banked together beyond the ban, but they were there, just the same. The moment the bells stopped, those banked masses broke and poured over the line like a vast black wave, and for as much as a half-hour it continued to flow, and then it solidified itself, and you could have walked upon a pavement of human heads to—well, miles.

We had a solemn stage-wait, now, for about twenty minutes—a thing I had counted on for effect; it is always good to let your audience have a chance to work up its expectancy. At length, out of the silence a noble Latin chant—men's voices—broke and swelled up and rolled away into the night, a majestic tide of melody. I had put that up, too, and it was one of the best effects I ever invented. When it was finished I stood up on the platform and extended my hands abroad, for two minutes, with my face uplifted—that always produces a dead hush— and then slowly pronounced this ghastly word with a kind of awfulness which caused hundreds to tremble, and many women to faint:

" Constantinopolitanischerdudelsackspfeifenmachersgesellschafft !"

Just as I was moaning out the closing hunks of that word, I touched off one of my electric connections, and all that murky world of people stood revealed in a hideous blue glare! It was immense—that effect! Lots of people shrieked, women curled up and quit in every direction, foundlings collapsed by platoons. The abbot and the monks crossed themselves nimbly and their lips fluttered with agitated prayers. Merlin held his grip, but he was astonished clear down to his corns; he had never seen anything to begin with that, before. Now was the time to pile in the effects. I lifted my hands and groaned out this word—as it were in agony:

" Nihilistendynamittheaterkaestchenssprengungsattentaets- versuchungen !"

—and turned on the red fire! You should have heard that Atlantic of people moan and howl when that crimson hell joined the blue! After sixty seconds I shouted:

" Transvaaltruppentropentransporttrampeltbier- treibertrauungsthraenentragoedie !"

—and lit up the green fire! After waiting only forty seconds this time, I spread my arms abroad and thundered out the devastating syllables of this word of words:

" Mekkamuselmannenmassenmench= enmoerdermohrenmuttermarmormonu= mentenmacher!"

—and whirled on the purple glare! There they were, all going at once, red, blue, green, purple!—four furious volcanoes pouring vast clouds of radiant smoke aloft, and spreading a blinding rainbowed noonday to the furthest confines of that valley. In the distance one could see that fellow on the pillar standing rigid against the background of sky, his seesaw stopped for the first time in twenty years. I knew the boys were at the pump now and ready. So I said to the abbot:

"The time is come, Father. I am about to pronounce the dread name and command the spell to dissolve. You want to brace up, and take hold of something." Then I shouted to the people: "Behold, in another minute the spell will be broken, or no mortal can break it. If it break, all will know it, for you will see the sacred water gush from the chapel door!"

I stood a few moments, to let the hearers have a chance to spread my announcement to those who couldn't hear, and so convey it to the furthest ranks, then I made a grand exhibition of extra posturing and gesturing, and shouted:

"Lo, I command the fell spirit that possesses the holy fountain to now disgorge into the skies all the infernal fires that still remain in him, and straightway dissolve his spell and flee hence to the pit, there to lie bound a thousand years. By his own dread name I command it—BGWJJILLIGKKK!"

Then I touched off the hogshead of rockets, and a vast fountain of dazzling lances of fire vomited itself toward the zenith with a hissing rush, and burst in mid-sky into a storm of flashing jewels! One mighty groan of terror started up from the massed people—then suddenly broke into a wild hosannah of joy—for there, fair and plain in the uncanny glare, they saw the freed water leaping forth! The old abbot could not speak a word, for tears and the chokings in his throat; without utterance of any sort, he folded me in his arms and mashed me. It was more eloquent than speech. And harder to get over, too, in a country where there were really no doctors that were worth a damaged nickel.

You should have seen those acres of people throw themselves down in that water and kiss it; kiss it, and pet it, and fondle it, and talk to it as if it were alive, and welcome it back with the dear names they gave their darlings, just as if it had been a friend who was long gone away and lost, and was come home again. Yes, it was pretty to see, and made me think more of them than I had done before.

I sent Merlin home on a shutter. He had caved in and gone down like a landslide when I pronounced that fearful name, and had never come to since. He never had heard that name before—neither had I—but to him it was the right one. Any jumble would have been the right one. He admitted, afterward, that that spirit's own mother could not have pronounced that name better than I did. He never could understand how I survived it, and I didn't tell him. It is only young magicians that give away a secret like that. Merlin spent three months working enchantments to try to find out the deep trick of how to pronounce that name and outlive it. But he didn't arrive.

When I started to the chapel, the populace uncovered and fell back reverently to make a wide way for me, as if I had been some kind of a superior being— and I was. I was aware of that. I took along a night shift of monks, and taught them the mystery of the pump, and set them to work, for it was plain that a good part of the people out there were going to sit up with the water all night, consequently it was but right that they should have all they wanted of it. To those monks that pump was a good deal of a miracle itself, and they were full of wonder over it; and of admiration, too, of the exceeding effectiveness of its performance.

It was a great night, an immense night. There was reputation in it. I could hardly get to sleep for glorying over it.

Chapter XXIV

A RIVAL MAGICIAN

MY INFLUENCE IN the Valley of Holiness was something prodigious now. It seemed worth while to try to turn it to some valuable account. The thought came to me the next morning, and was suggested by my seeing one of my knights who was in the soap line come riding in. According to history, the monks of this place two centuries before had been worldly-minded enough to want to wash. It might be that there was a leaven of this unrighteousness still remaining. So I sounded a Brother:

"Wouldn't you like a bath?"

He shuddered at the thought—the thought of the peril of it to the well—but he said with feeling:

"One needs not to ask that of a poor body who has not known that blessed refreshment sith that he was a boy. Would God I might wash me! but it may not be, fair sir, tempt me not; it is forbidden."

And then he sighed in such a sorrowful way that I was resolved he should have at least one layer of his real estate removed, if it sized up my whole influence and bankrupted the pile. So I went to the abbot and asked for a permit for this Brother. He blenched at the idea—I don't mean that you could see him blench, for of course you couldn't see it without you scraped him, and I didn't care enough about it to scrape him, but I knew the blench was there, just the same, and within a book-cover's thickness of the surface, too—blenched, and trembled. He said:

"Ah, son, ask aught else thou wilt, and it is thine, and freely granted out of a grateful heart—but this, oh, this! Would you drive away the blessed water again?"

"No, Father, I will not drive it away. I have mysterious knowledge which teaches me that there was an error that other time when it was thought the institution of the bath banished the fountain." A large interest began to show up in the old man's face. "My knowledge informs me that the bath was innocent of that misfortune, which was caused by quite another sort of sin."

"These are brave words—but—but right welcome, if they be true."

"They are true, indeed. Let me build the bath again, Father. Let me build it again, and the fountain shall flow forever."

"You promise this?—you promise it? Say the word—say you promise it !"

"I do promise it."

"Then will I have the first bath myself! Go—get ye to your work. Tarry not, tarry not, but go."

I and my boys were at work, straight off. The ruins of the old bath were there yet in the basement of the monastery, not a stone missing. They had been left just so, all these lifetimes, and avoided with a pious fear, as things accursed. In two days we had it all done and the water in—a spacious pool of clear pure

water that a body could swim in. It was running water, too. It came in, and
went out, through the ancient pipes. The old abbot kept his word, and was the
first to try it. He went down black and shaky, leaving the whole black community
above troubled and worried and full of bodings; but he came back white and
joyful, and the game was made! another triumph scored.

It was a good campaign that we made in that Valley of Holiness, and I was
very well satisfied, and ready to move on now, but I struck a disappointment.
I caught a heavy cold, and it started up an old lurking rheumatism of mine. Of
course the rheumatism hunted up my weakest place and located itself there. This
was the place where the abbot put his arms about me and mashed me, what time
he was moved to testify his gratitude to me with an embrace.

When at last I got out, I was a shadow. But everybody was full of attentions
and kindnesses, and these brought cheer back into my life, and were the right
medicine to help a convalescent swiftly up toward health and strength again; so
I gained fast.

Sandy was worn out with nursing, so I made up my mind to turn out and go
a cruise alone, leaving her at the nunnery to rest up. My idea was to disguise
myself as a freeman of peasant degree and wander through the country a week
or two on foot. This would give me a chance to eat and lodge with the lowliest
and poorest class of free citizens on equal terms. There was no other way to
inform myself perfectly of their every-day life and the operation of the laws
upon it. If I went among them as a gentleman, there would be restraints and
conventionalities which would shut me out from their private joys and troubles,
and I should get no further than the outside shell.

One morning I was out on a long walk to get up muscle for my trip, and had
climbed the ridge which bordered the northern extremity of the valley, when I
came upon an artificial opening in the face of a low precipice, and recognized
it by its location as a hermitage which had often been pointed out to me from
a distance as the den of a hermit of high renown for dirt and austerity. I knew
he had lately been offered a situation in the Great Sahara, where lions and
sandflies made the hermit life peculiarly attractive and difficult, and had gone
to Africa to take possession, so I thought I would look in and see how the
atmosphere of this den agreed with its reputation.

My surprise was great: the place was newly swept and scoured. Then there
was another surprise. Back in the gloom of the cavern I heard the clink of a
little bell, and then this exclamation:

"*Hello, Central! Is this you, Camelot?*—Behold, thou mayst glad thy heart
an thou hast faith to believe the wonderful when that it cometh in unexpected
guise and maketh itself manifest in impossible places—here standeth in the flesh
his mightiness The Boss, and with thine own ears shall ye hear him speak!"

Now what a radical revesal of things this was; what a jumbling together of
extravagant incongruities; what a fantastic conjunction of opposites and irrec-
oncilables—the home of the bogus miracle become the home of a real one, the
den of a medieval hermit turned into a telephone office!

The telephone clerk stepped into the light, and I recognized one of my young
fellows. I said:

"How long has this office been established here, Ulfius?"

"But since midnight, fair Sir Boss, an it please you. We saw many lights in
the valley, and so judged it well to make a station, for that where so many lights
be needs must they indicate a town of goodly size."

"Quite right. It isn't a town in the customary sense, but it's a good stand, anyway. Do you know where you are?"

"Of that I have had no time to make inquiry; for when as my comradeship moved hence upon their labors, leaving me in charge, I got me to needed rest, purposing to inquire when I waked, and report the place's name to Camelot for record."

"Well, this is the Valley of Holiness."

It didn't take; I mean, he didn't start at the name, as I had supposed he would. He merely said:

"I will so report it."

"Why, the surrounding regions are filled with the noise of late wonders that have happened here! You didn't hear of them?"

"An, ye will remember we move by night, and avoid speech with all. We learn naught but that we get by the telephone from Camelot."

"Why *they* know all about this thing. Haven't they told you anything about the great miracle of the restoration of a holy fountain?"

"Oh, *that*? Indeed yes. But the name of *this* valley doth woundily differ from the name of *that* one; indeed to differ wider were not pos—"

"What was that name, then?"

"The Valley of Hellishness."

"*That* explains it. Confound a telephone, anyway. It is the very demon for conveying similarities of sound that are miracles of divergence from similarity of sense. But no matter, you know the name of the place now. Call up Camelot."

He did it, and had Clarence sent for. It was good to hear my boy's voice again. It was like being home. After some affectionate interchanges, and some account of my late illness, I said:

"What is new?"

"The king and queen and many of the court do start even in this hour, to go to your valley to pay pious homage to the waters ye have restored, and cleanse themselves of sin, and see the place where the infernal spirit spouted true hell-flames to the clouds—an ye listen sharply ye may hear me wink and hear me likewise smile a smile, sith 'twas I that made selection of those flames from out our stock and sent them by your order."

"Does the king know the way to this place?"

"The king?—no, nor to any other in his realms, mayhap; but the lads that help you with your miracle will be his guide and lead the way, and appoint the places for rests at noon and sleeps at night."

"This will bring them here—when?"

"Mid-afternoon, or later, the third day."

"Anything else in the way of news?"

"The king hath begun the raising of the standing army ye suggested to him; one regiment is complete and officered."

"The mischief! I wanted a main hand in that myself. There is only one body of men in the kingdom that are fitted to officer a regular army."

"Yes—and now ye will marvel to know there's not so much as one West-Pointer in that regiment."

"What are you talking about? Are you in earnest?"

"It is truly as I have said."

"Why, this makes me uneasy. Who were chosen, and what was the method? Competitive examination?"

"Indeed, I know naught of the method. I but know this—these officers be all of noble family, and are born—what is it you call it?—chuckle-heads."

"There's something wrong, Clarence."

"Comfort yourself, then; for two candidates for a lieutenancy do travel hence with the king—young nobles both—and if you but wait where you are you will hear them questioned."

"That is news to the purpose. I will get one West-Pointer in, anyway. Mount a man and send him to that school with a message; let him kill horses, if necessary, but he must be there before sunset to-night and say—"

"There is no need. I have laid a ground-wire to the school. Prithee let me connect you with it."

It sounded good! In this atmosphere of telephones and lightning communication with distant regions, I was breathing the breath of life again after long suffocation. I realized, then, what a creepy, dull, inanimate horror this land had been to me all these years, and how I had been in such a stifled condition of mind as to have grown used to it almost beyond the power to notice it.

I gave my order to the superintendent of the Academy personally. I also asked him to bring me some paper and a fountain-pen and a box or so of safety matches. I was getting tired of doing without these conveniences. I could have them now, as I wasn't going to wear armor any more at present, and therefore could get at my pockets.

When I got back to the monastery, I found a thing of interest going on. The abbot and his monks were assembled in the great hall, observing with childish wonder and faith the performances of a new magician, a fresh arrival. His dress was the extreme of the fantastic; as showy and foolish as the sort of thing an Indian medicine-man wears. He was mowing, and mumbling, and gesticulating, and drawing mystical figures in the air and on the floor—the regular thing, you know. He was a celebrity from Asia—so he said, and that was enough. That sort of evidence was as good as gold, and passed current everywhere.

How easy and cheap it was to be a great magician on this fellow's terms. His specialty was to tell you what any individual on the face of the globe was doing at the moment; and what he had done at any time in the past, and what he would do at any time in the future. He asked if any would like to know what the Emperor of the East was doing now? The sparkling eyes and the delighted rubbing of hands made eloquent answer—this reverend crowd *would* like to know what that monarch was at, just at this moment. The fraud went through some more mummery, and then made grave announcement:

"The high and mighty Emperor of the East doth at this moment put money in the palm of a holy begging friar—one, two, three pieces, and they be all of silver."

A buzz of admiring exclamations broke out, all around:

"It is marvelous!" "Wonderful!" "What study, what labor, to have acquired a so amazing power as this!' '

Would they like to know what the Supreme Lord of Inde was doing? Yes. He told them what the Supreme Lord of Inde was doing. Then he told them what the Sultan of Egypt was at; also what the King of the Remote Seas was about. And so on and so on; and with each new marvel the astonishment at his accuracy rose higher and higher. They thought he must surely strike an uncertain place some time; but no, he never had to hesitate, he always knew, and always with unerring precision. I saw that if this thing went on I should lose my supremacy, this fellow would capture my following, I should be left out in the cold. I must put a cog in his wheel, and do it right away, too. I said:

"If I might ask, I should very greatly like to know what a certain person is doing."

"Speak, and freely. I will tell you."

"It will be difficult—perhaps impossible."

"My art knoweth not that word. The more difficult it is, the more certainly will I reveal it to you."

You see, I was working up the interest. It was getting pretty high, too; you could see that by the craning necks all around, and the half-suspended breathing. So now I climaxed it:

"If you make no mistake—if you tell me truly what I want to know—I will give you two hundred silver pennies."

"The fortune is mine! I will tell you what you would know."

"Then tell me what I am doing with my right hand."

"Ah-h!" There was a general gasp of surprise. It had not occurred to anybody in the crowd—that simple trick of inquiring about somebody who wasn't ten thousand miles away. The magician was hit hard; it was an emergency that had never happened in his experience before, and it corked him; he didn't know how to meet it. He looked stunned, confused; he couldn't say a word. "Come," I said, "what are you waiting for? Is it possible you can answer up, right off, and tell what anybody on the other side of the earth is doing, and yet can't tell what a person is doing who isn't three yards from you? Persons behind me know what I am doing with my right hand—they will indorse you if you tell correctly." He was still dumb. "Very well, I'll tell you why you don't speak up and tell; it is because you don't know. *You* a magician! Good friends, this tramp is a mere fraud and liar."

This distressed the monks and terrified them. They were not used to hearing these awful beings called names, and they did not know what might be the consequence. There was a dead silence now; superstitious bodings were in every mind. The magician began to pull his wits together, and when he presently smiled an easy, nonchalant smile, it spread a mighty relief around; for it indicated that his mood was not destructive. He said:

"It hath struck me speechless, the frivolity of this person's speech. Let all know, if perchance there be any who know it not, that enchanters of my degree deign not to concern themselves with the doings of any but kings, princes, emperors, them that be born in the purple and them only. Had ye asked me what Arthur the great king is doing, it were another matter, and I had told ye; but the doings of a subject interest me not."

"Oh, I misunderstood you. I thought you said 'anybody,' and so I supposed 'anybody' included—well, anybody; that is, everybody."

"It doth—anybody that is of lofty birth; and the better if he be royal."

"That, it meseemeth, might well be," said the abbot, who saw his opportunity to smooth things and avert disaster, "for it were not likely that so wonderful a gift as this would be conferred for the revelation of the concerns of lesser beings than such as be born near to the summits of greatness. Our Arthur the king—"

"Would you know of him?" broke in the enchanter.

"Most gladly, yea, and gratefully."

Everybody was full of awe and interest again right away, the incorrigible idiots. They watched the incantations absorbingly, and looked at me with a "There, now, what can you say to that?" air, when the announcement came:

"The king is weary with the chase, and lieth in his palace these two hours sleeping a dreamless sleep."

"God's benison upon him!" said the abbot, and crossed himself; "may that sleep be to the refreshment of his body and his soul."

"And so it might be, if he were sleeping," I said, "but the king is not sleeping, the king rides."

Here was trouble again—a conflict of authority. Nobody knew which of us to believe; I still had some reputation left. The magician's scorn was stirred, and he said:

"Lo, I have seen many wonderful soothsayers and prophets and magicians in my life days, but none before that could sit idle and see to the heart of things with never an incantation to help."

"You have lived in the woods, and lost much by it. I use incantations myself, as this good brotherhood are aware—but only on occasions of moment."

When it comes to sarcasming, I reckon I know how to keep my end up. That jab made this fellow squirm. The abbot inquired after the queen and the court, and got this information:

"They be all on sleep, being overcome by fatigue, like as to the king."

I said:

"That is merely another lie. Half of them are about their amusements, the queen and the other half are not sleeping, they ride. Now perhaps you can spread yourself a little, and tell us where the king and queen and all that are this moment riding with them are going?"

"They sleep now, as I said; but on the morrow they will ride, for they go a journey toward the sea."

"And where will they be the day after to-morrow at vespers?"

"Far to the north of Camelot, and half their journey will be done."

"That is another lie, by the space of a hundred and fifty miles. Their journey will not be merely half done, it will be all done, and they will be *here,* in this valley."

That was a noble shot! It set the abbot and the monks in a whirl of excitement, and it rocked the enchanter to his base. I followed the thing right up:

"If the king does not arrive, I will have myself ridden on a rail: if he does I will ride you on a rail instead."

Next day I went up to the telephone office and found that the king had passed through two towns that were on the line. I spotted his progress on the succeeding day in the same way. I kept these matters to myself. The third day's reports showed that if he kept up his gait he would arrive by four in the afternoon. There was still no sign anywhere of interest in his coming; there seemed to be no preparations making to receive him in state; a strange thing, truly. Only one thing could explain this: that other magician had been cutting under me, sure. This was true. I asked a friend of mine, a monk, about it, and he said, yes, the magician had tried some further enchantments and found out that the court had concluded to make no journey at all, but stay at home. Think of that! Observe how much a reputation was worth in such a country. These people had seen me do the very showiest bit of magic in history, and the only one within their memory that had a positive value, and yet here they were, ready to take up with an adventurer who could offer no evidence of his powers but his mere unproven word.

However, it was not good politics to let the king come without any fuss and feathers at all, so I went down and drummed up a procession of pilgrims and smoked out a batch of hermits and started them out at two o'clock to meet him. And that was the sort of state he arrived in. The abbot was helpless with rage and humiliation when I brought him out on a balcony and showed him the head of the state marching in and never a monk on hand to offer him welcome, and no stir of life or clang of joy-bell to glad his spirit. He took one look and then flew to rouse out his forces. The next minute the bells were dinning furiously, and the various buildings were vomiting monks and nuns, who went swarming in a rush toward the coming procession; and with them went that magician— and he was on a rail, too, by the abbot's order; and his reputation was in the mud, and mine was in the sky again. Yes, a man can keep his trade-mark current in such a country, but he can't sit around and do it; he has got to be on deck and attending to business right along.

Chapter XXV

A COMPETITIVE EXAMINATION

WHEN THE KING traveled for change of air, or made a progress, or visited a distant noble whom he wished to bankrupt with the cost of his keep, part of the administration moved with him. It was a fashion of the time. The Commission charged with the examination of candidates for posts in the army came with the king to the Valley, whereas they could have transacted their business just as well at home. And although this expedition was strictly a holiday excursion for the king, he kept some of his business functions going just the same. He touched for the evil, as usual; he held court in the gate at sunrise and tried cases, for he was himself Chief Justice of the King's Bench.

He shone very well in this latter office. He was a wise and humane judge, and he clearly did his honest best and fairest—according to his lights. That is a large reservation. His lights—I mean his rearing—often colored his decisions. Whenever there was a dispute between a noble or gentleman and a person of lower degree, the King's leanings and sympathies were for the former class always, whether he suspected it or not. It was impossible that this should be otherwise. The blunting effects of slavery upon the slaveholder's moral perceptions are known and conceded, the world over; and a privileged class, an aristocracy, is but a band of slaveholders under another name. This has a harsh sound, and yet should not be offensive to any—even to the noble himself—unless the fact itself be an offense: for the statement simply formulates a fact. The repulsive feature of slavery is the *thing,* not its name. One needs but to hear an aristocrat speak of the classes that are below him to recognize—and in but indifferently modified measure—the very air and tone of the actual slaveholder; and behind these are the slaveholder's spirit, the slaveholder's blunted feeling. They are the result of the same cause in both cases: the possessor's old and inbred custom of regarding himself as a superior being. The king's judgments wrought frequent injustices, but it was merely the fault of his training, his natural and unalterable sympathies. He was as unfitted for a judgeship as would be the average mother for the position of milk-distributer to starving children in famine-time; her own children would fare a shade better than the rest.

One very curious case came before the king. A young girl, an orphan, who had a considerable estate, married a fine young fellow who had nothing. The girl's property was within a seigniory held by the Church. The bishop of the diocese, an arrogant scion of the great nobility, claimed the girl's estate on the ground that she had married privately, and thus had cheated the Church out of one of its rights as lord of the seigniory—the one heretofore referred to as *le droit du seigneur*. The penalty of refusal or avoidance was confiscation. The girl's defense was, that the lordship of the seigniory was vested in the bishop, and the particular right here involved was not transferable, but must be exercised by the lord himself or stand vacated; and that an older law, of the Church itself, strictly barred the bishop from exercising it. It was a very odd case, indeed.

It reminded me of something I had read in my youth about the ingenious way in which the aldermen of London raised the money that built the Mansion House. A person who had not taken the Sacrament according to the Anglican rite could not stand as a candidate for sheriff of London. Thus Dissenters were ineligible; they could not run if asked, they could not serve if elected. The aldermen, who without any question were Yankees in disguise, hit upon this neat device: they passed a by-law imposing a fine of £400 upon any one who should refuse to be a candidate for sheriff, and a fine of £600 upon any person who, after being elected sheriff, refused to serve. Then they went to work and elected a lot of Dissenters, one after another, and kept it up until they had collected £15,000 in fines; and there stands the stately Mansion House to this day, to keep the blushing citizen in mind of a long past and lamented day when a band of Yankees slipped into London and played games of the sort that has given their race a unique and shady reputation among all truly good and holy peoples that be in the earth.

The girl's case seemed strong to me; the bishop's case was just as strong. I did not see how the king was going to get out of this hole. But he got out. I append his decision:

"Truly I find small difficulty here, the matter being even a child's affair for simpleness. An the young bride had conveyed notice, as in duty bound, to her feudal lord and proper master and protector the bishop, she had suffered no loss, for the said bishop could have got a dispensation making him, for temporary conveniency, eligible to the exercise of his said right, and thus would she have kept all she had. Whereas, failing in her first duty, she hath by that failure failed in all; for whoso, clinging to a rope, severeth it above his hands, must fall; it being no defense to claim that the rest of the rope is sound, neither any deliverance from his peril, as he shall find. Pardy, the woman's case is rotten at the source. It is the decree of the court that she forfeit to the said lord bishop all her goods, even to the last farthing that she doth possess, and be thereto mulcted in the costs. Next!"

Here was a tragic end to a beautiful honeymoon not yet three months old. Poor young creatures! They had lived these three months lapped to the lips in worldy comforts. These clothes and trinkets they were wearing were as fine and dainty as the shrewdest stretch of the sumptuary laws allowed to people of their degree; and in these pretty clothes, she crying on his shoulder, and he trying to comfort her with hopeful words set to the music of despair, they went from the judgment seat out into the world homeless, bedless, breadless; why, the very beggars by the roadsides were not so poor as they.

Well, the king was out of the hole; and on terms satisfactory to the Church and the rest of the aristocracy, no doubt. Men write many fine and plausible arguments in support of monarchy, but the fact remains that where every man in a state has a vote, brutal laws are impossible. Arthur's people were of course poor material for a republic, because they had been debased so long by monarchy; and yet even they would have been intelligent enough to make short work of that law which the king had just been administering if it had been submitted to their full and free vote. There is a phrase which has grown so common in the world's mouth that it has come to seem to have sense and meaning—the sense and meaning implied when it is used; that is the phrase which refers to this or that or the other nation as possibly being "capable of self-government"; and the implied sense of it is, that there has been a nation somewhere, some time or other, which *wasn't* capable of it—wasn't as able to govern itself as some self-appointed specialists were or would be to govern it. The master minds of all nations, in all ages, have sprung in affluent multitude from the mass of the nation, and from the mass of the nation only—not from its privileged classes; and so, no matter what the nation's intellectual grade was, whether high or low, the bulk of its ability was in the long ranks of its nameless and its poor, and so it never saw the day that it had not the material in abundance whereby to govern itself. Which is to assert an always selfproven fact: that even the best-governed and most free and most enlightened monarchy is still behind the best condition attainable by its people; and that the same is true of kindred governments of lower grades, all the way down to the lowest.

King Arthur had hurried up the army business altogether beyond my calculations. I had not supposed he would move in the matter while I was away; and so I had not mapped out a scheme for determining the merits of officers; I had only remarked that it would be wise to submit every candidate to a sharp and searching examination; and privately I meant to put together a list of military qualifications that nobody could answer to but my West-Pointers. That ought to have been attended to before I left; for the king was so taken with the idea of a standing army that he couldn't wait but must get about it at once, and get up as good a scheme of examination as he could invent out of his own head.

I was impatient to see what this was; and to show, too, how much more admirable was the one which I should display to the Examining Board. I intimated this, gently, to the king, and it fired his curiosity. When the Board was assembled, I followed him in, and behind us came the candidates. One of these candidates was a bright young West-Pointer of mine, and with him were a couple of my West Point professors.

When I saw the Board, I did not know whether to cry or to laugh. The head of it was the officer known to later centuries as Norroy King-at-Arms! The two other members were chiefs of bureaus in his department; and all three were priests, of course; all officials who had to know how to read and write were priests.

My candidate was called first, out of courtesy to me, and the head of the Board opened on him with official solemnity:

"Name?"

"Mal-ease."

"Son of?"

"Webster."

"Webster—Webster. H'm—I—my memory faileth to recall the name. Condition?"

"Weaver."

"Weaver!—God keep us!"

The king was staggered, from his summit to his foundations; one clerk fainted, and the others came near it. The chairman pulled himself together, and said indignantly:

"It is sufficient. Get you hence."

But I appealed to the king. I begged that my candidate might be examined. The king was willing, but the Board, who were all well-born folk, implored the king to spare them the indignity of examining the weaver's son. I knew they didn't know enough to examine him anyway, so I joined my prayers to theirs and the king turned the duty over to my professors. I had had a blackboard prepared, and it was put up now, and the circus began. It was beautiful to hear the lad lay out the science of war, and wallow in details of battle and siege, of supply, transportation, mining and countermining, grand tactics, big strategy and little strategy, signal service, infantry, cavalry, artillery, and all about siege-guns, field-guns, Gatling guns, rifled guns, smooth bores, musket practice, revolver practice—and not a solitary word of it all could these catfish make head or tail of, you understand—and it was handsome to see him chalk off mathematical nightmares on the blackboard that would stump the angels themselves, and do it like nothing, too—all about eclipses, and comets, and solstices, and constellations, and mean time, and sidereal time, and dinner-time, and bedtime, and every other imaginable thing above the clouds or under them that you could harry or bullyrag an enemy with and make him wish he hadn't come—and when the boy made his military salute and stood aside at last, I was proud enough to hug him, and all those other people were so dazed they looked partly petrified, partly drunk, and wholly caught out and snowed under. I judged that the cake was ours, and by a large majority.

Education is a great thing. This was the same youth who had come to West Point so ignorant that when I asked him, "If a general officer should have a horse shot under him on the field of battle, what ought he to do?" answered up naively and said:

"Get up and brush himself."

One of the young nobles was called up now. I thought I would question him a little myself. I said:

"Can your lordship read?"

His face flushed indignantly, and he fired this at me:

"Takest me for a clerk? I trow I am not of a blood that—"

"Answer the question!"

He crowded his wrath down and made out to answer "No."

"Can you write?"

He wanted to resent this, too, but I said:

"You will confine yourself to the questions, and make no comments. You are not here to air your blood or your graces, and nothing of the sort will be permitted. Can you write?"

"No."

"Do you know the multiplication table?"

"I wit not what ye refer to."

"How much is nine times six?"

"It is a mystery that is hidden from me by reason that the emergency requiring the fathoming of it hath not in my life-days occurred, and so, not having no need to know this thing, I abide barren of the knowledge."

"If A trade a barrel of onions to B, worth two-pence the bushel, in exchange for sheep worth four-pence and a dog worth a penny, and C kill the dog before delivery, because bitten by the same, who mistook him for D, what sum is still due to A from B, and which party pays for the dog, C or D, and who gets the money? If A, is the penny sufficient, or may he claim consequential damages in the form of additional money to represent the possible profit which might have inured from the dog, and classifiable as earned increment, that is to say, usufruct?"

"Verily, in the all-wise and unknowable providence of God, who moveth in mysterious ways His wonders to perform, have I never heard the fellow to this question for confusion of the mind and congestion of the ducts of thought. Wherefore I beseech you let the dog and the onions and these people of the strange and godless names work out their several salvations from their piteous and wonderful difficulties without help of mine, for indeed their trouble is sufficient as it is, whereas an I tried to help I should but damage their cause the more and yet mayhap not live myself to see the desolation wrought."

"What do you know of the laws of attraction and gravitation?"

"If there be such, mayhap his grace the king did promulgate them whilst that I lay sick about the beginning of the year and thereby failed to hear his proclamation."

"What do you know of the science of optics?"

"I know of governors of places, and seneschals of castles, and sheriffs of counties, and many like small offices and titles of honor, but him you call the Science of Optics I have not heard of before; peradventure it is a new dignity."

"Yes, in this country."

Try to conceive of this mollusk gravely applying for an official position, of any kind under the sun! Why, he had all the earmarks of a typewriter copyist, if you leave out the disposition to contribute uninvited emendations of your grammar and punctuation. It was unaccountable that he didn't attempt a little help of that sort out of his majestic supply of incapacity for the job. But that didn't prove that he hadn't material in him for the disposition, it only proved that he wasn't a typewriter copyist yet. After nagging him a little more, I let the professors loose on him and they turned him inside out, on the line of scientific war, and found him empty, of course. He knew somewhat about the warfare of the time—bushwhacking around for ogres, and bull-fights in the tournament ring, and such things—but otherwise he was empty and useless. Then we took the other young noble in hand, and he was the first one's twin, for ignorance and incapacity. I delivered them into the hands of the chairman of the Board with the comfortable consciousness that their cake was dough. They were examined in the previous order of precedence.

"Name, so please you?"

"Pertipole, son of Sir Pertipole, Baron of Barley Mash."

"Grandfather?"

"Also Sir Pertipole, Baron of Barley Mash."

"Great-grandfather?"

"The same name and title."

"Great-great-grandfather?"

"We had none, worshipful sir, the line failing before it had reached so far back."

"It mattereth not. It is a good four generations, and fulfilleth the requirements of the rule."

"Fulfils what rule?" I asked.

"The rule requiring four generations of nobility or else the candidate is not eligible."

"A man not eligible for a lieutenancy in the army unless he can prove four generations of noble descent?"

"Even so; neither lieutenant nor any other officer may be commissioned without that qualification."

"Oh, come, this is an astonishing thing. What good is such a qualification as that?"

"What good? It is a hardy question, fair sir and Boss, since it doth go far to impugn the wisdom of even our holy Mother Church herself."

"As how?"

"For that she hath established the selfsame rule regarding saints. By her law none may be canonized until he hath lain dead four generations."

"I see, I see—it is the same thing. It is wonderful. In the one case a man lies dead-alive four generations—mummified in ignorance and sloth—and that qualifies him to command live people, and take their weal and woe into his impotent hands; and in the other case, a man lies bedded with death and worms four generations, and that qualifies him for office in the celestial camp. Does the king's grace approve of this strange law?"

The king said:

"Why, truly I see naught about it that is strange. All places of honor and of profit do belong, by natural right, to them that be of noble blood, and so these dignities in the army are their property and would be so without this or any rule. The rule is but to mark a limit. Its purpose is to keep out too recent blood, which would bring into contempt these offices, and men of lofty lineage would turn their backs and scorn to take them. I were to blame an I permitted this calamity. *You* can permit it an you are minded so to do, for you have the delegated authority, but that the king should do it were a most strange madness and not comprehensible to any."

"I yield. Proceed, sir Chief of the Herald's College."

The chairman resumed as follows:

"By what illustrious achievement for the honor of the Throne and state did the founder of your great line lift himself to the sacred dignity of the British nobility?' '

"He built a brewery."

"Sire, the Board finds this candidate perfect in all the requirements and qualifications for military command, and doth hold his case open for decision after due examination of his competitor."

The competitor came forward and proved exactly four generations of nobility himself. So there was a tie in military qualifications that far.

He stood aside a moment, and Sir Pertipole was questioned further:

"Of what condition was the wife of the founder of your line?"

"She came of the highest landed gentry, yet she was not noble; she was gracious and pure and charitable, of a blameless life and character, insomuch that in these regards was she peer of the best lady in the land.''

"That will do. Stand down." He called up the competing lordling again, and asked: "What was the rank and condition of the great-grandmother who conferred British nobility upon your great house?"

"She was a king's leman and did climb to that splendid eminence by her own unholpen merit from the sewer where she was born."

"Ah, this, indeed, is true nobility, this is the right and perfect intermixture. The lieutenancy is yours, fair lord. Hold it not in contempt; it is the humble step which will lead to grandeurs more worthy of the splendor of an origin like to thine.''

I was down in the bottomless pit of humiliation. I had promised myself an easy and zenith-scouring triumph, and this was the outcome!

I was almost ashamed to look my poor disappointed cadet in the face. I told him to go home and be patient, this wasn't the end.

I had a private audience with the king, and made a proposition. I said it was quite right to officer that regiment with nobilities, and he couldn't have done a wiser thing. It would also be a good idea to add five hundred officers to it; in fact, add as many officers as there were nobles and relatives of nobles in the country, even if there should finally be five times as many officers as privates in it; and thus make it the crack regiment, the envied regiment, the King's Own regiment, and entitled to fight on its own hook and in its own way, and go whither it would and come when it pleased, in time of war, and be utterly swell and independent. This would make that regiment the heart's desire of all the nobility, and they would all be satisfied and happy. Then we would make up the rest of the standing army out of commonplace materials, and officer it with nobodies, as was proper—nobodies selected on a basis of mere efficiency—and we would make this regiment toe the line, allow it no aristocratic freedom from restraint, and force it to do all the work and persistent hammering, to the end that whenever the King's Own was tired and wanted to go off for a change and rummage around amongst ogres and have a good time, it could go without uneasiness, knowing that matters were in safe hands behind it, and business going to be continued at the old stand, same as usual. The king was charmed with the idea.

When I noticed that, it gave me a valuable notion. I thought I saw my way out of an old and stubborn difficulty at last. You see, the royalties of the Pendragon stock were a long-lived race and very fruitful. Whenever a child was born to any of these—and it was pretty often—there was wild joy in the nation's mouth, and piteous sorrow in the nation's heart. The joy was questionable, but the grief was honest. Because the event meant another call for a Royal Grant. Long was the list of these royalties, and they were a heavy and steadily increasing burden upon the treasury and a menace to the crown. Yet Arthur could not believe this latter fact, and he would not listen to any of my various projects for substituting something in the place of the royal grants. If I could have persuaded him to now and then provide a support for one of these outlying scions from his own pocket, I could have made a grand to-do over it, and it would have had a good effect with the nation; but no, he wouldn't hear of such a thing. He had something like a religious passion for royal grant; he seemed to look upon it as a sort of sacred swag, and one could not irritate him in any way so quickly and so surely as by an attack upon that venerable institution. If I ventured

to cautiously hint that there was not another respectable family in England that
would humble itself to hold out the hat—however, that is as far as I ever got;
he always cut me short there, and peremptorily, too.

But I believed I saw my chance at last. I would form this crack regiment out
of officers alone—not a single private. Half of it should consist of nobles, who
should fill all the places up to Major-General, and serve gratis and pay their
own expenses; and they would be glad to do this when they should learn that
the rest of the regiment would consist exclusively of princes of the blood. These
princes of the blood should range in rank from Lieutenant-General up to Field
Marshal, and be gorgeously salaried and equipped and fed by the state. Moreover—
and this was the master stroke—it should be decreed that these princely grandees
should be always addressed by a stunningly gaudy and awe-compelling title
(which I would presently invent), and they and they only in all England should
be so addressed. Finally, all princes of the blood should have free choice; join
that regiment, get that great title, and renounce the royal grant, or stay out and
receive a grant. Neatest touch of all: unborn but imminent princes of the blood
could be *born* into the regiment, and start fair, with good wages and a permanent
situation, upon due notice from the parents.

All the boys would join, I was sure of that; so, all existing grants would be
relinquished; that the newly born would always join was equally certain. Within
sixty days that quaint and bizarre anomaly, the Royal Grant, would cease to be
a living fact, and take its place among the curiosities of the past.

Chapter XXVI

THE FIRST NEWSPAPER

WHEN I TOLD the king I was going out disguised as a petty freeman to scour
the country and familiarize myself with the humbler life of the people, he was
all afire with the novelty of the thing in a minute, and was bound to take a
chance in the adventure himself—nothing should stop him—he would drop
everything and go along—it was the prettiest idea he had run across for many
a day. He wanted to glide out the back way and start at once; but I showed him
that that wouldn't answer. You see, he was billed for the king's-evil—to touch
for it, I mean—and it wouldn't be right to disappoint the house; and it wouldn't
make a delay worth considering, anyway, it was only a one-night stand. And I
thought he ought to tell the queen he was going away. He clouded up at that
and looked sad. I was sorry I had spoken, especially when he said mournfully:

"Thou forgettest that Launcelot is here; and where Launcelot is, she noteth
not the going forth of the king, nor what day he returneth."

Of course, I changed the subject. Yes, Guenever was beautiful, it is true, but
take her all around she was pretty slack. I never meddled in these matters, they
weren't my affair, but I did hate to see the way things were going on, and I
don't mind saying that much. Many's the time she had asked me, "Sir Boss,
hast seen Sir Launcelot about?" but if ever she went fretting around for the king
I didn't happen to be around at the time.

There was a very good lay-out for the king's-evil business—very tidy and creditable. The king sat under a canopy of state; about him were clustered a large body of the clergy in full canonicals. Conspicuous, both for location and personal outfit, stood Marinel, a hermit of the quack-doctor species, to introduce the sick. All abroad over the spacious floor, and clear down to the doors, in a thick jumble, lay or sat the scrofulous, under a strong light. It was as good as a tableau; in fact, it had all the look of being gotten up for that, though it wasn't. There were eight hundred sick people present. The work was slow; it lacked the interest of novelty for me, because I had seen the ceremonies before; the thing soon became tedious, but the proprieties required me to stick it out. The doctor was there for the reason that in all such crowds there were many people who only imagined something was the matter with them, and many who were consciously sound but wanted the immortal honor of fleshly contact with a king, and yet others who pretended to illness in order to get the piece of coin that went with the touch. Up to this time this coin had been a wee little gold piece worth about a third of a dollar. When you consider how much that amount of money would buy, in that age and country, and how usual it was to be scrofulous, when not dead, you would understand that the annual king's-evil appropriation was just the River and Harbor bill of that government for the grip it took on the treasury and the chance it afforded for skinning the surplus. So I had privately concluded to touch the treasury itself for the king's-evil. I covered six-sevenths of the appropriation into the treasury a week before starting from Camelot on my adventures, and ordered that the other seventh be inflated into five-cent nickels and delivered into the hands of the head clerk of the King's Evil Department; a nickel to take the place of each gold coin, you see, and do its work for it. It might strain the nickel some, but I judged it could stand it. As a rule, I do not approve of watering stock, but I considered it square enough in this case, for it was just a gift, anyway. Of course, you can water a gift as much as you want to; and I generally do. The old gold and silver coins of the country were of ancient and unknown origin, as a rule, but some of them were Roman; they were ill-shapen, and seldom rounder than a moon that is a week past the full; they were hammered, not minted, and they were so worn with use that the devices upon them were as illegible as blisters, and looked like them. I judged that a sharp, bright new nickel, with a first-rate likeness of the king on one side of it and Guenever on the other, and a blooming pious motto, would take the tuck out of scrofula as handy as a nobler coin and please the scrofulous fancy more; and I was right. This batch was the first it was tried on, and it worked to a charm. The saving in expense was a notable economy. You will see that by these figures: We touched a trifle over seven hundred of the eight hundred patients; at former rates, this would have cost the government about two hundred and forty dollars; at the new rate we pulled through for about thirty-five dollars, thus saving upward of two hundred dollars at one swoop. To appreciate the full magnitude of this stroke, consider these other figures: the annual expenses of a national government amount to the equivalent of a contribution of three days' average wages of every individual of the population, counting every individual as if he were a man. If you take a nation of sixty millions, where average wages are two dollars per day, three days' wages taken from each individual will provide three hundred and sixty million dollars and pay the government's expenses. In my day, in my own country, this money was collected from imposts, and the citizen imagined that the foreign importer paid it, and it made him comfortable to think so; whereas, in fact, it was paid by the American people, and was so equally and exactly distributed among them that the annual cost to the one-hundred-millionaire and the annual cost to the sucking child of the day-laborer was precisely the same—each paid six dollars. Nothing could be equaler than that, I reckon. Well, Scotland and Ireland were tributary to Arthur, and the united populations of the British Islands amounted to something less than one million. A mechanic's average wage was three cents a day, when he paid his own keep. By this rule the national government's expenses were ninety thousand dollars a year, or about two hundred and fifty dollars a day. Thus, by the substitution of nickels for gold on a king's-evil day, I not only injured no one, dissatisfied no one, but pleased all concerned and saved four-fifths of that day's national expense into the bargain—a saving which would have been the equivalent of eight hundred thousand dollars in my day in America. In making this substitution I had drawn upon the wisdom of a very remote source—the wisdom of my boyhood—for the true statesman does not despise any wisdom, howsoever lowly may be its origin: in my boyhood I had always saved my pennies and contributed buttons to the foreign missionary cause. The buttons would answer the ignorant savage as well as the coin, the coin would answer me better than the buttons; all hands were happy and nobody hurt.

Marinel took the patients as they came. He examined the candidate; if he couldn't qualify he was warned off; if he could he was passed along to the king. A priest pronounced the words, "They shall lay their hands on the sick, and they shall recover." Then the king stroked the ulcers, while the reading continued; finally, the patient graduated and got his nickel—the king hanging it around his neck himself—and was dismissed. Would you think that that would cure? It certainly did. Any mummery will cure if the patient's faith is strong in it. Up by Astolat there was a chapel where the Virgin had once appeared to a girl who used to herd geese around there—the girl said so herself—and they built the chapel upon that spot and hung a picture in it representing the occurrence—a picture which you would think it dangerous for a sick person to approach; whereas, on the contrary, thousands of the lame and the sick came and prayed before it every year and went away whole and sound; and even the well could look upon it and live. Of course, when I was told these things I did not believe them; but when I went there and saw them I had to succumb. I saw the cures effected myself; and they were real cures and not questionable. I saw cripples whom I had seen around Camelot for years on crutches, arrive and pray before that picture, and put down their crutches and walk off without a limp. There were piles of crutches there which had been left by such people as a testimony.

In other places people operated on a patient's mind, without saying a word to him, and cured him. In others, experts assembled patients in a room and prayed over them, and appealed to their faith, and those patients went away cured. Wherever you find a king who can't cure the king's-evil you can be sure that the most valuable superstition that supports his throne—the subject's belief in the divine appointment of his sovereign—has passed away. In my youth the monarchs of England had ceased to touch for the evil, but there was no occasion for this diffidence: they could have cured it forty-nine times in fifty.

Well, when the priest had been droning for three hours, and the good king polishing the evidences, and the sick were still pressing forward as plenty as ever, I got to feeling intolerably bored. I was sitting by an open window not far from the canopy of state. For the five hundredth time a patient stood forward to have his repulsivenesses stroked; again those words were being droned out:

"they shall lay their hands on the sick"—when outside there rang clear as a clarion a note that enchanted my soul and tumbled thirteen worthless centuries about my ears: "Camelot *Weekly Hosannah and Literary Volcano!*—latest irruption—only two cents—all about the big miracle in the Valley of Holiness!" One greater than kings had arrived—the newsboy. But I was the only person in all that throng who knew the meaning of this mighty birth, and what this imperial magician was come into the world to do.

I dropped a nickel out of the window and got my paper; the Adam-newsboy of the world went around the corner to get my change; is around the corner yet. It was delicious to see a newspaper again, yet I was conscious of a secret shock when my eye fell upon the first batch of display head-lines. I had lived in a clammy atmosphere of reverence, respect, deference, so long that they sent a quivery little cold wave through me:

HIGH TIMES IN THE VALLEY

OF HOLINESS!

———

THE WATER-WORKS CORKED!

———

BRER MERLIN WORKS HIS ARTS, BUT GETS

LEFT?

———

But the Boss scores on his first Innings!

———

The Miraculous Well Uncorked amid

awful outbursts of

INFERNAL FIRE AND SMOKE

ANDTHUNDER!

———

THE ꓭUZZARD-ROOST ASTONISHED!

———

UNPARALLELED REJOIBINGS!

———

—and so on, and so on. Yes, it was too loud. Once I could have enjoyed it and seen nothing out of the way about it, but now its note was discordant. It was good Arkansas journalism, but this was not Arkansas. Moreover, the next to the last line was calculated to give offense to the hermits, and perhaps lose us their advertising. Indeed, there was too lightsome a tone of flippancy all through the paper. It was plain I had undergone a considerable change without noticing it. I found myself unpleasantly affected by pert little irreverencies which would have seemed but proper and airy graces of speech at an earlier period of my life. There was an abundance of the following breed of items, and they discomforted me:

Sir Launceʃoʒ met up with old **King Vgrivance** of Ireland unexpectedly last **weok** over on the moor south of Sir Balmoral **le** Merveilleuse's hog **dasture.** The widow has been notified.

Expedition No. 3 will start adout **the first** of mext▪mgnth▪on a search f8r Sir **Sagramour** le Desirous. It **is** in com- **and of the** renowned Knight of the Red **Lawns,** assissted by **Sir** Persant of Inde, **who** is compete9t. intelligent, courte- **ous,** and in every ʍay a briᴄk, and fur- **tʜer** assisted **by** Sir Palamides the Sara- **cen,** who is no huckleberry hinself. This is no pic-nic, these boys ʍean **busine&s.**

The readers of the Hosannah will re- **gret** to learn that the hadndsome and **popular** Sir Charolais of Gaul, who dur- **ing** his four weeks' stay at the **Bull and** Halibut, this▪city, has won every **heart by** his polished manners and elegant **c¶nversation,** will pull out to-day for home.   Give us another call, Charley!

The bdsiness end of the funeral of the late Sir Dalliance the duke's son of Cornwall, killed in an encounter with the Giant of the Knotted Bludgeon last Juesday on the borders of the Plain of Enchantment was in the hands of the ever affable and eyycient ;Mumble, prince of un3ertakers, then whom there exists none by whom it were a more satisfying pleasure to have the last sad offices performed.   Give him a trial.

The cornial thanks of the Hosannah office are due, from editor down to devil, to the ever courteous and thought-ful Lord High Stew d of the Palace's Third Assistant V t for several sau-cets of ice crEam a quality calculated to make the ey of the recipients hu-mid with grt ude; and it done it. When this administration wants to chalk up a desirable name for early promotion, the Hosannah would like a chance to sudgest.

The Demoiselle Irene Ꟁewlap, of South Astolat, is visiting her uncle, the popular host of the Cattlemen's Boarding Ho&se, Liver Lane, this city.

Young Barker the bellows-mender iȝ hoMe again, and looks much improved by his vacation round-up among the ꭓut-lying smithies. Ƨee his ad.

Of course it was good enough journalism for a beginning; I knew that quite well, and yet it was somehow disappointing. The "Court Circular" pleased me better; indeed, its simple and dignified respectfulness was a distinct refreshment to me after all those disgraceful familiarities. But even it could have been improved. Do what one may, there is no getting an air of variety into a court circular, I acknowledge that. There is a profound monotonousness about its facts that baffles and defeats one's sincerest efforts to make them sparkle and enthuse. The best way to manage—in fact, the only sensible way—is to disguise repetitiousness of fact under variety of form: skin your fact each time and lay on a new cuticle of words. It deceives the eye; you think it is a new fact; it gives you the idea that the court is carrying on like everything; this excites you, and you drain the whole column, with a good appetite, and perhaps never notice that it's a barrel of soup made out of a single bean. Clarence's way was good, it was simple, it was dignified, it was direct and businesslike; all I say is, it was not the best way:

COURT CIRCULAR.

On Monday, the ꭓing rode in the park.
  " Tuesday,   "   "   "
  " Wendesday   "   "   "
  " Thursday   "   "   "
  " Friday,   "   "   "
  " Saturday   "   "   "
  " Sunday,   "   "   "

However, take the paper by and large, I was vastly pleased with it. Little crudities of a mechanical sort were observable here and there, but there were not enough of them to amount to anything, and it was good enough Arkansas proof-reading, anyhow, and better than was needed in Arthur's day and realm. As a rule, the grammar was leaky and the construction more or less lame; but I did not much mind these things. They are common defects of my own, and one mustn't criticize other people on grounds where he can't stand perpendicular himself.

I was hungry enough for literature to want to take down the whole paper at this one meal, but I got only a few bites, and then had to postpone, because the monks around me besieged me so with eager questions: What is this curious thing? What is it for? Is it a handkerchief?—saddle-blanket?—part of a shirt? What is it made of? How thin it is, and how dainty and frail; and how it rattles. Will it wear, do you think, and won't the rain injure it? Is it writing that appears on it, or is it only ornamentation? They suspected it was writing, because those among them who knew how to read Latin and had a smattering of Greek, recognized some of the letters, but they could make nothing out of the result as a whole. I put my information in the simplest form I could:

"It is a public journal; I will explain what that is, another time. It is not cloth, it is made of paper; some time I will explain what paper is. The lines on it are reading-matter; and not written by hand, but printed; by and by I will explain what printing is. A thousand of these sheets have been made, all exactly like this, in every minute detail—they can't be told apart." Then they all broke out with exclamations of surprise and admiration:

"A thousand! Verily a mighty work—a year's work for many men."

"No—merely a day's work for a man and a boy."

They crossed themselves, and whiffed out a protective prayer or two.

"Ah-h—a miracle, a wonder! Dark work of enchantment."

I let it go at that. Then I read in a low voice, to as many as could crowd their shaven heads within hearing distance, part of the account of the miracle of the restoration of the well, and was accompanied by astonished and reverent ejaculations all through: "Ah-h-h!" "How true!" "Amazing, amazing!" "These be the very haps as they happened, in marvelous exactness!" And might they take this strange thing in their hands, and feel of it and examine it?—they would be very careful. Yes. So they took it, handling it as cautiously and devoutly as if it had been some holy thing come from some supernatural region; and gently felt of its texture, caressed its pleasant smooth surface with lingering touch, and scanned the mysterious characters with fascinated eyes. These grouped bent heads, these charmed faces, these speaking eyes—how beautiful to me! For was not this my darling, and was not all this mute wonder and interest and homage a most eloquent tribute and unforced compliment to it? I knew, then, how a mother feels when women, whether strangers or friends, take her new baby, and close themselves about it with one eager impulse, and bend their heads over it in a tranced adoration that makes all the rest of the universe vanish out of their consciousness and be as if it were not, for that time. I knew how she feels, and that there is no other satisfied ambition, whether of king, conqueror, or poet, that ever reaches half-way to that serene far summit or yields half so divine a contentment.

During all the rest of the séance my paper traveled from group to group all up and down and about that huge hall, and my happy eye was upon it always, and I sat motionless, steeped in satisfaction, drunk with enjoyment. Yes, this was heaven; I was tasting it once, if I might never taste it more.

Chapter XXVII
THE YANKEE AND THE KING
TRAVEL INCOGNITO

ABOUT BEDTIME I took the king to my private quarters to cut his hair and help him get the hang of the lowly raiment he was to wear. The high classes wore their hair banged across the forehead but hanging to the shoulders the rest of the way around, whereas the lowest ranks of commoners were banged fore and aft both; the slaves were bangless, and allowed their hair free growth. So I inverted a bowl over his head and cut away all the locks that hung below it. I also trimmed his whiskers and mustache until they were only about a half-inch long; and tried to do it inartistically, and succeeded. It was a villainous disfigurement. When he got his lubberly sandals on, and his long robe of coarse brown linen cloth, which hung straight from his neck to his anklebones, he was no longer the comeliest man in his kingdom, but one of the unhandsomest and most commonplace and unattractive. We were dressed and barbered alike, and could pass for small farmers, or farm bailiffs, or shepherds, or carters; yes, or for village artisans, if we chose, our costume being in effect universal among the poor, because of its strength and cheapness. I don't mean that it was really cheap to a very poor person, but I do mean that it was the cheapest material there was for male attire—manufactured material, you understand.

We slipped away an hour before dawn, and by broad sun-up had made eight or ten miles, and were in the midst of a sparsely settled country. I had a pretty heavy knapsack; it was laden with provisions—provisions for the king to taper down on till he could take to the coarse fare of the country without damage.

I found a comfortable seat for the king by the roadside, and then gave him a morsel or two to stay his stomach with. Then I said I would find some water for him, and strolled away. Part of my project was to get out of sight and sit down and rest a little myself. It had always been my custom to stand when in his presence; even at the council board, except upon those rare occasions when the sitting was a very long one, extending over hours; then I had a trifling little backless thing which was like a reversed culvert and was as comfortable as the toothache. I didn't want to break him in suddenly, but do it by degrees. We should have to sit together now when in company, or people would notice; but it would not be good politics for me to be playing equality with him when there was no necessity for it.

I found the water some three hundred yards away, and had been resting about twenty minutes, when I heard voices. That is all right, I thought—peasants going to work; nobody else likely to be stirring this early. But the next moment these comers jingled into sight around a turn of the road—smartly clad people of quality, with luggage-mules and servants in their train! I was off like a shot, through the bushes, by the shortest cut. For a while it did seem that these people would pass the king before I could get to him; but desperation gives you wings, you know, and I canted my body forward, inflated my breast, and held my breath and flew. I arrived. And in plenty good enough time, too.

"Pardon, my king, but it's no time for ceremony—jump! Jump to your feet— some quality are coming!"

"Is that a marvel? Let them come."

"But my liege! You must not be seen sitting. Rise!—and stand in humble posture while they pass. You are a peasant, you know."

"True—I had forgot it, so lost was I in planning of a huge war with Gaul"— he was up by this time, but a farm could have got up quicker, if there was any kind of a boom in real estate—"and right-so a thought came randoming overthwart this majestic dream the which—"

"A humbler attitude, my lord the king—and quick! Duck your head!—more!— still more!—droop it!"

He did his honest best, but lord, it was no great things. He looked as humble as the leaning tower at Pisa. It is the most you could say of it. Indeed, it was such a thundering poor success that it raised wondering scowls all along the line, and a gorgeous flunkey at the tail end of it raised his whip; but I jumped in time and was under it when it fell; and under cover of the volley of coarse laughter which followed, I spoke up sharply and warned the king to take no notice. He mastered himself for the moment, but it was a sore tax; he wanted to eat up the procession. I said:

"It would end our adventures at the very start; and we, being without weapons, could do nothing with that armed gang. If we are going to succeed in our emprise, we must not only look the peasant but act the peasant."

"It is wisdom; none can gainsay it. Let us go on, Sir Boss. I will take note and learn, and do the best I may."

He kept his word. He did the best he could, but I've seen better. If you have ever seen an active, heedless, enterprising child going diligently out of one mischief and into another all day long, and an anxious mother at its heels all the while, and just saving it by a hair from drowning itself or breaking its neck with each new experiment, you've seen the king and me.

If I could have foreseen what the thing was going to be like, I should have said, No, if anybody wants to make his living exhibiting a king as a peasant, let him take the layout; I can do better with a menagerie, and last longer. And yet, during the first three days I never allowed him to enter a hut or other dwelling. If he could pass muster anywhere during his early novitiate, it would be in small inns and on the road; so to these places we confined ourselves. Yes, he certainly did the best he could, but what of that? He didn't improve a bit that I could see.

He was always frightening me, always breaking out with fresh astonishers, in new and unexpected places. Toward evening on the second day, what does he do but blandly fetch out a dirk from inside his robe!

"Great guns, my liege, where did you get that?"

"From a smuggler at the inn, yester eve."

"What in the world possessed you to buy it?"

"We have escaped divers dangers by wit—thy wit—but I have bethought me that it were but prudence if I bore a weapon, too. Thine might fail thee in some pinch."

"But people of our condition are not allowed to carry arms. What would a lord say—yes, or any other person of whatever condition—if he caught an upstart peasant with a dagger on his person?"

It was a lucky thing for us that nobody came along just then. I persuaded him to throw the dirk away; and it was as easy as persuading a child to give up some bright fresh new way of killing itself. We walked along, silent and thinking. Finally the king said:

"When ye know that I meditate a thing inconvenient, or that hath a peril in it, why do you not warn me to cease from that project?"

It was a startling question, and a puzzler. I didn't quite know how to take hold of it, or what to say, and so, of course, I ended by saying the natural thing:

"But, sire, how can *I* know what your thoughts are?"

The king stopped dead in his tracks, and stared at me.

"I believed thou wert greater than Merlin; and truly in magic thou art. But prophecy is greater than magic. Merlin is a prophet."

I saw I had made a blunder. I must get back my lost ground. After a deep reflection and careful planning, I said:

"Sire, I have been misunderstood. I will explain. There are two kinds of prophecy. One is the gift to foretell things that are but a little way off, the other is the gift to foretell things that are whole ages and centuries away. Which is the mightier gift, do you think?"

"Oh, the last, most surely!"

"True. Does Merlin possess it?"

"Partly, yes. He foretold mysteries about my birth and future kingship that were twenty years away."

"Has he ever gone beyond that?"

"He would not claim more, I think."

"It is probably his limit. All prophets have their limit. The limit of some of the great prophets has been a hundred years."

"These are few, I ween."

"There have been two still greater ones, whose limit was four hundred and six hundred years, and one whose limit compassed even seven hundred and twenty."

"Gramercy, it is marvelous!"

"But what are these in comparison with me? They are nothing."

"What? Canst thou truly look beyond even so vast a stretch of time as—"

"Seven hundred years? My liege, as clear as the vision of an eagle does my prophetic eye penetrate and lay bare the future of this world for nearly thirteen centuries and a half!"

My land, you should have seen the king's eyes spread slowly open, and lift the earth's entire atmosphere as much as an inch! That settled Brer Merlin. One never had any occasion to prove his facts, with these people; all he had to do was to state them. It never occurred to anybody to doubt the statement.

"Now, then," I continued, "I *could* work both kinds of prophecy—the long and the short—if I chose to take the trouble to keep in practice; but I seldom exercise any but the long kind, because the other is beneath my dignity. It is properer to Merlin's sort—stump-tail prophets, as we call them in the profession. Of course, I whet up now and then and flirt out a minor prophecy, but not often—hardly ever, in fact. You will remember that there was great talk, when you reached the Valley of Holiness, about my having prophesied your coming and the very hour of your arrival, two or three days beforehand."

"Indeed, yes, I mind it now."

"Well, I could have done it as much as forty times easier, and piled on a thousand times more detail into the bargain, if it had been five hundred years away instead of two or three days."

"How amazing that it should be so!"

"Yes, a genuine expert can always foretell a thing that is five hundred years away easier than he can a thing that's only five hundred seconds off."

"And yet in reason it should clearly be the other way; it should be five hundred times as easy to foretell the last as the first, for, indeed, it is so close by that one uninspired might almost see it. In truth, the law of prophecy doth contradict the likelihoods, most strangely making the difficult easy, and the easy difficult."

It was a wise head. A peasant's cap was no safe disguise for it; you could know it for a king's under a diving-bell, if you could hear it work its intellect.

I had a new trade now, and plenty of business in it. The king was as hungry to find out everything that was going to happen during the next thirteen centuries as if he were expecting to live in them. From that time out, I prophesied myself bald-headed trying to supply the demand. I have done some indiscreet things in my day, but this thing of playing myself for a prophet was the worst. Still, it had its ameliorations. A prophet doesn't have to have any brains. They are good to have, of course, for the ordinary exigencies of life, but they are no use in professional work. It is the restfulest vocation there is. When the spirit of prophecy comes upon you, you merely cake your intellect and lay it off in a cool place for a rest, and unship your jaw and leave it alone; it will work itself: the result is prophecy.

Every day a knight-errant or so came along, and the sight of them fired the king's martial spirit every time. He would have forgotten himself, sure, and said something to them in a style a suspicious shade or so above his ostensible degree, and so I always got him well out of the road in time. Then he would stand and look with all his eyes; and a proud light would flash from them, and his nostrils would inflate like a war-horse's, and I knew he was longing for a brush with them. But about noon of the third day I had stopped in the road to take a precaution which had been suggested by the whip-stroke that had fallen to my share two days before; a precaution which I had afterward decided to leave untaken, I was so loath to institute it; but now I had just had a fresh reminder: while striding heedlessly along, with jaw spread and intellect at rest, for I was prophesying, I stubbed my toe and fell sprawling. I was so pale I couldn't think for a moment; then I got softly and carefully up and unstrapped my knapsack. I had that dynamite bomb in it, done up in wool in a box. It was a good thing to have along; the time would come when I could do a valuable miracle with it, maybe, but it was a nervous thing to have about me, and I didn't like to ask the king to carry it. Yet I must either throw it away or think up some safe way to get along with its society. I got it out and slipped it into my scrip, and just then here came a couple of knights. The king stood, stately as a statue, gazing toward them—had forgotten himself again, of course—and before I could get a word of warning out, it was time for him to skip, and well that he did it, too. He supposed they would turn aside. Turn aside to avoid trampling peasant dirt under foot? When had he ever turned aside himself—or ever had the chance to do it, if a peasant saw him or any other noble knight in time to judiciously save him the trouble? The knights paid no attention to the king at all; it was his place to look out himself, and if he hadn't skipped he would have been placidly ridden down, and laughed at besides.

The king was in a flaming fury, and launched out his challenge and epithets with a most royal vigor. The knights were some little distance by now. They halted, greatly surprised, and turned in their saddles and looked back, as if wondering if it might be worth while to bother with such scum as we. Then they wheeled and started for us. Not a moment must be lost. I started for *them*. I passed them at a rattling gait, and as I went by I flung out a hair-lifting soul-scorching thirteen-jointed insult which made the king's effort poor and cheap by comparison. I got it out of the nineteenth century where they know how. They had such headway that they were nearly to the king before they could check up; then, frantic with rage, they stood up their horses on their hind hoofs and whirled them around, and the next moment here they came, breast to breast. I was seventy yards off, then, and scrambling up a great boulder at the roadside. When they were within thirty yards of me they let their long lances droop to a level, depressed their mailed heads, and so, with their horse-hair plumes streaming straight out behind, most gallant to see, this lightning express came tearing for me! When they were within fifteen yards, I sent that bomb with a sure aim, and it struck the ground under the horses' noses.

Yes, it was a neat thing, very neat and pretty to see. It resembled a steamboat explosion on the Mississippi; and during the next fifteen minutes we stood under a steady drizzle of microscopic fragments of knights and hardware and horse-flesh. I say we, for the king joined the audience, of course, as soon as he had got his breath again. There was a hole there which would afford steady work for all the people in that region for some years to come—in trying to explain it, I mean; as for filling it up, that service would be comparatively prompt, and would fall to the lot of a select few—peasants of that seigniory; and they wouldn't get anything for it, either.

But I explained it to the king myself. I said it was done with a dynamite bomb. This information did him no damage, because it left him as intelligent as he was before. However, it was a noble miracle, in his eyes, and was another settler for Merlin. I thought it well enough to explain that this was a miracle of so rare a sort that it couldn't be done except when the atmospheric conditions were just right. Otherwise he would be encoring it every time we had a good subject, and that would be inconvenient, because I hadn't any more bombs along.

Chapter XXVIII

DRILLING THE KING

ON THE MORNING of the fourth day, when it was just sunrise, and we had been tramping an hour in the chill dawn, I came to a resolution: the king *must* be drilled; things could not go on so, he must be taken in hand and deliberately and conscientiously drilled, or we couldn't ever venture to enter a dwelling; the very cats would know this masquerader for a humbug and no peasant. So I called a halt and said:

"Sire, as between clothes and countenance, you are all right, there is no discrepancy; but as between your clothes and your bearing, you are all wrong, there is a most noticeable discrepancy. Your soldierly stride, your lordly port—these will not do. You stand too straight, your looks are too high, too confident. The cares of a kingdom do not stoop the shoulders, they do not droop the chin, they do not depress the high level of the eye-glance, they do not put doubt and fear in the heart and hang out the signs of them in slouching body and unsure step. It is the sordid cares of the lowly born that do these things. You must learn the trick; you must imitate the trade-marks of poverty, misery, oppression, insult, and the other several and common inhumanities that sap the manliness out of a man and make him a loyal and proper and approved subject and a satisfaction to his masters, or the very infants will know you for better than your disguise, and we shall go to pieces at the first hut we stop at. Pray try to walk like this."

The king took careful note, and then tried an imitation.

"Pretty fair—pretty fair. Chin a little lower, please—there, very good. Eyes too high; pray don't look at the horizon, look at the ground, ten steps in front of you. Ah—that is better, that is very good. Wait, please; you betray too much vigor, too much decision; you want more of a shamble. Look at me, please—this is what I mean. . . . Now you are getting it; that is the idea—at least, it sort of approaches it. . . . Yes, that is pretty fair. *But!* There is a great big something wanting, I don't quite know what it is. Please walk thirty yards, so that I can get a perspective on the thing. . . . Now, then—your head's right, speed's right, shoulders right, eyes right, chin right, gait, carriage, general style right—everything's right! And yet the fact remains, the aggregate's wrong. The account don't balance. Do it again, please . . . *now* I think I begin to see what it is. Yes, I've struck it. You see, the genuine spiritlessness is wanting; that's what's the trouble. It's all *amateur*—mechanical details all right, almost to a hair; everything about the delusion perfect, except that it don't delude."

"What, then, must one do, to prevail?"

"Let me think. . . . I can't seem to quite get at it. In fact, there isn't anything that can right the matter but practice. This is a good place for it: roots and stony ground to break up your stately gait, a region not liable to interruption, only one field and one hut in sight, and they so far away that nobody could see us from there. It will be well to move a little off the road and put in the whole day drilling you, sire."

After the drill had gone on a little while, I said:

"Now, sire, imagine that we are at the door of the hut yonder, and the family are before us. Proceed, please—accost the head of the house."

The king unconsciously straightened up like a monument, and said, with frozen austerity:

"Varlet, bring a seat; and serve to me what cheer ye have."

"Ah, your grace, that is not well done."

"In what lacketh it?"

"These people do not call *each other* varlets."

"Nay, is that true?"

"Yes; only those above them call them so."

"Then must I try again. I will call him villein."

"No-no; for he may be a freeman."

"Ah—so. Then peradventure I should call him goodman."

"That would answer, your grace, but it would be still better if you said friend, or brother."

"Brother!—to dirt like that?"

"Ah, but *we* are pretending to be dirt like that, too."

"It is even true. I will say it. Brother, bring a seat, and thereto what cheer ye have, withal. *Now* 'tis right."

"Not quite, not wholly right. You have asked for one, not *us*—for one, not both; food for one, a seat for one."

The king looked puzzled—he wasn't a very heavy weight, intellectually. His head was an hour-glass; it could stow an idea, but it had to do it a grain at a time, not the whole idea at once.

"Would *you* have a seat also—and sit?"

"If I did not sit, the man would perceive that we were only pretending to be equals—and playing the deception pretty poorly, too."

"It is well and truly said! How wonderful is truth, come it in whatsoever unexpected form it may! Yes, he must bring out seats and food for both, and in serving us present not ewer and napkin with more show of respect to the one than to the other."

"And there is even yet a detail that needs correcting. He must bring nothing outside; we will go in—in among the dirt, and possibly other repulsive things— and take the food with the household, and after the fashion of the house, and all on equal terms, except the man be of the serf class; and finally, there will be no ewer and no napkin, whether he be serf or free. Please walk again, my liege. There—it is better—it is the best yet; but not perfect. The shoulders have known no ignobler burden than iron mail, and they will not stoop."

"Give me, then, the bag. I will learn the spirit that goeth with burdens that have not honor. It is the spirit that stoopeth the shoulders, I ween, and not the weight; for armor is heavy, yet it is a proud burden, and a man standeth straight in it. . . . Nay, but me no buts, offer me no objections. I will have the thing. Strap it upon my back."

He was complete now with that knapsack on, and looked as little like a king as any man I had ever seen. But it was an obstinate pair of shoulders; they could not seem to learn the trick of stooping with any sort of deceptive naturalness. The drill went on, I prompting and correcting:

"Now, make believe you are in debt, and eaten up by relentless creditors; you are out of work—which is horse-shoeing, let us say—and can get none; and your wife is sick, your children are crying because they are hungry—"

And so on, and so on. I drilled him as representing in turn all sorts of people out of luck and suffering dire privations and misfortunes. But lord, it was only just words, words—they meant nothing in the world to him, I might just as well have whistled. Words realize nothing, vivify nothing to you, unless you have suffered in your own person the thing which the words try to describe. There are wise people who talk ever so knowingly and complacently about "the working classes," and satisfy themselves that a day's hard intellectual work is very much harder than a day's hard manual toil, and is righteously entitled to much bigger pay. Why, they really think that, you know, because they know all about the one, but haven't tried the other. But I know all about both; and so far as I am concerned, there isn't money enough in the universe to hire me to swing a pickax thirty days, but I will do the hardest kind of intellectual work for just as near nothing as you can cipher it down—and I will be satisfied, too.

Intellectual "work" is misnamed; it is a pleasure, a dissipation, and is its own highest reward. The poorest paid architect, engineer, general, author, sculptor, painter, lecturer, advocate, legislator, actor, preacher, singer is constructively in heaven when he is at work; and as for the musician with the fiddle-bow in his hand who sits in the midst of a great orchestra with the ebbing and flowing tides of divine sound washing over him—why, certainly, he is at work, if you wish to call it that, but lord, it's a sarcasm just the same. The law of work does seem utterly unfair—but there it is, and nothing can change it: the higher the pay in enjoyment the worker gets out of it, the higher shall be his pay in cash, also. And it's also the very law of those transparent swindles, transmissible nobility and kingship.

Chapter XXIX

THE SMALLPOX HUT

WHEN WE ARRIVED at that hut at mid-afternoon, we saw no signs of life about it. The field near by had been denuded of its crop some time before, and had a skinned look, so exhaustively had it been harvested and gleaned. Fences, sheds, everything had a ruined look, and were eloquent of poverty. No animal was around anywhere, no living thing in sight. The stillness was awful, it was like the stillness of death. The cabin was a one-story one, whose thatch was black with age, and ragged from lack of repair.

The door stood a trifle ajar. We approached it stealthily—on tiptoe and at half-breath—for that is the way one's feeling makes him do, at such a time. The king knocked. We waited. No answer. Knocked again. No answer. I pushed the door softly open and looked in. I made out some dim forms, and a woman started up from the ground and stared at me, as one does who is wakened from sleep. Presently she found her voice:

"Have mercy!" she pleaded. "All is taken, nothing is left."

"I have not come to take anything, poor woman."

"You are not a priest?"

"No."

"Nor come not from the lord of the manor?"

"No, I am a stranger."

"Oh, then, for the fear of God, who visits with misery and death such as be harmless, tarry not here, but fly! This place is under his curse—and his Church's."

"Let me come in and help you—you are sick and in trouble."

I was better used to the dim light now. I could see her hollow eyes fixed upon me. I could see how emaciated she was.

"I tell you the place is under the Church's ban. Save yourself—and go, before some straggler see thee here, and report it."

"Give yourself no trouble about me; I don't care anything for the Church's curse. Let me help you."

"Now all good spirits—if there be any such—bless thee for that word. Would God I had a sup of water!—but hold, hold, forget I said it, and fly; for there is that here that even he that feareth not the Church must fear: this disease whereof we die. Leave us, thou brave, good stranger, and take with thee such whole and sincere blessing as them that be accursed can give."

But before this I had picked up a wooden bowl and was rushing past the king on my way to the brook. It was ten yards away. When I got back and entered, the king was within, and was opening the shutter that closed the window-hole, to let in air and light. The place was full of a foul stench. I put the bowl to the woman's lips, and as she gripped it with her eager talons the shutter came open and a strong light flooded her face. Smallpox!

I sprang to the king, and said in his ear:

"Out of the door on the instant, sire! the woman is dying of that disease that wasted the skirts of Camelot two years ago."

He did not budge.

"Of a truth I shall remain—and likewise help."

I whispered again:

"King, it must not be. You must go."

"Ye mean well, and ye speak not unwisely. But it were shame that a king should know fear, and shame that belted knight should withhold his hand where be such as need succor. Peace, I will not go. It is you who must go. The Church's ban is not upon me, but it forbiddeth you to be here, and she will deal with you with a heavy hand an word come to her of your trespass."

It was a desperate place for him to be in, and might cost him his life, but it was no use to argue with him. If he considered his knightly honor at stake here, that was the end of argument; he would stay, and nothing could prevent it; I was aware of that. And so I dropped the subject. The woman spoke:

"Fair sir, of your kindness will ye climb the ladder there, and bring me news of what ye find? Be not afraid to report, for times can come when even a mother's heart is past breaking—being already broke."

"Abide," said the king, "and give the woman to eat. I will go." And he put down the knapsack.

I turned to start, but the king had already started. He halted, and looked down upon a man who lay in a dim light, and had not noticed us thus far, or spoken.

"Is it your husband?" the king asked.

"Yes."

"Is he asleep?"

"God be thanked for that one charity, yes—these three hours. Where shall I pay to the full, my gratitude! for my heart is bursting with it for that sleep he sleepeth now."

I said:

"We will be careful. We will not wake him."

"Ah, no, that ye will not, for he is dead."

"Dead?"

"Yes, what triumph it is to know it! None can harm him, none insult him more. He is in heaven now, and happy; or if not there, he bides in hell and is content; for in that place he will find neither abbot nor yet bishop. We were boy and girl together; we were man and wife these five-and-twenty years, and never separated till this day. Think how long that is to love and suffer together. This morning was he out of his mind, and in his fancy we were boy and girl again and wandering in the happy fields; and so in that innocent glad converse wandered he far and farther, still lightly gossiping, and entered into those other fields we know not of, and was shut away from mortal sight. And so there was no parting, for in his fancy I went with him; he knew not but I went with him, my hand in his—my young soft hand, not this withered claw. Ah, yes, to go, and know it not; to separate and know it not; how could one go peacefuler than that? It was his reward for a cruel life patiently borne."

There was a slight noise from the direction of the dim corner where the ladder was. It was the king descending. I could see that he was bearing something in one arm, and assisting himself with the other. He came forward into the light; upon his breast lay a slender girl of fifteen. She was but half conscious; she was dying of smallpox. Here was heroism at its last and loftiest possibility, its utmost summit; this was challenging death in the open field unarmed, with all the odds against the challenger, no reward set upon the contest, and no admiring world in silks and cloth-of-gold to gaze and applaud; and yet the king's bearing was as serenely brave as it had always been in those cheaper contests where knight meets knight in equal fight and clothed in protecting steel. He was great now; sublimely great. The rude statues of his ancestors in his palace should have an addition—I would see to that; and it would not be a mailed king killing a giant or a dragon, like the rest, it would be a king in commoner's garb bearing death in his arms that a peasant mother might look her last upon her child and be comforted.

He laid the girl down by her mother, who poured out endearments and caresses from an overflowing heart, and one could detect a flickering faint light of response in the child's eyes, but that was all. The mother hung over her, kissing her, petting her, and imploring her to speak, but the lips only moved and no sound came. I snatched my liquor flask from my knapsack, but the woman forbade me, and said:

"No—she does not suffer; it is better so. It might bring her back to life. None that be so good and kind as ye are would do her that cruel hurt. For look you— what is left to live for? Her brothers are gone, her father is gone, her mother goeth, the Church's curse is upon her, and none may shelter or befriend her even though she lay perishing in the road. She is desolate. I have not asked you, good heart, if her sister be still on live, here overhead; I had no need; ye had gone back, else, and not left the poor thing forsaken—"

"She lieth at peace," interrupted the king, in a subdued voice.

"I would not change it. How rich is this day in happiness! An, my Annis, thou shalt join thy sister soon—thou'rt on thy way, and these be merciful friends that will not hinder."

And so she fell to murmuring and cooing over the girl again, and softly stroking her face and hair, and kissing her and calling her by endearing names; but there was scarcely sign of response now in the glazing eyes. I saw tears well from the king's eyes, and trickle down his face. The woman noticed them, too, and said:

"Ah, I know that sign: thou'st a wife at home, poor soul, and you and she have gone hungry to bed, many's the time, that the little ones might have your crust; you know what poverty is, and the daily insults of your betters, and the heavy hand of the Church and the king."

The king winced under this accidental home-shot, but kept still; he was learning his part; and he was playing it well, too, for a pretty dull beginner. I struck up a diversion. I offered the woman food and liquor, but she refused both. She would allow nothing to come between her and the release of death. Then I slipped away and brought the dead child from aloft, and laid it by her. This broke her down again, and there was another scene that was full of heartbreak. By and by I made another diversion, and beguiled her to sketch her story.

"Ye know it well yourselves, having suffered it—for truly none of our condition in Britain escape it. It is the old, weary tale. We fought and struggled and succeeded; meaning by success, that we lived and did not die; more than that is not to be claimed. No troubles came that we could not outlive, till this year brought them; then came they all at once, as one might say, and overwhelmed us. Years ago the lord of the manor planted certain fruit-trees on our farm; in the best part of it, too—a grievous wrong and shame—"

"But it was his right," interrupted the king.

"None denieth that, indeed; an the law mean anything, what is the lord's is his, and what is mine is his also. Our farm was ours by lease, therefore 'twas likewise his, to do with it as he would. Some little time ago, three of those trees were found hewn down. Our three grown sons ran frightened to report the crime. Well, in his lordship's dungeon there they lie, who saith there shall they lie and rot till they confess. They have naught to confess, being innocent, wherefore there will they remain until they die. Ye know that right well, I ween. Think how this left us; a man, a woman, and two children, to gather a crop that was planted by so much greater force, yes, and protect it night and day from pigeons and prowling animals that be sacred and must not be hurt by any of our sort. When my lord's crop was nearly ready for the harvest, so also was ours; when his bell rang to call us to his fields to harvest his crop for nothing, he would not allow that I and my two girls should count for our three captive sons, but for only two of them; so, for the lacking one were we daily fined. All this time our own crop was perishing through neglect; and so both the priest and his lordship fined us because their shares of it were suffering through damage. In the end the fines ate up our crop—and they took it all; they took it all and made us harvest it for them, without pay or food, and we starving. Then the worst came when I, being out of my mind with hunger and loss of my boys, and grief to see my husband and my little maids in rags and misery and despair, uttered a deep blasphemy—oh! a thousand of them!—against the Church and the Church's ways. It was ten days ago. I had fallen sick with this disease, and it was to the priest I said the words, for he was come to chide me for lack of due humility under the chastening hand of God. He carried my trespass to his betters; I was stubborn; wherefore, presently upon my head and upon all heads that were dear to me, fell the curse of Rome.

"Since that day we are avoided, shunned with horror. None has come near this hut to know whether we live or not. The rest of us were taken down. Then I roused me and got up, as wife and mother will. It was little they could have eaten in any case; it was less than little they had to eat. But there was water, and I gave them that. How they craved it! and how they blessed it! But the end came yesterday; my strength broke down. Yesterday was the last time I ever saw my husband and this youngest child alive. I have lain here all these hours— these ages, ye may say—listening, listening for any sound up there that—''

She gave a sharp quick glance at her eldest daughter, then cried out, ''Oh, my darling!'' and feebly gathered the stiffening form to her sheltering arms. She had recognized the death-rattle.

Chapter XXX

THE TRAGEDY OF THE MANOR-HOUSE

AT MIDNIGHT ALL was over, and we sat in the presence of four corpses. We covered them with such rags as we could find, and started away, fastening the door behind us. Their home must be these people's grave, for they could not have Christian burial, or be admitted to consecrated ground. They were as dogs, wild beasts, lepers, and no soul that valued its hope of eternal life would throw it away by meddling in any sort with these rebuked and smitten outcasts.

We had not moved four steps when I caught a sound as of footsteps upon gravel. My heart flew to my throat. We must not be seen coming from that house. I plucked at the king's robe and we drew back and took shelter behind the corner of the cabin.

''Now we are safe,'' I said, ''but it was a close call—so to speak. If the night had been lighter he might have seen us, no doubt, he seemed to be so near.''

''Mayhap it is but a beast and not a man at all.''

''True. But man or beast, it will be wise to stay here a minute and let it get by and out of the way.''

''Hark! It cometh hither.''

True again. The step was coming toward us—straight toward the hut. It must be a beast, then, and we might as well have saved our trepidation. I was going to step out, but the king laid his hand upon my arm. There was a moment of silence, then we heard a soft knock on the cabin door. It made me shiver. Presently the knock was repeated, and then we heard these words in a guarded voice:

''Mother! Father! Open—we have got free, and we bring news to pale your cheeks but glad your hearts; and we may not tarry, but must fly! And—but they answer not. Mother! father!—''

I drew the king toward the other end of the hut and whispered:

''Come—now we can get to the road.''

The king hesitated, was going to demur; but just then we heard the door give way, and knew that those desolate men were in the presence of their dead.

''Come, my liege! in a moment they will strike a light, and then will follow that which it would break your heart to hear.''

He did not hesitate this time. The moment we were in the road I ran; and after a moment he threw dignity aside and followed. I did not want to think of what was happening in the hut—I couldn't bear it; I wanted to drive it out of my mind; so I struck into the first subject that lay under that one in my mind:

"I have had the disease those people died of, and so have nothing to fear; but if you have not had it also—"

He broke in upon me to say he was in trouble, and it was his conscience that was troubling him:

"These young men have got free, they say—but *how*? It is not likely that their lord hath set them free."

"Oh, no, I make no doubt they escaped."

"That is my trouble; I have a fear that this is so, and your suspicion doth confirm it, you having the same fear."

"I should not call it by that name though. I do suspect that they escaped, but if they did, I am not sorry, certainly."

"I am not sorry, I *think*—but—"

"What is it? What is there for one to be troubled about?"

"*If* they did escape, then are we bound in duty to lay hands upon them and deliver them again to their lord; for it is not seemly that one of his quality should suffer a so insolent and high-handed outrage from persons of their base degree."

There it was again. He could see only one side of it. He was born so, educated so, his veins were full of ancestral blood that was rotten with this sort of unconscious brutality, brought down by inheritance from a long procession of hearts that had each done its share toward poisoning the stream. To imprison these men without proof, and starve their kindred, was no harm, for they were merely peasants and subject to the will and pleasure of their lord, no matter what fearful form it might take; but for these men to break out of unjust captivity was insult and outrage, and a thing not to be countenanced by any conscientious person who knew his duty to his sacred caste.

I worked more than half an hour before I got him to change the subject—and even then an outside matter did it for me. This was a something which caught our eyes as we struck the summit of a small hill—a red glow, a good way off.

"That's a fire," said I.

Fires interested me considerably, because I was getting a good deal of an insurance business started, and was also training some horses and building some steam fire-engines, with an eye to a paid fire department by and by. The priests opposed both my fire and life insurance, on the ground that it was an insolent attempt to hinder the decrees of God; and if you pointed out that they did not hinder the decrees in the least, but only modified the hard consequences of them if you took out policies and had luck, they retorted that that was gambling against the decrees of God, and was just as bad. So they managed to damage those industries more or less, but I got even on my Accident business. As a rule, a knight is a lummox, and sometimes even a labrick, and hence open to pretty poor arguments when they come glibly from a superstition-monger, but even *he* could see the practical side of a thing once in a while; and so of late you couldn't clean up a tournament and pile the result without finding one of my accident-tickets in every helmet.

We stood there awhile, in the thick darkness and stillness, looking toward the red blur in the distance, and trying to make out the meaning of a far-away murmur that rose and fell fitfully on the night. Sometimes it swelled up and for a moment seemed less remote; but when we were hopefully expecting it to betray its cause and nature, it dulled and sank again, carrying its mystery with it. We started down the hill in its direction, and the winding road plunged us at once into almost solid darkness—darkness that was packed and crammed in between two tall forest walls. We groped along down for half a mile, perhaps, that murmur growing more and more distinct all the time, the coming storm threatening more and more, with now and then a little shiver of wind, a faint show of lightning, and dull grumblings of distant thunder. I was in the lead. I ran against something—a soft heavy something which gave, slightly, to the impulse of my weight; at the same moment the lightning glared out, and within a foot of my face was the writhing face of a man who was hanging from the limb of a tree! That is, it seemed to be writhing, but it was not. It was a gruesome sight. Straightway there was an ear-splitting explosion of thunder, and the bottom of heaven fell out; the rain poured down in a deluge. No matter, we must try to cut this man down, on the chance that there might be life in him yet, mustn't we? The lightning came quick and sharp now, and the place was alternately noonday and midnight. One moment the man would be hanging before me in an intense light, and the next he was blotted out again in the darkness. I told the king we must cut him down. The king at once objected.

"If he hanged himself, he was willing to lose him property to his lord; so let him be. If others hanged him, belike they had the right—let him hang."

"But—"

"But me no buts, but even leave him as he is. And for yet another reason. When the lightning cometh again—there, look abroad."

Two others hanging, within fifty yards of us!

"It is not weather meet for doing useless courtesies unto dead folk. They are past thanking you. Come—it is unprofitable to tarry here."

There was reason in what he said, so we moved on. Within the next mile we counted six more hanging forms by the blaze of the lightning, and altogether it was a grisly excursion. That murmur was a murmur no longer, it was a roar; a roar of men's voices. A man came flying by now, dimly through the darkness, and other men chasing him. They disappeared. Presently another case of the kind occurred, and then another and another. Then a sudden turn of the road brought us in sight of that fire—it was a large manor-house, and little or nothing was left of it—and everywhere men were flying and other men raging after them in pursuit.

I warned the king that this was not a safe place for strangers. We would better get away from the light, until matters should improve. We stepped back a little, and hid in the edge of the wood. From this hiding-place we saw both men and women hunted by the mob. The fearful work went on until nearly dawn. Then, the fire being out and the storm spent, the voices and flying footsteps presently ceased, and darkness and stillness reigned again.

We ventured out, and hurried cautiously away; and although we were worn out and sleepy, we kept on until we had put this place some miles behind us. Then we asked hospitality at the hut of a charcoal-burner, and got what was to be had. A woman was up and about, but the man was still asleep, on a straw shake-down, on the clay floor. The woman seemed uneasy until I explained that we were travelers and had lost our way and been wandering in the woods all night. She became talkative, then, and asked if we had heard of the terrible goings-on at the manor-house of Abblasoure. Yes, we had heard of them, but what we wanted now was rest and sleep. The king broke in:

"Sell us the house and take yourselves away, for we be perilous company, being late come from people that died of the Spotted Death."

It was good of him, but unnecessay. One of the commonest decorations of the nation was the waffle-iron face. I had early noticed that the woman and her husband were both so decorated. She made us entirely welcome, and had no fears; and plainly she was immensely impressed by the king's proposition; for, of course, it was a good deal of an event in her life to run across a person of the king's humble appearance who was ready to buy a man's house for the sake of a night's lodging. It gave her a large respect for us, and she strained the lean possibilities of her hovel to the utmost to make us comfortable.

We slept till far into the afternoon, and then got up hungry enough to make cotter fare quite palatable to the king, the more particularly as it was scant in quantity. And also in variety; it consisted solely of onions, salt, and the national black bread—made out of horse-feed. The woman told us about the affair of the evening before. At ten or eleven at night, when everybody was in bed, the manor-house burst into flames. The country-side swarmed to the rescue, and the family were saved, with one exception, the master. He did not appear. Everybody was frantic over this loss, and two brave yeomen sacrificed their lives in ransacking the burning house seeking that valuable personage. But after a while he was found—what was left of him—which was his corpse. It was in a copse three hundred yards away, bound, gagged, stabbed in a dozen places.

Who had done this? Suspicion fell upon a humble family in the neighborhood who had been lately treated with peculiar harshness by the baron; and from these people the suspicion easily extended itself to their relatives and familiars. A suspicion was enough; my lord's liveried retainers proclaimed an instant crusade against these people, and were promptly joined by the community in general. The woman's husband had been active with the mob, and had not returned home until nearly dawn. He was gone now to find out what the general result had been. While we were still talking he came back from his quest. His report was revolting enough. Eighteen persons hanged or butchered, and two yeomen and thirteen prisoners lost in the fire.

"And how many prisoners were there altogether in the vaults?"

"Thirteen."

"Then every one of them was lost?"

"Yes, all."

"But the people arrived in time to save the family; how is it they could save none of the prisoners?"

The man looked puzzled, and said:

"Would one unlock the vaults at such a time? Marry, some would have escaped."

"Then you mean that nobody *did* unlock them?"

"None went near them, either to lock or unlock. It standeth to reason that the bolts were fast; wherefore it was only needful to establish a watch, so that if any broke the bonds he might not escape, but be taken. None were taken."

"Natheless, three did escape," said the king, "and ye will do well to publish it and set justice upon their track, for these murthered the baron and fired the house."

I was just expecting he would come out with that. For a moment the man and his wife showed an eager interest in this news and an impatience to go out and spread it; then a sudden something else betrayed itself in their faces, and they began to ask questions. I answered the questions myself, and narrowly watched the effects produced. I was soon satisfied that the knowledge of who these three prisoners were had somehow changed the atmosphere; that our hosts' continued eagerness to go and spread the news was now only pretended and not real. The king did not notice the change, and I was glad of that. I worked the conversation around toward other details of the night's proceedings, and noted that these people were relieved to have it take that direction.

The painful thing observable about all this business was the alacrity with which this oppressed community had turned their cruel hands against their own class in the interest of the common oppressor. This man and woman seemed to feel that in a quarrel between a person of their own class and his lord, it was the natural and proper and rightful thing for that poor devil's whole caste to side with the master and fight his battle for him, without ever stopping to inquire into the rights or wrongs of the matter. This man had been out helping to hang his neighbors, and had done his work with zeal, and yet was aware that there was nothing against them but a mere suspicion, with nothing back of it describable as evidence, still neither he nor his wife seemed to see anything horrible about it.

This was depressing—to a man with the dream of a republic in his head. It reminded me of a time thirteen centuries away, when the "poor whites" of our South who were always despised and frequently insulted by the slave-lords around them, and who owed their base condition simply to the presence of slavery in their midst, were yet pusillanimously ready to side with the slave-lords in all political moves for the upholding and perpetuating of slavery, and did also finally shoulder their muskets and pour out their lives in an effort to prevent the destruction of that very institution which degraded them. And there was only one redeeming feature connected with that pitiful piece of history; and that was, that secretly the "poor white" did detest the slave-lord, and did feel his own shame. That feeling was not brought to the surface, but the fact that it was there and could have been brought out, under favoring circumstances, was something—in fact, it was enough; for it showed that a man is at bottom a man, after all, even if it doesn't show on the outside.

Well, as it turned out, this charcoal-burner was just the twin of the Southern "poor white" of the far future. The king presently showed impatience, and said:

"An ye prattle here all the day, justice will miscarry. Think ye the criminals will abide in their father's house? They are fleeing, they are not waiting. You should look to it that a party of horse be set upon their track."

The woman paled slightly, but quite perceptibly, and the man looked flustered and irresolute. I said:

"Come, friend, I will walk a little way with you, and explain which direction I think they would try to take. If they were merely resisters of the gabelle or some kindred absurdity I would try to protect them from capture; but when men murder a person of high degree and likewise burn his house, that is another matter."

The last remark was for the king—to quiet him. On the road the man pulled his resolution together, and began the march with a steady gait, but there was no eagerness in it. By and by I said:

"What relation were these men to you—cousins?"

He turned as white as his layer of charcoal would let him, and stopped, trembling.

"Ah, my God, how know ye that?"

"I didn't know it; it was a chance guess."

"Poor lads, they are lost. And good lads they were, too."

"Were you actually going yonder to tell on them?"

He didn't quite know how to take that; but he said, hesitatingly:

"Ye-s."

"Then I think you are a damned scoundrel!"

It made him as glad as if I had called him an angel.

"Say the good words again, brother! for surely ye mean that ye would not betray me an I failed of my duty."

"Duty? There is no duty in the matter, except the duty to keep still and let those men get away. They've done a righteous deed."

He looked pleased; pleased, and touched with apprehension at the same time. He looked up and down the road to see that no one was coming, and then said in a cautious voice:

"From what land come you, brother, that you speak such perilous words, and seem not to be afraid?"

"They are not perilous words when spoken to one of my own caste, I take it. You would not tell anybody I said them?"

"I? I would be drawn asunder by wild horses first."

"Well, then, let me say my say. I have no fears of your repeating it. I think devil's work has been done last night upon those innocent poor people. That old baron got only what he deserved. If I had my way, all his kind should have the same luck."

Fear and depression vanished from the man's manner, and gratefulness and a brave animation took their place:

"Even though you be a spy, and your words a trap for my undoing, yet are they such refreshment that to hear them again and others like to them, I would go to the gallows happy, as having had one good feast at least in a starved life. And I will say my say now, and ye may report it if ye be so minded. I helped to hang my neighbors for that it were peril to my own life to show lack of zeal in the master's cause; the others helped for none other reason. All rejoice today that he is dead, but all do go about seemingly sorrowing, and shedding the hypocrite's tear, for in that lies safety. I have said the words, I have said the words! the only ones that have ever tasted good in my mouth, and the reward of that taste is sufficient. Lead on, an ye will, be it even to the scaffold, for I am ready."

There it was, you see. A man *is* a man, at bottom. Whole ages of abuse and oppression cannot crush the manhood clear out of him. Whoever thinks it a mistake is himself mistaken. Yes, there is plenty good enough material for a republic in the most degraded people that ever existed—even the Russians; plenty of manhood in them—even in the Germans—if one could but force it out of its timid and suspicious privacy, to overthrow and trample in the mud any throne that ever was set up and any nobility that ever supported it. We should see certain things yet, let us hope and believe. First, a modified monarchy, till Arthur's days were done, then the destruction of the throne, nobility abolished, every member of it bound out to some useful trade, universal suffrage instituted, and the whole government placed in the hands of the men and women of the nation there to remain. Yes, there was no occasion to give up my dream yet awhile.

Chapter XXXI

MARCO

WE STROLLED ALONG in a sufficiently indolent fashion now, and talked. We must dispose of about the amount of time it ought to take to go to the little hamlet of Abblasoure and put justice on the track of those murderers and get back home again. And meantime I had an auxiliary interest which had never paled yet, never lost its novelty for me since I had been in Arthur's kingdom: the behavior—born of nice and exact subdivisions of caste—of chance passersby toward each other. Toward the shaven monk who trudged along with his cowl tilted back and the sweat washing down his fat jowls, the coal-burner was deeply reverent; to the gentleman he was abject; with the small farmer and the free mechanic he was cordial and gossipy; and when a slave passed by with a countenance respectfully lowered, this chap's nose was in the air—he couldn't even see him. Well, there are times when one would like to hang the whole human race and finish the farce.

Presently we struck an incident. A small mob of half-naked boys and girls came tearing out of the woods, scared and shrieking. The eldest among them were not more than twelve or fourteen years old. They implored help, but they were so beside themselves that we couldn't make out what the matter was. However, we plunged into the wood, they scurrying in the lead, and the trouble was quickly revealed: they had hanged a little fellow with a bark rope, and he was kicking and struggling, in the process of choking to death. We rescued him, and fetched him around. It was some more human nature; the admiring little folk imitating their elders; they were playing mob, and had achieved a success which promised to be a good deal more serious than they had bargained for.

It was not a dull excursion for me. I managed to put in the time very well. I made various acquaintanceships, and in my quality of stranger was able to ask as many questions as I wanted to. A thing which naturally interested me, as a statesman, was the matter of wages. I picked up what I could under that head during the afternoon. A man who hasn't had much experience, and doesn't think, is apt to measure a nation's prosperity or lack of prosperity by the mere size of the prevailing wages; if the wages be high, the nation is prosperous; if low, it isn't. Which is an error. It isn't what sum you get, it's how much you can buy with it, that's the important thing; and it's that that tells whether your wages are high in fact or only high in name. I could remember how it was in the time of our great civil war in the nineteenth century. In the North a carpenter got three dollars a day, gold valuation; in the South he got fifty—payable in Confederate shinplasters worth a dollar a bushel. In the North a suit of overalls cost three dollars—a day's wages; in the South it cost seventy-five—which was two days' wages. Other things were in proportion. Consequently, wages were twice as high in the North as they were in the South, because the one wage had that much more purchasing power than the other had.

Yes, I made various acquaintances in the hamlet, and a thing that gratified me a good deal was to find our new coins in circulation—lots of milrays, lots of mills, lots of cents, a good many nickels, and some silver; all this among the artisans and commonalty generally; yes, and even some gold—but that was at the bank, that is to say, the goldsmith's. I dropped in there while Marco, the son of Marco, was haggling with a shopkeeper over a quarter of a pound of salt, and asked for change for a twenty-dollar gold piece. They furnished it—that is, after they had chewed the piece, and rung it on the counter, and tried acid on it, and asked me where I got it, and who I was, and where I was from, and where I was going to, and when I expected to get there, and perhaps a couple of hundred more questions; and when they got aground, I went right on and furnished them a lot of information voluntarily; told them I owned a dog, and his name was Watch, and my first wife was a Free Will Baptist, and her grandfather was a Prohibitionist, and I used to know a man who had two thumbs on each hand and a wart on the inside of his upper lip, and died in the hope of a glorious resurrection, and so on, and so on, and so on, till even that hungry village questioner began to look satisfied, and also a shade put out; but he had to respect a man of my financial strength, and so he didn't give me any lip, but I noticed he took it out of his underlings, which was a perfectly natural thing to do. Yes, they changed my twenty, but I judged it strained the bank a little, which was a thing to be expected, for it was the same as walkng into a paltry village store in the nineteenth century and requiring the boss of it to change a two-thousand-dollar bill for you all of a sudden. He could do it, maybe; but at the same time he would wonder how a small farmer happened to be carrying so much money around in his pocket; which was probably this goldsmith's thought, too; for he followed me to the door and stood there gazing after me with reverent admiration.

Our new money was not only handsomely circulating, but its language was already glibly in use; that is to say, people had dropped the names of the former moneys, and spoke of things as being worth so many dollars or cents or mills or milrays now. It was very gratifying. We were progressing, that was sure.

I got to know several master mechanics, but about the most interesting fellow among them was the blacksmith, Dowley. He was a live man and a brisk talker, and had two journeymen and three apprentices, and was doing a raging business. In fact, he was getting rich, hand over fist, and was vastly respected. Marco was very proud of having such a man for a friend. He had taken me there ostensibly to let me see the big establishment which bought so much of his charcoal, but really to let me see what easy and almost familiar terms he was on with this great man. Dowley and I fraternized at once; I had had just such picked men, splendid fellows, under me in the Colt Arms Factory. I was bound to see more of him, so I invited him to come out to Marco's Sunday, and dine with us. Marco was appalled, and held his breath; and when the grandee accepted, he was so grateful that he almost forgot to be astonished at the condescension.

Marco's joy was exuberant—but only for a moment; then he grew thoughtful, then sad; and when he heard me tell Dowley I should have Dickon, the boss mason, and Smug, the boss wheelwright, out there, too, the coal-dust on his face turned to chalk, and he lost his grip. But I knew what was the matter with him; it was the expense. He saw ruin before him; he judged that his financial days were numbered. However, on our way to invite the others, I said:

"You must allow me to have these friends come; and you must also allow me to pay the costs."

His face cleared, and he said with spirit:

"But not all of it, not all of it. Ye cannot well bear a burden like to this alone."

I stopped him, and said:

"Now let's understand each other on the spot, old friend. I am only a farm bailiff, it is true; but I am not poor, nevertheless. I have been very fortunate this year—you would be astonished to know how I have thriven. I tell you the honest truth when I say I could squander away as many as a dozen feasts like this and never care *that* for the expense!" and I snapped my fingers. I could see myself rise a foot at a time in Marco's estimation, and when I fetched out those last words I was become a very tower for style and altitude. "So you see, you must let me have my way. You can't contribute a cent to this orgy, that's *settled.*"

"It's grand and good of you—"

"No, it isn't. You've opened your house to Jones and me in the most generous way; Jones was remarking upon it to-day, just before you came back from the village; for although he wouldn't be likely to say such a thing to you—because Jones isn't a talker, and is diffident in society—he has a good heart and a grateful, and knows how to appreciate it when he is well treated; yes, you and your wife have been very hospitable toward us—"

"Ah, brother, 'tis nothing—*such* hospitality!"

"But it *is* something; the best a man has, freely given, is always something, and is as good as a prince can do, and ranks right along beside it—for even a prince can but do his best. And so we'll shop around and get up this layout now, and don't you worry about the expense. I'm one of the worst spendthrifts that ever was born. Why, do you know, sometimes in a single week I spend—but never mind about that—you'd never believe it anyway."

And so we went gadding along, dropping in here and there, pricing things, and gossiping with the shopkeepers about the riot, and now and then running across pathetic reminders of it, in the persons of shunned and tearful and houseless remnants of families whose homes had been taken from them and their parents butchered or hanged. The raiment of Marco and his wife was of coarse tow-linen and linseywoolsey respectively, and resembled township maps, it being made up pretty exclusively of patches which had been added, township by township, in the course of five or six years, until hardly a hand's-breadth of the original garments was surviving and present. Now I wanted to fit these people out with new suits, on account of that swell company, and I didn't know just how to get at it with delicacy, until at last it struck me that as I had already been liberal in inventing wordy gratitude for the king, it would be just the thing to back it up with evidence of a substantial sort; so I said:

"And Marco, there's another thing which you must permit—out of kindness for Jones—because you wouldn't want to offend him. He was very anxious to testify his appreciation in some way, but he is so diffident he couldn't venture it himself, and so he begged me to buy some little things and give them to you and Dame Phyllis and let him pay for them without your ever knowing they came from him—you know how a delicate person feels about that sort of thing—and so I said I would, and we would keep mum. Well, his idea was, a new outfit of clothes for you both—"

"Oh, it is wastefulness! It may not be, brother, it may not be. Consider the vastness of the sum—"

"Hang the vastness of the sum! Try to keep quiet for a moment, and see how it would seem; a body can't get in a word edgeways, you talk so much. You ought to cure that, Marco; it isn't good form, you know, and it will grow on you if you don't check it. Yes, we'll step in here now and price this man's stuff—and don't forget to remember to not let on to Jones that you know he had anything to do with it. You can't think how curiously sensitive and proud he is. He's a farmer—pretty fairly well-to-do farmer—and I'm his bailiff; *but* the imagination of that man! Why, sometimes when he forgets himself and gets to blowing off, you'd think he was one of the swells of the earth; and you might listen to him a hundred years and never take him for a farmer—especially if he talked agriculture. He *thinks* he's a Sheol of a farmer; thinks he's old Grayback from Wayback; but between you and me privately he don't know as much about farming as he does about running a kingdom—still, whatever he talks about, you want to drop your under-jaw and listen, the same as if you had never heard such incredible wisdom in all your life before, and were afraid you might die before you got enough of it. That will please Jones.''

It tickled Marco to the marrow to hear about such an odd character; but it also prepared him for accidents; and in my experience when you travel with a king who is letting on to be something else and can't remember it more than about half the time, you can't take too many precautions.

This was the best store we had come across yet; it had everything in it, in small quantities, from anvils and dry-goods all the way down to fish and pinchbeck jewelry. I concluded I would bunch my whole invoice right here, and not go pricing around any more. So I got rid of Marco, by sending him off to invite the mason and the wheelwright, which left the field free to me. For I never care to do a thing in a quiet way; it's got to be theatrical or I don't take any interest in it. I showed up money enough, in a careless way, to corral the shopkeeper's respect, and then I wrote down a list of the things I wanted, and handed it to him to see if he could read it. He could, and was proud to show that he could. He said he had been educated by a priest, and could both read and write. He ran it through, and remarked with satisfaction that it was a pretty heavy bill. Well, and so it was, for a little concern like that. I was not only providing a swell dinner, but some odds and ends of extras. I ordered that the things be carted out and delivered at the dwelling of Marco, the son of Marco, by Saturday evening, and send me the bill at dinner-time Sunday. He said I could depend upon his promptness and exactitude, it was the rule of the house. He also observed that he would throw in a couple of miller-guns for the Marcos gratis—that everybody was using them now. He had a mighty opinion of that clever device. I said:

''And please fill them up to the middle mark, too; and add that to the bill.''

He would, with pleasure. He filled them, and I took them with me. I couldn't venture to tell him that the miller-gun was a little invention of my own, and that I had officially ordered that every shopkeeper in the kingdom keep them on hand and sell them at government price—which was the merest trifle, and the shopkeeper got that, not the government. We furnished them for nothing.

The king had hardly missed us when we got back at nightfall. He had early dropped again into his dream of a grand invasion of Gaul with the whole strength of his kingdom at his back, and the afternoon had slipped away without his ever coming to himself again.

Chapter XXXII

DOWLEY'S HUMILIATION

WELL, WHEN THAT cargo arrived toward sunset, Saturday afternoon, I had my hands full to keep the Marcos from fainting. They were sure Jones and I were ruined past help, and they blamed themselves as accessories to this bankruptcy. You see, in addition to the dinner materials, which called for a sufficiently round sum, I had bought a lot of extras for the future comfort of the family: for instance, a big lot of wheat, a delicacy as rare to the tables of their class as was ice-cream to a hermit's; also a sizable deal dinner-table; also two entire pounds of salt, which was another piece of extravagance in those people's eyes; also crockery, stools, the clothes, a small cask of beer, and so on. I instructed the Marcos to keep quiet about this sumptuousness, so as to give me a chance to surprise the guests and show off a little. Concerning the new clothes, the simple couple were like children; they were up and down, all night, to see if it wasn't nearly daylight, so that they could put them on, and they were into them at last as much as an hour before dawn was due. Then their pleasure—not to say delirium—was so fresh and novel and inspiring that the sight of it paid me well for the interruptions which my sleep had suffered. The king had slept just as usual—like the dead. The Marcos could not thank him for their clothes, that being forbidden; but they tried every way they could think of to make him see how grateful they were. Which all went for nothing: he didn't notice any change.

It turned out to be one of those rich and rare fall days which is just a June day toned down to a degree where it is heaven to be out of doors. Toward noon the guests arrived, and we assembled under a great tree and were soon as sociable as old acquaintances. Even the king's reserve melted a little, though it was some little trouble to him to adjust himself to the name of Jones along at first. I had asked him to try to not forget that he was a farmer; but I had also considered it prudent to ask him to let the thing stand at that, and not elaborate it any. Because he was just the kind of person you could depend on to spoil a little thing like that if you didn't warn him, his tongue was so handy, and his spirit so willing, and his information so uncertain.

Dowley was in fine feather, and I early got him started, and then adroitly worked him around onto his own history for a text and himself for a hero, and then it was good to sit there and hear him hum. Self-made man, you know. They know how to talk. They do deserve more credit than any other breed of men, yes, that is true; and they are among the very first to find it out, too. He told how he had begin life an orphan lad without money and without friends able to help him; how he had lived as the slaves of the meanest master lived; how his day's work was from sixteen to eighteen hours long, and yielded him only enough black bread to keep him in a half-fed condition; how his faithful endeavors finally attracted the attention of a good blacksmith, who came near knocking him dead with kindness by suddenly offering, when he was totally unprepared, to take him as his bound apprentice for nine years and give him board and clothes and teach him the trade—or "mystery" as Dowley called it. That was his first great rise, his first gorgeous stroke of fortune; and you saw

629

that he couldn't yet speak of it without a sort of eloquent wonder and delight that such a gilded promotion should have fallen to the lot of a common human being. He got no new clothing during his apprenticeship, but on his graduation day his master tricked him out in spang-new tow-linens and made him feel unspeakably rich and fine.

"I remember me of that day!" the wheelwright sang out, with enthusiasm.

"And I likewise!" cried the mason. "I would not believe they were thine own; in faith I could not."

"Nor other!" shouted Dowley, with sparkling eyes. "I was like to lose my character, the neighbors wending I had mayhap been stealing. It was a great day, a great day; one forgetteth not days like that."

Yes, and his master was a fine man, and prosperous, and always had a great feast of meat twice in the year, and with it white bread, true wheaten bread; in fact, lived like a lord, so to speak. And in time Dowley succeeded to the business and married the daughter.

"And now consider what is come to pass," said he, impressively. "Two times in every month there is fresh meat upon my table." He made a pause here, to let that fact sink home, then added—"and eight times salt meat."

"It is even true," said the wheelwright, with bated breath.

"I know it of mine own knowledge," said the mason, in the same reverent fashion.

"On my table appeareth white bread every Sunday in the year," added the master smith, with solemmity. "I leave it to your own consciences, friends, if this is not also true?"

"By my head, yes," cried the mason.

"I can testify it—and I do," said the wheelwright.

"And as to furniture, ye shall say yourselves what mine equipment is." He waved his hand in fine gesture of granting frank and unhampered freedom of speech, and added: "Speak as ye are moved; speak as ye would speak an I were not here."

"Ye have five stools, and of the sweetest workmanship at that, albeit your family is but three," said the wheelwright, with deep respect.

"And six wooden goblets, and six platters of wood and two of pewter to eat and drink from withal," said the mason, impressively. "And I say it as knowing God is my judge, and we tarry not here alway, but must answer at the last day for the things said in the body, be they false or be they sooth."

"Now ye know what manner of man I am, brother Jones," said the smith, with a fine and friendly condescension, "and doubtless ye would look to find me a man jealous of his due of respect and but sparing of outgo to strangers till their rating and quality be assured, but trouble yourself not, as concerning that; wit ye well ye shall find me a man that regardeth not these matters but is willing to receive any he as his fellow and equal that carrieth a right heart in his body, be his worldly estate howsoever modest. And in token of it, here is my hand; and I say with my own mouth we are equals—equals"—and he smiled around on the company with the satisfaction of a god who is doing the handsome and gracious thing and is quite well aware of it.

The king took the hand with a poorly disguised reluctance, and let go of it as willingly as a lady lets go of a fish; all of which had a good effect, for it was mistaken for an embarrassment natural to one who was being beamed upon by greatness.

The dame brought out the table now, and set it under the tree. It caused a visible stir of surprise, it being brand new and a sumptuous article of deal. But the surprise rose higher still when the dame, with a body oozing easy indifference at every pore, but eyes that gave it all away by absolutely flaming with vanity, slowly unfolded an actual simon-pure table-cloth and spread it. That was a notch above even the blacksmith's domestic grandeurs, and it hit him hard; you could see it. But Marco was in Paradise; you could see that, too. Then the dame brought two fine new stools—whew! that was a sensation; it was visible in the eyes of every guest. Then she brought two more—as calmly as she could. Sensation again—with awed murmurs. Again she brought two—walking on air, she was so proud. The guests were petrified, and the mason muttered:

"There is that about earthly pomps which doth ever move to reverence."

As the dame turned away, Marco couldn't help slapping on the climax while the thing was hot; so he said with what was meant for a languid composure but was a poor imitation of it:

"These suffice; leave the rest."

So there were more yet! It was a fine effect. I couldn't have played the hand better myself.

From this out, the madam piled up the surprises with a rush that fired the general astonishment up to a hundred and fifty in the shade, and at the same time paralyzed expression of it down to gasped "Oh's" and "Ah's," and mute upliftings of hands and eyes. She fetched crockery—new, and plenty of it; new wooden goblets and other table furniture; and beer, fish, chicken, a goose, eggs, roast beef, roast mutton, a ham, a small roast pig, and a wealth of genuine white wheaten bread. Take it by and large, that spread laid everything far and away in the shade that ever that crowd had seen before. And while they sat there just simply stupefied with wonder and awe, I sort of waved my hand as if by accident, and the storekeeper's son emerged from space and said he had come to collect.

"That's all right," I said, indifferently. "What is the amount? Give us the items."

Then he read off this bill, while those three amazed men listened, and serene waves of satisfaction rolled over my soul and alternate waves of terror and admiration surged over Marco's:

2 pounds salt .	200
8 dozen pints beer, in the wood	800
3 bushels wheat	2,700
2 pounds fish .	100
3 hens	400
1 goose .	400
3 dozen eggs . .	150
1 roast of beef	450
1 roast of mutton	400
1 ham	800
1 sucking pig .	500
2 crockery dinner-sets	6,000
2 men's suits and underwear .	2,800
1 stuff and 1 linsey-woolsey gown and underwear	1,600
8 wooden goblets .	800
Various table furniture .	10,000

1 deal table	3,000
8 stools	4,000
2 miller-guns, loaded	3,000

He ceased. There was a pale and awful silence. Not a limb stirred. Not a nostril betrayed the passage of breath.

"Is that all?" I asked, in a voice of the most perfect calmness.

"All, fair sir, save that certain matters of light moment are placed together under a head hight sundries. If it would like you, I will sepa—"

"It is of no consequence," I said, accompanying the words with a gesture of the most utter indifference; "give me the grand total, please."

The clerk leaned against the tree to stay himself, and said:

"Thirty-nine thousand one hundred and fifty milrays!"

The wheelwright fell off his stool, the others grabbed the table to save themselves, and there was a deep and general ejaculation of:

"God be with us in the day of disaster!"

The clerk hastened to say:

"My father chargeth me to say he cannot honorably require you to pay it all at this time, and therefore only prayeth you—"

I paid no more heed than if it were the idle breeze, but, with an air of indifference amounting almost to weariness, got out my money and tossed four dollars onto the table. Ah, you should have seen them stare!

The clerk was astonished and charmed. He asked me to retain one of the dollars as security, until he could go to town and— I interrupted:

"What, and fetch back nine cents? Nonsense! Take the whole. Keep the change."

There was an amazed murmur to this effect:

"Verily this being is *made* of money! He throweth it away even as it were dirt."

The blacksmith was a crushed man.

The clerk took his money and reeled away drunk with fortune. I said to Marco and his wife:

"Good folk, here is a little trifle for you"—handing the miller-guns as if it were a matter of no consequence, though each of them contained fifteen cents in solid cash; and while the poor creatures went to pieces with astonishment and gratitude, I turned to the others and said as calmly as one would ask the time of day:

"Well, if we are all ready, I judge the dinner is. Come, fall to."

Ah, well, it was immense; yes, it was a daisy. I don't know that I ever put a situation together better, or got happier spectacular effects out of the materials available. The blacksmith—well, he was simply mashed. Land! I wouldn't have felt what that man was feeling, for anything in the world. Here he had been blowing and bragging about his grand meat-feast twice a year, and his fresh meat twice a month, and his salt meat twice a week, and his white bread every Sunday the year round—all for a family of three; the entire cost for the year not above 69.2.6 (sixty-nine cents, two mills, and six milrays), and all of a sudden here comes along a man who slashes out nearly four dollars on a single blow-out; and not only that, but acts as if it made him tired to handle such small sums. Yes, Dowley was a good deal wilted, and shrunk up and collapsed; he had the aspect of a bladder-balloon that's been stepped on by a cow.

Chapter XXXIII

SIXTH-CENTURY POLITICAL ECONOMY

HOWEVER, I MADE a dead set at him, and before the first third of the dinner was reached, I had him happy again. It was easy to do—in a country of ranks and castes. You see, in a country where they have ranks and castes, a man isn't ever a man, he is only part of a man, he can't ever get his full growth. You prove your superiority over him in station, or rank, or fortune, and that's the end of it—he knuckles down. You can't insult him after that. No, I don't mean quite that; of course you *can* insult him, I only mean it's difficult; and so, unless you've got a lot of useless time on your hands it doesn't pay to try. I had the smith's reverence now, because I was apparently immensely prosperous and rich; I could have had his adoration if I had had some little gimcrack title of nobility. And not only his, but any commoner's in the land, though he were the mightiest production of all the ages, in intellect, worth, and character, and I bankrupt in all three. This was to remain so, as long as England should exist in the earth. With the spirit of prophecy upon me, I could look into the future and see her erect statues and monuments to her unspeakable Georges and other royal and noble clothes-horses, and leave unhonored the creators of this world—after God—Gutenberg, Watt, Arkwright, Whitney, Morse, Stephenson, Bell.

The king got his cargo aboard, and then, the talk not turning upon battle, conquest, or iron-clad duel, he dulled down to drowsiness and went off to take a nap. Mrs. Marco cleared the table, placed the beerkeg handy, and went away to eat her dinner of leavings in humble privacy, and the rest of us soon drifted into matters near and dear to the hearts of our sort—business and wages, of course. At a first glance, things appeared to be exceeding prosperous in this little tributary kingdom—whose lord was King Bagdemagus—as compared with the state of things in my own region. They had the "protection" system in full force here, whereas we were working along down toward free trade, by easy stages, and were now about half-way. Before long, Dowley and I were doing all the talking, the others hungrily listening. Dowley warmed to his work, snuffed an advantage in the air, and began to put questions which he considered pretty awkward ones for me, and they did have something of that look:

"In your country, brother, what is the wage of a master bailiff, master hind, carter, shepherd, swineherd?"

"Twenty-five milrays a day; that is to say, a quarter of a cent."

The smith's face beamed with joy. He said:

"With us they are allowed the double of it! And what may a mechanic get—carpenter, dauber, mason, painter, blacksmith, wheelwright, and the like?"

"On the average, fifty milrays; half a cent a day."

"Ho-ho! With us they are allowed a hundred! With us any good mechanic is allowed a cent a day! I count out the tailor, but not the others—they are all allowed a cent a day, and in driving times they get more—yes, up to a hundred and ten and even fifteen milrays a day. I've paid a hundred and fifteen myself, within the week. 'Rah for protection—to Sheol with free trade!"

And his face shone upon the company like a sunburst. But I didn't scare at

633

all. I rigged up my pile-driver, and allowed myself fifteen minutes to drive him into the earth—drive him *all* in—drive him in till not even the curve of his skull should show above-ground. Here is the way I started in on him. I asked:

"What do you pay a pound for salt?"

"A hundred milrays."

"We pay forty. What do you pay for beef and mutton—when you buy it?" That was a neat hit; it made the color come.

"It varieth somewhat, but not much; one may say seventy-five milrays the pound."

"*We* pay thirty-three. What do you pay for eggs?"

"Fifty milrays the dozen."

"We pay twenty. What do you pay for beer?"

"It costeth us eight and one-half milrays the pint."

"We get it for four; twenty-five bottles for a cent. What do you pay for wheat?"

"At the rate of nine hundred milrays the bushel."

"We pay four hundred. What do you pay for a man's tow-linen suit?"

"Thirteen cents."

"We pay six. What do you pay for a stuff gown for the wife of the laborer or the mechanic?"

"We pay eight cents, four mills."

"Well, observe the difference: you pay eight cents and four mills, we pay only four cents." I prepared now to sock it to him. I said: "Look here, dear friend, *what's become of your high wages you were bragging so about a few minutes ago?*"—and I looked around on the company with placid satisfaction, for I had slipped up on him gradually and tied him hand and foot, you see, without his ever noticing that he was being tied at all. "What's become of those noble high wages of yours?—I seem to have knocked the stuffing all out of them, it appears to me."

But if you will believe me, he merely looked surprised, that is all! He didn't grasp the situation at all, didn't know he had walked into a trap, didn't discover that he was *in* a trap. I could have shot him, from sheer vexation. With cloudy eye and a struggling intellect he fetched this out:

"Marry, I seem not to understand. It is *proved* that our wages be double thine; how then may it be that thou'st knocked therefrom the stuffing?—an I miscall not the wonderly word, this being the first time under grace and providence of God it hath been granted me to hear it."

Well, I was stunned; partly with this unlooked-for stupidity on his part, and partly because his fellows so manifestly sided with him and were of his mind— if you might call it mind. My position was simple enough, plain enough; how could it ever be simplified more? However, I must try:

"Why, look here, brother Dowley, don't you see? Your wages are merely higher than ours in *name*, not in *fact*."

"Hear him! They are the *double*—ye have confessed it yourself."

"Yes-yes, I don't deny that at all. But that's got nothing to do with it; the *amount* of the wages in mere coins, with meaningless names attached to them to know them by, has got nothing to do with it. The thing is, how much can you *buy* with your wages?—that's the idea. While it is true that with you a good mechanic is allowed about three dollars and a half a year, and with us only about a dollar and seventy-five—"

"There—ye're confessing it again, ye're confessing it again!"

"Confound it, I've never denied it, I tell you! What I say is this. With us *half* a dollar buys more than a *dollar* buys with you— and *therefore* it stands to reason and the commonest kind of common sense, that our wages are *higher* than yours."

He looked dazed, and said, despairingly:

"Verily, I cannot make it out. Ye've just *said* ours are the higher, and with the same breath ye take it back."

"Oh, great Scott, isn't it possible to get such a simple thing through your head? Now look here—let me illustrate. We pay four cents for a woman's stuff gown, you pay eight cents four mills, which is four mills more than *double*. What do you allow a laboring-woman who works on a farm?"

"Two mills a day."

"Very good; we allow but half as much; we pay her only a tenth of a cent a day; and—"

"Again ye're conf—"

"Wait! Now, you see, the thing is very simple; this time you'll understand it. For instance, it takes your woman forty-two days to earn her gown, at two mills a day—seven weeks' work; but ours earns hers in forty days—two days *short* of seven weeks. Your woman has a gown, and her whole seven weeks' wages are gone; ours has a gown, and two days' wages left, to buy something else with. There—*now* you understand it!"

He looked—well, he merely looked dubious, it's the most I can say; so did the others. I waited—to let the thing work. Dowley spoke at last—and betrayed the fact that he actually hadn't gotten away from his rooted and grounded superstitions yet. He said, with a trifle of hesitancy:

"But—but—ye cannot fail to grant that two mills a day is better than one."

Shucks! Well, of course, I hated to give it up. So I chanced another flyer:

"Let us suppose a case. Suppose one of your journeymen goes out and buys the following articles:

> "1 pound of salt;
> 1 dozen eggs;
> 1 dozen pints of beer;
> 1 bushel of wheat;
> 1 tow-linen suit;
> 5 pounds of beef;
> 5 pounds of mutton.

"The lot will cost him thirty-two cents. It takes him thirty-two working days to earn the money—five weeks and two days. Let him come to us and work thirty-two days at *half* the wages; he can buy all those things for a shade under fourteen and a half cents; they will cost him a shade under twenty-nine days' work, and he will have about half a week's wages over. Carry it through the year; he would save nearly a week's wages every two months, *your* man nothing; thus saving five or six weeks' wages in a year, your man not a cent. *Now* I reckon you understand that 'high wages' and 'low wages' are phrases that don't mean anything in the world until you find out which of them will *buy* the most!"

It was a crusher.

But, alas! it didn't crush. No, I had to give it up. What those people valued was *high wages*; it didn't seem to be a matter of any consequence to them whether the high wages would buy anything or not. They stood for "protection," and swore by it, which was reasonable enough, because interested parties had gulled them into the notion that it was protection which had created their high wages. I proved to them that in a quarter of a century their wages had advanced but thirty per cent., while the cost of living had gone up one hundred; and that with us, in a shorter time, wages had advanced forty per cent. while the cost of living had gone steadily down. But it didn't do any good. Nothing could unseat their strange beliefs.

Well, I was smarting under a sense of defeat. Undeserved defeat, but what of that? That didn't soften the smart any. And to think of the circumstances! The first statesman of the age, the capablest man, the best-informed man in the entire world, the loftiest uncrowned head that had moved through the clouds of any political firmament for centuries, sitting here apparently defeated in argument by an ignorant country blacksmith! And I could see that those others were sorry for me!—which made me blush till I could smell my whiskers scorching. Put yourself in my place; feel as mean as I did, as ashamed as I felt—wouldn't *you* have struck below the belt to get even? Yes, you would; it is simply human nature. Well, that is what I did. I am not trying to justify it; I'm only saying that I was mad, and *anybody* would have done it.

Well, when I make up my mind to hit a man, I don't plan out a love-tap; no, that isn't my way; as long as I'm going to hit him at all, I'm going to hit him a lifter. And I don't jump at him all of a sudden, and risk making a blundering half-way business of it; no, I get away off yonder to one side, and work up on him gradually, so that he never suspects that I'm going to hit him at all; and by and by, all in a flash, he's flat on his back, and he can't tell for the life of him how it all happened. That is the way I went for brother Dowley. I started to talking lazy and comfortable, as if I was just talking to pass the time; and the oldest man in the world couldn't have taken the bearings of my starting-place and guessed where I was going to fetch up:

"Boys, there's a good many curious things about law, and custom, and usage, and all that sort of thing, when you come to look at it; yes, and about the drift and progress of human opinion and movement, too. There are written laws— they perish; but there are also unwritten laws—*they* are eternal. Take the unwritten law of wages: it says they've got to advance, little by little, straight through the centuries. And notice how it works. We know what wages are now, here and there and yonder; we strike an average, and say that's the wages of to-day. We know what the wages were a hundred years ago, and what they were two hundred years ago; that's as far back as we can get, but it suffices to give us the law of progress, the measure and rate of the periodical augmentation; and so, without a document to help us, we can come pretty close to determining what the wages were three and four and five hundred years ago. Good, so far. Do we stop there? No. We stop looking backward; we face around and apply the law to the future. My friends, I can tell you what people's wages are going to be at any date in the future you want to know, for hundreds and hundreds of years."

"What, goodman, what!"

"Yes. In seven hundred years wages will have risen to six times what they are now, here in your region, and farm-hands will be allowed three cents a day, and mechanics six."

"I would I might die now and live then!" interrupted Smug, the wheelwright, with a fine avaricious glow in his eye.

"And that isn't all; they'll get their board besides—such as it is: it won't bloat them. Two hundred and fifty years later—pay attention now—a mechanic's wages will be—mind you, this is law, not guesswork; a mechanic's wages will then be *twenty* cents a day!''

There was a general gasp of awed astonishment. Dickon the mason murmured, with raised eyes and hands:

"More than three weeks' pay for one day's work!''

"Riches!—of a truth, yes, riches!'' muttered Marco, his breath coming quick and short, with excitement.

"Wages will keep on rising, little by little, little by little, as steadily as a tree grows, and at the end of three hundred and forty years more there'll be at least *one* country where the mechanic's average wage will be *two hundred* cents a day!''

It knocked them absolutely dumb! Not a man of them could get his breath for upward of two minutes. Then the coal-burner said, prayerfully:

"Might I but live to see it!''

"It is the income of an earl!'' said Smug.

"An earl, say ye?'' said Dowley; "ye could say more than that and speak no lie; there's no earl in the realm of Bagdemagus that hath an income like to that. Income of an earl—mf! it's the income of an angel!''

"Now, then, that is what is going to happen as regards wages. In that remote day, that man will earn, with *one* week's work, that bill of goods which it takes you upward of *fifty* weeks to earn now. Some other pretty surprising things are going to happen, too. Brother Dowley, who is it that determines, every spring, what the particular wage of each kind of mechanic, laborer, and servant shall be for that year?' '

"Sometimes the courts, sometimes the town council; but most of all, the magistrate. Ye may say, in general terms, it is the magistrate that fixes the wages.''

"Doesn't ask any of those poor devils to *help* him fix their wages for them, does he?''

"Hm! That *were* an idea! The master that's to pay him the money is the one that's rightly concerned in that matter, ye will notice.''

"Yes—but I thought the other man might have some little trifle at stake in it, too; and even his wife and children, poor creatures. The masters are these: nobles, rich men, the prosperous generally. These few, who do no work, determine what pay the vast hive shall have who *do* work. You see? They're a 'combine'— a trade-union, to coin a new phrase—who band themselves together to force their lowly brother to take what they choose to give. Thirteen hundred years hence—so says the unwritten law—the 'combine' will be the other way, and then how these fine people's posterity will fume and fret and grit their teeth over the insolent tyranny of trade-unions! Yes, indeed! the magistrate will tranquilly arrange the wages from now clear away down into the nineteenth century; and then all of a sudden the wage-earner will consider that a couple of thousand years or so is enough of this one-sided sort of thing; and he will rise up and take a hand in fixing his wages himself. Ah, he will have a long and bitter account of wrong and humiliation to settle.''

"Do ye believe—''

"That he actually will help to fix his own wages? Yes, indeed. And he will be strong and able, then.''

"Brave times, brave times, of a truth!'' sneered the prosperous smith.

"Oh—and there's another detail. In that day, a master may hire a man for only just one day, or one week, or one month at a time, if he wants to."

"What?"

"It's true. Moreover, a magistrate won't be able to force a man to work for a master a whole year on a stretch whether the man wants to or not."

"Will there be *no* law or sense in that day?"

"Both of them, Dowley. In that day a man will be his own property, not the property of magistrate and master. And he can leave town whenever he wants to, if the wages don't suit him!—and they can't put him in the pillory for it."

"Perdition catch such an age!" shouted Dowley, in strong indignation. "An age of dogs, an age barren of reverence for superiors and respect for authority! The pillory—"

"Oh, wait, brother; say no good word for that institution. *I* think the pillory ought to be abolished."

"A most strange idea. Why?"

"Well, I'll tell you why. Is a man ever put in the pillory for a capital crime?"

"No."

"Is it right to condemn a man to a slight punishment for a small offense and then kill him?"

There was no answer. I had scored my first point! For the first time, the smith wasn't up and ready, The company noticed it. Good effect.

"You don't answer, brother. You were about to glorify the pillory a while ago, and shed some pity on a future age that isn't going to use it. *I* think the pillory ought to be abolished. What usually happens when a poor fellow is put in the pillory for some little offense that didn't amount to anything in the world? The mob try to have some fun with him, don't they?"

"Yes."

"They begin by clodding him; and they laugh themselves to pieces to see him try to dodge one clod and get hit with another?"

"Yes."

"Then they throw dead cats at him, don't they?"

"Yes."

"Well, then, suppose he has a few personal enemies in that mob—and here and there a man or a woman with a secret grudge against him—and suppose especially that he is unpopular in the community, for his pride, or his prosperity, or one thing or another—stones and bricks take the place of clods and cats presently, don't they?"

"There is no doubt of it."

"As a rule he is crippled for life, isn't he?—jaws broken, teeth smashed out?—or legs mutilated, gangrened, presently cut off?—or an eye knocked out, maybe both eyes?"

"It is true, God knoweth it."

"And if he is unpopular he can depend on *dying*, right there in the stocks, can't he?"

"He surely can! One may not deny it."

"I take it none of *you* are unpopular—by reason of pride or insolence, or conspicuous prosperity, or any of those things that excite envy and malice among the base scum of a village? *You* wouldn't think it much of a risk to take a chance in the stocks?"

Dowley winced, visibly. I judged he was hit. But he didn't betray it by any spoken word. As for the others, they spoke out plainly, and with strong feeling. They said they had seen enough of the stocks to know what a man's chance in them was, and they would never consent to enter them if they could compromise on a quick death by hanging.

"Well, to change the subject—for I think I've established my point that the stocks ought to be abolished. I think some of our laws are pretty unfair. For instance, if I do a thing which ought to deliver me to the stocks, and you know I did it and yet keep still and don't report me, *you* will get the stocks if anybody informs on you."

"Ah, but that would serve you but right," said Dowley, "for you *must* inform. So saith the law."

The others coincided.

"Well, all right, let it go, since you vote me down. But there's one thing which certainly isn't fair. The magistrate fixes a mechanic's wage at one cent a day, for instance. The law says that if any master shall venture, even under utmost press of business, to pay anything *over* that cent a day, even for a single day, he shall be both fined and pilloried for it; and whoever knows he did it and doesn't inform, they also shall be fined and pilloried. Now it seems to me unfair, Dowley, and a deadly peril to all of us, that because you thoughtlessly confessed, a while ago that within a week you have paid a cent and fifteen mil—"

Oh, I tell *you* it was a smasher! You ought to have seen them go to pieces, the whole gang. I had just slipped up on poor smiling and complacent Dowley so nice and easy and softly, that he never suspected anything was going to happen till the blow came crashing down and knocked him all to rags.

A fine effect. In fact, as fine as any I ever produced, with so little time to work it up in.

But I saw in a moment that I had overdone the thing a little. I was expecting to scare them, but I wasn't expecting to scare them to death. They were mighty near it, though. You see they had been a whole lifetime learning to appreciate the pillory; and to have that thing staring them in the face, and every one of them distinctly at the mercy of me, a stranger, if I chose to go and report— well, it was awful, and they couldn't seem to recover from the shock, they couldn't seem to pull themselves together. Pale, shaky, dumb, pitiful? Why, they weren't any better than so many dead men. It was very uncomfortable. Of course, I thought they would appeal to me to keep mum, and then we would shake hands, and take a drink all round, and laugh it off, and there an end. But no; you see I was an unknown person, among a cruelly oppressed and suspicious people, a people always accustomed to having advantage taken of their helplessness, and never expecting just or kind treatment from any but their own families and very closest intimates. Appeal to *me* to be gentle, to be fair, to be generous? Of course, they wanted to, but they couldn't dare.

Chapter XXXIV

THE YANKEE AND THE KING SOLD AS SLAVES

WELL, WHAT HAD I better do? Nothing in a hurry, sure. I must get up a diversion; anything to employ me while I could think, and while these poor fellows could have a chance to come to life again. There sat Marco, petrified in the act of trying to get the hang of his miller-gun—turned to stone, just in the attitude he was in when my pile-driver fell, the toy still gripped in his unconscious fingers. So I took it from him and proposed to explain its mystery. Mystery! a simple little thing like that; and yet it was mysterious enough, for that race and that age.

I never saw such an awkward people, with machinery; you see, they were totally unused to it. The miller-gun was a little double-barreled tube of toughened glass, with a neat little trick of a spring to it, which upon pressure would let a shot escape. But the shot wouldn't hurt anybody, it would only drop into your hand. In the gun were two sizes—wee mustard-seed shot, and another sort that were several times larger. They were money. The mustard-seed shot represented milrays, the larger ones mills. So the gun was a purse; and very handy, too; you could pay out money in the dark with it, with accuracy; and you could carry it in your mouth; or in your vest pocket, if you had one. I made them of several sizes—one size so large that it would carry the equivalent of a dollar. Using shot for money was a good thing for the government; the metal cost nothing, and the money couldn't be counterfeited, for I was the only person in the kingdom who knew how to manage a shot-tower. "Paying the shot" soon came to be a common phrase. Yes, and I knew it would still be passing men's lips, away down in the nineteenth century, yet none would suspect how and when it originated.

The king joined us, about this time, mightily refreshed by his nap, and feeling good. Anything could make me nervous now, I was so uneasy—for our lives were in danger; and so it worried me to detect a complacent something in the king's eye which seemed to indicate that he had been loading himself up for a performance of some kind or other; confound it, why must he go and choose such a time as this?

I was right. He began, straight off, in the most innocently artful, and transparent, and lubberly way, to lead up to the subject of agriculture. The cold sweat broke out all over me. I wanted to whisper in his ear, "Man, we are in awful danger! every moment is worth a principality till we get back these men's confidence; *don't* waste any of this golden time." But of course I couldn't do it. Whisper to him? It would look as if we were conspiring. So I had to sit there and look calm and pleasant while the king stood over that dynamite mine and mooned along about his damned onions and things. At first the tumult of my own thoughts, summoned by the danger-signal and swarming to the rescue from every quarter of my skull, kept up such a hurrah and confusion and fifing and drumming that I couldn't take in a word; but presently when my mob of gathering plans began to crystallize and fall into position and form line of battle, a sort of order and quiet ensued and I caught the boom of the king's batteries, as if out of remote distance:

—"were not the best way, methinks, albeit it is not to be denied that authorities differ as concerning this point, some contending that the onion is but an unwholesome berry when stricken early from the tree—"

The audience showed signs of life, and sought each other's eyes in a surprised and troubled way.

—"whileas others do yet maintain, with much show of reason, that this is not of necessity the case, instancing that plums and other like cereals do be always dug in the unripe state—"

The audience exhibited distinct distress; yes, and also fear.

—"yet are they clearly wholesome, the more especially when one doth assuage the asperities of their nature by admixture of the tranquilizing juice of the wayward cabbage—"

The wild light of terror began to glow in these men's eyes, and one of them muttered, "These be errors, every one—God hath surely smitten the mind of this farmer." I was in miserable apprehension; I sat upon thorns.

—"and further instancing the known truth that in the case of animals, the young, which may be called the green fruit of the creature, is the better, all confessing that when a goat is ripe, his fur doth heat and sore engame his flesh, the which defect, taken in connection with his several rancid habits, and fulsome appetites, and godless attitudes of mind, and bilious quality of morals—"

They rose and went for him! With a fierce shout, "The one would betray us, the other is mad! Kill them! Kill them!" they flung themselves upon us. What joy flamed up in the king's eye! He might be lame in agriculture, but this kind of thing was just in his line. He had been fasting long, he was hungry for a fight. He hit the blacksmith a crack under the jaw that lifted him clear off his feet and stretched him flat on his back. "St. George for Britain!" and he downed the wheelwright. The mason was big, but I laid him out like nothing. The three gathered themselves up and came again; went down again; came again; and kept on repeating this, with native British pluck, until they were battered to jelly, reeling with exhaustion, and so blind that they couldn't tell us from each other; and yet they kept right on, hammering away with what might was left in them. Hammering each other—for we stepped aside and looked on while they rolled, and struggled, and gouged, and pounded, and bit, with the strict and wordless attention to business of so many bulldogs. We looked on without apprehension, for they were fast getting past ability to go for help against us, and the arena was far enough from the public road to be safe from intrusion.

Well, while they were gradually playing out, it suddenly occurred to me to wonder what had become of Marco. I looked around; he was nowhere to be seen. Oh, but this was ominous! I pulled the king's sleeve, and we glided away and rushed for the hut. No Marco there, no Phyllis there! They had gone to the road for help, sure. I told the king to give his heels wings, and I would explain later. We made good time across the open ground, and as we darted into the shelter of the wood I glanced back and saw a mob of excited peasants swarm into view, with Marco and his wife at their head. They were making a world of noise, but that couldn't hurt anybody; the wood was dense, and as soon as we were well into its depths we would take to a tree and let them whistle. Ah, but then came another sound—dogs! Yes, that was quite another matter. It magnified our contract—we must find running water.

We tore along at a good gait, and soon left the sounds far behind and modified to a murmur. We struck a stream and darted into it. We waded swiftly down it, in the dim forest light, for as much as three hundred yards, and then came across an oak with a great bough sticking out over the water. We climbed up on this bough, and began to work our way along it to the body of the tree; now we began to hear those sounds more plainly; so the mob had struck our trail. For a while the sounds approached pretty fast. And then for another while they didn't. No doubt the dogs had found the place where we had entered the stream, and were now waltzing up and down the shores trying to pick up the trail again.

When we were snugly lodged in the tree and curtained with foliage, the king was satisfied, but I was doubtful. I believed we could crawl along a branch and get into the next tree, and I judged it worth while to try. We tried it, and made a success of it, though the king slipped, at the junction, and came near failing to connect. We got comfortable lodgment and satisfactory concealment among tho foliage, and then we had nothing to do but listen to the hunt.

Presently we heard it coming—and coming on the jump, too; yes, and down both sides of the stream. Louder—louder—next minute it swelled swiftly up into a roar of shoutings, barkings, tramplings, and swept by like a cyclone.

"I was afraid that the overhanging branch would suggest something to them," said I, "but I don't mind the disappointment. Come, my liege, it were well that we make good use of our time. We've flanked them. Dark is coming on, presently. If we can cross the stream and get a good start, and borrow a couple of horses from somebody's pasture to use for a few hours, we shall be safe enough."

We started down, and got nearly to the lowest limb, when we seemed to hear the hunt returning. We stopped to listen.

"Yes," said I, "they're baffled, they've given it up, they're on their way home. We will climb back to our roost again, and let them go by."

So we climbed back. The king listened a moment and said:

"They still search—I wit the sign. We did best to abide."

He was right. He knew more about hunting than I did. The noise approached steadily, but not with a rush. The king said:

"They reason that we were advantaged by no parlous start of them, and being on foot are as yet no mighty way from where we took the water."

"Yes, sire, that is about it, I am afraid, though I was hoping better things."

The noise drew nearer and nearer, and soon the van was drifting under us, on both sides of the water. A voice called a halt from the other bank, and said:

"An they were so minded, they could get to yon tree by this branch that overhangs, and yet not touch ground. Ye will do well to send a man up it."

"Marry, that we will do!"

I was obliged to admire my cuteness in foreseeing this very thing and swapping trees to beat it. But, don't you know, there are some things that can beat smartness and foresight? Awkwardness and stupidity can. The best swordsman in the world doesn't need to fear the second best swordsman in the world; no, the person for him to be afraid of is some ignorant antagonist who has never had a sword in his hand before; he doesn't do the thing he ought to do, and so the expert isn't prepared for him; he does the thing he ought not to do; and often it catches the expert out and ends him on the spot. Well, how could I, with all my gifts, make any valuable preparation against a near-sighted, cross-eyed, pudding-headed clown who would aim himself at the wrong tree and hit the right one? And that is what he did. He went for the wrong tree, which was, of course, the right one by mistake, and up he started.

Matters were serious now. We remained still, and awaited developments. The peasant toiled his difficult way up. The king raised himself up and stood; he made a leg ready, and when the comer's head arrived in reach of it there was a dull thud, and down went the man floundering to the ground. There was a wild outbreak of anger below, and the mob swarmed in from all around, and there we were treed, and prisoners. Another man started up; the bridging bough was detected, and a volunteer started up the tree that furnished the bridge. The king ordered me to play Horatius and keep the bridge. For a while the enemy came thick and fast; but no matter, the head man of each procession always got a buffet that dislodged him as soon as he came in reach. The king's spirits rose, his joy was limitless. He said that if nothing occurred to mar the prospect we should have a beautiful night, for on this line of tactics we could hold the tree against the whole country-side.

However, the mob soon came to that conclusion themselves; wherefore they called off the assault and began to debate other plans. They had no weapons, but there were plenty of stones, and stones might answer. We had no objections. A stone might possibly penetrate to us once in a while, but it wasn't very likely; we were well protected by boughs and foliage, and were not visible from any good aiming-point. If they would but waste half an hour in stone-throwing, the dark would come to our help. We were feeling very well satisfied. We could smile; almost laugh.

But we didn't; which was just as well, for we should have been interrupted. Before the stones had been raging through the leaves and bouncing from the boughs fifteen minutes, we began to notice a smell. A couple of sniffs of it was enough of an explanation: it was smoke! Our game was up at last. We recognized that. When smoke invites you, you have to come. They raised their pile of dry brush and damp weeds higher and higher, and when they saw the thick cloud begin to roll up and smother the tree, they broke out in a storm of joy-clamors. I got enough breath to say:

"Proceed, my liege; after you is manners."

The king gasped:

"Follow me down, and then back thyself against one side of the trunk, and leave me the other. Then will we fight. Let each pile his dead according to his own fashion and taste."

Then he descended, barking and coughing, and I followed. I struck the ground an instant after him; we sprang to our appointed places, and began to give and take with all our might. The powwow and racket were prodigious; it was a tempest of riot and confusion and thick-falling blows. Suddenly some horsemen tore into the midst of the crowd, and a voice shouted:

"Hold—or ye are dead men!"

How good it sounded! The owner of the voice bore all the marks of a gentleman: picturesque and costly raiment, the aspect of command, a hard countenance, with complexion and features marred by dissipation. The mob fell humbly back, like so many spaniels. The gentleman inspected us critically, then said sharply to the peasants:

"What are ye doing to these people?"

"They be madmen, worshipful sir, that have come wandering we know not whence, and—"

"Ye know not whence? Do ye pretend ye know them not?"

"Most honored sir, we speak but the truth. They are strangers and unknown to any in this region; and they be the most violent and blood-thirsty madmen that ever—''

"Peace! Ye know not what ye say. They are not mad. Who are ye? And whence are ye? Explain.''

"We are but peaceful strangers, sir,'' I said, "and traveling upon our own concerns. We are from a far country, and unacquainted here. We have purposed no harm; and yet but for your brave interference and protection these people would have killed us. As you have divined, sir, we are not mad; neither are we violent or bloodthirsty.''

The gentleman turned to his retinue and said calmly:

"Lash me these animals to their kennels!''

The mob vanished in an instant; and after them plunged the horsemen, laying about them with their whips and pitilessly riding down such as were witless enough to keep the road instead of taking to the bush. The shrieks and supplications presently died away in the distance, and soon the horsemen began to straggle back. Meantime the gentleman had been questioning us more closely, but had dug no particulars out of us. We were lavish of recognition of the service he was doing us, but we revealed nothing more than that we were friendless strangers from a far country. When the escort were all returned, the gentleman said to one of his servants:

"Bring the led-horses and mount these people.''

"Yes, my lord.''

We were placed toward the rear, among the servants. We traveled pretty fast, and finally drew rein some time after dark at a roadside inn some ten or twelve miles from the scene of our troubles. My lord went immediately to his room, after ordering his supper, and we saw no more of him. At dawn in the morning we breakfasted and made ready to start.

My lord's chief attendant sauntered forward at that moment with indolent grace, and said:

"Ye have said ye should continue upon this road, which is our direction likewise; wherefore my lord, the earl Grip, hath given commandment that ye retain the horses and ride, and that certain of us ride with ye a twenty mile to a fair town that hight Cambenet, whenso ye shall be out of peril.''

We could do nothing less than express our thanks and accept the offer. We jogged along, six in the party, at a moderate and comfortable gait, and in conversation learned that my lord Grip was a very great personage in his own region, which lay a day's journey beyond Cambenet. We loitered to such a degree that it was near the middle of the forenoon when we entered the market-square of the town. We dismounted, and left our thanks once more for my lord, and then approached a crowd assembled in the center of the square, to see what might be the object of interest. It was the remnant of that old peregrinating band of slaves! So they had been dragging their chains about, all this weary time. That poor husband was gone, and also many others; and some few purchases had been added to the gang. The king was not interested, and wanted to move along, but I was absorbed, and full of pity. I could not take my eyes away from these worn and wasted wrecks of humanity. There they sat, grouped upon the ground, silent, uncomplaining, with bowed heads, a pathetic sight. And by hideous contrast, a redundant orator was making a speech to another gathering not thirty steps away, in fulsome laudation of "our glorious British liberties!''

I was boiling. I had forgotten I was a plebeian, I was remembering I was a man. Cost what it might, I would mount that rostrum and—

Click! the king and I were handcuffed together! Our companions, those servants, had done it; my lord Grip stood looking on. The king burst out in a fury, and said:

"What meaneth this ill-mannered jest?"

My lord merely said to his head miscreant, coolly:

"Put up the slaves and sell them!"

Slaves! The word had a new sound—and how unspeakably awful! The king lifted his manacles and brought them down with a deadly force; but my lord was out of the way when they arrived. A dozen of the rascal's servants sprang forward, and in a moment we were helpless, with our hands bound behind us. We so loudly and so earnestly proclaimed ourselves freemen, that we got the interested attention of that liberty-mouthing orator and his patriotic crowd, and they gathered about us and assumed a very determined attitude. The orator said:

"If, indeed, ye are freemen, ye have naught to fear—the God-given liberties of Britain are about ye for your shield and shelter! [Applause.] Ye shall soon see. Bring forth your proofs."

"What proofs?"

"Proof that ye are freemen."

Ah—I remembered! I came to myself; I said nothing. But the king stormed out:

"Thou'rt insane, man. It were better, and more in reason, that this thief and scoundrel here prove that we are *not* freemen."

You see, he knew his own laws just as other people so often know the laws; by words, not by effects. They take a *meaning*, and get to be very vivid, when you come to apply them to yourself.

All hands shook their heads and looked disappointed; some turned away, no longer interested. The orator said—and this time in the tones of business, not of sentiment:

"An ye do not know your country's laws, it were time ye learned them. Ye are strangers to us; ye will not deny that. Ye may be freemen, we do not deny that; but also ye may be slaves. The law is clear: it doth not require the claimant to prove ye are slaves, it requireth you to prove ye are *not*."

I said:

"Dear sir, give us only time to send to Astolat; or give us only time to send to the Valley of Holiness—"

"Peace, good man, these are extraordinary requests, and you may not hope to have them granted. It would cost much time, and would unwarrantably inconvenience your master—"

"*Master*, idiot!" stormed the king. "I have no master, I myself am the m—"

"Silence, for God's sake!"

I got the words out in time to stop the king. We were in trouble enough already; it could not help us any to give these people the notion that we were lunatics.

There is no use in stringing out the details. The earl put us up and sold us at auction. This same infernal law had existed in our own South in my own time, more than thirteen hundred years later, and under it hundreds of freemen who could not prove that they were freemen had been sold into life-long slavery without the circumstance making any particular impression upon me; but the minute law and the auction block came into my personal experience, a thing which had been merely improper before became suddenly hellish. Well, that's the way we are made.

Yes, we were sold at auction, like swine. In a big town and an active market we should have brought a good price; but this place was utterly stagnant and so we sold at a figure which makes me ashamed, every time I think of it. The King of England brought seven dollars, and his prime minister nine; whereas the king was easily worth twelve dollars and I as easily worth fifteen. But that is the way things always go; if you force a sale on a dull market, I don't care what the property is, you are going to make a poor business of it, and you can make up your mind to it. If the earl had had wit enough to—

However, there is no occasion for my working my sympathies up on his account. Let him go, for the present; I took his number, so to speak.

The slave-dealer bought us both, and hitched us onto that long chain of his, and we constituted the rear of his procession. We took up our line of march and passed out of Cambenet at noon; and it seemed to me unaccountably strange and odd that the King of England and his chief minister, marching manacled and fettered and yoked, in a slave convoy, could move by all manner of idle men and women, and under windows where sat the sweet and the lovely, and yet never attract a curious eye, never provoke a single remark. Dear, dear, it only shows that there is nothing diviner about a king than there is about a tramp, after all. He is just a cheap and hollow artificiality when you don't know he is a king. But reveal his quality, and dear me it takes your very breath away to look at him. I reckon we are all fools. Born so, no doubt.

Chapter XXXV

A PITIFUL INCIDENT

IT'S A WORLD of surprises. The king brooded; this was natural. What would he brood about, should you say? Why, about the prodigious nature of his fall, of course—from the loftiest place in the world to the lowest; from the most illustrious station in the world to the obscurest; from the grandest vocation among men to the basest. No, I take my oath that the thing that graveled him most, to start with, was not this, but the price he had fetched! He couldn't seem to get over that seven dollars. Well, it stunned me so, when I first found it out, that I couldn't believe it; it didn't seem natural. But as soon as my mental sight cleared and I got a right focus on it, I saw I was mistaken; it *was* natural. For this reason: a king is a mere artificiality, and so a king's feelings, like the impulses of an automatic doll, are mere artificialities; but as a man, he is a reality, and his feelings, as a man, are real, not phantoms. It shames the average man to be valued below his own estimate of his worth; and the king certainly wasn't anything more than an average man, if he was up that high.

Confound him, he wearied me with arguments to show that in anything like a fair market he would have fetched twenty-five dollars, sure—a thing which was plainly nonsense, and full of the baldest conceit; I wasn't worth it myself.

But it was tender ground for me to argue on. In fact, I had to simply shirk argument and do the diplomatic instead. I had to throw conscience aside, and brazenly concede that he ought to have brought twenty-five dollars; whereas I was quite well aware that in all the ages, the world had never seen a king that was worth half the money, and during the next thirteen centuries wouldn't see one that was worth the fourth of it. Yes, he tired me. If he began to talk about the crops; or about the recent weather; or about the condition of politics; or about dogs, or cats, or morals, or theology—no matter what—I sighed, for I knew what was coming; he was going to get out of it a palliation of that tiresome seven-dollar sale. Wherever we halted where there was a crowd, he would give me a look which said plainly: "If that thing could be tried over again now, with this kind of folk, you would see a different result." Well, when he was first sold, it secretly tickled me to see him go for seven dollars; but before he was done with his sweating and worrying I wished he had fetched a hundred. The thing never got a chance to die, for every day, at one place or another, possible purchasers looked us over, and, as often as any other way, their comment on the king was something like this:

"Here's a two-dollar-and-a-half chump with a thirty-dollar style. Pity but style was marketable."

At last this sort of remark produced an evil result. Our owner was a practical person and he perceived that this defect must be mended if he hoped to find a purchaser for the king. So he went to work to take the style out of his sacred majesty. I could have given the man some valuable advice, but I didn't; you mustn't volunteer advice to a slave-driver unless you want to damage the cause you are arguing for. I had found it a sufficiently difficult job to reduce the king's style to a peasant's style, even when he was a willing and anxious pupil; now then, to undertake to reduce the king's style to a slave's style—and by force— go to! it was a stately contract. Never mind the details—it will save me trouble to let you imagine them. I will only remark that at the end of a week there was plenty of evidence that lash and club and fist had done their work well; the king's body was a sight to see—and to weep over; but his spirit?—why, it wasn't even phased. Even that dull clod of a slave-driver was able to see that there can be such a thing as a slave who will remain a man till he dies; whose bones you can break, but whose manhood you can't. This man found that from his first effort down to his latest, he couldn't ever come within reach of the king, but the king was ready to plunge for him, and did it. So he gave up at last, and left the king in possession of his style unimpaired. The fact is, the king was a good deal more than a king, he was a man; and when a man is a man, you can't knock it out of him.

We had a rough time for a month, tramping to and fro in the earth, and suffering. And what Englishman was the most interested in the slavery question by that time? His grace the king! Yes; from being the most indifferent, he was become the most interested. He was become the bitterest hater of the institution I had ever heard talk. And so I ventured to ask once more a question which I had asked years before and had gotten such a sharp answer that I had not thought it prudent to meddle in the matter further. Would he abolish slavery?

His answer was as sharp as before, but it was music this time; I shouldn't ever wish to hear pleasanter, though the profanity was not good, being awkwardly put together, and with the crash-word almost in the middle instead of at the end, where, of course, it ought to have been.

I was ready and willing to get free now; I hadn't wanted to get free any sooner. No, I cannot quite say that. I had wanted to, but I had not been willing to take desperate chances, and had always dissuaded the king from them. But now— ah, it was a new atmosphere! Liberty would be worth any cost that might be put upon it now. I set about a plan, and was straightway charmed with it. It would require time, yes, and patience, too, a great deal of both. One could invent quicker ways, and fully as sure ones; but none that would be as picturesque as this; none that could be made so dramatic. And so I was not going to give this one up. It might delay us months, but no matter, I would carry it out or break something.

Now and then we had an adventure. One night we were overtaken by a snow-storm while still a mile from the village we were making for. Almost instantly we were shut up as in a fog, the driving snow was so thick. You couldn't see a thing, and we were soon lost. The slave-driver lashed us desperately, for he saw ruin before him, but his lashings only made matters worse, for they drove us further from the road and from likelihood of succor. So we had to stop at last and slump down in the snow where we were. The storm continued until toward midnight, then ceased. By this time two of our feebler men and three of our women were dead, and others past moving and threatened with death. Our master was nearly beside himself. He stirred up the living, and made us stand, jump, slap ourselves, to restore our circulation, and he helped as well as he could with his whip.

Now came a diversion. We heard shrieks and yells, and soon a woman came running and crying; and seeing our group, she flung herself into our midst and begged for protection. A mob of people came tearing after her, some with torches, and they said she was a witch who had caused several cows to die by a strange disease, and practised her arts by help of a devil in the form of a black cat. This poor woman had been stoned until she hardly looked human, she was so battered and bloody. The mob wanted to burn her.

Well, now, what do you suppose our master did? When we closed around this poor creature to shelter her, he saw his chance. He said, burn her here, or they shouldn't have her at all. Imagine that! They were willing. They fastened her to a post; they brought wood and piled it about her; they applied the torch while she shrieked and pleaded and strained her two young daughters to her breast; and our brute, with a heart solely for business, lashed us into position about the stake and warmed us into life and commercial value by the same fire which took away the innocent life of that poor harmless mother. That was the sort of master we had. I took *his* number. That snow-storm cost him nine of his flock; and he was more brutal to us than ever, after that, for many days together, he was so enraged over his loss.

We had adventures all along. One day we ran into a procession. And such a procession! All the riffraff of the kingdom seemed to be comprehended in it; and all drunk at that. In the van was a cart with a coffin in it, and on the coffin sat a comely young girl of about eighteen suckling a baby, which she squeezed to her breast in a passion of love every little while, and every little while wiped from its face the tears which her eyes rained down upon it; and always the foolish little thing smiled up at her, happy and content, kneading her breast with its dimpled fat hand, which she patted and fondled right over her breaking heart.

Men and women, boys and girls, trotted along beside or after the cart, hooting, shouting profane and ribald remarks, singing snatches of foul song, skipping, dancing—a very holiday of hellions, a sickening sight. We had struck a suburb of London, outside the walls, and this was a sample of one sort of London society. Our master secured a good place for us near the gallows. A priest was in attendance, and he helped the girl climb up, and said comforting words to her, and made the under-sheriff provide a stool for her. Then he stood there by her on the gallows, and for a moment looked down upon the mass of upturned faces at his feet, then out over the solid pavement of heads that stretched away on every side occupying the vacancies far and near, and then began to tell the story of the case. And there was pity in his voice—how seldom a sound that was in that ignorant and savage land! I remember every detail of what he said, except the words he said it in; and so I change it into my own words:

"Law is intended to mete out justice. Sometimes it fails. This cannot be helped. We can only grieve, and be resigned, and pray for the soul of him who falls unfairly by the arm of the law, and that his fellows may be few. A law sends this poor young thing to death—and it is right. But another law had placed her where she must commit her crime or starve with her child—and before God that law is responsible for both her crime and her ignominious death!

"A little while ago this young thing, this child of eighteen years, was as happy a wife and mother as any in England; and her lips were blithe with song, which is the native speech of glad and innocent hearts. Her young husband was as happy as she; for he was doing his whole duty, he worked early and late at his handicraft, his bread was honest bread well and fairly earned, he was prospering, he was furnishing shelter and sustenance to his family, he was adding his mite to the wealth of the nation. By consent of a treacherous law, instant destruction fell upon this holy home and swept it away! That young husband was waylaid and impressed, and sent to sea. The wife knew nothing of it. She sought him everywhere, she moved the hardest hearts with the supplications of her tears, the broken eloquence of her despair. Weeks dragged by, she watching, waiting, hoping, her mind going slowly to wreck under the burden of her misery. Little by little all her small possessions went for food. When she could no longer pay her rent, they turned her out of doors. She begged, while she had strength; when she was starving at last, and her milk failing, she stole a piece of linen cloth of the value of a fourth part of a cent, thinking to sell it and save her child. But she was seen by the owner of the cloth. She was put in jail and brought to trial. The man testified to the facts. A plea was made for her, and her sorrowful story was told in her behalf. She spoke, too, by permission, and said she did steal the cloth, but that her mind was so disordered of late by trouble that when she was overborne with hunger all acts, criminal or other, swam meaningless through her brain and she knew nothing rightly, except that she was *so* hungry! For a moment all were touched, and there was disposition to deal mercifully with her, seeing that she was so young and friendless, and her case so piteous, and the law that robbed her of her support to blame as being the first and only cause of her transgression; but the prosecuting officer replied that whereas these things were all true, and most pitiful as well, still there was much small theft in these days, and mistimed mercy here would be a danger to property—oh, my God, is there no property in ruined homes, and orphaned babes, and broken hearts that British law holds precious!—and so he must require sentence.

"When the judge put on his black cap, the owner of the stolen linen rose trembling up, his lip quivering, his face as gray as ashes; and when the awful words came, he cried out, 'Oh, poor child, poor child, I did not know it was death!' and fell as a tree falls. When they lifted him up his reason was gone; before the sun was set, he had taken his own life. A kindly man; a man whose heart was right, at bottom; add his murder to this that is to be now done here; and charge them both where they belong—to the rulers and the bitter laws of Britain. The time is come, my child; let me pray over thee—not *for* thee, dear abused poor heart and innocent, but for them that be guilty of thy ruin and death, who need it more.''

After his prayer they put the noose around the young girl's neck, and they had great trouble to adjust the knot under her ear, because she was devouring the baby all the time, wildly kissing it, and snatching it to her face and her breast, and drenching it with tears, and half moaning, half shrieking all the while, and the baby crowing, and laughing, and kicking its feet with delight over what it took for romp and play. Even the hangman couldn't stand it, but turned away. When all was ready the priest gently pulled and tugged and forced the child out of the mother's arms, and stepped quickly out of her reach; but she clasped her hands, and made a wild spring toward him, with a shriek; but the rope—and the under-sheriff—held her short. Then she went on her knees and stretched out her hands and cried:

''One more kiss—oh, my God, one more, one more—it is the dying that begs it!''

She got it; she almost smothered the little thing. And when they got it away again, she cried out:

''Oh, my child, my darling, it will die! It has no home, it has no father, no friend, no mother—''

''It has them all!'' said that good priest. ''All these will I be to it till I die.''

You should have seen her face then! Gratitude? Lord, what do you want with words to express that? Words are only painted fire; a look is the fire itself. She gave that look, and carried it away to the treasury of heaven, where all things that are divine belong.

Chapter XXXVI

AN ENCOUNTER IN THE DARK

LONDON—TO A slave—was a sufficiently interesting place. It was merely a great big village; and mainly mud and thatch. The streets were muddy, crooked, unpaved. The populace was an ever flocking and drifting swarm of rags, and splendors, of nodding plumes and shining armor. The king had a palace there; he saw the outside of it. It made him sigh; yes, and swear a little, in a poor juvenile sixth-century way. We saw knights and grandees whom we knew, but they didn't know us in our rags and dirt and raw welts and bruises, and wouldn't have recognized us if we had hailed them, nor stopped to answer, either, it being unlawful to speak with slaves on a chain. Sandy passed within ten yards of me on a mule—hunting for me, I imagined. But the thing which clean broke my heart was something which happened in front of our old barrack in a square, while we were enduring the spectacle of a man being boiled to death in oil for counterfeiting pennies. It was the sight of a newsboy—and I couldn't get at him!

Still, I had one comfort; here was proof that Clarence was still alive and banging away. I meant to be with him before long; the thought was full of cheer.

I had one little glimpse of another thing, one day, which gave me a great uplift. It was a wire stretching from housetop to housetop. Telegraph or telephone, sure. I did very much wish I had a little piece of it. It was just what I needed, in order to carry out my project of escape. My idea was to get loose some night, along with the king, then gag and bind our master, change clothes with him, batter him into the aspect of a stranger, hitch him to the slave-chain, assume possession of the property, march to Camelot, and—

But you get my idea; you see what a stunning dramatic surprise I would wind up with at the palace. It was all feasible, if I could only get hold of a slender piece of iron which I could shape into a lock-pick. I could then undo the lumbering padlocks with which our chains were fastened, whenever I might choose. But I never had any luck; no such thing ever happened to fall in my way. However, my chance came at last. A gentleman who had come twice before to dicker for me, without result, or indeed any approach to a result, came again. I was far from expecting ever to belong to him, for the price asked for me from the time I was first enslaved was exorbitant, and always provoked either anger or derision, yet my master stuck stubbornly to it—twenty-two dollars. He wouldn't bate a cent. The king was greatly admired, because of his grand physique, but his kingly style was against him, and he wasn't salable; nobody wanted that kind of a slave. I considered myself safe from parting from him because of my extravagant price. No, I was not expecting to ever belong to this genleman whom I have spoken of, but he had something which I expected would belong to me eventually, if he would but visit us often enough. It was a steel thing with a long pin to it, with which his long cloth outside garment was fastened together in front. There were three of them. He had disappointed me twice, because he did not come quite close enough to me to make my project entirely safe; but this time I succeeded; I captured the lower clasp of the three, and when he missed it he thought he had lost it on the way.

I had a chance to be glad about a minute, then straightway a chance to be sad again. For when the purchase was about to fail, as usual, the master suddenly spoke up and said what would be worded thus—in modern English:

"I'll tell you what I'll do. I'm tired supporting these two for no good. Give me twenty-two dollars for this one, and I'll throw the other one in."

The king couldn't get his breath, he was in such a fury. He began to choke and gag, and meantime the master and the gentleman moved away discussing.

"An ye will keep the offer open—"

"'Tis open till the morrow at this hour."

"Then I will answer you at that time," said the gentleman, and disappeared, the master following him.

I had a time of it to cool the king down, but I managed it. I whispered in his ear, to this effect:

"Your grace *will* go for nothing, but after another fashion. And so shall I. To-night we shall both be free."

"Ah! How is that?"

"With this thing which I have stolen, I will unlock these locks and cast off these chains to-night. When he comes about nine-thirty to inspect us for the night, we will seize him, gag him, batter him, and early in the morning we will march out of this town, proprietors of this caravan of slaves."

That was as far as I went, but the king was charmed and satisfied. That evening we waited patiently for our fellow-slaves to get to sleep and signify it by the usual sign, for you must not take many chances on those poor fellows if you can avoid it. It is best to keep your own secrets. No doubt they fidgeted only about as usual, but it didn't seem so to me. It seemed to me that they were going to be forever getting down to their regular snoring. As the time dragged on I got nervously afraid we shouldn't have enough of it left for our needs; so I made several premature attempts, and merely delayed things by it; for I couldn't seem to touch a padlock, there in the dark, without starting a rattle out of it which interrupted somebody's sleep and made him turn over and wake some more of the gang.

But finally I did get my last iron off, and was a free man once more. I took a good breath of relief, and reached for the king's irons. Too late! in comes the master, with a light in one hand and his heavy walking-staff in the other. I snuggled close among the wallow of snorers, to conceal as nearly as possible that I was naked of irons; and I kept a sharp lookout and prepared to spring for my man the moment he should bend over me.

But he didn't approach. He stopped, gazed absently toward our dusky mass a minute, evidently thinking about something else; then set down his light, moved musingly toward the door, and before a body could imagine what he was going to do, he was out of the door and had closed it behind him.

"Quick!" said the king. "Fetch him back!"

Of course, it was the thing to do, and I was up and out in a moment. But, dear me, there were no lamps in those days, and it was a dark night. But I glimpsed a dim figure a few steps away. I darted for it, threw myself upon it, and then there was a state of things and lively! We fought and scuffled and struggled, and drew a crowd in no time. They took an immense interest in the fight and encouraged us all they could, and, in fact, couldn't have been pleasanter or more cordial if it had been their own fight. Then a tremendous row broke out behind us, and as much as half of our audience left us, with a rush, to invest some sympathy in that. Lanterns began to swing in all directions; it was the watch gathering from far and near. Presently a halberd fell across my back, as a reminder, and I knew what it meant. I was in custody. So was my adversary. We were marched off toward prison, one on each side of the watchman. Here was disaster, here was a fine scheme gone to sudden destruction! I tried to imagine what would happen when the master should discover that it was I who had been fighting him; and what would happen if they jailed us together in the general apartment for brawlers and petty law-breakers, as was the custom; and what might—

Just then my antagonist turned his face around in my direction, the freckled light from the watchman's tin lantern fell on it, and by George, he was the wrong man!

Chapter XXXVII

AN AWFUL PREDICAMENT

SLEEP? IT WAS impossible. It would naturally have been impossible in that noisome cavern of a jail, with its mangy crowd of drunken, quarrelsome, and song-singing rapscallions. But the thing that made sleep all the more a thing not to be dreamed of, was my racking impatience to get out of this place and find out the whole size of what might have happened yonder in the slave-quarters in consequence of that intolerable miscarriage of mine.

It was a long night, but the morning got around at last. I made a full and frank explanation to the court. I said I was a slave, the property of the great Earl Grip, who had arrived just after dark at the Tabard inn in the village on the other side of the water, and had stopped there overnight, by compulsion, he being taken deadly sick with a strange and sudden disorder. I had been ordered to cross to the city in all haste and bring the best physician; I was doing my best; naturally I was running with all my might; the night was dark, I ran against this common person here, who seized me by the throat and began to pummel me, although I told him my errand, and implored him, for the sake of the great earl my master's mortal peril—

The common person interrupted and said it was a lie; and was going to explain how I rushed upon him and attacked him without a word—

"Silence, sirrah!" from the court. "Take him hence and give him a few stripes whereby to teach him how to treat the servant of a nobleman after a different fashion another time. Go!"

Then the court begged my pardon, and hoped I would not fail to tell his lordship it was in no wise the court's fault that this high-handed thing had happened. I said I would make it all right, and so took my leave. Took it just in time, too; he was starting to ask me why I didn't fetch out these facts the moment I was arrested. I said I would if I had thought of it—which was true—but that I was so battered by that man that all my wit was knocked out of me—and so forth and so on, and got myself away, still mumbling.

I didn't wait for breakfast. No grass grew under my feet. I was soon at the slave quarters. Empty—everybody gone! That is, everybody except one body—the slave-master's. It lay there all battered to pulp; and all about were the evidences of a terrific fight. There was a rude board coffin on a cart at the door, and workmen, assisted by the police, were thinning a road through the gaping crowd in order that they might bring it in.

I picked out a man humble enough in life to condescend to talk with one so shabby as I, and got his account of the matter.

"There were sixteen slaves here. They rose against their master in the night, and thou seest how it ended."

"Yes. How did it begin?"

"There was no witness but the slaves. They said the slave that was most valuable got free of his bonds and escaped in some strange way—by magic arts 'twas thought, by reason that he had no key, and the locks were neither broke nor in any wise injured. When the master discovered his loss, he was mad with despair, and threw himself upon his people with his heavy stick, who resisted and brake his back and in other and divers ways did give him hurts that brought him swiftly to his end.''

"This is dreadful. It will go hard with the slaves, no doubt, upon the trial."

"Marry, the trial is over."

"Over!"

"Would they be a week, think you—and the matter so simple? They were not the half of a quarter of an hour at it."

"Why, I don't see how they could determine which were the guilty ones in so short a time."

"*Which* ones? Indeed, they considered not particulars like to that. They condemned them in a body. Wit ye not the law?—which men say the Romans left behind them here when they went—that if one slave killeth his master all the slaves of that man must die for it."

"True. I had forgotten. And when will these die?"

"Belike within a four and twenty hours; albeit some say they will wait a pair of days more, if peradventure they may find the missing one meantime."

The missing one! It made me feel uncomfortable.

"Is it likely they will find him?"

"Before the day is spent—yes. They seek him everywhere. They stand at the gates of the town, with certain of the slaves who will discover him to them if he cometh, and none can pass out but he will be first examined."

"Might one see the place where the rest are confined?"

"The outside of it—yes. The inside of it—but ye will not want to see that."

I took the address of that prison for future reference and then sauntered off. At the first second-hand clothing shop I came to, up a back street, I got a rough rig suitable for a common seaman who might be going on a cold voyage, and bound up my face with a liberal bandage, saying I had a toothache. This concealed my worst bruises. It was a transformation. I no longer resembled my former self. Then I struck out for that wire, found it and followed it to its den. It was a little room over a butcher's shop—which meant that business wasn't very brisk in the telegraphic line. The young chap in charge was drowsing at his table. I locked the door and put the vast key in my bosom. This alarmed the young fellow, and he was going to make a noise; but I said:

"Save your wind; if you open your mouth you are dead, sure. Tackle your instrument. Lively, now! Call Camelot."

"This doth amaze me! How should such as you know aught of such matters as—"

"Call Camelot! I am a desperate man. Call Camelot, or get away from the instrument and I will do it myself."

"What—you?"

"Yes—certainly. Stop gabbling. Call the palace."

He made the call.

"Now, then, call Clarence."

"Clarence *who?*"

"Never mind Clarence who. Say you want Clarence; you'll get an answer."

He did so. We waited five nerve-straining minutes—ten minutes—how long it did seem!—and then came a click that was as familiar to me as a human voice; for Clarence had been my own pupil.

"Now, my lad, vacate! They would have known *my* touch, maybe, and so your call was surest; but I'm all right now."

He vacated the place and cocked his ear to listen—but it didn't win. I used a cipher. I didn't waste any time in sociabilities with Clarence, but squared away for business, straight-off—thus:

"The king is here and in danger. We were captured and brought here as slaves. We should not be able to prove our identity—and the fact is, I am not in a position to try. Send a telegram for the palace here which will carry conviction with it."

His answer came straight back:

"They don't know anything about the telegraph; they haven't had any experience yet, the line to London is so new. Better not venture that. They might hang you. Think up something else."

Might hang us! Little he knew how closely he was crowding the facts. I couldn't think up anything for the moment. Then an idea struck me, and I started it along:

"Send five hundred picked knights with Launcelot in the lead; and send them on the jump. Let them enter by the southwest gate, and look out for the man with a white cloth around his right arm."

The answer was prompt:

"They shall start in half an hour."

"All right, Clarence; now tell this lad here that I'm a friend of yours and a dead-head; and that he must be discreet and say nothing about this visit of mine."

The instrument began to talk to the youth and I hurried away. I fell to ciphering. In half an hour it would be nine o'clock. Knights and horses in heavy armor couldn't travel very fast. These would make the best time they could, and now that the ground was in good condition, and no snow or mud, they would probably make a seven-mile gait; they would have to change horses a couple of times; they would arrive about six, or a little after; it would still be plenty light enough; they would see the white cloth which I should tie around my right arm, and I would take command. We would surround that prison and have the king out in no time. It would be showy and picturesque enough, all things considered, though I would have preferred noonday, on account of the more theatrical aspect the thing would have.

Now, then, in order to increase the strings to my bow, I thought I would look up some of those people whom I had formerly recognized, and make myself known. That would help us out of our scrape, without the knights. But I must proceed cautiously, for it was a risky business. I must get into sumptuous raiment, and it wouldn't do to run and jump into it. No, I must work up to it by degrees, buying suit after suit of clothes, in shops wide apart, and getting a little finer article with each change, until I should finally reach silk and velvet, and be ready for my project. So I started.

But the scheme fell through like scat! The first corner I turned, I came plump upon one of our slaves, snooping around with a watchman. I coughed at the moment, and he gave me a sudden look that bit right into my marrow. I judge he thought he had heard that cough before. I turned immediately into a shop and worked along down the counter, pricing things and watching out of the corner of my eye. Those people had stopped, and were talking together and looking in at the door. I made up my mind to get out the back way, if there was a back way, and I asked the shopwoman if I could step out there and look for the escaped slave, who was believed to be in hiding back there somewhere, and said I was an officer in disguise, and my pard was yonder at the door with one of the murderers in charge, and would she be good enough to step there and tell him he needn't wait, but had better go at once to the further end of the back alley and be ready to head him off when I rousted him out.

She was blazing with eagerness to see one of those already celebrated murderers, and she started on the errand at once. I slipped out the back way, locked the door behind me, put the key in my pocket and started off, chuckling to myself and comfortable.

Well, I had gone and spoiled it again, made another mistake. A double one, in fact. There were plenty of ways to get rid of that officer by some simple and plausible device, but no, I must pick out a picturesque one; it is the crying defect of my character. And then, I had ordered my procedure upon what the officer, being human, would *naturally* do; whereas when you are least expecting it, a man will now and then go and do the very thing which it's *not* natural for him to do. The natural thing for the officer to do, in this case, was to follow straight on my heels; he would find a stout oaken door, securely locked, between him and me; before he could break it down, I should be far away and engaged in slipping into a succession of baffling disguises which would soon get me into a sort of raiment which was a surer protection from meddling law-dogs in Britain than any amount of mere innocence and purity of character. But instead of doing the natural thing, the officer took me at my word, and followed my instructions. And so, as I came trotting out of that *cul de sac,* full of satisfaction with my own cleverness, he turned the corner and I walked right into his handcuffs. If I had known it was a *cul de sac*—however, there isn't any excusing a blunder like that, let it go. Charge it up to profit and loss.

Of course, I was indignant, and swore I had just come ashore from a long voyage, and all that sort of thing—just to see, you know, if it would deceive that slave. But it didn't. He knew me. Then I reproached him for betraying me. He was more surprised than hurt. He stretched his eyes wide, and said:

"What, wouldst have me let thee, of all men, escape and not hang with us, when thou'rt the very *cause* of our hanging? Go to!"

"Go to" was their way of saying, "I should smile!" or "I like that!" Queer talkers, those people.

Well, there was a sort of bastard justice in his view of the case, and so I dropped the matter. When you can't cure a disaster by argument, what is the use to argue? It isn't my way. So I only said:

"You're not going to be hanged. None of us are."

Both men laughed, and the slave said:

"Ye have not ranked as a fool—before. You might better keep your reputation, seeing the strain would not be for long."

"It will stand it, I reckon. Before to-morrow we shall be out of prison, and free to go where we will, besides."

The witty officer lifted at his left ear with his thumb, made a rasping noise in his throat, and said:

"Out of prison—yes—ye say true. And free likewise to go where ye will, so ye wander not out of his grace the Devil's sultry realm."

I kept my temper, and said, indifferently:

"Now I suppose you really think we are going to hang within a day or two."

"I thought it not many minutes ago, for so the thing was decided and proclaimed."

"Ah, then you've changed your mind, is that it?"

"Even that. I only *thought,* then; I *know,* now."

I felt sarcastical, so I said:

"Oh, sapient servant of the law, condescend to tell us, then, what you *know."*

"That ye will all be hanged *to-day,* at mid-afternoon! Oho! that shot hit home! Lean upon me."

The fact is I did need to lean upon somebody. My knights couldn't arrive in time. They would be as much as three hours too late. Nothing in the world could save the King of England; nor me, which was more important. More important, not merely to me, but to the nation—the only nation on earth standing ready to blossom into civilization. I was sick. I said no more, there wasn't anything to say. I knew what the man meant; that, if the missing slave was found, the postponement would be revoked, the execution take place to-day. Well, the missing slave was found.

Chapter XXXVIII

SIR LAUNCELOT AND KNIGHTS TO THE RESCUE

NEARING FOUR IN the afternoon. The scene was just outside the walls of London. A cool,, comfortable, superb day, with a brilliant sun; the kind of day to make one want to live, not die. The multitude was prodigious and far-reaching; and yet we fifteen poor devils hadn't a friend in it. There was something painful in that thought, look at it how you might. There we sat, on our tall scaffold, the butt of the hate and mockery of all those enemies. We were being made a holiday spectacle. They had built a sort of grand-stand for the nobility and gentry, and these were there in full force, with their ladies. We recognized a good many of them.

The crowd got a brief and unexpected dash of diversion out of the king. The moment we were freed of our bonds he sprang up, in his fantastic rags, with face bruised out of all recognition, and proclaimed himself Arthur, King of Britain, and denounced the awful penalties of treason upon every soul there present if hair of his sacred head were touched. It startled and surprised him to hear them break into a vast roar of laughter. It wounded his dignity, and he locked himself up in silence, then, although the crowd begged him to go on, and tried to provoke him to it by catcalls, jeers, and shouts of:

"Let him speak! The king! The king! his humble subjects hunger and thirst for words of wisdom out of the mouth of their master his Serene and Sacred Raggedness!"

But it went for nothing. He put on all his majesty and sat under this rain of contempt and insult unmoved. He certainly was great in his way. Absently, I had taken off my white bandage and wound it about my right arm. When the crowd noticed this, they began upon me. They said:

"Doubtless this sailor-man is his minister—observe his costly badge of office!"

I let them go on until they got tired, and then I said:

"Yes, I am his minister, The Boss; and to-morrow you will hear that from Camelot which—"

I got no further. They drowned me out with joyous derision. But presently there was silence; for the sheriffs of London, in their official robes, with their subordinates, began to make a stir which indicated that business was about to begin. In the hush which followed, our crime was recited, the death-warrant read, then everybody uncovered while a priest uttered a prayer.

Then a slave was blindfolded; the hangman unslung his rope. There lay the smooth road below us, we upon one side of it, the banked multitude walling its other side—a good clear road, and kept free by the police—how good it would be to see my five hundred horsemen come tearing down it! But no, it was out of the possibilities. I followed its receding thread out into the distance—not a horseman on it, or sign of one.

There was a jerk, and the slave hung dangling; dangling and hideously squirming, for his limbs were not tied.

A second rope was unslung, in a moment another slave was dangling.

In a minute a third slave was struggling in the air. It was dreadful. I turned away my head a moment, and when I turned back I missed the king! They were blindfolding him! I was paralyzed; I couldn't move, I was choking, my tongue was petrified. They finished blindfolding him, they led him under the rope. I couldn't shake off that clinging impotence. But when I saw them put the noose around his neck, then everything let go in me and I made a spring to the rescue—and as I made it I shot one more glance abroad—by George! here they came, a-tilting!—five hundred mailed and belted knights on bicycles!

The grandest sight that ever was seen. Lord, how the plumes streamed, how the sun flamed and flashed from the endless procession of webby wheels!

I waved my right arm as Launcelot swept in—he recognized my rag—I tore away noose and bandage, and shouted:

"On your knees, every rascal of you, and salute the king! Who fails shall sup in hell to-night!"

I always use that high style when I'm climaxing an effect. Well, it was noble to see Launcelot and the boys swarm up onto that scaffold and heave sheriffs and such overboard. And it was fine to see that astonished multitude go down on their knees and beg their lives of the king they had just been deriding and insulting. And as he stood apart there, receiving this homage in rags, I thought to myself, well, really there *is* something peculiarly grand about the gait and bearing of a king, after all.

I was immensely satisfied. Take the whole situation all around, it was one of the gaudiest effects I ever instigated.

And presently up comes Clarence, his own self! and winks, and says, very modernly:

"Good deal of a surprise, wasn't it? I knew you'd like it. I've had the boys practising this long time, privately; and just hungry for a chance to show off."

Chapter XXXIX

THE YANKEE'S FIGHT WITH THE KNIGHTS

HOME AGAIN, AT Camelot. A morning or two later I found the paper, damp from the press, by my plate at the breakfast-table. I turned to the advertising columns, knowing I should find something of personal interest to me there. It was this:

DE PAR LE ROI.

Know that the great lord and illustrious Knight, SIR SAGRAMOR LE DESIROUS having condescended to meet the King's Minister, Hank Morgan, the which is surnamed The Boss, for satisfgetion of offence anciently given, these will engage in the lists by Camelot about the fourth hour of the morning of the sixteenth day of this next succeeding month. The battle will be à l outrance, sith the said offence was of a deadly sort, admitting of no comPosition.

DE PAR LE ROI

Clarence's editorial reference to this affair was to this effect:

thdrew.
work maintained
there since, soon
lastic have wity
oked interest
upon the esen-
ve been m..d
by the an..ns,
ent out ch..y by
pterian B..1, and
e some y..ng men
of our under the
1 guidance of tha
t or aid in a.known
the great enterprise
of making pure;
esenj
movement had its
origin in preven-
has ever been a
sions id our
on the Wis-
other one
ospel,
by-
e
The
the same
to represent
ized thirty of
needs and hear-
which, years age!
..esgn was osgan-
ing, the missions,
so that both had
to withdraw' and
much to their
grief,

It will be observed, by a glance at our advertising columns, that the community is to be favored with a treat of unusual interest in the tournament line. The names of the artists are warrant of good entertamment. The box-office will be open at noon of the 13th; admission 3 cents, reserved seats 5; proceeds to go to the hospital fund. The royal pair and all the Court will be present. With these exceptions, and the press and the clergy, the free list is strictly suspended. Parties are hereby warned against buying tickets of speculators; they will not be good at the door. Everybody knows and likes The Boss, everybody knows and likes Sir Sag.; come, let us give tne lads a good send-off. ReMember, tne proceeds go to a great and free charity, and one whose broad begevolence stretches out its helping hand, warm with the blood of a loving heart, to all that suffer, regardless of race, creed, condition or color—the only charity yet established in the earth which has no politico-religious stopcock on its compassion, but says Here flows the stream, let *all* come and drink! Turn out, all hands! fetch along your doughnuts and your gum drops and have a good time. Pie for sale on the grounds, and rocks to crack it with; also circus-lemonade—three drops of lime juice to a barrel of water.

N. B. *This is the first tournament under the new law, which allow each combatant to use any weapon he may prefer.* You want to make a note of that.

our disappointment
promptly and —|
two of their fek
erlain, and othe
ers have already
spoken, you b
furnished for
their use, m
make and
the kind
letters
of introd
duction whi
they are unin
ing friends to u,
ried, and leave the
thot kind words and
which you my joy-
hind; and it is a
home matter of b
it is our durp
direct them to
now under the
g fields as are
These young men
are warm-hearted
azirl, regions b..
not to "build a
ond,', and the
der instructi
ons of our
another man
founhati's on.,
ociety, which
They go un-
say that "inr
ionaries to mon
say sending miss

Up to the day set, there was no talk in all Britain of anything but this combat. All other topics sank into insignificance and passed out of men's thoughts and interest. It was not because a tournament was a great matter; it was not because Sir Sagramor had found the Holy Grail, for he had not, but had failed; it was not because the second (official) personage in the kingdom was one of the duelists; no, all these features were commonplace. Yet there was abundant reason for the extraordinary interest which this coming fight was creating. It was born of the fact that all the nation knew that this was not to be a duel between mere men, so to speak, but a duel between two mighty magicians; a duel not of muscle but of mind, not of human skill but of superhuman art and craft; a final struggle for supremacy between the two master enchanters of the age. It was realized that the most prodigious achievements of the most renowned knights could not be worthy of comparison with a spectacle like this; they could be but child's play, contrasted with this mysterious and awful battle of the gods. Yes, all the world knew it was going to be in reality a duel between Merlin and me, a measuring of his magic powers against mine. It was known that Merlin had been busy whole days and nights together, imbuing Sir Sagramor's arms and armor with supernal powers of offense and defense, and that he had procured for him from the spirits of the air a fleecy veil which would render the wearer invisible to his antagonist while still visible to other men. Against Sir Sagramor, so weaponed and protected, a thousand knights could accomplish nothing; against him no known enchantments could prevail. These facts were sure; regarding them there was no doubt, no reason for doubt. There was but one question: might there be still other enchantments, *unknown* to Merlin, which could render Sir Sagramor's veil transparent to me, and make his enchanted mail vulnerable to my weapons? This was the one thing to be decided in the lists. Until then the world must remain in suspense.

So the world thought there was a vast matter at stake here, and the world was right, but it was not the one they had in their minds. No, a far vaster one was upon the cast of this die: *the life of knight-errantry.* I was a champion, it was true, but not the champion of the frivolous black arts, I was the champion of hard unsentimental common sense and reason. I was entering the lists to either destroy knight-errantry or be its victim.

Vast as the show-grounds were, there were no vacant spaces in them outside of the lists, at ten o'clock on the morning of the 16th. The mammoth grandstand was clothed in flags, streamers, and rich tapestries, and packed with several acres of small-fry tributary kings, their suites, and the British aristocracy; with our own royal gang in the chief place, and each and every individual a flashing prism of gaudy silks and velvets—well, I never saw anything to begin with it but a fight between an Upper Mississippi sunset and the aurora borealis. The huge camp of beflagged and gay-colored tents at one end of the lists, with a stiff-standing sentinel at every door and a shining shield hanging by him for challenge, was another fine sight. You see, every knight was there who had any ambition or any caste feeling; for my feeling toward their order was not much of a secret, and so here was their chance. If I won my fight with Sir Sagramor, others would have the right to call me out as long as I might be willing to respond.

Down at our end there were but two tents; one for me, and another for my servants. At the appointed hour the king made a sign, and the heralds, in their tabards, appeared and made proclamation, naming the combatants and stating the cause of quarrel. There was a pause, then a ringing bugle-blast, which was the signal for us to come forth. All the multitude caught their breath, and an eager curiosity flashed into every face.

Out from his tent rode great Sir Sagramor, an imposing tower of iron, stately and rigid, his huge spear standing upright in its socket and grasped in his strong hand, his grand horse's face and breast cased in steel, his body clothed in rich trappings that almost dragged the ground—oh, a most noble picture. A great shout went up, of welcome and admiration.

And then out I came. But I didn't get any shout. There was a wondering and eloquent silence for a moment, then a great wave of laughter began to sweep along that human sea, but a warning bugle-blast cut its career short. I was in the simplest and comfortablest of gymnast costumes—flesh-colored tights from neck to heel, with blue silk puffings about my loins, and bareheaded. My horse was not above medium size, but he was alert, slender-limbed, muscled with watch-springs, and just a greyhound to go. He was a beauty, glossy as silk, and naked as he was when he was born, except for bridle and ranger-saddle.

The iron tower and the gorgeous bed-quilt came cumbrously but gracefully pirouetting down the lists, and we tripped lightly up to meet them. We halted; the tower saluted, I responded; then we wheeled and rode side by side to the grand-stand and faced our king and queen, to whom we made obeisance. The queen exclaimed:

"Alack, Sir Boss, wilt fight naked, and without lance or sword or—"

But the king checked her and made her understand, with a polite phrase or two, that this was none of her business. The bugles rang again; and we separated and rode to the ends of the lists, and took position. Now old Merlin stepped into view and cast a dainty web of gossamer threads over Sir Sagramor which turned him into Hamlet's ghost; the king made a sign, the bugles blew, Sir Sagramor laid his great lance in rest, and the next moment here he came thundering down the course with his veil flying out behind, and I went whistling through the air like an arrow to meet him—cocking my ear the while, as if noting the invisible knight's position and progress by hearing, not sight. A chorus of encouraging shouts burst out for him, and one brave voice flung out a heartening word for me—said;

"Go it, slim Jim!"

It was an even bet that Clarence had procured that favor for me—and furnished the language, too. When that formidable lance-point was within a yard and a half of my breast I twitched my horse aside without an effort, and the big knight swept by, scoring a blank. I got plenty of applause that time. We turned, braced up, and down we came again. Another blank for the knight, a roar of applause for me. This same thing was repeated once more; and it fetched such a whirlwind of applause that Sir Sagramor lost his temper, and at once changed his tactics and set himself the task of chasing me down. Why, he hadn't any show in the world at that; it was a game of tag, with all the advantage on my side; I whirled out of his path with ease whenever I chose, and once I slapped him on the back as I went to the rear. Finally I took the chase into my own hands; and after that, turn, or twist, or do what he would, he was never able to get behind me again; he found himself always in front at the end of his manœuver. So he gave up that business and retired to his end of the lists. His temper was clear gone now, and he forgot himself and flung an insult at me which disposed of mine. I slipped my lasso from the horn of my saddle, and grasped the coil in my right hand.

This time you should have seen him come!—it was a business trip, sure; by his gait there was blood in his eye. I was sitting my horse at ease, and swinging the great loop of my lasso in wide circles about my head; the moment he was under way, I started for him; when the space between us had narrowed to forty feet, I sent the snaky spirals of the rope a-cleaving through the air, then darted aside and faced about and brought my trained animal to a halt with all his feet braced under him for a surge. The next moment the rope sprang taut and yanked Sir Sagramor out of the saddle! Great Scott, but there was a sensation!

Unquestionably, the popular thing in this world is novelty. These people had never seen anything of that cowboy business before, and it carried them clear off their feet with delight. From all around and everywhere, the shout went up:

"Encore! encore!"

I wondered where they got the word, but there was no time to cipher on philological matters, because the whole knight-errantry hive was just humming now, and my prospect for trade couldn't have been better. The moment my lasso was released and Sir Sagramor had been assisted to his tent, I hauled in the slack, took my station and began to swing my loop around my head again. I was sure to have use for it as soon as they could elect a successor for Sir Sagramor, and that couldn't take long where there were so many hungry candidates. Indeed, they elected one straight off—Sir Hervis de Revel.

Bzz! Here he came, like a house afire; I dodged: he passed like a flash, with my horse-hair coils settling around his neck; a second or so later, *fst!* his saddle was empty.

I got another encore; and another, and another, and still another. When I had snaked five men out, things began to look serious to the ironclads, and they stopped and consulted together. As a result, they decided that it was time to waive etiquette and send their greatest and best against me. To the astonishment of that little world, I lassoed Sir Lamorak de Galis, and after him Sir Galahad. So you see there was simply nothing to be done now, but play their right bower—bring out the superbest of the superb, the mightiest of the mighty, the great Sir Launcelot himself!

A proud moment for me? I should think so. Yonder was Arthur, King of Britain; yonder was Guinever; yes, and whole tribes of little provincial kings and kinglets; and in the tented camp yonder, renowned knights from many lands; and likewise the selectest body known to chivalry, the Knights of the Table Round, the most illustrious in Christendom; and biggest fact of all, the very sun of their shining system was yonder couching his lance, the focal point of forty thousand adoring eyes; and all by myself, here was I laying for him. Across my mind flitted the dear image of a certain hello-girl of West Hartford, and I wished she could see me now. In that moment, down came the Invincible, with the rush of a whirlwind—the courtly world rose to its feet and bent forward—the fateful coils went circling through the air, and before you could wink I was towing Sir Launcelot across the field on his back, and kissing my hand to the storm of waving kerchiefs and the thunder-crash of applause that greeted me!

Said I to myself, as I coiled my lariat and hung it on my saddle-horn, and sat there drunk with glory, "The victory is perfect—no other will venture against me—knight-errantry is dead." Now imagine my astonishment—and everybody else's, too—to hear the peculiar bugle-call which announces that another competitor is about to enter the lists! There was a mystery here; I couldn't account for this thing. Next, I noticed Merlin gliding away from me; and then I noticed that my lasso was gone! The old sleight-of-hand expert had stolen it, sure, and slipped it under his robe.

The bugle blew again. I looked, and down came Sagramor riding again, with his dust brushed off and his veil nicely rearranged. I trotted up to meet him, and pretended to find him by the sound of his horse's hoofs. He said:

"Thou'rt quick of ear, but it will not save thee from this!" and he touched the hilt of his great sword. "An ye are not able to see it, because of the influence of the veil, know that it is no cumbrous lance, but a sword—and I ween ye will not be able to avoid it."

His visor was up; there was death in his smile. I should never be able to dodge his sword, that was plain. Somebody was going to die this time. If he got the drop on me, I could name the corpse. We rode forward together, and saluted the royalties. This time the king was disturbed. He said:

"Where is thy strange weapon?"

"It is stolen, sire,"

"Hast another at hand?"

"No, sire, I brought only the one."

Then Merlin mixed in:

"He brought but the one because there was but the one to bring. There exists none other but that one. It belongeth to the king of the Demons of the Sea. This man is a pretender, and ignorant; else he had known that that weapon can be used in but eight bouts only, and then it vanisheth away to its home under the sea."

"Then is he weaponless," said the king. "Sir Sagramor, ye will grant him leave to borrow."

"And I will lend!" said Sir Launcelot, limping up. "He is as brave a knight of his hands as any that be on live, and he shall have mine."

He put his hand on his sword to draw it, but Sir Sagramor said:

"Stay, it may not be. He shall fight with his own weapons; it was his privilege to choose them and bring them. If he has erred, on his head be it."

"Knight!" said the king. "Thou'rt overwrought with passion; it disorders thy mind. Wouldst kill a naked man?"

"An he do it, he shall answer it to me," said Sir Launcelot.

"I will answer it to any he that desireth!" retorted Sir Sagramor hotly.

Merlin broke in, rubbing his hands and smiling his low-downest smile of malicious gratication:

"'Tis well said, right well said! And 'tis enough of parleying, let my lord the king deliver the battle signal."

The king had to yield. The bugle made proclamation, and we turned apart and rode to our stations. There we stood, a hundred yards apart, facing each other, rigid and motionless, like horsed statues. And so we remained, in a soundless hush, as much as a full minute, everybody gazing, nobody stirring. It seemed as if the king could not take heart to give the signal. But at last he lifted his hand, the clear note of a bugle followed, Sir Sagramor's long blade described a flashing curve in the air, and it was superb to see him come. I sat still. On he came. I did not move. People got so excited that they shouted to me:

"Fly, fly! Save thyself! This is murther!"

I never budged so much as an inch till that thundering apparition had got within fifteen paces of me; then I snatched a dragoon revolver out of my holster, there was a flash and a roar, and the revolver was back in the holster before anybody could tell what had happened.

Here was a riderless horse plunging by, and yonder lay Sir Sagramor, stone dead.

The people that ran to him were stricken dumb to find that the life was actually gone out of the man and no reason for it visible, no hurt upon his body, nothing like a wound. There was a hole through the breast of his chain-mail, but they attached no importance to a little thing like that; and as a bullet-wound there produces but little blood, none came in sight because of the clothing and swaddlings under the armor. The body was dragged over to let the king and the swells look down upon it. They were stupefied with astonishment naturally. I was requested to come and explain the miracle. But I remained in my tracks, like a statue, and said:

"If it is a command, I will come, but my lord the king knows that I am where the laws of combat require me to remain while any desire to come against me."

I waited. Nobody challenged. Then I said:

"If there are any who doubt that this field is well and fairly won, I do not wait for them to challenge me, I challenge them."

"It is a gallant offer," said the king, "and well beseems you. Whom will you name first?"

"I name none, I challenge all! Here I stand, and dare the chivalry of England to come against me—not by individuals, but in mass!"

"What!" shouted a score of knights.

"You have heard the challenge. Take it, or I proclaim you recreant knights and vanquished, every one!"

It was a "bluff" you know. At such a time it is sound judgment to put on a bold face and play your hand for a hundred times what it is worth; forty-nine times out of fifty nobody dares to "call," and you rake in the chips. But just this once—well, things looked squally! In just no time, five hundred knights were scrambling into their saddles, and before you could wink a widely scattering drove were under way and clattering down upon me. I snatched both revolvers from the holsters and began to measure distances and calculate chances.

Bang! One saddle empty. Bang! another one. Bang—bang, and I bagged two. Well, it was nip and tuck with us, and I knew it. If I spent the eleventh shot without convincing these people, the twelfth man would kill me, sure. And so I never did feel so happy as I did when my ninth downed its man and I detected the wavering in the crowd which is premonitory of panic. An instant lost now could knock out my last chance. But I didn't lose it. I raised both revolvers and pointed them—the halted host stood their ground just about one good square moment, then broke and fled.

The day was mine. Knight-errantry was a doomed institution. The march of civilization was begun. How did I feel? Ah, you never could imagine it.

And Brer Merlin? His stock was flat again. Somehow, every time the magic of fol-de-rol tried conclusions with the magic of science, the magic of fol-de-rol got left.

Chapter XL

THREE YEARS LATER

WHEN I BROKE the back of knight-errantry that time, I no longer felt obliged to work in secret. So, the very next day I exposed my hidden schools, my mines, and my vast system of clandestine factories and workshops to an astonished world. That is to say, I exposed the nineteenth century to the inspection of the sixth.

Well, it is always a good plan to follow up an advantage promptly. The knights were temporarily down, but if I would keep them so I must just simply paralyze them—nothing short of that would answer. You see, I was ''bluffing'' that last time in the field; it would be natural for them to work around to that conclusion, if I gave them a chance. So I must not give them time; and I didn't.

I renewed my challenge, engraved it on brass, posted it up where any priest could read it to them, and also kept it standing in the advertising columns of the paper.

I not only renewed it, but added to its proportions. I said, name the day, and I would take fifty assistants and stand up *against the massed chivalry of the whole earth and destroy it.*

I was not bluffing this time. I meant what I said; I could do what I promised. There wasn't any way to misunderstand the language of that challenge. Even the dullest of the chivalry perceived that this was a plain case of ''put up, or shut up.'' They were wise and did the latter. In all the next three years they gave me no trouble worth mentioning.

Consider the three years sped. Now look around on England. A happy and prosperous country, and strangely altered. Schools everywhere, and several colleges; a number of pretty good newspapers. Even authorship was taking a start; Sir Dinadan the Humorist was first in the field, with a volume of gray-headed jokes which I had been familiar with during thirteen centuries. If he had left out that old rancid one about the lecturer I wouldn't have said anything; but I couldn't stand that one. I suppressed the book and hanged the author.

Slavery was dead and gone; all men were equal before the law; taxation had been equalized. The telegraph, the telephone, the phonograph, the typewriter, the sewing-machine, and all the thousand willing and handy servants of steam and electricity were working their way into favor. We had a steamboat or two on the Thames, we had steam war-ships, and the beginnings of a steam commercial marine; I was getting ready to send out an expedition to discover America.

We were building several lines of railway, and our line from Camelot to London was already finished and in operation. I was shrewd enough to make all offices connected with the passenger service places of high and distinguished honor. My idea was to attract the chivalry and nobility, and make them useful and keep them out of mischief. The plan worked very well, the competition for the places was hot. The conductor of the 4.33 express was a duke; there wasn't a passenger conductor on the line below the degree of earl. They were good men, every one, but they had two defects which I couldn't cure, and so had to wink at: they wouldn't lay aside their armor, and they would "knock down" fare—I mean rob the company.

There was hardly a knight in all the land who wasn't in some useful employment. They were going from end to end of the country in all manner of useful missionary capacities; their penchant for wandering, and their experience in it, made them altogether the most effective spreaders of civilization we had. They went clothed in steel and equipped with sword and lance and battle-ax, and if they couldn't persuade a person to try a sewing-machine on the instalment plan, or a melodeon, or a barbed-wire fence, or a prohibition journal, or any of the other thousand and one things they canvassed for, they removed him and passed on.

I was very happy. Things were working steadily toward a secretly longed-for point. You see, I had two schemes in my head which were the vastest of all my projects. The one was to overthrow the Catholic Church and set up the Protestant faith on its ruins—not as an Established Church, but a go-as-you-please one; and the other project was to get a decree issued by and by, commanding that upon Arthur's death unlimited suffrage should be introduced, and given to men and women alike—at any rate to all men, wise or unwise, and to all mothers who at middle age should be found to know nearly as much as their sons at twenty-one. Arthur was good for thirty years yet, he being about my own age—that is to say, forty—and I believed that in that time I could easily have the active part of the population of that day ready and eager for an event which should be the first of its kind in the history of the world—a rounded and complete governmental revolution without bloodshed. The result to be a republic. Well, I may as well confess, though I do feel ashamed when I think of it: I was beginning to have a base hankering to be its first president myself. Yes, there was more or less human nature in me; I found that out.

Clarence was with me as concerned the revolution, but in a modified way. His idea was a republic, without privileged orders, but with a hereditary royal family at the head of it instead of an elective chief magistrate. He believed that no nation that had ever known the joy of worshiping a royal family could ever be robbed of it and not fade away and die of melancholy. I urged that kings were dangerous. He said, then have cats. He was sure that a royal family of cats would answer every purpose. They would be as useful as any other royal family, they would know as much, they would have the same virtues and the same treacheries, the same disposition to get up shindies with other royal cats, they would be laughably vain and absurd and never know it, they would be wholly inexpensive; finally, they would have as sound a divine right as any other royal house, and "Tom VII., or Tom XI., or Tom XIV. by the grace of God King," would sound as well as it would when applied to the ordinary royal tom-cat with tights on. "And as a rule," said he, in his neat modern English, "the character of these cats would be considerably above the character of the average king, and this would be an immense moral advantage to the nation, for the reason that a nation always models its morals after its monarch's. The worship of royalty being founded in unreason, these graceful and harmless cats would easily become as sacred as any other royalties, and indeed more so, because it would presently be noticed that they hanged nobody, beheaded nobody, imprisoned nobody, inflicted no cruelties or injustices of any sort, and so must be worthy of a deeper love and reverence than the customary human king, and would certainly get it. The eyes of the whole harried world would soon be fixed upon this humane and gentle system, and royal butchers would presently begin to disappear; their subjects would fill the vacancies with catlings from our own royal house; we should become a factory; we should supply the thrones of the world; within forty years all Europe would be governed by cats, and we should furnish the cats. The reign of universal peace would begin then, to end no more forever. . . . *Me-e-e-yow-ow-ow-ow—fzt!—wow!''*

Hang him, I supposed he was in earnest, and was beginning to be persuaded by him, until he exploded that cat-howl and startled me almost out of my clothes. But he never could be in earnest. He didn't know what it was. He had pictured a distinct and perfectly rational and feasible improvement upon constitutional monarchy, but he was too feather-headed to know it, or care anything about it, either. I was going to give him a scolding, but Sandy came flying in at that moment, wild with terror, and so choked with sobs that for a minute she could not get her voice. I ran and took her in my arms, and lavished caresses upon her and said, beseechingly:

"Speak, darling, speak! What is it?"

Her head fell limp upon my bosom, and she gasped, almost inaudibly:

"HELLO-CENTRAL!"

"Quick!" I shouted to Clarence; "telephone the king's homeopath to come!"

In two minutes I was kneeling by the child's crib, and Sandy was despatching servants here, there, and everywhere, all over the palace. I took in the situation almost at a glance—membranous croup! I bent down and whispered:

"Wake up, sweetheart! Hello-Central!"

She opened her soft eyes languidly, and made out to say:

"Papa."

That was a comfort. She was far from dead yet. I sent for preparations of sulphur, I rousted out the croup-kettle myself; for I don't sit down and wait for doctors when Sandy or the child is sick. I knew how to nurse both of them, and had had experience. This little chap had lived in my arms a good part of its small life, and often I could soothe away its troubles and get it to laugh through the tear-dews on its eyelashes when even its mother couldn't.

Sir Launcelot, in his richest armor, came striding along the great hall now on his way to the stock-board; he was president of the stock-board, and occupied the Siege Perilous, which he had bought of Sir Galahad; for the stock-board consisted of the Knights of the Round Table, and they used the Round Table for business purposes now. Seats at it were worth—well, you would never believe the figure, so it is no use to state it. Sir Launcelot was a bear, and he had put up a corner in one of the new lines, and was just getting ready to squeeze the shorts to-day; but what of that? He was the same old Launcelot, and when he glanced in as he was passing the door and found out that his pet was sick, that was enough for him; bulls and bears might fight it out their own way for all him, he would come right in here and stand by little Hello-Central for all he was worth. And that was what he did. He shied his helmet into the corner, and in half a minute he had a new wick in the alcohol lamp and was firing up on the croup-kettle. By this time Sandy had built a blanket canopy over the crib, and everything was ready.

Sir Launcelot got up steam, he and I loaded up the kettle with unslaked lime and carbolic acid, with a touch of lactic acid added thereto, then filled the thing up with water and inserted the steam-spout under the canopy. Everything was shipshape now, and we sat down on either side of the crib to stand our watch. Sandy was so grateful and so comforted that she charged a couple of churchwardens with willow-bark and sumach-tobacco for us, and told us to smoke as much as we pleased, it couldn't get under the canopy, and she was used to smoke, being the first lady in the land who had ever seen a cloud blown. Well, there couldn't be a more contented or comfortable sight than Sir Launcelot in his noble armor sitting in gracious serenity at the end of a yard of snowy church-warden. He was a beautiful man, a lovely man, and was just intended to make a wife and children happy. But, of course, Guenever—however, it's no use to cry over what's done and can't be helped.

Well, he stood watch-and-watch with me, right straight through, for three days and nights, till the child was out of danger; then he took her up in his great arms and kissed her, with his plumes falling about her golden head, then laid her softly in Sandy's lap again and took his stately way down the vast hall, between the ranks of admiring men-at-arms and menials, and so disappeared. And no instinct warned me that I should never look upon him again in this world! Lord, what a world of heartbreak it is.

The doctors said we must take the child away, if we would coax her back to health and strength again. And she must have sea-air. So we took a man-of-war, and a suite of two hundred and sixty persons, and went cruising about, and after a fortnight of this we stepped ashore on the French coast, and the doctors thought it would be a good idea to make something of a stay there. The little king of that region offered us his hospitalities, and we were glad to accept. If he had had as many conveniences as he lacked, we should have been plenty comfortable enough; even as it was, we made out very well, in his queer old castle, by the help of comforts and luxuries from the ship.

At the end of a month I sent the vessel home for fresh supplies, and for news. We expected her back in three or four days. She would bring me, along with other news, the result of a certain experiment which I had been starting. It was a project of mine to replace the tournament with something which might furnish an escape for the extra steam of the chivalry, keep those bucks entertained and out of mischief, and at the same time preserve the best thing in them, which was their hardy spirit of emulation. I had had a choice band of them in private training for some time, and the date was now arriving for their first public effort.

This experiment was baseball. In order to give the thing vogue from the start, and place it out of the reach of criticism, I chose my nines by rank, not capacity. There wasn't a knight in either team who wasn't a sceptered sovereign. As for material of this sort, there was a glut of it always around Arthur. You couldn't throw a brick in any direction and not cripple a king. Of course, I couldn't get these people to leave off their armor; they wouldn't do that when they bathed. They consented to differentiate the armor so that a body could tell one team from the other, but that was the most they would do. So, one of the teams wore chain-mail ulsters, and the other wore plate armor made of my new Bessemer steel. Their practice in the field was the most fantastic thing I ever saw. Being ball-proof, they never skipped out of the way, but stood still and took the result; when a Bessemer was at the bat and a ball hit him, it would bound a hundred and fifty yards sometimes. And when a man was running, and threw himself on his stomach to slide to his base, it was like an ironclad coming into port. At first I appointed men of no rank to act as umpires, but I had to discontinue that. These people were no easier to please than other nines. The umpire's first decision was usually his last; they broke him in two with a bat, and his friends toted him home on a shutter. When it was noticed that no umpire ever survived a game, umpiring got to be unpopular. So I was obliged to appoint somebody whose rank and lofty position under the government would protect him.

Here are the names of the nines:

BESSEMERS	ULSTERS
KING ARTHUR.	EMPEROR LUCIUS.
KING LOT OF LOTHIAN.	KING LOGRIS.
KING OF NORTHGALIS.	KING MARHALT OF IRELAND.
KING MARSIL.	KING MORGANORE.
KING OF LITTLE BRITAIN.	KING MARK OF CORNWALL.
KING LABOR.	KING NENTRES OF GARLOT.
KING PELLAM OF LISTENGESE.	KING MELIODAS OF LIONES.
KING BAGDEMAGUS.	KING OF THE LAKE.
KING TOLLEME LA FEINTES.	THE SOWDAN OF SYRIA

Umpire—CLARENCE.

The first public game would certainly draw fifty thousand people; and for solid fun would be worth going around the world to see. Everything would be favorable; it was balmy and beautiful spring weather now, and Nature was all tailored out in her new clothes.

Chapter XLI

THE INTERDICT

HOWEVER, MY ATTENTION was suddenly snatched from such matters; our child began to lose ground again, and we had to go to sitting up with her, her case became so serious. We couldn't bear to allow anybody to help in this service, so we two stood watch-and-watch, day in and day out. Ah, Sandy, what a right heart she had, how simple, and genuine, and good she was! She was a flawless wife and mother; and yet I had married her for no other particular reasons, except that by the customs of chivalry she was my property until some knight should win her from me in the field. She had hunted Britain over for me; had found me at the hanging-bout outside of London, and had straightway resumed her old place at my side in the placidest way and as of right. I was a New-Englander, and in my opinion this sort of partnership would compromise her, sooner or later. She couldn't see how, but I cut argument short and we had a wedding.

Now I didn't know I was drawing a prize, yet that was what I did draw. Within the twelvemonth I became her worshiper; and ours was the dearest and perfectest comradeship that ever was. People talk about beautiful friendships between two persons of the same sex. What is the best of that sort, as compared with the friendship of man and wife, where the best impulses and highest ideals of both are the same? There is no place for comparison between the two friendships; the one is earthly, the other divine.

In my dreams, along at first, I still wandered thirteen centuries away, and my unsatisfied spirit went calling and harking all up and down the unreplying vacancies of a vanished world. Many a time Sandy heard that imploring cry come from my lips in my sleep. With a grand magnanimity she saddled that cry of mine upon our child, conceiving it to be the name of some lost darling of mine. It touched me to tears, and it also nearly knocked me off my feet, too, when she smiled up in my face for an earned reward, and played her quaint and pretty surprise upon me:

"The name of one who was dear to thee is here preserved, here made holy, and the music of it will abide always in our ears. Now thou'lt kiss me, as knowing the name I have given the child."

But I didn't know it, all the same. I hadn't an idea in the world; but it would have been cruel to confess it and spoil her pretty game; so I never let on, but said:

"Yes, I know, sweetheart—how dear and good it is of you, too! But I want to hear these lips of yours, which are also mine, utter it first—then its music will be perfect."

Pleased to the marrow, she murmured:

"HELLO-CENTRAL!"

I didn't laugh—I am always thankful for that—but the strain ruptured every cartilage in me, and for weeks afterward I could hear my bones clack when I walked. She never found out her mistake. The first time she heard that form of salute used at the telephone she was surprised, and not pleased; but I told her I had given order for it: that henceforth and forever the telephone must always be invoked with that reverent formality, in perpetual honor and remembrance of my lost friend and her small namesake. This was not true. But it answered.

Well, during two weeks and a half we watched by the crib, and in our deep solicitude we were unconscious of any world outside of that sick-room. Then our reward came: the center of the universe turned the corner and began to mend. Grateful? It isn't the term. There *isn't* any term for it. You know that yourself, if you've watched your child through the Valley of the Shadow and seen it come back to life and sweep night out of the earth with one all-illuminating smile that you could cover with your hand.

Why, we were back in this world in one instant! Then we looked the same startled thought into each other's eyes at the same moment; more than two weeks gone, and that ship not back yet!

In another minute I appeared in the presence of my train. They had been steeped in troubled bodings all this time—their faces showed it. I called an escort and we galloped five miles to a hilltop overlooking the sea. Where was my great commerce that so lately had made these glistening expanses populous and beautiful with its white-winged flocks? Vanished, every one! Not a sail, from verge to verge, not a smoke-bank—just a dead and empty solitude, in place of all that brisk and breezy life.

I went swiftly back, saying not a word to anybody. I told Sandy this ghastly news. We could imagine no explanation that would begin to explain. Had there been an invasion? an earthquake? a pestilence? Had the nation been swept out of existence? But guessing was profitless. I must go—at once. I borrowed the king's navy—a "ship" no bigger than a steam-launch—and was soon ready.

The parting—ah, yes, that was hard. As I was devouring the child with last kisses, it brisked up and jabbered out its vocabulary!—the first time in more than two weeks, and it made fools of us for joy. The darling mispronunciations of childhood!—dear me, there's no music that can touch it; and how one grieves when it wastes away and dissolves into correctness, knowing it will never visit his bereaved ear again. Well, how good it was to be able to carry that gracious memory away with me!

I approached England the next morning, with the wide highway of salt-water all to myself. There were ships in the harbor, at Dover, but they were naked as to sails, and there was no sign of life about them. It was Sunday; yet at Canterbury the streets were empty; strangest of all, there was not even a priest in sight, and no stroke of a bell fell upon my ear. The mournfulness of death was everywhere. I couldn't understand it. At last, in the further edge of that town I saw a small funeral procession—just a family and a few friends following a coffin—no priest; a funeral without bell, book, or candle; there was a church there close at hand, but they passed it by weeping, and did not enter it; I glanced up at the belfry, and there hung the bell, shrouded in black, and its tongue tied back. Now I knew! Now I understood the stupendous calamity that had overtaken England. Invasion? Invasion is a triviality to it. It was the INTERDICT!

I asked no questions; I didn't need to ask any. The Church had struck; the thing for me to do was to get into a disguise, and go warily. One of my servants gave me a suit of clothes, and when we were safe beyond the town I put them on, and from that time I traveled alone; I could not risk the embarrassment of company.

A miserable journey. A desolate silence everywhere. Even in London itself. Traffic had ceased; men did not talk or laugh, or go in groups, or even in couples; they moved aimlessly about, each man by himself, with his head down, and woe and terror at his heart. The Tower showed recent war-scars. Verily, much had been happening.

Of course, I meant to take the train for Camelot. Train! Why, the station was as vacant as a cavern. I moved on. The journey to Camelot was a repetition of what I had already seen. The Monday and the Tuesday differed in no way from the Sunday. I arrived far in the night. From being the best electric-lighted town in the kingdom and the most like a recumbent sun of anything you ever saw, it was become simply a blot—a blot upon darkness—that is to say, it was darker and solider than the rest of the darkness, and so you could see it a little better; it made me feel as if maybe it was symbolical—a sort of sign that the Church was going to *keep* the upper hand now, and snuff out all my beautiful civilization just like that. I found no life stirring in the somber streets. I groped my way with a heavy heart. The vast castle loomed black upon the hilltop, not a spark visible about it. The drawbridge was down, the great gate stood wide, I entered without challenge, my own heels making the only sound I heard—and it was sepulchral enough, in those huge vacant courts.

Chapter XLII

WAR!

I FOUND CLARENCE alone in his quarters, drowned in melancholy; and in place of the electric light, he had reinstituted the ancient rag-lamp, and sat there in a

grisly twilight with all curtains drawn tight. He sprang up and rushed for me
eagerly, saying:

"Oh, it's worth a billion milays to look upon a live person again!"

He knew me as easily as if I hadn't been disguised at all. Which frightened
me; one may easily believe that.

"Quick, now, tell me the meaning of this fearful disaster," I said. "How did
it come about?"

"Well, if there hadn't been any Queen Guenever, it wouldn't have come so
early; but it would have come, anyway. It would have come on your own account
by and by; by luck, it happened to come on the queen's."

"*And* Sir Launcelot's?"

"Just so."

"Give me the details."

"I reckon you will grant that during some years there has been only one pair
of eyes in these kingdoms that has not been looking steadily askance at the queen
and Sir Launcelot—"

"Yes, King Arthur's."

—"and only one heart that was without suspicion—"

"Yes—the king's; a heart that isn't capable of thinking evil of a friend."

"Well, the king might have gone on, still happy and unsuspecting, to the end
of his days, but for one of your modern improvements—the stock-board. When
you left, three miles of the London, Canterbury and Dover were ready for the
rails, and also ready and ripe for manipulation in the stock-market. It was wildcat,
and everybody knew it. The stock was for sale at a give-away. What does Sir
Launcelot do, but—"

"Yes, I know; he quietly picked up nearly all of it for a song; then he bought
about twice as much more, deliverable upon call; and he was about to call when
I left."

"Very well, he did call. The boys couldn't deliver. Oh, he had them—and
he just settled his grip and squeezed them. They were laughing in their sleeves
over their smartness in selling stock to him at fifteen and sixteen and along there
that wasn't worth ten. Well, when they had laughed long enough on that side
of their mouths, they rested up that side by shifting the laugh to the other side.
That was when they compromised with the Invincible at two hundred and eighty-
three!"

"Good land!"

"He skinned them alive, and they deserved it—anyway, the whole kingdom
rejoiced. Well, among the flayed were Sir Agravaine and Sir Mordred, nephews
to the king. End of the first act. Act second, scene first, an apartment in Carlisle
castle, where the court had gone for a few days' hunting. Persons present, the
whole tribe of the king's nephews. Mordred and Agravaine propose to call the
guileless Arthur's attention to Guenever and Sir Launcelot. Sir Gawaine, Sir
Gareth, and Sir Gaheris will have nothing to do with it. A dispute ensues, with
loud talk; in the midst of it enter the king. Mordred and Agravaine spring their
devastating tale upon him. *Tableau*. A trap is laid for Launcelot, by the king's
command, and Sir Launcelot walks into it. He made it sufficiently uncomfortable
for the ambushed witnesses—to wit, Mordred, Agravaine, and twelve knights
of lesser rank, for he killed every one of them but Mordred; but of course that
couldn't straighten matters between Launcelot and the king, and didn't."

"Oh, dear, only one thing could result—I see that. War, and the knights of the realm divided into a king's party and a Sir Launcelot's party."

"Yes—that was the way of it. The king sent the queen to the stake, proposing to purify her with fire. Launcelot and his knights rescued her, and in doing it slew certain good old friends of yours and mine—in fact, some of the best we ever had; to wit, Sir Belias le Orgulous, Sir Segwarides, Sir Griflet le Fils de Dieu, Sir Brandiles, Sir Aglovale—"

"Oh, you tear out my heartstrings."

—"wait, I'm not done yet—Sir Tor, Sir Gauter, Sir Gillimer—"

"The very best man in my subordinate nine. What a handy right-fielder he was!"

—"Sir Reynold's three brothers, Sir Damus, Sir Priamus, Sir Kay the stranger—"

"My peerless short-stop! I've seen him catch a daisy-cutter in his teeth. Come, I can't stand this!"

—"Sir Driant, Sir Lambegus, Sir Herminde, Sir Pertilope, Sir Perimones, and—whom do you think?"

"Rush! Go on."

"Sir Gaheris, and Sir Gareth—both!"

"Oh, incredible! Their love for Launcelot was indestructible."

"Well, it was an accident. They were simply on-lookers; they were unarmed, and were merely there to witness the queen's punishment. Sir Launcelot smote down whoever came in the way of his blind fury, and he killed these without noticing who they were. Here is an instantaneous photograph one of our boys got of the battle; it's for sale on every newsstand. There—the figures nearest the queen are Sir Launcelot with his sword up, and Sir Gareth gasping his latest breath. You can catch the agony in the queen's face through the curling smoke. It's a rattling battle-picture."

"Indeed, it is. We must take good care of it; its historical value is incalculable. Go on."

"Well, the rest of the tale is just war, pure and simple. Launcelot retreated to his town and castle of Joyous Gard, and gathered there a great following of knights. The king, with a great host, went there, and there was desperate fighting during several days, and, as a result, all the plain around was paved with corpses and cast-iron. Then the Church patched up a peace between Arthur and Launcelot and the queen and everybody—everybody but Sir Gawaine. He was bitter about the slaying of his brothers, Gareth and Gaheris, and would not be appeased. He notified Launcelot to get him thence, and make swift preparation, and look to be soon attacked. So Launcelot sailed to his Duchy of Guienne with his following, and Gawaine soon followed with an army, and he beguiled Arthur to go with him. Arthur left the kingdom in Sir Mordred's hands until you should return—"

"Ah—a king's customary wisdom!"

"Yes. Sir Mordred set himself at once to work to make his kingship permanent. He was going to marry Guenever, as a first move; but she fled and shut herself up in the Tower of London. Mordred attacked; the Bishop of Canterbury dropped down on him with the Interdict. The king returned; Mordred fought him at Dover, at Canterbury, and again at Barham Down. Then there was talk of peace and a composition. Terms, Mordred to have Cornwall and Kent during Arthur's life, and the whole kingdom afterward."

"Well, upon my word! My dream of a republic to *be* a dream, and so remain."

"Yes. The two armies lay near Salisbury. Gawaine—Gawaine's head is at Dover Castle, he fell in the fight there—Gawaine appeared to Arthur in a dream, at least his ghost did, and warned him to refrain from conflict for a month, let the delay cost what it might. But battle was precipitated by an accident. Arthur had given order that if a sword was raised during the consultation over the proposed treaty with Mordred, sound the trumpet and fall on! for he had no confidence in Mordred. Mordred had given a similar order to *his* people. Well, by and by an adder bit a knight's heel; the knight forgot all about the order, and made a slash at the adder with his sword. Inside of half a minute those two prodigious hosts came together with a crash! They butchered away all day. Then the king—however, we have started something fresh since you left—our paper has."

"No? What is that?"

"War correspondence!"

"Why, that's good."

"Yes, the paper was booming right along, for the Interdict made no impression, got no grip, while the war lasted. I had war correspondents with both armies. I will finish that battle by reading you what one of the boys says:

> Then the king looked about him, and then was he aware of all his host and of all his good knights were left no more on live but two knights, that was Sir Lucan de Butlere, and his brother Sir Bedivere: and they were full sore wounded. Jesu mercy, said the king, where are all my noble knights becomen? Alas that ever I should see this doleful day. For now, said Arthur, I am come to mine end. But would to God that I wist where were that traitor Sir Mordred, that hath caused all this mischief. Then was King Arthur ware where Sir Mordred leaned upon his sword among a great heap of dead men. Now give me my spear, said Arthur unto Sir Lucan, for yonder I have espied the traitor that all this woe hath wrought. Sir, let him be, said Sir Lucan, for he is unhappy; and if ye pass this unhappy day, ye shall be right well revenged upon him. Good lord, remember ye of your night's dream, and what the spirit of Sir Gawaine told you this night, yet God of his great goodness hath preserved you hitherto. Therefore, for God's sake, my lord, leave off by this. For blessed be God ye have won the field: for here we be three on live, and with Sir Mordred is none on live. And if ye leave off now, this wicked day of destiny is past. Tide me death, betide me life, saith the king, now I see him yonder alone, he shall never escape mine hands, for at a better avail shall I never have him. God speed you well, said Sir Bedivere. Then the king gat his spear in both his hands, and ran toward Sir Mordred crying, Traitor, now is thy death day come. And when Sir Mordred heard Sir Arthur, he ran until him with his sword drawn in his hand. And then King Arthur smote Sir Mordred under the shield, with a foin of his spear throughout the body more than a fathom. And when Sir Mordred felt that he had his death's wound, he thrust himself, with the might that he had, up to the butt of King Arthur's spear. And right so he smote his father Arthur with his sword holden in both his hands, on the side of the head, that the sword pierced the helmet and the brain-pan, and therewithal

Sir Mordred fell stark dead to the earth. And the noble Arthur fell in a swoon to the earth, and there he swooned ofttimes.

"That is a good piece of war correspondence, Clarence; you are a first-rate newspaper man. Well—is the king all right? Did he get well?"

"Poor soul, no. He is dead."

I was utterly stunned; it had not seemed to me that any wound could be mortal to him.

"And the queen, Clarence?"

"She is a nun, in Almesbury."

"What changes! and in such a short while. It is inconceivable. What next, I wonder?"

"I can tell you what next."

"Well?' '

"Stake our lives and stand by them!"

"What do you mean by that?"

"The Church is master now. The Interdict included you with Mordred; it is not to be removed while you remain alive. The clans are gathering. The Church has gathered all the knights that are left alive, and as soon as you are discovered we shall have business on our hands."

"Stuff! With our deadly scientific war material; with our hosts of trained—"

"Save your breath—we haven't sixty faithful left!"

"What are you saying? Our schools, our colleges, our vast workshops, our—"

"When those knights come, those establishments will empty themselves and go over to the enemy. Did you think you had educated the superstition out of those people?"

"I certainly did think it."

"Well, then, you may unthink it. They stood every strain easily—until the Interdict. Since then, they merely put on a bold outside—at heart they are quaking. Make up your mind to it—when the armies come, the mask will fall."

"It's hard news. We are lost. They will turn our own science against us."

"No they won't."

"Why?"

"Because I and a handful of the faithful have blocked that game. I'll tell you what I've done, and what moved me to it. Smart as you are, the Church was smarter. It was the Church that sent you cruising—through her servants, the doctors."

"Clarence!"

"It is the truth. I know it. Every officer of your ship was the Church's picked servant, and so was every man of the crew."

"Oh, come!"

"It is just as I tell you. I did not find out these things at once, but I found them out finally. Did you send me verbal information, by the commander of the ship, to the effect that upon his return to you, with supplies, you were going to leave Cadiz—"

"Cadiz! I haven't been at Cadiz at all!"

—"going to leave Cadiz and cruise in distant seas indefinitely, for the health of your family? Did you send me that word?"

"Of course not. I would have written, wouldn't I?"

"Naturally. I was troubled and suspicious. When the commander sailed again I managed to ship a spy with him. I have never heard of vessel or spy since. I gave myself two weeks to hear from you in. Then I resolved to send a ship to Cadiz. There was a reason why I didn't."

"What was that?"

"Our navy had suddenly and mysteriously disappeared! Also, as suddenly and as mysteriously, the railway and telegraph and telephone service ceased, the men all deserted, poles were cut down, the Church laid a ban upon the electric light! I had to be up and doing—and straight off. Your life was safe—nobody in these kingdoms but Merlin would venture to touch such a magician as you without ten thousand men at his back—I had nothing to think of but how to put preparations in the best trim against your coming. I felt safe myself—nobody would be anxious to touch a pet of yours. So this is what I did. From our various works I selected all the men—boys I mean—whose faithfulness under whatsoever pressure I could swear to, and I called them together secretly and gave them their instructions. There are fifty-two of them; none younger than fourteen, and none above seventeen years old."

"Why did you select boys?"

"Because all the others were born in an atmosphere of superstition and reared in it. It is in their blood and bones. We imagined we had educated it out of them; they thought so, too; the Interdict woke them up like a thunderclap! It revealed them to themselves, and it revealed them to me, too. With boys it was different. Such as have been under our training from seven to ten years have had no acquaintance with the Church's terrors, and it was among these that I found my fifty-two. As a next move, I paid a private visit to that old cave of Merlin's—not the small one—the big one—"

"Yes, the one where we secretly established our first great electric plant when I was projecting a miracle."

"Just so. And as that miracle hadn't become necessary then, I thought it might be a good idea to utilize the plant now. I've provisioned the cave for a siege—"

"A good idea, a first-rate idea."

"I think so. I placed four of my boys there as a guard—inside, and out of sight. Nobody was to be hurt—while outside; but any attempt to enter—well, we said just let anybody try it! Then I went out into the hills and uncovered and cut the secret wires which connected your bedroom with the wires that go to the dynamite deposits under all our vast factories, mills, workshops, magazines, etc., and about midnight I and my boys turned out and connected that wire with the cave, and nobody but you and I suspects where the other end of it goes to. We laid it under ground, of course, and it was all finished in a couple of hours or so. We sha'n't have to leave our fortress now when we want to blow up our civilization."

"It was the right move—and the natural one; a military necessity, in the changed condition of things. Well, what changes *have* come! We expectcd to be besieged in the palace some time or other, but—however, go on."

"Next, we built a wire fence."

"Wire fence?"

"Yes. You dropped the hint of it yourself, two or three years ago."

"Oh, I remember—the time the Church tried her strength against us the first time, and presently thought it wise to wait for a hopefuler season. Well, how have you arranged the fence?''

''I start twelve immensely strong wires—naked, not insulated—from a big dynamo in the cave—dynamo with no brushes except a positive and a negative one—''

''Yes, that's right.''

''The wires go out from the cave and fence in a circle of level ground a hundred yards in diameter; they make twelve independent fences, ten feet apart— that is to say, twelve circles within circles—and their ends come into the cave again.''

''Right; go on.''

''The fences are fastened to heavy oaken posts only three feet apart, and these posts are sunk five feet in the ground.''

''That is good and strong.''

''Yes. The wires have no ground-connection outside of the cave. They go out from the positive brush of the dynamo; there is a ground-connection through the negative brush; the other ends of the wire return to the cave, and each is grounded independently.''

''No-no, that won't do!''

''Why?''

''It's too expensive—uses up force for nothing. You don't want any ground-connection except the one through the negative brush. The other end of every wire must be brought back into the cave and fastened independently, and *without* any ground-connection. Now, then, observe the economy of it. A cavalry charge hurls itself against the fence; you are using no power, you are spending no money, for there is only one ground-connection till those horses come against the wire; the moment they touch it they form a connection with the negative brush *through the ground,* and drop dead. Don't you see?—you are using no energy until it is needed; your lightning is there, and ready, like the load in a gun; but it isn't costing you a cent till you touch it off. Oh, yes, the single ground-connection—''

''Of course! I don't know how I overlooked that. It's not only cheaper, but it's more effectual than the other way, for if wires break or get tangled, no harm is done.''

''No, especially if we have a telltale in the cave and disconnect the broken wire. Well, go on. The Gatlings?''

''Yes—that's arranged. In the center of the inner circle, on a spacious platform six feet high, I've grouped a battery of thirteen Gatling guns, and provided plenty of ammunition.''

''That's it. They command every approach, and when the Church's knights arrive, there's going to be music. The brow of the precipice over the cave—''

''I've got a wire fence there, and a Gatling. They won't drop any rocks down on us.''

''Well, and the glass-cylinder dynamite torpedoes?''

''That's attended to. It's the prettiest garden that was ever planted. It's a belt forty feet wide, and goes around the outer fence—distance between it and the fence one hundred yards—kind of neutral ground that space is. There isn't a single square yard of that whole belt but is equipped with a torpedo. We laid them on the surface of the ground, and sprinkled a layer of sand over them. It's an innocent-looking garden, but you let a man start in to hoe it once, and you'll see.''

"You tested the torpedoes?"

"Well, I was going to, but—"

"But what? Why, it's an immense oversight not to apply a—"

"Test? Yes, I know; but they're all right; I laid a few in the public road beyond our line and they've been tested.''

"Oh, that alters the case. Who did it?"

"A Church committee."

"How kind!"

"Yes. They came to command us to make submission. You see they didn't really come to test the torpedoes; that was merely an incident.''

"Did the committee make a report?"

"Yes, they made one. You could have heard it a mile."

"Unanimous?"

"That was the nature of it. After that I put up some signs, for the protection of future committees, and we have had no intruders since.''

"Clarence, you've done a world of work, and done it perfectly."

"We had plenty of time for it; there wasn't any occasion for hurry."

We sat silent awhile, thinking. Then my mind was made up, and I said:

"Yes, everything is ready; everything is ship-shape, no detail is wanting. I know what to do now.''

"So do I; sit down and wait."

"No, *sir!* rise up and *strike!*''

"Do you mean it?"

"Yes, indeed! The *de*fensive isn't in my line, and the *of*fensive is. That is, when I hold a fair hand—two-thirds as good a hand as the enemy. Oh, yes, we'll rise up and strike; that's our game.''

"A hundred to one you are right. When does the performance begin?"

"*Now!* We'll proclaim the Republic."

"Well, that *will* precipitate things, sure enough!"

"It will make them buzz, *I* tell you! England will be a hornets' nest before noon to-morrow, if the Church's hand hasn't lost its cunning—and we know it hasn't. Now you write and I'll dictate thus:

"PROCLAMATION

"BE IT KNOWN UNTO ALL. Whereas the king having died and left no heir, it becomes my duty to continue the executive authority vested in me, until a government shall have been created and set in motion. The monarchy has lapsed, it no longer exists. By consequence, all political power has reverted to its original source, the people of the nation. With the monarchy, its several adjuncts died also; wherefore there is no longer a nobility, no longer a privileged class, no longer an Established Church; all men are become exactly equal; they are upon one common level, and religion is free. *A Republic is hereby proclaimed,* as being the natural estate of a nation when other authority has ceased. It is the duty of the British people to meet together immediately, and by their votes elect representatives and deliver into their hands the government.''

I signed it "The Boss," and dated it from Merlin's Cave. Clarence said: "Why, that tells where we are, and invites them to call right away.''

"That is the idea. We *strike*—by the Proclamation—then it's their innings. Now have the thing set up and printed and posted, right off; that is, give the order; then, if you've got a couple of bicycles handy at the foot of the hill, ho for Merlin's Cave!"

"I shall be ready in ten minutes. What a cyclone there is going to be to-morrow when this piece of paper gets to work! . . . It's a pleasant old palace, this is; I wonder if we shall ever again—but never mind about that."

Chapter XLIII

THE BATTLE OF THE SAND-BELT

IN MERLIN'S CAVE—Clarence and I and fifty-two fresh, bright, well-educated, clean-minded young British boys. At dawn I sent an order to the factories and to all our great works to stop operations and remove all life to a safe distance, as everything was going to be blown up by secret mines, *"and no telling at what moment—therefore, vacate at once."* These people knew me, and had confidence in my word. They would clear out without waiting to part their hair, and I could take my own time about dating the explosion. You couldn't hire one of them to go back during the century, if the explosion was still impending.

We had a week of waiting. It was not dull for me, because I was writing all the time. During the first three days, I finished turning my old diary into this narrative form; it only required a chapter or so to bring it down to date. The rest of the week I took up in writing letters to my wife. It was always my habit to write to Sandy every day, whenever we were separate, and now I kept up the habit for love of it, and of her, though I couldn't do anything with the letters, of course, after I had written them. But it put in the time, you see, and was almost like talking; it was almost as if I was saying, "Sandy, if you and Hello-Central were here in the cave, instead of only your photographs, what good times we could have!" And then, you know, I could imagine the baby goo-gooing something out in reply, with its fists in its mouth and itself stretched across its mother's lap on its back, and she a-laughing and admiring and worshiping, and now and then tickling under the baby's chin to set it cackling, and then maybe throwing in a word of answer to me herself—and so on and so on—well, don't you know, I could sit there in the cave with my pen, and keep it up, that way, by the hour with them. Why, it was almost like having us all together again.

I had spies out every night, of course, to get news. Every report made things look more and more impressive. The hosts were gathering, gathering; down all the roads and paths of England the knights were riding, and priests rode with them, to hearten these original Crusaders, this being the Church's war. All the nobilities, big and little, were on their way, and all the gentry. This was all as was expected. We should thin out this sort of folk to such a degree that the people would have nothing to do but just step to the front with their republic and—

Ah, what a donkey I was! Toward the end of the week I began to get this large and disenchanting fact through my head: that the mass of the nation had swung their caps and shouted for the republic for about one day, and there an end! The Church, the nobles, and the gentry then turned one grand, all-disapproving frown upon them and shriveled them into sheep! From that moment the sheep had begun to gather to the fold—that is to say, the camps—and offer their valueless lives and their valuable wool to the "righteous cause." Why, even the very men who had lately been slaves were in the "righteous cause," and glorifying it, praying for it, sentimentally slabbering over it, just like all the other commoners. Imagine such human muck as this; conceive of this folly!

Yes, it was now "Death to the Republic!" everywhere—not a dissenting voice. All England was marching against us! Truly, this was more than I had bargained for.

I watched my fifty-two boys narrowly; watched their faces, their walk, their unconscious attitudes: for all these are a language—a language given us purposely that it may betray us in times of emergency, when we have secrets which we want to keep. I knew that that thought would keep saying itself over and over again in their minds and hearts, *All England is marching against us!* and ever more strenuously imploring attention with each repetition, ever more sharply realizing itself to their imaginations, until even in their sleep they would find no rest from it, but hear the vague and flitting creatures of the dreams say, *All England—*ALL ENGLAND!—*is marching against you!* I knew all this would happen; I knew that ultimately the pressure would become so great that it would compel utterance; therefore, I must be ready with an answer at that time—an answer well chosen and tranquilizing.

I was right. The time came. They *had* to speak. Poor lads, it was pitiful to see, they were so pale, so worn, so troubled. At first their spokesman could hardly find voice or words; but he presently got both. This is what he said—and he put it in the neat modern English taught him in my schools:

"We have tried to forget what we are—English boys! We have tried to put reason before sentiment, duty before love; our minds approve, but our hearts reproach us. While apparently it was only the nobility, only the gentry, only the twenty-five or thirty thousand knights left alive out of the late wars, we were of one mind, and undisturbed by any troubling doubt; each and every one of these fifty-two lads who stand here before you, said, 'They have chosen—it is their affair.' But think!—the matter is altered—*all England is marching against us!* Oh, sir, consider!—reflect!—these people are our people, they are bone of our bone, flesh of our flesh, we love them—do not ask us to destroy our nation!"

Well, it shows the value of looking ahead, and being ready for a thing when it happens. If I hadn't foreseen this thing and been fixed, that boy would have had me!—I couldn't have said a word. But I *was* fixed. I said:

"My boys, your hearts are in the right place, you have thought the worthy thought, you have done the worthy thing. You are English boys, you will remain English boys, and you will keep that name unsmirched. Give yourselves no further concern, let your minds be at peace. Consider this: while all England *is* marching against us, who is in the van? Who, by the commonest rules of war, will march in the front? Answer me."

"The mounted host of mailed knights."

"True. They are thirty thousand strong. Acres deep they will march. Now, observe: none but *they* will ever strike the sand-belt! Then there will be an episode! Immediately after, the civilian multitude in the rear will retire, to meet business engagements elsewhere. None but nobles and gentry are knights, and *none but these* will remain to dance to our music after that episode. It is absolutely true that we shall have to fight nobody but these thirty thousand knights. Now speak, and it shall be as you decide. Shall we avoid the battle, retire from the field?''

''NO!!!''

The shout was unanimous and hearty.

''Are you—are you—well, afraid of these thirty thousand knights?''

That joke brought out a good laugh, the boys' troubles vanished away, and they went gaily to their posts. Ah, they were a darling fifty-two! As pretty as girls, too.

I was ready for the enemy now. Let the approaching big day come along—it would find us on deck.

The big day arrived on time. At dawn the sentry on watch in the corral came into the cave and reported a moving black mass under the horizon, and a faint sound which he thought to be military music. Breakfast was just ready; we sat down and ate it.

This over, I made the boys a little speech, and then sent out a detail to man the battery, with Clarence in command of it.

The sun rose presently and sent its unobstructed splendors over the land, and we saw a prodigious host moving slowly toward us, with the steady drift and aligned front of a wave of the sea. Nearer and nearer it came, and more and more sublimely imposing became its aspect; yes, all England was there, apparently. Soon we could see the innumerable banners fluttering, and then the sun struck the sea of armor and set it all aflash. Yes, it was a fine sight; I hadn't ever seen anything to beat it.

At last we could make out details. All the front ranks, no telling how many acres deep, were horsemen—plumed knights in armor. Suddenly we heard the blare of trumpets; the slow walk burst into a gallop, and then—well, it was wonderful to see! Down swept that vast horse-shoe wave—it approached the sand-belt—my breath stood still; nearer, nearer—the strip of green turf beyond the yellow belt grew narrow—narrower still—became a mere ribbon in front of the horses—then disappeared under their hoofs. Great Scott! Why, the whole front of that host shot into the sky with a thunder-crash, and became a whirling tempest of rags and fragments; and along the ground lay a thick wall of smoke that hid what was left of the multitude from our sight.

Time for the second step in the plan of campaign! I touched a button, and shook the bones of England loose from her spine!

In that explosion all our noble civilization-factories went up in the air and disappeared from the earth. It was a pity, but it was necessary. We could not afford to let the enemy turn our own weapons against us.

Now ensued one of the dullest quarter-hours I had ever endured. We waited in a silent solitude inclosed by our circles of wire, and by a circle of heavy smoke outside of these. We couldn't see over the wall of smoke, and we couldn't see through it. But at last it began to shred away lazily, and by the end of another quarter-hour the land was clear and our curiosity was enabled to satisfy itself. No living creature was in sight! We now perceived that additions had been made to our defenses. The dynamite had dug a ditch more than a hundred feet wide, all around us, and cast up an embankment some twenty-five feet high on both borders of it. As to destruction of life, it was amazing. Moreover, it was beyond estimate. Of course, we could not *count* the dead, because they did not exist as

"THE SUN STRUCK THE SEA OF ARMOR AND SET IT ALL AFLASH"

individuals, but merely as homogeneous protoplasm, with alloys of iron and buttons.

No life was in sight, but necessarily there must have been some wounded in the rear ranks, who were carried off the field under cover of the wall of smoke; there would be sickness among the others—there always is, after an episode like that. But there would be no reinforcements; this was the last stand of the chivalry of England; it was all that was left of the order, after the recent annihilating wars. So I felt quite safe in believing that the utmost force that could for the future be brought against us would be but small; that is, of knights. I therefore issued a congratulatory proclamation to my army in these words:

> SOLDIERS, CHAMPIONS OF HUMAN LIBERTY AND EQUALITY: Your General congratulates you! In the pride of his strength and the vanity of his renown, an arrogant enemy came against you. You were ready. The conflict was brief; on your side, glorious. This mighty victory, having been achieved utterly without loss, stands without example in history. So long as the planets shall continue to move in their orbits, the BATTLE OF THE SAND-BELT will not perish out of the memories of men.
>
> THE BOSS.

I read it well, and the applause I got was very gratiying to me. I then wound up with these remarks:

"The war with the English nation, as a nation, is at an end. The nation has retired from the field and the war. Before it can be persuaded to return, war will have ceased. This campaign is the only one that is going to be fought. It will be brief—the briefest in history. Also the most destructive to life, considered from the standpoint of proportion of casualties to numbers engaged. We are done with the nation; henceforth we deal only with the knights. English knights can be killed, but they cannot be conquered. We know what is before us. While one of these men remains alive, our task is not finished, the war is not ended. We will kill them all." [Loud and long-continued applause.]

I picketed the great embankments thrown up around our lines by the dynamite explosion—merely a lookout of a couple of boys to announce the enemy when he should appear again.

Next, I sent an engineer and forty men to a point just beyond our lines on the south, to turn a mountain brook that was there, and bring it within our lines and under our command, arranging it in such a way that I could make instant use of it in an emergency. The forty men were divided into two shifts of twenty each, and were to relieve each other every two hours. In ten hours the work was accomplished.

It was nightfall now, and I withdrew my pickets. The one who had had the northern outlook reported a camp in sight, but visible with the glass only. He also reported that a few knights had been feeling their way toward us, and had driven some cattle across our lines, but that the knights themselves had not come very near. That was what I had been expecting. They were feeling us, you see; they wanted to know if we were going to play that red terror on them again. They would grow bolder in the night, perhaps. I believed I knew what project they would attempt, because it was plainly the thing I would attempt myself if I were in their places and as ignorant as they were. I mentioned it to Clarence.

"I think you are right," said he; "it is the obvious thing for them to try."

"Well, then," I said, "if they do it they are doomed."

"Certainly."

"They won't have the slightest show in the world."

"Of course they won't."

"It's dreadful, Clarence. It seems an awful pity."

The thing disturbed me so that I couldn't get any peace of mind for thinking of it and worrying over it. So, at last, to quiet my conscience, I framed this message to the knights:

> To the Honorable the Commander of the Insurgent Chivalry of England: You fight in vain. We know your strength—if one may call it by that name. We know that at the utmost you cannot bring against us above five-and-twenty thousand knights. Therefore, you have no chance—none whatever. Reflect: we are well equipped, well fortified, we number 54. Fifty-four what? Men? No, *minds*—the capablest in the world; a force against which mere animal might may no more hope to prevail than may the idle waves of the sea hope to prevail against the granite barriers of England. Be advised. We offer you your lives; for the sake of your families, do not reject the gift. We offer you this chance, and it is the last: throw down your arms; surrender unconditionally to the Republic, and all will be forgiven.
>
>   (Signed)   The Boss.

I read it to Clarence, and said I proposed to send it by a flag of truce. He laughed the sarcastic laugh he was born with, and said:

"Somehow it seems impossible for you to ever fully realize what these nobilities are. Now let us save a little time and trouble. Consider me the commander of the knights yonder. Now, then, you are the flag of truce; approach and deliver me your message, and I will give you your answer."

I humored the idea. I came forward under an imaginary guard of the enemy's soldiers, produced my paper, and read it through. For answer, Clarence struck the paper out of my hand, pursed up a scornful lip and said with lofty disdain:

"Dismember me this animal, and return him in a basket to the base-born knave who sent him; other answer have I none!"

How empty is theory in presence of fact! And this was just fact, and nothing else. It was the thing that would have happened, there was no getting around that. I tore up the paper and granted my mistimed sentimentalities a permanent rest.

Then, to business. I tested the electric signals from the Gatling platform to the cave, and made sure that they were all right; I tested and retested those which commanded the fences—these were signals whereby I could break and renew the electric current in each fence independently of the others at will. I placed the brook-connection under the guard and authority of three of my best boys, who would alternate in two-hour watches all night and promptly obey my signal, if I should have occasion to give it—three revolver-shots in quick succession. Sentry duty was discarded for the night, and the corral left empty of life; I ordered that quiet be maintained in the cave, and the electric lights turned down to a glimmer.

As soon as it was good and dark, I shut off the current from all the fences, and then groped my way out to the embankment bordering our side of the great dynamite ditch. I crept to the top of it and lay there on the slant of the muck to watch. But it was too dark to see anything. As for sounds, there were none. The stillness was deathlike. True, there were the usual night sounds of the country—the whir of night birds, the buzzing of insects, the barking of distant dogs, the mellow lowing of far-off kine—but these didn't seem to break the stillness, they only intensified it, and added a gruesome melancholy to it into the bargain.

I presently gave up looking, the night shut down so black, but I kept my ears strained to catch the least suspicious sound, for I judged I had only to wait, and I shouldn't be disappointed. However, I had to wait a long time. At last I caught what you may call indistinct glimpses of sound—dulled metallic sound. I pricked up my ears, then, and held my breath, for this was the sort of thing I had been waiting for. This sound thickened, and approached—from toward the north. Presently, I heard it at my own level—the ridge-top of the opposite embankment, a hundred feet or more away. Then I seemed to see a row of black dots appear along that ridge—human heads? I couldn't tell; it mightn't be anything at all; you can't depend on your eyes when your imagination is out of focus. However, the question was soon settled. I heard that metallic noise descending into the great ditch. It augmented fast, it spread all along, and it unmistakably furnished me this fact: an armed host was taking up its quarters in the ditch. Yes, these people were arranging a little surprise party for us. We could expect entertainment about dawn, possibly earlier.

I groped my way back to the corral now; I had seen enough. I went to the platform and signaled to turn the current on to the two inner fences. Then I went into the cave, and found everything satisfactory there—nobody awake but the working-watch. I woke Clarence and told him the great ditch was filling up with men, and that I believed all the knights were coming for us in a body. It was my notion that as soon as dawn approached we could expect the ditch's ambuscaded thousands to swarm up over the embankment and make an assault, and be followed immediately by the rest of their army.

Clarence said:

"They will be wanting to send a scout or two in the dark to make preliminary observations. Why not take the lightning off the outer fences, and give them a chance?"

"I've already done it, Clarence. Did you ever know me to be inhospitable?"

"No, you are a good heart. I want to go and—"

"Be a reception committee? I will go, too."

We crossed the corral and lay down together between the two inside fences. Even the dim light of the cave had disordered our eyesight somewhat, but the focus straightway began to regulate itself and soon it was adjusted for present circumstances. We had had to feel our way before, but we could make out to see the fence-posts now. We started a whispered conversation, but suddenly Clarence broke off and said:

"What is that?"

"What is what?"

"That thing yonder."

"What thing—where?"

"There beyond you a little piece—a dark something—a dull shape of some kind—against the second fence."

I gazed and he gazed. I said:

"Could it be a man, Clarence?"

"No, I think not. If you notice, it looks a lit—why, it *is* a man!—leaning on the fence."

"I certainly believe it is; let us go and see."

We crept along on our hands and knees until we were pretty close, and then looked up. Yes, it was a man—a dim great figure in armor, standing erect, with both hands on the upper wire—and, of course, there was a smell of burning flesh. Poor fellow, dead as a door-nail, and never knew what hurt him. He stood there like a statue—no motion about him, except that his plumes swished about a little in the night wind. We rose up and looked in through the bars of his visor, but couldn't make out whether we knew him or not—features too dim and shadowed.

We heard muffled sounds approaching, and we sank down to the ground where we were. We made out another knight vaguely; he was coming very stealthily, and feeling his way. He was near enough now for us to see him put out a hand, find an upper wire, then bend and step under it and over the lower one. Now he arrived at the first knight—and started slightly when he discovered him. He stood a moment—no doubt wondering why the other one didn't move on; then he said, in a low voice, "Why dreamest thou here, good Sir Mar—" then he laid his hand on the corpse's shoulder—and just uttered a little soft moan and sunk down dead. Killed by a dead man, you see—killed by a dead friend, in fact. There was something awful about it.

These early birds came scattering along after each other, about one every five minutes in our vicinity, during half an hour. They brought no armor of offense but their swords; as a rule, they carried the sword ready in the hand, and put it forward and found the wires with it. We would now and then see a blue spark when the knight that caused it was so far away as to be invisible to us; but we knew what had happened, all the same; poor fellow, he had touched a charged wire with his sword and been elected. We had brief intervals of grim stillness, interrupted with piteous regularity by the clash made by the falling of an ironclad; and this sort of thing was going on, right along, and was very creepy there in the dark and lonesomeness.

We concluded to make a tour between the inner fences. We elected to walk upright, for convenience' sake; we argued that if discerned, we should be taken for friends rather than enemies, and in any case we should be out of reach of swords, and these gentry did not seem to have any spears along. Well, it was a curious trip. Everywhere dead men were lying outside the second fence—not plainly visible, but still visible; and we counted fifteen of those pathetic statues— dead knights standing with their hands on the upper wire.

One thing seemed to be sufficiently demonstrated: our current was so tremendous that it killed before the victim could cry out. Pretty soon we detected a muffled and heavy sound, and next moment we guessed what it was. It was a surprise in force coming! I whispered Clarence to go and wake the army, and notify it to wait in silence in the cave for further orders. He was soon back, and we stood by the inner fence and watched the silent lightning do its awful work upon that swarming host. One could make out but little of detail; but he could note that a black mass was piling itself up beyond the second fence. That swelling bulk was dead men! Our camp was inclosed with a solid wall of the dead—a bulwark, a breastwork, of corpses, you may say. One terrible thing about this thing was the absence of human voices; there were no cheers, no war-cries; being intent upon a surprise, these men moved as noiselessly as they could; and always when the front rank was near enough to their goal to make it proper for them to begin to get a shout ready, of course they struck the fatal line and went down without testifying.

I sent a current through the third fence now; and almost immediately through the fourth and fifth, so quickly were the gaps filled up. I believed the time was come now for my climax; I believed that that whole army was in our trap. Anyway, it was high time to find out. So I touched a button and set fifty electric suns aflame on the top of our precipice.

Land, what a sight! We were inclosed in three walls of dead men! All the other fences were pretty nearly filled with the living, who were stealthily working their way forward through the wires. The sudden glare paralyzed this host, petrified them, you may say, with astonishment; there was just one instant for me to utilize their immobility in, and I didn't lose the chance. You see, in another instant they would have recovered their faculties, then they'd have burst into a cheer and made a rush, and my wires would have gone down before it; but that lost instant lost them their opportunity forever; while even that slight fragment of time was still unspent, I shot the current through all the fences and struck the whole host dead in their tracks! *There* was a groan you could *hear!* It voiced the death-pang of eleven thousand men. It swelled out on the night with awful pathos.

A glance showed that the rest of the enemy—perhaps ten thousand strong— were between us and the encircling ditch, and pressing forward to the assault. Consequently we had them *all!* and had them past help. Time for the last act of the tragedy. I fired the three appointed revolver-shots—which meant:

"Turn on the water!"

There was a sudden rush and roar, and in a minute the mountain brook was raging through the big ditch and creating a river a hundred feet wide and twenty-five deep.

"Stand to your guns, men! Open fire!"

The thirteen Gatlings began to vomit death into the fated ten thousand. They halted, they stood their ground a moment against that withering deluge of fire, then they broke, faced about and swept toward the ditch like chaff before a gale. A full fourth part of their force never reached the top of the lofty embankment; the three-fourths reached it and lunged over—to death by drowning.

Within ten short minutes after we had opened fire, armed resistance was totally anninilated, the campaign was ended, we fifty-four were masters of England! Twenty-five thousand men lay dead around us.

But how treacherous is fortune! In a little while—say an hour—happened a thing, by my own fault, which—but I have no heart to write that. Let the record end here.

Chapter XLIV

A POSTSCRIPT BY CLARENCE

I, CLARENCE, MUST write it for him. He proposed that we two go out and see if any help could be accorded the wounded. I was strenuous against the project. I said that if there were many, we could do but little for them; and it would not be wise for us to trust ourselves among them, anyway. But he could seldom be turned from a purpose once formed; so we shut off the electric current from the fences, took an escort along, climbed over the inclosing ramparts of dead knights, and moved out upon the field. The first wounded man who appealed for help was sitting with his back against a dead comrade. When The Boss bent over him and spoke to him, the man recognized him and stabbed him. That knight was Sir Meliagraunce, as I found out by tearing off his helmet. He will not ask for help any more.

We carried The Boss to the cave and gave his wound, which was not very serious, the best care we could. In this service we had the help of Merlin, though we did not know it. He was disguised as a woman, and appeared to be a simple old peasant goodwife. In this disguise, with brown-stained face and smooth-shaven, he had appeared a few days after The Boss was hurt, and offered to cook for us, saying her people had gone off to join certain new camps which the enemy were forming, and that she was starving. The Boss had been getting along very well, and had amused himself with finishing up his record.

We were glad to have this woman, for we were short-handed. We were in a trap, you see—a trap of our own making. If we stayed where we were, our dead would kill us; if we moved out of our defenses, we should no longer be invincible. We had conquered; in turn we were conquered. The Boss recognized this; we all recognized it. If we could go to one of those new camps and patch up some kind of terms with the enemy—yes, but The Boss could not go, and neither could I, for I was among the first that were made sick by the poisonous air bred by those dead thousands. Others were taken down, and still others. To-morrow—

To-morrow. It is here. And with it the end. About midnight I awoke, and saw that hag making curious passes in the air about The Boss's head and face, and wondered what it meant. Everybody but the dynamo-watch lay steeped in sleep; there was no sound. The woman ceased from her mysterious foolery, and started tiptoeing toward the door. I called out:

"Stop! What have you been doing?"

She halted, and said with an accent of malicious satisfaction:

"Ye were conquerors; ye are conquered? These others are perishing—you also. Ye shall all die in this place—every one—except *him*. He sleepeth now—and shall sleep thirteen centuries. I am Merlin!"

Then such a delirium of silly laughter overtook him that he reeled about like a drunken man, and presently fetched up against one of our wires. His mouth is spread open yet; apparently he is still laughing. I suppose the face will retain that petrified laugh until the corpse turns to dust.

The Boss has never stirred—sleeps like a stone. If he does not wake to-day we shall understand what kind of a sleep it is, and his body will then be borne to a place in one of the remote recesses of the cave where none will ever find it to desecrate it. As for the rest of us—well, it is agreed that if any one of us ever escapes alive from this place, he will write the fact here, and loyally hide this Manuscript with The Boss, our dear good chief, whose property it is, be he alive or dead.

THE END OF MANUSCRIPT

FINAL P. S. BY M. T.

THE DAWN WAS come when I laid the Manuscript aside. The rain had almost ceased, the world was gray and sad, the exhausted storm was sighing and sobbing itself to rest. I went to the stranger's room, and listened at his door, which was slightly ajar. I could hear his voice, and so I knocked. There was no answer, but I still heard the voice. I peeped in. The man lay on his back in bed, talking brokenly but with spirit, and punctuating with his arms, which he thrashed about, restlessly, as sick people do in delirium. I slipped in softly and bent over him. His mutterings and ejaculations went on. I spoke—merely a word, to call his attention. His glassy eyes and his ashy face were alight in an instant with pleasure, gratitude, gladness, welcome:

"Oh, Sandy, you are come at last—how I have longed for you! Sit by me— do not leave me—never leave me again, Sandy, never again. Where is your hand?—give it me, dear, let me hold it—there—now all is well, all is peace, and I am happy again—*we* are happy again, isn't it so, Sandy? You are so dim, so vague, you are but a mist, a cloud, but you are *here*, and that is blessedness sufficient; and I have your hand; don't take it away—it is for only a little while, I shall not require it long. . . . Was that the child? . . . Hello-Central! . . . She doesn't answer. Asleep, perhaps? Bring her when she wakes, and let me touch her hands, her face, her hair, and tell her good-by. . . . Sandy! . . . Yes, you are there. I lost myself a moment, and I thought you were gone. . . . Have I been sick long? It must be so; it seems months to me. And such dreams! such strange and awful dreams, Sandy! Dreams that were as real as reality—delirium, of course, but *so* real! Why, I thought the king was dead, I thought you were in Gaul and couldn't get home, I thought there was a revolution; in the fantastic frenzy of these dreams, I thought that Clarence and I and a handful of my cadets fought and exterminated the whole chivalry of England! But even that was not the strangest. I seemed to be a creature out of a remote unborn age, centuries hence, and even *that* was as real as the rest! Yes, I seemed to have flown back out of that age into this of ours, and then forward to it again, and was set down, a stranger and forlorn in that strange England, with an abyss of thirteen centuries yawning between me and you! between me and my home and my friends! between me and all that is dear to me, all that could make life worth the living! It was awful—awfuler than you can ever imagine, Sandy. Ah, watch by me, Sandy— stay by me every moment—*don't* let me go out of my mind again; death is nothing, let it come, but not with those dreams, not with the torture of those hideous dreams—I cannot endure *that* again. . . . Sandy? . . ."

He lay muttering incoherently some little time; then for a time he lay silent, and apparently sinking away toward death. Presently his fingers began to pick busily at the coverlet, and by that sign I knew that his end was at hand. With the first suggestion of the death-rattle in his throat he started up slightly, and seemed to listen: then he said:

"A bugle? . . . It is the king! The drawbridge, there! Man the battlements!—turn out the—"

He was getting up his last "effect"; but he never finished it.

THE END

Roughing It

PREFATORY

THIS book is merely a personal narrative and not a pretentious history or a philosophical dissertation. It is a record of several years of variegated vagabondizing, and its object is rather to help the resting reader while away an idle hour than afflict him with metaphysics, or goad him with science. Still, there is information in the volume; information concerning an interesting episode in the history of the Far West, about which no books have been written by persons who were on the ground in person, and saw the happenings of the time with their own eyes. I allude to the rise, growth and culmination of the silver-mining fever in Nevada— a curious episode, in some respects; the only one, of its peculiar kind, that has occurred in the land; and the only one, indeed, that is likely to occur in it.

Yes, take it all around, there is quite a good deal of information in the book. I regret this very much; but really it could not be helped: information appears to stew out of me naturally, like the precious ottar of roses out of the otter. Sometimes it has seemed to me that I would give worlds if I could retain my facts; but it cannot be. The more I calk up the sources, and the tighter I get, the more I leak wisdom. Therefore, I can only claim indulgence at the hands of the reader, not justification.

THE AUTHOR.

TO
CALVIN H. HIGBIE,
Of California,
an Honest Man, a Genial Comrade, and a Steadfast Friend.
THIS BOOK IS INSCRIBED
By the Author,
In Memory of the Curious Time
When We Two
WERE MILLIONAIRES FOR TEN DAYS.

Chapter I

MY BROTHER HAD just been appointed Secretary of Nevada Territory—an office of such majesty that it concentrated in itself the duties and dignities of Treasurer, Comptroller, Secretary of State, and Acting Governor in the Governor's absence. A salary of eighteen hundred dollars a year and the title of "Mr. Secretary" gave to the great position an air of wild and imposing grandeur. I was young and ignorant, and I envied my brother. I coveted his distinction and his financial splendor, but particularly and especially the long, strange journey he was going to make, and the curious new world he was going to explore. He was going to travel! I never had been away from home, and that word "travel" had a seductive charm for me. Pretty soon he would be hundreds and hundreds of miles away on the great plains and deserts, and among the mountains of the Far West, and would see buffaloes and Indians, and prairie dogs, and antelopes, and have all kinds of adventures, and maybe get hanged or scalped, and have ever such a fine time, and write home and tell us all about it, and be a hero. And he would see the gold mines and the silver mines, and maybe go about of an afternoon when his work was done, and pick up two or three pailfuls of shining slugs, and nuggets of gold and silver on the hillside. And by and by he would become very rich, and return home by sea, and be able to talk as calmly about San Francisco and the ocean, and "the isthmus" as if it was nothing of any consequence to have seen those marvels face to face. What I suffered in contemplating his happiness, pen cannot describe. And so, when he offered me, in cold blood, the sublime position of private secretary under him, it appeared to me that the heavens and the earth passed away, and the firmament was rolled together as a scroll! I had nothing more to desire. My contentment was complete. At the end of an hour or two I was ready for the journey. Not much packing up was necessary, because we were going in the overland stage from the Missouri frontier to Nevada, and passengers were only allowed a small quantity of baggage apiece. There was no Pacific railroad in those fine times of ten or twelve years ago—not a single rail of it.

I only proposed to stay in Nevada three months—I had no thought of staying longer than that. I meant to see all I could that was new and strange, and then hurry home to business. I little thought that I would not see the end of that three-month pleasure excursion for six or seven uncommonly long years!

I dreamed all night about Indians, deserts, and silver bars, and in due time, next day, we took shipping at the St. Louis wharf on board a steamboat bound up the Missouri River.

We were six days going from St. Louis to "St. Joe"—a trip that was so dull, and sleepy, and eventless that it has left no more impression on my memory than if its duration had been six minutes instead of that many days. No record is left in my mind, now, concerning it, but a confused jumble of savage-looking snags, which we deliberately walked over with one wheel or the other; and of reefs which we butted and butted, and then retired from and climbed over in some softer place; and of sand-bars which we roosted on occasionally, and rested, and then got out our crutches and sparred over. In fact, the boat might almost as well have gone to St. Joe by land, for she was walking most of the time, anyhow—climbing over reefs and clambering over snags patiently and laboriously all day long. The captain said she was a "bully" boat, and all she wanted was more "shear" and a bigger wheel. I thought she wanted a pair of stilts, but I had the deep sagacity not to say so.

Chapter II

THE FIRST THING we did on that glad evening that landed us at St. Joseph was to hunt up the stage-office, and pay a hundred and fifty dollars apiece for tickets per overland coach to Carson City, Nevada.

The next morning, bright and early, we took a hasty breakfast, and hurried to the starting-place. Then an inconvenience presented itself which we had not properly appreciated before, namely, that one cannot make a heavy traveling trunk stand for twenty-five pounds of baggage—because it weighs a good deal more. But that was all we could take—twenty-five pounds each. So we had to snatch our trunks open, and make a selection in a good deal of a hurry. We put our lawful twenty-five pounds apiece all in one valise, and shipped the trunks back to St. Louis again. It was a sad parting, for now we had no swallow-tail coats and white kid gloves to wear at Pawnee receptions in the Rocky Mountains, and no stovepipe hats nor patent-leather boots, nor anything else necessary to make life calm and peaceful. We were reduced to a war footing. Each of us put on a rough, heavy suit of clothing, woolen army shirt and "stogy" boots included; and into the valise we crowded a few white shirts, some under-clothing and such things. My brother, the Secretary, took along about four pounds of United States statutes and six pounds of Unabridged Dictionary; for we did not know—poor innocents—that such things could be bought in San Francisco on one day and received in Carson City the next. I was armed to the teeth with a pitiful little Smith & Wesson's seven-shooter, which carried a ball like a homœopathic pill, and it took the whole seven to make a dose for an adult. But I thought it was grand. It appeared to me to be a dangerous weapon. It only had one fault—you could not hit anything with it. One of our "conductors" practiced awhile on a cow with it, and as long as she stood still and behaved herself she was safe; but as soon as she went to moving about, and he got to shooting at other things, she came to grief. The Secretary had a small-sized Colt's revolver strapped around him for protection against the Indians, and to guard against accidents he carried it uncapped. Mr. George Bemis was dismally formidable. George Bemis was our fellow-traveler. We had never seen him before. He wore in his belt an old original "Allen" revolver, such as irreverent people called a "pepperbox." Simply drawing the trigger back, cocked and fired the pistol. As the trigger came back, the hammer would begin to rise and the barrel to turn over, and presently down would drop the hammer, and away would speed the ball. To aim along the turning barrel and hit the thing aimed at was a feat which was probably never done with an "Allen" in the world. But George's was a reliable weapon, nevertheless, because, as one of the stage-drivers afterward said, "If she didn't get what she went after, she would fetch something else." And so she did. She went after a deuce of spades nailed against a tree, once, and fetched a mule standing about thirty yards to the left of it. Bemis did not want the mule; but the owner came out with a double-barreled shotgun and persuaded him to buy it, anyhow. It was a cheerful weapon—the "Allen." Sometimes all its six barrels would go off at once, and then there was no safe place in all the region round about, but behind it.

We took two or three blankets for protection against frosty weather in the mountains. In the matter of luxuries we were modest—we took none along but some pipes and five pounds of smoking tobacco. We had two large canteens to carry water in, between stations on the Plains, and we also took with us a little shot-bag of silver coin for daily expenses in the way of breakfasts and dinners.

By eight o'clock everything was ready, and we were on the other side of the river. We jumped into the stage, the driver cracked his whip, and we bowled away and left "the States" behind us. It was a superb summer morning, and all the landscape was brilliant with sunshine. There was a freshness and breeziness, too, and an exhilarating sense of emancipation from all sorts of cares and responsibilities, that almost made us feel that the years we had spent in the close, hot city, toiling and slaving, had been wasted and thrown away. We were spinning along through Kansas, and in the course of an hour and a half we were fairly abroad on the great Plains. Just here the land was rolling—a grand sweep of regular elevations and depressions as far as the eye could reach—like the stately heave and swell of the ocean's bosom after a storm. And everywhere were cornfields, accenting with squares of deeper green, this limitless expanse of grassy land. But presently this sea upon dry ground was to lose its "rolling" character and stretch away for seven hundred miles as level as a floor!

Our coach was a great swinging and swaying stage, of the most sumptuous description—an imposing cradle on wheels. It was drawn by six handsome horses, and by the side of the driver sat the "conductor," the legitimate captain of the craft; for it was his business to take charge and care of the mails, baggage, express matter, and passengers. We three were the only passengers this trip. We sat on the back seat, inside. About all the rest of the coach was full of mail bags—for we had three days' delayed mails with us. Almost touching our knees, a perpendicular wall of mail matter rose up to the roof. There was a great pile of it strapped on top of the stage, and both the fore and hind boots were full. We had twenty-seven hundred pounds of it aboard, the driver said—"a little for Brigham, and Carson, and 'Frisco, but the heft of it for the Injuns, which is powerful troublesome 'thout they get plenty of truck to read." But as he just then got up a fearful convulsion of his countenance which was suggestive of a wink being swallowed by an earthquake, we guessed that his remark was intended to be facetious, and to mean that we would unload the most of our mail matter somewhere on the Plains and leave it to the Indians, or whosoever wanted it.

We changed horses every ten miles, all day long, and fairly flew over the hard, level road. We jumped out and stretched our legs every time the coach stopped, and so the night found us still vivacious and unfatigued.

After supper a woman got in, who lived about fifty miles further on, and we three had to take turns at sitting outside with the driver and conductor. Apparently she was not a talkative woman. She would sit there in the gathering twilight and fasten her steadfast eyes on a mosquito rooting into her arm, and slowly she would raise her other hand till she had got his range, and then she would launch a slap at him that would have jolted a cow; and after that she would sit and contemplate the corpse with tranquil satisfaction—for she never missed her mosquito; she was a dead shot at short range. She never removed a carcass, but left them there for bait. I sat by this grim Sphinx and watched her kill thirty or forty mosquitoes—watched her, and waited for her to say something, but she never did. So I finally opened the conversation myself. I said:

"The mosquitoes are pretty bad about here, madam."

"You bet!"

"What did I understand you to say, madam?"

"You BET!"

Then she cheered up, and faced around and said:

"Danged if I didn't begin to think you fellers was deef and dumb. I did, b' gosh. Here I've sot, and sot, and sot, a-bust'n muskeeters and wonderin' what was ailin' ye. Fust I thot you was deef and dumb, then I thot you was sick or crazy, or suthin', and then by and by I begin to reckon you was a passel of sickly fools that couldn't think of nothing to say. Wher'd ye come from?"

The Sphinx was a Sphinx no more! The fountains of her great deep were broken up, and she rained the nine parts of speech forty days and forty nights, metaphorically speaking, and buried us under a desolating deluge of trivial gossip that left not a crag or pinnacle of rejoinder projecting above the tossing waste of dislocated grammar and decomposed pronunciation!

How we suffered, suffered, suffered! She went on, hour after hour, till I was sorry I ever opened the mosquito question and gave her a start. She never did stop again until she got to her journey's end toward daylight; and then she stirred

PLEASING NEWS.

us up as she was leaving the stage (for we were nodding, by that time), and said:

"Now you git out at Cottonwood, you fellers, and lay over a couple o' days, and I'll be along sometime to-night, and if I can do ye any good by edgin' in a word now and then, I'm right thar. Folks 'll tell you 't I've always ben kind o' offish and partic'lar for a gal that's raised in the woods, and I *am*, with the rag-tag and bob-tail, and a gal *has* to be, if she wants to *be* anything, but when people comes along which is my equals, I reckon I'm a pretty sociable heifer after all."

We resolved not to "lay by at Cottonwood."

Chapter III

ABOUT AN HOUR and a half before daylight we were bowling along smoothly over the road—so smoothly that our cradle only rocked in a gentle, lulling way, that was gradually soothing us to sleep, and dulling our consciousness—when something gave away under us! We were dimly aware of it, but indifferent to it. The coach stopped. We heard the driver and conductor talking together outside, and rummaging for a lantern, and swearing because they could not find it—but we had no interest in whatever had happened, and it only added to our comfort to think of those people out there at work in the murky night, and we snug in our nest with the curtains drawn. But presently, by the sounds, there seemed to be an examination going on, and then the driver's voice said:

"By George, the thoroughbrace is broke!"

This startled me broad awake—as an undefined sense of calamity is always apt to do. I said to myself: "Now, a thoroughbrace is probably part of a horse; and doubtless a vital part, too, from the dismay in the driver's voice. Leg, maybe—and yet how could he break his leg waltzing along such a road as this? No, it can't be his leg. That is impossible, unless he was reaching for the driver. Now, what can be the thoroughbrace of a horse, I wonder? Well, whatever comes, I shall not air my ignorance in this crowd, anyway."

Just then the conductor's face appeared at a lifted curtain, and his lantern glared in on us and our wall of mail matter. He said:

"Gents, you'll have to turn out a spell. Thoroughbrace is broke."

We climbed out into a chill drizzle, and felt ever so homeless and dreary. When I found that the thing they called a 'thoroughbrace" was the massive combination of belts and springs which the coach rocks itself in, I said to the driver:

"I never saw a thoroughbrace used up like that before, that I can remember. How did it happen?"

"Why, it happened by trying to make one coach carry three days' mail— that's how it happened," said he. "And right here is the very direction which is wrote on all the newspaper-bags which was to be put out for the Injuns for to keep 'em quiet. It's most uncommon lucky, becuz it's so nation dark I should 'a' gone by unbeknowns if that air thoroughbrace hadn't broke."

I knew that he was in labor with another of those winks of his, though I could not see his face, because he was bent down at work; and wishing him a safe delivery, I turned to and helped the rest get out the mail-sacks. It made a great pyramid by the roadside when it was all out. When they had mended the thorough-brace we filled the two boots again, but put no mail on top, and only half as much inside as there was before. The conductor bent all the seat backs down, and then filled the coach just half full of mail-bags from end to end. We objected loudly to this, for it left us no seats. But the conductor was wiser than we, and said a bed was better than seats, and moreover, this plan would protect his thoroughbraces. We never wanted any seats after that. The lazy bed was infinitely preferable. I had many an exciting day, subsequently, lying on it reading the statutes and the dictionary, and wondering how the characters would turn out.

The conductor said he would send back a guard from the next station to take charge of the abandoned mail-bags, and we drove on.

It was now just dawn; and as we stretched our cramped legs full length on the mail sacks, and gazed out through the windows across the wide wastes of greensward clad in cool, powdery mist, to where there was an expectant look in the eastern horizon, our perfect enjoyment took the form of a tranquil and contented ecstasy. The stage whirled along at a spanking gait, the breeze flapping curtains and suspended coats in a most exhilarating way; the cradle swayed and swung luxuriously; the pattering of the horses' hoofs, the cracking of the driver's whip, and his "Hi-yi! g'lang!" were music; the spinning ground and the waltzing trees appeared to give us a mute hurrah as we went by, and then slack up and look after us with interest, or envy, or something; and as we lay and smoked the pipe of peace and compared all this luxury with the years of tiresome city life that had gone before it, we felt that there was only one complete and satisfying happiness in the world, and we had found it.

After breakfast, at some station whose name I have forgotten, we three climbed up on the seat behind the driver, and let the conductor have our bed for a nap. And by and by, when the sun made me drowsy, I lay down on my face on top of the coach, grasping the slender iron railing, and slept for an hour or more. That will give one an appreciable idea of those matchless roads. Instinct will make a sleeping man grip a fast hold of the railing when the stage jolts, but when it only swings and sways, no grip is necessary. Overland drivers and conductors used to sit in their places and sleep thirty or forty minutes at a time, on good roads, while spinning along at the rate of eight or ten miles an hour. I saw them do it, often. There was no danger about it; a sleeping man *will* seize the irons in time when the coach jolts. These men were hard worked, and it was not possible for them to stay awake all the time.

By and by we passed through Marysville, and over the Big Blue and Little Sandy; thence about a mile, and entered Nebraska. About a mile further on, we came to the Big Sandy—one hundred and eighty miles from St. Joseph.

As the sun was going down, we saw the first specimen of an animal known familiarly over two thousand miles of mountain and desert—from Kansas clear to the Pacific Ocean—as the "jackass rabbit." He is well named. He is just like any other rabbit, except that he is from one third to twice as large, has longer legs in proportion to his size, and has the most preposterous ears that ever were mounted on any creature *but* a jackass. When he is sitting quiet, thinking about his sins, or is absent-minded or unapprehensive of danger, his majestic ears project above him conspicuously; but the breaking of a twig will scare him nearly to death, and then he tilts his ears back gently and starts for home. All you can see, then, for the next minute, is his long gray form stretched out straight and "streaking it" through the low sage-brush, head erect, eyes right, and ears just canted a little to the rear, but showing you where the animal is, all the time, the same as if he carried a jib. Now and then he makes a marvelous spring with his long legs, high over the stunted sage-brush, and scores a leap that would make a horse envious. Presently he comes down to a long, graceful "lope," and shortly he mysteriously disappears. He has crouched behind a sage-bush, and will sit there and listen and tremble until you get within six feet of him, when he will get under way again. But one must shoot at this creature once, if he wishes to see him throw his heart into his heels, and do the best he knows how. He is frightened clear through, now, and he lays his long ears down on his back, straightens himself out like a yard-stick every spring he makes, and scatters miles behind him with an easy indifference that is enchanting.

Our party made this specimen "hump himself," as the conductor said. The secretary started him with a shot from the Colt; I commenced spitting at him with my weapon; and all in the same instant the old "Allen's" whole broadside let go with a rattling crash, and it is not putting it too strong to say that the rabbit was frantic! He dropped his ears, set up his tail, and left for San Francisco at a speed which can only be described as a flash and a vanish! Long after he was out of sight we could hear him whiz.

I do not remember where we first came across "sage-brush," but as I have been speaking of it I may as well describe it. This is easily done, for if the reader can imagine a gnarled and venerable live oak tree reduced to a little shrub two feet high, with its rough bark, its foliage, its twisted boughs, all complete, he can picture the "sage-brush" exactly. Often, on lazy afternoons in the mountains, I have lain on the ground with my face under a sage-bush, and entertained myself with fancying that the gnats among its foliage were liliputian birds, and that the ants marching and countermarching about its base were liliputian flocks and herds, and myself some vast loafer from Brobdignag waiting to catch a little citizen and eat him.

It is an imposing monarch of the forest in exquisite miniature, is the "sage-brush." Its foliage is a grayish green, and gives that tint to desert and mountain. It smells like our domestic sage, and "sage-tea" made from it tastes like the sage-tea which all boys are so well acquainted with. The sage-brush is a singularly hardy plant, and grows right in the midst of deep sand, and among barren rocks, where nothing else in the vegetable world would try to grow, except "bunch-grass."* The sage-bushes grow from three to six or seven feet apart, all over the mountains and deserts of the Far West, clear to the borders of California. There is not a tree of any kind in the deserts, for hundreds of miles—there is no vegetation at all in a regular desert, except the sage-brush and its cousin the "greasewood," which is so much like the sage-brush that the difference amounts to little. Camp-fires and hot suppers in the deserts would be impossible but for the friendly sage-brush. Its trunk is as large as a boy's wrist (and from that up

---

* "Bunch-grass" grows on the bleak mountain-sides of Nevada and neighboring territories, and offers excellent feed for stock, even in the dead of winter, wherever the snow is blown aside and exposes it; notwithstanding its unpromising home, bunch-grass is a better and more nutritious diet for cattle and horses than almost any other hay or grass that is known—so stock-men say.

to a man's arm), and its crooked branches are half as large as its trunk—all good, sound, hard wood, very like oak.

When a party camps, the first thing to be done is to cut sage-brush; and in a few minutes there is an opulent pile of it ready for use. A hole a foot wide, two feet deep, and two feet long, is dug, and sage-brush chopped up and burned in it till it is full to the brim with glowing coals. Then the cooking begins, and there is no smoke, and consequently no swearing. Such a fire will keep all night, with very little replenishing; and it makes a very sociable camp-fire, and one around which the most impossible reminiscences sound plausible, instructive, and profoundly entertaining.

Sage-brush is very fair fuel, but as a vegetable it is a distinguished failure. Nothing can abide the taste of it but the jackass and his illegitimate child the mule. But their testimony to its nutritiousness is worth nothing, for they will eat pine knots, or anthracite coal, or brass filings, or lead pipe, or old bottles, or anything that comes handy, and then go off looking as grateful as if they had had oysters for dinner. Mules and donkeys and camels have appetites that anything will relieve temporarily, but nothing satisfy. In Syria, once, at the head-waters of the Jordan, a camel took charge of my overcoat while the tents were being pitched, and examined it with a critical eye, all over, with as much interest as if he had an idea of getting one made like it; and then, after he was done figuring on it as an article of apparel, he began to contemplate it as an article of diet. He put his foot on it, and lifted one of the sleeves out with his teeth, and chewed and chewed at it, gradually taking it in, and all the while opening and closing his eyes in a kind of religious ecstasy, as if he had never tasted anything as good as an overcoat before, in his life. Then he smacked his lips once or twice, and reached after the other sleeve. Next he tried the velvet collar, and smiled a smile of such contentment that it was plain to see that he regarded that as the daintiest thing about an overcoat. The tails went next, along with some percussion caps and cough candy, and some fig-paste from Constantinople. And then my newspaper correspondence dropped out, and he took a chance in that—manuscript letters written for the home papers. But he was treading on dangerous ground now. He began to come across solid wisdom in those documents that was rather weighty on his stomach; and occasionally he would take a joke that would shake him up till it loosened his teeth; it was getting to be perilous times with him, but he held his grip with good courage and hopefully, till at last he began to stumble on statements that not even a camel could swallow with impunity. He began to gag and gasp, and his eyes to stand out, and his forelegs to spread, and in about a quarter of a minute he fell over as stiff as a carpenter's work-bench, and died a death of indescribable agony. I went and pulled the manuscript out of his mouth, and found that the sensitive creature had choked to death on one of the mildest and gentlest statements of fact that I ever laid before a trusting public.

I was about to say, when diverted from my subject, that occasionally one finds sage-bushes five or six feet high, and with a spread of branch and foliage in proportion, but two or two and a half feet is the usual height.

Chapter IV

As THE SUN went down and the evening chill came on, we made preparation for bed. We stirred up the hard leather letter-sacks, and the knotty canvas bags of printed matter (knotty and uneven because of projecting ends and corners of magazines, boxes, and books). We stirred them up and redisposed them in such a way as to make our bed as level as possible. And we *did* improve it, too, though after all our work it had an upheaved and billowy look about it, like a little piece of a stormy sea. Next we hunted up our boots from odd nooks among the mail-bags where they had settled, and put them on. Then we got down our coats, vests, pantaloons, and heavy woolen shirts, from the arm-loops where they had been swinging all day, and clothed ourselves in them—for, there being no ladies either at the stations or in the coach, and the weather being hot, we had looked to our comfort by stripping to our underclothing, at nine o'clock in the morning. All things being now ready, we stowed the uneasy dictionary where it would lie as quiet as possible, and placed the water-canteens and pistols where we could find them in the dark. Then we smoked a final pipe, and swapped a final yarn; after which, we put the pipes, tobacco and bag of coin in snug holes and caves among the mail-bags, and then fastened down the coach curtains all around, and made the place as "dark as the inside of a cow," as the conductor phrased it in his picturesque way. It was certainly as dark as any place could be—nothing was even dimly visible in it. And finally, we rolled ourselves up like silk-worms, each person in his own blanket, and sank peacefully to sleep.

Whenever the stage stopped to change horses, we would wake up, and try to recollect where we were—and succeed—and in a minute or two the stage would be off again, and we likewise. We began to get into country, now, threaded here and there with little streams. These had high, steep banks on each side, and every time we flew down one bank and scrambled up the other, our party inside got mixed somewhat. First we would all be down in a pile at the forward end of the stage, nearly in a sitting posture, and in a second we would shoot to the other end, and stand on our heads. And we would sprawl and kick, too, and ward off ends and corners of mail-bags that came lumbering over us and about us; and as the dust rose from the tumult, we would all sneeze in chorus, and the majority of us would grumble, and probably say some hasty thing, like: "Take your elbow out of my ribs! Can't you quit crowding?"

Every time we avalanched from one end of the stage to the other, the Unabridged Dictionary would come too; and every time it came it damaged somebody. One trip it "barked" the Secretary's elbow; the next trip it hurt me in the stomach, and the third it tilted Bemis's nose up till he could look down his nostrils—he said. The pistols and coin soon settled to the bottom, but the pipes, pipe-stems, tobacco, and canteens clattered and floundered after the Dictionary every time it made an assault on us, and aided and abetted the book by spilling tobacco in our eyes, and water down our backs.

Still, all things considered, it was a very comfortable night. It wore gradually away, and when at last a cold gray light was visible through the puckers and chinks in the curtains, we yawned and stretched with satisfaction, shed our cocoons, and felt that we had slept as much as was necessary. By and by, as the sun rose up and warmed the world, we pulled off our clothes and got ready for breakfast. We were just pleasantly in time, for five minutes afterward the driver sent the weird music of his bugle winding over the grassy solitudes, and presently we detected a low hut or two in the distance. Then the rattling of the coach, the clatter of our six horses' hoofs, and the driver's crisp commands, awoke to a louder and stronger emphasis, and we went sweeping down on the station at our smartest speed. It was fascinating—that old overland stage-coaching.

We jumped out in undress uniform. The driver tossed his gathered reins out on the ground, gaped and stretched complacently, drew off his heavy buckskin gloves with great deliberation and insufferable dignity—taking not the slightest notice of a dozen solicitous inquiries after his health, and humbly facetious and flattering accostings, and obsequious tenders of service, from five or six hairy and half-civilized station-keepers and hostlers who were nimbly unhitching our steeds and bringing the fresh team out of the stables—for in the eyes of the stage-driver of that day, station-keepers and hostlers were a sort of good enough low creatures, useful in their place, and helping to make up a world, but not the kind of beings which a person of distinction could afford to concern himself with; while, on the contrary, in the eyes of the station-keeper and the hostler, the stage-driver was a hero—a great and shining dignitary, the world's favorite son, the envy of the people, the observed of the nations. When they spoke to him they received his insolent silence meekly, and as being the natural and proper conduct of so great a man; when he opened his lips they all hung on his words with admiration (he never honored a particular individual with a remark, but addressed it with a broad generality to the horses, the stables, the surrounding country *and* the human underlings); when he discharged a facetious insulting personality at a hostler, that hostler was happy for the day; when he uttered his one jest—old as the hills, coarse, profane, witless, and inflicted on the same audience, in the same language, every time his coach drove up there—the varlets roared, and slapped their thighs, and swore it was the best thing they'd ever heard in all their lives. And how they would fly around when he wanted a basin of water, a gourd of the same, or a light for his pipe!—but they would instantly insult a passenger if he so far forgot himself as to crave a favor at their hands. They could do that sort of insolence as well as the driver they copied it from—for, let it be borne in mind, the overland driver had but little less contempt for his passengers than he had for his hostlers.

The hostlers and station-keepers treated the really powerful *conductor* of the coach merely with the best of what was their idea of civility, but the *driver* was the only being they bowed down to and worshiped. How admiringly they would gaze up at him in his high seat as he gloved himself with lingering deliberation, while some happy hostler held the bunch of reins aloft, and waited patiently for him to take it! And how they would bombard him with glorifying ejaculations as he cracked his long whip and went careering away.

The station buildings were long, low huts, made of sun-dried, mud-colored bricks, laid up without mortar (*adobes*, the Spaniards call these bricks, and Americans shorten it to *'dobies*.) The roofs, which had no slant to them worth speaking of, were thatched and then sodded or covered with a thick layer of earth, and from this sprang a pretty rank growth of weeds and grass. It was the first time we had ever seen a man's front yard on top of his house. The buildings consisted of barns, stable-room for twelve or fifteen horses, and a hut for an eating-room for passengers. This latter had bunks in it for the station-keeper and a hostler or two. You could rest your elbow on its eaves, and you had to bend in order to get in at the door. In place of a window there was a square hole about large enough for a man to crawl through, but this had no glass in it. There was no flooring, but the ground was packed hard. There was no stove, but the fire-place served all needful purposes. There were no shelves, no cupboards, no closets. In a corner stood an open sack of flour, and nestling against its base were a couple of black and venerable tin coffee-pots, a tin teapot, a little bag of salt, and a side of bacon.

By the door of the station-keeper's den, outside, was a tin wash-basin, on the ground. Near it was a pail of water and a piece of yellow bar soap, and from the eaves hung a hoary blue woolen shirt, significantly—but this latter was the station-keeper's private towel, and only two persons in all the party might venture to use it—the stage-driver and the conductor. The latter would not, from a sense of decency; the former would not, because he did not choose to encourage the advances of a station-keeper. We had towels—in the valise; they might as well have been in Sodom and Gomorrah. We (and the conductor) used our handkerchiefs, and the driver his pantaloons and sleeves. By the door, inside, was fastened a small old-fashioned looking-glass frame, with two little fragments of the original mirror lodged down in one corner of it. This arrangement afforded a pleasant double-barreled portrait of you when you looked into it, with one half of your head set up a couple of inches above the other half. From the glass frame hung the half of a comb by a string—but if I had to describe that patriarch or die, I believe I would order some sample coffins. It had come down from Esau and Samson, and had been accumulating hair ever since—along with certain impurities. In one corner of the room stood three or four rifles and muskets, together with horns and pouches of ammunition. The station men wore pantaloons of coarse, country-woven stuff, and into the seat and the inside of the legs were sewed ample additions of buckskin, to do duty in place of leggings, when the man rode horseback—so the pants were half dull blue and half yellow, and unspeakably picturesque. The pants were stuffed into the tops of high boots, the heels whereof were armed with great Spanish spurs, whose little iron clogs and chains jingled with every step. The man wore a huge beard and mustachios, an old slouch hat, a blue woolen shirt, no suspenders, no vest, no coat—in a leathern sheath in his belt, a great long "navy" revolver (slung on right side, hammer to the front), and projecting from his boot a horn-handled bowie-knife. The furniture of the hut was neither gorgeous nor much in the way. The rocking-chairs and sofas were not present, and never had been, but they were represented by two three-legged stools, a pine-board bench four feet long, and two empty candle-boxes. The table was a greasy board on stilts, and the table-cloth and napkins had not come—and they were not looking for them, either. A battered tin platter, a knife and fork, and a tin pint cup, were at each man's place, and the driver had a queens-ware saucer that had seen better days. Of course this duke sat at the head of the table. There was one isolated piece of table furniture that bore about it a touching air of grandeur in misfortune. This was the caster. It was German silver, and crippled and rusty, but it was so preposterously out of place there that it was suggestive of a tattered exiled king among barbarians, and the majesty of its native position compelled respect even in its degradation. There was only one cruet left, and that was a stopperless, fly-specked, broken-necked thing, with two inches of vinegar in it, and a dozen preserved flies with their heels up and looking sorry they had invested there.

The station-keeper up-ended a disk of last week's bread, of the shape and size of an old-time cheese, and carved some slabs from it which were as good as Nicholson pavement, and tenderer.

He sliced off a piece of bacon for each man, but only the experienced old hands made out to eat it, for it was condemned army bacon which the United States would not feed to its soldiers in the forts, and the stage company had bought it cheap for the sustenance of their passengers and employés. We may have found this condemned army bacon further out on the plains than the section I am locating it in, but we *found* it—there is no gainsaying that.

Then he poured for us a beverage which he called "*Slumgullion*," and it is hard to think he was not inspired when he named it. It really pretended to be tea, but there was too much dish-rag, and sand, and old bacon-rind in it to deceive the intelligent traveler. He had no sugar and no milk—not even a spoon to stir the ingredients with.

We could not eat the bread or the meat, nor drink the "slumgullion." And when I looked at that melancholy-vinegar cruet, I thought of the anecdote (a very, very old one, even at that day) of the traveler who sat down to a table which had nothing on it but a mackerel and a pot of mustard. He asked the landlord if this was all. The landlord said:

"*All!* Why, thunder and lightning, I should think there was mackerel enough there for six."

"But I don't like mackerel."

"Oh—then help yourself to the mustard."

In other days I had considered it a good, a very good, anecdote, but there was a dismal plausibility about it, here, that took all the humor out of it.

Our breakfast was before us, but our teeth were idle.

I tasted and smelled, and said I would take coffee, I believed. The station-boss stopped dead still, and glared at me speechless. At last, when he came to, he turned away and said, as one who communes with himself upon a matter too vast to grasp:

"*Coffee!* Well, if that don't go clean ahead of me, I'm d——d!"

We could not eat, and there was no conversation among the hostlers and herdsmen—we all sat at the same board. At least there was no conversation

DRINKING SLUMGULLION.

further than a single hurried request, now and then, from one employé to another. It was always in the same form, and always gruffly friendly. Its Western freshness and novelty startled me, at first, and interested me; but it presently grew monotonous, and lost its charm. It was:

"Pass the bread, you son of a skunk!" No, I forget—skunk was not the word; it seems to me it was still stronger than that; I know it was, in fact, but it is gone from my memory, apparently. However, it is no matter—probably it was too strong for print, anyway. It is the landmark in my memory which tells me where I first encountered the vigorous new vernacular of the occidental plains and mountains.

We gave up the breakfast, and paid our dollar apiece and went back to our mail-bag bed in the coach, and found comfort in our pipes. Right here we suffered the first diminution of our princely state. We left our six fine horses and took six mules in their place. But they were wild Mexican fellows, and a man had to stand at the head of each of them and hold him fast while the driver gloved and got himself ready. And when at last he grasped the reins and gave the word, the men sprung suddenly away from the mules' heads and the coach shot from the station as if it had issued from a cannon. How the frantic animals did scamper! It was a fierce and furious gallop—and the gait never altered for a moment till we reeled off ten or twelve miles and swept up to the next collection of little station huts and stables.

So we flew along all day. At 2 P.M. the belt of timber that fringes the North Platte and marks its windings through the vast level floor of the Plains came in sight. At 4 P.M. we crossed a branch of the river, and at 5 P.M. we crossed the Platte itself, and landed at Fort Kearney, *fifty-six hours out from St. Joe*—THREE HUNDRED MILES!

Now that was stagecoaching on the great overland, ten or twelve years ago, when perhaps not more than ten men in America, all told, expected to live to see a railroad follow that route to the Pacific. But the railroad is there, now, and it pictures a thousand odd comparisons and contrasts in my mind to read the following sketch, in The New York *Times*, of a recent trip over almost the very ground I have been describing. I can scarcely comprehend the new state of things:

"ACROSS THE CONTINENT"

"At 4.20 P.M., Sunday, we rolled out of the station at Omaha, and started westward on our long jaunt. A couple of hours out, dinner was announced—an "event" to those of us who had yet to experience what it is to eat in one of Pullman's hotels on wheels; so, stepping into the car next forward of our sleeping palace, we found ourselves in the dining-car. It was a revelation to us, that first dinner on Sunday. And though we continued to dine for four days, and had as many breakfasts and suppers, our whole party never ceased to admire the perfection of the arrangements, and the marvelous results achieved. Upon tables covered with snowy linen, and garnished with services of solid silver, Ethiop waiters, flitting about in spotless white, placed as by magic a repast at which Delmonico himself could have had no occasion to blush; and, indeed, in some respects it would be hard for that distinguished *chef* to match our *menu;* for, in addition to all that ordinarily makes up a first-chop dinner, had we not our antelope steak (the gormand who has not experienced this—bah! what does he know of the feast of fat things?) our delicious mountain-brook trout, and choice fruits and berries, and (sauce piquant and unpurchasable!) our sweet-scented, appetite-compelling air of the prairies? You may depend upon it, we all did justice to the good things, and as we washed them down with bumpers of sparkling Krug, whilst we sped along at the rate of thirty miles an hour, agreed it was the *fastest* living we had ever experienced. (We beat that, however, two days afterward when we made *twenty-seven miles in twenty-seven minutes*, while our Champagne glasses filled to the brim spilled not a drop!) After dinner we repaired to our drawing-room car, and, as it was Sabbath eve, intoned some of the grand old hymns—"Praise God from whom," etc.; "Shining Shore," "Coronation," etc.—the voices of the men singers and of the women singers blending sweetly in the evening air, while our train, with its great, glaring Polyphemus eye, lighting up long vistas of prairie, rushed into the night and the Wild. Then to bed in luxurious couches, where we slept the sleep of the just and only awoke the next morning (Monday) at eight o'clock, to find ourselves at the crossing of the North Platte, three hundred miles from Omaha—*fifteen hours and forty minutes out.*"

Chapter V

ANOTHER NIGHT OF alternate tranquillity and turmoil. But morning came, by and by. It was another glad awakening to fresh breezes, vast expanses of level greensward, bright sunlight, an impressive solitude utterly without visible human beings or human habitations, and an atmosphere of such amazing magnifying properties that trees that seemed close at hand were more than three miles away. We resumed undress uniform, climbed atop of the flying coach, dangled our legs over the side, shouted occasionally at our frantic mules, merely to see them lay their ears back and scamper faster, tied our hats on to keep our hair from blowing away, and leveled an outlook over the world-wide carpet about us for things new and strange to gaze at. Even at this day it thrills me through and through to think of the life, the gladness, and the wild sense of freedom that used to make the blood dance in my veins on those fine overland mornings!

Along about an hour after breakfast we saw the first prairie-dog villages, the first antelope, and the first wolf. If I remember rightly, this latter was the regular *cayote* (pronounced ky-*o*-te) of the farther deserts. And if it *was*, he was not a pretty creature or respectable either, for I got well acquainted with his race afterward, and can speak with confidence. The cayote is a long, slim, sick and sorry-looking skeleton, with a gray wolfskin stretched over it, a tolerably bushy tail that forever sags down with a despairing expression of forsakenness and misery, a furtive and evil eye, and a long, sharp face, with slightly lifted lip and exposed teeth. He has a general slinking expression all over. The cayote is a living, breathing allegory of Want. He is *always* hungry. He is always poor, out of luck, and friendless. The meanest creatures despise him, and even the fleas would desert him for a velocipede. He is so spiritless and cowardly that even while his exposed teeth are pretending a threat, the rest of his face is apologizing for it. And he is *so* homely!—so scrawny, and ribby, and coarse-haired, and pitiful. When he sees you he lifts his lip and lets a flash of his teeth out, and then turns a little out of the course he was pursuing, depresses his head a bit, and strikes a long, soft-footed trot through the sage-brush, glancing over his shoulder at you, from time to time, till he is about out of easy pistol range, and then he stops and takes a deliberate survey of you; he will trot fifty yards and stop again—another fifty and stop again; and finally the gray of his gliding body blends with the gray of the sage-brush, and he disappears. All this is when you make no demonstration against him; but if you do, he develops a livelier interest in his journey, and instantly electrifies his heels and puts such a deal of real estate between himself and your weapon, that by the time you have raised the hammer you see that you need a minie rifle, and by the time you have got him in line you need a rifled cannon, and by the time you have "drawn a bead" on him you see well enough that nothing but an unusually long-winded streak of lightning could reach him where he is now. But if you start a swift-footed dog after him, you will enjoy it ever so much—especially if it is a dog that has a good opinion of himself, and has been brought up to think he knows something about speed. The cayote will go swinging gently off on that deceitful trot of his, and every little while he will smile a fraudful smile over his shoulder that will fill that dog entirely full of encouragement and worldly ambition, and make him lay his head still lower to the ground, and stretch his neck further to the front, and pant more fiercely, and stick his tail out straighter behind, and move his furious legs with a yet wilder frenzy, and leave a broader and broader, and higher and denser cloud of desert sand smoking behind, and marking his long wake across the level plain! And all this time the dog is only a short twenty feet behind the cayote, and to save the soul of him he cannot understand why it is that he cannot get perceptibly closer; and he begins to get aggravated, and it makes him madder and madder to see how gently the cayote glides along and never pants or sweats or ceases to smile; and he grows still more and more incensed to see how shamefully he has been taken in by an entire stranger, and what an ignoble swindle that long, calm, soft-footed trot is; and next he notices that he is getting fagged, and that the cayote actually has to slacken speed a little to keep from running away from him—and *then* that town-dog is mad in earnest, and he begins to strain and weep and swear, and paw the sand higher than ever, and reach for the cayote with concentrated and desperate energy. This "spurt" finds him six feet behind the gliding enemy, and two miles from his friends. And then, in the instant that a wild new hope is lighting up his face, the cayote turns and smiles blandly upon him once more, and with a something about it which seems to say: "Well, I shall have to tear myself away from you, bub—business is business, and it will not do for me to be fooling along this way all day"—and forthwith there is a rushing sound, and the sudden splitting of a long crack through the atmosphere, and behold that dog is solitary and alone in the midst of a vast solitude!

It makes his head swim. He stops, and looks all around; climbs the nearest sand mound, and gazes into the distance; shakes his head reflectively, and then, without a word, he turns and jogs along back to his train, and takes up a humble position under the hindmost wagon, and feels unspeakably mean, and looks ashamed, and hangs his tail at half-mast for a week. And for as much as a year after that, whenever there is a great hue and cry after a cayote, that dog will merely glance in that direction without emotion, and apparently observe to himself, "I believe I do not wish any of the pie."

The cayote lives chiefly in the most desolate and forbidding deserts, along with the lizard, the jackass-rabbit, and the raven, and gets an uncertain and precarious living, and earns it. He seems to subsist almost wholly on the carcasses of oxen, mules and horses that have dropped out of emigrant trains and died, and upon windfalls of carrion, and occasional legacies of offal bequeathed to him by white men who have been opulent enough to have something better to butcher than condemned army bacon. He will eat anything in the world that his first cousins, the desert-frequenting tribes of Indians will, and they will eat anything they can bite. It is a curious fact that these latter are the only creatures known to history who will eat nitro-glycerine and ask for more if they survive.

The cayote of the deserts beyond the Rocky Mountains has a peculiarly hard time of it, owing to the fact that his relations, the Indians, are just as apt to be the first to detect a seductive scent on the desert breeze, and follow the fragrance to the late ox it emanated from, as he is himself; and when this occurs he has to content himself with sitting off at a little distance watching those people strip off and dig out everything edible, and walk off with it. Then he and the waiting ravens explore the skeleton and polish the bones. It is considered that the cayote, and the obscene bird, and the Indian of the desert, testify their blood kinship with each other in that they live together in the waste places of the earth on terms of perfect confidence and friendship, while hating all other creatures and yearning to assist at their funerals. He does not mind going a hundred miles to breakfast, and a hundred and fifty to dinner, because he is sure to have three or four days between meals, and he can just as well be traveling and looking at the scenery as lying around doing nothing and adding to the burdens of his parents.

We soon learned to recognize the sharp, vicious bark of the cayote as it came across the murky plain at night to disturb our dreams among the mail-sacks; and remembering his forlorn aspect and his hard fortune, made shift to wish him the blessed novelty of a long day's good luck and a limitless larder the morrow.

Chapter VI

OUR NEW CONDUCTOR (just shipped) had been without sleep for twenty hours. Such a thing was very frequent. From St. Joseph, Missouri, to Sacramento, California, by stage-coach, was nearly nineteen hundred miles, and the trip was often made in fifteen days (the cars do it in four and a half, now), but the time specified in the mail contracts, and required by the schedule, was eighteen or nineteen days, if I remember rightly. This was to make fair allowance for winter storms and snows, and other unavoidable causes of detention. The stage company had everything under strict discipline and good system. Over each two hundred and fifty miles of road they placed an agent or superintendent, and invested him with great authority. His beat or jurisdiction of two hundred and fifty miles was called a "division." He purchased horses, mules' harness, and food for men and beasts, and distributed these things among his stage stations, from time to time, according to his judgment of what each station needed. He erected station buildings and dug wells. He attended to the paying of the station-keepers, hostlers, drivers, and blacksmiths, and discharged them whenever he chose. He was a very, very great man in his "division"—a kind of Grand Mogul, a Sultan of the Indies, in whose presence common men were modest of speech and manner, and in the glare of whose greatness even the dazzling stage-driver dwindled to a penny dip. There were about eight of these kings, all told, on the overland route.

Next in rank and importance to the division-agent came the "conductor." His beat was the same length as the agent's—two hundred and fifty miles. He sat with the driver, and (when necessary) rode that fearful distance, night and day, without other rest or sleep than what he could get perched thus on top of the flying vehicle. Think of it! He had absolute charge of the mails, express matter, passengers and stagecoach, until he delivered them to the next conductor, and got his receipt for them. Consequently he had to be a man of intelligence, decision, and considerable executive ability. He was usually a quiet, pleasant man, who attended closely to his duties, and was a good deal of a gentleman. It was not absolutely necessary that the division-agent should be a gentleman, and occasionally he wasn't. But he was always a general in administrative ability, and a bulldog in courage and determination—otherwise the chieftainship over the lawless underlings of the overland service would never in any instance have been to him anything but an equivalent for a month of insolence and distress and a bullet and a coffin at the end of it. There were about sixteen or eighteen conductors on the overland, for there was a daily stage each way, and a conductor on every stage.

Next in *real* and official rank and importance, *after* the conductor, came my delight, the driver—next in real but not in *apparent* importance—for we have seen that in the eyes of the common herd the driver was to the conductor as an admiral is to the captain of the flag-ship. The driver's beat was pretty long, and his sleeping-time at the stations pretty short, sometimes; and so, but for the grandeur of his position his would have been a sorry life, as well as a hard and a wearing one. We took a new driver every day or every night (for they drove backward and forward over the same piece of road all the time), and therefore we never got as well acquainted with them as we did with the conductors; and besides, they would have been above being familiar with such rubbish as passengers, anyhow, as a general thing. Still, we were always eager to get a sight of each and every new driver as soon as the watch changed, for each and every day we were either anxious to get rid of an unpleasant one, or loath to part with a driver we had learned to like and had come to be sociable and friendly with. And so the first question we asked the conductor whenever we got to where we were to exchange drivers, was always, "Which is him?" The grammar was faulty, maybe, but we could not know, then, that it would go into a book some day. As long as everything went smoothly, the overland driver was well enough situated, but if a fellow driver got sick suddenly it made trouble, for the coach *must* go on, and so the potentate who was about to climb down and take a luxurious rest after his long night's siege in the midst of wind and rain and darkness, had to stay where he was and do the sick man's work. Once, in the Rocky Mountains, when I found a driver sound asleep on the box, and the mules going at the usual break-neck pace, the conductor said never mind him, there was no danger, and he was doing double duty—had driven seventy-five miles on one coach, and was now going back over it on this without rest or sleep. A hundred and fifty miles of holding back of six vindictive mules and keeping them from climbing the trees! It sounds incredible, but I remember that statement well enough.

The station-keepers, hostlers, etc., were low, rough characters, as already described; and from western Nebraska to Nevada a considerable sprinkling of them might be fairly set down as outlaws—fugitives from justice, criminals whose best security was a section of country which was without law and without even the pretense of it. When the "division-agent" issued an order to one of these parties he did it with the full understanding that he might have to enforce it with a navy six-shooter, and so he always went "fixed" to make things go along smoothly. Now and then a division-agent was really obliged to shoot a hostler through the head to teach him some simple matter that he could have taught him with a club if his circumstances and surroundings had been different. But they were snappy, able men, those division-agents, and when they tried to teach a subordinate anything, that subordinate generally "got it through his head."

A great portion of this vast machinery—these hundreds of men and coaches, and thousands of mules and homes—was in the hands of Mr. Ben Holliday. All the western half of the business was in his hands. This reminds me of an incident of Palestine travel which is pertinent here, and so I will transfer it just in the language in which I find it set down in my Holy Land note-book:

> No doubt everybody has heard of Ben Holliday—a man of prodigious energy, who used to send mails and passengers flying across the continent in his overland stage-coaches like a very whirlwind—two thousand long miles in fifteen days and a half, by the watch! But this fragment of history is not about Ben Holliday, but about a young New York boy by the name of Jack, who traveled with our small party of pilgrims in the Holy Land (and who had traveled to California in Mr. Holliday's overland coaches three years before, and had by no means forgotten it or lost his gushing admiration of Mr. H.). Aged nineteen, Jack was a good boy—a good-

THE SUPERINTENDENT AS A TEACHER.

hearted and always well-meaning boy, who had been reared in the city
of New York, and although he was bright and knew a great many useful
things, his Scriptural education had been a good deal neglected—to such
a degree, indeed, that all Holy Land history was fresh and new to him,
and all Bible names mysteries that had never disturbed his virgin ear.
Also in our party was an elderly pilgrim who was the reverse of Jack,
in that he was learned in the Scriptures and an enthusiast concerning
them. He was our encyclopedia, and we were never tired of listening to
his speeches, nor he of making them. He never passed a celebrated
locality, from Bashan to Bethlehem, without illuminating it with an
oration. One day, when camped near the ruins of Jericho, he burst forth
with something like this:

"Jack, do you see that range of mountains over yonder that bounds
the Jordan valley? The mountains of Moab, Jack! Think of it, my boy—
the actual mountains of Moab—renowned in Scripture history! We are
actually standing face to face with those illustrious crags and peaks—
and for all we know" [dropping his voice impressively], "*our eyes may
be resting at this very moment upon the spot* WHERE LIES THE MYSTERIOUS
GRAVE OF MOSES! Think of it, Jack!"

"Moses *who?*" (falling inflection).

"Moses *who!* Jack, you ought to be ashamed of yourself—you ought
to be ashamed of such criminal ignorance. Why, Moses, the great guide,
soldier, poet, lawgiver of ancient Israel! Jack, from this spot where we
stand, to Egypt, stretches a fearful desert three hundred miles in extent—
and across that desert that wonderful man brought the children of Israel!—
guiding them with unfailing sagacity for forty years over the sandy desolation
and among the obstructing rocks and hills, and landed them at last, safe
and sound, with insight of this very spot; and where we now stand they
entered the Promised Land with anthems of rejoicing! It was a wonderful,
wonderful thing to do, Jack! Think of it!"

"*Forty years? Only three hundred miles?* Humph! Ben Holliday would
have fetched them through in thirty-six hours!"

The boy meant no harm. He did not know that he had said anything
that was wrong or irreverent. And so no one scolded him or felt offended
with him—and nobody *could* but some ungenerous spirit incapable of
excusing the heedless blunders of a boy.

At noon on the fifth day out, we arrived at the "Crossing of the South Platte,"
alias "Julesburg," *alias* "Overland City," four hundred and seventy miles from
St. Joseph—the strangest, quaintest, funniest frontier town that our untraveled
eyes had ever stared at and been astonished with.

Chapter VII

IT DID SEEM strange enough to see a town again after what appeared to us such
a long acquaintance with deep, still, almost lifeless and houseless solitude! We
tumbled out into the busy street feeling like meteoric people crumbled off the

corner of some other world, and wakened up suddenly in this. For an hour we took as much interest in Overland City as if we had never seen a town before. The reason we had an hour to spare was because we had to change our stage (for a less sumptuous affair, called a "mud-wagon") and transfer our freight of mails.

Presently we got under way again. We came to the shallow, yellow, muddy South Platte, with its low banks and its scattering flat sand-bars and pygmy islands—a melancholy stream straggling through the center of the enormous flat plain, and only saved from being impossible to find with the naked eye by its sentinel rank of scattering trees standing on either bank. The Platte was "up," they said—which made me wish I could see it when it was down, if it could look any sicker and sorrier. They said it was a dangerous stream to cross, now, because its quicksands were liable to swallow up horses, coach and passengers if an attempt was made to ford it. But the mails had to go, and we made the attempt. Once or twice in midstream the wheels sunk into the yielding sands so threateningly that we half believed we had dreaded and avoided the sea all our lives to be shipwrecked in a "mud-wagon" in the middle of a desert at last. But we dragged through and sped away toward the setting sun.

Next morning, just before dawn, when about five hundred and fifty miles from St. Joseph, our mud-wagon broke down. We were to be delayed five or six hours, and therefore we took horses, by invitation, and joined a party who were just starting on a buffalo hunt. It was noble sport galloping over the plain in the dewy freshness of the morning, but our part of the hunt ended in disaster and disgrace, for a wounded buffalo bull chased the passenger Bemis nearly two miles, and then he forsook his horse and took to a lone tree. He was very sullen about the matter for some twenty-four hours, but at last he began to soften little by little, and finally he said:

"Well, it was not funny, and there was no sense in those gawks making themselves so facetious over it. I tell you I was angry in earnest for a while. I should have shot that long gangly lubber they called Hank, if I could have done it without crippling six or seven other people—but of course I couldn't, the old 'Allen's' so confounded comprehensive. I wish those loafers had been up in the

AN INHUMAN SPECTACLE.

tree; they wouldn't have wanted to laugh so. If I had had a horse worth a cent—but no, the minute he saw that buffalo bull wheel on him and give a bellow, he raised straight up in the air and stood on his heels. The saddle began to slip, and I took him round the neck and laid close to him, and began to pray. Then he came down and stood up on the other end awhile, and the bull actually stopped pawing sand and bellowing to contemplate the inhuman spectacle. Then the bull made a pass at him and uttered a bellow that sounded perfectly frightful, it was so close to me, and that seemed to literally prostrate my horse's reason, and make a raving distracted maniac of him, and I wish I may die if he didn't stand on his head for a quarter of a minute and shed tears. He was absolutely out of his mind—he was, as sure as truth itself, and he really didn't know what he was doing. Then the bull came charging at us, and my horse dropped down on all fours and took a fresh start—and then for the next ten minutes he would actually throw one hand-spring after another so fast that the bull began to get unsettled, too, and didn't know where to start in—and so he stood there sneezing, and shoveling dust over his back, and bellowing every now and then, and thinking he had got a fifteen-hundred-dollar circus horse for breakfast, certain. Well, I was first out on his neck—the horse's, not the bull's—and then underneath, and next on his rump, and sometimes head up, and sometimes heels—but I tell you it seemed solemn and awful to be ripping and tearing and carrying on so in the presence of death, as you might say. Pretty soon the bull made a snatch for us and brought away some of my horse's tail (I suppose, but do not know, being pretty busy at the time), but *something* made him hungry for solitude and suggested to him to get up and hunt for it. And then you ought to have seen that spider-legged old skeleton go! and you ought to have seen the bull cut out after him, too—head down, tongue out, tail up, bellowing like everything, and actually mowing down the weeds, and tearing up the earth, and boosting up the sand like a whirlwind! By George, it was a hot race! I and the saddle were back on the rump, and I had the bridle in my teeth and holding onto the pommel with both hands. First we left the dogs behind; then we passed a jackass rabbit; then we overtook a cayote, and were gaining on an antelope when the rotten girth let go and threw me about thirty yards off to the left, and as the saddle went down over the horse's rump he gave it a lift with his heels that sent it more than four hundred yards up in the air, I wish I may die in a minute if he didn't. I fell at the foot of the only solitary tree there was in nine counties adjacent (as any creature could see with the naked eye), and the next second I had hold of the bark with four sets of nails and my teeth, and the next second after that I was astraddle of the main limb and blaspheming my luck in a way that made my breath smell of brimstone. I *had* the bull, now, if he did not think of *one* thing. But that one thing I dreaded. I dreaded it very seriously. There was a possibility that the bull might not think of it, but there were greater chances that he would. I made up my mind what I would do in case he did. It was a little over forty feet to the ground from where I sat. I cautiously unwound the lariat from the pommel of my saddle—"

"Your *saddle?* Did you take your saddle up in the tree with you?"

"Take it up in the tree with me? Why, how you talk. Of course I didn't. No man could do that. It *fell* in the tree when it came down."

"Oh—exactly."

"Certainly. I unwound the lariat, and fastened one end of it to the limb. It was the best green raw-hide, and capable of sustaining tons. I made a slip noose in the other end, and then hung it down to see the length. It reached down twenty-two feet—half way to the ground. I then loaded every barrel of the Allen with a double charge. I felt satisfied. I said to myself, if he never thinks of that one thing that I dread, all right—but if he does, all right anyhow—I am fixed for him. But don't you know that the very thing a man dreads is the thing that always happens? Indeed it is so. I watched the bull, now, with anxiety—anxiety which no one can conceive of who has not been in such a situation and felt that at any moment death might come. Presently a thought came into the bull's eye. I knew it! said I—if my nerve fails now, I am lost. Sure enough, it was just as I had dreaded, he started in to climb the tree—"

"What, the bull?"

"Of course—who else?"

"But a bull can't climb a tree."

"He can't, can't he? Since you know so much about it, did you ever see a bull try?"

"No! I never dreamt of such a thing."

"Well, then, what is the use of your talking that way, then? Because you never saw a thing done, is that any reason why it can't be done?"

"Well, all right—go on. What did you do?"

"The bull started up, and got along well for about ten feet, then slipped and slid back. I breathed easier. He tried it again—got up a little higher—slipped again. But he came at it once more, and this time he was careful. He got gradually higher and higher, and my spirits went down more and more. Up he came—an inch at a time—with his eyes hot, and his tongue hanging out. Higher and higher—hitched his foot over the stump of a limb, and looked up, as much as to say, 'You are my meat, friend.' Up again—higher and higher, and getting more excited the closer he got. He was within ten feet of me! I took a long breath,—and then said I, 'It is now or never.' I had the coil of the lariat all ready; I paid it out slowly, till it hung right over his head; all of a sudden I let go of the slack, and the slip noose fell fairly round his neck! Quicker than lightning I out with the Allen and let him have it in the face. It was an awful roar, and must have scared the bull out of his senses. When the smoke cleared away, there he was, dangling in the air, twenty foot from the ground, and going out of one convulsion into another faster than you could count! I didn't stop to count, anyhow—I shinned down the tree and shot for home."

"Bemis, is all that true, just as you have stated it?"

"I wish I may rot in my tracks and die the death of a dog if it isn't."

"Well, we can't refuse to believe it, and we don't. But if there were some proofs—"

"Proofs! Did I bring back my lariat?"

"No."

"Did I bring back my horse?"

"No."

"Did you ever see the bull again?"

"No."

"Well, then, what more do you want? I never saw anybody as particular as you are about a little thing like that."

I made up my mind that if this man was not a liar he only missed it by the skin of his teeth. This episode reminds me of an incident of my brief sojourn in Siam, years afterward. The European citizens of a town in the neighborhood

of Bangkok had a prodigy among them by the name of Eckert, an Englishman—
a person famous for the number, ingenuity, and imposing magnitude of his lies.
They were always repeating his most celebrated falsehoods, and always trying
to "draw him out" before strangers; but they seldom succeeded. Twice he was
invited to the house where I was visiting, but nothing could seduce him into a
specimen lie. One day a planter named Bascom, an influential man, and a proud
and sometimes irascible one, invited me to ride over with him and call on Eckert.
As we jogged along, said he:

"Now, do you know where the fault lies? It lies in putting Eckert on his
guard. The minute the boys go to pumping at Eckert he knows perfectly well
what they are after, and of course he shuts up his shell. Anybody might know
he would. But when we get there, we must play him finer than that. Let him
shape the conversation to suit himself—let him drop it or change it whenever
he wants to. Let him see that nobody is trying to draw him out. Just let him
have his own way. He will soon forget himself and begin to grind out lies like
a mill. Don't get impatient—just keep quiet, and let me play him. I will make
him lie. It does seem to me that the boys must be blind to overlook such an
obvious and simple trick as that."

Eckert received us heartily—a pleasant-spoken, gentle-mannered creature. We
sat in the veranda an hour, sipping English ale, and talking about the king, and
the sacred white elephant, the Sleeping Idol, and all manner of things; and I
noticed that my comrade never led the conversation himself or shaped it, but
simply followed Eckert's lead, and betrayed no solicitude and no anxiety about
anything. The effect was shortly perceptible. Eckert began to grow communicative;
he grew more and more at his ease, and more and more talkative and sociable.
Another hour passed in the same way, and then all of a sudden Eckert said:

"Oh, by the way! I came near forgetting. I have got a thing here to astonish
you. Such a thing as neither you nor any other man ever heard of—I've got a
cat that will eat cocoanut! Common green cocoanut—and not only eat the meat,
but drink the milk. It is so—I'll swear to it."

A quick glance from Bascom—a glance that I understood—then:

"Why, bless my soul, I never heard of such a thing. Man, it is impossible."

"I knew you would say it. I'll fetch the cat."

He went in the house. Bascom said:

"There—what did I tell you? Now, that is the way to handle Eckert. You
see, I have petted him along patiently, and put his suspicions to sleep. I am glad
we came. You tell the boys about it when you go back. Cat eat a cocoanut—
oh, my! Now, that is just his way, exactly—he will tell the absurdest lie, and
trust to luck to get out of it again. Cat eat a cocoanut—the innocent fool!"

Eckert approached with his cat, sure enough.

Bascom smiled. Said he:

"I'll hold the cat—you bring a cocoanut."

Eckert split one open, and chopped up some pieces. Bascom smuggled a wink
to me, and proffered a slice of the fruit to puss. She snatched it, swallowed it
ravenously, and asked for more!

We rode our two miles in silence, and wide apart. At least I was silent, though
Bascom cuffed his horse and cursed him a good deal, notwithstanding the horse
was behaving well enough. When I branched off homeward, Bascom said:

"Keep the horse till morning. And—you need not speak of this——foolishness
to the boys."

Chapter VIII

IN A LITTLE while all interest was taken up in stretching our necks and watching for the "pony-rider"—the fleet messenger who sped across the continent from St. Joe to Sacramento, carrying letters nineteen hundred miles in eight days! Think of that for perishable horse and human flesh and blood to do! The pony-rider was usually a little bit of a man, brimful of spirit and endurance. No matter what time of the day or night his watch came on, and no matter whether it was winter or summer, raining, snowing, hailing, or sleeting, or whether his "beat" was a level straight road or a crazy trail over mountain crags and precipices, or whether it led through peaceful regions or regions that swarmed with hostile Indians, he must be always ready to leap into the saddle and be off like the wind! There was no idling time for a pony-rider on duty. He rode fifty miles without stopping, by daylight, moonlight, starlight, or through the blackness of darkness—just as it happened. He rode a splendid horse that was born for a racer and fed and lodged like a gentleman; kept him at his utmost speed for ten miles, and then, as he came crashing up to the station where stood two men holding fast a fresh, impatient steed, the transfer of rider and mail-bag was made in the twinkling of an eye, and away flew the eager pair and were out of sight before the spectator could get hardly the ghost of a look. Both rider and horse went "flying light." The rider's dress was thin, and fitted close; he wore a "round-about," and a skull-cap, and tucked his pantaloons into his boot-tops like a race-rider. He carried no arms—he carried nothing that was not absolutely necessary, for even the postage on his literary freight was worth *five dollars a letter*. He got but little frivolous correspondence to carry—his bag had business letters in it, mostly. His horse was stripped of all unnecessary weight, too. He wore a little wafer of a racing-saddle, and no visible blanket. He wore light shoes, or none at all. The little flat mail pockets strapped under the rider's thighs would each hold about the bulk of a child's primer. They held many and many an important business chapter and newspaper letter, but these were written on paper as airy and thin as gold-leaf, nearly, and thus bulk and weight were economized. The stage-coach traveled about a hundred to a hundred and twenty-five miles a day (twenty-four hours), the pony-rider about two hundred and fifty. There were about eighty pony-riders in the saddle all the time, night and day, stretching in a long, scattering procession from Missouri to California, forty flying eastward, and forty toward the west, and among them making four hundred gallant horses earn a stirring livelihood and see a deal of scenery every single day in the year.

We had had a consuming desire, from the beginning, to see a pony-rider, but somehow or other all that passed us and all that met us managed to streak by in the night, and so we heard only a whiz and a hail, and the swift phantom of the desert was gone before we could get our heads out of the windows. But now we were expecting one along every moment, and would see him in broad daylight. Presently the driver exclaims:

"HERE HE COMES!"

Every neck is stretched further, and every eye strained wider. Away across the endless dead level of the prairie a black speck appears against the sky, and

716

it is plain that it moves. Well, I should think so! In a second or two it becomes a horse and rider, rising and falling, rising and falling—sweeping toward us nearer and nearer—growing more and more distinct, more and more sharply defined—nearer and still nearer, and the flutter of the hoofs comes faintly to the ear—another instant a whoop and a hurrah from our upper deck, a wave of the rider's hand, but no reply, and man and horse burst past our excited faces, and go winging away like a belated fragment of a storm!

So sudden is it all, and so like a flash of unreal fancy, that but for the flake of white foam left quivering and perishing on a mail-sack after the vision had flashed by and disappeared, we might have doubted whether we had seen any actual horse and man at all, maybe.

We rattled through Scott's Bluffs Pass, by and by. It was along here somewhere that we first came across genuine and unmistakable alkali water in the road, and we cordially hailed it as a first-class curiosity, and a thing to be mentioned with eclat in letters to the ignorant at home. This water gave the road a soapy appearance, and in many places the ground looked as if it had been whitewashed. I think the strange alkali water excited us as much as any wonder we had come upon yet, and I know we felt very complacent and conceited, and better satisfied with life after we had added it to our list of things which *we* had seen and some other people had not. In a small way we were the same sort of simpletons as those who climb unnecessarily the perilous peaks of Mont Blanc and the Matterhorn, and derive no pleasure from it except the reflection that it isn't a common experience. But once in a while one of those parties trips and comes darting down the long mountain-crags in a sitting posture, making the crusted snow smoke behind him, flitting from bench to bench, and from terrace to terrace, jarring the earth where he strikes, and still glancing and flitting on again, sticking an iceberg into himself every now and then, and tearing his clothes, snatching at things to save himself, taking hold of trees and fetching them along with him, roots and all, starting little rocks now and then, then big boulders, then acres of ice and snow and patches of forest, gathering and still gathering as he goes, adding and still adding to his massed and sweeping grandeur as he nears a three-thousand-foot precipice, till at last he waves his hat magnificently and rides into eternity on the back of a raging and tossing avalanche!

This is all very fine, but let us not be carried away by excitement, but ask calmly, how does this person feel about it in his cooler moments next day, with six or seven thousand feet of snow and stuff on top of him?

We crossed the sand hills near the scene of the Indian mail robbery and massacre of 1856, wherein the driver and conductor perished, and also all the passengers but one, it was supposed; but this must have been a mistake, for at different times afterward on the Pacific coast I was personally acquainted with a hundred and thirty-three or four people who were wounded during that massacre, and barely escaped with their lives. There was no doubt of the truth of it—I had it from their own lips. One of these parties told me that he kept coming across arrow-heads in his system for nearly seven years after the massacre; and another of them told me that he was struck so literally full of arrows that after the Indians were gone and he could raise up and examine himself, he could not restrain his tears, for his clothes were completely ruined.

The most trustworthy tradition avers, however, that only one man, a person named Babbitt, survived the massacre, and that he was desperately wounded.

RIDING THE AVALANCHE.

He dragged himself on his hand and knee (for one leg was broken) to a station several miles away. He did it during portions of two nights, lying concealed one day and part of another, and for more than forty hours suffering unimaginable anguish from hunger, thirst, and bodily pain. The Indians robbed the coach of everything it contained, including quite an amount of treasure.

Chapter IX

WE PASSED FORT LARAMIE in the night, and on the seventh morning out we found ourselves in the Black Hills, with Laramie Peak at our elbow (apparently) looming vast and solitary—a deep, dark, rich indigo blue in hue, so portentously did the old colossus frown under his beetling brows of storm cloud. He was thirty or forty miles away, in reality, but he only seemed removed a little beyond the low ridge at our right. We breakfasted at Horse-Shoe Station, six hundred and seventy-six miles out from St. Joseph. We had now reached hostile Indian country, and during the afternoon we passed Laparelle Station, and enjoyed great discomfort all the time we were in the neighborhood, being aware that many of the trees we dashed by at arm's length concealed a lurking Indian or two. During the preceding night an ambushed savage had sent a bullet through the pony-rider's jacket, but he had ridden on, just the same, because pony-riders were not allowed to stop and inquire into such things except when killed. As long as they had life enough left in them they had to stick to the horse and ride, even if the Indians had been waiting for them a week, and were entirely out of patience. About two hours and a half before we arrived at Laparelle Station, the keeper in charge of it had fired four times at an Indian, but he said with an injured air that the Indian had "skipped around so's to spile everything and ammunition's blamed skurse, too." The most natural inference conveyed by his manner of speaking was, that in "skipping around," the Indian had taken an unfair advantage. The coach we were in had a neat hole through its front—a reminiscence of its last trip through this region. The bullet that made it wounded the driver slightly, but he did not mind it much. He said the place to keep a man "huffy" was down on the Southern Overland, among the Apaches, before the company moved the stage line up on the northern route. He said the Apaches used to annoy him all the time down there, and that he came as near as anything to starving to death in the midst of abundance, because they kept him so leaky with bullet holes that he "couldn't hold his vittles." This person's statements were not generally believed.

We shut the blinds down very tightly that first night in the hostile Indian country, and lay on our arms. We slept on them some, but most of the time we only lay on them. We did not talk much, but kept quiet and listened. It was an inky-black night, and occasionally rainy. We were among woods and rocks, hills and gorges—so shut in, in fact, that when we peeped through a chink in a curtain, we could discern nothing. The driver and conductor on top were still, too, or only spoke at long intervals, in low tones, as is the way of men in the midst of invisible dangers. We listened to rain-drops pattering on the roof; and the grinding of the wheels through the muddy gravel; and the low wailing of the wind; and all the time we had that absurd sense upon us, inseparable from travel at night in a close-curtained vehicle, the sense of remaining perfectly still in one place, notwithstanding the jolting and swaying of the vehicle, the trampling of the horses, and the grinding of the wheels. We listened a long time, with intent faculties and bated breath; every time one of us would relax, and draw a long sigh of relief and start to say something, a comrade would be sure to utter a sudden "Hark!" 'and instantly the experimenter was rigid and listening again. So that the tiresome minutes and decades of minutes dragged away, until at last our tense forms filmed over with a dulled consciousness, and we slept, if one might call such a condition by so strong a name—for it was a sleep set with a hair-trigger. It was a sleep seething and teeming with a weird and distressful confusion of shreds and fag-ends of dreams—a sleep that was a chaos. Presently, dreams and sleep and the sullen hush of the night were startled by a ringing report, and cloven by *such* a long, wild, agonizing shriek! Then we heard—ten steps from the stage—

"Help! help! help!" [It was our driver's voice.]

"Kill him! Kill him like a dog!"

"I'm being murdered! Will no man lend me a pistol?"

"Look out! head him off! head him off!"

[Two pistol shots; a confusion of voices and the trampling of many feet, as if a crowd were closing and surging together around some object; several heavy, dull blows, as with a club; a voice that said appealingly, "Don't, gentlemen, please don't—I'm a dead man!" Then a fainter groan, and another blow, and away sped the stage into the darkness, and left the grisly mystery behind us.]

What a startle it was! Eight seconds would amply cover the time it occupied—maybe even five would do it. We only had time to plunge at a curtain and unbuckle and unbutton part of it in an awkward and hindering flurry, when our whip cracked sharply overhead, and we went rumbling and thundering away, down a mountain "grade."

We fed on that mystery the rest of the night—what was left of it, for it was waning fast. It had to remain a present mystery, for all we could get from the conductor in answer to our hails was something that sounded, through the clatter of the wheels, like "Tell you in the morning!"

So we lit our pipes and opened the corner of a curtain for a chimney, and lay there in the dark, listening to each other's story of how he first felt and how many thousand Indians he first thought had hurled themselves upon us, and what his remembrance of the subsequent sounds was, and the order of their occurrence. And we theorized, too, but there was never a theory that would account for our driver's voice being out there, nor yet account for his Indian murderers talking such good English, if they *were* Indians.

So we chatted and smoked the rest of the night comfortably away, our boding anxiety being somehow marvelously dissipated by the real presence of something to be anxious *about*.

We never did get much satisfaction about that dark occurrence. All that we could make out of the odds and ends of the information we gathered in the morning, was that the disturbance occurred at a station; that we changed drivers there, and that the driver that got off there had been talking roughly about some of the outlaws that infested the region ("for there wasn't a man around there but had a price on his head and didn't dare show himself in the settlements," the conductor said); he had talked roughly about these characters, and ought to have "drove up there with his pistol cocked and ready on the seat alongside of him, and begun business himself, because any softy would know they would be laying for him."

That was all we could gather, and we could see that neither the conductor nor the new driver was much concerned about the matter. They plainly had little respect for a man who would deliver offensive opinions of people and then be so simple as to come into their presence unprepared to "back his judgment," as they pleasantly phrased the killing of any fellow, being who did not like said opinions. And likewise they plainly had a contempt for the man's poor discretion in venturing to rouse the wrath of such utterly reckless wild beasts as those outlaws—and the conductor added:

"I tell you it's as much as Slade himself wants to do!"

This remark created an entire revolution in my curiosity. I cared nothing now about the Indians, and even lost interest in the murdered driver. There was such magic in that name, SLADE. Day or night, now, I stood always ready to drop any subject in hand, to listen to something new about Slade and his ghastly exploits. Even before we got to Overland City, we had begun to hear about Slade and his "division" (for he was a "division-agent") on the Overland; and from the hour we had left Overland City we had heard drivers and conductors talk about only three things—"Californy," the Nevada silver mines, and this desperado Slade. And a deal the most of the talk was about Slade. We had gradually come to have a realizing sense of the fact that Slade was a man whose heart and hands and soul were steeped in the blood of offenders against his dignity; a man who awfully avenged all injuries, affronts, insults or slights, of whatever kind—on the spot if he could, years afterward if lack of earlier opportunity compelled it; a man whose hate tortured him day and night till vengeance appeased it—and not an ordinary vengeance either, but his enemy's absolute death— nothing less; a man whose face would light up with a terrible joy when he surprised a foe and had him at a disadvantage. A high and efficient servant of the Overland, an outlaw among outlaws and yet their relentless scourge, Slade was at once the most bloody, the most dangerous, and the most valuable citizen that inhabited the savage fastnesses of the mountains.

Chapter X

REALLY AND TRULY, two thirds of the talk of drivers and conductors had been about this man Slade, ever since the day before we reached Julesburg. In order that the eastern reader may have a clear conception of what a Rocky Mountain desperado is, in his highest state of development, I will reduce all this mass of overland gossip to one straightforward narrative, and present it in the following shape:

Slade was born in Illinois, of good parentage. At about twenty-six years of age he killed a man in a quarrel and fled the country. At St. Joseph, Missouri, he joined one of the early California-bound emigrant trains, and was given the post of train-master. One day on the plains he had an angry dispute with one of his wagon-drivers, and both drew their revolvers. But the driver was the quicker artist, and had his weapon cocked first. So Slade said it was a pity to waste life on so small a matter, and proposed that the pistols be thrown on the ground and the quarrel settled by a fist-fight. The unsuspecting driver agreed, and threw down his pistol—whereupon Slade laughed at his simplicity, and shot him dead!

He made his escape, and lived a wild life for awhile, dividing his time between fighting Indians and avoiding an Illinois sheriff, who had been sent to arrest him for his first murder. It is said that in one Indian battle he killed three savages with his own hand, and afterward cut their ears off and sent them, with his compliments, to the chief of the tribe.

Slade soon gained a name for fearless resolution, and this was sufficient merit to procure for him the important post of overland division-agent at Julesburg, in place of Mr. Jules, removed. For some time previously, the company's horses had been frequently stolen, and the coaches delayed, by gangs of outlaws, who were wont to laugh at the idea of any man's having the temerity to resent such outrages. Slade resented them promptly. The outlaws soon found that the new agent was a man who did not fear anything that breathed the breath of life. He made short work of all offenders. The result was that delays ceased, the company's property was let alone, and no matter what happened or who suffered, Slade's coaches went through, every time! True, in order to bring about this wholesome change, Slade had to kill several men—some say three, others say four, and others six—but the world was the richer for their loss. The first prominent difficulty he had was with the ex-agent Jules, who bore the reputation of being a reckless and desperate man himself. Jules hated Slade for supplanting him, and a good fair occasion for a fight was all he was waiting for. By and by Slade dared to employ a man whom Jules had once discharged. Next, Slade seized a team of stage-horses which he accused Jules of having driven off and hidden somewhere for his own use. War was declared, and for a day or two the two men walked warily about the streets, seeking each other, Jules armed with a double-barreled shot gun, and Slade with his history-creating revolver. Finally, as Slade stepped into a store, Jules poured the contents of his gun into him from behind the door. Slade was plucky, and Jules got several bad pistol wounds in return. Then both men fell, and were carried to their respective lodgings, both swearing that better aim should do deadlier work next time. Both were bedridden a long time, but Jules got on his feet first, and gathering his possessions together,

721

packed them on a couple of mules, and fled to the Rocky Mountains to gather strength in safety against the day of reckoning. For many months he was not seen or heard of, and was gradually dropped out of the remembrance of all save Slade himself. But Slade was not the man to forget him. On the contrary, common report said that Slade kept a reward standing for his capture, dead or alive!

After a while, seeing that Slade's energetic administration had restored peace and order to one of the worst divisions of the road, the overland stage company transferred him to the Rocky Ridge division in the Rocky Mountains, to see if he could perform a like miracle there. It was the very paradise of outlaws and desperadoes. There was absolutely no semblance of law there. Violence was the rule. Force was the only recognized authority. The commonest misunderstandings were settled on the spot with the revolver or the knife. Murders were done in open day, and with sparkling frequency, and nobody thought of inquiring into them. It was considered that the parties who did the killing had their private reasons for it; for other people to meddle would have been looked upon as indelicate. After a murder, all that Rocky Mountain etiquette required of a spectator was, that he should help the gentleman bury his game—otherwise his churlishness would surely be remembered against him the first time he killed a man himself and needed a neighborly turn in interring him.

Slade took up his residence sweetly and peacefully in the midst of this hive of horse thieves and assassins, and the very first time one of them aired his insolent swaggerings in his presence he shot him dead! He began a raid on the outlaws, and in a singularly short space of time he had completely stopped their depredations on the stage stock, recovered a large number of stolen horses, killed several of the worst desperadoes of the district, and gained such a dread ascendancy over the rest that they respected him, admired him, feared him, obeyed him! He wrought the same marvelous change in the ways of the community that had marked his administration at Overland City. He captured two men who had stolen overland stock, and with his own hands he hanged them. He was supreme judge in his district, and he was jury and executioner likewise—and not only in the case of offenses against his employers, but against passing emigrants as well. On one occasion some emigrants had their stock lost or stolen, and told Slade, who chanced to visit their camp. With a single companion he rode to a ranch, the owners of which he suspected, and opening the door, commenced firing, killing three, and wounding the fourth.

From a bloodthirstily interesting little Montana book* I take this paragraph:

> While on the road, Slade held absolute sway. He would ride down to a station, get into a quarrel, turn the house out of windows, and maltreat the occupants most cruelly. The unfortunates had no means of redress, and were compelled to recuperate as best they could. On one of these occasions, it is said he killed the father of the fine little half-breed boy Jemmy, whom he adopted, and who lived with his widow after his execution. Stories of Slade's hanging men, and of innumerable assaults, shootings, stabbings, and beatings, in which he was a principal actor, form part of the legends of the stage line. As for minor quarrels and

---

* "The Vigilantes of Montana," by Prof. Thos. J. Dimsdale.

SLADE AS EXECUTIONER.

shootings, it is absolutely certain that a minute history of Slade's life would be one long record of such practices.

Slade was a matchless marksman with a navy revolver. The legends say that one morning at Rocky Ridge, when he was feeling comfortable, he saw a man approaching who had offended him some days before—observe the fine memory he had for matters like that—and, "Gentlemen," said Slade, drawing, "it is a good twenty-yard shot—I'll clip the third button on his coat!" Which he did. The bystanders all admired it. And they all attended the funeral, too.

On one occasion a man who kept a little whisky-shelf at the station did something which angered Slade—and went and made his will. A day or two afterward Slade came in and called for some brandy. The man reached under the counter (ostensibly to get a bottle—possibly to get something else), but Slade smiled upon him that peculiarly bland and satisfied smile of his which the neighbors had long ago learned to recognize as a death-warrant in disguise, and told him to "none of that!—pass out the high-priced article." So the poor bar-keeper had to turn his back and get the high-priced brandy from the shelf; and when he faced around again he was looking into the muzzle of Slade's pistol. "And the next instant," added my informant, impressively, "he was one of the deadest men that ever lived."

The stage-drivers and conductors told us that sometimes Slade would leave a hated enemy wholly unmolested, unnoticed, and unmentioned, for weeks together—had done it once or twice at any rate. And some said they believed he did it in order to lull the victims into unwatchfulness, so that he could get the advantage of them, and others said they believed he saved up an enemy that way, just as a schoolboy saves up a cake, and made the pleasure go as far as it would by gloating over the anticipation. One of these cases was that of a Frenchman who had offended Slade. To the surprise of everybody Slade did not kill him on the spot, but let him alone for a considerable time. Finally, however, he went to the Frenchman's house very late one night, knocked, and when his enemy opened the door, shot him dead—pushed the corpse inside the door with his foot, set the house on fire, and burned up the dead man, his widow and three children! I heard this story from several different people, and they evidently believed what they were saying. It may be true, and it may not. "Give a dog a bad name," etc.

Slade was captured, once, by a party of men who intended to lynch him. They disarmed him, and shut him up in a strong log-house, and placed a guard over him. He prevailed on his captors to send for his wife, so that he might have a last interview with her. She was a brave, loving, spirited woman. She jumped on a horse and rode for life and death. When she arrived they let her in without searching her, and before the door could be closed she whipped out a couple of revolvers, and she and her lord marched forth defying the party. And then, under a brisk fire, they mounted double and galloped away unharmed!

In the fullness of time Slade's myrmidons captured his ancient enemy Jules, whom they found in a well-chosen hiding-place in the remote fastnesses of the mountains, gaining a precarious livelihood with his rifle. They brought him to Rocky Ridge, bound hand and foot, and deposited him in the middle of the cattle-yard with his back against a post. It is said that the pleasure that lit Slade's face when he heard of it was something fearful to contemplate. He examined his enemy to see that he was securely tied, and then went to bed, content to wait till morning before enjoying the luxury of killing him. Jules spent the night in the cattle-yard, and it is a region where warm nights are never known. In the morning Slade practiced on him with his revolver, nipping the flesh here and there, and occasionally clipping off a finger, while Jules begged him to kill him outright and put him out of his misery. Finally Slade reloaded, and walking up close to his victim, made some characteristic remarks and then dispatched him. The body lay there half a day, nobody venturing to touch it without orders, and then Slade detailed a party and assisted at the burial himself. But he first cut off the dead man's ears and put them in his vest pocket, where he carried them for some time with great satisfaction. That is the story as I have frequently heard it told and seen it in print in California newspapers. It is doubtless correct in all essential particulars.

In due time we rattled up to a stage-station, and sat down to breakfast with a half-savage, half-civilized company of armed and bearded mountaineers, ranchmen, and station employees. The most gentlemanly-appearing, quiet, and affable officer we had yet found along the road in the Overland Company's service was the person who sat at the head of the table, at my elbow. Never youth stared and shivered as I did when I heard them call him SLADE!

Here was romance, and I sitting face to face with it!—looking upon it—touching it—hobnobbing with it, as it were! Here, right by my side, was the actual ogre who, in fights and brawls and various ways, *had taken the lives of twenty-six human beings*, or all men lied about him! I suppose I was the proudest stripling that ever traveled to see strange lands and wonderful people.

He was so friendly and so gentle-spoken that I warmed to him in spite of his awful history. It was hardly possible to realize that this pleasant person was the pitiless scourge of the outlaws, the raw-head-and-bloody-bones the nursing mothers of the mountains terrified their children with. And to this day I can remember nothing remarkable about Slade except that his face was rather broad across the cheek-bones, and that the cheek-bones were low and the lips peculiarly thin and straight. But that was enough to leave something of an effect upon me, for since then I seldom see a face possessing those characteristics without fancying that the owner of it is a dangerous man.

The coffee ran out. At least it was reduced to one tin-cupful, and Slade was about to take it when he saw that my cup was empty. He politely offered to fill it, but although I wanted it, I politely declined. I was afraid he had not killed anybody that morning, and might be needing diversion. But still with firm politeness he insisted on filling my cup, and said I had traveled all night and better deserved it than he—and while he talked he placidly poured the fluid, to the last drop. I thanked him and drank it, but it gave me no comfort, for I could not feel sure that he would not be sorry, presently, that he had given it away, and proceed to kill me to distract his thoughts from the loss. But nothing of the kind occurred. We left him with only twenty-six dead people to account for, and I felt a tranquil satisfaction in the thought that in so judiciously taking care of No. 1 at that breakfast-table I had pleasantly escaped being No. 27. Slade came out to the coach and saw us off, first ordering certain reärrangements of the mail-bags for our comfort, and then we took leave of him, satisfied that we should hear of him again, some day, and wondering in what connection.

Chapter XI

AND SURE ENOUGH, two or three years afterward, we did hear of him again. News came to the Pacific coast that the Vigilance Committee in Montana (whither Slade had removed from Rocky Ridge) had hanged him. I find an account of the affair in the thrilling little book I quoted a paragraph from in the last chapter— "The Vigilantes of Montana; being a Reliable Account of the Capture, Trial and Execution of Henry Plummer's Notorious Road Agent Band- By Prof. Thos. J. Dimsdale, Virginia City, M. T." Mr. Dimsdale's chapter is well worth reading, as a specimen of how the people of the frontier deal with criminals when the courts of law prove inefficient. Mr. Dimsdale makes two remarks about Slade, both of which are accurately descriptive, and one of which is exceedingly picturesque: "Those who saw him in his natural state only, would pronounce him to be a kind husband, a most hospitable host and a courteous gentleman; on the contrary, those who met him when maddened with liquor and surrounded by a gang of armed roughs, would pronounce him a fiend incarnate." And this: "From Fort Kearney, west, he was feared *a great deal more than the Almighty.*" For compactness, simplicity, and vigor of expression, I will "back" that sentence against anything in literature. Mr. Dimsdale's narrative is as follows. In all places where italics occur, they are mine:

> After the execution of the five men on the 14th of January, the Vigilantes considered that their work was nearly ended. They had freed the country of highwaymen and murderers to a great extent, and they determined that in the absence of the regular civil authority they would establish a People's Court where all offenders should be tried by judge and jury. This was the nearest approach to social order that the circumstances permitted, and, though strict legal authority was wanting, yet the people were firmly determined to maintain its efficiency, and to enforce its decrees. It may here be mentioned that the overt act which was the last round on the fatal ladder leading to the scaffold on which Slade perished, *was the tearing in pieces and stamping upon a writ of this court, followed*

by his arrest of the judge, Alex. Davis, by authority of a presented Derringer, and with his own hands.

J. A. Slade was himself, we have been informed, a Vigilante; he openly boasted of it, and said he knew all that they knew. He was never accused, or even suspected, of either murder or robbery, committed in this Territory (the latter crime was never laid to his charge, in any place); but that he had killed several men in other localities was notorious, and his bad reputation in this respect was a most powerful argument in determining his fate, when he was finally arrested for the offense above mentioned. On returning from Milk River he became more and more addicted to drinking, until at last it was a common feat for him and his friends to "take the town." He and a couple of his dependents might often be seen on one horse, galloping through the streets, shouting and yelling, firing revolvers, etc. On many occasions he would ride his horse into stores, break up bars, toss the scales out of doors and use most insulting language to parties present. Just previous to the day of his arrest, he had given a fearful beating to one of his followers; but such was his influence over them that the man wept bitterly at the gallows, and begged for his life with all his power. *It had become quite common, when Slade was on a spree, for the shop-keepers and citizens to close the stores and put out all the lights;* being fearful of some outrage at his hands. For his wanton destruction of goods and furniture, he was always ready to pay, when sober, if he had money; but there were not a few who regarded payment as small satisfaction for the outrage, and these men were his personal enemies.

From time to time Slade received warnings from men that he well knew would not deceive him, of the certain end of his conduct. There was not a moment, for weeks previous to his arrest, in which the public did not expect to hear of some bloody outrage. The dread of his very name, and the presence of the armed band of hangers-on who followed him alone prevented a resistance which must certainly have ended in the instant murder or mutilation of the opposing party.

Slade was frequently arrested by order of the court whose organization we have described, and had treated it with respect by paying one or two fines and promising to pay the rest when he had money; but in the transaction that occurred at this crisis, he forgot even this caution, and goaded by passion and the hatred of restraint, he sprang into the embrace of death.

Slade had been drunk and "cutting up" all night. He and his companions had made the town a perfect hell. In the morning, J. M. Fox, the sheriff, met him, arrested him, took him into court and commenced reading a warrant that he had for his arrest, by way of arraignment. He became uncontrollably furious, and *seizing the writ, he tore it up, threw it on the ground and stamped on it.* The clicking of the locks of his companions' revolvers was instantly heard, and a crisis was expected. The sheriff did not attempt his retention; but being at least as prudent as he was valiant, he succumbed, leaving Slade the *master of the situation and the conqueror and the ruler of the courts, law and law-makers.* This was a declaration of war, and was so accepted. The Vigilance Committee now felt that the question of social order and the preponderance of the law-abiding citizens had then and there to be decided. They knew the character of Slade, and they were well aware that they must submit to his rule without murmur, or else that he must be dealt with in such fashion as would prevent his being able to wreak his vengeance on the committee, who could never have hoped to live in the Territory secure from outrage or death, and who could never leave it without encountering his friends, whom his victory would have emboldened and stimulated to a pitch that would have rendered them reckless of consequences. The day previous he had ridden into Dorris's store, and on being requested to leave, he drew his revolver and threatened to kill the gentleman who spoke to him. Another saloon he had led his horse into, and buying a bottle of wine, he tried to make the animal drink it. This was not considered an uncommon performance, as he had often entered saloons and commenced firing at the lamps, causing a wild stampede.

A leading member of the committee met Slade, and informed him in the quiet, earnest manner of one who feels the importance of what he is saying: "Slade, get your horse at once, and go home, or there will be—
——to pay." Slade started and took a long look, with his dark and piercing eyes, at the gentleman. "What do you mean?" said he. "You have no right to ask me what I mean," was the quiet reply, "get your horse at once, and remember what I tell you." After a short pause he promised to do so, and actually got into the saddle; but, being still intoxicated, he began calling aloud to one after another of his friends, and at last seemed to have forgotten the warning he had received and became again uproarious, shouting the name of a well-known courtesan in company with those of two men whom he considered heads of the committee, as a sort of challenge; perhaps, however, as a simple act of bravado. It seems probable that the intimation of personal danger he had received had not been forgotten entirely; though fatally for him, he took a foolish way of showing his remembrance of it. He sought out Alexander Davis, the Judge of the Court, and drawing a cocked Derringer, he presented it at his head, and told him that he should hold him as a hostage for his own safety. As the judge stood perfectly quiet, and offered no resistance to his captor, no further outrage followed on this score. Previous to this, on account of the critical state of affairs, the committee had met, and at last resolved to arrest him. His execution had not been agreed upon, and, at that time, would have been negatived, most assuredly. A messenger rode down to Nevada to inform the leading men of what was on hand, as it was desirable to show that there was a feeling of unanimity on the subject, all along the gulch.

The miners turned out almost *en masse*, leaving their work and forming in solid column. About six hundred strong, armed to the teeth, they marched up to Virginia. The leader of the body well knew the temper of his men on the subject. He spurred on ahead of them, and hastily calling a meeting of the executive, he told them plainly that the miners meant "business," and that, if they came up, they would not stand in the street to be shot down by Slade's friends; but that they would take him and hang him. The meeting was small, as the Virginia men were loath to act at all. This momentous announcement of the feeling of the

Lower Town was made to a cluster of men, who were deliberating behind a wagon, at the rear of a store on Main Street.

The committee were most unwilling to proceed to extremities. All the duty they had ever performed seemed as nothing to the task before them; but they had to decide, and that quicky. It was finally agreed that if the whole body of the miners were of the opinion that he should be hanged, that the committee left it in their hands to deal with him. Off, at hot speed, rode the leader of the Nevada men to join his command.

Slade had found out what was intended, and the news sobered him instantly. He went into P. S. Pfouts' store, where Davis was, and apologized for his conduct, saying that he would take it all back.

The head of the column now wheeled into Wallace Street and marched up at quick time. Halting in front of the store, the executive officer of the committee stepped forward and arrested Slade, who was at once informed of his doom, and inquiry was made as to whether he had any business to settle. Several parties spoke to him on the subject; but to all such inquiries he turned a deaf ear, being entirely absorbed in the terrifying reflections on his own awful position. He never ceased his entreaties for life, and to see his dear wife. The unfortunate lady referred to, between whom and Slade there existed a warm affection, was at this time living at their ranch on the Madison. She was possessed of considerable personal attractions; tall, well-formed, of graceful carriage, pleasing manners, and was, withal, an accomplished horsewoman.

A messenger from Slade rode at full speed to inform her of her husband's arrest. In an instant she was in the saddle, and with all the energy that love and despair could lend to an ardent temperament and a strong physique, she urged her fleet charger over the twelve miles of rough and rocky ground that intervened between her and the object of her passionate devotion.

Meanwhile a party of volunteers had made the necessary preparations for the execution, in the valley traversed by the branch. Beneath the site of Pfouts' and Russell's stone building there was a corral, the gate-posts of which were strong and high. Across the top was laid a beam, to which the rope was fastened, and a dry-goods box served for the platform. To this place Slade was marched, surrounded by a guard, composed of the best armed and most numerous force that has ever appeared in Montana Territory.

The doomed man had so exhausted himself by tears, prayers and lamentations, that he had scarcely strength left to stand under the fatal beam. He repeatedly exclaimed, "My God! my God! must I die? Oh, my dear wife!"

On the return of the fatigue party, they encountered some friends of Slade, staunch and reliable citizens and members of the committee, but who were personally attached to the condemned. On hearing of his sentence, one of them, a stout-hearted man, pulled out his handkerchief and walked away, weeping like a child. Slade still begged to see his wife, most piteously, and it seemed hard to deny his request; but the bloody consequences that were sure to follow the inevitable attempt at a rescue, that her presence and entreaties would have certainly incited, forbade the granting of his request. Several gentlemen were sent for to see him, in his last moments, one of whom (Judge Davis) made a short address to the people; but in such low tones as to be inaudible, save to a few in his immediate vicinity. One of his friends, after exhausting his powers of entreaty, threw off his coat and declared that the prisoner could not be hanged until he himself was killed. A hundred guns were instantly leveled at him; whereupon he turned and fled; but, being brought back, he was compelled to resume his coat, and to give a promise of future peaceable demeanor.

Scarcely a leading man in Virginia could be found, though numbers of the citizens joined the ranks of the guard when the arrest was made. All lamented the stern necessity which dictated the execution.

Everything being ready, the command was given, "Men, do your duty," and the box being instantly slipped from beneath his feet, he died almost instantaneously.

The body was cut down and carried to the Virginia Hotel, where, in a darkened room, it was scarcely laid out when the unfortunate and bereaved companion of the deceased arrived, at headlong speed, to find that all was over, and that she was a widow. Her grief and heart-piercing cries were terrible evidences of the depth of her attachment for her lost husband, and a considerable period elapsed before she could regain the command of her excited feelings.

There is something about the desperado-nature that is wholly unaccountable— at least it looks unaccountable. It is this. The true desperado is gifted with splendid courage, and yet he will take the most infamous advantage of his enemy; armed and free, he will stand up before a host and fight until he is shot all to pieces, and yet when he is under the gallows and helpless he will cry and plead like a child. Words are cheap, and it is easy to call Slade a coward (all executed men who do not "die game" are promptly called cowards by unreflecting people), and when we read of Slade that he "had so exhausted himself by tears, prayers and lamentations, that he had scarcely strength left to stand under the fatal beam," the disgraceful word suggests itself in a moment—yet in frequently defying and inviting the vengeance of banded Rocky Mountain cut-throats by shooting down their comrades and leaders, and never offering to hide or fly, Slade showed that he was a man of peerless bravery. No coward would dare that. Many a notorious coward, many a chicken-livered poltroon, coarse, brutal, degraded, has made his dying speech without a quaver in his voice and been swung into eternity with what looked like the calmest fortitude, and so we are justified in believing, from the low intellect of such a creature, that it was not *moral* courage that enabled him to do it. Then, if moral courage is not the requisite quality, what could it have been that this stout-hearted Slade lacked?—this bloody, desperate, kindly-mannered, urbane gentleman, who never hesitated to warn his most ruffianly enemies that he would kill them whenever or wherever he came across them next! I think it is a conundrum worth investigating.

Chapter XII

JUST BEYOND THE breakfast-station we overtook a Mormon emigrant train of thirty-three wagons; and tramping wearily along and driving their herd of loose cows, were dozens of coarse-clad and sad-looking men, women, and children, who had walked as they were walking now, day after day for eight lingering weeks, and in that time had compassed the distance our stage had come in *eight days and three hours*—seven hundred and ninety-eight miles! They were dusty and uncombed, hatless, bonnetless and ragged, and they did look so tired!

After breakfast, we bathed in Horse Creek, a (previously) limpid, sparkling stream—an appreciated luxury, for it was very seldom that our furious coach halted long enough for an indulgence of that kind. We changed horses ten or twelve times in every twenty-four hours—changed mules, rather—six mules— and did it nearly every time in *four minutes*. It was lively work. As our coach rattled up to each station six harnessed mules stepped gaily from the stable; and in the twinkling of an eye, almost, the old team was out, and the new one in and we off and away again.

During the afternoon we passed Sweetwater Creek, Independence Rock, Devil's Gate and the Devil's Gap. The latter were wild specimens of rugged scenery, and full of interest—*we were in the heart of the Rocky Mountains, now*. And we also passed by "Alkali" or "Soda Lake," and we woke up to the fact that our journey had stretched a long way across the world when the driver said that the Mormons often came there from Great Salt Lake City to haul away saleratus. He said that a few days gone by they had shoveled up enough pure saleratus from the ground (it was a *dry* lake) to load two wagons, and that when they got these two wagon-loads of a drug that cost them nothing, to Salt Lake, they could sell it for twenty-five cents a pound.

In the night we sailed by a most notable curiosity, and one we had been hearing a good deal about for a day or two, and were suffering to see. This was what might be called a natural ice house. It was August, now, and sweltering weather in the daytime, yet at one of the stations the men could scrape the soil on the hill-side under the lee of a range of boulders, and at a depth of six inches cut out pure blocks of ice—hard, compactly frozen, and clear as crystal!

Toward dawn we got under way again, and presently as we sat with raised curtains enjoying our early-morning smoke and contemplating the first splendor of the rising sun as it swept down the long array of mountain peaks, flushing and gilding crag after crag and summit after summit, as if the invisible Creator reviewed his gray veterans and they saluted with a smile, we hove in sight of South Pass City. The hotel-keeper, the postmaster, the blacksmith, the mayor, the constable, the city marshal and the principal citizen and property holder, all came out and greeted us cheerily, and we gave him good day. He gave us a little Indian news, and a little Rocky Mountain news, and we gave him some Plains information in return. He then retired to his lonely grandeur and we climbed on up among the bristling peaks and the ragged clouds. South Pass City consisted of four log cabins, one of which was unfinished, and the gentleman with all those offices and titles was the chiefest of the ten citizens of the place. Think of hotel-keeper, postmaster, blacksmith, mayor, constable, city marshal, and principal citizen all condensed into one person and crammed into one skin. Bemis said he was "a perfect Allen's revolver of dignities." And he said that if he were to die as postmaster, or as blacksmith, or as postmaster and blacksmith both, the people might stand it, but if he were to die all over, it would be a frightful loss to the community.

Two miles beyond South Pass City we saw for the first time that mysterious marvel which all Western untraveled boys have heard of and fully believe in, but are sure to be astounded at when they see it with their own eyes, nevertheless— banks of snow in dead summer time. We were now far up toward the sky, and knew all the time that we must presently encounter lofty summits clad in the "eternal snow" which was so commonplace a matter of mention in books, and yet when I did see it glittering in the sun on stately domes in the distance and knew the month was August and that my coat was hanging up because it was too warm to wear it, I was full as much amazed as if I never had heard of snow in August before. Truly, "seeing is believing"—and many a man lives a long life through, *thinking* he believes certain universally received and well-established things, and yet never suspects that if he were confronted by those things once, he would discover that he did not *really* believe them before, but only thought he believed them.

In a little while quite a number of peaks swung into view with long claws of glittering snow clasping them; and with here and there, in the shade, down the mountain side, a little solitary patch of snow looking no larger than a lady's pocket-handkerchief, but being in reality as large as a "public square."

And now, at last, we were fairly in the renowned SOUTH PASS, and whirling gaily along high above the common world. We were perched upon the extreme summit of the great range of the Rocky Mountains, toward which we had been climbing, patiently climbing, ceaselessly climbing, for days and nights together— and about us was gathered a convention of Nature's kings that stood ten, twelve, and even thirteen thousand feet high—grand old fellows who would have to stoop to see Mount Washington, in the twilight. We were in such an airy elevation above the creeping populations of the earth, that now and then when the obstructing crags stood out of the way it seemed that we could look around and abroad and contemplate the whole great globe, with its dissolving views of mountains, seas, and continents stretching away through the mystery of the summer haze.

As a general thing the Pass was more suggestive of a valley than a suspension bridge in the clouds—but it strongly suggested the latter at one spot. At that place the upper third of one or two majestic purple domes projected above our level on either hand and gave us a sense of a hidden great deep of mountains and plains and valleys down about their bases which we fancied we might see if we could step to the edge and look over. These Sultans of the fastnesses were turbaned with tumbled volumes of cloud, which shredded away from time to time and drifted off fringed and torn, trailing their continents of shadow after them; and catching presently on an intercepting peak, wrapped it about and brooded there—then shredded away again and left the purple peak, as they had left the purple domes, downy and white with new-laid snow. In passing, these monstrous rags of cloud hung low and swept along right over the spectator's head, swinging their tatters so nearly in his face that his impulse was to shrink when they came closest. In the one place I speak of, one could look below him upon a world of diminishing crags and canyons leading down, down, and away to a vague plain with a thread in it which was a road, and bunches of feathers in it which were trees—a pretty picture sleeping in the sunlight—but with a darkness stealing over it and glooming its features deeper and deeper under the frown of a coming storm; and then, while no film or shadow marred the noon brightness of his high perch, he could watch the tempest break forth down there and see the lightnings leap from crag to crag and the sheeted rain drive along the canyon-sides, and hear the thunder peal and crash and roar. We had this spectacle; a familiar one to many, but to us a novelty.

We bowled along cheerily, and presently, at the very summit (though it had been all summit to us, and all equally level, for half an hour or more), we came to a spring which spent its water through two outlets and set it in opposite directions. The conductor said that one of those streams which we were looking at, was just starting on a journey westward to the Gulf of California and the Pacific Ocean, through hundreds and even thousands of miles of desert solitudes. He said that the other was just leaving its home among the snow peaks on a similar journey eastward—and we knew that long after we should have forgotten the simple rivulet it would still be plodding its patient way down the mountain sides, and canyon-beds, and between the banks of the Yellowstone; and by and by would join the broad Missouri and flow through unknown plains and deserts and unvisited wildernesses; and add a long and troubled pilgrimage among snags and wrecks and sand bars; and enter the Mississippi, touch the wharves of St. Louis and still drift on, traversing shoals and rocky channels, then endless chains of bottomless and ample bends, walled with unbroken forests, then mysterious byways and secret passages among woody islands, then the chained bends again, bordered with wide levels of shining sugar-cane in place of the somber forests; then by New Orleans and still other chains of bends—and finally, after two long months of daily and nightly harassment, excitement, enjoyment, adventure, and awful peril of parched throats, pumps and evaporation, pass the Gulf and enter into its rest upon the bosom of the tropic sea, never to look upon its snow-peaks again or regret them.

I freighted a leaf with a mental message for the friends at home, and dropped it in the stream. But I put no stamp on it and it was held for postage somewhere.

On the summit we overtook an emigrant train of many wagons, many tired men and women, and many a disgusted sheep and cow. In the woefully dusty

IT SPOILED THE MELON.

horseman in charge of the expedition I recognized John ———. Of all persons in the world to meet on top of the Rocky Mountains thousands of miles from home, he was the last one I should have looked for. We were school boys together and warm friends for years. But a boyish prank of mine had disruptured this friendship and it had never been renewed. The act of which I speak was this. I had been accustomed to visit occasionally an editor whose room was in the third story of a building and overlooked the street. One day this editor gave me a watermelon which I made preparations to devour on the spot, but chancing to look out of the window, I saw John standing directly under it and an irresistible desire came upon me to drop the melon on his head, which I immediately did. I was the loser, for it spoiled the melon, and John never forgave me and we dropped all intercourse and parted, but now met again under these circumstances.

We recognized each other simultaneously, and hands were grasped as warmly as if no coldness had ever existed between us, and no allusion was made to any. All animosities were buried and the simple fact of meeting a familiar face in that isolated spot so far from home, was sufficient to make us forget all things but pleasant ones, and we parted again with sincere "good byes" and "God bless you" from both.

We had been climbing up the long shoulders of the Rocky Mountains for many tedious hours—we started *down* them, now. And we went spinning away at a round rate too.

We left the snowy Wind River Mountains and Uinta Mountains behind, and sped away, always through splendid scenery but occasionally through long ranks of white skeletons of mules and oxen—monuments of the huge emigration of other days—and here and there were up-ended boards or small piles of stones which the driver said marked the resting-place of more precious remains. It was the loneliest land for a grave! A land given over to the cayote and the raven— which is but another name for desolation and utter solitude. On damp, murky nights, these scattered skeletons gave forth a soft, hideous glow, like very faint spots of moonlight starring the vague desert. It was because of the phosphorus in the bones. But no scientific explanation could keep a body from shivering when he drifted by one of those ghostly lights and knew that a skull held it.

At midnight it began to rain, and I never saw anything like it—indeed, I did not even see this, for it was too dark. We fastened down the curtains and even caulked them with clothing, but the rain streamed in in twenty places, notwithstanding. There was no escape. If one moved his feet out of a stream, he brought his body under one; and if he moved his body he caught one somewhere clse. If he struggled out of the drenched blankets and sat up, he was bound to get one down the back of his neck. Meantime the stage was wandering about a plain with gaping gullies in it, for the driver could not see an inch before his face nor keep the road, and the storm pelted so pitilessly that there was no keeping the horses still. With the first abatement the conductor turned out with lanterns to look for the road, and the first dash he made was into a chasm about fourteen feet deep, his lantern following like a meteor. As soon as he touched bottom he sang out frantically:

"Don't come here!"

To which the driver, who was looking over the precipice where he had disappeared, replied, with an injured air: "Think I'm a dam fool?"

The conductor was more than an hour finding the road—a matter which showed us how far we had wandered and what chances we had been taking. He traced our wheel tracks to the imminent verge of danger, in two places. I have always been glad that we were not killed that night. I do not know any particular reason, but I have always been glad.

In the morning, the tenth day out, we crossed Green River, a fine, large, limpid stream—stuck in it, with the water just up to the top of our mail-bed, and waited till extra teams were put on to haul us up the steep bank. But it was nice cool water, and besides it could not find any fresh place on us to wet.

At the Green River station we had breakfast—hot biscuits, fresh antelope steaks, and coffee—the only decent meal we tasted between the United States and Great Salt Lake City, and the only one we were ever really thankful for. Think of the monotonous execrableness of the thirty that went before it, to leave this one simple breakfast looming up in my memory like a shot-tower after all these years have gone by!

At 5 P.M. we reached Fort Bridger, one hundred and seventeen miles from the South Pass, and one thousand and twenty-five miles from St. Joseph. Fifty-two miles further on, near the head of Echo Canyon, we met sixty United States soldiers from Camp Floyd. The day before, they had fired upon three hundred or four hundred Indians, whom they supposed gathered together for no good purpose. In the fight that had ensued, four Indians were captured, and the main body chased four miles, but nobody killed. This looked like business. We had a notion to get out and join the sixty soldiers, but upon reflecting that there were four hundred of the Indians, we concluded to go on and join the Indians.

Echo Canyon is twenty miles long. It was like a long, smooth, narrow street, with a gradual descending grade, and shut in by enormous perpendicular walls of coarse conglomerate, four hundred feet high in many places, and turreted like mediæaeval castles. This was the most faultless piece of road in the mountains, and the driver said he would "let his team out." He did, and if the Pacific express trains whiz through there now any faster than we did then in the stage-coach, I envy the passengers the exhilaration of it. We fairly seemed to pick up our wheels and fly—and the mail matter was lifted up free from everything and held in solution! I am not given to exaggeration, and when I say a thing I mean it.

However, time presses. At four in the afternoon we arrived on the summit of Big Mountain, fifteen miles from Salt Lake City, when all the world was glorified with the setting sun, and the most stupendous panorama of mountain peaks yet encountered burst on our sight. We looked out upon this sublime spectacle from under the arch of a brilliant rainbow! Even the overland stage-driver stopped his horses and gazed!

Half an hour or an hour later, we changed horses, and took supper with a Mormon "Destroying Angel." "Destroying Angels," as I understand it, are Latter-Day Saints who are set apart by the Church to conduct permanent disappearances of obnoxious citizens. I had heard a deal about these Mormon Destroying Angels and the dark and bloody deeds they had done, and when I entered this one's house I had my shudder all ready. But alas for all our romances, he was nothing but a loud, profane, offensive, old blackguard! He was murderous enough, possibly, to fill the bill of a Destroyer, but would you have *any* kind of an Angel devoid of dignity? Could you abide an Angel in an unclean shirt and no suspenders? Could you respect an angel with a horse-laugh and a swagger like a buccaneer?

There were other blackguards present—comrades of this one. And there was one person that looked like a gentleman—Heber C. Kimball's son, tall and well made, and thirty years old, perhaps. A lot of slatternly women flitted hither and thither in a hurry, with coffee-pots, plates of bread, and other appurtenances to supper, and these were said to be the wives of the Angel—or some of them, at least. And of course they were; for if they had been hired "help" they would not have let an angel from above storm and swear at them as he did, let alone one from the place this one hailed from.

This was our first experience of the western "peculiar institution," and it was not very prepossessing. We did not tarry long to observe it, but hurried on to the home of the Latter-Day Saints, the stronghold of the prophets, the capital of the only absolute monarchy in America—Great Salt Lake City. As the night closed in we took sanctuary in the Salt Lake House and unpacked our baggage.

Chapter XIII

WE HAD A fine supper, of the freshest meats and fowls and vegetables—a great variety and as great abundance. We walked about the streets some, afterward, and glanced in at shops and stores; and there was fascination in surreptitiously staring at every creature we took to be a Mormon. This was fairy-land to us, to all intents and purposes—a land of enchantment, and goblins, and awful mystery. We felt a curiosity to ask every child how many mothers it had, and if it could tell them apart; and we experienced a thrill every time a dwelling-house door opened and shut as we passed, disclosing a glimpse of human heads and backs and shoulders—for we so longed to have a good satisfying look at a Mormon family in all its comprehensive ampleness, disposed in the customary concentric rings of its home circle.

By and by the Acting Governor of the Territory introduced us to other "Gentiles," and we spent a sociable hour with them. "Gentiles" are people who are not Mormons. Our fellow-passenger, Bemis, took care of himself, during this part of the evening, and did not make an overpowering success of it, either, for he came into our room in the hotel about eleven o'clock, full of cheerfulness, and talking loosely, disjointedly and indiscriminately, and every now and then tugging out a ragged word by the roots that had more hiccups than syllables in it. This, together with his hanging his coat on the floor on one side of a chair, and his vest on the floor on the other side, and piling his pants on the floor just in front of the same chair, and then contemplating the general result with superstitious awe, and finally pronouncing it "too many for *him*" and going to bed with his boots on, led us to fear that something he had eaten had not agreed with him.

But we knew afterward that it was something he had been drinking. It was the exclusively Mormon refresher, "valley tan." Valley tan (or, at least, one form of valley tan) is a kind of whisky, or first cousin to it; is of Mormon invention and manufactured only in Utah. Tradition says it is made of (imported) fire and brimstone. If I remember rightly no public drinking saloons were allowed in the kingdom by Brigham Young, and no private drinking permitted among the faithful, except they confined themselves to "valley tan."

Next day we strolled about everywhere through the broad, straight, level streets, and enjoyed the pleasant strangeness of a city of fifteen thousand inhabitants

EFFECTS OF "VALLEY TAN."

with no loafers perceptible in it; aad no visible drunkards or noisy people; a limpid stream rippling and dancing through every street in place of a filthy gutter; block after block of trim dwellings, built of "frame" and sunburned brick—a great thriving orchard and garden behind every one of them, apparently—branches from the street stream winding and sparkling among the garden beds and fruit trees—and a grand general air of neatness, repair, thrift and comfort, around and about and over the whole. And everywhere were workshops, factories, and all manner of industries; and intent faces and busy hands were to be seen wherever one looked; and in one's ears was the ceaseless clink of hammers, the buzz of trade and the contented hum of drums and fly-wheels.

The armorial crest of my own State consisted of two dissolute bears holding up the head of a dead and gone cask between them and marking the pertinent remark, "UNITED, WE STAND—(hic!)—DIVIDED, WE FALL." It was always too figurative for the author of this book. But the Mormon crest was easy. And it was simple, unostentatious, and fitted like a glove. It was a representation of a GOLDEN BEEHIVE, with the bees all at work!

The city lies in the edge of a level plain as broad as the State of Connecticut, and crouches close down to the ground under a curving wall of mighty mountains whose heads are hidden in the clouds, and whose shoulders bear relics of the snows of winter all the summer long. Seen from one of these dizzy heights, twelve or fifteen miles off, Great Salt Lake City is toned down and diminished till it is suggestive of a child's toy-village reposing under the majestic protection of the Chinese wall.

On some of those mountains, to the southwest, it had been raining every day for two weeks, but not a drop had fallen in the city. And on hot days in late spring and early autumn the citizens could quit fanning and growling and go out and cool off by looking at the luxury of a glorious snow-storm going on in the mountains. They could enjoy it at a distance, at those seasons, every day, though no snow would fall in their streets, or anywhere near them.

Salt Lake City was healthy—an extremely healthy city. They declared there was only one physician in the place and he was arrested every week regularly and held to answer under the vagrant act for having "no visible means of support." They always give you a good substantial article of truth in Salt Lake, and good measure and good weight, too. Very often, if you wished to weigh one of their airiest little commonplace statements, you would want the hay scales.]

We desired to visit the famous inland sea, the American "Dead Sea," the great Salt Lake—seventeen miles, horseback, from the city—for we had dreamed about it, and thought about it, and talked about it, and yearned to see it, all the first part of our trip; but now when it was only arm's length away it had suddenly lost nearly every bit of its interest. And so we put it off, in a sort of general way, till next day—and that was the last we ever thought of it. We dined with some hospitable Gentiles; and visited the foundation of the prodigious temple; and talked long with that shrewd Connecticut Yankee, Heber C. Kimball (since deceased), a saint of high degree and a mighty man of commerce. We saw the "Tithing-House," and the "Lion House," and I do not know or remember how many more church and government buildings of various kinds and curious names. We flitted hither and thither and enjoyed every hour, and picked up a great deal of useful information and entertaining nonsense, and went to bed at night satisfied.

The second day, we made the acquaintance of Mr. Street (since deceased) and put on white shirts and went and paid a state visit to the king. He seemed a quiet, kindly, easy-mannered, dignified, self-possessed old gentleman of fifty-five or sixty, and had a gentle craft in his eye that probably belonged there. He was very simply dressed and was just taking off a straw hat as we entered. He talked about Utah, and the Indians, and Nevada, and general American matters and questions, with our secretary and certain government officials who came with us. But he never paid any attention to me, notwithstanding I made several attempts to "draw him out" on federal politics and his high handed attitude toward Congress. I thought some of the things I said were rather fine. But he merely looked around at me, at distant intervals, somewhat as I have seen a benignant old cat look around to see which kitten was meddling with her tail. By and by I subsided into an indignant silence, and so sat until the end, hot and flushed, and execrating him in my heart for an ignorant savage. But he was calm. His conversation with those gentlemen flowed on as sweetly and peacefully and musically as any summer brook. When the audience was ended and we were retiring from the presence, he put his hand on my head, beamed down on me in an admiring way, and said to my brother:

"Ah—your child, I presume? Boy, or girl?"

Chapter XIV

MR. STREET WAS very busy with his telegraphic matters—and considering that he had eight or nine hundred miles of rugged, snowy, uninhabited mountains, and waterless, treeless, melancholy deserts to traverse with his wire, it was natural and needful that he should be as busy as possible. He could not go comfortably along and cut his poles by the roadside, either, but they had to be hauled by ox teams across those exhausting deserts—and it was two days' journey from water to water, in one or two of them. Mr. Street's contract was a vast work, every way one looked at it; and yet to comprehend what the vague words "eight hundred miles of rugged mountains and dismal deserts" mean, one must go over the ground in person—pen-and-ink descriptions cannot convey the dreary reality to the reader. And after all, Mr. S.'s mightiest difficulty turned out to be one which he had never taken into the account at all. Unto Mormons he had sub-let the hardest and heaviest half of his great undertaking, and all of a sudden they concluded that they were going to make little or nothing, and so they tranquilly threw their poles overboard in mountain or desert, just as it happened when they took the notion, and drove home and went about their customary business! They were under written contract to Mr. Street, but they did not care anything for that. They said they would "admire" to see a "Gentile" force a Mormon to fulfill a losing contract in Utah! And they made themselves very merry over the matter. Street said—for it was he that told us these things:

"I was in dismay. I was under heavy bonds to complete my contract in a given time, and this disaster looked very much like ruin. It was an astounding thing; it was such a wholly unlooked-for difficulty, that I was entirely nonplussed. I am a business man—have always been a business man—do not know anything *but* business—and so you can imagine how like being struck by lightning it was to find myself in a country where *written contracts were worthless!*—that main security, that sheet-anchor, that absolute necessity, of business. My confidence left me. There was no use in making new contracts—that was plain. I talked with first one prominent citizen and then another. They all sympathized with me, first rate, but they did not know how to help me. But at last a Gentile said, 'Go to Brigham Young! —these small fry cannot do you any good.' I did not think much of the idea, for if the *law* could not help me, what could an individual do who had not even anything to do with either making the laws or executing them? He might be a very good patriarch of a church and preacher in its tabernacle, but something sterner than religion and moral suasion was needed to handle a hundred refractory, half-civilized sub-contractors. But what was a man to do? I thought if Mr. Young could not do anything else, he might probably be able to give me some advice and a valuable hint or two, and so I went straight to him and laid the whole case before him. He said very little, but he showed strong interest all the way through. He examined all the papers in detail, and whenever there seemed anything like a hitch, either in the papers or my statement, he would go back and take up the thread and follow it patiently out to an intelligent and satisfactory result. Then he made a list of the contractors' names. Finally he said:

" 'Mr. Street, this is all perfectly plain. These contracts are strictly and legally drawn, and are duly signed and certified. These men manifestly entered into them with their eyes open. I see no fault or flaw anywhere.'

"Then Mr. Young turned to a man waiting at the other end of the room and said: 'Take this list of names to So-and-so, and tell him to have these men here at such-and-such an hour.'

"They were there, to the minute. So was I. Mr. Young asked them a number of questions, and their answers made my statement good. Then he said to them:

" 'You signed these contracts and assumed these obligations of your own free will and accord?'

" 'Yes.'

" 'Then carry them out to the letter, if it makes paupers of you! Go!'

"And they *did* go, too! They are strung across the deserts now, working like bees. And I never hear a word out of them. There is a batch of governors, and judges, and other officials here, shipped from Washington, and they maintain the semblance of a republican form of government—but the petrified truth is that Utah is an absolute monarchy and Brigham Young is king!''

Mr. Street was a fine man, and I believe his story. I knew him well during several years afterward in San Francisco.

Our stay in Salt Lake City amounted to only two days, and therefore we had no time to make the customary inquisition into the workings of polygamy and get up the usual statistics and deductions preparatory to calling the attention of the nation at large once more to the matter. I had the will to do it. With the gushing self-sufficiency of youth I was feverish to plunge in headlong and achieve a great reform here—until I saw the Mormon women. Then I was touched. My heart was wiser than my head. It warmed toward these poor, ungainly and pathetically ''homely'' creatures, and as I turned to hide the generous moisture in my eyes, I said, ''No—the man that marries one of them has done an act of Christian charity which entitles him to the kindly applause of mankind, not their harsh censure—and the man that marries sixty of them has done a deed of open-handed generosity so sublime that the nations should stand uncovered in his presence and worship in silence.''

Chapter XV

IT IS A luscious country for thrilling evening stories about assassinations of intractable Gentiles. I cannot easily conceive of anything more cozy than the night in Salt Lake which we spent in a Gentile den, smoking pipes and listening to tales of how Burton galloped in among the pleading and defenseless ''Morisites'' and shot them down, men and women, like so many dogs. And how Bill Hickman, a Destroying Angel, shot Drown and Arnold dead for bringing suit against him for a debt. And how Porter Rockwell did this and that dreadful thing. And how heedless people often come to Utah and make remarks about Brigham, or polygamy, or some other sacred matter, and the very next morning at daylight such parties are sure to be found lying up some back alley, contentedly waiting for the hearse.

I WAS TOUCHED.

And the next most interesting thing is to sit and listen to these Gentiles talk about polygamy; and how some portly old frog of an elder, or a bishop, marries a girl—likes her, marries her sister—likes her, marries another sister—likes her, takes another—likes her, marries her mother—likes her, marries her father, grandfather, great-grandfather, and then comes back hungry and asks for more. And how the pert young thing of eleven will chance to be the favorite wife and her own venerable grandmother have to rank away down toward D 4 in their mutual husband's esteem, and have to sleep in the kitchen, as like as not. And how this dreadful sort of thing, this hiving together in one foul nest of mother and daughters, and the making a young daughter superior to her own mother in rank and authority, are things which Mormon women submit to because their religion teaches them that the more wives a man has on earth, and the more children he rears, the higher the place they will all have in the world to come— and the warmer, maybe, though they do not seem to say anything about that.

According to these Gentile friends of ours, Brigham Young's harem contains twenty or thirty wives. They said that some of them had grown old and gone out of active service, but were comfortably housed and cared for in the henery— or the Lion House, as it is strangely named. Along with each wife were her children—fifty altogether. The house was perfectly quiet and orderly, when the children were still. They all took their meals in one room, and a happy and home-like sight it was pronounced to be. None of our party got an opportunity to take dinner with Mr. Young, but a Gentile by the name of Johnson professed to have enjoyed a sociable breakfast in the Lion House. He gave a preposterous account of the "calling of the roll," and other preliminaries, and the carnage that ensued when the buckwheat cakes came in. But he embellished rather too much. He said that Mr. Young told him several smart sayings of certain of his "two-year-olds," observing with some pride that for many years he had been the heaviest contributor in that line to one of the Eastern magazines; and then he wanted to show Mr. Johnson one of the pets that had said the last good thing, but he could not find the child. He searched the faces of the children in detail, but could not decide which one it was. Finally he gave it up with a sigh and said:

"I thought I would know the little cub again but I don't." Mr. Johnson said

NEEDED MARKING.

further that Mr. Young observed that life was a sad, sad thing—"because the joy of every new marriage a man contracted was so apt to be blighted by the inopportune funeral of a less recent bride." And Mr. Johnson said that while he and Mr. Young were pleasantly conversing in private, one of the Mrs. Youngs came in and demanded a breast-pin, remarking that she had found out that he had been giving a breast-pin to No. 6, and *she*, for one, did not propose to let this partiality go on without making a satisfactory amount of trouble about it. Mr. Young reminded her that there was a stranger present. Mrs. Young said that if the state of things inside the house was not agreeable to the stranger, he could find room outside. Mr. Young promised the breast-pin, and she went away. But in a minute or two another Mrs. Young came in and demanded a breast-pin. Mr. Young began a remonstrance, but Mrs. Young cut him short. She said No. 6 had got one, and No. 11 was promised one, and it was "no use for him to try to impose on her—she hoped she knew her rights." He gave his promise, and she went. And presently three Mrs. Youngs entered in a body and opened on their husband a tempest of tears, abuse, and entreaty. They had heard all about No. 6, No. 11, and No. 14. Three more breast-pins were promised. They were hardly gone when nine more Mrs. Youngs filed into the presence, and a new tempest burst forth and raged round about the prophet and his guest. Nine breast-pins were promised, and the weird sisters filed out again. And in came eleven more, weeping and wailing and gnashing their teeth. Eleven promised breast-pins purchased peace once more.

"That is a specimen," said Mr. Young. "You see how it is. You see what a life I lead. A man *can't* be wise all the time. In a heedless moment I gave my darling No. 6—excuse my calling her thus, as her other name has escaped me for the moment—a breast-pin. It was only worth twenty-five dollars—that is, *apparently* that was its whole cost—but its ultimate cost was inevitably bound to be a good deal more. You yourself have seen it climb up to six hundred and fifty dollars—and alas, even that is not the end! For I have wives all over this Territory of Utah. I have dozens of wives whose *numbers*, even, I do not know without looking in the family Bible. They are scattered far and wide among the mountains and valleys of my realm. And mark you, every solitary one of them will hear of this wretched breast-pin, and every last one of them will have one or die. No. 6's breast-pin will cost me twenty-five hundred dollars before I see the end of it. And these creatures will compare these pins together, and if one is a shade finer than the rest, they will all be thrown on my hands, and I will have to order a new lot to keep peace in the family. Sir, you probably did not know it, but all the time you were present with my children your every movement was watched by vigilant servitors of mine. If you had offered to give a child a dime, or a stick of candy, or any trifle of the kind, you would have been snatched out of the house instantly, provided it could be done before your gift left your hand. Otherwise it would be absolutely necessary for you to make an exactly similar gift to all my children—and knowing by experience the importance of the thing, I would have stood by and seen to it myself that you did it, and did it thoroughly. Once a gentleman gave one of my children a tin whistle—a veritable invention of Satan, sir, and one which I have an unspeakable horror of, and so would you if you had eighty or ninety children in your house. But the deed was done—the man escaped. I knew what the result was going to be, and I thirsted for vengeance. I ordered out a flock of Destroying Angels, and they hunted the man far into the fastnesses of the Nevada mountains. But they never caught him. I am not cruel, sir—I am not vindictive except when sorely outraged—but if I had caught him, sir, so help me Joseph Smith, I would have locked him into the nursery till the brats whistled him to death. By the slaughtered body of St. Parley Pratt (whom God assoil!) there was never anything on this earth like it! *I* knew who gave the whistle to the child, but I could not make these jealous mothers believe me. They believed *I* did it, and the result was just what any man of reflection could have foreseen: I had to order a hundred and ten whistles—I think we had a hundred and ten children in the house then, but some of them are off at college now—I had to order a hundred and ten of those shrieking things, and I wish I may never speak another word if we didn't have to talk on our fingers entirely, from that time forth until the children got tired of the whistles. And if ever another man gives a whistle to a child of mine and I get my hands on him, I will hang him higher than Haman! That is the word with the bark on it! Shade of Nephi! *You* don't know anything about married life. I am rich, and everybody knows it. I am benevolent, and everybody takes advantage of it. I have a strong fatherly instinct and all the foundlings are foisted on me. Every time a woman wants to do well by her darling, she puzzles her brain to cipher out some scheme for getting it into my hands. Why, sir, a woman came here once with a child of a curious lifeless sort of complexion (and so had the woman), and swore that the child was mine and she my wife—that I had married her at such-and-such a time in such-and-such a place, but she had forgotten her number, and of course I could not remember her name. Well, sir, she called my attention to the fact that the child looked like me, and really it did seem to resemble me—a common thing in the Territory—and, to cut the story short, I put it in my nursery, and she left. And by the ghost of Orson Hyde, when they came to wash the paint off that child it was an Injun! Bless my soul, you don't know anything about married life. It is a perfect dog's life, sir—a perfect dog's life. You can't economize. It isn't possible. I have tried keeping one set of bridal attire for all occasions. But it is of no use. First you'll marry a combination of calico and consumption that's as thin as a rail, and next you'll get a creature that's nothing more than the dropsy in disguise, and then you've got to eke out that bridal dress with an old balloon. That is the way it goes. And think of the wash-bill—(excuse these tears)—nine hundred and eighty-four pieces a week! No, sir, there is no such a thing as economy in a family like mine. Why, just the one item of cradles—think of it! And vermifuge! Soothing syrup! Teething rings! And 'papa's watches' for the babies to play with! And things to scratch the furniture with! And lucifer matches for them to eat, and pieces of glass to cut themselves with! The item of glass alone would support *your* family, I venture to say, sir. Let me scrimp and squeeze all I can, I still can't get ahead as fast as I feel I ought to, with my opportunities. Bless you, sir, at a time when I had seventy-two wives in this house, I groaned under the pressure of keeping thousands of dollars tied up in seventy-two bedsteads when the money ought to have been out at interest; and I just sold out the whole stock, sir, at a sacrifice, and built a bedstead seven feet long and ninety-six feet wide. But it was a failure, sir. I could *not* sleep. It appeared to me that the whole seventy-two women snored at once. The roar was deafening. And then the danger of it! That was what I was looking at. They would all draw in their breath at once, and you could actually see the walls of the house suck in—and then they would all exhale their breath at once, and you could see the walls swell out, and strain, and hear the rafters crack, and the shingles grind together. My friend, take an old man's advice, and *don't* encumber yourself with a large family—mind, I tell you, don't do it. In a small family, and in a small family only, you will find that comfort and that peace of mind which are the best at last of the blessings this world is able to afford us, and for the lack of which no accumulation of wealth, and no acquisition of fame, power, and greatness can ever compensate us. Take my word for it, ten or eleven wives is all you need—never go over it."

Some instinct or other made me set this Johnson down as being unreliable. And yet he was a very entertaining person, and I doubt if some of the information he gave us could have been acquired from any other source. He was a pleasant contrast to those reticent Mormons.

Chapter XVI

ALL MEN HAVE heard of the Mormon Bible, but few except the "elect" have seen it, or, at least, taken the trouble to read it. I brought away a copy from Salt Lake. The book is a curiosity to me, it is such a pretentious affair, and yet so "slow," so sleepy; such an insipid mess of inspiration. It is chloroform in print. If Joseph Smith composed this book, the act was a miracle—keeping awake while he did it was, at any rate. If he, according to tradition, merely translated it from certain ancient and mysteriously engraved plates of copper, which he declares he found under a stone in an out-of-the-way locality, the work of translating was equally a miracle, for the same reason.

The book seems to be merely a prosy detail of imaginary history, with the Old Testament for a model; followed by a tedious plagiarism of the New Testament. The author labored to give his words and phrases the quaint, old-fashioned sound and structure of our King James's translation of the Scriptures; and the result is a mongrel—half modern glibness, and half ancient simplicity and gravity. The latter is awkward and constrained; the former natural, but grotesque by the contrast. Whenever he found his speech growing too modern—which was about every sentence or two—he ladled in a few such Scriptural phrases as "exceeding sore," "and it came to pass," etc., and made things satisfactory again. "And it came to pass" was his pet. If he had left that out, his Bible would have been only a pamphlet.

The title-page reads as follows:

THE BOOK OF MORMON: AN ACCOUNT WRITTEN BY THE HAND OF MOR-MON, UPON PLATES TAKEN FROM THE PLATES OF NEPHI.

Wherefore it is an abridgment of the record of the people of Nephi, and also of the Lamanites; written to the Lamanites, who are a remnant of the House of Israel; and also to Jew and Gentile; written by way of commandment, and also by the spirit of prophecy and of revelation. Written and sealed up, and hid up unto the Lord, that they might not be destroyed; to come forth by the gift and power of God unto the interpretation thereof; sealed by the hand of Moroni, and hid up unto the Lord, to come forth in due time by the way of Gentile; the interpretation thereof by the gift of God. An abridgment taken from the Book of Ether also; which

is a record of the people of Jared; who were scattered at the time the
Lord confounded the language of the people when they were building a
tower to get to Heaven.

"Hid up" is good. And so is "wherefore"—though why "wherefore"? Any
other word would have answered as well—though in truth it would not have
sounded so Scriptural.

Next comes:

THE TESTIMONY OF THREE WITNESSES

Be it known unto all nations, kindreds, tongues, and people unto whom
this work shall come, that we, through the grace of God the Father, and
our Lord Jesus Christ, have seen the plates which contain this record,
which is a record of the people of Nephi, and also of the Lamanites,
their brethren, and also of the people of Jared, who came from the tower
of which hath been spoken; and we also know that they have been
translated by the gift and power of God, for His voice hath declared it
unto us; wherefore we know of a surety that the work is true. And we
also testify that we have seen the engravings which are upon the plates;
and they have been shown unto us by the power of God, and not of man.
And we declare with words of soberness, that an angel of God came
down from heaven, and he brought and laid before our eyes, that we
beheld and saw the plates, and the engravings thereon; and we know that
it is by the grace of God the Father, and our Lord Jesus Christ, that we
beheld and bear record that these things are true; and it is marvelous in
our eyes; nevertheless the voice of the Lord commanded us that we should
bear record of it; wherefore, to be obedient unto the commandments of
God, we bear testimony of these things. And we know that if we are
faithful in Christ, we shall rid our garments of the blood of all men, and
be found spotless before the judgment-seat of Christ, and shall dwell
with Him eternally in the heavens. And the honor be to the Father, and
to the Son, and to the Holy Ghost, which is one God. Amen.

OLIVER COWDERY.
DAVID WHITMER.
MARTIN HARRIS.

Some people have to have a world of evidence before they can come anywhere
in the neighborhood of believing anything; but for me, when a man tells me that
he has "seen the engravings which are upon the plates," and not only that, but
an angel was there at the time, and saw him see them, and probably took his
receipt for it, I am very far on the road to conviction, no matter whether I ever
heard of that man before or not, and even if I do not know the name of the
angel, or his nationality either.

Next is this:

AND ALSO THE TESTIMONY OF EIGHT WITNESSES.

Be it known unto all nations, kindreds, tongues, and people unto whom
this work shall come, that Joseph Smith, Jr., the translator of this work,

has shown unto us the plates of which hath been spoken, which have the appearance of gold; and as many of the leaves as the said Smith has translated, we did handle with our hands; and we also saw the engravings thereon, all of which has the appearance of ancient work, and of curious workmanship. And this we bear record with words of soberness, that the said Smith has shown unto us, for we have seen and hefted, and know of a surety that the said Smith has got the plates of which we have spoken. And we give our names unto the world, to witness unto the world that which we have seen; and we lie not, God bearing witness of it.

CHRISTIAN WHITMER,	HIRAM PAGE,
JACOB WHITMER,	JOSEPH SMITH, SR.,
PETER WHITMER,	JR., HYRUM SMITH,
JOHN WHITMER,	SAMUEL H. SMITH.

And when I am far on the road to conviction, and eight men, be they grammatical or otherwise, come forward and tell me that they have seen the plates too; and not only seen those plates but "hefted" them, I *am* convinced. I could not feel more satisfied and at rest if the entire Whitmer family had testified.

The Mormon Bible consists of fifteen "books"—being the books of Jacob, Enos, Jarom, Omni, Mosiah, Zeniff, Alma, Helaman, Ether, Moroni, two "books" of Mormon, and three of Nephi.

In the first book of Nephi is a plagiarism of the Old Testament, which gives an account of the exodus from Jerusalem of the "children of Lehi"; and it goes on to tell of their wanderings in the wilderness, during eight years, and their supernatural protection by one of their number, a party by the name of Nephi. They finally reached the land of "Bountiful," and camped by the sea. After they had remained there "for the space of many days"—which is more Scriptural than definite—Nephi was commanded from on high to build a ship wherein to "carry the people across the waters." He travestied Noah's ark—but he obeyed orders in the matter of the plan. He finished the ship *in a single day*, while his brethren stood by and made fun of it—and of him, too—"saying, our brother is a fool, for he thinketh that he can build a ship." They did not wait for the timbers to dry, but the whole tribe or nation sailed the next day. Then a bit of genuine nature cropped out, and is revealed by outspoken Nephi with Scriptural frankness—they all got on a spree! They, "and also their wives, began to make themselves merry, insomuch that they began to dance, and to sing, and to speak with much rudeness; yea, they were lifted up unto exceeding rudeness."

Nephi tried to stop these scandalous proceedings; but they tied him neck and heels, and went on with their lark. But observe how Nephi the prophet circumvented them by the aid of the invisible powers:

> And it came to pass that after they had bound me, insomuch that I could not move, the compass, which had been prepared of the Lord, did cease to work; wherefore, they knew not whither they should steer the ship, insomuch that there arose a great storm, yea, a great and terrible tempest, and we were driven back upon the waters for the space of three days; and they began to be frightened exceedingly, lest they should be drowned in the sea; nevertheless they did not loose me. And on the fourth day, which we had been driven back, the tempest began to be exceeding sore.

> And it came to pass that we were about to be swallowed up in the depths of the sea.

Then they untied him.

> And it came to pass after they had loosed me, behold, I took the compass, and it did work whither I desired it. And it came to pass that I prayed unto the Lord; and after I had prayed, the winds did cease, and the storm did cease, and there was a great calm.

Equipped with their compass, these ancients appear to have had the advantage of Noah.

Their voyage was toward a "promised land"—the only name they give it. They reached it in safety.

Polygamy is a recent feature in the Mormon religion, and was added by Brigham Young after Joseph Smith's death. Before that, it was regarded as an "abomination." This verse from the Mormon Bible occurs in Chapter II of the book of Jacob:

> For behold, thus saith the Lord, this people begin to wax in iniquity; they understand not the Scriptures; for they seek to excuse themselves in committing whoredoms, because of the things which were written concerning David, and Solomon his son. Behold, David and Solomon truly had many wives and concubines, which thing was abominable before me, saith the Lord; wherefore, thus saith the Lord, I have led this people forth out of the land of Jerusalem, by the power of mine arm, that I might raise up unto me a righteous branch from the fruit of the loins of Joseph. Wherefore, I the Lord God, will not suffer that this people shall do like unto them of old.

However, the project failed—or at least the modern Mormon end of it—for Brigham "suffers" it. This verse is from the same chapter:

> Behold, the Lamanites your brethren, whom ye hate, because of their filthiness and the cursings which hath come upon their skins, are more righteous than you; for they have not forgotten the commandment of the Lord, which was given unto our fathers, that they should have, save it were one wife; and concubines they should have none.

The following verse (from Chapter IX of the Book of Nephi) appears to contain information not familiar to everybody:

> And now it came to pass that when Jesus had ascended into heaven, the multitude did disperse, and every man did take his wife and his children, and did return to his own home.
>
> And it came to pass that on the morrow, when the multitude was gathered together, behold, Nephi and his brother whom he had raised from the dead, whose name was Timothy, and also his son, whose name was Jonas, and also Mathoni, and Mathonihah, his brother, and Kumen, and Kumenonhi, and Jeremiah, and Shemnon, and Jonas, and Zedekiah,

and Isaiah; now these were the names of the disciples whom Jesus had chosen.

In order that the reader may observe how much more grandeur and picturesqueness (as seen by these Mormon twelve) accompanied one of the tenderest episodes in the life of our Saviour than other eyes seem to have been aware of, I quote the following from the same "book"—Nephi:

> And it came to pass that Jesus spake unto them, and bade them arise. And they arose from the earth, and He said unto them, Blessed are ye because of your faith. And now behold, My joy is full. And when He had said these words, He wept, and the multitude bear record of it, and He took their little children, one by one, and blessed them, and prayed unto the Father for them. And when He had done this He wept again, and He spake unto the multitude, and saith unto them, Behold your little ones. And as they looked to behold, they cast their eyes toward heaven, and they saw the heavens open, and they saw angels descending out of heaven as it were, in the midst of fire; and they came down and encircled those little ones about, and they were encircled about with fire; and the angels did minister unto them, and the multitude did see and hear and bear record; and they know that their record is true, for they all of them did see and hear, every man for himself; and they were in number about two thousand and five hundred souls; and they did consist of men, women, and children.

And what else would they be likely to consist of?

The Book of Ether is an incomprehensible medley of "history," much of it relating to battles and sieges among peoples whom the reader has possibly never heard of; and who inhabited a country which is not set down in the geography. There was a king with the remarkable name of Coriantumr, and he warred with Shared, and Lib, and Shiz, and others, in the "plains of Heshlon"; and the "valley of Gilgal"; and the "wilderness of Akish"; and the "land of Moran"; and the "plains of Agosh"; and "Ogath," and "Ramah," and the "land of Corihor," and the "hill Comnor," by "the waters of Ripliancum," etc., etc., etc. "And it came to pass," after a deal of fighting, that Coriantumr, upon making calculation of his losses, found that "there had been slain two millions of mighty men, and also their wives and their children"—say 5,000,000 or 6,000,000 in all—"and he began to sorrow in his heart." Unquestionably it was time. So he wrote to Shiz, asking a cessation of hostilities, and offering to give up his kingdom to save his people. Shiz declined, except upon condition that Coriantumr would come and let him cut his head off first—a thing which Coriantumr would not do. Then there was more fighting for a season; then *four years* were devoted to gathering the forces for a final struggle—after which ensued a battle which, I take it, is the most remarkable set forth in history,—except, perhaps, that of the Kilkenny cats, which it resembles in some respects. This is the account of the gathering and the battle:

> 7. And it came to pass that they did gather together all the people, upon all the face of the land, who had not been slain, save it was Ether. And it came to pass that Ether did behold all the doings of the people;

and he beheld that the people who were for Coriantumr, were gathered together to the army of Coriantumr; and the people who were for Shiz, were gathered together to the army of Shiz; wherefore they were for the space of four years gathering together the people, that they might get all who were upon the face of the land, and that they might receive all the strength which it was possible that they could receive. And it came to pass that when they were all gathered together, every one to the army which he would, with their wives and their children; both men, women, and children being armed with weapons of war, having shields, and breast-plates, and head-plates, and being clothed after the manner of war, they did march forth one against another, to battle; and they fought all that day, and conquered not. And it came to pass that when it was night they were weary, and retired to their camps; and after they had retired to their camps, they took up a howling and a lamentation for the loss of the slain of their people; and so great were their cries, their howling and lamentations, that it did rend the air exceedingly. And it came to pass that on the morrow they did go again to battle, and great and terrible was that day; nevertheless they conquered not, and when the night came again, they did rend the air with their cries, and their howlings, and their mournings, for the loss of the slain of their people.

8. And it came to pass that Coriantumr wrote again an epistle unto Shiz, desiring that he would not come again to battle, but that he would take the kingdom, and spare the lives of the people. But behold, the Spirit of the Lord had ceased striving with them, and Satan had full power over the hearts of the people, for they were given up unto the hardness of their hearts, and the blindness of their minds that they might be destroyed; wherefore they went again to battle. And it came to pass that they fought all that day, and when the night came they slept upon their swords; and on the morrow they fought even until the night came; and when the night came they were drunken with anger, even as a man who is drunken with wine; and they slept again upon their swords; and on the morrow they fought again; and when the night came they had all fallen by the sword save it were fifty and two of the people of Coriantumr, and sixty and nine of the people of Shiz. And it came to pass that they slept upon their swords that night, and on the morrow they fought again, and they contended in their mights with their swords, and with their shields, all that day; and when the night came there were thirty and two of the people of Shiz, and twenty and seven of the people of Coriantumr.

9. And it came to pass that they ate and slept, and prepared for death on the morrow. And they were large and mighty men, as to the strength of men. And it came to pass that they fought for the space of three hours, and they fainted with the loss of blood. And it came to pass that when the men of Coriantumr had received sufficient strength, that they could walk, they were about to flee for their lives, but behold, Shiz arose, and also his men, and he swore in his wrath that he would slay Coriantumr, or he would perish by the sword: wherefore he did pursue them, and on the morrow he did overtake them; and they fought again with the sword. And it came to pass that when they had all fallen by the sword, save it were Coriantumr and Shiz, behold Shiz had fainted with loss of blood. And it came to pass that when Coriantumr had leaned upon his sword,

that he rested a little, he smote off the head of Shiz. And it came to pass that after he had smote off the head of Shiz, that Shiz raised upon his hands and fell; and after that he had struggled for breath, he died. And it came to pass that Coriantumr fell to the earth, and became as if he had no life. And the Lord spake unto Ether, and said unto him, go forth. And he went forth, and beheld that the words of the Lord had all been fulfilled; and he finished his record; and the hundredth part I have not written.

It seems a pity he did not finish, for after all his dreary former chapters of commonplace, he stopped just as he was in danger of becoming interesting.

The Mormon Bible is rather stupid and tiresome to read, but there is nothing vicious in its teachings. Its code of morals is unobjectionable—it is "smouched" * from the New Testament and no credit given.

Chapter XVII

AT THE END of our two days' sojourn, we left Great Salt Lake City hearty and well fed and happy—physically superb but not so very much wiser, as regards the "Mormon question," than we were when we arrived, perhaps. We had a deal more "information" than we had before, of course, but we did not know what portion of it was reliable and what was not—for it all came from acquaintances of a day—strangers, strictly speaking. We were told, for instance, that the dreadful "Mountain Meadows Massacre" was the work of the Indians entirely, and that the Gentiles had meanly tried to fasten it upon the Mormons; we were told, likewise, that the Indians were to blame, partly, and partly the Mormons; and we were told, likewise, and just as positively, that the Mormons were almost if not wholly and completely responsible for that most treacherous and pitiless butchery. We got the story in all these different shapes, but it was not till several years afterward that Mrs. Waite's book, "The Mormon Prophet," came out with Judge Cradlebaugh's trial of the accused parties in it and revealed the truth that the latter version was the correct one and that the Mormons *were* the assassins. All our "information" had three sides to it, and so I gave up the idea that I could settle the "Mormon question" in two days. Still, I have seen newspaper correspondents do it in one.

I left Great Salt Lake a good deal confused as to what state of things existed there—and sometimes even questioning in my own mind whether a state of things existed there at all or not. But presently I remembered with a lightening sense of relief that we had learned two or three trivial things there which we could be certain of; and so the two days were not wholly lost. For instance, we had learned that we were at last in a pioneer land, in absolute and tangible reality. The high prices charged for trifles were eloquent of high freights and bewildering distances of freightage. In the east, in those days, the smallest moneyed denomination was a penny, and it represented the smallest purchasable quantity of any

---

*Milton.

THREE SIDES TO A QUESTION.

commodity. West of Cincinnati the smallest coin in use was the silver five-cent piece and no smaller quantity of an article could be bought than "five cents' worth." In Overland City the lowest coin appeared to be the ten-cent piece; but in Salt Lake there did not seem to be any money in circulation smaller than a quarter, or any smaller quantity purchasable of any commodity than twenty-five cents' worth. We had always been used to half dimes and "five cents' worth" as the minimum of financial negotiations; but in Salt Lake if one wanted a cigar, it was a quarter; if he wanted a chalk pipe, it was a quarter; if he wanted a peach, or a candle, or a newspaper, or a shave, or a little Gentile whiskey to rub on his corns to arrest indigestion and keep him from having the toothache, twenty-five cents was the price, every time. When we looked at the shot-bag of silver, now and then, we seemed to be wasting our substance in riotous living, but if we referred to the expense account we could see that we had not been doing anything of the kind. But people easily get reconciled to big money and big prices, and fond and vain of both—it is a descent to little coins and cheap prices that is hardest to bear and slowest to take hold upon one's toleration. After a month's acquaintance with the twenty-five-cent minimum, the average human being is ready to blush every time he thinks of his despicable five-cent days. How sunburned with blushes I used to get in gaudy Nevada, every time I thought of my first financial experience in Salt Lake. It was on this wise (which is a favorite expression of great authors, and a very neat one, too, but I never hear anybody *say* on this wise when they are talking). A young half-breed with a complexion like a yellow-jacket asked me if I would have my boots blacked. It was at the Salt Lake House the morning after we arrived. I said yes, and he blacked them. Then I handed him a silver five-cent piece, with the benevolent air of a person who is conferring wealth and blessedness upon poverty and suffering. The yellow-jacket took it with what I judged to be suppressed emotion, and laid it reverently down in the middle of his broad hand. Then he began to contemplate it, much as a philosopher contemplates a gnat's ear in the ample field of his microscope. Several mountaineers, teamsters, stage-drivers, etc., drew near and dropped into the tableau and fell to surveying the money with that attractive indifference to formality which is noticeable in the hardy pioneer. Presently the yellow-jacket handed the half dime back to me and told me I ought to keep my money in my pocket-book instead of in my soul, and then I wouldn't get it cramped and shriveled up so!

What a roar of vulgar laughter there was! I destroyed the mongrel reptile on the spot, but I smiled and smiled all the time I was detaching his scalp, for the remark he made *was* good for an "Injun."

Yes, we had learned in Salt Lake to be charged great prices without letting the inward shudder appear on the surface—for even already we had overheard and noted the tenor of conversations among drivers, conductors, and hostlers, and finally among citizens of Salt Lake, until we were well aware that these superior beings despised "emigrants." We permitted no tell-tale shudders and winces in our countenances, for we wanted to seem pioneers, or Mormons, half-breeds, teamsters, stage-drivers, Mountain Meadow assassins—anything in the world that the plains and Utah respected and admired—but we were wretchedly ashamed of being "emigrants," and sorry enough that we had white shirts and could not swear in the presence of ladies without looking the other way.

And many a time in Nevada, afterward, we had occasion to remember with humiliation that we were "emigrants," and consequently a low and inferior sort of creatures. Perhaps the reader has visited Utah, Nevada, or California, even in these latter days, and while communing with himself upon the sorrowful banishment of those countries from what he considers "the world," has had his wings clipped by finding that *he* is the one to be pitied, and that there are entire populations around him ready and willing to do it for him—yea, who are complacently doing it for him already, wherever he steps his foot. Poor thing, they are making fun of his hat; and the cut of his New York coat; and his conscientiousness about his grammar; and his feeble profanity; and his consumingly ludicrous ignorance of ores, shafts, tunnels, and other things which he never saw before, and never felt enough interest in to read about. And all the time that he is thinking what a sad fate it is to be exiled to that far country, that lonely land, the citizens around him are looking down on him with a blighting compassion because he is an "emigrant" instead of that proudest and blessedest creature that exists on all the earth, a "FORTY-NINER."

The accustomed coach life began again, now, and by midnight it almost seemed as if we never had been out of our snuggery among the mail sacks at all. We had made one alteration, however. We had provided enough bread, boiled ham, and hard-boiled eggs to last double the six hundred miles of staging we had still to do.

And it was comfort in those succeeding days to sit up and contemplate the majestic panorama of mountains and valleys spread out below us and eat ham and hard boiled eggs while our spiritual natures revelled alternately in rainbows, thunderstorms, and peerless sunsets. Nothing helps scenery like ham and eggs. Ham and eggs, and after these a pipe—an old, rank, delicious pipe—ham and eggs and scenery, a "down grade," a flying coach, a fragrant pipe and a contented heart—these make happiness. It is what all the ages have struggled for.

Chapter XVIII

AT EIGHT IN the morning we reached the remnant and ruin of what had been the important military station of "Camp Floyd," some forty-five or fifty miles from Salt Lake City. At four P.M. we had doubled our distance and were ninety or a hundred miles from Salt Lake. And now we entered upon one of that species of deserts whose concentrated hideousness shames the diffused and diluted horrors of Sahara—an *"alkali"* desert. For sixty-eight miles there was but one break in it. I do not remember that this was really a break; indeed it seems to me that it was nothing but a watering depot *in the midst* of the stretch of sixty-eight miles. If my memory serves me, there was no well or spring at this place, but the water was hauled there by mule and ox teams from the farther side of the desert. There was a stage station there. It was forty-five miles from the beginning of the desert, and twenty-three from the end of it.

We plowed and dragged and groped along, the whole live-long night, and at the end of this uncomfortable twelve hours we finished the forty-five-mile part of the desert and got to the stage station where the imported water was. The sun was just rising. It was easy enough to cross a desert in the night while we were asleep; and it was pleasant to reflect, in the morning, that we in actual person *had* encountered an absolute desert and could always speak knowingly of deserts in presence of the ignorant thenceforward. And it was pleasant also to reflect that this was not an obscure, back country desert, but a very celebrated one, the metropolis itself, as you may say. All this was very well and very comfortable and satisfactory—but now we were to cross a desert in *daylight*. This was fine—novel—romantic—dramatically adventurous—*this*, indeed, was worth living for, worth traveling for! We would write home all about it.

This enthusiasm, this stern thirst for adventure, wilted under the sultry August sun and did not last above one hour. One poor little hour—and then we were ashamed that we had "gushed" so. The poetry was all in the anticipation—there is none in the reality. Imagine a vast, waveless ocean stricken dead and turned to ashes; imagine this solemn waste tufted with ash-dusted sage-bushes; imagine the lifeless silence and solitude that belong to such a place; imagine a coach, creeping like a bug through the midst of this shoreless level, and sending up tumbled volumes of dust as if it were a bug that went by steam; imagine this aching monotony of tolling and plowing kept up hour after hour, and the shore still as far away as ever, apparently; imagine team, driver, coach, and passengers so deeply coated with ashes that they are all one colorless color; imagine ash-drifts roosting above moustaches and eyebrows like snow accumulations on boughs and bushes. This is the reality of it.

The sun beats down with dead, blistering, relentless malignity; the perspiration is welling from every pore in man and beast, but scarcely a sign of it finds its way to the surface—it is absorbed before it gets there; there is not the faintest breath of air stirring; there is not a merciful shred of cloud in all the brilliant firmament; there is not a living creature visible in any direction whither one searches the blank level that stretches its monotonous miles on every hand; there is not a sound—not a sigh—not a whisper—not a buzz, or a whir of wings, or distant pipe of bird—not even a sob from the lost souls that doubtless people that dead air. And so the occasional sneezing of the resting mules, and the champing of the bits, grate harshly on the grim stillness, not dissipating the spell but accenting it and making one feel more lonesome and forsaken than before.

The mules, under violent swearing, coaxing, and whip-cracking, would make at stated intervals a "spurt," and drag the coach a hundred or maybe two hundred yards, stirring up a billowy cloud of dust that rolled back, enveloping the vehicle to the wheel-tops or higher, and making it seem afloat in a fog. Then a rest followed, with the usual sneezing and bit-champing. Then another "spurt" of a hundred yards and another rest at the end of it. All day long we kept this up, without water for the mules and without ever changing the team. At least we kept it up ten hours, which, I take it, is a day, and a pretty honest one, in an alkali desert. It was from four in the morning till two in the afternoon. And it was so hot! and so close! and our water canteens went dry in the middle of the day and we got so thirsty! It was so stupid and tiresome and dull! and the tedious hours did lag and drag and limp along with such a cruel deliberation! It was so trying to give one's watch a good long undisturbed spell and then take it out and find that it had been fooling away the time and not trying to get ahead any! The alkali dust cut through our lips, it persecuted our eyes, it ate through the delicate membranes and made our noses bleed and *kept* them bleeding—and truly and seriously the romance all faded far away and disappeared, and left the desert trip nothing but a harsh reality—a thirsty, sweltering, longing, hateful reality!

Two miles and a quarter an hour for ten hours—that was what we accomplished. It was hard to bring the comprehension away down to such a snail-pace as that, when we had been used to making eight and ten miles an hour. When we reached the station on the farther verge of the desert, we were glad, for the first time, that the dictionary was along, because we never could have found language to tell how glad we were, in any sort of dictionary but an unabridged one with pictures in it. But there could not have been found in a whole library of dictionaries language sufficient to tell how tired those mules were after their twenty-three mile pull. To try to give the reader an idea of how *thirsty* they were, would be to "gild refined gold or paint the lily."

Somehow, now that it is there, the quotation does not seem to fit—but no matter, let it stay, anyhow. I think it is a graceful and attractive thing, and therefore have tried time and time again to work it in where it *would* fit, but could not succeed. These efforts have kept my mind distracted and ill at ease, and made my narrative seem broken and disjointed, in places. Under these circumstances it seems to me best to leave it in, as above, since this will afford at least a temporary respite from the wear and tear of trying to "lead up" to this really apt and beautiful quotation.

Chapter XIX

ON THE MORNING of the sixteenth day out from St. Joseph we arrived at the entrance of Rocky Canyon, two hundred and fifty miles from Salt Lake. It was along in this wild country somewhere, and far from any habitation of white men, except the stage stations, that we came across the wretchedest type of mankind

I have ever seen, up to this writing. I refer to the Goshoot Indians. From what we could see and all we could learn, they are very considerably inferior to even the despised Digger Indians of California; inferior to all races of savages on our continent; inferior to even the Tierra del Fuegans; inferior to the Hottentots, and actually inferior in some respects to the Kytches of Africa. Indeed, I have been obliged to look the bulky volumes of Wood's "Uncivilized Races of Men" clear through in order to find a savage tribe degraded enough to take rank with the Goshoots. I find but one people fairly open to that shameful verdict. It is the Bosjesmans (Bushmen) of South Africa. Such of the Goshoots as we saw, along the road and hanging about the stations, were small, lean, "scrawny" creatures; in complexion a dull black like the ordinary American Negro; their faces and hands bearing dirt which they had been hoarding and accumulating for months, years, and even generations, according to the age of the proprietor; a silent, sneaking, treacherous looking race; taking note of everything, covertly, like all the other "Noble Red Men" that we (do not) read about, and betraying no sign in their countenances: indolent, everlastingly patient and tireless, like all other Indians; prideless beggars—for if the beggar instinct were left out of an Indian he would not "go," any more than a clock without a pendulum; hungry, always hungry, and yet never refusing anything that a hog would eat, though often eating what a hog would decline; hunters, but having no higher ambition than to kill and eat jackass rabbits, crickets, and grasshoppers, and embezzle carrion from the buzzards and cayotes; savages who, when asked if they have the common Indian belief in a Great Spirit show a something which almost amounts to emotion, thinking whiskey is referred to; a thin, scattering race of almost naked black children, these Goshoots are, who produce nothing at all, and have no villages, and no gatherings together into strictly defined tribal communities— a people whose only shelter is a rag cast on a bush to keep off a portion of the snow, and yet who inhabit one of the most rocky, wintry, repulsive wastes that our country or any other can exhibit.

The Bushmen and our Goshoots are manifestly descended from the self-same gorilla, or kangaroo, or Norway rat, whichever animal-Adam the Darwinians trace them to.

One would as soon expect the rabbits to fight as the Goshoots and yet they

GOSHOOT INDIANS HANGING AROUND STATIONS.

used to live off the offal and refuse of the stations a few months and then come some dark night when no mischief was expected, and burn down the buildings and kill the men from ambush as they rushed out. And once, in the night, they attacked the stage-coach when a District Judge, of Nevada Territory, was the only passenger, and with their first volley of arrows (and a bullet or two) they riddled the stage curtains, wounded a horse or two and mortally wounded the driver. The latter was full of pluck, and so was his passenger. At the driver's call Judge Mott swung himself out, clambered to the box and seized the reins of the team, and away they plunged, through the racing mob of skeletons and under a hurtling storm of missiles. The stricken driver had sunk down on the boot as soon as he was wounded, but had held onto the reins and said he would manage to keep hold of them until relieved. And after they were taken from his relaxing grasp, he lay with his head between Judge Mott's feet, and tranquilly gave directions about the road; he said he believed he could live till the miscreants were out-run and left behind, and that if he managed that, the main difficulty would be at an end, and then if the Judge drove so and so (giving directions about bad places in the road, and general course) he would reach the next station without trouble. The Judge distanced the enemy and at last rattled up to the station and knew that the night's perils were done; but there was no comrade-in-arms for him to rejoice with, for the soldierly driver was dead.

Let us forget that we have been saying harsh things about the Overland drivers, now. The disgust which the Goshoots gave me, a disciple of Cooper and a worshiper of the Red Man—even of the scholarly savages in "The Last of the Mohicans" who are fittingly associated with backswoodsmen who divide each sentence into two equal parts: one part critically grammatical, refined and choice of language, and the other part just such an attempt to talk like a hunter or a mountaineer, as a Broadway clerk might make after eating an edition of Emerson Bennett's works and studying frontier life at the Bowery Theatre a couple of weeks—I say that the nausea which the Goshoots gave me, an Indian worshiper, set me to examining authorities, to see if perchance I had been overestimating the Red Man while viewing him through the mellow moonshine of romance. The revelations that came were disenchanting. It was curious to see how quickly the paint and tinsel fell away from him and left him treacherous, filthy and repulsive—and how quickly the evidence accumulated that wherever one finds an Indian tribe he has only found Goshoots more or less modified by circumstances and surroundings—but Goshoots, after all. They deserve pity, poor creatures; and they can have mine—at this distance. Nearer by, they never get anybody's.

There is an impression abroad that the Baltimore and Washington Railroad Company and many of its employés are Goshoots; but it is an error. There is only a plausible resemblance, which, while it is apt enough to mislead the ignorant, cannot deceive parties who have contemplated both tribes. But seriously, it was not only poor wit, but very wrong to start the report referred to above; for however innocent the motive may have been, the necessary effect was to injure the reputation of a class who have a hard enough time of it in the pitiless deserts of the Rocky Mountains, Heaven knows! If we cannot find it in our hearts to give those poor naked creatures our Christian sympathy and compassion, in God's name let us at least not throw mud at them.

Chapter XX

ON THE SEVENTEENTH day we passed the highest mountain peaks we had yet seen, and although the day was very warm the night that followed upon its heels was wintry cold and blankets were next to useless.

On the eighteenth day we encountered the eastward-bound telegraph-constructors at Reese River station and sent a message to His Excellency Gov. Nye at Carson City (distant one hundred and fifty-six miles).

On the nineteenth day we crossed the Great American Desert—forty memorable miles of bottomless sand, into which the coach wheels sunk from six inches to a foot. We worked our passage most of the way across. That is to say, we got out and walked. It was a dreary pull and a long and thirsty one, for we had no water. From one extremity of this desert to the other, the road was white with the bones of oxen and horses. It would hardly be an exaggeration to say that we could have walked the forty miles and set our feet on a bone at every step! The desert was one prodigious graveyard. And the log-chains, wagon tyres, and rotting wrecks of vehicles were almost as thick as the bones. I think we saw log-chains enough rusting there in the desert, to reach across any state in the Union. Do not these relics suggest something of an idea of the fearful suffering and privation the early emigrants to California endured?

At the border of the Desert lies Carson Lake, or The "Sink" of the Carson, a shallow, melancholy sheet of water some eighty or a hundred miles in circumference. Carson River empties into it and is lost—sinks mysteriously into the earth and never appears in the light of the sun again—for the lake has no outlet whatever.

There are several rivers in Nevada, and they all have this mysterious fate. They end in various lakes or "sinks," and that is the last of them. Carson Lake, Humboldt Lake, Walker Lake, Mono Lake, are all great sheets of water without any visible outlet. Water is always flowing into them; none is ever seen to flow out of them, and yet they remain always level full, neither receding nor overflowing. What they do with their surplus is known only to the Creator.

On the western verge of the Desert we halted a moment at Ragtown. It consisted of one log-house and is not set down on the map.

This reminds me of a circumstance. Just after we left Julesburg, on the Platte, I was sitting with the driver, and he said:

"I can tell you a most laughable thing indeed, if you would like to listen to it. Horace Greeley went over this road once. When he was leaving Carson City he told the driver, Hank Monk, that he had an engagement to lecture at Placerville and was very anxious to go through quick. Hank Monk cracked his whip and started off at an awful pace. The coach bounced up and down in such a terrific way that it jolted the buttons all off of Horace's coat, and finally shot his head clean through the roof of the stage, and then he yelled at Hank Monk and begged him to go easier—said he warn't in as much of a hurry as he was awhile ago. But Hank Monk said, 'Keep your seat, Horace, and I'll get you there on time'— and you bet you he did, too, what was left of him!"

A day or two after that we picked up a Denver man at the cross roads, and he told us a good deal about the country and the Gregory Diggings. He seemed

756

a very entertaining person and a man well posted in the affairs of Colorado. By and by he remarked:

"I can tell you a most laughable thing indeed, if you would like to listen to it. Horace Greeley went over this road once. When he was leaving Carson City he told the driver, Hank Monk, that he had an engagement to lecture at Placerville and was very anxious to go through quick. Hank Monk cracked his whip and started off at an awful pace. The coach bounced up and down in such a terrific way that it jolted the buttons all off of Horace's coat, and finally shot his head clean through the roof of the stage, and then he yelled at Hank Monk and begged him to go easier—said he warn't in as much of a hurry as he was a while ago. But Hank Monk said, 'Keep your seat, Horace, and I'll get you there on time!'— and you bet you he did, too, what was left of him!''

At Fort Bridger, some days after this, we took on board a cavalry sergeant, a very proper and soldierly person indeed. From no other man during the whole journey, did we gather such a store of concise and well-arranged military information. It was surprising to find in the desolate wilds of our country a man so thoroughly acquainted with everything useful to know in his line of life, and yet of such inferior rank and unpretentious bearing. For as much as three hours we listened to him with unabated interest. Finally he got upon the subject of trans-continental travel, and presently said:

"I can tell you a very laughable thing indeed, if you would like to listen to it. Horace Greeley went over this road once. When he was leaving Carson City he told the driver, Hank Monk, that he had an engagement to lecture at Placerville and was very anxious to go through quick. Hank Monk cracked his whip and started off at an awful pace. The coach bounced up and down in such a terrific way that it jolted the buttons all off of Horace's coat, and finally shot his head clean through the roof of the stage, and then he yelled at Hank Monk and begged him to go easier—said he warn't in as much of a hurry as he was a while ago. But Hank Monk said, 'Keep your seat, Horace, and I'll get you there on time!'— and you bet you he did, too, what was left of him!''

When we were eight hours out from Salt Lake City a Mormon preacher got in with us at a way station—a gentle, soft-spoken, kindly man, and one whom any stranger would warm to at first sight. I can never forget the pathos that was in his voice as he told, in simple language, the story of his people's wanderings and unpitied sufferings. No pulpit eloquence was ever so moving and so beautiful as this outcast's picture of the first Mormon pilgrimage across the plains, struggling sorrowfully onward to the land of its banishment and marking its desolate way with graves and watering it with tears. His words so wrought upon us that it was a relief to us all when the conversation drifted into a more cheerful channel and the natural features of the curious country we were in came under treatment. One matter after another was pleasantly discussed, and at length the stranger said:

"I can tell you a most laughable thing indeed, if you would like to listen to it. Horace Greeley went over this road once. When he was leaving Carson City he told the driver, Hank Monk, that he had an engagement to lecture in Placerville, and was very anxious to go through quick. Hank Monk cracked his whip and started off at an awful pace. The coach bounced up and down in such a terrific way that it jolted the buttons all off of Horace's coat, and finally shot his head clean through the roof of the stage, and then he yelled at Hank Monk and begged him to go easier—said he warn't in as much of a hurry as he was a while ago.

But Hank Monk said, 'Keep your seat, Horace, and I'll get you there on time!'—
and you bet you he did, too, what was left of him!''

Ten miles out of Ragtown we found a poor wanderer who had lain down to
die. He had walked as long as he could, but his limbs had failed him at last.
Hunger and fatigue had conquered him. It would have been inhuman to leave
him there. We paid his fare to Carson and lifted him into the coach. It was some
little time before he showed any very decided signs of life; but by dint of chafing
him and pouring brandy between his lips we finally brought him to a languid
consciousness. Then we fed him a little, and by and by he seemed to comprehend
the situation and a grateful light softened his eye. We made his mail-sack bed
as comfortable as possible, and constructed a pillow for him with our coats. He
seemed very thankful. Then he looked up in our faces, and said in a feeble voice
that had a tremble of honest emotion in it:

''Gentlemen, I know not who you are, but you have saved my life; and although
I can never be able to repay you for it, I feel that I can at least make one hour
of your long journey lighter. I take it you are strangers to this great thoroughfare,
but I am entirely familiar with it. In this connection I can tell you a most laughable
thing indeed, if you would like to listen to it. Horace Greeley—''

I said, impressively:

''Suffering stranger, proceed at your peril. You see in me the melancholy
wreck of a once stalwart and magnificent manhood. What has brought me to
this? That thing which you are about to tell. Gradually but surely, that tiresome
old anecdote has sapped my strength, undermined my constitution, withered my
life. Pity my helplessness. Spare me only just this once, and tell me about young
George Washington and his little hatchet for a change.''

We were saved. But not so the invalid. In trying to retain the anecdote in his
system he strained himself and died in our arms.

I am aware, now, that I ought not to have asked of the sturdiest citizen of all
that region, what I asked of that mere shadow of a man; for, after seven years'
residence on the Pacific coast, I know that no passenger or driver on the Overland
ever corked that anecdote in, when a stranger was by, and survived. Within a
period of six years I crossed and recrossed the Sierras between Nevada and
California thirteen times by stage and listened to that deathless incident four
hundred and eighty-one or eighty-two times. I have the list somewhere. Drivers
always told it, conductors told it, landlords told it, chance passengers told it,
the very Chinamen and vagrant Indians recounted it. I have had the same driver
tell it to me two or three times in the same afternoon. It has come to me in all
the multitude of tongues that Babel bequeathed to earth, and flavored with
whiskey, brandy, beer, cologne, sozodont, tobacco, garlic, onions, grasshoppers—
everything that has a fragrance to it through all the long list of things that are
gorged or guzzled by the sons of men. I never have smelled any anecdote as
often as I have smelled that one; never have smelled any anecdote that smelled
so variegated as that one. And you never could learn to know it by its smell,
because every time you thought you had learned the smell of it, it would turn
up with a different smell. Bayard Taylor has written about this hoary anecdote,
Richardson has published it; so have Jones, Smith, Johnson, Ross Browne, and
every other correspondence-inditing being that ever set his foot upon the great
overland road anywhere between Julesburg and San Francisco; and I have heard
that it is in the Talmud. I have seen it in print in nine different foreign languages;
I have been told that it is employed in the inquisition in Rome; and I now learn

with regret that it is going to be set to music. I do not think that such things are right.

Stage-coaching on the Overland is no more, and stage-drivers are a race defunct. I wonder if they bequeathed that bald-headed anecdote to their successors, the railroad brake-men and conductors, and if these latter still persecute the helpless passenger with it until he concludes, as did many a tourist of other days, that the real grandeurs of the Pacific coast are not Yo Semite and the Big Trees, but Hank Monk and his adventure with Horace Greeley.*

Chapter XXI

WE WERE APPROACHING the end of our long journey. It was the morning of the twentieth day. At noon we would reach Carson City, the capital of Nevada Territory. We were not glad, but sorry. It had been a fine pleasure trip; we had fed fat on wonders every day; and we were now well accustomed to stage life, and very fond of it; so the idea of coming to a stand-still and settling down to a humdrum existence in a village was not agreeable, but on the contrary depressing.

Visibly our new home was a desert, walled in by barren, snow-clad mountains. There was not a tree in sight. There was no vegetation but the endless sage-brush and greasewood. All nature was gray with it. We were plowing through great deeps of powdery alkali dust that rose in thick clouds and floated across the plain like smoke from a burning house. We were coated with it like millers; so were the coach, the mules, the mail-bags, the driver—we and the sage-brush and the other scenery were all one monotonous color. Long trains of freight wagons in the distance enveloped in ascending masses of dust suggested pictures of prairies on fire. These teams and their masters were the only life we saw. Otherwise we moved in the midst of solitude, silence and desolation. Every twenty steps we passed the skeleton of some dead beast of burden, with its dust-coated skin stretched tightly over its empty ribs. Frequently a solemn raven sat upon the skull or the hips and contemplated the passing coach with meditative serenity.

By and by Carson City was pointed out to us. It nestled in the edge of a great plain and was a sufficient number of miles away to look like an assemblage of mere white spots in the shadow of a grim range of mountains overlooking it, whose summits seemed lifted clear out of companionship and consciousness of earthly things.

We arrived, disembarked, and the stage went on. It was a "wooden" town; its population two thousand souls. The main street consisted of four or five blocks of little white frame stores which were too high to sit down on, but not

---

* And what makes that worn anecdote the more aggravating is, that the adventure it celebrates *never occurred*. If it were a good anecdote, that seeming demerit would be its chiefest virtue, for creative power belongs to greatness; but what ought to be done to a man who would wantonly contrive so flat a one as this? If *I* were to suggest what ought to be done to him, I should be called extravagant—but what does the sixteenth chapter of Daniel say? Aha!

too high for various other purposes; in fact, hardly high enough. They were packed close together, side by side, as if room were scarce in that mighty plain. The sidewalk was of boards that were more or less loose and inclined to rattle when walked upon. In the middle of the town, opposite the stores, was the "plaza" which is native to all towns beyond the Rocky Mountains—a large, unfenced, level vacancy, with a liberty pole in it, and very useful as a place for public auctions, horse trades, and mass meetings, and likewise for teamsters to camp in. Two other sides of the plaza were faced by stores, offices, and stables. The rest of Carson City was pretty scattering.

We were introduced to several citizens, at the stage-office and on the way up to the Governor's from the hotel—among others, to a Mr. Harris, who was on horseback; he began to say something, but interrupted himself with the remark:

"I'll have to get you to excuse me a minute; yonder is the witness that swore I helped to rob the California coach—a piece of impertinent intermeddling, sir, for I am not even acquainted with the man."

Then he rode over and began to rebuke the stranger with a six-shooter, and the stranger began to explain with another. When the pistols were emptied, the stranger resumed his work (mending a whip-lash), and Mr. Harris rode by with a polite nod, homeward bound, with a bullet through one of his lungs, and several in his hips; and from them issued little rivulets of blood that coursed down the horse's sides and made the animal look quite picturesque. I never saw Harris shoot a man after that but it recalled to mind that first day in Carson.

This was all we saw that day, for it was two o'clock, now, and according to custom the daily "Washoe Zephyr" set in; a soaring dust-drift about the size of the United States set up edgewise came with it, and the capital of Nevada Territory disappeared from view. Still, there were sights to be seen which were not wholly uninteresting to new comers; for the vast dust cloud was thickly freckled with things strange to the upper air—things living and dead, that flitted hither and thither, going and coming, appearing and disappearing among the rolling billows of dust—hats, chickens and parasols sailing in the remote heavens; blankets, tin signs, sage-brush and shingles a shade lower; door-mats and buffalo robes lower still; shovels and coal scuttles on the next grade; glass doors, cats and little children on the next; disrupted lumber yards, light buggies, and wheelbarrows on the next; and down only thirty or forty feet above ground was a scurrying storm of emigrating roofs and vacant lots.

It was something to see that much. I could have seen more, if I could have kept the dust out of my eyes.

But seriously a Washoe wind is by no means a trifling matter. It blows flimsy houses down, lifts shingle roofs occasionally, rolls up tin ones like sheet music, now and then blows a stage-coach over and spills the passengers; and tradition says the reason there are so many bald people there, is, that the wind blows the hair off their heads while they are looking skyward after their hats. Carson streets seldom look inactive on summer afternoons, because there are so many citizens skipping around their escaping hats, like chambermaids trying to head off a spider.

The "Washoe Zephyr" (Washoe is a pet nickname for Nevada) is a peculiarly Scriptural wind, in that no man knoweth "whence it cometh." That is to say, where it *originates*. It comes right over the mountains from the West, but when one crosses the ridge he does not find any of it on the other side! It probably is manufactured on the mountain-top for the occasion, and starts from there. It is a pretty regular wind, in the summer time. Its office hours are from two in the afternoon till two the next morning; and anybody venturing abroad during those twelve hours needs to allow for the wind or he will bring up a mile or two to leeward of the point he is aiming at. And yet the first complaint a Washoe visitor to San Francisco makes, is that the sea winds blow so, there! There is a good deal of human nature in that.

We found the state palace of the Governor of Nevada Territory to consist of a white frame one-story house with two small rooms in it and a stanchion-supported shed in front—for grandeur—it compelled the respect of the citizen and inspired the Indians with awe. The newly arrived Chief and Associate Justices of the Territory, and other machinery of the government, were domiciled with less splendor. They were boarding around privately, and had their offices in their bedrooms.

The Secretary and I took quarters in the "ranch" of a worthy French lady by the name of Bridget O'Flannigan, a camp follower of his Excellency the Governor. She had known him in his prosperity as commander-in-chief of the Metropolitan Police of New York, and she would not desert him in his adversity as Governor of Nevada. Our room was on the lower floor, facing the plaza, and when we had got our bed, a small table, two chairs, the government fire-proof safe, and the Unabridged Dictionary into it, there was still room enough left for a visitor—may be two, but not without straining the walls. But the walls could stand it—at least the partitions could, for they consisted simply of one thickness of white "cotton domestic" stretched from corner to corner of the room. This was the rule in Carson—any other kind of partition was the rare exception. And if you stood in a dark room and your neighbors in the next had lights, the shadows on your canvas told queer secrets sometimes! Very often these partitions were made of old flour sacks basted together; and then the difference between the common herd and the aristocracy was, that the common herd had unornamented sacks, while the walls of the aristocrat were overpowering with rudimental fresco—*i.e.,* red and blue mill brands on the flour sacks. Occasionally, also, the better classes embellished their canvas by pasting pictures from *Harper's Weekly* on them. In many cases, too, the wealthy and the cultured rose to spittoons and other evidences of a sumptuous and luxurious taste.* We had a carpet and a genuine queen's-ware washbowl. Consequently we were hated without reserve by the other tenants of the O'Flannigan "ranch." When we added a painted oilcloth window curtain, we simply took our lives into our own hands. To prevent bloodshed I removed upstairs and took up quarters with the untitled plebeians in one of the fourteen white pine cot-bedsteads that stood in two long ranks in the one sole room of which the second story consisted.

It was a jolly company, the fourteen. They were principally voluntary camp-followers of the Governor, who had joined his retinue by their own election at New York and San Francisco and came along, feeling that in the scuffle for little territorial crumbs and offices they could not make their condition more precarious than it was, and might reasonably expect to make it better. They were popularly known as the "Irish Brigade," though there were only four or five

---

* Washoe people take a joke so hard that I must explain that the above description was only the rule; there were many honorable exceptions in Carson—plastered ceilings and houses that had considerable furniture in them.—M. T.

Irishmen among all the Governor's retainers. His good-natured Excellency was much annoyed at the gossip his henchmen created—especially when there arose a rumor that they were paid assassins of his, brought along to quietly reduce the democratic vote when desirable!

Mrs. O'Flannigan was boarding and lodging them at ten dollars a week apiece, and they were cheerfully giving their notes for it. They were perfectly satisfied, but Bridget presently found that notes that could not be discounted were but a feeble constitution for a Carson boarding-house. So she began to harry the Governor to find employment for the "Brigade." Her importunities and theirs together drove him to a gentle desperation at last, and he finally summoned the Brigade to the presence. Then, said he:

"Gentlemen, I have planned a lucrative and useful service for you—a service which will provide you with recreation amid noble landscapes, and afford you never ceasing opportunities for enriching your minds by observation and study. I want you to survey a railroad from Carson City westward to a certain point! When the legislature meets I will have the necessary bill passed and the remuneration arranged."

"What, a railroad over the Sierra Nevada Mountains?"

"Well, then, survey it eastward to a certain point!"

He converted them into surveyors, chain-bearers and so on, and turned them loose in the desert. It was "recreation" with a vengeance! Recreation on foot, lugging chains through sand and sage-brush, under a sultry sun and among cattle bones, cayotes, and tarantulas. "Romantic adventure" could go no further. They surveyed very slowly, very deliberately, very carefully. They returned every night during the first week, dusty, footsore, tired, and hungry, but very jolly. They brought in great store of prodigious hairy spiders—tarantulas—and imprisoned them in covered tumblers upstairs in the "ranch." After the first week, they had to camp on the field, for they were getting well eastward. They made a good many inquiries as to the location of that indefinite "certain point," but got no information. At last, to a peculiarly urgent inqury of "How far eastward?" Governor Nye telegraphed back:

"To the Atlantic Ocean, blast you!—and then bridge it and go on!"

This brought back the dusty toilers, who sent in a report and ceased from

THE IRISH BRIGADE.

their labors. The Governor was always comfortable about it; he said Mrs. O'Flannigan would hold him for the Brigade's board anyhow, and he intended to get what entertainment he could out of the boys; he said, with his old-time pleasant twinkle, that he meant to survey them into Utah and then telegraph Brigham to hang them for trespass!

The surveyors brought back more tarantulas with them, and so we had quite a menagerie arranged along the shelves of the room. Some of these spiders could straddle over a common saucer with their hairy, muscular legs, and when their feelings were hurt, or their dignity offended, they were the wickedest-looking desperados the animal world can furnish. If their glass prison-houses were touched ever so lightly they were up and spoiling for a fight in a minute. Starchy?—proud? Indeed, they would take up a straw and pick their teeth like a member of Congress. There was as usual a furious "zephyr" blowing the first night of the Brigade's return, and about midnight the roof of an adjoining stable blew off, and a corner of it came crashing through the side of our ranch. There was a simultaneous awakening, and a tumultuous muster of the brigade in the dark, and a general tumbling and sprawling over each other in the narrow aisle between the bed-rows. In the midst of the turmoil, Bob H—— sprung up out of a sound sleep, and knocked down a shelf with his head. Instantly he shouted:

"Turn out, boys—the tarantulas is loose!"

No warning ever sounded so dreadful. Nobody tried, any longer, to leave the room, lest he might step on a tarantula. Every man groped for a trunk or a bed, and jumped on it. Then followed the strangest silence—a silence of grisly suspense it was, too—waiting, expectancy, fear. It was as dark as pitch, and one had to imagine the spectacle of those fourteen scant-clad men roosting gingerly on trunks and beds, for not a thing could be seen. Then came occasional little interruptions of the silence, and one could recognize a man and tell his locality by his voice, or locate any other sound a sufferer made by his gropings or changes of position. The occasional voices were not given to much speaking—you simply heard a gentle ejaculation of "Ow!" followed by a solid thump, and you knew the gentleman had felt a hairy blanket or something touch his bare skin and had skipped from a bed to the floor. Another silence. Presently you would hear a gasping voice say:

"Su-su-something's crawling up the back of my neck!"

Every now and then you could hear a little subdued scramble and a sorrowful "O Lord!" and then you knew that somebody was getting away from something he took for a tarantula, and not losing any time about it, either. Directly a voice in the corner rang out wild and clear:

"I've got him! I've got him!" [Pause, and probable change of circumstances.] "No, he's got me! Oh, ain't they *never* going to fetch a lantern!"

The lantern came at that moment, in the hands of Mrs. O'Flannigan, whose anxiety to know the amount of damage done by the assaulting roof had not prevented her waiting a judicious interval, after getting out of bed and lighting up, to see if the wind was done, now, up stairs, or had a larger contract.

The landscape presented when the lantern flashed into the room was picturesque, and might have been funny to some people, but was not to us. Although we were perched so strangely upon boxes, trunks and beds, and so strangely attired, too, we were too earnestly distressed and too genuinely miserable to see any fun about it, and there was not the semblance of a smile anywhere visible. I know I am not capable of suffering more than I did during those few minutes of suspense in the dark, surrounded by those creeping, bloody-minded tarantulas. I had skipped from bed to bed and from box to box in a cold agony, and every time I touched anything that was furry I fancied I felt the fangs. I had rather go to war than live that episode over again. Nobody was hurt. The man who thought a tarantula had "got him" was mistaken—only a crack in a box had caught his finger. Not one of those escaped tarantulas was ever seen again. There were ten or twelve of them. We took candles and hunted the place high and low for them, but with no success. Did we go back to bed then? We did nothing of the kind. Money could not have persuaded us to do it. We sat up the rest of the night playing cribbage and keeping a sharp lookout for the enemy.

Chapter XXII

IT WAS THE end of August, and the skies were cloudless and the weather superb. In two or three weeks I had grown wonderfully fascinated with the curious new country, and concluded to put off my return to "the States" awhile. I had grown well accustomed to wearing a damaged slouch hat, blue woolen shirt, and pants crammed into boot-tops, and gloried in the absence of coat, vest, and braces. I felt rowdyish and "bully," (as the historian Josephus phrases it, in his fine chapter upon the destruction of the Temple). It seemed to me that nothing could be so fine and so romantic. I had become an officer of the government, but that was for mere sublimity. The office was a unique sinecure. I had nothing to do and no salary. I was private Secretary to his majesty the Secretary and there was not yet writing enough for two of us. So Johnny K—— and I devoted our time to amusement. He was the young son of an Ohio nabob and was out there for recreation. He got it. We had heard a world of talk about the marvelous beauty of Lake Tahoe, and finally curiosity drove us thither to see it. Three or four members of the Brigade had been there and located some timber lands on its shores and stored up a quantity of provisions in their camp. We strapped a couple of blankets on our shoulders and took an ax apiece and started—for we intended to take up a wood ranch or so ourselves and become wealthy. We were on foot. The reader will find it advantageous to go horseback. We were told that the distance was eleven miles. We tramped a long time on level ground, and then toiled laboriously up a mountain about a thousand miles high and looked over. No lake there. We descended on the other side, crossed the valley and toiled up another mountain three or four thousand miles high, apparently, and looked over again. No lake yet. We sat down tired and perspiring, and hired a couple of Chinamen to curse those people who had beguiled us. Thus refreshed, we presently resumed the march with renewed vigor and determination. We plodded on, two or three hours longer, and at last the Lake burst upon us—a noble sheet of blue water lifted six thousand three hundred feet above the level of the sea, and walled in by a rim of snow-clad mountain peaks that towered aloft full three thousand feet higher still! It was a vast oval, and one would have to use up eighty or a hundred good miles in traveling around it. As it lay there with the shadows of the mountains brilliantly photographed upon its still surface, I thought it must surely be the fairest picture the whole earth affords.

We found the small skiff belonging to the Brigade boys, and without loss of time set out across a deep bend of the lake toward the landmarks that signified the locality of the camp. I got Johnny to row—not because I mind exertion myself, but because it makes me sick to ride backward when I am at work. But I steered. A three-mile pull brought us to the camp just as the night fell, and we stepped ashore very tired and wolfishly hungry. In a "cache" among the rocks we found the provisions and the cooking utensils, and then, all fatigued as I was, I sat down on a boulder and superintended while Johnny gathered wood and cooked supper. Many a man who had gone through what I had would have wanted to rest.

It was a delicious supper—hot bread, fried bacon, and black coffee. It was a delicious solitude we were in, too. Three miles away was a saw-mill and some workmen, but there were not fifteen other human beings throughout the wide circumference of the lake. As the darkness closed down and the stars came out and spangled the great mirror with jewels, we smoked meditatively in the solemn hush and forgot our troubles and our pains. In due time we spread our blankets in the warm sand between two large boulders and soon fell asleep, careless of the procession of ants that passed in through rents in our clothing and explored our persons. Nothing could disturb the sleep that fettered us, for it had been fairly earned, and if our consciences had any sins on them they had to adjourn court for that night, any way. The wind rose just as we were losing consciousness, and we were lulled to sleep by the beating of the surf upon the shore.

It is always very cold on that lake shore in the night, but we had plenty of blankets and were warm enough. We never moved a muscle all night, but waked at early dawn in the original positions, and got up at once, thoroughly refreshed, free from soreness, and brim full of friskiness. There is no end of wholesome medicine in such an experience. That morning we could have whipped ten such people as we were the day before—sick ones at any rate. But the world is slow, and people will go to "water cures" and "movement cures" and to foreign lands for health. Three months of camp life on Lake Tahoe would restore an Egyptian mummy to his pristine vigor, and give him an appetite like an alligator. I do not mean the oldest and driest mummies, of course, but the fresher ones. The air up there in the clouds is very pure and fine, bracing and delicious. And why shouldn't it be?—it is the same the angels breathe. I think that hardly any amount of fatigue can be gathered together that a man cannot sleep off in one night on the sand by its side. Not under a roof, but under the sky; it seldom or never rains there in the summer time. I know a man who went there to die. But he made a failure of it. He was a skeleton when he came, and could barely stand. He had no appetite and did nothing but read tracts and reflect on the future. Three months later he was sleeping out of doors regularly, eating all he could hold, three times a day, and chasing game over mountains three thousand feet high for recreation. And he was a skeleton no longer, but weighed part of a ton. This is no fancy sketch, but the truth. His disease was consumption. I confidently commend his experience to other skeletons.

I superintended again, and as soon as we had eaten breakfast we got in the boat and skirted along the lake shore about three miles and disembarked. We liked the appearance of the place, and so we claimed some three hundred acres of it and stuck our "notices" on a tree. It was yellow pine timber land—a dense forest of trees a hundred feet high and from one to five feet through at the butt. It was necessary to fence our property or we could not hold it. That is to say, it was necessary to cut down trees here and there and make them fall in such a way as to form a sort of enclosure (with pretty wide gaps in it). We cut down three trees apiece, and found it such heart-breaking work that we decided to "rest our case" on those; if they held the property, well and good; if they didn't, let the property spill out through the gaps and go; it was no use to work ourselves to death merely to save a few acres of land. Next day we came back to build a house—for a house was also necessary, in order to hold the property. We decided to build a substantial log-house and excite the envy of the Brigade boys; but by the time we had cut and trimmed the first log it seemed unnecessary to be so elaborate, and so we concluded to build it of saplings. However, two saplings, duly cut and trimmed, compelled recognition of the fact that a still modester architecture would satisfy the law, and so we concluded to build a "brush" house. We devoted the next day to this work, but we did so much "sitting around" and discussing, that by the middle of the afternoon we had achieved only a half-way sort of affair which one of us had to watch while the other cut brush, lest if both turned our backs we might not be able to find it again, it had such a strong family resemblance to the surrounding vegetation. But we were satisfied with it.

We were land owners now, duly seized and possessed, and within the protection of the law. Therefore we decided to take up our residence on our own domain and enjoy that large sense of independence which only such an experience can bring. Late the next afternoon, after a good long rest, we sailed away from the Brigade camp with all the provisions and cooking utensils we could carry off— borrow is the more accurate word—and just as the night was falling we beached the boat at our own landing.

Chapter XXIII

IF THERE IS any life that is happier than the life we led on our timber ranch for the next two or three weeks, it must be a sort of life which I have not read of in books or experienced in person. We did not see a human being but ourselves during the time, or hear any sounds but those that were made by the wind and the waves, the sighing of the pines, and now and then the far-off thunder of an avalanche. The forest about us was dense and cool, the sky above us was cloudless and brilliant with sunshine, the broad lake before us was glassy and clear, or rippled and breezy, or black and storm-tossed, according to Nature's mood; and its circling border of mountain domes, clothed with forests, scarred with land-slides, cloven by canyons and valleys, and helmeted with glittering snow, fitly framed and finished the noble picture. The view was always fascinating, bewitching, entrancing. The eye was never tired of gazing, night or day, in calm or storm; it suffered but one grief, and that was that it could not look always, but must close sometimes in sleep.

We slept in the sand close to the water's edge, between two protecting boulders, which took care of the stormy night winds for us. We never took any paregoric to make us sleep. At the first break of dawn we were always up and running foot-races to tone down excess of physical vigor and exuberance of spirits. That is, Johnny was—but I held his hat. While smoking the pipe of peace after breakfast we watched the sentinel peaks put on the glory of the sun, and followed the conquering light as it swept down among the shadows, and set the captive crags and forests free. We watched the tinted pictures grow and brighten upon the water till every little detail of forest, precipice and pinnacle was wrought in and finished, and the miracle of the enchanter complete. Then to "business."

That is, drifting around in the boat. We were on the north shore. There, the rocks on the bottom are sometimes gray, sometimes white. This gives the marvelous transparency of the water a fuller advantage than it has elsewhere on the lake. We usually pushed out a hundred yards or so from shore, and then lay down on the thwarts, in the sun, and let the boat drift by the hour whither it would. We seldom talked. It interrupted the Sabbath stillness, and marred the dreams the luxurious rest and indolence brought. The shore all along was indented with deep, curved bays and coves, bordered by narrow sand-beaches; and where the sand ended, the steep mountain-sides rose right up aloft into space—rose up like a vast wall a little out of the perpendicular, and thickly wooded with tall pines.

So singularly clear was the water, that when it was only twenty or thirty feet deep the bottom was so perfectly distinct that the boat seemed floating in the air! Yes, where it was even *eighty* feet deep. Every little pebble was distinct, every specked trout, every hand's-breadth of sand. Often, as we lay on our faces, a granite boulder, as large as a village church, would start out of the bottom apparently, and seem climbing up rapidly to the surface, till presently it threatened to touch our faces, and we could not resist the impulse to seize an oar and avert the danger. But the boat would float on, and the boulder descend again, and then we could see that when we had been exactly above it, it must still have been twenty or thirty feet below the surface. Down through the transparency of these great depths, the water was not *merely* transparent, but dazzlingly, brilliantly so. All objects seen through it had a bright, strong vividness, not only of outline, but of every minute detail, which they would not have had when seen simply through the same depth of atmosphere. So empty and airy did all spaces seem below us, and so strong was the sense of floating high aloft in mid-nothingness, that we called these boat excursions "balloon-voyages."

We fished a good deal, but we did not average one fish a week. We could see trout by the thousand winging about in the emptiness under us, or sleeping in shoals on the bottom, but they would not bite—they could see the line too plainly, perhaps. We frequently selected the trout we wanted, and rested the bait patiently and persistently on the end of his nose at a depth of eighty feet, but he would only shake it off with an annoyed manner, and shift his position.

We bathed occasionally, but the water was rather chilly, for all it looked so sunny. Sometimes we rowed out to the "blue water," a mile or two from shore. It was as dead blue as indigo there, because of the immense depth. By official measurement the lake in its center is one thousand five hundred and twenty-five feet deep!

Sometimes, on lazy afternoons, we lolled on the sand in camp, and smoked pipes and read some old well-worn novels. At night, by the camp-fire, we played euchre and seven-up to strengthen the mind—and played them with cards so greasy and defaced that only a whole summer's acquaintance with them could enable the student to tell the ace of clubs from the jack of diamonds.

We never slept in our "house." It never recurred to us, for one thing; and besides, it was built to hold the ground, and that was enough. We did not wish to strain it.

By and by our provisions began to run short, and we went back to the old camp and laid in a new supply. We were gone all day, and reached home again about night-fall, pretty tired and hungry. While Johnny was carrying the main bulk of the provisions up to our "house" for future use, I took the loaf of bread, some slices of bacon, and the coffee-pot, ashore, set them down by a tree, lit a fire, and went back to the boat to get the frying-pan. While I was at this, I heard a shout from Johnny, and looking up I saw that my fire was galloping all over the premises!

Johnny was on the other side of it. He had to run through the flames to get to the lake shore, and then we stood helpless and watched the devastation.

The ground was deeply carpeted with dry pine-needles, and the fire touched them off as if they were gunpowder. It was wonderful to see with what fierce speed the tall sheet of flame traveled! My coffee-pot was gone, and everything with it. In a minute and a half the fire seized upon a dense growth of dry manzanita chaparral six or eight feet high, and then the roaring and popping and crackling was something terrific. We were driven to the boat by the intense heat, and there we remained, spell-bound.

Within half an hour all before us was a tossing, blinding tempest of flame! It went surging up adjacent ridges—surmounted them and disappeared in the canyons beyond—burst into view upon higher and farther ridges, presently— shed a grander illumination abroad, and dove again—flamed out again, directly, higher and still higher up the mountain-side—threw out skirmishing parties of fire here and there, and sent them trailing their crimson spirals away among remote ramparts and ribs and gorges, till as far as the eye could reach the lofty mountain-fronts were webbed as it were with a tangled network of red lava streams. Away across the water the crags and domes were lit with a ruddy glare, and the firmament above was a reflected hell!

Every feature of the spectacle was repeated in the glowing mirror of the lake! Both pictures were sublime, both were beautiful; but that in the lake had a bewildering richness about it that enchanted the eye and held it with the stronger fascination.

We sat absorbed and motionless through four long hours. We never thought of supper, and never felt fatigue. But at eleven o'clock the conflagration had traveled beyond our range of vision, and then darkness stole down upon the landscape again.

Hunger asserted itself now, but there was nothing to eat. The provisions were all cooked, no doubt, but we did not go to see. We were homeless wanderers again, without any property. Our fence was gone, our house burned down; no insurance. Our pine forest was well scorched, the dead trees all burned up, and our broad acres of manzanita swept away. Our blankets were on our usual sand- bed, however, and so we lay down and went to sleep. The next morning we started back to the old camp, but while out a long way from shore, so great a storm came up that we dared not try to land. So I baled out the seas we shipped, and Johnny pulled heavily through the billows till we had reached a point three or four miles beyond the camp. The storm was increasing, and it became evident that it was better to take the hazard of beaching the boat than go down in a hundred fathoms of water; so we ran in, with tall white-caps following, and I sat down in the stern sheets and pointed her head-on to the shore. The instant the bow struck, a wave came over the stern that washed crew and cargo ashore, and saved a deal of trouble. We shivered in the lee of a boulder all the rest of the day, and froze all the night through. In the morning the tempest had gone down, and we paddled down to the camp without any unnecessary delay. We were so starved that we ate up the rest of the Brigade's provisions, and then set out to Carson to tell them about it and ask their forgiveness. It was accorded, upon payment of damages.

We made many trips to the lake after that, and had many a hair-breadth escape and blood-curdling adventure which will never be recorded in any history.

Chapter XXIV

I RESOLVED TO have a horse to ride. I had never seen such wild, free, magnificent horsemanship outside of a circus as these picturesquely-clad Mexicans, Californians and Mexicanized Americans displayed in Carson streets every day. How they rode! Leaning just gently forward out of the perpendicular, easy and nonchalant, with broad slouch-hat brim blown square up in front, and long *riata* swinging above the head, they swept through the town like the wind! The next minute they were only a sailing puff of dust on the far desert. If they trotted, they sat up gallantly and gracefully, and seemed part of the horse; did not go jiggering up and down after the silly Miss-Nancy fashion of the riding-schools. I had quickly learned to tell a horse from a cow, and was full of anxiety to learn more. I was resolved to buy a horse.

While the thought was rankling in my mind, the auctioneer came scurrying through the plaza on a black beast that had as many humps and corners on him as a dromedary, and was necessarily uncomely; but he was "going, going, at twenty-two!—horse, saddle and bridle at twenty-two dollars, gentlemen!" and I could hardly resist.

A man whom I did not know (he turned out to be the auctioneer's brother) noticed the wistful look in my eye, and observed that that was a very remarkable horse to be going at such a price; and added that the saddle alone was worth the money. It was a Spanish saddle, with ponderous *tapidaros,* and furnished with the ungainly sole-leather covering with the unspellable name. I said I had half a notion to bid. Then this keen-eyed person appeared to me to be "taking my measure"; but I dismissed the suspicion when he spoke, for his manner was full of guileless candor and truthfulness. Said he:

"I know that horse—know him well. You are a stranger, I take it, and so you might think he was an American horse, maybe, but I assure you he is not. He is nothing of the kind; but—excuse my speaking in a low voice, other people being near—he is, without the shadow of a doubt, a Genuine Mexican Plug!"

I did not know what a Genuine Mexican Plug was, but there was something about this man's way of saying it, that made me swear inwardly that I would own a Genuine Mexican Plug, or die.

"Has he any other—er—advantages?" I inquired, suppressing what eagerness I could.

He hooked his forefinger in the pocket of my army-shirt, led me to one side, and breathed in my ear impressively these words:

"He can out-buck anything in America!"

"Going, going, going—at *twent-ty*-four dollars and a half, gen—"

"Twenty-seven!" I shouted, in a frenzy.

"And sold!" said the auctioneer, and passed over the Genuine Mexican Plug to me.

I could scarcely contain my exultation. I paid the money, and put the animal in a neighboring livery-stable to dine and rest himself.

In the afternoon I brought the creature into the plaza, and certain citizens held him by the head, and others by the tail, while I mounted him. As soon as they let go, he placed all his feet in a bunch together, lowered his back, and then suddenly arched it upward, and shot me straight into the air a matter of three or four feet! I came as straight down again, lit in the saddle, went instantly up again, came down almost on the high pommel, shot up again, and came down on the horse's neck—all in the space of three or four seconds. Then he rose and stood almost straight up on his hind feet, and I, clasping his lean neck desperately, slid back into the saddle, and held on. He came down, and immediately hoisted his heels into the air, delivering a vicious kick at the sky, and stood on his forefeet. And then down he came once more, and began the original exercise of shooting me straight up again. The third time I went up I heard a stranger say:

"Oh, *don't* he buck, though!"

While I was up, somebody struck the horse a sounding thwack with a leathern strap, and when I arrived again the Genuine Mexican Plug was not there. A Californian youth chased him up and caught him, and asked if he might have a ride. I granted him that luxury. He mounted the Genuine, got lifted into the air once, but sent his spurs home as he descended, and the horse darted away like a telegram. He soared over three fences like a bird, and disappeared down the road toward the Washoe Valley.

I sat down on a stone, with a sigh, and by a natural impulse one of my hands sought my forehead, and the other the base of my stomach. I believe I never appreciated, till then, the poverty of the human machinery—for I still needed a hand or two to place elsewhere. Pen cannot describe how I was jolted up. Imagination cannot conceive how disjointed I was—how internally, externally, and universally I was unsettled, mixed up, and ruptured. There was a sympathetic crowd around me, though.

One elderly-looking comforter said:

"Stranger, you've been taken in. Everybody in this camp knows that horse.

UNEXPECTED ELEVATION.

Any child, any Injun, could have told you that he'd buck; he is the very worst devil to buck on the continent of America. You hear *me*. I'm Curry. *Old* Curry. Old *Abe* Curry. And moreover, he is a simon-pure, out-and-out, genuine d—d Mexican plug, and an uncommon mean one at that, too. Why, you turnip, if you had laid low and kept dark, there's chances to buy an *American* horse for mighty little more than you paid for that bloody old foreign relic."

I gave no sign; but I made up my mind that if the auctioneer's brother's funeral took place while I was in the Territory I would postpone all other recreations and attend it.

After a gallop of sixteen miles the Californian youth and the Genuine Mexican Plug came tearing into town again, shedding foam-flakes like the spume-spray that drives before a typhoon, and, with one final skip over a wheelbarrow and a Chinaman, cast anchor in front of the "ranch."

Such panting and blowing! Such spreading and contracting of the red equine nostrils, and glaring of the wild equine eye! But was the imperial beast subjugated? Indeed he was not. His lordship the Speaker of the House thought he was, and mounted him to go down to the Capitol; but the first dash the creature made was over a pile of telegraph poles half as high as a church; and his time to the Capitol—one mile and three quarters—remains unbeaten to this day. But then he took an advantage—he left out the mile, and only did the three quarters. That is to say, he made a straight cut across lots, preferring fences and ditches to a crooked road; and when the Speaker got to the Capitol he said he had been in the air so much he felt as if he had made the trip on a comet.

In the evening the Speaker came home afoot for exercise, and got the Genuine towed back behind a quartz wagon. The next day I loaned the animal to the clerk of the House to go down to the Dana silver mine, six miles, and *he* walked back for exercise, and got the horse towed. Everybody I loaned him to always walked back; they never could get enough exercise any other way. Still, I continued to loan him to anybody who was willing to borrow him, my idea being to get him crippled, and throw him on the borrower's hands, or killed, and make the borrower pay for him. But somehow nothing ever happened to him. He took chances that no other horse ever took and survived, but he always came out safe. It was his daily habit to try experiments that had always before been considered impossible, but he always got through. Sometimes he miscalculated a little, and did not get his rider through intact, but *he* always got through himself. Of course I had tried to sell him; but that was a stretch of simplicity which met with little sympathy. The auctioneer stormed up and down the streets on him for four days, dispersing the populace, interrupting business, and destroying children, and never got a bid—at least never any but the eighteen-dollar one he hired a notoriously substanceless bummer to make. The people only smiled pleasantly, and restrained their desire to buy, if they had any. Then the auctioneer brought in his bill, and I withdrew the horse from the market. We tried to trade him off at private vendue next, offering him at a sacrifice for second-hand tombstones, old iron, temperance tracts—any kind of property. But holders were stiff, and we retired from the market again. I never tried to ride the horse any more. Walking was good enough exercise for a man like me, that had nothing the matter with him except ruptures, internal injuries, and such things. Finally I tried to *give* him away. But it was a failure. Parties said earthquakes were handy enough on the Pacific coast—they did not wish to own one. As a last resort I offered him to the Governor for the use of the "Brigade." His face lit up eagerly at first, but toned down again, and he said the thing would be too palpable.

Just then the livery-stable man brought in his bill for six weeks' keeping—stall-room for the horse, fifteen dollars; hay for the horse, two hundred and fifty! The Genuine Mexican Plug had eaten a ton of the article, and the man said he would have eaten a hundred if he had let him.

I will remark here, in all seriousness, that the regular price of hay during that year and a part of the next was really two hundred and fifty dollars a ton. During a part of the previous year it had sold at five hundred a ton, in gold, and during the winter before that there was such scarcity of the article that in several instances small quantities had brought eight hundred dollars a ton in coin! The consequence might be guessed without my telling it: people turned their stock loose to starve, and before the spring arrived Carson and Eagle valleys were almost literally carpeted with their carcasses! Any old settler there will verify these statements.

I managed to pay the livery bill, and that same day I gave the Genuine Mexican Plug to a passing Arkansas emigrant whom fortune delivered into my hand. If this ever meets his eye, he will doubtless remember the donation.

Now whoever has had the luck to ride a real Mexican plug will recognize the animal depicted in this chapter, and hardly consider him exaggerated—but the uninitiated will feel justified in regarding his portrait as a fancy sketch, perhaps.

Chapter XXV

ORIGINALLY, NEVADA WAS a part of Utah and was called Carson County; and a pretty large county it was, too. Certain of its valleys produced no end of hay, and this attracted small colonies of Mormon stock-raisers and farmers to them. A few orthodox Americans straggled in from California, but no love was lost between the two classes of colonists. There was little or no friendly intercourse; each party stayed to itself. The Mormons were largely in the majority, and had the additional advantage of being peculiarly under the protection of the Mormon government of the Territory. Therefore they could afford to be distant and even peremptory toward their neighbors. One of the traditions of Carson Valley illustrates the condition of things that prevailed at the time I speak of. The hired girl of one of the American families was Irish, and a Catholic; yet it was noted with surprise that she was the only person outside of the Mormon ring who could get favors from the Mormons. She asked kindnesses of them often, and always got them. It was a mystery to everybody. But one day as she was passing out at the door, a large bowie knife dropped from under her apron, and when her mistress asked for an explanation she observed that she was going out to "borry a wash-tub from the Mormons!"

In 1858 silver lodes were discovered in "Carson County," and then the aspect of things changed. Californians began to flock in, and the American element was soon in the majority. Allegiance to Brigham Young and Utah was renounced, and a temporary territorial government for "Washoe" was instituted by the citizens. Governor Roop was the first and only chief magistrate of it. In due course of time Congress passed a bill to organize "Nevada Territory," and President Lincoln sent out Governor Nye to supplant Roop.

At this time the population of the territory was about twelve or fifteen thousand, and rapidly increasing. Silver mines were being vigorously developed and silver mills erected. Business of all kinds was active and prosperous and growing more so day by day.

The people were glad to have a legitimately constituted government, but did not particularly enjoy having strangers from distant states put in authority over them—a sentiment that was natural enough. They thought the officials should have been chosen from among themselves—from among prominent citizens who had earned a right to such promotion, and who would be in sympathy with the populace and likewise thoroughly acquainted with the needs of the Territory. They were right in viewing the matter thus, without doubt. The new officers were "emigrants," and that was no title to anybody's affection or admiration either.

The new government was received with considerable coolness. It was not only a foreign intruder, but a poor one. It was not even worth plucking—except by the smallest of small fry office seekers and such. Everybody knew that Congress had appropriated only twenty thousand dollars a year in green-backs for its support—about money enough to run a quartz mill a month. And everybody knew, also, that the first year's money was still in Washington, and that the getting hold of it would be a tedious and difficult process. Carson City was too wary and too wise to open up a credit account with the imported bantling with anything like indecent haste.

There is something solemnly funny about the struggles of a newborn Territorial government to get a start in this world. Ours had a trying time of it. The Organic Act and the "instructions" from the State Department commanded that a legislature should be elected at such-and-such a time, and its sittings inaugurated at such-and-such a date. It was easy to get legislators, even at three dollars a day, although board was four dollars and fifty cents, for distinction has its charm in Nevada as well as elsewhere, and there were plenty of patriotic souls out of employment; but to get a legislative hall for them to meet in was another matter altogether. Carson blandly declined to give a room rent-free, or let one to the government on credit.

But when Curry heard of the difficulty, he came forward, solitary and alone, and shouldered the Ship of State over the bar and got her afloat again. I refer to "Curry—*Old* Curry—Old *Abe* Curry." But for him the legislature would have been obliged to sit in the desert. He offered his large stone building just outside the capital limits, rent-free, and it was gladly accepted. Then he built a horse-railroad from town to the capitol, and carried the legislators gratis. He also furnished pine benches and chairs for the legislature, and covered the floors with clean saw-dust by way of carpet and spittoon combined. But for Curry the government would have died in its tender infancy. A canvas partition to separate the Senate from the House of Representatives was put up by the Secretary, at a cost of three dollars and forty cents, but the United States declined to pay for it. Upon being reminded that the "instructions" permitted the payment of a liberal rent for a legislative hall, and that that money was saved to the country by Mr. Curry's generosity, the United States said that did not alter the matter, and the three dollars and forty cents would be subtracted from the Secretary's eighteen-hundred-dollar salary—and it *was!*

The matter of printing was from the beginning an interesting feature of the new government's difficulties. The Secretary was sworn to obey his volume of written "instructions," and these commanded him to do two certain things without fail, viz.:

1. Get the House and Senate journals printed; and,

2. For this work, pay one dollar and fifty cents per "thousand" for composition, and one dollar and fifty cents per "token" for press-work, in greenbacks.

It was easy to swear to do these two things, but it was entirely impossible to do more than one of them. When greenbacks had gone down to forty cents on the dollar, the prices regularly charged everybody by printing establishments were one dollar and fifty cents per "thousand" and one dollar and fifty cents per "token," in *gold*. The "instructions" commanded that the Secretary regard a paper dollar issued by the government as equal to any other dollar issued by the government. Hence the printing of the journals was discontinued. Then the United States sternly rebuked the Secretary for disregarding the "instructions," and warned him to correct his ways. Wherefore he got some printing done, forwarded the bill to Washington with full exhibits of the high prices of things in the Territory, and called attention to a printed market report wherein it would be observed that even hay was two hundred and fifty dollars a ton. The United States responded by subtracting the printing-bill from the Secretary's suffering salary—and moreover remarked with dense gravity that he would find nothing in his "instructions" requiring him to purchase hay!

Nothing in this world is pailed in such impenetrable obscurity as a U. S. Treasury Comptroller's understanding. The very fires of the hereafter could get up nothing more than a fitful glimmer in it. In the days I speak of he never could be made to comprehend why it was that twenty thousand dollars would not go as far in Nevada, where all commodities ranged at an enormous figure, as it would in the other Territories, where exceeding cheapness was the rule. He was an officer who looked out for the little expenses all the time. The Secretary of the Territory kept his office in his bedroom, as I before remarked; and he charged the United States no rent, although his "instructions" provided for that item and he could have justly taken advantage of it (a thing which I would have done with more than lightning promptness if I had been Secretary myself). But the United States never applauded this devotion. Indeed, I think my country was ashamed to have so improvident a person in its employ.

Those "instructions" (we used to read a chapter from them every morning, as intellectual gymnastics, and a couple of chapters in Sunday school every Sabbath, for they treated of all subjects under the sun and had much valuable religious matter in them along with the other statistics) those "instructions" commanded that pen-knives, envelopes, pens, and writing-paper be furnished the members of the legislature. So the Secretary made the purchase and the distribution. The knives cost three dollars apiece. There was one too many, and the Secretary gave it to the Clerk of the House of Representatives. The United States said the Clerk of the House was not a "member" of the legislature, and took that three dollars out of the Secretary's salary, as usual.

White men charged three or four dollars a "load" for sawing up stove-wood. The Secretary was sagacious enough to know that the United States would never pay any such price as that; so he got an Indian to saw up a load of office wood at one dollar and a half. He made out the usual voucher, but signed no name to it—simply appended a note explaining that an Indian had done the work, and had done it in a very capable and satisfactory way, but could not sign the voucher owing to lack of ability in the necessary direction. The Secretary had to pay that dollar and a half. He thought the United States would admire both his economy and his honesty in getting the work done at half price and not putting a pretended Indian's signature to the voucher, but the United States did not see it in that light. The United States was too much accustomed to employing dollar-and-a-half thieves in all manner of official capacities to regard his explanation of the voucher as having any foundation in fact.

But the next time the Indian sawed wood for us I taught him to make a cross at the bottom of the voucher—it looked like a cross that had been drunk a year— and then I "witnessed" it and it went through all right. The United States never said a word. I was sorry I had not made the voucher for a thousand loads of wood instead of one. The government of my country snubs honest simplicity but fondles artistic villainy, and I think I might have developed into a very capable pickpocket if I had remained in the public service a year or two.

That was a fine collection of sovereigns, that first Nevada legislature. They

NEEDS PRAYING FOR.

levied taxes to the amount of thirty or forty thousand dollars and ordered expenditures to the extent of about a million. Yet they had their little periodical explosions of economy like all other bodies of the kind. A member proposed to save three dollars a day to the nation by dispensing with the Chaplain. And yet that short-sighted man needed the Chaplain more than any other member, perhaps, for he generally sat with his feet on his desk, eating raw turnips, during the morning prayer.

The legislature sat sixty days, and passed private toll-road franchises all the time. When they adjourned it was estimated that every citizen owned about three franchises, and it was believed that unless Congress gave the Territory another degree of longitude there would not be room enough to accommodate the toll-roads. The ends of them were hanging over the boundary line everywhere like a fringe.

The fact is, the freighting business had grown to such important proportions that there was nearly as much excitement over suddenly acquired toll-road fortunes as over the wonderful silver mines.

Chapter XXVI

BY AND BY I was smitten with the silver fever. "Prospecting parties" were leaving for the mountains every day, and discovering and taking possession of rich silver-bearing lodes and ledges of quartz. Plainly this was the road to fortune. The great "Gould and Curry" mine was held at three or four hundred dollars a foot when we arrived; but in two months it had sprung up to eight hundred. The "Ophir" had been worth only a mere trifle, a year gone by, and now it was selling at nearly *four thousand dollars a foot!* Not a mine could be named that had not experienced an astonishing advance in value within a short time. Everybody was talking about these marvels. Go where you would, you heard nothing else, from morning till far into the night. Tom So-and-So had sold out of the "Amanda Smith" for $40,000—hadn't a cent when he "took up" the ledge six months ago. John Jones had sold half his interest in the "Bald Eagle and Mary Ann" for $65,000, gold coin, and gone to the States for his family. The widow Brewster had "struck it rich" in the "Golden Fleece" and sold ten feet for $18,000— hadn't money enough to buy a crape bonnet when Sing-Sing Tommy killed her husband at Baldy Johnson's wake last spring. The "Last Chance" had found a "clay casing" and knew they were "right on the ledge"—consequence, "feet" that went begging yesterday were worth a brick house apiece to-day, and seedy owners who could not get trusted for a drink at any bar in the country yesterday were roaring drunk on champagne to-day and had hosts of warm personal friends in a town where they had forgotten how to bow or shake hands from long-continued want of practice. Johnny Morgan, a common loafer, had gone to sleep in the gutter and waked up worth a hundred thousand dollars, in consequence of the decision in the "Lady Franklin and Rough and Ready" lawsuit. And so on—day in and day out the talk pelted our ears and the excitement waxed hotter and hotter around us.

I would have been more or less than human if I had not gone mad like the rest. Cart-loads of solid silver bricks, as large as pigs of lead, were arriving from the mills every day, and such sights as that gave substance to the wild talk about me. I succumbed and grew as frenzied as the craziest.

Every few days news would come of the discovery of a brand-new mining region; immediately the papers would teem with accounts of its richness, and away the surplus population would scamper to take possession. By the time I was fairly inoculated with the disease, "Esmeralda" had just had a run and "Humboldt" was beginning to shriek for attention. "Humboldt! Humboldt!" was the new cry, and straightway Humboldt, the newest of the new, the richest of the rich, the most marvelous of the marvelous discoveries in silver-land, was occupying two columns of the public prints to "Esmeralda's" one. I was just on the point of starting to Esmeralda, but turned with the tide and got ready for Humboldt. That the reader may see what moved me, and what would as surely have moved him had he been there, I insert here one of the newspaper letters of the day. It and several other letters from the same calm hand were the main means of converting me. I shall not garble the extract, but put it in just as it appeared in the *Daily Territorial Enterprise:*

> But what about our mines? I shall be candid with you. I shall express an honest opinion, based upon a thorough examination. Humboldt county is the richest mineral region upon God's footstool. Each mountain range is gorged with the precious ores. Humboldt is the true Golconda.
>
> The other day an assay of mere *croppings* yielded exceeding *four thousand dollars to the ton.* A week or two ago an assay of just such surface developments made returns of *seven thousand* dollars to the ton. Our mountains are full of rambling prospectors. Each day and almost every hour reveals new and more startling evidences of the profuse and intensified wealth of our favored county. The metal is not silver alone. There are distinct ledges of auriferous ore. A late discovery plainly evinces cinnabar. The coarser metals are in gross abundance. Lately evidences of bituminous coal have been detected. My theory has ever been that coal is a ligneous formation. I told Col. Whitman, in times past, that the neighborhood of Dayton (Nevada) betrayed no present or previous manifestations of a ligneous foundation, and that hence I had no confidence in his lauded coal mines. I repeated the same doctrine to the exultant coal discoverers of Humboldt. I talked with my friend Captain Burch on the subject. My pyrhanism vanished upon his statement that in the very region referred to he had seen petrified trees of the length of two hundred feet. Then is the fact established that huge forests once cast their grim shadows over this remote section. I am firm in the coal faith. Have no fears of the mineral resources of Humboldt county. They are immense—incalculable.

Let me state one or two things which will help the reader to better comprehend certain items in the above. At this time, our near neighbor, Gold Hill, was the most successful silver-mining locality in Nevada. It was from there that more than half the daily shipments of silver bricks came. "Very rich" (and scarce) Gold Hill ore yielded from $100 to $400 to the ton; but the usual yield was only $20 to $40 per ton—that is to say, each hundred pounds of ore yielded from one dollar to two dollars. But the reader will perceive by the above extract, that in Humboldt from one fourth to nearly half the mass was silver! That is to say,

every one hundred pounds of the ore had from *two hundred* dollars up to about
three hundred and fifty in it. Some days later this same correspondent wrote:

> I have spoken of the vast and almost fabulous wealth of this region—
> it is incredible. The intestines of our mountains are gorged with precious
> ore to plethora. I have said that nature has so shaped our mountains as
> to furnish most excellent facilities for the working of our mines. I have
> also told you that the country about here is pregnant with the finest mill
> sites in the world. But what is the mining history of Humboldt? The
> Sheba mine is in the hands of energetic San Francisco capitalists. It
> would seem that the ore is combined with metals that render it difficult
> of reduction with our imperfect mountain machinery. The proprietors
> have combined the capital and labor hinted at in my exordium. They are
> toiling and probing. Their tunnel has reached the length of one hundred
> feet. From primal assays alone, coupled with the development of the
> mine and public confidence in the continuance of effort, the stock had
> reared itself to eight hundred dollars market value. I do not know that
> one ton of the ore has been converted into current metal. I do know that
> there are many lodes in this section that surpass the Sheba in primal assay
> value. Listen a moment to the calculations of the Sheba operators. They
> purpose transporting the ore concentrated to Europe. The conveyance
> from Star City (its locality) to Virginia City will cost seventy dollars per
> ton; from Virginia to San Francisco, forty dollars per ton; from thence
> to Liverpool, its destination, ten dollars per ton. Their idea is that its
> conglomerate metals will reimburse them their cost of original extraction,
> the price of transportation, and the expense of reduction, and that then
> a ton of the raw ore will net them twelve hundred dollars. The estimate
> may be extravagant. Cut it in twain, and the product is enormous, far
> transcending any previous developments of our racy Territory.
>
> A very common calculation is that many of our mines will yield five
> hundred dollars to the ton. Such fecundity throws the Gould & Curry,
> the Ophir and the Mexican, of your neighborhood, in the darkest shadow.
> I have given you the estimate of the value of a single developed mine.
> Its richness is indexed by its market valuation. The people of Humboldt
> county are *feet* crazy. As I write, our towns are near deserted. They look
> as languid as a consumptive girl. What has become of our sinewy and
> athletic fellow-citizens? They are coursing through ravines and over
> mountain tops. Their tracks are visible in every direction. Occasionally
> a horseman will dash among us. His steed betrays hard usage. He alights
> before his adobe dwelling, hastily exchanges courtesies with his townsmen,
> hurries to an assay office and from thence to the District Recorder's. In
> the morning, having renewed his provisional supplies, he is off again on
> his wild and unbeaten route. Why, the fellow numbers already his feet
> by the thousands. He is the horse-leech. He has the craving stomach of
> the shark or anaconda. He would conquer metallic worlds.

This was enough. The instant we had finished reading the above article, four
of us decided to go to Humboldt. We commenced getting ready at once. And
we also commenced upbraiding ourselves for not deciding sooner—for we were
in terror lest all the rich mines would be found and secured before we got there,

and we might have to put up with ledges that would not yield more than two or three hundred dollars a ton, maybe. An hour before, I would have felt opulent if I had owned ten feet in a Gold Hill mine whose ore produced twenty-five dollars to the ton; now I was already annoyed at the prospect of having to put up with mines the poorest of which would be a marvel in Gold Hill.

Chapter XXVII

HURRY, WAS THE word! We wasted no time. Our party consisted of four persons—a blacksmith sixty years of age, two young lawyers, and myself. We bought a wagon and two miserable old horses. We put eighteen hundred pounds of provisions and mining tools in the wagon and drove out of Carson on a chilly December afternoon. The horses were so weak and old that we soon found that it would be better if one or two of us got out and walked. It was an improvement. Next, we found that it would be better if a third man got out. That was an improvement also. It was at this time that I volunteered to drive, although I had never driven a harnessed horse before and many a man in such a position would have felt fairly excused from such a responsibility. But in a little while it was found that it would be a fine thing if the driver got out and walked also. It was at this time that I resigned the position of driver, and never resumed it again. Within the hour, we found that it would not only be better, but was absolutely necessary, that we four, taking turns, two at a time, should put our hands against the end of the wagon and push it through the sand, leaving the feeble horses little to do but keep out of the way and hold up the tongue. Perhaps it is well for one to know his fate at first, and get reconciled to it. We had learned ours in one afternoon. It was plain that we had to walk through the sand and shove that wagon and those horses two hundred miles. So we accepted the situation, and from that time forth we never rode. More than that, we stood regular and nearly constant watches pushing up behind.

We made seven miles and camped in the desert. Young Clagett (now member of Congress from Montana) unharnessed and fed and watered the horses; Oliphant and I cut sage-brush, built the fire, and brought water to cook with; and old Mr. Ballou the blacksmith did the cooking. This division of labor, and this appointment, was adhered to throughout the journey. We had no tent, and so we slept under our blankets in the open plain. We were so tired that we slept soundly.

We were fifteen days making the trip—two hundred miles; thirteen, rather, for we lay by a couple of days, in one place, to let the horses rest. We could really have accomplished the journey in ten days if we had towed the horses behind the wagon, but we did not think of that until it was too late, and so went on shoving the horses and the wagon too when we might have saved half the labor. Parties who met us, occasionally, advised us to put the horses *in* the wagon, but Mr. Ballou, through whose iron-clad earnestness no sarcasm could pierce, said that that would not do, because the provisions were exposed and would suffer, the horses being "bituminous from long deprivation." The reader will excuse me from translating. What Mr. Ballou customarily meant, when he used a long word, was a secret between himself and his Maker. He was one of the best and kindest hearted men that ever graced a humble sphere of life. He was gentleness and simplicity itself—and unselfishness, too. Although he was more than twice as old as the eldest of us, he never gave himself any airs, privileges, or exemptions on that account. He did a *young* man's share of the work; and did his share of conversing and entertaining from the general standpoint of *any* age—not from the arrogant, overawing summit-height of sixty years. His one striking peculiarity was his Partingtonian fashion of loving and using big words *for their own sakes*, and independent of any bearing they might have upon the thought he was purposing to convey. He always let his ponderous syllables fall with an easy unconsciousness that left them wholly without offensiveness. In truth his air was so natural and so simple that one was always catching himself accepting his stately sentences as meaning something, when they really meant nothing in the world. If a word was long and grand and resonant, that was sufficient to win the old man's love, and he would drop that word into the most out-of-the-way place in a sentence or a subject, and be as pleased with it as if it were perfectly luminous with meaning.

We four always spread our common stock of blankets together on the frozen ground, and slept side by side; and finding that our foolish, long-legged hound pup had a deal of animal heat in him, Oliphant got to admitting him to the bed, between himself and Mr. Ballou, hugging the dog's warm back to his breast and finding great comfort in it. But in the night the pup would get stretchy and brace his feet against the old man's back and shove, grunting complacently the while; and now and then, being warm and snug, grateful and happy, he would paw the old man's back simply in excess of comfort; and at yet other times he would dream of the chase and in his sleep tug at the old man's back hair and bark in his ear. The old gentleman complained mildly about these familiarities, at last, and when he got through with his statement he said that such a dog as that was not a proper animal to admit to bed with tired men, because he was "so meretricious in his movements and so organic in his emotions." We turned the dog out.

It was a hard, wearing, toilsome journey, but it had its bright side; for after each day was done and our wolfish hunger appeased with a hot supper of fried bacon, bread, molasses, and black coffee, the pipe-smoking, song-singing, and yarn-spinning around the evening camp-fire in the still solitudes of the desert was a happy, care-free sort of recreation that seemed the very summit and culmination of earthly luxury. It is a kind of life that has a potent charm for all men, whether city or country-bred. We are descended from desert-lounging Arabs, and countless ages of growth toward perfect civilization have failed to root out of us the nomadic instinct. We all confess to a gratified thrill at the thought of "camping out."

Once we made twenty-five miles in a day, and once we made forty miles (through the Great American Desert), and ten miles beyond—fifty in all—in twenty-three hours, without halting to eat, drink or rest. To stretch out and go to sleep, even on stony and frozen ground, after pushing a wagon and two horses fifty miles, is a delight so supreme that for the moment it almost seems cheap at the price.

We camped two days in the neighborhood of the "Sink of the Humboldt." We tried to use the strong alkaline water of the Sink, but it would not answer. It was like drinking lye, and not weak lye, either. It left a taste in the mouth, bitter and every way execrable, and a burning in the stomach that was very uncomfortable. We put molasses in it, but that helped it very little; we added a pickle, yet the alkali was the prominent taste, and so it was unfit for drinking. The coffee we made of this water was the meanest compound man has yet invented. It was really viler to the taste than the unameliorated water itself. Mr. Ballou, being the architect and builder of the beverage felt constrained to endorse and uphold it, and so drank half a cup, by little sips, making shift to praise it faintly the while, but finally threw out the remainder, and said frankly it was "too technical for *him*."

But presently we found a spring of fresh water, convenient, and then, with nothing to mar our enjoyment, and no stragglers to interrupt it, we entered into our rest.

Chapter XXVIII

AFTER LEAVING THE Sink, we traveled along the Humboldt River a little way. People accustomed to the monster mile-wide Mississippi grow accustomed to associating the term "river" with a high degree of watery grandeur. Consequently, such people feel rather disappointed when they stand on the shores of the Humboldt or the Carson and find that a "river" in Nevada is a sickly rivulet which is just the counterpart of the Erie canal in all respects save that the canal is twice as long and four times as deep. One of the pleasantest and most invigorating exercises one can contrive is to run and jump across the Humboldt River till he is overheated, and then drink it dry.

On the fifteenth day we completed our march of two hundred miles and entered Unionville, Humboldt county, in the midst of a driving snow-storm. Unionville consisted of eleven cabins and a liberty-pole. Six of the cabins were strung along one side of the deep canyon, and the other five faced them. The rest of the landscape was made up of bleak mountain walls that rose so high into the sky from both sides of the canyon that the village was left, as it were, far down in the bottom of a crevice. It was always daylight on the mountain tops a long time before the darkness lifted and revealed Unionville.

PLEASURES OF CAMPING OUT.

We built a small, rude cabin in the side of the crevice and roofed it with canvas, leaving a corner open to serve as a chimney, through which the cattle used to tumble occasionally, at night, and mash our furniture and interrupt our sleep. It was very cold weather and fuel was scarce. Indians brought brush and bushes several miles on their backs; and when we could catch a laden Indian it was well—and when we could not (which was the rule, not the exception), we shivered and bore it.

I confess, without shame, that I expected to find masses of silver lying all about the ground. I expected to see it glittering in the sun on the mountain summits. I said nothing about this, for some instinct told me that I might possibly have an exaggerated idea about it, and so if I betrayed my thought I might bring derision upon myself. Yet I was as perfectly satisfied in my own mind as I could be of anything, that I was going to gather up, in a day or two, or at furthest a week or two, silver enough to make me satisfactorily wealthy—and so my fancy was already busy with plans for spending this money. The first opportunity that offered, I sauntered carelessly away from the cabin, keeping an eye on the other boys, and stopping and contemplating the sky when they seemed to be observing me; but as soon as the coast was manifestly clear, I fled away as guiltily as a thief might have done and never halted till I was far beyond sight and call. Then I began my search with a feverish excitement that was brimful of expectation— almost of certainty. I crawled about the ground, seizing and examining bits of stone, blowing the dust from them or rubbing them on my clothes, and then peering at them with anxious hope. Presently I found a bright fragment and my heart bounded! I hid behind a boulder and polished it and scrutinized it with a nervous eagerness and a delight that was more pronounced than absolute certainty itself could have afforded. The more I examined the fragment, the more I was convinced that I had found the door to fortune. I marked the spot and carried away my specimen. Up and down the rugged mountain side I searched, with always increasing interest and always augmenting gratitude that I had come to Humboldt and come in time. Of all the experiences of my life, this secret search among the hidden treasures of silver-land was the nearest to unmarred ecstasy. It was a delirious revel. By and by, in the bed of a shallow rivulet, I found a deposit of shining yellow scales, and my breath almost forsook me! A gold mine, and in my simplicity I had been content with vulgar silver! I was so excited that I half believed my overwrought imagination was deceiving me. Then a fear came upon me that people might be observing me and would guess my secret. Moved by this thought, I made a circuit of the place, and ascended a knoll to reconnoiter. Solitude. No creature was near. Then I returned to my mine, fortifying myself against possible disappointment, but my fears were groundless—the shining scales were still there. I set about scooping them out, and for an hour I toiled down the windings of the stream and robbed its bed. But at last the descending sun warned me to give up the quest, and I turned homeward laden with wealth. As I walked along I could not help smiling at the thought of my being so excited over my fragment of silver when a nobler metal was almost under my nose. In this little time the former had so fallen in my estimation that once or twice I was on the point of throwing it away.

The boys were as hungry as usual, but I could eat nothing. Neither could I talk. I was full of dreams and far away. Their conversation interrupted the flow of my fancy somewhat, and annoyed me a little, too. I despised the sordid and commonplace things they talked about. But as they proceeded, it began to amuse me. It grew to be rare fun to hear them planning their poor little economies and sighing over possible privations and distresses when a gold mine, all our own, lay within sight of the cabin and I could point it out at any moment. Smothered hilarity began to oppress me, presently. It was hard to resist the impulse to burst out with exultation and reveal everything; but I did resist. I said within myself that I would filter the great news through my lips calmly and be serene as a summer morning while I watched its effect in their faces. I said:

"Where have you all been?"

"Prospecting."

"What did you find?"

"Nothing."

"Nothing? What do you think of the country?"

"Can't tell, yet," said Mr. Ballou, who was an old gold miner, and had likewise had considerable experience among the silver mines.

"Well, haven't you formed any sort of opinion?"

"Yes, a sort of a one. It's fair enough here, may be, but overrated. Seven-thousand-dollar ledges are scarce, though. That Sheba may be rich enough, but we don't own it; and besides, the rock is so full of base metals that all the science in the world can't work it. We'll not starve, here, but we'll not get rich, I'm afraid."

"So you think the prospect is pretty poor?"

"No name for it!"

"Well, we'd better go back, hadn't we?"

"Oh, not yet—of course not. We'll try it a riffle, first."

"Suppose, now—this is merely a supposition, you know—suppose you could find a ledge that would yield, say, a hundred and fifty dollars a ton—would that satisfy you?"

"Try us once!" from the whole party.

"Or suppose—merely a supposition, of course—suppose you were to find a ledge that would yield two thousand dollars a ton—would *that* satisfy you?"

"Here—what do you mean? What are you coming at? Is there some mystery behind all this?"

"Never mind. I am not saying anything. You know perfectly well there are no rich mines here—of course you do. Because you have been around and examined for yourselves. Anybody would know that, that had been around. But just for the sake of argument, suppose—in a kind of general way—suppose some person were to tell you that two-thousand-dollar ledges were simply contemptible—contemptible, understand—and that right yonder in sight of this very cabin there were piles of pure gold and pure silver—oceans of it—enough to make you all rich in twenty-four hours! Come!"

"I should say he was as crazy as a loon!" said old Ballou, but wild with excitement, nevertheless.

"Gentlemen," said I, "I don't say anything—*I* haven't been around, you know, and of course don't know anything—but all I ask of you is to cast your eye on *that*, for instance, and tell me what you think of it!" and I tossed my treasure before them.

There was an eager scramble for it, and a closing of heads together over it under the candle-light. Then old Ballou said:

"Think of it? I think it is nothing but a lot of granite rubbish and nasty glittering mica that isn't worth ten cents an acre!"

So vanished my dream. So melted my wealth away. So toppled my airy castle to the earth and left me stricken and forlorn.

Moralizing, I observed, then, that "all that glitters is not gold."

Mr. Ballou said I could go further than that, and lay it up among my treasures of knowledge, that *nothing* that glitters is gold. So I learned then, once for all, that gold in its native state is but dull, unornamental stuff, and that only low-born metals excite the admiration of the ignorant with an ostentatious glitter. However, like the rest of the world, I still go on underrating men of gold and glorifying men of mica. Commonplace human nature cannot rise above that.

Chapter XXIX

TRUE KNOWLEDGE OF the nature of silver mining came fast enough. We went out "prospecting" with Mr. Ballou. We climbed the mountain sides, and clambered among sage-brush, rocks and snow till we were ready to drop with exhaustion, but found no silver—nor yet any gold. Day after day we did this. Now and then we came upon holes burrowed a few feet into the declivities and apparently abandoned; and now and then we found one or two listless men still burrowing. But there was no appearance of silver. These holes were the beginnings of tunnels, and the purpose was to drive them hundreds of feet into the mountain, and some day tap the hidden ledge where the silver was. Some day! It seemed far enough away, and very hopeless and dreary. Day after day we toiled, and climbed and searched, and we younger partners grew sicker and still sicker of the promiseless toil. At last we halted under a beetling rampart of rock which projected from the earth high upon the mountain. Mr. Ballou broke off some fragments with a hammer, and examined them long and attentively with a small eye-glass; threw them away and broke off more; said this rock was quartz, and quartz was the sort of rock that contained silver. *Contained* it! I had thought that at least it would be caked on the outside of it like a kind of veneering. He still broke off pieces and critically examined them, now and then wetting the piece with his tongue and applying the glass. At last he exclaimed:

"We've got it!"

We were full of anxiety in a moment. The rock was clean and white, where it was broken, and across it ran a ragged thread of blue. He said that that little thread had silver in it, mixed with base metals, such as lead and antimony, and other rubbish, and that there was a speck or two of gold visible. After a great deal of effort we managed to discern some little fine yellow specks, and judged that a couple of tons of them massed together might make a gold dollar, possibly. We were not jubilant, but Mr. Ballou said there were worse ledges in the world than that. He saved what he called the "richest" piece of the rock, in order to determine its value by the process called the "fire-assay." Then we named the mine "Monarch of the Mountains" (modesty of nomenclature is not a prominent feature in the mines), and Mr. Ballou wrote out and stuck up the following "notice," preserving a copy to be entered upon the books in the mining recorder's office in the town.

"NOTICE"

"We the undersigned claim three claims, of three hundred feet each (and one for discovery), on this silver-bearing quartz lead or lode, extending north and south from this notice, with all its dips, spurs, and angles, variations and sinuosities, together with fifty feet of ground on either side for working the same."

We put our names to it and tried to feel that our fortunes were made. But when we talked the matter all over with Mr. Ballou, we felt depressed and dubious. He said that this surface quartz was not all there was to our mine; but that the wall or ledge of rock called the "Monarch of the Mountains," extended down hundreds and hundreds of feet into the earth—he illustrated by saying it was like a curb-stone, and maintained a nearly uniform thickness—say twenty feet—away down into the bowels of the earth, and was perfectly distinct from the casing rock on each side of it; and that it kept to itself, and maintained its distinctive character always, no matter how deep it extended into the earth or how far it stretched itself through and across the hills and valleys. He said it might be a mile deep and ten miles long, for all we knew; and that wherever we bored into it above ground or below, we would find gold and silver in it, but no gold or silver in the meaner rock it was cased between. And he said that down in the great depths of the ledge was its richness, and the deeper it went the richer it grew. Therefore, instead of working here on the surface, we must either bore down into the rock with a shaft till we came to where it was rich— say a hundred feet or so—or else we must go down into the valley and bore a long tunnel into the mountain side and tap the ledge far under the earth. To do either was plainly the labor of months; for we could blast and bore only a few feet a day—some five or six. But this was not all. He said that after we got the ore out it must be hauled in wagons to a distant silver-mill, ground up, and the silver extracted by a tedious and costly process. Our fortune seemed a century away!

But we went to work. We decided to sink a shaft. So, for a week we climbed the mountain, laden with picks, drills, gads, crowbars, shovels, cans of blasting powder and coils of fuse and strove with might and main. At first the rock was broken and loose and we dug it up with picks and threw it out with shovels, and the hole progressed very well. But the rock became more compact, presently, and gads and crowbars came into play. But shortly nothing could make an impression but blasting powder. That was the weariest work! One of us held the iron drill in its place and another would strike with an eight-pound sledge—it was like driving nails on a large scale. In the course of an hour or two the drill would reach a depth of two or three feet, making a hole a couple of inches in diameter. We would put in a charge of powder, insert half a yard of fuse, pour in sand and gravel and ram it down, then light the fuse and run. When the explosion came and the rocks and smoke shot into the air, we would go back and find about a bushel of that hard, rebellious quartz jolted out. Nothing more. One week of this satisfied me. I resigned. Clagget and Oliphant followed. Our shaft was only twelve feet deep. We decided that a tunnel was the thing we wanted.

So we went down the mountain side and worked a week; at the end of which time we had blasted a tunnel about deep enough to hide a hogshead in, and

INCIPIENT MILLIONAIRES.

judged that about nine hundred feet more of it would reach the ledge. I resigned again, and the other boys only held out one day longer. We decided that a tunnel was not what we wanted. We wanted a ledge that was already "developed." There were none in the camp.

We dropped the "Monarch" for the time being.

Meantime the camp was filling up with people, and there was a constantly growing excitement about our Humboldt mines. We fell victims to the epidemic and strained every nerve to acquire more "feet." We prospected and took up new claims, put "notices" on them and gave them grandiloquent names. We traded some of our "feet" for "feet" in other people's claims. In a little while we owned largely in the "Gray Eagle," the "Columbiana," the "Branch Mint," the "Maria Jane," the "Universe," the "Root-Hog-or-Die," the "Samson and Delilah," the "Treasure Trove," the "Golconda," the "Sultana," the "Boomerang," the "Great Republic," the "Grand Mogul," and fifty other "mines" that had never been molested by a shovel or scratched with a pick. We had not less than thirty thousand "feet" apiece in the "richest mines on earth" as the frenzied cant phrased it—and were in debt to the butcher. We were stark mad with excitement—drunk with happiness—smothered under mountains of prospective wealth—arrogantly compassionate toward the plodding millions who knew not our marvellous canyon—but our credit was not good at the grocer's.

It was the strangest phase of life one can imagine. It was a beggars' revel. There was nothing doing in the district—no mining—no milling—no productive effort—no income—and not enough money in the entire camp to buy a corner lot in an eastern village, hardly; and yet a stranger would have supposed he was walking among bloated millionaires. Prospecting parties swarmed out of town with the first flush of dawn, and swarmed in again at nightfall laden with spoil—rocks. Nothing but rocks. Every man's pockets were full of them; the floor of his cabin was littered with them; they were disposed in labeled rows on his shelves.

Chapter XXX

I MET MEN at every turn who owned from one thousand to thirty thousand "feet" in undeveloped silver mines, every single foot of which they believed would shortly be worth from fifty to a thousand dollars—and as often as any other way they were men who had not twenty-five dollars in the world. Every man you met had his new mine to boast of, and his "specimens" ready; and if the opportunity offered, he would infallibly back you into a corner and offer as a favor to *you,* not to *him,* to part with just a few feet in the "Golden Age," or the "Sarah Jane," or some other unknown stack of croppings, for money enough to get a "square meal" with, as the phrase went. And you were never to reveal that he had made you the offer at such a ruinous price, for it was only out of friendship for you that he was willing to make the sacrifice. Then he would fish a piece of rock out of his pocket, and after looking mysteriously around as if he feared he might be waylaid and robbed if caught with such wealth in his possession, he would dab the rock against his tongue, clap an eye-glass to it, and exclaim:

"Look at that! Right there in that red dirt! See it? See the specks of gold? And the streak of silver? That's from the 'Uncle Abe.' There's a hundred thousand tons like that in sight! Right in sight, mind you! And when we get down on it and the ledge comes in solid, it will be the richest thing in the world! Look at the assay! I don't want you to believe *me*—look at the assay!"

Then he would get out a greasy sheet of paper which showed that the portion of rock assayed had given evidence of containing silver and gold in the proportion of so many hundreds or thousands of dollars to the ton. I little knew, then, that the custom was to hunt out the *richest* piece of rock and get it assayed! Very often, that piece, the size of a filbert, was the only fragment in a ton that had a particle of metal in it—and yet the assay made it pretend to represent the average value of the ton of rubbish it came from!

On such a system of assaying as that, the Humboldt world had gone crazy. On the authority of such assays its newspaper correspondents were frothing about rock worth four and seven thousand dollars a ton!

And does the reader remember, a few pages back, the calculations, of a quoted correspondent, whereby the ore is to be mined and shipped all the way to England, the metals extracted, and the gold and silver contents received back by the miners as clear profit, the copper, antimony and other things in the ore being sufficient to pay all the expenses incurred? Everybody's head was full of such "calculations" as those—such raving insanity, rather. Few people took *work* into their calculations—or outlay of money either; except the work and expenditures of other people.

We never touched our tunnel or our shaft again. Why? Because we judged that we had learned the *real* secret of success in silver mining—which was, *not* to mine the silver ourselves by the sweat of our brows and the labor of our hands, but to *sell* the ledges to the dull slaves of toil and let them do the mining!

Before leaving Carson, the Secretary and I had purchased "feet" from various Esmeralda stragglers. We had expected immediate returns of bullion, but were only afflicted with regular and constant "assessments" instead—demands for money wherewith to develop the said mines. These assessments had grown so oppressive that it seemed necessary to look into the matter personally. Therefore I projected a pilgrimage to Carson and thence to Esmeralda. I bought a horse and started, in company with Mr. Ballou and a gentleman named Ollendorff, a Prussian—not the party who has inflicted so much suffering on the world with his wretched foreign grammars, with their interminable repetitions of questions which never have occurred and are never likely to occur in any conversation among human beings. We rode through a snow-storm for two or three days, and arrived at "Honey Lake Smith's," a sort of isolated inn on the Carson river. It was a two-story log house situated on a small knoll in the midst of the vast basin or desert through which the sickly Carson winds its melancholy way. Close to the house were the Overland stage stables, built of sun-dried bricks. There was not another building within several leagues of the place. Toward sunset about twenty hay-wagons arrived and camped around the house and all the teamsters came in to supper—a very, very rough set. There were one or two Overland stage drivers there, also, and half a dozen vagabonds and stragglers; consequently the house was well crowded.

We walked out, after supper, and visited a small Indian camp in the vicinity. The Indians were in a great hurry about something, and were packing up and getting away as fast as they could. In their broken English they said, "By'm-by, heap water!" and by the help of signs made us understand that in their opinion a flood was coming. The weather was perfectly clear, and this was not the rainy season. There was about a foot of water in the insignificant river—or maybe two feet; the stream was not wider than a back alley in a village, and its banks were scarcely higher than a man's head. So, where was the flood to come from? We canvassed the subject awhile and then concluded it was a ruse, and that the Indians had some better reason for leaving in a hurry than fears of a flood in such an exceedingly dry time.

At seven in the evening we went to bed in the second story—with our clothes on, as usual, and all three in the same bed, for every available space on the floors, chairs, etc., was in request, and even then there was barely room for the housing of the inn's guests. An hour later we were awakened by a great turmoil, and springing out of bed we picked our way nimbly among the ranks of snoring teamsters on the floor and got to the front windows of the long room. A glance revealed a strange spectacle, under the moonlight. The crooked Carson was full to the brim, and its waters were raging and foaming in the wildest way—sweeping around the sharp bends at a furious speed, and bearing on their surface a chaos of logs, brush and all sorts of rubbish. A depression, where its bed had once been, in other times, was already filling, and in one or two places the water was beginning to wash over the main bank. Men were flying hither and thither, bringing cattle and wagons close up to the house, for the spot of high ground on which it stood extended only some thirty feet in front and about a hundred in the rear. Close to the old river bed just spoken of, stood a little log stable, and in this our horses were lodged. While we looked, the waters increased so fast in this place that in a few minutes a torrent was roaring by the little stable and its margin encroaching steadily on the logs. We suddenly realized that this flood was not a mere holiday spectacle, but meant damage—and not only to the small log stable but to the Overland buildings close to the main river, for the waves had now come ashore and were creeping about the foundations and invading the great hay-corral adjoining. We ran down and joined the crowd of excited men and frightened animals. We waded knee-deep into the log stable, unfastened the horses and waded out almost *waist*-deep, so fast the waters increased. Then the crowd rushed in a body to the hay-corral and began to tumble down the huge stacks of baled hay and roll the bales up on the high ground by the house. Meantime it was discovered that Owens, an Overland driver, was missing, and a man ran to the large stable, and wading in, boot-top deep, discovered him asleep in his bed, awoke him, and waded out again. But Owens was drowsy and resumed his nap; but only for a minute or two, for presently he turned in his bed, his hand dropped over the side and came in contact with the cold water! It was up level with the mattress! He waded out, breast-deep, almost, and the next moment the sun-burned bricks melted down like sugar and the big building crumbled to a ruin and was washed away in a twinkling.

At eleven o'clock only the roof of the little log stable was out of water, and our inn was on an island in mid-ocean. As far as the eye could reach, in the moonlight, there was no desert visible, but only a level waste of shining water. The Indians were true prophets, but how did they get their information? I am not able to answer the question.

We remained cooped up eight days and nights with that curious crew. Swearing, drinking, and card playing were the order of the day, and occasionally a fight was thrown in for variety. Dirt and vermin—but let us forget those features; their profusion is simply inconceivable—it is better that they remain so.

There were two men—however, this chapter is long enough.

Chapter XXXI

THERE WERE TWO men in the company who caused me particular discomfort. One was a little Swede, about twenty-five years old, who knew only one song, and he was forever singing it. By day we were all crowded into one small, stifling bar-room, and so there was no escaping this person's music. Through all the profanity, whisky-guzzling, "old sledge" and quarreling, his monotonous song meandered with never a variation in its tiresome sameness, and it seemed to me, at last, that I would be content to die, in order to be rid of the torture. The other man was a stalwart ruffian called "Arkansas," who carried two revolvers in his belt and a bowie knife projecting from his boot, and who was always drunk and always suffering for a fight. But he was so feared, that nobody would accommodate him. He would try all manner of little wary ruses to entrap somebody into an offensive remark, and his face would light up now and then when he fancied he was fairly on the scent of a fight, but invariably his victim would elude his toils and then he would show a disappointment that was almost pathetic. The landlord, Johnson, was a meek, well-meaning fellow, and Arkansas fastened on him early, as a promising subject, and gave him no rest day or night, for a while. On the fourth morning, Arkansas got drunk and sat himself down to wait for an opportunity. Presently Johnson came in, just comfortably sociable with whisky, and said:

"I reckon the Pennsylvania 'lection—"

Arkansas raised his finger impressively and Johnson stopped. Arkansas rose unsteadily and confronted him. Said he:

"Wha-what do you know a-about Pennsylvania? Answer me that. Wha-what do you know 'bout Pennsylvania?"

"I was only goin' to say—"

"You was only goin' to *say. You* was! You was only goin' to say—*what* was you goin' to say? That's it! That's what *I* want to know. *I* want to know wha-what you ('*ic*) what you know about Pennsylvania, since you're makin' yourself so d—d free. Answer me that!"

"Mr. Arkansas, if you'd only let me—"

"Who's a henderin' you? Don't you insinuate nothing agin me!—don't you do it. Don't you come in here bullyin' around, and cussin' and goin' on like a lunatic—don't you do it. 'Coz *I* won't *stand* it. If fight's what you want, out with it! I'm your man! Out with it!"

Said Johnson, backing into a corner, Arkansas following, menacingly:

"Why, *I* never said nothing, Mr. Arkansas. You don't give a man no chance. I was only goin' to say that Pennsylvania was goin' to have an election next week—that was all—that was everything I was goin' to say—I wish I may never stir if it wasn't."

"Well then why d'n't you say it? What did you come swellin' around that way for, and tryin' to raise trouble?"

"Why *I* didn't come swellin' around, Mr. Arkansas—I just—"

"I'm a liar am I! Ger-reat Cæsar's ghost—"

"Oh, please, Mr. Arkansas, I never meant such a thing as that, I wish I may die if I did. All the boys will tell you that I've always spoke well of you, and respected you more'n any man in the house. Ask Smith. Ain't it so, Smith? Didn't I say, no longer ago than last night, that for a man that was a gentleman *all* the time and every way you took him, give me Arkansas? I'll leave it to any gentleman here if them warn't the very words I used. Come, now, Mr. Arkansas, le's take a drink—le's shake hands and take a drink. Come up—everybody! It's my treat. Come up, Bill, Tom, Bob, Scotty—come up. I want you all to take a drink with me and Arkansas—*old* Arkansas, I call him—bully old Arkansas. Gimme your hand agin. Look at him, boys—just take a *look* at him. Thar stands the whitest man in America!—and the man that denies it has got to fight *me,* that's all. Gimme that old flipper agin!"

They embraced, with drunken affection on the landlord's part and unresponsive toleration on the part of Arkansas, who, bribed by a drink, was disappointed of his prey once more. But the foolish landlord was so happy to have escaped butchery, that he went on talking when he ought to have marched himself out of danger. The consequence was that Arkansas shortly began to glower upon him dangerously, and presently said:

"Lan'lord, will you p-please make that remark over agin if you please?"

"I was a-sayin' to Scotty that my father was up'ards of eighty year old when he died."

"Was that *all* that you said?"

"Yes, that was all."

"Didn't say nothing but that?"

"No—nothing."

Then an uncomfortable silence.

Arkansas played with his glass a moment, lolling on his elbows on the counter. Then he meditatively scratched his left shin with his right boot, while the awkward silence continued. But presently he loafed away toward the stove, looking dissatisfied; roughly shouldered two or three men out of a comfortable position; occupied it himself, gave a sleeping dog a kick that sent him howling under a bench, then spread his long legs and his blanket-coat tails apart and proceeded to warm his back. In a little while he fell to grumbling to himself, and soon he slouched back to the bar and said:

"Lan'lord, what's your idea for rakin' up old personalities and blowin' about your father? Ain't this company agreeable to you? Ain't it? If this company ain't agreeable to you, p'r'aps we'd better leave. Is that your idea? Is that what you're coming at?"

"Why bless your soul, Arkansas, I warn't thinking of such a thing. My father and my mother—"

"Lan'lord, *don't* crowd a man! Don't do it. If nothing'll do you but a disturbance, out with it like a man (*'ic*)—but *don't* rake up old bygones and fling 'em in the teeth of a passel of people that wants to be peaceable if they could git a chance. What's the matter with you this mornin', anyway? I never see a man carry on so."

"Arkansas, I reely didn't mean no harm, and I won't go on with it if it's onpleasant to you. I reckon my licker's got into my head, and what with the flood, and havin' so many to feed and look out for—"

"So *that's* what's a-ranklin' in your heart, is it? You want us to leave do you? There's too many of us. You want us to pack up and swim. Is that it? Come!"

"Please be reasonable, Arkansas. Now *you* know that I ain't the man to—"

"Are you a threatenin' me? Are you? By George, the man don't live that can skeer me! Don't you try to come that game, my chicken—'cuz I can stand a good deal, but I won't stand that. Come out from behind that bar till I clean you! You want to drive us out, do you, you sneakin' underhanded hound! Come out from behind that bar! *I'll* learn you to bully and badger and browbeat a gentleman that's forever trying to befriend you and keep you out of trouble!"

"Please, Arkansas, please don't shoot! If there's got to be bloodshed—"

"Do you hear that, gentlemen? Do you hear him talk about bloodshed? So it's blood you want, is it, you ravin' desperado! You'd made up your mind to murder somebody this mornin'—I knowed it perfectly well. I'm the man, am I? It's me you're goin' to murder, is it? But you can't do it 'thout I get one chance first, you thievin' black-hearted, white-livered son of a nigger! Draw your weepon!"

With that, Arkansas began to shoot, and the landlord to clamber over benches, men and every sort of obstacle in a frantic desire to escape. In the midst of the wild hubbub the landlord crashed through a glass door, and as Arkansas charged after him the landlord's wife suddenly appeared in the doorway and confronted the desperado with a pair of scissors! Her fury was magnificent. With head erect and flashing eye she stood a moment and then advanced, with her weapon raised. The astonished ruffian hesitated, and then fell back a step. She followed. She backed him step by step into the middle of the bar-room, and then, while the wondering crowd closed up and gazed, she gave him such another tongue-lashing as never a cowed and shamefaced braggart got before, perhaps! As she finished and retired victorious, a roar of applause shook the house, and every man ordered "drinks for the crowd" in one and the same breath.

The lesson was entirely sufficient. The reign of terror was over, and the Arkansas domination broken for good. During the rest of the season of island

AN ARMED ALLY.

captivity, there was one man who sat apart in a state of permanent humiliation, never mixing in any quarrel or uttering a boast, and never resenting the insults the once cringing crew now constantly leveled at him, and that man was ''Arkansas.''

By the fifth or sixth morning the waters had subsided from the land, but the stream in the old river bed was still high and swift and there was no possibility of crossing it. On the eighth it was still too high for an entirely safe passage, but life in the inn had become next to insupportable by reason of the dirt, drunkenness, fighting, etc., and so we made an effort to get away. In the midst of a heavy snow-storm we embarked in a canoe, taking our saddles aboard and towing our horses after us by their halters. The Prussian, Ollendorff, was in the bow with a paddle, Ballou paddled in the middle, and I sat in the stern holding the halters. When the horses lost their footing and began to swim, Ollendorff got frightened, for there was great danger that the horses would make our aim uncertain, and it was plain that if we failed to land at a certain spot the current would throw us off and almost surely cast us into the main Carson, which was a boiling torrent, now. Such a catastrophe would be death, in all probability, for we would be swept to sea in the ''Sink'' or overturned and drowned. We warned Ollendorff to keep his wits about him and handle himself carefully, but it was useless; the moment the bow touched the bank, he made a spring and the canoe whirled upside down in ten-foot water. Ollendorff seized some brush and dragged himself ashore, but Ballou and I had to swim for it, encumbered with our overcoats. But we held onto the canoe, and although we were washed down nearly to the Carson, we managed to push the boat ashore and make a safe landing. We were cold and water-soaked, but safe. The horses made a landing, too, but our saddles were gone, of course. We tied the animals in the sage-brush and there they had to stay for twenty-four hours. We baled out the canoe and ferried over some food and blankets for them, but we slept one more night in the inn before making another venture on our journey.

The next morning it was still snowing furiously when we got away with our new stock of saddles and accoutrements. We mounted and started. The snow lay so deep on the ground that there was no sign of a road perceptible, and the snow-fall was so thick that we could not see more than a hundred yards ahead, else we could have guided our course by the mountain ranges. The case looked dubious, but Ollendorff said his intinct was as sensitive as any compass, and that he could "strike a bee-line" for Carson City and never diverge from it. He said that if he were to straggle a single point out of the true line his instinct would assail him like an outraged conscience. Consequently we dropped into his wake happy and content. For half an hour we poked along warily enough, but at the end of that time we came upon a fresh trail, and Ollendorff shouted proudly:

"I knew I was as dead certain as a compass, boys! Here we are, right in somebody's tracks that will hunt the way for us without any trouble. Let's hurry up and join company with the party."

So we put the horses into as much of a trot as the deep snow would allow, and before long it was evident that we were gaining on our predecessors, for the tracks grew more distinct. We hurried along, and at the end of an hour the tracks looked still newer and fresher—but what surprised us was, that the *number* of travelers in advance of us seemed to steadily increase. We wondered how so large a party came to be traveling at such a time and in such a solitude. Somebody suggested that it must be a company of soldiers from the fort, and so we accepted that solution and jogged along a little faster still, for they could not be far off now. But the tracks still multiplied, and we began to think the platoon of soldiers was miraculously expanding into a regiment—Ballou said they had already increased to five hundred! Presently he stopped his horse and said:

"Boys, these are our own tracks, and we're actually been circussing round and round in a circle for more than two hours, out here in this blind desert! By George this is perfectly hydraulic!"

Then the old man waxed wroth and abusive. He called Ollendorff all manner of hard names—said he never saw such a lurid fool as he was, and ended with the peculiarly venomous opinion that he "did not know as much as a logarythm!"

We certainly had been following our own tracks. Ollendorff and his "mental compass" were in disgrace from that moment. After all our hard travel, here we were on the bank of the stream again, with the inn beyond dimly outlined through the driving snow-fall. While we were considering what to do, the young Swede landed from the canoe and took his pedestrian way Carson-wards, singing his same tiresome song about his "sister and his brother" and "the child in the grave with its mother," and in a short minute faded and disappeared in the white oblivion. He was never heard of again. He no doubt got bewildered and lost, and Fatigue delivered him over to Sleep and Sleep betrayed him to Death. Possibly he followed our treacherous tracks till he became exhausted and dropped.

Presently the Overland stage forded the now fast receding stream and started toward Carson in its first trip since the flood came. We hesitated no longer, now, but took up our march in its wake, and trotted merrily along, for we had good confidence in the driver's bump of locality. But our horses were no match for the fresh stage team. We were soon left out of sight; but it was no matter, for we had the deep ruts the wheels made for a guide. By this time it was three in the afternoon, and consequently it was not very long before night came—and not with a lingering twilight, but with a sudden shutting down like a cellar door, as is its habit in that country. The snow-fall was still as thick as ever, and of course we could not see fifteen steps before us; but all about us the white glare of the snow-bed enabled us to discern the smooth sugar-loaf mounds made by the covered sage-bushes, and just in front of us the two faint grooves which we knew were the steadily filling and slowly disappearing wheel-tracks.

Now those sage-bushes were all about the same height—three or four feet; they stood just about seven feet apart, all over the vast desert; each of them was a mere snow-mound, now; in *any* direction that you proceeded (the same as in a well laid out orchard) you would find yourself moving down a distinctly defined avenue, with a row of these snow-mounds on either side of it—an avenue the customary width of a road, nice and level in its breadth, and rising at the sides in the most natural way, by reason of the mounds. But we had not thought of this. Then imagine the chilly thrill that shot through us when it finally occurred to us, far in the night, that since the last faint trace of the wheel tracks had long ago been buried from sight, we might now be wandering down a mere sage-brush avenue, miles away from the road and diverging further and further away from it all the time. Having a cake of ice slipped down one's back is placid comfort compared to it. There was a sudden leap and stir of blood that had been asleep for an hour, and as sudden a rousing of all the drowsing activities in our minds and bodies. We were alive and awake at once—and shaking and quaking with consternation, too. There was an instant halting and dismounting, a bending low and an anxious scanning of the road-bed. Useless, of course; for if a faint depression could not be discerned from an altitude of four or five feet above it, it certainly could not with one's nose nearly against it.

Chapter XXXII

WE SEEMED TO be in a road, but that was no proof. We tested this by walking off in various directions—the regular snow-mounds and the regular avenues between them convinced each man that *he* had found the true road, and that the others had found only false ones. Plainly the situation was desperate. We were cold and stiff and the horses were tired. We decided to build a sage-brush fire and camp out till morning. This was wise, because if we were wandering from the right road and the snow-storm continued another day our case would be the next thing to hopeless if we kept on.

All agreed that a camp fire was what would come nearest to saving us, now, and so we set about building it. We could find no matches, and so we tried to make shift with the pistols. Not a man in the party had ever tried to do such a thing before, but not a man in the party doubted that it *could* be done, and without any trouble—because every man in the party had read about it in books many a time and had naturally come to believe it, with trusting simplicity, just as he had long ago accepted and believed *that other* common book-fraud about Indians and lost hunters making a fire by rubbing two dry sticks together.

We huddled together on our knees in the deep snow, and the horses put their noses together and bowed their patient heads over us; and while the feathery flakes eddied down and turned us into a group of white statuary, we proceeded with the momentous experiment. We broke twigs from a sage bush and piled them on a little cleared place in the shelter of our bodies. In the course of ten or fifteen minutes all was ready, and then, while conversation ceased and our pulses beat low with anxious suspense, Ollendorff applied his revolver, pulled the trigger, and blew the pile clear out of the county! It was the flattest failure that ever was.

This was distressing, but it paled before a greater horror—the horses were gone! I had been appointed to hold the bridles, but in my absorbing anxiety over the pistol experiment I had unconsciously dropped them and the released animals had walked off in the storm. It was useless to try to follow them, for their footfalls could make no sound, and one could pass within two yards of the creatures and never see them. We gave them up without an effort at recovering them, and cursed the lying books that said horses would stay by their masters for protection and companionship in a distressful time like ours.

We were miserable enough, before; we felt still more forlorn, now. Patiently, but with blighted hope, we broke more sticks and piled them, and once more the Prussian shot them into annihilation. Plainly, to light a fire with a pistol was an art requiring practice and experience, and the middle of a desert at midnight in a snow-storm was not a good place or time for the acquiring of the accomplishment. We gave it up and tried the other. Each man took a couple of sticks and fell to chafing them together. At the end of half an hour we were thoroughly chilled, and so were the sticks. We bitterly execrated the Indians, the hunters and the books that had betrayed us with the silly device, and wondered dismally what was next to be done. At this critical moment Mr. Ballou fished out four matches from the rubbish of an overlooked pocket. To have found four gold bars would have seemed poor and cheap good luck compared to this. One cannot think how good a match looks under such circumstances—or how lovable and precious, and sacredly beautiful to the eye. This time we gathered sticks with high hopes; and when Mr. Ballou prepared to light the first match, there was an amount of interest centred upon him that pages of writing could not describe. The match burned hopefully a moment, and then went out. It could not have carried more regret with it if it had been a human life. The next match simply flashed and died. The wind puffed the third one out just as it was on the imminent verge of success. We gathered together closer than ever, and developed a solicitude that was rapt and painful, as Mr. Ballou scratched our last hope on his leg. It lit, burned blue and sickly, and then budded into a robust flame. Shading it with his hands, the old gentleman bent gradually down and every heart went with him—everybody, too, for that matter—and blood and breath stood still. The flame touched the sticks at last, took gradual hold upon them—hesitated—took a stronger hold—hesitated again—held its breath five heart-breaking seconds, then gave a sort of human gasp and went out.

Nobody said a word for several minutes. It was a solemn sort of silence; even the wind put on a stealthy, sinister quiet, and made no more noise than the falling flakes of snow. Finally a sad-voiced conversation began, and it was soon apparent that in each of our hearts lay the conviction that this was our last night with the living. I had so hoped that I was the only one who felt so. When the others calmly acknowledged their conviction, it sounded like the summons itself. Ollendorff said:

"Brothers, let us die together. And let us go without one hard feeling towards each other. Let us forget and forgive bygones. I know that you have felt hard towards me for turning over the canoe, and for knowing too much and leading you round and round in the snow—but I meant well; forgive me. I acknowledge freely that I have had hard feelings against Mr. Ballou for abusing me and calling me a logarythm, which is a thing I do not know what, but no doubt a thing considered disgraceful and unbecoming in America, and it has scarcely been out of my mind and has hurt me a great deal—but let it go; I forgive Mr. Ballou with all my heart, and—''

Poor Ollendorff broke down and the tears came. He was not alone, for I was crying too, and so was Mr. Ballou. Ollendorff got his voice again and forgave me for things I had done and said. Then he got out his bottle of whisky and said that whether he lived or died he would never touch another drop. He said he had given up all hope of life, and although ill-prepared, was ready to submit humbly to his fate; that he wished he could be spared a little longer, not for any selfish reason, but to make a thorough reform in his character, and by devoting himself to helping the poor, nursing the sick, and pleading with the people to guard themselves against the evils of intemperance, make his life a beneficent example to the young, and lay it down at last with the precious reflection that it had not been lived in vain. He ended by saying that his reform should begin at this moment, even here in the presence of death, since no longer time was to be vouchsafed wherein to prosecute it to men's help and benefit—and with that he threw away the bottle of whisky.

Mr. Ballou made remarks of similar purport, and began the reform he could not live to continue, by throwing away the ancient pack of cards that had solaced our captivity during the flood and made it bearable. He said he never gambled, but still was satisfied that the meddling with cards in any way was immoral and injurious, and no man could be wholly pure and blemishless without eschewing them. ''And therefore,'' continued he, ''in doing this act I already feel more in sympathy with that spiritual saturnalia necessary to entire and obsolete reform.'' These rolling syllables touched him as no intelligible eloquence could have done, and the old man sobbed with a mournfulness not unmingled with satisfaction.

My own remarks were of the same tenor as those of my comrades, and I know that the feelings that prompted them were heartfelt and sincere. We were all sincere, and all deeply moved and earnest, for we were in the presence of death and without hope. I threw away my pipe, and in doing it felt that at last I was free of a hated vice and one that had ridden me like a tyrant all my days. While I yet talked, the thought of the good I might have done in the world and the still greater good I might *now* do, with these new incentives and higher and better aims to guide me if I could only be spared a few years longer, overcame me and the tears came again. We put our arms about each other's necks and awaited the warning drowsiness that precedes death by freezing.

It came stealing over us presently, and then we bade each other a last farewell. A delicious dreaminess wrought its web about my yielding senses, while the snow-flakes wove a winding sheet about my conquered body. Oblivion came. The battle of life was done.

Chapter XXXIII

I DO NOT know how long I was in a state of forgetfulness, but it seemed an age. A vague consciousness grew upon me by degrees, and then came a gathering anguish of pain in my limbs and through all my body. I shuddered. The thought flitted through my brain, ''this is death—this is the hereafter.''

Then came a white upheaval at my side, and a voice said, with bitterness: "Will some gentleman be so good as to kick me behind?"

It was Ballou—at least it was a towzled snow image in a sitting posture, with Ballou's voice.

I rose up, and there in the gray dawn, not fifteen steps from us, were the frame buildings of a stage station, and under a shed stood our still saddled and bridled horses!

An arched snow-drift broke up, now, and Ollendorff emerged from it, and the three of us sat and stared at the houses without speaking a word. We really had nothing to say. We were like the profane man who could not "do the subject justice," the whole situation was so painfully ridiculous and humiliating that words were tame and we did not know where to commence anyhow.

The joy in our hearts at our deliverance was poisoned; well-nigh dissipated, indeed. We presently began to grow pettish by degrees, and sullen; and then, angry at each other, angry at ourselves, angry at everything in general, we moodily dusted the snow from our clothing and in unsociable single file plowed our way to the horses, unsaddled them, and sought shelter in the station.

I have scarcely exaggerated a detail of this curious and absurd adventure. It occurred almost exactly as I have stated it. We actually went into camp in a snow-drift in a desert, at midnight in a storm, forlorn and hopeless, within fifteen steps of a comfortable inn.

For two hours we sat apart in the station and ruminated in disgust. The mystery was gone, now, and it was plain enough why the horses had deserted us. Without a doubt they were under that shed a quarter of a minute after they had left us, and they must have overheard and enjoyed all our confessions and lamentations.

After breakfast we felt better, and the zest of life soon came back. The world looked bright again, and existence was as dear to us as ever. Presently an uneasiness came over me—grew upon me—assailed me without ceasing. Alas, my regeneration was not complete—I wanted to smoke! I resisted with all my strength, but the flesh was weak. I wandered away alone and wrestled with myself an hour. I recalled my promises of reform and preached to myself persuasively, upbraidingly, exhaustively. But it was all vain, I shortly found myself sneaking among the snow-drifts hunting for my pipe. I discovered it after a considerable search, and crept away to hide myself and enjoy it. I remained behind the barn a good while, asking myself how I would feel if my braver, stronger, truer comrades should catch me in my degradation. At last I lit the pipe, and no human being can feel meaner and baser than I did then. I was ashamed of being in my own pitiful company. Still dreading discovery, I felt that perhaps the further side of the barn would be somewhat safer, and so I turned the corner. As I turned the one corner, smoking, Ollendorff turned the other with his bottle to his lips, and between us sat unconscious Ballou deep in a game of "solitaire" with the old greasy cards!

Absurdity could go no farther. We shook hands and agreed to say no more about "reform" and "examples to the rising generation."

The station we were at was at the verge of the Twenty-six-Mile Desert. If we had approached it half an hour earlier the night before, we must have heard men shouting there and firing pistols; for they were expecting some sheep drovers and their flocks and knew that they would infallibly get lost and wander out of reach of help unless guided by sounds. While we remained at the station, three

of the drovers arrived, nearly exhausted with their wanderings, but two others
of their party were never heard of afterward.

We reached Carson in due time, and took a rest. This rest, together with
preparations for the journey to Esmeralda, kept us there a week, and the delay
gave us the opportunity to be present at the trial of the great land-slide case of
Hyde *vs*. Morgan—an episode which is famous in Nevada to this day. After a
word or two of necessary explanation, I will set down the history of this singular
affair just as it transpired.

Chapter XXXIV

THE MOUNTAINS ARE very high and steep about Carson, Eagle and Washoe
Valleys—very high and very steep, and so when the snow gets to melting off
fast in the Spring and the warm surface-earth begins to moisten and soften, the
disastrous land-slides commence. The reader cannot know what a land-slide is,
unless he has lived in that country and seen the whole side of a mountain taken
off some fine morning and deposited down in the valley, leaving a vast, treeless,
unsightly scar upon the mountain's front to keep the circumstance fresh in his
memory all the years that he may go on living within seventy miles of that place.

General Buncombe was shipped out to Nevada in the invoice of Territorial
officers, to be United States Attorney. He considered himself a lawyer of parts,
and he very much wanted an opportunity to manifest it—partly for the pure
gratification of it and partly because his salary was Territorially meagre (which
is a strong expression). Now the older citizens of a new territory look down
upon the rest of the world with a calm, benevolent compassion, as long as it
keeps out of the way—when it gets in the way they snub it. Sometimes this
latter takes the shape of a practical joke.

One morning Dick Hyde rode furiously up to General Buncombe's door in
Carson City and rushed into his presence without stopping to tie his horse. He
seemed much excited. He told the general that he wanted him to conduct a suit
for him and would pay him five hundred dollars if he achieved a victory. And
then, with violent gestures and a world of profanity, he poured out his griefs.
He said it was pretty well known that for some years he had been farming (or
ranching as the more customary term is) in Washoe District, and making a
successful thing of it, and furthermore it was known that his ranch was situated
just in the edge of the valley, and that Tom Morgan owned a ranch immediately
above it on the mountain side. And now the trouble was, that one of those hated
and dreaded land-slides had come and slid Morgan's ranch, fences, cabins, cattle,
barns and everything down on top of *his* ranch and exactly covered up every
single vestige of his property, to a depth of about thirty-eight feet. Morgan was
in possession and refused to vacate the premises—said he was occupying his
own cabin and not interfering with anybody else's—and said the cabin was
standing on the same dirt and same ranch it had always stood on, and he would
like to see anybody make him vacate.

"And when I reminded him," said Hyde, weeping, "that it was on top of
my ranch and that he was trespassing, he had the infernal meanness to ask me
why didn't I *stay* on my ranch and hold possession when I see him a-coming!

Why didn't I *stay* on it, the blathering lunatic—by George, when I heard that racket and looked up that hill it was just like the whole world was a-ripping and a-tearing down that mountain side—splinters, and cord-wood, thunder and lightning, hail and snow, odds and ends of hay stacks, and awful clouds of dust!—trees going end over end in the air, rocks as big as a house jumping 'bout a thousand feet high and busting into ten million pieces, cattle turned inside out and a-coming head on with their tails hanging out between their teeth!—and in the midst of all that wrack and destruction sot that cussed Morgan on his gate-post, a-wondering why I didn't *stay and hold possession!* Laws bless me, I just took one glimpse, General, and lit out'n the county in three jumps exactly.

"But what grinds me is that that Morgan hangs on there and won't move off'n that ranch—says it's his'n and he's going to keep it—likes it better'n he did when it was higher up the hill. Mad! Well, I've been so mad for two days I couldn't find my way to town—been wandering around in the brush in a starving condition—got anything here to drink, General? But I'm here *now,* and I'm a-going to law. You hear *me!*"

Never in all the world, perhaps, were a man's feelings so outraged as were the General's. He said he had never heard of such high-handed conduct in all his life as this Morgan's. And he said there was no use in going to law—Morgan had no shadow of right to remain where he was—nobody in the wide world would uphold him in it, and no lawyer would take his case and no judge listen to it. Hyde said that right there was where he was mistaken—everybody in town sustained Morgan; Hal Brayton, a very smart lawyer, had taken his case; the courts being in vacation, it was to be tried before a referee, and ex-Governor Roop had already been appointed to that office and would open his court in a large public hall near the hotel at two that afternoon.

The General was amazed. He said he had suspected before that the people of that Territory were fools, and now he knew it. But he said rest easy, rest easy and collect the witnesses, for the victory was just as certain as if the conflict were already over. Hyde wiped away his tears and left.

At two in the afternoon referee Roop's court opened, and Roop appeared throned among his sheriffs, the witnesses, and spectators, and wearing upon his face a solemnity so awe-inspiring that some of his fellow-conspirators had misgivings that maybe he had not comprehended, after all, that this was merely a joke. An unearthly stillness prevailed, for at the slightest noise the judge uttered sternly the command:

"Order in the Court!"

And the sheriffs promptly echoed it. Presently the General elbowed his way through the crowd of spectators, with his arms full of law-books, and on his ears fell an order from the judge which was the first respectful recognition of his high official dignity that had ever saluted them, and it trickled pleasantly through his whole system:

"Way for the United States Attorney!"

The witnesses were called—legislators, high government officers, ranchmen, miners, Indians, Chinamen, negroes. Three fourths of them were called by the defendant Morgan, but no matter, their testimony invariably went in favor of the plaintiff Hyde. Each new witness only added new testimony to the absurdity of a man's claiming to own another man's property because his farm had slid down on top of it. Then the Morgan lawyers made their speeches, and seemed to make singularly weak ones—they did really nothing to help the Morgan cause.

And now the General, with exultation in his face, got up and made an impassioned effort; he pounded the table, he banged the law-books, he shouted, and roared, and howled, he quoted from everything and everybody, poetry, sarcasm, statistics, history, pathos, bathos, blasphemy, and wound up with a grand war-whoop for free speech, freedom of the press, free schools, the Glorious Bird of America and the principles of eternal justice! [Applause.]

When the General sat down, he did it with the conviction that if there was anything in good strong testimony, a great speech and believing and admiring countenances all around, Mr. Morgan's case was killed. Ex-Governor Roop leaned his head upon his hand for some minutes, thinking, and the still audience waited for his decision. Then he got up and stood erect, with bended head, and thought again. Then he walked the floor with long, deliberate strides, his chin in his hand, and still the audience waited. At last he returned to his throne, seated himself, and began, impressively:

"Gentlemen, I feel the great responsibility that rests upon me this day. This is no ordinary case. On the contrary it is plain that it is the most solemn and awful that ever man was called upon to decide. Gentlemen, I have listened attentively to the evidence, and have perceived that the weight of it, the over-whelming weight of it, is in favor of the plaintiff Hyde. I have listened also to the remarks of counsel, with high interest—and especially will I commend the masterly and irrefutable logic of the distinguished gentleman who represents the plaintiff. But gentlemen, let us beware how we allow mere human testimony, human ingenuity in argument and human ideas of equity, to influence us at a moment so solemn as this. Gentlemen, it ill becomes us, worms as we are, to meddle with the decrees of Heaven. It is plain to me that Heaven, in its inscrutable wisdom, has seen fit to move this defendant's ranch for a purpose. We are but creatures, and we must submit. If Heaven has chosen to favor the defendant Morgan in this marked and wonderful manner; and if Heaven, dissatisfied with the position of the Morgan ranch upon the mountain side, has chosen to remove it to a position more eligible and more advantageous for its owner, it ill becomes us, insects as we are, to question the legality of the act or inquire into the reasons that prompted it. No—Heaven created the ranches and it is Heaven's prerogative to rearrange them, to experiment with them, to shift them around at its pleasure. It is for us to submit, without repining. I warn you that this thing which has happened is a thing with which the sacrilegious hands and brains and tongues of men must not meddle. Gentlemen, it is the verdict of this court that the plaintiff, Richard Hyde, has been deprived of his ranch by the visitation of God! And from this decision there is no appeal."

Buncombe seized his cargo of law-books and plunged out of the court-room frantic with indignation. He pronounced Roop to be a miraculous fool, an inspired idiot. In all good faith he returned at night and remonstrated with Roop upon his extravagant decision, and implored him to walk the floor and think for half an hour, and see if he could not figure out some sort of modification of the verdict. Roop yielded at last and got up to walk. He walked two hours and a half, and at last his face lit up happily and he told Buncombe it had occurred to him that the ranch underneath the new Morgan ranch still belonged to Hyde, that his title to the ground was just as good as it had ever been, and therefore he was of opinion that Hyde had a right to dig it out from under there and—

The General never waited to hear the end of it. He was always an impatient and irascible man, that way. At the end of two months the fact that he had been played upon with a joke had managed to bore itself, like another Hoosac Tunnel, through the solid adamant of his understanding.

Chapter XXXV

WHEN WE FINALLY left for Esmeralda, horseback, we had an addition to the company in the person of Capt. John Nye, the Governor's brother. He had a good memory, and a tongue hung in the middle. This is a combination which gives immortality to conversation. Capt. John never suffered the talk to flag or falter once during the hundred and twenty miles of the journey. In addition to his conversational powers, he had one or two other endowments of a marked character. One was a singular "handiness" about doing anything and everything, from laying out a railroad or organizing a political party, down to sewing on buttons, shoeing a horse, or setting a broken leg, or a hen. Another was a spirit of accommodation that prompted him to take the needs, difficulties and perplexities of anybody and everybody upon his own shoulders at any and all times, and dispose of them with admirable facility and alacrity—hence he always managed to find vacant beds in crowded inns, and plenty to eat in the emptiest larders. And finally, wherever he met a man, woman, or child, in camp, inn, or desert, he either knew such parties personally or had been acquainted with a relative of the same. Such another traveling comrade was never seen before. I cannot forbear giving a specimen of the way in which he overcame difficulties. On the second day out, we arrived, very tired and hungry, at a poor little inn in the desert, and were told that the house was full, no provisions on hand, and neither hay nor barley to spare for the horses—we must move on. The rest of us wanted to hurry on while it was yet light, but Capt. John insisted on stopping awhile. We dismounted and entered. There was no welcome for us on any face. Capt. John began his blandishments, and within twenty minutes he had accomplished the following things, viz.: found old acquaintances in three teamsters; discovered that he used to go to school with the landlord's mother; recognized his wife as a lady whose life he had saved once in California, by stopping her runaway horse; mended a child's broken toy and won the favor of its mother, a guest of the inn; helped the hostler bleed a horse, and prescribed for another horse that had the "heaves"; treated the entire party three times at the landlord's bar; produced a later paper than anybody had seen for a week and sat himself down to read the news to a deeply interested audience. The result, summed up, was as follows: The hostler found plenty of feed for our horses; we had a trout supper, an exceedingly sociable time after it, good beds to sleep in, and a surprising breakfast in the morning—and when we left, we left lamented by all! Capt. John had some bad traits, but he had some uncommonly valuable ones to offset them with.

Esmeralda was in many respects another Humboldt, but in a little more forward state. The claims we had been paying assessments on were entirely worthless, and we threw them away. The principal one cropped out of the top of a knoll that was fourteen feet high, and the inspired Board of Directors were running a tunnel under that knoll to strike the ledge. The tunnel would have to be seventy feet long, and would then strike the ledge at the same depth that a *shaft* twelve feet deep would have reached! The Board were living on the "assessments." [N.B.—This hint comes too late for the enlightenment of New York silver miners; they have already learned all about this neat trick by experience.] The Board had no desire to strike the ledge, knowing that it was as barren of silver as a curbstone. This reminiscence calls to mind Jim Townsend's tunnel. He had paid assessments on a mine called the "Daley" till he was well-nigh penniless. Finally an assessment was levied to run a tunnel two hundred and fifty feet on the Daley, and Townsend went up on the hill to look into matters. He found the Daley cropping out of the apex of an exceedingly sharp-pointed peak, and a couple of men up there "facing" the proposed tunnel. Townsend made a calculation. Then he said to the men:

"So you have taken a contract to run a tunnel into this hill two hundred and fifty feet to strike this ledge?"

"Yes, sir."

"Well, do you know that you have got one of the most expensive and arduous undertakings before you that was ever conceived by man?"

"Why no—how is that?"

"Because this hill is only twenty-five feet through from side to side; and so you have got to build two hundred and twenty-five feet of your tunnel on trestle-work!"

The ways of silver mining Boards are exceedingly dark and sinuous.

We took up various claims, and *commenced* shafts and tunnels on them, but never finished any of them. We had to do a certain amount of work on each to "hold" it, else other parties could seize our property after the expiration of ten days. We were always hunting up new claims and doing a little work on them and then waiting for a buyer—who never came. We never found any ore that would yield more than fifty dollars a ton; and as the mills charged fifty dollars a ton for *working* ore and extracting the silver, our pocket-money melted steadily away and none returned to take its place. We lived in a little cabin and cooked for ourselves; and altogether it was a hard life, though a hopeful one—for we never ceased to expect fortune and a customer to burst upon us some day.

At last, when flour reached a dollar a pound, and money could not be borrowed on the best security at less than *eight per cent a month* (I being without the security, too), I abandoned mining and went to milling. That is to say, I went to work as a common laborer in a quartz mill, at ten dollars a week and board.

Chapter XXXVI

I HAD ALREADY learned how hard and long and dismal a task it is to burrow down into the bowels of the earth and get out the coveted ore; and now I learned that the burrowing was only half the work; and that to get the silver out of the ore was the dreary and laborious other half of it. We had to turn out at six in the morning and keep at it till dark. This mill was a six-stamp affair, driven by steam. Six tall, upright rods of iron, as large as a man's ankle, and heavily shod with a mass of iron and steel at their lower ends, were framed together like a gate, and these rose and fell, one after the other, in a ponderous dance, in an iron box called a "battery." Each of these rods or stamps weighed six hundred pounds. One of us stood by the battery all day long, breaking up masses of silver-bearing rock with a sledge and shoveling it into the battery. The ceaseless dance of the stamps pulverized the rock to powder, and a stream of water that trickled into the battery turned it to a creamy paste. The minutest particles were driven through a fine wire screen which fitted close around the battery, and were washed into great tubs warmed by super-heated steam—amalgamating pans, they are called. The mass of pulp in the pans was kept constantly stirred up by revolving "mullers." A quantity of quicksilver was kept always in the battery, and this seized some of the liberated gold and silver particles and held on to them; quicksilver was shaken in a fine shower into the pans, also, about every half hour, through a buckskin sack. Quantities of coarse salt and sulphate of copper were added, from time to time to assist the amalgamation by destroying base metals which coated the gold and silver and would not let it unite with the quicksilver. All these tiresome things we had to attend to constantly. Streams of dirty water flowed always from the pans and were carried off in broad wooden troughs to the ravine. One would not suppose that atoms of gold and silver would float on top of six inches of water, but they did; and in order to catch them, coarse blankets were laid in the troughs, and little obstructing "riffles" charged with quicksilver were placed here and there across the troughs also. These riffles had to be cleaned and the blankets washed out every evening, to get their precious accumulations—and after all this eternity of trouble one third of the silver and gold in a ton of rock would find its way to the end of the troughs in the ravine at last and have to be worked over again some day. There is nothing so aggravating as silver milling. There never was any idle time in that mill. There was always something to do. It is a pity that Adam could not have gone straight out of Eden into a quartz mill, in order to understand the full force of his doom to "earn his bread by the sweat of his brow." Every now and then, during the day, we had to scoop some pulp out of the pans, and tediously "wash" it in a horn spoon—wash it little by little over the edge till at last nothing was left but some little dull globules of quicksilver in the bottom. If they were soft and yielding, the pan needed some salt or some sulphate of copper or some other chemical rubbish to assist digestion; if they were crisp to the touch and would retain a dint, they were freighted with all the silver and gold they could seize and hold, and consequently the pans needed a fresh charge of quicksilver. When there was nothing else to do, one could always "screen tailings." That is to say, he could shovel up the dried sand that had washed down to the ravine through the troughs and dash it against an upright wire screen to free it from pebbles and prepare it for working over. The process of amalgamation differed in the various mills, and this included changes in style of pans and other machinery, and a great diversity of opinion existed as to the best in use, but none of the methods employed involved the principle of drilling ore without "screening the tailings." Of all recreations in the world, screening tailings on a hot day, with a long-handled shovel, is the most undesirable.

At the end of the week the machinery was stopped and we "cleaned up." That is to say, we got the pulp out of the pans and batteries, and washed the mud patiently away till nothing was left but the long accumulating mass of quicksilver, with its imprisoned treasures. This we made into heavy, compact snow-balls, and piled them up in a bright, luxurious heap for inspection. Making these snow-balls cost me a fine gold ring—that and ignorance together; for the quicksilver invaded the ring with the same facility with which water saturates a sponge—separated its particles and the ring crumbled to pieces.

We put our pile of quicksilver balls into an iron retort that had a pipe leading from it to a pail of water, and then applied a roasting heat. The quicksilver turned to vapor, escaped through the pipe into the pail, and the water turned it into good wholesome quicksilver again. Quicksilver is very costly, and they never waste it. On opening the retort, there was our week's work—a lump of pure white, frosty looking silver, twice as large as a man's head. Perhaps a fifth of the mass was gold, but the color of it did not show—would not have shown if two thirds of it had been gold. We melted it up and made a solid brick of it by pouring it into an iron brick-mould.

By such a tedious and laborious process were silver bricks obtained. This mill was but one of many others in operation at the time. The first one in Nevada was built at Egan Canyon and was a small insignificant affair and compared most unfavorably with some of the immense establishments afterwards located at Virginia City and elsewhere.

From our bricks a little corner was chipped off for the "fire-assay"—a method used to determine the proportions of gold, silver and base metals in the mass. This is an interesting process. The chip is hammered out as thin as paper and weighed on scales so fine and sensitive that if you weigh a two-inch scrap of paper on them and then write your name on the paper with a coarse, soft pencil and weigh it again, the scales will take marked notice of the addition. Then a little lead (also weighed) is rolled up with the flake of silver and the two are melted at a great heat in a small vessel called a cupel, made by compressing bone ashes into a cup-shape in a steel mold. The base metals oxydize and are absorbed with the lead into the pores of the cupel. A button or globule of perfectly pure gold and silver is left behind, and by weighing it and noting the loss, the assayer knows the proportion of base metal the brick contains. He has to separate the gold from the silver now. The button is hammered out flat and thin, put in the furnace and kept some time at a red heat; after cooling it off it is rolled up like a quill and heated in a glass vessel containing nitric acid; the acid dissolves the silver and leaves the gold pure and ready to be weighed on its own merits. Then salt water is poured into the vessel containing the dissolved silver and the silver returns to palpable form again and sinks to the bottom. Nothing now remains but to weigh it; then the proportions of the several metals contained in the brick are known, and the assayer stamps the value of the brick upon its surface.

The sagacious reader will know now, without being told, that the speculative miner, in getting a "fire-assay" made of a piece of rock from his mine (to help him sell the same), was not in the habit of picking out the least valuable fragment of rock on his dump-pile, but quite the contrary. I have seen men hunt over a pile of nearly worthless quartz for an hour, and at last find a little piece as large as a filbert, which was rich in gold and silver—and this was reserved for a fire-assay! Of course the fire-assay would demonstrate that a ton of such rock would yield hundreds of dollars—and on such assays many an utterly worthless mine was sold.

Assaying was a good business, and so some men engaged in it, occasionally, who were not strictly scientific and capable. One assayer got such rich results out of all specimens brought to him that in time he acquired almost a monopoly of the business. But like all men who achieve success, he became an object of envy and suspicion. The other assayers entered into a conspiracy against him, and let some prominent citizens into the secret in order to show that they meant fairly. Then they broke a little fragment off a carpenter's grindstone and got a stranger to take it to the popular scientist and get it assayed. In the course of an hour the result came—whereby it appeared that a ton of that rock would yield $1,284.40 in silver and $366.36 in gold!

Due publication of the whole matter was made in the paper, and the popular assayer left town "between two days."

I will remark, in passing, that I only remained in the milling business one week. I told my employer I could not stay longer without an advance in my wages; that I liked quartz milling, indeed was infatuated with it; that I had never before grown so tenderly attached to an occupation in so short a time; that nothing, it seemed to me, gave such scope to intellectual activity as feeding a battery and screening tailings, and nothing so stimulated the moral attributes as retorting bullion and washing blankets—still, I felt constrained to ask an increase of salary.

He said he was paying me ten dollars a week, and thought it a good round sum. How much did I want?

I said about four hundred thousand dollars a month, and board, was about all I could reasonably ask, considering the hard times.

I was ordered off the premises! And yet, when I look back to those days and call to mind the exceeding hardness of the labor I performed in that mill, I only regret that I did not ask him seven hundred thousand.

Shortly after this I began to grow crazy, along with the rest of the population, about the mysterious and wonderful "cement mine," and to make preparations to take advantage of any opportunity that might offer to go and help hunt for it.

Chapter XXXVII

IT WAS SOMEWHERE in the neighborhood of Mono Lake that the marvelous Whiteman cement mine was supposed to lie. Every now and then it would be reported that Mr. W. had passed stealthily through Esmeralda at dead of night, in disguise, and then we would have a wild excitement—because he must be steering for his secret mine, and now was the time to follow him. In less than three hours after daylight all the horses and mules and donkeys in the vicinity would be bought, hired or stolen, and half the community would be off for the mountains, following in the wake of Whiteman. But W. would drift about through the mountain gorges for days together, in a purposeless sort of way, until the provisions of the miners ran out, and they would have to go back home. I have known it reported at eleven at night, in a large mining camp, that Whiteman had just passed through, and in two hours the streets, so quiet before, would be swarming with men and animals. Every individual would be trying to be very secret, but yet venturing to whisper to just one neighbor that W. had passed through. And long before daylight—this in the dead of winter—the stampede would be complete, the camp deserted, and the whole population gone chasing after W.

The tradition was that in the early immigration, more than twenty years ago, three young Germans, brothers, who had survived an Indian massacre on the Plains, wandered on foot through the deserts, avoiding all trails and roads, and simply holding a westerly direction and hoping to find California before they starved, or died of fatigue. And in a gorge in the mountains they sat down to rest one day, when one of them noticed a curious vein of cement running along the ground, shot full of lumps of dull yellow metal. They saw that it was gold, and that here was a fortune to be acquired in a single day. The vein was about as wide as a curbstone, and fully two thirds of it was pure gold. Every pound of the wonderful cement was worth well-nigh $200. Each of the brothers loaded himself with about twenty-five pounds of it, and then they covered up all traces of the vein, made a rude drawing of the locality and the principal landmarks in the vicinity, and started westward again. But troubles thickened about them. In their wanderings one brother fell and broke his leg, and the others were obliged to go on and leave him to die in the wilderness. Another, worn out and starving, gave up by and by, and laid down to die, but after two or three weeks of incredible hardships, the third reached the settlements of California exhausted, sick, and his mind deranged by his sufferings. He had thrown away all his cement but a few fragments, but these were sufficient to set everybody wild with excitement. However, he had had enough of the cement country, and nothing could induce him to lead a party thither. He was entirely content to work on a farm for wages. But he gave Whiteman his map, and described the cement region as well as he could, and thus transferred the curse to that gentleman—for when I had my one accidental glimpse of Mr. W. in Esmeralda he had been hunting for the lost mine, in hunger and thirst, poverty and sickness, for twelve or thirteen years. Some people believed he had found it, but most people believed he had not. I saw a piece of cement as large as my fist which was said to have been given to Whiteman by the young German, and it was of a seductive nature. Lumps of virgin gold were as thick in it as raisins in a slice of fruit cake. The privilege of working such a mine one week would be sufficient for a man of reasonable desires.

A new partner of ours, a Mr. Higbie, knew Whiteman well by sight, and a friend of ours, a Mr. Van Dorn, was well acquainted with him, and not only

THE SAVED BROTHER

that, but had Whiteman's promise that he should have a private hint in time to enable him to join the next cement expedition. Van Dorn had promised to extend the hint to us. One evening Higbie came in greatly excited, and said he felt certain he had recognized Whiteman, up town, disguised and in a pretended state of intoxication. In a little while Van Dorn arrived and confirmed the news; and so we gathered in our cabin and with heads close together arranged our plans in impressive whispers.

We were to leave town quietly, after midnight, in two or three small parties, so as not to attract attention, and meet at dawn on the "divide" overlooking Mono Lake, eight or nine miles distant. We were to make no noise after starting, and not speak above a whisper under any circumstances. It was believed that for once Whiteman's presence was unknown in the town and his expedition unsuspected. Our conclave broke up at nine o'clock, and we set about our preparations diligently and with profound secrecy. At eleven o'clock we saddled our horses, hitched them with their long *riatas* (or lassos), and then brought out a side of bacon, a sack of beans, a small sack of coffee, some sugar, a hundred pounds of flour in sacks, some tin cups and a coffee pot, frying pan and some few other necessary articles. All these things were "packed" on the back of a led horse—and whoever has not been taught, by a Spanish adept, to pack an animal, let him never hope to do the thing by natural smartness. That is impossible. Higbie had had some experience, but was not perfect. He put on the pack saddle (a thing like a saw-buck), piled the property on it and then wound a rope all over and about it and under it, "every which way," taking a hitch in it every now and then, and occasionally surging back on it till the horse's sides sunk in and he gasped for breath—but every time the lashings grew tight in one place they loosened in another. We never did get the load tight all over, but we got it so that it would do, after a fashion, and then we started, in single file, close order, and without a word. It was a dark night. We kept to the middle of the road, and proceeded in a slow walk past the rows of cabins, and whenever a miner came to his door I trembled for fear the light would shine on us and excite curiosity. But nothing happened. We began the long winding ascent of the canyon, toward the "divide," and presently the cabins began to grow infrequent, and the intervals between them wider and wider, and then I began to breathe tolerantly freely and feel less like a thief and a murderer. I was in the rear, leading the pack horse. As the ascent grew steeper he grew proportionately less satisfied with his cargo, and began to pull back on his *riata* occasionally and delay progress. My comrades were passing out of sight in the gloom. I was getting anxious. I coaxed and bullied the pack horse till I presently got him into a trot, and then the tin cups and pans strung about his person frightened him and he ran. His *riata* was wound around the pommel of my saddle, and so, as he went by he dragged me from my horse and the two animals traveled briskly on without me. But I was not alone—the loosened cargo tumbled overboard from the pack horse and fell close to me. It was abreast of almost the last cabin. A miner came out and said:

"Hello!"

I was thirty steps from him, and knew he could not see me, it was so very dark in the shadow of the mountain. So I lay still. Another head appeared in the light of the cabin door, and presently the two men walked toward me. They stopped within ten steps of me, and one said:

"'St! Listen."

I could not have been in a more distressed state if I had been escaping justice with a price on my head. Then the miners appeared to sit down on a boulder, though I could not see them distinctly enough to be very sure what they did. One said:

"I heard a noise, as plain as I ever heard anything. It seemed to be about there—"

A stone whizzed by my head. I flattened myself out in the dust like a postage stamp, and thought to myself if he mended his aim ever so little he would probably hear another noise. In my heart, now, I execrated secret expeditions. I promised myself that this should be my last, though the Sierras were ribbed with cement veins. Then one of the men said:

"I'll tell you what! Welch knew what he was talking about when he said he saw Whiteman to-day. I heard horses—that was the noise. I am going down to Welch's, right away."

They left and I was glad. I did not care whither they went, so they went. I was willing they should visit Welch, and the sooner the better.

As soon as they closed their cabin door my comrades emerged from the gloom; they had caught the horses and were waiting for a clear coast again. We remounted the cargo on the pack horse and got under way, and as day broke we reached the "divide" and joined Van Dorn. Then we journeyed down into the valley of the Lake, and feeling secure, we halted to cook breakfast, for we were tired and sleepy and hungry. Three hours later the rest of the population filed over the "divide" in a long procession, and drifted off out of sight around the borders of the Lake!

Whether or not my accident had produced this result we never knew, but at least one thing was certain—the secret was out and Whiteman would not enter upon a search for the cement mine this time. We were filled with chagrin.

We held a council and decided to make the best of our misfortune and enjoy a week's holiday on the borders of the curious Lake. Mono, it is sometimes called, and sometimes the "Dead Sea of California." It is one of the strangest freaks of Nature to be found in any land, but it is hardly ever mentioned in print and very seldom visited, because it lies away off the usual routes of travel and besides is so difficult to get at that only men content to endure the roughest life will consent to take upon themselves the discomforts of such a trip. On the morning of our second day, we traveled around to a remote and particularly wild spot on the borders of the Lake, where a stream of fresh, ice-cold water entered it from the mountainside, and then we went regularly into camp. We hired a large boat and two shot-guns from a lonely ranchman who lived some ten miles further on, and made ready for comfort and recreation. We soon got thoroughly acquainted with the Lake and all its peculiarities.

Chapter XXXVIII

MONO LAKE LIES in a lifeless, treeless, hideous desert, eight thousand feet above the level of the sea, and is guarded by mountains two thousand feet higher, whose summits are always clothed in clouds. This solemn, silent, sailless sea—this lonely tenant of the loneliest spot on earth—is little graced with the picturesque.

It is an unpretending expanse of grayish water, about a hundred miles in circumference, with two islands in its center, mere upheavals of rent and scorched
and blistered lava, snowed over with gray banks and drifts of pumice stone and
ashes, the winding sheet of the dead volcano, whose vast crater the lake has
seized upon and occupied.

The lake is two hundred feet deep, and its sluggish waters are so strong with
alkali that if you only dip the most hopelessly soiled garment into them once or
twice, and wring it out, it will be found as clean as if it had been through the
ablest of washerwomen's hands. While we camped there our laundry work was
easy. We tied the week's washing astern of our boat, and sailed a quarter of a
mile, and the job was complete, all to the wringing out. If we threw the water
on our heads and gave them a rub or so, the white lather would pile up three
inches high. This water is not good for bruised places and abrasions of the skin.
We had a valuable dog. He had raw places on him. He had more raw places on
him than sound ones. He was the rawest dog I almost ever saw. He jumped
overboard one day to get away from the flies. But it was bad judgment. In his
condition, it would have been just as comfortable to jump into the fire. The
alkali water nipped him in all the raw places simultaneously, and he struck out
for the shore with considerable interest. He yelped and barked and howled as
he went—and by the time he got to the shore there was no bark to him—for he
had barked the bark all out of his inside, and the alkali water had cleaned the
bark all off his outside, and he probably wished he had never embarked in any
such enterprise. He ran round and round in a circle, and pawed the earth and
clawed the air, and threw double somersaults, sometimes backward and sometimes
forward, in the most extraordinary manner. He was not a demonstrative dog, as
a general thing, but rather of a grave and serious turn of mind, and I never saw
him take so much interest in anything before. He finally struck out over the
mountains, at a gait which we estimated at about two hundred and fifty miles
an hour, and he is going yet. This was about nine years ago. We look for what
is left of him along here every day.

A white man cannot drink the water of Mono Lake, for it is nearly pure lye.
It is said that the Indians in the vicinity drink it sometimes, though. It is not
improbable, for they are among the purest liars I ever saw. [There will be no
additional charge for this joke, except to parties requiring an explanation of it.
This joke has received high commendation from some of the ablest minds of
the age.]

There are no fish in Mono Lake—no frogs, no snakes, no polliwigs—nothing,
in fact, that goes to make life desirable. Millions of wild ducks and sea-gulls
swim about the surface, but no living thing exists *under* the surface, except a
white feathery sort of worm, one half an inch long, which looks like a bit of
white thread frayed out at the sides. If you dip up a gallon of water, you will
get about fifteen thousand of these. They give to the water a sort of grayish-
white appearance. Then there is a fly, which looks something like our house
fly. These settle on the beach to eat the worms that wash ashore—and any time,
you can see there a belt of flies an inch deep and six feet wide, and this belt
extends clear around the lake—a belt of flies one hundred miles long. If you
throw a stone among them, they swarm up so thick that they look dense, like a
cloud. You can hold them under water as long as you please—they do not mind
it—they are only proud of it. When you let them go, they pop up to the surface
as dry as a patent-office report, and walk off as unconcernedly as if they had

been educated especially with a view to affording instructive entertainment to man in that particular way. Providence leaves nothing to go by chance. All things have their uses and their part and proper place in Nature's economy: the ducks eat the flies—the flies eat the worms—the Indians eat all three—the wild cats eat the Indians—the white folks eat the wild cats—and thus all things are lovely.

Mono Lake is a hundred miles in a straight line from the ocean—and between it and the ocean are one or two ranges of mountains—yet thousands of sea-gulls go there every season to lay their eggs and rear their young. One would as soon expect to find sea-gulls in Kansas. And in this connection let us observe another instance of Nature's wisdom. The islands in the lake being merely huge masses of lava, coated over with ashes and pumice-stone, and utterly innocent of vegetation or anything that would burn; and sea-gull's eggs being entirely useless to anybody unless they be cooked, Nature has provided an unfailing spring of boiling water on the largest island, and you can put your eggs in there, and in four minutes you can boil them as hard as any statement I have made during the past fifteen years. Within ten feet of the boiling spring is a spring of pure cold water, sweet and wholesome. So, in that island you get your board and washing free of charge—and if nature had gone further and furnished a nice American hotel clerk who was crusty and disobliging, and didn't know anything about the time tables, or the railroad routes—or—anything—and was proud of it—I would not wish for a more desirable boarding-house.

Half a dozen little mountain brooks flow into Mono Lake, but *not a stream of any kind flows out of it*. It neither rises nor falls, apparently, and what it does with its surplus water is a dark and bloody mystery.

There are only two seasons in the region round about Mono Lake—and these are, the breaking up of one Winter and the beginning of the next. More than once (in Esmeralda) I have seen a perfectly blistering morning open up with the thermometer at ninety degrees at eight o'clock, and seen the snow fall fourteen inches deep and that same identical thermometer go down to forty-four degrees under shelter, before nine o'clock at night. Under favorable circumstances it snows at least once in every single month in the year, in the little town of Mono. So uncertain is the climate in Summer that a lady who goes out visiting cannot hope to be prepared for all emergencies unless she takes her fan under one arm and her snow shoes under the other. When they have a Fourth of July procession it generally snows on them, and they do say that as a general thing when a man calls for a brandy toddy there, the bar keeper chops it off with a hatchet and wraps it up in a paper, like maple sugar. And it is further reported that the old soakers haven't any teeth—wore them out eating gin cocktails and brandy punches. I do not endorse that statement—I simply give it for what it is worth—and it is worth—well, I should say, millions, to any man who can believe it without straining himself. But I do endorse the snow on the Fourth of July—because I know that to be true.

Chapter XXXIX

ABOUT SEVEN O'CLOCK one blistering hot morning—for it was now dead summertime—Higbie and I took the boat and started on a voyage of discovery to the two islands. We had often longed to do this, but had been deterred by the fear of storms; for they were frequent, and severe enough to capsize an ordinary row-boat like ours without great difficulty—and once capsized, death would ensue in spite of the bravest swimming, for that venomous water would eat a man's eyes out like fire, and burn him out inside, too, if he shipped a sea. It was called twelve miles, straight out to the islands—a long pull and a warm one—but the morning was so quiet and sunny, and the lake so smooth and glassy and dead, that we could not resist the temptation. So we filled two large tin canteens with water (since we were not acquainted with the locality of the spring said to exist on the large island), and started. Higbie's brawny muscles gave the boat good speed, but by the time we reached our destination we judged that we had pulled nearer fifteen miles than twelve.

We landed on the big island and went ashore. We tried the water in the canteens, now, and found that the sun had spoiled it; it was so brackish that we could not drink it; so we poured it out and began a search for the spring—for thirst augments fast as soon as it is apparent that one has no means at hand of quenching it. The island was a long, moderately high hill of ashes—nothing but gray ashes and pumice-stone, in which we sunk to our knees at every step—and all around the top was a forbidding wall of scorched and blasted rocks. When we reached the top and got within the wall, we found simply a shallow, far-reaching basin, carpeted with ashes, and here and there a patch of fine sand. In places, picturesque jets of steam shot up out of crevices, giving evidence that although this ancient crater had gone out of active business, there was still some fire left in its furnaces. Close to one of these jets of steam stood the only tree on the island—a small pine of most graceful shape and most faultless symmetry; its color was a brilliant green, for the steam drifted unceasingly through its branches and kept them always moist. It contrasted strangely enough, did this vigorous and beautiful outcast, with its dead and dismal surroundings. It was like a cheerful spirit in a mourning household.

We hunted for the spring everywhere, traversing the full length of the island (two or three miles), and crossing it twice—climbing ash-hills patiently, and then sliding down the other side in a sitting posture, plowing up smothering volumes of gray dust. But we found nothing but solitude, ashes and a heart-breaking silence. Finally we noticed that the wind had risen, and we forgot our thirst in a solicitude of greater importance; for, the lake being quiet, we had not taken pains about securing the boat. We hurried back to a point overlooking our landing place, and then—but mere words cannot describe our dismay—the boat was gone! The chances were that there was not another boat on the entire lake. The situation was not comfortable—in truth, to speak plainly, it was frightful. We were prisoners on a desolate island, in aggravating proximity to friends who were for the present helpless to aid us; and what was still more uncomfortable was the reflection that we had neither food nor water. But presently we sighted the boat. It was drifting along, leisurely, about fifty yards from shore, tossing in a foamy sea. It drifted, and continued to drift, but at the same safe distance from land, and we walked along abreast it and waited for fortune to favor us. At the end of an hour it approached a jutting cape, and Higbie ran ahead and posted himself on the utmost verge and prepared for the assault. If we failed there, there was no hope for us. It was driving gradually shoreward all the time, now; but whether it was driving fast enough to make the connection or not was the momentous question. When it got within thirty steps of Higbie I was so excited that I fancied I could hear my own heart beat. When, a little later, it dragged slowly along and seemed about to go by, only one little yard out of reach, it seemed as if my heart stood still; and when it was exactly abreast him and began to widen away, and he still standing like a watching statue, I knew my heart did stop. But when he gave a great spring, the next instant, and lit fairly in the stern, I discharged a war-whoop that woke the solitudes!

But it dulled my enthusiasm, presently, when he told me he had not been caring whether the boat came within jumping distance or not, so that it passed within eight or ten yards of him, for he had made up his mind to shut his eyes and mouth and swim that trifling distance. Imbecile that I was, I had not thought of that. It was only a long swim that could be fatal.

The sea was running high and the storm increasing. It was growing late, too—three or four in the afternoon. Whether to venture toward the mainland or not, was a question of some moment. But we were so distressed by thirst that we decided to try it, and so Higbie fell to work and I took the steering-oar. When we had pulled a mile, laboriously, we were evidently in serious peril, for the storm had greatly augmented; the billows ran very high and were capped with foaming crests, the heavens were hung with black, and the wind blew with great fury. We would have gone back, now, but we did not dare to turn the boat around, because as soon as she got in the trough of the sea she would upset, of course. Our only hope lay in keeping her head-on to the seas. It was hard work to do this, she plunged so, and so beat and belabored the billows with her rising and falling bows. Now and then one of Higbie's oars would trip on the top of a wave, and the other one would snatch the boat half around in spite of my cumbersome steering apparatus. We were drenched by the sprays constantly, and the boat occasionally shipped water. By and by, powerful as my comrade was, his great exertions began to tell on him, and he was anxious that I should change places with him till he could rest a little. But I told him this was impossible; for if the steering oar were dropped a moment while we changed, the boat would slue around into the trough of the sea, capsize, and in less than five minutes we would have a hundred gallons of soap-suds in us and be eaten up so quickly that we could not even be present at our own inquest.

But things cannot last always. Just as the darkness shut down we came booming into port, head on. Higbie dropped his oars to hurrah—I dropped mine to help—the sea gave the boat a twist, and over she went!

The agony that alkali water inflicts on bruises, chafes and blistered hands, is unspeakable, and nothing but greasing all over will modify it—but we ate, drank and slept well, that night, notwithstanding.

In speaking of the peculiarities of Mono Lake, I ought to have mentioned that at intervals all around its shores stand picturesque turret-looking masses and clusters of a whitish, coarse-grained rock that resembles inferior mortar dried hard; and if one breaks off fragments of this rock he will find perfectly shaped and thoroughly petrified gulls' eggs deeply embedded in the mass. How did they get there? I simply state the fact—for it is a fact—and leave the geological reader to crack the nut at his leisure and solve the problem after his own fashion.

At the end of a week we adjourned to the Sierras on a fishing excursion, and spent several days in camp under snowy Castle Peak, and fished successfully for trout in a bright, miniature lake whose surface was between ten and eleven thousand feet above the level of the sea; cooling ourselves during the hot August noons by sitting on snow banks ten feet deep, under whose sheltering edges *fine grass and dainty flowers flourished luxuriously;* and at night entertaining ourselves by almost freezing to death. Then we returned to Mono Lake, and finding that the cement excitement was over for the present, packed up and went back to Esmeralda. Mr. Ballou reconnoitered awhile, and not liking the prospect, set out alone for Humboldt.

About this time occurred a little incident which has always had a sort of interest to me, from the fact that it came so near "instigating" my funeral. At a time when an Indian attack had been expected, the citizens hid their gunpowder where it would be safe and yet convenient to hand when wanted. A neighbor of ours hid six cans of rifle powder in the bake-oven of an old discarded cooking stove which stood on the open ground near a frame out-house or shed, and from and after that day never thought of it again. We hired a half-tamed Indian to do some washing for us, and he took up quarters under the shed with his tub. The ancient stove reposed within six feet of him, and before his face. Finally it occurred to him that hot water would be better than cold, and he went out and fired up under that forgotten powder magazine and set on a kettle of water. Then he returned to his tub. I entered the shed presently and threw down some more clothes, and was about to speak to him when the stove blew up with a prodigious crash, and disappeared, leaving not a splinter behind. Fragments of it fell in the streets full two hundred yards away. Nearly a third of the shed roof over our heads was destroyed, and one of the stove lids, after cutting a small stanchion half in two in front of the Indian, whizzed between us and drove partly through the weather-boarding beyond. I was as white as a sheet and as weak as a kitten and speechless. But the Indian betrayed no trepidation, no distress, not even discomfort. He simply stopped washing, leaned forward, and surveyed the clean, blank ground a moment, and then remarked:

"STOVE HEAP GONE."

"Mph! Dam stove heap gone!"—and resumed his scrubbing as placidly as if it were an entirely customary thing for a stove to do. I will explain, that "heap" is "Injun-English" for "very much." The reader will perceive the exhaustive expressiveness of it in the present instance.

Chapter XL

I NOW COME to a curious episode—the most curious, I think, that had yet accented my slothful, valueless, heedless career. Out of a hillside toward the upper end of the town, projected a wall of reddish looking quartz-croppings, the exposed comb of a silver-bearing ledge that extended deep down into the earth, of course. It was owned by a company entitled the "Wide West." There was a shaft sixty or seventy feet deep on the under side of the croppings, and everybody was acquainted with the rock that came from it—and tolerably rich rock it was, too, but nothing extraordinary. I will remark here, that although to the inexperienced stranger all the quartz of a particular "district" looks about alike, an old resident of the camp can take a glance at a mixed pile of rock, separate the fragments and tell you which mine each came from, as easily as a confectioner can separate and classify the various kinds and qualities of candy in a mixed heap of the article.

All at once the town was thrown into a state of extraordinary excitement. In mining parlance the Wide West had "struck it rich!" Everybody went to see the new developments, and for some days there was such a crowd of people about the Wide West shaft that a stranger would have supposed there was a mass meeting in session there. No other topic was discussed but the rich strike, and nobody thought or dreamed about anything else. Every man brought away a specimen, ground it up in a hand mortar, washed it out in his horn spoon, and glared speechless upon the marvelous result. It was not hard rock, but black, decomposed stuff which could be crumbled in the hand like a baked potato, and when spread out on a paper exhibited a thick sprinkling of gold and particles of "native" silver. Higbie brought a handful to the cabin, and when he had washed it out his amazement was beyond description. Wide West stock soared skywards. It was said that repeated offers had been made for it at a thousand dollars a foot, and promptly refused. We have all had the "blues"—the mere sky-blues—but mine were indigo, now—because I did not own in the Wide West. The world seemed hollow to me, and existence a grief. I lost my appetite, and ceased to take an interest in anything. Still I had to stay, and listen to other people's rejoicings, because I had no money to get out of the camp with.

The Wide West company put a stop to the carrying away of "specimens," and well they might, for every handful of the ore was worth a sum of some consequence. To show the exceeding value of the ore, I will remark that a sixteen-hundred-pounds parcel of it was sold, just as it lay, at the mouth of the shaft, at *one dollar a pound;* and the man who bought it "packed" it on mules a hundred and fifty or two hundred miles, over the mountains, to San Francisco, satisfied that it would yield at a rate that would richly compensate him for his trouble. The Wide West people also commanded their foreman to refuse any but their own operatives permission to enter the mine at any time or for any purpose. I kept up my "blue" meditations and Higbie kept up a deal of thinking, too, but of a different sort. He puzzled over the "rock," examined it with a glass, inspected it in different lights and from different points of view, and after each experiment delivered himself, in soliloquy, of one and the same unvarying opinion in the same unvarying formula:

"It is *not* Wide West rock!"

He said once or twice that he meant to have a look into the Wide West shaft if he got shot for it. I was wretched, and did not care whether he got a look into it or not. He failed that day, and tried again at night; failed again; got up at dawn and tried, and failed again. Then he lay in ambush in the sage-brush hour after hour, waiting for the two or three hands to adjourn to the shade of a boulder for dinner; made a start once, but was premature—one of the men came back for something; tried it again, but when almost at the mouth of the shaft, another of the men rose up from behind the boulders as if to reconnoitre, and he dropped on the ground and lay quiet; presently he crawled on his hands and knees to the mouth of the shaft, gave a quick glance around, then seized the rope and slid down the shaft. He disappeared in the gloom of a "side drift" just as a head appeared in the mouth of the shaft and somebody shouted "Hello!"—which he did not answer. He was not disturbed any more. An hour later he entered the cabin, hot, red, and ready to burst with smothered excitement, and exclaimed in a stage whisper:

"I knew it! We are rich! IT'S A BLIND LEAD!"

I thought the very earth reeled under me. Doubt—conviction—doubt again—exultation—hope, amazement, belief, unbelief—every emotion imaginable swept in wild procession through my heart and brain, and I could not speak a word. After a moment or two of this mental fury, I shook myself to rights, and said:

"Say it again!"

"It's a blind lead!"

"Cal., let's—let's burn the house—or kill somebody! Let's get out where there's room to hurrah! But what is the use? It is a hundred times too good to be true."

"It's a blind lead, for a million!—hanging wall—foot wall—clay casings—everything complete!" He swung his hat and gave three cheers, and I cast doubt to the winds and chimed in with a will. For I was worth a million dollars, and did not care "whether school kept or not!"

But perhaps I ought to explain. A "blind lead" is a lead or ledge that does not "crop out" above the surface. A miner does not know where to look for such leads, but they are often stumbled upon by accident in the course of driving a tuunel or sinking a shaft. Higbie knew the Wide West rock perfectly well, and the more he had examined the new developments the more he was satisfied that the ore could not have come from the Wide West vein. And so had it occurred to him alone, of all the camp, that there was a blind lead down in the shaft, and that even the Wide West people themselves did not suspect it. He was right. When he went down the shaft, he found that the blind lead held its independent way through the Wide West vein, cutting it diagonally, and that it was enclosed in its own well-defined casing-rocks and clay. Hence it was public property. Both leads being perfectly well defined, it was easy for any miner to see which one belonged to the Wide West and which did not.

We thought it well to have a strong friend, and therefore we brought the foreman of the Wide West to our cabin that night and revealed the great surprise to him. Higbie said:

"We are going to take possession of this blind lead, record it and establish ownership, and then forbid the Wide West company to take out any more of the rock. You cannot help your company in this matter—nobody can help them. I will go into the shaft with you and prove to your entire satisfaction that it *is* a blind lead. Now we propose to take you in with us, and claim the blind lead in our three names. What do you say?"

What could a man say who had an opportunity to simply stretch forth his hand and take possession of a fortune without risk of any kind and without wronging any one or attaching the least taint of dishonor to his name? He could only say, "Agreed."

The notice was put up that night, and duly spread upon the recorder's books before ten o'clock. We claimed two hundred feet each—six hundred feet in all—the smallest and compactest organization in the district, and the easiest to manage.

No one can be so thoughtless as to suppose that we slept, that night. Higbie and I went to bed at midnight, but it was only to lie broad awake and think, dream, scheme. The floorless, tumble-down cabin was a palace, the ragged gray blankets silk, the furniture rosewood and mahogany. Each new splendor that burst out of my visions of the future whirled me bodily over in bed or jerked me to a sitting posture just as if an electric battery had been applied to me. We shot fragments of conversation back and forth at each other. Once Higbie said:

"When are you going home—to the States?"

"To-morrow!"—with an evolution or two, ending with a sitting position. "Well—no—but next month, at furthest."

"We'll go in the same steamer."

"Agreed."

A pause.

"Steamer of the 10th?"

"Yes. No, the 1st."

"All right."

Another pause.

"Where are you going to live?" said Higbie.

"San Francisco."

"That's me!" Pause. "Too high—too much climbing"—from Higbie. "What is?" "I was thinking of Russian Hill—building a house up there."

"Too much climbing? Shan't you keep a carriage?"

"Of course. I forgot that."

Pause.

"Cal., what kind of a house are you going to build?"

"I was thinking about that. Three-story and an attic."

"But what *kind?*"

"Well, I don't hardly know. Brick, I suppose."

"Brick—bosh."

"Why? What is your idea?"

"Brown stone front—French plate glass—billiard-room off the dining-room—statuary and paintings—shrubbery and two-acre grass plat—greenhouse—iron dog on the front stoop—gray horses—landau, and a coachman with a bug on his hat!"

"By George!"

MILLIONAIRES LAYING PLANS.

A long pause.

"Cal., when are you going to Europe?"

"Well—I hadn't thought of that. When are you?"

"In the Spring."

"Going to be gone all summer?"

"All summer! I shall remain there three years."

"No—but are you in earnest?"

"Indeed I am."

"I will go along too."

"Why of course you will."

"What part of Europe shall you go to?"

"All parts. France, England, Germany—Spain, Italy, Switzerland, Syria, Greece, Palestine, Arabia, Persia, Egypt—all over—everywhere."

"I'm agreed."

"All right."

"Won't it be a swell trip!"

"We'll spend forty or fifty thousand dollars trying to make it one, anyway."

Another long pause.

"Higbie, we owe the butcher six dollars, and he has been threatening to stop our—"

"Hang the butcher!"

"Amen."

And so it went on. By three o'clock we found it was no use, and so we got up and played cribbage and smoked pipes till sunrise. It was my week to cook. I always hated cooking—now, I abhorred it.

The news was all over town. The former excitement was great—this one was greater still. I walked the streets serene and happy. Higbie said the foreman had been offered two hundred thousand dollars for his third of the mine. I said I would like to see myself selling for any such price. My ideas were lofty. My figure was a million. Still, I honestly believe that if I had been offered it, it would have had no other effect than to make me hold off for more.

I found abundant enjoyment in being rich. A man offered me a three-hundred-dollar horse, and wanted to take my simple, unendorsed note for it. That brought the most realizing sense I had yet had that I was actually rich, beyond shadow of doubt. It was followed by numerous other evidences of a similar nature— among which I may mention the fact of the butcher leaving us a double supply of meat and saying nothing about money.

By the laws of the district, the "locators" or claimants of a ledge were obliged to do a fair and reasonable amount of work on their new property within ten days after the date of the location, or the property was forfeited, and anybody could go and seize it that chose. So we determined to go to work the next day. About the middle of the afternoon, as I was coming out of the post office, I met a Mr. Gardiner, who told me that Capt. John Nye was lying dangerously ill at his place (the "Nine-Mile Ranch"), and that he and his wife were not able to give him nearly as much care and attention as his case demanded. I said if he would wait for me a moment, I would go down and help in the sick room. I ran to the cabin to tell Higbie. He was not there, but I left a note on the table for him, and a few minutes later I left town in Gardiner's wagon.

Chapter XLI

CAPTAIN NYE WAS very ill indeed, with spasmodic rheumatism. But the old gentleman was himself—which is to say, he was kind-hearted and agreeable when comfortable, but a singularly violent wild-cat when things did not go well. He would be smiling along pleasantly enough, when a sudden spasm of his disease would take him and he would go out of his smile into a perfect fury. He would groan and wail and howl with the anguish, and fill up the odd chinks with the most elaborate profanity that strong convictions and a fine fancy could contrive. With fair opportunity he could swear very well and handle his adjectives with considerable judgment; but when the spasm was on him it was painful to listen to him, he was so awkward. However, I had seen him nurse a sick man himself and put up patiently with the inconveniences of the situation, and consequently I was willing that he should have full license now that his own turn had come. He could not disturb me, with all his raving and ranting, for my mind had work on hand, and it labored on diligently, night and day, whether my hands were idle or employed. I was altering and amending the plans for my house, and thinking over the propriety of having the billiard-room in the attic, instead of on the same floor with the dining-room; also, I was trying to decide between green and blue for the upholstery of the drawing room, for, although my preference was blue I feared it was a color that would be too easily damaged by dust and sunlight; likewise while I was content to put the coach-man in a modest livery, I was uncertain about a footman—I needed one, and was even resolved to have one, but wished he could properly appear and perform his functions out of livery, for I somewhat dreaded so much show; and yet, inasmuch as my late grandfather had had a coachman and such things, but no liveries, I felt rather drawn to beat him;—or beat his ghost, at any rate; I was also systematizing the European trip, and managed to get it all laid out, as to route and length of time to be devoted to it—everything, with one exception—namely, whether to cross the desert from Cairo to Jerusalem per camel, or go by sea to Beirut, and thence down through the country per caravan. Meantime I was writing to the friends at home every

day, instructing them concerning all my plans and intentions, and directing them
to look up a handsome homestead for my mother and agree upon a price for it
against my coming, and also directing them to sell my share of the Tennessee
land and tender the proceeds to the widows' and orphans' fund of the typographical
union of which I had long been a member in good standing. [This Tennessee
land had been in the possession of the family many years, and promised to confer
high fortune upon us some day; it still promises it, but in a less violent way.]

When I had been nursing the Captain nine days he was somewhat better, but
very feeble. During the afternoon we lifted him into a chair and gave him an
alcoholic vapor bath, and then set about putting him on the bed again. We had
to be exceedingly careful, for the least jar produced pain. Gardiner had his
shoulders and I his legs; in an unfortunate moment I stumbled and the patient
fell heavily on the bed in an agony of torture. I never heard a man swear so in
my life. He raved like a maniac, and tried to snatch a revolver from the table—
but I got it. He ordered me out of the house, and swore a world of oaths that
he would kill me wherever he caught me when he got on his feet again. It was
simply a passing fury, and meant nothing. I knew he would forget it in an hour,
and maybe be sorry for it, too; but it angered me a little, at the moment. So
much so, indeed, that I determined to go back to Esmeralda. I thought he was
able to get along alone, now, since he was on the war path. I took supper, and
as soon as the moon rose, began my nine-mile journey, on foot. Even millionaires
needed no horses, in those days, for a mere nine-mile jaunt without baggage.

As I "raised the hill" overlooking the town, it lacked fifteen minutes of
twelve. I glanced at the hill over beyond the canyon, and in the bright moonlight
saw what appeared to be about half the population of the village massed on and
around the Wide West croppings. My heart gave an exulting bound, and I said
to myself, "They have made a new strike to-night—and struck it richer than
ever, no doubt." I started over there, but gave it up. I said the "strike" would
keep, and I had climbed hills enough for one night. I went on down through the
town, and as I was passing a little German bakery, a woman ran out and begged
me to come in and help her. She said her husband had a fit. I went in, and
judged she was right—he appeared to have a hundred of them, compressed into
one. Two Germans were there, trying to hold him, and not making much of a
success of it. I ran up the street half a block or so and routed out a sleeping
doctor, brought him down half dressed, and we four wrestled with the maniac,
and doctored, drenched and bled him, for more than an hour, and the poor
German woman did the crying. He grew quiet, now, and the doctor and I
withdrew and left him to his friends.

It was a little after one o'clock. As I entered the cabin door, tired but jolly,
the dingy light of a tallow candle revealed Higbie, sitting by the pine table gazing
stupidly at my note, which he held in his fingers, and looking pale, old, and
haggard. I halted, and looked at him. He looked at me, stolidly. I said:

"Higbie, what—what is it?"

"We're ruined—we didn't do the work—THE BLIND LEAD'S RELOCATED!"

It was enough. I sat down sick, grieved—broken-hearted, indeed. A minute
before, I was rich and brimful of vanity; I was a pauper now, and very meek.
We sat still an hour, busy with thought, busy with vain and useless self-upbraidings,
busy with "Why *didn't* I do this, and why *didn't* I do that," but neither spoke
a word. Then we dropped into mutual explanations, and the mystery was cleared
away. It came out that Higbie had depended on me, as I had on him, and as

WORTH NOTHING.

both of us had on the foreman. The folly of it! It was the first time that ever staid and steadfast Higbie had left an important matter to chance or failed to be true to his full share of a responsibility.

But he had never seen my note till this moment, and this moment was the first time he had been in the cabin since the day he had seen me last. He, also, had left a note for me, on that same fatal afternoon—had ridden up on horseback, and looked through the window, and being in a hurry and not seeing me, had tossed the note into the cabin through a broken pane. Here it was, on the floor, where it had remained undisturbed for nine days:

> "Don't fail to do the work before the ten days expire. W. has passed
> through and given me notice. I am to join him at Mono Lake, and we
> shall go on from there to-night. He says he will find it this time, sure.
> CAL."

"W." meant Whiteman, of course. That thrice accursed "cement!"

That was the way of it. An old miner, like Higbie, could no more withstand the fascination of a mysterious mining excitement like this "cement" foolishness, than he could refrain from eating when he was famishing. Higbie had been dreaming about the marvelous cement for months; and now, against his better judgment, he had gone off and "taken the chances" on my keeping secure a mine worth a million undiscovered cement veins. They had not been followed this time. His riding out of town in broad daylight was such a common-place thing to do that it had not attracted any attention. He said they prosecuted their search in the fastnesses of the mountains during nine days, without success; they could not find the cement. Then a ghastly fear came over him that something might have happened to prevent the doing of the necessary work to hold the blind lead (though indeed he thought such a thing hardly possible), and forthwith he started home with all speed. He would have reached Esmeralda in time, but his horse broke down and he had to walk a great part of the distance. And so it happened that as he came into Esmeralda by one road, I entered it by another. His was the superior energy, however, for he went straight to the Wide West, instead of turning aside as I had done—and he arrived there about five or ten minutes too late! The "notice" was already up, the "relocation" of our mine completed beyond recall, and the crowd rapidly dispersing. He learned some facts before he left the ground. The foreman had not been seen about the streets since the night we had located the mine—a telegram had called him to California on a matter of life and death, it was said. At any rate he had done no work and the watchful eyes of the community were taking note of the fact. At midnight of this woeful tenth day, the ledge would be "relocatable," and by eleven o'clock the hill was black with men prepared to do the relocating. That was the crowd I had seen when I fancied a new "strike" had been made—idiot that I was. [We three had the same right to relocate the lead that other people had, provided we were quick enough.] As midnight was announced, fourteen men, duly armed and ready to back their proceedings, put up their "notice" and proclaimed their ownership of the blind lead, under the new name of the "Johnson." But A. D. Allen our partner (the foreman) put in a sudden appearance about that time, with a cocked revolver in his hand, and said his name must be added to the list, or he would "thin out the Johnson company some." He was a manly, splendid, determined fellow, and known to be as good as his word, and therefore a compromise was effected. They put in his name for a hundred feet, reserving to themselves the customary two hundred feet each. Such was the history of the night's events, as Higbie gathered from a friend on the way home.

Higbie and I cleared out on a new mining excitement the next morning, glad to get away from the scene of our sufferings, and after a month or two of hardship and disappointment, returned to Esmeralda once more. Then we learned that the Wide West and the Johnson companies had consolidated; that the stock, thus united, comprised five thousand feet, or shares; that the foreman, apprehending tiresome litigation, and considering such a huge concern unwieldy, had sold his hundred feet for ninety thousand dollars in gold and gone home to the States to enjoy it. If the stock was worth such a gallant figure, with five thousand shares in the corporation, it makes me dizzy to think what it would have been worth with only our original six hundred in it. It was the difference between six hundred men owning a house and five thousand owning it. We would have been millionaires if we had only worked with pick and spade one little day on our property and so secured our ownership!

It reads like a wild fancy sketch, but the evidence of many witnesses, and likewise that of the official records of Esmeralda District, is easily obtainable in proof that it is a true history. I can always have it to say that I was absolutely and unquestionably worth a million dollars, once, for ten days.

A year ago my esteemed and in every way estimable old millionaire partner, Higbie, wrote me from an obscure little mining camp in California that after nine or ten years of buffetings and hard striving, he was at last in a position where he could command twenty-five hundred dollars, and said he meant to go into the fruit business in a modest way. How such a thought would have insulted him the night we lay in our cabin planning European trips and brown stone houses on Russian Hill!

Chapter XLII

WHAT TO DO next?

It was a momentous question. I had gone out into the world to shift for myself, at the age of thirteen (for my father had endorsed for friends; and although he left us a sumptuous legacy of pride in his fine Virginian stock and its national distinction, I presently found that I could not live on that alone without occasional bread to wash it down with). I had gained a livelihood in various vocations, but had not dazzled anybody with my successes; still the list was before me, and the amplest liberty in the matter of choosing, provided I wanted to work—which I did not, after being so wealthy. I had once been a grocery clerk, for one day, but had consumed so much sugar in that time that I was relieved from further duty by the proprietor; said he wanted me outside, so that he could have my custom. I had studied law an entire week, and then given it up because it was so prosy and tiresome. I had engaged briefly in the study of blacksmithing, but wasted so much time trying to fix the bellows so that it would blow itself, that the master turned me adrift in disgrace, and told me I would come to no good. I had been a bookseller's clerk for awhile, but the customers bothered me so much I could not read with any comfort, and so the proprietor gave me a furlough and forgot to put a limit to it. I had clerked in a drug store part of a summer, but my prescriptions were unlucky, and we appeared to sell more stomach pumps than soda water. So I had to go. I had made of myself a tolerable printer, under the impression that I would be another Franklin someday, but some how had missed the connection thus far. There was no berth open in the Esmeralda *Union*, and besides I had always been such a slow compositor that I looked with envy upon the achievements of apprentices of two years' standing; and when I took a "take," foremen were in the habit of suggesting that it would be wanted "some time during the year." I was a good average St. Louis and New Orleans pilot and by no means ashamed of my abilities in that line; wages were two hundred and fifty dollars a month and no board to pay, and I did long to stand behind a wheel again and never roam any more—but I had been making such an ass of myself lately in grandiloquent letters home about my blind lead and my European excursion that I did what many and many a poor disappointed miner had done before; said "It is all over with me now, and I will never go back home to be pitied—and snubbed." I had been a private secretary, a silver miner and a silver mill operative, and amounted to less than nothing in each, and now—

What to do next?

I yielded to Higbie's appeals and consented to try the mining once more. We climbed far up on the mountain side and went to work on a little rubbishy claim of ours that had a shaft on it eight feet deep. Higbie descended into it and worked bravely with his pick till he had loosened up a deal of rock and dirt and then I went down with a long-handled shovel (the most awkward invention yet contrived by man) to throw it out. You must brace the shovel forward with the side of your knee till it is full, and then, with a skilful toss, throw it backward over your left shoulder. I made the toss, and landed the mess just on the edge of the shaft and it all came back on my head and down the back of my neck. I never said a word, but climbed out and walked home. I inwardly resolved that I would starve before I would make a target of myself and shoot rubbish at it with a long-handled shovel. I sat down, in the cabin, and gave myself up to solid misery—so to speak. Now in pleasanter days I had amused myself with writing letters to the chief paper of the Territory, the Virginia *Daily Territorial Enterprise*, and had always been surprised when they appeared in print. My good opinion of the editors had steadily declined; for it seemed to me that they might have found something better to fill up with than my literature. I had found a letter in the post office as I came home from the hill side, and finally I opened it. Eureka! [I never did know what Eureka meant, but it seems to be as proper a word to heave in as any when no other that sounds pretty offers.] It was a deliberate offer to me of Twenty-Five Dollars a week to come up to Virginia and be city editor of the *Enterprise*.

I would have challenged the publisher in the "blind lead" days—I wanted to fall down and worship him, now. Twenty-Five Dollars a week—it looked like bloated luxury—a fortune, a sinful and lavish waste of money. But my transports cooled when I thought of my inexperience and consequent unfitness for the position—and straightway, on top of this, my long array of failures rose up before me. Yet if I refused this place I must presently become dependent upon somebody for my bread, a thing necessarily distasteful to a man who had never experienced such a humiliation since he was thirteen years old. Not much to be proud of, since it is so common—but then it was all I had to *be* proud of. So I was scared into being city editor. I would have declined, otherwise. Necessity is the mother of "taking chances." I do not doubt that if, at that time, I had been offered a salary to translate the Talmud from the original Hebrew, I would have accepted—albeit with diffidence and some misgivings—and thrown as much variety into it as I could for the money.

I went up to Virginia and entered upon my new vocation. I was a rusty looking city editor, I am free to confess—coatless, slouch hat, blue woolen shirt, pantaloons stuffed into boot tops, whiskered half down to the waist, and the universal navy revolver slung to my belt. But I secured a more Christian costume and discarded the revolver. I had never had occasion to kill anybody, nor ever felt a desire to do so, but had worn the thing in deference to popular sentiment, and in order

AS CITY EDITOR.

that I might not, by its absence, be offensively conspicuous, and a subject of remark. But the other editors, and all the printers, carried revolvers. I asked the chief editor and proprietor (Mr. Goodman, I will call him, since it describes him as well as any name could do) for some instructions with regard to my duties, and he told me to go all over town and ask all sorts of people all sorts of questions, make notes of the information gained, and write them out for publication. And he added:

"Never say 'We learn' so-and-so, or 'It is reported,' or 'It is rumored,' or 'We understand' so-and-so, but go to headquarters and get the absolute facts, and then speak out and say 'It *is* so-and-so.' Otherwise, people will not put confidence in your news. Unassailable certainty is the thing that gives a newspaper the firmest and most valuable reputation."

It was the whole thing in a nut-shell; and to this day when I find a reporter commencing his article with "We understand," I gather a suspicion that he has not taken as much pains to inform himself as he ought to have done. I moralize well, but I did not always practice well when I was a city editor; I let fancy get the upper hand of fact too often when there was a dearth of news. I can never forget my first day's experience as a reporter. I wandered about town questioning everybody, boring everybody, and finding out that nobody knew anything. At the end of five hours my notebook was still barren. I spoke to Mr. Goodman. He said:

"Dan used to make a good thing out of the hay wagons in a dry time when there were no fires or inquests. Are there no hay wagons in from the Truckee? If there are, you might speak of the renewed activity and all that sort of thing, in the hay business, you know. It isn't sensational or exciting, but it fills up and looks business like."

I canvassed the city again and found one wretched old hay truck dragging in from the country. But I made affluent use of it. I multiplied it by sixteen, brought it into town from sixteen different directions, made sixteen separate items out of it, and got up such another sweat about hay as Virginia City had never seen in the world before.

This was encouraging. Two nonpareil columns had to be filled, and I was getting along. Presently, when things began to look dismal again, a desperado killed a man in a saloon and joy returned once more. I never was so glad over any mere trifle before in my life. I said to the murderer:

"Sir, you are a stranger to me, but you have done me a kindness this day which I can never forget. If whole years of gratitude can be to you any slight compensation, they shall be yours. I was in trouble and you have relieved me nobly and at a time when all seemed dark and drear. Count me your friend from this time forth, for I am not a man to forget a favor."

If I did not really say that to him I at least felt a sort of itching desire to do it. I wrote up the murder with a hungry attention to details, and when it was finished experienced but one regret—namely, that they had not hanged my benefactor on the spot, so that I could work him up too.

Next I discovered some emigrant wagons going into camp on the plaza and found that they had lately come through the hostile Indian country and had fared rather roughly. I made the best of the item that the circumstances permitted, and felt that if I were not confined within rigid limits by the presence of the reporters of the other papers I could add particulars that would make the article much more interesting. However, I found one wagon that was going on to California, and made some judicious inquiries of the proprietor. When I learned, through his short and surly answers to my cross-questioning, that he was certainly going on and would not be in the city next day to make trouble, I got ahead of the other papers, for I took down his list of names and added his party to the killed and wounded. Having more scope here, I put this wagon through an Indian fight that to this day has no parallel in history.

My two columns were filled. When I read them over in the morning I felt that I had found my legitimate occupation at last. I reasoned within myself that news, and stirring news, too, was what a paper needed, and I felt that I was peculiarly endowed with the ability to furnish it. Mr. Goodman said that I was as good a reporter as Dan. I desired no higher commendation. With encouragement like that, I felt that I could take my pen and murder all the immigrants on the plains if need be and the interests of the paper demanded it.

Chapter XLIII

HOWEVER AS I grew better acquainted with the business and learned the run of the sources of information I ceased to require the aid of fancy to any large extent, and became able to fill my columns without diverging noticeably from the domain of fact.

I struck up friendships with the reporters of the other journals, and we swapped "regulars" with each other and thus economized work. "Regulars" are permanent sources of news, like courts, bullion returns, "clean-ups" at the quartz mills, and inquests. Inasmuch as everybody went armed, we had an inquest about every day, and so this department was naturally set down among the "regulars." We had lively papers in those days. My great competitor among the reporters was Boggs of the *Union*. He was an excellent reporter. Once in three or four months he would get a little intoxicated, but as a general thing he was a wary and cautious drinker although always ready to tamper a little with the enemy. He had the advantage of me in one thing; he could get the monthly public school report and I could not, because the principal hated the *Enterprise*. One snowy night when the report was due, I started out sadly wondering how I was going to get it. Presently, a few steps up the almost deserted street I stumbled on Boggs and asked him where he was going.

"After the school report."

"I'll go along with you."

"No, *sir*. I'll excuse you."

"Just as you say."

A saloon-keeper's boy passed by with a steaming pitcher of hot punch, and Boggs snuffed the fragrance gratefully. He gazed fondly after the boy and saw him start up the *Enterprise* stairs. I said:

"I wish you could help me get that school business, but since you can't, I must run up to the *Union* office and see if I can get them to let me have a proof of it after they have set it up, though I don't begin to suppose they will. Good night."

"Hold on a minute. I don't mind getting the report and sitting around with the boys a little, while you copy it, if you're willing to drop down to the principal's with me.''

"Now you talk like a rational being. Come along.''

We plowed a couple of blocks through the snow, got the report, and returned to our office. It was a short document and soon copied. Meantime Boggs helped himself to the punch. I gave the manuscript back to him and we started out to get an inquest, for we heard pistol shots near by. We got the particulars with little loss of time, for it was only an inferior sort of bar-room murder, and of little interest to the public, and then we separated. Away at three o'clock in the morning, when we had gone to press and were having a relaxing concert as usual—for some of the printers were good singers and others good performers on the guitar and on that atrocity the accordion—the proprietor of the *Union* strode in and desired to know if anybody had heard anything of Boggs or the school report. We stated the case, and all turned out to help hunt for the delinquent. We found him standing on a table in a saloon, with an old tin lantern in one hand and the school report in the other, haranguing a gang of intoxicated Cornish miners on the iniquity of squandering the public moneys on education "when hundreds and hundreds of honest hard-working men are literally starving for whiskey.'' [Riotous applause.] He had been assisting in a regal spree with those parties for hours. We dragged him away and put him to bed.

Of course there was no school report in the *Union*, and Boggs held me accountable, though I was innocent of any intention or desire to compass its absence from that paper and was as sorry as anyone that the misfortune had occurred.

But we were perfectly friendly. The day that the school report was next due, the proprietor of the "Genessee" mine furnished us a buggy and asked us to go down and write something about the property—a very common request and one always gladly acceded to when people furnished buggies, for we were as fond of pleasure excursions as other people. In due time we arrived at the "mine"— nothing but a hole in the ground ninety feet deep, and no way of getting down into it but by holding on to a rope and being lowered with a windlass. The workmen had just gone off somewhere to dinner. I was not strong enough to lower Boggs's bulk; so I took an unlighted candle in my teeth, made a loop for my foot in the end of the rope, implored Boggs not to go to sleep or let the windlass get the start of him, and then swung out over the shaft. I reached the bottom muddy and bruised about the elbows, but safe. I lit the candle, made an examination of the rock, selected some specimens and shouted to Boggs to hoist away. No answer. Presently a head appeared in the circle of daylight away aloft, and a voice came down:

"Are you all set?''

"All set—hoist away.''

"Are you comfortable?''

"Perfectly.''

"Could you wait a little?''

"Oh certainly—no particular hurry.''

"Well—good by.''

"Why? Where are you going?''

"After the school report!''

And he did. I staid down there an hour, and surprised the workmen when they hauled up and found a man on the rope instead of a bucket of rock. I walked home, too—five miles—up hill. We had no school report next morning; but the *Union* had.

Six months after my entry into journalism the grand "flush times" of Silverland began, and they continued with unabated splendor for three years. All difficulty about filling up the "local department" ceased, and the only trouble now was how to make the lengthened columns hold the world of incidents and happenings that came to our literary net every day. Virginia had grown to be the "livest" town, for its age and population, that America had ever produced. The sidewalks swarmed with people—to such an extent, indeed, that it was generally no easy matter to stem the human tide. The streets themselves were just as crowded with quartz wagons, freight teams and other vehicles. The procession was endless. So great was the pack, that buggies frequently had to wait half an hour for an opportunity to cross the principal street. Joy sat on every countenance, and there was a glad, almost fierce, intensity in every eye, that told of the money-getting schemes that were seething in every brain and the high hope that held sway in every heart. Money was as plenty as dust; every individual considered himself wealthy, and a melancholy countenance was nowhere to be seen. There were military companies, fire companies, brass bands, banks, hotels, theatres, "hurdy-gurdy houses," wide-open gambling palaces, political pow-wows, civic processions, street fights, murders, inquests, riots, a whiskey mill every fifteen steps, a Board of Aldermen, a Mayor, a City Surveyor, a City Engineer, a Chief of the Fire Department, with First, Second and Third Assistants, a Chief of Police, City Marshal and a large police force, two Boards of Mining Brokers, a dozen breweries and half a dozen jails and station houses in full operation, and some talk of building a church. The "flush times" were in magnificent flower! Large fire-proof brick buildings were going up in the principal streets, and the wooden suburbs were spreading out in all directions. Town lots soared up to prices that were amazing.

The great "Comstock lode" stretched its opulent length straight through the town from north to south, and every mine on it was in diligent process of development. One of these mines alone employed six hundred and seventy-five men, and in the matter of elections the adage was, "as the 'Gould and Curry' goes, so goes the city." Laboring men's wages were four and six dollars a day, and they worked in three "shifts" or gangs, and the blasting and picking and shoveling went on without ceasing, night and day.

The "city" of Virginia roosted royally midway up the steep side of Mount Davidson, seven thousand two hundred feet above the level of the sea, and in the clear Nevada atmosphere was visible from a distance of fifty miles! It claimed a population of fifteen thousand to eighteen thousand, and all day long half of this little army swarmed the streets like bees and the other half swarmed among the drifts and tunnels of the "Comstock," hundreds of feet down in the earth directly under those same streets. Often we felt our chairs jar, and heard the faint boom of a blast down in the bowels of the earth under the office.

The mountain side was so steep that the entire town had a slant to it like a roof. Each street was a terrace, and from each to the next street below the descent was forty or fifty feet. The fronts of the houses were level with the street they faced, but their rear first floors were propped on lofty stilts; a man could stand at a rear first floor window of a C street house and look down the chimneys of the row of houses below him facing D street. It was a laborious climb, in that thin atmosphere, to ascend from D to A street, and you were panting and out of breath when you got there; but you could turn around and go down again like a house a-fire—so to speak. The atmosphere was so rarified, on account of the great altitude, that one's blood lay near the surface always, and the scratch of a pin was a disaster worth worrying about, for the chances were that a grievous erysipelas would ensue. But to offset this, the thin atmosphere seemed to carry healing to gunshot wounds, and therefore, to simply shoot your adversary through both lungs was a thing not likely to afford you any permanent satisfaction, for he would be nearly certain to be around looking for you within the month, and not with an opera glass, either.

From Virginia's airy situation one could look over a vast, far-reaching panorama of mountain ranges and deserts; and whether the day was bright or overcast, whether the sun was rising or setting, or flaming in the zenith, or whether night and the moon held sway, the spectacle was always impressive and beautiful. Over your head Mount Davidson lifted its gray dome, and before and below you a rugged canyon clove the battlemented hills, making a sombre gateway through which a soft-tinted desert was glimpsed, with the silver thread of a river winding through it, bordered with trees which many miles of distance diminished to a delicate fringe; and still further away the snowy mountains rose up and stretched their long barrier to the filmy horizon—far enough beyond a lake that burned in the desert like a fallen sun, though that, itself, lay fifty miles removed. Look from your window where you would, there was fascination in the picture. At rare intervals—but very rare—there were clouds in our skies, and then the setting sun would gild and flush and glorify this mighty expanse of scenery with a bewildering pomp of color that held the eye like a spell and moved the spirit like music.

Chapter XLIV

MY SALARY WAS increased to forty dollars a week. But I seldom drew it. I had plenty of other resources, and what were two broad twenty-dollar gold pieces to a man who had his pockets full of such and a cumbersome abundance of bright half dollars besides? [Paper money has never come into use on the Pacific coast.] Reporting was lucrative, and every man in the town was lavish with his money and his "feet." The city and all the great mountainside were riddled with mining shafts. There were more mines than miners. True, not ten of these mines were yielding rock worth hauling to a mill, but everybody said, "Wait till the shaft gets down where the ledge comes in solid, and then you will see!" So nobody was discouraged. These were nearly all "wild cat" mines, and wholly worthless, but nobody believed it then. The "Ophir," the "Gould & Curry," the "Mexican," and other great mines on the Comstock lead in Virginia and Gold Hill were turning out huge piles of rich rock every day, and every man believed that his little wild cat claim was as good as any on the "main lead" and would infallibly be worth a thousand dollars a foot when he "got down where it came in solid." Poor fellow, he was blessedly blind to the fact that he never would see that day. So the thousand wild cat shafts burrowed deeper and deeper into the earth day by day, and all men were beside themselves with hope and happiness. How they labored, prophesied, exulted! Surely nothing like it was ever seen before since the world began. Every one of these wild cat mines—not mines, but holes in the ground over imaginary mines—was incorporated and had handsomely engraved "stock" and the stock was salable, too. It was bought and sold with a feverish avidity in the boards every day. You could go up on the mountain side, scratch around and find a ledge (there was no lack of them), put up a "notice" with a grandiloquent name in it, start a shaft, get your stock printed, and with nothing whatever to prove that your mine was worth a straw, you could put your stock on the market and sell out for hundreds and even thousands of dollars. To make money, and make it fast, was as easy as it was to eat your dinner. Every man owned "feet" in fifty different wild cat mines and considered his fortune made. Think of a city with not one solitary poor man in it! One would suppose that when month after month went by and still not a wild cat mine [by wild cat I mean, in general terms, *any* claim not located on the mother vein, *i.e.*, the "Comstock"] yielded a ton of rock worth crushing, the people would begin to wonder if they were not putting too much faith in their prospective riches; but there was not a thought of such a thing. They burrowed away, bought and sold, and were happy.

New claims were taken up daily, and it was the friendly custom to run straight to the newspaper offices, give the reporter forty or fifty "feet," and get them to go and examine the mine and publish a notice of it. They did not care a fig what you said about the property so long as you said something. Consequently we generally said a word or two to the effect that the "indications" were good, or that the ledge was "six feet wide," or that the rock "resembled the Comstock" (and so it did—but as general thing the resemblance was not startling enough to knock you down). If the rock was moderately promising, we followed the custom of the country, used strong adjectives and frothed at the mouth as if a very marvel in silver discoveries had transpired. If the mine was a "developed" one, and had no pay ore to show (and of course it hadn't), we praised the tunnel; said it was one of the most infatuating tunnels in the land; driveled and driveled about the tunnel till we ran entirely out of ecstasies—but never said a word about the rock. We would squander half a column of adulation on a shaft, or a new wire rope, or a dressed pine windlass, or a fascinating force pump, and close with a burst of admiration of the "gentlemanly and efficient Superintendent" of the mine—but never utter a whisper about the rock. And those people were always pleased, always satisfied. Occasionally we patched up and varnished our reputation for discrimination and stern, undeviating accuracy, by giving some old abandoned claim a blast that ought to have made its dry bones rattle—and then somebody would seize it and sell it on the fleeting notoriety thus conferred upon it.

There was *nothing* in the shape of a mining claim that was not salable. We received presents of "feet" every day. If we needed a hundred dollars or so, we sold some; if not, we hoarded it away, satisfied that it would ultimately be worth a thousand dollars a foot. I had a trunk about half full of "stock." When a claim made a stir in the market and went up to a high figure, I searched through my pile to see if I had any of its stock—and generally found it.

The prices rose and fell constantly; but still a fall disturbed us little, because a thousand dollars a foot was our figure, and so we were content to let it fluctuate as much as it pleased till it reached it. My pile of stock was not all given to me by people who wished their claims "noticed." At least half of it was given me by persons who had no thought of such a thing, and looked for nothing more than a simple verbal "thank you;" and you were not even obliged by law to furnish that. If you are coming up the street with a couple of baskets of apples in your hands, and you meet a friend, you naturally invite him to take a few. That describes the condition of things in Virginia in the "flush times." Every man had his pockets full of stock, and it was the actual *custom* of the country to part with small quantities of it to friends without the asking. Very often it was a good idea to close the transaction instantly, when a man offered a stock present to a friend, for the offer was only good and binding at that moment, and if the price went to a high figure shortly afterward the procrastination was a thing to be regretted. Mr. Stewart (Senator, now, from Nevada) one day told me he would give me twenty feet of "Justis" stock if I would walk over to his office. It was worth five or ten dollars a foot. I asked him to make the offer good for next day, as I was just going to dinner. He said he would not be in town; so I risked it and took my dinner instead of the stock. Within the week the price went up to seventy dollars and afterward to a hundred and fifty, but nothing could make that man yield. I suppose he sold that stock of mine and placed the guilty proceeds in his own pocket. [My revenge will be found in the accompanying portrait.] I met three friends one afternoon, who said they had been buying "Overman" stock at auction at eight dollars a foot. One said if I would come up to his office he would give me fifteen feet; another said he would add fifteen; the third said he would do the same. But I was going after an inquest and could not stop. A few weeks afterward they sold all their "Overman" at six hundred dollars a foot and generously came around to tell me about it—and also to urge me to accept of the next forty-five feet of it that people tried to force on me. These are actual facts, and I could make the list a long one and still confine myself strictly to the truth. Many a time friends gave us as much as twenty-five feet of stock that was selling at twenty-five dollars a foot, and they thought no more of it than they would of offering a guest a cigar. These were "flush times" indeed! I thought they were going to last always, but somehow I never was much of a prophet.

To show what a wild spirit possessed the mining brain of the community, I will remark that "claims" were actually "located" in excavations for cellars, where the pick had exposed what seemed to be quartz veins—and not cellars in the suburbs, either, but in the very heart of the city; and forthwith stock would be issued and thrown on the market. It was small matter who the cellar belonged to—the "ledge" belonged to the finder, and unless the United States government interfered (inasmuch as the government holds the primary right to mines of the noble metals in Nevada—or at least did then), it was considered to be his privilege to work it. Imagine a stranger staking out a mining claim among the costly shrubbery in your front yard and calmly proceeding to lay waste the ground with pick and shovel and blasting powder! It has been often done in California. In the middle of one of the principal business streets of Virginia, a man "located" a mining claim and began a shaft on it. He gave me a hundred feet of the stock and I sold it for a fine suit of clothes because I was afraid somebody would fall down the shaft and sue for damages. I owned in another claim that was located in the middle of another street; and to show how absurd people can be, that "East India" stock (as it was called) sold briskly although there was an ancient tunnel running directly under the claim and any man could go into it and see that it did not cut a quartz ledge or anything that remotely resembled one.

One plan of acquiring sudden wealth was to "salt" a wild cat claim and sell

SELLING A MINE.

out while the excitement was up. The process was simple. The schemer located a worthless ledge, sunk a shaft on it, bought a wagon load of rich "Comstock" ore, dumped a portion of it into the shaft and piled the rest by its side, above ground. Then he showed the property to a simpleton and sold it to him at a high figure. Of course the wagon load of rich ore was all that the victim ever got out of his purchase. A most remarkable case of "salting" was that of the "North Ophir." It was claimed that this vein was a remote "extension" of the original "Ophir," a valuable mine on the "Comstock." For a few days everybody was talking about the rich developments in the North Ophir. It was said that it yielded perfectly pure silver in small, solid lumps. I went to the place with the owners, and found a shaft six or eight feet deep, in the bottom of which was a badly shattered vein of dull, yellowish, unpromising rock. One would as soon expect to find silver in a grindstone. We got out a pan of the rubbish and washed it in a puddle, and sure enough, among the sediment we found half a dozen black, bullet-looking pellets of unimpeachable "native" silver. Nobody had ever heard of such a thing before; science could not account for such a queer novelty. The stock rose to sixty-five dollars a foot, and at this figure the world-renowned tragedian, McKean Buchanan, bought a commanding interest and prepared to quit the stage once more—he was always doing that. And then it transpired that the mine had been "salted"—and not in any hackneyed way, either, but in a singularly bold, barefaced and peculiarly original and outrageous fashion. On one of the lumps of "native" silver was discovered the minted legend, "TED STATES OF," and then it was plainly apparent that the mine had been "salted" with melted half-dollars! The lumps thus obtained had been blackened till they resembled native silver, and were then mixed with the shattered rock in the bottom of the shaft. It is literally true. Of course the price of the stock at once fell to nothing, and the tragedian was ruined. But for this calamity we might have lost McKean Buchanan from the stage.

Chapter XLV

THE "FLUSH TIMES" held bravely on. Something over two years before, Mr. Goodman and another journeyman printer, had borrowed forty dollars and set out from San Francisco to try their fortunes in the new city of Virginia. They found the *Territorial Enterprise*, a poverty-stricken weekly journal, gasping for breath and likely to die. They bought it, type, fixtures, good-will and all, for a thousand dollars, on long time. The editorial sanctum, news-room, press-room, publication office, bed-chamber, parlor, and kitchen were all compressed into one apartment and it was a small one, too. The editors and printers slept on the floor, a Chinaman did their cooking, and the "imposing-stone" was the general dinner table. But now things were changed. The paper was a great daily, printed by steam; there were five editors and twenty-three compositors; the subscription price was sixteen dollars a year; the advertising rates were exorbitant, and the columns crowded. The paper was clearing from six to ten thousand dollars a month, and the "Enterprise Building" was finished and ready for occupation— a stately fire-proof brick. Every day from five all the way up to eleven columns of "live" advertisements were left out or crowded into spasmodic and irregular "supplements."

The "Gould & Curry" company were erecting a monster hundred-stamp mill at a cost that ultimately fell little short of a million dollars. Gould & Curry stock paid heavy dividends—a rare thing, and an experience confined to the dozen or fifteen claims located on the "main lead," the "Comstock." The Superintendent of the Gould & Curry lived, rent free, in a fine house built and furnished by the company. He drove a fine pair of horses which were a present from the company, and his salary was twelve thousand dollars a year. The superintendent of another of the great mines traveled in grand state, had a salary of twenty-eight thousand dollars a year, and in a law suit in after days claimed that he was to have had one per cent. on the gross yield of the bullion likewise.

Money was wonderfully plenty. The trouble was, not how to get it,—but how to spend it, how to lavish it, get rid of it, squander it. And so it was a happy thing that just at this juncture the news came over the wires that a great United States Sanitary Commission had been formed and money was wanted for the relief of the wounded sailors and soldiers of the Union languishing in the Eastern hospitals. Right on the heels of it came word that San Francisco had responded superbly before the telegram was half a day old. Virginia rose as one man! A Sanitary Committee was hurriedly organized, and its chairman mounted a vacant cart in C street and tried to make the clamorous multitude understand that the rest of the committee were flying hither and thither and working with all their might and main, and that if the town would only wait an hour, an office would be ready, books opened, and the Commission prepared to receive contributions. His voice was drowned and his information lost in a ceaseless roar of cheers, and demands that the money be received *now*—they swore they would not wait. The chairman pleaded and argued, but, deaf to all entreaty, men plowed their way through the throng and rained checks of gold coin into the cart and scurried away for more. Hands clutching money, were thrust aloft out of the jam by men who hoped this eloquent appeal would cleave a road their strugglings could not open. The very Chinamen and Indians caught the excitement and dashed their half dollars into the cart without knowing or caring what it was all about. Women plunged into the crowd, trimly attired, fought their way to the cart with their coin, and emerged again, by and by, with their apparel in a state of hopeless dilapidation. It was the wildest mob Virginia had ever seen and the most determined and ungovernable; and when at last it abated its fury and dispersed, it had not a penny in its pocket. To use its own phraseology, it came there "flush" and went away "busted."

After that, the Commission got itself into systematic working order, and for weeks the contributions flowed into its treasury in a generous stream. Individuals and all sorts of organizations levied upon themselves a regular weekly tax for the Sanitary fund, graduated according to their means, and there was not another grand universal outburst till the famous "Sanitary Flour Sack" came our way. Its history is peculiar and interesting. A former schoolmate of mine, by the name of Reuel Gridley, was living at the little city of Austin, in the Reese river country, at this time, and was the Democratic candidate for mayor. He and the Republican candidate made an agreement that the defeated man should be publicly presented with a fifty-pound sack of flour by the successful one, and should carry it home on his shoulder. Gridley was defeated. The new mayor gave him the sack of flour, and he shouldered it and carried it a mile or two, from Lower Austin to his home in Upper Austin, attended by a band of music and the whole population. Arrived there, he said he did not need the flour, and asked what the people thought he had better do with it. A voice said:

"Sell it to the highest bidder, for the benefit of the Sanitary fund."

The suggestion was greeted with a round of applause, and Gridley mounted a dry-goods box and assumed the role of auctioneer. The bids went higher and higher, as the sympathies of the pioneers awoke and expanded, till at last the sack was knocked down to a mill man at two hundred and fifty dollars, and his check taken. He was asked where he would have the flour delivered, and he said:

"Nowhere—sell it again."

Now the cheers went up royally, and the multitude were fairly in the spirit of the thing. So Gridley stood there and shouted and perspired till the sun went down; and when the crowd dispersed he had sold the sack to three hundred different people, and had taken in eight thousand dollars in gold. And still the flour sack was in his possession.

The news came to Virginia, and a telegram went back:

"Fetch along your flour sack!"

Thirty-six hours afterward Gridley arrived, and an afternoon mass meeting was held in the Opera House, and the auction began. But the sack had come sooner than it was expected; the people were not thoroughly aroused, and the sale dragged. At nightfall only five thousand dollars had been secured, and there was a crestfallen feeling in the community. However, there was no disposition to let the matter rest here and acknowledge vanquishment at the hands of the village of Austin. Till late in the night the principal citizens were at work arranging the morrow's campaign, and when they went to bed they had no fears for the result. At eleven the next morning a procession of open carriages, attended by clamorous bands of music and adorned with a moving display of flags, filed along C street and was soon in danger of blockade by a huzzaing multitude of citizens. In the first carriage sat Gridley, with the flour sack in prominent view,

THE GREAT FLOUR SACK PROCESSION.

the latter splendid with bright paint and gilt lettering; also in the same carriage
sat the mayor and the recorder. The other carriages contained the Common
Council, the editors and reporters, and other people of imposing consequence.
The crowd pressed to the corner of C and Taylor streets, expecting the sale to
begin there, but they were disappointed, and also unspeakably surprised; for the
cavalcade moved on as if Virginia had ceased to be of importance, and took its
way over the "divide," toward the small town of Gold Hill. Telegrams had
gone ahead to Gold Hill, Silver City and Dayton, and those communities were
at fever heat and rife for the conflict. It was a very hot day, and wonderfully
dusty. At the end of a short half hour we descended into Gold Hill with drums
beating and colors flying, and enveloped in imposing clouds of dust. The whole
population—men, women and children, Chinamen and Indians, were massed in
the main street, all the flags in town were at the mast head, and the blare of the
bands was drowned in cheers. Gridley stood up and asked who would make the
first bid for the National Sanitary Flour Sack. Gen. W. said:

"The Yellow Jacket silver mining company offers a thousand dollars, coin!"

A tempest of applause followed. A telegram carried the news to Virginia, and
fifteen minutes afterward that city's population was massed in the streets devouring
the tidings—for it was part of the programme that the bulletin boards should do
a good work that day. Every few minutes a new dispatch was bulletined from
Gold Hill, and still the excitement grew. Telegrams began to return to us from
Virginia beseeching Gridley to bring back the flour sack; but such was not the
plan of the campaign. At the end of an hour Gold Hill's small population had
paid a figure for the flour sack that awoke all the enthusiasm of Virginia when
the grand total was displayed upon the bulletin boards. Then the Gridley cavalcade
moved on, a giant refreshed with new lager beer and plenty of it—for the people
brought it to the carriages without waiting to measure it—and within three hours
more the expedition had carried Silver City and Dayton by storm and was on
its way back covered with glory. Every move had been telegraphed and bulletined,
and as the procession entered Virginia and filed down C street at half past eight
in the evening the town was abroad in the thoroughfares, torches were glaring,
flags flying, bands playing, cheer on cheer cleaving the air, and the city ready
to surrender at discretion. The auction began, every bid was greeted with bursts
of applause, and at the end of two hours and a half a population of fifteen
thousand souls had paid in coin for a fifty-pound sack of flour a sum equal to
forty thousand dollars in greenbacks! It was at a rate in the neigborhood of three
dollars for each man, woman and child of the population. The grand total would
have been twice as large, but the streets were very narrow, and hundreds who
wanted to bid could not get within a block of the stand, and could not make
themselves heard. These grew tired of waiting and many of them went home
long before the auction was over. This was the greatest day Virginia ever saw,
perhaps.

Gridley sold the sack in Carson City and several California towns; also in San
Francisco. Then he took it east and sold it in one or two Atlantic cities, I think.
I am not sure of that, but I know that he finally carried it to St. Louis, where
a monster Sanitary Fair was being held, and after selling it there for a large sum
and helping on the enthusiasm by displaying the portly silver bricks which
Nevada's donation had produced, he had the flour baked up into small cakes
and retailed them at high prices.

It was estimated that when the flour sack's mission was ended it had been sold for a grand total of a hundred and fifty thousand dollars in greenbacks! This is probably the only instance on record where common family flour brought three thousand dollars a pound in the public market.

It is due to Mr. Gridley's memory to mention that the expenses of his Sanitary flour sack expedition of fifteen thousand miles, going and returning, were paid in large part, if not entirely, out of his own pocket. The time he gave to it was not less than three months. Mr. Gridley was a soldier in the Mexican war and a pioneer Californian. He died at Stockton, California, in December, 1870, greatly regretted.

Chapter XLVI

THERE WERE NABOBS in those days—in the "flush times," I mean. Every rich strike in the mines created one or two. I call to mind several of these. They were careless, easy-going fellows, as a general thing, and the community at large was as much benefited by their riches as they were themselves—possibly more, in some cases.

Two cousins, teamsters, did some hauling for a man and had to take a small segregated portion of a silver mine in lieu of $300 cash. They gave an outsider a third to open the mine, and they went on teaming. But not long. Ten months afterward the mine was out of debt and paying each owner $8,000 to $10,000 a month—say $100,000 a year.

One of the earliest nabobs that Nevada was delivered of wore $6,000 worth of diamonds in his bosom, and swore he was unhappy because he could not spend his money as fast as he made it.

Another Nevada nabob boasted an income that often reached $16,000 a month; and he used to love to tell how he had worked in the very mine that yielded it, for five dollars a day, when he first came to the country.

The silver and sage-brush State has knowledge of another of these pets of fortune—lifted from actual poverty to affluence almost in a single night—who was able to offer $100,000 for a position of high official distinction, shortly afterward, and did offer it—but failed to get it, his politics not being as sound as his bank account.

Then there was John Smith. He was a good, honest, kind-hearted soul, born and reared in the lower ranks of life, and miraculously ignorant. He drove a team, and owned a small ranch—a ranch that paid him a comfortable living, for although it yielded but little hay, what little it did yield was worth from $250 to $300 in gold per ton in the market. Presently Smith traded a few acres of the ranch for a small undeveloped silver mine in Gold Hill. He opened the mine and built a little unpretending ten-stamp mill. Eighteen months afterward he retired from the hay business, for his mining income had reached a most comfortable figure. Some people said it was $30,000 a month, and others said it was $60,000. Smith was very rich at any rate.

And then he went to Europe and traveled. And when he came back he was never tired of telling about the fine hogs he had seen in England, and the gorgeous sheep he had seen in Spain, and the fine cattle he had noticed in the vicinity of Rome. He was full of the wonders of the old world, and advised everybody to travel. He said a man never imagined what surprising things there were in the world till he had traveled.

One day, on board ship, the passengers made up a pool of $500, which was to be the property of the man who should come nearest to guessing the run of the vessel for the next twenty-four hours. Next day, toward noon, the figures were all in the purser's hands in sealed envelopes. Smith was serene and happy, for he had been bribing the engineer. But another party won the prize! Smith said:

"Here, that won't do! He guessed two miles wider of the mark than I did."

The purser said, "Mr. Smith, you missed it further than any man on board. We traveled two hundred and eight miles yesterday."

"Well, sir," said Smith, "that's just where I've got you, for I guessed two hundred and nine. If you'll look at my figgers again you'll find a 2 and two 0's, which stands for 200, don't it?—and after 'em you'll find a 9 (2009), which stands for two hundred and nine. I reckon I'll take that money, if you please."

The Gould & Curry claim comprised twelve hundred feet, and it all belonged originally to the two men whose names it bears. Mr. Curry owned two thirds of it—and he said that he sold it out for twenty-five hundred dollars in cash, and an old plug horse that ate up his market value in hay and barley in seventeen days by the watch. And he said that Gould sold out for a pair of second-hand government blankets and a bottle of whiskey that killed nine men in three hours, and that an unoffending stranger that smelled the cork was disabled for life. Four years afterward the mine thus disposed of was worth in the San Francisco market seven millions six hundred thousand dollars in gold coin.

In the early days a poverty-stricken Mexican who lived in a canyon directly back of Virginia City, had a stream of water as large as a man's wrist trickling from the hill-side on his premises. The Ophir Company segregated a hundred feet of their mine and traded it to him for the stream of water. The hundred feet proved to be the richest part of the entire mine; four years after the swap, its market value (including its mill) was $1,500,000.

An individual who owned twenty feet in the Ophir mine before its great riches were revealed to men, traded it for a horse, and a very sorry looking brute he was, too. A year or so afterward, when Ophir stock went up to $3,000 a foot, this man, who had not a cent, used to say he was the most startling example of magnificence and misery the world had ever seen—because he was able to ride a sixty-thousand-dollar horse—yet could not scrape up cash enough to buy a saddle, and was obliged to borrow one or ride bareback. He said if fortune were to give him another sixty-thousand-dollar horse it would ruin him.

A youth of nineteen, who was a telegraph operator in Virginia on a salary of a hundred dollars a month, and who, when he could not make out German names in the list of San Francisco steamer arrivals, used to ingeniously select and supply substitutes for them out of an old Berlin city directory, made himself rich by watching the mining telegrams that passed through his hands and buying and selling stocks accordingly, through a friend in San Francisco. Once when a private dispatch was sent from Virginia announcing a rich strike in a prominent mine and advising that the matter be kept secret till a large amount of the stock could be secured, he bought forty "feet" of the stock at twenty dollars a foot, and afterward sold half of it at eight hundred dollars a foot and the rest at double that figure. Within three months he was worth $150,000 and had resigned his telegraphic position.

MAGNIFICENCE AND MISERY.

Another telegraph operator who had been discharged by the company for divulging the secrets of the office, agreed with a moneyed man in San Francisco to furnish him the result of a great Virginia mining lawsuit within an hour after its private reception by the parties to it in San Francisco. For this he was to have a large percentage of the profits on purchases and sales made on it by his fellow-conspirator. So he went, disguised as a teamster, to a little wayside telegraph office in the mountains, got acquainted with the operator, and sat in the office day after day, smoking his pipe, complaining that his team was fagged out and unable to travel—and meantime listening to the dispatches as they passed clicking through the machine from Virginia. Finally the private dispatch announcing the result of the lawsuit sped over the wires, and as soon as he heard it he telegraphed his friend in San Francisco:

"Am tired waiting. Shall sell the team and go home."

It was the signal agreed upon. The word "waiting" left out, would have signified that the suit had gone the other way. The mock teamster's friend picked up a deal of the mining stock, at low figures, before the news became public, and a fortune was the result.

For a long time after one of the great Virginia mines had been incorporated, about fifty feet of the original location were still in the hands of a man who had never signed the incorporation papers. The stock became very valuable, and every effort was made to find this man, but he had disappeared. Once it was heard that he was in New York, and one or two speculators went east but failed to find him. Once the news came that he was in the Bermudas, and straightway a speculator or two hurried east and sailed for Bermuda—but he was not there. Finally he was heard of in Mexico, and a friend of his, a bar-keeper on a salary, scraped together a little money and sought him out, bought his "feet" for a hundred dollars, returned and sold the property for $75,000.

But why go on? The traditions of Silverland are filled with instances like these, and I would never get through enumerating them were I to attempt to do it. I only desired to give the reader an idea of a peculiarity of the "flush times" which I could not present so strikingly in any other way, and which some mention of was necessary to a realizing comprehension of the time and the country.

I was personally acquainted with the majority of the nabobs I have referred to, and so, for old acquaintance sake, I have shifted their occupations and experiences around in such a way as to keep the Pacific public from recognizing these once notorious men. No longer notorious, for the majority of them have drifted back into poverty and obscurity again.

In Nevada there used to be current the story of an adventure of two of her nabobs, which may or may not have occurred. I give it for what it is worth:

Col. Jim had seen somewhat of the world, and knew more or less of its ways; but Col. Jack was from the back settlements of the States, had led a life of arduous toil, and had never seen a city. These two, blessed with sudden wealth, projected a visit to New York,—Col. Jack to see the sights, and Col. Jim to guard his unsophistication from misfortune. They reached San Francisco in the night, and sailed in the morning. Arrived in New York, Col. Jack said:

"I've heard tell of carriages all my life, and now I mean to have a ride in one; I don't care what it costs. Come along."

They stepped out on the sidewalk, and Col. Jim called a stylish barouche. But Col. Jack said:

"*No*, sir! None of your cheap-John turn-outs for me. I'm here to have a good time, and money ain't any object. I mean to have the nobbiest rig that's going. Now here comes the very trick. Stop that yaller one with the pictures on it— don't you fret—I'll stand all the expenses myself."

So Col. Jim stopped an empty omnibus, and they got in. Said Col. Jack:

"Ain't it gay, though? Oh, no, I reckon not! Cushions, and windows, and pictures, till you can't rest. What would the boys say if they could see us cutting a swell like this in New York? By George, I wish they *could* see us."

Then he put his head out of the window, and shouted to the driver:

"Say, Johnny, this suits *me!*—suits yours truly, you bet, you! I want this shebang all day. I'm *on* it, old man! Let 'em out! Make 'em go! We'll make it all right with *you*, sonny!"

The driver passed his hand through the strap-hole, and tapped for his fare— it was before the gongs came into common use. Col. Jack took the hand, and shook it cordially. He said:

"You twig me, old pard! All right between gents. Smell of *that*, and see how you like it!"

And he put a twenty-dollar gold piece in the driver's hand. After a moment the driver said he could not make change.

"Bother the change! Ride it out. Put it in your pocket."

Then to Col. Jim, with a sounding slap on his thigh:

"*Ain't* it style, though? Hanged if I don't hire this thing every day for a week."

The omnibus stopped, and a young lady got in. Col. Jack stared a moment, then nudged Col. Jim with his elbow:

"Don't say a word," he whispered. "Let her ride, if she wants to. Gracious, there's room enough."

The young lady got out her porte-monnaie, and handed her fare to Col. Jack.

"What's this for?" said he.

"Give it to the driver, please."

"Take back your money, madam. We can't allow it. You're welcome to ride here as long as you please, but this shebang's chartered, and we can't let you pay a cent."

The girl shrunk into a corner, bewildered. An old lady with a basket climbed in, and proffered her fare.

"Excuse me," said Colonel Jack. "You're perfectly welcome here, madam, but we can't allow you to pay. Set right down there, mum, and don't you be the least uneasy. Make yourself just as free as if you was in your own turnout."

Within two minutes, three gentlemen, two fat women, and a couple of children entered.

"Come right along, friends," said Col. Jack; "don't mind *us*. This is a free blow-out." Then he whispered to Col. Jim, "New York ain't no sociable place, I don't reckon—it ain't no *name* for it!"

He resisted every effort to pass fares to the driver, and made everybody cordially welcome. The situation dawned on the people, and they pocketed their money, and delivered themselves up to covert enjoyment of the episode. Half a dozen more passengers entered.

"Oh, there's *plenty* of room," said Col. Jack. "Walk right in, and make yourselves at home. A blow-out ain't worth anything *as* a blow-out, unless a body has company." Then in a whisper to Col. Jim: "But *ain't* these New Yorkers friendly? And ain't they cool about it, too? Icebergs ain't anywhere. I reckon they'd tackle a hearse, if it was going their way."

More passengers got in; more yet, and still more. Both seats were filled, and a file of men were standing up, holding on to the cleats overhead. Parties with baskets and bundles were climbing up on the roof. Half-suppressed laughter rippled up from all sides.

"Well, for clean, cool, out-and-out cheek, if this don't bang anything that ever I saw, I'm an Injun!" whispered Col. Jack.

A Chinaman crowded his way in.

"I weaken!" said Col. Jack. "Hold on, driver! Keep your seats, ladies and gents. Just make yourselves free—everything's paid for. Driver, rustle these folks around as long as they're a mind to go—friends of ours, you know. Take them everywheres—and if you want more money, come to the St. Nicholas, and we'll make it all right. Pleasant journey to you, ladies and gents—go it just as long as you please—it shan't cost you a cent!"

The two comrades got out, and Col. Jack said:

"Jimmy, it's the sociablest place *I* ever saw. The Chinaman waltzed in as comfortable as anybody. If we'd stayed awhile, I reckon we'd had some niggers. B' George, we'll have to barricade our doors to-night, or some of these ducks will be trying to sleep with us."

Chapter XLVII

SOMEBODY HAS SAID that in order to know a community, one must observe the style of its funerals and know what manner of men they bury with most ceremony. I cannot say which class we buried with most eclat in our "flush times," the distinguished public benefactor or the distinguished rough—possibly the two chief grades or grand divisions of society honored their illustrious dead about equally; and hence, no doubt the philosopher I have quoted from would have needed to see two representative funerals in Virginia before forming his estimate of the people.

There was a grand time over Buck Fanshaw when he died. He was a representative citizen. He had "killed his man"—not in his own quarrel, it is true, but in defence of a stranger unfairly beset by numbers. He had kept a sumptuous saloon. He had been the proprietor of a dashing helpmeet whom he could have discarded without the formality of a divorce. He had held a high position in the fire department and been a very Warwick in politics. When he died there was great lamentation throughout the town, but especially in the vast bottom-stratum of society.

On the inquest it was shown that Buck Fanshaw, in the delirium of a wasting typhoid fever, had taken arsenic, shot himself through the body, cut his throat, and jumped out of a four-story window and broken his neck—and after due deliberation, the jury, sad and tearful, but with intelligence unblinded by its sorrow, brought in a verdict of death "by the visitation of God." What could the world do without juries?

Prodigious preparations were made for the funeral. All the vehicles in town were hired, all the saloons put in mourning, all the municipal and fire-company flags hung at half-mast, and all the firemen ordered to muster in uniform and bring their machines duly draped in black. Now—let us remark in parenthesis—as all the peoples of the earth had representative adventurers in the Silverland, and as each adventurer had brought the slang of his nation or his locality with him, the combination made the slang of Nevada the richest and the most infinitely varied and copious that had ever existed anywhere in the world, perhaps, except in the mines of California in the "early days." Slang was the language of Nevada. It was hard to preach a sermon without it, and be understood. Such phrases as "You bet!" "Oh, no, I reckon not!" "No Irish need apply," and a hundred others, became so common as to fall from the lips of a speaker unconsciously—and very often when they did not touch the subject under discussion and consequently failed to mean anything.

After Buck Fanshaw's inquest, a meeting of the short-haired brotherhood was held, for nothing can be done on the Pacific coast without a public meeting and an expression of sentiment. Regretful resolutions were passed and various committees appointed; among others, a committee of one was deputed to call on the minister, a fragile, gentle, spiritual new fledgling from an Eastern theological seminary, and as yet unacquainted with the ways of the mines. The committeeman, "Scotty" Briggs, made his visit; and in after days it was worth something to hear the minister tell about it. Scotty was a stalwart rough, whose customary suit, when on weighty official business, like committee work, was a fire helmet, flaming red flannel shirt, patent leather belt with spanner and revolver attached, coat hung over arm, and pants stuffed into boot tops. He formed something of a contrast to the pale theological student. It is fair to say of Scotty, however, in passing, that he had a warm heart, and a strong love for his friends, and never entered into a quarrel when he could reasonably keep out of it. Indeed, it was commonly said that whenever one of Scotty's fights was investigated, it always turned out that it had originally been no affair of his, but that out of native goodheartedness he had dropped in of his own accord to help the man who was getting the worst of it. He and Buck Fanshaw were bosom friends for years, and had often taken adventurous "pot-luck" together. On one occasion, they had thrown off their coats and taken the weaker side in a fight among strangers, and after gaining a hard-earned victory, turned and found that the men they were helping had deserted early, and not only that, but had stolen their coats and made off with them! But to return to Scotty's visit to the minister. He was on a sorrowful mission, now, and his face was the picture of woe. Being admitted to the presence he sat down before the clergyman, placed his fire-hat on an unfinished manuscript sermon under the minister's nose, took from it a red silk handkerchief, wiped his brow and heaved a sigh of dismal impressiveness, explanatory of his business. He choked, and even shed tears; but with an effort he mastered his voice and said in lugubrious tones:

"Are you the duck that runs the gospel-mill next door?"

"Am I the—pardon me, I believe I do not understand?"

With another sigh and a half-sob, Scotty rejoined:

"Why you see we are in a bit of trouble, and the boys thought maybe you would give us a lift, if we'd tackle you—that is, if I've got the rights of it and you are the head clerk of the doxology-works next door."

"I am the shepherd in charge of the flock whose fold is next door."

"The which?"

"The spiritual adviser of the little company of believers whose sanctuary adjoins these premises."

Scotty scratched his head, reflected a moment, and then said:

"You ruther hold over me, pard. I reckon I can't call that hand. Ante and pass the buck."

"How? I beg pardon. What did I understand you to say?"

"Well, you've ruther got the bulge on me. Or maybe we've both got the bulge, somehow. You don't smoke me and I don't smoke you. You see, one of the boys has passed in his checks and we want to give him a good send-off, and so the thing I'm on now is to roust out somebody to jerk a little chin-music for us and waltz him through handsome."

"My friend, I seem to grow more and more bewildered. Your observations are wholly incomprehensible to me. Cannot you simplify them in some way? At first I thought perhaps I understood you, but I grope now. Would it not expedite matters if you restricted yourself to categorical statements of fact unencumbered with obstructing accumulations of metaphor and allegory?"

Another pause, and more reflection. Then, said Scotty:

"I'll have to pass, I judge."

"How?"

"You've raised me out, pard."

"I still fail to catch your meaning."

"Why, that last lead of yourn is too many for me—that's the idea. I can't neither trump nor follow suit."

The clergyman sank back in his chair perplexed. Scotty leaned his head on his hand and gave himself up to thought. Presently his face came up, sorrowful but confident.

"I've got it now, so's you can savvy," he said. "What we want is a gospel-sharp. See?"

"A what?"

"Gospel-sharp. Parson."

"Oh! Why did you not say so before? I am a clergyman—a parson."

"Now you talk! You see my blind and straddle it like a man. Put it there!"—

extending a brawny paw, which closed over the minister's small hand and gave it a shake indicative of fraternal sympathy and fervent gratification.

"Now we're all right, pard. Let's start fresh. Don't you mind my snuffling a little—becuz we're in a power of trouble. You see, one of the boys has gone up the flume—"

"Gone where?"

"Up the flume—throwed up the sponge, you understand."

"Thrown up the sponge?"

"Yes—kicked the bucket—"

"Ah—has departed to that mysterious country from whose bourne no traveler returns."

"Return! I reckon not. Why pard, he's *dead!*"

"Yes, I understand."

"Oh, you do? Well I thought maybe you might be getting tangled some more. Yes, you see he's dead again—"

"*Again?* Why, has he ever been dead before?"

"Dead before? No! Do you reckon a man has got as many lives as a cat? But you bet you he's awful dead now, poor old boy, and I wish I'd never seen this day. I don't want no better friend than Buck Fanshaw. I knowed him by the back; and when I know a man and like him, I freeze to him—you hear *me*. Take him all round, pard, there never was a bullier man in the mines. No man ever knowed Buck Fanshaw to go back on a friend. But it's all up, you know, it's all up. It ain't no use. They've scooped him."

"Scooped him?"

"Yes—death has. Well, well, well, we've got to give him up. Yes indeed. It's a kind of a hard world, after all, *ain't* it? But pard, he was a rustler! You ought to seen him get started once. He was a bully boy with a glass eye! Just spit in his face and give him room according to his strength, and it was just beautiful to see him peel and go in. He was the worst son of a thief that ever drawed breath. Pard, he was *on* it! He was on it bigger than an Injun!"

"On it? On what?"

"On the shoot. On the shoulder. On the fight, you understand. *He* didn't give a continental for *any*body. *Beg* your pardon, friend, for coming so near saying a cuss-word—but you see I'm on an awful strain, in this palaver, on account of having to cramp down and draw everything so mild. But we've got to give him up. There ain't any getting around that, I don't reckon. Now if we can get you to help plant him   "

"Preach the funeral discourse? Assist at the obsequies?"

"Obs'quies is good. Yes. That's it—that's our little game. We are going to get the thing up regardless, you know. He was always nifty himself, and so you bet you his funeral ain't going to be no slouch—solid silver door-plate on his coffin, six plumes on the hearse, and a nigger on the box in a biled shirt and a plug hat—how's that for high? And we'll take care of *you*, pard. We'll fix you all right. There'll be a kerridge for you; and whatever you want, you just 'scape out and we'll 'tend to it. We've got a shebang fixed up for you to stand behind, in No. 1's house, and don't you be afraid. Just go in and toot your horn, if you don't sell a clam. Put Buck through as bully as you can, pard, for anybody that knowed him will tell you that he was one of the whitest men that was ever in the mines. You can't draw it too strong. He never could stand it to see things going wrong. He's done more to make this town quiet and peaceable than any man in it. I've seen him lick four Greasers in eleven minutes, myself. If a thing wanted regulating, *he* warn't a man to go browsing around after somebody to do it, but he would prance in and regulate it himself. He warn't a Catholic. Scasely. He was down on 'em. His word was, 'No Irish need apply!' But it didn't make no difference about that when it came down to what a man's rights was—and so, when some roughs jumped the Catholic bone-yard and started in to stake out town-lots in it he *went* for 'em! And he *cleaned* 'em, too! I was there, pard, and I seen it myself.''

"That was very well indeed—at least the impulse was—whether the act was strictly defensible or not. Had deceased any religious convictions? That is to say, did he feel a dependence upon, or acknowledge allegiance to a higher power?''

More reflection.

"I reckon you've stumped me again, pard. Could you say it over once more, and say it slow?''

"Well, to simplify it somewhat, was he, or rather had he ever been connected with any organization sequestered from secular concerns and devoted to self-sacrifice in the interests of morality?''

"All down but nine—set 'em up on the other alley, pard.''

"What did I understand you to say?''

"Why, you're most too many for me, you know. When you get in with your left I hunt grass every time. Every time you draw, you fill; but I don't seem to have any luck. Let's have a new deal.''

"How? Begin again?''

"That's it.''

"Very well. Was he a good man, and—''

"There—I see that; don't put up another chip till I look at my hand. A good man, says you? Pard, it ain't no name for it. He was the best man that ever—pard, you would have doted on that man. He could lam any galoot of his inches in America. It was him that put down the riot last election before it got a start; and everybody said he was the only man that could have done it. He waltzed in with a spanner in one hand and a trumpet in the other, and sent fourteen men home on a shutter in less than three minutes. He had that riot all broke up and

SCOTTY REGULATING MATTERS.

prevented nice before anybody ever got a chance to strike a blow. He was always for peace, and he would *have* peace—he could not stand disturbances. Pard, he was a great loss to this town. It would please the boys if you could chip in something like that and do him justice. Here once when the Micks got to throwing stones through the Methodis' Sunday-school windows, Buck Fanshaw, all of his own notion, shut up his saloon and took a couple of six-shooters and mounted guard over the Sunday school. Says he, 'No Irish need apply!' And they didn't. He was the bulliest man in the mountains, pard! He could run faster, jump higher, hit harder, and hold more tangle-foot whisky without spilling it than any man in seventeen counties. Put that in, pard—it'll please the boys more than anything you could say. And you can say, pard, that he never shook his mother.''

"Never shook his mother?"

"That's it—any of the boys will tell you so."

"Well, but why *should* he shake her?"

"That's what *I* say—but some people does."

"Not people of any repute?"

"Well, some that averages pretty so-so."

"In my opinion the man that would offer personal violence to his own mother, ought to—"

"Cheese it, pard; you've banked your ball clean outside the string. What I was a drivin' at, was, that he never *throwed off* on his mother—don't you see? No indeedy. He give her a house to live in, and town lots, and plenty of money; and he looked after her and took care of her all the time; and when she was down with the small-pox I'm d—d if he didn't set up nights and nuss her himself! *Beg* your pardon for saying it, but it hopped out too quick for yours truly. You've treated me like a gentleman, pard, and I ain't the man to hurt your feelings intentional. I think you're white. I think you're a square man, pard. I like you, and I'll lick any man that don't. I'll lick him till he can't tell himself from a last year's corpse! Put it *there!*" [Another fraternal handshake—and exit.]

The obsequies were all that "the boys" could desire. Such a marvel of funeral pomp had never been seen in Virginia. The plumed hearse, the dirge-breathing brass bands, the closed marts of business, the flags drooping at half-mast, the long, plodding procession of uniformed secret societies, military battalions and fire companies, draped engines, carriages of officials, and citizens in vehicles and on foot, attracted multitudes of spectators to the sidewalks, roofs and windows; and for years afterward, the degree of grandeur attained by any civic display in Virginia was determined by comparison with Buck Fanshaw's funeral.

Scotty Briggs, as a pall-bearer and a mourner, occupied a prominent place at the funeral, and when the sermon was finished and the last sentence of the prayer for the dead man's soul ascended, he responded, in a low voice, but with feeling:

"AMEN. No Irish need apply."

As the bulk of the response was without apparent relevancy, it was probably nothing more than a humble tribute to the memory of the friend that was gone; for, as Scotty had once said, it was "his word."

Scotty Briggs, in after days, achieved the distinction of becoming the only convert to religion that was ever gathered from the Virginia roughs; and it transpired that the man who had it in him to espouse the quarrel of the weak out of inborn nobility of spirit was no mean timber whereof to construct a Christian. The making him one did not warp his generosity or diminish his courage; on the contrary it gave intelligent direction to the one and a broader field to the other. If his Sunday-school class progressed faster than the other classes, was it matter for wonder? I think not. He talked to his pioneer small-fry in a language they understood! It was my large privilege, a month before he died, to hear him tell the beautiful story of Joseph and his brethren to his class "without looking at the book." I leave it to the reader to fancy what it was like, as it fell, riddled with slang, from the lips of that grave, earnest teacher, and was listened to by his little learners with a consuming interest that showed that they were as unconscious as he was that any violence was being done to the sacred proprieties!

Chapter XLVIII

THE FIRST TWENTY-SIX graves in the Virginia cemetery were occupied by *murdered* men. So everybody said, so everybody believed, and so they will always say and believe. The reason why there was so much slaughtering done was that in a new mining district the rough element predominates, and a person is not respected until he has "killed his man." That was the very expression used.

If an unkown individual arrived, they did not inquire if he was capable, honest, industrious, but—had he killed his man? If he had not, he gravitated to his natural and proper position, that of a man of small consequence; if he had, the cordiality of his reception was graduated according to the number of his dead. It was tedious work struggling up to a position of influence with bloodless hands; but when a man came with the blood of half a dozen men on his soul, his worth was recognized at once and his acquaintance sought.

In Nevada, for a time, the lawyer, the editor, the banker, the chief desperado, the chief gambler, and the saloon-keeper, occupied the same level in society, and it was the highest. The cheapest and easiest way to become an influential man and be looked up to by the community at large, was to stand behind a bar, wear a cluster-diamond pin, and sell whisky. I am not sure but that the saloon-keeper held a shade higher rank than any other member of society. His opinion had weight. It was his privilege to say how the elections should go. No great movement could succeed without the countenance and direction of the saloon-keepers. It was a high favor when the chief saloon-keeper consented to serve in the legislature or the board of aldermen. Youthful ambition hardly aspired so much to the honors of the law, or the army and navy as to the dignity of proprietorship in a saloon.

To be a saloon-keeper and kill a man was to be illustrious. Hence the reader will not be surprised to learn that more than one man was killed in Nevada under hardly the pretext of provocation, so impatient was the slayer to achieve reputation and throw off the galling sense of being held in indifferent repute by his associates. I knew two youths who tried to "kill their men" for no other reason—and got killed themselves for their pains. "There goes the man that killed Bill Adams" was higher praise and a sweeter sound in the ears of this sort of people than any other speech that admiring lips could utter.

The men who murdered Virginia's original twenty-six cemetery-occupants were never punished. Why? Because Alfred the Great, when he invented trial by jury, and knew that he had admirably framed it to secure justice in his age

THE MAN WHO HAD KILLED A DOZEN.

of the world, was not aware that in the nineteenth century the condition of things would be so entirely changed that unless he rose from the grave and altered the jury plan to meet the emergency, it would prove the most ingenious and infallible agency for *defeating* justice that human wisdom could contrive. For how could he imagine that we simpletons would go on using his jury plan after circumstances had stripped it of its usefulness, any more than he could imagine that we would go on using his candle-clock after we had invented chronometers? In his day news could not travel fast, and hence he could easily find a jury of honest, intelligent men who had not heard of the case they were called to try—but in our day of telegraphs and newspapers his plan compels us to swear in juries composed of fools and rascals, because the system rigidly excludes honest men and men of brains.

I remember one of those sorrowful farces, in Virginia, which we call a jury trial. A noted desperado killed Mr. B., a good citizen, in the most wanton and cold-blooded way. Of course the papers were full of it, and all men capable of reading, read about it. And of course all men not deaf and dumb and idiotic, talked about it. A jury list was made out, and Mr. B. L., a prominent banker and a valued citizen, was questioned precisely as he would have been questioned in any court in America:

"Have you heard of this homicide?"

"Yes."

"Have you held conversations upon the subject?"

"Yes."

"Have you formed or expressed opinions about it?"

"Yes."

"Have you read the newspaper accounts of it?"

"Yes."

"We do not want you."

A minister, intelligent, esteemed, and greatly respected; a merchant of high character and known probity; a mining superintendent of intelligence and un-blemished reputation; a quartz mill owner of excellent standing, were all questioned in the same way, and all set aside. Each said the public talk and the newspaper reports had not so biased his mind but that sworn testimony would overthrow his previously formed opinions and enable him to render a verdict without prejudice and in accordance with the facts. But of course such men could not be trusted with the case. Ignoramuses alone could mete out unsullied justice.

When the peremptory challenges were all exhausted, a jury of twelve men was impaneled—a jury who swore they had neither heard, read, talked about, nor expressed an opinion concerning a murder which the very cattle in the corrals, the Indians in the sage-brush and the stones in the streets were cognizant of! It was a jury composed of two desperadoes, two low beer-house politicians, three bar-keepers, two ranchmen who could not read, and three dull, stupid, human donkeys! It actually came out afterward, that one of these latter thought that incest and arson were the same thing.

The verdict rendered by this jury was, Not Guilty. What else could one expect?

The jury system puts a ban upon intelligence and honesty, and a premium upon ignorance, stupidity and perjury. It is a shame that we must continue to use a worthless system because it *was* good a thousand years ago. In this age, when a gentleman of high social standing, intelligence and probity, swears that testimony given under solemn oath will outweigh, with him, street talk and newspaper reports based upon mere hearsay, he is worth a hundred jurymen who will swear to their own ignorance and stupidity, and justice would be far safer in his hands than in theirs. Why could not the jury law be so altered as to give men of brains and honesty an *equal chance* with fools and miscreants? Is it right to show the present favoritism to one class of men and inflict a disability on another, in a land whose boast is that all its citizens are free and equal? I am a candidate for the legislature. I desire to tamper with the jury law. I wish to so alter it as to put a premium on intelligence and character, and close the jury box against idiots, blacklegs, and people who do not read newspapers. But no doubt I shall be defeated—every effort I make to save the country "misses fire."

My idea, when I began this chapter, was to say something about desperadoism in the "flush times" of Nevada. To attempt a portrayal of that era and that land, and leave out the blood and carnage, would be like portraying Mormondom and leaving out polygamy. The desperado stalked the streets with a swagger graded according to the number of his homicides, and a nod of recognition from him was sufficient to make a humble admirer happy for the rest of the day. The deference that was paid to a desperado of wide reputation, and who "kept his private graveyard," as the phrase went, was marked, and cheerfully accorded. When he moved along the sidewalk in his excessively long-tailed frock-coat, shiny stump-toed boots, and with dainty little slouch hat tipped over left eye, the small-fry roughs made room for his majesty; when he entered the restaurant, the waiters deserted bankers and merchants to overwhelm him with obsequious service; when he shouldered his way to a bar, the shouldered parties wheeled indignantly, recognized him, and—apologized. They got a look in return that froze their marrow, and by that time a curled and breast-pinned bar keeper was beaming over the counter, proud of the established acquaintanceship that permitted such a familiar form of speech as:

"How're ye, Billy, old fel? Glad to see you. What'll you take—the old thing?"

The "old thing" meant his customary drink, of course.

The best known names in the Territory of Nevada were those belonging to these long-tailed heroes of the revolver. Orators, Governors, capitalists and leaders of the legislature enjoyed a degree of fame, but it seemed local and meagre when contrasted with the fame of such men as Sam Brown, Jack Williams,

Billy Mulligan, Farmer Pease, Sugarfoot Mike, Pock-Marked Jake, El Dorado Johnny, Jack McNabb, Joe McGee, Jack Harris, Six-fingered Pete, etc., etc. There was a long list of them. They were brave, reckless men, and traveled with their lives in their hands. To give them their due, they did their killing principally among themselves, and seldom molested peaceable citizens, for they considered it small credit to add to their trophies so cheap a bauble as the death of a man who was "not on the shoot," as they phrased it. They killed each other on slight provocation, and hoped and expected to be killed themselves— for they held it almost shame to die otherwise than "with their boots on," as they expressed it.

I remember an instance of a desperado's contempt for such small game as a private citizen's life. I was taking a late supper in a restaurant one night, with two reporters and a little printer named—Brown, for instance—any name will do. Presently a stranger with a long-tailed coat on came in, and not noticing Brown's hat, which was lying in a chair, sat down on it. Little Brown sprang up and became abusive in a moment. The stranger smiled, smoothed out the hat, and offered it to Brown with profuse apologies couched in caustic sarcasm, and begged Brown not to destroy him. Brown threw off his coat and challenged the man to fight—abused him, threatened him, impeached his courage, and urged and even implored him to fight; and in the meantime the smiling stranger placed himself under our protection in mock distress. But presently he assumed a serious tone, and said:

"Very well, gentlemen, if we must fight, we must, I suppose. But don't rush into danger and then say I gave you no warning. I am more than a match for all of you when I get started. I will give you proofs, and then if my friend here still insists, I will try to accommodate him."

The table we were sitting at was about five feet long, and unusually cumbersome and heavy. He asked us to put our hands on the dishes and hold them in their places a moment—one of them was a large oval dish with a portly roast on it. Then he sat down, tilted up one end of the table, set two of the legs on his knees, took the end of the table between his teeth, took his hands away, and pulled down with his teeth till the table came up to a level position, dishes and all! He said he could lift a keg of nails with his teeth. He picked up a common glass tumbler and bit a semi-circle out of it. Then he opened his bosom and showed us a net-work of knife and bullet scars; showed us more on his arms and face, and said he believed he had bullets enough in his body to make a pig of lead. He was armed to the teeth. He closed with the remark that he was Mr.—— of Cariboo—a celebrated name whereat we shook in our shoes. I would publish the name, but for the suspicion that he might come and carve me. He finally inquired if Brown still thirsted for blood. Brown turned the thing over in his mind a moment, and then—asked him to supper.

With the permission of the reader, I will group together, in the next chapter, some samples of life in our small mountain village in the old days of desperadoism. I was there at the time. The reader will observe peculiarities in our *official* society; and he will observe also, an instance of how, in new countries, murders breed murders.

Chapter XLIX

AN EXTRACT OR two from the newspapers of the day will furnish a photograph that can need no embellishment:

> FATAL SHOOTING AFFRAY.—An affray occurred, last evening, in a billiard saloon on C street, between *Deputy Marshal Jack Williams* and Wm. Brown, which resulted in the immediate death of the latter. There had been some difficulty between the parties for several months.
>
> An inquest was immediately held, and the following testimony adduced: Officer GEO. BIRDSALL, sworn, says:—I was told Wm. Brown was drunk and was looking for Jack Williams; so soon as I heard that I started for the parties to prevent a collision; went into the billiard saloon; saw Billy Brown running around, saying if anybody had anything against him to show cause; he was talking in a boisterous manner, and officer Perry took him to the other end of the room to talk to him; Brown came back to me; remarked to me that he thought he was as good as anybody, and knew how to take care of himself; he passed by me and went to the bar; don't know whether he drank or not; Williams was at the end of the billiard-table, next to the stairway; Brown, after going to the bar, came back and said he was as good as any man in the world; he had then walked out to the end of the first billiard-table from the bar; I moved closer to them, supposing there would be a fight; as Brown drew his pistol I caught hold of it; he had fired one shot at Williams; don't know the effect of it; caught hold of him with one hand, and took hold of the pistol and turned it up; think he fired once after I caught hold of the pistol; I wrenched the pistol from him; walked to the end of the billiard-table and told a party that I had Brown's pistol, and to stop shooting; I think four shots were fired in all; after walking out, Mr. Foster remarked that Brown was shot dead.

Oh, there was no excitement about it—he merely "remarked" the small circumstance!

Four months later the following item appeared in the same paper (the *Enterprise*). In this item the name of one of the city officers above referred to (*Deputy Marshal Jack Williams*) occurs again:

> ROBBERY AND DESPERATE AFFRAY.—On Tuesday night, a German named Charles Hurtzal, engineer in a mill at Silver City, came to this place, and visited the hurdy-gurdy house on B street. The music, dancing and Teutonic maidens awakened memories of Faderland until our German friend was carried away with rapture. He evidently had money, and was spending it freely. Late in the evening Jack Williams and Andy Blessington invited him down stairs to take a cup of coffee. Williams proposed a game of cards and went up stairs to procure a deck, but not finding any returned. On the stairway he met the German, and drawing his pistol knocked him down and rifled his pockets of some seventy dollars. Hurtzal

850

dared give no alarm, as he was told, with a pistol at his head, if he made any noise or exposed them, they would blow his brains out. So effectually was he frightened that he made no complaint, until his friends forced him. Yesterday a warrant was issued, but the culprits had disappeared.

This efficient city officer, Jack Williams, had the common reputation of being a burglar, a highwayman and a desperado. It was said that he had several times drawn his revolver and levied money contributions on citizens at dead of night in the public streets of Virginia.

Five months after the above item appeared, Williams was assassinated while sitting at a card table one night; a gun was thrust through the crack of the door and Williams dropped from his chair riddled with balls. It was said, at the time, that Williams had been for some time aware that a party of his own sort (desperadoes) had sworn away his life; and it was generally believed among the people that Williams's friends and enemies would make the assassination memorable—and useful, too—by a wholesale destruction of each other.*

It did not so happen, but still, times were not dull during the next twenty-four hours, for within that time a woman was killed by a pistol shot, a man was brained with a slung shot, and a man named Reeder was also disposed of permanently. Some matters in the *Enterprise* account of the killing of Reeder are worth noting—especially the accommodating complaisance of a Virginia justice of the peace. The italics in the following narrative are mine:

> MORE CUTTING AND SHOOTING.—The devil seems to have again broken loose in our town. Pistols and guns explode and knives gleam in our streets as in early times. When there has been a long season of quiet, people are slow to wet their hands in blood; but once blood is spilled, cutting and shooting come easy. Night before last Jack Williams was assassinated, and yesterday forenoon we had more bloody work, growing out of the killing of Williams, and on the same street in which he met

---

* However, one prophecy was verified, at any rate. It was asserted by the desperadoes that one of their brethren (Joe McGee, *a special policeman*) was known to be the conspirator chosen by lot to assassinate Williams; and they also asserted that doom had been pronounced against McGee, and that he would be assassinated in exactly the same manner that had been adopted for the destruction of Williams—a prophecy which came true a year later. After twelve months of distress (for McGee saw a fancied assassin in every man that approached him), he made the last of many efforts to get out of the country unwatched. He went to Carson and sat down in a saloon to wait for the stage—it would leave at four in the morning. But as the night waned and the crowd thinned, he grew uneasy, and told the bar-keeper that assassins were on his track. The bar-keeper told him to stay in the middle of the room, then, and not to go near the door, or the window by the stove. But a fatal fascination seduced him to the neighborhood of the stove every now and then, and repeatedly the bar-keeper brought him back to the middle of the room and warned him to remain there. But he could not. At three in the morning he again returned to the stove and sat down by a stranger. Before the bar-keeper could get to him with another warning whisper, some one outside fired through the window and riddled McGee's breast with slugs, killing him almost instantly. By the same discharge the stranger at McGee's side also received attentions which proved fatal in the course of two or three days.

his death. It appears that Tom Reeder, a friend of Williams, and George Gumbert were talking, at the meat market of the latter, about the killing of Williams the previous night, when Reeder said it was a most cowardly act to shoot a man in such a way, giving him "no show." Gumbert said that Williams had "as good a show as he gave Billy Brown," meaning the man killed by Williams last March. Reeder said it was a d—d lie, that Williams had no show at all. At this, Gumbert drew a knife and stabbed Reeder, cutting him in two places in the back. One stroke of the knife cut into the sleeve of Reeder's coat and passed downward in a slanting direction through his clothing, and entered his body at the small of the back; another blow struck more squarely, and made a much more dangerous wound. Gumbert gave himself up to the officers of justice, and was shortly after discharged by Justice Atwill, *on his own recognizance,* to appear for trial at six o'clock in the evening. In the meantime Reeder had been taken into the office of Dr. Owens, where his wounds were properly dressed. *One of his wounds was considered quite dangerous, and it was thought by many that it would prove fatal. But being considerably under the influence of liquor, Reeder did not feel his wounds as he otherwise would, and he got up and went into the street.* He went to the meat market and renewed his quarrel with Gumbert, threatening his life. Friends tried to interfere to put a stop to the quarrel and get the parties away from each other. In the Fashion Saloon Reeder made threats against the life of Gumbert, saying he would kill him, and it is said that *he requested the officers not to arrest Gumbert, as he intended to kill him.* After these threats Gumbert went off and procured a double-barreled shot gun, loaded with buck-shot or revolver balls, and went after Reeder. Two or three persons were assisting him along the street, trying to get him home, and had him just in front of the store of Klopstock & Harris, when Gumbert came across toward him from the opposite side of the street with his gun. He came up within about ten or fifteen feet of Reeder, and called out to those with him to "look out! get out of the way!" and they had only time to heed the warning, when he fired. Reeder was at the time attempting to screen himself behind a large cask, which stood against the awning post of Klopstock & Harris's store, but some of the balls took effect in the lower part of his breast, and he reeled around forward and fell in front of the cask. Gumbert then raised his gun and fired the second barrel, which missed Reeder and entered the ground. At the time that this occurred, there were a great many persons on the street in the vicinity, and a number of them called out to Gumbert, when they saw him raise his gun, to "hold on," and "don't shoot!" The cutting took place about ten o'clock and the shooting about twelve. After the shooting the street was instantly crowded with inhabitants of that part of the town, some appearing much excited and laughing—declaring that it looked like the "good old times of '60." Marshal Perry and officer Birdsall were near when the shooting occurred, and Gumbert was immediately arrested and his gun taken from him, when he was marched off to jail. Many persons who were attracted to the spot where this bloody work had just taken place, looked bewildered and seemed to be asking themselves what was to happen next, appearing in doubt as to whether the killing mania had reached its climax, or whether we were to turn in and have a grand killing spell, shooting whoever might have given us offence. It was whispered around that it was not all over yet—five or six more were to be killed before night. Reeder was taken to the Virginia City Hotel, and doctors called in to examine his wounds. They found that two or three balls had entered his right side; one of them appeared to have passed through the substance of the lungs, while another passed into the liver. Two balls were also found to have struck one of his legs. As some of the balls struck the cask, the wounds in Reeder's leg were probably from these, glancing downwards, though they might have been caused by the second shot fired. After being shot, Reeder said when he got on his feet—smiling as he spoke—"It will take better shooting than that to kill me." The doctors consider it almost impossible for him to recover, but as he has an excellent constitution he may survive, notwithstanding the number and dangerous character of the wounds he has received. The town appears to be perfectly quiet at present, as though the late stormy times had cleared our moral atmosphere; but who can tell in what quarter clouds are lowering or plots ripening?

Reeder—or at least what was left of him—survived his wounds two days! Nothing was ever done with Gumbert.

Trial by jury is the palladium of our liberties. I do not know what a palladium is, having never seen a palladium, but it is a good thing no doubt at any rate. Not less than a hundred men have been murdered in Nevada—perhaps I would be within bounds if I said three hundred—and as far as I can learn, only two persons have suffered the death penalty there. However, four or five who had no money and no political influence have been punished by imprisonment—one languished in prison as much as eight months, I think. However, I do not desire to be extravagant—it may have been less.

Chapter L

THESE MURDER AND jury statistics remind me of a certain very extraordinary trial and execution of twenty years ago; it is a scrap of history familiar to all old Californians, and worthy to be known by other peoples of the earth that love simple, straightforward justice unencumbered with nonsense. I would apologize for this digression but for the fact that the information I am about to offer is apology enough in itself. And since I digress constantly anyhow, perhaps it is as well to eschew apologies altogether and thus prevent their growing irksome.

Capt. Ned Blakely—that name will answer as well as any other fictitious one (for he was still with the living at last accounts, and may not desire to be famous)—sailed ships out of the harbor of San Francisco for many years. He was a stalwart, warm-hearted, eagle-eyed veteran, who had been a sailor nearly fifty years—a sailor from early boyhood. He was a rough, honest creature, full of pluck, and just as full of hard-headed simplicity, too. He hated trifling conventionalities—"business" was the word, with him. He had all a sailor's vindictiveness against the quips and quirks of the law, and steadfastly believed that the first and last aim and object of the law and lawyers was to defeat justice.

He sailed for the Chincha Islands in command of a guano ship. He had a fine crew, but his negro mate was his pet—on him he had for years lavished his admiration and esteem. It was Capt. Ned's first voyage to the Chinchas, but his fame had gone before him—the fame of being a man who would fight at the dropping of a handkerchief, when imposed upon, and would stand no nonsense. It was a fame well earned. Arrived in the islands, he found that the staple of conversation was the exploits of one Bill Noakes, a bully, the mate of a trading ship. This man had created a small reign of terror there. At nine o'clock at night, Capt. Ned, all alone, was pacing his deck in the starlight. A form ascended the side, and approached him. Capt. Ned said:

"Who goes there?"

"I'm Bill Noakes, the best man in the islands."

"What do you want aboard this ship?"

"I've heard of Capt. Ned Blakely, and one of us is a better man than 'tother—I'll know which, before I go ashore."

"You've come to the right shop—I'm your man. I'll learn you to come aboard this ship without an *in*vite."

He seized Noakes, backed him against the mainmast, pounded his face to a pulp, and then threw him overboard.

Noakes was not convinced. He returned the next night, got the pulp renewed, and went overboard head first, as before. He was satisfied.

A week after this, while Noakes was carousing with a sailor crowd on shore, at noonday, Capt. Ned's colored mate came along, and Noakes tried to pick a quarrel with him. The negro evaded the trap, and tried to get away. Noakes followed him up; the negro began to run; Noakes fired on him with a revolver and killed him. Half a dozen sea-captains witnessed the whole affair. Noakes retreated to the small after-cabin of his ship, with two other bullies, and gave out that death would be the portion of any man that intruded there. There was no attempt made to follow the villains; there was no disposition to do it, and indeed very little thought of such an enterprise. There were no courts and no officers; there was no government; the islands belonged to Peru, and Peru was far away; she had no official representative on the ground; and neither had any other nation.

However, Capt. Ned was not perplexing his head about such things. They concerned him not. He was boiling with rage and furious for justice. At nine o'clock at night he loaded a double-barreled gun with slugs, fished out a pair of handcuffs, got a ship's lantern, summoned his quartermaster, and went ashore. He said:

"Do you see that ship there at the dock?"

"Ay-ay, sir."

"It's the Venus."

"Ay-ay, sir."

"You—you know *me*."

"Aye-ay, sir."

"Very well, then. Take the lantern. Carry it just under your chin. I'll walk behind you and rest this gun-barrel on your shoulder, p'inting forward—so. Keep your lantern well up, so's I can see things ahead of you good. I'm going to march in on Noakes—and take him—and jug the other chaps. If you flinch—well, you know *me*."

"Ay-ay, sir."

In this order they filed aboard softly, arrived at Noakes's den, the quartermaster pushed the door open, and the lantern revealed the three desperadoes sitting on the floor. Capt. Ned said:

"I'm Ned Blakely. I've got you under fire. Don't you move without orders—any of you. You two kneel down in the corner; faces to the wall—now. Bill Noakes, put these handcuffs on; now come up close. Quartermaster, fasten 'em. All right. Don't stir, sir. Quartermaster, put the key in the outside of the door. Now, men, I'm going to lock you two in; and if you try to burst through this door—well, you've heard of *me*. Bill Noakes, fall in ahead, and march. All set. Quartermaster, lock the door."

Noakes spent the night on board Blakely's ship, a prisoner under strict guard. Early in the morning Capt. Ned called in all the sea-captains in the harbor and invited them, with nautical ceremony, to be present on board his ship at nine o'clock to witness the hanging of Noakes at the yard-arm!

"What! The man has not been tried."

"Of course he hasn't. But didn't he kill the nigger?"

"Certainly he did; but you are not thinking of hanging him without a trial?"

"*Trial!* What do I want to try him for, if he killed the nigger?"

"Oh, Capt. Ned, this will *never* do. Think how it will sound."

"Sound be hanged! *Didn't he kill the nigger?*"

"Certainly, certainly, Capt. Ned,—nobody denies that,—but—"

"Then I'm going to *hang* him, that's all. Everybody I've talked to talks just the same way you do. Everybody says he killed the nigger, everybody knows he killed the nigger, and yet every lubber of you wants him *tried* for it. I don't understand such bloody foolishness as that. *Tried!* Mind you, I don't object to trying him, if it's got to be done to give satisfaction; and I'll be there, and chip in and help, too; but put it off till afternoon—put it off till afternoon, for I'll have my hands middling full till after the burying—"

"Why, what do you mean? Are you going to hang him *any how*—and try him afterward?"

"Didn't I *say* I was going to hang him? I never saw such people as you. What's the difference? You ask a favor, and then you ain't satisfied when you get it. Before or after's all one—*you* know how the trial will go. He killed the nigger. Say—I must be going. If your mate would like to come to the hanging, fetch him along. I like him."

There was a stir in the camp. The captains came in a body and pleaded with Capt. Ned not to do this rash thing. They promised that they would create a court composed of captains of the best character; they would empanel a jury; they would conduct everything in a way becoming the serious nature of the business in hand, and give the case an impartial hearing and the accused a fair trial. And they said it would be murder, and punishable by the American courts if he persisted and hung the accused on his ship. They pleaded hard. Capt. Ned said:

"Gentlemen, I'm not stubborn and I'm not unreasonable. I'm always willing to do just as near right as I can. How long will it take?"

"Probably only a little while."

"And can I take him up the shore and hang him as soon as you are done?"

"If he is proven guilty he shall be hanged without unnecessary delay."

"*If* he's proven guilty. Great Neptune, *ain't* he guilty? This beats my time. Why you all *know* he's guilty."

But at last they satisfied him that they were projecting nothing underhanded. Then he said:

"Well, all right. You go on and try him and I'll go down and overhaul his conscience and prepare him to go—like enough he needs it, and I don't want to send him off without a show for hereafter."

This was another obstacle. They finally convinced him that it was necessary to have the accused in court. Then they said they would send a guard to bring him.

"No, sir, I prefer to fetch him myself—he don't get out of *my* hands. Besides, I've got to go to the ship to get a rope, anyway."

The court assembled with due ceremony, empaneled a jury, and presently Capt. Ned entered, leading the prisoner with one hand and carrying a Bible and a rope in the other. He seated himself by the side of his captive and told the court to "up anchor and make sail." Then he turned a searching eye on the jury, and detected Noakes's friends, the two bullies. He strode over and said to them confidentially:

"You're here to interfere, you see. Now you vote right, do you hear?—or else there'll be a double-barreled inquest here when this trial's off, and your remainders will go home in a couple of baskets."

The caution was not without fruit. The jury was a unit—the verdict, "Guilty."

Capt. Ned sprung to his feet and said:

"Come along—you're my meat *now,* my lad, anyway. Gentlemen, you've done yourselves proud. I invite you all to come and see that I do it all straight. Follow me to the canyon, a mile above here."

The court informed him that a sheriff had been appointed to do the hanging, and—

Capt. Ned's patience was at an end. His wrath was boundless, The subject of a sheriff was judiciously dropped.

When the crowd arrived at the canyon, Capt. Ned climbed a tree and arranged the halter, then came down and noosed his man. He opened his Bible, and laid aside his hat. Selecting a chapter at random, he read it through, in a deep bass voice and with sincere solemnity. Then he said:

"Lad, you are about to go aloft and give an account of yourself; and the lighter a man's manifest is, as far as sin's concerned, the better for him. Make a clean breast, man, and carry a log with you that'll bear inspection. You killed the nigger?"

No reply. A long pause.

The captain read another chapter, pausing, from time to time, to impress the effect. Then he talked an earnest, persuasive sermon to him, and ended by repeating the question:

"Did you kill the nigger?"

No reply—other than a malignant scowl. The captain now read the first and second chapters of Genesis, with deep feeling—paused a moment, closed the book reverently, and said with a perceptible savor of satisfaction:

"There. Four chapters. There's few that would have took the pains with you that I have."

Then he swung up the condemned, and made the rope fast; stood by and timed him half an hour with his watch, and then delivered the body to the court. A little after, as he stood contemplating the motionless figure, a doubt came into his face; evidently he felt a twinge of conscience—a misgiving—and he said with a sigh:

"Well, p'raps I ought to burnt him, maybe. But I was trying to do for the best."

When the history of this affair reached California (it was in the "early days") it made a deal of talk, but did not diminish the captain's popularity in any degree. It increased it, indeed. California had a population then that "inflicted" justice after a fashion that was simplicity and primitiveness itself, and could therefore admire appreciatively when the same fashion was followed elsewhere.

Chapter LI

VICE FLOURISHED LUXURIANTLY during the hey-day of our "flush times." The saloons were overburdened with customers; so were the police courts, the gambling dens, the brothels and the jails—unfailing signs of high prosperity in a mining region—in any region for that matter. Is it not so? A crowded police court docket is the surest of all signs that trade is brisk and money plenty. Still, there is one other sign; it comes last, but when it does come it establishes beyond cavil that the "flush times" are at the flood. This is the birth of the "literary" paper. The *Weekly Occidental,* "devoted to literature," made its appearance in Virginia. All the literary people were engaged to write for it. Mr. F. was to edit it. He was a felicitous skirmisher with a pen, and a man who could say happy things in a crisp, neat way. Once, while editor of the *Union,* he had disposed of a labored, incoherent, two-column attack made upon him by a contemporary, with a single line, which, at first glance, seemed to contain a solemn and tremendous compliment—viz.: "THE LOGIC OF OUR ADVERSARY RESEMBLES THE PEACE OF GOD,"—and left it to the reader's memory and after-thought to invest the remark with another and "more different" meaning by supplying for himself and at his own leisure the rest of the Scripture—*"in that it passeth understanding."* He once said of a little, half-starved, wayside community that had no subsistence except what they could get by preying upon chance passengers who stopped over with them a day when traveling by the overland stage, that in their Church service they had altered the Lord's Prayer to read: "Give us this day our daily stranger!"

We expected great things of the *Occidental.* Of course it could not get along without an original novel, and so we made arrangements to hurl into the work the full strength of the company. Mrs. F. was an able romancist of the ineffable school—I know no other name to apply to a school whose heroes are all dainty and all perfect. She wrote the opening chapter, and introduced a lovely blonde simpleton who talked nothing but pearls and poetry and who was virtuous to the verge of eccentricity. She also introduced a young French Duke of aggravated refinement, in love with the blonde. Mr. F. followed next week, with a brilliant lawyer who set about getting the Duke's estates into trouble, and a sparkling young lady of high society who fell to fascinating the Duke and impairing the appetite of the blonde. Mr. D., a dark and bloody editor of one of the dailies, followed Mr. F., the third week, introducing a mysterious Rosicrucian who transmuted metals, held consultations with the devil in a cave at dead of night, and cast the horoscope of the several heroes and heroines in such a way as to provide plenty of trouble for their future careers and breed a solemn and awful public interest in the novel. He also introduced a cloaked and masked melodramatic miscreant, put him on a salary and set him on the midnight tract of the Duke with a poisoned dagger. He also created an Irish coachman with a rich brogue and placed him in the service of the society-young-lady with an ulterior mission to carry billet-doux to the Duke.

About this time there arrived in Virginia a dissolute stranger with a literary turn of mind—rather seedy he was, but very quiet and unassuming; almost diffident, indeed. He was so gentle, and his manners were so pleasing and kindly, whether he was sober or intoxicated, that he made friends of all who came in contact with him. He applied for literary work, offered conclusive evidence that he wielded an easy and practiced pen, and so Mr. F. engaged him at once to help write the novel. His chapter was to follow Mr. D.'s, and mine was to come next. Now what does this fellow do but go off and get drunk and then proceed to his quarters and set to work with his imagination in a state of chaos, and that chaos in a condition of extravagant activity. The result may be guessed. He scanned the chapters of his predecessors, found plenty of heroes and heroines already created, and was satisfied with them; he decided to introduce no more; with all the confidence that whisky inspires and all the easy complacency it gives to its servant, he then launched himself lovingly into his work: he married the coachman to the society-young-lady for the sake of the scandal; married the Duke to the blonde's stepmother, for the sake of the sensation; stopped the desperado's salary; created a misunderstanding between the devil and the Rosicrucian; threw the Duke's property into the wicked lawyer's hands; made the lawyer's upbraiding conscience drive him to drink, thence to *delirium tremens*, thence to suicide; broke the coachman's neck; let his widow succumb to contumely, neglect, poverty and consumption; caused the blonde to drown herself, leaving her clothes on the bank with the customary note pinned to them forgiving the Duke and hoping he would be happy; revealed to the Duke, by means of the usual strawberry mark on left arm, that he had married his own long-lost mother and destroyed his long-lost sister; instituted the proper and necessary suicide of the Duke and the Duchess in order to compass poetical justice; opened the earth

THE HEROES AND HEROINES OF THE STORY.

and let the Roscicrucian through, accompanied with the accustomed smoke and thunder and smell of brimstone, and finished with the promise that in the next chapter, after holding a general inquest, he would take up the surviving character of the novel and tell what became of the devil!

It read with singular smoothness, and with a "dead" earnestness that was funny enough to suffocate a body. But there was war when it came in. The other novelists were furious. The mild stranger, not yet more than half sober, stood there, under a scathing fire of vituperation, meek and bewildered, looking from one to another of his assailants, and wondering what he could have done to invoke such a storm. When a lull came at last, he said his say gently and appealingly—said he did not rightly remember what he had written, but was sure he had tried to do the best he could, and knew his object had been to make the novel not only pleasant and plausible but instructive and—

The bombardment began again. The novelists assailed his ill-chosen adjectives and demolished them with a storm of denunciation and ridicule. And so the siege went on. Every time the stranger tried to appease the enemy he only made matters worse. Finally he offered to rewrite the chapter. This arrested hostilities. The indignation gradually quieted down, peace reigned again and the sufferer retired in safety and got him to his own citadel.

But on the way thither the evil angel tempted him and he got drunk again. And again his imagination went mad. He led the heroes and heroines a wilder dance than ever; and yet all through it ran that same convincing air of honesty and earnestness that had marked his first work. He got the characters into the most extraordinary situations, put them through the most surprising performances, and made them talk the strangest talk! But the chapter cannot be described. It was symmetrically crazy; it was artistically absurd; and it had explanatory footnotes that were fully as curious as the text. I remember one of the "situations," and will offer it as an example of the whole. He altered the character of the brilliant lawyer, and made him a great-hearted, splendid fellow; gave him fame and riches, and set his age at thirty-three years. Then he made the blonde discover, through the help of the Rosicrucian and the melodramatic miscreant, that while the Duke loved her money ardently and wanted it, he secretly felt a sort of leaning toward the society-young-lady. Stung to the quick, she tore her affections from him and bestowed them with tenfold power upon the lawyer, who responded with consuming zeal. But the parents would none of it. What they wanted in the family was a Duke; and a Duke they were determined to have; though they confessed that next to the Duke the lawyer had their preference. Necessarily the blonde now went into a decline. The parents were alarmed. They pleaded with her to marry the Duke, but she steadfastly refused, and pined on. Then they laid a plan. They told her to wait a year and a day, and if at the end of that time she still felt that she could not marry the Duke, she might marry the lawyer with their full consent. The result was as they had foreseen: gladness came again, and the flush of returning health. Then the parents took the next step in their scheme. They had the family physician recommend a long sea voyage and much land travel for the thorough restoration of the blonde's strength; and they invited the Duke to be of the party. They judged that the Duke's constant presence and the lawyer's protracted absence would do the rest—for they did not invite the lawyer.

So they set sail in a steamer for America—and the third day out, when their sea-sickness called truce and permitted them to take their first meal at the public table, behold there sat the lawyer! The Duke and party made the best of an awkward situation; the voyage progressed, and the vessel neared America. But, by and by, two hundred miles off New Bedford, the ship took fire; she burned to the water's edge; of all her crew and passengers, only thirty were saved. They floated about the sea half an afternoon and all night long. Among them were our friends. The lawyer, by superhuman exertions, had saved the blonde and her parents, swimming back and forth two hundred yards and bringing one each time—(the girl first). The Duke had saved himself. In the morning two whale ships arrived on the scene and sent their boats. The weather was stormy and the embarkation was attended with much confusion and excitement. The lawyer did his duty like a man; helped his exhausted and insensible blonde, her parents and some others into a boat (the Duke helped himself in); then a child fell overboard at the other end of the raft and the lawyer rushed thither and helped half a dozen people fish it out, under the stimulus of its mother's screams. When he ran back—a few seconds too late—the blonde's boat was under way. So he had to take the other boat, and go to the other ship. The storm increased and drove the vessels out of sight of each other—drove them whither it would. When it calmed, at the end of three days, the blonde's ship was seven hundred miles north of Boston and the other about seven hundred south of that port. The blonde's captain was bound on a whaling cruise in the North Atlantic and could not go back such a distance or make a port without orders; such being nautical law. The lawyer's captain was to cruise in the North Pacific, and *he* could not go back or make a port without orders. All the lawyer's money and baggage were in the blonde's boat and went to the blonde's ship—so his captain made him work his passage as a common sailor. When both ships had been cruising nearly a year, the one was off the coast of Greenland and the other in the Behring's Strait. The blonde had long ago been well-nigh persuaded that her lawyer had been washed overboard and lost just before the whale ships reached the raft, and now, under the pleadings of her parents and the Duke she was at last beginning to nerve herself for the doom of the covenant, and prepare for the hated marriage. But she would not yield a day before the date set. The weeks dragged on, the time narrowed, orders were given to deck the ship for the wedding—a wedding at sea among icebergs and walruses. Five days more and all would be over. So the blonde reflected, with a sigh and a tear. Oh where was her true love—and why, why did he not come and save her? At that moment he was lifting his harpoon to strike a whale in the Behring's Strait, five thousand miles away, by the way of the Arctic Ocean, or twenty thousand by the way of the Horn—that was the reason. He struck, but not with perfect aim—his foot slipped and he fell in the whale's mouth and went down his throat. He was insensible five days. Then he came to himself and heard voices; daylight was streaming through a hole cut in the whale's roof. He climbed out and astonished the sailors who were hoisting blubber up a ship's side. He recognized the vessel, flew aboard, surprised the wedding party at the altar and exclaimed:

"Stop the proceedings—I'm here! Come to my arms, my own!"

There were foot-notes to this extravagant piece of literature wherein the author endeavored to show that the whole thing was within the possibilities; he said he got the incident of the whale traveling from the Behring's Strait to the coast of Greenland, five thousand miles in five days, through the Arctic Ocean, from Charles Reade's "Love Me Little Love Me Long," and considered that that established the fact that the thing could be done; and he instanced Jonah's adventure as proof that a man could live in a whale's belly, and added that if a preacher could stand it three days a lawyer could surely stand it five!

There was a fiercer storm than ever in the editorial sanctum now, and the stranger was peremptorily discharged, and his manuscript flung at his head. But he had already delayed things so much that there was not time for someone else to rewrite the chapter, and so the paper came out without any novel in it. It was but a feeble, struggling, stupid journal, and the absence of the novel probably shook public confidence; at any rate, before the first side of the next issue went to press, the *Weekly Occidental* died as peacefully as an infant.

An effort was made to resurrect it, with the proposed advantage of a telling new title, and Mr. F. said that *The Phoenix* would be just the name for it, because it would give the idea of a resurrection from its dead ashes in a new and undreamed of condition of splendor; but some low-priced smarty on one of the dailies suggested that we call it the *Lazarus;* and inasmuch as the people were not profound in Scriptural matters but thought the resurrected Lazarus and the dilapidated mendicant that begged in the rich man's gateway were one and the same person, the name became the laughing stock of the town, and killed the paper for good and all.

I was sorry enough, for I was very proud of being connected with a literary paper—prouder than I have ever been on anything since, perhaps. I had written some rhymes for it—poetry I considered it—and it was a great grief to me that the production was on the "first side" of the issue that was not completed, and hence did not see the light. But time brings its revenges—I can put it in here; it will answer in place of a tear dropped to the memory of the lost *Occidental*. The idea (not the chief idea, but the vehicle that bears it) was probably suggested by the old song called "The Raging Canal," but I cannot remember now. I do remember, though, that at that time I thought my doggerel was one of the ablest poems of the age:

THE AGED PILOT MAN

On the Erie Canal, it was,
    All on a summer's day,
I sailed forth with my parents
    Far away to Albany.

From out the clouds at noon that day
    There came a dreadful storm,
That piled the billows high about,
    And filled us with alarm.

A man came rushing from a house,
    Saying, "Snub up your boat I pray,
Snub up your boat, snub up, alas,
    Snub up while yet you may."

Our captain cast one glance astern,
    Then forward glanced he,
And said, "My wife and little ones
    I never more shall see."

Said Dollinger the pilot man,
  In noble words, but few,—
"Fear not, but lean on Dollinger,
  And he will fetch you through."

The boat drove down on, frightened mules
  Tore through the rain and wind,
And bravely still, in danger's post,
  The whip-boy strode behind.

"Come 'board, come 'board," the captain cried,
  "Nor tempt so wild a storm;"
But still the raging mules advanced,
  And still the boy strode on.

Then said the captain to us all,
  "Alas, 'tis plain to me,
The greater danger is not there,
  But here upon the sea.

So let us strive, while life remains,
  To save all souls on board,
And then if die at last we must,
  Let . . . . I *cannot* speak the word!"

Said Dollinger the pilot man,
  Tow'ring above the crew,
"Fear not, but trust in Dollinger,
  And he will fetch you through."

"Low bridge! low bridge!" all heads went down,
  The laboring bark sped on;
A mill we passed, we passed a church,
  Hamlets, and fields of corn ;
And all the world came out to see,
  And chased along the shore

Crying, "Alas, alas, the sheeted rain,
  The wind, the tempest's roar!
Alas, the gallant ship and crew,
  Can *nothing* help them more?"

And from our deck sad eyes looked out
  Across the stormy scene:
The tossing wake of billows aft,
  The bending forests green,

The chickens sheltered under carts
  In lee of barn the cows,

The skurrying swine with straw in mouth,
 The wild spray from our bows!

 "She balances!
 She wavers!
Now let her go about!
 If she misses stays and broaches to,
We're all"—[then with a shout,]
 "Huray! huray!
 Avast! belay!
 Take in more sail!
 Lord, what a gale!
Ho, boy, haul taut on the hind mule's tail!"
Ho! lighten ship! ho! man the pump!
 Ho, hostler, heave the lead!

"A quarter-three!—'tis shoaling fast!
 Three feet large!—t-h-r-e-e feet!—
Three feet scant!" I cried in fright
 "Oh, is there *no* retreat?"

Said Dollinger, the pilot man,
 As on the vessel flew,
"Fear not, but trust in Dollinger,
 And he will fetch you through."

"Sever the tow-line! Cripple the mules!"
 The boldest cheek turned pale ;
For plain to all, this shoaling said
A leak had burst the ditch's bed!
And, straight as bolt from crossbow sped,
Our ship swept on, with shoaling lead,
 Before the fearful gale!

"Sever the tow-line! Cripple the mules!"
 Too late! . . . . . There comes a shock!
Another length, and the fated craft
 Would have swum in the saving lock!

Then gathered together the shipwrecked crew
 And took one last embrace,
While sorrowful tears from despairing eyes
 Ran down each hopeless face;
And some did think of their little ones
 Whom they never more might see,
And others of waiting wives at home,
 And mothers that grieved would be.

But of all the children of misery there
 On that poor sinking frame,

But one spake words of hope and faith,
    And I worshipped as they came:
Said Dollinger the pilot man,—
    (O brave heart, strong and true!)—
"Fear not, but trust in Dollinger,
    For he will fetch you through."

Lo! scarce the words have passed his lips
    The dauntless prophet say'th,
When every soul about him seeth
    A wonder crown his faith!

And count ye all, both great and small,
    As numbered with the dead!
For mariner for forty year,
    On Erie, boy and man,
I never yet saw such a storm,
    Or one 't with it began!"

So overboard a keg of nails
    And anvils three we threw,
Likewise four bales of gunny-sacks,
    Two hundred pounds of glue,
Two sacks of corn, four ditto wheat,
    A box of books, a cow,
A violin, Lord Byron's works,
    A rip-saw and a sow.

A curve! a curve! the danger grow!
"Labbord!—stabbord!—s-t-e-a-d-y!—so!—
Hard-a-port, Do!—hellum-a-lee!
    Haw the head mule!—the aft one gee!
Luff!—bring her to the wind!"

For straight a farmer brought a plank,—
    (Mysteriously inspired)—
And laying it unto the ship,
    In silent awe retired.

Then every sufferer stood amazed
    That pilot man before;
A moment stood. Then wondering turned,
    and speechless walked ashore.

Chapter LII

SINCE I DESIRE, in this chapter, to say an instructive word or two about the silver mines, the reader may take this fair warning and skip, if he chooses. The year 1863 was perhaps the very top blossom and culmination of the "flush times." Virginia swarmed with men and vehicles to that degree that the place looked like a very hive—that is when one's vision could pierce through the thick fog of alkali dust that was generally blowing in summer. I will say, concerning this dust, that if you drove ten miles through it, you and your horses would be coated with it a sixteenth of an inch thick and present an outside appearance that was a uniform pale yellow color, and your buggy would have three inches of dust in it, thrown there by the wheels. The delicate scales used by the assayers were inclosed in glass cases intended to be air-tight, and yet some of this dust was so impalpable and so invisibly fine that it would get in, somehow, and impair the accuracy of those scales.

Speculation ran riot, and yet there was a world of substantial business going on, too. All freights were brought over the mountains from California (150 miles) by pack-train partly, and partly in huge wagons drawn by such long mule teams that each team amounted to a procession, and it did seem, sometimes, that the grand combined procession of animals stretched unbroken from Virginia to California. Its long route was traceable clear across the deserts of the Territory by the writhing serpent of dust it lifted up. By these wagons, freights over that hundred and fifty miles were $200 a ton for small lots (same price for all express matter brought by stage), and $100 a ton for full loads. One Virginia firm received one hundred tons of freight a month, and paid $10,000 a month freightage. In the winter the freights were much higher. All the bullion was shipped in bars by stage to San Francisco (a bar was usually about twice the size of a pig of lead and contained from $1,500 to $3,000 according to the amount of gold mixed with the silver), and the freight on it (when the shipment was large) was one and a quarter per cent. of its intrinsic value. So, the freight on these bars probably averaged something more than $25 each. Small shippers paid two per cent. There were three stages a day, each way, and I have seen the outgoing stages carry away a third of a ton of bullion each, and more than once I saw them divide a two-ton lot and take it off. However, these were extraordinary events.* Two

---

* Mr. Valentine, Wells Fargo's agent, has handled all the bullion shipped through the Virginia office for many a month. To his memory—which is excellent—we are indebted for the following exhibit of the company's business in the Virginia since the first of January, 1862: From January 1st to April 1st, about $270,000 worth of bullion passed through that office; during the next quarter, $570,000; next quarter, $800,000; next quarter, $956,000; next quarter, $1,275,000; and for the quarter ending on the 30th of last June, about $1,600,000. Thus in a year and a half, the Virginia office only shipped $5,330,000 in bullion. During the year 1862 they shipped $2,615,000, so we perceive the average shipments have more than doubled in the last six months. This gives us room to promise for the Virginia office $500,000 a month for the year 1863 (though perhaps, judging by the steady increase in the business, we are under estimating, somewhat). This

tons of silver bullion would be in the neighborhood of forty bars, and the freight on it over $1,000. Each coach always carried a deal of ordinary express matter beside, and also from fifteen to twenty passengers at from $25 to $30 a head. With six stages going all the time, Wells-Fargo and Co.'s Virginia City business was important and lucrative.

All along under the center of Virginia and Gold Hill, for a couple of miles, ran the great Comstock silver lode—a vein of ore from fifty to eighty feet thick between its solid walls of rock—a vein as wide as some of New York's streets. I will remind the reader that in Pennsylvania a coal vein only eight feet wide is considered ample.

Virginia was a busy city of streets and houses above ground. Under it was another busy city, down in the bowels of the earth, where a great population of men thronged in and out among the intricate maze of tunnels and drifts, flitting hither and thither under a winking sparkle of lights, and over their heads towered a vast web of interlocking timbers that held the walls of the gutted Comstock apart. These timbers were as large as a man's body, and the framework stretched upward so far that no eye could pierce to its top through the closing gloom. It was like peering up through the clean-picked ribs and bones of some colossal skeleton. Imagine such a framework two miles long, sixty feet wide, and higher than any church spire in America. Imagine this stately lattice-work stretching down Broadway, from the St. Nicholas to Wall street, and a Fourth of July procession, reduced to pigmies, parading on top of it and flaunting their flags, high above the pinnacle of Trinity steeple. One can imagine that, but he cannot well imagine what that forest of timbers cost, from the time they were felled in the pineries beyond Washoe Lake, hauled up and around Mount Davidson at atrocious rates of freightage, then squared, let down into the deep maw of the mine and built up there. Twenty ample fortunes would not timber one of the greatest of those silver mines. The Spanish proverb says it requires a gold mine to "run" a silver one, and it is true. A beggar with a silver mine is a pitiable pauper indeed if he cannot sell.

I spoke of the underground Virginia as a city. The Gould and Curry is only one single mine under there, among a great many others; yet the Gould and Curry's streets of dismal drifts and tunnels were five miles in extent, altogether, and its population five hundred miners. Taken as a whole, the underground city had some thirty miles of streets and a population of five or six thousand. In this

---

gives us $6,000,000 for the year. Gold Hill and Silver City together can beat us—we will give them $10,000,000. To Dayton, Empire City, Ophir and Carson City, we will allow an aggregate of $8,000,000, which is not over the mark, perhaps, and may possibly be a little under it. To Esmeralda we give $4,000,000. To Reese River and Humboldt $2,000,000, which is liberal now, but may not be before the year is out. So we prognosticate that the yield of bullion this year will be about $30,000,000. Placing the number of mills in the Territory at one hundred, this gives to each the labor of producing $300,000 in bullion during the twelve months. Allowing them to run three hundred days in the year (which none of them more than do), this makes their work average $1,000 a day. Say the mill averages twenty tons rock a day and this rock is worth $50 as a general thing, and you have the actual work of our one hundred mills figured down "to a spot"— $1,000 a day each, and $30,000,000 a year in the aggregate.—*Enterprise*.
[A considerable over estimate—M.T.]

present day some of those populations are at work from twelve to sixteen hundred feet under Virginia and Gold Hill, and the signal-bells that tell them what the superintendent above ground desires them to do are struck by telegraph as we strike a fire alarm. Sometimes men fall down a shaft, there, a thousand feet deep. In such cases, the usual plan is to hold an inquest.

If you wish to visit one of those mines, you may walk through a tunnel about half a mile long if you prefer it, or you may take the quicker plan of shooting like a dart down a shaft, on a small platform. It is like tumbling down through an empty steeple, feet first. When you reach the bottom, you take a candle and tramp through drifts and tunnels where throngs of men are digging and blasting; you watch them send up tubs full of great lumps of stone—silver ore; you select choice specimens from the mass, as souvenirs; you admire the world of skeleton timbering; you reflect frequently that you are buried under a mountain, a thousand feet below daylight; being in the bottom of the mine you climb from "gallery" to "gallery," up endless ladders that stand straight up and down; when your legs fail you at last, you lie down in a small box-car in a cramped "incline" like a half-up-ended sewer and are dragged up to daylight feeling as if you are crawling through a coffin that has no end to it. Arrived at the top, you find a busy crowd of men receiving the ascending cars and tubs and dumping the ore from an elevation into long rows of bins capable of holding half a dozen tons each; under the bins are rows of wagons loading from chutes and trap-doors in the bins, and down the long street is a procession of these wagons wending toward the silver mills with their rich freight. It is all "done," now, and there you are. You need never go down again, for you have seen it all. If you have forgotten the process of reducing the ore in the mill and making the silver bars, you can go back and find it again in my Esmeralda chapters if so disposed.

Of course these mines cave in, in places, occasionally, and then it is worth one's while to take the risk of descending into them and observing the crushing power exerted by the pressing weight of a settling mountain. I published such an experience in the *Enterprise,* once, and from it I will take an extract:

AN HOUR IN THE CAVED MINES.—We journeyed down into the Ophir mine, yesterday, to see the earthquake. We could not go down the deep incline, because it still has a propensity to cave in places. Therefore we traveled through the long tunnel which enters the hill above the Ophir office, and then by means of a series of long ladders, climbed away down from the first to the fourth gallery. Traversing a drift, we came to the Spanish line, passed five sets of timbers still uninjured, and found the earthquake. Here was as complete a chaos as ever was seen—vast masses of earth and splintered and broken timbers piled confusedly together, with scarcely an aperture left large enough for a cat to creep through. Rubbish was still falling at intervals from above, and one timber which had braced others earlier in the day, was *now* crushed down out of its former position, showing that the caving and settling of the tremendous mass was still going on. We were in that portion of the Ophir known as the "north mines." Returning to the surface, we entered a tunnel leading into the Central, for the purpose of getting into the main Ophir. Descending a long incline in this tunnel, we traversed a drift or so, and then went down a deep shaft from whence we proceeded into the fifth gallery of the Ophir. From a side-drift we crawled through a small hole and got into the midst of the earthquake again—earth and broken timbers mingled together without regard to grace or symmetry. A large portion of the second, third and fourth galleries had caved in and gone to destruction— the two latter at seven o'clock on the previous evening.

At the turn-table, near the northern extremity of the fifth gallery, two big piles of rubbish had forced their way through from the fifth gallery, and from the looks of the timbers, more was about to come. These beams are solid—eighteen inches square; first, a great beam is laid on the floor, then upright ones, five feet high, stand on it, supporting another horizontal beam, and so on, square above square, like the framework of a window. The superincumbent weight was sufficient to mash the ends of those great upright beams fairly into the solid wood of the horizontal ones three inches, compressing and bending the upright beam till it curved like a bow. Before the Spanish caved in, some of their twelve-inch horizontal timbers were compressed in this way until they were only five inches thick! Imagine the power it must take to squeeze a solid log together in that way. Here, also, was a range of timbers, for a distance of twenty feet, tilted six inches out of the perpendicular by the weight resting upon them from the caved galleries above. You could hear things cracking and giving way, and it was not pleasant to know that the world overhead was slowly and silently sinking down upon you. The men down in the mine do not mind it, however.

Returning along the fifth gallery, we struck the safe part of the Ophir incline, and went down it to the sixth; but we found ten inches of water there, and had to come back. In repairing the damage done to the incline, the pump had to be stopped for two hours, and in the meantime the water gained about a foot. However, the pump was at work again, and the floodwater was decreasing. We climbed up to the fifth gallery again and sought a deep shaft, whereby we might descend to another part of the sixth, out of reach of the water, but suffered disappointment, as the men had gone to dinner, and there was no one to man the windlass. So, having seen the earthquake, we climbed out at the Union incline and tunnel, and adjourned, all dripping with candle grease and perspiration, to lunch at the Ophir office.

During the great flush year of 1863, Nevada [claims to have] produced $25,000,000 in bullion—almost, if not quite, a round million to each thousand inhabitants, which is very well, considering that she was without agriculture and manufactures.* Silver mining was her sole productive industry.

---

* Since the above was in type, I learn from an offical source that the above figure is too high, and that the yield for 1863 did not exceed $20,000,000. However, the day for large figures is approaching; the Sutro Tunnel is to plow through the Comstock lode from end to end, at a depth of two thousand feet, and then mining will be easy and comparatively inexpensive; and the momentous matters of drainage, and hoisting and hauling of ore will cease to be burdensome. This vast work will absorb many years, and millions of dollars, in its completion; but it will early yield money, for that desirable epoch will begin as soon as it strikes the first end of the vein. The tunnel will be some eight miles long, and will develop astonishing riches. Cars will carry the ore through the tunnel and dump it in the mills and thus do away with the present costly system of double handling

EVERY NOW AND then, in these days, the boys used to tell me I ought to get one Jim Blaine to tell me the stirring story of his grandfather's old ram—but they always added that I must not mention the matter unless Jim was drunk at the time—just comfortably and sociably drunk. They kept this up until my curiosity was on the rack to hear the story. I got to haunting Blaine; but it was of no use, the boys always found fault with his condition; he was often moderately but never satisfactorily drunk. I never watched a man's condition with such absorbing interest, such anxious solicitude; I never so pined to see a man uncompromisingly drunk before. At last, one evening I hurried to his cabin, for I learned that this time his situation was such that even the most fastidious could find no fault with it—he was tranquilly, serenely, symmetrically drunk—not a hiccup to mar his voice, not a cloud upon his brain thick enough to obscure his memory. As I entered, he was sitting upon an empty powder-keg, with a clay pipe in one hand and the other raised to command silence. His face was round, red, and very serious; his throat was bare and his hair tumbled; in general appearance and costume he was a stalwart miner of the period. On the pine table stood a candle, and its dim light revealed "the boys" sitting here and there on bunks, candle-boxes, powder-kegs, etc. They said:

"Sh—! Don't speak—he's going to commence."

THE STORY OF THE OLD RAM.

I found a seat at once, and Blaine said:

"I don't reckon them times will ever come again. There never was a more bullier old ram than what he was. Grandfather fetched him from Illinois—got him of a man by the name of Yates—Bill Yates—maybe you might have heard of him; his father was a deacon—Baptist—and he was a rustler, too; a man had to get up ruther early to get the start of old Thankful Yates; it was him that put the Greens up to jining teams with my grandfather when he moved west. Seth Green was prob'ly the pick of the flock; he married a Wilkerson—Sarah Wilkerson—good cretur, she was—one of the likeliest heifers that was ever raised in old Stoddard, everybody said that knowed her. She could heft a bar'l of flour as easy as I can flirt a flapjack. And spin? Don't mention it! Independent? Humph! When Sile Hawkins come a browsing around her, she let him know that for all his tin he couldn't trot in harness alongside of *her*. You see, Sile Hawkins was—no, it warn't Sile Hawkins, after all—it was a galoot by the name of Filkins—I disremember his first name; but he *was* a stump—come into pra'r meeting drunk, one night, hooraying for Nixon, becuz he thought it was a primary; and old deacon Ferguson up and scooted him through the window and he lit on old Miss Jefferson's head, poor old filly. She was a good soul—had a glass eye and

___

power for the mills. Mr. Sutro, the originator of this prodigious enterprise, is one of the few men in the world who is gifted with the pluck and perseverance necessary to follow up and hound such an undertaking to its completion. He has converted several obstinate Congresses to a deserved friendliness toward his important work, and has gone up and down and to and fro in Europe until he has enlisted a great moneyed interest in it there.

used to lend it to old Miss Wagner, that hadn't any, to receive company in; it warn't big enough, and when Miss Wagner warn't noticing, it would get twisted around in the socket, and look up, maybe, or out to one side, and every which way, while t' other one was looking as straight ahead as a spy-glass. Grown people didn't mind it, but it most always made the children cry, it was so sort of scary. She tried packing it in raw cotton, but it wouldn't work, somehow— the cotton would get loose and stick out and look so kind of awful that the children couldn't stand it no way. She was always dropping it out, and turning up her old dead-light on the company empty, and making them oncomfortable, becuz *she* never could tell when it hopped out, being blind on that side, you see. So somebody would have to hunch her and say, "Your game eye has fetched loose, Miss Wagner dear"—and then all of them would have to sit and wait till she jammed it in again—wrong side before, as a general thing, and green as a bird's egg, being a bashful cretur and easy sot back before company. But being wrong side before warn't much difference, anyway, becuz her own eye was sky-blue and the glass one was yaller on the front side, so whichever way she turned it it didn't match nohow. Old Miss Wagner was considerable on the borrow, she was. When she had a quilting, or Dorcas S'iety at her house she gen'ally borrowed Miss Higgins's wooden leg to stump around on; it was considerable shorter than her other pin, but much *she* minded that. She said she couldn't abide crutches when she had company, becuz they were so slow; said when she had company and things had to be done, she wanted to get up and hump herself. She was as bald as a jug, and so she used to borrow Miss Jacops's wig—Miss Jacops was the coffin-peddler's wife—a ratty old buzzard, he was, that used to go roosting around where people was sick, waiting for 'em; and there that old rip would sit all day, in the shade, on a coffin that he judged would fit the can'idate; and if it was a slow customer and kind of uncertain, he'd fetch his rations and a blanket along and sleep in the coffin nights. He was anchored out that way, in frosty weather, for about three weeks, once, before old Robbins's place, waiting for him; and after that, for as much as two years, Jacops was not on speaking terms with the old man, on account of his disapp'inting him. He got one of his feet froze, and lost money, too, becuz old Robbins took a favorable turn and got well. The next time Robbins got sick, Jacops tried to make up with him, and varnished up the same old coffin and fetched it along; but old Robbins was too many for him; he had him in, and 'peared to be powerful weak; he bought the coffin for ten dollars and Jacops was to pay it back and twenty-five more besides if Robbins didn't like the coffin after he'd tried it. And then Robbins died, and at the funeral he bursted off the lid and riz up in his shroud and told the parson to let up on the performances, becuz he could *not* stand such a coffin as that. You see he had been in a trance once before, when he was young, and he took the chances of another, cal'lating that if he made the trip it was money in his pocket, and if he missed fire he couldn't lose a cent. And by George he sued Jacops for the rhino and got jedgment; and he set up the coffin his back parlor and said he 'lowed to take his time, now. It was always an aggravation to Jacops, the way that miserable old thing acted. He moved back to Indiany pretty soon—went to Wellsville—Wellsville was the place the Hogadorns was from. Mighty fine family. Old Maryland stock. Old Squire Hogadorn could carry around more mixed licker, and cuss better than most any man I ever see. His second wife was the widder Billings—she that was Becky Martin; her dam was deacon Dunlap's first wife. Her oldest child, Maria, married a missionary and died in grace—et up by the savages. They et *him,* too, poor feller—biled him. It warn't the custom, so they say, but they explained to friends of his'n that went down there to bring away his things, that they'd tried missionaries every other way and never could get any good out of 'em—and so it annoyed all his relations to find out that that man's life was fooled away just out of a dern'd experiment, so to speak. But mind you, there ain't anything ever reely lost; everything that people can't understand and don't see the reason of does good if you only hold on and give it a fair shake; Prov'dence don't fire no blank ca'tridges, boys. That there missionary's substance, unbeknowns to himself, actu'ly converted every last one of them heathens that took a chance at the barbacue. Nothing ever fetched them but that. Don't tell *me* it was an accident that he was biled. There ain't no such a thing as an accident. When my uncle Lem was leaning up agin a scaffolding once, sick, or drunk, or suthin, an Irishman with a hod full of bricks fell on him out of the third story and broke the old man's back in two places. People said it was an accident. Much accident there was about that. He didn't know what he was there for, but he was there for a good object. If he hadn't been there the Irishman would have been killed. Nobody can ever make me believe anything different from that. Uncle Lem's dog was there. Why didn't the Irishman fall on the dog? Becuz the dog would a seen him a coming and stood from under. That's the reason the dog warn't appinted. A dog can't be depended on to carry out a special providence. Mark my words it was a put-up thing. Accidents don't happen, boys. Uncle Lem's dog—I wish you could a seen that dog. He was a reglar shepherd—or ruther he was part bull and part shepherd—splendid animal; belonged to parson Hagar before Uncle Lem got him. Parson Hagar belonged to the Western Reserve Hagars; prime family; his mother was a Watson; one of his sisters married a Wheeler; they settled in Morgan County, and he got nipped by the machinery in a carpet factory and went through in less than a quarter of a minute; his widder bought the piece of carpet that had his remains wove in, and people come a hundred mile to 'tend the funeral. There was fourteen yards in the piece. She wouldn't let them roll him up, but planted him just so—full length. The church was middling small where they preached the funeral, and they had to let one end of the coffin stick out of the window. They didn't bury him—they planted one end, and let him stand up, same as a monument. And they nailed a sign on it and put—put on— put on it—sacred to—the m-e-m-o-r-y—of fourteen y-a-r-d-s—of three-ply— car—pet—containing all that was—m-o-r-t-a-l—of—of—W-i-l-l-i-a-m—W-h- e—''

Jim Blaine had been growing gradually drowsy and drowsier—his head nodded, once, twice, three times—dropped peacefully upon his breast, and he fell tranquilly asleep. The tears were running down the boys' cheeks—they were suffocating with suppressed laughter—and had been from the start, though I had never noticed it. I perceived that I was ''sold.'' I learned then that Jim Blaine's peculiarity was that whenever he reached a certain stage of intoxication, no human power could keep him from setting out, with impressive unction, to tell about a wonderful adventure which he had once had with his grandfather's old ram—and the mention of the ram in the first sentence was as far as any man had ever heard him get, concerning it. He always maundered off, interminably, from one thing to another, till his whisky got the best of him and he fell asleep. What the thing was that happened to him and his grandfather's old ram is a dark mystery to this day, for nobody has ever yet found out.

WAITING FOR A CUSTOMER.

Chapter LIV

OF COURSE THERE was a large Chinese population in Virginia—it is the case with every town and city on the Pacific coast. They are a harmless race when white men either let them alone or treat them no worse than dogs; in fact they are almost entirely harmless anyhow, for they seldom think of resenting the vilest insults or the cruelest injuries. They are quiet, peaceable, tractable, free from drunkenness, and they are as industrious as the day is long. A disorderly Chinaman is rare, and a lazy one does not exist. So long as a Chinaman has strength to use his hands he needs no support from anybody; white men often complain of want of work, but a Chinaman offers no such complaint; he always manages to find something to do. He is a great convenience to everybody— even to the worst class of white men, for he bears the most of their sins, suffering fines for their petty thefts, imprisonment for their robberies, and death for their murders. Any white man can swear a Chinaman's life away in the courts, but no Chinaman can testify against a white man. Ours is the "land of the free"— nobody denies that—nobody challenges it. [Maybe it is because we won't let other people testify.] As I write, news comes that in broad daylight in San Francisco, some boys have stoned an inoffensive Chinaman to death, and that although a large crowd witnessed the shameful deed, no one interfered.

There are seventy thousand (and possibly one hundred thousand) Chinamen on the Pacific coast. There were about a thousand in Virginia. They were penned into a "Chinese quarter"—a thing which they do not particularly object to, as they are fond of herding together. Their buildings were of wood; usually only one story high, and set thickly together along streets scarcely wide enough for a wagon to pass through. Their quarter was a little removed from the rest of the town. The chief employment of Chinamen in towns is to wash clothing. They always send a bill, like this below, pinned to the clothes. It is mere ceremony, for it does not enlighten the customer much. Their price for washing was $2.50 per dozen—rather cheaper than white people could afford to wash for at that

872

time. A very common sign on the Chinese houses was: "See Yup, Washer and Ironer"; "Hong Wo, Washer"; "Sam Sing W & Ah Hop, Washing." The house servants, cooks, etc., in California and Nevada, were chiefly Chinamen. There were few white servants and no Chinawomen so employed. Chinamen make good house servants, being quick, obedient, patient, quick to learn and tirelessly industrious. They do not need to be taught a thing twice as a general thing. They are imitative. If a Chinaman were to see his master break up a centre table, in a passion, and kindle a fire with it, that Chinaman would be likely to resort to the furniture for fuel forever afterward.

All Chinamen can read, write and cipher with easy facility—pity but all our petted *voters* could. In California they rent little patches of ground and do a deal of gardening. They will raise surprising crops of vegetables on a sand pile. They waste nothing. What is rubbish to a Christian, a Chinaman carefully preserves and makes useful in one way or another. He gathers up all the old oyster and sardine cans that white people throw away, and procures marketable tin and solder from them by melting. He gathers up old bones and turns them into manure. In California he gets a living out of old mining claims that white men have abandoned as exhausted and worthless—and then the officers come down on him once a month with an exorbitant swindle to which the legislature has given the broad, general name of "foreign" mining tax, but it is usually inflicted on no foreigners but Chinamen. This swindle has in some cases been repeated once or twice on the same victim in the course of the same month—but the public treasury was not additionally enriched by it, probably.

Chinamen hold their dead in great reverence—they worship their departed ancestors, in fact. Hence, in China, a man's front yard, back yard, or any other part of his premises, is made his family burying ground, in order that he may visit the graves at any and all times. Therefore that huge empire is one mighty cemetery; it is ridged and wringled from its centre to its circumference with graves—and inasmuch as every foot of ground must be made to do its utmost, in China, lest the swarming population suffer for food, the very graves are cultivated and yield a harvest, custom holding this to be no dishonor to the dead. Since the departed are held in such worshipful reverence, a Chinaman cannot bear that any indignity be offered the places where they sleep. Mr. Burlingame

said that herein lay China's bitter opposition to railroads; a road could not be
built anywhere in the empire without disturbing the graves of their ancestors or
friends.

A Chinaman hardly believes he could enjoy the hereafter except his body lay
in his beloved China; also, he desires to receive, himself, after death, that worship
with which he has honored his dead that preceded him. Therefore, if he visits
a foreign country, he makes arrangements to have his bones returned to China
in case he dies; if he hires to go to a foreign country on a labor contract, there
is always a stipulation that his body shall be taken back to China if he dies; if
the government sells a gang of Coolies to a foreigner for the usual five-year
term, it is specified in the contract that their bodies shall be restored to China
in case of death. On the Pacific coast the Chinamen all belong to one or another
of several great companies or organizations, and these companies keep track of
their members, register their names, and ship their bodies home when they die.
The See Yup Company is held to be the largest of these. The Ning Yeong
Company is next, and numbers eighteen thousand members on the coast. Its
headquarters are at San Francisco, where it has a costly temple, several great
officers (one of whom keeps regal state in seclusion and cannot be approached
by common humanity), and a numerous priesthood. In it I was shown a register
of its members, with the dead and the date of their shipment to China duly
marked. Every ship that sails from San Francisco carries away a heavy freight
of Chinese corpses—or did, at least, until the legislature, with an ingenious
refinement of Christian cruelty, forbade the shipments, as a neat underhanded
way of deterring Chinese immigration. The bill was offered, whether it passed
or not. It is my impression that it passed. There was another bill—it became a
law—compelling every incoming Chinaman to be vaccinated on the wharf and
pay a duly appointed quack (no decent doctor would defile himself with such
legalized robbery) ten dollars for it. As few importers of Chinese would want
to go to an expense like that, the lawmakers thought this would be another heavy
blow to Chinese immigration.

What the Chinese quarter of Virginia was like—or, indeed, what the Chinese
quarter of any Pacific coast town was and is like—may be gathered from this
item which I printed in the *Enterprise* while reporting for that paper:

> CHINATOWN.—Accompanied by a fellow reporter, we made a trip
> through our Chinese quarter the other night. The Chinese have built their
> portion of the city to suit themselves; and as they keep neither carriages
> nor wagons, their streets are not wide enough, as a general thing, to
> admit of the passage of vehicles. At ten o'clock at night the Chinaman
> may be seen in all his glory. In every little cooped-up, dingy cavern of
> a hut, faint with the odor of burning Josh-lights and with nothing to see
> the gloom by save the sickly, guttering tallow candle, were two or three
> yellow, long-tailed vagabonds, coiled up on a sort of short truckle-bed,
> smoking opium, motionless and with their lustreless eyes turned inward
> from excess of satisfaction—or rather the recent smoker looks thus,
> immediately after having passed the pipe to his neighbor—for opium-
> smoking is a comfortless operation, and requires constant attention. A
> lamp sits on the bed, the length of the long pipe-stem from the smoker's
> mouth; he puts a pellet of opium on the end of a wire, sets it on fire,
> and plasters it into the pipe much as a Christian would fill a hole with

putty; then he applies the bowl to the lamp and proceeds to smoke—and the stewing and frying of the drug and the gurgling of the juices in the stem would wellnigh turn the stomach of a statue. John likes it, though; it soothes him, he takes about two dozen whiffs, and then rolls over to dream, Heaven only knows what, for we could not imagine by looking at the soggy creature. Possibly in his visions he travels far away from the gross world and his regular washing, and feasts on succulent rats and birds'-nests in Paradise.

Mr. Ah Sing keeps a general grocery and provision store at No. 13 Wang street. He lavished his hospitality upon our party in the friendliest way. He had various kinds of colored and colorless wines and brandies, with unpronounceable names, imported from China in little crockery jugs, and which he offered to us in dainty little miniature wash-basins of porcelain. He offered us a mess of birds'-nests; also, small, neat sausages, of which we could have swallowed several yards if we had chosen to try, but we suspected that each link contained the corpse of a mouse, and therefore refrained. Mr. Sing had in his store a thousand articles of merchandise, curious to behold, impossible to imagine the uses of, and beyond our ability to describe.

His ducks, however, and his eggs, we could understand; the former were split open and flattened out like codfish, and came from China in that shape, and the latter were plastered over with some kind of paste which kept them fresh and palatable through the long voyage.

We found Mr. Hong Wo, No. 37 Chow-chow street, making up a lottery scheme—in fact we found a dozen others occupied in the same way in various parts of the quarter, for about every third Chinaman runs a lottery, and the balance of the tribe "buck" at it. "Tom," who speaks faultless English, and used to be chief and only cook to the *Territorial Enterprise,* when the establishment kept bachelor's hall two years ago, said that "Sometime Chinaman buy ticket one dollar hap, ketch um two tree hundred, sometime no ketch um anyting; lottery like one man fight um seventy—may-be he whip, may-be he get whip heself, welly good." However, the percentage being sixty-nine against him, the chances are, as a general thing, that "he get whip heself." We could not see that these lotteries differed in any respect from our own, save that the figures being Chinese, no ignorant white man might ever hope to succeed in telling "t'other from which;" the manner of drawing is similar to ours.

Mr. See Yup keeps a fancy store on Live Fox street. He sold us fans of white feathers, gorgeously ornamented; perfumery that smelled like Limburger cheese, Chinese pens, and watch-charms made of a stone unscratchable with steel instruments, yet polished and tinted like the inner coat of a sea-shell.* As tokens of his esteem, See Yup presented the party with gaudy plumes made of gold tinsel and trimmed with peacocks' feathers.

We ate chow-chow with chop-sticks in the celestial restaurants; our comrade chided the moon-eyed damsels in front of the houses for their want of feminine reserve; we received protecting Josh-lights from our

---

* A peculiar species of the "jade-stone"—to a Chinaman peculiarly precious.

CHINESE LOTTERY.

hosts and "dickered" for a pagan God or two. Finally, we were impressed
with the genius of a Chinese book-keeper; he figured up his accounts on
a machine like a grid-iron with buttons strung on its bars; the different
rows represented units, tens, hundreds and thousands. He fingered them
with incredible rapidity—in fact, he pushed them from place to place as
fast as a musical professor's fingers travel over the keys of a piano.

They are a kindly disposed, well-meaning race, and are respected and well
treated by the upper classes, all over the Pacific coast. No Californian *gentleman
or lady* ever abuses or oppresses a Chinaman, under any circumstances, an
explanation that seems to be much needed in the East. Only the scum of the
population do it—they and their children; they, and, naturally and consistently,
the policemen and politicians, likewise, for these are the dust-licking pimps and
slaves of the scum, there as well as elsewhere in America.

Chapter LV

I BEGAN TO get tired of staying in one place so long. There was no longer
satisfying variety in going down to Carson to report the proceedings of the
legislature once a year, and horse-races and pumpkin-shows once in three months,
(they had got to raising pumpkins and potatoes in Washoe Valley, and of course
one of the first achievements of the legislature was to institute a ten-thousand-
dollar Agricultural Fair to show off forty dollars' worth of those pumpkins in—
however, the territorial legislature was usually spoken of as the "asylum"). I
wanted to see San Francisco. I wanted to go somewhere. I wanted—I did not
know *what* I wanted. I had the "spring fever" and wanted a change, principally,
no doubt. Besides, a convention had framed a State Constitution; nine men out
of every ten wanted an office; I believed that these gentlemen would "treat"
the moneyless and the irresponsible among the population into adopting the
constitution and thus wellnigh killing the country (it could not well carry such

a load as a State government, since it had nothing to tax that could stand a tax, for undeveloped mines could not, and there were not fifty developed ones in the land, there was but little realty to tax, and it did seem as if nobody was ever going to think of the simple salvation of inflicting a money penalty on murder). I believed that a State government would destroy the "flush times," and I wanted to get away. I believed that the mining stocks I had on hand would soon be worth $100,000, and thought if they reached that before the Constitution was adopted, I would sell out and make myself secure from the crash the change of government was going to bring. I considered $100,000 sufficient to go home with decently, though it was but a small amount compared to what I had been expecting to return with. I felt rather down-hearted about it, but I tried to comfort myself with the reflection that with such a sum I could not fall into want. About this time a schoolmate of mine whom I had not seen since boyhood, came tramping in on foot from Reese River, a very allegory of Poverty. The son of wealthy parents, here he was, in a strange land, hungry, bootless, mantled in an ancient horse-blanket, roofed with a brimless hat, and so generally and so extravagantly dilapidated that he could have "taken the shine out of the Prodigal Son himself," as he pleasantly remarked. He wanted to borrow forty-six dollars— twenty-six to take him to San Francisco, and twenty for something else; to buy some soap with, maybe, for he needed it. I found I had but little more than the amount wanted, in my pocket; so I stepped in and borrowed forty-six dollars of a banker (on twenty days' time, without the formality of a note), and gave it him, rather than walk half a block to the office, where I had some specie laid up. If anybody had told me that it would take me two years to pay back that forty-six dollars to the banker (for I did not expect it of the Prodigal, and was not disappointed), I would have felt injured. And so would the banker.

I wanted a change. I wanted variety of some kind. It came. Mr. Goodman went away for a week and left me the post of chief editor. It destroyed me. The first day, I wrote my "leader" in the forenoon. The second day, I had no subject and put it off till the afternoon. The third day I put it off till evening, and then copied an elaborate editorial out of the "American Cyclopedia," that steadfast friend of the editor, all over this land. The fourth day I "fooled around" till midnight, and then fell back on the Cyclopedia again. The fifth day I cudgeled

AN OLD FRIEND.

my brain till midnight, and then kept the press waiting while I penned some bitter personalities on six different people. The sixth day I labored in anguish till far into the night and brought forth—nothing. The paper went to press without an editorial. The seventh day I resigned. On the eighth, Mr. Goodman returned and found six duels on his hands—my personalities had borne fruit.

Nobody, except he has tried it, knows what it is to be an editor. It is easy to scribble local rubbish, with the facts all before you; it is easy to clip selections from other papers; it is easy to string out a correspondence from any locality; but it is unspeakable hardship to write editorials. *Subjects* are the trouble—the dreary lack of them, I mean. Every day, it is drag, drag, drag—think, and worry and suffer—all the world is a dull blank, and yet the editorial columns *must* be filled. Only give the editor a *subject,* and his work is done—it is no trouble to write it up; but fancy how you would feel if you had to pump your brains dry every day in the week, fifty-two weeks in the year. It makes one low spirited simply to think of it. The matter that each editor of a daily paper in America writes in the course of a year would fill from four to eight bulky volumes like this book! Fancy what a library an editor's work would make, after twenty or thirty years' service. Yet people often marvel that Dickens, Scott, Bulwer, Dumas, etc., have been able to produce so many books. If these authors had wrought as voluminously as newspaper editors do, the result would be something to marvel at, indeed. How editors can continue this tremendous labor, this exhausting consumption of brain fibre (for their work is creative, and not a mere mechanical laying-up of facts, like reporting), day after day and year after year, is incomprehensible. Preachers take two months' holiday in midsummer, for they find that to produce two sermons a week is wearing, in the long run. In truth it must be so, and is so; and therefore, how an editor can take from ten to twenty texts and build upon them from ten to twenty painstaking editorials a week and keep it up all the year round, is farther beyond comprehension than ever. Ever since I survived my week as editor, I have found at least one pleasure in any newspaper that comes to my hand; it is in admiring the long columns of editorial, and wondering to myself how in the mischief he did it!

Mr. Goodman's return relieved me of employment, unless I chose to become a reporter again. I could not do that; I could not serve in the ranks after being General of the army. So I thought I would depart and go abroad into the world somewhere. Just at this juncture, Dan, my associate in the reportorial department, told me, casually, that two citizens had been trying to persuade him to go with them to New York and aid in selling a rich silver mine which they had discovered and secured in a new mining district in our neighborhood. He said they offered to pay his expenses and give him one third of the proceeds of the sale. He had refused to go. It was the very opportunity I wanted. I abused him for keeping so quiet about it, and not mentioning it sooner. He said it had not occurred to him that I would like to go, and so he had recommended them to apply to Marshall, the reporter of the other paper. I asked Dan if it was a good, honest mine, and no swindle. He said the men had shown him nine tons of the rock, which they had got out to take to New York, and he could cheerfully say that he had seen but little rock in Nevada that was richer; and moreover, he said that they had secured a tract of valuable timber and a mill-site, near the mine. My first idea was to kill Dan. But I changed my mind, notwithstanding I was so angry, for I thought maybe the chance was not yet lost. Dan said it was by no means lost; that the men were absent at the mine again, and would not be in

Virginia to leave for the East for some ten days; that they had requested him to do the talking to Marshall, and he had promised that he would either secure Marshall or somebody else for them by the time they got back; he would now say nothing to anybody till they returned, and then fulfil his promise by furnishing me to them.

It was splendid. I went to bed all on fire with excitement; for nobody had yet gone East to sell a Nevada silver mine, and the field was white for the sickle. I felt that such a mine as the one described by Dan would bring a princely sum in New York, and sell without delay or difficulty. I could not sleep, my fancy so rioted through its castles in the air. It was the "blind lead" come again.

Next day I got away, on the coach, with the usual eclat attending departures of old citizens,—for if you have only half a dozen friends out there they will make noise for a hundred rather than let you seem to go away neglected and unregretted—and Dan promised to keep strict watch for the men that had the mine to sell.

The trip was signalized but by one little incident, and that occurred just as we were about to start. A very seedy looking vagabond passenger got out of the stage a moment to wait till the usual ballast of silver bricks was thrown in. He was standing on the pavement, when an awkward express employé, carrying a brick weighing a hundred pounds, stumbled and let it fall on the bummer's foot. He instantly dropped on the ground and began to howl in the most heart-breaking way. A sympathizing crowd gathered around and were going to pull his boot off; but he screamed louder than ever and they desisted; then he fell to gasping, and between the gasps ejaculated "Brandy! for Heaven's sake, brandy!" They poured half a pint down him, and it wonderfully restored and comforted him. Then he begged the people to assist him to the stage, which was done. The express people urged him to have a doctor at their expense, but he declined, and said that if he only had a little brandy to take along with him, to soothe his paroxysms of pain when they came on, he would be grateful and content. He was quickly supplied with two bottles, and we drove off. He was so smiling and happy after that, that I could not refrain from asking him how he could possibly be so comfortable with a crushed foot.

"Well," said he, "I hadn't had a drink for twelve hours, and hadn't a cent to my name. I was most perishing—and so, when that duffer dropped that hundred-pounder on my foot, I see my chance. Got a cork leg, you know!" and he pulled up his pantaloons and proved it.

He was as drunk as a lord all day long, and full of chucklings over his timely ingenuity.

One drunken man necessarily reminds one of another. I once heard a gentleman tell about an incident which he witnessed in a Californian bar-room. He entitled it "Ye Modest Man Taketh a Drink." It was nothing but a bit of acting, but it seemed to me a perfect rendering, and worthy of Toodles himself. The modest man, tolerably far gone with beer and other matters, enters a saloon (twenty-five cents is the price for anything and everything, and specie the only money used) and lays down a half dollar; calls for whiskey and drinks it; the bar-keeper makes change and lays the quarter in a wet place on the counter; the modest man fumbles at it with nerveless fingers, but it slips and the water holds it; he contemplates it, and tries again; same result; observes that people are interested in what he is at, blushes; fumbles at the quarter again—blushes—puts his forefinger carefully, slowly down, to make sure of his aim—pushes the coin toward the bar-keeper, and says with a sigh:

"('ic!) Gimme a cigar!"

Naturally, another gentleman present told about another drunken man. He said he reeled toward home late at night; made a mistake and entered the wrong gate; thought he saw a dog on the stoop; and it was—an iron one. He stopped and considered; wondered if it was a dangerous dog; ventured to say "Be (hic) begone!" No effect. Then he approached warily, and adopted conciliation; pursed up his lips and tried to whistle, but failed; still approached, saying, "Poor dog!— doggy, doggy, doggy!—poor doggy-dog!" Got up on the stoop, still petting with fond names; still master of the advantages; then exclaimed, "Leave, you thief!"—planted a vindictive kick in his ribs, and went head-over-heels overboard, of course. A pause; a sigh or two of pain, and then a remark in a reflective voice:

"Awful solid dog. What could he ben eating? ('ic!) Rocks, p'raps. Such animals is dangerous. 'At's what *I* say—they're dangerous. If a man—('ic!)— if a man wants to feed a dog on rocks, let him *feed* him on rocks; 'at's all right; but let him keep him at *home*—not have him layin' round promiscuous, where ('ic!) where people's liable to stumble over him when they ain't noticin'!''

It was not without regret that I took a last look at the tiny flag (it was thirty-five feet long and ten feet wide) fluttering like a lady's handkerchief from the topmost peak of Mount Davidson, two thousand feet above Virginia's roofs, and felt that doubtless I was bidding a permanent farewell to a city which had afforded me the most vigorous enjoyment of life I had ever experienced. And this reminds me of an incident which the dullest memory Virginia could boast at the time it happened must vividly recall, at times, till its possessor dies. Late one summer afternoon we had a rain shower. That was astonishing enough, in itself, to set the whole town buzzing, for it only rains (during a week or two weeks) in the winter in Nevada, and even then not enough at a time to make it worth while for any merchant to keep umbrellas for sale. But the rain was not the chief wonder. It only lasted five or ten minutes; while the people were still talking about it all the heavens gathered to themselves a dense blackness as of midnight. All the vast eastern front of Mount Davidson, overlooking the city, put on such a funereal gloom that only the nearness and solidity of the mountain made its outlines even faintly distinguishable from the dead blackness of the heavens they rested against. This unaccustomed sight turned all eyes toward the mountain; and as they looked, a little tongue of rich golden flame was seen waving and quivering in the heart of the midnight, away up on the extreme summit! In a few minutes the streets were packed with people, gazing with hardly an uttered word, at the one brilliant mote in the brooding world of darkness. It flicked like a candle-flame, and looked no larger; but with such a background it was wonderfully bright, small as it was. It was the flag!—though no one suspected it at first, it seemed so like a supernatural visitor of some kind—a mysterious messenger of good tidings, some were fain to believe. It was the nation's emblem transfigured by the departing rays of a sun that was entirely palled from view; and on no other object did the glory fall, in all the broad panorama of mountain ranges and deserts. Not even upon the staff of the flag—for that, a needle in the distance at any time, was now untouched by the light and undistinguishable in the gloom. For a whole hour the weird visitor winked and burned in its lofty solitude, and still the thousands of uplifted eyes watched it with fascinated interest. How the people were wrought up! The superstition grew apace that this was a mystic courier come with great news from the war—the poetry of the idea excusing and commending it—and on it spread, from heart to heart, from lip to lip and from street to street, till there was a general impulse to have out the military and welcome the bright waif with a salvo of artillery!

And all that time one sorely tried man, the telegraph operator sworn to official secrecy, had to lock his lips and chain his tongue with a silence that was like to rend them; for he, and he only, of all the speculating multitude, knew the great things this sinking sun had seen that day in the east—Vicksburg fallen, and the Union arms victorious at Gettysburg!

But for the journalistic monopoly that forbade the slightest revealment of eastern news till a day after its publication in the California papers, the glorified flag on Mount Davidson would have been saluted and re-saluted, that memorable evening, as long as there was a charge of powder to thunder with; the city would have been illuminated, and every man that had any respect for himself would have got drunk,—as was the custom of the country on all occasions of public moment. Even at this distant day I cannot think of this needlessly marred supreme opportunity without regret. What a time we might have had!

Chapter LVI

WE RUMBLED OVER the plains and valleys, climbed the Sierras to the clouds, and looked down upon summer-clad California. And I will remark here, in passing, that all scenery in California requires *distance* to give it its highest charm. The mountains are imposing in their sublimity and their majesty of form and altitude, from any point of view—but one must have distance to soften their ruggedness and enrich their tintings; a Californian forest is best at a little distance, for there is a sad poverty of variety in species, the trees being chiefly of one monotonous family—redwood, pine, spruce, fir—and so, at a near view there is a wearisome sameness of attitude in their rigid arms, stretched downward and outward in one continued and reiterated appeal to all men to "Sh!—don't say a word!—you might disturb somebody!" Close at hand, too, there is a reliefless and relentless smell of pitch and turpentine; there is a ceaseless melancholy in their sighing and complaining foliage; one walks over a soundless carpet of beaten yellow bark and dead spines of the foliage till he feels like a wandering spirit bereft of a footfall; he tires of the endless tufts of needles and yearns for substantial, shapely leaves; he looks for moss and grass to loll upon, and finds none, for where there is no bark there is naked clay and dirt, enemies to pensive musing and clean apparel. Often a grassy plain in California, is what it should be, but often, too, it is best contemplated at a distance, because although its grass blades are tall, they stand up vindictively straight and self-sufficient, and are unsociably wide apart, with uncomely spots of barren sand between.

One of the queerest things I know of, is to hear tourists from "the States" go into ecstasies over the loveliness of "ever-blooming California." And they always do go into that sort of ecstasies. But perhaps they would modify them if they knew how old Californians, with the memory full upon them of the dust-

covered and questionable summer greens of Californian "verdure," stand astonished, and filled with worshiping admiration, in the presence of the lavish
richness, the brilliant green, the infinite freshness, the spendthrift variety of form
and species and foliage that make an Eastern landscape a vision of Paradise
itself. The idea of a man falling into raptures over grave and sombre California,
when that man has seen New England's meadow-expanses and her maples, oaks
and cathedral-windowed elms decked in summer attire, or the opaline splendors
of autumn descending upon her forests, comes very near being funny—would
be, in fact, but that it is so pathetic. No land with an unvarying climate can be
very beautiful. The tropics are not, for all the sentiment that is wasted on them.
They seem beautiful at first, but sameness impairs the charm by and by. *Change*
is the handmaiden Nature requires to do her miracles with. The land that has
four well-defined seasons, cannot lack beauty, or pall with monotony. Each
season brings a world of enjoyment and interest in the watching of its unfolding,
its gradual, harmonious development, its culminating graces—and just as one
begins to tire of it, it passes away and a radical change comes, with new witcheries
and new glories in its train. And I think that to one in sympathy with nature,
each season, in its turn, seems the loveliest.

San Francisco, a truly fascinating city to live in, is stately and handsome at
a fair distance, but close at hand one notes that the architecture is mostly old-
fashioned, many streets are made up of decaying, smoke-grimed, wooden houses,
and the barren sand-hills toward the outskirts obtrude themselves too prominently.
Even the kindly climate is sometimes pleasanter when read about than personally
experienced, for a lovely, cloudless sky wears out its welcome by and by, and
then when the longed for rain does come it *stays*. Even the playful earthquake
is better contemplated at a dis—

However there are varying opinions about that.

The climate of San Francisco is mild and singularly equable. The thermometer
stands at about seventy degrees the year round. It hardly changes at all. You
sleep under one or two light blankets Summer and Winter, and never use a
mosquito bar. Nobody ever wears Summer clothing. You wear black broadcloth—
if you have it—in August and January, just the same. It is no colder, and no
warmer, in the one month than the other. You do not use overcoats and you do
not use fans. It is as pleasant a climate as could well be contrived, take it all
around, and is doubtless the most unvarying in the whole world. The wind blows
there a good deal in the Summer months, but then you can go over to Oakland,
if you choose—three or four miles away—it does not blow there. It has only
snowed twice in San Francisco in nineteen years, and then it only remained on
the ground long enough to astonish the children, and set them to wondering
what the feathery stuff was.

During eight months of the year, straight along, the skies are bright and
cloudless, and never a drop of rain falls. But when the other four months come
along, you will need to go and steal an umbrella. Because you will require it.
Not just one day, but one hundred and twenty days in hardly varying succession.
When you want to go visiting, or attend church, or the theatre, you never look
up at the clouds to see whether it is likely to rain or not—you look at the almanac.
If it is Winter, it will *rain*—and if it is Summer, it *won't* rain, and you cannot
help it. You never need a lightning-rod, because it never thunders and it never
lightens. And after you have listened for six or eight weeks, every night, to the
dismal monotony of those quiet rains, you will wish in your heart the thunder

would leap and crash and roar along those drowsy skies once, and make everything alive—you will wish the prisoned lightnings *would* cleave the dull firmament asunder and light it with a blinding glare for *one* little instant. You would give *anything* to hear the old familiar thunder again and see the lightning strike somebody. And along in the Summer, when you have suffered about four months of lustrous, pitiless sunshine, you are ready to go down on your knees and plead for rain—hail—snow—thunder and lightning—anything to break the monotony— you will take an earthquake, if you cannot do any better. And the chances are that you'll get it, too.

San Francisco is built on sand hills, but they are prolific sand hills. They yield a generous vegetation. All the rare flowers which people in "the States" rear with such patient care in parlor flower-pots and green-houses, flourish luxuriantly in the open air there all the year round. Calla lilies, all sorts of geraniums, passion flowers, moss roses—I do not know the names of a tenth part of them. I only know that while New Yorkers are burdened with banks and drifts of snow, Californians are burdened with banks and drifts of flowers, if they only keep their hands off and let them grow. And I have heard that they have also that rarest and most curious of all the flowers, the beautiful *Espiritu Santo,* as the Spaniards call it—or flower of the Holy Spirit—though I thought it grew only in Central America—down on the Isthmus. In its cup is the daintiest little fac-simile of a dove, as pure as snow. The Spaniards have a superstitious reverence for it. The blossom has been conveyed to the States, submerged in ether; and the bulb has been taken thither also, but every attempt to make it bloom after it arrived, has failed.

I have elsewhere spoken of the endless Winter of Mono, California, and but this moment of the eternal Spring of San Francisco. Now if we travel a hundred miles in a straight line, we come to the eternal Summer of Sacramento. One never sees Summer-clothing or mosquitoes in San Francisco—but they can be found in Sacramento. Not always and unvaryingly, but about one hundred and forty-three months out of twelve years, perhaps. Flowers bloom there, always, the reader can easily believe—people suffer and sweat, and swear, morning, noon and night, and wear out their stanchest energies fanning themselves. It gets hot there, but if you go down to Fort Yuma you will find it hotter. Fort Yuma is probably the hottest place on earth. The thermometer stays at one hundred and twenty in the shade there all the time—except when it varies and goes higher. It is a U.S. military post, and its occupants get so used to the terrific heat that they suffer without it. There is a tradition (attributed to John Phenix*) that a very, very wicked soldier died there, once, and of course, went straight to the hottest corner of perdition,—and the next day he *telegraphed back for his blankets*. There is no doubt about the truth of this statement—there can be no doubt about it. I have seen the place where that soldier used to board. In Sacramento it is fiery Summer always, and you can gather roses, and eat strawberries and ice-cream, and wear white linen clothes, and pant and perspire, at eight or nine o'clock in the morning, and then take the cars, and at noon put on your furs and your skates, and go skimming over frozen Donner Lake, seven thousand feet above the valley, among snow banks fifteen feet deep, and in the shadow

---

* It has been purloined by fifty different scribblers who were too poor to invent a fancy but not ashamed to steal one.—M. T.

of grand mountain peaks that lift their frosty crags ten thousand feet above the level of the sea. There is a transition for you! Where will you find another like it in the Western hemisphere? And some of us have swept around snow-walled curves of the Pacific Railroad in that vicinity, six thousand feet above the sea, and looked down as the birds do, upon the deathless Summer of the Sacramento Valley, with its fruitful fields, its feathery foliage, its silver streams, all slumbering in the mellow haze of its enchanted atmosphere, and all infinitely softened and spiritualized by distance—a dreamy, exquisite glimpse of fairyland, made all the more charming and striking that it was caught through a forbidden gateway of ice and snow, and savage crags and precipices.

Chapter LVII

IT WAS IN this Sacramento Valley, just referred to, that a deal of the most lucrative of the early gold mining was done, and you may still see, in places, its grassy slopes and levels torn and guttered and disfigured by the avaricious spoilers of fifteen and twenty years ago. You may see such disfigurements far and wide over California—and in some such places, where only meadows and forests are visible—not a living creature, not a house, no stick or stone or remnant of a ruin, and not a sound, not even a whisper to disturb the Sabbath stillness—you will find it hard to believe that there stood at one time a fiercely-flourishing little city, of two thousand or three thousand souls, with its newspaper, fire company, brass band, volunteer militia, bank, hotels, noisy Fourth of July processions and speeches, gambling halls crammed with tobacco smoke, profanity, and rough-bearded men of all nations and colors, with tables heaped with gold dust sufficient for the revenues of a German principality—streets crowded and rife with business—town lots worth four hundred dollars a front foot—labor, laughter, music, dancing, swearing, fighting, shooting, stabbing—a bloody inquest and a man for breakfast every morning—*everything* that delights and adorns existence—all the appointments and appurtenances of a thriving and prosperous

SACRAMENTO.

and promising young city,—and *now* nothing is left of it all but a lifeless, homeless solitude. The men are gone, the houses have vanished, even the *name* of the place is forgotten. In no other land, in modern times, have towns so absolutely died and disappeared, as in the old mining regions of California.

It was a driving, vigorous, restless population in those days. It was a *curious* population. It was the *only* population of the kind that the world has ever seen gathered together, and it is not likely that the world will ever see its like again. For, observe, it was an assemblage of two hundred thousand *young* men—not simpering, dainty, kid-gloved weaklings, but stalwart, muscular, dauntless young braves, brimful of push and energy, and royally endowed with every attribute that goes to make up a peerless and magnificent manhood—the very pick and choice of the world's glorious ones. No women, no children, no gray and stooping veterans,—none but erect, bright-eyed, quick-moving, strong-handed young giants—the strangest population, the finest population, the most gallant host that ever trooped down the startled solitudes of an unpeopled land. And where are they now? Scattered to the ends of the earth—or prematurely aged and decrepit— or shot or stabbed in street affrays—or dead of disappointed hopes and broken hearts—all gone, or nearly all—victims devoted upon the altar of the golden calf—the noblest holocaust that ever wafted its sacrificial incense heavenward. It is pitiful to think upon.

It was a splendid population—for all the slow, sleepy, sluggish-brained sloths staid at home—you never find that sort of people among pioneers—you cannot build pioneers out of that sort of material. It was that population that gave to California a name for getting up astounding enterprises and rushing them through with a magnificent dash and daring and a recklessness of cost or consequences, which she bears unto this day—and when she projects a new surprise, the grave world smiles as usual, and says, "Well, that is California all over."

But they were rough in those times! They fairly reveled in gold, whisky, fights, and fandangoes, and were unspeakably happy. The honest miner raked from a hundred to a thousand dollars out of his claim a day, and what with the gambling dens and the other entertainments, he hadn't a cent the next morning, if he had any sort of luck. They cooked their own bacon and beans, sewed on their own buttons, washed their own shirts—blue woollen ones; and if a man wanted a fight on his hands without any annoying delay, all he had to do was to appear in public in a white shirt or a stove-pipe hat, and he would be accommodated. For those people hated aristocrats. They had a particular and malignant animosity toward what they called a "biled shirt."

It was a wild, free, disorderly, grotesque society! *Men*—only swarming hosts of stalwart *men*—nothing juvenile, nothing feminine, visible anywhere!

In those days miners would flock in crowds to catch a glimpse of that rare and blessed spectacle, a woman! Old inhabitants tell how, in a certain camp, the news went abroad early in the morning that a woman was come! They had seen a calico dress hanging out of a wagon down at the camping-ground—sign of emigrants from over the great plains. Everybody went down there, and a shout went up when an actual, bona fide dress was discovered fluttering in the wind! The male emigrant was visible. The miners said:

"Fetch her out!"

He said: "It is my wife, gentlemen—she is sick—we have been robbed of money, provisions, everything, by the Indians—we want to rest."

"Fetch her out! We've got to see her!"

"But, gentlemen, the poor thing, she—"

"FETCH HER OUT!"

He "fetched her out," and they swung their hats and sent up three rousing cheers and a tiger; and they crowded around and gazed at her, and touched her dress, and listened to her voice with the look of men who listened to a *memory* rather than a present reality—and then they collected twenty-five hundred dollars in gold and gave it to the man, and swung their hats again and gave three more cheers, and went home satisfied.

Once I dined in San Francisco with the family of a pioneer, and talked with his daughter, a young lady whose first experience in San Francisco was an adventure, though she herself did not remember it, as she was only two or three years old at the time. Her father said that, after landing from the ship, they were walking up the street, a servant leading the party with the little girl in her arms. And presently a huge miner, bearded, belted, spurred, and bristling with deadly weapons—just down from a long campaign in the mountains, evidently—barred the way, stopped the servant, and stood gazing, with a face all alive with gratification and astonishment. Then he said, reverently:

"Well, if it ain't a child!" And then he snatched a little leather sack out of his pocket and said to the servant:

"There's a hundred and fifty dollars in dust, there, and I'll give it to you to let me kiss the child!"

That anecdote is *true*.

But see how things change. Sitting at that dinner-table, listening to that anecdote, if I had offered double the money for the privilege of kissing the same child, I would have been refused. Seventeen added years have far more than doubled the price.

And while upon this subject I will remark that once in Star City, in the Humboldt Mountains, I took my place in a sort of long, post-office single file of miners, to patiently await my chance to peep through a crack in the cabin and get a sight of the splendid new sensation—a genuine, live Woman! And at the end of half of an hour my turn came, and I put my eye to the crack, and there she was, with one arm akimbo, and tossing flap-jacks in a frying-pan with the other. And she was one hundred and sixty-five* years old, and hadn't a tooth in her head.

Chapter LVIII

FOR A FEW months I enjoyed what to me was an entirely new phase of existence— a butterfly idleness; nothing to do, nobody to be responsible to, and untroubled with financial uneasiness. I fell in love with the most cordial and sociable city in the Union. After the sage-brush and alkali deserts of Washoe, San Francisco was Paradise to me. I lived at the best hotel, exhibited my clothes in the most conspicuous places, infested the opera, and learned to seem enraptured with music which oftener afflicted my ignorant ear than enchanted it, if I had had

---

* Being in calmer mood, now, I voluntarily knock off a hundred from that.—M. T.

the vulgar honesty to confess it. However, I suppose I was not greatly worse than the most of my countrymen in that. I had longed to be a butterfly, and I was one at last. I attended private parties in sumptuous evening dress, simpered and aired my graces like a born beau, and polked and schottisched with a step peculiar to myself—and the kangaroo. In a word, I kept the due state of a man worth a hundred thousand dollars (prospectively,) and likely to reach absolute affluence when that silver-mine sale should be ultimately achieved in the East. I spent money with a free hand, and meantime watched the stock sales with an interested eye and looked to see what might happen in Nevada.

Something very important happened. The property holders of Nevada voted against the State Constitution; but the folks who had nothing to lose were in the majority, and carried the measure over their heads. But after all it did not immediately look like a disaster, though unquestionably it was one. I hesitated, calculated the chances, and then concluded not to sell. Stocks went on rising; speculation went mad; bankers, merchants, lawyers, doctors, mechanics, laborers, even the very washerwomen and servant girls, were putting up their earnings on silver stocks, and every sun that rose in the morning went down on paupers enriched and rich men beggared. What a gambling carnival it was! Gould and Curry soared to six thousand three hundred dollars a foot! And then—all of a sudden, out went the bottom and everything and everybody went to ruin and destruction! The wreck was complete. The bubble scarcely left a microscopic moisture behind it. I was an early beggar and a thorough one. My hoarded stocks were not worth the paper they were printed on. I threw them all away. I, the cheerful idiot that had been squandering money like water, and thought myself beyond the reach of misfortune, had not now as much as fifty dollars when I gathered together my various debts and paid them. I removed from the hotel to a very private boarding house. I took a reporter's berth and went to work. I was not entirely broken in spirit, for I was building confidently on the sale of the silver mine in the east. But I could not hear from Dan. My letters miscarried or were not answered.

One day I did not feel vigorous and remained away from the office. The next day I went down toward noon as usual, and found a note on my desk which had been there twenty-four hours. It was signed "Marshall"—the Virginia re-

THE GRACE OF A KANGAROO.

porter—and contained a request that I should call at the hotel and see him and a friend or two that night, as they would sail for the east in the morning. A postscript added that their errand was a big mining speculation! I was hardly ever so sick in my life. I abused myself for leaving Virginia and entrusting to another man a matter I ought to have attended to myself; I abused myself for remaining away from the office on the one day of all the year that I should have been there. And thus berating myself I trotted a mile to the steamer wharf and arrived just in time to be too late. The ship was in the stream and under way.

I comforted myself with the thought that maybe the speculation would amount to nothing—poor comfort at best—and then went back to my slavery, resolved to put up with my thirty-five dollars a week and forget all about it.

A month afterward I enjoyed my first earthquake. It was one which was long called the "great" earthquake, and is doubtless so distinguished till this day. It was just after noon, on a bright October day. I was coming down Third street. The only objects in motion anywhere in sight in that thickly built and populous quarter, were a man in a buggy behind me, and a street car wending slowly up the cross street. Otherwise, all was solitude and a Sabbath stillness. As I turned the corner, around a frame house, there was a great rattle and jar, and it occurred to me that here was an item!—no doubt a fight in that house. Before I could turn and seek the door, there came a really terrific shock; the ground seemed to roll under me in waves, interrupted by a violent joggling up and down, and there was a heavy grinding noise as of brick houses rubbing together. I fell up against the frame house and hurt my elbow. I knew what it was, now, and from mere reportorial instinct, nothing else, took out my watch and noted the time of day; at that moment a third and still severer shock came, and as I reeled about on the pavement trying to keep my footing, I saw a sight! The entire front of a tall four-story brick building in Third street sprung outward like a door and fell sprawling across the street, raising a dust like a great volume of smoke! And here came the buggy—overboard went the man, and in less time than I can tell it the vehicle was distributed in small fragments along three hundred yards of street. One could have fancied that somebody had fired a charge of chair-rounds and rags down the thoroughfare. The street car had stopped, the horses were rearing and plunging, the passengers were pouring out at both ends, and one fat man had crashed half way through a glass window on one side of the car, got wedged fast and was squirming and screaming like an impaled madman. Every door, of every house, as far as the eye could reach, was vomiting a stream of human beings; and almost before one could execute a wink and begin another, there was a massed multitude of people stretching in endless procession down every street my position commanded. Never was solemn solitude turned into teeming life quicker.

Of the wonders wrought by "the great earthquake," these were all that came under my eye; but the tricks it did, elsewhere, and far and wide over the town, made toothsome gossip for nine days. The destruction of property was trifling—the injury to it was wide-spread and somewhat serious.

The "curiosities" of the earthquake were simply endless. Gentlemen and ladies who were sick, or were taking a siesta, or had dissipated till a late hour and were making up lost sleep, thronged into the public streets in all sorts of queer apparel, and some without any at all. One woman who had been washing a naked child, ran down the street holding it by the ankles as if it were a dressed turkey. Prominent citizens who were supposed to keep the Sabbath strictly, rushed out of saloons in their shirt-sleeves, with billiard cues in their hands. Dozens of men with necks swathed in napkins, rushed from barber-shops, lathered to the eyes or with one cheek clean shaved and the other still bearing a hairy stubble. Horses broke from stables, and a frightened dog rushed up a short attic ladder and out onto a roof, and when his scare was over had not the nerve to go down again the same way he had gone up. A prominent editor flew down stairs, in the principal hotel, with nothing on but one brief undergarment—met a chambermaid, and exclaimed:

"Oh, what *shall* I do! Where shall I go!"

She responded with naive serenity:

"If you have no choice, you might try a clothing-store!"

A certain foreign consul's lady was the acknowledged leader of fashion, and every time she appeared in anything new or extraordinary, the ladies in the vicinity made a raid on their husbands' purses and arrayed themselves similarly. One man who had suffered considerably and growled accordingly, was standing at the window when the shocks came, and the next instant the consul's wife, just out of the bath, fled by with no other apology for clothing than—a bath towel! The sufferer rose superior to the terrors of the earthquake, and said to his wife:

"Now *that* is something I *like*! Get out your towel, my dear!"

The plastering that fell from ceilings in San Francisco that day, would have covered several acres of ground. For some days afterward, groups of eyeing and pointing men stood about many a building, looking at long zig-zag cracks that extended from the eaves to the ground. Four feet of the tops of three chimneys on one house were broken square off and turned around in such a way as to completely stop the draft. A crack a hundred feet long gaped open six inches wide in the middle of one street and then shut together again with such force, as to ridge up the meeting earth like a slender grave. A lady sitting in her rocking and quaking parlor, saw the wall part at the ceiling, open and shut twice, like a mouth, and then drop the end of a brick on the floor like a tooth. She was a woman easily disgusted with foolishness, and she arose and went out of there. One lady who was coming down stairs was astonished to see a bronze Hercules lean forward on its pedestal as if to strike her with its club. They both reached the bottom of the flight at the same time,—the woman insensible from the fright. Her child, born some little time afterward, was club-footed. However—on second thought,—if the reader sees any coincidence in this, he must do it at his own risk.

The first shock brought down two or three huge organ-pipes in one of the churches. The minister, with uplifted hands, was just closing the services. He glanced up, hesitated, and said:

"However, we will omit the benediction!"—and the next instant there was a vacancy in the atmosphere where he had stood.

After the first shock, an Oakland minister said:

"Keep your seats! There is no better place to die than this"—

And added, after the third:

"But outside is good enough!" He then skipped out at the back door.

Such another destruction of mantel ornaments and toilet bottles as the earthquake created, San Francisco never saw before. There was hardly a girl or a matron in the city but suffered losses of this kind. Suspended pictures were thrown down, but oftener still, by a curious freak of the earthquake's humor, they were whirled completely around with their faces to the wall! There was great difference of opinion, at first, as to the course or direction the earthquake traveled, but water that splashed out of various tanks and buckets settled that. Thousands of people were made so sea-sick by the rolling and pitching of floors and streets that they were weak and bed-ridden for hours, and some few for even days afterward.— Hardly an individual escaped nausea entirely.

The queer earthquake—episodes that formed the staple of San Francisco gossip for the next week would fill a much larger book than this, and so I will diverge from the subject.

By and by, in the due course of things, I picked up a copy of the *Enterprise* one day, and fell under this cruel blow:

> NEVADA MINES IN NEW YORK.—G. M. Marshall, Sheba Hurst and Amos H. Rose, who left San Francisco last July for New York City, with ores from mines in Pine Wood District, Humboldt County, and on the Reese River range, have disposed of a mine containing six thousand feet and called the Pine Mountains Consolidated, for the sum of $3,000,000. The stamps on the deed, which is now on its way to Humboldt County, from New York, for record, amounted to $3,000, which is said to be the largest amount of stamps ever placed on one document. A working capital of $1,000,000 has been paid into the treasury, and machinery has already been purchased for a large quartz mill, which will be put up as soon as possible. The stock in this company is all full paid and entirely unassessable. The ores of the mines in this district somewhat resemble those of the Sheba mine in Humboldt. Sheba Hurst, the discoverer of the mines, with his friends corralled all the best leads and all the land and timber they desired before making public their whereabouts. Ores from there, assayed in this city, showed them to be exceedingly rich in silver and gold—silver predominating. There is an abundance of wood and water in the District. We are glad to know that New York capital has been enlisted in the development of the mines of this region. Having seen the ores and assays, we are satisfied that the mines of the District are very valuable—anything but wild-cat.

Once more native imbecility had carried the day, and I had lost a million! It was the "blind lead" over again.

Let us not dwell on this miserable matter. If I were inventing these things, I could be wonderfully humorous over them; but they are too true to be talked of with hearty levity, even at this distant day.* Suffice it that I so lost heart, and so yielded myself up to repinings and sighings and foolish regrets, that I neglected my duties and became about worthless, as a reporter for a brisk newspaper. And at last one of the proprietors took me aside, with a charity I still remember with

---

* True, and yet not exactly as given in the above figures, possibly. I saw Marshall, months afterward, and although he had plenty of money he did not claim to have captured an entire *million*. In fact I gathered that he had not then received $50,000. Beyond that figure his fortune appeared to consist of uncertain vast expectations rather than prodigious certainties. However, when the above item appeared in print I put full faith in it, and incontinently wilted and went to seed under it.

considerable respect, and gave me an opportunity to resign my berth and so save myself the disgrace of a dismissal.

Chapter LIX

FOR A TIME I wrote literary screeds for the *Golden Era*. C.H. Webb had established a very excellent literary weekly called the *Californian,* but high merit was no guaranty of success; it languished, and he sold out to three printers, and Bret Harte became editor at $20 a week, and I was employed to contribute an article a week at $12. But the journal still languished, and the printers sold out to Captain Ogden, a rich man and a pleasant gentleman who chose to amuse himself with such an expensive luxury without much caring about the cost of it. When he grew tired of the novelty, he re-sold to the printers, the paper presently died a peaceful death, and I was out of work again. I would not mention these things but for the fact that they so aptly illustrate the ups and downs that characterize life on the Pacific coast. A man could hardly stumble into such a variety of queer vicissitudes in any other country.

For two months my sole occupation was avoiding acquaintances; for during that time I did not earn a penny, or buy an article of any kind, or pay my board. I became a very adept at ''slinking.'' I slunk from back street to back street, I slunk away from approaching faces that looked familiar, I slunk to my meals, ate them humbly and with a mute apology for every mouthful I robbed my generous landlady of, and at midnight, after wanderings that were but slinkings away from cheerfulness and light, I slunk to my bed. I felt meaner, and lowlier, and more despicable than the worms. During all this time I had but one piece of money—a silver ten cent piece—and I held to it and would not spend it on any account, lest the consciousness coming strong upon me that I was *entirely* penniless, might suggest suicide. I had pawned every thing but the clothes I had on; so I clung to my dime desperately, till it was smooth with handling.

However, I am forgetting. I did have one other occupation beside that of

SLINKING.

"slinking." It was the entertaining of a collector (and being entertained by him), who had in his hands the Virginia banker's bill for the forty-six dollars which I had loaned my schoolmate, the "Prodigal." This man used to call regularly once a week and dun me, and sometimes oftener. He did it from sheer force of habit, for he knew he could get nothing. He would get out his bill, calculate the interest for me, at five per cent a month, and show me clearly that there was no attempt at fraud in it and no mistakes; and then plead, and argue and dun with all his might for any sum—any little trifle—even a dollar—even half a dollar, on account. Then his duty was accomplished and his conscience free. He immediately dropped the subject there always; got out a couple of cigars and divided, put his feet in the window, and then we would have a long, luxurious talk about everything and everybody, and he would furnish me a world of curious dunning adventures out of the ample store in his memory. By and by he would clap his hat on his head, shake hands and say briskly:

"Well, business is business—can't stay with you always!"—and was off in a second.

The idea of pining for a dun! And yet I used to long for him to come, and would get as uneasy as any mother if the day went by without his visit, when I was expecting him. But he never collected that bill, at last nor any part of it. I lived to pay it to the banker myself.

Misery loves company. Now and then at night, in out-of-the-way, dimly lighted places, I found myself happening on another child of misfortune. He looked so seedy and forlorn, so homeless and friendless and forsaken, that I yearned toward him as a brother. I wanted to claim kinship with him and go about and enjoy our wretchedness together. The drawing toward each other must have been mutual; at any rate we got to falling together oftener, though still seemingly by accident; and although we did not speak or evince any recognition, I think the dull anxiety passed out of both of us when we saw each other, and then for several hours we would idle along contentedly, wide apart, and glancing furtively in at home lights and fireside gatherings, out of the night shadows, and very much enjoying our dumb companionship.

Finally we spoke, and were inseparable after that. For our woes were identical, almost. He had been a reporter too, and lost his berth, and this was his experience, as nearly as I can recollect it. After losing his berth, he had gone down, down, down, with never a halt: from a boarding house on Russian Hill to a boarding house in Kearney street; from thence to Dupont; from thence to a low sailor den; and from thence to lodgings in goods boxes and empty hogsheads near the wharves. Then, for a while, he had gained a meagre living by sewing up bursted sacks of grain on the piers; when that failed he had found food here and there as chance threw it in his way. He had ceased to show his face in daylight, now, for a reporter knows everybody, rich and poor, high and low, and cannot well avoid familiar faces in the broad light of day.

This mendicant Blucher—I call him that for convenience—was a splendid creature. He was full of hope, pluck and philosophy; he was well read and a man of cultivated taste; he had a bright wit and was a master of satire; his kindliness and his generous spirit made him royal in my eyes and changed his curb-stone seat to a throne and his damaged hat to a crown.

He had an adventure, once, which sticks fast in my memory as the most pleasantly grotesque that ever touched my sympathies. He had been without a penny for two months. He had shirked about obscure streets, among friendly dim lights, till the thing had become second nature to him. But at last he was driven abroad in daylight. The cause was sufficient; *he had not tasted food for forty-eight hours,* and he could not endure the misery of his hunger in idle hiding. He came along a back street, glowering at the loaves in bake-shop windows, and feeling that he could trade his life away for a morsel to eat. The sight of the bread doubled his hunger; but it was good to look at it, any how, and imagine what one might do if one only had it. Presently, in the middle of the street he saw a shining spot—looked again—did not, and could not, believe his eyes— turned away, to try them, then looked again. It was a verity—no vain, hunger- inspired delusion—it was a silver dime! He snatched it—gloated over it; doubted it—bit it—found it genuine—choked his heart down, and smothered a hallelujah. Then he looked around—saw that nobody was looking at him—threw the dime down where it was before—walked away a few steps, and approached again, pretending he did not know it was there, so that he could re-enjoy the luxury of finding it. He walked around it, viewing it from different points; then sauntered about with his hands in his pockets, looking up at the signs and now and then glancing at it and feeling the old thrill again. Finally he took it up, and went away, fondling it in his pocket. He idled through unfrequented streets, stopping in doorways and corners to take it out and look at it. By and by he went home to his lodgings—an empty queensware hogshead,—and employed himself till night trying to make up his mind what to buy with it. But it was hard to do. To get the most for it was the idea. He knew that at the Miner's Restaurant he could get a plate of beans and a piece of bread for ten cents; or a fish-ball and some few trifles, but they gave "no bread with one fish-ball" there. At French Pete's he could get a veal cutlet, plain, and some radishes and bread, for ten cents; or a cup of coffee—a pint at least—and a slice of bread; but the slice was not thick enough by the eighth of an inch, and sometimes they were still more criminal than that in the cutting of it. At seven o'clock his hunger was wolfish; and still his mind was not made up. He turned out and went up Merchant street, still ciphering; and chewing a bit of stick, as is the way of starving men. He passed before the lights of Martin's restaurant, the most aristocratic in the city, and stopped. It was a place where he had often dined, in better days, and Martin knew him well. Standing aside, just out of the range of the light, he worshiped the quails and steaks in the show window, and imagined that may be the fairy times were not gone yet and some prince in disguise would come along presently and tell him to go in there and take whatever he wanted. He chewed his stick with a hungry interest as he warmed to his subject. Just at this juncture he was conscious of someone at his side, sure enough; and then a finger touched his arm. He looked up, over his shoulder, and saw an apparition—a very allegory of Hunger! It was a man six feet high, gaunt, unshaven, hung with rags; with a haggard face and sunken cheeks, and eyes that pleaded piteously. This phantom said:

"Come with me—please."

He locked his arm in Blucher's and walked up the street to where the passengers were few and the light not strong, and then facing about, put out his hands in a beseeching way, and said:

"Friend—stranger—look at me! Life is easy to you—you go about, placid and content, as I did once, in my day—you have been in there, and eaten your sumptuous supper, and picked your teeth, and hummed your tune, and thought your pleasant thoughts, and said to yourself it is a good world—but you've never

suffered! You don't know what trouble is—you don't know what misery is—
nor hunger! Look at me! Stranger have pity on a poor friendless, homeless dog!
As God is my judge, I have not tasted food for eight and forty hours!—look in
my eyes and see if I lie! Give me the least trifle in the world to keep me from
starving—anything—twenty-five cents! Do it, stranger—do it, *please*. It will be
nothing to you, but life to me. Do it, and I will go down on my knees and lick
the dust before you! I will kiss your footprints—I will worship the very ground
you walk on! Only twenty-five cents! I am famishing—perishing—starving by
inches! For God's sake don't desert me!''

Blucher was bewildered—and touched, too—stirred to the depths. He reflected.
Thought again. Then an idea struck him, and he said:

"Come with me."

He took the outcast's arm, walked him down to Martin's restaurant, seated
him at a marble table, placed the bill of fare before him, and said:

"Order what you want, friend. Charge it to me, Mr. Martin."

"All right, Mr. Blucher," said Martin.

Then Blucher stepped back and leaned against the counter and watched the
man stow away cargo after cargo of buckwheat cakes at seventy-five cents a
plate; cup after cup of coffee, and porter house steaks worth two dollars apiece;
and when six dollars and a half's worth of destruction had been accomplished,
and the stranger's hunger appeased, Blucher went down to French Pete's, bought
a veal cutlet plain, a slice of bread, and three radishes, with his dime, and set
to and feasted like a king!

Take the episode all around, it was as odd as any that can be culled from the
myriad curiosities of Californian life, perhaps.

Chapter LX

BY AND BY, an old friend of mine, a miner, came down from one of the decayed
mining camps of Tuolumne, California, and I went back with him. We lived in
a small cabin on a verdant hillside, and there were not five other cabins in view
over the wide expanse of hill and forest. Yet a flourishing city of two or three
thousand population had occupied this grassy dead solitude during the flush times
of twelve or fifteen years before, and where our cabin stood had once been the
heart of the teeming hive, the center of the city. When the mines gave out the
town fell into decay, and in a few years wholly disappeared—streets, dwellings,
shops, eveything—and left no sign. The grassy slopes were as green and smooth
and desolate of life as if they had never been disturbed. The mere handful of
miners still remaining, had seen the town spring up, spread, grow and flourish
in its pride; and they had seen it sicken and die, and pass away like a dream.
With it their hopes had died, and their zest of life. They had long ago resigned
themselves to their exile, and ceased to correspond with their distant friends or
turn longing eyes toward their early homes. They had accepted banishment,
forgotten the world and been forgotten of the world. They were far from telegraphs
and railroads, and they stood, as it were, in a living grave, dead to the events
that stirred the globe's great populations, dead to the common interests of men,
isolated and outcast from brotherhood with their kind. It was the most singular,

and almost the most touching and melancholy exile that fancy can imagine.—
One of my associates in this locality, for two or three months, was a man who
had had a university education; but now for eighteen years he had decayed there
by inches, a bearded, rough-clad, clay-stained miner, and at times, among his
sighings and soliloquizings, he unconsciously interjected vaguely remembered
Latin and Greek sentences—dead and musty tongues, meet vehicles for the
thoughts of one whose dreams were all of the past, whose life was a failure; a
tired man, burdened with the present, and indifferent to the future; a man without
ties, hopes, interests, waiting for rest and the end.

In that one little corner of California is found a species of mining which is
seldom or never mentioned in print. It is called "pocket mining" and I am not
aware that any of it is done outside of that little corner. The gold is not evenly
distributed through the surface dirt, as in ordinary placer mines, but is collected
in little spots, and they are very wide apart and exceedingly hard to find, but
when you do find one you reap a rich and sudden harvest. There are not now
more than twenty pocket miners in that entire little region. I think I know every
one of them personally. I have known one of them to hunt patiently about the
hill-sides every day for eight months without finding gold enough to make a
snuff-box—his grocery bill running up relentlessly all the time—and then find
a pocket and take out of it two thousand dollars in two dips of his shovel. I have
known him to take out three thousand dollars in two hours, and go and pay up
every cent of his indebtedness, then enter on a dazzling spree that finished the
last of his treasure before the night was gone. And the next day he bought his
groceries on credit as usual, and shouldered his pan and shovel and went off to
the hills hunting pockets again happy and content. This is the most fascinating
of all the different kinds of mining, and furnishes a very handsome percentage
of victims to the lunatic asylum.

Pocket hunting is an ingenious process. You take a spadeful of earth from the
hill-side and put it in a large tin pan and dissolve and wash it gradually away
till nothing is left but a teaspoonful of fine sediment. Whatever gold was in that
earth has remained, because, being the heaviest, it has sought the bottom. Among
the sediment you will find half a dozen yellow particles no larger than pin-heads.
You are delighted. You move off to one side and wash another pan. If you find
gold again, you move to one side further, and wash a third pan. If you find *no*
gold this time, you are delighted again, because you know you are on the right
scent. You lay an imaginary plan, shaped like a fan, with its handle up the hill—
for just where the end of the handle is, you argue that the rich deposit lies hidden,
whose vagrant grains of gold have escaped and been washed down the hill,
spreading farther and farther apart as they wandered. And so you proceed up
the hill, washing the earth and narrowing your lines every time the absence of
gold in the pan shows that you are outside the spread of the fan; and at last,
twenty yards up the hill your lines have converged to a point—a single foot from
that point you cannot find any gold. Your breath comes short and quick, you
are feverish with excitement; the dinner bell may ring its clapper off, you pay
no attention; friends may die, weddings transpire, houses burn down, they are
nothing to you; you sweat and dig and delve with a frantic interest—and all at
once you strike it! Up comes a spadeful of earth and quartz that is all lovely
with soiled lumps and leaves and sprays of gold. Sometimes that one spadeful
is all—$500. Sometimes the nest contains $10,000, and it takes you three or
four days to get it all out. The pocket-miners tell of one nest that yielded $60,000

and two men exhausted it in two weeks, and then sold the ground for $10,000 to a party who never got $300 out of it afterward.

The hogs are good pocket hunters. All the summer they root around the bushes, and turn up a thousand little piles of dirt, and then the miners long for the rains; for the rains beat upon these little piles and wash them down and expose the gold, possibly right over a pocket. Two pockets were found in this way by the same man in one day. One had $5,000 in it and the other $8,000. That man could appreciate it, for he hadn't had a cent for about a year.

In Tuolumne lived two miners who used to go to the neighboring village in the afternoon and return every night with household supplies. Part of the distance they traversed a trail, and nearly always sat down to rest on a great boulder that lay beside the path. In the course of thirteen years they had worn that boulder tolerably smooth, sitting on it. By and by two vagrant Mexicans came along and occupied the seat. They began to amuse themselves by chipping off flakes from the boulder with a sledge-hammer. They examined one of these flakes and found it rich with gold. That boulder paid them $800 afterward. But the aggravating circumstance was that these "Greasers" knew that there must be more gold where that boulder came from, and so they went panning up the hill and found what was probably the richest pocket that region has yet produced. It took three months to exhaust it, and it yielded $120,000. The two American miners who used to sit on the boulder are poor yet, and they take turn about in getting up early in the morning to curse those Mexicans—and when it comes down to pure ornamental cursing, the native American is gifted above the sons of men.

I have dwelt at some length upon this matter of pocket mining because it is a subject that is seldom referred to in print, and therefore I judged that it would have for the reader that interest which naturally attaches to novelty.

Chapter LXI

ONE OF MY comrades there—another of those victims of eighteen years of unrequited toil and blighted hopes—was one of the gentlest spirits that ever bore its patient cross in a weary exile: grave and simple Dick Baker, pocket-miner of Dead-House Gulch.—He was forty-six, gray as a rat, earnest, thoughtful, slenderly educated, slouchily dressed and clay-soiled, but his heart was finer metal than any gold his shovel ever brought to light—than any, indeed, that ever was mined or minted.

Whenever he was out of luck and a little down-hearted, he would fall to mourning over the loss of a wonderful cat he used to own (for where women and children are not, men of kindly impulses take up with pets, for they must love something). And he always spoke of the strange sagacity of that cat with the air of a man who believed in his secret heart that there was something human about it—may be even supernatural.

I heard him talking about this animal once. He said:

"Gentlemen, I used to have a cat here, by the name of Tom Quartz, which you'd a took an interest in I reckon—most any body would. I had him here eight year—and he was the remarkablest cat *I* ever see. He was a large gray one of the Tom specie, an' he had more hard, natchral sense than any man in the camp—'n' a *power* of dignity—he wouldn't let the Gov'ner of Californy be familiar with him. He never ketched a rat in his life—'peared to be above it. He never cared for nothing but mining. He knowed more about mining, that cat did, than any man *I* ever, ever see. You couldn't tell *him* noth'n' 'bout placer diggin's—'n' as for pocket mining, why he was just born for it. He would dig out after me an' Jim when we went over the hills prospect'n', and he would trot along behind us for as much as five mile, if we went so fur. An' he had the best judgment about mining ground—why you never see anything like it. When we went to work, he'd scatter a glance around, 'n' if he didn't think much of the indications, he would give a look as much as to say, 'Well, I'll have to get you to excuse *me*,' 'n' without another word he'd hyste his nose into the air 'n' shove for home. But if the ground suited him, he would lay low 'n' keep dark till the first pan was washed, 'n' then he would sidle up 'n' take a look, an' if there was about six or seven grains of gold *he* was satisfied—he didn't want no better prospect 'n' that—'n' then he would lay down on our coats and snore like a steamboat till we'd struck the pocket, an' then get up 'n' superintend. He was nearly lightnin' on superintending.

"Well, bye an' bye, up comes this yer quartz excitement. Every body was into it—every body was pick'n' 'n' blast'n' instead of shovelin' dirt on the hill side—every body was put'n' down a shaft instead of scrapin' the surface. Noth'n' would do Jim, but *we* must tackle the ledges, too, 'n' so we did. We commenced put'n' down a shaft, 'n' Tom Quartz he begin to wonder what in the Dickens it was all about. *He* hadn't ever seen any mining like that before, 'n' he was all upset, as you may say—he couldn't come to a right understanding of it no way— it was too many for *him*. He was down on it, too, you bet you—he was down on it powerful—'n' always appeared to consider it the cussedest foolishness out. But that cat, you know, was *always* agin new fangled arrangements—somehow he never could abide 'em. *You* know how it is with old habits. But by an' by Tom Quartz begin to git sort of reconciled a little, though he never *could* altogether understand that eternal sinkin' of a shaft an' never pannin' out anyhing. At last he got to comin' down in the shaft, hisself, to try to cipher it out. An' when he'd git the blues, 'n' feel kind o' scruffy, 'n' aggravated 'n' disgusted— knowin' as he did, that the bills was runnin' up all the time an' we warn't makin' a cent—he would curl up on a gunny sack in the corner an' go to sleep. Well, one day when the shaft was down about eight foot, the rock got so hard that we had to put in a blast—the first blast'n' we'd ever done since Tom Quartz was born. An' then we lit the fuse 'n' clumb out 'n' got off 'bout fifty yards—'n' forgot 'n' left Tom Quartz sound asleep on the gunny sack. In 'bout a minute we seen a puff of smoke bust up out of the hole, 'n' then everything let go with an awful crash, 'n' about four million ton of rocks 'n' dirt 'n' smoke 'n' splinters shot up 'bout a mile an' a half into the air, an' by George, right in the dead centre of it was old Tom Quartz a goin' end over end, an' a snortin' an' a sneez'n', an' a clawin' an' a reachin' for things like all possessed. But it warn't no use, you know, it warn't no use. An' that was the last we see of *him* for about two minutes 'n' a half, an' then all of a sudden it begin to rain rocks and rubbage, an' directly he come down ker-whop about ten foot off f'm where we stood. Well, I reckon he was p'raps the orneriest lookin' beast you ever see. One ear was sot back on his neck, 'n' his tail was stove up, 'n' his eye-winkers was swinged off, 'n' he was all blacked up with powder an' smoke, an' all sloppy with mud 'n' slush f'm one end to the other. Well sir, it warn't no use to try to apologize—we couldn't say a word. He took a sort of a disgusted look at hisself, 'n' then he looked at us—an' it was just exactly the same as if he had said—'Gents, may be *you* think it's smart to take advantage of a cat that 'ain't had no experience of quartz minin', but *I* think *different*'—an' then he turned on his heel 'n' marched off home without ever saying another word.

"That was jest his style. An' maybe you won't believe it, but after that you never see a cat so prejudiced agin quartz mining as what he was. An' by an' bye when he *did* get to goin' down in the shaft agin, you'd 'a been astonished at his sagacity. The minute we'd tetch off a blast 'n' the fuse'd begin to sizzle, he'd give a look as much as to say: 'Well, I'll have to git you to excuse *me*,' an' it was surpris'n' the way he'd shin out of that hole 'n' go f'r a tree. Sagacity? It ain't no name for it. 'Twas *inspiration*!"

I said, "Well, Mr. Baker, his prejudice against quartz-mining *was* remarkable, considering how he came by it. Couldn't you ever cure him of it?"

"*Cure him!* No! When Tom Quartz was sot once, he was *always* sot—and you might a blowed him up as much as three million times 'n' you'd never a broken him of his cussed prejudice agin quartz mining."

The affection and the pride that lit up Baker's face when he delivered this tribute to the firmness of his humble friend of other days, will always be a vivid memory with me.

At the end of two months we had never "struck" a pocket. We had panned up and down the hillsides till they looked plowed like a field; we could have put in a crop of grain, then, but there would have been no way to get it to market. We got many good "prospects," but when the gold gave out in the pan and we dug down, hoping and longing, we found only emptiness—the pocket that should have been there was as barren as our own.—At last we shouldered our pans and shovels and struck out over the hills to try new localities. We prospected around Angel's Camp, in Calaveras county, during three weeks, but had no success. Then we wandered on foot among the mountains, sleeping under the trees at night, for the weather was mild, but still we remained as centless as the last rose of summer. That is a poor joke, but it is in pathetic harmony with the circumstances, since we were so poor ourselves. In accordance with the custom of the country, our door had always stood open and our board welcome to tramping miners—they drifted along nearly every day, dumped their paust shovels by the threshold and took "pot luck" with us—and now on our own tramp we never found cold hospitality.

Our wanderings were wide and in many directions; and now I could give the reader a vivid description of the Big Trees and the marvels of the Yo Semite—

Some of the phrases in the above are mining technicalities, purely, and may be a little obscure to the general reader. In *"placer diggings"* the gold is scattered all through the surface dirt; in *"pocket"* diggings it is concentrated in one little spot; in *"quartz"* the gold is in a solid, continuous vein of rock, enclosed between distinct walls of some other kind of stone—and this is the most laborious and expensive of all the different kinds of mining. *"Prospecting"* is hunting for a *"placer"*; *"indications"* are signs of its presence; *"panning out"* refers to the washing process by which the grains of gold are separated from the dirt; a *"prospect"* is what one finds in the first panful of dirt—and its value determines whether it is a good or a bad prospect, and whether it is worth while to tarry there or seek further.

but what has this reader done to me that I should persecute him? I will deliver him into the hands of less conscientious tourists and take his blessing. Let me be charitable, though I fail in all virtues else.

Chapter LXII

AFTER A THREE months' absence, I found myself in San Francisco again, without a cent. When my credit was about exhausted (for I had become too mean and lazy, now, to work on a morning paper, and there were no vacancies on the evening journals), I was created San Francisco correspondent of the *Enterprise,* and at the end of five months I was out of debt, but my interest in my work was gone; for my correspondence being a daily one, without rest or respite, I got unspeakably tired of it. I wanted another change. The vagabond instinct was strong upon me. Fortune favored and I got a new berth and a delightful one. It was to go down to the Sandwich Islands and write some letters for the Sacramento *Union,* an excellent journal and liberal with employés.

We sailed in the propeller *Ajax,* in the middle of winter. The almanac called it winter, distinctly enough, but the weather was a compromise between spring and summer. Six days out of port, it became summer altogether. We had some thirty passengers; among them a cheerful soul by the name of Williams, and three sea-worn old whaleship captains going down to join their vessels. These latter played euchre in the smoking room day and night, drank astonishing quantities of raw whiskey without being in the least affected by it, and were the happiest people I think I ever saw. And then there was "the old Admiral"—a retired whaleman. He was a roaring, terrific combination of wind and lightning and thunder, and earnest, whole-souled profanity. But nevertheless he was tenderhearted as a girl. He was a raving, deafening, devastating typhoon, laying waste the cowering seas but with an unvexed refuge in the centre where all comers were safe and at rest. Nobody could know the "Admiral" without liking him; and in a sudden and dire emergency I think no friend of his would know which to choose—to be cursed by him or prayed for by a less efficient person.

His title of "Admiral" was more strictly "official" than any ever worn by a naval officer before or since, perhaps—for it was the voluntary offering of a whole nation, and came direct from the *people* themselves without any intermediate red tape—the people of the Sandwich Islands. It was a title that came to him freighted with affection, and honor, and appreciation of his unpretending merit. And in testimony of the genuineness of the title it was publicly ordained that an exclusive flag should be devised for him and used solely to welcome his coming and wave him God-speed in his going. From that time forth, whenever his ship was signaled in the offing, or he catted his anchor and stood out to sea, that ensign streamed from the royal halliards on the parliament house and the nation lifted their hats to it with spontaneous accord.

Yet he had never fired a gun or fought a battle in his life. When I knew him on board the *Ajax,* he was seventy-two years old and had plowed the salt water sixty-one of them. For sixteen years he had gone in and out of the harbor of Honolulu in command of a whaleship, and for sixteen more had been captain of a San Francisco and Sandwich Island passenger packet and had never had an accident or lost a vessel. The simple natives knew him for a friend who never failed them, and regarded him as children regard a father. It was a dangerous thing to oppress them when the roaring Admiral was around.

Two years before I knew the Admiral, he had retired from the sea on a competence, and had sworn a colossal nine-jointed oath that he would "never go within *smelling* distance of the salt water again as long as he lived." And he had conscientiously kept it. That is to say, *he* considered he had kept it, and it would have been more than dangerous to suggest to him, even in the gentlest way, that making eleven long sea voyages, as a passenger, during the two years that had transpired since he "retired," was only keeping the general spirit of it and not the strict letter.

The Admiral knew only one narrow line of conduct to pursue in any and all cases where there was a fight, and that was to shoulder his way straight in without an inquiry as to the rights or the merits of it, and take the part of the weaker side. And this was the reason why he was always sure to be present at the trial of any universally execrated criminal to oppress and intimidate the jury with a vindictive pantomime of what he would do to them if he ever caught them out of the box. And this was why harried cats and outlawed dogs that knew him confidently took sanctuary under his chair in time of trouble. In the beginning he was the most frantic and bloodthirsty Union man that drew breath in the shadow of the flag; but the instant the Southerners began to go down before the sweep of the Northern armies, he ran up the Confederate colors and from that time till the end was a rampant and inexorable secessionist.

He hated intemperance with a more uncompromising animosity than any individual I have ever met, of either sex; and he was never tired of storming against it and beseeching friends and strangers alike to be wary and drink with moderation. And yet if any creature had been guileless enough to intimate that his absorbing nine gallons of "straight" whiskey during our voyage was any fraction short of rigid or inflexible abstemiousness, in that self-same moment the old man would have spun him to the uttermost parts of the earth in the whirlwind of his wrath. Mind, I am not saying his whisky ever affected his head or his legs, for it did not, in even the slightest degree. He was a capacious container, but he did not hold enough for that. He took a level tumblerful of whisky every morning before he put his clothes on—"to sweeten his bilgewater," he said.—He took another after he got the most of his clothes on, "to settle his mind and give him his bearings." He then shaved and put on a clean shirt, after which he recited the Lord's Prayer in a fervent, thundering bass that shook the ship to her kelson and suspended all conversation in the main cabin. Then, at this stage, being invariably "by the head," or "by the stern," or "listed to port or starboard," he took one more to "put him on an even keel so that he would mind his hellum and not miss stays and go about, every time he came up in the wind." —And now, his state-room door swung open and the sun of his benignant face beamed redly out upon men and women and children, and he roared his "Shipmets a'hoy!" in a way that was calculated to wake the dead and precipitate the final resurrection; and forth he strode, a picture to look at and a presence to enforce attention. Stalwart and portly; not a gray hair; broad-brimmed slouch hat; semi-sailor toggery of blue navy flannel—roomy and ample; a stately expanse of shirt-front and a liberal amount of black silk neck-cloth tied with a sailor knot; large chain and imposing seals impending from his fob; awe-inspiring feet, and "a hand like the hand of Providence," as his whaling brethren expressed it; wrist-bands and sleeves pushed back half way to the elbow, out of respect for the warm weather, and exposing hairy arms, gaudy with red and blue anchors, ships, and goddesses of liberty tattooed in India ink. But these details were only secondary matters—his face was the lodestone that chained the eye. It was a sultry disk, glowing determinedly out through a weather beaten mask of mahogany, and studded with warts, seamed with scars, "blazed" all over with unfailing fresh slips of the razor; and with cheery eyes, under shaggy brows, contemplating the world from over the back of a gnarled crag of a nose that loomed vast and lonely out of the undulating immensity that spread away from its foundations. At his heels frisked the darling of his bachelor estate, his terrier "Fan," a creature no larger than a squirrel. The main part of his daily life was occupied in looking after "Fan," in a motherly way, and doctoring her for a hundred ailments which existed only in his imagination.

The Admiral seldom read newspapers; and when he did he never believed anything they said. He read nothing, and believed in nothing, but "The Old Guard," a secession periodical published in New York. He carried a dozen copies of it with him, always, and referred to them for all required information. If it was not there, he supplied it himself out of a bountiful fancy, inventing history, names, dates, and everything else necessary to make his point good in an argument. Consequently he was a formidable antagonist in a dispute. Whenever he swung clear of the record and began to create history, the enemy was helpless and had to surrender. Indeed, the enemy could not keep from betraying some little spark of indignation at his manufactured history—and when it came to indignation, that was the Admiral's very "best hold." He was always ready for a political argument, and if nobody started one he would do it himself. With his third retort his temper would begin to rise, and within five minutes he would be blowing a gale, and within fifteen his smoking-room audience would be utterly stormed away and the old man left solitary and alone, banging the table with his fist, kicking the chairs, and roaring a hurricane of profanity. It got so, after a while, that whenever the Admiral approached, with politics in his eye, the passengers would drop out with quiet accord, afraid to meet him; and he would camp on a deserted field.

But he found his match at last, and before a full company. At one time or another, everybody had entered the lists against him and been routed, except the quiet passenger Williams. He had never been able to get an expression of opinion out of him on politics. But now, just as the Admiral drew near the door and the company were about to slip out, Williams said:

"Admiral, are you *certain* about that circumstance concerning the clergymen you mentioned the other day?"—referring to a piece of the Admiral's manufactured history.

Every one was amazed at the man's rashness. The idea of deliberately inviting annihilation was a thing incomprehensible. The retreat came to a halt; then everybody sat down again wondering, to await the upshot of it. The Admiral himself was as surprised as any one. He paused in the door, with his red handkerchief half raised to his sweating face, and contemplated the daring reptile in the corner.

"*Certain* of it? Am I *certain* of it? Do you think I've been lying about it? What do you take me for? Anybody that don't know the circumstance, don't know anything; a child ought to know it. Read up your history! Read it up—

——————— —————— ————, and don't come asking a man if he's *certain* about
a bit of A B C stuff that the very Southern niggers know all about.''

Here the Admiral's fires began to wax hot, the atmosphere thickened, the
coming earthquake rumbled, he began to thunder and lighten. Within three
minutes his voice was in full irruption and he was discharging flames and ashes
of indignation, belching black volumes of foul history aloft, and vomiting red-
hot torrents of profanity from his crater. Meantime Williams sat silent, and
apparently deeply and earnestly interested in what the old man was saying. By
and by, when the lull came, he said in the most deferential way, and with the
gratified air of a man who has had a mystery cleared up which had been puzzling
him uncomfortably:

"*Now* I understand it. I always thought I knew that piece of history well
enough, but was still afraid to trust it, because there was not that convincing
particularity about it that one likes to have in history; but when you mentioned
every name, the other day, and every date, and every little circumstance, in their
just order and sequence, I said to myself, *this* sounds something like—*this* is
history—*this* is putting it in a shape that gives a man confidence; and I said to
myself afterward, I will just ask the Admiral if he is perfectly certain about the
details, and if he is I will come out and thank him for clearing this matter up
for me. And that is what I want to do now—for until you set that matter right
it was nothing but just a confusion in my mind, without head or tail to it.''

Nobody ever saw the Admiral look so mollified before, and so pleased. Nobody
had ever received his bogus history as gospel before; its genuineness had always
been called in question either by words or looks; but here was a man that not
only swallowed it all down, but was grateful for the dose. He was taken a back;
he hardly knew what to say; even his profanity failed him. Now, Williams
continued, modestly and earnestly:

"But Admiral, in saying that this was the first stone thrown, and that this
precipitated the war, you have overlooked a circumstance which you are perfectly
familiar with, but which has escaped your memory. Now I grant you that what
you have stated is correct in every detail—to wit: that on the 16th of October,
1860, two Massachusetts clergymen, named Waite and Granger, went in disguise
to the house of John Moody, in Rockport, at dead of night, and dragged forth
two southern women and their two little children, and after tarring and feathering
them conveyed them to Boston and burned them alive in the State House square;
and I also grant your proposition that this deed is what led to the secession of
South Carolina on the 20th of December following. Very well." [Here the
company were pleasantly surprised to hear Williams proceed to come back at
the Admiral with his own invincible weapon—clean, pure, *manufactured history,*
without a word of truth in it.] "Very well, I say. But Admiral, why overlook
the Willis and Morgan case in South Carolina? You are too well informed a
man not to know all about that circumstance. Your arguments and your conversations
have shown you to be intimately conversant with every detail of this national
quarrel. You develop matters of history every day that show plainly that you
are no smatterer in it, content to nibble about the surface, but a man who has
searched the depths and possessed yourself of everything that has a bearing upon
the great question. Therefore, let me just recall to your mind that Willis and
Morgan case—though I see by your face that the whole thing is already passing
through your memory at this moment. On the 12th of August, 1860, *two months*
before the Waite and Granger affair, two South Carolina clergymen, named John

H. Morgan and Winthrop L. Willis, one a Methodist and the other an Old School
Baptist, disguised themselves, and went at midnight to the house of a planter
named Thompson—Archibald F. Thompson, Vice President under Thomas Jefferson—and took thence, at midnight, his widowed aunt (a Northern woman),
and her adopted child, an orphan named Mortimer Highie, affiicted with epilepsy
and suffering at the time from white swelling on one of his legs, and compelled
to walk on crutches in consequence; and the two ministers, in spite of the
pleadings of the victims, dragged them to the bush, tarred and feathered them,
and afterward burned them at the stake in the city of Charleston. You remember
perfectly well what a stir it made; you remember perfectly well that even the
Charleston *Courier* stigmatized the act as being unpleasant, of questionable
propriety, and scarcely justifiable, and likewise that it would not be matter of
surprise if retaliation ensued. And you remember also that this thing was the
cause of the Massachusetts outrage. Who, indeed, were the two Massachusetts
ministers? and who were the two Southern women they burned? I do not need
to remind *you*, Admiral, with your intimate knowledge of history, that Waite
was the nephew of the woman burned in Charleston; that Granger was her cousin
in the second degree, and that the woman they burned in Boston was the wife
of John H. Morgan, and the still loved but divorced wife of Winthrop L. Willis.
Now, Admiral, it is only fair that you should acknowledge that the first provocation
came from the Southern preachers and that the Northern ones were justified in
retaliating. In your arguments you never yet have shown the least disposition to
withhold a just verdict or be in anywise unfair, when authoritative history condemned
your position, and therefore I have no hesitation in asking you to take the original
blame from the Massachusetts ministers, in this matter, and transfer it to the
South Carolina clergymen where it justly belongs.''

The Admiral was conquered. This sweet spoken creature who swallowed his
fraudulent history as if it were the bread of life; basked in his furious blasphemy
as if it were generous sunshine; found only calm, even-handed justice in his
rampart partisanship; and flooded him with invented history so sugar-coated with
flattery and deference that there was no rejecting it, was "too many" for him.
He stammered some awkward, profane sentences about the———— —— —— Willis
and Morgan business having escaped his memory, but that he "remembered it
now," and then, under pretense of giving Fan some medicine for an imaginary
cough, drew out of the battle and went away, a vanquished man. Then cheers
and laughter went up, and Williams, the ship's benefactor, was a hero. The
news went about the vessel, champagne was ordered, an enthusiastic reception
instituted in the smoking room, and everybody flocked thither to shake hands
with the conqueror. The wheelsman said afterward that the Admiral stood up
behind the pilot house and "ripped and cursed all to himself" till he loosened
the smokestack guys and becalmed the mainsail.

The Admiral's power was broken. After that, if he began an argument, somebody
would bring Williams, and the old man would grow weak and begin to quiet
down at once. And as soon as he was done, Williams, in his dulcet, insinuating
way, would invent some history (referring for proofs to the old man's own
excellent memory and to copies of "The Old Guard" known not to be in his
possession) that would turn the tables completely and leave the Admiral all
abroad and helpless. By and by he came to so dread Williams and his gilded
tongue that he would stop talking when he saw him approach, and finally ceased
to mention politics altogether, and from that time forward there was entire peace
and serenity in the ship.

Chapter LXIII

ON A CERTAIN bright morning the Islands hove in sight, lying low on the lonely sea, and everybody climbed to the upper deck to look. After two thousand miles of watery solitude the vision was a welcome one. As we approached, the imposing promontory of Diamond Head rose up out of the ocean, its rugged front softened by the hazy distance, and presently the details of the land began to make themselves manifest: first the line of beach; then the plumed coacoanut trees of the tropics; then cabins of the natives; then the white town of Honolulu, said to contain between twelve and fifteen thousand inhabitants spread over a dead level; with streets from twenty to thirty feet wide, solid and level as a floor, most of them straight as a line and few as crooked as a corkscrew.

The further I traveled through the town the better I liked it. Every step revealed a new contrast—disclosed something I was unaccustomed to. In place of the grand mud-colored brown fronts of San Francisco, I saw dwellings built of straw, adobes, and cream-colored pebble-and-shell-conglomerated coral, cut into oblong blocks and laid in cement; also a great number of neat white cottages, with green window shutters; in place of front yards like billiard-tables with iron fences around them, I saw these homes surrounded by ample yards, thickly clad with green grass, and shaded by tall trees, through whose dense foliage the sun could scarcely penetrate; in place of the customary geranium, calla lily, etc., languishing in dust and general debility, I saw luxurious banks and thickets of flowers, fresh as a meadow after a rain, and glowing with the richest dyes; in place of the dingy horrors of San Francisco's pleasure grove, the "Willows," I saw huge-bodied, wide-spreading forest trees, with strange names and stranger appearance—trees that cast a shadow like a thundercloud, and were able to stand alone without being tied to green poles; in place of gold fish, wiggling around in glass globes, assuming countless shades and degrees of distortion through the magnifying and diminishing qualities of their transparent prison houses, I saw cats—Tomcats, Mary Ann cats, long-tailed cats, bob-tailed cats, blind cats, one-eyed cats, wall-

SCENES ON THE ISLANDS.

eyed cats, cross-eyed cats, gray cats, black cats, white cats, yellow cats, striped cats, spotted cats, tame cats, wild cats, singed cats, individual cats, groups of cats, platoons of cats, companies of cats, regiments of cats, armies of cats, multitudes of cats, millions of cats, and all of them sleek, fat, lazy, and sound asleep.

I looked on a multitude of people, some white, in white coats, vests, pantaloons, even white cloth shoes, made snowy with chalk duly laid on every morning; but the majority of the people were almost as dark as Negroes—women with comely features, fine black eyes, rounded forms, inclining to the voluptuous, clad in a single bright red or white garment that fell free and unconfined from shoulder to heel, long black hair falling loose, gypsy hats, encircled with wreaths of natural flowers of a brilliant carmine tint; plenty of dark men in various costumes, and some with nothing on but a battered stove-pipe hat tilted on the nose, and a very scant breech-clout; certain smoke-dried children were clothed in nothing but sunshine—a very neat fitting and picturesque apparel indeed.

In place of roughs and rowdies staring and blackguarding on the corners, I saw long-haired, saddle-colored Sandwich Island maidens sitting on the ground

FASHIONABLE ATTIRE.

in the shade of corner houses, gazing indolently at whatever or whoever happened along; instead of wretched cobble-stone pavements, I walked on a firm foundation of coral, built up from the bottom of the sea by the absurd but persevering insect of that name, with a light layer of lava and cinders overlying the coral, belched up out of fathomless perdition long ago through the seared and blackened crater that stands dead and harmless in the distance now; instead of cramped and crowded street-cars, I met dusky native women sweeping by, free as the wind, on fleet horses and astride, with gaudy riding-sashes streaming like banners behind them; instead of the combined stenches of Chinadom and Brannan street slaughter-houses, I breathed the balmy fragrance of jessamine, oleander, and the Pride of India; in place of the hurry and bustle and noisy confusion of San Francisco, I moved in the midst of a Summer calm as tranquil as dawn in the Garden of Eden; in place of the Golden City's skirting sand hills and the placid bay, I saw on the one side a frame-work of tall, precipitous mountains close at hand, clad in refreshing green, and cleft by deep, cool, chasm-like valleys— and in front the grand sweep of the ocean: a brilliant, transparent green near the shore, bound and bordered by a long white line of foamy spray dashing against the reef, and further out the dead blue water of the deep sea, flecked with "white caps," and in the far horizon a single, lonely sail—a mere accent-mark to emphasize a slumberous calm and a solitude that were without sound or limit. When the sun sunk down—the one intruder from other realms and persistent in suggestions of them—it was tranced luxury to sit in the perfumed air and forget that there was any world but these enchanted islands.

It was such ecstasy to dream, and dream—till you got a bite. A scorpion bite. Then the first duty was to get up out of the grass and kill the scorpion; and the next to bathe the bitten place with alcohol or brandy; and the next to resolve to keep out of the grass in future. Then came an adjournment to the bedchamber and the pastime of writing up the day's journal with one hand and the destruction of mosquitoes with the other—a whole community of them at a slap. Then, observing an enemy approaching—a hairy tarantula on stilts—why not set the spittoon on him? It is done, and the projecting ends of his paws give a luminous idea of the magnitude of his reach. Then to bed and become a promenade for a centipede with forty-two legs on a side and every foot hot enough to burn a hole though a raw-hide. More soaking with alcohol, and a resolution to examine the bed before entering it, in future. Then wait, and suffer, till all the mosquitoes in the neighborhood have crawled in under the bar, then slip out quickly, shut them in, and sleep peacefully on the floor till morning. Meantime it is comforting to curse the tropics in occasional wakeful intervals.

We had an abundance of fruit in Honolulu, of course. Oranges, pine-apples, bananas, strawberries, lemons, limes, mangoes, guavas, melons, and a rare and curious luxury called the chirimoya, which is deliciousness itself. Then there is the tamarind. I thought tamarinds were made to eat, but that was probably not the idea. I ate several, and it seemed to me that they were rather sour that year. They pursed up my lips, till they resembled the stem-end of a tomato, and I had to take my sustenance through a quill for twenty-four hours. They sharpened my teeth till I could have shaved with them, and gave them a "wire edge" that I was afraid would stay; but a citizen said, "no, it will come off when the enamel does"—which was comforting, at any rate. I found, afterward, that only strangers eat tamarinds—but they only eat them once.

Chapter LXIV

IN MY DIARY of our third day in Honolulu, I find this: I am probably the most sensitive man in Hawaii to-night—especially about sitting down in the presence of my betters. I have ridden fifteen or twenty miles on horse-back since 5 P.M. and to tell the honest truth, I have a delicacy about sitting down at all.

An excursion to Diamond Head and the King's Coacoanut Grove was planned to-day—time, 4:30 P.M.—the party to consist of half a dozen gentlemen and three ladies. They all started at the appointed hour except myself. I was at the Government prison (with Captain Fish and another whaleship-skipper, Captain Phillips), and got so interested in its examination that I did not notice how quickly the time was passing. Somebody remarked that it was twenty minutes past five o'clock, and that woke me up. It was a fortunate circumstance that

Captain Phillips was along with his "turnout," as he calls a top-buggy that
Captain Cook brought here in 1778, and a horse that was here when Captain
Cook came. Captain Phillips takes a just pride in his driving and in the speed
of his horse, and to his passion for displaying them I owe it that we were only
sixteen minutes coming from the prison to the American Hotel—a distance which
has been estimated to be over half a mile. But it took some fearful driving. The
Captain's whip came down fast, and the blows started so much dust out of the
horse's hide that during the last half of the journey we rode through an impenetrable
fog, and ran by a pocket compass in the hands of Captain Fish, a whaler of
twenty-six years experience, who sat there through the perilous voyage as self-
possessed as if he had been on the euchre-deck of his own ship, and calmly
sald, "Port your helm—port," from time to time, and "Hold her a little free—
steady—so-o," and "Luff—hard down to starboard!" and never once lost his
presence of mind or betrayed the least anxiety by voice or manner. When we
came to anchor at last, and Captain Phillips looked at his watch and said, "Sixteen
minutes—I told you it was in her! that's over three miles an hour!" I could see
he felt entitled to a compliment, and so I said I had never seen lightning go like
that horse. And I never had.

The landlord of the American said the party had been gone nearly an hour,
but that he could give me my choice of several horses that could overtake them.
I said, never mind—I preferred a safe horse to a fast one—I would like to have
an excessively gentle horse—a horse with no spirit whatever—a lame one, if he
had such a thing. Inside of five minutes I was mounted, and perfectly satisfied
with my outfit. I had no time to label him 'This is a horse," and so if the public
took him for a sheep I cannot help it. I was satisfied, and that was the main
thing. I could see that he had as many fine points as any man's horse, and so I
hung my hat on one of them, behind the saddle, and swabbed the perspiration
from my face and started. I named him after this island, "Oahu" (pronounced
O-waw-hee). The first gate he came to he started in; I had neither whip nor spur,
and so I simply argued the case with him. He resisted argument, but ultimately
yielded to insult and abuse. He backed out of that gate and steered for another
one on the other side of the street. I triumphed by my former process. Within
the next six hundred yards he crossed the street fourteen times and attempted
thirteen gates, and in the meantime the tropical sun was beating down and
threatening to cave the top of my head in, and I was literally dripping with
perspiration. He abandoned the gate business after that and went along peaceably
enough, but absorbed in meditation. I noticed this latter circumstance, and it
soon began to fill me with apprehension. I said to myself, this creature is planning
some new outrage, some fresh deviltry or other—no horse ever thought over a
subject so profoundly as this one is doing just for nothing. The more this thing
preyed upon my mind the more uneasy I became, until the suspense became
almost unbearable and I dismounted to see if there was anything wild in his
eye—for I had heard that the eye of this noblest of our domestic animals is very
expressive. I cannot describe what a load of anxiety was lifted from my mind
when I found that he was only asleep. I woke him up and started him into a
faster walk, and then the villainy of his nature came out again. He tried to climb
over a stone wall, five or six feet high. I saw that I must apply force to this
horse, and that I might as well begin first as last. I plucked a stout switch from
a tamarind tree, and the moment he saw it, he surrendered. He broke into a
convulsive sort of canter, which had three short steps in it and one long one,

and reminded me alternately of the clattering shake of the great earthquake and the sweeping plunging of the Ajax in a storm.

And now there can be no fitter occasion than the present to pronounce a left-handed blessing upon the man who invented the American saddle. There is no seat to speak of about it—one might as well sit in a shovel—and the stirrups are nothing but an ornamental nuisance. If I were to write down here all the abuse I expended on those stirrups, it would make a large book, even without pictures. Sometimes I got one foot so far through, that the stirrup partook of the nature of an anklet; sometimes both feet were through, and I was handcuffed by the legs; and sometimes my feet got clear out and left the stirrups wildly dangling about my shins. Even when I was in proper position and carefully balanced upon the balls of my feet, there was no comfort in it, on account of my nervous dread that they were going to slip one way or the other in a moment. But the subject is too exasperating to write about.

A mile and a half from town, I came to a grove of tall cocoa-nut trees, with clean, branchless stems reaching straight up sixty or seventy feet and topped with a spray of green foliage sheltering clusters of cocoa-nuts—not more picturesque than a forest of colossal ragged parasols, with bunches of magnified grapes under them, would be. I once heard a grouty northern invalid say that a cocoa-nut tree might be poetical, possibly it was; but it looked like a feather-duster struck by lightning. I think that describes it better than a picture—and yet, without any question, there is something fascinating about a cocoa-nut tree—and graceful, too.

About a dozen cottages, some frame and the others of native grass, nestled sleepily in the shade here and there. The grass cabins are of a grayish color, are shaped much like our own cottages, only with higher and steeper roofs usually, and are made of some kind of weed strongly bound together in bundles. The roofs are very thick, and so are the walls; the latter have square holes in them for windows. At a little distance these cabins have a furry appearance, as if they might be made of bear skins. They are very cool and pleasant inside. The King's flag was flying from the roof of one of the cottages, and His Majesty was probably within. He owns the whole concern thereabouts, and passes his time there frequently, on sultry days "laying off." The spot is called "The King's Grove."

Nearby is an interesting ruin—the meagre remains of an ancient heathen temple—a place where human sacrifices were offered up in those old bygone days when the simple child of nature, yielding momentarily to sin when sorely tempted, acknowledged his error when calm reflection had shown it him, and came forward with noble frankness and offered up his grandmother as an atoning sacrifice—in those old days when the luckless sinner could keep on cleansing his conscience and achieving periodical happiness as long as his relations held out; long, long before the missionaries braved a thousand privations to come and make them permanently miserable by telling them how beautiful and how blissful a place heaven is, and how nearly impossible it is to get there; and showed the poor native how dreary a place perdition is and what unnecessarily liberal facilities there are for going to it; showed him how, in his ignorance he had gone and fooled away all his kinfolks to no purpose; showed him what rapture it is to work all day long for fifty cents to buy food for next day with, as compared with fishing for pastime and lolling in the shade through eternal Summer, and eating of the bounty that nobody labored to provide but Nature.

How sad it is to think of the multitudes who have gone to their graves in this beautiful island and never knew there was a hell!

This ancient temple was built of rough blocks of lava, and was simply a roofless inclosure a hundred and thirty feet long and seventy wide—nothing but naked walls, very thick, but not much higher than a man's head. They will last for ages no doubt, if left unmolested. Its three altars and other sacred appurtenances have crumbled and passed away years ago. It is said that in the old times thousands of human beings were slaughtered here, in the presence of naked and howling savages. If these mute stones could speak, what tales they could tell, what pictures they could describe, of fettered victims writhing under the knife; of massed forms straining forward out of the gloom, with ferocious faces lit up by the sacrificial fires; of the background of ghostly trees; of the dark pyramid of Diamond Head standing sentinel over the uncanny scene, and the peaceful moon looking down upon it through rifts in the cloud-rack!

When Kamehameha (pronounced Ka-may-ha-may-ah) the Great—who was a sort of a Napoleon in military genius and uniform success—invaded this island of Oahu three quarters of a century ago, and exterminated the army sent to oppose him, and took full and final possession of the country, he searched out the dead body of the King of Oahu, and those of the principal chiefs, and impaled their heads on the walls of this temple.

Those were savage times when this old slaughter-house was in its prime. The King and the chiefs ruled the common herd with a rod of iron; made them gather all the provisions the masters needed; build all the houses and temples; stand all the expenses, of whatever kind; take kicks and cuffs for thanks; drag out lives well flavored with misery, and then suffer death for trifling offenses or yield up their lives on the sacrificial altars to purchase favors from the gods for their hard rulers. The missionaries have clothed them, educated them, broken up the tyrannous authority of their chiefs, and given them freedom and the right to enjoy whatever their hands and brains produce with equal laws for all, and punishment for all alike who transgress them. The contrast is so strong—the benefit conferred upon this people by the missionaries is so prominent, so palpable and so unquestionable— that the frankest compliment I can pay them, and the best, is simply to point to the condition of the Sandwich Islanders of Captain Cook's time, and their condition to-day. Their work speaks for itself.

Chapter LXV

BY AND BY, after a rugged climb, we halted on the summit of a hill which commanded a far-reaching view. The moon rose and flooded mountain and valley and ocean with a mellow radiance, and out of the shadows of the foliage the distant lights of Honolulu glinted like an encampment of fireflies. The air was heavy with the fragrance of flowers. The halt was brief. Gayly laughing and talking, the party galloped on, and I clung to the pommel and cantered after. Presently we came to a place where no grass grew—a wide expanse of deep sand. They said it was an old battle-ground. All around everywhere, not three feet apart, the bleached bones of men gleamed white in the moonlight. We picked up a lot of them for mementos. I got quite a number of arm bones and leg bones—of great chiefs, may be, who had fought savagely in that fearful battle in the old days, when blood flowed like wine where we now stood—and wore the choicest of them out on Oahu afterward, trying to make him go. All sorts of bones could be found, except skulls; but a citizen said, irreverently, that there had been an unusual number of "skull-hunters" there lately—a species of sportsmen I had never heard of before.

Nothing whatever is known about this place—its story is a secret that will never be revealed. The oldest natives make no pretense of being possessed of its history. They say these bones were here when they were children. They were here when their grandfathers were children—but how they came here, they can only conjecture. Many people believe this spot to be an ancient battle-ground, and it is usual to call it so; and they believe that these skeletons have lain for ages just where their proprietors fell in the great fight. Other people believe that Kamehameha I. fought his first battle here. On this point, I have heard a story, which may have been taken from one of the numerous books which have been written concerning these islands—I do not know where the narrator got it. He said that when Kamehameha (who was at first merely a subordinate chief on the island of Hawaii), landed here, he brought a large army with him and encamped at Waikiki. The Oahuans marched against him, and so confident were they of success that they readily acceded to a demand of their priests that they should draw a line where these bones now lie, and take an oath that, if forced to retreat at all, they would never retreat beyond this boundary. The priests told them that death and everlasting punishment would overtake any who violated the oath, and the march was resumed. Kamehameha drove them back step by step; the priests fought in the front rank and exhorted them both by voice and inspiriting example to remember their oath—to die, if need be, but never cross the fatal line. The struggle was manfully maintained, but at last the chief priest fell, pierced to the heart with a spear, and the unlucky omen fell like a blight upon the brave souls at his back; with a triumphant shout the invaders pressed forward— the line was crossed—the offended gods deserted the despairing army, and, accepting the doom their perjury had brought upon them, they broke and fled over the plain where Honolulu stands now—up the beautiful Nuuanu Valley— paused a moment, hemmed in by precipitous mountains on either hand and the frightful precipice of the Pari in front, and then were driven over—a sheer plunge of six hundred feet!

The story is pretty enough, but Mr. Jarves' excellent history says the Oahuans were entrenched in Nuuanu Valley; that Kamehameha ousted them, routed them, pursued them up the valley, and drove them over the precipice. He makes no mention of our boneyard at all in his book.

Impressed by the profound silence and repose that rested over the beautiful landscape, and being, as usual, in the rear, I gave voice to my thoughts. I said:

"What a picture is here slumbering in the solemn glory of the moon! How strong the rugged outlines of the dead volcano stand out against the clear sky! What a snowy fringe marks the bursting of the surf over the long, curved reef! How calmly the dim city sleeps yonder in the plain! How soft the shadows lie upon the stately mountains that border the dream-haunted Manoa Valley! What a grand pyramid of billowy clouds towers above the storied Pari! How the grim warriors of the past seem flocking in ghostly squadrons to their ancient battlefield again—how the walls of the dying well up from the——"

At this point the horse called Oahu sat down in the sand. Sat down to listen,

I suppose. Never mind what he heard, I stopped apostrophising and convinced him that I was not a man to allow contempt of Court on the part of a horse. I broke the back-bone of a chief over his rump and set out to join the cavalcade again.

Very considerably fagged out we arrived in town at 9 o'clock at night, myself in the lead—for when my horse finally came to understand that he was homeward bound and hadn't far to go, he turned his attention strictly to business.

This is a good time to drop in a paragraph of information. There is no regular livery stable in Honolulu, or, indeed, in any part of the kingdom of Hawaii; therefore unless you are acquainted with wealthy residents (who all have good horses), you must hire animals of the wretchedest description from the Kanakas (i.e., natives). Any horse you hire, even though it be from a white man, is not often of much account, because it wlll be brought in for you from some ranch, and has necessarily been leading a hard llfe. If the Kanakas who have been caring for him (inveterate riders they are) have not ridden him half to death every day themselves, you can depend upon it they have been doing the same thing by proxy, by clandestinely hiring him out. At least, so I am informed. The result is, that no horse has a chance to eat, drink, rest, recuperate, or look well or feel well, and so strangers go about the Islands mounted as I was to-day.

In hiring a horse from a Kanaka, you must have all your eyes about you, because you can rest satisfied that you are dealing with a shrewd, unprincipled rascal. You may leave your door open and your trunk unlocked as long as you please, and he will not meddle with your property; he has no important vices and no inclination to commit robbery on a large scale; but if he can get ahead of you in the horse business, he will take a genuine delight in doing it. This trait is characteristic of horse jockeys the world over, is it not? He will overcharge you if he can; he will hire you a fine-looking horse at night (anybody's—may be the King's, if the royal steed be in convenient view), and bring you the mate to my Oahu in the morning, and contend that it is the same animal. If you make trouble, he will get out by saying it was not himself who made the bargain with you, but his brother, "who went out in the country this morning." They have always got a "brother" to shift the responsibility upon. A victim said to one of these fellows one day:

"But I know I hired the horse of you, because I noticed that scar on your cheek."

The reply was not bad: "Oh, yes—yes—my brother all same—we twins!"

A friend of mine, J. Smith, hired a horse yesterday, the Kanaka warranting him to be in excellent condition. Smith had a saddle and blanket of his own, and he ordered the Kanaka to put these on the horse. The Kanaka protested that he was perfectly willing to trust the gentleman with the saddle that was already on the animal, but Smith refused to use it. The change was made; then Smith noticed that the Kanaka had only changed the saddles, and had left the original blanket on the horse; he said he forgot to change the blankets, and so, to cut the bother short, Smith mounted and rode away. The horse went lame a mile from town, and afterward got to cutting up some extraordinary capers. Smith got down and took off the saddle, but the blanket stuck fast to the horse—glued to a procession of raw places. The Kanaka's mysterious conduct stood explained.

Another friend of mine bought a pretty good horse from a native, a day or two ago, after a tolerably thorough examination of the animal. He discovered

MY BROTHER—WE TWINS.

today that the horse was as blind as a bat, in one eye. He meant to have examined that eye, and came home with a general notion that he had done it; but he remembers now that every time he made the attempt his attention was called to something else by his victmizer.

One more instance, and then I will pass to something else. I am informed that when a certain Mr. L., a visiting stranger, was here, he bought a pair of very respectable-looking match horses from a native. They were in a little stable with a partition through the middle of it—one horse in each apartment. Mr. L. examined one of them critically through a window (the Kanaka's "brother" having gone to the country with the key), and then went around the house and examined the other through a window on the other side. He said it was the neatest match he had ever seen, and paid for the horses on the spot. Whereupon the Kanaka departed to join his brother in the country. The fellow had shamefully swindled L. There was only one "match" horse, and he had examined his starboard side through one window and his port side through another! I decline to believe this story, but I give it because it is worth something as a fanciful illustration of a fixed fact—namely, that the Kanaka horse-jockey is fertile in invention and elastic in conscience.

You can buy a pretty good horse for forty or fifty dollars, and a good enough horse for all practical purposes for two dollars and a half. I estimate "Oahu" to be worth somewhere in the neighborhood of thirty-five cents. A good deal better animal than he is was sold here day before yesterday for a dollar and seventy-five cents, and sold again today for two dollars and twenty-five cents; Williams bought a handsome and lively little pony yesterday for ten dollars; and about the best common horse on the island (and he is a really good one) sold yesterday, with Mexican saddle and bridle, for seventy dollars—a horse which is well and widely known, and greatly respected for his speed, good disposition, and everlasting bottom. You give your horse a little grain once a day; it comes from San Francisco, and is worth about two cents a pound; and you give him as much hay as he wants; it is cut and brought to the market by natives, and is not very good; it is baled into long, round bundles, about the size of a large man; one of them is stuck by the middle on each end of a six-foot pole, and the Kanaka shoulders the pole and walks about the streets between the upright bales in search of customers. These hay bales, thus carried, have a general resemblance to a colossal capital H.

The hay bundles cost twenty-five cents apiece, and one will last a horse about a day. You can get a horse for a song, a week's hay for another song, and you can turn your animal loose among the luxuriant grass in your neighbor's broad front yard without a song at all—you do it at midnight, and stable the beast again before morning. You have been at no expense thus far, but when you come to buy a saddle and bridle they will cost you from twenty to thirty-five dollars. You can hire a horse, saddle, and bridle at from seven to ten dollars a week, and the owner will take care of them at his own expense.

It is time to close this day's record—bed time. As I prepare for sleep, a rich voice rises out of the still night, and, far as this ocean rock is toward the ends of the earth, I recognize a familiar home air. But the words seem somewhat out of joint:

"Waikiki lantoniœ Kaa hooly hooly wawhoo."

Translated, that means "When we were marching through Georgia."

Chapter LXVI

PASSING THROUGH THE marketplace we saw that feature of Honolulu under its most favorable auspices—that is, in the full glory of Saturday afternoon, which is a festive day with the natives. The native girls by twos and threes and parties of a dozen, and sometimes in whole platoons and companies, went cantering up and down the neighboring streets astride of fleet but homely horses, and with their gaudy riding habits streaming like banners behind them. Such a troop of free and easy riders, in their natural home, the saddle, makes a gay and graceful spectacle. The riding habit I speak of is simply a long, broad scarf, like a tavern table cloth brilliantly colored, wrapped around the loins once, then apparently passed between the limbs and each end thrown backward over the same, and floating and flapping behind on both sides beyond the horse's tail like a couple of fancy flags; then, slipping the stirrup-irons between her toes, the girl throws her chest forward, sits up like a Major General, and goes sweeping by like the wind.

The girls put on all the finery they can on Saturday afternoon—fine black silk robes; flowing red ones that nearly put your eyes out; others as white as snow; still others that discount the rainbow; and they wear their hair in nets, and trim their jaunty hats with fresh flowers, and encircle their dusky throats with home-made necklaces of the brilliant vermillion-tinted blossom of the *ohia*; and they fill the markets and the adjacent streets with their bright presences, and smell like a rag factory on fire with their offensive cocoanut oil.

Occasionally you see a heathen from the sunny isles away down in the South Seas, with his face and neck tattooed till he looks like the customary mendicant from Washoe who has been blown up in a mine. Some are tattooed a dead blue color down to the upper lip—masked, as it were—leaving the natural light yellow skin of Micronesia unstained from thence down; some with broad marks drawn down from hair to neck, on both sides of the face, and a strip of the original yellow skin, two inches wide, down the center—a gridiron with a spoke broken out; and some with the entire face discolored with the popular mortification tint, relieved only by one or two thin, wavy threads of natural yellow running across the face from ear to ear, and eyes twinkling out of this darkness, from under shadowing hat-brims, like stars in the dark of the moon.

Moving among the stirring crowds, you come to the poi merchants, squatting in the shade on their hams, in true native fashion, and surrounded by purchasers. (The Sandwich Islanders always squat on their hams, and who knows but they may be the old original "ham sandwiches?" The thought is pregnant with interest.) The poi looks like common flour paste, and is kept in large bowls formed of a species of gourd and capable of holding from one to three or four gallons. Poi is the chief article of food among the natives, and is prepared from the *taro* plant. The taro root looks like a thick, or, if you please, a corpulent sweet potato, in shape, but is of a light purple color when boiled. When boiled it answers as a passable substitute for bread. The buck Kanakas bake it underground, then mash it up well with a heavy lava pestle, mix water with it until it becomes a paste, set it aside and let it ferment, and then it is poi—and an unseductive mixture it is, almost tasteless before it ferments and too sour for a luxury afterward. But nothing is more nutritious. When solely used, however, it produces acrid humors, a fact which sufficiently accounts for the humorous character of the Kanakas. I think there must be as much of a knack in handling poi as there is in eating with chopsticks. The forefinger is thrust into the mess and stirred quickly round several times and drawn as quickly out, thickly coated, just as if it were poulticed; the head is thrown back, the finger inserted in the mouth, and the delicacy stripped off and swallowed—the eye closing gently, meanwhile, in a languid sort of ecstasy. Many a different finger goes into the same bowl and many a different kind of dirt and shade and quality of flavor is added to the virtues of its contents.

Around a small shanty was collected a crowd of natives buying the *awa* root. It is said that but for the use of this root the destruction of the people in former times by certain imported diseases would have been far greater than it was, and by others it is said that this is merely a fancy. All agree that poi will rejuvenate

SANDWICH ISLAND GIRLS.

a man who is used up and his vitality almost annihilated by hard drinking, and that in some kinds of diseases it will restore health after all medicines have failed; but all are not willing to allow to the *awa* the virtues claimed for it. The natives manufacture an intoxicating drink from it which is fearful in its effects when persistently indulged in. It covers the body with dry, white scales, inflames the eyes, and causes premature decrepitude. Although the man before whose establishment we stopped has to pay a government license of eight hundred dollars a year for the exclusive right to sell *awa* root, it is said that he makes a small fortune every twelve-month; while saloon keepers, who pay a thousand dollars a year for the privilege of retailing whiskey, etc., only make a bare living.

We found the fish market crowded; for the native is very fond of fish, and *eats the article raw and alive!* Let us change the subject.

In old times here Saturday was a grand gala day indeed. All the native population of the town forsook their labors, and those of the surrounding country journeyed to the city. Then the white folks had to stay indoors, for every street was so packed with charging cavaliers and cavalieresses that it was next to impossible to thread one's way through the cavalcades without getting crippled.

At night they feasted and the girls danced the lascivious *hula hula*—a dance that is said to exhibit the very perfection of educated motion of limb and arm, hand, head and body, and the exactest uniformity of movement and accuracy of "time." It was performed by a circle of girls with no raiment on them to speak of, who went through an infinite variety of motions and figures without prompting, and yet so true was their "time," and in such perfect concert did they move, that when they were placed in a straight line, hands, arms, bodies, limbs, and heads waved, swayed, gesticulated, bowed, stooped, whirled, squirmed, twisted, and undulated as if they were part and parcel of a single individual; and it was difficult to believe they were not moved in a body by some exquisite piece of mechanism.

Of late years, however, Saturday has lost most of its quondam gala features. This weekly stampede of the natives interfered too much with labor and the interests of the white folks, and by sticking in a law here, and preaching a sermon there, and by various other means, they gradually broke it up. The demoralizing *hula hula* was forbidden to be performed, save at night, with closed doors, in presence of few spectators, and only by permission duly procured from the authorities and the payment of ten dollars for the same. There are few girls now-a-days able to dance this ancient national dance in the highest perfection of the art.

The missionaries have christianized and educated all the natives. They all belong to the Church, and there is not one of them, above the age of eight years, but can read and write with facility in the native tongue. It is the most universally educated race of people outside of China. They have any quantity of books, printed in the Kanaka language, and all the natives are fond of reading. They are inveterate church-goers—nothing can keep them away. All this ameliorating cultivation has at last built up in the native women a profound respect for chastity—in other people. Perhaps that is enough to say on that head. The national sin will die out when the race does, but perhaps not earlier.—But doubtless this purifying is not far off, when we reflect that contact with civilization and the whites has reduced the native population from *four hundred thousand* (Captain Cook's estimate,) to *fifty-five thousand* in something over eighty years!

Society is a queer medley in this notable missionary, whaling, and governmental centre. If you get into conversation with a stranger and experience that natural desire to know what sort of ground you are treading on by finding out what manner of man your stranger is, strike out boldly and address him as "Captain." Watch him narrowly, and if you see by his countenance that you are on the wrong tack, ask him where he preaches. It is a safe bet that he is either a missionary or captain of a whaler. I am now personally acquainted with seventy-two captains and ninety-six missionaries. The captains and ministers form one half of the population; the third fourth is composed of common Kanakas and mercantile foreigners and their families, and the final fourth is made up of high officers of the Hawaiian Government. And there are just about cats enough for three apiece all around.

A solemn stranger met me in the suburbs the other day, and said:

"Good morning, your reverence. Preach in the stone church yonder, no doubt?"

"No, I don't. I'm not a preacher."

"Really, I beg your pardon, Captain. I trust you had a good season. How much oil"—

"Oil? What do you take me for? I'm not a whaler."

"Oh, I beg a thousand pardons, your Excellency. Major General in the household troops, no doubt? Minister of the Interior, likely? Secretary of war? First Gentleman of the Bed-chamber? Commissioner of the Royal"—

"Stuff! I'm no official. I'm not connected in any way with the Government."

"Bless my life! Then, who the mischief are you? what the mischief are you? and how the mischief did you get here, and where in thunder did you come from?"

"I'm only a private personage—an unassuming stranger—lately arrived from America."

"No? Not a missionary! Not a whaler! Not a member of his Majesty's Government! Not even Secretary of the Navy! Ah, Heaven! it is too blissful to be true; alas, I do but dream. And yet that noble, honest countenance—those oblique, ingenuous eyes—that massive head, incapable of—of—anything; your hand; give me your hand, bright waif. Excuse these tears. For sixteen weary years I have yearned for a moment like this, and"—

Here his feelings were too much for him, and he swooned away. I pitied this poor creature from the bottom of my heart. I was deeply moved. I shed a few tears on him and kissed him for his mother. I then took what small change he had and "shoved."

Chapter LXVII

I STILL QUOTE from my journal:

I found the national Legislature to consist of half a dozen white men and some thirty or forty natives. It was a dark assemblage. The nobles and ministers (about a dozen of them altogether) occupied the extreme left of the hall, with David Kalakaua (the King's Chamberlain) and Prince William at the head. The President of the Assembly, His Royal Highness M. Kekuanaoa,* and the Vice-President (the latter a white man) sat in the pulpit, if I may so term it.

---

*Since dead.

The President is the King's father. He is an erect, strongly built, massive featured, white-haired, tawny old gentleman of eighty years of age or thereabouts. He was simply but well dressed, in a blue cloth coat and white vest, and white pantaloons, without spot, dust, or blemish upon them. He bears himself with a calm, stately dignity and is a man of noble presence. He was a young man and a distinguished warrior under that terrific fighter, Kamehameha I., more than half a century ago. A knowledge of his career suggested some such thought as this: "This man, naked as the day he was born, and war-club and spear in hand, has charged at the head of a horde of savages against other hordes of savages more than a generation and a half ago, and reveled in slaughter and carnage; has worshiped wooden images on his devout knees; has seen hundreds of his race offered up in heathen temples as sacrifices to wooden idols, at a time when no missionary's foot had ever pressed this soil, and he had never heard of the white man's God; has believed his enemy could secretly pray him to death; has seen the day, in his childhood, when it was a crime punishable by death for a man to eat with his wife, or for a plebeian to let his shadow fall upon the King— and now look at him; an educated Christian; neatly and handsomely dressed; a high-minded, elegant gentleman; a traveler, in some degree, and one who has been the honored guest of royalty in Europe; a man practiced in holding the reins of an enlightened government, and well versed in the politics of his country and in general, practical information. Look at him, sitting there presiding over the deliberations of a legislative body, among whom are white men—a grave, dignified, statesmanlike personage, and as seemingly natural and fitted to the place as if he had been born in it and had never been out of it in his life time. How the experiences of this old man's eventful life shame the cheap inventions of romance!"

Kekuanaoa is not of the blood royal. He derives his princely rank from his wife, who was a daughter of Kamehameha the Great. Under other monarchies the male line takes precedence of the female in tracing genealogies, but here the opposite is the case—the female line takes precedence. Their reason for this is exceedingly sensible, and I recommend it to the aristocracy of Europe: They say it is easy to know who a man's mother was, but, etc., etc.

The christianizing of the natives has hardly even weakened some of their barbarian superstitions, much less destroyed them. I have just referred to one of these. It is still a popular belief that if your enemy can get hold of any article belonging to you he can get down on his knees over it and *pray you to death*. Therefore many a native gives up and dies merely because he *imagines* that some enemy is putting him through a course of damaging prayer. This praying an individual to death seems absurd enough at a first glance, but then when we call to mind some of the pulpit efforts of certain of our own ministers the thing looks plausible.

In former times, among the Islanders, not only a plurality of wives was customary, but a *plurality of husbands* likewise. Some native women of noble rank had as many as six husbands. A woman thus supplied did not reside with all her husbands at once, but lived several months with each in turn. An understood sign hung at her door during these months. When the sign was taken down, it meant "NEXT."

In those days woman was rigidly taught to "know her place." Her place was to do all the work, take all the cuffs, provide all the food, and content herself with what was left after her lord had finished his dinner. She was not only forbidden, by ancient law, and under penalty of death, to eat with her husband or enter a canoe, but was debarred, under the same penalty, from eating bananas, pine-apples, oranges, and other choice fruits at any time or in any place. She had to confine herself pretty strictly to "poi" and hard work. These poor ignorant heathen seem to have had a sort of groping idea of what came of woman eating fruit in the Garden of Eden, and they did not choose to take any more chances. But the missionaries broke up this satisfactory arrangement of things. They liberated woman and made her the equal of man.

The natives had a romantic fashion of burying some of their children alive when the family became larger than necessary. The missionaries interfered in this matter too, and stopped it.

To this day the natives are able to *lie down and die whenever they want to,* whether there is anything the matter with them or not. If a Kanaka takes a notion to die, that is the end of him; nobody can persuade him to hold on; all the doctors in the world could not save him.

A luxury which they enjoy more than anything else is a large funeral. If a person wants to get rid of a troublesome native, it is only necessary to promise him a fine funeral and name the hour and he will be on hand to the minute—at least his remains will.

All the natives are Christians, now, but many of them still desert to the Great Shark God for temporary succor in time of trouble. An irruption of the great volcano of Kilauea, or an earthquake, always brings a deal of latent loyalty to the Great Shark God to the surface. It is common report that the King, educated, cultivated, and refined Christian gentleman as he undoubtedly is, still turns to the idols of his fathers for help when disaster threatens. A planter caught a shark, and one of his christianized natives testified his emancipation from the thrall of ancient superstition by assisting to dissect the shark after a fashion forbidden by his abandoned creed. But remorse shortly began to torture him. He grew moody and sought solitude; brooded over his sin, refused food, and finally said he must die and ought to die, for he had sinned against the Great Shark God and could never know peace any more. He was proof against persuasion and ridicule, and in the course of a day or two took to his bed and died, although he showed no symptom of disease. His young daughter followed his lead and suffered a like fate within the week. Superstition is ingrained in the native blood and bone, and it is only natural that it should crop out in time of distress. Wherever one goes in the Islands, he will find small piles of stones by the wayside, covered with leafy offerings, placed there by the natives to appease evil spirits or honor local deities belonging to the mythology of former days.

In the rural districts of any of the Islands, the traveler hourly comes upon parties of dusky maidens bathing in the streams or in the sea without any clothing on and exhibiting no very intemperate zeal in the matter of hiding their nakedness. When the missionaries first took up their residence in Honolulu, the native women would pay their families frequent friendly visits, day by day, not even clothed with a blush. It was found a hard matter to convince them that this was rather indelicate. Finally the missionaries provided them with long, loose calico robes, and that ended the difficulty—for the women would troop through the town, stark naked, with their robes folded under their arms, march to the missionary houses, and then proceed to dress! The natives soon manifested a strong proclivity for clothing, but it was shortly apparent that they only wanted it for grandeur. The missionaries imported a quantity of hats, bonnets, and other male and female wearing apparel, instituted a general distribution, and begged the people not to come to church naked, next Sunday, as usual. And they did not; but the national spirit of unselfishness led them to divide up with neighbors who were not at the distribution, and next Sabbath the poor preachers could hardly keep countenance before their vast congregations. In the midst of the reading of a hymn a brown, stately dame would sweep up the aisle with a world of airs, with nothing in the world on but a "stove-pipe" hat and a pair of cheap gloves; another dame would follow, tricked out in a man's shirt, and nothing else; another one would enter with a flourish, with simply the sleeves of a bright calico dress tied around her waist and the rest of the garment dragging behind like a peacock's tail off duty; a stately "buck" Kanaka would stalk in with a woman's bonnet on, wrong side before—only this, and nothing more; after him would stride his fellow, with the legs of a pair of pantaloons tied around his neck, the rest of his person untrammeled; in his rear would come another gentleman simply gotten up in a fiery neck-tie and a striped vest. The poor creatures were beaming with complacency and wholly unconscious of any absurdity in their appearance. They gazed at each other with happy admiration, and it was plain to see that the young girls were taking note of what each other had on, as naturally as if they had always lived in a land of Bibles and knew what churches were made for; here was the evidence of a dawning civilization. The spectacle which the congregation presented was so extraordinary and withal so moving that the missionaries found it difficult to keep to the text and go on with the services; and by and by when the simple children of the sun began a general swapping of garments in open meeting and produced some irresistibly grotesque effects in the course of re-dressing, there was nothing for it but to cut the thing short with the benediction and dismiss the fantastic assemblage.

In our country, children play "keep house;" and in the same high-sounding but miniature way the grown folk here, with the poor little material of slender territory and meagre population, play "empire." There is his royal Majesty the King, with a New York detective's income of thirty or thirty-five thousand dollars a year from the "royal civil list" and the "royal domain." He lives in a two-story frame "palace."

And there is the "royal family"—the customary hive of royal brothers, sisters,

FULL CHURCH DRESS.

cousins, and other noble drones and vagrants usual to monarchy,—all with a spoon in the national pap-dish, and all bearing such titles as his or her Royal Highness the Prince or Princess So-and-so. Few of them can carry their royal splendors far enough to ride in carriages, however; they sport the economical Kanaka horse or "hoof it"* with the plebeians.

Then there is His Excellency the "royal Chamberlain"—a sinecure, for his majesty dresses himself with his own hands, except when he is ruralizing at Waikiki and then he requires no dressing.

Next we have his Excellency the Commander-in-chief of the Household Troops, whose forces consist of about the number of soldiers usually placed under a corporal in other lands.

Next comes the royal Steward and the Grand Equerry in Waiting—high dignitaries with modest salaries and little to do.

Then we have his Excellency the First Gentleman of the Bed-chamber—an office as easy as it is magnificent.

Next we come to his Excellency the Prime Minister, a renegade American from New Hampshire, all jaw, vanity, bombast, and ignorance, a lawyer of "shyster" calibre, a fraud by nature, a humble worshiper of the sceptre above him, a reptile never tired of sneering at the land of his birth or glorifying the ten-acre kingdom that has adopted him—salary, $4,000 a year, vast consequence, and no perquisites.

Then we have his Excellency the Imperial Minister of Finance, who handles a million dollars of public money a year, sends in his annual "budget" with great ceremony, talks prodigiously of "finance," suggests imposing schemes for paying off the "national debt" (of $150,000), and does it all for $4,000 a year and unimaginable glory.

Next we have his Excellency the Minister of War, who holds sway over the royal armies—they consist of two hundred and thirty uniformed Kanakas, mostly Brigadier Generals, and if the country ever gets into trouble with a foreign power we shall probably hear from them. I knew an American whose copper-plate visiting card bore this impressive legend: "Lieutenant-Colonel in the Royal Infantry." To say that he was proud of this distinction is stating it but tamely. The Minister of War has also in his charge some venerable swivels on Punch-bowl Hill wherewith royal salutes are fired when foreign vessels of war enter the port.

Next comes his Excellency the Minister of the Navy—a nabob who rules the "royal fleet" (a steam-tug and a sixty-ton schooner.)

And next comes his Grace the Lord Bishop of Honolulu, the chief dignitary of the "Established Church"—for when the American Presbyterian missionaries had completed the reduction of the nation to a compact condition of Christianity, native royalty stepped in and erected the grand dignity of an "Established (Episcopal) Church" over it, and imported a cheap, ready-made Bishop from England to take charge. The chagrin of the missionaries has never been comprehensively expressed, to this day, profanity not being admissible.

Next comes his Excellency the Minister of Public Instruction.

Next, their Excellencies the Governors of Oahu, Hawaii, etc., and after them a string of High Sheriffs and other small fry too numerous for computation.

---

*Missionary phrase.

Then there are their Excellencies the Envoy Extraordinary and Minister Plen-
ipotentiary of His Imperial Majesty the Emperor of the French; her British
Majesty's Minister; the Minister Resident, of the United States; and some six
or eight representatives of other foreign nations, all with sounding titles, imposing
dignity and prodigious but economical state.

Imagine all this grandeur in a play-house "kingdom" whose population falls
absolutely short of sixty thousand souls!

The people are so accustomed to nine-jointed titles and colossal magnates that
a foreign prince makes very little more stir in Honolulu than a Western Congressman
does in New York.

And let it be borne in mind that there is a strictly defined "court costume"
of so "stunning" a nature that it would make the clown in a circus look tame
and commonplace by comparison; and each Hawaiian official dignitary has a
gorgeous vari-colored, gold-laced uniform peculiar to his office—no two of them
are alike, and it is hard to tell which one is the "loudest." The King had a
"drawing room" at stated intervals, like other monarchs, and when these varied
uniforms congregate there weak-eyed people have to contemplate the spectacle
through smoked glass. Is there not a gratifying contrast between this latter-day
exhibition and the one the ancestors of some of these magnates afforded the
missionaries the Sunday after the old-time distribution of clothing? Behold what
religion and civilization have wrought!

Chapter LXVIII

WHILE I WAS in Honolulu I witnessed the ceremonious funeral of the King's
sister, her Royal Highness the Princess Victoria. According to the royal custom,
the remains had lain in state at the palace *thirty days,* watched day and night by
a guard of honor. And during all that time a great multitude of natives from the
several islands had kept the palace grounds well crowded and had made the place
a pandemonium every night with their howlings and wailings, beating of tom-
toms, and dancing of the (at other times) forbidden "hula-hula" by half-clad
maidens to the music of songs of questionable decency chanted in honor of the
deceased. The printed programme of the funeral procession interested me at the
time; and after what I have just said of Hawaiian grandiloquence in the matter
of "playing empire," I was persuaded that a perusal of it may interest the reader:

After reading the long list of dignitaries, etc., and remembering the sparseness of the
population, one is almost inclined to wonder where the material for that portion of the
procession devoted to "Hawaiian Population Generally" is going to be procured:

Undertaker.

Royal School.　Kawaiahao School.　Roman Catholic School.　Miæmæ School.

Honolulu Fire Department.

Mechanics' Benefit Union.

Attending Physicians.

Konohikis (Superintendents) of the Crown Lands, Konohikis of the Private Lands
of His Majesty, Konohikis of Private Lands of Her late Royal Highness.

Governor of Oahu and Staff.

Hulumanu (Military Company).

Household Troops.
The Prince of Hawaii's Own (Military Company).
The King's household servants.
Servants of Her late Royal Highness.
Protestant Clergy. The Clergy of the Roman Catholic Church.
His Lordship Louis Maigret, The Right Rev. Bishop of Arathea, Vicar-Apostolic
of the Hawaiian Islands.
The Clergy of the Hawaiian Reformed Catholic Church.
His Lordship the Right Rev. Bishop of Honolulu.

Escort Hawaiian Cavalry.
Large Kahilis.*
Small Kahilis.
Pall Bearers.

[HEARSE.]

Her Majesty Queen Emma's Carriage.
His Majesty's Staff.
Carriage of Her late Royal Highness.
Carriage of Her Majesty the Queen Dowager.
The King's Chancellor.
Cabinet Ministers.
His Excellency the Minister Resident of the United States.
H. I. M's Commissioner.
H. B. M's Acting Commissioner.
Judges of Supreme Court.
Privy Councillors.
Members of Legislative Assembly.
Consular Corps.
Circuit Judges.
Clerks of Government Departments.
Members of the Bar.
Collector General, Custom-house Officers and Officers of the Customs.
Marshal and Sheriffs of the different Islands.
King's Yeomanry.
Foreign Residents.
Ahahui Kaahumanu.
Hawaiian Population Generally.
Hawaiian Cavalry.
Police Force.

I resume my journal at the point where the procession arrived at the royal
mausoleum:

As the procession filed through the gate, the military deployed handsomely
to the right and left and formed an avenue through which the long column
of mourners passed to the tomb. The coffin was borne through the door
of the mausoleum, followed by the King and his chiefs, the great officers

---

* Ranks of long-handled mops made of gaudy feathers—sacred to royalty. They are stuck
in the ground around the tomb and left there.

of the kingdom, foreign Consuls, Embassadors, and distinguished guests (Burlingame and General Van Valkenburgh). Several of the kahilis were then fastened to a frame-work in front of the tomb, there to remain until they decay and fall to pieces, or, forestalling this, until another scion of royalty dies. At this point of the proceedings the multitude set up such a heart-broken wailing as I hope never to hear again. The soldiers fired three volleys of musketry—the wailing being previously silenced to permit of the guns being heard. His Highness Prince William, in a showy military uniform (the "true prince," this—scion of the house over-thrown by the present dynasty—he was formerly betrothed to the Princess but was not allowed to marry her), stood guard and paced back and forth within the door. The privileged few who followed the coffin into the mausoleum remained some time, but the King soon came out and stood in the door and near one side of it. A stranger could have guessed his rank (although he was so simply and unpretentiously dressed) by the profound deference paid him by all persons in his vicinity; by seeing his high officers receive his quiet orders and suggestions with bowed and uncovered heads; and by observing how careful those persons who came out of the mausoleum were to avoid "crowding" him (although there was room enough in the doorway for a wagon to pass, for that matter); how respectfully they edged out sideways, scraping their back against the wall and always presenting a front view of their persons to his Majesty, and never putting their hats on until they were well out of the royal presence.

He was dressed entirely in black—dress coat and silk hat—and looked rather democratic in the midst of the showy uniforms about him. On his breast he wore a large gold star, which was half hidden by the lapel of his coat. He remained at the door a half hour, and occasionally gave an order to the men who were erecting the *kahilis* before the tomb. He had the good taste to make one of them substitute black crape for the ordinary hempen rope he was about to tie one of them to the framework with. Finally he entered his carriage and drove away, and the populace shortly began to drop into his wake. While he was in view there was but one man who attracted more attention than himself, and that was Harris (the Yankee Prime Minister). This feeble personage had crape enough around his hat to express the grief of an entire nation, and as usual he neglected no opportunity of making himself conspicuous and exciting the admiration of the simple Kanakas. Oh! noble ambition of this modern Richelieu!

It is interesting to contrast the funeral ceremonies of the Princess Victoria with those of her noted ancestor Kamehameha the Conqueror, who died fifty years ago—in 1819, the year before the first missionaries came.

On the 8th of May, 1819, at the age of sixty-six, he died, as he had lived, in the faith of his country. It was his misfortune not to have come in contact with men who could have rightly influenced his religious aspirations. Judged by his advantages and compared with the most eminent of his countrymen he may be justly styled not only great, but good. To this day his memory warms the heart and elevates the national feelings of Hawaiians. They are proud of their old warrior King; they love his name; his deeds form their historical age; and an enthusiasm everywhere prevails, shared even by foreigners who knew his worth, that constitutes the firmest pillar of the throne of his dynasty.

"In lieu of human victims (the custom of that age), a sacrifice of three hundred dogs attended his obsequies—no mean holocaust when their national value and the estimation in which they were held are considered. The bones of Kamehameha, after being kept for a while, were so carefully concealed that all knowledge of their final resting place is now lost. There was a proverb current among the common people that the bones of a cruel King could not be hid; they made fishhooks and arrows of them, upon which, in using them, they vented their abhorrence of his memory in bitter execrations."

The account of the circumstances of his death, as written by the native historians, is full of minute detail, but there is scarcely a line of it which does not mention or illustrate some by-gone custom of the country. In this respect it is the most comprehensive document I have yet met with. I will quote it entire:

"When Kamehameha was dangerously sick, and the priests were unable to cure him, they said: 'Be of good courage and build a house for the god' (his own private god or idol), 'that thou mayest recover.' The chiefs corroborated this advice of the priests, and a place of worship was prepared for Kukailimoku, and consecrated in the evening. They proposed also to the King, with a view to prolong his life, that human victims should be sacrificed to his deity; upon which the greater part of the people absconded through fear of death, and concealed themselves in hiding places till the *tabu** in which destruction impended, was past. It is doubtful whether Kamehameha approved of the plan of the chiefs and priests to sacrifice men, as he was known to say, 'The men are sacred for the King'; meaning that they were for the service of his successor. This information was derived from Liholiho, his son.

After this, his sickness increased to such a degree that he had not strength to turn himself in his bed. When another season, consecrated for worship at the new temple *(heiau),* arrived, he said to his son, Liholiho, 'Go thou and make supplication to thy god; I am not able to go, and will offer my prayers at home.' When his devotions to his feathered god, Kukailimoku, were concluded, a certain religiously disposed individual, who had a bird god, suggested to the king that through its influence his sickness might be removed. The name of this god was Pua; its body was made of a bird, now eaten by the Hawaiians, and called in their language *alae.* Kamehameha was willing that a trial should be made, and two houses were constructed to facilitate the experiment; but while dwelling in them he became so very weak as not to receive food. After lying there three days, his wives, children and chiefs, perceiving that he was very low, returned him to his own house. In the evening he was

---

* *Tabu* (pronounced tah-boo,) means prohibition (we have borrowed it,) or sacred. The tabu was sometimes permanent, sometimes temporary; and the person or thing placed under tabu was for the time being sacred to the purpose for which it was set apart. In the above case the victims selected under the tabu would be sacred to the sacrifice.

carried to the eating house,† where he took a little food in his mouth which he did not swallow; also a cup of water. The chiefs requested him to give them his counsel; but he made no reply, and was carried back to the dwelling house; but when near midnight—ten o'clock, perhaps—he was carried again to the place to eat; but, as before, he merely tasted of what was presented to him. Then Kaikioewa addressed him thus: 'Here we all are, your younger brethren, your son Liholiho and your foreigner; impart to us your dying charge, that Liholiho and Kaahumanu may hear.' Then Kamehameha inquired, 'What do you say?' Kaikioewa repeated, 'Your counsels for us.' He then said, 'Move on in my good way and—' He could proceed no further. The foreigner, Mr. Young, embraced and kissed him. Hoapili also embraced him, whispering something in his ear, after which he was taken back to the house. About twelve he was carried once more to the house for eating, into which his head entered, while his body was in the dwelling house immediately adjoining. It should be remarked that this frequent carrying of a sick chief from one house to another resulted from the *tabu* system, then in force. There were at that time six houses (huts) connected with an establishment—one was for worship, one for the man to eat in, an eating house for the women, a house to sleep in, a house in which to manufacture kapa (native cloth) and one where, at certain intervals, the women might dwell in seclusion.

The sick was once more taken to his house, when he expired; this was at two o'clock, a circumstance from which Leleiohoku derived his name. As he breathed his last, Kalaimoku came to the eating house to order those in it to go out. There were two aged persons thus directed to depart; one went, the other remained on account of love to the King, by whom he had formerly been kindly sustained. The children also were sent away. Then Kalaimoku came to the house, and the chiefs had a consultation. One of them spoke thus: 'This is my thought—we will eat him raw.'** Kaahumanu (one of the dead King's widows) replied, 'Perhaps his body is not at our disposal; that is more properly with his successor. Our part in him—his breath—has departed; his remains will be disposed of by Liholiho.'

"After this conversation the body was taken into the consecrated house for the performance of the proper rites by the priest and the new King. The name of this ceremony is *uko;* and when the sacred hog was baked the priest offered it to the dead body, and it became a god, the King at the same time repeating the customary prayers.

"Then the priest, addressing himself to the king and chiefs, said: 'I will now make known to you the rules to be observed respecting persons to be sacrificed on the burial of this body. If you obtain one man before the corpse is removed, one will be sufficient; but after it leaves this house

---

† It was deemed pollution to eat in the same hut a person slept in—the fact that the patient was dying could not modify the rigid etiquette.
** This sounds suspicious, in view of the fact that all Sandwich Island historians, white and black, protest that cannibalism never existed in the Islands. However, since they only proposed to "eat him raw" we "don't count that." But it would certainly have been cannibalism if they had cooked him.—[M. T.]

four will be required. If delayed until we carry the corpse to the grave
there must be ten; but after it is deposited in the grave there must be
fifteen. To-morrow morning there will be a *tabu,* and, if the sacrifice be
delayed until that time, forty men must die.'

"Then the high priest, Hewahewa, inquired of the chiefs, 'Where shall
be the residence of King Liholiho?' They replied, 'Where, indeed? You,
of all men, ought to know.' Then the priest observed, 'There are two
suitable places; one is Kau, the other is Kohala.' The chiefs preferred
the latter, as it was more thickly inhabited. The priest added, 'These are
proper places for the King's residence; but he must not remain in Kona,
for it is polluted.' This was agreed to. It was now break of day. As he
was being carried to the place of burial the people perceived that their
King was dead, and they wailed. When the corpse was removed from
the house to the tomb, a distance of one chain, the procession was met
by a certain man who was ardently attached to the deceased. He leaped
upon the chiefs who were carrying the King's body; he desired to die
with him on account of his love. The chiefs drove him away. He persisted
in making numerous attempts, which were unavailing. Kalaimoku also
had it in his heart to die with him, but was prevented by Hookio.

"The morning following Kamehameha's death, Liholiho and his train
departed for Kohala, according to the suggestions of the priest, to avoid
the defilement occasioned by the dead. At this time if a chief died the
land was polluted, and the heirs sought a residence in another part of
the country until the corpse was dissected and the bones tied in a bundle,
which being done, the season of defilement terminated. If the deceased
were not a chief, the house only was defiled which became pure again
on the burial of the body. Such were the laws on this subject.

"On the morning on which Liholiho sailed in his canoe for Kohala,
the chiefs and people mourned after their manner on occasion of a chief's
death, conducting themselves like madmen and like beasts. Their conduct
was such as to forbid description. The priests, also, put into action the
sorcery apparatus, that the person who had prayed the King to death
might die; for it was not believed that Kamehameha's departure was the
effect either of sickness or old age. When the sorcerers set up by their
fire-places sticks with a strip of kapa flying at the top, the chief Keeaumoku,
Kaahumanu's brother, came in a state of intoxication and broke the flagstaff of the sorcerers, from which it was inferred that Kaahumanu and
her friends had been instrumental in the King's death. On this account
they were subjected to abuse."

You have the contrast, now, and a strange one it is. This great Queen, Kaahumanu, who was "subjected to abuse" during the frightful orgies that followed
the king's death, in accordance with ancient custom, afterward became a devout
Christian and a steadfast and powerful friend of the missionaries.

Dogs were, and still are, reared and fattened for food, by the natives—hence
the reference to their value in one of the above paragraphs.

Forty years ago it was the custom in the Islands to suspend all law for a certain
number of days after the death of a royal personage; and then a saturnalia ensued
which one may picture to himself after a fashion, but not in the full horror of
the reality. The people shaved their heads, knocked out a tooth or two, plucked

out an eye sometimes, cut, bruised, mutilated, or burned their flesh, got drunk, burned each other's huts, maimed or murdered one another according to the caprice of the moment, and both sexes gave themselves up to brutal and unbridled licentiousness. And after it all, came a torpor from which the nation slowly emerged bewildered and dazed, as if from a hideous half-remembered nightmare. They were not the salt of the earth, those "gentle children of the sun."

The natives still keep up an old custom of theirs which cannot be comforting to an invalid. When they think a sick friend is going to die, a couple of dozen neighbors surround his hut and keep up a deafening wailing night and day till he either dies or gets well. No doubt this arrangement has helped many a subject to a shroud before his appointed time.

They surround a hut and wail in the same heart-broken way when its occupant returns from a journey. This is their dismal idea of a welcome. A very little of it would go a great way with most of us.

Chapter LXIX

BOUND FOR HAWAII (a hundred and fifty miles distant) to visit the great volcano and behold the other notable things which distinguish that island above the remainder of the group, we sailed from Honolulu on a certain Saturday afternoon, in the good schooner *Boomerang*.

The Boomerang was about as long as two street cars, and about as wide as one. She was so small (though she was larger than the majority of the inter-island coasters) that when I stood on her deck I felt but little smaller than the Colossus of Rhodes must have felt when he had a man-of-war under him. I could reach the water when she lay over under a strong breeze. When the Captain and my comrade (a Mr. Billings), myself, and four other persons were all assembled on the little after portion of the deck which is sacred to the cabin

FORMER FUNERAL ORGIES.

passengers, it was full—there was not room for any more quality folks. Another section of the deck, twice as large as ours, was full of natives of both sexes, with their customary dogs, mats, blankets, pipes, calabashes of poi, fleas, and other luxuries and baggage of minor importance. As soon as we set sail the natives all lay down on the deck as thick as negroes in a slave-pen, and smoked, conversed, and spit on each other, and were truly sociable.

The little low-ceiled cabin below was rather larger than a hearse and as dark as a vault. It had two coffins on each side—I mean two bunks. A small table, capable of accommodating three persons at dinner, stood against the forward bulkhead, and over it hung the dingiest whale oil lantern that ever peopled the obscurity of a dungeon with ghostly shapes. The floor room unoccupied was not extensive. One might swing a cat in it, perhaps, but not a long cat. Tbe hold forward of the bulkhead had but little freight in it, and from morning till night a portly old rooster, with a voice like Baalam's ass, and the same disposition to use it, strutted up and down in that part of the vessel and crowed. He usually took dinner at six o'clock, and then, after an hour devoted to meditation, he mounted a barrel and crowed a good part of the night. He got hoarser and hoarser all the time, but he scorned to allow any personal consideration to interfere with his duty and kept up his labors in defiance of threatened diphtheria.

Sleeping was out of the question when he was on watch. He was a source of genuine aggravation and annoyance. It was worse than useless to shout at him or apply offensive epithets to him—he only took these things for applause and strained himself to make more noise. Occasionally, during the day, I threw potatoes at him through an aperture in the bulkhead, but he only dodged and went on crowing.

The first night, as I lay in my coffin, idly watching the dim lamp swinging to the rolling of the ship, and snuffing the nauseous odors of bilge water, I felt something gallop over me. I turned out promptly. However, I turned in again when I found it was only a rat. Presently something galloped over me once more. I knew it was not a rat this time, and I thought it might be a centipede, because the Captain had killed one on deck in the afternoon. I turned out. The first glance at the pillow showed me a repulsive sentinel perched upon each end of it—cockroaches as large as peach leaves—fellows with long, quivering antennae and fiery, malignant eyes. They were grating their teeth like tobacco worms, and appeared to be dissatisfied about something. I had often heard that these reptiles were in the habit of eating off sleeping sailors' toe nails down to the quick, and I would not get in the bunk anymore. I lay down on the floor. But a rat came and bothered me, and shortly afterward a procession of cockroaches arrived and camped in my hair. In a few moments the rooster was crowing with uncommon spirit and a party of fleas were throwing double somersaults about my person in the wildest disorder, and taking a bite every time they struck. I was beginning to feel really annoyed. I got up and put my clothes on and went on deck.

The above is not overdrawn; it is a truthful sketch of inter-island schooner life. There is no such thing as keeping a vessel in elegant condition when she carries molasses and Kanakas.

It was compensation for my sufferings to come unexpectedly upon so beautiful a scene as met my eye—to step suddenly out of the sepulchral gloom of the cabin and stand under the strong light of the moon—in the centre, as it were, of a glittering sea of liquid silver—to see the broad sails straining in the gale, the ship keeled over on her side, the angry foam hissing past her lee bulwarks, and sparkling sheets of spray dashing high over her bows and raining upon her decks; to brace myself and hang fast to the first object that presented itself, with hat jammed down and coat tails whipping in the breeze, and feel that exhilaration that thrills in one's hair and quivers down his backbone when he knows that every inch of canvas is drawing and the vessel cleaving through the waves at her utmost speed. There was no darkness, no dimness, no obscurity there. All was brightness, every object was vividly defined. Every prostrate Kanaka; every coil of rope; every calabash of poi; every puppy; every seam in the flooring; every bolthead; every object, however minute, showed sharp and distinct in its every outline; and the shadow of the broad mainsail lay black as a pall upon the deck, leaving Billings's white, upturned face glorified and his body in a total eclipse.

Monday morning we were close to the island of Hawaii. Two of its high mountains were in view—Mauna Loa and Hualaiai. The latter is an imposing peak, but being only ten thousand feet high is seldom mentioned or heard of. Mauna Loa is said to be sixteen thousand feet high. The rays of glittering snow and ice, that clasped its summit like a claw, looked refreshing when viewed from the blistering climate we were in. One could stand on that mountain (wrapped up in blankets and furs to keep warm), and while he nibbled a snowball or an icicle to quench his thirst he could look down the long sweep of its sides and see spots where plants are growing that grow only where the bitter cold of Winter prevails; lower down he could see sections devoted to productions that thrive in the temperate zone alone; and at the bottom of the mountain he could see the home of the tufted cocoa-palms and other species of vegetation that grow only in the sultry atmosphere of eternal Summer. He could see all the climes of the world at a single glance of the eye, and that glance would only pass over a distance of four or five miles as the bird flies!

By and by we took boat and went ashore at Kailua, designing to ride horseback through the pleasant orange and coffee region of Kona, and rejoin the vessel at a point some leagues distant. This journey is well worth taking. The trail passes along on high ground—say a thousand feet above sea level—and usually about a mile distant from the ocean, which is always in sight, save that occasionally you find yourself buried in the forest in the midst of a rank tropical vegetation and a dense growth of trees, whose great bows overarch the road and shut out sun and sea and everything, and leave you in a dim, shady tunnel, haunted with invisible singing birds and fragrant with the odor of flowers. It was pleasant to ride occasionally in the warm sun, and feast the eye upon the ever-changing panorama of the forest (beyond and below us), with its many tints, its softened lights and shadows, its billowy undulations sweeping gently down from the mountain to the sea. It was pleasant also, at intervals, to leave the sultry sun and pass into the cool, green depths of this forest and indulge in sentimental reflections under the inspiration of its brooding twilight and its whispering foliage.

We rode through one orange grove that had ten thousand trees in it! They were all laden with fruit.

At one farmhouse we got some large peaches of excellent flavor. This fruit, as a general thing, does not do well in the Sandwich Islands. It takes a sort of almond shape, and is small and bitter. It needs frost, they say, and perhaps it does; if this be so, it will have a good opportunity to go on needing it, as it will not be likely to get it. The trees from which the fine fruit I have spoken of, came, had been planted and replanted *sixteen times,* and to this treatment the proprietor of the orchard attributed his success.

We passed several sugar plantations—new ones and not very extensive. The crops were, in most cases, third rattoons. [NOTE.—The first crop is called "plant cane;" subsequent crops which spring from the original roots, without replanting, are called "rattoons."] Almost everywhere on the island of Hawaii sugar-cane matures in twelve months, both rattoons and plant, and although it ought to be taken off as soon as it tassels, no doubt, it is not absolutely necessary to do it until about four months afterward. In Kona, the average yield of an acre of ground is *two tons* of sugar, they say. This is only a moderate yield for these islands, but would be astounding for Louisiana and most other sugar-growing countries. The plantations in Kona being on pretty high ground—up among the light and frequent rains—no irrigation whatever is required.

Chapter LXX

WE STOPPED SOME time at one of the plantations, to rest ourselves and refresh the horses. We had a chatty conversation with several gentlemen present; but there was one person, a middle-aged man, with an absent look in his face, who simply glanced up, gave us good-day and lapsed again into the meditations which our coming had interrupted. The planters whispered us not to mind him—crazy. They said he was in the Islands for his health; was a preacher; his home, Michigan. They said that if he woke up presently and fell to talking about a correspondence which he had some time held with Mr. Greeley about a trifle of some kind, we must humor him and listen with interest; and we must humor his fancy that this correspondence was the talk of the world.

It was easy to see that he was a gentle creature and that his madness had nothing vicious in it. He looked pale, and a little worn, as if with perplexing thought and anxiety of mind. He sat a long time, looking at the floor, and at intervals muttering to himself and nodding his head acquiescingly or shaking it in mild protest. He was lost in his thought, or in his memories. We continued our talk with the planters, branching from subiect to subject. But at last the word "circumstance," casually dropped, in the course of conversation, attracted his attention and brought an eager look into his countenance. He faced about in his chair and said:

"Circumstance? What circumstance? Ah, I know—I know too well. So you. have heard of it, too." [With a sigh.] "Well, no matter—all the world has heard of it. All the world. The whole world. It is a large world, too, for a thing to travel so far in—now isn't it? Yes, yes—the Greeley correspondence with Erickson has created the saddest and bitterest controversy on both sides of the ocean— and still they keep it up! It makes us famous, but at what a sorrowful sacrifice! I was so sorry when I heard that it had caused that bloody and distressful war over there in Italy. It was little comfort to me, after so much bloodshed, to know that the victors sided with me, and the vanquished with Greeley.—It is little comfort to know that Horace Greeley is responsible for the battle of Sadowa, and not me. Queen Victoria wrote me that she felt just as I did about it—she said that as much as she was opposed to Greeley and the spirit he showed in

THE DEMENTED.

the correspondence with me, she would not have had Sadowa happen for hundreds of dollars. I can show you her letter, if you would like to see it. But gentlemen, much as you may think you know about that unhappy correspondence, you cannot know the *straight* of it till you hear it from my lips. It has always been garbled in the journals, and even in history. Yes, even in history—think of it! Let me—*please* let me, give you the matter, exactly as it occurred. I truly will not abuse your confidence.''

Then he leaned forward, all interest, all earnestness, and told his story—and told it appealingly, too, and yet in the simplest and most unpretentious way; indeed, in such a way as to suggest to one, all the time, that this was a faithful, honorable witness, giving evidence in the sacred interest of justice, and under oath. He said:

''Mrs. Beazeley—Mrs. Jackson Beazeley, widow, of the village of Campbellton, Kansas,—wrote me about a matter which was near her heart—a matter which many might think trivial, but to her it was a thing of deep concern. I was living in Michigan, then—serving in the ministry. She was, and is, an estimable woman— a woman to whom poverty and hardship have proven incentives to industry, in place of discouragements. Her only treasure was her son William, a youth just verging upon manhood; religious, amiable, and sincerely attached to agriculture. He was the widow's comfort and her pride. And so, moved by her love for him, she wrote me about a matter, as I have said before, which lay near her heart— because it lay near her boy's. She desired me to confer with Mr. Greeley about turnips. Turnips were the dream of her child's young ambition. While other youths were frittering away in frivolous amusements the precious years of budding vigor which God had given them for useful preparation, this boy was patiently enriching his mind with information concerning turnips. The sentiment which he felt toward the turnip was akin to adoration. He could not think of the turnip without emotion; he could not speak of it calmly; he could not contemplate it without exaltation. He could not eat it without shedding tears. All the poetry in his sensitive nature was in sympathy with the gracious vegetable. With the earliest pipe of dawn he sought his patch, and when the curtaining night drove him from it he shut himself up with his books and garnered statistics till sleep overcame him. On rainy days he sat and talked hours together with his mother about turnips. When company came, he made it his loving duty to put aside everything else and converse with them all the day long of his great joy in the turnip. And yet, was this joy rounded and complete? Was there no secret alloy of unhappiness in it? Alas, there was. There was a canker gnawing at his heart; the noblest inspiration of his soul eluded his endeavor—viz: he could not make of the turnip a climbing vine. Months went by; the bloom forsook his cheek, the fire faded out of his eye; sighings and abstraction usurped the place of smiles and cheerful converse. But a watchful eye noted these things and in time a motherly sympathy unsealed the secret. Hence the letter to me. She pleaded for attention—she said her boy was dying by inches.

"I was a stranger to Mr. Greeley, but what of that? The matter was urgent. I wrote and begged him to solve the difficult problem if possible and save the student's life. My interest grew, until it partook of the anxiety of the mother. I waited in much suspense.—At last the answer came.

"I found that I could not read it readily, the handwriting being unfamiliar and my emotions somewhat wrought up. It seemed to refer in part to the boy's case, but chiefly to other and irrelevant matters—such as paving-stones, electricity, oysters, and something which I took to be 'absolution' or 'agrarianism,' I could not be certain which; still, these appeared to be simply casual mentions, nothing more; friendly in spirit, without doubt, but lacking the connection or coherence necessary to make them useful.—I judged that my understanding was affected by my feelings, and so laid the letter away till morning.

"In the morning I read it again, but with difficulty and uncertainty still, for I had lost some little rest and my mental vision seemed clouded. The note was more connected, now, but did not meet the emergency it was expected to meet. It was too discursive. It appeared to read as follows, though I was not certain of some of the words:

> 'Polygamy dissembles majesty; extracts redeem polarity; causes hitherto
> exist. Ovations pursue wisdom, or warts inherit and condemn. Boston,
> botany, cakes, folony undertakes, but who shall allay? We fear not.
> Yrxwly,   HEVACE EVEELOJ.'

"But there did not seem to be a word about turnips. There seemed to be no suggestion as to how they might be made to grow like vines. There was not even a reference to the Beazeleys. I slept upon the matter; I ate no supper, neither any breakfast next morning. So I resumed my work with a brain refreshed, and was very hopeful. *Now* the letter took a different aspect—all save the signature, which latter I judged to be only a harmless affectation of Hebrew. The epistle was necessarily from Mr. Greeley, for it bore the printed heading of *The Tribune,* and I had written to no one else there. The letter, I say, had taken a different aspect, but still its language was eccentric and avoided the issue. It now appeared to say:

> 'Bolivia extemporizes mackerel; borax esteems polygamy; sausages
> wither in the east. Creation perdu, is done; for woes inherent one can
> damn. Buttons, buttons, corks, geology underrates but we shall allay.
> My beer's out. Yrxwly,

"I was evidently overworked. My comprehension was impaired. Therefore I gave two days to recreation, and then returned to my task greatly refreshed. The letter now took this form:

'Poultices do sometimes choke swine; tulips reduce posterity; causes leather to resist. Our notions empower wisdom, her let's afford while we can. Butter but any cakes, fill any undertaker, we'll wean him from his filly. We feel hot.

Yrxwly,   HEVACE EVEELOJ.'

"I was still not satisfied. These generalities did not meet the question. They were crisp, and vigorous, and delivered with a confidence that almost compelled conviction; but at such a time as this, with a human life at stake, they seemed inappropriate, worldly, and in bad taste. At any other time I would have been not only glad, but proud, to receive from a man like Mr. Greeley a letter of this kind, and would have studied it earnestly and tried to improve myself all I could; but now, with that poor boy in his far home languishing for relief, I had not heart for learning.

"Three days passed by, and I read the note again. Again its tenor had changed. It now appeared to say:

'Potations do sometimes wake wines; turnips restrain passion; causes necessary to state. Infest the poor widow; her lord's effects will be void. But dirt, bathing, etc., etc., followed unfairly, will worm him from his folly—so swear not.

Yrxwly,   HEVACE EVEELOJ.'

"This was more like it. But I was unable to proceed. I was much too worn. The word 'turnips' brought temporary joy and encouragement, but my strength was so much impaired, and the delay might be so perilous for the boy, that I relinquished the idea of pursuing the translation further and resolved to do what I ought to have done at first. I sat down and wrote Mr. Greeley as follows:

"DEAR SIR: I fear I do not entirely comprehend your kind note. It cannot be possible, Sir, that 'turnips restrain passion'—at least the study or contemplation of turnips cannot—for it is this very employment that has scorched our poor friend's mind and sapped his bodily strength.— But if they *do* restrain it, will you bear with us a little further and explain how they should be prepared? I observe that you say 'causes necessary to state,' but you have omitted to state them.

"Under a misapprehension, you seem to attribute to me interested motives in this matter—to call it by no harsher term. But I assure you, dear sir, that if I seem to be 'infesting the widow,' it is all *seeming,* and void of reality. It is from no seeking of mine that I am in this position. She asked me, herself, to write you. I never have infested her—indeed I scarcely know her. I do not infest anybody. I try to go along, in my humble way, doing as near right as I can, never harming anybody, and never *throwing out insinuations*. As for 'her lord and his effects,' they are of no interest to me. I trust I have effects enough of my own—shall endeavor to get along with them, at any rate, and not go mousing around to get hold of somebody's that are 'void.' But do you not see?—this woman is a *widow*—she has no 'lord.' He is dead—or pretended to be, when they buried him. Therefore, no amount of 'dirt, bathing, etc., etc.,' howsoever 'unfairly followed' will be likely to 'worm him from his folly'—if being dead and a ghost is 'folly.' Your closing remark is as unkind as it was uncalled for; and if report says true you might have applied it to yourself, sir, with more point and less impropriety.

Very Truly Yours,   SIMON ERICKSON.

"In the course of a few days, Mr. Greeley did what would have saved a world of trouble, and much mental and bodily suffering and misunderstanding, if he had done it sooner. To-wit, he sent an intelligible rescript or translation of his original note, made in a plain hand by his clerk. Then the mystery cleared, and I saw that his heart had been right, all the time. I will recite the note in its clarified form:

[Translation.]

'Potatoes do sometimes make vines; turnips remain passive: cause unnecessary to state. Inform the poor widow her lad's efforts will be vain. But diet, bathing, etc. etc., followed uniformly, will wean him from his folly—so fear not.

Yours,   HORACE GREELEY.'

"But alas, it was too late, gentlemen—too late. The criminal delay had done its work—young Beazeley was no more. His spirit had taken its flight to a land where all anxieties shall be charmed away, all desires gratified, all ambitions realized. Poor lad, they laid him to his rest with a turnip in each hand."

So ended Erickson, and lapsed again into nodding, mumbling, and abstraction. The company broke up, and left him so. . . . But they did not say what drove him crazy. In the momentary confusion, I forgot to ask.

Chapter LXXI

AT FOUR O'CLOCK in the afternoon we were winding down a mountain of dreary and desolate lava to the sea, and closing our pleasant land journey. This lava is the accumulation of ages; one torrent of fire after another has rolled down here in old times, and built up the island structure higher and higher. Underneath, it is honey-combed with caves; it would be of no use to dig wells in such a place; they would not hold water—you would not find any for them to hold, for that matter. Consequently, the planters depend upon cisterns.

The last lava flow occurred here so long ago that there are none now living who witnessed it. In one place it enclosed and burned down a grove of cocoa-nut trees, and the holes in the lava where the trunks stood are still visible; their sides retain the impression of the bark; the trees fell upon the burning river, and becoming partly submerged, left in it the perfect counterpart of every knot and branch and leaf, and even nut, for curiosity seekers of a long distant day to gaze upon and wonder at.

There were doubtless plenty of Kanaka sentinels on guard hereabouts at that time, but they did not leave casts of their figures in the lava as the Roman sentinels at Herculaneum and Pompeii did. It is a pity it is so, because such things are so interesting; but so it is. They probably went away. They went away early, perhaps. However, they had their merits; the Romans exhibited the higher pluck, but the Kanakas showed the sounder judgment.

Shortly we came in sight of that spot whose history is so familiar to every school-boy in the wide world—Kealakekua Bay—the place where Captain Cook, the great circumnavigator, was killed by the natives, nearly a hundred years ago. The setting sun was flaming upon it, a Summer shower was falling, and it was spanned by two magnificent rainbows. Two men who were in advance of us rode through one of these and for a moment their garments shone with a more than regal splendor. Why did not Captain Cook have taste enough to call his great discovery the Rainbow Islands? These charming spectacles are present to you at every turn; they are common in all the islands; they are visible every day, and frequently at night also—not the silvery bow we see once in an age in the States, by moonlight, but barred with all bright and beautiful colors, like the children of the sun and rain. I saw one of them a few nights ago. What the sailors call "rain dogs"—little patches of rainbow—are often seen drifting about the heavens in these latitudes, like stained cathedral windows.

Kealakekua Bay is a little curve like the last kink of a snail-shell, winding deep into the land, seemingly not more than a mile wide from shore to shore. It is bounded on one side—where the murder was done—by a little flat plain, on which stands a cocoanut grove and some ruined houses; a steep wall of lava, a thousand feet high at the upper end and three or four hundred at the lower, comes down from the mountain and bounds the inner extremity of it. From this wall the place takes its name, *Kealakekua,* which in the native tongue signifies "The Pathway of the Gods." They say, (and still believe, in spite of their liberal education in Christianity), that the great god *Lono,* who used to live upon the hill-side, always traveled that causeway when urgent business connected with heavenly affairs called him down to the seashore in a hurry.

As the red sun looked across the placid ocean through the tall, clean stems of the cocoanut trees, like a blooming whiskey bloat through the bars of a city prison, I went and stood in the edge of the water on the flat rock pressed by Captain Cook's feet when the blow was dealt which took away his life, and tried to picture in my mind the doomed man struggling in the midst of the multitude of exasperated savages—the men in the ship crowding to the vessel's side and gazing in anxious dismay toward the shore—the—but I discovered that I could not do it.

It was growing dark, the rain began to fall, we could see that the distant Boomerang was helplessly becalmed at sea, and so I adjourned to the cheerless little box of a warehouse and sat down to smoke and think, and wish the ship would make the land—for we had not eaten much for ten hours and were viciously hungry.

Plain unvarnished history takes the romance out of Captain Cook's assassination, and renders a deliberate verdict of justifiable homicide. Wherever he went among

KEALAKEKUA BAY AND COOK'S MONUMENT.

the islands, he was cordially received and welcomed by the inhabitants, and his ships lavishly supplied with all manner of food. He returned these kindnesses with insult and ill-treatment. Perceiving that the people took him for the long vanished and lamented god Lono, he encouraged them in the delusion for the sake of the limitless power it gave him; but during the famous disturbance at this spot, and while he and his comrades were surrounded by fifteen thousand maddened savages, he received a hurt and betrayed his earthly origin with a groan. It was his death-warrant. Instantly a shout went up: "He groans!—he is not a god!" So they closed in upon him and dispatched him.

His flesh was stripped from the bones and burned (except nine pounds of it which were sent on board the ships). The heart was hung up in a native hut, where it was found and eaten by three children, who mistook it for the heart of a dog. One of these children grew to be a very old man, and died in Honolulu a few years ago. Some of Cook's bones were recovered and consigned to the deep by the officers of the ships.

Small blame should attach to the natives for the killing of Cook. They treated him well. In return, he abused them. He and his men inflicted bodily injury upon many of them at different times, and killed at least three of them before they offered any proportionate retaliation.

Near the shore we found "Cook's Monument"—only a cocoanut stump, four feet high and about a foot in diameter at the butt. It had lava boulders piled around its base to hold it up and keep it in its place, and it was entirely sheathed over, from top to bottom, with rough, discolored sheets of copper, such as ships' bottoms are coppered with. Each sheet had a rude inscription scratched upon it—with a nail, apparently—and in every case the execution was wretched. Most of these merely recorded the visits of British naval commanders to the spot, but one of them bore this legend:

"Near this spot fell
CAPTAIN JAMES COOK,
The Distinguished Circumnavigator, who Discovered these
Islands A. D. 1778.

After Cook's murder, his second in command, on board the ship, opened fire upon the swarms of natives on the beach, and one of his cannon balls cut this cocoanut tree short off and left this monumental stump standing. It looked sad and lonely enough to us, out there in the rainy twilight. But there is no other monument to Captain Cook. True, up on the mountain side we had passed by a large inclosure like an ample hog-pen, built of lava blocks, which marks the spot where Cook's flesh was stripped from his bones and burned; but this is not properly a monument, since it was erected by the natives themselves, and less to do honor to the circumnavigator than for the sake of convenience in roasting him. A thing like a guide-board was elevated above this pen on a tall pole, and formerly there was an inscription upon it describing the memorable occurrence that had there taken place; but the sun and the wind have long ago so defaced it as to render it illegible.

Toward midnight a fine breeze sprang up and the schooner soon worked herself into the bay and cast anchor. The boat came ashore for us, and in a little while the clouds and the rain were all gone. The moon was beaming tranquilly down on land and sea, and we two were stretched upon the deck sleeping the refreshing sleep and dreaming the happy dreams that are only vouchsafed to the weary and the innocent.

Chapter LXXII

In the breezy morning we went ashore and visited the ruined temple of the last god Lono. The high chief cook of this temple—the priest who presided over it and roasted the human sacrifices—was uncle to Obookia, and at one time that youth was an apprentice-priest under him. Obookia was a young native of fine mind, who, together with three other native boys, was taken to New England by the captain of a whaleship during the reign of Kamehameha I, and they were the means of attracting the attention of the religious world to their country. This resulted in the sending of missionaries there. And this Obookia was the very same sensitive savage who sat down on the church steps and wept because his people did not have the Bible. That incident has been very elaborately painted in many a charming Sunday School book—aye, and told so plaintively and so tenderly that I have cried over it in Sunday School myself, on general principles, although at a time when I did not know much and could not understand why the people of the Sandwich Islands needed to worry so much about it as long as they did not know there was a Bible at all.

Obookia was converted and educated, and was to have returned to his native land with the first missionaries, had he lived. The other native youths made the voyage, and two of them did good service, but the third, William Kanui, fell from grace afterward, for a time, and when the gold excitement broke out in California he journeyed thither and went to mining, although he was fifty years old. He succeeded pretty well, but the failure of Page, Bacon & Co. relieved him of six thousand dollars, and then, to all intents and purposes, he was a bankrupt in his old age and he resumed service in the pulpit again. He died in Honolulu in 1864.

Quite a broad tract of land near the temple, extending from the sea to the mountain top, was sacred to the god Lono in olden times—so sacred that if a common native set his sacrilegious foot upon it it was judicious for him to make his will, because his time had come. He might go around it by water, but he could not cross it. It was well sprinkled with pagan temples and stocked with awkward, homely idols carved out of logs of wood. There was a temple devoted to prayers for rain—and with fine sagacity it was placed at a point so well up on the mountain side that if you prayed there twenty-four times a day for rain you would be likely to get it every time. You would seldom get to your Amen before you would have to hoist your umbrella.

And there was a large temple near at hand which was built in a single night, in the midst of storm and thunder and rain, by the ghastly hands of dead men! Tradition says that by the weird glare of the lightning a noiseless multitude of phantoms were seen at their strange labor far up the mountain side at dead of night—flitting hither and thither and bearing great lava-blocks clasped in their nerveless fingers—appearing and disappearing as the pallid lustre fell upon their forms and faded away again. Even to this day, it is said, the natives hold this dread structure in awe and reverence, and will not pass by it in the night.

At noon I observed a bevy of nude native young ladies bathing in the sea, and went and sat down on their clothes to keep them from being stolen. I begged them to come out, for the sea was rising and I was satisfied that they were running some risk. But they were not afraid, and presently went on with their sport. They were finished swimmers and divers, and enjoyed themselves to the last degree. They swam races, splashed and ducked and tumbled each other about, and filled the air with their laughter. It is said that the first thing an Islander learns is how to swim; learning to walk being a matter of smaller consequence, comes afterward. One hears tales of native men and women swimming ashore from vessels many miles at sea—more miles, indeed, than I dare vouch for or even mention. And they tell of a native diver who went down in thirty or forty-foot waters and brought up an anvil! I think he swallowed the anvil afterward, if my memory serves me. However I will not urge this point.

I have spoken, several times, of the god Lono—I may as well furnish two or three sentences concerning him.

The idol the natives worshiped for him was a slender, unornamented staff twelve feet long. Tradition says he was a favorite god on the Island of Hawaii—a great king who had been deified for meritorious services—just our own fashion of rewarding heroes, with the difference that we would have made him a Postmaster instead of a god, no doubt. In an angry moment he slew his wife, a goddess named Kaikilani Aiii. Remorse of conscience drove him mad, and tradition presents us the singular spectacle of a god traveling "on the shoulder;" for in his gnawing grief he wandered about from place to place boxing and wrestling with all whom he met. Of course this pastime soon lost its novelty, inasmuch as it must necessarily have been the case that when so powerful a deity sent a frail human opponent "to grass" he never came back any more. Therefore, he instituted games called makahiki, and ordered that they should be held in his honor, and then sailed for foreign lands on a three-cornered raft, stating that he would return some day—and that was the last of Lono. He was never seen any more; his raft got swamped, perhaps. But the people always expected his return, and thus they were easily led to accept Captain Cook as the restored god.

Some of the old natives believed Cook was Lono to the day of their death; but many did not, for they could not understand how he could die if he was a god.

Only a mile or so from Kealakekua Bay is a spot of historic interest—the place where the last battle was fought for idolatry. Of course we visited it, and came away as wise as most people do who go and gaze upon such mementos of the past when in an unreflective mood.

While the first missionaries were on their way around the Horn, the idolatrous customs which had obtained in the island, as far back as tradition reached were suddenly broken up. Old Kamehameha I., was dead, and his son, Liholiho, the new King, was a free liver, a roystering, dissolute fellow, and hated the restraints of the ancient *tabu*. His assistant in the Government, Kaahumanu, the Queen dowager, was proud and high-spirited, and hated the *tabu* because it restricted the privileges of her sex and degraded all women very nearly to the level of brutes. So the case stood. Liholiho had half a mind to put his foot down, Kaahumahu had a whole mind to badger him into doing it, and whiskey did the rest. It was probably the rest. It was probably the first time whiskey ever prominently figured as an aid to civilization. Liholiho came up to Kailua as drunk as a piper, and attended a great feast; the determined Queen spurred his drunken courage up to a reckless pitch, and then, while all the multitude stared in blank dismay, he moved deliberately forward and sat down with the women! They saw him eat from the same vessel with them, and were appalled! Terrible moments drifted slowly by, and still the King ate, still he lived, still the lightnings of the insulted gods were withheld! Then conviction came like a revelation—the superstitions of a hundred generations passed from before the people like a cloud, and a shout went up, "the *tabu* is broken! the *tabu* is broken!"

Thus did King Liholiho and his dreadful whiskey preach the first sermon and prepare the way for the new gospel that was speeding southward over the waves of the Atlantic.

The *tabu* broken and destruction failing to follow the awful sacrilege, the people, with that childlike precipitancy which has always characterized them, jumped to the conclusion that their gods were a weak and wretched swindle, just as they formerly jumped to the conclusion that Captain Cook was no god, merely because he groaned, and promptly killed him without stopping to inquire whether a god might not groan as well as a man if it suited his convenience to do it; and satisfied that the idols were powerless to protect themselves they went

THE TABU BROKEN.

to work at once and pulled them down—hacked them to pieces—applied the torch—annihilated them!

The pagan priests were furious. And well they might be; they had held the fattest offices in the land, and now they were beggared; they had been great—they had stood above the chiefs—and now they were vagabonds. They raised a revolt; they scared a number of people into joining their standard, and Bekuokalani, an ambitious offshoot of royalty, was easily persuaded to become their leader.

In the first skirmish the idolaters triumphed over the royal army sent against them, and full of confidence they resolved to march upon Kailua. The King sent an envoy to try and conciliate them, and came very near being an envoy short by the operation; the savages not only refused to listen to him, but wanted to kill him. So the King sent his men forth under Major General Kalaimoku and the two hosts met at Kuamoo. The battle was long and fierce—men and women fighting side by side, as was the custom—and when the day was done the rebels were flying in every direction in hopeless panic, and idolatry and the *tabu* were dead in the land!

The royalists marched gayly home to Kailua glorifying the new dispensation. ''There is no power in the gods,'' said they; ''they are a vanity and a lie. The army with idols was weak; the army without idols was strong and victorious!''

The nation was without a religion.

The missionary ship arrived in safety shortly afterward, timed by providential exactness to meet the emergency, and the Gospel was planted as in a virgin soil.

Chapter LXXIII

AT NOON, WE hired a Kanaka to take us down to the ancient ruins at Honaunau in his canoe—price two dollars—reasonable enough, for a sea voyage of eight miles, counting both ways.

The native canoe is an irresponsible looking contrivance. I cannot think of anything to liken it to but a boy's sled runner hollowed out, and that does not quite convey the correct idea. It is about fifteen feet long, high and pointed at both ends, is a foot and a half or two feet deep, and so narrow that if you wedged a fat man into it you might not get him out again. It sits on top of the water like a duck, but it has an outrigger and does not upset easily, if you keep still. This outrigger is formed of two long bent sticks like plow handles, which project from one side, and to their outer ends is bound a curved beam composed of an extremely light wood, which skims along the surface of the water and thus saves you from an upset on that side, while the outrigger's weight is not so easily lifted as to make an upset on the other side a thing to be greatly feared. Still, until one gets used to sitting perched upon this knife-blade, he is apt to reason within himself that it would be more comfortable if there were just an outrigger or so on the other side also.

I had the bow seat, and Billings sat amidships and faced the Kanaka, who occupied the stern of the craft and did the paddling. With the first stroke the trim shell of a thing shot out from the shore like an arrow. There was not much to see. While we were on the shallow water of the reef, it was pastime to look down into the limpid depths at the large bunches of branching coral—the unique

SURF-BATHING—SUCCESS.

shrubbery of the sea. We lost that, though, when we got out into the dead blue water of the deep. But we had the picture of the surf, then, dashing angrily against the crag-bound shore and sending a foaming spray high into the air. There was interest in this beetling border, too, for it was honey-combed with quaint caves and arches and tunnels, and had a rude semblance of the dilapidated architecture of ruined keeps and castles rising out of the restless sea. When this novelty ceased to be a novelty, we turned our eyes shoreward and gazed at the long mountain with its rich green forests stretching up into the curtaining clouds, and at the specks of houses in the rearward distance and the diminished schooner riding sleepily at anchor. And when these grew tiresome we dashed boldly into the midst of a school of huge, beastly porpoises engaged at their eternal game of arching over a wave and disappearing, and then doing it over again and keeping it up—always circling over, in that way, like so many well-submerged wheels. But the porpoises wheeled themselves away, and then we were thrown upon our own resources. It did not take many minutes to discover that the sun was blazing like a bonfire, and that the weather was of a melting temperature. It had a drowsing effect, too.

In one place we came upon a large company of naked natives, of both sexes and all ages, amusing themselves with the national pastime of surf-bathing. Each heathen would paddle three or four hundred yards out to sea, (taking a short board with him), then face the shore and wait for a particularly prodigious billow to come along; at the right moment he would fling his board upon its foamy crest and himself upon the board, and here he would come whizzing by like a bombshell! It did not seem that a lightning express train could shoot along at a more hair-lifting speed. I tried surf-bathing once, subsequently, but made a failure of it. I got the board placed right, and at the right moment, too; but missed the connection myself.—The board struck the shore in three quarters of a second, without any cargo, and I struck the bottom about the same time, with a couple of barrels of water in me. None but natives ever master the art of surf-bathing thoroughly.

At the end of an hour, we had made the four miles, and landed on a level point of land, upon which was a wide extent of old ruins, with many a tall cocoanut tree growing among them. Here was the ancient City of Refuge—a

SURF-BATHING—FAILURE.

vast inclosure, whose stone walls were twenty feet thick at the base, and fifteen feet high; an oblong square, a thousand and forty feet one way and a fraction under seven hundred the other. Within this inclosure, in early times, had been three rude temples; each two hundred and ten feet long by one hundred wide, and thirteen high.

In those days, if a man killed another anywhere on the island the relatives were privileged to take the murderer's life; and then a chase for life and liberty began—the outlawed criminal flying through pathless forests and over mountain and plain, with his hopes fixed upon the protecting walls of the City of Refuge, and the avenger of blood following hotly after him! Sometimes the race was kept up to the very gates of the temple, and the panting pair sped through long files of excited natives, who watched the contest with flashing eye and dilated nostril, encouraging the hunted refugee with sharp, inspiriting ejaculations, and sending up a ringing shout of exultation when the saving gates closed upon him and the cheated pursuer sank exhausted at the threshold. But sometimes the flying criminal fell under the hand of the avenger at the very door, when one more brave stride, one more brief second of time would have brought his feet upon the sacred ground and barred him against all harm. Where did these isolated pagans get this idea of a City of Refuge—this ancient Oriental custom?

This old sanctuary was sacred to all—even to rebels in arms and invading armies. Once within its walls, and confession made to the priest and absolution obtained, the wretch with a price upon his head could go forth without fear and without danger—he was *tabu,* and to harm him was death. The routed rebels in the lost battle for idolatry fled to this place to claim sanctuary, and many were thus saved.

Close to the corner of the great inclosure is a round structure of stone, some six or eight feet high, with a level top about ten or twelve in diameter. This was the place of execution. A high palisade of cocoanut piles shut out the cruel scenes from the vulgar multitude. Here criminals were killed, the flesh stripped from the bones and burned, and the bones secreted in holes in the body of the structure. If the man had been guilty of a high crime, the entire corpse was burned.

The walls of the temple are a study. The same food for speculation that is offered the visitor to the Pyramids of Egypt he will find here—the mystery of how they were constructed by a people unacquainted with science and mechanics. The natives have no invention of their own for hoisting heavy weights, they had no beasts of burden, and they have never even shown any knowledge of the properties of the lever. Yet some of the lava blocks quarried out, brought over rough, broken ground, and built into this wall, six or seven feet from the ground, are of prodigious size and would weigh tons. How did they transport and how raise them?

Both the inner and outer surfaces of the walls present a smooth front and are very creditable specimens of masonry. The blocks are of all manner of shapes and sizes, but yet are fitted together with the neatest exactness. The gradual narrowing of the wall from the base upward is accurately preserved.

No cement was used, but the edifice is firm and compact and is capable of resisting storm and decay for centuries. Who built this temple, and how was it built, and when, are mysteries that may never be unraveled.

Outside of these ancient walls lies a sort of coffin-shaped stone eleven feet four inches long and three feet square at the small end (it would weigh a few thousand pounds), which the high chief who held sway over this district many centuries ago brought thither on his shoulder one day to use as a lounge! This circumstance is established by the most reliable traditions. He used to lie down on it, in his indolent way, and keep an eye on his subjects at work for him and see that there was no "soldiering" done. And no doubt there was not any done to speak of, because he was a man of that sort of build that incites to attention to business on the part of an employee. He was fourteen or fifteen feet high. When he stretched himself at full length on his lounge, his legs hung down over the end, and when he snored he woke the dead. These facts are all attested by irrefragable tradition.

On the other side of the temple is a monstrous seven-ton rock, eleven feet long, seven feet wide and three feet thick. It is raised a foot or a foot and a half above the ground, and rests upon half a dozen little stony pedestals. The same old fourteen-footer brought it down from the mountain, merely for fun (he had his own notions about fun), and propped it up as we find it now and as others may find it a century hence, for it would take a score of horses to budge it from its position. They say that fifty or sixty years ago the proud Queen Kaahumanu used to fly to this rock for safety, whenever she had been making trouble with her fierce husband, and hide under it until his wrath was appeased. But these Kanakas will lie, and this statement is one of their ablest efforts—for Kaahumanu was six feet high—she was bulky—she was built like an ox—and she could no more have squeezed herself under that rock than she could have passed between the cylinders of a sugar mill. What could she gain by it, even if she succeeded? To be chased and abused by a savage husband could not be otherwise than humiliating to her high spirit, yet it could never make her feel so flat as an hour's repose under that rock would.

We walked a mile over a raised macadamized road of uniform width; a road paved with flat stones and exhibiting in its every detail a considerable degree of engineering skill. Some say that that wise old pagan, Kamehameha I. planned and built it, but others say it was built so long before his time that the knowledge of who constructed it has passed out of the traditions. In either case, however, as the handiwork of an untaught and degraded race it is a thing of pleasing interest. The stones are worn and smooth, and pushed apart in places, so that the road has the exact appearance of those ancient paved highways leading out of Rome which one sees in pictures.

The object of our tramp was to visit a great natural curiosity at the base of the foothills—a congealed cascade of lava. Some old forgotten volcanic eruption sent its broad river of fire down the mountain side here, and it poured down in a great torrent from an overhanging bluff some fifty feet high to the ground below. The flaming torrent cooled in the winds from the sea, and remains there to-day, all seamed, and frothed and rippled a petrified Niagara. It is very picturesque, and withal so natural that one might almost imagine it still flowed. A smaller stream trickled over the cliff and built up an isolated pyramid about thirty feet high, which has the semblance of a mass of large gnarled and knotted vines and roots and stems intricately twisted and woven together.

We passed in behind the cascade and the pyramid, and found the bluff pierced by several cavernous tunnels, whose crooked courses we followed a long distance.

Two of these winding tunnels stand as proof of Nature's mining abilities. Their floors are level, they are seven feet wide, and their roofs are gently arched. Their height is not uniform, however. We passed through one a hundred feet long, which leads through a spur of the hill and opens out well up in the sheer wall of a precipice whose foot rests in the waves of the sea. It is a commodious tunnel, except that there are occasional places in it where one must stoop to pass under. The roof is lava, of course, and is thickly studded with little lava-pointed icicles an inch long, which hardened as they dripped. They project as closely together as the iron teeth of a corn-sheller, and if one will stand up straight and walk any distance there, he can get his hair combed free of charge.

Chapter LXXIV

WE GOT BACK to the schooner in good time, and then sailed down to Kau, where we disembarked and took final leave of the vessel. Next day we bought horses and bent our way over the summer-clad mountain-terraces, toward the great volcano of Kilauea (Ke-low-way-ah). We made nearly a two days' journey of it, but that was on account of laziness. Toward sunset on the second day, we reached an elevation of some four thousand feet above sea level, and as we picked our careful way through billowy wastes of lava long generations ago stricken dead and cold in the climax of its tossing fury, we began to come upon signs of the near presence of the volcano—signs in the nature of ragged fissures that discharged jets of sulphurous vapor into the air, hot from the molten ocean down in the bowels of the mountain.

Shortly the crater came into view. I have seen Vesuvius since, but it was a mere toy, a child's volcano, a soup-kettle, compared to this. Mount Vesuvius is a shapely cone thirty-six hundred feet high; its crater an inverted cone only three hundred feet deep, and not more than a thousand feet in diameter, if as much as that; its fires meagre, modest, and docile.—But here was a vast, perpendicular, walled cellar, nine hundred feet deep in some places, thirteen hundred in others, level-floored, and *ten miles in circumference!* Here was a yawning pit upon whose floor the armies of Russia could camp, and have room to spare.

Perched upon the edge of the crater, at the opposite end from where we stood, was a small lookout house—say three miles away. It assisted us, by comparison, to comprehend and appreciate the great depth of the basin—it looked like a tiny martin-box clinging at the eaves of a cathedral. After some little time spent in resting and looking and ciphering, we hurried on to the hotel.

By the path it is half a mile from the Volcano House to the lookout house. After a hearty supper we waited until it was thoroughly dark and then started to the crater. The first glance in that direction revealed a scene of wild beauty. There was a heavy fog over the crater and it was splendidly illuminated by the glare from the fires below. The illumination was two miles wide and a mile high, perhaps; and if you ever, on a dark night and at a distance beheld the light from thirty or forty blocks of distant buildings all on fire at once, reflected strongly against overhanging clouds, you can form a fair idea of what this looked like.

A colossal column of cloud towered to a great height in the air immediately above the crater, and the outer swell of every one of its vast folds was dyed with a rich crimson lustre, which was subdued to a pale rose tint in the depressions between. It glowed like a muffled torch and stretched upward to a dizzy height toward the zenith. I thought it just possible that its like had not been seen since the children of Israel wandered on their long march through the desert so many centuries ago over a path illuminated by the mysterious "pillar of fire." And I was sure that I now had a vivid conception of what the majestic "pillar of fire" was like, which almost amounted to a revelation.

Arrived at the little thatched lookout house, we rested our elbows on the railing in front and looked abroad over the wide crater and down over the sheer precipice at the seething fires beneath us. The view was a startling improvement on my daylight experience. I turned to see the effect on the balance of the company and found the reddest-faced set of men I almost ever saw. In the strong light every countenance glowed like red-hot iron, every shoulder was suffused with crimson and shaded rearward into dingy, shapeless obscurity! The place below looked like the infernal regions and these men like half-cooled devils just come up on a furlough.

I turned my eyes upon the volcano again. The "cellar" was tolerably well lighted up. For a mile and a half in front of us and half a mile on either side, the floor of the abyss was magnificently illuminated; beyond these limits the mists hung down their gauzy curtains and cast a deceptive gloom over all that made the twinkling fires in the remote corners of the crater seem countless leagues removed—made them seem like the camp-fires of a great army far away. Here was room for the imagination to work! You could imagine those lights the width of a continent away—and that hidden under the intervening darkness were hills, and winding rivers, and weary wastes of plain and desert—and even then the tremendous vista stretched on, and on, and on!—to the fires and far beyond! You could not compass it—it was the idea of eternity made tangible—and the longest end of it made visible to the naked eye!

The greater part of the vast floor of the desert under us was as black as ink, and apparently smooth and level; but over a mile square of it was ringed and streaked and striped with a thousand branching streams of liquid and gorgeously brilliant fire! It looked like a colossal railroad map of the State of Massachusetts done in chain lightning on a midnight sky. Imagine it—imagine a coal-black sky shivered into a tangled net-work of angry fire!

Here and there were gleaming holes a hundred feet in diameter, broken in the dark crust, and in them the melted lava—the color a dazzling white just tinged with yellow—was boiling and surging furiously; and from these holes branched numberless bright torrents in many directions, like the spokes of a wheel, and kept a tolerably straight course for a while and then swept round in huge rainbow curves, or made a long succession of sharp worm-fence angles, which looked precisely like the fiercest jagged lightning. These streams met other streams, and they mingled with and crossed and recrossed each other in every conceivable direction, like skate tracks on a popular skating ground. Sometimes streams twenty or thirty feet wide flowed from the holes to some distance without dividing—and through the opera glasses we could see that they ran down small, steep hills and were genuine cataracts of fire, white at their source, but soon cooling and turning to the richest red, grained with alternate lines of black and gold. Every now and then masses of the dark crust broke away and floated slowly down these streams like rafts down a river. Occasionally the molten lava flowing under the superincumbent crust broke through—split a dazzling streak, from five hundred to a thousand feet long, like a sudden flash of lightning, and then acre after acre of the cold lava parted into fragments, turned up edgewise like cakes of ice when a great river breaks up, plunged downward and were swallowed in the crimson cauldron. Then the wide expanse of the "thaw" maintained a ruddy glow for a while, but shortly cooled and became black and level again. During a "thaw," every dismembered cage was marked by a glittering white border which was superbly shaded inward by aurora borealis rays, which were a flaming yellow where they joined the white border, and from thence toward their points tapered into glowing crimson, then into a rich, pale carmine, and finally into a faint blush that held its own a moment and then dimmed and turned black. Some of the streams preferred to mingle together in a tangle of fantastic circles, and then they looked something like the confusion of ropes one sees on a ship's deck when she has just taken in sail and dropped anchor—provided one can imagine those ropes on fire.

Through the glasses, the little fountains scattered about looked very beautiful. They boiled, and coughed, and spluttered, and discharged sprays of stringy red fire—of about the consistency of mush, for instance—from ten to fifteen feet into the air, along with a shower of brilliant white sparks—a quaint and unnatural mingling of gouts of blood and snow-flakes!

We had circles and serpents and streaks of lightning all twined and wreathed and tied together, without a break throughout an area more than a mile square (that amount of ground was covered, though it was not strictly "square"), and it was with a feeling of placid exultation that we reflected that many years had elapsed since any visitor had seen such a splendid display—since any visitor had seen anything more than the now snubbed and insignificant "North" and "South" lakes in action. We had been reading old files of Hawaiian newspapers and the "Record Book" at the Volcano House, and were posted.

I could see the North Lake lying out on the black floor away off in the outer edge of our panorama, and knitted to it by a web-work of lava streams. In its individual capacity it looked very little more respectable than a schoolhouse on fire. True, it was about nine hundred feet long and two or three hundred wide, but then, under the present circumstances, it necessarily appeared rather insignificant, and besides it was so distant from us.

I forgot to say that the noise made by the bubbling lava is not great, heard as we heard it from our lofty perch. It makes three distinct sounds—a rushing, a hissing, and a coughing or puffing sound; and if you stand on the brink and close your eyes it is no trick at all to imagine that you are sweeping down a river on a large low-pressure steamer, and that you hear the hissing of the steam about her boilers, the puffing from her escape-pipes and the churning rush of the water abaft her wheels. The smell of sulphur is strong, but not unpleasant to a sinner.

We left the lookout house at ten o'clock in a half cooked condition, because of the heat from Pele's furnaces, and wrapping up in blankets, for the night was cold, we returned to our Hotel.

Chapter LXXV

THE NEXT NIGHT was appointed for a visit to the bottom of the crater, for we desired to traverse its floor and see the "North Lake" (of fire) which lay two miles away, toward the further wall. After dark half a dozen of us set out, with lanterns and native guides, and climbed down a crazy, thousand-foot pathway in a crevice fractured in the crater wall, and reached the bottom in safety.

The irruption of the previous evening had spent its force and the floor looked black and cold; but when we ran out upon it we found it hot yet, to the feet, and it was likewise riven with crevices which revealed the underlying fires gleaming vindictively. A neighboring cauldron was threatening to overflow, and this added to the dubiousness of the situation. So the native guides refused to continue the venture, and then every body deserted except a stranger named Marlette. He said he had been in the crater a dozen times in daylight and believed he could find his way through it at night. He thought that a run of three hundred yards would carry us over the hottest part of the floor and leave us our shoe-soles. His pluck gave me back-bone. We took one lantern and instructed the guides to hang the other to the roof of the lookout house to serve as a beacon for us in case we got lost, and then the party started back up the precipice and Marlette and I made our run. We skipped over the hot floor and over the red crevices with brisk dispatch and reached the cold lava safe but with pretty warm feet. Then we took things leisurely and comfortably, jumping tolerably wide and probably bottomless chasms, and threading our way through picturesque lava upheavals with considerable confidence. When we got fairly away from the cauldrons of boiling fire, we seemed to be in a gloomy desert, and a suffocatingly dark one, surrounded by dim walls that seemed to tower to the sky. The only cheerful objects were the glinting stars high overhead.

By and by Marlette shouted "Stop!" I never stopped quicker in my life. I asked what the matter was. He said we were out of the path. He said we must not try to go on till we found it again, for we were surrounded with beds of rotten lava through which we could easily break and plunge down a thousand feet. I thought eight hundred would answer for me, and was about to say so when Marlette partly proved his statement by accidently crushing through and disappearing to his arm-pits. He got out and we hunted for the path with the lantern. He said there was only one path and that it was but vaguely defined. We could not find it. The lava surface was all alike in the lantern light. But he was an ingenious man. He said it was not the lantern that had informed him that we were out of the path, but his *feet*. He had noticed a crisp grinding of fine lava-needles under his feet, and some instinct reminded him that in the path these were all worn away. So he put the lantern behind him, and began to search with his boots instead of his eyes. It was good sagacity. The first time his foot touched a surface that did not grind under it he announced that the trail was found again; and after that we kept up a sharp listening for the rasping sound and it always warned us in time.

It was a long tramp, but an exciting one. We reached the North Lake between ten and eleven o'clock, and sat down on a huge overhanging lava-shelf, tired but satisfied. The spectacle presented was worth coming double the distance to see. Under us, and stretching away before us, was a heaving sea of molten fire of seemingly limitless extent. The glare from it was so blinding that it was some time before we could bear to look upon it steadily. It was like gazing at the sun at noon-day, except that the glare was not quite so white. At unequal distances all around the shores of the lake were nearly white-hot chimneys or hollow drums of lava, four or five feet high, and up through them were bursting gorgeous sprays of lava-gouts and gem spangles, some white, some red, and some golden— a ceaseless bombardment, and one that fascinated the eye with its unapproachable splendor. The more distant jets, sparkling up through an intervening gossamer veil of vapor, seemed miles away; and the further the curving ranks of fiery fountains receded, the more fairy-like and beautiful they appeared.

Now and then the surging bosom of the lake under our noses would calm down ominously and seem to be gathering strength for an enterprise; and then all of a sudden a red dome of lava of the bulk of an ordinary dwelling would heave itself aloft like an escaping balloon, then burst asunder, and out of its heart would flit a pale-green film of vapor, and float upward and vanish in the darkness—a released soul soaring homeward from captivity with the damned, no doubt. The crashing plunge of the ruined dome into the lake again would send a world of seething billows lashing against the shores and shaking the foundations of our perch. By and by, a loosened mass of the hanging shelf we sat on tumbled into the lake, jarring the surroundings like an earthquake and delivering a suggestion that may have been intended for a hint, and may not. We did not wait to see.

FIRE FOUNTAINS.

We got lost again on our way back, and were more than an hour hunting for the path. We were where we could see the beacon lantern at the lookout house at the time, but thought it was a star and paid no attention to it. We reached the hotel at two o'clock in the morning pretty well fagged out.

Kilauea never overflows its vast crater, but bursts a passage for its lava through the mountain side when relief is necessary, and then the destruction is fearful. About 1840 it rent its overburdened stomach and sent a broad river of fire careering down to the sea, which swept away forests, huts, plantations, and every thing else that lay in its path. The stream was *five miles broad,* in places, and *two hundred feet deep,* and the distance it traveled was forty miles. It tore up and bore away acre-patches of land on its bosom like rafts—rocks, trees and all intact. At night the red glare was visible a hundred miles at sea; and at a distance of forty miles fine print could be read at midnight. The atmosphere was poisoned with sulphurous vapors and choked with falling ashes, pumice stones and cinders; countless columns of smoke rose up and blended together in a tumbled canopy that hid the heavens and glowed with a ruddy flush reflected from the fires below; here and there jets of lava sprung hundreds of feet into the air and burst into rocket-sprays that returned to earth in a crimson rain; and all the while the laboring mountain shook with Nature's great palsy and voiced its distress in moanings and the muffled booming of subterranean thunders.

Fishes were killed for twenty miles along the shore, where the lava entered the sea. The earthquakes caused some loss of human life, and a prodigious tidal-wave swept inland, carrying every thing before it and drowning a number of natives. The devastation consummated along the route traversed by the river of lava was complete and incalculable. Only a Pompeii and a Herculaneum were needed at the foot of Kilauea to make the story of the irruption immortal.

Chapter LXXVI

WE RODE HORSEBACK all around the island of Hawaii (the crooked road making the distance two hundred miles), and enjoyed the journey very much. We were more than a week making the trip, because our Kanaka horses would not go by a house or a hut without stopping—whip and spur could not alter their minds about it, and so we finally found that it economized time to let them have their way. Upon inquiry the mystery was explained: the natives are such thorough-going gossips that they never pass a house without stopping to swap news, and consequently their horses learn to regard that sort of thing as an essential part of the whole duty of man, and his salvation not to be compassed without it. However, at a former crisis of my life I had once taken an aristocratic young lady out driving, behind a horse that had just retired from a long and honorable career as the moving impulse of a milk wagon, and so this present experience awoke a reminiscent sadness in me in place of the exasperation more natural to the occasion. I remembered how helpless I was that day, and how humiliated; how ashamed I was of having intimated to the girl that I had always owned the horse and was accustomed to grandeur; how hard I tried to appear easy, and even vivacious, under suffering that was consuming my vitals; how placidly and maliciously the girl smiled, and kept on smiling, while my hot blushes baked

themselves into a permanent blood-pudding in my face; how the horse ambled
from one side of the street to the other and waited complacently before every
third house two minutes and a quarter while I belabored his back and reviled
him in my heart; how I tried to keep him from turning corners, and failed; how
I moved heaven and earth to get him out of town, and did not succeed; how he
traversed the entire settlement and delivered imaginary milk at a hundred and
sixty-two different domiciles, and how he finally brought up at a dairy depot
and refused to budge further, thus rounding and completing the revealment of
what the plebeian service of his life had been; how, in eloquent silence, I walked
the girl home, and how, when I took leave of her, her parting remark scorched
my soul and appeared to blister me all over: she said that my horse was a fine,
capable animal, and I must have taken great comfort in him in my time—but
that if I would take along some milk-tickets next time, and appear to deliver
them at the various halting places, it might expedite his movements a little.
There was a coolness between us after that.

In one place in the island of Hawaii, we saw a laced and ruffled cataract of
limpid water leaping from a sheer precipice fifteen hundred feet high; but that
sort of scenery finds its stanchest ally in the arithmetic rather than in spectacular
effect. If one desires to be so stirred by a poem of Nature wrought in the happily
commingled graces of picturesque rocks, glimpsed distances, foliage, color,
shifting lights and shadows, and falling water, that the tears almost come into
his eyes so potent is the charm exerted, he need not go away from America to
enjoy such an experience. The Rainbow Fall, in Watkins Glen (N.Y.), on the
Erie railway, is an example. It would recede into pitiable insignificance if the
callous tourist drew an arithmetic on it; but left to compete for the honors simply
on scenic grace and beauty—the grand, the august and the sublime being barred
the contest—it could challenge the old world and the new to produce its peer.

In one locality, on our journey, we saw some horses that had been born and
reared on top of mountains, above the range of running water, and consequently
they had never drank that fluid in their lives, but had been always accustomed
to quenching their thirst by eating dew-laden or shower-wetted leaves. And now
it was destructively funny to see them sniff suspiciously at a pail of water, and
then put in their noses and try to take a *bite* out of the fluid, as if it were a solid.

TRIP ON THE MILKY WAY.

Finding it liquid, they would snatch away their heads and fall to trembling, snorting and showing other evidences of fright. When they became convinced at last that the water was friendly and harmless, they thrust in their noses up to their eyes, brought out a mouthful of the water, and proceeded to *chew* it complacently. We saw a man coax, kick, and spur one of them five or ten minutes before he could make it cross a running stream. It spread its nostrils, distended its eyes and trembled all over, just as horses customarily do in the presence of a serpent—and for aught I know it thought the crawling stream *was* a serpent.

In due course of time our journey came to an end at Kawaehae (usually pronounced To-a-*hi*—and before we find fault with this elaborate orthographical method of arriving at such an unostentatious result, let us lop off the *ugh* from our word "though"). I made this horseback trip on a mule. I paid ten dollars for him at Kau (Kah-oo), added four to get him shod, rode him two hundred miles, and then sold him for fifteen dollars. I mark the circumstances with a white stone (in the absence of chalk—for I never saw a white stone that a body could mark anything with, though out of respect for the ancients I have tried it often enough); for up to that day and date it was the first strictly commercial transaction I had ever entered into, and come out winner. We returned to Honolulu, and from thence sailed to the island of Maui, and spent several weeks there very pleasantly. I still remember, with a sense of indolent luxury, a picnicking excursion up a romantic gorge there, called the Iao Valley. The trail lay along the edge of a brawling stream in the bottom of the gorge—a shady route, for it was well roofed with the verdant domes of forest trees. Through openings in the foliage we glimpsed picturesque scenery that revealed ceaseless changes and new charms with every step of our progress. Perpendicular walls from one to three thousand feet high guarded the way, and were sumptuously plumed with varied foliage in places, and in places swathed in waving ferns. Passing shreds of cloud trailed their shadows across these shining fronts, mottling them with blots; billowy masses of white vapor hid the turreted summits, and far above the vapor swelled a background of gleaming green crags and cones that came and went, through the veiling mists, like islands drifting in a fog; sometimes the cloudy curtain descended till half the cañon wall was hidden, then shredded gradually away till only airy glimpses of the ferny front appeared through it—then swept aloft and left it glorified in the sun again. Now and then, as our position changed, rocky bastions swung out from the wall, a mimic ruin of castellated ramparts and crumbling towers clothed with mosses and hung with garlands of swaying vines, and as we moved on they swung back again and hid themselves once more in the foliage. Presently a verdure-clad needle of stone, a thousand feet high, stepped out from behind a corner, and mounted guard over the mysteries of the valley. It seemed to me that if Captain Cook needed a monument, here was one ready made—therefore, why not put his sign here, and sell out the venerable cocoanut stump?

But the chief pride of Maui is her dead volcano of Haleakala—which means, translated, "the house of the sun." We climbed a thousand feet up the side of this isolated colossus one afternoon; then camped, and next day climbed the remaining nine thousand feet, and anchored on the summit, where we built a fire and froze and roasted by turns, all night. With the first pallor of dawn we got up and saw things that were new to us. Mounted on a commanding pinnacle, we watched Nature work her silent wonders. The sea was spread abroad on every hand, its tumbled surface seeming only wrinkled and dimpled in the distance. A broad valley below appeared like an ample checker-board, its velvety green sugar plantations alternating with dun squares of barrenness and groves of trees diminished to mossy tufts. Beyond the valley were mountains picturesquely grouped together; but bear in mind, we fancied that we were looking *up* at these things—not down. We seemed to sit in the bottom of a symmetrical bowl ten thousand feet deep, with the valley and the skirting sea lifted away into the sky above us! It was curious; and not only curious, but aggravating; for it was having our trouble all for nothing, to climb ten thousand feet toward heaven and then have to look *up* at our scenery. However, we had to be content with it and make the best of it; for all we could do we could not coax our landscape down out of the clouds. Formerly, when I had read an article in which Poe treated of this singular fraud perpetrated upon the eye by isolated great altitudes, I had looked upon the matter as an invention of his own fancy.

I have spoken of the outside view—but we had an inside one, too. That was the yawning dead crater, into which we now and then tumbled rocks, half as large as a barrel, from our perch, and saw them go careering down the almost perpendicular sides, bounding three hundred feet at a jump; kicking up dust-clouds wherever they struck; diminishing to our view as they sped farther into distance; growing invisible, finally, and only betraying their course by faint little puffs of dust; and coming to a halt at last in the bottom of the abyss, two thousand five hundred feet down from where they started! It was magnificent sport. We wore ourselves out at it.

The crater of Vesuvius, as I have before remarked, is a modest pit about a thousand feet deep and three thousand in circumference; that of Kilauea is somewhat deeper, and *ten miles* in circumference. But what are either of them compared to the vacant stomach of Haleakala? I will not offer any figures of my own, but give official ones—those of Commander Wilkes, U.S.N., who surveyed it and testifies that it is *twenty-seven miles in circumference!* If it had a level bottom it would make a fine site for a city like London. It must have afforded a spectacle worth contemplating in the old days when its furnaces gave full rein to their anger.

Presently vagrant white clouds came drifting along, high over the sea and the valley; then they came in couples and groups; then in imposing squadrons; gradually joining their forces, they banked themselves solidly together, a thousand feet under us, and *totally shut out land and ocean*—not a vestige of *anything* was left in view but just a little of the rim of the crater, circling away from the pinnacle whereon we sat (for a ghostly procession of wanderers from the filmy hosts without had drifted through a chasm in the crater wall and filed round and round, and gathered and sunk and blended together till the abyss was stored to the brim with a fleecy fog). Thus banked, motion ceased, and silence reigned. Clear to the horizon, league on league, the snowy floor stretched without a break—not level, but in rounded folds, with shallow creases between, and with here and there stately piles of vapory architecture lifting themselves aloft out of the common plain—some near at hand, some in the middle distances, and others relieving the monotony of the remote solitudes. There was little conversation, for the impressive scene overawed speech. I felt like the Last Man, neglected of the judgment, and left pinnacled in mid-heaven, a forgotten relic of a vanished world.

While the hush yet brooded, the messengers of the coming resurrection appeared

in the East. A growing warmth suffused the horizon, and soon the sun emerged
and looked out over the cloud-waste, flinging bars of ruddy light across it,
staining its folds and billow-caps with blushes, purpling the shaded troughs
between, and glorifying the massy vapor-palaces and cathedrals with a wasteful
splendor of all blendings and combinations of rich coloring.

It was the sublimest spectacle I ever witnessed, and I think the memory of it
will remain with me always.

Chapter LXXVII

I STUMBLED UPON one curious character in the Island of Maui. He became a
sore annoyance to me in the course of time. My first glimpse of him was in a
sort of public room in the town of Lahaina. He occupied a chair at the opposite
side of the apartment, and sat eying our party with interest for some minutes,
and listening as critically to what we were saying as if he fancied we were talking
to him and expecting him to reply. I thought it very sociable in a stranger.
Presently, in the course of conversation, I made a statement bearing upon the
subject under discussion—and I made it with due modesty, for there was nothing
extraordinary about it, and it was only put forth in illustration of a point at issue.
I had barely finished when this person spoke out with rapid utterance and feverish
anxiety:

"Oh, that was certainly remarkable, after a fashion, but you ought to have
seen *my* chimney—you ought to have seen *my* chimney, sir! Smoke! I wish I
may hang if—Mr. Jones, *you* remember that chimney—you *must* remember that
chimney! No, no—I recollect, now, you warn't living on this side of the island
then. But I am telling you nothing but the truth, and I wish I may never draw
another breath if that chimney didn't smoke so that the smoke actually got *caked*
in it and I had to dig it out with a pickaxe! You may smile, gentlemen, but the
High Sheriff's got a hunk of it which I dug out before his eyes, and so it's
perfectly easy for you to go and examine for yourselves."

The interruption broke up the conversation, which had already begun to lag,
and we presently hired some natives and an outrigger canoe or two, and went
out to overlook a grand surf-bathing contest.

Two weeks after this, while talking in a company, I looked up and detected
this same man boring through and through me with his intense eye, and noted
again his twitching muscles and his feverish anxiety to speak. The moment I
paused, he said:

"*Beg* your pardon, sir, beg your pardon, but it can only be considered remarkable
when brought into strong outline by isolation. Sir, contrasted with a circumstance
which occurred in my own experience, it instantly becomes commonplace. No,
not that—for I will not speak so discourteously of any experience in the career
of a stranger and a gentleman—but I am *obliged* to say that you could not, and
you *would* not ever again refer to this tree as a *large* one, if you could behold,
as I have, the great Yakmatack tree, in the island of Ounaska, sea of Kamchatka—
a tree, sir, not one inch less than four hundred and fifteen feet in solid diameter!—
and I wish I may die in a minute if it isn't so! Oh, you needn't look so questioning,

gentlemen; here's old Cap Saltmarsh can say whether I know what I'm talking about or not. I showed him the tree.''

Captain Saltmarsh.—''Come, now, cat your anchor, lad—you're heaving too taut. You *promised* to show me that stunner, and I walked more than eleven mile with you through the cussedest jungle *I* ever see, a hunting for it; but the tree you showed me finally warn't as big around as a beer cask, and *you* know that your own self, Markiss.''

''Hear the man talk! Of *course* the tree was reduced that way, but didn't I *explain* it? Answer me, didn't I? Didn't I say I wished you could have seen it when *I* first saw it? When you got up on your ear and called me names, and said I had brought you eleven miles to look at a sapling, didn't I *explain* to you that all the whaleships in the North Seas had been wooding off of it for more than twenty-seven years? And did you s'pose the tree could last for-*ever*, con*found* it? I don't see why you want to keep back things that way, and try to injure a person that's never done *you* any harm.''

Somehow this man's presence made me uncomfortable, and I was glad when a native arrived at that moment to say that Muckawow, the most companionable and luxurious among the rude war-chiefs of the Islands, desired us to come over and help him enjoy a missionary whom he had found trespassing on his grounds.

I think it was about ten days afterward that, as I finished a statement I was making for the instruction of a group of friends and acquaintants, and which made no pretence of being extraordinary, a familiar voice chimed instantly in on the heels of my last word, and said:

''But, my dear sir, there was *nothing* remarkable about that horse, or the circumstance either—nothing in the world! I mean no sort of offence when I say it, sir, but you really do not know anything whatever about speed. Bless your heart, if you could only have seen my mare Margaretta; *there* was a beast!— *there* was lightning for you! Trot! Trot is no name for it—she flew! How she *could* whirl a buggy along! I started her out once, sir—Colonel Bilgewater, *you* recollect that animal perfectly well—I started her out about thirty or thirty-five yards ahead of the awfullest storm I ever saw in my life, and it chased us upwards of eighteen miles! It did, by the everlasting hills! And I'm telling you nothing but the unvarnished truth when I say that not one single drop of rain fell on me—not a single *drop*, sir! And I swear to it! But my dog was a-swimming behind the wagon all the way!''

For a week or two I stayed mostly within doors, for I seemed to meet this person everywhere, and he had become utterly hateful to me. But one evening I dropped in on Captain Perkins and his friends, and we had a sociable time. About ten o'clock I chanced to be talking about a merchant friend of mine, and without really intending it, the remark slipped out that he was a little mean and parsimonious about paying his workmen. Instantly, through the steam of a hot whiskey punch on the opposite side of the room, a remembered voice shot— and for a moment I trembled on the imminent verge of profanity:

''Oh, my dear sir, really you expose yourself when you parade *that* as a surprising circumstance. Bless your heart and hide, you are ignorant of the very A B C of meanness! ignorant as the unborn babe! ignorant as unborn *twins!* You don't know *any thing* about it! It is pitiable to see you, sir, a well-spoken and prepossessing stranger, making such an enormous pow-wow here about a subject concerning which your ignorance is perfectly humiliating! Look me in the eye, if you please; look me in the eye. John James Godfrey was the son of poor but

LEAVING WORK.

honest parents in the State of Mississippi—boyhood friend of mine—bosom comrade in later years. Heaven rest his noble spirit, he is gone from us now. John James Godfrey was hired by the Hayblossom Mining Company in California to do some blasting for them—the "Incorporated Company of Mean Men," the boys used to call it. Well, one day he drilled a hole about four feet deep and put in an awful blast of powder, and was standing over it ramming it down with an iron crowbar about nine foot long, when the cussed thing struck a spark and fired the powder, and scat! away John Godfrey whizzed like a sky-rocket, him and his crowbar! Well, sir, he kept on going up in the air higher and higher, till he didn't look any bigger than a boy—and he kept going on up higher and higher, till he didn't look any bigger than a doll—and he kept on going up higher and higher, till he didn't look any bigger than a little small bee—and then he went out of sight! Presently he came in sight again, looking like a little small bee—and he came along down further and further, till he looked as big as a doll again—and down further and further, till he was as big as a boy again—and further and further, till he was a full-sized man once more; and then him and his crowbar came a wh-izzing down and lit right exactly in the same old tracks and went to r-ramming down, and r-ramming down, and r-ramming down again, just the same as if nothing had happened! Now do you know, that poor cuss warn't gone only sixteen minutes, and yet that Incorporated Company of Mean Men DOCKED HIM FOR THE LOST TIME!''

I said I had the headache, and so excused myself and went home. And on my diary I entered "another night spoiled" by this offensive loafer. And a fervent curse was set down with it to keep the item company. And the next day I packed up, out of all patience, and left the Island.

Almost from the very beginning, I regarded that man as a liar.

. . . .

The line of points represents an interval of years. At the end of which time the opinion hazarded in that last sentence came to be gratifyingly and remarkably endorsed, and by wholly disinterested persons. The man Markiss was found one morning hanging to a beam of his own bedroom (the doors and windows securely fastened on the inside), dead; and on his breast was pinned a paper in his own handwriting begging his friends to suspect no innocent person of having any thing to do with his death, for that it was the work of his own hands entirely. Yet the jury brought in the astounding verdict that deceased came to his death "by the hands of some person or persons unknown!" They explained that the perfectly undeviating consistency of Markiss's character for thirty years towered aloft as colossal and indestructible testimony, that whatever statement he chose to make was entitled to instant and unquestioning acceptance as a *lie*. And they furthermore stated their belief that he was not dead, and instanced the strong circumstantial evidence of his own word that he *was* dead—and beseeched the coroner to delay the funeral as long as possible, which was done. And so in the tropical climate of Lahaina the coffin stood open for seven days, and then even the loyal jury gave him up. But they sat on him again, and changed their verdict to "suicide induced by mental aberration"—because, said they, with penetration, "he said he was dead, and he *was* dead; and would he have told the truth if he had been in his right mind? *No*, sir."

Chapter LXXVIII

AFTER HALF A year's luxurious vagrancy in the islands, I took shipping in a sailing vessel, and regretfully returned to San Francisco—a voyage in every way delightful, but without incident: unless lying two long weeks in a dead calm, eighteen hundred miles from the nearest land, may rank as an incident. Schools of whales grew so tame that day after day they played about the ship among the porpoises and the sharks without the least apparent fear of us, and we pelted them with empty bottles for lack of better sport. Twenty-four hours afterward these bottles would be still lying on the glassy water under our noses, showing that the ship had not moved out of her place in all that time. The calm was absolutely breathless, and the surface of the sea absolutely without a wrinkle. For a whole day and part of a night we lay so close to another ship that had drifted to our vicinity, that we carried on conversations with her passengers, introduced each other by name, and became pretty intimately acquainted with people we had never heard of before, and have never heard of since. This was the only vessel we saw during the whole lonely voyage. We had fifteen passengers, and to show how hard pressed they were at last for occupation and amusement, I will mention that the gentlemen gave a good part of their time every day, during the calm, to trying to sit on an empty champagne bottle (lying on its side), and thread a needle without touching their heels to the deck, or falling over; and the ladies sat in the shade of the mainsail, and watched the enterprise with absorbing interest. We were at sea five Sundays; and yet, but for the almanac, we never would have known but that all the other days were Sundays too.

I was home again, in San Francisco, without means and without employment. I tortured my brain for a saving scheme of some kind, and at last a public lecture occurred to me! I sat down and wrote one, in a fever of hopeful anticipation. I showed it to several friends, but they all shook their heads. They said nobody would come to hear me, and I would make a humiliating failure of it. They said that as I had never spoken in public, I would break down in the delivery, anyhow. I was disconsolate now. But at last an editor slapped me on the back and told me to "go ahead." He said, "Take the largest house in town, and charge a dollar a ticket." The audacity of the proposition was charming; it seemed fraught with practical worldly wisdom, however. The proprietor of the several theatres endorsed the advice, and said I might have his handsome new opera-house at half price—fifty dollars. In sheer desperation I took it—on credit, for sufficient reasons. In three days I did a hundred and fifty dollars' worth of printing and advertising, and was the most distressed and frightened creature on the Pacific coast. I could not sleep—who could, under such circumstances? For other people there was facetiousness in the last line of my posters, but to me it was plaintive with a pang when I wrote it:

"Doors open at 7 1/2. The trouble will begin at 8."

That line has done good service since. Showmen have borrowed it frequently. I have even seen it appended to a newspaper advertisement reminding school pupils in vacation what time next term would begin. As those three days of suspense dragged by, I grew more and more unhappy. I had sold two hundred tickets among my personal friends, but I feared they might not come. My lecture, which had seemed "humorous" to me, at first, grew steadily more and more dreary, till not a vestige of fun seemed left, and I grieved that I could not bring a coffin on the stage and turn the thing into a funeral. I was so panic-stricken, at last, that I went to three old friends, giants in stature, cordial by nature, and stormy-voiced, and said:

"This thing is going to be a failure; the jokes in it are so dim that nobody will ever see them; I would like to have you sit in the parquette, and help me through."

They said they would. Then I went to the wife of a popular citizen, and said that if she was willing to do me a very geat kindness, I would be glad if she and her husband would sit prominently in the left-hand stage-box, where the whole house could see them. I explained that I should need help, and would turn toward her and smile, as a signal, when I had been delivered of an obscure joke—"and then," I added, "don't wait to investigate, but *respond!*"

She promised. Down the street I met a man I never had seen before. He had been drinking, and was beaming with smiles and good nature. He said:

"My name's Sawyer. You don't know me, but that don't matter. I haven't got a cent, but if you knew how bad I wanted to laugh, you'd give me a ticket. Come, now, what do you say?"

"Is your laugh hung on a hair-trigger?—that is, is it critical, or can you get it off *easy?*"

My drawling infirmity of speech so affected him that he laughed a specimen or two that struck me as being about the article I wanted, and I gave him a ticket, and appointed him to sit in the second circle, in the centre, and be responsible for that division of the house. I gave him minute instructions about how to detect indistinct jokes, and then went away, and left him chuckling placidly over the novelty of the idea.

I ate nothing on the last of the three eventful days—I only suffered. I had advertised that on this third day the box-office would be opened for the sale of reserved seats. I crept down to the theatre at four in the afternoon to see if any sales had been made. The ticket seller was gone, the box-office was locked up. I had to swallow suddenly, or my heart would have got out. "No sales," I said

SEVERE CASE OF STAGE-FRIGHT.

to myself; "I might have known it." I thought of suicide, pretended illness, flight. I thought of these things in earnest, for I was very miserable and scared. But of course I had to drive them away, and prepare to meet my fate. I could not wait for half-past seven—I wanted to face the horror, and end it—the feeing of many a man doomed to hang, no doubt. I went down back streets at six o'clock, and entered the theatre by the back door. I stumbled my way in the dark among the ranks of canvas scenery, and stood on the stage. The house was gloomy and silent, and its emptiness depressing. I went into the dark among the scenes again, and for an hour and a half gave myself up to the horrors, wholly unconscious of everything else. Then I heard a murmur; it rose higher and higher, and ended in a crash, mingled with cheers. It made my hair raise, it was so close to me, and so loud. There was a pause, and then another; presently came a third, and before I well knew what I was about, I was in the middle of the stage, staring at a sea of faces, bewildered by the fierce glare of the lights, and quaking in every limb with a terror that seemed like to take my life away. The house was full, aisles and all!

The tumult in my heart and brain and legs continued a full minute before I could gain any command over myself. Then I recognized the charity and friendliness in the faces before me, and little by little my fright melted away, and I began to talk. Within three or four minutes I was comfortable, and even content. My three chief allies, with three auxiliaries, were on hand, in the parquette, all sitting together, all armed with bludgeons, and all ready to make an onslaught upon the feeblest joke that might show its head. And whenever a joke did fall, their bludgeons came down and their faces seemed to split from ear to ear; Sawyer, whose hearty countenance was seen looming redly in the centre of the second circle, took it up, and the house was carried handsomely. Inferior jokes never fared so royally before. Presently I delivered a bit of serious matter with impressive unction (it was my pet), and the audience listened with an absorbed hush that gratified me more than any applause; and as I dropped the last word of the clause, I happened to turn and catch Mrs. ----'s intent and waiting eye; my conversation with her flashed upon me, and in spite of all I could do I smiled. She took it for the signal, and promptly delivered a mellow laugh that touched off the whole audience; and the explosion that followed was the triumph of the evening. I thought that that honest man Sawyer would choke himself; and as for the bludgeons, they performed like pile-drivers. But my poor little morsel of pathos was ruined. It was taken in good faith as an intentional joke, and the prize one of the entertainment, and I wisely let it go at that.

All the papers were kind in the morning; my appetite returned; I had abundance of money. All's well that ends well.

Chapter LXXIX

I LAUNCHED OUT as a lecturer, now, with great boldness. I had the field all to myself, for public lectures were almost an unknown commodity in the Pacific market. They are not so rare, now, I suppose. I took an old personal friend along to play agent for me, and for two or three weeks we roamed through Nevada and California and had a very cheerful time of it. Two days before I lectured in Virginia City, two stage-coaches were robbed within two miles of the town. The daring act was committed just at dawn, by six masked men, who sprang up alongside the coaches, presented revolvers at the heads of the drivers and passengers, and commanded a general dismount. Everybody climbed down, and the robbers took their watches and every cent they had. Then they took gunpowder and blew up the express specie boxes and got their contents. The leader of the robbers was a small, quick-spoken man, and the fame of his vigorous manner and his intrepidity was in everybody's mouth when we arrived.

The night after instructing Virginia, I walked over the desolate "divide" and down to Gold Hill, and lectured there. The lecture done, I stopped to talk with a friend, and did not start back till eleven. The "divide" was high, unoccupied ground, between the towns, the scene of twenty midnight murders and a hundred robberies. As we climbed up and stepped out on this eminence, the Gold Hill lights dropped out of sight at our backs, and the night closed down gloomy and dismal. A sharp wind swept the place, too, and chilled our perspiring bodies through.

"I tell you I don't like this place at night," said Mike the agent.

"Well, don't speak so loud," I said. "You needn't remind anybody that we are here."

Just then a dim figure approached me from the direction of Virginia—a man, evidently. He came straight at me, and I stepped aside to let him pass; he stepped in the way and confronted me again. Then I saw that he had a mask on and was holding something in my face—I heard a click-click and recognized a revolver in dim outline. I pushed the barrel aside with my hand and said:

"Don't!"

He ejaculated sharply:

"Your watch! Your money!"

I said:

"You can have them with pleasure—but take the pistol away from my face, please. It makes me shiver."

"No remarks! Hand out your money!"

"Certainly—I—"

"Put up your hands! Don't you go for a weapon! Put 'em up! Higher!"

I held them above my head.

A pause. Then:

"Are you going to hand out your money or not?"

I dropped my hands to my pockets and said:

"Certainly! I—"

"Put up your *hands!* Do you want your head blown off? Higher!"

I put them above my head again.

Another pause.

"*Are* you going to hand out your money or *not?* Ah-ah—again? Put up your hands! By George, you want the head shot off you awful bad!"

"Well, friend, I'm trying my best to please you. You tell me to give up my money, and when I reach for it you tell me to put up my hands. If you would only—. Oh, now—don't! All six of you at me! That other man will get away while.—Now please take some of those revolvers out of my face—*do,* if you *please!* Every time one of them clicks, my liver comes up into my throat! If you have a mother—any of you—or if any of you have ever *had* a mother—or a—grandmother—or a—"

"Cheese it! *Will* you give up your money, or have we got to—. There-there—none of that! Put up your *hands!*"

"Gentlemen—I know you are gentlemen by your—"

"Silence! If you want to be facetious, young man, there are times and places more fitting. *This* is a serious business."

"You prick the marrow of my opinion. The funerals I have attended in my time were comedies compared to it. Now *I* think—"

"Curse your palaver! Your money!—your money!—your money! Hold!—put up your hands!"

"Gentlemen, listen to reason. You *see* how I am situated—now *don't* put those pistols so close—I smell the powder. You see how I am situated. If I had four hands—so that I could hold up two and—"

"Throttle him! Gag him! Kill him!"

"Gentlemen, *don't!* Nobody's watching the other fellow. Why don't some of you—. Ouch! Take it away, please! Gentlemen, you see that I've got to hold up my hands; and so I can't take out my money—but if you'll be so kind as to take it out for me, I will do as much for you some—"

"Search him Beauregard—and stop his jaw with a bullet, quick, if he wags it again. Help Beauregard, Stonewall."

Then three of them, with the small, spry leader, adjourned to Mike and fell to searching him. I was so excited that my lawless fancy tortured me to ask my two men all manner of facetious questions about their rebel brother-generals of the South, but, considering the order they had received, it was but common prudence to keep still. When everything had been taken from me,—watch, money, and a multitude of trifles of small value,—I supposed I was free, and forthwith put my cold hands into my empty pockets and began an inoffensive jig to warm my feet and stir up some latent courage—but instantly all pistols were at my head, and the order came again:

"Be still! Put up your hands! And *keep* them up!"

They stood Mike up alongside of me, with strict orders to keep his hands above his head, too, and then the chief highwayman said:

"Beauregard, hide behind that boulder; Phil Sheridan, you hide behind that other one; Stonewall Jackson, put yourself behind that sage-bush there. Keep your pistols bearing on these fellows, and if they take down their hands within ten minutes, or move a single peg, let them have it!''

Then three disappeared in the gloom toward the several ambushes, and the other three disappeared down the road toward Virginia.

It was depressingly still, and miserably cold. Now this whole thing was a practical joke, and the robbers were personal friends of ours in disguise, and twenty more lay hidden within ten feet of us during the whole operation, listening. Mike knew all this, and was in the joke, but I suspected nothing of it. To me it was most uncomfortably genuine.

When we had stood there in the middle of the road five minutes, like a couple of idiots, with our hands aloft, freezing to death by inches, Mike's interest in the joke began to wane. He said:

''The time's up, now, ain't it?''

''No, you keep still. Do you want to take any chances with those bloody savages?''

Presently Mike said:

''*Now* the time's up, anyway. I'm freezing.''

''Well freeze. Better freeze than carry your brains home in a basket. Maybe the time *is* up, but how do *we* know?—got no watch to tell by. I mean to give them good measure. I calculate to stand here fifteen minutes or die. Don't you move.''

So, without knowing it, I was making one joker very sick of his contract. When we took our arms down at last, they were aching with cold and fatigue, and when we went sneaking off, the dread I was in that the time might not yet be up and that we would feel bullets in a moment, was not sufficient to draw all my attention from the misery that racked my stiffened body.

The joke of these highwayman friends of ours was mainly a joke upon themselves; for they had waited for me on the cold hill-top two full hours before I came, and there was very little fun in that; they were so chilled that it took them a couple of weeks to get warm again. Moreover, I never had a thought that they would kill me to get money which it was so perfectly easy to get without any such folly, and so they did not really frighten me bad enough to make their enjoyment worth the trouble they had taken. I was only afraid that their weapons would go off accidentally. Their very numbers inspired me with confidence that no blood would be intentionally spilled. They were not smart; they ought to have sent only *one* highwayman, with a double-barrelled shot gun, if they desired to see the author of this volume climb a tree.

However, I suppose that in the long run I got the largest share of the joke at last; and in a shape not foreseen by the highwaymen; for the chilly exposure of the ''divide'' while I was in a perspiration gave me a cold which developed itself into a troublesome disease and kept my hands idle some three months, besides costing me quite a sum in doctor's bills. Since then I play no practical jokes on people and generally lose my temper when one is played on me.

When I returned to San Francisco I projected a pleasure journey to Japan and thence westward around the world; but a desire to see home again changed my mind, and I took a berth in the steamship, bade good bye to the friendliest land and livest, heartiest community on our continent, and came by the way of the Isthmus to New York—a trip that was not much of a pic-nic excursion, for the cholera broke out among us on the passage and we buried two or three bodies at sea every day. I found home a dreary place after my long absence; for half

BEST PART OF THE JOKE.

the children I had known were now wearing whiskers or waterfalls, and few of the grown people I had been acquainted with remained at their hearthstones prosperous and happy—some of them had wandered to other scenes, some were in jail, and the rest had been hanged. These changes touched me deeply, and I went away and joined the famous Quaker City European Excursion and carried my tears to foreign lands.

Thus, after seven years of vicissitudes, ended a "pleasure trip" to the silver mines of Nevada which had originally been intended to occupy only three months. However, I usually miss my calculations further than that.

MORAL

If the reader thinks he is done, now, and that this book has no moral to it, he is in error. The moral of it is this: If you are of any account, stay at home and make your way by faithful diligence; but if you are "no account," go away from home, and then you will *have* to work, whether you want to or not. Thus you become a blessing to your friends by ceasing to be a nuisance to them—if the people you go among suffer by the operation.